THE COMPLETE DISRUPTION TRILOGY

Thrillers by
R. E. McDermott

Published by R.E. McDermott

Copyright © 2018 by R.E. McDermott

Under A Tell-Tale Sky, copyright © 2015 by R.E. McDermott

Push Back, copyright © 2016 by R.E. McDermott

Promises To Keep, copyright © 2017 by R.E. McDermott

ISBN: 978-1-7320976-1-2

For more information about the author, please visit
www.remcdermott.com

Cover design by Lieu Pham, **www.covertopia.com**
Layout by Guido Henkel, **www.guidohenkel.com**

UNDER A TELL-TALE SKY

To the men and women of
The U.S. Coast Guard
Past, Present, & Future

Semper Paratus

THE EVENT

1 April 2020

The world ended on a Wednesday.

Not *physically*, of course, but the world as most knew it. The Big Blue Marble continued to spin on its axis and orbit the sun, and neither the indigenous people of the Amazon River Basin nor the Papuan tribes of New Guinea noted anything amiss. But the 'civilized' world, the modern world of cheap abundant electrical power and all the wonders it provided, regressed a century and a half in the blink of an eye.

It was fitting Wednesday was also April Fool's Day. As if on cue, world governments responded foolishly, dithering over the wording of last minute press releases on the eve of the Apocalypse, sending mixed signals to an oblivious public. Don't panic. Everything is under control. Business as usual. Communications went down before most advisories were transmitted.

A few warnings did get through, but the unfortunate timing and muted official response led many to conclude it WAS an elaborate April Fool's Day prank. Witty anchor people cocked eyebrows and shared the joke, accompanied by a clip dug from the archives, featuring a rustic gentleman with a single tooth and a tin-foil hat, discussing The End of The World as We Know It (to say nothing of his recent colonoscopy at the hands of extraterrestrials).

But events would prove the gentleman with dental hygiene issues and aluminum head wear to be right after all. The world would never be the same again. But what would it become and who would rule it? An open question, it seemed, but if bureaucrats the world over had been shortsighted in regard to disaster preparation, guns and ammunition were available in abundance. They might not understand preparedness, but they certainly understood power and control.

Desperate times call for desperate measures, and extraordinary circumstances produce heroes and villains in equal measure. Sometimes it's difficult to tell the difference.

CHAPTER ONE

M/V *Pecos Trader*
Buckeye Marine Terminal
Wilmington, North Carolina

Day 1, Impact

Dan Gowan stood bent at the waist, forearms resting on the ship's rail. The lightening eastern sky was bringing the first hints of the coming day. The terminal was a vivid contrast of light and dark shadows as powerful dock lights reflected off enormous stark white storage tanks. He shifted a plug of tobacco from one cheek to the other and squirted tobacco juice over the rail to arc into the dark shadows between the ship and the dock. Beside him, Captain Jordan Hughes shook his head.

"Damned engineers. If it's not grease, it's tobacco juice," Hughes said. "Get that nasty stuff on my nice clean deck, you're gonna clean it up."

Gowan looked over with a lump-cheeked grin. "Don't worry, Cap, I always hit what I aim for." The engineer straightened and glanced down the deck toward the cargo manifold. "And when we gonna start pumping? We've been hooked up over two hours."

Hughes looked at his watch. "It's just after four. These third-shift guys won't get in too much of a hurry. I'm betting they'll drag things out to make sure they don't get stuck with the disconnect at the end of the discharge. They'll likely screw the pooch a few hours before they let us start pumping, just to make sure." He shrugged. "No skin off our ass. We gave them written notice of readiness, so any delays are on them." He paused. "Besides, what's it to you? Why aren't you in your bunk sleeping instead of worrying the hell out of me about something that doesn't concern you?"

"I just kept tossing and turning. Figured I might as well get up."

Hughes grinned. "Short-timer fever, huh? Don't worry, Chief, we'll be back in Beaumont this time next week. You'll start your vacation on time."

"We better be, or Trixie's gonna have my ass."

Hughes cocked an eyebrow. "I thought the divorce was final."

Gowan reddened. "It is, but we're trying to... to work some things out."

"Uh, didn't you already try to reconcile a couple of times already?"

"It's complicated," Gowan said, changing the subject by nodding toward a slightly built black man approaching from the deckhouse, a backpack slung over one shoulder. "Looks like Levi is headed home."

Hughes turned. Levi Jenkins was a qualified member of the engine department, or QMED for short, and had been on the ship longer than anyone else except Hughes himself. Even-tempered and a hard worker, Jenkins was universally liked and generally known as a 'good shipmate.' There was no higher accolade.

"Evenin', Capt'n, Chief," said Levi, focusing his gaze on Gowan.

"Chief, if it's okay with you, Jimmy's gonna cover for me today so I can go home. I already cleared it with the first engineer, but he said to double-check with you before I left."

"No problem as long as your job's covered, and the First runs the engine room, so that's his call. Just make sure you get back before we sail." Gowan grinned. "But there is the usual condition."

Levi grinned back. "Peanut butter or chocolate chip?"

"Some of each would be nice," Gowan said.

Levi laughed and nodded toward the distant parking area, where they could just make out a figure leaning against the front fender of a vintage Ford pickup. "I expect Celia's already got the cookie dough mixed up."

Gowan shook his head. "Now that, my friend, is outstanding. Trixie stopped picking me up at the dock about six months after the honeymoon, and she NEVER showed up at four in the morning."

Levi shrugged. "We want to get through Wilmington traffic before rush hour. We don't call at Wilmington often, and when I got less than a day to spend with the family, I don't want to spend any of it tied up in traffic."

"And we're keeping you," Hughes said, "so take off and enjoy your day, Levi."

"But don't forget the cookies," Gowan added.

"I won't. Anyway, Celia knows if she was to send me back aboard empty-handed there might be a mutiny." Levi laughed and moved toward the gangway.

Gowan called after him, "And when are you going to get rid of that old beater and get a decent truck anyway? Celia deserves more dependable transportation."

"Celia's just fine with that truck," Levi called back over his shoulder, "and they don't get more reliable than Old Blue. If it ain't broke, don't fix it, Chief."

"Good man," Hughes said as he watched Jenkins' departure.

Gowan nodded. "The best unlicensed guy I have in the engine room. I've been bugging him forever to take the license exam, but I can't convince him. Says he's happy right where he is. He does have a few strange ideas, though," Gowan added quietly before turning back to Hughes. "Now when the hell are they gonna let us start pumping?"

Hughes rolled his eyes. "Soon, I hope. Otherwise I'll have to go ashore and start opening valves myself, just to shut you up."

***

An hour later, Hughes and Gowan were in the officers' mess when they heard the familiar whine of the cargo pumps.

"Finally!" Gowan said, checking his watch. "I thought maybe they'd all gone home. This'll put us finishing when, mid-morning tomorrow?"

Hughes nodded. "Give or take, even with a delay we should get out of here on the evening tide."

"It won't be soon enough for —"

The radio squawked, "Captain Hughes, Captain Hughes."

Hughes put the mike to his mouth and pressed the transmit button. "This is Hughes. Over."

"Cap, you might want to come out on deck," said the chief mate.

"On my way," Hughes said, rising from his seat with Gowan close behind.

They arrived on the open deck to stare in wonder. The predawn sky in all directions was awash with shimmering colors, vivid greens, reds, and blues and all shades in between, dancing across the sky from horizon to horizon.

Gowan's mouth hung open. "What the hell —"

"It's... it's the Northern Lights," Hughes gasped.

"In friggin' North Carolina?"

"I saw them once in Alaska," Hughes said. "Trust me, this is them. And enjoy them while you can. It'll be sunrise in half an hour, and they'll fade with full daylight."

They stood mesmerized, soon joined by others of the crew, both working and non-watch seamen, wakened by their shipmates to see the spectacle. As Hughes predicted, the light show began to fade with the dawn.

"Well, I guess the show's over," Hughes said as the last curtain of shimmering green disappeared. "Time to get back to—"

He was interrupted by a thunderous bang and a flash as a transformer on a utility pole ashore exploded, followed by more explosions in the distance along utility lines, one after another like a string of firecrackers. Lights on the dock winked out in response to the explosions, while on board *Pecos Trader* , the hydraulic cargo pumps continued their high-pitched whine.

"They've lost power ashore!" said Hughes. "We have to stop pumping!"

Just as he spoke, the ship lost power as well, and they heard the telltale sound of the pumps winding down.

"Well, that takes care of the pumps," Gowan said.

"What the hell is going on, Chief?" Hughes asked.

"Damned if I know, Cap, but it's not good."

"Go check—" Hughes began, but he was already talking to Gowan's back as the engineer rushed across the deck toward the deckhouse and the engine room below, tugging an ever-present flashlight from his pocket as he ran.

US HIGHWAY 421
NORTHBOUND

Levi Jenkins gripped the wheel tightly as they sped north on US 421. His headlights bored a tunnel through the darkness at ground level as a dazzling display of shimmering colors lit the upper reaches of the predawn sky.

"It's so beautiful." Celia stared into the sky a moment longer, then turned back to him. "Do… do you think this is really it? One of those big solar storms you've been worried about?"

"I can't be sure," Levi said. "I've never seen the Northern Lights, but this can't be anything else, and everything I've read says they're caused by solar activity. If we're seeing the Northern Lights in North Carolina, I'm thinking it's a LOT of solar activity."

Celia gestured to their right at the lights of Wilmington. "The lights are still on."

Levi shook his head. "We're turned away from the sun now, so the lights in the sky may just be from the solar storm, kind of washing around the edges. But it'll be sunrise soon and we'll be taking the full force of the blast. If anything is gonna happen, it'll happen then." He moved into the left lane and passed a slow-moving truck before continuing. "I'm just glad traffic is light. I don't know what's going to happen, but I don't feel good about this and I damn sure want to get across the bridge at Peter Point before sunrise. Even with light traffic, it doesn't take much to jam that bridge. If we get stuck south of the river, it will be tough to get home anytime soon."

"Will all the cars stop working?" Celia asked.

Levi shook his head. "I don't think so, not from a solar flare, anyway. But it really doesn't matter. If the power grid goes down and stays down, there won't be any way to refine and distribute fuel anyway." He glanced at the colors dancing across the lightening sky and increased speed. "A worry for another day. Right now, we just need to get across that bridge."

Celia leaned over and looked at the speedometer. "You're going twenty miles an hour over the limit now. If we get pulled over, we may not make it across the bridge at all."

"Calculated risk," Levi said, but eased off the accelerator a bit.

Ten minutes later they crossed the bridge. Levi heaved a relieved sigh and slowed to the posted limit as he drove northwest through a mixture of woodlands, vacant fields, and industrial development along US 17/421. It wouldn't do to get pulled over at this point. Traffic was getting heavier as he encountered the first of the morning commuters headed into work. Levi looked once again at the lightening sky.

"The kids with your folks?"

She smiled. "You know they are."

It was a standard ritual. Whenever Levi made port in Wilmington with an anticipated nighttime arrival, Celia arranged for their two children to sleep over at her parents' house next door. Thus, they were never alone when she went to collect Levi, and the adults could enjoy some 'private time' before the kids woke up.

"You think your folks are up yet?"

Celia laughed. "Are you kidding? They'll be mostly through a pot of coffee by now. Why?"

"Better call your momma. Tell her if the lights go out, to wake up the kids and start getting ready to move to the river."

"You really think that's necessary? Shouldn't we wait a bit —"

"We've talked about this, Celia. If we lose power after these lights in the sky, I'm thinking this is the real deal. We need to get out of harm's way while everyone else is confused."

"I know, but then it just seemed... I don't know... theoretical."

Levi shot another look skyward. "Well, we're about to find out just how theoretical it is, so you better make the call now while we still have cell service. Another five miles and we'll be in a dead zone."

Celia nodded and dug her phone from her purse. Levi listened as she made the call. It was obvious from Celia's side of the conversation her mother wasn't particularly receptive to the idea.

"I know, Mom, I know. But you don't have to do it unless the power goes out. Yes, I'll tell him. Love you too. See you soon."

"Tell me what?" Levi asked as Celia put her phone away.

"That she loves you, but you irritate the hell out of her, scaring everybody with all this 'end of the world stuff,'" Celia said.

"But she's gonna do —"

KA-BOOM! Sparks cascaded into the roadway as a transformer exploded on a utility pole, followed immediately by similar explosions all along the power line in the distance. Levi flinched and jerked the wheel, inadvertently sending the old truck into a skid. He fought the truck back under control, but two hundred yards ahead of them, a startled motorist veered from the northbound lane into the path of an oncoming car with a resulting thunderous crash. Similar events happened along the length of the highway, and Levi stood on the brakes to bring Old Blue to a shuddering halt at the side of the road, only a few feet away from the wreckage of the nearest collision. He and Celia jumped from the truck and rushed to help.

The northbound vehicle causing the crash was older, either without an air bag or with one that failed to deploy. Nor had the driver been wearing his seat belt. He'd gone through the windshield head first and was draped across the smashed hood of the car like a bloody and boneless rag doll. There was no doubt he was dead. Levi rushed to the other mangled car, where Celia was tugging frantically, and unsuccessfully, at the driver's side door. Inside the vehicle, two young women slumped in their seat belts, deflated air bags lying across their laps. Both were dazed but conscious, and he ran around to try the passenger-side door as Celia continued to jerk frantically on the driver's door.

"Hurry," Celia yelled. "I smell gas!"

Levi's nose was assaulted by the pungent smell as he tugged at the passenger door. It was locked.

"Unlock the doors," he screamed, beating on the window, but the only response from the passenger was a glassy-eyed stare.

He searched the ground and spotted a fist-sized rock in the grass just off the road. It was too small to hold and use as a hammer, so he backed off and threw it at the passenger window with all his might. It produced a crack but little else, rebounding off the glass to fly out of sight into the tall grass. The gas smell was almost overpowering now. Levi weighed his chance of finding the rock, just as the woman passenger began to scream. Levi moved back to the window.

"Unlock the door," he screamed, but the woman was in hysterics.

Desperate now, he leaned his back against the cracked window and hammered the weakened glass with his bare elbow. It yielded on the third blow, showering the screaming passenger with glass. Levi whirled and thrust his hand through the broken window to unlock the door and jerk it open. Still screaming, the terrified and confused woman fought Levi as he attempted to unfasten her seat belt.

"Easy, easy." Levi groped one-handed for the belt buckle, fending off her attacks with the other. "You've been in a car wreck. I'm trying to get you out. Don't fight me!"

Finally it registered. The woman allowed Levi to help her from the car. Celia was there now, and Levi passed the woman to her.

"Get her away from here and over by our truck. I'll get the driver out."

"Hurry, Levi! The gas —"

"I know, get out of here, now!" Levi dug in his pocket and handed her the truck keys. "And back the truck away from here as quick as you can."

Celia started toward the truck, dragging the rescued woman along in a stumbling run. Levi dived through the passenger door to reach across the now lucid driver and unlock the driver's side door. He reached for her buckle, but she beat him to it.

"I'll get your door open —" Levi began, but she was already tugging at the door handle.

"Jammed!" she cried and clawed her way from behind the wheel and over the center console as Levi backed out of the car to give her room. He helped her scramble out the open passenger door.

"Can you walk?" Levi asked.

"I can run. Which way?"

Levi grabbed her arm and ran toward where Celia had backed the truck fifty yards away. They were halfway there when the wreckage ignited with a whoosh.

The first victim was sitting on the open tailgate, obviously in shock. Levi helped the driver sit beside her friend. He retrieved two bottles of water from behind the truck seat and carried them back to the women. The driver accepted both gratefully, but the passenger continued to stare off into space.

"You're bleeding, Levi," Celia said.

Levi looked at his bloody right elbow. "Must have done it on the window."

"I'll get the first aid kit."

Celia moved to the cab and returned with the small box and another bottle of water to wash the wound. She got it as clean as possible before she smeared it with antiseptic cream and bandaged it.

"That'll have to do for now." She lowered her voice. "What are we going to do about them?"

Levi's face hardened. He looked down the road. There were two more wrecks in the distance and it was obvious cars were still moving, but traffic was beginning to back up.

"We leave them. We can't wait for help. Emergency services will be totally maxed out, even assuming there's any way to contact them. If we don't get through this mess fast and make the turn onto Route 1114, we'll be stuck here for hours. And between the Northern Lights and all these transformers popping, it's obvious something is wrong. If we're lucky, it's localized, but we have to assume the worst. We have to get the family to safety, now!"

"We can't just leave them here, Levi! One of them is in shock. She may have serious internal injuries."

"She might, but what can we do about it? We saved their lives, but now we have to worry about our own family." He nodded toward the women on the tailgate. "They're on their own. You know I'm right, Celia."

Celia hesitated, then gave a reluctant nod. Levi hugged her, then fished more water and some protein bars from behind the truck seat and moved back to the tailgate.

"I'm sorry, ladies, but we have to leave. Our kids are home alone. I expect with all the accidents, the police and EMTs will be here shortly," he lied. "We'll leave you some more water and protein bars, but then we have to leave."

The driver stood and helped her friend stand as well. Levi set the meager supplies at their feet.

"I understand," the driver said as Levi closed the tailgate. "And thank you so much. We'd both be dead if not for you."

"No problem," Levi said, "I'm sure you would have done the same for us."

They all stood in awkward silence until Levi nodded and moved towards the driver's door. Celia hesitated a moment and then nodded and moved toward the passenger side. Levi opened his door, muttered a curse under his breath, and called back to the women.

"Where do y'all live?"

"About seven miles north, in a subdivision a half mile off 421. We were on our way to work," the driver said.

"Is that before the turn for Route 1114?" Levi asked.

"Yes. Our road is about a mile before the turn."

"Well, we're going that way, so we can give you a ride home," Levi said.

"But my car... and that... that other car... is the driver..."

"I'm sorry, ma'am, but he's beyond help," Levi said gently, moving back toward the tailgate as Celia matched his movements on the other side of the truck.

"It's really best if you let us take you home," Levi said.

"But... I can't leave the scene of an accident, and Brenda's not right. She needs to go to a hospital, I think... I just can't..."

Levi and Celia were both by the women now.

"Ma'am, despite what I said, I'm pretty sure no one's coming, at least any time soon. Y'all need to get off the road," Levi said.

"But the police... I mean isn't it a crime to leave the scene of an accident..."

"The other car isn't burning," Celia said. "I have some paper and a pen in the glove box. Leave your name and number on the other car and the police can contact you when they arrive. How's that?"

"I guess so," the woman said.

Celia retrieved an old envelope and a pen from the truck and scrawled a note. Levi trotted over and jammed it under the wiper on the intact passenger side of the windshield, doing his best to avoid looking at the corpse draped across the crumpled hood. Moments later they were all squeezed into the cab of Old Blue as Levi wound through wrecks and cars that had stopped to help. Twenty minutes after that they helped the women into the driver's house and were back on US 17/421 headed north.

"I'm glad we helped them, Levi," Celia said softly. "It was the Christian thing to do."

Levi didn't respond immediately.

"I'm glad we could help too," he said finally, "but I expect the world's just become a crueler place, Celia, and it's likely charity, Christian or otherwise, may not have much of a place in it. And my family will survive, no matter what I have to do."

CHAPTER TWO

THE WHITE HOUSE
SITUATION ROOM

DAY 3
3 APRIL 2020

The Honorable Theodore M. Gleason, President of the United States of America, glared down the long table at the Secretary of Energy. The man didn't meet his gaze, but continued reading, tension in his voice.

"Between 0500 Eastern Daylight Time on 1 April and 1700 Eastern Daylight Time yesterday, 2 April 2020, a solar storm of unprecedented magnitude released a series of massive coronal mass ejections, all of which struck Earth. The number of impacts is unknown, as the first events destroyed measuring instrumentation. Global damage is severe."

The Secretary paused. A glance at the President was met with a stony stare. He quickly continued.

"Damage assessment of the North American power grid is ongoing, but in excess of sixty percent of the two thousand one hundred high voltage transformers are confirmed damaged beyond repair. Percentages for medium voltage transformers are similar. Damage to millions of smaller distribution transformers to residential and commercial service drops is more difficult to assess, but sampling suggests a failure rate over seventy percent. Power is out across all of North and Central America. Though the transformers were a known vulnerability—"

"Then why weren't they addressed?" The question was quiet, for all its career-killing potential.

The Secretary of Energy stalled. "Excuse me, Mr. President?"

"It's a simple question, John. If these transformers were so damned vital, why wasn't the issue addressed?"

"With respect, Mr. President, everyone in this room knows why. Those transformers are forty-five feet tall with a footprint of over two thousand square feet—larger than most single-family homes. We have to close roads to move even one of them. And they're custom built for each site, so it's not just a matter of keeping a few interchangeable spares on hand; 'addressing the issue' requires one hundred percent spares. Even if the government mandated one hundred percent spares, the private utilities would have to raise rates by three hundred percent or more to pay for it, and neither the utility industry nor their various regulators have ever deemed rate increases of that magnitude politically feasible. Both parties have been kicking this particular can down the road for a long, long time, Mr. President. Time has run out."

Gleason visibly struggled to contain his rage, and the room grew silent, awaiting his outburst. It never came.

"Very well," he said, "there'll be time enough to get into causes later. What's important now is restoring power. How long are we looking at, bottom line?"

The Secretary of Energy took a deep breath. "Bottom line, Mr. President? Years. Spares to recover in the short term simply don't exist, nor does the capability to produce or ship them. Most are, or I should say were, manufactured in Germany and South Korea, and even if limited manufacturing capability is restored, global demand will be tremendous. Every country that restores or develops manufacturing capability will undoubtedly restrict exports until domestic needs are met, which means we have to develop our own capability in the midst of this chaos. There are only five manufacturing plants in all of North America even capable of manufacturing HVTs, and three are in Canada. Our current most optimistic estimate is power restoration to forty to fifty percent of the US within a decade—"

BANG! Coffee cups jumped in their saucers as Gleason slapped the table.

"UNACCEPTABLE! Don't sit at this table and tell me what CAN'T be done! Get off your ass and start finding me solutions to this problem." Gleason looked at his watch. "It's a bit after nine. We'll reconvene at three and I expect a plan from you for getting power back in months, not years. Is that clear?"

"Yes, Mr. President," the Secretary of Energy said, stuffing papers into his briefcase.

Gleason nodded at the rest of his cabinet. "All right, ladies and gentlemen, this meeting is adjourned. Be back here at three p.m., prepared to update us in your various areas of interest." He looked at his Chief of Staff and the Secretary of Homeland Security. "Doug, Ollie, stay back please."

The pair nodded and kept their seats while the rest of the cabinet members rose and filed from the room. When the door closed behind the last to leave, Gleason turned to Oliver Crawford, Secretary of Homeland Security.

"How bad is it, Ollie?"

"It's bad, Mr. President. Within forty-eight hours every major city in the US will be ungovernable. We need to get you up to Camp David Compound and soon. The First Family will go via chopper, of course, but the others will go by motorcade with armed escort. If we wait much longer, they may have to fight their way out of the city."

Gleason nodded and turned to his Chief of Staff. "Okay, Doug, work with Ollie's people to start the move but not until we finish our meetings today."

Doug Jergens nodded and scribbled on a legal pad.

"Mr. President, we should go ahead and get the Vice President and his group headed toward the NORAD Complex in Cheyenne Mountain, in accordance with the Continuity of Government plan," Crawford said.

"Good idea," Gleason agreed. "How about the Mount Weather complex? Is FEMA ready to open for business?"

"It'll be tight, but we can accommodate senior military, members of Congress, and their families and staff. Not all underground, but the surface complex is huge too. We'll manage, providing we can round them all up."

Gleason shot him a questioning look.

"Easter recess, Mr. President. It was to start today, but there were no major votes scheduled in either house, and a lot of legislators took off last weekend. No telling where they all are now, and with comms down, they might be tough to locate."

Doug Jergens nodded. "Most of them probably wanted to get some campaigning time in."

Gleason snorted. "Elections! We'll be lucky to have a friggin' country in November."

"Ah… about that, sir," Secretary Crawford said, "have you thought about the way forward."

Gleason's eyes narrowed. "What do you mean?"

Crawford took a deep breath. "The only way I see surviving this with any sort of national government intact will likely require using the Constitution as toilet paper, something damn near impossible without a cooperative legislature. We both know there's a pretty fair chance we might not be holding elections in seven months. If that happens, whoever shows up here and now is going to be in power a long time. We have some control now, and we'd be foolish not to use it."

"You're suggesting I just abandon any legislator who might present future problems?"

Crawford shook his head. "Not at all. If a legislator is in town, we put them, their family, and staff on the bus for Mount Weather, regardless of their party or perspective. But I'm betting that will be a minority. And if they're NOT here, or don't contact us, I see nothing wrong with restricting use of our very limited resources to finding and transporting those members of Congress we believe to be most beneficial to the country's recovery. It's all about the national interest."

15

"As dictated by us?"

"Well, yes, sir, but I'd probably avoid that particular verb," Crawford said.

"Point taken. Both points taken, actually." Gleason turned to his Chief of Staff. "Doug?"

"Yes, Mr. President?"

"Draw up a priority list of our favorite legislators and render all possible aid in getting them up to Mount Weather."

The White House
Situation Room

3:00 P.M.

Gleason walked into the room, motioning his cabinet secretaries to keep their seats. They stood anyway and waited for him to settle into his own seat before they sat back down.

"All right, folks," Gleason said, "let's get started. I want a brief, and I stress brief, overview of the situation from the viewpoint of your particular problems and challenges. Is that clear?"

There were nods around the table.

"All right, we'll start with State." Gleason gestured to a woman sitting to his right. "You're up, Dot."

Dorothy Suarez, Secretary of State, nodded. "Thank you, Mr. President. All of our embassies have hardened backup generators and radio stations. We've heard from all of them. In brief, the global situation mirrors our own, especially in the northern hemisphere. Civil unrest is accelerating. Our facilities are all on high alert. Our foreign counterparts are, like us, currently assessing the way forward. Initial indications are the southern hemisphere may have escaped the brunt of the impact. Specifically, the southern portions of both Chile and Argentina, all of Uruguay, Paraguay, much of Sub-Saharan Africa, Australia, and New Zealand are reported to have electrical power. Rio Grande do Sol, the southernmost state of Brazil, may also have escaped relatively unscathed."

"Threats?" Gleason asked.

"I've consulted with both the Agency and Defense." She nodded toward the Secretary of Defense. "Secretary Ballard will touch on that as well, but our consensus is there are no immediate foreign threats. Frankly our biggest concern at State right now is getting our people home."

"Understood. Sounds like we should hear from Defense next." Gleason nodded toward the Secretary of Defense.

"No one is in a position to launch a conventional attack," the Secretary said, "and the consensus is a nuclear attack would be pointless, as we would meet it with an overwhelming response from our submarine-based nukes. However, long-term viability of our overseas bases is dependent upon the infrastructure in the host country, and that's impossible to assess. After consultation with the Joint Chiefs, our recommendation is the repatriation of US military personnel by the most expeditious means, leaving behind only a skeleton force to maintain and secure the bases pending our eventual return. We can start repatriation of both military and State Department personnel and dependents via navy ships."

"How about equipment?" Gleason asked.

The Secretary of Defense grimaced. "Anything we can't fly or sail home will be at risk, Mr. President. We will bring away all our forward-deployed tactical nukes and as much other equipment as possible. But we'll have to leave a lot. Armor, missile batteries, or other equipment will be pre-rigged with demolition charges so the 'stay behind' force can destroy them quickly if necessary to keep them from falling into the hands of those who might use the equipment against us."

"How are you going to resupply the stay-behind force?"

"The numbers will be small, Mr. President, and we'll leave them enough resources for several months. We'll reassess sixty days down the road and decide whether to pull them out or resupply them. We didn't feel we could in good conscience abandon our entire overseas infrastructure with incomplete intelligence and seventy-two hours of study."

Gleason nodded. "It sounds like a prudent approach, so proceed. But you said use the navy ships to 'start' repatriation. Does that mean you don't have sufficient transport capacity?"

"That's correct Mr. President. Accommodation space is tight on navy ships already, and we'll have to make multiple trips. Quite frankly, I doubt things will hold together long enough to allow that. My next suggestion was to authorize military commanders on scene to charter commercial vessels and purchase food and stores. The question then becomes payment and what to do if ship masters or bunker suppliers refuse our offers."

Gleason reflected a moment. "Payment will be by voucher, guaranteed by the full faith and trust of the US government. Should anyone refuse to accept vouchers, use all necessary force. Just try not to piss off anyone with nukes."

The Secretary of Defense nodded, and the President looked across the table. "Agriculture."

"Domestically, this couldn't have hit us at a worse time, Mr. President," said the Secretary of Agriculture. "We have limited stocks of recently harvested winter wheat and barley, but less than five percent of this year's grain crop has been sown. Getting the rest of the crop in and cultivating it all is going to be tough with fuel shortages. Internationally, things look better. It's just past harvest in the southern hemisphere, and there are substantial crop surpluses in southern Latin America, Southern Africa, and Australia/New Zealand. We're trying to get grain purchase contracts in place. The big unknown is cost."

Gleason shook his head. "I won't be gouged. Stick to Latin American stocks and buy all they have, paying in gold from our reserves, and at the market price prevailing the last day international commodity markets were open. If they won't accept that, we'll take the food by force if necessary." He looked at the Secretary of Defense. "I want nuclear carrier battle groups off both coasts of South America. Any food cargoes leaving South American ports will be bound for the US or no place at all."

The Defense Secretary nodded and Gleason turned back to the Secretary of State. "Before we evacuate our embassies in Russia and China, have our ambassadors assure those governments we have no designs on any surplus food stocks in Africa or Australia/New Zealand."

"Yes, Mr. President," Secretary Suarez said.

Gleason nodded and turned to the Secretary of Energy.

"Okay, John," Gleason said, "your turn. And I hope you have something better to offer than you did this morning."

"Ahh... yes, sir, I believe I do." He cleared his throat. "While our capacity to produce electrical power remains largely intact, the lack of transformers severely limits our ability to efficiently distribute that power. The key word being 'efficiently.' Even without the transformers, we can still use the power within a limited distance from the source. By designating certain nuclear power plants as manufacturing hubs, we'll dedicate remaining resources to converting nearby facilities to manufacture transformers. Simply put, we will bring the manufacturing facilities to the power. With nuclear, fuel supply won't be a problem. As we produce transformers, we'll rebuild the grid outward from the nuclear plants." He hesitated.

"Go on," Gleason said.

"There are... significant challenges, Mr. President. Not only will such an accelerated effort require a tremendous share of our remaining labor force and industrial resources for the foreseeable future, but it will require nationalization on an unprecedented and massive scale—the national electrical grid, all power plants, all related manufacturing facilities, as well as all private assets within a designated radius of each plant will become government property. It's never been done before, sir, and quite frankly, I question the legality."

"Well, the world never ended before, John, so I suppose an unprecedented disaster requires an equally unprecedented response. And starting three days ago, it's legal if I... if we... say it's legal. Now. How long before we get the lights back on?"

The Energy Secretary set his jaw. "Unknown, Mr. President. And it will still be unknown, even if you demand a time. I simply do not know, nor does anyone else. We'll work just as hard as possible to make this happen, but I still believe it will be years and not months. You may replace me with someone who'll tell you what you want, or demand, to hear, but that won't change facts."

Gleason had been leaning forward in his chair, but he slowly sat back, the glare on his face dissolving. After a moment, he nodded. "You're right. But I want a timetable. I'll give you thirty days to begin implementation and then we'll reassess and set deadlines. Deadlines you will meet. Are we clear on that?"

"Yes, Mr. President."

"Good," Gleason said, nodding at Oliver Crawford. "Let's hear from Homeland Security. All right, Ollie. Bring us up to date on the unrest."

"It's not good, Mr. President. The blackout overwhelmed first responders. Rioting and looting is widespread in all major cities. It's the typical blackout scenario, focusing on looting of consumer goods, but that will change. The average city has less than a week's supply of food on hand. Escalation of violence is inevitable as people begin to compete for dwindling but vital resources. Our most optimistic estimate is millions of deaths in the next six months, from violence and other blackout-related causes. The elderly and the chronically ill requiring maintenance medication are the most vulnerable. Hunger, polluted drinking water, and disease will take the rest."

There was silence around the big table, broken by the Secretary of Defense.

"My God," he said. "We have to try to get ahead of this. Call out the National Guard—"

Gleason raised a hand to cut him off. "First we have to fully understand our options." He turned back to Crawford. "How many millions?"

"Unknown, Mr. President, but perhaps as much as half the population."

The room grew quiet again. Gleason shook his head.

"That can't be right! I understand violence and casualties among the 'at-risk' population with the medical infrastructure overwhelmed, but half the population? Mass starvation? What about FEMA stockpiles? We've spent a lot of taxpayer dollars on disaster preparedness, are you telling me that bought us nothing?"

"On the contrary, Mr. President, we're well prepared for disasters, but not an apocalyptic event. Our models call for stockpiles sufficient for three separate but simultaneous regional disasters, each of thirty days' duration. They further assume impacted regional populations of twenty-five million, since a disaster would not impact all regional inhabitants. Thus we have supplies for seventy-five million people for thirty days distributed among regional FEMA warehouses, with the bulk prepositioned near the coasts. The military maintains its own emergency stockpile, and the figures above are for FEMA stockpiles only. However, it's likely FEMA stockpiles might be needed to support military personnel at some future point."

"Sounds like a lot," Gleason said.

"The population is over three hundred thirty million, Mr. President. Even supposing we could meet the enormous distribution challenges, FEMA stockpiles wouldn't last more than a week, ten days at most. The previously mentioned stores of winter wheat and barley could help, again assuming we seize that grain in the national interest." Crawford paused. "There is no realistic scenario that sees us feeding the majority of the US population long enough to harvest a crop in the fall, or even hold out until the arrival of the foreign grain shipments we've been discussing."

The President looked around the room, studying the shocked faces of his cabinet secretaries. He wasn't encouraged.

"All right," Gleason said. "We obviously have to give this more thought. We'll adjourn now and I'd like you all to begin immediate implementation of the plans we've discussed so far. We'll reconvene here tomorrow at—"

Doug Jergens, the Chief of Staff, cleared his throat. Gleason shot him an annoyed look.

"Ah. Sorry to interrupt, sir," Jergens said, "but the transfer…"

"Oh, right," Gleason said. "We'll meet tomorrow morning at seven o'clock at Camp David."

THE WHITE HOUSE
OVAL OFFICE

SAME DAY, 6:00 P.M.

Gleason slumped in the armchair, staring into his glass as he swirled the amber liquid. Oliver Crawford sat on the sofa across from him, sipping from his ever-present bottle of water. Gleason wondered for what must have been the thousandth time whether or not he really trusted a man who wouldn't take an occasional drink.

"How many?"

"Approximately ten million, Mr. President," Crawford replied, "not counting the military and assuming we have to sustain our civilian core group no longer than six months, eight at the outside. I figured in a small contingency in case the harvest is worse than average or the foreign grain imports are inadequate."

"Will that be enough?" Gleason asked.

"It will have to be. It's the most people we can keep fed, sheltered, and productive, and the absolute minimum we'll need to keep the power-restoration project going forward until we get a crop in, along with government workers to administer it all," Crawford said.

"What's the breakdown?"

"Approximately two hundred thousand government administrative employees and twice that number of security personnel. Everyone else will be dedicated to either power restoration or agriculture, the bulk of them agriculture. There'll be a lot of manual labor needed there."

Gleason nodded and stared into his drink.

"If I may ask, Mr. President, why are you assigning me these various tasks? I'm happy to take them on, but a lot of them rightly fall under the responsibilities of the other cabinet members. There may be... problems."

Gleason looked up. "Because this can't be run by a goddamned committee, that's why. I could sense it this afternoon, and I'm sure you could as well. We've both been reading people a long time, Ollie, and despite all the 'Yes, Mr. Presidents,' I sensed a great reluctance to make the hard choices demanded of us. You're the only one who seemed to immediately appreciate what we're up against. I need someone to help me run things."

"The Vice President—"

"The Vice President is on his way to a hole under Cheyenne Mountain, and there he'll stay."

"Yes, Mr. President," Crawford said, his face impassive.

Gleason drained his glass and held it out. Crawford leaned over and accepted the glass and rose and walked to the sideboard, where he replenished the President's drink. He returned and handed the drink to Gleason before resuming his seat.

"Thank you, Ollie," Gleason said, "and you know I'm right. How do you think Agriculture will react when he hears we're nationalizing all grain and seed stocks and all agricultural holdings and farm equipment, or Labor when she hears we're recruiting our migrant farmworker force out of state refugee camps on a 'no work—no food' basis? What's that name you came up with? The Civilian Agricultural Initiative?" Gleason snorted. "We can pretty it up all we want, but I doubt we'll fool anyone."

"We're not nationalizing ALL land," Crawford temporized, "only holdings larger than five hundred acres. Family farmers on smaller holdings will produce fruits and vegetables on the truck gardening model. We'll even provide starter seed and fertilizer if available, as well as providing labor—"

"And take ninety percent of their crop in return."

"Which will still likely leave them more food than most people," Crawford said. "I KNOW we could sell the whole program to Secretary Jackson—"

"That's the damned point, Ollie! I don't have to SELL programs to anyone, especially someone who works for ME! This isn't a debating society, we just don't have the time. YOU understand what's necessary and are on board with the program, so I'm putting you in charge. That's that. Now, what's your plan on lodging the workforce?"

"My initial thoughts are to quarter the power workers on site in redevelopment zones centered on each of the nuclear plants we're bringing back on line. The agricultural workforce will have to be more transient with the crop and the season. I'm thinking a dozen semipermanent regional camps with temporary satellite camps as and when needed. We'll need perimeter security on all of them. We don't want to lose trained workers at peak labor periods."

Gleason nodded. "What about the administration workers?"

"Staying in the cities is a nonstarter. I was thinking cruise ships, maybe anchored off Annapolis. They'll be self-contained offices and living quarters with plenty of amenities and a lot easier to defend at anchor. And we can move them around if we need to set up regional HQs," Crawford said. "And what's more, they'll mostly be out of sight of the general population. There's bound to be resentment, and there's no need to advertise the fact that government workers are living in decent conditions."

"Good idea," Gleason said. "Actually a damn good idea. They should be thick out of the Florida ports and the Caribbean this time of year. Try chartering them on payment guarantees like we're doing overseas, but if that doesn't work, just seize them by force. And speaking of force, how do you think our friends in uniform are going to take all this?"

Crawford didn't answer immediately, but when he did, it was obvious he'd already considered the question.

"It's my greatest fear, actually. The worst-case scenario is for the military, either collectively or individually, to decide these very necessary steps are unacceptable. If we send them out to put down civil unrest, I think there's a good chance they'll turn against us. No one's going to be happy firing on starving refugees. The last thing we need is a bunch of disaffected military personnel deserting and taking their weapons and training with them," Crawford said.

"What choice do we have? I can't see how any of this works without them."

"First, we get rid of any potential troublemakers. I'd say anyone who wants to leave, we grant an immediate discharge. Let them leave with their personal possessions and maybe a few days rations. Not only do we lose a lot of problems, but also extend military food and water reserves, at least in the longer term. Service personnel with families on base will likely stay, and we can beef up security around the base perimeter and also take in as many dependents of remaining troops as possible. We clear a quarter-mile security perimeter around all bases, both to provide clear fields of fire and prevent refugee camps from springing up next to the bases. And finally, we have to discourage fraternization with the civilian population completely, and immediately discharge any military personnel caught doing it. To the degree possible, we need to build a psychological wall between the troops and the civilian population. The civilians will grow to resent those inside the wire, and the troops will feel doubly protective of both the base and their families the base is sheltering. In six months, possibly less, the military will be with us completely—presuming we don't drive them away in the short term."

"Just great, Ollie, but what do we do in the interim? Use the National Guard—"

Crawford was already shaking his head. "The Guard's too close to their respective communities, and for the same reason, we shouldn't let Defense mobilize the reserves. We're trying to sever connections between the civilians and the military, not build them." Crawford paused. "I have another idea."

Gleason cocked an eyebrow. "Mercenaries?"

"Private security contractors," Crawford corrected. "Most are very experienced in chaotic conditions in third world countries. They'll have no problem doing whatever needs to be done. We can use the regular military for overseas missions like the South American thing, or maybe duties not likely to be challenging, like guarding the power plants. But if something looks likely to be domestic and messy, we'll use the contractors. They'll be the tip of the spear."

"We can't just send in armed thugs," Gleason said.

"They'll all be members of a FEMA Special Reaction Force, something I've been working on for a while. I can have it up and running in forty-eight hours."

"You'll have enough merc… contractors?"

"I'll have enough to form the backbone of the unit and get things started. They'll set the tone; then we'll fill the unit out by selective recruitment from the regular forces," Crawford said. "We'll restrict it to single individuals and then station them in SRF units far from their regular units and in places where they have no former ties to the civilian community. They'll be isolated, and the SRF will become their home—and if they fail to adapt, we'll strip them of weapons and equipment and 'discharge' them into the civilian population."

"How are you going to recruit them in the first place?" Gleason asked. "I can't see too many of our regular troops being eager to join a 'contractor' force set up to keep the lid on civilian unrest."

Crawford smiled. "I'm going to lie, of course."

Crawford glanced at his watch. "It's almost time for you to be off, Mr. President. I think the chopper is—"

"Going to leave when I'm ready to leave, Ollie, and there's one more thing I'd like to set in motion ASAP."

"Yes, Mr. President, what did I miss?"

"Spin, Ollie. Any of our citizens who survive on their own over the next months are going to be mad as hell. So if we end up with a nation of say fifty or a hundred million angry citizens, we have no chance of governing even if we restore electrical power. We have to make sure we give them someone other than us to hate."

Crawford nodded. "Makes sense, but how?"

"By making state and local officials the face of a failed relief effort. I want your folks on the horn, assuring governors and other state officials that stores are tight, but we can meet the near-term requirements and that distribution will begin immediately. Tell them we're not calling out the National Guard at the federal level, because we don't want to 'panic the population' or some such excuse. Make up something plausible, you're good at that sort of thing. Then tell state officials FEMA is going to take a secondary and supportive role and encourage the governors to call their own Guard out for state service to set up state-run shelters and distribute the FEMA-supplied stores. Invite the governors and other state officials to join the appeal for calm and make sure they get plenty of airtime on the Emergency Broadcast System to do it. I think those guys will all jump at the chance of being heroes."

"So THEY'LL own the relief effort when it goes belly up?"

"Exactly," Gleason said. "I also want you contacting all the 'administration friendly' news anchors and entertainment celebrities you can reach. Give them jobs at DHS Public Affairs Office, and find places for them and their families on those cruise ships. Got it?"

Crawford nodded again, impressed. "You're thinking when we need to get the word out on something, we use spokespersons the public already trusts? But what happens if they come aboard and then develop journalistic conscience?"

Gleason shrugged. "Then we terminate their employment and evict them from their cushy new quarters. I'm sure we can arrange to establish some brigs on these cruise ships. They'll fall in line, trust me."

Gleason continued. "When public outrage boils over at the incompetence at the state level, FEMA will supply the worst trouble spots with a few days' supply of water and food. Package the whole affair as state and local government missteps corrected by the prompt FEMA intervention. Have our celebrity spokespersons on hand to report on FEMA saving the day via the Emergency Broadcast System. The narrative will be the feds were doing their best, but state and local governments screwed up. Then we refuse the state governments any access to the Emergency Broadcast System so they'll have no means to counter our story."

"It makes sense," Crawford said. "People always want a focus for their anger. If we can direct it elsewhere, we're ahead of the game."

"This recovery effort's going to take years," Gleason said, "and if we have a hope in hell of getting continued cooperation, we have to spin the inevitable famine in such a way to legitimize the federal

government in the minds of the survivors. And who knows? If the governors are convincing enough, they might even help keep things calmed down a bit for a few days so it will be easier to start getting the rest of the programs in place."

Gleason finished just as Doug Jergens stuck his head into the Oval Office.

"Marine One is standing by on the helipad at your pleasure, Mr. President," Jergens said.

Gleason nodded and rose. "All right, Ollie. You've got your work cut out for you. See you at Camp David tomorrow morning."

CHAPTER THREE

5 April 2020

RECIPIENTS' EYES ONLY

From: POTUS
Distribution: All Cabinet Members
Secondary Distribution: PROHIBITED

Subject: Disruption of National Power Grid - The Way Back

First let me say how relieved I was to learn most of your family members made it to Camp David or otherwise found shelter in secure government facilities. Gina and I are keeping those still unaccounted for in our hearts and prayers, in hopes all will reach safety soon.

By this time, I know all of you have had time to absorb the assessment of our situation Secretary Crawford shared with us Friday and then discussed in more depth at yesterday morning's cabinet meeting here at Camp David. I feel sure you found it as disturbing as I did. The situation seems bleak and the actions necessary are beyond frightening, and all things I would reject out of hand in most circumstances. That said, I can see no real alternatives if we are to survive as a nation, and after prayerful deliberation, I have concluded we have little choice but to implement the initiatives presented by Secretary Crawford. I have issued executive orders directing full implementation of all such measures. Also, given the overall role the Department of Homeland Security must play in our recovery efforts, I'm sure you all understand why I've delegated oversight and management of that effort to Secretary Crawford. Please consider any requests or directions from Secretary Crawford as carrying the full weight and approval of the Office of the President.

On a slightly related subject, while I know a number of you disagree on constitutional grounds with some or all of the actions we're taking, your full cooperation is expected and appreciated. For those of you who indicated an intention to resign as a matter of conscience, I respect that decision and harbor no ill will. I will ensure Presidential Transport places helicopters at your disposal to return you and your dependents to a location of your choosing.

For those of you staying the course, you have my profound thanks, as the road ahead will be anything but smooth. As you all know, both the Speaker of the House and the President pro tempore of the Senate are currently sheltering with their families at FEMA Headquarters at Mount Weather, and I had a conference call with them this morning. As expected, both Congressman Tremble and Senator Leddy objected vociferously to our planned action, but neither offered viable alternatives. At the conclusion of the conversation I had little choice but to direct Secretary Crawford to have FEMA security personnel confine both Speaker Tremble and Senator Leddy to their quarters to be held incommunicado. My fervent hope is, in time, they'll recognize the necessity for my actions.

May God have mercy upon us all.
Theodore Gleason
President of the United States

* * *

PRESIDENTIAL QUARTERS
CAMP DAVID COMPLEX
MARYLAND

DAY 5
5 APRIL 2020

"Are any of them giving you trouble?" Gleason asked.

"Nothing I can't deal with, Mr. President," Crawford replied. "The three secretaries making noise about resigning had a change of heart. I'd say your memo did the trick."

"Well, watch them. If they aren't contributing, we may have to replace them anyway, and if they do leave the facility, it goes without saying they know a bit too much. We'll have to consider that," Gleason said.

"As cabinet members, they all signed National Security nondisclosure agreements—"

Gleason snorted. "Seriously, Ollie? And you really think that's sufficient under current conditions?"

Crawford flushed. "No, sir, obviously not. But I want to be clear. You want me to..."

"I want you to be aware of the potential problem and take care of it should it arise. I've placed you in charge, so take charge. And don't bother me with the details. That isn't the sort of thing I need to know. I've given you a great deal of power, Ollie, and power comes at a price. Clear enough?"

"Yes, Mr. President. I'll handle it."

CHAPTER FOUR

DAY 5

Johnson looked up from his crossword and pulled cotton out of his right ear. "What's a five-letter word for 'occupied, as a table,' beginning with s?"

Broussard threw the paperback on the desk and pulled out one of his own earplugs.

"What?" he asked.

"I said, what's a five-letter word for 'occupied, as a table,' beginning with s?"

"How the hell should I know?" Broussard turned his head toward the cell block. "God, can't those assholes shut up for even a minute? They've been howling twenty-four hours straight."

Johnson shrugged. "Animals being animals ain't surprising. They been locked down five days straight and it must be a hundred plus in there. Whatever genius designed a building for south Texas with no natural ventilation and a crappy little backup generator too small to run air-conditioning was obviously some fat-ass politician's not-too-bright nephew or something."

"Well, it's not like it's much better in here," Broussard said, nodding at the cheap box fan laboring in the corner of the control room. "That damn thing's just blowing around hot air; it's probably ninety in here. And you could use a shower."

"You're no damned petunia yourself," Johnson responded. "Now go make a round."

"I went last time!"

"And you'll go next time if I say so. That's why I got these here sergeant's stripes on my sleeve," Johnson said.

"The toilets are starting to back up. It's getting really nasty in there. On my last round one of the assholes threw shit at me. Son of a bitch almost hit me."

Johnson nodded. "After Hurricane Rita it was like this for a month." He nodded toward the cell block. "I was new then, and they started doing the same stuff, hollering and moaning and throwing crap. But ole Sergeant Thompson, he just walked out calm as you please and told 'em there'd be no food or water for anyone for two days. They calmed right down." He paused. "Which reminds me, what did that food services guy say when he brought the food yesterday."

"He said they're down to baloney sandwiches on stale heels, and not much of that," Broussard said.

"Well, whatever," Johnson said, "when you only got baloney, you don't want to lose it, so go over to food services and tell them not to bother for a couple of days, then see how those animals in there like it."

Broussard hesitated. "Only one problem, Sarge. From the smell of the sandwiches yesterday, I doubt that baloney's gonna last two days."

CHAPTER FIVE

DAY 6

Jordan Hughes contemplated the three senior officers clustered around the seating area of his day room, half-finished cups of coffee on the low table in front of them. The last days had taken their toll, and all looked worried and sleep deprived; Hughes knew he didn't look any better. He directed the first question at Gowan.

"How're things looking down below, Chief?"

Gowan shrugged. "We're keeping the lights on. Other than the initial blackout, all the machinery seems to be okay, but I'm getting a few intermittent faults in the electronic controls. It could be totally unrelated to this whole solar-flare thing. I mean, we've had control problems before. However, this is WAY outside my experience, and under the circumstances, I'm concerned."

He shook his head. "I just don't fully trust the automation yet. We're running everything in manual mode and I've got us on the emergency generator for now." He nodded toward Rich Martin, the first engineer. "Rich and I will be going through all the systems, but we're stretched thin. The automation was designed to reduce manning, and if it's not working reliably, we just don't have the manpower to compensate. I'd rather find that out alongside the dock than in the middle of the ocean."

"We're on the same page there," Hughes said. "Do what you have to do."

He turned to the chief mate. "Any movement ashore, Georgia?"

Georgia Howell shook her head. "No change. Not a soul in the terminal."

Hughes nodded. The dock foreman came aboard about four hours after the blackout to report almost none of the day shift had showed up for work, and those that did went home after confirming there was no power in the terminal. The man was obviously worried about his family and conflicted by a pressing need to get home and a reluctance to leave the terminal unmanned. Concern for his family prevailed. He'd assured Hughes he'd return and left, not to be seen again.

"How're the fires?" Hughes asked. Shortly after the blackout, smoke rose across the city, likely fires caused by massive electrical surges. They burned out of control as the sheer number of blazes overwhelmed the city's firefighting resources. Intermittent rain over several days had dampened but not completely extinguished the fires, and based on the growing columns of smoke now billowing in the distance, they were raging once again.

"Tex is keeping an eye on them. They're not any closer and the wind has them traveling in the other direction for now, but—"

She was interrupted by the sound of sustained gunfire in the distance.

"Damn! That's beginning to sound like World War Three," Gowan said.

"And it's getting closer," Rich Martin added as the others nodded agreement.

"Which brings up my next point," the chief mate said. "Bob and I walked up to the street this morning, and the main gate's standing wide open. It's on a drive chain, and the security guard probably couldn't close it without power and just headed for the hills."

Hughes nodded. "Good point. When we finish here, take some guys and tools and manhandle it closed. Bust the drive linkage if you have to, but get it closed. And take some chain and a padlock too. We're off the beaten track in an industrial area, and we can't really be seen from the streets because of the terminal tanks, but better safe than sorry. I don't like the sound of things and the radio traffic isn't very encouraging either."

"What's the latest?" Gowan asked.

"Confused," Hughes said. "There was the national alert about a solar storm on the NOAA Weather Radio frequencies, but it kept breaking up, and reception was crap until earlier today. I'm thinking since the Northern Lights didn't start fading until last night there was still a lot of atmospheric interference, but communications are improving. I've been scanning all the frequencies and picking up bits and pieces. Best I can tell, what's happening here in Wilmington is being repeated everywhere. Scumbags are seizing the opportunity to do whatever they want, and desperate people are just trying to make sure their families survive. The police are losing control, if they ever had it. There's no cell service and not much on the marine frequencies, though it sounds like the Coasties at Oak Island Station are still in business. They answered my call but told me to get off the air unless I had an emergency. I tried the pilots too, but I couldn't raise anyone." Hughes shrugged. "Basically, I think we're on our own."

"It's all over the country?" Georgia Howell asked.

Hughes shrugged. "I think it must be."

The group grew quiet until Rich Martin broke the silence. "I wish there was some way to contact our families."

"I'm sure we all do, First," Hughes said, "but we just have to have faith they'll be okay and figure out what to do next."

"Well, one thing's for sure," Gowan said, nodding towards shore. "We're a hell of a lot better off than those poor bastards out there. We got power and hot showers and at least a few months of food and water."

"Yeah, and I'm thinking someone might figure that out," Hughes said. "It's only a matter of time. We can't be seen from the street and the locked gate might discourage the curious, but we can be seen from the river, so starting immediately we're going to set blackout discipline. I want all blackout curtains closed on all windows. We don't show any lights at night. None. Is that clear?"

"Absolutely. Good idea," Gowan replied.

"What about noise?" Rich asked. "With power down and no traffic, you can probably hear the emergency genny running a long way."

"We're quite a ways from the gate," Georgia said, "so I doubt the street's a problem, but sound carries pretty far over water. I'll set an extra security watch and tell them to keep a sharp eye on the river, especially upstream toward downtown Wilmington." She sighed. "Then I guess we just have to hope none of the looters decide to become river pirates."

"And if they do," Gowan asked, "just exactly how do we discourage them?"

"They'd have difficulty from the river side, so they'd probably land at the dock and come up the gangway," Hughes said. "Georgia, when you get back from locking the gate let's take in the gangway. If they can't get on board, they may just go away."

There were nods around the table. Captain Hughes rose. "Okay, folks, time to get back to work."

The others stood and moved towards the door, but Gowan held back a bit.

"Uh, Cap?"

"Yes, Chief?" Hughes asked.

"I'm thinking the looters might be after easy pickings now, but sooner or later one of them is gonna be smart enough to think of all the fuel in these shore tanks, not to mention the thirty-five thousand tons of diesel and gasoline we're hauling." Gowan paused. "To say nothing of the problem of being tied up next to a terminal full of gasoline and diesel if those fires shift direction."

"That already occurred to me, Chief, but one way or another, I don't plan on us being here much longer."

LEVI JENKINS' FISHING CAMP
BLACK RIVER, NORTH CAROLINA

DAY 6

The ax bit into the wood with a satisfying thump and Levi Jenkins grinned to himself as the log separated cleanly, the pieces clattering down on either side of the chopping block. Moisture gleamed on the hard muscles of his ebony torso in the warmth of early spring, and he set down the ax to swat away a drop of sweat forming on the tip of his nose. It was liberating to lose himself in the mindless work and put aside the constant worry of the last few days.

He looked at the wood scattered around the chopping block and judged he had enough. He nodded to Little Tony, his nine-year-old son, who leapt from where he was standing to one side and began gathering the wood to carry it to the neatly stacked woodpile beside the outdoor kitchen. Though 'kitchen' was a bit of a stretch, Levi thought.

Basically it was an open-air structure with a rough wooden floor and a shingled roof supported by four stout corner posts. From the roof protruded the stovepipe for the enormous wood cookstove, and each of the four corner posts was fitted with tie-down points so sides of the structure could be either enclosed by roll-down tarps to block the wind or left open to take advantage of a cooling breeze. A sink with running water with counter space down two sides completed the layout, and a simple wooden worktable graced the center of the structure to provide more work area. It was rough, but functional, and during the warmer months avoided the necessity of heating up the main house while cooking. An additional wood stove in the 'regular' kitchen of the main house got a good workout in the colder months when it was too cold to cook outside, and when the heat was a welcome addition to the small home's interior.

Levi heard footsteps and turned to see his father-in-law approaching from the direction of the river. Anthony McCoy looked past Levi to his grandson and namesake stacking the wood, and beamed.

"Well, looks like you got a hardworking helper there, Levi," Anthony said. "That is one fine woodpile. Good job, Tony."

"Thanks, Grandpa. And guess what? Dad says when I finish all my chores, we can go fishing. Wanna come?"

The old man looked upward, as if concentrating on something, and stroked his neatly trimmed goatee, its snow-white stubble a stark contrast to his face. "Well, let's see, now that I think about it, I don't believe I have any prior engagements, so yes, I believe I will go along." He looked back at the boy and smiled. "And if you promise not to tell anyone, I'll show you my very favorite place to dig night crawlers."

"Okay, deal," the boy said, returning the smile.

"And that would be AFTER chores, and I believe there are a few left on the list," Levi said.

"Yes, sir," little Tony said, and started toward the chicken coop.

"Where you going?" Levi asked. "I thought gathering the eggs was on your sister's chore list."

"It was," Tony said, "but Sally claims she's afraid of the chickens, so I switched with her. She's making my bed instead." The little boy rolled his eyes so expressively Levi had to stifle a laugh. "Besides," Tony continued, "she don't wanna do nothing since she got here but mope around and gripe about how dumb it is to be here, but I think it's awesome."

Levi laughed. "Well, thank you for your support. Now get those eggs in to your mom and grandma."

Tony nodded and hurried away, and Levi turned back toward his father-in-law.

"See anything on the river?" Levi asked.

"Not a thing," Anthony responded, "and I took the kayak a mile in each direction. There wasn't any activity at either of the camps you can see from the river, so I don't think anyone's moved into them yet. Likely they won't now, so I suspect we're the only ones around for several miles. I also had another look at our inlet from the river. Those willows you planted a few years back are perfect. They hang right down to the water like a curtain, and you can't even tell the inlet is there. And we're so far back off the river, as long as we mind how we show lights at night, I don't think anyone will know we're here."

The older man gave an involuntary shudder. "My only problem with that willow curtain is thinking about a big ol' cottonmouth laying up in the branches when we're going through, just ready to drop on my head."

Levi shuddered as well. "Damn. I hadn't thought about that. I must've been through there fifty times without a care, but now I'll be nervous as hell every time." Levi paused. "What say we hide one of those long cane poles somewhere on either side of the willows so we can poke in ahead of us and shake it around before we go through? That should scare any sunning snakes into the water."

"Damn good idea," Anthony agreed. "I do hate snakes."

Levi nodded and looked back toward the neat little homestead, surveying his handiwork of many years. A wisp of smoke rose from the stovepipe of the outdoor kitchen, no doubt from the remains of the fire the women had kindled to cook breakfast, and Levi's face once again took on the look of worry he'd had so many times since the blackout.

"You got your worry scowl on again," Anthony said. "What you worried about now?"

Levi sighed. "Everything, Anthony. But just now I was thinking about smoke. If we keep the wood dry and learn to control the air, we can keep it pretty clear, but I reckon it will still have a wood-smoke smell. I was just wondering if it's likely to give us away."

The older man shrugged. "These woods are thick as hell and stretch at least ten miles in every direction, with poor roads. Maybe a small plane or helicopter could pinpoint the smoke, but that would be about the only way. And if anyone is flying over, they'd see the clearing and maybe a reflection off the solar panels anyway. But I don't think anyone's gonna find us coming overland. Even if they smell smoke, it could be coming from anywhere. Hell, you got that twisty road coming in here camouflaged so well I can't hardly find it myself, and I helped you build it."

"I know, I know. But I still worry," Levi said.

"I know you do, but you need to stop. You've done a wonderful job here. We got a tight, snug house, as much electricity as we need, and hot and cold running water. In a month's time, there's not going to be many folks can take a hot shower and use a real toilet. You got food laid by for us all for a year and extra to boot, seeds and a good garden spot, and with the rabbits and chickens we brought from the house, we'll have meat and eggs, even if huntin' an' fishin' is poor." He paused. "Hell, you hit a home run in my book."

"If someone doesn't try to take it all away from us," Levi said. "There's just me and you to protect the family and there's gonna be a whole lot of really desperate folks out there, Anthony. I wish there were more of us, not only for defense, but for the social side of things. Little Sally already thinks I ruined her life, and truth be known, Celia and Jo aren't really happy to be here either. I mean I know they UNDERSTAND why we have to be here, but I can tell the isolation is already starting to get to them."

Anthony nodded. "It's a fact women are social creatures. I think men can be much more content in isolation. But what exactly were we supposed to do? We couldn't go blabbing around about our plans, and no one trustworthy seemed interested. You got no family to speak of but us, and Celia's our only living child. And I SURE as hell don't want to be spending the apocalypse with none of my no-account relatives, nor Josephine's either."

Levi hesitated. "That prepper group over at Bryson's Corners. We might still hook up with them if..."

Anthony was already shaking his head. "There's good people and bad people, black and white," he said, "and you know I'm not one to be hollerin' 'racist' every time some white man opens his mouth before he engages his brain. Black people say pretty dumb stuff sometimes, and for sure, no race has a monopoly on stupid. I go mostly by how I see folks actin' more than what they say. I suspect most of the members there are good folks, but there's a few of them who make me uncomfortable, no matter how friendly they might seem. I don't want to be the only black family in that group. At least not yet." He paused. "We gotta play the hand we've been dealt. I expect we'll do just fine as hidden river rats."

Levi nodded and grew pensive.

"What?" Anthony asked. "I've seen that look before. C'mon, out with it."

Levi hesitated. "There are some people I trust completely, not far away."

"The folks on your ship?" Anthony asked, and Levi nodded.

"You sure you can trust them? And why would they want to come here anyway? And what about food, will ours stretch?"

"First, yes, I trust them completely" Levi replied, "most of them, anyway. And I'm not sure any would want to come here, but some might, at least the single folks might come temporarily. There's food aboard, so we could probably barter for a bit extra if any of the guys come back with us, and even if we don't, I think we can stretch what we have over at least two or three more people, especially if hunting and fishing are even marginal."

"You sure you've thought this out, Levi?"

"Actually, I've been thinking about it since we got here. It didn't seem right to desert the ship, but the family came first. And this has possibilities, even if they are a bit remote. These folks are used to operating independently and they all have practical skills we can use. There aren't any repair shops at sea. Anybody I invite here will be able to pull their weight."

Anthony looked skeptical. "How do you know the ship's even there anymore, it's been six days?"

"I don't for sure," Levi said, "but the radio's getting clearer. I didn't want to transmit, but I can risk a quick call to see if they're still docked in Wilmington."

"And if they are, what then?"

"One thing at a time, Anthony. One thing at a time."

Levi Jenkins' Fishing Camp

Day 6, 8:00 p.m.

Levi and Anthony stood beside the flat-bottom aluminum boat, surveying their handiwork in the fading light. The sun had just dipped below the tree line and would be fully set in half an hour. The pair were going over everything one last time. They both had sidearms and holsters, along with an AR-15 and Anthony's old Model 12 Winchester shotgun. Two pairs of night-vision goggles lay on the boat seats.

Levi always planned on the river as their main access. Water didn't leave tracks and he could move on the river stealthily. Mounted on the boat's stern was a twenty-horsepower outboard, the model and brand chosen for its quietness rather than speed or power. At Anthony's suggestion, Levi muted the motor even more with a layer of adhesive Ensolite insulation under the cowling. A large bow-mounted trolling motor powered by two deep-cycle marine batteries completed the propulsion options. He'd had to compromise, as the older model outboards wouldn't meet his noise requirements and none of the newer models were completely free of electronics. Nor did the older trolling motors have near the power he needed. He'd solved the problem by opting for the newer models and shielding both the outboard and trolling motor in makeshift Faraday cages made of old oil drums lined with plywood. Overkill, as it turned out, since Levi had planned for the worst-case scenario of an electronics-frying EMP, and the damage from the solar storm was largely confined to the power grid. Better safe than sorry, he thought, as he looked at the outfitted boat.

Anthony broke Levi's reverie. "That about it?"

"Almost," Levi said. "I'm bringing a thirty-eight revolver and the old twenty gauge, along with ammo. We don't have much for those anyway and they're mismatches to everything else we have. I figure they'll need some protection, and other than maybe a thirty-eight in the Old Man's safe, there are no guns aboard."

"Gettin' kind of generous, aren't you? Guns and ammo will be more valuable than gold about now, I expect."

"I'm not GIVING them away. I'll be looking for a fair trade. Besides, if we bring back recruits, it might make Captain Hughes a bit more willing to send along some extra food with them."

"Fair enough," Anthony said. "They expecting us?"

Levi nodded. "I got a light signal arranged so they don't think we're river pirates and try to drop something on our heads when we come alongside. We'll leave here just after midnight. If there's anyone along the river between here and there, I want to give them plenty of time to get to sleep. My biggest concern is downtown Wilmington. I'd like to pass there in the wee hours, when folks are likely to be sleeping the soundest."

"How long you figure?"

Levi shook his head. "I've never run the river at low speed in the dark with night-vision goggles, so your guess is as good as mine. I'm figuring four hours max."

"It'll be longer coming back against the current, and the boat will be heavier." Anthony paused. "Well, hopefully it'll be heavier."

"Yeah, but even at that, if we start back at midnight tomorrow night, we should still make it back here before daylight."

Anthony nodded. "Well, I guess you've thought of everything. Make that almost everything. I'm gonna go get a long cane pole and put it in the boat. And by the way, stealth or no stealth, when we're going out through those damned willows we WILL have the spotlight on high beam. I'm not dancin' with no snake in the dark."

DAY 6, 8:00 P.M.

Hughes called the senior officers together again that evening to announce his intentions. He tried to suppress his anxiety as he glanced around the coffee table, awaiting their reactions. Gowan spoke first.

"You'll get no argument from me," the chief engineer said. "I live in the area."

"All of us here do, or at least we live closer to Beaumont than here," Georgia Howell said, "but the problem is how it will play out with the rest of the crew. We might not exactly be a democracy, but I believe there'll be some push back." She looked at Hughes. "How you planning on selling this, Captain?"

Hughes ran a hand through his hair. "Well, I won't lie. I want to get home like everyone else, but Beaumont is our only logical destination regardless. I can't reach anyone in the company, and I doubt I will. Things here are generally going to hell, and Beaumont is the closest company terminal. I'm still responsible for the ship and cargo. If we eventually have to leave the ship, I want to at least leave it secured to the company dock."

"Things might not be any better in Texas," Rich Martin pointed out.

Hughes shrugged. "They're probably not, but at least it's worth a shot and will get most of us closer to home."

"I think the 'most of us' is key," Dan Gowan agreed. "It'll get the majority of the crew near home, but what do we do if some refuse. We're stretched pretty thin in the best of circumstances, and with the automation down, we really can't afford to lose anyone."

"Well, I can't force anyone to go," Hughes said. "This isn't the navy. Legally, we're in a US port and anyone can sign off at any time; all I can do is shake his or her hand and pay them off. I figure sooner or later all this uncertainty is going to get the better of folks, and they'll strike off for home on their own anyway. If we wait too long, we won't be able to move the ship." He paused. "Any thoughts on who we might lose?"

"Of the deck officers, probably only Tex," Georgia said. "Her folks live in western New Jersey and she's very close. I doubt she'll sail in the opposite direction. Among the unlicensed guys in the deck department, a couple are from somewhere here on the East Coast, but they've only been aboard a few weeks, so I don't know much about them. I think everyone in the steward's department lives close to Beaumont, so that won't likely be a problem. I'll let Rich speak for the engine gang."

"We'll lose Bill Wiggins, the second engineer, for sure," Rich Martin said. "He lives in Maine with his wife and kid and another on the way. In fact, he was about to get off on vacation to be home for the delivery. No way he's heading south voluntarily. On the unlicensed side, Jimmy the pumpman lives in Virginia, but I don't really know which way he'd lean. The rest of the engine department would be okay with the trip south." He paused. "Except, of course, for Levi. He's home, and not likely to be going anywhere else. And speaking of Levi, when is he supposed to be here?"

"He was a bit vague on the radio," Hughes said, "but I expect him in the wee hours." He turned to Georgia Howell. "The watch straight on the light signal?"

She nodded. "Two longs, one short, three longs."

"All right, I guess that's it. We'll deal with being shorthanded if and when the problem arises. I want to hear what Levi has to say, since he's been out in the world. Let's tentatively plan on calling the whole crew together tomorrow after breakfast."

The others nodded and rose, and Hughes followed them towards the office door and closed it behind them before walking back to his desk. He picked up his favorite picture of his wife, Laura, smiling out at him, her long auburn hair framing a beautiful face accented by lovely brown eyes, and her arms around their twin daughters, one on either side of her, mugging for the camera. He set the picture down gently and mentally sent up what must be the thousandth prayer for their safety, then walked slowly toward his bedroom, knowing even as he did so sleep was unlikely to come.

Hughes' Residence
Pecan Grove
Oleander, Texas

Day 6, 11:30 p.m.

Laura Hughes held Jordan's picture and murmured another short prayer for his safety. He'd called from Wilmington as he always did if he had cell service and the hour wasn't too late. This time he'd called from anchor as they awaited a pilot, knowing she'd likely be fast asleep by the time the ship docked. He was considerate like that, though she'd told him repeatedly that hearing his voice was worth being awakened.

She gazed at the picture, her favorite photo of him. He was totally camera shy, and she joked in posed family pictures he always looked like his underwear was a few sizes too tight. This was a candid shot on the bridge of his ship, Jordan's dark hair flecked with just the right amount of gray and a bit mussed by a breeze, his slight squint as he stared into the far distance unable to obscure his clear blue eyes. He looked tan and fit and in charge; she called it his 'captain's' picture. She'd received it out of the blue in an envelope with Dan Gowan's return address and with a sticky note reading, "Thought you might like this picture of Cap I took when he wasn't looking. It's the only one I've seen where he doesn't look like he has a stick up his ass. Best, Dan." She laughed every time she thought of it.

A small desk lamp kept the dark at bay, and she could hear the low throb of the generator in its enclosure behind the garage. Jordan had installed the generator after one too many hurricanes left them without power for three weeks. It was a compromise between capacity and fuel consumption: big enough to run limited lights, the well pump, and the fridge and freezer. On hot southeast Texas nights, she temporarily diverted power from the freezer to two small window air conditioners in the master and guest bedrooms. She smiled, the guest-room unit was another 'compromise,' as the twins each wanted the unit in their own bedrooms. Jordan had issued a Solomon-like decision and installed the unit in 'neutral territory.' The girls were informed they could double bunk in the guest room during power outages or sweat. He called it a 'compromise,' but the twins characterized it as a 'decree.'

She looked at the pile of unpaid bills and sighed. Oh well, with power down, there was likely no one at work to pay anyway; not a pressing problem in the scheme of things. Truthfully, other than Jordan's absence, they had no major concerns. Water was no problem as long as she could run the well pump, and the generator ran on propane. She'd just had the tank filled last week to take advantage of low off-season prices. They were always prepared for hurricanes, and the ample kitchen pantry was well stocked. And if push came to shove, they could always eat pecans until the garden started producing more.

The sturdy old farmhouse built by her great-grandparents sat well off the blacktop, nestled in a grove of ninety-year-old pecan trees from which the property took its name. Laura thought naming property was pretentious in the extreme, and the practice always conjured up visions of yuppie assholes named 'J Something the Third' with overpriced McMansions built on one-acre lots in trendy suburbs. Houses the owners named 'Long Ridge' or 'Beechwood' prior to adding ostentatious driveway entrances suggesting Camelot lay within.

But unlike those efforts to fabricate a past that never was, Pecan Grove was a name bestowed not by the owners, but by area inhabitants. A name arising over time as the towering pecan trees grew to a landmark of note in the otherwise flat pastures and rice fields of Southeast Texas. A point of reference, such that 'out by the Pecan Grove' or 'about a mile past the Pecan Grove' became common directions. So common, in fact, Laura's ancestors finally adopted the term as the name for home, without the least bit of pretension or posturing. It was always just 'home' to them, with 'the' omitted for convenience and 'Pecan Grove' becoming a place instead of a feature of the landscape.

And those old trees still produced a bountiful crop each year, a small side business to Laura's large animal veterinary practice. All the proceeds of bulk pecan sales went into the girls' college funds, and the ten-acre pecan grove in most years provided sufficient surplus for a seemingly never-ending supply of pecans for home consumption and gifts to family and friends. Laura's honey-glazed roasted pecans were a coveted Christmas gift.

No, they weren't likely to starve, regardless of the length of the power outage, and her only real concern was Jordan. Was he safe, and when would he get home?

CHAPTER SIX

DAY 7, 2:00 A.M.

The best-laid plans, thought Levi, as he watched the river in front of the boat, the landscape a dull green in the NV goggles. Dull green but clear as day, thanks to a full moon. He'd counted on moonlight, and though a trial night river run had been on his 'preparation to-do list,' like many things, it had remained undone. He hadn't really appreciated just how much visibility the moonlight reflecting off the water would provide. It made things much easier—and much riskier. The moon was so bright, the NV goggles made the trip like navigating in broad daylight, and they'd made much better time than he'd planned. They quickly reached the point where the Black River became the Cape Fear, and the Peter Point highway bridge loomed across the river in the distance ahead. Levi cut the outboard and the muted muttering died, leaving only the sounds of the river around them.

"Let's switch to the trolling motor," Levi said softly. Sounds carried a long way over the water.

"Isn't it a little early," Anthony whispered back. "We're still a half mile from the first bridge."

"With this moon, anyone looking can see us, and I don't want to take a chance the noise will get them looking," Levi said.

Anthony bobbed his head and lowered the trolling motor.

They moved more slowly on the electric trolling motor, but still at a respectable clip with the current behind them. Soon they glided silently under the first bridge and a few minutes later saw the old battleship *USS North Carolina* on their right in her permanent berth. On the east bank, scattered fires burned in the distance in Wilmington proper, and much closer, Levi detected movement in the upscale shopping district lining the river's edge.

Well, so much for everyone sleeping. Evidently looters didn't keep regular hours. Ahead of him at the trolling motor controls, Anthony cast nervous glances to his left—he'd seen the movement too. Levi looked astern. They moved silently at three or four knots, leaving a wake visible in the moonlight, pointing at them like a telltale arrow. He glanced at the eastern shore again and then ahead to the Cape Fear Memorial Bridge towering above the river's surface. Downstream of the bridge, the restaurants and trendy businesses of the Wilmington riverfront gave way to industrial areas, and Eagle Island on the west bank held nothing but a dredge spoils area where the US Army Corp of Engineers dumped years' worth of muck dredged from the river bottom. If they could make it past Memorial Bridge unseen, they'd have smooth sailing to the *Pecos Trader* .

It seemed to take forever to reach the bridge. Just as they started under the span, a large heavy object fell from the sky, striking the water with a tremendous splash, narrowly missing the boat and soaking both men.

"What the hell—" Anthony gasped as he flinched away from the impact by reflex, inadvertently pulling the trolling motor tiller hard over and radically altering the boat's course—a chance event that saved them. The boat exited the shadow of the bridge several feet off her original course, and the assailant waiting on the downstream side was unable to adjust in time. The heavy steel pipe he released speared the water just aft of the boat, soaking Levi a second time as he cranked the outboard.

"Pull up the trolling motor, Anthony," Levi yelled. "They know we're here."

Above him he heard shouted curses and loud arguing as the assailants blamed each other for the failed attack. The little outboard coughed to life, and Levi ran it up to full speed, such as it was, and immediately started zigzagging downstream as he heard semiautomatic gunfire above and behind him. Fortunately, their attackers' marksmanship was no more accurate than their makeshift bombardment, and the thunderous assault resulted in multiple splashes around them, but none seemed to hit the boat. It was over in seconds, and Levi swallowed his heart.

"You… you okay, Anthony?" he called when they were out of range.

"I might have to clean out my pants, but other than that, yeah, I'm okay," the older man replied. "You?"

"Yeah, I'm okay. I just… damn!"

"You hit?" Anthony called, concern in his voice.

"Not me. But there's water in the boat. They hit us somewhere."

"What are we going to do?" Anthony asked.

"Haul ass and pray. We're only a couple of miles from the ship. You take the flashlight and see if you can find the leak and plug it with something. If we start taking on water too badly, I'll run the boat to the bank and we'll continue on foot if we have to."

"This is a fine how do you do," Anthony said. "If the boat sinks, how the hell are we going to get home?"

"We'll cross that bridge when we come to it," Levi said.

"Huh," Anthony muttered. "If you don't mind, I'd just as soon steer clear of bridges from now on."

M/V PECOS TRADER
BUCKEYE MARINE TERMINAL
WILMINGTON, NORTH CAROLINA

DAY 7, 3:05 A.M.

"There it is," the sailor said, pointing.

His watch partner followed his pointing finger.

"That's the signal all right. Flash him back, then help me get the pilot ladder out," the second man said, as his shipmate moved to comply.

Minutes later, an aluminum boat with two men aboard pulled into the beams of their flashlights and moved sluggishly to press its length against the ship's hull, just below the dangling ladder. The men in the boat were standing ankle deep in water.

"Damn, Levi," one of the sailors said, "you're damn near sunk."

"Obviously," Levi said, "get us lines down here so we can tie her off bow and stern to the ship's rail. We can save her if she doesn't sink!"

The sailors ran to grab rope from the nearby deck locker and, minutes later, had the boat safe from immediate danger. They threw down additional lines to allow Levi to tie off gear in the boat to be hoisted aboard. When satisfied they'd done all they could, Levi took a last look around and nodded, and both newcomers climbed the swaying rope ladder to the main deck. They reached the deck just as the chief mate arrived, summoned by radio.

"Good to see you, Levi," Georgia Howell said, offering her hand. "Who's your friend?"

"Thanks, ma'am," Levi said, returning her handshake. "This is my father-in-law, Anthony McCoy. Anthony, this is Georgia Howell, the chief mate." Levi grinned and nodded at the two sailors. "And these two deck apes are Charlie Lynch and Pete Sonnier."

Anthony shook hands all around as Levi turned back to the chief mate.

"Which brings me to another point," Hughes said. "If you do run into trouble, I'd really prefer it if you break contact and not lead an army of bloodthirsty gangbangers back on your heels. The only thing keeping us fairly safe is no one knows we're here."

Kinsey nodded. "Understood. How about this? On the way there, we have to pass the main gate to the container terminal upstream anyway, and we'll make sure it's passable. I'll move our boat upstream to the container dock and if we're coming out with bad guys on our tail, I'll radio ahead and the boat can be standing by to haul ass as soon as we reach them. I might not be able to prevent leading any bad guys back to your neighborhood, but maybe I can avoid leading them right to your front door."

"You do realize if they look downstream from the container docks, they may see us sitting here anyway?"

Kinsey shook his head. "The container dock is really long, so we'll board as far upstream as possible then head farther upstream and across the river to keep their attention focused away from you. We'll hang out just in sight across the river until sundown and then move downstream under the cover of darkness. That's the best I can do."

"Better than nothing," Hughes said, "but let's just hope you don't meet any bad guys."

EAST BOUND ON SHIPYARD BOULEVARD
WILMINGTON, NORTH CAROLINA

DAY 8, 1:00 P.M.

Senior Chief Boatswain's Mate Matt Kinsey, USCG, was conflicted as he sat in the golf cart rolling down the deserted street at a blinding ten miles per hour. It was infinitely preferable to walking and they'd get to their destination much faster, but four men in full body armor and carrying automatic rifles looked a bit ridiculous perched in golf carts. Oh well, maybe if they did encounter opposition, they could take them out while they were still laughing.

The number of burned-out buildings increased as they traveled east. Some still smoldered, and the stench of rain-soaked ashes hung heavy in the air. There were no moving vehicles, and the few pedestrians scouring the pathetic ruins scurried into hiding at the sight of armed men. The whole tragic scene reminded Kinsey of television newscasts from some war-torn third world country, not Wilmington, North Carolina; the improbable comparison made even more apt by the furtive actions of the residents. If civilians were already scattering at the sight of armed men, even four assholes in golf carts, it said a lot about what they'd endured in the short time since the blackout. It also made Kinsey increasingly uneasy about riding exposed down the middle of the street.

"It's the next left," he said.

Jeff Baker nodded. "I've been to HQ before, Chief."

Kinsey bit back a reply and nodded as Baker turned the wheel hard to make the sharp turn onto Carolina Beach Road, heading northwest. Another quarter mile on this road and then right on Medical Center Drive for a quarter of a mile, and they'd be there.

"What's that up ahead?" Baker asked, and Kinsey felt the cart slow.

"Stop," Kinsey said as he clawed a monocular from his pocket to glass the intersection ahead.

"Looks like a Humvee blocking the intersection," Kinsey said, sitting the monocular on the seat beside him and keying his shoulder-mounted microphone.

"Jackson, do you copy?" he said.

"Go ahead," came the reply from the following cart.

"Hold where you are. I think these are the good guys, but Baker and I are going to check it out. Copy?"

"I copy," said Jackson.

Kinsey nodded to Baker and they started forward. As they approached the roadblock, the gunner on top of the vehicle tracked them with an M2 .50-caliber machine gun. When they were a hundred feet from the roadblock, a soldier clad in body armor and carrying an M4 stepped from behind the Humvee, his hand raised.

"Stop right there," he called. "Exit your vehicle. Leave your weapons in your vehicle. Tell your friends back there to approach slowly and do the same. This is an order, not a request. Be advised you are covered from multiple locations and we will open fire if you fail to obey. You have ten seconds to comply."

Kinsey looked around and spotted the muzzle of another machine gun peeking through some low shrubs on the left side of the road just ahead, and he suspected there were more he didn't see.

"All right. Don't shoot," he called, and keyed his mike to call Jackson forward.

Three minutes later, all four Coasties were standing by their golf carts, awaiting further instructions, and the soldier at the roadblock called out again.

"All right. Approach slowly with your hands in the air. Do not make any sudden moves."

The four started forward, and when they were halfway to the roadblock, the soldier halted them and instructed Kinsey to approach alone.

Pretty smart, thought Kinsey, he's separated us from our vehicles and weapons and is keeping the majority at a distance while he questions one of us. It looked like the guy had danced this dance before.

The soldier waved Kinsey to a stop ten feet away and the two studied each other silently. Kinsey noted sergeant's stripes on the soldier's ACUs, and the man seemed to relax when he spotted the insignia on Kinsey's coveralls. The sergeant's face split into a grin.

"I heard you Coasties were on a tight budget," he said, "but golf carts? Seriously? Is the clown car in the shop?"

Kinsey returned the grin. "Small service, big job," he replied. "Wear it out, fix it up, make it work. That's our motto."

"I thought it was *Semper Paratus* —Always Prepared," the soldier said.

Kinsey's smile faded. "That too, though I don't feel very friggin' prepared for this."

"None of us were," the soldier said, closing the distance and extending his hand. "Josh Wright, North Carolina National Guard. Now, Chief, what brings y'all into our fair city. If you're looking for the golf course, you're headed the wrong way."

Kinsey took the offered hand. "Matt Kinsey." He glanced pointedly up at the machine gunner.

"Oh, right," Wright said, releasing Kinsey's hand. "Y'all can point those elsewhere, boys," he called to the gunners. "They don't appear to be hostile." He then waved to the other Coasties. "Y'all come on in."

Wright turned back to Kinsey as the other Coasties approached. "So again, Chief, what the hell are you doing running around Wilmington in golf carts?"

"We're from the Oak Island Station, and we're trying to get over to the command center. We got as close as we could on the river, and the golf carts were the only transportation we could find," Kinsey explained.

Wright hesitated. "You don't know?"

"Know what?" Kinsey asked.

"The Coast Guard building was attacked two nights ago. It burned to the ground."

"What? Who the hell would attack the Coast Guard HQ? And why? We HELP people, for Christ's sake! I can see if it was a food store or…" He broke off, unable to articulate his confusion. "This… this just doesn't make sense. What about our people? Was anyone hurt? Where did they set up?"

Wright just shook his head and looked at the ground, unable to meet Kinsey's eye. It took a moment to sink in.

"All… all of them? Are you saying they're all dead?" Kinsey demanded.

"As far as we know," Wright said. "We got a Mayday from your folks and saw the fire from the armory. We sent out a team immediately, but by the time we got there, the building was already completely engulfed and we couldn't get close. We found a dozen bodies in the ruins yesterday, but the building is unsafe and we couldn't search thoroughly." He hesitated again. "They… they had their hands tied behind their backs. It appeared they'd all been killed execution style."

Red began to flood Kinsey's vision and his heart raced as Wright continued.

"The 'why' I can't answer, but as far as the 'who' goes, it was likely gangbangers. When the lights didn't come on by the second day and it became pretty obvious law enforcement and everything else was being overwhelmed, the stronger gangs saw an opportunity and took it. They have a 'command structure,' so to speak, and filled the power vacuum. And to be honest, they were a helluva lot more effective than the police. I mean, there's probably only three or four hundred police officers and sheriff's deputies combined, and with everything else going to hell, there's no way they could handle a gangbanger uprising too, so the gangs sort of took over. Let's face it, if you've got no problem murdering anyone that gives you any trouble right on the spot, it tends to get folks' attention. By the time the governor called out the guard and those of us who could respond mobilized, the police were already overwhelmed and were forted up in various places with their families and loved ones. We were already outnumbered and playing defense when we got here."

"But what's that got to do with the Coast Guard? Why were they attacked?" Kinsey asked.

Wright shrugged. "Who knows how these bastards think? I guess maybe the Coasties wore uniforms and represented governmental authority, and it's not like they were a hardened target. I mean, it was an office building with open parking lots all the way around it and multiple entrances. There wasn't even a damn fence! I mean, I know our CO was in touch with your CO and wanted him to move over to the armory since it's at least somewhat defensible, but your guy was reluctant."

"Why?" Kinsey asked.

"Well, it kind of makes sense in a way. I think your skipper was a pretty stand-up guy and he was trying to figure out some way to make a difference in an impossible situation. He apparently had pretty good backup generator capability and all his coms were concentrated there in the command center, so if he moved, he was sure to lose some of whatever capability remained. Also, with the media down and communications being as piss poor as they were, there was no way to spread the word if they moved, and more of your people were straggling in as they were able. If he moved, they likely wouldn't know where to report." Wright paused. "And I guess like you, he didn't figure anyone would be targeting the Coast Guard."

"Who the hell does this?" muttered Baker.

"The same stupid worthless assholes that torch their own neighborhoods and then shoot at the firefighters who come to put it out," Jackson said.

The men nodded agreement and then fell silent, processing what they'd just heard. Kinsey broke the silence.

"What's the status here? Are you guys making any headway?"

Wright shook his head. "Negative. We're forted up ourselves, back in the armory about a mile up the road. We push out patrols like this one up all the major cross streets every morning to show the flag and maybe give folks a bit of hope, but come nighttime, we'll be back behind the barbed wire. Most of us are fortunate enough to live outside the city, so at least we don't have to worry about our families facing gang violence. Some of the guys that live in the city brought their families inside. The CO said no at first, but it became pretty obvious the families stayed or the guys were leaving, so he eased up. We've got a storage tank with a couple of thousand gallons of drinking water and there are a couple of little lakes over by the armory. We suck water out of them with a tank truck for flushing toilets and taking outdoor showers. We got maybe ten days of MREs and twice that of diesel fuel, depending on how we conserve it. If we don't get resupplied before then, I guess it's game over."

"What do you hear from up the chain of command?" Kinsey asked. "Surely there's some sort of recovery plan?"

"Maybe on paper, but from where I'm standing here on the ground, it's not working," Wright said. "I mean, the governor's office screwed around over two days before calling up the Guard, but with communications being spotty and all the media down, very few of the notifications got through anyway. And even if they did, enough of them didn't that 'no notification' is a pretty good excuse and what person wants to go off and leave their family when all hell is breaking loose? I mean, I figured we'd be needed and left my wife and kids with my brother's family and reported on my own, but way less than fifty percent of my unit showed up, and to be honest, I'm starting to feel like a chump. It would be different if we could make a difference, but all we're really doing is trying to stay alive ourselves."

"How about the regular army," Kinsey said, "or FEMA?"

"Ah yes, FEMA," Wright said, spitting the acronym out like a curse word. "We had a visit from a FEMA official. He came in by chopper to 'brief us on the recovery effort.' His main concern seemed to be he couldn't get his laptop to boot up so he could show us his PowerPoint presentation. Apparently he couldn't answer any questions without his presentation, so he spent two hours telling us nothing in great detail then got on his chopper and left, never to be seen again. I wouldn't count on FEMA.

"And as far as the regular army goes," Wright continued, "that's way above my pay grade, but I do know they have to be called out by the President after he declares a disaster. I figure if anything qualifies as a disaster, it's this. But the thing is, where they gonna stage from? I mean, if there's a hurricane or flood or whatever, they stage from places that aren't impacted and move resources to the disaster. But what do you do if the friggin' disaster is EVERYWHERE? And part of the unwritten deal with soldiers is the security of their families. It's one thing to expect troops from Fort Campbell or Fort Bragg to deploy to the sandbox with their families safe and sound at home, and it's quite another to ask them to leave their loved ones in danger. And besides, the way I look at it, there's no need to deploy troops. There's plenty of disaster to go around. What would be gained by moving troops from one place where things are going to hell to another place where things are going to hell? At least if troops are providing relief services around their home bases, they're helping friends and family." He shook his head. "I'm thinking the cavalry isn't coming to the party."

"You're just a little ray of sunshine, aren't you," Kinsey said.

"Just realistic," Wright said. "If you'd seen what I've seen in the last few days, you'd feel the same."

Kinsey nodded and sighed. "I expect you're right. Well, I guess we need to get out of your hair."

"You headed back to your boat?"

Kinsey hesitated and looked at his men before responding. "We're only a quarter of a mile from HQ, and we all had friends there. I think we all want to at least go have a look."

Wright nodded. "Tell you what, it's not like we were accomplishing anything here. We'll run you over there."

"Thanks," Kinsey said, but Wright was already turning to speak into his radio.

"All Bird Dog units, this is Bird Dog Actual," Wright said. "Mount up, repeat, mount up."

Kinsey heard the Humvee rumble to life beside him and then another, and glanced over to see a second vehicle he'd missed parked across a parking lot in the shadow of a Bojangles restaurant. Meanwhile three soldiers emerged from the shrubbery on the west side of the street, one of them carrying the machine gun he'd noticed earlier and the other two armed with M-4s. The second Humvee just drove across the grass strip and sidewalk, and the soldiers started moving towards the two vehicles, but Wright called out last minute instructions rearranging them between the two vehicles as Kinsey and his men walked back to the golf carts to retrieve their weapons.

"Y'all can ride with me," Wright said from the open passenger-side door of his Humvee as they returned. "Plenty of room."

The Coasties mumbled their thanks and climbed into the vehicle. Less than a minute later, they pulled into the parking lot of their former headquarters. The building was a blackened ruin, one wall had collapsed in places along the top floor and portions of the roof were visible sagging in the gaps. The burned smell was almost overpowering and mixed with it was a sickly sweet odor that didn't bear thinking about.

"Don't try to go inside," Wright warned. "All the bodies we recovered were on the ground floor, but we had to get out when a section of ceiling and a piece of a support wall collapsed on us. One of our guys was hurt pretty badly."

Kinsey just stared at the building a moment. "Thanks for trying," he said quietly. "Can we have a moment?"

"Absolutely," said Wright, and the Coast Guardsmen all got out of the vehicle and moved closer to the building as Wright keyed his mike and ordered his two machine gunners to cover the street in opposite directions. The remainder of the soldiers dismounted and stood near their vehicles, covering the Coast Guardsmen from a respectful distance.

Kinsey stared into the ruins, his grief and his rage as black as the ravaged building. He had almost thirty years in the Coast Guard and it was a small service, almost like a large, extended family. If you stayed in long enough, it seemed like you knew, or at least knew of, almost everyone, and the men and women in that blackened ruin weren't just fellow service members. They were shipmates with whom he'd weathered raging storms, and rescue chopper crews, and veterans of arctic ice breakers, and rescue swimmers, and men and women of a dozen other specialties. They were people he'd worked with and played with, gotten drunk and been hungover with. He'd danced at their weddings and commiserated with more than a few when they divorced, their relationship unable to withstand the demands of the service. He'd toasted the birth of their children as they had toasted his. He'd shared their triumphs and defeats, and most of all a sense of purpose and quiet pride in their chosen calling. They were as tough as they had to be and wielded necessary force when appropriate, but mostly they were life savers and not life takers, and that's what they'd signed up for. They were his friends, and he felt their loss on a visceral level he was utterly incapable of articulating to anyone who wasn't a Coastie.

He dropped to one knee, grounded his weapon, and bowed his head in a silent prayer. When he rose, wiping his cheek with the back of his hand, he looked over to see Baker observing him with glistening eyes.

"You thinking what I'm thinking?" Baker asked.

Kinsey nodded. "You know how to do it?"

"We can manage," Baker said, and stepped toward the other two Coast Guardsmen and spoke to them quietly. Kinsey saw their heads bob in affirmation.

Kinsey looked back at the building a moment, then drew himself up to attention and executed a parade ground perfect right face toward the other men.

"DETAIL FALL IN!" he bellowed in his best parade-ground voice, as the three men snapped to attention in a straight line.

"READY."

"AIM."

"FIRE."

The movements of the first salute were clumsy and the volley a bit ragged, but the second was better and the third and last perfect as the men obeyed Kinsey's shouted orders.

"PREEE-SENT ARMS," Kinsey then bellowed, and the men brought their rifles to the salute position in slow motion while Kinsey performed a hand salute equally slowly.

"OOOR-DER ARMS," Kinsey continued, and the men slowly brought their rifles to order arms as Kinsey matched their speed in releasing his hand salute.

"DETAIL DISMISSED," Kinsey called and the men just stood a moment looking at the ruins.

He turned to find all of Wright's dismounted men standing at present arms. Kinsey returned the salute and Wright called his men to order arms. They all immediately glanced toward the two machine gunners, who were staring in opposite directions down the road, vigilant guards to the impromptu ceremony.

"Mount up!" Wright yelled, and the men began climbing back into the vehicles.

A minute later, they were back at the intersection where they met. Wright spoke from the front passenger seat.

"Well, unless y'all are really attached to your clown cars, I'll give you a lift back to your boat."

"That would be outstanding," Kinsey said, and his men added their thanks.

"Just point us in the right direction," Wright said.

Kinsey briefly considered going directly back to the *Pecos Trader*, but he had agreed with Hughes to avoid revealing his location. He didn't really think that would be a problem with Wright, but neither was it absolutely necessary.

"Head to the main gate of the container terminal on Shipyard Boulevard," Kinsey said. "Our boat's at the container dock."

The driver nodded, no further instructions needed, and Kinsey radioed the boat to tell them he was coming in with friendlies in a Humvee. Five minutes later, they were rolling through the container terminal. Wright's head was on a swivel and they passed row upon row of brightly colored shipping containers.

"Hmmm? I wonder what's in all these containers?" Wright said.

"All manner of useful stuff, I'd guess," Kinsey said. "The custody transfer is all computerized, but I suspect there are some paper copies of the cargo manifests somewhere in one of these office buildings."

Wright looked thoughtful. "Overall this isn't a bad location. Pretty good fence, river to your back, and it wouldn't take much to rearrange these containers into a defensive wall, presuming some of these container transporters are still running. Not much in the way of shelter or power, though."

"I don't know," Kinsey said. "I suspect there are tugs, ferries, tour boats, and maybe other abandoned craft up and down the river that might have generating capacity and berths, and you've got a damned long dock to tie them up. Some of the larger vessels might have water distillers as well."

"Yeah, if we just had the fuel to run them."

Kinsey hesitated, then thought what the hell, Wright was a smart cookie and he'd figure things out quickly anyway.

"Matter of fact, the product terminal just downstream has great big tanks full of fuel. Food for thought," Kinsey said.

Wright was still looking around. "Damn right it is," he said, just as they reached the river and saw the Coast Guard boat moving in to where a recessed ladder extended from the dock down to the surface of the water.

The men all got out of the vehicles and handshakes were exchanged all around before the Coasties moved toward the ladder.

"A word before you go, Chief?" said Wright as he moved down the dock away from both the vehicles with Kinsey in tow. When they were well away from the others, Kinsey spoke.

"What's up?" he asked.

"Just a little chat, NCO to NCO," Wright said, then hesitated as if choosing his words carefully.

"You just took a helluva sucker punch, right between the eyes, and you likely need to process that a bit. The thing is, you also have to make some hard decisions, and fast, and you don't have the luxury of time to grieve."

Kinsey bridled. "Look, Wright, I appreciate the help, but I don't need you to tell me —"

Wright raised his hand in a calming gesture. "Hear me out. I'm not trying to tell you what to do, but I want you to fully appreciate the situation, because as negative as you think I was before, I was actually holding back in front of the other guys." He paused for emphasis. "This is a complete and total shit show," he said slowly. "We got a Humpty Dumpty situation here. You know, as in an 'all the king's horses and all the king's men couldn't put Humpty together again' situation."

"Yeah, I got that," Kinsey said.

Wright shook his head. "Maybe, maybe not. What I'm telling you is the guys calling the shots on a national level couldn't find their own assholes with both hands and a mirror on a stick, and there ain't no way anything is ever going to be the same again. There just aren't the smarts or the resources to make this better at a national level even if everyone played nice, and as you may recall, the country was pretty polarized before this happened. It's unlikely to improve with folks starving to death and killing each other. Even if the powers that be do manage to mobilize the Army or the other services, what can they do but kill people to keep them from killing each other over a dwindling supply of food and water? And in the end, they'll be killing people to take the resources for themselves, because that's the only way they'll survive."

Kinsey nodded. "Okay, but what's your point?"

"My point is most people are going to die, and it's gonna be up to guys like me and you to survive and help as many other people survive as possible, and we have to use our own best judgment, right or wrong. If we wait for orders or follow stupid ones, more folks are going to die, and we might be among them. Also, if I'm gonna try to save anyone, my family's got to be at the top of the list. Until five minutes ago, my plan was to haul ass with those of my guys who wanted to go and two Humvees, to collect our families and make it up to my uncle's farm about twenty miles north of here." He gestured around the terminal. "But you got me thinking we might be able to establish a foothold here, so I'm going to at least put that plan to the major before I take off.

"But my real point is this," Wright continued, "I'm just a weekend warrior, so I might be more willing to head for the hills than you career types, but y'all all need to be thinking of yourselves and your families too. However you do that, you can always help as many other people as you can too. It's sort of like that Marine Corps general said back in Korea when he was surrounded by the Chinese, 'We're not retreating. We're attacking in another direction.'"

Wright fell silent and Kinsey just looked at him for a minute.

"Who you trying to convince, Wright?" Kinsey asked. "Me or you?"

Wright took off his helmet and ran his hand through his hair before giving Kinsey a sheepish grin.

"Both of us, I reckon," he said.

Kinsey nodded. "Definitely food for thought," he said. "Let's exchange radio frequencies and call signs. I suspect we might hook up again."

Wright nodded and produced a small notebook and pen from a shoulder pocket, and the two men exchanged contact information before Kinsey extended his hand.

"Good luck to you, Sarge," Kinsey said as Wright gripped his hand.

"And to you, Chief," Wright replied.

UNITED BLOOD NATION HQ
(FORMERLY NEW HANOVER COUNTY
DEPARTMENT OF SOCIAL SERVICES)
1650 GREENFIELD STREET
WILMINGTON, NC

DAY 8, 3:00 P.M.

Kwintell Banks, first superior of the SMM (Sex, Money, Murder) 'set' of the United Blood Nation, sat in the committee meeting and surveyed the small conference room attached to the director's office of the new HQ he now occupied by right of conquest. All in all, it was fairly shabby, and he knew they could and would do better in the future, but there was symbolism at play here, and despite his lack of a formal education, Kwintell was nobody's fool. People were already trained to come to the Department of Social Services to bow and scrape for the meager government handouts that defined their miserable lives, so why not take advantage of that? And what better signal to all concerned there was a new order—a new regime controlling their lives — than usurping the government's administration center? The only difference was, the new regime had teeth, and the populace could either fall in line — or die.

He shook himself from his reverie and refocused on Darren Mosley, his Minister of Information.

"... and then they rode off with the soldiers down to the river," said Mosley.

"That's it?" Kwintell demanded. "They just showed up at the building and shot their guns in the air? What kind of crazy cracker shit is that?"

"No, it wasn't just like poppin' off in the air," Mosley said. "It was like at a funeral, you know, a salute like."

Kwintell considered a moment. "Like for all them mofos we capped there two days ago?"

Mosley nodded. "True dat."

"And where we didn't get shit. You the Minister of Information, Darren, and you said there was some good stuff there, but we didn't get a dozen gats out of the whole deal, even after we started capping the mofos." He paused for effect. "Which ain't very good information."

Mosley shifted in his chair. "Straight up, Kwintell, I thought there was shit there. One of the Pee Wees be choppin' it up 'bout how his cousin in the Coast Guard and how they have all kinda gats at the HQ. Machine guns and grenades and shit. I —"

Kwintell waved Mosley silent. "Ight, ight, just don't be slippin' no mo. Now what up with the soldiers?"

"No change," Mosley said. "They go out in the morning and sit in the road and go back in at night."

"They messin' with us anywhere?"

Mosley shook his head. "We been leavin' them alone, they be leaving us alone. Ain't very many of them, but they got them machine guns and tanks. Why, you thinkin' we need to be bangin' them?"

Kwintell shook his head. "No. They run out of food and water and they'll leave. No point gettin' any of our soldiers shot."

"You think maybe the regular army be comin', or they might be sending supplies?"

Kwintell bit back his anger at having to provide 'intelligence' to his subordinate who was supposed to be providing it to him. It was early days, and Mosley still commanded respect in the set, more for his violent courage than his intelligence. Kwintell would have to be careful in replacing him. He shook his head again.

"Been eight days, and the radio say this happenin' all over. If they was gonna send help or supplies, they'd be here by now. I'm thinkin' this is how it's gonna be, and we need to move fast to make sure UBN take our share now."

There were murmurs of 'straight up' and 'true dat' around the small table, and Kwintell turned this attention to Keyshaun Jackson, his Minister of Food.

"What up with the food?" he asked.

"All good," Keyshaun said. "Most everything was stripped in the 'hood, but I got copies of the yellow pages so we could hit all the food stores and divided up the city, putting a lieutenant in charge of each section. We sittin' on most of the food in the city, but it's spread out, so I'm thinkin' we need to move it all to one place where we can guard it. The yellow pages gave me an idea too, and I started havin' them sit on the bottled water companies too."

Kwintell nodded approval and turned his attention further down the table.

"Desmond, help Keyshaun out if he needs more soldiers to sit on the food. Use baby gangstas if need be, just to sit on the stores 'til we get it moved. And use that yellow pages idea — but look for gas stations, gun stores, beer and soft drink distributors, shit like that, you know, anything we gonna need.

"And one more thing," Kwintell continued, "I see all you niggas smilin' when I said beer distributors, so let's be straight up here. I ain't playing around and I don't want nobody forgetting that! Last week we all seen people running around, acting the fool and looting liquor stores and stealing TVs that ain't never gonna work again. We in this for the long run, and if I see a UBN soldier doing that shit, I will cap his ass right there on the street and I expect you to do the same. Is that clear?"

The rest of the committee members traded hesitant looks, then one by one, nodded their concurrence.

"Good," Kwintell said, then turned to the last member of the committee. "Jermaine, where we at on recruitment?"

"Way more than we can handle," Jermaine said, "leastwise more than we can initiate anytime soon, and since we got a truce going on with the Crips and everyone else and the cops aren't out, they ain't really nobody for the recruits to take out to earn membership."

"How many you figure waiting to join?" Kwintell asked.

"Couple of thousand, easy," Jermaine said, "and probably anybody we want when the food runs out and we got all that's left."

Kwintell was silent a moment and when he spoke again, he addressed his question to Keyshaun Jackson, the Minister of Food.

"How many others have food?" he asked.

Keyshaun shrugged. "The Crips be sitting on the Food Lion over on Oleander and a bunch of convenience stores, and the Sure Shots and Gaza maybe got half a dozen convenience stores and gas stations between 'em. Ain't none of the other gangs big enough to matter. Mostly the gangs all just loot and leave, but the Crips and the others started trying to occupy places a couple of days ago, copying us, I think."

Kwintell nodded and turned back to Jermain.

"Okay," he said, "we gonna change the rules a bit. Accept every prospective member that come and make them all 'probationary recruits.' Divide them up in groups of at least fifty and put one of our baby gangstas in charge. Send a group against every rival gang location—that's the initiation, they have to take the location and cap all the rival gangstas there. The group succeeds or fails as a group, and if one group fails, have another standing by to go right in. This way we initiate the recruits and get rid of those other mofos without risking any experienced soldiers."

There was silence around the table.

"Wh-what about the truces?" Mosley asked.

"FUCK THE TRUCES!" shouted Kwintell as he pounded the table with his fist. "We got no time for truces! We got the advantage now and we gonna use it to wipe them out so we don't have to be looking over our shoulder all the time. This is a new world, homies, and we gonna be the kings!"

"What about the cops?" Jermaine this time.

"They'll slip away, just like the soldiers, we give them half a chance," Kwintell said. "Hell, most of them don't even live in the county, much less the city. We'll leave 'em be for now and concentrate on wiping out the other gangs and controlling all the food and water. After that, we take out all the crackers and toms. A lot of them are armed, but they're not organized, so we can overwhelm them. We'll use the baby gangsta swarms again. I'm sure we'll be getting more recruits that need initiation anyway."

"What if anyone surrenders?" Jermaine asked. "We gonna cap 'em anyway?"

Kwintell smiled. "Maybe not. I got my eye on a real nice place in Forest Hills, so maybe I'll keep the mayor around as my yard boy."

M/V PECOS TRADER
CAPTAIN'S OFFICE

DAY 8, 8:30 P.M.

Hughes once again sat across from Matt Kinsey, who was gazing down into the half-finished cup of coffee grown cold on the low table between them. The Coasties had accepted Hughes' hospitality, unable to resist the offer of hot showers, a good meal, and a bunk with clean sheets. Kinsey had radioed back to Oak Island to confirm they would return to base in the morning, and Hughes had bedded four of them down in the ship's hospital while two kept a security watch on their boat tied up alongside *Pecos Trader* . As an added benefit, they'd gone to dinner clad in the disposable Tyvek coveralls used aboard for tank cleaning and other dirty tasks, and Hughes had arranged for the steward to wash and dry their clothes, all luxuries hard to come by in their crowded base at Oak Island.

"That must have been hard," Hughes said, referring to Kinsey's just recounted visit to Coast Guard HQ.

"Yeah, it was," Kinsey said, and Hughes nodded towards Kinsey's half-finished coffee.

"Care for something a bit stronger?" Hughes asked.

Kinsey hesitated, then said, "Don't mind if I do."

Hughes rose and retrieved a bottle from his lower desk drawer and two short water glasses from the cabinet behind his desk. He walked over, set the two glasses on the coffee table, and poured an inch of amber liquid in the bottom of each.

"Purely medicinal, of course," Hughes said.

Kinsey grinned. "Of course."

As Hughes resumed his seat, Kinsey raised his glass and said, "Absent friends."

Hughes joined the toast, and both men took a swallow then settled back in their chairs.

"So where's home and family, Chief?" Hughes asked.

Kinsey shrugged. "Wisconsin originally, but when you've been in the Coast Guard almost thirty years, you find out pretty quick home is anywhere the Coast Guard says it is. I'm an only child and my folks passed, so I don't really have any strong connections to Wisconsin. My wife is… was from near Baton Rouge and has family there; they're pretty much my family now. That's where I'm planning… or at least WAS planning… to retire. Our son's in the 101st Airborne in Fort Campbell, Kentucky, so there's no telling where he might end up in all this mess. Our daughter is a freshman at LSU in Baton Rouge, full boat scholarship for soccer," he added, pride in his voice. "School's out, but she was taking summer courses and staying with my sister-in-law, so I think she should be okay."

"So you're not married now?" Hughes asked.

"Widowed, two years now." Kinsey didn't elaborate and Hughes sensed it was a painful subject.

"When are… or were… you planning to retire?"

"I hit thirty years last week, and I already put in the paperwork. No clue what I was going to do for a second career." He took another sip and shrugged. "But I guess we're all going to be frigging farmers now— or dead."

Hughes smiled at the gallows humor. "So what now?"

"Damned if I know," Kinsey said. "But there are over fifty of us all told at Oak Island and I have to figure something out. I'm responsible for them."

"I wouldn't have thought so many," Hughes said.

"Well, we only had the duty section on station at the time of the blackout, but when it hit the fan, everybody who could make it in did so. Most of my guys live relatively close to the station. When it became obvious everything was going to hell, I let families on station as well. We're basically camping out in the office and support spaces. There's a limited solar system from a 'green initiative' the Coast Guard put in place a couple of years ago, and the water's still running, though who knows for how long. Everyone stripped their cupboards and brought their food, and we're fishing as well, but it won't last more than another week, two at most. I'm hearing rumblings people are going to take off, and I can't blame them." He shrugged. "To be honest, Cap, I've no clue what to do."

Hughes fell silent a moment, mentally parsing the possibilities.

"Come with us," he said finally.

Kinsey looked confused. "Come with you where?"

"Beaumont, Texas," Hughes said. "We're sailing day after tomorrow. Beaumont's close to Baton Rouge, or at least it's a hell of a lot closer than Wilmington. You and any of your folks are welcome to join us."

Kinsey rubbed his chin. "I don't know, Captain. I'm the unit CO and that kind of seems like desertion."

"Look, we're shorthanded, and we could really use the extra manpower," Hughes said. "And besides, isn't one of your missions protection of shipping? Well, we're shipping, and we sure as hell could use some protection. And besides, you're retiring anyway, so I suspect your relief, or at least someone qualified to relieve you, is probably already on station, right?"

Kinsey was mulling it over when he thought of Wright's comment about 'attacking in a different direction.' That tipped the balance. "All right," he said. "I can't speak for the others, but I'll come. We'll go downriver at first light and come back with anyone else who wants to come. When do you plan on leaving again?"

"Day after tomorrow. I want to leave the dock midafternoon at low slack water. That way I figure the incoming tide will mitigate the current in the river, especially down at the Battery Island Turn, and if we go aground between here and there, the rising tide will help us off. We should be at sea before nightfall," Hughes said. "Supposing I don't put her into the riverbank."

MAYPORT NAVAL STATION
JACKSONVILLE, FLORIDA

DAY 8, 11:00 A.M.

Lieutenant Luke Kinsey, formerly of the 101st Airborne and currently a member of the newly formed Special Reaction Force, squinted in the bright sunlight as he watched the UH-60 Black Hawk settle in the landing zone a hundred yards away, partially obscured by wavy lines of heat steaming off the tarmac. Near noon in north Florida always seemed like summer, even in early April. The T-shirt under his ACUs was already soaked.

"So when do we change to the black uniforms?" asked Sergeant Joel Washington, staring at a group of eight black-clad soldiers a short distance away.

Luke followed the sergeant's gaze as the third man in their group commented.

"I'm fine with our old uniforms," Long said. "They look like losers in a Johnny Cash look-alike contest. I don't want to wear that crap."

Luke stifled a laugh and managed to snarl at Long. "Knock it off, Long. We all volunteered and these guys are all part of our new unit. And when they get more of the new uniforms in, I expect you to wear yours without any bitching. Is that clear?"

Beside Luke, Washington laughed. "You're dreaming, LT," Washington said, pronouncing the title 'el-tee' in the typical verbal shorthand of an enlisted man for a lieutenant. "Long here was born bitching. Why, if he couldn't bitch, he wouldn't be able to talk at all."

Long reddened. "Oh, and I suppose you just love the Johnny Cash look, huh, Washington. And I did volunteer, LT, but I did it mostly 'cause I was tired of twiddling my thumbs in barracks and I wanted to do something to help people. Nobody told me most of this so-called 'Special Reaction Force' was just a bunch of damned mercs. I haven't met over a handful of regular troops since we've been here, and some of these 'private security' guys seem pretty shady."

"And we've been here, what, all of twenty-four hours?" Luke asked. When Long didn't reply, he continued, "So I expect you should crank it down a notch or two, Long. Just because some of these guys were previously private contractors doesn't mean they're bad troops. Private security pays well, and a lot of first-rate guys leave the service to go private."

"Yeah, well, these ain't those guys," Long muttered. "These are the assholes that used to be guarding drug shipments in Colombia and blowing up villages in East Shithole, Africa."

"Chill, Long," Washington whispered. "Here comes the captain."

Luke looked up to see their new commanding officer approaching. He was well over six feet and of indeterminate age, and moved with a grace made somehow sinister by the solid black battle utilities he wore. At odds with the strict grooming standards Luke was accustomed to as a member of the Screaming Eagles, his new boss wore a thick, but neatly trimmed blond goatee, which reminded Luke somehow of a pirate. The pirate illusion was enhanced by the ropelike welt of scar tissue emanating from the outer corner of the man's eye, obscuring most of his left cheek and marring an otherwise handsome face. Captain Rorke exuded a quiet menace that signaled in no uncertain terms he was not a man to be crossed.

As he approached, the three former Screaming Eagles came to attention and Luke saluted crisply. Rorke looked surprised. A derisive smile tugged at the corners of his mouth before he responded with something between a wave and an aborted high five.

"We don't do much of that, Kinsey," Rorke said, "but it is kind of refreshing. Maybe it'll rub off on the rest of the boys."

"Yes, sir," Luke said, dropping his salute.

Rorke looked them over. "Sorry we couldn't get you a uniform issued just yet, but the mission comes first and we're way understaffed. Today it's a 'come as you are' party."

"Not a problem, sir," Luke said.

"Okay," Rorke said, "this is your first time out, so just follow my lead. We're flying to Miami to board a cruise ship the government has chartered. The passengers are refusing to leave, and our job is to clear the ship. We did one here in Jacksonville yesterday, and one in Charleston the day before."

"Cruise ships? What's the government… oh, I get it, housing," Luke said. "But can they do that? Just kick the people off, I mean. Don't they have some sort of obligation to the passengers or something?"

Rorke glared. "That would be both well outside your 'need to know' and also way above your pay grade, Kinsey. Now, do you have any questions of an OPERATIONAL nature?"

Luke said nothing for a moment, then responded, "Yes, sir. Did you have… ah… any trouble with the other boats?"

Rorke shook his head. "Nothing substantial. When well-armed operators show up in full battle rattle, it tends to put a damper on any opposition. We did have a few loudmouth assholes with hero complexes yesterday, but that turned out to be beneficial." He smirked. "You'd be surprised how a couple of publicly administered beat downs and a little blood speeds people toward the exits."

Over Rorke's shoulder, Luke saw Washington and Long exchange concerned glances as Rorke continued.

"Shouldn't be a problem this time, though, our orders are to lighten up. We're going with a charm offensive. Matter of fact, it looks like the head charmer just arrived."

Luke turned to follow Rorke's gaze across the tarmac.

A woman approached at a fast walk. She was slim and even at a distance it was apparent she was attractive, with long dark hair swaying from side to side. The dark lightweight FEMA coveralls she wore did nothing to conceal her femininity, and as she drew nearer, Luke thought she looked vaguely familiar. Apparently he wasn't the only one.

"Is she famous or something?" Washington asked. "She looks familiar."

"Maria Velasquez," Rorke said. "She's a local news anchor in Miami, but her reports get picked up nationally. That's probably where you saw her. She is, or was anyway, a rising star. Now she works for FEMA."

The woman reached the group and studied them a moment before spotting Rorke's rank insignia.

"Captain Rorke?"

"That would be me," Rorke said, extending his hand. "Nice to meet you, Ms. Velasquez, I'm an admirer."

She favored Rorke with a dazzling smile and he continued without bothering to introduce Luke or the others.

"I presume you've been briefed?"

"Oh yes," she said, "and I have a script committed to memory. I'm sure we can resolve the situation without unpleasantness."

"Excellent," Rorke replied. "Let's be off, then. Sit next to me and we can discuss the situation more fully on the flight down."

She bobbed her head and Rorke rested an unnecessary hand on her waist to guide her toward the chopper, leaving the other three to trail behind.

"Secondary mission objective," Luke heard Long whisper to Washington, "getting into *chiquita*'s pants."

Luke's attempt to communicate his displeasure via a hard look was somewhat defeated by his inability to suppress a grin.

An hour and a half later, they were hovering over the Port of Miami on Dodge Island, gazing down at almost empty docks and little movement except aboard a large white cruise ship at one of the cruise terminals. Rorke directed the pilot to land, and the chopper flared over an empty parking lot and settled to the pavement. They were scrambling out before the blades stopped turning, moving behind Rorke and Velasquez toward the cruise terminal.

They passed empty shuttle buses in front of the terminal and found the terminal itself practically deserted except for a scattering of people in FEMA T-shirts and a few terminal personnel pressed into service to tie up the ship and deploy the gangway. Luke wondered where they got the power to deploy the gangway, then heard the muted throb of a generator somewhere in the near distance. He almost bumped into Rorke's back as his new boss stopped and watched one of the FEMA people hasten toward them.

"So what's the story?" Rorke asked. "Any change?"

The man shook his head. "Not really. The captain and crew are cooperating. I mean, the captain's pissed we're basically confiscating his ship, but he agreed to sign the charter on behalf of his company after I assured him we wouldn't kick the crew off if they don't cause trouble. The problem is the passengers. It was a seniors' cruise with several veterans' groups, mainly from the Korean and Vietnam wars, and a scattering of World War Two vets. Hell, a couple of the old farts look like they might have survived the Civil War." He paused. "Anyway, they were in St. Thomas when the blackouts hit, and I guess things got nasty there in a hurry. A shore excursion was surrounded by a mob and they were all robbed at gunpoint and verbally and physically abused. Several of the old guys who attempted to defend the group were beaten for their efforts before local police intervened and got the group back to the ship. They've heard a lot of conflicting reports since and they're confused and scared and not inclined to believe anything I tell them."

He shook his head. "The captain managed to convince them to leave their luggage outside their staterooms this morning, and the crew went around and gave them all baggage claim checks, but that's where things bogged down. I guess a lot of them figured out no matter how anxious they are to get home, conditions on the ship might be a lot better than they are anywhere else. They'll be a pretty tough sell, I'm afraid."

Rorke nodded. "Understood. Is there any place where Ms. Velasquez here can address all the passengers in person?"

"Not in person, at least where everyone can see her directly," the man said, "but I had the captain ask all passengers to gather on the embarkation deck for an update on the situation ashore. That area runs most of the length of the ship, and there are large flat-screen TV monitors every few feet. Ms. Velasquez can address everyone from the ship's communications center. If she gets them moving, we'll funnel them right down the gangway and across the terminal to the buses."

Rorke nodded again and turned to Luke. "I'll accompany Ms. Velasquez to the comm center. You take the rest of the men aboard and space them out along the embarkation deck to keep things moving after they start. Spread six of them out evenly along the deck, but pick three men to stay with you near the gangway. That's the potential bottleneck, so keep it moving. Do NOT let things back up there, is that clear?"

"Yes, sir," Luke said, and Rorke turned and started toward the ship.

Once aboard, Rorke and Velasquez disappeared into the crowd and Luke picked six of Rorke's men to spread out along the deck, retaining both of his own men and a private named Grogan to stay with him near the gangway. When he was satisfied everyone was in position, he surveyed the crowd. As the FEMA man indicated, they were seniors, and while most seemed reasonably fit, there were many canes and walkers, and not a few wheelchairs, as well as scattered passengers with oxygen tubes clipped in their noses. The mood was tense and subdued. Suddenly the undercurrent of hushed conversation stopped as the TV monitors all sprang to life with the identical images of a handsome blond man of late middle age whose shirt displayed the four-stripe shoulder boards of a captain.

"Good day, ladies and gentlemen. As I'm sure you know by now"—he showed perfect white teeth in a smile—"I am Captain Larson. I apologize for what I know has been a frustrating lack of information, but in truth we have had very little information to share. I know you all have questions regarding the situation ashore. So, I'm very pleased we now have on board representatives of the US Federal Emergency Management Agency, or FEMA, who can address your various concerns."

The captain stepped to one side, and Maria Velasquez took his place, somehow managing to look professional while favoring her viewing audience with a radiant smile. From the murmurs rippling through the assembled passengers, it was obvious to Luke many recognized Velasquez and were informing their less-enlightened shipmates of her identity.

"Hi, folks, I'm Maria Velasquez, and some of you might recognize me from my work on both local and national news teams. However, today I'm here on behalf of FEMA. As I'm sure you've figured out by now, most of the media infrastructure was badly damaged by the recent disaster, so when FEMA reached out to media professionals and offered us a way to serve our viewers, or perhaps I should say former viewers, most of us gladly accepted the opportunity to do our part.

"First, the situation. Eight days ago a massive solar storm released a series of what are called 'coronal mass ejections' at earth. Without going into too much technical mumbo jumbo, the bottom line is there were blackouts, not just across the US and Canada, but the world. Obviously, there has been chaos and confusion, but the good news is, here in the US anyway, the authorities have control of the situation. Food and water is going out to folks who need it, even as we speak, so don't worry about your loved ones."

Washington looked over at Luke, who merely returned his puzzled look and shrugged his shoulders.

"But the bad news," Velasquez continued, "is the power is still out. However, all of the utilities are working on the problem, with the full assistance of the federal government, and they are confident they can restore the power within the week in some places, but perhaps two to three weeks in most." There were groans from the audience and evidently the comm center was close enough for Velasquez to hear them, because she responded with a sympathetic smile and allowed the groaning to dissipate on its own.

"Now," she said, "as far as your situations go, it's another big mixture of the good news/bad news thing, I'm afraid. The bad news is air travel is disrupted, and gasoline and fuel of all kinds are currently in really short supply—again both things the federal government is working on correcting—but that doesn't help you folks much in the near term. The good news is we're working on charter flights to get you where you need to go, but the bad news is it's going to take a few days. More good news is you'll get to extend your vacation a few days at government expense because we're going to put you all up in some of Miami's great hotels. The bad news is they're not so awesome these days, because most are operating with limited power on backup generators."

There was grumbling from the crowd now, but a few chuckles as well, as the information gave the listeners a greater sense of understanding, and Velasquez's earnest but somewhat light-hearted delivery seemed to make the situation more tolerable. Though Luke doubted the veracity of some of her claims, he figured they were at least partial truths, and having the crowd disembark voluntarily was a hell of a lot better than the alternative.

"More good news," Velasquez said, continuing her monologue, "is all of your food and drink will be taken care of, but the bad news, I'm afraid, is it will be in the form of FEMA emergency provisions. However, even that's good news in a way, as the many veterans among you will be able to satisfy what I'm sure is your curiosity as to whether the new meals ready-to-eat, or MREs, are superior to the old rations you may remember from your own gallant service." She paused for effect. "The bad news is current soldiers refer to the MREs as 'meals, rarely edible.'"

The laughter was spontaneous and widespread this time, mixed with good-natured groans, and Luke had to admit Velasquez was a pro when it came to winning over a crowd. The tension in the crowd was significantly lower than when they'd arrived. Velasquez waited for the laughter to subside, and continued.

"So here's the deal, folks. We have buses standing by outside to transport you to your hotels. You don't have to worry about your baggage, as the crew will collect it and we will transport it to your hotel. We have crew members standing by to assist those of you who require assistance in disembarking—"

"Why can't we just stay here until the flights are ready? The chow's a hell of a lot better and we got power," yelled a voice from the crowd. There was another voice of agreement followed almost immediately by a chorus of noisy agreement, drowning out Velasquez's words as she continued to speak on the screens. She continued to speak for a while and then stopped and looked a bit confused, as if she'd heard the noise but not the specific question. She then looked off camera and it was obvious she was listening to someone; then she turned back to the camera and made calming gestures. Eventually, the crowd noise subsided.

"I understand some of you have asked why you can't just stay aboard," she said. "That's a reasonable question and I apologize for not addressing it first. The fact is, the captain informs me there is less than a day's food left on board, so we are reduced to emergency rations regardless of where you are quartered. As far as staying here, the ship is also almost out of fuel, and it will be a long time before any more is available. With no power, the ship will be even less pleasant than the hotels ashore, so it's better to leave now while we have resources in place to accommodate the transfer." She paused. "And I have to stress here, folks, there are a lot of people needing help, not only people on other cruise ships like this one, but other people in the community at large. We are here now and ready to help you, but if you turn down our offer, you will be completely on your own as far as getting back to your homes."

Luke doubted the last assertion. The government wasn't 'chartering' a ship to leave it sitting at a dock empty and without fuel. However, he couldn't help feeling relieved as he saw heads nod here and there in the crowd, his disgust at the blatant manipulation mitigated by the rising hope he wouldn't have to participate in a forcible eviction of a crowd of senior citizens. Velasquez gave her announcement a moment to sink in and then continued.

"Now as I was saying, we have crew members standing by to assist those of you who need help disembarking. Unfortunately we only have the single gangway in use, so we ask crewmen assisting wheelchair-bound passengers to stay to the right during disembarkation to allow walking passengers to pass to your left. Thank you for your cooperation, ladies and gentlemen, and I wish you all a safe journey to your homes."

Velasquez's face blanked from all the screens and Luke saw ship's officers around the embarkation deck begin to dispatch Filipino crewmen into the crowd to assist wheelchair-bound passengers. Like magic, other crewmen arrived with folding wheelchairs, encouraging passengers with walkers or canes to accept a wheelchair ride to the buses. A few seemed resistant, but in the end all accepted the assistance.

Somewhat unsure of his role, Luke positioned himself on one side of the gangway entrance with Long and nodded for Washington and Grogan to take the other side as the crowd converged on the gangway entrance. It wasn't a line exactly, but it was orderly, as people at the front of the pack politely waited their turn to move onto the gangway, generally making way for the wheelchairs pushed by the Filipino seamen to move on the gangway and start down in a slower moving line, hugging the right rail as faster walking passengers filled the left side of the gangway.

As the gangway filled, two wheelchairs moved on to the gangway side by side, obviously an elderly couple, with the woman clinging to her husband's hand. When the seaman pushing the woman's chair tried to move ahead to form a single line, his passenger grew visibly agitated and refused to release her husband's hand. The Filipino seaman relented and it became obvious they intended to transit the gangway abreast.

"Shit!" muttered Grogan as he shouldered the little Filipino aside and shoved the woman's chair forward, the unexpected move breaking her grip on her husband's hand as Grogan pushed her chair to the right.

"Frank! Frank!" the old woman screamed, terror in her voice.

But Grogan hadn't counted on the husband behind him, who grabbed the cane stowed upright between his knees and propelled it forward between Grogan's legs, crooked end up, then jerked back savagely, hooking it into Grogan's crotch, to stop him in mid-stride before the old man lost his grip on the cane.

"Jesus," gasped Grogan as he released the wheelchair and stumbled to the rail. The cane clattered to the gangway at his feet. Grogan straightened and whirled, face red with rage and fist raised—to face Washington, who had swiftly inserted himself between Grogan and the old man.

All the while, the old woman's piteous screams continued.

"Stand down, Grogan!" Luke shouted, then motioned the seaman pushing the old man's chair forward so the couple could be reunited.

Grogan glared at Luke. "But he—"

"I said stand down and get off the gangway, now!" Luke said, and after a moment's hesitation, Grogan complied and Luke stepped forward toward the reunited couple as Washington scooped the old man's cane up off the gangway.

The woman was calmer now, though still agitated, and her husband was holding both her hands and speaking to her softly. "It's fine, sweetheart. I'm right here and I'm not going anyplace. You're safe now."

"Is she all right, sir?" Luke asked.

The old man looked up, his eyes moist. "She gets… confused sometimes and doesn't know where she is. When that happens I can't be out of her sight without her getting upset. It was only happening once in a while, but all this stress made it worse."

Luke nodded, and when the old man disengaged his left hand from his wife's grip in order to accept his cane from Washington, Luke notice the man's baseball cap for the first time. It bore a Screaming Eagles patch over the logo 101st Airborne, with a small enamel pin depicting sergeant's stripes. Another small circular pin said "Charter Member" in the center, with script around the outside reading "The Battered Bastards of Bastogne." Luke saw Washington do a double take when he noticed the cap. On the front of the old man's shirt was a temporary name tag, likely one he'd neglected to remove after some previous shipboard gathering. Written in a spidery, old man's hand was the name Frank Hastings.

"Sergeant Washington," Luke said, "would you and Private Long be good enough to escort Sergeant Hastings and his lady to the end of the gangway?"

"It would be our honor and privilege, sir," Washington said, and motioned Long over to help.

Luke watched them start down the gangway, his men pushing the wheelchairs abreast as the old couple held hands and the attending seamen trailed along, as if unsure what to do. He turned and walked the few steps back to the ship where Grogan waited. As soon as he stepped off the gangway, Grogan motioned the waiting passengers forward.

"Disregard that," Luke said to the waiting passengers, raising his hand. Then he turned to Grogan. "Let's let them get far enough along that people aren't breathing down their necks."

"But the captain said—"

"As you were, PRIVATE," Luke said, and Grogan glared at him.

When the couple was halfway down the gangway, Luke nodded at Grogan and motioned the waiting passengers forward. As they passed him, the other veterans who'd seen the incident on the gangway favored him with nods or murmured words of approval, making him feel even guiltier given his role in the con job.

He took some comfort in the fact at least they were getting the people to their homes, however bad the situations might be when they got there.

He kept a watch down the gangway and saw Washington and Long release the Hastings into the care of the Filipino seamen at the bottom of the gangway, and watched the couple roll out of sight, still hand in hand. Via hand signals, he directed Washington and Long to remain at the bottom of the gangway.

The rest of the disembarkation went without incident, and his other men trailed the shrinking crowd to the gangway, so when the last of the passengers moved off the ship, Luke had all his troops together with the exception of Washington and Long. Rorke made a brief appearance and indicated he had 'matters to attend to on board' and Luke should take the rest of the men and wait for him at the chopper.

At the chopper, Luke put the men at ease, and they broke into groups of two or three to talk, segregating themselves based on past friendships or shared experiences, with Washington and Long together near him. Not good, thought Luke, knowing if they were to develop any sort of unit identity they had to start integrating themselves on all levels. He saw Grogan wander even further afield to bum a smoke from one of the FEMA drivers, and Luke watched as the two chatted like old friends while passengers boarded the last bus. The FEMA driver dropped his cigarette and ground it out underfoot, to board the bus himself just as Luke got a radio call from Rorke, directing him to board the chopper and have the pilots start their preflight checks for departure in ten minutes.

Washington and Long sat near him in the chopper, looking subdued as the pilots ran through their preflights.

"It's a bad situation," Luke said, "but at least they're headed home."

Washington and Long nodded as across the chopper, Grogan tried unsuccessfully to stifle a snort.

"You got something to say, Grogan?" Washington asked.

"Seriously? You didn't buy all that happy horseshit she was spouting, did you?"

"What are you getting at? It sounded legit to me," Washington said.

"Except there ain't no flights, man, and there hasn't been a hotel with emergency power in Miami in three or four days, except the ones currently occupied by bunches of gangbangers," Grogan said. "And you might not have noticed, but things are frigging grim, and I'm thinking FEMA's not wasting any food on those people. I mean, let's face it, they're all likely to be dead in a month no matter what happens."

"Bullshit," Long snorted. "How could you know that? Does FEMA consult you about their relief plans?"

"Because my cousin's driving one of those FEMA buses, genius," Grogan said, "and he says they're only pumping out bullshit to get the passengers away from the dock and out of the way. Randy told me this was his second trip today, and his orders are to ride at least twenty minutes and then pick out someplace that looks reasonable from the outside. He just dumps them in front of whatever hotel he wants, and by the time the old farts hobble into the lobby and find it deserted, or maybe full of gangbangers, he's already hauled ass back here to the terminal."

Luke sat in shock as Washington and Long turned to him, seeking assurances he didn't have.

Finally Washington spoke.

"This is messed up, LT! Like REALLY messed up!"

Luke could only nod.

CHAPTER EIGHT

Day 9, 4:00 p.m.

"That was fast," Hughes said, standing on the deck with Howell and Gowan staring downstream at the approaching flotilla.

There were two of the forty-five-foot patrol boats they'd seen earlier as well as two smaller boats that appeared to be semirigid inflatables, each about twenty-five feet long, and all carried the distinctive markings of the US Coast Guard. Following them, and setting the somewhat sedate pace of the flotilla, was a much larger barge-shaped vessel with a cube-like deckhouse and a large flat deck dominated by a large crane near the bow. Numerous people were visible on both the larger patrol boats and the barge.

True to his word, Kinsey had left at first light and raced downriver. He'd radioed back to the ship that he'd be returning with his group of volunteers the same day, as soon as he'd 'arranged a few things.' Hughes glanced at his watch and then looked to the west. The early spring day promised at least four more hours of daylight. His only concern was the noise and activity might invite unwelcome attention.

"More people than we figured," Georgia Howell said. "We might be hard-pressed to accommodate them."

"We'll make it work," Hughes said somewhat absently as he gazed downstream. "Why in the hell did they bring a buoy tender barge?"

"Beats me," Dan Gowan responded, squinting downriver himself. "There's a pile of stuff on deck. Maybe they brought us a present."

"We'll find out soon enough," Hughes said, turning to Georgia Howell. "Mate, that's a lot of folks and they'll probably all have baggage, so the pilot ladder will be a bottleneck. Would you please deploy the accommodation ladder?"

"Right away, Captain," she said, "and I'll get some lines out over the side so the boats can tie off while they wait to unload. No point in having them waste fuel holding station against the current."

"Good idea, Georgia," Hughes said, and she started across the deck, calling for the bosun as she did so.

***

Kinsey was first aboard, followed up the accommodation ladder by six other men in Coast Guard coveralls. He waved to Georgia Howell where she was supervising the welcome of his little flotilla, then looked around and moved toward Hughes and Gowan, his men following close behind.

"Welcome aboard," Hughes said as Gowan nodded his concurrence. "That's quite a crew. They all signing on?"

Kinsey grinned and shook his head. "No, some are just here to help. However, these guys" — he inclined his head toward the men with him — "are your new shipmates. They're from Corpus Christi to Mobile, and all of them want to get a bit closer to home."

"We're glad to have you," Hughes said. "I'm Jordan Hughes, the captain, and this is Dan Gowan, the chief engineer."

The men all nodded and Kinsey introduced each along with their occupational specialties. When the group turned out to be all petty officers, including two machinery technicians and one electrician's mate, Gowan's face split into a wide grin.

"Out-fucking-standing!" Gowan said, and Kinsey cocked his head at Hughes.

"It takes so little to make engineers happy," Hughes deadpanned, "and apparently new playmates are high on the list." He grinned. "Seriously, gentlemen, we're pleased to have you all, and as soon as you've settled in, we can surely use your help." He glanced over at Gowan. "Though for those of you unfortunate enough to be engineers, I'm not sure the chief here is willing to wait that long."

One of the men, a petty officer second class whose name Hughes hadn't yet committed to memory, spoke directly to Dan Gowan. "We're ready to turn to right away if you need us, Chief." He shifted his gaze to Kinsey. "That is, presuming Chief Kinsey can get by without us and see our gear and families get aboard okay."

"Done," Kinsey said. "Go help Chief Gowan."

"REALLY out-fucking-standing!" Gowan said.

"And I assure you," Hughes added, "he really does have a much larger vocabulary."

Gowan turned red, grinned as everyone else laughed, motioned for the newest members of his engine gang to follow and headed toward the deckhouse. Kinsey detailed the remaining Coasties to assist with the boarding of the families and loading of gear, then turned back to Hughes.

"How many altogether?" Hughes asked.

"Seven men, counting myself, five wives, and nine kids. Twenty-one in all," Kinsey said.

Hughes nodded. "We're tight on accommodations. I can double up some crew, use the hospital and the owner's room, and probably put some cots in the public spaces like the officers' lounge. It won't be the most comfortable accommodations, but you'll all have a place to sleep, access to toilet and showers, and three meals a day." He paused. "But speaking of food, did you bring any with you? This more than doubles our head count and effectively cuts our rations in half. We're probably all right for eight to ten weeks, but after that, we got nothing."

Kinsey shook his head. "The accommodations are no problem, and we have inflatable mattresses if they're needed, but the food's a different story. I'm leaving over thirty people here, without much food to start with, so I didn't feel right taking any. Our leaving will double their food supply, but that's maybe three weeks at most." He hesitated. "Besides, I've got an idea regarding provisions, which may solve everyone's problems, but I'd like to hold off discussing it for a bit, if you don't mind."

Hughes raised an eyebrow. "That's a bit cryptic," he said, gesturing at the various vessels alongside. "Does it have anything to do with your little fleet here? If you're just bringing people and baggage, I figure you could have crammed them into the two bigger patrol boats and saved a lot of fuel."

"I didn't say we came empty-handed." Kinsey pointed past the accommodation ladder where Georgia Howell was greeting new arrivals and sending them with crewmen to get settled.

Hughes followed Kinsey's finger to the buoy tender barge. Stacked on the open deck were boxes and cases of various sizes along with an empty boat trailer. Hughes looked back at Kinsey, obviously confused.

"Okay, I see a boat trailer and some boxes. What's in the boxes and what good is a trailer going to do us?"

"The trailer by itself, nothing," Kinsey said. "But we're going to hoist it on board, tie it down securely, and use it as a transport cradle for THAT!"

Again Hughes followed Kinsey's pointing finger to one of the smaller patrol boats.

"Which is not, as you might think, a nice little inflatable boat, but a Defender-class Response Boat, with an aluminum hull and a rigid foam-filled flotation collar, and with a range of one hundred seventy-five nautical miles and a speed of forty-six knots," Kinsey said. "And we're taking her."

Hughes seemed stunned and Kinsey continued. "And those boxes contain, among other things, two M240 machine guns, along with ten M4 carbines, and of course, ammunition for all of the above."

Hughes just stared at Kinsey, wide-eyed.

"Well, say something, dammit! You look like you're about to have a stroke," Kinsey said.

Hughes burst out laughing. "All I can think of," he said when he'd recovered, "is out-fucking-standing! I guess... guess I've been sailing with Dan too long."

Then Hughes cast an appraising eye at the stack of boxes down on the barge.

"But all those boxes can't be just guns and ammunition," he said.

"Oh, I almost forgot," Kinsey said, "the big boxes are solar panels."

"All of them? There must be a dozen boxes there?"

"Fifteen, actually," Kinsey said. "Station Oak Island is, or was, I guess now, home to an Aids to Navigation Team maintaining buoys and lights up and down a sector of the Intracoastal Waterway. Most of those navaids are solar powered, and we received a big shipment of the latest model solar panels right before the blackout." He paused. "Given the situation, I suspect navaid maintenance isn't going to be very high on anyone's list of priorities anytime soon."

"What are we going to do with them?" Hughes asked.

Kinsey shrugged. "I don't know, but something tells me they'll come in handy. They're reliable as hell and meant to work unattended in the salt air and in the middle of nowhere, to say nothing of being covered with seagull droppings—that stuff is corrosive as hell, you know."

"I'll say one thing, Kinsey, when you commit, you go all in," Hughes said. "The guys you're leaving behind all right with you taking all this stuff? You know if things start getting back to normal in a few months, this is all going to look like a very bad idea."

"If things get back to normal, I'll take the heat for any decisions I make, and be thankful to do it," Kinsey said, shaking his head, "but I honestly can't see that happening. And as far as the other guys, they agreed to a fifty-fifty split on resources, as long as they kept the food and we documented everything." He smiled. "I haven't been in the service this long without learning how to cover my ass when necessary. Mike Butler is the chief in charge of the Aids to Navigation Team, and he's taking over as CO of the Oak Island Station. We filled out the paperwork and had a short 'change of command' ceremony this morning. Me and the other guys going with you all officially requested transfers to the Marine Safety Unit in Port Arthur, Texas, which in his role of commanding officer, Mike provisionally approved since we aren't in contact with anyone to say no. We followed the time-honored concept it's better to apologize than ask permission."

Hughes grinned appreciatively. "Pretty slick, but what about all the stuff?"

"We're one of the first units to receive our allotment of the new solar panels, and it would be selfish of us not to share them with our unit in Port Arthur during this time of scarcity," Kinsey said piously. "Nor can we in good conscience see valuable government property or, for that matter, this private vessel, which we have an obligation to safeguard, sail unprotected in this increasingly lawless environment. Therefore, we have drawn sufficient armaments and resources to execute that protective mission. Further to the execution of the mission, and in the US Coast Guard's best tradition of making maximum use of limited resources, we are pursuing those multiple missions efficiently, by cost effectively transporting personnel, equipment, and dependents to their new duty station while simultaneously conducting said protective mission."

Hughes shook his head, still grinning. "I gotta hand it to you, Chief, you're full of surprises."

Kinsey grinned back. "Oh, you haven't seen them all yet, Captain. Matter of fact, I think we can expect visitors any time—"

Kenny Nunez, the bosun, shouted across the deck from where he was standing at the ship side next to the terminal. "Captain, there's some sort of armored car with a machine gun on top coming this way through the terminal!"

"I was getting to that," Kinsey said. "Now about those provisions..."

M/V PECOS TRADER
CONFERENCE ROOM

DAY 9, 5:00 P.M.

Hughes' chair squeaked a bit as he leaned to his left and whispered to Georgia Howell, "Any word from Tex?"

She shook her head and whispered back, "No, but it shouldn't be long. She'll either find something or she won't, and I told her to call me on the radio, either way."

Hughes nodded and turned his attention to the group crowded elbow to elbow around the rectangular table that nearly filled the small conference room. He sat at the head, nominal host to the impromptu meeting, and opposite him at the far end sat a man of early middle age with chestnut hair shot with streaks of gray Hughes suspected weren't there a week earlier. Dark circles under the man's eyes gave testimony to lack of sleep. His ACUs bore the insignia of a major, and he was flanked on one side by a younger black man wearing lieutenant's bars and on the other by a sergeant.

On Hughes' end of the table sat his three senior officers, and in the middle on either side were the two senior Coast Guardsmen, Kinsey representing the group sailing with the ship, and Chief Boatswain's Mate Mike Butler as the new CO of Station Oak Island. Also summoned to the meeting at the suggestion of Dan Gowan (and looking decidedly ill at ease) was Levi Jenkins.

Major Douglas Hunnicutt shook his head. "It's a good location, but there's no way we have enough people to secure it. We're down to fifty combat effectives, maybe seventy-five if we multitask support people, and between the container terminal and oil terminal, there's just too much perimeter fence. And we've still got over three hundred civilians depending on us." He sighed. "I'd like to save those people at least. I'm thinking the wisest course of action is to get out of the city while we still have the means, and hope FEMA resupplies us."

"But we don't really have to defend it all, sir," Sergeant Josh Wright countered. "It's ten feet high topped with razor wire, so we just have to control the gates and patrol the rest, while we use the containers to build an interior strong point if we need to fall back. If the Coasties move up and join us like Chief Kinsey and I discussed," he added, warming to the argument, "we'll have our back to the river and they'll be protecting that. Besides, I'd rather take a chance on whatever is in these containers than FEMA. There must be a thousand containers here, and there's BOUND to be some food in some of them."

"You don't know WHAT'S in those containers, Sergeant," the major countered, "and we don't have the manpower to start a treasure hunt. And as far as moving the containers, we don't even know if any of the equipment in the terminal is operable or if we have anyone who can operate it even if it—"

"Sorry to interrupt, Major," Hughes said, "but there are at least SEVERAL thousand containers in the terminal, and I suspect the sergeant's right about the food. The US imports a lot, and it just makes sense some percentage of these boxes contain canned goods." The major glared at him for interrupting and was about to cut him off when Hughes raised a hand. "But we'll know soon enough. Our Coast Guard friends here were kind enough to ferry our third mate to the terminal. She's sailed container ships and she'll search the terminal offices for cargo manifests. We should know pretty quickly what's in each box and exactly where it's located in the terminal. There won't be any need for a treasure hunt."

Hunnicutt sighed and settled back in his chair, then looked back and forth between Hughes and Wright. "Even presuming we identify useful resources, what you're suggesting is looting, the prevention of which is one of our primary missions. The contents of those containers doesn't belong to us, and I have no authority to appropriate private property. My orders are to prevent looting with any force necessary."

The room fell silent for a long moment until Dan Gowan spoke from Hughes' right.

"How's that 'looting prevention' thing working out for you?"

Hunnicutt glared at the chief engineer and was about to reply when Hughes cut him off.

"Look, Major," Hughes said. "I understand your position, but when did you last receive any orders you have even a remote chance of successfully executing?"

Hunnicutt shifted uncomfortably in his chair. "I haven't gotten any orders that made sense since this whole fiasco started" — his face hardened — "but that doesn't mean we should quit trying to execute our —"

"*Pecos Trader* , *Pecos Trader* , this is Tex. Do you copy?" squawked Georgia Howell's radio.

"We copy, Tex," Georgia said into her own unit. "Find anything?"

"The mother lode," came the reply, "but you really need to see this for yourself. I'm on the way back, be there in ten. Tex out."

***

Fifteen minutes later, the group watched impatiently while Georgia Howell leafed quickly through a thick stack of paper brought in by Shyla Texeira, the third mate. Tex retreated to the corner and leaned against the bulkhead, her arms crossed as she waited and watched.

"Dammit, Mate," Hughes said, when Howell was about a third of the way through the thick stack, "what's the deal?"

"Oh, sorry," said Howell, looking up. "There's tons of stuff here. I'm only scanning for food, but so far I'd guess at least a hundred containers, maybe more. Canned seafood of all sorts, pine nuts, water chestnuts and other Asian veggies… it's just… a lot," she finished, unable to articulate the sheer magnitude of their discovery.

Hughes looked at Hunnicutt. "Well, Major, there's obviously food here. What now?"

Hunnicutt nodded. "Under those circumstances, I suppose it does make sense to secure this area as our new base of operations. We'll use what we need to sustain ourselves and distribute food to the civilian population until FEMA can get its act together and the power is restored —"

"The power's not coming back, at least not for a long time. Maybe never."

Everyone turned to where Levi sat, looking nervous at the sudden attention.

"And how do you figure that?" the major asked, then looked back and forth between Levi and Hughes. "And who the hell are you, exactly? I can understand the role of everyone else here, but I can't quite figure out what qualifies you to be in this meeting."

Levi opened his mouth to respond, but Hughes beat him to it.

"Mr. Jenkins is a trusted member of my crew," Hughes said. "And of all the people here, he's the only one who's been consistently right about what to expect since this whole mess began." He paused. "So to answer your question, Major, he's likely the only guy in this room with a clue, so my advice is to listen to him. Go ahead, Levi."

Levi hesitated, looking back and forth between Hughes and Hunnicutt. He took a deep breath and started to speak.

"I'm no expert," he said, "but I've been reading about this stuff a long time. Solar storms are sometimes accompanied by coronal mass ejections, or CMEs for short, which generate power spikes in the electrical distribution grid. In this case, we've been hit by multiple CMEs. The way I understand it, the long transmission lines act like antennas to collect power, and it pretty much burns out anything connected to them, specifically the big transformers. Those transformers are big and expensive, and there are minimal spares. If the solar storm smoked even ten or twenty percent of those big transformers, power could be down for months or even years.

"So ask yourself, where are they going to get those spares if there's no power to the plants that make them? And supposing they did miraculously get spares, who's going to install them? It's not like a hurricane, where linemen from Maine or Nebraska or Washington State roll in to help out. This disaster is everywhere, and even supposing there was enough fuel in the right places to get repair crews on the road, all those linemen are trying to make sure their own families don't starve. No one is going to voluntarily leave their family in danger or their own community in the dark to go help restore power somewhere else."

Levi shook his head again. "It took a century for electrical distribution to reach the stage it's at now, or was a week ago anyway, and right now, we're back to 1900. I think the power grid's down for the count, and the quicker everyone accepts that, the better off they'll be. Waiting for the lights to come on is right up there with waiting for Santa Claus, in my opinion."

The room fell silent.

"That's a pretty grim assessment," Hunnicutt said at last, "and with all due respect, I'm not particularly inclined to base my actions on the theory of some random seaman. But supposing for the sake of argument you're correct, what do you propose?"

Levi shrugged. "We all saw those transformers exploding like a string of firecrackers, and we all saw the Northern Lights, so believe what you want, Major," he said. "And I'm not proposing anything, because all this is way above my pay grade. I'm going to take care of me and mine, and that's all I can really do. I just want y'all to go into things with your eyes open, that's all."

Mike Butler spoke for the first time, nodding at Levi, "I just met most of the people in this room an hour ago, Major, but for my money, this guy makes more sense than anything else I've heard since this whole mess started. The way I look at it, we've got nothing to lose by assuming he's right and acting accordingly, as in 'plan for the worst, hope for the best.' And speaking for the Coast Guard, we don't have enough people to maintain a presence down at Oak Island and one here to guard what is apparently our only source of supply, so I'm moving my people and their dependents up here and forting up somehow, whatever you decide to do. There's more than enough here to last us, all of us, for the foreseeable future, no matter what happens."

"Don't think all these goodies y'all found are going to last forever," Levi interrupted, "not the fuel in this ship and the terminal tanks, or the food in the containers. All of it has a shelf life."

"He's right about the fuel at least," Dan Gowan added. "This gas and diesel will last a year or two without stabilizer before it starts degrading, and there isn't any way you're going to come up with enough additive to stabilize it all. It will be useless in three years at the outside." He shrugged. "I don't know about the canned food, but I doubt it would last much longer."

"I can't speak for anyone else," Georgia Howell said, "but I'm not particularly thrilled about eating anything processed in China anyway, even if it was canned last week."

Laughter rippled through the group, easing the tension somewhat.

"All right," Hunnicutt said. "I'm not sold on this, but it does seem to be the only sensible plan at the moment." He turned to the lieutenant beside him. "Lieutenant Arnold, set up a guard rotation for the gates both here at the oil terminal and also for the container terminal next door. One Humvee with a fifty caliber and two troops at each gate at all times. Knock a hole in the fence between the two terminals and keep two extra men and one of the civilian vehicles as a reserve force to support either location or respond to threats elsewhere on the perimeter. There are no apparent threats for the moment, so we'll forgo full perimeter patrols until we get everyone inside and some sort of routine established. Also set up a schedule to ferry our troops and civilians here. I'd like everyone inside and things buttoned up by" — he looked at his wristwatch — "twenty-two hundred."

Arnold nodded. "Yes, sir, but that's pretty quick. There'll be some bitching from the civilians."

"Let 'em bitch all they want, but make sure they understand we're moving, and if they want to move with us and be protected during the move, they better be ready. If not, they get left behind and make their way here the best they can."

"Yes, sir," Lieutenant Arnold said, and Hunnicutt turned to Sergeant Wright. "Sergeant, since this was all your idea, I suggest you start looking at the office buildings in both terminals and figure out how we're going to turn them into accommodations." He looked over at Mike Butler. "And since we're sharing space with the Coast Guard, I suspect you need to coordinate with Chief Butler here."

"Yes, sir," Wright said, "about that. It's going to be pretty tight. However, there's that RV dealership down Carolina Beach Boulevard. I bet there are a hundred RVs and trailers just sitting there, and a lot of them even have their own generators. Since fuel's no longer a problem, I think they could be real useful."

Hunnicutt glared at him momentarily and then sighed.

"What the hell. I guess if we're going to be looters, we may as well be thorough," Hunnicutt said. "Take what you need from wherever you find it, under one iron-clad condition. Under no circumstances are you to take anything occupied or actively claimed by civilians, even if you suspect they may have acquired it by less than legal means. We're not in the confiscation business. All those poor bastards out there are having it hard enough without us adding to it. Are we clear on that?"

"Crystal, sir," Wright said.

"There is one more thing we need to discuss," Mike Butler interjected. "We haven't talked about water. We've still got water at Oak Island, but I suspect that's only because there's a pretty big water tower for a fairly small population. However, we checked the buildings in the terminal and it looks like everything is drained here in Wilmington. I suppose we can boil and filter river water if we have to, but it will take some time to jury-rig some means of filtering and sterilizing water on a sizable scale." He looked at Hunnicutt. "Y'all have any water to spare?"

Hunnicutt looked at Wright, who shook his head. "A week or ten days drinking water for our own group. I don't know—"

"I think we can help you out there," Hughes said, nodding toward Dan Gowan. "How about it, Chief? Can we spot our friends here some water?"

"Sure," Gowan said. "We came in almost full, and I'll be able to make some more on the way down to Texas. I could probably let you have two hundred tons with no problem."

"Ahh... how much is that in gallons?" Wright asked.

"A bit more than fifty thousand," Gowan said, "though I don't know where you're going to put it all."

"Don't worry about that," Wright said. "You pump it and we'll find a place to put it."

CHAPTER NINE

M/V Pecos Trader
Main Deck
Wilmington Container Terminal

Day 10, 4:00 p.m.

Gowan leaned his elbows on the ship's rail and squirted tobacco juice into the void between the ship's side and the dock.

"Damned if he didn't do it," Gowan said, watching a mixed group of North Carolina National Guardsmen and US Coast Guardsmen wrestle a heavy hose into an aboveground swimming pool erected on the dock near the stern of *Pecos Trader* . Two identical filled swimming pools rested in line with the pool currently filling, covers in place to protect the precious drinking water. Two Coasties were adding a fourth pool to the line, erecting it rapidly with a practiced ease gained from assembly of the first units.

"Sergeant Wright is nothing if not resourceful," Hughes said. "Will he be able to take the whole two hundred tons?"

"He found a whole damned container full of those pools," Gowan said, "and he wants to erect two more. That'll give him capacity for almost two hundred and fifty tons, and I've a mind to give him the extra if you have no objection, Cap? I can distill almost that much on our southbound passage, and these guys are going to have their plate pretty full without having to immediately solve the water problem. Besides, it's not like we're not making out on the deal."

Hughes nodded and looked down the deck where the bosun was sitting in the cab of the hose-handling crane, watching Georgia Howell at the ship's side and waiting for her hand signals to lift a load aboard. On the dock below the dangling crane hook, two sailors were rigging a twenty-foot container for lifting. Other partially filled twenty footers stood open on the dock nearby, across from several open and densely packed forty-foot containers. Chief Cook Jake Kadowski, aka 'Polak,' scurried between them all, directing sailors from the deck and steward's departments in transferring stores from the forty-footers and stuffing the twenty footers with the most useful provisions.

They'd found the empty twenty-foot containers in the terminal, a fortunate find since they could be handled with the limited capacity and reach of the ship's hose-handling crane. Hughes was hoping to get six or even eight of the smaller containers aboard. Far more food than they could conceivably use, but in the new world in which they found themselves, something told him there was no such thing as too much food.

"That was good thinking on shifting over to this dock, by the way," Gowan said. "We had the main engine all set to go, but I'm glad we didn't need it."

Hughes grinned. "The first law of wing-walking. Never let go of one handhold until you have a firm grasp on another."

When they'd decided to move upstream the short distance to the container terminal, the Coasties helped them out by running a mooring line over to the container dock with one of their patrol boats, and a long line of National Guardsmen had taken the end and heaved the massive rope up on the dock and put the eye on one of the mooring bits. Hughes had pulled the ship forward by heaving in on the line with the ship's mooring winch, keeping the bow off the container dock during the approach by using his bow thruster. He'd made the move 'dead ship' without using the ship's main engine.

"And speaking of shifting," Gowan said, "when do you think we'll get out of here?"

"Tomorrow maybe, the day after at the outside," Hughes said. "Later than I wanted, but worth the delay, considering how much better off we'll be when we leave."

Hughes looked out over the bustling terminal, the National Guardsmen had moved in camping trailers and RVs parked in neat rows, and elsewhere erected large tents to serve as field kitchens and a mess tent. Several container transporters worked feverishly, rearranging those containers identified as having food to where they were all at ground level and accessible.

"It's amazing how much has been accomplished in twenty-four hours," Hughes said.

"Thanks to Tex for a lot of that," Gowan said, nodding down to the dock where the slender third mate held a clipboard and was now conferring with the chief cook. "Bringing in the terminal guys was frigging brilliant."

"That it was," Hughes said, smiling at the memory of Tex speaking up just before yesterday's meeting broke up, pointing out she'd found the contact list with the names and addresses of terminal personnel when she was searching for the cargo manifests, and that all those terminal employees were likely 'scared shitless' just like everyone else. Everyone had shrugged, until she suggested those with homes within easy reach of Major Hunnicutt's Humvees would likely be amenable to joining the group with their families, trading food and shelter for their knowledge of, you know, how all this stuff actually worked. Everyone jumped at the idea, and she'd further pointed out there was probably a similar list in the offices of the product terminal. A quick search proved her correct.

So Major Hunnicutt had 're-tasked some assets,' and by the following morning the little group of Coasties, National Guardsmen, and assorted civilians was joined by nine container terminal employees and two product terminal employees, with their families, five dogs, three cats, and a goldfish. Major Hunnicutt had a rather loud discussion with Sergeant Wright concerning the arrival of the pets, whereupon Sergeant Wright suggested perhaps the major might like to explain to the various children why their pets were being abandoned. The major dropped the subject. The point soon became moot in any event, as before the day was out, one of the cats ate the goldfish, then ran off along with both the other cats, and everyone liked the dogs.

"How about Levi?" Gowan asked. "You think he's going to stay with these folks? I'm sure they could use him."

Hughes looked across the deck where Levi and his father-in-law, Anthony, stood examining their aluminum boat.

He shrugged. "I know Chief Butler and Sergeant Wright are trying to talk him into bringing his family in, though I think Major Hunnicutt's not a big Levi fan just yet. However, Levi's gonna do what he thinks is best for him and his family, and you can't blame him."

* * *

"A hundred things can happen," Anthony McCoy said, "and ninety-nine of them are bad. I'm for keeping our distance."

Levi nodded. "I feel the same, but what if these folks do make a go of it? We wouldn't be so isolated and Celia and Jo and the kids would be part of a community. There's something to be said for that." He paused. "And besides, we don't have to worry about being the only black folks in the group. Between the Coasties and the National Guard and their families, it looks like almost a third of the group is black."

"I'll grant you it's tempting," Anthony said, "and it looks like food won't be a problem for a while anyway, but they're not exactly low profile, and guns or not, I reckon someone, or a lot of someones, is gonna take a shot at taking what they have. Our whole idea was to be invisible, and they're just the opposite."

"I know, I know," Levi said, then fell silent.

"All right, boy, what's eatin' you? Seems like this is bothering you way more than it should."

"It's just there are a lot of things they haven't considered," Levi said. "I mean, they just can't go handing out food without a plan. Yes, they need to help folks because a lot of stuff is likely to go bad before they can eat it anyway, but if they set up a feeding station, it needs to be some distance away or else they'll have a huge refugee camp right on their doorstep. And all those folks attracted by the food are going to be a sanitation nightmare, completely aside from the fact the folks here in the terminal haven't even considered the sanitation issue for their OWN group. And what about water? *Pecos Trader* probably left them enough for three months, but by then, they need to have some sort —"

"And you think you're gonna solve all the problems for them, huh?" Anthony asked. "All these folks looking up to the great Levi after you been hearing folks giggle up their sleeves about your 'prepper ways' all this time. Think maybe there might be a little bit of ego involved here, Levi?"

Levi bristled and started to reply; then he relaxed and nodded. "Yeah, maybe a little."

"Understandable," Anthony said, "but you can't let that get in the way of taking care of the family."

"I won't, but I do think I could help these people."

"I think you could too," Anthony said, "but how about this. We help them on a 'commuter' basis. We can stay in our hidey-hole but keep in touch with them on a regular basis by radio. If we use the Brunswick, we can get here fairly quickly and avoid passing through Wilmington. When we learn all the cutoffs and shortcuts, I think it might be not much more than an hour's run with the outboard. You come down here and help them out a couple of days a week, and maybe get paid in food. When hunting's good, we can also bring them in deer and pigs to trade. If everything seems to be safe, we can bring the family in maybe once every couple of weeks, just like farm families went to town in the old days. Difference is, we don't let NOBODY know where our home place is.

"In time," Anthony continued, "we may even decide it's safe enough to move into the group, but we ALWAYS keep our bug-out place stocked and ready, so we can take off if need be. How's that sound?"

"Sounds like a plan," Levi said.

CHAPTER TEN

M/V Pecos Trader
Starboard Bridge Wing
Wilmington Container Terminal

Day 11, 2:00 p.m.

Hughes paced the bridge wing and stared down at the main deck, where his crewmen and their new Coast Guard shipmates swarmed over the containers, securing them for sea under the watchful eye of Georgia Howell. Despite his nervousness, he had to suppress a smile when he saw Polak approaching her, arms waving. The chief cook was known for his excitability, and 'getting Polak spun up' was a favorite pastime among the unlicensed crew. Hughes heard a footstep on the deck behind him and turned to find Matt Kinsey standing there, a sympathetic look on his face.

"Nervous, Cap?" he asked.

Hughes sighed and ran a hand through his hair. "As a whore in church," he admitted. "I've practically memorized the damn chart, but I don't mind telling you I'm terrified. I never thought I'd make my debut as a harbor pilot taking a fully loaded tanker downstream with no tugs and a following current. I'm beginning to wonder if this is such a good idea."

"Well, at least you're timing the tide right. Besides," Kinsey said, "it's either this or stay here, right?"

Hughes nodded and was about to reply when his radio squawked.

"Mate to bridge. Over," came Georgia Howell's voice over the radio.

"Bridge, go ahead, Georgia," Hughes replied.

"Captain, Polak says one of the twenties he had marked didn't get loaded aboard —"

"What the hell is he talking about? He supervised the stuffing of those containers himself," Hughes demanded, and then belatedly added, "Over."

"This was a twenty he found on the inventory that didn't need re-stuffing," Georgia replied, "but I guess the terminal guys got overwhelmed and didn't bring it to the dock. He wants to hold up until we can get —"

"Absolutely not," Hughes said. "We have to leave here within the hour to hit the Battery Island turn at full flood tide, and it's going to be hairy enough at that. Nothing is important enough to delay that, so tell Polak to suck it up and figure something out. He's got eight containers full of extra food. Over."

Hughes turned back and looked over the wind dodger as he spoke, gazing down to where Polak was standing in front of Georgia Howell, arms waving. He saw the mate raise the microphone to her mouth again.

"Uh, Captain," said Howell, "Polak says it's not food. Over."

"Okay, what's so critical we can't live without it?"

"Uh, toilet paper," came the reply.

Hughes cursed under his breath. He heard a strangling sound behind him and turned to see Kinsey struggling unsuccessfully to keep from laughing. He snarled into his radio.

"You tell Polak to get his ass ashore and organize getting that container alongside. This vessel is leaving the dock in forty-five minutes and not one minute later, container or no container. Is that clear? Over."

"Yes sir," Howell replied, and Hughes saw her speak to Polak, who then raced for the gangway.

"Toilet paper!" Hughes muttered as he resumed pacing the bridge wing.

M/V PECOS TRADER
BRIDGE
WILMINGTON CONTAINER TERMINAL

DAY 11, 2:40 P.M.

"You okay down there, Dan?" Hughes asked into the telephone.

"Ready as we'll ever be," Gowan replied, adding after a short pause, "Don't worry Jordan, you can do this."

"Your lips to God's ear, friend," Hughes said. "Should be any time now."

Hughes hung up and turned as Levi Jenkins and the other three departing crewmen came through the stairwell door. He smiled and nodded.

"Looks like this is it, folks," Hughes said. "I'm sorry to lose you all, but I understand your decisions, and wish you all good luck and Godspeed getting back to your families."

"Same to you, Captain," Levi said, extending his hand.

Hughes shook first Levi's hand, then Bill Wiggins, the departing second engineer's. He turned to Singletary, but before he extended his hand, the man gave him a curt nod and Hughes didn't press it. When he turned to Shyla Texiera, she brushed his hand aside and took him off guard by folding him in a fierce hug before stepping back, her eyes glistening.

"Captain, if it wasn't for my folks—"

He held up a hand to stop her. "We know that, Tex. We're going to miss you, but no one faults you for leaving." He included them all with his glance. "Any of you. Family comes first."

Levi pulled a folded piece of paper from his pocket and handed it over. "I don't know what's going to happen, Captain, but here are radio frequencies I'll be monitoring and the days and times I'll be listening if you ever want to establish contact. I'd like to keep in touch if we can."

"As would I, Levi," Hughes said and slipped the paper into his pocket.

The group stood quietly for a few moments until Hughes broke the awkward silence.

He smiled sadly. "Well, folks, all ashore that's going ashore. Otherwise you'll be taking a trip downriver."

With more murmured goodbyes, the group turned for the stairwell door, and when the last one was through it, Hughes took a brief moment to compose himself and then moved forward to gaze out the wide wheelhouse windows as the last container dropped into place on deck under the watchful eye of the mate. He called her on his radio and saw her raise her own mike to her mouth.

"Bridge, this is the mate. Over."

"Georgia," Hughes said, "our departing folks are headed ashore. Please take the gangway in as soon as they're off. Leave the Coasties to secure the last container and gangway, and have our deck gang turn to fore and aft. I want you and Boats on the bow during transit and both anchors backed out ready to drop if necessary. Attend to that first and let me know when you're done, please. Then stand by to single up lines on my order. Over."

"Understood, Captain," she replied, looking back up at the bridge window. "I'll let you know when we're ready. Mate out."

Hughes nodded, and he saw her head bob in an answering nod far below.

"Just a suggestion, but you might want to have her rig the pilot ladder on the offshore side," said a voice behind him.

He whirled to see Kinsey standing there grinning.

"What the hell are you talking about?"

Kinsey's grin widened and he jerked his head toward the port bridge wing and started that way, a confused Hughes on his heels. When they got to the bridge wing, Kinsey pointed downstream to where one of the smaller Coast Guard patrol boats was approaching at top speed, with three people aboard.

"So? Who are those people?" Hughes asked.

"Well, two of them are Coasties," Kinsey said, "but the third, well, the third is Captain Randall Ewing, retired Wilmington harbor pilot and fishing buddy of my good friend Chief Butler. Mike convinced him, via some inducement that shall remain confidential, to come out of retirement for one last transit."

"What? Why the hell didn't you tell me, Goddamn it!" Hughes demanded. "I've been sweating bullets here."

"Because Mike didn't even know if Captain Ewing was still at his house on the river, and we couldn't spare the guys to go look until this morning." Kinsey paused. "We've been sort of busy if you'll recall?"

Hughes nodded, unable to speak.

"Anyway, we didn't even want to mention the possibility until we were sure it was going to happen, as we figured you were pretty stressed as it was, and it might really screw with your head if you thought you might get a pilot and then found out it wasn't happening at the last minute. Mike called me about ten minutes ago and said they were headed upriver." Kinsey grinned again. "So like I said, we better get the pilot ladder rigged."

"Kinsey, I could kiss you!" Hughes said.

The Coastie took a step back. "I'd just as soon you didn't, if it's all the same to you."

M/V PECOS TRADER
CAPE FEAR RIVER — SOUTHBOUND

DAY 11, 5:00 P.M.

Captain Randall Ewing glanced ahead to starboard, squinting in the bright sunlight at a substantial concrete wharf along the western riverbank.

"That's the northern wharf of the Military Ocean Terminal," he said, nodding toward the riverbank, "and this is where things start getting a bit tricky. The channel narrows from six hundred to four hundred feet soon, and the current picks up quite a bit, even on the incoming tide."

Hughes only nodded, a tight-lipped frown on his face.

Randall Ewing's eyes never left the river, but a slight smile tugged at the corners of his mouth.

"You can relax at least a little, Captain Hughes," Ewing said. "This isn't my first transit, or even my first transit without tugs. I'll get you to the sea buoy all right."

"Sorry. Is it that obvious?"

Ewing chuckled. "You're as nervous as a nine-tailed cat in a room full of rocking chairs, and I suspect your fingerprints are probably permanently pressed into that rail."

Hughes laughed, the tension easing a bit. "Well, I'd be a hell of a lot more nervous if you hadn't turned up, I can tell you that. I'll bet you didn't figure you'd be coming out of retirement like this."

Ewing shrugged, eyes still on the river. "Didn't figure on coming out of retirement at all. I've got a nice place along the river and I was happy as a clam — until the power went out, anyway."

"What are you going to do now?" Hughes asked.

"Survive, I guess," Ewing responded. "We don't have it too bad, at least compared to most folks. I've got a nice place on the river, up in a little cove, actually, secluded like. Our two kids and grandkids made it there, so at least the immediate family's okay, and that's a blessing. We're on a well and have a septic system, and there's also an older well on the place with a hand pump. I kept it as a curiosity, really—our kids and then our grandkids liked to pump the handle and watch the water come out. Damn glad I got it now. My wife's always been into gardening and canning, so we're pretty well stocked up for a while." He smiled. "And it looks like we'll be eating a lot of fish.

"And as far as power goes," he continued, "I got a small generator after the last hurricane scare, and the Coasties"—he nodded to starboard where the Coast Guard patrol boat was moving along with the ship—"are hooking me up with some of those solar panels of theirs. That was my pilotage fee for getting you out of here."

"Cheap at several times the price," Hughes said.

Ewing grinned. "Glad you feel that way, because I'm looking for a little contribution from you too. How about a case of coffee? We can't grow that."

"Done," Hughes said.

Conversation lapsed as they both studied the river ahead, the silence broken only by occasional helm orders from Ewing. Then the pilot walked out to the bridge wing to study the bank a bit more intently and returned to the wheelhouse.

"Okay," Ewing said, "it's going to get a bit hairier from this point on. In half an hour we'll be going into Battery Island Turn, which means a ninety-five-degree turn to port, and I have to keep enough speed on her to maintain steerage way or the current will set us hard into the bank."

Half an hour later, Matt Kinsey stepped on to the bridge to find Fort Caswell to starboard as *Pecos Trader* cleared the channel, her bow pointed toward the open sea.

"Thank God," he heard Hughes say as Captain Ewing nodded in obvious agreement.

Kinsey looked toward the open sea and his mouth dropped open. Spread out in the nearby anchorage were a dozen ships of various sizes and types. "Damn, would you look at that," he said.

"Make's sense," Ewing said. "The port's been closed, what, eleven days now. It was unusually empty when the blackout hit, but there had to be inbound traffic, and here it is."

"Tanker outbound, tanker outbound," the radio squawked, "do you have a pilot aboard? This is the container vessel *Maersk Tangier* . We urgently require a pilot—"

"Tanker outbound, tanker outbound, any pilot aboard tanker outbound. This is the container vessel *Hanjin Wilmington* ," broke in a Korean-accented voice. "We at anchor and I claim priority—"

"US Coast Guard vessel with outbound tanker," said a Greek-accented voice, "this is the bulk carrier *Sabrina* , inbound with thirty thousand metric tons of wheat. I have a fuel emergency with less than twenty-four hours of fuel remaining. I must proceed to berth or have a bunker barge immediately."

The chaotic calls increased as more of the ships at anchor spotted the outbound tanker and pressed their claims for attention. Hughes reached over to turn down the volume on the VHF radio, then shook his head in amazement.

Wheels turned in Kinsey's head.

"What do you think about that?" Hughes asked.

"I think," Kinsey said, turning toward Ewing, "Captain Ewing here just started the first successful 'post blackout' small business, and Chief Butler and Major Hunnicutt just got several shiploads full of early Christmas presents. We just have to sort out what's waiting out here and pass the word back so they can tell Captain Ewing here what they want first, and where. You okay with that Captain Ewing?"

The old pilot shrugged. "I don't know what's in the containers, but I see another tanker and also at least two bulkers, and they're likely full of grain. I can't see leaving stuff out here that might feed or otherwise help people. It'll take a few days, 'cause we can only do daylight transits, but with the Coasties help, I can likely find at least a couple of other pilots. We can probably get all this stuff inside in a week or so." He paused.

"Thing is, I expect at least a few more ships will show up, especially northbound grain cargoes from South America, as they're normally two weeks or more in transit."

Hughes nodded. "Well, we'll leave that for you and the guys in Wilmington to figure out."

Ewing returned his nod as a slow smile spread over his face.

"What are you grinning about, Captain?" Kinsey asked.

"Just realizing I won't be running out of coffee anytime soon," Ewing replied.

An hour later, after a rough assessment of the ships at anchor and a radio exchange with Wilmington, Kinsey and Hughes stood on the bridge wing and watched the Coast Guard patrol boat pull away from the ship's side, bound for the Greek bulk carrier *Sabrina* .

"Distributing raw grain is going to be challenging," Hughes said.

"They'll figure something out," Kinsey said, "and it's a lot better problem to have than trying to figure out how you're going to survive with nothing."

Hughes nodded, seemingly distracted.

"Why so glum?" Kinsey asked. "The river transit's behind us and we're ready to head south."

"Just thinking ahead," Hughes said, "because when we get to Texas, we're going to be the one's out at the mouth of the river with no pilot."

MAYPORT NAVAL STATION
JACKSONVILLE, FLORIDA

DAY 11, 1:00 P.M.

Sergeant Joel Washington squinted against the midday sun and looked out across the growing ranks of temporary shelters rapidly transforming the former golf course into a sizable town. Mayport had been tight on housing anyway, and with families of the shipboard sailors now required to live within the base perimeter—also in temporary shelters—there'd been no choice but to expand the base, and the adjacent country club had been the logical choice. They'd set up portable toilets and shower facilities as well, with a pump providing salt water from the inlet in unlimited quantities anytime but with a three-minute fresh water rinse available twice a week. Most of the members of the newly formed Special Reaction Force preferred to combine the two, so twice weekly showers had become the norm. Combined with the heat and humidity of north Florida and the increasing stench of the portable toilets, personal hygiene (or lack thereof) contributed greatly to the growing 'ambiance' of the camp.

Washington flicked a bead of sweat off his forehead. It didn't help that the new black uniforms could double as solar collectors, and he wondered for the hundredth time what genius had decided black was a good color for operations in the southern US in the summer, or anytime for that matter? Then again he strongly suspected the color was chosen to intimidate rather than conceal, for despite the recruitment pitch about 'serving the nation in time of crisis,' there was growing awareness among the newly recruited that the SRF were meant to be shock troops—insurance against civil unrest. The recent word the assignment was permanent rather than temporary as promised hadn't been well-received among the 'volunteers,' but no one had chosen the 'honorable discharge' option, or at least any 'takers' had been removed quietly. The consequences of being disarmed and dropped into the growing refugee population, far from friends or former comrades, didn't bear thinking about.

He heard distant whoops and laughter and turned toward a yet to be developed area of the golf course, where several men had stripped to their skivvies and were using one of the former water hazards as a swimming hole. That was technically against standing orders, but discipline was considerably more relaxed in the SRF than it ever was in the 101st Airborne and he was quickly learning to pick his battles. Maybe an alligator would eat their asses, he thought, and turned a blind eye to the swimming hole before he ducked into a shelter. He stood in the comparative gloom, waiting for his eyes to adjust. Corporal Neal Long was bitching as usual.

"I been eatin' this garbage five days now, and I haven't had a decent crap in three," Long said, staring down morosely at the contents of an MRE spread before him.

"Meals-refusal-to-exit, dude," said the man seated next to Long, with a shake of his head, "and it ain't gonna get any better unless you can score a few of those chili mac meals. Those things will set you free."

"And they distribute them like one in ten or twelve and every swinging dick in this camp is gonna hoard them, Gibson, so the 'chili mac exit strategy' isn't exactly a workable solution. And besides," Long said, "this is bullshit. In a camp this size there should be a kitchen and dining tent. Even you jarheads are that civilized."

Gibson shook his head. "When I left Lejeune, they were already running out of regular chow and switching to MREs, and it's the same thing here. I talked to some of the fleet Marines on the ships here and they told me the same story. Only difference is the galley squids heat up all the packages at once and set 'em out for the guys to grab when they go through the chow line."

"And you should be glad you have it, Long," Washington said from his spot near the entrance, "so quit your bitching. There are a lot of folks out there going hungry."

Long sighed and looked back down at the food packets. "I know, Sergeant, but some of this stuff is just nasty."

"Washington's right," said Grogan from where he sat on the opposite side of the shelter. "Save all the nasty stuff. Just give it a couple of more weeks for reality to set in good and you'll be able to trade it for all the 'fugee pussy you want." He grinned at the men on either side of him. "Ain't that right, boys?"

Washington crossed the floor to loom over Grogan and glared down at him.

"That's SERGEANT Washington, Grogan, and leaving aside how despicable that statement was, you seem to forget there's a 'no fraternization' policy in effect. You stay the hell away from civilians except in the line of duty. You got that?"

Grogan rose to his feet and looked Washington in the eye with an expression just short of a sneer. "Well, 'Sergeant,' I believe if you'll check, you'll find that 'no frat' rule is for regular troops, not us. And since the only pay we're likely to get in this wonderful new world is a place to bunk and these crappy MREs, I reckon we have to take our fringe benefits where we find them. And FYI, 'Sergeant,' me and the boys here"—he nodded at his two companions—"have been with Rorke through a lot of shit shows, and I can tell you from experience he don't sweat the small shit as long as it keeps the troops happy."

"Yeah, well, you take orders from me now, and I take mine from Lieutenant Kinsey, so you better get used to it," Washington said.

"And you better tell that prick Kinsey to lighten up," Grogan said, "or someone might roll a surprise into his quarters some dark night."

Washington's face hardened and he shoved his nose an inch from Grogan's.

"Did I just hear you threaten an officer in front of witnesses, Grogan?"

Grogan shrugged. "Just sayin' we live in dangerous times," He grinned. "But if you'd like to bring me up on charges, go ahead. I'm pretty sure I know how that would play out."

Washington stood dumbstruck by the blatant insubordination, and Grogan took a step back and moved toward the shelter exit.

"Come on, boys," Grogan said to his two companions, "let's go take a swim."

QUARTERS OF CAPTAIN QUENTIN RORKE
MAYPORT NAVAL STATION
JACKSONVILLE, FLORIDA

DAY 11, 9:00 P.M.

First Lieutenant Luke Kinsey closed his eyes and sighed as the breeze from the room air conditioner washed over him, then opened them to look at the remains of what was the best meal he'd eaten in a week—or maybe ever—spread out on the table in the flickering light of half a dozen candles.

"That was a fantastic meal, thank you, Maria," he said, as across from him, Maria Velasquez beamed at the compliment. As always, she looked as if she were about to step in front of a camera, and Luke marveled at her ability to maintain her appearance in the chaotic hell the world was becoming.

Beside Maria, Rorke reached over and covered her hand with his on the white linen tablecloth. "My Maria is a woman of varied and remarkable talents," he said, and Maria's smile widened.

"And," Rorke said, as he grinned and disengaged his hand to top off Luke's wineglass, "notwithstanding Maria's outstanding culinary talents, I suspect the air-conditioning added to our enjoyment."

"How'd you manage that, by the way? Friends in high places?" Luke asked.

Rorke laughed. "Or low places. There are two units, actually, and they were already here when we moved in, one in each bedroom. We just relocated the one in the second bedroom here to the living/dining room area. The generator's big enough to run one of them at a time and still keep the refrigerator cool, as long as we opt for candlelight."

"Which is more romantic anyway," Maria added, leaning over to nibble on Rorke's ear.

Rorke turned his face toward Maria's for a light kiss, then turned back to Luke.

"An unanticipated benefit of taking over navy enlisted quarters. We have AC and the regular officer's housing with big central units don't," Rorke said. "I was also able to scrounge a big propane grill for the garage. We just crack the garage door when we're cooking."

"So these units were empty?"

Rorke shrugged. "Rank has its privileges, Kinsey. You know that. The enlisted dependents who lived here were relocated to the temporary structures closer to the docks. It's been decided Mayport's going to be the main SRF base for the Southeast, so things have to be restructured a bit. We'll need officer's quarters, and housing inside the wire is tight. These units are now designated as housing for captains and above, which brings me to why I asked you to dinner. One of them is yours if you want it."

Luke said nothing as Rorke gazed at him in the flickering light.

"I'm not a captain," Luke replied.

"You will be if I say so," Rorke said. "We're growing daily and will be at brigade strength within two weeks. I've been given the brigade and a promotion to lieutenant colonel." He smiled at Luke's expression. "Yeah, we're going to do things a little differently in the SRF. I'm skipping the whole 'major' thing.

"Anyway," Rorke continued, "I'll need company commanders. I want you to be one of them."

"Why me?"

"Because you're smart, and you follow orders, most of the time anyway. You have a natural leadership ability. So presuming I can make sure you understand the new realities, I think you'll be an asset," Rorke said.

"What new realities?" Luke asked.

"That it's not getting any better, ever, and in fact, it will get a whole lot worse," Rorke said. "That the only ones who will prosper, or even survive, are those strong enough to take what they need and defend what they take. People are beginning to see this as The End of the World as We Know It, but that's not quite correct. It may be the end as far as YOU knew it, or as most people knew it, but it's pretty much business as usual for me and the men who currently form a big part of this force. We've been soldiering in shit holes all over the world for a lot of years. Places where we make the rules. We made large sums of money and then came back to civilization to enjoy it, but it turns out that was all just a dress rehearsal for the real thing." He grinned. "I've been training for this my whole life, I just didn't know it."

"I don't know," Luke said, after a long pause. "I'm not sure I accept your 'realities,' and even if I do, I signed up to help people, not exploit them."

Rorke's face hardened. "But you did sign up, and as you've probably figured out by now, this is a bit like the French Foreign Legion, only your hitch is forever. The only way you get out is being stripped of weapons and dropped among the 'fugees to fend for yourself. And if you stay, I can not only promote you to captain, I can also bust you back to private. So it's up to you to decide what kind of life you want."

Rorke motioned to the remains of the meal as he continued. "Where do you think that chicken and the fresh vegetables and the tomatoes for the salad you just ate came from? And what about the wine, and the generator running that air conditioner, and the gasoline running it? I've had a dozen of my guys out scrounging from the beginning, and I don't care where they find stuff or who they take it from. They take a share and pass on half to me, no questions asked. Then as long as they follow my orders, I protect them, no matter what they do. And as long as I meet the objectives set out for the SRF, FEMA doesn't give a damn either."

Luke said nothing.

"Well, what's it gonna be, Kinsey? I only make an offer once, and there are plenty of people to take the job if you don't. So you don't get to ponder it or think on it or sleep on it. I want your answer now. In or out? Captain or private?"

Luke sighed. "I guess I'll go with captain."

Rorke's face split into a grin. "Excellent choice," he said, turning to Velasquez. "This calls for a celebration. Break out the good stuff."

She nodded and moved to a sideboard, bringing back a cut-crystal decanter full of amber liquid and three squat glasses, then poured an inch of whiskey into each glass and set them within reach.

"A toast," Rorke said, raising his glass, "to Captain Kinsey."

"To Captain Kinsey," Velasquez echoed, and raised her glass.

It was the first of many toasts—one of Luke's new duties was apparently to be Rorke's drinking buddy. The decanter was quickly drained and replaced by a full bottle of whiskey of equal pedigree. By the second hour, Rorke was starting to slur his words a bit and Velasquez was openly groping him beneath the table, as well as occasionally stretching her leg out to run her toes along Luke's calf. They were both outdrinking him two or three to one, but he was definitely feeling the alcohol.

"…couldn't believe they could be so frigging stupid," Rorke said. "I mean, it's like a mercenary leader's wet dream. FEMA collects all the trained single guys motivated enough to volunteer and then just gives them to me. I get to decide to keep them or not, and anyone I can't turn into a follower gets a one-way trip to 'Fugeeville, courtesy of FEMA Air. It's a brigade now, but I'll have a regiment in two months, and in a year, an army. I'll be unstoppable, and all I gotta do is make nice with FEMA while they build, equip and feed my army."

"So what then? You set up your own kingdom?" Luke asked. "The regular military is a thousand times stronger, and they have air power. They'll crush us like bugs if we desert or go rogue."

Rorke's face split into a drunken lopsided grin. "But, Captain Kinsey, why would we ever desert or go rogue? Perish the thought! We'll do everything our FEMA superiors task us with, and they'll continue to build and support our force. And in two years or so the gas will start going bad, and spare parts will be in short supply…" He stopped and looked at Luke as if sidetracked by a random thought.

"Do you know how many friggin' spare parts and maintenance people it takes to keep those jets and choppers flying, Kinsey?" Rorke asked, his slur becoming more pronounced.

Luke shook his head.

"Me neither," Rorke said, whiskey slopping from his glass as he took a drink. "But it's a load, Kinsey. A SHIT LOAD! In two years, three at the outside, there ain't gonna be any 'air power,' and in ten or fifteen years, we'll be transitioning to horseback for most of the force."

"We'll still be outnumbered by regular troops," Luke said.

Rorke snorted. "You think so? FEMA's terrified to use them to do the dirty work, so they keep them close to base. Just sitting there with their dependents, sucking up resources and getting stale and less capable as we siphon more and more troops from them. Sooner or later FEMA's gonna cut 'em off, and they'll just dissolve or 'go rogue' themselves. Then we'll be the government's only 'enforcers,' with no counterbalance." Rorke smiled, "And we'll see who really cares about 'accountability to civilian authorities' then. Here's a hint—it won't be me. Time is on our side, Kinsey, no matter how you slice it."

"A military coup, then?" Luke asked. "But what if the government's plan is successful, and FEMA does succeed in a partial restoration of power and gets food production going? Then they can keep supporting the regular forces and there WILL be a counterbalance. What then, civil war?"

Rorke shrugged. "They may have some partial success, but even if they do, so what? It's a big country, Kinsey, and even if they have some success, they won't have the resources to control it all without us. If we can't take over what they manage to build, we'll just leave and establish our own operation outside of their control. It's all about options. And as far as civil war goes, that's inevitable, isn't it? You don't seriously think I'm the only 'ex-private security contractor' in the SFR who's figured this out, do you?"

Luke didn't answer immediately, sobered by the implications of Rorke's drunken revelations.

"So you're saying the government and FEMA are essentially creating a whole bunch of warlords," Luke said at last, "and you figure sooner or later it's going to be rival warlords fighting over whatever is left."

Rorke nodded. "For want of a better term, yes. My plan is to grow faster than the rest by becoming FEMA's fair-haired boy. After all, I've already got my own public relations department." He gave Velasquez a lascivious grin and she melted against him for an open-mouthed kiss.

The pair broke from the kiss, and Rorke turned back to Luke.

"It's like this, Kinsey," Rorke said, reaching for his glass. "If you think things are screwed up now, wait a year or two. We'll be talking medieval Genghis Khan shit, and I plan on being on top of that pile, whatever it takes. Are you with me?"

Luke hesitated and then raised his glass toward Rorke in a toast. "All hail the Great Khan!"

Two hours later, Maria Velasquez lay in bed, propped up on an elbow as she pressed her naked body against Rorke and stroked his chest hair, watching her lover in the moonlight washing in from the window.

"Do you trust him?" she asked.

"Trust is relative, my sweet. No one is trustworthy unless their interests align with my own. In Kinsey's case, I'm trying to make that happen, because I need him, and men like him."

"Why not just promote Grogan or any of the others you already know and trust?"

Rorke laughed. "I don't TRUST Grogan or any of those other idiots any more than I would trust an attack dog. I've already promoted the few who possess any leadership skills at all, and the rest are just barbarians— blunt instruments I manage and control. They're useful enough on the front line, and fine for controlling and terrorizing helpless fools in some Third World backwater, but sooner or later we may have to confront disciplined opposition, and when that happens, I'll need an officer corps. No, I need Kinsey, and men with his skills."

"Still, it seems a risk," she said. "How can you be sure of him, or anyone?"

"By starting slow," he replied. "I'll make sure each unit is a mix of my longtime mercenaries and new recruits, and send them out on nearby 'foraging' missions. If Kinsey and others like him can rein in the barbarians a bit, I have no problem with that, but my thinking is the influence will be in the opposite direction. Moral standards decline in chaos, and power corrupts—in six months, any high ideals our new recruits may have held will be long gone, and any who haven't adapted will be obvious and can be 'honorably discharged' in accordance with the guidelines our FEMA friends have so thoughtfully provided."

"What if they just leave?"

"Ahh, but that's the beauty of it," he said. "They have nowhere to go, now do they? They're all far from any support network and the FEMA guidelines ensure no organized command still functioning will take them in. If they strike out on their own, they'll be branded rogues and deserters and cut off completely, without a continuing source of food and water, to say nothing of ammunition and fuel—unless they scavenge and steal from the civilian/refugee population. So, they're going to be 'takers' in any event, because there isn't any other way they can survive. The intelligent ones like Kinsey will realize that, whether they like it or not. As much as they may be repelled by the idea, they will also come to realize if they're going to be 'marauders,' doing so with 'official' sanction is the least objectionable option."

CHAPTER ELEVEN

DAY 12, 11:00 A.M.

"Are you sure disabling the AIS was a good move?" asked Hughes, staring westward through the binoculars. "Won't it look kind of suspicious if anyone sees us and we aren't transmitting a signal?"

Hughes lowered the glasses and turned toward Kinsey, who stood beside him on the bridge wing. The Coastie shrugged. "Maybe. Maybe not. The solar storm did weird and unpredictable things, so knocking out your Automatic Identification System transmitter isn't that far-fetched. At least, it won't be dismissed as an immediate lie. Given our cargo, it's best to keep a low profile."

"You think the government would commandeer the ship?" Hughes asked.

Kinsey shrugged again. "Right now a tanker full of fuel will be mighty tempting. We might find ourselves drafted into becoming floating storage for the navy or FEMA. That may happen in Texas anyway, but at least we'll all be closer to home. We won't have a problem if we can just get past Jacksonville and Key West.

"Mayport Naval Station at Jacksonville is home port for more than a dozen navy ships, and I'm sure they can use the fuel. If they pick us up, we can probably expect a visit. But we're well offshore, so we have at least a shot at slipping past. I'm more worried about Coast Guard Station Key West. We'll have to come close inshore to transit the Florida Strait, and our cover story is a bit thin."

Kinsey had just finished speaking when they heard a familiar drone. They scanned the skies, searching for an approaching aircraft.

"And speaking of our navy friends at Jacksonville," Kinsey said, "apparently we aren't quite far enough offshore. I believe that will be them now."

"Will they board?" Hughes asked.

Kinsey shook his head. "Doubtful, at least for now. It's a fixed wing so they'll circle and take pictures, or maybe hail us and report back. If they're interested, they'll send a chopper for a closer look, but we're at extreme chopper range, so they won't be able to hang around. If they decide to board, we're screwed anyway."

Both men stared as the P-3 Orion dropped lower into a long looping orbit above the ship. On the third pass, the VHF squawked.

"Southbound tanker, southbound tanker, this is the US Navy aircraft over you. Do you copy? Over."

Hughes stepped inside and lifted the mike.

"US Navy, this is the tanker *Pecos Trader* . We copy, go ahead. Over."

"*Pecos Trader* , state your destination and cargo. Over."

"We are bound for Beaumont, Texas, under command and control of the US Coast Guard. I repeat our destination is Beaumont, Texas, and we are under command and control of the US Coast Guard. Do you copy? Over."

"*Pecos Trader* , we copy. What is your cargo? Over."

"Off specification diesel rejected by receiving facility to be pumped to slops and reclaimed. Over."

"*Pecos Trader* , say again. Over."

"Off spec diesel, repeat, off spec diesel. We experienced an internal pipeline leak and our entire cargo was contaminated with gasoline and rejected by the receiver in Wilmington, North Carolina. Our last orders prior to the blackout were to return the cargo to the refinery for reclamation. Over."

"Affirmative, *Pecos Trader* , we copy. Please let me speak to senior Coast Guard officer aboard. Over."

Hughes passed the mike to Matt Kinsey.

"US Navy, this is Senior Chief Petty Officer Matt Kinsey, US Coast Guard. Over."

"Chief, we have no information on your vessel, please state your mission. Over."

"We are transferring personnel and equipment from Oak Island Station, North Carolina, to the Coast Guard MSU in Port Arthur, Texas. Our orders are to proceed by most expeditious means. *Pecos Trader* was the only ride available. You can see our patrol boat on deck. Over."

"Affirmative, Chief. Why have you disabled the vessel AIS? Over."

"Negative, Navy. I say again, negative. We did not disable the AIS. Captain reports it malfunctioned during the solar storm, exact cause and extent of damage unknown."

"We copy *Pecos Trader* . Wait one. Over."

"What now?" Hughes asked.

"They'll run this all by Jacksonville for orders," Kinsey said. "If they order us in, I hope that contaminated diesel story holds up."

"That's the beauty of it," Hughes said. "It can't be confirmed one way or another. I doubt any testing labs are operational these days, so it's just my word against anyone else's opinion. It's like putting a poison sign on a water hole; no one's likely to want to take a drink to check it out."

Kinsey nodded but looked uneasy.

"What's the matter, Chief?" Hughes asked.

"I've spent thirty years following orders, so this 'make stuff up as you go along' operation is pretty stressful."

"I understand," Hughes said, "but there's no shortage of people needing help, and you can help just as many people where we're going as you could where you were, and *Pecos Trader* is our only ride home. After we get there, we can decide what to do with the fuel."

Kinsey was about to reply when the VHF radio cut him off.

"*Pecos Trader* , *Pecos Trader* , this transmission is for Chief Kinsey. Do you copy? Over."

"We copy, Navy. This is Kinsey, go ahead. Over."

"Chief, when did you receive orders to deploy to Texas, and is your chain of command aware you are en route? Over."

"Four days ago, repeat, four days ago. My chain of command is aware of transit plan, but we lost comms prior to departure, so they do not know current status. Over."

"*Pecos Trader* , we copy and you are cleared to proceed as we have no orders to supersede your current ones. However, be advised two days ago, the US Coast Guard was subordinated to FEMA for the duration of the current emergency and is now the cognizant authority controlling coastal and inland marine traffic. When you transit the Florida Strait, please check in with US Coast Guard Station Key West for any updates to current orders. We will alert them to expect you. God speed, *Pecos Trader* . US Navy out!"

"Thank you, Navy," Kinsey said into the mike. "*Pecos Trader* out."

He cradled the mike, looking as if he'd just been slapped.

"What's the problem, Chief?" Hughes asked.

"The problem is the Coasties in Key West now have over twenty-four hours to check out my little fairy tale, and they know we're coming. A bigger problem is there are several patrol boats and a cutter at Station

R.E. McDermott

Key West, and a balloon-borne radar at Cudjoe Key covering the entire strait and its approaches. I've no doubt they'll want to have a little chat 'up close and personal,' all of which boils down to us being screwed."

TERMINAL OFFICE BUILDING
WILMINGTON CONTAINER TERMINAL
WILMINGTON, NORTH CAROLINA

DAY 12, 12 NOON

The battered office chair squeaked as Levi shifted his weight, the high-pitched noise filling the small office he and his father-in-law shared as quarters since the *Pecos Trader* sailed.

"We've got to get back to the river camp today, Anthony," Levi said. "We've been here five days now, which is three days longer than I told Celia we'd be gone. Despite radio updates, I'm sure she's fit to be tied."

The older man nodded. "I expect Jo's right there with her, holding the rope. Like as not it'll be us that's tied when we get back to the river." He paused. "What about the others? Who's going with us?"

"I think just Bill Wiggins and Tex." Levi said, "Jimmy the Pumpman decided to stay here in Wilmington now that the Coasties and National Guard guys are setting up shop. I'd been counting on him to join us, but I don't feel too bad about it, considering the possibilities of them making a go of it here in the terminal. Anyway, he'll be close by and we can invite him to join us if things go to hell here."

"What about Singletary?"

Levi shook his head. "I promised Captain Hughes I'd get him started to Baltimore, but that was when he'd have no place to go when the ship sailed. Now that we're not leaving him on his own, I have no intention of taking him to our place. Anyway, his best chance of getting back to Baltimore is grabbing an abandoned boat from one of the marinas and heading up the inland waterway. That's what I'll advise him to do, though what he's likely to find in Baltimore is anyone's guess. I doubt it's going to be pretty."

"That's a fact," Anthony said, "and I'm glad you said that. There's something off about the guy. I don't trust him any further than I could throw him. Maybe not that far."

"Me neither," Levi said. "I'll go get Bill and Tex, and I think we need to keep the Coasties in the loop because we need their help. Will you see if you can find Chief Butler and then meet us in that little conference room down the hall?"

"Will do," Anthony said.

A half hour later, Levi had most of the attendees gathered in the conference room, awaiting the arrival of Anthony and Chief Mike Butler. The group awaiting Butler was larger than Levi had intended. With lodging space tight, Bill Wiggins was sharing an office turned bedroom with Jimmy Barrios and Jerome Singletary. The two had tagged along to the meeting, and Levi could think of no graceful way to 'uninvite' them. He looked up as Anthony entered the room with a haggard Mike Butler.

"Thanks for joining us, Chief Butler," Levi said. "I know you're busy. I'll try to make this quick."

"No problem, Mr. Jenkins," Butler replied, "you've been a big help to us and I'm glad to return the favor. What do you need?"

"Maybe just some extra fuel and some logistical support if you can handle it," Levi said, "but I'll get to that in a minute. Right now I need to make sure we're all on the same page."

Butler nodded, and Levi turned to the others.

"Bill, Tex, first off, Anthony and I have stayed here as long as we can. I'm assuming you're both anxious to get headed back to your folks, and if you want our help, now is the time."

They both nodded, and Levi spread a road map on the table.

83

"Okay then, we need to take you both to our place on the river by boat and you can leave from there. That'll let you bypass any possible problems getting out of Wilmington. Anthony and I've been talking it over, and our family has four cars between us, which is about three more than we need now. We left a later model SUV in our barn at home. It runs, or it did when we left it, anyway. We can let you have that, and with the help of our Coast Guard friends here, enough gas to get you pretty far along your way, if not all the way to your destinations."

Wiggins and Tex looked shocked.

"I don't know what to say, Levi," Bill Wiggins said, "that's incredibly generous." Tex nodded agreement.

Levi shrugged. "Given how hard it's likely to be to get fuel and parts from now on, automobiles are back to being a luxury used only when necessary. Having four is an extravagance no one's likely to be able to afford, and the newer cars will only last until something goes wrong with the computers, then they're toast. We're keeping the old, reliable vehicles that are easy to work on, so it's really not all that generous—just realistic. We're not likely to use the car, so I got no problem helping shipmates get home."

"Still, thank you," Tex said.

Levi and Anthony seemed embarrassed by the thanks, so Bill Wiggins moved to break the uncomfortable silence.

"You said the car was in your barn, is that on the river too?" he asked.

Levi shook his head and bent over to point out a spot on the map. "No, the barn's at our old place, just outside of Currie. Anthony and I will take you to it in my old truck and you can leave from there."

"Look's good," Wiggins said. "We can cut across on secondary roads to I-40 and that'll take us right into I-95 North."

"Negative," Levi said, "way too many big cities and people along the I-95 corridor. You'll never make it through unharmed."

"I'm with Bill on this one, Levi," Shyla Texeira said, "95 North's the most direct route to both my folks' place in New Jersey and Bill's home in Maine. We can circle the cities."

Levi shook his head. "Even the suburbs have way too many people, and by now they're all starving. I'm sure the interstates are all jammed with abandoned cars as well, because by all reports, folks are fleeing the cities, and maybe not thinking too clearly. If you're running AWAY from a city on the interstate system, it means you're running TOWARD another one. If they abandoned their cars on the interstate when they ran out of gas, or just realized their error and moved off onto nearby secondary roads, there's likely a huge mass of desperate, hungry people not only in the cities, but spread out within corridors several miles wide along both sides of the interstate system. If you're driving by, winding your way through stalled cars, you might as well be carrying a big sign reading 'we got gas, we got food.' Trust me, you'll never make your destinations along major roads."

"How, then?" Wiggins asked, gesturing to the map. "The kind of roads you're talking about don't show up on a road map of the Eastern US, and we sure can't be stopping to ask directions."

Levi smiled and reached down into a backpack on the floor at his feet and produced a small paperback book and a thick stack of maps bound with a rubber band. He laid both on the table.

"The book's a guide to the Appalachian Trail, and the bundle contains state and local maps from here to Canada," he said.

"But how did you…" Tex began, looking confused, and Levi laughed.

"I'm one of those crazy preppers, remember," he said, "and one who spent half of each year far from home, mostly traveling up and down the East Coast." He nodded down at the backpack. "I kept my 'getting home' bag with me on the ship at all times, and I have a route home planned out in my head from every port between Corpus Christi, Texas and St. Johns, Newfoundland. You just reverse one of my planned routes."

"But the Appalachian Trail is a hiking trail. We can't drive on it. Are you saying I have to walk all the way to Maine?" Wiggins asked.

"Not unless you have to," Levi said, "but yeah, that's plan B. But let me explain; the AT runs within twenty or thirty miles of both of your destinations, and in most cases it's paralleled by nearby roads. Sometimes they're not much more than dirt or gravel tracks, but they're drivable and they'll keep you both close to the AT and more importantly, away from people and close to water sources. If for some reason, you have to abandon the vehicle, you can continue on foot along the trail. There are shelters every eight miles or so, and more importantly game and natural sources of safe drinking water, all marked in the guide. The guide also has information on the towns you'll pass, how far off the trail, how big they are, or were anyway, and services they had before the blackout. If you're afoot on the trail, that might give you the best idea about where it might be possible to pick up another vehicle, or at least a clue to what you might expect if you go into the town." Levi shrugged. "It's not perfect and it's still going to be a hard trip, but I think you'll have a much better chance sticking to the boonies than trying to transit the more populated areas."

Wiggins and Tex nodded, clearly impressed.

"Again, I don't know what to say, Levi," Wiggins said. "This is terrific, thank you."

"Don't thank me yet," Levi said. "It's gonna be harder than you've ever imagined, and I'm pretty sure you'll be afoot before it's all over. And remember, this is a plan and theoretical, so it's not like I've made the trip."

"Still," Tex said, "it's far better than we could have done on our own, and it's obvious you've given it a lot of thought."

"Speaking of which," Singletary said, "did you have a plan for getting home from Baltimore I can use in the reverse direction, hopefully something that doesn't involve walking through the woods, picking ticks off my ass?"

"As a matter of fact, I did," Levi said. "I figured if I was caught anywhere between Miami and Baltimore, I'd try to get a boat and head up or down the inland waterway to Wilmington, and up the river from here. It's all very populated, but I figure most of the traffic will be on land and not water. Even if you have to row or paddle, it's a helluva lot faster than walking with a pack on your back."

"Okay," Singletary said, "but where am I gonna get a boat?"

Levi looked at Butler. "This wasn't the reason I asked you to attend, Chief Butler, but since Singletary brought it up, can you help us out here? There are several marinas upstream, and any boats still there belong to owners who aren't likely to need them anymore."

Butler hesitated. "Yeah, okay," he said at last, "I suppose I could send the guys up to have a look around. There ought to be something up there he could use, and we can load him up with gas cans to extend the range if need be."

"I'll need a gun too," Singletary said, but Butler was already shaking his head.

"Sorry, but no way I'm giving up any of our weapons. We'll probably need everything we have at some point," Butler said.

"I have a thirty-eight revolver and half a box of ammo I can let you have before I leave," Levi said. "It's a snub nose and not very accurate, but it's better than being defenseless."

Singletary nodded, seemingly satisfied for once. Levi turned back to Butler.

"Which brings me to my last request, Chief Butler," Levi said. "We found some Jerry cans here in the container terminal, and there's plenty of fuel in the product terminal next door. I want to send Bill and Tex off with fifty gallons of gas. Between that, the four of us, the extra food for their trip, and the extra food and fuel for our own use, we'll have to make multiple trips in our boat unless you can help us out."

"No problem," Butler said. "Is there less than four feet of water anywhere you want to go?"

"No," Levi said. "We've got that much even in our inlet."

Butler nodded. "Then we'll use the forty-five. She can even carry extra if you need, and tow you up to your place if you want." He leaned over the spread-out road map. "You said it was what, on the Black River? Can you show me the approximate location on the road map?"

Levi hesitated for the slightest moment and glanced toward Singletary. "It's easier to see on the actual river chart, and I don't have it with me," Levi said. "I'll show you later."

Butler caught the hesitation and nodded. "What time do you want to get out of here?"

Levi glanced at his watch. "It's almost one. If we start packing up now, we can get out of here by five and make it home before dark."

MAXIMUM SECURITY UNIT
FEDERAL CORRECTIONAL COMPLEX
KNAUTH ROAD
BEAUMONT, TEXAS

DAY 12, 3:00 P.M.

"What we gonna do, Sarge?" asked Broussard, a note of accusation in his voice. "There's only two of us left here in Max. The warden said when they released the inmates over on the low security unit, those COs would come over here and spell us. That was three days ago, and we haven't seen a soul except the food service guy who came over with the crap they stripped out of the commissary."

"What do you want me to tell you?" Johnson asked. "I've been here with you, right from the time the warden showed up with the air mattresses and the 'help is on the way' pep talk. You think I got a friggin' crystal ball?"

Broussard sighed and settled back in his chair, and looked up to where the few security monitors still working displayed the unimaginable squalor of the various cell blocks. "Well, at least we're away from the stink except when we have to feed 'em."

Johnson grunted and nodded toward the dwindling stack of cardboard boxes full of snack food in the corner of the cramped control room. "Yeah, well, I reckon we won't have that problem much longer. Not that a daily ration of a package of snack crackers and a bottle of water is doing much but delaying the inevitable."

"Well, I suspect plenty of ordinary decent people are going hungry too," Broussard said, "so the way I figure it, these assholes got it coming. Besides, the MREs they gave us suck too. I'd almost rather eat stale crackers out of the commissary."

"Let's see how you feel when the MREs are gone in a—"

"Shit," Johnson said as he stared up at one working monitor showing the prison exterior. The camera was mounted over the main entrance and focused on the approach from the now mostly empty employee parking lot and the grassy circle in the center of the lot behind the entrance. On the ground in the grassy circle was a body, features indistinct, but definitely clad in a correction officer's uniform with dark stains on it.

"When the hell did he get there?" Broussard asked.

Johnson shook his head. "I wasn't watching, but he's definitely a CO, and that looks like blood."

"We gotta get help. Are the inside phones still working?" Broussard asked.

"They were this morning, but who knows?" Johnson said, reaching for the phone. He tried several presets before shaking his head.

"Anything?" Broussard asked.

"Negative," Johnson replied, hanging up the phone, "I tried the main admin building, the medium-security unit, and the main gate. The phones ring, but no one answers." He sighed. "I guess I need to go see if I can help him."

"Uhh... we're supposed to keep two COs here at all times," Broussard said.

Johnson sneered, "Well, maybe you missed it, but things aren't exactly normal, so I think maybe bending the rules a bit more is okay. Besides" — he nodded toward the monitors covering the cell blocks — "those bastards in there can hardly lift their heads, so I don't think they're planning a prison break."

"All right," Broussard said, "but be careful."

"Yes, mother," Johnson said, walking over to retrieve a shotgun leaning against the wall, one of a pair. Normally guns in this area of the prison were prohibited, but given the circumstances, the two officers had accessed the armory without asking permission, and armed themselves with both shotguns and sidearms.

"Keep an eye on the monitor," Johnson said as he moved toward the door.

"Yeah," Broussard replied, "I pretty much had that part figured out." He paused and grew serious. "And try not to get in trouble, 'cause it's not like I have any reinforcements to call."

Johnson nodded and exited the control room to move through the now nonfunctioning double-door mantrap separating the secure area from the administrative side of the maximum-security unit, disabled because Johnson had no one to man the security checkpoint. He moved swiftly through the halls of the administration office area and exited the building to cross the open yard and enter the deserted receiving facility built into the stout prison wall. Here too, the mantrap was left open due to a lack of personnel — not that it mattered with the main entrance locked down. He crossed through the building, unlocked the heavy glass door, and pushed it open. There, across the perimeter road that circled the prison walls, lay the inert form of a corrections officer. The red smears in the bright sunlight confirming the stains he'd seen on the monochrome display were indeed blood.

"Shit," Johnson muttered, and looked around for any threat. Seeing none, he hurried across the road toward his fallen comrade.

Darren McComb, aka federal inmate number 26852-278, aka 'Spike,' doing a triple life sentence and captain of the Aryan Brotherhood of Texas, lay sweating in the grass, with growing concerns the sweat running down his arms would wash away the dead badge's blood he'd smeared over his tattoos. It was fate that had him in a holding cell in the medium-security unit when the power went out, awaiting transfer back to max security after extraction of an abscessed tooth. More good luck allowed him to take advantage of deteriorating security measures as fewer and fewer badges showed up for work. Feigning death and luring the inexperienced rookie into his cell had almost been child's play. Freeing the others and killing the few remaining COs in medium security had been easy as well, and then they'd fallen on the central administration complex like a pack of wolves. He smiled into the grass; dealing with the warden had been particularly enjoyable, and informative as well. It was good to know there were only two badges left in the whole of max security; all he had to do was get the heavy security door open at the main entrance, and it was a done deal.

McComb stiffened as he heard the sound of an opening door, and opened his eyes to thin slits to look down his body toward the badge rushing toward him from the building. He closed his eyes tight as the CO approached, the man's breathing labored from the exertion of the short run. The man knelt beside him and McComb felt a hand on his shoulder begin to roll him face up.

"Are you all righ —"

The badge's question died on his lips as McComb drove the concealed knife into his throat, spraying them both with bright arterial blood. The man collapsed on top of McComb, the shotgun in his free hand tumbling to the grass. McComb held the man close, savoring the kill as he waited for him to stop struggling. When the badge went limp, McComb rolled him to one side and grabbed the shotgun before standing and placing two fingers in his mouth to emit a long high-pitched whistle. Two dozen figures in convict khaki, armed with assorted weaponry from the looted armory of the medium-security unit, rose from behind cars scattered throughout the parking lot and began to converge on Spike's position.

Broussard sat sipping a bottle of tepid water as he watched the grainy monitor. Then Johnson collapsed over the fallen CO, and Broussard was momentarily confused as the man he'd thought dead or injured rose with Johnson's shotgun. Confusion was replaced by near paralytic fear as armed convicts entered the picture from off screen and converged toward the main entrance of the max-security unit. The water bottle slipped from his trembling fingers and water gushed out around his feet as he stared at the monitor in disbelief.

He knew he couldn't beat them to the main entrance security door, so in a panic, he scooped up his shotgun and a box of shells and went in search of a defensible hiding place. He had no illusion he could stop them; his only hope for survival was to hide where they couldn't find him or if they did find him, make it too costly to get to him. Faced with losses to dig him out of his hole, they might ignore him, free the others, and clear out.

But time was not his friend, and by the time he made it through the nonfunctional mantrap into the administration area, he heard them slamming through doors on the opposite end of the building, howling like a pack of wolves. Out of options, he ducked into a large storage closet, reaching up with his shotgun to smash the bare light bulb as he entered, then pulled the door closed and backed himself into the far corner, shotgun positioned to blast any target silhouetted in the doorway if it opened.

McComb was at the front of the pack, head on a swivel, alert for the presence of the last CO. The dying warden had told him the last two badges were in Central Control, but McComb figured the surviving CO had witnessed his partner's death and might be anywhere. He led his men through the open mantrap and slowed as he neared the glass-enclosed control room. There was no one visible through the glass, but the badge might be crouched down behind the waist-high solid wall. McComb nodded to his two closest subordinates to follow him, then burst through the door of Central Control, bringing his shotgun to bear on the previously concealed portion of the wall. He heaved a sigh of relief when he found the control room empty and more of his followers crowded into the space.

"Okay, the last badge ain't here, and I want to take care of him before we get out of here. So far no one's escaped to rat us out, and I want to keep it that way, so spread out and find him," McComb said.

The man closest to him gave a gap-toothed smile. "Shouldn't be too tough," he said, pointing to the overturned water bottle and the wet footprints on the floor.

McComb grinned back and pushed through the crowd, backtracking and following the water trail. The footprints were obliterated by the cons' own entrance, but the water was still there, pointing like an arrow to the closed door of the storage closet.

"Anybody bring any of them flash bangs from the armory?" he asked quietly.

Several men nodded.

"Okay," McComb said, still keeping his voice down and pointing at the men with the flash bangs, "you three get ready to chuck those in when the door is open. You," he said, pointing to another man, "snatch the door open and jump out of the way, quick like so these three can toss in their packages. He's probably in there laying for us, so all you knuckleheads stay out of the open door until the flash bangs go off, got it?"

There were head nods all around, and McComb continued, looking around and spotting a couple of men armed with shotguns. "You two jump to the doorway as soon as the flash bangs go off and sweep the room with your shotguns. Don't stop until you empty the magazines and cover every square inch of the room. It ain't nothin' but a closet and I want to make damn sure he don't survive. Got it?"

The pair grinned their understanding.

"Shock and awe, baby!" McComb said. "Now everybody get ready."

The men moved into position quickly and executed the plan on McComb's hand signals. Thirty violent seconds later, he stood in the half light of the storage closet, looking down at the bloody remains of the last CO. He gave a satisfied nod then returned to the hallway and gathered his men around him.

"Okay," he said, "same drill as in medium security. Let our guys out, and any other whites willing to pledge allegiance to the ABT, but make sure they understand what'll happen to them if they try to punk out."

There were grunts of approval as he continued, "Leave the niggers and greasers," he said. "No point in wastin' ammo when we can just let 'em starve to death."

There was laughter, followed by a question from his gap-toothed lieutenant.

"What're you going to do, Spike?" the man asked.

"Oh, I'm gonna pay someone a little visit," McComb said.

Five minutes later, McComb was squatting on his haunches, sipping water from a plastic bottle as he stared through the bars at Daris Jefferson, leader of the Gangsta Killa Blood set of the United Blood Nation.

"Just wanted to stop by and say goodbye before me and the boys go on jackrabbit parole," McComb said.

Jefferson glared back, his eyes two burning embers of hatred in an emaciated face. "I see yo keeping yo distance, cracker. Get a little closer, and I'll beat that smile off yo pasty-ass face."

"Oh, I wouldn't want you to get all tuckered out trying, boy. You need to save your strength so it takes a long, long time to die. And here's a little something to remember me by." McComb rose from his haunches and leaned in a bit. "I hear thirst is worse than hunger, so while you're in there dying of thirst, I want you to look at this bottle and think about me." He hocked up something from deep in his throat and theatrically dripped it from his mouth into the open neck of the half-filled bottle, then set the bottle on the floor out of reach. "In a few days, you'll be looking at this bottle and dreaming of drinking my spit, and when you do, remember I wouldn't piss on you if you were on fire." McComb grinned. "So enjoy the rest of your miserable life, Buckwheat."

Jefferson tried to spit in McComb's face, but he was so dehydrated he had no saliva, and the failed effort looked almost as if he were blowing a kiss. McComb's laughter echoed through the half-empty cell block as he walked away, eager to make his mark in what he knew would be a predator's paradise.

CHAPTER TWELVE

DAY 13, 2:00 A.M.

Levi kept the lights off and avoided the brakes as he kept Old Blue at a steady forty miles an hour, the county road an eerie green in his night-vision goggles. Anthony road shotgun, literally, with his trusty old shotgun upright between his knees, squeezed against the passenger door by the presence of Bill Wiggins and Tex in the center of the bench seat. The old truck wasn't designed for four passengers.

They'd gotten back to the fishing camp just before dusk, and Levi was pretty sure only the presence of strangers had saved him and Anthony from a dressing-down from Celia and Josephine. Despite the women's restrained anger over the longer-than-promised absence, they were both far too gracious to make guests feel uncomfortable by venting their anger. And the kids had been excited and happy about anything that broke up what, for them, was becoming a very boring existence.

Levi and Anthony had debated the wisdom of bringing the Coast Guard boat all the way into their hideaway, but in the end, there was just too much cargo to be shifted to allow for any other solution. Concerned about giving offense, but more worried about security, they'd discussed their concerns with Chief Butler, who, to their relief, was not at all offended. He'd volunteered to pilot the Coast Guard boat himself and brought along his most trusted subordinate, assuring both Levi and Anthony the secret of their location was safe.

That only left Wiggins and Tex, and though he trusted them completely, there was always the chance they might run in with bad people and be forced or coerced into revealing the source of the ample supplies they were carrying. But they couldn't reveal what they didn't know. Levi glanced to his right, past his two ex-shipmates to where Anthony rode at the passenger door, looking insect-like in his own set of NV goggles.

"I'm sorry we only had two sets of night-vision glasses," Levi said, "but since Anthony's riding shotgun, I figured he needed them."

"No problem," Wiggins said, "though I have to say, riding down the road in the pitch dark is a pretty uncomfortable feeling."

Beside him, Tex laughed. "I'll say."

"We'll be there soon," Levi said.

True to his word, a few minutes later Levi pulled into the long gravel drive of the five acres he and Celia shared with her parents, and eased down between the two houses to the barn. As Anthony exited the truck wordlessly to open the barn door, Levi looked around the property in the green glow of the NV goggles and wondered again if the move to the river had been premature. After all, it had been almost two weeks since the power went out, and the place seemed undisturbed. Then he shook his head again. Country road or not, it was still a paved road that saw traffic, and the houses were just too visible and hard to defend. No, moving to the river was the right call.

"Are we there?" Tex asked.

"Oh, yeah, sorry," Levi said. "I forgot you guys can't see. Anthony's opening the barn door now, and when we get inside, we'll crank up a couple of lanterns."

Anthony swung the barn door wide, and Levi nosed the car into the barn beside an SUV.

"Everybody out," Levi said as Anthony closed the barn door and walked over to take down two lanterns from where they hung on nails in the wall. In moments, light filled the barn, accompanied by the soft hiss of the lanterns. Wiggins and Tex blinked in the light and checked out the SUV, a ten-year-old Toyota Highlander that looked showroom new.

"That's still some gift, Levi," Wiggins said.

"Don't worry about it," Levi said. "Like I said before, it's not really as generous as you think. Everything's running now, but when all these newer cars and planes and helicopters and what have you start breaking down, there won't be any fixing them, at least not easily. They're all just about impossible to work on without sophisticated diagnostic equipment. We're much better off keeping the old, simple cars we can work on ourselves. I've got no problem letting shipmates use something we're likely to have little use for anyway. That's all." Levi tapped the map with his finger. "Now, we got a lot to go over, and Anthony and I want to be back in the woods before daylight, so let's get to it."

Tex and Wiggins moved beside Levi as he pointed at the map. "You need to stay off the main roads and get near the Appalachian Trail as soon as possible. That's likely going to be the most dangerous part, because the AT doesn't start paralleling the Blue Ridge Parkway until just north of Roanoke, Virginia. I've traced out a route on the North Carolina map from here to Linnville, where you can pick up the Blue Ridge Parkway north. It's about three hundred miles, which you could make in six hours in normal times, but now, who knows? However, I figure if you leave at first light and given the lengthening days, you ought to get to the parkway before dark. I've tried to keep you on secondary roads, so they should be okay, but whoever isn't driving needs to be looking at the county maps I've included so if you find a problem, you can get around it. Always be thinking of a plan B before you need it, understand?"

Both the travelers nodded and Levi continued. "You'll intersect the AT the first time about two hundred miles up the Blue Ridge Parkway at a little place called Black Horse Gap. Then the two routes stay more or less together until the parkway ends about a hundred miles north at Afton, Virginia. It actually doesn't 'end,' though. It just turns into another scenic road called Skyline Drive that continues a hundred miles or so to Front Royal. The AT parallels Skyline Drive as well. After that, you'll have to pick out secondary roads, logging roads, etc., that parallel the AT." He paused. "And just to be clear, I use the term 'parallel' loosely. Actually the AT cuts back and forth across these and the other roads you'll use to head north, but in some places it might veer away from the nearest road by ten or twenty miles. So this is important, ALWAYS know where the access points to the AT are, and how far it is back to the last one you passed, and how far it is ahead to the next one."

"Uhh… isn't this a little overkill, Levi?" Wiggins asked. "I mean, striking off on foot into the woods is about the last thing I want to do. We just want to get home."

"And I'm trying to make sure you get there, Bill," Levi said. "If things are as bad as I think and y'all run into trouble, hoofing it into the woods might be your only option. Also, that little AT guidebook lists locations where you can find good water, which may be like liquid gold, and all of the land the AT traverses is mostly state or national forest, which means there will be plenty of game if you end up needing it, 'cause you sure as hell will need to avoid grocery stores, assuming there are any that haven't been stripped."

"Is that even legal?" Wiggins asked, and Levi saw Tex suppress a smile. Anthony was less restrained.

"Seriously?" he snorted. "You think there are still game wardens running around, worried about folks shooting rabbits?"

Wiggins' face reddened in the lamplight. "I guess not. Stupid comment. Sorry."

Levi shook his head. "No need to apologize, and I know I'm coming on strong, but you need to understand the AT's your lifeline and your 'Mega Plan B.' 'Cause I got a sneaking suspicion you both, but you especially, Bill, are so worried about your families that as soon as you roll out of that driveway, you're thinking about heading north by the most direct route possible, caution be damned."

No one spoke and the uncomfortable silence grew.

"All right, I'll admit it," Wiggins said. "Tex and I've been considering some other routes."

"Well, stop considering them," Levi said, "because they'll likely get you killed."

Tex sighed. "How long you figure, Levi?"

"Getting you to Jersey, four or five days, and that much longer for Bill to get to Maine, assuming you can drive the whole way."

"Ten days! That can't be right," Wiggins said. "Even at thirty miles an hour on this convoluted path, I should be able to make it to Maine in three or four days tops, driving straight through."

"But you're not going straight through, because we've got no night vision to give you, and driving at night lit up like a Christmas tree is an invitation to be ambushed," Levi said. "Any bad guys can see you coming a long, long way off, and way before you know they're even there. You're gonna plan each day's trip, including a stopping point, and get there in plenty of time to check out the site, hide the car, and make camp away from the road so, if you need a fire, neither it or what you're cooking can be seen or smelled." Levi paused for emphasis. "Now get this straight. If you're not moving, you're hiding. You're most vulnerable when you're stationary, and you need to act accordingly."

Both Wiggins and Tex nodded slowly, resigned rather than enthusiastic, and Levi walked over to Old Blue and returned with a small backpack. He fished in the pack and produced an automatic pistol in a holster as well as what looked like a plastic rifle stock and laid both on top of the road map spread over the hood of the SUV. Several boxes of ammunition followed.

"Either of you have any experience with handguns?" Levi asked.

"I've been to the range a few times," Wiggins said.

"Uhh… actually, I used to shoot competitively," Tex said.

Levi reached for the Glock. He ejected the magazine then racked the slide back and left the action open before handing the nine millimeter pistol to Tex. "Winner, winner, chicken dinner," he said. "Tex will carry the main defensive armament when you're outside the vehicle. When you're moving, whoever isn't driving will have the pistol out and ready."

Tex nodded, and Levi and Anthony watched with approval as she examined the pistol expertly, closed the action, and then checked and inserted the magazine before checking out the holster. Wiggins was looking less sure, instinctively reacting to a perceived slight to his manhood.

"This is perfect, actually," Levi said. "Tex, that's a small-of-the-back holster. Do you have an overshirt you can wear with the tail out?" Tex nodded and Levi looked back and forth between Tex and Wiggins. "Good. If you're attacked by surprise, it will likely be when you're out of the car, and any attackers are unlikely to perceive Tex as a threat. They'll move on Bill first, and that may give you the edge."

Wiggins nodded, on board now, and then pointed toward the plastic rifle stock. "And what's that?"

Levi picked up the plastic stock and pried a rubber boot off the butt, revealing various items stored neatly inside. "This is a Henry survival rifle, which will bring home the bacon, or more likely the rabbit, if you need it."

Levi deftly assembled the little rifle in seconds, and then pointed out the two small magazines.

"It's a twenty-two-caliber semiautomatic and it comes with two eight-round magazines. I suggest you keep both fully loaded at all times. You'll notice there's a good supply of two different types of ammo. The stuff in the blue box is 'quiet' loads, reduced power for low noise, but it's fine for taking small game at any distance you'll likely be shooting. The advantage is if you DO have to hunt, the gunshots won't draw attention to you. The downside is these rounds don't have enough recoil to cycle the bolt, so when you're shooting them, the rifle isn't semiautomatic—you'll have to cycle the bolt manually between shots. The other ammo is regular twenty-two long rifle, and if you have to use the rifle for defense, that's what you need to use. A twenty-two doesn't have much stopping power, but in semiautomatic mode, it can at least make someone think twice about charging you. But like I said, it's mainly a hunting weapon."

"What's with the red dot?" Wiggins pointed to one of the magazines.

"I was getting to that," Levi said. "I put a dot of nail polish on one, so you could tell the mags apart in an emergency, and I loaded the one with the red dot with the regular rounds and the other one with the low-noise rounds. I suggest you maintain that so you can switch out quickly if needed."

"Sound's good," Wiggins said, "but to be honest, I hope I don't have to use either."

"I do too," Levi said, "and if everything goes well, you won't. The gas tank's full, and you've got fifty gallons in Jerry cans. I don't like to see you carrying all that gas inside the car, but there really isn't an option. You got food and water for twelve days, a bit longer if you need to stretch it. I've also packed both of you 'escape packs,' because if you do have to abandon the car and haul ass, you likely will be doing it under duress. Mostly it's food, gallon ziplock bags full of crushed noodles and pasta for carbs, nuts for fat, and jerky for protein, along with three liter camel packs of water and a small bottle of bleach for disinfecting water if need be. I also threw in some other odds and ends, which you'll figure out if you need it, lighters, space blankets, paracord, stuff like that. Don't mess with the bags, just keep them handy. And don't forget to take the AT guide, maps, and ammo —"

Wiggins smiled and held up his hand to stop Levi. "You know you told us all this before, Levi. I think we have it. Really."

Levi hesitated. "Well, okay. Let's get the stuff loaded, then."

There were nods all around, and the group began transferring the supplies from Old Blue to the Toyota. Fifteen minutes later, the task was complete, and everyone stood silently in the middle of the barn, reluctant to part ways.

Anthony broke the silence. "Well, good luck and God's speed."

Tex stepped over and wrapped him in a hug. "You take care of these folks, Anthony," she whispered into his ear, and Anthony squeezed her tight before she let him go and transferred her embrace to Levi. "Thank you, shipmate," she said softly, and Levi only nodded, unable to speak.

Tex let go of Levi and stepped back to let the men exchange handshakes.

"Oh yeah," Levi said, extracting a piece of paper from his pocket, "I almost forgot. These are the radio frequencies we worked out with the *Pecos Trader* and the Coasties in Wilmington, as well as the times we'll all be listening and some security codes. When you get home, try to let us know you got there safely and then keep in touch."

Wiggins and Tex nodded, and after another short awkward silence, Wiggins spoke. "I'll kill the lanterns."

"I'll get the barn door," Tex added, and Levi and Anthony got into the cab of Old Blue.

Ten minutes later, Levi was driving through the darkness, lost in thought, when he felt Anthony's hand on his shoulder.

"Don't you fret, Levi," the older man said. "You did all you could."

"Let's just hope it was enough," Levi said.

M/V PECOS TRADER
FLORIDA STRAIT

DAY 13, 2:00 P.M.

Hughes pressed the binoculars to his eyes and strained to make out more detail of the line of white marking the ocean's surface to the east, where the gentle swell was breaking over a barely submerged reef.

He heaved a sigh of relief and lowered the glasses. "I think that's Elbow Cay behind us, so at least I can scratch running aground off my list of things to worry about today."

Beside him, Chief Matt Kinsey chuckled. "Which still makes the list pretty long, I imagine."

"You mean like staying as far away from the US coast as possible and hugging the Bahamian shallows, with absolutely no working navigational aids while simultaneously hoping to avoid detection by US radar and stay clear of Cuban waters?"

"Well, you're two for two, so far," Kinsey said. "You've managed to avoid grounding in Bahamian waters, despite lack of navaids, and my Coast Guard folks haven't hailed us yet, so I'm thinking that's a good indication the alert from the navy at Jacksonville got lost in the confusion."

"Yeah, I have to say I'm pleasantly surprised," Hughes said. "What do you make of that?"

Kinsey shrugged. "I'm thinking everybody's shorthanded. If they haven't hailed us by now, we might have a shot at sliding by unnoticed, as long as we stay as far south as possible."

"I'm thinking the same thing," Hughes said. "All in all, I'm starting to feel a lot better about this."

"Captain! I think you'll want to see this," called Georgia Howell from the radar.

"What is it?" Hughes asked as he and Kinsey crossed the bridge toward the radar.

"I've got a small, fast target approaching from the south," Howell said, "making better than forty knots and headed right for us. ETA approximately ten minutes." She moved aside to let Hughes take her place.

"What do you make of that, Matt?" Hughes asked.

"Smuggler maybe? Some well-heeled Cuban-American taking advantage of the chaos to reunite more of the family?"

"Maybe," Howell said, "but then why isn't he headed straight for the Florida coast?"

"Well, we'll find out soon enough," Hughes said, and walked to the port side of the bridge to stare south through his binoculars.

A few minutes later, he spotted a speck on the sea, growing in his binoculars as it raced toward the ship. It was a fast patrol boat, similar to the Coast Guard boat they carried as deck cargo, with several uniformed men aboard and a menacing-looking bow-mounted machine gun.

"Oh shit," Hughes said, "that's a Cuban patrol boat."

"What the hell do they want?" Georgia Howell said. "We're a good ten miles outside Cuban waters."

"Maybe they don't see it that way." Kinsey turned to Hughes. "What are you going to do, Captain?"

"Well, normally I'd call the Coast Guard, but now? Who the hell knows?"

"Ahh… I think I'd rather be on a FEMA storage tanker just about anywhere than in a Cuban prison," Georgia Howell said, "because given what's going on, I don't think anyone's going to be spending any resources trying to get us back."

"Good point," Hughes said, moving to the VHF. He keyed the mike and started to transmit. "US Coast Guard, US Coast Guard. This is —"

Everyone dropped to the deck instinctively as the port bridge windows shattered and spiderwebbed from a well-placed burst of machine-gun fire, followed immediately by an amplified voice with a thick Spanish accent.

"AMERICAN TANKER! AMERICAN TANKER! STOP TRANSMITTING IMMEDIATELY AND STOP YOUR VESSEL OR WE WILL OPEN FIRE!"

"I think you already did, asshole," Hughes muttered.

Kinsey and Howell crouched with him on the deck. A few feet away, Pete Sonnier, the AB on watch, squatted near the steering stand. "They seem pretty serious to me, Cap," he said.

Hughes nodded and looked back and forth between Kinsey and Howell. "Don't stand on ceremony," Hughes said, "'cause it's not like I have a clue what to do here." He nodded to where the VHF mike dangled on its cord a few inches off the deck. "I don't think they can hit us here, so I can probably continue to call the Coast Guard before they can get aboard. I'm sure the Coasties can have an armed chopper over us before they can force us into Cuban waters."

"Presuming anyone answers our call in a timely manner," Kinsey said. "Remember they're shorthanded as hell and low on resources. And if we do play that card and no one responds, I'm pretty sure our new amigos are going to be pretty pissed."

"AMERICAN TANKER! DO NOT TRANSMIT AND STOP YOUR VESSEL AT ONCE OR WE WILL OPEN FIRE! BE ADVISED WE ARE EQUIPPED WITH ROCKET-PROPELLED GRENADES AND WILL USE THEM! REPEAT, STOP YOUR VESSEL AT ONCE!"

"All right, that's it," Hughes said. "Georgia, ring the engine room and tell them to stop the engine. I'm going to have to talk to this asshole."

Howell nodded and duckwalked over to the control console and reached up for the phone. Within seconds, they felt the vibration change as the big diesel rumbled to a halt and the ship started to slow. When he was confident the patrol boat had seen the ship slowing, Hughes rose and walked toward the port bridge wing, motioning the others to stay back out of sight.

He approached the side of the bridge wing with his arms raised so they'd have no doubt he was surrendering. When he spotted the boat approximately a hundred feet off the port side, the first thing he saw were armed men, one at the stern with an RPG and another manning the machine gun in the bow. Both weapons were pointed directly at *Pecos Trader*'s bridge—and him. Midships in the boat near the small glass-windowed pilothouse stood another man, obviously in charge, with the bullhorn in his hand and a pistol on his hip. There was a fourth man in the pilothouse at the wheel. All four wore the uniforms of the Cuban Border Guards. The officer type raised the bullhorn to his mouth.

"AMERICAN TANKER! YOU HAVE ENTERED OUR WATERS WITHOUT PERMISSION AND HAVE VIOLATED OUR SOVEREIGNTY. COME TO A COMPLETE STOP AT ONCE AND DEPLOY YOUR PILOT LADDER. DO NOT, REPEAT, DO NOT ATTEMPT TO USE YOUR RADIO OR WE WILL OPEN FIRE. LOWER BOTH YOUR ARMS AND THEN RAISE YOUR RIGHT ARM IF YOU UNDERSTAND!"

Hughes considered shouting a protest in return, but suspected it would be useless. He dutifully lowered both arms, then raised his right arm as instructed.

"GOOD! NOW DEPLOY YOUR PILOT LADDER AND PREPARE TO BE BOARDED. YOU HAVE FIVE MINUTES TO COMPLY. LOWER AND RAISE YOUR RIGHT ARM AGAIN IF YOU UNDERSTAND."

Hughes did as instructed and waited a moment to see if there were further instructions. When there were none, he turned and went back into the wheelhouse.

"You heard?" he asked Kinsey and Howell as he approached their position back in the chart room, out of sight from the patrol boat.

They both nodded, and Hughes continued, "Anybody got any ideas, or should we all start brushing up on our Spanish?"

"Well, obviously we aren't in Cuban waters, and he doesn't want us to use the radio, or use it himself," Howell said, "which I'm figuring is why he's using the bullhorn; he doesn't want to attract anyone's attention."

"I agree," Kinsey said, "and as screwed up as things are in the States, I suspect it's ten times worse in Cuba. These guys, with or without Cuban government authorization, probably figured they can take advantage of US inattention to snag as many resources transiting near their island as possible. Kind of make sense, actually."

"Question is," Hughes said, "what are we going to do? They can't get on board easily until we lower the pilot ladder, but if we don't let them on, they'll just stand off and machine gun us or hit us with RPGs. The cargo is inerted, so they probably can't blow us up, but even if we evacuate the bridge and keep everyone locked down in the house, a couple of RPGs into the bridge would probably wipe out all our controls and we're toast anyway. But on the other hand, if they DO get on board, we're screwed too, because they'll force us into a Cuban port."

"Not necessarily," Kinsey said, "could you see how many they have aboard?"

"Four," Hughes said. "An officer type and three others, one at the helm and two handling weapons."

Kinsey considered a moment, then said, "Okay, I think we can handle that, but I need a bit of time. How long can you stall them?"

"AMERICAN TANKER! YOU HAVE TWO MINUTES TO DEPLOY YOUR PILOT LADDER OR WE WILL OPEN FIRE!" came the amplified voice.

"Obviously not long," Hughes said, turning to Howell. "Georgia, get some of the deck gang and start rigging the pilot ladder, be as visibly awkward and clumsy as possible. How long do you think you can drag it out without being too obvious?"

She shrugged. "Ten minutes anyway, maybe fifteen."

Hughes looked at Kinsey.

"That will have to do," Kinsey said. "Let me get my guys lined up."

Once again, the amplified voice rose from the ship's side.

"AMERICAN TANKER! YOU HAVE ONE MINUTE TO DEPLOY YOUR PILOT LADDER OR WE WILL OPEN FIRE!"

Howell nodded and started for the stairwell door as Hughes looked toward the port bridge wing. "I better show myself to keep this guy calmed down until he sees us working on the pilot ladder."

Kinsey nodded and started for the stairs behind Howell as Hughes moved out on the bridge wing again to motion to the Cubans that work was in progress.

Ten minutes later, Hughes stood at the ship's side on the main deck, watching Georgia Howell direct the final securing and deployment of the pilot ladder as the Cuban boat floated twenty feet away, the Cuban officer on the small boat visibly irritated by the delay. Finally the rope ladder unrolled down the ship's side, and the little boat nosed in toward it. The officer motioned a man to lead the way up the ladder while he and the second Cuban sailor hung back, waiting their turn. Hughes stepped away from the side of the ship and moved toward the open watertight door of the deckhouse, where Matt Kinsey waited just out of sight.

"Looks like three out of the four in the boarding party," Hughes said softly, "the officer and two sailors. The officer has a sidearm, and the other two have what look like AKs."

"Good," Kinsey replied. "I figure the officer type will place himself on the bridge and send at least one guy to the engine control room. They don't have enough people to completely contain and control the crew, so I'm thinking he's just going to control the bridge and engine room and get us into actual Cuban waters ASAP. He'll probably call help from there. Now we just need to figure out where he decides to put the third guy, and we can take them down fast. If we can achieve complete surprise, this might be painless for all concerned."

"What about the boat? If he gets away or calls for help, there's no way we're outrunning any reinforcements at our blinding top speed of fifteen knots."

"Well, the officer used the bull horn, so I'm counting on the fact they're probably under orders to maintain radio silence outside of Cuban waters," Kinsey said, "and as far as the boat getting away, I've got that covered. Trust me on that."

"I sure as hell hope so," Hughes said. "Now I gotta go greet our visitors. When I figure out what's up, I'll pass the word."

"Okay, but remember, if any shooting starts—"

"I know, hit the deck. Everybody knows." Hughes moved back to the ship's side near the top of the pilot ladder.

He reached it just as the first Cuban stepped on the deck, his head on a swivel as he unslung his assault rifle and motioned the Americans away from the ladder. The officer was next, and after a quick glance at the assembled Americans—that lingered on Georgia Howell a bit too long—he stepped over in front of Hughes.

"You are the *capitan*?" he asked.

Hughes extended his hand. "Yes, I'm Captain Jordan Hughes."

The Cuban ignored the outstretched hand. "I am Lieutenant Hector Ramos of the *Tropas Guarda Fronteras* or, as I believe you *yanquis* refer to us, the Cuban Border Guard. You have entered the waters of the sovereign Republic of Cuba without authorization, *Capitan*, so I regret to inform you I must place your vessel under arrest. We will proceed at once to the nearest Cuban port, which is in this case Matanzas, where you will stand trial. If it is found your trespass was unintentional, you and your crew may be returned to the United States, but unfortunately your vessel and your cargo will be forfeited." He smiled for the first time. "And you appear to be fully loaded, so exactly what is your cargo?"

"There must be some mistake," Hughes said. "We're at least ten miles from Cuban—"

The Cuban's face clouded. "There is indeed a mistake, *Capitan*, and you have made—"

"*Teniente, mira el barco alli!*" said the last Cuban to board.

Ramos's gaze followed the pointing finger of his subordinate to the bright orange hull of the Coast Guard boat stowed on deck some distance away. Unconsciously he rested his hand on his sidearm.

"You are a military vessel? You have US Coast Guard aboard?" They were accusations rather than questions.

"No, no," Hughes said. "We are only carrying the boat as cargo. We're supposed to deliver it to the Coast Guard station near our destination in Texas."

Ramos studied the boat for a moment, then smiled. "It is a fine boat, *Capitan*. Unfortunately you will not be able to make delivery as intended, but I can assure you it will make a welcome addition to our little fleet and we will make good use of it, after an appropriate change of color, of course. Now, I repeat, what is your cargo? It is unusual to see a loaded tanker southbound in these waters."

Hughes shrugged. "These are unusual times. We are carrying diesel and gasoline. We were unable to enter port at Wilmington due to lack of a pilot, so we decided to return to Texas, as most of the crew lives near there."

"A most fortunate decision for the people of Cuba," the Cuban said, pleased by the unexpected bonus of the patrol boat and somewhat more relaxed. He turned and spit out some rapid-fire Spanish.

"Now, *Capitan*," he said, "please have an officer escort one of my men to the engine room and instruct the crew there not to make any trouble. Then I will go with you to the bridge and we will be on our way. Understand?"

Hughes nodded and motioned Howell over. When she arrived, he said, "Please take one of these guys to the engine room and tell Dan not to try anything funny."

She nodded and Hughes looked at the Cuban, who nodded in turn and directed one of his men to follow Howell.

"Now, *Capitan*, the bridge, if you please," the Cuban said, and Hughes led the way across the main deck to the deckhouse entrance to start the long climb up to the bridge. He noted with satisfaction both the remaining Cubans were following him.

On the bridge they found an anxious Pete Sonnier peering out the port bridge window to where the Cuban patrol boat had moved out a few hundred feet from the ship. The AB turned when he heard the door open and blanched when he saw the two armed Cubans with the captain.

"Everything's cool, Pete," Hughes said. "We'll get through this."

Sonnier nodded and moved to the steering stand.

"Is she still on the mike?" Hughes asked.

"Oh… yeah, I guess so," Sonnier said. "When the mate called down and stopped the engine, I didn't even think about the autopilot."

"Yeah, me neither," Hughes said. "I guess we were a bit distracted."

He turned to Ramos. "With your permission, I will have the helmsman take the ship off autopilot, as I presume you intend to give us a new course."

"Exactly so, *Capitan* , and after you do that, please call the engine room, as I wish to speak to my man there."

Hughes nodded. "Take her off the mike, Pete," he said, then walked over to the console and called the engine room.

"Engine room, Chief speaking," Dan Gowan answered.

"Is the Cuban down there with you, Dan? The guy up here wants to speak to him."

"I'll put him on," Gowan said, and Hughes handed the phone to the Cuban officer.

There was a short exchange in Spanish, which seemed to satisfy Ramos, and he hung up the phone.

"Very well, *Capitan* ," he said, "please order the engine back up to sea speed and come to a new course of two hundred ten degrees true."

Hughes nodded and did as instructed. Vibrations throbbed through the hull as the massive ship slowly built speed back up. They rode in silence, Sonnier behind the wheel, staring ahead except for occasional glances at the gyro repeater, and Hughes studying the Cubans as they, in turn, studied the bridge console and instrumentation. After ten minutes Hughes broke the silence.

"You said if we were found not guilty, we would be returned to the US. How?"

Ramos shrugged. "That is not my concern."

Prick, thought Hughes, but rather than punching the guy, he returned the shrug and smiled. "It will work out, I suppose. Would you like something to eat? We have plenty and my cook makes very good sandwiches. Roast beef? Ham and cheese?"

The look on the Cuban's face was a combination of greed and suspicion.

"Don't worry," Hughes said. "I'm not trying to poison you. How about I have a variety sent up and you choose which one you would like me to eat first? Would that be satisfactory?

Ramos considered it for a moment, his hunger obvious. "Yes. That would be acceptable… and thank you."

"No problem." Hughes walked to the phone to call the galley.

"Yeah, Polak," he said into the phone. "Send up an assortment of sandwiches to the bridge. Yeah, mix 'em up. Enough for Sonnier and I and our two guests. Oh, and while you're at it, send some down to the engine room for the chief and our guest down there."

"Got it. Two on the bridge, one in the engine room," said Kinsey in Hughes' ear, "which side is the patrol boat on?"

"I'm not sure when we'll make port, Polak. Several hours at least," Hughes said into the phone.

"I copy, the boat is on the PORT side of the ship," Kinsey said, "glance at the bridge clock NOW and in exactly five minutes, create some diversion to get the Cubans to the STARBOARD side of the bridge and well out of sight of the boat. Do you copy?"

"Copy that Polak, and send some spicy brown mustard up with the sandwiches, okay? Great, we'll be waiting." Hughes hung up.

Ramos raised his eyebrows. "I must say, *Capitan* , you are taking your arrest remarkably well."

Hughes shrugged. "I learned long ago life is less stressful when you don't worry about what you can't control."

"A very intelligent philosophy," the Cuban said.

They lapsed back into silence as Hughes kept watch on the bridge clock in his peripheral vision. At approximately the four-minute mark, he strolled over and studied the radar screen, then screwed up his face in a look of puzzled concern.

"What is it?" Ramos asked, moving toward the radar.

Hughes shook his head as Ramos joined him at the radar. "I don't know. Some sort of radar contact, but it's intermittent. There!" He pointed to a nonexistent blip. "Did you see it?"

"I saw nothing," Ramos said as Hughes moved from behind the radar to retrieve his binoculars from the storage box by the bridge window, then turned and started out the door to the starboard bridge wing.

"Where are you going?" Ramos demanded.

"There's something to starboard. I'm going to check it out." Hughes hurried out the door before the Cuban could object.

He rushed to the far side of the bridge wing, binoculars pressed to his eyes as he scanned the open ocean for the nonexistent radar contact. He heard Ramos approach behind him, and he lowered the binoculars and shot a quick glance back at the Cuban. Ramos was scowling as he approached, and behind him, Hughes could see the second Cuban was also interested and was standing in the wheelhouse door, watching the confrontation about to unfold between his superior and the *yanqui capitan* .

Hughes turned and pressed the binoculars back to his eyes.

"There is nothing! Come back inside at once, or I will —"

"There!" Hughes lowered the glasses and pointed into the distance. "See for yourself." He offered the binoculars to Ramos.

Ramos put the glasses to his eyes and looked out over the open ocean.

"And what exactly am I looking for?"

Matt Kinsey stood with the door from the stairwell to the chartroom slightly cracked, straining to hear the conversation on the bridge. When he heard Hughes exit the wheelhouse over the Cuban's objection, he waited a few seconds and then eased the door open quietly to enter the chartroom, crouched low behind the large chart table, two of his men close behind. They were all armed with pistols.

He peeked around the chartroom curtain and cursed. Both Cubans were on the starboard side, but one was in the wheelhouse door, blocking access to the second. They had to take the first man swiftly and silently to subdue the second before he could react. And there was no time; Hughes couldn't distract the Cuban officer forever.

Kinsey flashed a signal, and one of his men holstered his sidearm and drew a stun gun. Kinsey and his backup charged, widely separated so they both had clear shots at the Cuban in the doorway with his back to them, while the Coastie with the stun gun circled far left, approaching the Cuban swiftly while staying out of the other two men's fields of fire.

The man with the stun gun leaped on the Cuban, placing his left arm around the man, pinning the AK tight against the man's body by hugging him close. He jammed the stun gun electrodes into the Cuban's neck, intent on incapacitating him and dragging him from the doorway without alerting the Cuban officer.

It almost worked.

Unfortunately, the young Cuban was a very recent conscript, pressed into service only after the blackout. Long on enthusiasm if short on training, not only was the young Cuban holding his finger inside the trigger guard, he'd inadvertently moved the fire selector switch to 'full auto' mode. Electricity coursing through his nervous system contracted the muscles in his trigger finger, sending a loud burst of automatic fire ricocheting off the bridge wing deck. The surprised young Cuban, and his equally surprised assailant, collapsed in a tangled heap in the wheelhouse door, foiling Kinsey's plan to rush the bridge wing.

Hughes flinched and ducked instinctively as something stung his left ear and all hell broke loose behind him. His ears rang from the unexpected gunfire, and things seemed to move in slow motion. He spun to see Kinsey just inside the wheelhouse door, staring in horror at a tangle of arms and legs blocking the doorway. Then Kinsey pointed a gun at Ramos, who dropped the binoculars and began to claw his sidearm from its holster. Hughes rose from his crouch, partially spinning as he put all his weight and strength into the right elbow he hammered into the Cuban's face. Something gave under his elbow, and Ramos collapsed, his pistol still in the holster.

Hughes steadied himself on the bridge rail and watched as Kinsey and his men cleared the young Cuban from the door and then rushed out to subdue Ramos. The Coasties fell on the two Cubans with duct tape, and as they were trussing them up, Hughes heard Pete Sonnier call from the wheelhouse, his voice cracking from stress.

"The boat heard, Captain. She's circling our stern!" Sonnier yelled.

"Shit!" Hughes said, looking at Kinsey. "What now?"

Kinsey looked up at the top of the wheelhouse. "TORRES!" he shouted. "THE BOAT'S CIRCLING ASTERN. YOU GOT THIS?"

"I'M ON IT, CHIEF!" came the reply, and Hughes looked up to see a face peeking over the edge of the deck on top of the wheelhouse, obviously one of the Coasties lying prone to keep from being spotted by the boat.

"LIKE WE TALKED ABOUT, TAKE OUT ANY COMMS FIRST."

"PIECE OF CAKE, CHIEF. I ALREADY CHECKED IT OUT WHEN THE BOAT WAS ON THE OTHER SIDE. TWO ANTENNAS."

"ROGER THAT! YOU ARE WEAPONS FREE!"

Hughes saw the man nod, then the head disappeared to be replaced by a thin pipe. It took him a moment to realize it was a rifle barrel.

"What happens if he runs?" Hughes asked. "You gonna shoot the boat driver?"

"Only if he makes us," Kinsey said. "Now let's get inside. The less he can see, the closer he may come to try to figure out what's going on, and that will make it easier for Torres. He's good, but he's not a magician."

Hughes nodded and followed Kinsey back into the wheelhouse.

"That's got to be a pretty tough shot," Hughes said, when they were back out of sight.

Kinsey shook his head. "Not a problem. Torres is cross-trained as a chopper gunner. He used to fly with the HITRON squadron out of Jacksonville and his job was to incapacitate the 'go fast' smuggling boats. And among the equipment we're 'transferring' to MSU Port Arthur, there just happens to be two fifty-caliber Barrett sniper rifles. He'll get the job done."

Just as he finished speaking, the boat pulled into view, steering a parallel course two hundred yards to starboard. The boat held station for several minutes, and it was apparent it would come no closer.

"Doesn't look like he's gonna take the bait," Kinsey said. "Torres will have to take his shot —"

A shot rang out and the top of the wheelhouse on the boat erupted as the shot took out one of the antennas. In less than two seconds, a second shot wiped out the remaining antenna.

A rooster tail shot up behind the boat as the driver rammed both throttles to full speed and turned to race directly away from *Pecos Trader* . No shots followed.

Hughes tensed, waiting for another shot, and the boat opened the distance at almost fifty knots.

"He's getting away —"

The shot shattered the silence as the big slug tore into the starboard outboard, shutting it down forever as the boat suddenly swung to starboard and slowed abruptly. The driver struggled to compensate for the now uneven thrust, wrestling the wheel as the boat continued on an erratic corkscrew track. A final shot sounded and the port outboard coughed smoke and died, the boat drifting powerless several hundred yards from this ship.

"I take it back," Kinsey said, "maybe he is a magician."

WARDEN'S OFFICE
FEDERAL CORRECTIONAL COMPLEX
BEAUMONT, TEXAS

DAY 13, 5:00 P.M.

Spike McComb leaned back in the chair, put his feet up on the warden's desk, and smiled. He had on a relatively clean correctional officer's uniform and his hair was neatly trimmed. Across from him sat Owen Fairchild, aka 'Snaggle' for his dental issues, similarly dressed and barbered.

"Some of the boys are pissed, Spike," Snaggle said. "You said we was goin' on jackrabbit parole and we're still here."

"'Cause I ain't a dumb ass," Spike said. "It didn't come to me right off, but I finally figured out this is the best place we could be."

Snaggle shook his head. "Don't seem right, breakin' out of the joint and then hangin' around. There ain't much law around, and lots of easy pickings."

"And after we take what we want, where we gonna keep it? And when all these dumb asses get all boozed up and are lyin' around drunk, what's to keep a bunch of other assholes from sneaking up and blowing 'em 'way? Answer me that, genius."

Snaggle shrugged and said nothing. McComb pointed in the direction of the maximum-security unit. "Over there at max security, we got about the closest thing to a castle we're likely to find. Razor-wire-topped fence AND big thick walls with guard towers all around and one way in and out. All those things designed to keep us in is just as good to keep people out. Not only that, but we got all the cells we need to keep people to work for us and we got plenty of guns, for now anyway."

McComb smiled. "And the beautiful part is, until we're strong enough, no one's the wiser. Where else would you expect cons to be but in a prison? We both been out to have a look, and you know I'm right. The law's spread pretty thin, but there's still a few around. We just stay low profile until we're strong enough to take over."

Snaggle nodded as realization dawned. "Okay," he said, "but what about the mud people in max security? It's gonna start stinkin' even worse if they die and are lying around in all the heat. Nobody's likely to want to hole up anywhere near there."

"Move 'em over to medium security and leave them to rot," McComb said. "Do it now while they can still move on their own."

"Why don't we make them clean the place up before we move them out?"

McComb shook his head. "Most of them are too far gone, plus they know we ain't gonna let 'em go, so no telling what they might try. We'll get more work out of fresh civilians. Besides, they'll be easier to keep in line."

Snaggle nodded. "I gotta hand it to you, Spike, that's pretty smart."

McComb smirked. "That's why I'm the captain. Now what's the final head count?"

"We got almost a hundred soldiers, and all of them are getting cleaned up like you said. Lucky one of the guys used to work in the barbershop, so the haircuts don't look too bad. We pieced together about a dozen uniforms off the dead COs—the rest of the stuff was too bloody. We can also dress a few guys in civvies we took off bodies here in the admin complex—oh yeah, that reminds me, since we're staying, what do you want to do with all the bodies? They're gonna start stinking too."

"Pile them up over in the admin area of medium security. We'll bury them after we 'recruit' our workforce," McComb said. "Then put together patrols to go out tonight and scavenge for food and supplies. Use the prison vans we found over in the motor pool. Is there enough gas?"

Snaggle nodded. "A couple of hundred gallons and most of the vehicles have some gas in the tanks. It won't last long. And where they gonna find supplies? I figure most of the stores have been stripped by now, and the law is probably all over what's left."

"That's why they're going at night. Put two 'COs' per van, and the story if they're stopped is they're looking for an escaped prisoner. Have 'em cruise residential areas, looking for lights or the sound of generators. Anybody with a generator like as not has both food and fuel. This is hurricane country, so I expect they'll find more than a few. Bring anybody they find so there ain't any witnesses left. We can use 'em to start our workforce. Oh yeah, have them bring the generators too."

Snaggle rose from his chair. "Anything else?"

"Yeah, remind the boys I get first shot at any women they bring back. It's been a long season without rain."

CHAPTER THIRTEEN

M/V Pecos Trader
Gulf of Mexico
West of Dry Tortugas

Day 14, 6:00 a.m.

Hughes stood on the starboard bridge wing, staring down in the early morning light at Georgia Howell as she supervised the offloading of the Cuban patrol boat. He watched her raise her hand to signal Nunez in the cab of the hose-handling crane, and the boat descended further and settled gently on the calm blue sea. Hughes glanced to the lightening sky in the east and willed the mate to hurry.

"Second-guessing yourself?"

Hughes turned to see Matt Kinsey walking out the wheelhouse door.

"Not really," Hughes said. "We couldn't leave them floating around that close to Cuba. If they got picked up before we got out of range, we were screwed, and we sure as hell can't take them with us. Short of shooting them, marooning them somewhere with a chance of making their way back to civilization seemed the only choice."

"If there's any civilization left," Kinsey said.

"You know what I meant."

"I know, just jerking your chain a bit, Cap," Kinsey said and looked east toward Dry Tortugas. "Though I doubt our passengers will be excited about your choice of disembarkation ports."

"Well, I'm pushing the envelope as it is, and this is as close to Key West as I'm willing to get," Hughes said. "We're leaving them food and water, and Dan broke up some old pallets and made them multiple paddles. They can land on Dry Tortugas and make their plan and then all they have to do is follow the rising sun to the Marquesas Keys and then island-hop up the keys until they get to Key West. They should be able to make it in three or four days, a week max."

Kinsey nodded. "I'm sure dumping the useless outboards made the boat considerably lighter and easier to paddle."

"That was the idea." Hughes looked distracted. "My only real concern is if they make it to Key West and start raving to your Coastie buddies about the *Pecos Trader* . We've been lucky enough to slip past, and I'd just as soon our name didn't come up again."

"I don't think you need to worry," Kinsey said. "In normal times, four Cubans paddling into port in a disabled patrol craft with a tall tale would likely be front-page news, but today there's so many things going down, I doubt it would even register."

"That's probably true," Hughes said, "but all things considered, I could have really done without this whole experience."

Kinsey grinned. "Look at the bright side, we got another machine gun, an RPG launcher and four grenades, three AKs and a pistol out of the deal, along with a lot of ammunition. The Cubans might be short on food, but they seem to have plenty of hardware."

"There is that." Hughes turned to look down at the deck. "Seems it's time to wish our guests 'bon voyage.' Care to join me?"

"Wouldn't miss it for the world," Kinsey said.

When Hughes and Kinsey arrived on the main deck, they found the Cubans lined up, hands still bound with duct tape. Georgia Howell was instructing Lieutenant Ramos as to his location and the easterly route necessary to reach the inhabited area of the Keys. The three enlisted Cubans were standing docilely, unsure what to expect and obviously frightened, but Ramos's face was red with rage, in stark contrast to the white of the tape the second mate had used to stabilize his broken nose. When the Cuban saw Hughes approach, he turned and vented.

"This is an act of piracy, an outrage!" he hissed. "You cannot abandon us here. How do you expect us to return to Cuba?"

Hughes shrugged. "As someone said to me very recently, that is not my concern."

"You will pay for this *Yanqui* !"

"I already have, Ramos," Hughes said, "by taking the time to drop your sorry ass here instead of just casting you adrift. However, that's still an option, so if you'd like to be dropped off in the middle of the Gulf of Mexico instead of spitting distance from land, just keep talking."

The Cuban glared at Hughes but held his tongue, and Hughes motioned to the armed Coasties to escort the Cubans to the pilot ladder. At the top of the ladder, Georgia Howell produced a pocketknife and cut the duct tape from each man's hands to allow him to descend to the waiting boat. Ramos was the last down, and as soon as he was aboard the small boat, Howell motioned for Kenny Nunez to cast the boat off and begin hauling the pilot ladder back on board.

Hughes walked to the ship's side and stood beside Howell, staring down at the boat as it paddled away.

"Good riddance," Howell said.

"I'll second that," Hughes said. "Did you give them plenty of stores?"

"Twenty gallons of water and two cases of Spam," she replied.

Hughes burst out laughing. "Seriou—seriously?" he asked.

"Serves the bastard right for checking out my ass when he thought I wasn't looking," Howell said. "Now let's get this ship to Texas."

"I'm with you, Mate," Hughes said, and they started for the bridge.

MAYPORT NAVAL STATION
JACKSONVILLE, FLORIDA

DAY 14, 6:00 A.M.

"How are the new guys?" Luke asked. "Jarheads, right?"

Washington nodded. "From Lejeune. Corley and Abrams are their names. Gibson knows them both and says they're good troops."

Luke grinned. "Corley and Abrams? Sounds like a friggin' law firm."

A smile flitted across Washington's face, disappearing as quickly to be replaced by what was becoming a perpetual worried frown.

"So what's the drill, LT," he asked, "another 'recon patrol? What are we supposed to steal today?"

"It's a tough one," Luke said. "Evidently my efforts to restrict our 'acquisitions' to things abandoned hasn't gone unnoticed. Rorke came to me last night and 'reminded' me we're to concentrate on food. He pointed out his other 'recon teams' were producing much more and he expected today's mission into a new area to 'yield significant results.' All of which means we can no longer just go through the motions."

Washington shook his head. "I... I don't think I can steal food out of folks' mouths."

Luke sighed. "I don't like it any better than you do, Sergeant, but if we don't do it, someone else will, likely someone more aggressive about it than us. Besides, we both took an oath, and as screwed up as this is, we're still following the orders of our lawfully appointed superiors. We don't get to choose which orders we follow." He relented a bit. "It's not like we have a lot of options here, Washington."

Washington looked unconvinced, but nodded. "Who you want to take?"

Luke considered a moment. "Long, Gibson, and the two new jarheads. And I suppose we need to take at least a couple of the others. I guess Grogan and one more. Which one do you want?"

Washington shrugged. "Six of one, they're all assholes. Morton, I guess."

"All right. We'll roll out at oh eight hundred," Luke said.

***

Luke stared out the window as the Humvee moved along US 17 North, aka Main Street North. There were cars stopped in the middle of the road where they ran out of gas, but the drivers of most had coasted to the right shoulder, no doubt sure they would come back 'when things got back to normal' to retrieve their vehicles. The two Humvees were traveling at a steady clip of thirty to thirty-five miles per hour, with two commandeered civilian pickups sandwiched between them, all maintaining their safety intervals to allow them reaction time if the driver ahead had to swerve around obstacles in the road.

He'd chosen US 17 in preference to I-95 a bit further to the west, because intelligence from chopper flyovers indicated I-95 was a parking lot, with refugees straggling its entire length, heading north. Luke wondered briefly what would happen when the northbound refugees met the no doubt equally desperate southbound horde from Savannah. By all accounts, the situation was dire, with bodies beside the interstate, bloating in the Florida sun. Impromptu refugee camps had sprung up around both abutments of the Nassau River bridge, where people too exhausted or discouraged to move on were fighting for the limited shade of scrubby trees and drinking the near brackish river water. It wasn't something he was eager to see—each foray 'outside the wire' brought fresh scenes of horror.

Nor was this route free of horrors. His driver swerved around a late model BMW with both front doors open, blocking the view ahead, then swerved again to avoid the bodies of an elderly couple lying in the road, their mangled skulls leaving no doubt they'd met a violent end.

"Jesus!" Long said, instinctively slowing the vehicle. "Should I stop, LT?"

Luke shook his head. "They're beyond help, and unfortunately I suspect that's a sight we'll be seeing a lot more of. But call back and advise the others to watch it when they pass the BMW."

Long complied and Luke studied the passing landscape, mostly pine forest on the left with scattered residential neighborhoods on the right. His orders were to bypass them all and go straight north to the town of Yulee, turning east there on A1A toward Amelia Island and Fernandina Beach. Rorke seemed to think the A1A corridor was far enough from Jacksonville proper to hold 'greater promise,' and Luke was instructed to find and work the most promising subdivisions while identifying others for attention by additional 'recon teams.' It hadn't escaped his notice the area was also far enough away from any FEMA command presence for Rorke's 'off the book' operations to go largely unnoticed. FEMA would likely turn a blind eye in any event, but Luke sensed Rorke was being careful to avoid anything that might create a conflict with his benefactors.

***

Thirty minutes later they were headed east on A1A when they reached a commercial retail area on the left, a long row of fast-food outlets and chain restaurants lining the road in front of expansive parking lots serving big-box stores of various types. Luke spotted the sign for a Publix supermarket and directed Long to pull into the parking lot. It was a long shot at this point, but if they could scrape together a reasonable yield from the supermarket, they might minimize the civilian contact he was dreading. The rest of the little convoy followed his vehicle into the deserted parking lot and came to rest in front of the supermarket.

"Long, get up on the Ma Deuce and keep your eyes open," Luke said. "I don't think we should have any problems, but let's be careful."

"Roger that, LT," Long said, as Luke dismounted.

Washington walked up as Luke was getting out of the Humvee, a look of doubt on his face.

"I know, I know," Luke said. "It's probably stripped, but it doesn't hurt to look. Take two guys and do a quick recon. If the shelves are bare, check to see if there's anything left in back."

"Roger that," Washington said, then yelled, "Gibson, Abrams, you're with me. Move your asses."

The three men disappeared into the building and came out a few minutes later. Washington emerged last and gave Luke a shake of his head as he approached.

"Damn, it stinks in there," Washington said.

"Rotten meat and fish?" Luke asked.

"Among other things. It's bad in there, LT—three bodies, two women and a man. Looks like the women were shot and the man's head was beat in with a can of creamed corn. The can busted and it's lying there in his blood."

Luke suppressed a shudder. "I don't suppose there was any food?"

"Not a crumb anywhere—unless you count the creamed corn," Washington said.

"All right, I guess we have to do this. Leave Long on the Ma Deuce and get everyone else down here so we can go over the op."

Washington nodded and began shouting orders and the men gathered around Luke.

"All right, given all the commercial development, I'm thinking there are plenty of subdivisions nearby. We're going to head south at the last intersection we went through and find the first one. I'll drive one Humvee with Long up top and Sergeant Washington will drive the second one with Gibson on the Ma Deuce there. We'll stay in reserve to respond with overwhelming force if need be. I doubt we need it, but better safe than sorry."

There were nods of agreement as Luke continued. "Grogan, I want you and Morton in one pickup and Corley and Abrams in the other. You guys will be going door-to-door in pairs to collect, one street at a time. Washington's Humvee will take a position at the entrance to the street being worked by Grogan and Morton, and Long and I will support Corley and Abrams. If either group runs into a big problem, specifically armed resistance, I want BOTH Humvees to respond, and the collection team that's temporarily unsupported is just to hold in place. Is that clear?"

Again there were nods before Luke continued, "Now get this straight, we're not going in and stripping these people of all their food. I want you to go door-to-door, identify yourselves as members of the FEMA Special Reaction Force and politely but firmly inform residents there is a mandatory food collection operation in process. Tell them though we are authorized to seize all food and fuel, we will only requisition fifty percent of their stores at this time, assuming they cooperate. Tell them they have ten minutes to collect their contribution and bring it curbside to load into the pickup, then move on to the next house. Inform them if we believe they're holding back, we will enter their homes to verify the amounts. Further inform them if verification shows they failed to deliver fifty percent of their stores, we will take it all. You are to stay together and you are NOT to threaten them, harm them in any way beyond the warning I have indicated, or enter their houses. Is that clear?"

"That's bullshit," Grogan said. "This ain't a food drive. They'll just give as little as they think they can get away with and it'll all be crappy stuff. This ain't what Colonel Rorke wants and you know it, Kinsey."

Washington moved towards Grogan, but Luke waved him off. "We may get less than half of what they have," Luke said, "but I'm betting there are plenty of houses and we'll get enough to fill these two pickups before the day is out, and without harming anyone or leaving them completely without food. Since that's all we can carry anyway, that seems like a win for all concerned or, at least, less of a loss." Luke's voice hardened, "And that PRIVATE Grogan, is the first and last time I ever intend to explain an order to you. And you will address me as sir or lieutenant, or Lieutenant Kinsey, or even LT, but if you ever disrespect me again, it will be the last time you disrespect anyone. Is that clear?"

Grogan glared and, after a long moment, bobbed his head once.

"I didn't hear you, Private. I asked you if that was clear?"

"Yes, SIR," hissed Grogan between clenched teeth.

"Good, now are there any other questions?" Luke asked.

Corley, one of the new men, raised his hand and Luke nodded.

"Ahh… what if no one answers the door, LT?"

Luke considered a moment. "In that case," he said, "pound on the door with the butt of your weapon and announce loudly you assume the house is abandoned and you're going to break in. Give anyone inside a couple of minutes to respond. If no one responds, notify us you have a potential breach situation and then breach the door. That is the ONLY circumstance under which you will enter a home without a specific direct order from either myself or Sergeant Washington. Is that clear?"

There was a muted chorus of 'yes, sirs,' and Luke nodded at Washington.

"All right," Washington yelled, "let's mount up and get to it."

***

They found the first residential area a half mile south of the intersection on the left side of the road, where what had been a carefully landscaped side road marked the entrance to an upscale subdivision of large new homes on spacious lots between the main thoroughfare and a man-made lake. Homes backing on to the busier main street were protected by a handsome brick privacy wall at least twelve feet high.

The little convoy turned into the subdivision entrance and immediately encountered conditions requiring a plan modification. The entrance yielded on to a small traffic circle with streets branching off to the left and right. After a hurried consultation between Luke and Washington, they decided both Humvees would maintain station at the traffic circle, with Grogan and Morton working the street to the south while Corley and Abrams took the street to the north.

The two collection teams parked their pickups a half-dozen houses down their respective streets and started canvassing. The civilian responses varied from tentative to argumentative, but politely meeting resistance with a few minutes of interaction before dropping the not-so-veiled threat of total confiscation and then moving on was working well. After reflection, all of the residents decided giving up something under their control was much preferable to having these intruders in their homes. In a few minutes, sullen residents emerged from their homes with plastic grocery bags and cardboard boxes, usually small, to cast resentful looks at the Humvees as they deposited their meager offerings into the bed of the waiting pickups. The process was slow, but it was undoubtedly faster and less stressful than having a confrontation at every house. The threat of entering nonresponsive houses was also effective, as several homeowners answered their doors just before Luke authorized breaches.

"So far, so good," said Luke, as he stood with Washington in the little traffic circle next to the two Humvees.

Washington grunted, "True, but that asshole Grogan was right about one thing. I suspect we're getting a ton of creamed spinach and pickled beets."

Luke shrugged. "Rorke said food, he wasn't specific."

Washington chuckled. Every fifteen or twenty minutes, the collection teams moved the slowly filling pickups a few houses down the street, diverging in opposite directions from the Humvees. At the ninety-minute mark, the Corley and Abrams team still had a long stretch of straight street visible ahead, but the pickup assigned to Grogan and Morton was moving abreast of an intersection. Washington climbed into the driver's seat of the Humvee and keyed the mike on the radio.

"Shopping Cart Four, this is Shopping Cart Two, do you copy? Over," Washington said.

"Shopping Cart Two, this is Shopping Cart Four, go ahead. Over," came Grogan's voice over the speaker.

"Four, what is the status of the side street? Is it a through street? Over."

"Negative Two, I say again negative. It's a cul-de-sac. Over."

"We copy, Four, intersection is a cul-de-sac. Leave your vehicle parked on this street where we can keep it under observation and have residents carry their… their…" Washington was momentarily stumped as to what to call the food they were collecting. Donations? Contributions? Tribute? After a moment he punted, "Their stuff out to the truck."

"Shopping Cart Two this is Shopping Cart Four. We copy. Anything else? Over."

"Yes, Four, please say estimated time to clear the cul-de-sac. Over," Washington said.

"About a dozen houses. At five minutes a house, I estimate one hour minimum. Over," Grogan said.

"Two, I copy. We will not have a visual on you, so if you run into problems, get on the horn ASAP. Over."

"Affirmative Two. Shopping Cart Four out," Grogan said.

Washington racked the mike and crawled out of the Humvee to stand beside Luke.

"You heard?" Washington asked.

Luke nodded.

"You think I should move down and cover them in the cul-de-sac?" Washington asked.

Luke looked down the road in both directions and then back at the entrance to the subdivision.

"No," he said, "because it's just dawning on me this might not be the best place to be. We got a lake on one side and a pretty stout brick wall on the other, and this entrance is the only way through the wall we know of. We could probably bust through if need be, but I don't see any place to get a running start. So no, Sergeant, I'm fine with both the Humvees here watching our six unless we actually need to provide close support. Better safe than sorry."

Washington nodded. "I agree. Hopefully we'll have the trucks full in another couple of hours and we can get the hell out of here."

* * *

"This blows," Morton said as he and Grogan trudged across the lawn of the first house on the left in the neat cul-de-sac. "We'll be dicking around for hours doing this touchy-feely shit, and we could have already filled both trucks up a couple of times over if we just cleaned out the first six or eight houses we hit. Publix and those other stores aren't far away, and if these assholes are still all hunkered down in these houses, I'm thinking they got at least some of the loot. I'm betting they got plenty stashed."

"Tell me about it," Grogan said. "Kinsey's a prick. Him and his crap rules… hey, I just thought of something!"

"What?"

"Since they can't see us, let's speed things up. Washington's expecting us to be here an hour at least, so we can ditch all that nicey-nice crap and work all these houses and then take a break."

"Sounds good to me, bro," Morton replied just as they reached the front door of the house.

Grogan grinned and pulled open the storm door to hammer on the inner door with the butt of his weapon, leaving dents in the beautifully stained wooden door.

"OPEN UP! FEMA! OFFICIAL BUSINESS!" he yelled. Beside him, Morton smirked.

The door opened tentatively to the full width allowed by the security chain and an elderly woman's face appeared in the crack at waist level. "Y-yes? What is it?" she asked, fear in her voice.

"You got five minutes to get half your food and any fuel to the pickup truck at the entrance to the cul-de-sac," Grogan snarled. "If it's not out there in time, we're coming back and taking everything you got. Any questions?"

"B-but I don't have much—"

"Not my problem," Grogan said, "comply or we'll come back and take it all."

"I-I'm in a wheelchair. I can't get it out to the stree—"

"Again, not my problem, grandma," Grogan said. "But if it ain't out to the truck in five, we'll be back to help you, and I guarantee you won't like it. You have a nice fucking day!"

Morton burst out laughing as the two turned to cut across the yard to the next house.

"Outstanding," Morton said.

Grogan smirked, pleased with himself. "Did you time me?"

"A minute, more or less."

"I'm gonna try to do the next one in forty-five," Grogan said.

"Shit no, man! Let's take turns," Morton said. "I bet I make the next one in under thirty."

"All right, that'll make it interesting. What's the bet?"

Morton thought for a minute. "I got two six packs of brew stashed. How about you?"

"You're on. I got half a bottle of Jack Black squirreled away. Fastest time takes it all."

The two raced from house to house down the same side of the street, circling the cul-de-sac as they delivered their ever briefer ultimatums with cheerful brutality, until they arrived back at the entrance to the cul-de-sac across the street from the old woman's house.

"I still think you cheated," Grogan grumbled.

"Seventeen seconds, bro," Morton chortled, "that Jack is gonna go down so smooth—"

"Watch it, man! You want Washington to see us?" Grogan said, grabbing Morton's arm and pulling him back as he neared the main road.

Morton grinned. "Sorry, bro, just thinking about that Jack. How much time we got?"

Grogan looked at his watch as Morton eyed the steady stream of residents carrying parcels to the pickup, noting with satisfaction the 'contributions' seemed much more substantial.

"That only took us fifteen minutes," Grogan said. "We got at least forty-five left, easy."

"This is gonna finish filling the truck," Morton said. "Maybe we should blow off the break and just report back. Besides, I do want to get me a taste of that Jack."

"Don't be a dumb ass. If we show back up in fifteen or twenty minutes, Kinsey's gonna know we didn't follow his stupid rules, and give us a ration of shit. We just gotta chill till he's expecting us. I'm gonna sit my ass down right over there under that big shade tree."

Morton nodded and the two started across the yard, until Morton grabbed Grogan's arm and dragged him down behind a hedge.

"Whoa! Dude, check it out!" Morton said, and nodded across the street to the old lady's house as he peeked up over the hedge.

Grogan followed suit and saw a slim young woman in a sundress carrying two plastic grocery bags and walking down the old lady's sidewalk, headed for the pickup at the entrance to the cul-de-sac.

"I guess Granny's 'I'm all alone in my wheelchair' story was bullshit," Morton said.

Grogan nodded as he eyed the woman hungrily. She was in her late teens or early twenties, and the simple sundress did nothing to hide the curves of her slim body. She had long blond hair pulled back in a ponytail.

"Now that is one fine piece of ass," Grogan said as he watched the woman deposit the bags in the pickup and start back toward her house, hurrying now, as she looked in all directions. "You reckon it's just her and the old lady?"

"That's my guess," Morton said, "'cause I'm thinking if there was a husband or father or brother, he'd have hauled the stuff to the truck."

"You thinking what I'm thinking?" Grogan asked.

"If you're thinking you know how to spend the rest of our little break, I believe I am," Morton said, then added, "First dibs."

"Screw you, Morton! You already got my whiskey, so I got first dibs on the woman. Besides, you probably only need about seventeen seconds anyway, seeing as how you're so fast and all."

"Screw you back, Grogan," Morton said, but he was laughing as the two men rose and moved toward the old lady's house.

"What's up, Sergeant?" Luke asked as Washington lowered the binoculars.

"I don't know," Washington said, "but it doesn't seem right. A bunch of people started dropping off food in the pickup not long after Grogan and Morton started canvassing. That's way faster than I expected, and now there hasn't been anyone there for the last fifteen minutes."

"You think you should —"

Gunfire sounded down the street from the direction of the cul-de-sac, a few individual shots, possibly a handgun, followed after a brief pause by semiautomatic rifle fire.

"Shit!" Washington said as he swung into the driver's seat on the Humvee and grabbed the mike.

"Shopping Cart Four this is Shopping Cart two. Sitrep, NOW. Over," Washington said.

"We're taking fire, repeat, we're taking fire. Grogan is down, repeat, Grogan is down. I am withdrawing to the pickup. Over," came Morton's voice.

"We copy, Four. Support is on the way. Over."

Washington looked at Luke, who was already in the driver's seat of his own Humvee, picking up the mike. "Shopping Cart Three, this is Shopping Cart Actual. Suspend your current operation and move pickup to our current position to assume control of the subdivision entrance. Shopping Cart Actual and Shopping Cart Two are moving in support of Shopping Cart Four. Confirm. Over."

"This is Shopping Cart Three, we copy. On the way, LT," Abrams said.

Luke cranked up the Humvee and started after Washington, who was already racing toward Grogan and Morton's pickup. They arrived within seconds of each other, bracketing the pickup, just as Morton ran across a lawn and ducked behind the truck, rising to shoot toward the house, then moving into the more secure area behind Washington's Humvee. Gibson and Long manned the M2s, searching for threats, as Luke and Washington exited their vehicles on the sides away from the house and moved beside Morton.

"What the hell happened, Morton?" Washington demanded.

"Me and Grogan heard screaming coming from that house. We got there and found the door kicked in and stumbled upon a bunch of gangbangers, must be a dozen of them, maybe more. Anyway, we got in a firefight and Grogan got hit. They almost got me too. I had to leave him; there was too many of them," Morton said.

"Is Grogan dead?" Luke asked.

Morton nodded. "Absolutely, LT. He took a round in the head. I hated to leave him, but it was just too hot. I think there may be more of them. We need to get out of here 'cause this place will be crawling with bangers in a few minutes."

"We're not leaving anyone." Luke moved to peer around the Humvee at the house. "Damn! The place is on fire. There's smoke coming out the windows."

"The dude is DEAD," Morton said, "and we shouldn't risk anyone just to recover a body."

Luke kept his face impassive. "All right, Morton, settle down. Take cover behind the pickup and keep an eye on the front door. I have to think about this."

"The dude is DEAD," Morton repeated, but assumed the position behind the truck as ordered.

Luke nodded at Washington and stepped away as far as possible. "What do you think of that story?" he asked softly.

"It's a fairy tale. The gunfire we heard wasn't nearly sustained enough to be a firefight, and if there were bangers in there, they'd be opening up on us. They're all trigger-happy assholes with no fire discipline at all, and the only one shooting when we got here was Morton." Washington looked toward the house. "And if we want to find out what went down, we don't have much time before it goes up in smoke."

Luke nodded and drew his sidearm. "Get Long down here, but leave Gibson on the Ma Deuce just in case there's a miracle and this asshole is telling the truth."

Washington nodded and hurried to carry out those orders as Luke walked back over to Morton. Morton stiffened when he saw the handgun and Luke saw the man's weapon move a bit.

"Don't even think about it, Morton. Set your weapon down gently against the truck, face away from me and put both hands on the back of your head."

"What the fuc—"

Luke leveled the gun at Morton's head. "I'm not going to ask twice, and it's well within my authority to shoot you for disobeying a direct order while in contact with the enemy."

"All right, all right," Morton said as Long climbed out of the Humvee.

"Long, zip-tie Private Morton's hands and sit him down behind the pickup. If he makes an aggressive move, shoot him. Got it?" Luke asked.

"Absolutely," Long replied.

Luke looked at Washington. "Okay, Sergeant, let's go take out these gangbangers."

Washington nodded and they approached the house on opposite zigzag paths, taking advantage of available cover to stack up on opposite sides of the splintered front door.

Washington pulled out a flash bang and looked a question at Luke, who nodded, and the big man activated it and tossed it into the house. Both men rushed in on the heels of the explosion and found the house—empty—or at least not occupied by the living. The smoke was emanating from smoldering curtains in the family room, evidently set on fire by Morton before his hasty retreat. Washington pulled them down and dragged them through a patio door to toss them into an inground pool with green scummy water, then returned, leaving the patio door open to help clear the room.

Luke stared at the scene, rage rising within him. Grogan was dead, sure enough, lying face up with his pants and underwear around his ankles, his face disfigured by the exit wound of a gunshot. There was also an old woman on the floor beside a wheelchair, dead of multiple gunshot wounds, and a young girl near the woman, dead of the same cause. The girl was naked and there were angry red marks on her body from where her underwear had been ripped from her body. There was a Colt 1911 on the floor beside the girl.

Luke looked at Washington, who only shook his head, as if incapable of speech, and both men turned and left the house. At the Humvees, Luke stood staring down at Morton.

"Let's hear it, Morton," he said.

"It was an accident, LT. We didn't mean to kill 'em. We just wanted to have a little fun, you know."

"Go on," Luke said, his face a mask.

"Well, I taped the old lady's trap to shut her up and taped her hands to the wheelchair and then rolled her out of the way into a bedroom, but the old bitch got loose somehow. The next thing I know, I'm watching Grogan do his business and she rolls out with a Colt and shoots Grogan in the head. Right there in front of me, for Christ's sake. Then she starts shooting at me, but I've stripped off most of my gear and I have to dive behind the couch, and by the time I can get to my gun and shoot the old bitch, the girl got out from under Grogan. Then when I cap the old lady, the girl picks up the gun and starts shooting at me, so I have to shoot her too. I mean, I didn't have a choice, it was self-defense."

"So you figure you'll just make up this fairy tale and burn down the house, and we're all cool, huh?" Luke asked.

Morton shrugged. "It seemed like a good idea at the time." Then he continued, "Look, LT, I know we screwed up and I'm sorry I didn't come clean. I'm willing to take any punishment you want. Why, when Grogan and I screwed up in Uganda, Rorke had us on all the shit details for six months and—"

"So you've done this before?"

"No, not exactly like this, but some chick's kid brother got pissed off and tried to kill us, so we had to defend ourselves, and Rorke had to smooth it over with the head dude in the village. I think he bought him a bunch of goats or something—"

"Shut your mouth, you sick bastard," Washington said. "I heard enough."

Washington stalked away, jerking his head for Luke to follow. He stopped some distance from the Humvees and turned to Luke.

"What are we gonna do, LT? If we take that piece of shit back, you know Rorke's gonna let him off with a slap on the wrist. Five will get you ten, he'll pay lip service to 'severe punishment' and a few weeks from now Morton will just be in another unit. This is messed up."

Luke said nothing as Washington articulated his own worst fears. He looked over at Morton on his knees and the truck full of looted food. Beyond the truck he could see people starting to emerge from houses along the cul-de-sac, their body language telegraphing their fear, even at a distance. And here and there, he saw angry gestures and an occasional pistol or hunting rifle. None of the residents understood what had happened just yet, but when they did, a conflict was inevitable.

What had Rorke called it, 'medieval Genghis Khan shit'? A lawless time with no rules, except those made by men with power for their own benefit. Was that a system he could live under, even under duress? He turned back to Washington and looked him in the eye.

"WE aren't going to do anything, Sergeant. This is entirely MY responsibility and if it goes sideways, no blame will be on you or any other member of this unit. Is that clear?"

"But, LT—"

"Sergeant Washington, please confirm your understanding of the difference between your responsibilities and mine by saying yes, sir."

Washington came almost to attention. "Yes, sir!"

"Very good, Sergeant." Luke turned and marched back to Morton.

"Private Morton, you have confirmed you killed the two women in the house across the street, is that correct?"

Morton looked confused. "Yeah, like I said, I shot them in self-defense—"

"Private Morton, you stand convicted by your own testimony of two criminal acts against the civilian population, specifically violations of Article 118 of the Uniform Code of Military Justice, or murder. Furthermore, and also by your own testimony, both such criminal acts occurred during the commission of a violation of Article 120 of the Uniform Code of Military Justice, specifically rape, making these crimes especially vile in nature. The penalty for these crimes is death. Accordingly, by the legal precedent which allows for the summary execution of soldiers in emergency situations with no recourse to legal process, and in light of your own confession, I hereby inform you of my intention to carry out that execution."

Luke drew his sidearm. "Do you have any last words?"

"Wh-what do you mean?"

"I mean I'm about to blow your sorry ass away, but you get to say something first."

"You can't do this!"

Luke shot Morton between the eyes.

"Yes, I can," he whispered as he looked down at Morton's lifeless body, "and I wish I'd done it a lot sooner." He straightened.

"Sergeant Washington!"

"Yes, sir?"

"Sergeant, throw Morton's remains on the pickup truck and then take Private Long and go collect Grogan. We've done enough to these people without leaving them our garbage to deal with. Then I want Long to drive the pickup and we'll all withdraw to the traffic circle and pick up Shopping Cart Three as we exit the subdivision. We need to get out of here ASAP before anyone else is hurt. We'll rally in the Publix parking lot. Clear?"

"Yes, sir," Washington said, and nodded to Long as he stooped to pick up Morton's body.

Thirty minutes later, Luke directed the four vehicles to form a hollow square in the center of the Publix parking lot. Everyone dismounted in the center except for Gibson, who stayed on the Ma Deuce, scanning for threats.

"Can you hear me okay up there, Gibson?" asked Luke from the center of the square.

"Yes, sir."

"Good. Okay, people, listen up. As you know, this is a confused situation, and we're all doing the best we can. We all volunteered for the SRF on the understanding we'd be helping in the recovery, and no one told us at the time the transfer was permanent, or we'd be 'discharged' if we attempted to resign from the SRF. I can no longer in good conscience follow the orders I'm being given, but I sure as hell am not going to let them disarm me and dump me God knows where. I'm taking one of the Humvees and a share of the stores and leaving. Anyone who wants to come with me is welcome, and anyone who wants to return to base can do so in the other vehicles. Your call."

"But where you gonna go, LT?" Long asked. "I heard standing orders are anybody who bugs out is classed a deserter."

"I can't answer that question because I don't have a plan, but I do know I'd rather be a deserter than associated with this mercenary scum they're pairing us with, following orders I believe are criminal. My dad's in the Coast Guard up in Wilmington, so I guess I'll head that way." He paused. "But I want all of you to think VERY hard before you decide to come with me or just strike off on your own. I have no hard feelings either way, and after you commit, there's no turning back."

There was murmuring and head nods, but after the briefest of pauses, Washington spoke.

"I'm with you, LT."

"Make it three," Long said.

"Four," Gibson called down from the Ma Deuce. "My folks' place is just northeast of Wilmington anyway, so that works for me. I'll stay with you at least that far, LT."

Gibson's agreement was followed quickly by nods from the other two Marines.

Luke nodded. "All right then, gentlemen, I guess we're all officially rogues and outlaws."

There was a long silence as they all reflected on his words, but slowly Washington's face split into a grin.

"Hell, LT, this is the best I felt since the friggin' lights went out!"

FORT BOX
WILMINGTON CONTAINER TERMINAL
WILMINGTON, NORTH CAROLINA

DAY 14, 9:00 A.M.

Chief Boatswain's Mate Mike Butler watched from his raised vantage point on the deck of the container ship as across the terminal, large forklifts stacked empty containers into a makeshift wall a hundred feet inside the chain-link fence surrounding the terminal.

"Fort Box, huh? Accurate, but not real original."

Beside him, Sergeant Josh Wright grunted. "I'm more interested in defensible than original. We couldn't defend the entire terminal perimeter now anyway, even with the crew-served weapons. This way, we limit the wall to what we can defend and expand it as the need arises and we have more manpower. And we can set up inside the fence, leaving good fields of fire between the new wall and the original fence. We just concentrate the ships on one section of the dock and just build out from there. The added bonus is there aren't any nearby buildings high enough to let the gangbangers, or anyone else, snipe at us inside the new walls."

Butler nodded and followed Wright's gaze down the length of the dock. Three other fully loaded container ships were tied up bow to stern, just forward of the ship he was on, and two grain carriers, with full cargoes of corn and wheat respectively, rested forward of the farthest container ship. The container ships were tied up with their starboard sides directly to the dock, so they could all be worked by the terminal cranes, but the grain carriers were rafted side by side with one tied off abreast of the other to reduce the length of dock the ships occupied and thus minimize the length of defensive wall to be constructed. Two loaded product tankers were similarly rafted together side by side, sharing the single berth in the product terminal just downriver, previously occupied by *Pecos Trader* . Given the importance of fuel, 'Fort Box' was being extended downstream to include the product terminal within its protective walls. The few ships carrying cement, paper, and other bulk cargoes of no immediate use had been moored at various docks downstream, outside the defensive perimeter of the fledgling fort. Food, water, and defense of same were priorities now. Anything else was a distant second.

Butler turned his gaze to the substantial but increasingly crowded patch of asphalt being enclosed by the growing wall of containers.

"Well, expansion can't be too soon for me, since our 'defensible' area is already chockablock with RVs, travel trailers, your swimming pool waterworks, and God knows what all," Butler said. "You know we still need room to get the stuff OFF the ships and some place to put it, and the transporters need room to move around—"

Wright held up his hand. "And we're leaving you plenty of room next to each ship and a lane to get the containers out of the defended area. You'll just have to store them out beyond the wall until the stuff is needed. They'll be behind the fence and in sight and within coverage of the M2s on the wall. It's not like the bangers can steal a whole container. They got no clue what's in which box anyway. Hell, we got the manifests, and it's still tough to find stuff among all these boxes. It's getting easier, though, now that we got a few folks assigned full time." Wright nodded. "We're in a hell of a lot better shape than I ever thought possible."

"That we are," Butler said. "It's an embarrassment of riches, really. We need to start distributing some of this stuff."

"Just as soon as we have a defensible perimeter and the ability to safeguard what we have. I agree with Major Hunnicutt on this one—if we try to start helping people before we're prepared, everything could go tits up in a hurry. I'm thinking another three or four days max, then we can start on a relief/feeding station. "

"Where?" Butler asked.

"We're leaning toward Pine Valley Country Club. It's a straight shot up Shipyard Boulevard on a wide open road with no pinch points or likely places for the bangers to ambush us. We can set up another small container fort there in the middle of one of the golf courses and maintain open fields of fire. Then we can install a field kitchen and forward supply dump for food and water with enough guys to defend it. We won't need many because we're only a radio call and a ten- or twelve-minute ride away. We set up mess tents outside the secure area of the new fort and have the people file through to be fed. It's inevitable a refugee population is going to gravitate there, but there's a lot of open land on the golf courses. Also it's far enough away that we don't have to worry about attracting a shanty town around us here at Fort Box. We have to maintain clear fields of fire if we have any chance of holding this place against an attack, by the bangers or anyone else."

"Sounds like you got it worked out," Butler said.

"Mostly, but sanitation and water issues are gonna be a problem. But hell, we haven't even solved those here, at least in the long run."

"I think our water problems may be solved. Our snipes were talking to the engineers on the *Maersk Tangier* . They figure they can run the ships' evaporators. There may be health concerns using the river for feed water, but beggars can't be choosers. They're working on a way to convert some of the ship's heat exchangers to raise and hold the outlet water at a high enough temperature to kill any remaining bacteria, just to be on the safe side. If it works, I think you can count on your little swimming pool waterworks staying full no matter how hard you pump it. Sanitation is a different issue. We can't just be dumping our sewage in the river, especially right by where we're gonna be taking in our drinking water feedstock, but they're working on it."

"How're the ships' crews taking their new forced residence?"

Butler shrugged. "The Americans seem to be okay with it. I mean, no one's forcing them to stay, and if they want to head overland back to their homes, we offered to supply them and wish them Godspeed. The foreign crews are a different story, since they're pretty much stuck here. We'll just have to see how that plays out."

Wright nodded and they lapsed into silence until Butler spotted Singletary moving along the docks, looking up at the ships.

"Damn!" Butler said, pulling back from where he'd been leaning with his forearms resting on the ship's rail.

"BUTLER! WAIT UP!" came the cry from below.

Butler backed away from the rail to ensure he wasn't visible from the dock below.

"NO NEED TRYING TO DODGE ME AGAIN, BUTLER," Singletary yelled up. "I KNOW YOU'RE UP THERE AND AIN'T BUT ONE WAY OFF THAT SHIP. SO I'M JUST GONNA SIT MY ASS DOWN HERE AT THE BOTTOM OF THE GANGWAY 'TIL YOU DECIDE TO COME ON DOWN."

Wright grinned. "Looks like you're busted. What's all that about?"

Butler sighed. "In a moment of weakness I promised Levi I'd help this asshole find a boat to get back to Baltimore. Like I didn't have enough to do already. Anyway, he's been bugging me for two days straight now, so I guess I'd better take care of it and get him out of my hair."

"He probably just wants to get home to his family, like everyone else."

"Yeah, maybe, but that's not the vibe he gives off. It's not like he's worried, but more like he's—I don't know, afraid he's missing out on something, I guess is the best way to describe it. Kind of 'entitled' somehow. Anyway, it just doesn't feel right," Butler said.

"All the more reason to get rid of the bastard," Wright said. "If he's trouble, we don't want him around. Besides, how long can it take to find a boat, load him up with fuel and supplies and wish him bon voyage?"

"I don't know, something tells me it's not going to be that easy," Butler said, moving toward the gangway.

***

Butler stood outside the small cabin of the patrol boat and looked upstream at the Cape Fear Memorial Bridge looming over the river. He spotted movement and raised his binoculars. Sure enough there were two figures on the bridge, one pointing at the patrol boat. The second figure nodded and jumped on a motorcycle to speed off in the direction of Wilmington. Butler keyed his throat mike so he could be heard over the roar of the outboards by both the helmsman and the machine gunner in the bow.

"We may have a welcoming committee, so punch it up to full speed, and zigzag so they can't be sure where we're going to cross under the bridge. These are probably the same assholes who tried to bombard Levi and Anthony."

"Roger that," the helmsman replied.

"Guns, possible threat on the bridge. Do you see him?" Butler asked.

"I got him, Chief," the gunner replied.

"Roger that, Guns. Track him, but only fire on my order."

"Roger that, Chief."

The boat began to zigzag and Singletary stuck his head out the cabin door.

"What's going on? Why we zigzagging?"

"Possible threat on the bridge. Don't worry about it, Singletary. Just stay in the cabin."

Singletary muttered under his breath and pulled his head back in. Butler resumed his watch of the solitary figure on the bridge, surprised to see the man now had binoculars trained on the boat. The man let the glasses fall to his chest on the neck strap and raised an assault rifle.

"Shooter! Weapons free!" Butler said into the throat mike, and the M240 machine gun on the bow spoke at once, silencing the threat before the man got off a single round.

Butler heard movement beside him and turned to see Singletary in the cabin door.

"GET BACK IN THE CABIN, SINGLETARY!"

Then they were under the bridge, zigzagging up the river.

"Helm, maintain full speed and secure zigzagging. Keep us on the west side of the river as far away from Wilmington as possible."

"Roger that," came the reply, and Butler heard the distant sound of motorcycles from the Wilmington side of the bridge. No doubt their reception on the return trip would be a bit warmer.

Five minutes later they passed the battleship USS *North Carolina* in her permanent berth, and a few minutes later, they stayed right when the river split, now hugging the west bank of the Northeast Cape Fear River. They continued upstream until the lift bridge serving US 74 came into view, and in its shadow, the marinas lining the eastern bank of the river. Butler raised his binoculars and glassed the length of the bridge, but it seemed clear.

"Helm, cut your speed. We need to go boat shopping. Guns, stay alert. I don't know who those guys on the bridge were, but they know we're on the river, so they might come looking for us."

Butler got affirmative replies and stuck his head into the cabin.

"Get on out here, Mr. Singletary, and let's find you a boat. I don't want to hang around here too long."

Singletary grunted an acknowledgment and exited the cabin to stand at Butler's side as the boat slowed to a crawl along a long stretch of floating docks jammed with boats.

"We should be able to find something here," Butler said. "I'd like to avoid transiting under the bridge."

Singletary grunted again, looking down the long line of boats.

"Most of 'em look to be sailboats."

"True, but there are quite a few powerboats. There's a nice little Boston Whaler over there—"

"Ain't got no cabin, in fact, none of these powerboats have a cabin. I'm probably gonna have to live in this thing when I get to Baltimore, you know," Singletary said.

I guess the asshole's got a point, thought Butler.

"All right, Mr. Singletary, let's have a look upstream on the other side of the bridge," Butler said, and keyed his throat mike.

"Haul ass under the bridge at full power and go on by the docks nearest to the bridge. Guns, get the sniper rifle and come back to the stern. Any threat's likely to come from the bridge and you can't cover that with the M2 on the bow when we're headed upstream. I want you scanning for threats, but especially the bridge. Do you copy?"

"Roger that," said the gunner, moving aft as the helmsman accelerated to blast under the bridge.

Two hundred yards past the bridge, Butler ordered the boat to slow again and began cruising along another extensive stretch of floating docks. Butler spotted something and motioned the helmsman to pull alongside a moored vessel.

"Here we go, Mr. Singletary," Butler said, "this looks like just what the doctor ordered. About twenty-five feet, I'd say, a nice little cuddy cabin, twin outboards so you'll have a backup if one breaks down, and I'm pretty sure we'll find a berth as well as a galley and a head. Looks perfect."

Singletary was looking further up the dock. "What about that one?"

Butler followed Singletary's pointing finger to a power yacht occupying a long length of the dock several berths away. It was sixty or seventy feet long and obviously a custom-built luxury vessel. He looked back at Singletary. "You're not serious?"

"Damn right I'm serious. Why wouldn't I be serious?"

"That's a lot of boat for one man to handle, and I expect it burns through fuel pretty fast," Butler said.

"Let me worry about handling it," Singletary said, "and you said I could have all the fuel I needed. It ain't like you don't have tanks of it sitting around."

"I'm talking about AFTER you get to Baltimore," Butler said. "You won't have access to fuel. Besides, that's way more boat than you need to get to Baltimore or to even live on after you get there. This cuddy boat is a better choice, anyway."

"Oh, I see, y'all don't have any problem taking RVs and trailers and such, but if I want to pick out my own boat, then you decide it's too good for me. What's your problem, Butler, it ain't like it's your boat."

Butler's face hardened. "There's a big difference between taking a twenty- or thirty-thousand-dollar trailer to house a family or a group of single guys and stealing a half-million-dollar yacht. You want to take the yacht? Hop out now and be my guest, but just keep on trucking when you pass our docks because I'm not giving you jack. I agreed to help you get home, not outfit you like a friggin' Saudi prince."

"That ain't fair!"

"Tough. You want the cuddy boat or not? Make up your mind, because in two minutes, we're headed back downriver, with you or without you."

Singletary glared at Butler. "Fine. I'll take the friggin' cuddy boat."

"Then hop out and check it out. I suspect you'll have to break into the cabin and I doubt there's a key around. You got any problem hot-wiring the ignition?"

"I think I can handle it," Singletary said.

"I figured you probably could," Butler said, earning him another glare from Singletary.

A few minutes later, Singletary had the engines running on the boat, and Butler nodded approval.

"You got enough fuel to get back? I want to go the long way around and avoid trouble at the bridge," Butler yelled across to Singletary.

"Easy," Singletary replied, and Butler nodded and motioned for the helmsman to move the Coast Guard boat back into the river. As he did so, the gunner resumed his place at the bow machine gun, and Singletary cast off and fell in behind the Coasties.

The Coast Guard boat roared downstream at full power, dropping speed a bit only when Singletary was falling behind. At Peter Point, they turned hard to starboard, continuing up the Cape Fear River and bypassing downtown Wilmington and whatever reception committee might be awaiting them atop the Cape Fear Memorial Bridge. They continued up the Cape Fear River until its juncture with the Brunswick, and then turned south downstream on the Brunswick until it once again intersected the Cape Fear River, some distance downstream from the container terminal. It tripled the length of the trip, but given the speed of both of the boats, it wasn't a real issue. It was early afternoon when they turned into the Cape Fear River and headed upstream to the newly christened Fort Box.

SAME DAY, 4:00 P.M.

"I don't know, Singletary," Mike Butler said, "I think I'd wait and leave in the morning. You can't really travel at night with all the navigational aids out, so you're not going to get very far tonight. If you leave at first light, that would give you time to get in a good day's run and plenty of time to find a good anchorage for the night."

"Why don't you let me worry about that? I got the fuel topped up and plenty of extra, and all the food and water is loaded, so I'm ready to go. And I'm tired of all your crap anyway."

"Yeah, you're welcome," Butler said, and turned his back to walk away from the dock.

Singletary shot the finger at the retreating Coastie's back, moved down the vertical ladder to where his boat rested beneath the high container dock, and cast off, happy to finally be on his own. The boat was laboring a bit, loaded down as it was with all he could possibly get aboard. However, even at that he figured he'd reach his destination with a couple of hours of daylight left; plenty of time to get his stores shifted over and prepare for an early departure tomorrow morning. He smiled. Maybe he should have thanked Butler for showing him a way not only around the bridge, but also around 'Fort Box' and its collection of assholes.

As he approached the mouth of the Brunswick River, he began a long sweeping turn to starboard and started upstream. He knew where he was spending the night, all right, and it wasn't anchored in the weeds on some Godforsaken mosquito-infested stretch of the Intracoastal Waterway. He figured his new yacht would have a pretty nice master bedroom.

SAME DAY, 8:00 P.M.

Singletary looked around the main salon, not believing his good fortune. He'd been over the yacht from stem to stern, and been even more delighted to discover the tanks were topped up with diesel. That had been a worry, since all the extra fuel he'd taken from Fort Box was gasoline. He'd figured he might have to scavenge fuel from the other diesel-powered boats in the marina, but that would take time. Without that worry, he was free to depart at first light.

All of his stores were aboard, and he cursed once again at a lost opportunity. If Butler hadn't been such a prick about the yacht, he'd have been able to take a lot more stores. He'd also loaded the extra gasoline from the cuddy boat aboard the yacht. Even though he couldn't use it directly, he figured it would be useful to barter.

Nothing to do now but relax, and he walked over and examined the fully stocked bar—an unexpected bonus. The former owner of the boat had exceptional—and expensive—tastes. Singletary reached up and slipped a brandy snifter from the rack and lifted a bottle of Courvoisier from the recessed hole that secured it against movement of the boat. He poured himself an ample measure and held the snifter to his nose, savoring the aroma, then took a tiny sip, allowing the taste to spread through his mouth before it slipped down his throat. He reached over to set the bottle back in the recess, thought better of it, and carried both the bottle and the snifter to the table beside a leather-upholstered easy chair. He knew he was going to have more than one, and there was no need to strain himself by getting up and down, now was there?

***

He was the captain at last, and not of some crappy tanker stinking of gasoline and diesel, but a luxury yacht, crewed by all those fools and stuck-up bitches from his old neighborhood. He called the shots and they did exactly like he said or they didn't eat. How did they like that shit? Everything was going along just fine until... until some fool was poking him in the forehead with something hard. What the hell...

Singletary opened his eyes to stare at a huge gun held perhaps two inches away from the bridge of his nose, the hole in the barrel looking as big as a half dollar. He followed the gun to the hand that held it, and then up a long arm to stare into the face of the meanest looking black dude he'd ever seen.

"Wh-who are you?"

"I'm Kwintell Banks, nigga, but the question is who are YOU, and what you doin' on MY boat, drinkin' MY booze."

"I… I'm Jerome Singletary, and I didn't know it was your boat… I mean, I didn't know it was anyone's… I was just looking for a place to sleep…"

"That so? Looks like to me you was getting ready to steal my boat. That right? Best tell the truth, or it'll go hard on you," Banks said.

"Yes, but I didn't know it was yours. I'm very sorry. I'll pick another boat."

"You see, that's the thing. They're ALL my boats, including the one you and those crackers stole earlier. Though I do thank you for bringing it back, all filled up with nice things. Just for that, I'm gonna kill you fast so you don't suffer too much."

Banks backed away, and Singletary became fully aware of his surroundings for the first time. Lights were on in the cabin, and he saw four men with Banks, all heavily armed. He saw Banks holster his pistol and then point at him with his free hand.

"Take this fool into the middle of the river and then shoot him in the head. We got enough dead people stinking things up around here without adding another one."

Two of the men nodded and dragged Singletary out of the chair and toward the door, deflecting his efforts to resist as if he were a child.

"Wait, wait! I have information. I can help you."

Banks held up his hand and his underlings stopped but retained their grip on the squirming Singletary.

"So what you gonna tell me, Singletary? You gonna tell me about those crazy crackers and their tame Toms, building their little fort down on the docks? We watching 'em all the time, and I know how many they got and what they doing. It don't matter because they got those machine guns and grenades, so we ain't dumb enough to start a fight with them. No need anyhow. If they want to stay inside their little fort, that's fine by me. We got everything else and we're already spreading out into the country, figuring ways to put people to work growing food. We might even let them keep a little. Not too much, mind you, but just enough to make sure they stay alive so they can keep working for us. So you see, you don't really know nothing."

Banks nodded at his two underlings, and they started for the door once again.

"Wait, I know other things. There's… there's this guy named Levi with a hideout near here with a lot of food. Guns and ammunition too, and a generator, I think. And a lot of other stuff, gold and silver too. I… I know where it is. He tries to keep it quiet, but I heard him talking. I'll tell you, just let me go."

Banks stopped his henchmen again and rubbed his chin, deliberating. After a moment he nodded and his men returned Singletary and dumped him down on the couch.

"All right," Banks said, "start talking. And it better be good or your death ain't gonna be near as easy as the one you just avoided."

SKYLINE DRIVE—NORTHBOUND
APPROACHING FRONT ROYAL, VA

DAY 14, 1:00 P.M.

Bill Wiggins gripped the wheel, white-knuckled as he negotiated the twisting switchback, tires squealing on the asphalt. Tex looked up from the map.

"You're not going to do your family any good piled up at the bottom of a cliff in the back of beyond."

"Sorry," Wiggins said as he came out of the turn and focused on the next one. "I guess that thirty-five mile an hour speed limit might be pushing the envelope on some of these turns. I thought the Blue Ridge Parkway was winding, but this damn thing's a corkscrew. I bet there's not a hundred yards of straight level pavement on the whole drive."

Tex smiled. "Yeah, it might even be enjoyable if we weren't trying to get home in the middle of the apocalypse.

"That would be if you're not driving."

"Hey, I offered," Tex said.

"You did, sorry for bitching. But anyway, you're the mate. That naturally makes you the navigator."

Tex nodded, and they lapsed into silence as Bill's mind wandered back over the last thirty-six hours. As Levi predicted, the run to the Blue Ridge Parkway had been the most harrowing leg of the journey thus far. Two weeks into the power outage, gasoline was scarce and the roadside littered with stalled cars, making a moving vehicle all the more conspicuous. Even on secondary roads they encountered haggard pedestrians, undoubtedly refugees leaking into the countryside from the nearby interstates and major highways. They were a mixed bag, both individuals and family groups, many with haunted looks as if they no longer had a destination, but continued in the forlorn expectation wherever they were going was better than where they'd been. The children were the worst, crying from hunger or thirst, or both. It was all Bill and Tex could do to resist stopping and sharing their food.

At stream crossings, camps had sprung up — odd collections of tents and shelters improvised of plastic or blankets, as if some had concluded there really wasn't any better place, and they could best cheat death a bit longer by conserving their energy. Mostly they flew by these places, transiting before the residents knew they were there. Mostly. At one small bridge they'd been confronted by a human chain, four dirty desperate men spread across the road, armed with a collection of hunting rifles and pistols. Bill floored it as Tex leaned out the window, firing the Glock over their heads to scatter them as the Highlander roared over the bridge. They rode on in silence for some time, each aware it could easily have been them on the roadside were it not for Levi's generosity.

They reached the Blue Ridge Parkway with three hours of daylight left on the first day, and again as Levi predicted, found the route empty. The popularity of a twisting, scenic road-to-nowhere wasn't great during a disaster. Their next major concern had been near Roanoke, where the parkway skirted the more congested urban area. They pressed on the first day and stopped for the night fifty miles south of Roanoke, pulling well off the road into the trees. Feeling a bit foolish, they'd strung fishing line knee high between trees and attached bells as a crude 'early warning system.' They ate a cold supper to avoid a fire, then sacked out in the hammocks Levi provided. They both slept fitfully and were on the road north at first light, transiting the Roanoke area without incident.

Bill brought himself back to the present as they passed a mileage sign for Front Royal, Virginia. Tex still had her nose buried in the map.

"Front Royal in five miles. That's the northern terminus for Skyline Drive. Where to, navigator?"

Tex looked up. "It's complicated. Find an overlook to stop and I'll show you."

Bill snorted. "Shouldn't be a problem. There's one about every ten feet on this damn road."

Sure enough, they rounded a sharp curve and he pulled into a scenic overlook. He put the car in park and leaned over to study the map Tex spread out on the seat between them.

She traced a route on the map with her finger. "We're about eight miles west of the AT at Front Royal, but it starts running northeast at this point, through a couple of state parks to where it crosses US 50 near Paris, then continues northeast to cross Virginia State Route 7 just west of Bluemont. Our best bet is to go through Front Royal and take Happy Creek Road out of town. That'll get us under I-66 at a place where the road passes under the interstate with no interchange and gets us to the Shenandoah River. There are a series of interconnecting rural roads paralleling the river, which also parallels the AT. Our access point to the AT will be everywhere a substantial road intersects both the river and the AT. At those points, we can jump on the road, go a mile or two east, and have access to the AT as a backup, just like Levi said. That works as far as Bluemont. After that, we'll take another look."

"You think we'll have any problem getting through Front Royal?"

She shrugged. "Who knows? It's not real big, maybe fifteen thousand. I'm actually more concerned about I-66 because we're only about sixty or seventy miles out of DC. Given what we've seen on the secondary roads, I gotta think the I-66 corridor is a horror show. What I like about this route is this Happy Creek Road approaches and leaves the interstate at a right angle and transits under it with no interchange. If we're lucky, maybe we can blow right under the interstate in a hurry, with minimal contact."

"Sounds like a plan." Bill started the car.

Five minutes later, he exited Skyline Drive to turn north on the broad expanse of Stonewall Jackson Highway. There was the usual collection of convenience stores, fast-food restaurants, and motels increasing in density as they neared Front Royal, all closed, of course. There were hollow-eyed pedestrians as well, some registering surprise at the moving car, but most moving mindlessly to some undetermined destination.

"Notice anything strange about the pedestrians?" Bill asked.

Tex nodded. "They're all walking away from town. That can't be good."

Two miles up the highway, just past the intersection with State Route 55 East, two police cars were drawn across the road. A police officer got out of one of the cars and raised his hand as Bill approached and stopped fifty feet from the roadblock. The cop approached, well to the side, his hand on the butt of his holstered sidearm. A cop got out of the other car and approached from Tex's side. Both men's uniforms were rumpled and dirty, and neither looked as if they'd shaved in several days.

"This doesn't look promising," Bill said, as he rolled down his window. "Is there a problem, officer?"

The officer grunted. "Yeah, there's a lot of problems. You interested in one in particular, or would you like a list?"

Bill smiled. "Sorry, I guess I meant is there any problem with us coming through?"

The officer shook his head. "No refugees. I'm gonna have to ask you folks to turn around and go back the way you came."

"We're not refugees," Bill said. "We're headed north. We just want to go as far as Happy Creek Road and take it out of town. If you'll let us by, we won't even slow down in Front Royal."

"Yeah, that's what they all say."

"No, really. How about you escort us? That way you can make sure."

"And does it look to you as if we have enough manpower to be providing 'private escorts' through town? Walt and I've been here over twenty-four hours without relief. So again, I ask you to turn around."

"I understand, but we really don't want to stay. If you'll just let us—"

"Sir, you DON'T understand. Nobody's getting into Front Royal who doesn't belong here. We tried to help at first, what with all those folks fleeing DC and running out of gas, coming down from the interstate on foot. They were grateful for a day or two, and then more people kept showing up and they stopped asking and started demanding, and it got real ugly. A lot of good folks got killed before we sorted it out, and there's plenty of hard feelings. So even if I was to LET you past, driving a car full of who knows what, I reckon you wouldn't make it out of town alive, so you might say I'm doing you a favor. Now TURN AROUND."

Tex leaned across the seat and looked up at the cop. "Is there any other way north, officer?"

"None I'd recommend," he said. "You can take State Route 55 East to US 17, but 55 parallels the interstate for five or six miles at least, and it's like the Wild West out there. The gangs started coming out from DC, hitting the outlying communities as long as the gas held out, and we didn't have enough manpower to do anything but establish control here in town. Even now, they're still coming out on motorbikes and hitting farms and homes near the interstate. A moving car at this point might as well have a sign saying 'Good Stuff—Take Me.'"

Bill looked at Tex. She shrugged. "I guess we take 55 East and hope for the best."

"Your funeral," the cop said, and Bill backed the car around and turned east at the intersection as Tex stuck her head back in the map. In the distance, Bill saw another police cruiser on the side of the road, positioned to observe all of the cross streets leading off of State Route 55. He had no doubt if he attempted to turn north into town, the police would be on him in short order.

Bill passed the cop and watched in his mirror until he was out of sight. They were just passing Remount Road.

"I assume you're working on plan B?"

"Absolutely. If they're spread as thin as he says, the cops can't be everywhere. I see one last shot at getting up to Happy Creek Road. The third street ahead on the left should be Jamestown Road. It connects to a lot of surface streets winding through subdivisions on the east side of town. It's convoluted, but it should get us where we need to go."

Bill nodded and began to study the left side of the road. He saw Jamestown Road about half a mile later and made the left. They hadn't gone a hundred yards when the center of the windshield shattered with a heart-stopping crack. He slammed on the brakes, throwing them forward against their seat belts, staring at the hole in the middle of the shattered glass.

"Crap!" Bill said as he jammed the gear shift into reverse and stomped the gas, looking over his shoulder as they raced backwards and another round struck the front of the car.

He slammed on the brakes again when he hit the highway, barely managing to avoid crashing into the opposite ditch as the tires squealed and the car shuddered to a halt. He slammed the transmission into drive and raced east on 55, not stopping until they were a mile out of town with nothing on either side but trees. He sat there, afraid to let go of the wheel because he knew his hands would be shaking.

"Are you all right, Tex?" he asked.

"I... I think so, but what the hell was that? No 'turn around' or 'halt' or anything."

"I guess the cop was right," Bill said. "That's a town full of pissed-off people. One thing for sure, we're not going through any part of Front Royal. Is there any other way to get over to the river?"

She shook her head and reached for the map. "I don't think so, but I'll have another look."

"Okay. I'll see if that second shot hit anything vital."

Bill got out and was relieved to find the second round buried in the composite bumper. Had he been just a bit slower, the bullet would have likely gone through the radiator and then done more damage in the engine compartment. As it was, they got off light with a hole in the windshield and a bullet in the bumper. A few inches either way and one of them would be dead or the vehicle disabled. He was beginning to appreciate Levi's caution. It was amazing how being shot at clarified the mind.

He got back in the car. Tex was frowning.

"We're screwed," she said. "Like the cop said, in a couple of miles this road veers north and converges with I-66, running right beside the interstate for almost six miles, in places no more than a hundred yards away. Whatever bad guys came out of DC likely used the interstate, and a lot of them might still be there. If we run that gauntlet successfully, then we head back north on US 17 to Paris, where we can take US 50 a few miles west and get back on our 'parallel the Shenandoah' plan. The problem is, US 17 is also a major road, so I'm thinking it may have attracted its share of desperate people leaking off from the interstate. That's the bad news."

"There's good news?"

"The whole distance back up to Paris is like eighteen miles on good straight roads. If you wind this baby up to seventy or eighty and bob and weave around any obstacles, and I get ready to hang out the window and pop some warning shots off at anybody who looks like they might even be thinking about stopping us, we could be back on track in half an hour."

Even under the circumstances, Bill couldn't suppress a smile. "Wow, you're getting into the postapocalyptic stuff. That's like Mad Max in a Toyota Highlander."

Tex bristled a moment, then chuckled. "Eat your heart out, Tina Turner."

"How about access points to the AT? Given what's happened in the last hour, I'm a bit less skeptical about Levi's paranoia."

"The next one's actually on this road, about four miles east and smack in the middle of the area where this road parallels I-66. The AT emerges from the woods and crosses under the interstate, running due north on Turner's Lane, then branches off back into the woods about a quarter mile north. Then it runs through two state parks. The next access is where it crosses US 50, west of Paris and after we run the gauntlet."

"How about behind us?"

"All the way back by Front Royal and back up Skyline Drive about five miles, which would mean we'd have to hike at least a half day to get back to the I-66 crossing just ahead of us, and still have to cross under the interstate in the open and on foot," Tex said.

"Well, that's not happening," Bill said. "I guess it's Mad Max. You ready, Tina?"

"Ready as I'll ever be, I guess."

Bill nodded and pulled back on the road, accelerating eastbound. The road was empty and he was doing eighty a few minutes later when Tex pointed out the AT crossing at Turner Lane. Almost immediately thereafter they began to encounter stalled cars, a few in the middle of the road, mixed with scattered pedestrians, forcing him to slow. However, he was able to maintain a steady fifty miles an hour as he slalomed around the obstacles, hoping no pedestrian wandered out from between the stationary cars. Not that they seemed so inclined. In fact, their heads rose sharply at the sound of the approaching engine, and the refugees hurried away from the roadway.

"Not exactly Mad Max," Tex said as they wound through the obstacle course, "but I guess it'll work."

Just as she finished speaking, the woods on the right opened up on a vast expanse of pasture jammed with refugees and a mass of crudely constructed shelters.

"What the hell—"

Tex glanced down at the map. "Water," she said. "Looks like a pretty substantial creek parallels the road. I guess all these poor bastards gravitated here for the water."

A sickening smell wafted through the open windows, redolent of too many humans living together without benefit of basic services or hygiene. They shuddered as hundreds of refugees turned toward the sound of the car, their body language telegraphing anxiety, even at a distance.

"I'm not liking this at all," Bill said as he swerved around another car. "What's ahead?"

Tex glanced down at the map. "There's an interchange just ahead at a wide spot in the road called Markham. There's not much there but a vineyard. Then we've got three or four miles of this before we head north on US 17. No guarantee what we're gonna find there either."

Bill nodded and kept driving, pushing the speed up to sixty as he wound down the highway.

They saw a sign announcing their approach to State Route 688, then passed a large attractive building on the right, with a sign identifying it as the vineyard sales office. There were multiple vehicles in the parking lot. They whizzed by and then heard engines cough to life behind them.

"Motorcycles?" Tex asked.

Bill glanced in his mirror as two motorcycles rocketed out of the parking lot, engines snarling.

"Motorcycles," he confirmed, and accelerated.

Tex turned in her seat. "Maybe they just want to talk—"

They both cringed as the back window of the SUV shattered.

"Or maybe not," she finished, unbuckling her seat belt and crawling between the seats into the back. "I guess this really is Mad Max shit."

The back of the SUV was piled high with stores, and Tex crawled across on elbows and knees, pitching with the car as Bill swerved around stationary vehicles. She steadied herself with her right hand and balled her left fist to hammer at the shattered safety glass, managing to dislodge a large sheet, which hit the pavement behind the car in a dazzling display of flying glass shards flashing in the sunlight. Only then did she reach behind and draw the Glock from its holster and assess the situation.

Which sucked.

She was on a swaying, bouncing platform, shooting a handgun at equally (and unpredictably) mobile targets. The only upside was the targets were getting closer, but since they were armed, that was a somewhat dubious benefit. But their attackers had challenges as well. Steering a motorcycle one-handed while negotiating obstacles and shooting with the other hand wasn't easy. When they shot, they had to slow a bit, negating the added agility of their vehicles and allowing Bill to draw ahead. After their initial (and lucky) fusillade with no return fire, they'd apparently decided to concentrate on closing the distance. That would change as soon as they started taking fire. She had to take them out quickly.

Tex watched a moment. They were mobile, but the obstacles they were negotiating were not. If she concentrated her fire on the front corner of a stalled car just as one of the motorcycles swerved around it, they'd move into her field of fire. She steadied herself as she felt Bill swerve around a car, and as it came into view behind her, she targeted the right front headlight. When the lead cyclist was almost abreast of the front of the car, she fired a half-dozen shots in rapid succession just as the man swerved back toward the middle of the road — directly into her field of fire.

She'd been hoping for center-mass hits, but she was a bit high. A single round penetrated her attacker's face shield, driving him backwards off the bike directly in the path of the remaining cyclist. The front wheel of the second man's bike struck the body of his fallen comrade and the driver fought to maintain control — and lost. He slammed into a stalled car straight on at over fifty miles an hour and rocketed through the air to land some distance away, unmoving.

Tex holstered the Glock and clawed her way back to the front, squeezing between the seats just as they flew past the highway interchange. She glanced forward to see the road was suddenly free of stalled cars, and felt the SUV accelerate as Bill split his attention between the road ahead and quick glances in the rearview mirror.

"Damn! Remind me never to piss you off."

"Lucky shot," Tex said.

"Uh-oh! Let's hope your luck holds."

Tex turned back to the road, to see a big tractor trailer rig moving across the road from a side street a quarter mile ahead of them. Two cars pulling across the road in front of the big rig left no doubt it was a roadblock.

"Looks like they have radios!" Tex said as she felt the SUV decelerate rapidly, and another round punctured the windshield and several more struck the front of the car.

"And assault rifles! Get down!" Bill yelled as he stomped the brakes even harder and twisted the wheel, causing the SUV to swap ends, skidding backwards toward their attackers as Bill once again stomped the gas and smoke billowed off the screaming tires before they finally grabbed and the car shot back the way they'd come.

"Where the hell did you learn that?"

"Empty parking lots when I was a teenager," Bill said. "There's not a hell of a lot to do in small towns in the middle of the Maine woods."

Tex twisted in her seat and stared back at the roadblock.

"More cycles?" Bill asked.

"Negative. Looks like a jacked-up four-wheel-drive pickup with a bed full of shooters," Tex said.

Just then, steam or smoke billowed from under the hood, and Bill glanced down at the dash.

"The engine temp's going straight up! They must have hit the radiator," he said.

"What are we gonna do?"

"What can we do but ride and hope? How far ahead is that AT access we passed?"

"Three miles at least. Can we make it?"

"Who the hell knows. I should be able to stay ahead of these assholes through the obstacle course as long as we can keep moving. I've had a little experience now and that jacked-up truck has a high center of gravity. He can't bob and weave too quickly."

A round shattered the passenger-side mirror, and they both flinched.

"Should I return fire?"

Bill shook his head. "Not much point now. We don't really have a fighting chance to escape unless we make the AT. If they do end up catching us, it might be better if we haven't killed quite as many of them."

Tex watched as Bill hurtled down the road, all caution gone now as the SUV caromed along the congested path, missing some cars by inches and glancing off others. She twisted in her seat and stared back.

"You're opening up a lead, a pretty good one."

Bill nodded, then frowned as horrible sounds started coming from under the hood. He glanced down at the instrument panel again.

"We're red-lined on the engine temp and the oil pressure isn't looking too great either. Say a little prayer this'll all hold together long enough to make Turner Lane. Maybe if we can build up a big enough lead, we can be out of sight when we make the turn. What's the road look like there, you remember?"

Tex jerked out the map and pulled it open. "Mostly straight and open, but there is a slight curve. It's not much, but we might be out of their sight a couple of minutes. The only problem is when they round that curve, the road runs straight for a long way. If they don't see us, it'll be obvious we turned off somewhere and Turner Lane is the only option."

"Let's just hope they aren't as smart as you," Bill said.

Tex twisted back to watch their pursuers, shutting out the ever-increasing din of the dying engine and willing their lead to increase. Finally she watched the truck fade out of sight as the angle between the vehicles changed. She snapped her head to the front. Turner Lane was in the near distance.

"There it is," Bill said. "Can they see us?"

"No. We just lost visual contact."

"I make it a quarter of a mile to the turn. Were they further back than that?"

"I don't know. Maybe," Tex said.

"Just keep looking. Hopefully we'll be under the interstate before they spot us."

Tex kept her eyes fixed behind them and felt Bill braking hard as he ran up to the intersection at almost full speed, the engine shrieking, accompanied now by a burning smell. She gripped the seat back as he cornered on two wheels, then whipped her head to the right to look out the passenger window back the way they'd come. They roared north on Turner Lane, and were almost past a farmhouse when she glimpsed the nose of the truck rounding the curve.

"Did they see us?" Bill demanded.

"I don't know, but I saw them for a second, so we have to assume they did. Besides, if they get much closer, they'll be able to track us by sound. We're not exactly inconspicuous."

Bill nodded as they sped under I-66, engine shrieking and smoking. "How far is the AT access?"

Tex was fumbling with the AT guidebook. "Should be just after Walker Ridge Road forks off to the right. I don't know how well it's marked. It might be just a blaze on a tree or something."

"Guess we'll find out. We're going to go off road whether we find it or not. If they see the abandoned car, they'll just run us down—"

"There!" Tex pointed to white blazes on a tree, barely visible across a small open meadow.

Bill veered off the road without slowing and they bounced through a shallow drainage ditch to rumble across the meadow, trailing smoke. In seconds they plunged into the trees, following a narrow walking path through thick foliage, branches slapping against the side of the car.

"What's ahead!"

Tex fumbled with the guidebook. "It says a small footbridge over a stream—"

The foliage opened somewhat, revealing the bridge not more than thirty feet away, a neat little structure perhaps three feet wide with handrails, the depth of the stream it crossed unknown.

"Hold on!" Bill shouted and floored the accelerator as he jerked the wheel to the right. They bounced through the shallow stream and up the other bank, back on the narrow hiking trail winding its way up a steep hillside. A hundred yards up the hill, the Toyota shuddered and died.

They sat in the sudden calm, the smells of the dying engine thick in their nostrils, the silence broken only by the tick of the overheated engine cooling for the final time.

The sound of the pickup grew behind them, then faded away to the north.

"They went past," Bill said, relief in his voice. "Where does Tucker's Lane go and how soon before they figure out we're not still ahead of them?" Tex was already studying the map.

"It dead-ends about five miles up. That's the bad news. The good news is it has at least a dozen side roads that dead-end off of it. It should take them quite some time to figure out where we gave them the slip."

"All right, I guess we ought to grab Levi's escape packs and get the hell out of here. Let's do a quick check and take some extra food if we have room. But we ought to be out of here in ten minutes tops."

"Agreed," Tex said.

They climbed out of the SUV and did a quick inventory, adding things to the packs as they could fit them, and eight minutes later they shouldered their packs and started north.

"Just out of curiosity," Bill said as they labored up the steep hill under the unfamiliar weight of the packs, "did you happen to notice how far it is to Maine on this friggin' goat track?"

"Twelve hundred and one miles to Mount Katahdin," Tex said, "but I think probably only around eleven hundred to where you're headed."

"Wonderful. Just friggin' wonderful!"

CHAPTER FOURTEEN

DAY 15, 10:00 A.M.

Jerome Singletary fought back the pain and lifted his face from the blood-spattered road map spread in front of him.

"I CAN'T show you on the map! I've never been there that way, so I don't know the way by the road."

Kwintell Banks glared. "Then show me on the river. The river shows on the map."

Singletary shook his head, causing more blood to escape his flattened nose and drop on the map. "It's not the same. This here's a road map. Where it shows the river isn't accurate."

Singletary had no idea if that was true, but it made no difference since he had only the vaguest idea where that asshole Levi's camp was anyway. He did know if Banks concluded he didn't know, or figured he could get there without help, Singletary was a dead man.

"So what you saying? We need some sort of special map?"

Singletary nodded. "A river chart. Maybe we can find one on one of the boats. I'll help, if you let me go."

Banks scoffed. "You know that ain't happening."

"Then put me with some of your men to look, or you might as well shoot me now, 'cause you can't beat something out of me I don't know."

Banks dropped his hand to his holstered pistol and glared. Singletary began to shake, fearful he'd overplayed it.

Then Banks relaxed a bit. "All right. I'll put two soldiers on your ass, and you go look for this map. But you try to run, you gonna wish you were already dead. Understand?"

"Absolutely," Singletary said, "but one other thing—"

Banks' hand went back to his side. "What 'other' thing would that be?"

"Even when we find the chart, you need a guide. I mean, the chart will get you close, but all that riverbank looks alike. You need someone who's been there before. And you can't just roar up in some big-ass noisy boats, he'll hear and maybe ambush you. You need fishing boats with electric motors so you can sneak up on him quiet like. I can help with all that stuff."

Banks cocked an eye. "How you know so much about this? I thought you was a city boy?"

In truth, all Singletary knew was what he gleaned from eavesdropping, but that fact seemed unlikely to keep him alive.

"I learned from Levi. He wanted me to stay with 'em on the river, but I need to get back to Baltimore. Before I left his place, he showed me everything. I know the whole setup," Singletary lied.

"I don't know. Special maps. Special boats. Might all be more trouble than it's worth. Maybe I'll just cap yo' ass and be done with it."

"It's worth it, man! Levi's got all sorts of shit! He's real tight with them soldiers and Coast Guard guys. They was even talking about giving him some grenades."

"Grenades? Why the hell didn't you say something before?"

"'Cause I'm not sure," Singletary said, "but I am sure it's worth your while, grenades or not. He's got a lot of stuff there."

Banks hesitated, then nodded to two men standing nearby. They moved to each side of Singletary, hooking him under the arms and dragging him to his feet.

"Okay," Banks said, "you go find the stuff you need. And I hope you ain't bullshittin' me, 'cause if you are…"

Relief surged through Singletary. "Don't you worry a bit. I won't let you down…"

But Banks had already turned his back as the two thugs dragged Singletary into the hall and started toward the door to the street, unaware their captive was already plotting his next move. He might not know where to find Levi, but he did know his chances of escape were much better on the river.

FEMA
EMERGENCY OPERATIONS CENTER
MOUNT WEATHER
NEAR BLUEMONT, VA

DAY 15, 10:00 A.M.

The Honorable Theodore M. Gleason, President of the United States, sipped his coffee then set the bone-china cup back into its saucer on the walnut table. He was the only occupant of the well-appointed conference room. He wore khaki trousers and an open collar golf shirt, but for all its informality, the look he cultivated was studied and deliberate. He sat not at the head of the huge table but midway down its length and closest to the door into the room. He would greet his guest personally and as equals, without the barrier of the table or by subtle implication any other barriers between them. A part of an artful lie, of course, but he hoped a convincing one.

It was what he did. He was a politician, and a good one. Some might consider that a pejorative, but he cared not at all, for he was a student of history. Statesmen might be venerated in the history books, but it was politicians who made things work. To his mind, his was the noblest of professions, and he was a proud practitioner of the political arts.

He looked up as the door opened. Representative Simon Tremble looked rumpled and sleep-deprived. He was badly in need of a haircut and sported a two-day growth of beard. Gleason rose with a practiced smile and outstretched hand.

"Simon, thank you for coming."

Tremble ignored Gleason's hand and looked him in the eye. "I had a choice?"

Gleason's smile flickered only slightly as he dropped his hand. "Oh, there's always a choice, Simon. But have a seat." He gestured to a chair beside his own. "Coffee?"

Tremble shook his head and dropped into the offered seat as Gleason took his own chair.

"Simon, I just wanted to let you know how much I regret the necessity —"

Tremble arched his eyebrows. "Necessity? Arresting the Speaker of the House and the President Pro Tem of the Senate was a 'necessity'? For God's sake, Ted, we're from your own party! It's not like we were wild-eyed anarchists!"

Gleason's face hardened. "I gave you an opportunity —"

"Opportunity? Is that what you call it? Sorry, but from where we were sitting, it looked a whole lot like an ultimatum."

Gleason tried another tack. "I understand, Simon, I really do, but this is a disaster of unprecedented scope. I had to be decisive and must continue to be. There's just no time for business as usual."

Tremble shook his head. "I might buy the argument we need to streamline things and take immediate action, even to the point of stretching constitutional safeguards to near breaking. But what you and Crawford are implementing, totally without oversight or regard for dissenting opinion, is an absolute outrage."

Gleason spoke through clenched teeth. "I had to do it."

"That would be a hell of a lot easier for me to believe if you hadn't been quite so eager to declare yourself king, Mr. President. Or should I say Your Majesty?"

Gleason's face reddened, but he recovered his composure quickly. "I guess we'll just have to agree to disagree on the necessity, Simon, but I didn't ask you here to debate. What's done is done, and I hope we CAN agree it's in the nation's best interest to get power restored as soon as possible. So I'm asking for your public support. It will go a long ways towards reassuring folks out there if you join me in some of the emergency broadcasts."

"Un-frigging-believable! You lock me and my son up without access to a soul, and now expect me to endorse your coup? But why talk to me one on one? I figured you'd want Senator Leddy in on the deal too, along with anyone else you've had under house arrest. What's the problem, did Jim turn you down?"

Gleason hesitated. "I'm sorry to say Jim Leddy died five days ago."

Tremble sat shocked. "H-how did he die?"

"Very suddenly. A brain aneurysm. But he didn't suffer, thank God."

"Is there... was there a service? I'd like to pay my respects."

"We thought it best not to upset the public with news of yet another loss. There's been so much bad news as it is. There was a cremation and a small family service."

Tremble glared. "How thoughtful of you. What about Linda? How is she holding up?"

Gleason shrugged. "She was upset, as you would expect."

"Was?"

"I haven't seen her since the memorial service," Gleason said.

"And why is that?"

"As you know, Mount Weather shelters the national leadership and their dependents. With Jim's unfortunate passing, Linda no longer qualifies. It's tragic, but these are difficult times. Linda was provided air transport to her and Jim's last home of record," Gleason said.

"YOU DROPPED A DEFENSELESS WOMAN IN THE MIDDLE OF SAINT LOUIS?"

"She was disembarked with her luggage at the St. Louis airport. It was all according to established policy, of course," Gleason said. "I'd think you would be all for established policies. After all, my deviation from policies to take 'unilateral action' seems to have upset you no end."

Tremble's face clouded and he clenched his fists as he half-rose from his chair.

Gleason continued quickly. "But let's talk about something more pleasant. How's Keith, by the way? What is he, eighteen now?" Gleason paused. "Oh, to be eighteen again, even in these troubled times. I do hope we can avoid mandatory conscription, but then again, we all have to do our part. I'm sure a patriotic young man like Keith would make a valuable addition to the new Special Reaction Force. Of course, a young man with a father in the national leadership always has options, assuming you decide to stay, of course."

Tremble sank back into his chair and glared at Gleason.

"Food for thought, Simon," said Gleason as he reached over and patted Tremble's knee, "just food for thought."

Gleason flashed his perfect white teeth in another million-dollar smile and rose.

"I'll give you some time to think. Help yourself to the coffee on the sideboard, and let the fellow at the door know if you'd like anything to snack on. We try to keep things civilized, even in the midst of disaster. I'll be back in an hour or so for your decision."

WARDEN'S OFFICE
FEDERAL CORRECTIONAL COMPLEX
BEAUMONT, TEXAS

DAY 15, 1:00 P.M.

McComb leaned back in the warden's chair, his feet on the desk.

"So how'd it work?"

Snaggle flashed his gap-toothed grin. "Slicker 'n snot on a doorknob. I gotta hand it to ya Spike, bustin' the guys outta Stiles was genius. We drove right up in the federal CO uniforms and prison vans in broad daylight and those dumb-ass state assholes let us in easy as you please. Weren't many of 'em left anyway, so it didn't take long to take care of 'em. We had a lot more brothers in the state lockup too."

"How many we free?"

"Just over two hundred Aryan Brotherhood of Texas, and maybe that many more new recruits. Like you said, we only took recruits who seemed hardcore, and left the others locked up with the jigs and beaners." Snaggle smirked. "I expect the rest of the whites will be a mite more enthusiastic after a day or so without any food or water. They wasn't gettin' much anyway, but the state assholes seemed to be doing a bit better about feeding 'em than they was doing by us."

McComb shook his head. "We're tight on food and such anyway, and better off to have committed ABT soldiers we know we can trust, so we'll look at recruits hard from here on. Any of the whites that don't measure up we'll use in the labor gang unless they look to be trouble, then we just leave 'em to rot with the mud people. Everything set up now at Stiles?"

Snaggle nodded. "We left guys in the Texas state CO uniforms running the place, so it looks normal if anyone checks, or at least normal considerin' what's going on. The brothers we freed are setting up quarters in the admin buildings, and I left a few of our guys in charge to run things. Nobody at Stiles outranked you in the Brotherhood, but I brought the three or four top guys over here to our group so we can keep an eye on 'em, just in case. We don't want nobody gettin' no wrong ideas on who's in charge."

"Good man. How's the scavenging going?"

"Could be better, but we're building up the stores a little at a time. It would go a lot faster if we could just blow through and take stuff, but we're keepin' it low key, like you want."

"Any problems?"

"Not with the scavenging, the boys are getting pretty good at it. They just drive up in uniform and one of 'em knocks at the door politely. When folks answer the door, they give 'em the old 'be on the lookout for escaped prisoners' and then check out the situation while the other guys circle around the house. Then they either bust in and take everything or pull back and figure out the best way to take 'em. They ain't leavin' no witnesses behind, and so far it's all been smooth along those lines, but..." Snaggle hesitated.

"Out with it. What's the problem?"

"Well, we're still short of women. I mean, me and you and the rest of the top guys have our pick. And I ain't caught up by a damn sight, but I'm feelin' a lot better in that department. But the problem is, we ain't got enough women to go around yet, especially good-lookin' ones, and it's causing some problems. I mean, some of the junior guys go out and grab some good-lookin' bitch, and the next thing he knows, he brings her back here and he goes to the end of the line. Some of 'em are starting to grumble, and to be honest, I don't think it's good for morale."

"All right, I get it. We'll have to cool it with the rank thing and make sure everybody gets a fair shot at the women." McComb smiled. "In a few weeks when we control everything, women will be crawling up the road begging us to take 'em, so I guess we can be patient. I mean, now that we've had a little taste to hold us awhile."

"Good call, I think," Snaggle said. "Just one more thing. One of the scavenging teams ran into a deputy sheriff patrol last night —"

"Goddammit, I told you to avoid —"

Snaggle held up his hands. "It's cool, Spike, we got it handled. They took 'em out before they got on the radio, and they brought the cruiser back here. We got it hid in the motor pool."

McComb struggled to contain himself, but slowly calmed. "I suppose it was gonna happen sooner or later. What about the bodies?"

"Body," Snaggle said, "we stripped the uniform and dumped him with the others in the medium-security administration building. They took the second deputy alive, and one of the guys recognized him. Seems like the asshole busted him some time back, and he wanted payback. They got him over in max security, having a little fun with him. I made 'em strip him to his skivvies first. I figure we might be able to use the uniform."

"All right," McComb said, "just as long as nobody saw…" He trailed off.

"What's up, Spike? What're you thinking?"

But McComb was already on his feet, moving toward the door, and Snaggle fell in behind, hurrying to keep up as McComb raced out of the building. Five minutes later they rushed through the entrance to the max-security unit, where an ABT soldier in a CO uniform manned the security checkpoint.

"Where's the cop?" McComb demanded.

The soldier smirked. "In the dining hall so everybody could watch."

McComb raced for the dining hall, with Snaggle trailing, and burst in to find the deputy tied to a chair, blood covering his battered face as he slumped forward with his chin on his chest, and convicts lined up before him, each apparently waiting their turn to beat the man. Others cheered them on, and a few enterprising souls were taking bets on which blow would finish the cop off.

"All right, all right, knock it off!" McComb yelled as he walked into the room. His order was met with jeers and catcalls. But he leveled a stony gaze at the audience and the jeering stopped as abruptly as it began.

"I got better use for this asshole," McComb said, "supposing you morons ain't killed him." He walked over and raised a bloody eyelid with his thumb and poked a finger in the cop's eye, and the cop's head jerked back at this latest and unexpected assault.

McComb nodded and turned to Snaggle. "All right, he's alive, or alive enough, anyway. Get him in one of the private offices and send somebody over to the motor pool for a car battery and a pair of jumper cables, and make sure the battery has a good hot charge. Matter of fact, better have 'em bring a couple of extra batteries as backups."

***

Two hours later, McComb straightened, handed the jumper cable leads to Snaggle, and wiped the sweat from his forehead with the back of his hand.

"That's all he knows. Shoot him in the head and throw him with the others."

"He's still alive, maybe we should give him back to the boys," Snaggle said. "You know, just for morale."

"I don't give a damn, do what you want. I doubt he lasts another ten minutes anyway, and he served my purpose."

"You think he was tellin' the truth about FEMA? And what about the National Guard? Don't sound right they ain't together. I mean, I thought they would be actin' more like after one of the hurricanes."

McComb shrugged. "It kinda makes sense in a way. The FEMA assholes are all concentrating on that nuke plant over by Bay City, probably trying to get the power back. That's fine by me, it's over a hundred and fifty miles from here with Houston in between. And with almost all the National Guard units in East Texas detailed to help out in Houston and Dallas, that mostly leaves the local yokels and a few state troopers minding the store here." He smiled. "Which is gonna make this a lot easier."

JACK BROOKS REGIONAL AIRPORT
US HIGHWAY 69
NEDERLAND, TEXAS

DAY 15, 5:00 P.M.

Snaggle looked around nervously, checking the setup for the tenth time. The Bureau of Prisons' transport bus was a hundred yards down the entrance road to the airport, pitched forward into the shallow ditch, not quite at a right angle to the road. A dozen ABT soldiers still dressed as prisoners and carrying guns of various types stood around, talking and smoking, ready to play their parts.

Spike McComb stood next to him, both men uniformed as federal corrections officers, as were six of their fellow prisoners. To complete the ruse, two prisoners wore the uniforms of the most recently deceased Jefferson County sheriff's deputies. All ten men stood behind the deputies' captured cruiser and two of the Bureau of Prison's sedans, the three vehicles drawn across the road to form a roadblock to prevent the escape of the prison bus—or so it seemed.

"I don't know, Spike, this seems a bit risky," Snaggle said. "I mean, what if too many of 'em show up at once?"

"Relax, you heard what the guy said. There ain't that many of 'em left to patrol at any one time. Hell, I'm worried we won't draw up enough of 'em. I figure where we are, we'll most likely get a few Port Arthur cops and county deputies. I hope it'll be enough to go to the next part of the plan, 'cause I don't think we can pull this off twice. Even cops ain't that friggin' dumb."

Snaggle nodded, and McComb turned, cupping his hands to yell over the fake roadblock. "Okay, boys, get ready and make it look good. Start shootin' when you see the cop cars arrive, and make damn sure you're shootin' high because if any one of us gets hit, whoever fired the shot is a dead man."

There were waves and sarcastic comments as the men followed orders and crawled under the bus, and McComb gathered the other men around for final instructions.

"Okay, minimum blood. I don't want the uniforms messed up. We take 'em down from behind with the stun guns and then cap 'em with the little twenty-two to the head at close range. Everybody got that?"

There were nods of understanding.

"Okay, boys, showtime!" McComb said. He walked to the deputies' car and reached in for the radio mike.

"OFFICER DOWN! SHOTS FIRED! OFFICER DOWN ON US 69 IN NEDERLAND AT THE ENTRANCE TO THE AIRPORT. REQUEST IMMEDIATE ASSISTANCE FROM ALL UNITS IN THE VICINITY. REPEAT. OFFICER DOWN! SHOTS FIRED! OFFICER DOWN ON US 69 IN NEDERLAND AT THE ENTRANCE TO THE AIRPORT. REQUEST IMMEDIATE ASSISTANCE FROM ALL UNITS IN THE VICINITY."

He replaced the mike and listened, but didn't respond to the flood of requests for more information. He knew those units that could respond would, because nothing had a greater priority than 'officer down,' and the less they knew, the more confused they'd be when they arrived. He listened for units responding along with their ETAs, and held up fingers for each separate response he heard so his men would know as well. In moments he'd registered five responding units, with arrivals spread over the next fifteen minutes, and he heard the first siren in the distance.

It went like clockwork as the cons under the bus kept up a steady fire and their fake police colleagues crouched behind the roadblock, rising sporadically to return fire. The officers in each responding unit interpreted the scene exactly as intended and parked their cruisers to rush to McComb's side, peering over the roadblock at the prison bus as McComb's men took a step back and jammed stun guns into their necks. The helpless would-be rescuers were then dragged out of sight on the opposite side of the roadblock and dispatched with a single small-caliber round to the head, as all the while the radio shrieked requests for status updates.

It was over in twenty minutes and McComb counted the dead and inventoried his spoils—four Port Arthur cops, three Jefferson County deputy sheriffs, and two Beaumont cops, along with five captured police cars. All the radios were active now as dispatchers sought more information, and McComb knew they had to move quickly.

"All right, Snag, just like we planned, get the guys out of the bus and into these dead cop's uniforms now—no, wait—have six of 'em dress out, but leave one dead cop from each service in uniform and throw 'em in the cruisers. They'll respond better if they think one of their own is down. We have to hit the Port Arthur Police Department and the sheriff's department office in Port Arthur together, 'cause they're closest and only a block apart. We'll split the guys into two teams; you take the sheriff's office and I'll take the police department. You know the story, the only change is you carry the dead deputy in with the first guys, so it looks like he's hurt and you're helping him in. No lights and sirens until we're half a block away, then light 'em up and raise holy hell. Be fast, don't give 'em a chance to figure things out, and take out the dispatcher first thing. Got it?"

Snaggle nodded and set about his tasks. Ten minutes later a convoy of police cars was streaming towards downtown Port Arthur, packed with fake cops and correction officers. The Bureau of Prisons' sedans with the remainder of the cons followed a half mile back. When the convoy reached the corner of Procter Street and Beaumont Avenue, McComb lit up the lights and siren, signaling all units to do the same, and the convoy split to complete their separate missions.

McComb led his three-car force to a skidding halt in the police department parking lot, disgorging his men. McComb and one of his cons grabbed the dead policeman and hurried into the building in front of the group, blood trailing down the dead man's shirt from the head wound. They burst into the lightly manned police station, with McComb screaming an alarm.

"THERE'S BEEN A MASS ESCAPE FROM THE FEDERAL PRISON! THERE MUST BE TWO HUNDRED OF THEM AND THEY'RE ARMED AND HEADED THIS WAY. GET EVERYBODY OUT HERE RIGHT NOW AND START LOCKING DOWN THE BUILDING! THEY'RE RIGHT BEHIND US!"

The cops would have figured it out, given half a chance, but McComb didn't give them one. In the two minutes of confusion generated by his arrival, his men swarmed through the lightly manned police station, killing without warning or mercy. The dispatcher was the first to go, and by the five-minute mark, the cons were in total control. McComb dispatched an underling to bring the rest of the force in the prison sedans in to help with the cleanup, and another to check on Snaggle's progress at the sheriff's department.

Five minutes later, Snaggle showed up in person, grinning from ear to ear.

"Fish in a barrel, Spike," Snaggle said, "we got 'em all."

"The dispatcher?"

"Got her myself first thing. Nothing went out."

"All right, we still gotta move fast. We leave uniformed guys at each place to deal with any who straggle in from patrol or shift change or whatever. We got guys standing by at the prison to reinforce here, so when we go back by there, we send a dozen more down for each office. Right now, we gotta get up to Beaumont. We still got the sheriff's office there, as well as the Beaumont PD and the highway patrol office out on Eastex Freeway." McComb looked at his watch. "We should be done in two hours."

"I don't know, Spike, we done real good here. I think maybe we just ought to wait—"

McComb glared at his underling. "Thinking's my department. Yours is doing what you're told. That 'officer down' call likely went everywhere and they're all tense and nervous now, probably not thinkin' too good. We give 'em time, they're gonna figure things out, so we strike fast before that happens. Now I want everybody ready to roll in ten minutes. Got it?"

TEXAS DEPARTMENT OF PUBLIC SAFETY
REGION II, DISTRICT B
7200 EASTEX FREEWAY
BEAUMONT, TEXAS

DAY 15, 7:00 P.M.

The Texas Highway Patrol troopers had been the last to fall and the hardest to take down, even though they had the least manpower. They'd been the most suspicious, and McComb's men ended up fighting a pitched battle with the holdouts, losing four men in the process. Fortunately, they had managed to take out the dispatcher quickly. That was especially important to McComb, as the highway patrol would be the most likely to transmit a distress call to authorities at the state level.

Nonetheless, he was pleased. They'd managed to take down all remaining law enforcement in the entire county in an afternoon, and if their luck held, no one would be the wiser for a while. For sure the state authorities, assuming there actually were any state authorities left, would have their plate full, and it looked like FEMA only cared about the nuclear plant over in Bay City. The National Guard was up to their asses in alligators in Houston and Dallas, so that pretty much left Jefferson County, Texas, as his new kingdom.

He nodded as Snaggle walked up. "Good work, Snag, and pass that on to the boys. We need to get these three locations in Beaumont fully manned. We can surprise any stragglers and take care of them as they drift in, but I had another idea too. We got all the personnel records, so I want to put someone on checking out where every cop of any kind lives. I reckon some of them haven't come in to work for one reason or another, but we gotta take 'em out, just to be on the safe side. Send guys in state trooper uniforms to each local cop's house and check it out. That way, the local cops won't necessarily pick up on it if they don't recognize the state troopers. Then you send guys in local cops' uniforms to the state troopers' homes for the same reason. If they find the cop, take 'em out and don't leave no witnesses. Then search and bring back all their guns, spare uniforms, and what have you. In a few days, we can make sure every uniformed cop in these parts is one of our guys. Then we don't have to lay low and can pretty much do what we please. We make the two prisons our strongholds and consolidate our loot and prisoners there, so we always have a place to fall back to and defend if things go sideways. Other than that, we take what we want and live like we want."

McComb's grin widened. "I think I'm gonna like being chief of PO-lice."

M/V PECOS TRADER
GULF OF MEXICO—WESTBOUND
EAST OF SABINE PASS, TEXAS

DAY 15, 7:00 P.M.

Hughes leaned on the wind dodger in the fading light, staring at the western horizon.

"They'll be all right," said Dan Gowan, standing beside him.

Hughes turned, a sheepish smile on his face. "Was it that obvious?"

Gowan shrugged. "It doesn't take a mind reader to figure out a man would be worried about his family with all the craziness going on. But Laura's a smart lady, and y'all are pretty well supplied for emergencies. Like I said, they're all right." The chief engineer shook his head. "But Trixie's a different story. I do believe that woman wakes up in a new world every day, bless her heart. I am a bit anxious about her."

"Well, we'll find out soon enough, I guess. I figure we'll be hitting Sabine bar right at daybreak."

"You figured out what you gonna do when we get there?" Gowan asked.

"Yeah, I'd kinda like to know that myself, Captain," said Matt Kinsey as he stepped out the wheelhouse door onto the bridge wing.

Hughes sighed. "A day ago I'd say it depended on what we find when we get there, but the more I've been thinking about it, I've come to the conclusion it doesn't matter. For sure there'll be some ships anchored out, and I'm presuming there won't be a pilot. I mean, why would there be? Most of the traffic is tankers, and with no power to the refineries, there's no need for crude inbound, and no petroleum products outbound. So I'm thinking there'll be ships stacked up, not knowing what to do. I'm not gonna join that circus. I've timed our arrival for first light and we'll just head between the jetties and go upriver."

"No pilot? You seemed pretty worried about that at Wilmington," Kinsey said.

"I still am," Hughes said, "but this is a lot different. There's not that much current to contend with and we'll be heading into what little there is, which is a hell of a lot different than Wilmington. And while I've been to Wilmington maybe a dozen times, I've made the Sabine-Neches transit many times, probably pushing a hundred. I know all the waypoints and landmarks cold. I'll be nervous as hell, but it's not nearly as scary as coming down the Cape Fear River with a four- or five-knot current behind you. My biggest worry is what to do when we get where we're going."

Kinsey looked confused. "What do you mean? I figured you'd just tie up at your refinery dock."

"I have a couple of concerns. When we put the gangway down, it runs both ways. With resources in short supply, being a tanker loaded with fuel with containers full of food aboard makes us a pretty tempting target. My second concern is the crew."

Kinsey shrugged. "What about them?"

"They're all civilians, with families nearby they want to check on. I put that gangway down and we're liable to have an immediate exodus, and there isn't anything I can do about it. For that matter, I'm pretty sure you and your guys are thinking the same thing. But if everyone hauls ass with the ship tied to the dock, we can neither move it nor defend it," Hughes said. "I can't blame them, really. I certainly intend to go look for my family."

"Then don't tie up," Gowan said.

Hughes stroked his chin and nodded. "I guess we could anchor, not many places with enough water, though, since we're loaded. I'm thinking the Sun Lower Anchorage is probably the best. We've poked our bow in there to turn around often enough when fully loaded."

"Sounds like the best choice," Gowan agreed. "Then nobody can get to us except by boat, and it's plus twenty feet from the water to the main deck. We use the fast rescue boat or the Coasties' patrol boat to get back and forth to shore, and we can land pretty much where we want, out of sight of the ship. If anyone sees us, they can't really tell where we came from. And we can set up some sort of structured rotation for going ashore to look for families. The guys might not like it, but if you're controlling the boats to and from shore, they can't just say screw you and run down the gangway."

"That's it, then," Hughes said, turning to Kinsey. "Now we just have to worry about the Coasties and the navy. You think they're just gonna let us do what we please?"

Kinsey shrugged. "I guess we'll find out at daybreak tomorrow, won't we?"

CHAPTER FIFTEEN

M/V *Pecos Trader*
Approaching Sabine Pass, Texas

Day 16, 5:00 a.m.

Hughes studied the radar as *Pecos Trader* moved toward the sea buoy at reduced speed. Two dozen ships crowded the anchorage ahead, their Automatic Identification System transmissions broadcasting many familiar names — other tankers, all in ballast. Their presence was both expected and disappointing. Someone cleared their throat behind him, and Kinsey moved up beside him at the radar screen.

"Looks like Wilmington, Act 2," Kinsey said. "Any luck with a pilot?"

Hughes shook his head as he stepped to the VHF and picked up the mike. "I tried twice. Let's see if anyone is home at the Coasties' house."

He spoke into the mike. "Port Arthur Traffic, Port Arthur Traffic, this is the tanker *Pecos Trader* . My ETA at Sabine Bank Buoy is zero five thirty and I require a pilot. Repeat, this is the tanker *Pecos Trader* . My ETA at Sabine Bank Buoy is zero five thirty and I require a pilot. Over."

There was no answer and Hughes repeated the call, with the same response. He shook his head. "With all the ships at anchor, even if Port Arthur VTS doesn't respond, I'd think someone at anchor would be butting in to let us know what's going on —"

"Tanker *Pecos Trader* , repeat, tanker *Pecos Trader* , this is the tanker *Ambrose Channel* . Do you copy? Over."

"Now that's more like what I expected," Hughes said, and keyed the mike.

"*Ambrose Channel* , this is *Pecos Trader.* We copy. Over."

"*Pecos Trader* , be advised there is no pilot service and Port Arthur VTS is nonoperational. At least they haven't responded to any calls from anchorage in the ten days we've been here. Over."

"We copy, *Ambrose Channel* . What's going on? Over."

"Who knows? Most of us have no loading orders. A navy ship came by five days ago and instructed us to wait here at anchor. I guess they're trying to figure out where they might need us. So here we sit, at least as long as we have fuel and stores, which might not be very long. Welcome to the club. Over."

"Thank you, *Ambrose Channel* , but I don't think I want to join. This is *Pecos Trader* , out."

Hughes reracked the mike and looked over at Chief Mate Georgia Howell.

"You ready to do this, Mate?"

"Do I have a choice?"

Hughes sighed. "Not really."

***

Hughes was sweating, despite the early hour, as he kept *Pecos Trader* in the middle of the channel and crawled upstream at a fraction of the speed an experienced pilot might employ. Periodically he moved from one bridge wing to the other, looking down the side of the ship to gauge his position relative to the shore from different perspectives. If he put her aground, there'd be no tugs to pull her off. He had Pete Sonnier, his best helmsman, on the wheel, and Georgia Howell was handling engine orders, but despite the presence of his 'A Team,' the stress was palpable. Kinsey was on the bridge in case they encountered the Coast Guard, but Kinsey seemed to sense the tension and was keeping to the chartroom, available if needed, but out of the way.

For all Hughes' anxiety, things were going well. He'd timed their arrival and transit at high slack water to avoid the strong westerly set of the current, and successfully negotiated the known shallow spot on the inside of the turn some distance from the entrance to the jetties. They were in protected waters now, less subject to the vagaries of wind and current, and he let himself relax a bit as he walked to the port bridge wing. They passed the Sabine Pilot Docks on the west bank, the pilot boats all tied up and the small parking lot completely empty.

"CHIEF KINSEY," he shouted back towards the wheelhouse, "COAST GUARD STATION COMING UP. YOU MIGHT WANT TO HAVE A LOOK."

Kinsey was at his side in seconds, and they watched as the ship drew abreast of the Coast Guard station, a neatly kept jewel in the otherwise scruffy industrial blight of the shoreline. The building was a sparkling white in the Spanish style with a red tile roof, and set in a broad expanse of verdant green lawn. But even at a distance, the beginnings of decay were obvious; the St. Augustine grass was overgrown and encroaching on the sidewalks, and there were no cars in the parking lot or boats at the dock. The place looked abandoned.

"Looks like nobody's home," Hughes said.

Kinsey nodded. "They must've been re-tasked somewhere, especially since the boats are gone. If they'd just taken off on their own, I doubt it would have been by boat, so I'm thinking they probably got reassigned to the Houston-Galveston area. There's a lot more marine traffic there, especially if the refineries here in Beaumont and Port Arthur are shut down." He shrugged. "But that's just a guess."

"Good a guess as any," Hughes said, "and at least we don't have to worry about having to finesse our way around another obstacle."

Kinsey looked relieved, and Hughes moved back into the wheelhouse, leaving Kinsey alone on the bridge wing.

Things continued smoothly, and apart from some anxiety when transiting the highway bridge just north of Texas Island, Hughes was growing confident he might actually reach the anchorage without going aground. They'd seen zero activity ashore, but given both the circumstances and the early hour, he wasn't surprised. That changed as they drew abreast of downtown Port Arthur and Hughes caught movement ashore out of the corner of his eye. He took a quick look at the arrow-straight section of the channel ahead, then moved out to the port bridge wing, grabbing the binoculars from their storage box on the way out the wheelhouse door.

"What we got, Chief?" he asked Kinsey.

"Looks like cops, so maybe things haven't gone completely to hell here."

Hughes nodded and raised the glasses. A police cruiser was stopped on the road paralleling the channel, with two officers standing at the open doors and staring at the ship.

"Sheriff's deputies based on the car and the uniforms," Hughes said.

He watched the men jump back in the car and race along the road, lights flashing and siren wailing, to a small waterfront park in the far distance well ahead of the ship. The cops exited the car and left the lights flashing to race out on to a small dock projecting slightly into the channel.

"What the hell…"

"Well, this is a first," Kinsey said. "I think they want you to pull over."

"Those friggin' idiots! Don't they realize I can't…" He trailed off and shot Kinsey an exasperated look.

"Probably not." Kinsey shrugged. "Your call, Cap, but stupid though they may be, they might represent the only authority around here. It might not be wise to piss 'em off at this point."

Hughes looked at the channel again. He had plenty of water depth and no traffic in a straight channel, and he was only creeping along. He could probably accommodate them without too much risk. He nodded and handed Kinsey the binoculars before stomping back into the wheelhouse.

"STOP!" he called out to Georgia Howell.

She looked startled, but after a moment's hesitation confirmed the order and passed it to the engine room while Hughes gave the helm orders to edge the *Pecos Trader* a bit closer to the west bank of the channel.

"HALF ASTERN!" Hughes ordered, and the ship began to slow from its already snail-like pace. Moments later he ordered 'STOP' again and nodded with satisfaction as the big ship drifted to a halt about fifty feet off the dock where the two cops stood. He turned to Georgia Howell.

"Mate, keep an eye on things while I talk to these knuckleheads. If it looks like we're drifting into trouble, let me know."

"Yes, sir," she replied, and Hughes hurried back out on the bridge wing.

"Y'ALL COME ON IN AND TIE UP," shouted one of the cops.

Hughes suppressed a curse. "I CAN'T TIE UP TO THAT, IT'S A FISHING DOCK," he called. "IF I PUT THIS SHIP ALONGSIDE, I'LL CRUSH IT LIKE AN EGG. BESIDES, WHY DO YOU WANT US TO TIE UP?"

There was a discussion between the cops, as if they were unsure. The spokesman turned and yelled back to the ship, "WE NEED TO SEARCH Y'ALL FOR CONTRABAND AND HOARDED GOODS. ALL SUPPLIES ARE BEING CENTRALIZED BY THE COUNTY GOVERNMENT FOR THE RELIEF EFFORT."

Beside Hughes, Kinsey studied the cops through the binoculars. "Unless the cops are okay with swastika neck tattoos," he said under his breath, "I suspect those guys aren't really cops."

Hughes nodded slightly and improvised.

"WELL, I CAN'T TIE UP HERE," he yelled back down, "SO WHAT DO YOU SUGGEST?"

Another conversation between the fake cops.

"TIE UP AT THE FIRST DOCK THAT WILL TAKE YOU. WE'LL FOLLOW YOU THERE," the spokesman said.

"THAT WOULD BE WHERE WE'RE GOING ANYWAY," Hughes yelled back. "WE NEED REPAIRS. DO YOU KNOW THE BLUDWORTH MARINE SHIPYARD IN ORANGE?"

"NO, BUT WE'LL JUST FOLLOW YOU."

"WELL, GOOD LUCK WITH THAT UNLESS YOUR CRUISER'S A MARSH BUGGY BECAUSE THE ROAD DOESN'T RUN BESIDE THE CHANNEL. BESIDES, IT'S NOT EXACTLY LIKE WE CAN RUN AWAY FROM YOU."

More conversation ashore.

"ALL RIGHT, WE'LL MEET YOU AT THIS SHIPYARD, BUT DON'T TRY NO TRICKS," the spokesman said.

"FINE, WE'LL SEE YOU THERE IN THREE HOURS," Hughes yelled back.

The pair moved to their car, and Hughes flashed Kinsey a smile. "I guess those boys aren't from around here."

"I'm not from around here either, but I know there's no way a ship this size is getting anywhere near Orange. That's a tug and barge yard anyway. Why'd you pick that?"

"Because it's the farthest place away I could think of that might sound reasonable to someone without a clue. Right now they're probably rushing to look it up in the phone book or someplace. It'll be listed as a shipyard, and they don't exactly strike me as the sharpest tacks in the box, so I'm hoping they'll haul ass for Orange. If they're as dumb as I think they are, they probably won't figure it out even after they get there, so they'll sit around and wait for us to show up, for a while at least. By that time, we ought to be safe in our anchorage."

***

"What kind of ship? A navy ship. A cargo ship? What?"

"Hell, I don't know, Spike! A big one."

Spike McComb looked at the pair before him and suppressed an urge to kill them.

"So lemme get this straight. You two spot a big-ass ship comin' up the channel and lose it? How do you lose a friggin' ship, for Christ's sake?"

"There was one of them orange Coast Guard boats on the deck and one of the guys on board had on a uniform of some kind," the second of the pair volunteered.

"Shit!" McComb said. "That ain't good. We don't need the Coast Guard around here messin' things up."

"Maybe they stole the Coast Guard boat," Snaggle said, joining the conversation. "WE got uniforms, so that don't necessarily mean nothing."

McComb rubbed his chin. "Could be you're right, but I still don't like it. We need tight control of our territory and I don't like the idea of no Coast Guard pukes running around. Hell, they're as bad as cops, worse maybe 'cause they got better guns. And for all we know, this ship's full of prime cargo of some kind."

He thought about it a moment longer and then turned to Snaggle.

"Snag, get on top of this. It ain't like there are a lot of places to hide a big ship. Figure out where it might be and start lookin' for it."

"Okay, Spike, whatever you say. But things are goin' pretty smooth and we're really bringin' in the loot now that we got 'police backup,'" Snaggle said. "You want me to pull some boys off scavengin' and put 'em looking for this ship?"

"Maybe we should do both. We got anybody lookin' at the river? You know, houseboats, marinas, places like that? A lot of them boats have generators, so there's likely people living aboard. Might be a whole new source of loot and labor."

"I never thought of that," Snaggle said. "The sheriff's department has a boat somewhere, maybe we'll start up the Marine Patrol again."

"Get it done," McComb said.

STATE HIGHWAY 11
WEST OF CURRIE, NC

DAY 16, 10:00 A.M.

Luke studied the thick woods on either side of the road ahead, alert for an ambush. They'd looped far inland, avoiding interstate corridors and population centers, keeping to local roads and the occasional small town, stretching the four-hundred-mile trip to twice that, and lengthening it farther by traveling only during daylight. They'd consolidated all their stores into a single pickup to save fuel and abandoned the second truck in the Publix parking lot along with the two bodies. Plenty of good people were going unburied, and none of the now ex-SRF troopers had the slightest remorse about dumping the remains of the dead mercenaries like the trash they were.

Two nights running, they set up the vehicles in a triangular laager well off the road, with trip wires and noise makers all around and someone keeping watch on one of the Ma Deuces. Keeping to the hinterland had been a wise choice—one they'd debated at some length given their Humvees' thirst for diesel. They'd maintained a constant watch for abandoned gas stations along their route, and possible sources of residual fuel in underground storage tanks. As it turned out, stations farther off the beaten path weren't yet scavenged as thoroughly as those in more populated areas.

Fuel wasn't plentiful, but it was adequate, helped no doubt by scavengers concentrating on gasoline rather than the diesel their Humvees guzzled. Luke smiled at the memory of their only 'armed confrontation' at a dilapidated country store as they hand-pumped diesel into their Jerry cans. An older gentleman had appeared, brandishing a shotgun and less than happy over the theft of fuel. Some placating discussion and allowing him his choice of the contents of the stores truck ended the affair without bloodshed.

"Won't be long now," Gibson said from behind the wheel. "My folks' place is just past this intersection with fifty-three."

"Anxious to get home?" Luke asked.

Gibson gave a solemn nod. "And kind of afraid of what I might find. My folks' farm is back here in the sticks, though, so I ain't too worried. I joined the Corps 'cause I never much wanted to be a farmer, but I gotta admit, when times get tough, at least country folks have something to eat."

"That's a fact," Luke said, just as they passed the intersection, another paved rural road leading off to the left at an angle. Ahead he could just make out the guardrails of a fairly substantial bridge of some sort, but Gibson slowed and made a right turn onto a gravel track before they reached the bridge.

"This leads to my folks' place. My family owns a pretty fair strip of land between this road and the river beyond the trees to our left. Almost four hundred acres all told. Been in the family since before the war," Gibson said. Despite his professed aversion to farming, Luke could hear pride of ownership in the young man's voice.

"World War Two?"

Gibson laughed. "The War Between the States."

"There have been a few since then, you know," Luke said.

"Yeah, but none of 'em happened in North Carolina," Gibson replied, still smiling. Then his smile faded. "Leastwise, not until now."

Luke nodded and they rode in silence for a couple of minutes until Gibson took his foot off the gas and let the vehicle roll to a stop.

"What's up?" Luke asked.

"Our driveway's about a hundred yards ahead on the left. Might be better if I went ahead on foot. My dad's a veteran, but he ain't a real big fan of the government in the best of times. No tellin' how he might take it if two armed Humvees roll in, especially with these uniforms. If there are SRF units up here, and they got 'em doing what we was doing in Florida, I think we got about a fifty-fifty chance of a warm reception."

"How's that going to be any different if you go in alone? You're still wearing the uniform," Luke said.

"Because I'm walking up the driveway with my helmet off and my hands up, yelling 'Dad, don't shoot,' that's why."

"And what happens if someone other than your folks are there and they're not friendly?" Luke shook his head. "I don't like it, Gibson. You do it your way, but I'm trailing behind out of sight to lay down some covering fire in case you gotta turn around and beat feet out of there."

"Look, LT, I know you mean well, but —"

"No buts, Gibson. I can't stop you from going in like you want, but you can't stop me from providing backup. That's just the way it is."

Gibson sighed. "Okay, LT, I'll give you the layout, but be careful. Even with me there, Dad's not gonna take kindly to anyone pointing a gun at him."

The feeling's mutual, thought Luke, but he only nodded.

They exited their vehicle and Gibson described the entrance to his family's farm and briefed the others before he set off for the house with only his sidearm. His helmet was off and suspended from his web gear. Luke let him get fifty yards ahead and started through the tall grass in the field to his left, heading for the sunken creek Gibson told him ran roughly parallel to the road. He hit it and jogged upstream, hidden by the creek banks. He rounded a bend to see a large culvert ahead where the driveway crossed the creek. He redoubled his efforts, splashing through the shallow creek to the culvert and then crawling up the left bank, to peek over and see Gibson's back as he walked, hands above his head, toward an ancient, but well-maintained farmhouse with a large barn nearby. Luke sighted his assault rifle on the house in the distance beyond Gibson.

"HELLO IN THE HOUSE! DON'T SHOOT! IT'S ME, DONNY!"

For a long minute, nothing happened, then the door of the house opened, followed by the squeak of the wooden screen door. A man appeared holding a rifle. His body language was tentative as he peered into the distance.

"DONNY? PRAISE GOD! IS THAT REALLY YOU, BOY?"

"IT'S ME, DAD—"

Luke heard the squawk of a radio and he watched in his scope as the man raised a walkie-talkie to his face, but he was too far away to hear what was said. The man on the porch looked up, his body language changing from tentative to tense.

"DONNY! GET DOWN!" the man shouted, and the dirt immediately in front of Luke exploded in his face from the impact of a three-round burst. He jerked his head back below the bank just as another burst shredded the earth where his head had been. In the near distance behind him, he heard the Humvees firing up, no doubt intent on bringing their Ma Deuces to bear if the Gibson homestead was occupied by bad guys. This was going to hell in a hurry, thought Luke as he chanced another quick 'peek and duck,' rewarded by another three-round burst.

"DAD! RICHARD! STOP SHOOTING! THEY'RE FRIENDS!"

Luke heard footsteps pounding toward him and ducked into the metal culvert under the driveway, just to be on the safe side.

"LT? LT? Are you hit?" came Gibson's voice above him.

"Not yet," Luke said as he moved out of the culvert and looked up, "but I'm not sure I like my odds. Are they done shooting at me yet?"

Gibson moved to the side of the stream and reached down a hand. "Yeah, and you're lucky. My brother, Richard, don't miss too often."

Luke took Gibson's offered hand and pulled himself up the steep creek bank just as the little convoy roared around the turn into the driveway. Luke signaled them to hold in place and turned to follow Gibson back toward the farmhouse and Gibson's father, who was now off the porch and halfway down the long driveway, running to meet them. In the distance over the approaching man's shoulder, Luke saw another figure exit the barn and rush toward them, a rifle slung across his back.

Gibson's dad reached them and wrapped his son in a hug. "Donny! Thank God you're home, boy. Your mom's been worried sick ever since the lights went out." The man straightened and released his son. "I'm sure glad to see you, but what are y'all doing here?"

"It's a long story, Dad. But first meet Lieutenant Kinsey. LT, this is my dad," Gibson said.

The older man extended his hand to Luke. "Vern Gibson, Lieutenant, and sorry about before. We thought you was holding a gun on Donny."

"Understandable, Mr. Gibson and no harm done. And call me Luke. I expect I'm not a lieutenant anymore anyway."

Vern Gibson eyed their uniforms. "I was wonderin' about that, but I expect we'll get to—"

"Damn, Donny! If it weren't bad enough you was a jarhead, it looks like you done changed sides again," Richard Gibson said as he approached, the fierce hug he gave his brother giving lie to his taunt.

Luke assessed the newcomer quickly. He was an inch or so taller and perhaps a decade older than Donny Gibson, but there could be no mistaking they were brothers. Richard Gibson moved with the quiet confidence of a soldier, or at least a former soldier, but there was something a bit awkward in the hug. It took a moment to realize Richard's gloved left hand was actually a prosthetic.

Donny Gibson returned his brother's hug and then pushed him back and grinned. "Well, you ought to get along well with the LT here, aside from almost killin' him, I mean. He's one of you idiots who jumps out of perfectly good aircraft."

Richard looked at Luke and smiled. "Sorry about that, but I have to say this is about the only time I've been happy I'm not quite as accurate as I was before I lost the hand." He held up the prosthetic left hand and then extended his real right hand to Luke. "Richard Gibson, formerly of the 82nd Airborne."

"Luke Kinsey, 101st… formerly of the 101st Airborne."

"Dopes on ropes?" Richard asked, his wide grin taking the sting out of his words.

Luke laughed. "Can't say I haven't felt like it at times." Then he grew serious as he nodded at the other man's prosthetic. "Sandbox?"

Richard nodded. "IED in Anbar Province. I got off lucky compared to —"

"DONNY!" a small woman screamed, and then launched herself at Donny Gibson, hugging him fiercely and laughing and crying simultaneously. "Oh, thank you, Jesus! You've brought my baby home to me safe and sound."

Luke watched as the woman continued to hang on to Donny Gibson for all she was worth, rocking on her feet and overcome with emotion, unable to speak. Young Gibson returned her fierce hug then gradually tried to release her as his face colored in embarrassment, but his mother was clamped tight. After a long moment he whispered something in her ear and gently but firmly pushed her back. Anger flashed across her face.

"Well, you may not be a baby, young man, but you're MY baby and don't you forget it…"

She turned and saw the men all grinning at her, joined now by an attractive younger woman, joining the group in the first woman's wake.

"What are you grinning at, Vernon Gibson? And just when did you plan on coming to tell me Donny was home? Or were you just planning on leaving me and Evie down in that hidey-hole until it dawned on you I might be a little interested my youngest son was home?"

"I'm sorry, Virginia. I was just —"

"You were just out here having a 'man talk' without concern as to what it was like for Evie and me stuck down in the dark, listening to gunfire and not knowin' if you two were alive or dead. THAT's what you were doing."

"I'm sorry, Virginia, but —"

"Don't you 'I'm sorry' me, Mr. Vernon Gibson. And I'll tell you another thing! That is the LAST time I'm goin' in that hole. I can shoot near as good as you and Richard, and if there's a threat, I'm gonna be right beside you defendin' this place. Is that clear?"

Vern Gibson sighed. "Yes, ma'am."

Virginia Gibson sniffed and turned to Luke.

"And who might you be, young man?"

"Luke Kinsey, ma'am. I'm —"

"Anyone who can bring my son home safe and sound in these troubled times is welcome in my home," she said, looking over his shoulder and down the driveway. "And I suppose those men and trucks belong with you. How many of y'all are there?"

"Six counting Gibs… six counting Donny," Luke said.

"Well, I suspect y'all are hungry, seems like everybody is these days. Come on in and I'll fix y'all a home-cooked meal. Have to be breakfast this late in the morning and on short notice, but I'll feed y'all enough to hold you until supper time and then do something special to celebrate Donny's homecoming." She turned back to her husband without waiting for a reply.

"Vernon, best git them army trucks out of sight in the barn before somebody comes by and gets nosy, then show these fellas where to wash up. Richard, bring in some more wood and stir the fire up in the cookstove, then bring in all the extra eggs and some more of that bacon. Eva and I are going to start making biscuits."

She motioned to the other woman and they both started for the house, heads together as they planned the impromptu meal. Luke watched them go, a bit shell-shocked at the sudden turn of events.

"We best git movin', Lieutenant," Vern Gibson said. "Virginia can get real mean when she's riled up."

"She's not riled up yet?"

Vern Gibson laughed. "Oh, hell no. Not by a long shot."

***

The meal was simple and bountiful—huge platters of scrambled eggs and bacon, accompanied by heaped plates of biscuits with small crocks of fresh butter and homemade preserves, all of which the two women kept constantly refilled, and washed down with cold milk from heavy stoneware pitchers. Except for Donny Gibson, the men ate tentatively at first, feeling guilty about depleting the family's stores. However, repeated assurances there was 'plenty more' and the temptation of the best food they'd seen in weeks soon ate through their restraint. They began shoveling it down while Virginia Gibson looked on with approval, ready to refill the platters.

Finally Sergeant Joel Washington had his fill and leaned back in his chair.

"Ma'am, I do believe that was the best meal I've ever eaten in my entire life."

There was a chorus of agreement around the table as Virginia Gibson blushed. "It's nothing special, just eggs and such," she said. "I expect y'all were just hungry is all."

"We were that," Luke said, "but the meal was outstanding nonetheless. However, I'm still concerned we're depleting your stores. We didn't mean to come in and eat you out of house and home."

"Not a problem," Vern Gibson said. "We always had extra milk and eggs we sold, but we been keeping close to home what with things the way they are. Most folks around here been doing likewise, so y'all just ate up what was likely to go bad anyway."

"How do you keep the milk cold?" Neal Long asked. "You got a generator?"

Vern Gibson nodded. "We got a little generator in the barn, but we only use it when we have to. But folks was keepin' milk cold a long time before we got electricity in these parts. We got a springhouse that's been here almost two hundred years. It's the same spring where we get our drinking water."

"Looks like you've got a pretty good setup," Luke said.

Vern nodded again. "Too good maybe. This ain't been goin' on all that long, but I'm worried as it gets worse we're going to see more folks comin' around trying to take what don't belong to 'em. As a matter of fact, there's only two other farms on this road and yesterday we all agreed to plow up the gravel road from the state highway until our driveway and let it go back natural, just to keep strangers from poking their noses down the road. Ain't no point in invitin' trouble. Most of the farms here border the river, and we figure we can use it for transportation and tradin' among ourselves, just like folks did in the old days."

"Sounds like a plan," Luke said, smiling as he nodded toward Donny Gibson, "and you've got another good man to help with defense."

Donny Gibson flushed as his father nodded. "And we're obliged for you helping him get home. Y'all can stay here as long as you like. There ain't room in the house for everybody, but we can make the barn pretty comfortable this time of the year, and I'm sure we can find another woodstove before winter sets in. I figure farming's gonna get a lot more labor intensive, and Lord knows we can use the extra firepower if things get bad." He smiled. "And it ain't a bad place for outlaws to hang out. I reckon nobody's gonna be lookin' for you here."

Luke nodded. "That's a generous offer and we, or at least some of us, might take you up on it. But I really want to try to connect with my dad first. He's at the Coast Guard station down at Oak Island."

"Family's important," Vern agreed. "How you figure to get there?"

"That's a problem," Luke said. "I think we've been pushing our luck a bit, riding around in the Humvees and these uniforms. We haven't had any problems in the countryside, but I don't know exactly what to expect closer to a population center. For sure, we'll attract more notice, and if it's of the 'official' variety, we'll either get in a shootout or have to surrender. Even if we run into troops who don't know we're AWOL, they're likely gonna want to conscript us and our vehicles into their operation—not too many military commanders would warm to the idea of a lieutenant running around doing whatever he pleases. Do you have any idea what's going on in the city?"

"Not a real good idea, but we do have kind of a grapevine," Vern said. "I hear it's pretty bad with no law left to speak of. The gangs are runnin' things and they're starting to spread out from the city. One of our neighbors took his boat down quiet like one night and said there's some soldiers around the docks and a Coast Guard patrol boat in the river, but he didn't contact 'em. He just looked around a bit and came home."

Luke sat up straighter at the mention of the boat. "If we can contact the Coast Guard boat, I might be able to get word to my dad."

Vern nodded. "We got a couple of boats and I can take you downriver. Between me, Richard, and Donny, I reckon we can get you all into civvies. If we get stopped by the wrong folks, you're just farmers from upriver, comin' in to check out the situation."

"Sounds like a plan," Luke said.

APPALACHIAN TRAIL
MILE MARKER 998.6 NORTHBOUND
EAST OF BLUEMONT, VIRGINIA

DAY 16, 3:00 P.M.

Bill Wiggins stopped to catch his breath, trying to ignore the pack straps cutting into his shoulders and his aching back and feet. Tex stepped up beside him and looked up the hill.

She flashed a weary smile. "Only another half mile."

Wiggins snorted. "It's not the half mile I mind. It's the three-hundred-foot vertical part."

She nodded and took the lead. He fell in behind her to trudge up the incline.

It was their second full day afoot and they'd covered barely twenty-five miles total. The afternoon they'd fled, the first three miles were a steep climb, and he immediately doubted the wisdom of overloading their packs. They reached the ridgetop and only two miles further when by mutual agreement, they moved off the trail and made cold camp. They'd used the remaining daylight to empty and reload their packs, abandoning heavier items they'd grabbed in their hasty flight. The only consolation was eating their fill of food they would have otherwise left behind. They started the next day on full stomachs.

They made twelve miles the second day, crossing US 50 at Ashby Gap and continuing four miles to the Rod Hollow shelter, arriving with two hours of daylight remaining. They were limping by the time they made camp in the woods, well away from the shelter, Wiggins more than Tex. They boiled pasta in the little pot of the ultralight camp stove Levi had included in the pack. They wolfed it down plain, carbs to balance the nuts and jerky they'd eaten through the day. The little AT guidebook was already proving invaluable, for its list of water sources alone. They topped their camel packs at the shelter before retreating to their hidden campsite and stringing their bell-studded fishing line through the trees.

When Wiggins removed his boots to massage his aching feet, he'd found the nails of both big toes purplish and tender to the touch. Roomy, steel-toed work boots were fine for standing on the engine-room deck plates for long hours, but far from ideal for hiking. Tex was having similar problems, though her toenails weren't yet discolored. But exhaustion proved an effective anesthetic and they'd crawled into their hammocks with the setting sun and slept like the dead to rise, stiff and sore, at first light.

They breakfasted on leftover cold pasta, jerky, and a handful of nuts, then donned extra pairs of socks to pad their aching feet. They laced their boots extra tight across the insteps, seeking to protect their battered toes, and started north with the rising sun—to find even more challenging terrain. Yesterday was long grueling climbs followed by equally long descents, but the past hours had been a roller coaster in comparison: a seemingly endless series of steep climbs with equally steep downhill grades, jamming their toes despite the tightness of the laces.

Wiggins was close to hobbling, and despite having made only ten miles for the day and with several hours of daylight remaining, he'd readily agreed to Tex's suggestion they start looking for a place to camp. He limped up the hill behind her now, trying not to fixate on their poor progress—two and a half days to make twenty-five miles—at this rate it would take him over four months to reach his family, provided his feet held out. He shook off the gloom and spoke to Tex's back.

"So what does the guidebook say about this Bear's Den place?"

"It looks to be a fairly substantial facility," she said. "It's a state park and listed as 'the premier hiker's hostel on the AT.' Looks like they have showers and food service, though I doubt if there's anyone there at this point. I'm just hoping we can liberate some toilet paper and... other things. Levi was a bit stingy with paper goods. We can hunt food, but we can't make toilet paper and I'm not a big fan of leaves."

"You think we'll run into anyone?" he asked.

"I'm thinking no," she said back over her shoulder, "but it's probably more likely there than other places. It is a park off a paved road."

"Wait up," Wiggins said, and Tex complied, her eyebrows raised in a question as Wiggins caught up with her.

"Let's leave our packs hidden back here off the trail and approach this place cautiously. If we have to run, we're not doing it with packs on our back. We can loop back later and get them. For that matter, maybe we ought to just keep to the woods and bypass this place."

Tex shook her head. "My camel pack ran dry a mile back and the next water source beyond Bear's Den is at least two hours, given our rate of travel. And what if it's dry? How's your water?"

"I'm almost dry too," he admitted. "All right, then I guess it's the 'cautious approach' scenario. Let's get a little closer to the top, then ditch our packs. I'm thinking we don't walk into the place from the trail but circle around and give it a good look from cover first."

Tex grinned. "You're getting so damned paranoid; Levi would be proud."

"I became a convert as soon as people started shooting at us."

Tex nodded and started back up the hill. When the trees began to thin, they moved off the trail and took off their packs. Wiggins opened his and pulled out the little survival rifle, quickly assembling it and slapping in a magazine.

"Going squirrel hunting?" Tex asked.

"Hey, it's better than nothing. You got the Glock?"

Tex reached around and patted the small of her back. "It hasn't been out of reach since the first shots were fired."

Wiggins nodded and they moved through the woods to the edge of a clearing. There in the center stood an impressive stone lodge built into the side of a low hill with a door to a daylight or 'walk out' basement in the rear. They kept to the woods and crept all the way around the building, alert for any signs of habitation.

"No activity, no cars," Wiggins whispered. "I'd say no one's home."

"I agree," Tex said. "Let's go back around. That basement door is supposed to be the hikers' entrance, accessible twenty-four hours a day."

Wiggins nodded and they emerged from the clearing and walked to the rear of the lodge. Sure enough, the door had a keypad.

"What's up with that?" Wiggins asked.

"According to the guidebook, you're supposed to enter the 'mileage code' for access. Not that it matters, since there's no power."

Wiggins was looking around. He spotted what he was looking for and returned with a large rock and smashed a window.

"I don't think that's what they had in mind for 'hiker access,'" Tex said.

"Hey, we got our share of the payoff money from the ship, I'll leave a couple of hundred bucks."

"Works for me," Tex said as Wiggins tapped glass shards from the window frame with the rock and reached inside to unlock the window.

"I'm smaller," Tex said. "Boost me in and I'll unlock the door."

Moments later they were inside, examining a row of bunk beds and a lounge with basic amenities. Wiggins followed Tex down a hall to a bathroom, and heard her emit a relieved sigh. He followed her gaze to a tampon dispenser on the wall and suppressed a smile. Couldn't really fault Levi for not putting that essential in his 'getting home' bag, he thought.

He walked to the sink and turned the faucet, surprised when water gushed out. Pressure was low, but adequate and he let it run a long moment to make sure it wasn't just residual water in the line.

"Damn! Running water. I'm thinking that must mean gravity flow from a tank—"

"And I'm thinking SHOWERS! Try the hot water," Tex said.

"Fat chance," Wiggins said as he twisted the knob. Warm water gushed across his hand.

"Well, I'll be damned. Must be solar."

"Hallelujah!" Tex said, and Wiggins laughed and nodded to a shelf piled with towels and personal-sized soap and shampoo.

"Ladies first," he said. "I'll have a look around and stand watch out here just to make sure no one catches us by surprise. After you've showered, you can return the favor. But first, let's go back and grab our packs."

An hour later, they had both finished their showers and were sitting in the lounge area of the hiker hostel.

"We still have daylight left, and I'm feeling much better," Wiggins said. "Should we try to put a few more miles behind us?"

Tex shook her head. "I think both our feet could use the rest. I also think we have to face facts. We can't continue like this. We've been hiking less than three days and we're both near crippled. We HAVE to get better footwear, or we're unlikely to make it at all."

"And how we gonna do that? It's not like there's an REI or a Cabela's on the trail."

Tex flipped through the guidebook. "There's a general store in Bluemont, and this is hiking country. They might have something. Even sneakers or running shoes would be better than these work boots."

"Okay, how far to Bluemont?"

"A mile and a half as the crow flies, but about three times that overland. We can take the AT down to Snicker's Gap, but then we'd have to get on the road. From the switchbacks, I'm guessing it will be a hell of a climb up the road to Bluemont."

"I don't know, Tex. An eight- or nine-mile round trip that doesn't get us any closer to home, to check out a store that's surely not open and probably doesn't have what we need if it is? That doesn't sound promising."

"We can use your patented 'rock method' to open it, and we just leave money if we find what we need." She sighed. "But you're right, anyway you hack it, it's the better part of a day's trip and doesn't get us any closer to home."

"What's the next possibility?"

"Harpers Ferry. A bit over twenty miles, but that's a fairly populous area, and I'm a bit worried about straying off the trail there. In fact, I was already worried about Harpers Ferry anyway."

"Why?"

"Because we cross both the Shenandoah and the Potomac rivers there, and given what we saw at Front Royal, I'm guessing there'll be roadblocks on the bridges. And a boat's pretty much a nonstarter, even if we could find one, because both rivers are full of rapids at that point. It's bridges or nothing."

"So is there any good news?"

Tex looked over at the rows of bunks. "Well, if we stay here tonight we don't have to sack out in those damned hammocks. I mean, they're better than sleeping on the ground with the creepy crawlies and they are light to carry, but they're getting old real quick. I could use a good night's sleep on a mattress."

Wiggins looked skeptical. "I'd love to sack out in a real bed too, but we're sitting ducks if anyone stumbles in here when we're sleeping."

"If anyone shows up, it will likely be from the road, and they'll break in the front and we'll hear them. And just to be on the safe side, we'll barricade the door from the upstairs down here to the basement to buy some more time, and keep our packs by our bunks and ready to go. At the first sign of trouble, we'll wake up, grab our gear, and be back in the woods before anyone even knows we were here."

"It's tempting," said Wiggins, "but I think it would be a mistake."

Tex looked crestfallen, but she nodded. "Yeah, you're right."

Then Wiggins smiled. "But the mattresses aren't nailed to the bunks. There's nothing says we can't carry a couple of them out into the woods a ways and set up our camp there. We can always drag 'em back in the morning if we want to be stand-up citizens. We'll need to come in and top up our water anyway."

Tex grinned. "And use a real toilet as long as it's available."

"Sounds like a plan," Wiggins said.

HUGHES' RESIDENCE
PECAN GROVE
OLEANDER, TEXAS

DAY 16, 4:00 P.M.

"This stinks, Mom. And it's hot! How much more do we have to do?"

Laura Hughes wiped the sweat from her forehead with the back of a gloved hand. She looked across the large garden to where her daughter Jana rested on her knees, her fifteen-year-old face contorted in anguish at the latest perceived injustice. Laura sighed.

"All right, just finish those two rows and we'll call it a day. We've made a good dent and it's not like the weeds won't be here tomorrow."

"TWO ROWS? REALLY? That's not fair! I've done TWICE as much as Julie. Why does SHE get to stay inside just because she's sunburned? You TOLD her to use sunblock. Now she gets to stay inside while I work like a SLAVE. And I did what you told me to. It's not fair."

Laura suppressed her anger, something she was having to do more frequently as the days dragged. She took a calming breath.

"You're right, Jana, it's not fair, but neither is life, so you'd best learn to deal with it. Regardless of how Julie got sunburned, she IS burned and that can't be undone. If she gets back out in this sun too soon, she could get seriously ill and we have no way to handle that. That leaves just the two of us. To keep eating, we need to keep the garden in good shape and I can't do it by myself, so fair or not, you have to help me. And it's not like Julie isn't working. She's washing all the clothes by hand and I've given her ALL of your inside chores." She paused and her voice softened, sounding weary to the bone. "I'm doing the best I can, honey, and it's not fair to me either, but help me out here a little, please."

Jana stared at her mother for a long moment and then a single tear rolled down her cheek. Her shoulders began to shake in silent sobs. Laura was on her feet in an instant, stepping over the rows separating them, to kneel at her daughter's side and fold her into an embrace.

"It's okay, honey, it's okay," she said, patting Jana's back. "I didn't mean to upset you."

"N-no, Mom," Jana stuttered between sobs, "it… it's ME who… who should be sorry. You… you're working so hard… and Dad's gone and we don't know… we don't know whe… when he's coming home… or even if he's okay. And the power's out and we don't even know if it's coming back… and we haven't seen any of our friends… and people are getting really mean and it just SUCKS so bad." Jana took a ragged breath, tears flowing freely now. "Mom, I'm just so scared, and Julie is too." She sniffed loudly, and Laura released her to peel off her own gloves and dig a crumpled handkerchief from the pocket of her jeans.

"Blow," she said as she held the handkerchief to Jana's nose.

Her daughter complied and Laura smiled. "You haven't done that since you were a little girl."

Jana smiled back through the tears. "I remember."

Laura pulled her close in a fierce hug. "Then remember I took care of you then, and I'll take care of you now."

Laura released her daughter and stood, then reached down to grab a hand and pull Jana up after her. "And on second thought, I think we've done enough today. What say we go in and have a big glass of iced tea?"

Jana nodded emphatically. "Thank God for the generator. I don't think I could stand this without ice. And since making tea is an INSIDE job, I do believe the sunburn queen can SERVE me my tea."

Laura burst out laughing. "You just talked me out of an hour of weeding, so don't push your luck. I am NOT going to spend my OWN goof off time refereeing another fight between you two. I get to play hooky a bit too, you know."

TEXAS STATE HIGHWAY 124
WESTBOUND

DAY 16, 5:00 P.M.

"There ain't nothin' out here, Willard," said Kyle Morgan. "We ain't seen jack since we went through that shitty little town a while back. We need to go back and check that out. There's likely some loot to be had there."

"Would you just shut the hell up and do what I tell you," said Willard Jukes. "Who's in charge here, anyway?"

"I'm just sayin'—"

"And I'm just sayin' shut the hell up! We been over it. We find an isolated place nobody's likely to find; otherwise it's too risky," Jukes said.

"I know, Willard, but I been thinking. Maybe we should just loot like usual. If Snag or Spike find out—"

"Don't you go gettin' chickenshit on me now. You're just as pissed as I am about bringin' in all the good stuff and having it dripped back to us like we're some sort of pimply-faced jerk-off kids on an allowance. And I'm doubly pissed off about the pussy. We brought in eight or ten of them bitches our own selves, so we should at least get one apiece for our very own, and the pick of the lot too, leastwise of the ones we brung in."

"I know, Willard, but if we get caught…"

"For the umpteenth time, we AIN'T gonna get caught. We just find us an isolated place on one of these crappy country roads and take it. Then when we find some good stuff or really smokin' hot bitches, we bring 'em here along with our share of the loot and take the rest of the stuff back to Spike. We'll lock the women up first until we got 'em broke in good, then we have 'em run the place. We visit when we want. And here's the beauty part, if anyone gets suspicious, we just close down and 'find' the location and bring all the loot back to the prison. The women won't say nothin' 'cause they know we'll kill 'em if they do. Matter of fact, we can kill one of 'em ahead of time, just to show the others we mean business."

Jukes paused and looked at Morgan. "It's just like skimmin' in the old days except now there ain't no cash involved. I used to do it all the time and I never got caught, for that anyway."

Morgan said nothing, but gave an unconvincing nod.

They rode in silence a few minutes until they approached a minor intersection.

"Take that road to the left," Jukes said, and Morgan complied.

"This don't look like it goes nowhere," Morgan said.

"Every road goes somewhere, it's just a question of what's at the end of it," Jukes said, "and in this case, I'm thinking this one will take us to that buncha trees way over yonder."

Morgan followed Jukes' pointing finger to a dark green blot far across the flat pastureland.

"Why there?" Morgan asked.

"'Cause if we can see 'em this far away, that means they're damn big trees. Trees like that don't just spring up in the middle of this flat pastureland. They gotta be planted and a long time ago at that. Like as not, there's a house there, and maybe a pretty big one. And you can't get a whole lot more isolated. Must be ten miles to the nearest neighbor, easy."

They rode in silence, broken only by the road noise outside the car, barely audible through the closed windows over the welcome hum of the air conditioner. The green blot grew in the windshield, and as they neared, they saw a large white farmhouse nestled in the edge of the trees and a barn and other outbuildings nearby. Jukes looked at Morgan and grinned as the car turned up the long drive.

"Now this might be just the ticket," Jukes said.

HUGHES' RESIDENCE
PECAN GROVE
OLEANDER, TEXAS

DAY 16, 6:15 P.M.

Laura was in the kitchen, putting together a salad for supper as the car turned up the drive. She'd decided to let the girls goof off a bit more, and they were in the air-conditioned guest room, playing video games. It wasn't the best use of generator fuel, but the social isolation was especially hard on the girls. She was learning allowances from time to time made their new lives tolerable.

She looked up at the sound of the tires on gravel and parted the curtains over the sink. Her heart almost stopped at the sight of the police car. A hundred scenarios played out in her mind since the power outage, and among those were half-formed and quickly dismissed visions of official notification of something bad happening to Jordan.

Panic set in as she watched the cop car roll to a stop, and she gripped the edge of the kitchen counter and squeezed her eyes shut to say a short but fervent prayer for her husband's safety. She opened her eyes to look out the window again, studying the car more closely—Jefferson County Sheriff's Department—now that was strange. Two deputies got out of the car and moved towards her front door. She hurried to meet them.

The front door was open in an attempt to catch a bit of a breeze. As she hurried across the living room, she studied the approaching deputies through the latched screen door. They were both large men, their uniforms stretched tightly across muscled shoulders, the short sleeves of their khaki uniform shirts straining around bulging biceps. Both had heavily tattooed forearms. She sensed something was wrong immediately, despite the disarming manner of the first deputy up on the porch. She didn't open the screen door.

"Afternoon, ma'am. How are you?" the deputy asked through the screen.

"I'm fine, officer. How can I help you?" she replied.

"Well, it's us who hope to do the helping," he said. "We're just visiting folks to make sure they got what they need and to see if there's anything we can do to assist."

"Quite commendable," Laura said, "but I'm a bit confused. Y'all crossed the county line about three miles back. This is Chambers County."

The man hesitated only a fraction of a second, then smiled and nodded. "Times like these, we all gotta help each other out, so county lines don't mean much. If folks need help, we'll do our best to give it. Protect and serve, that's what it's all about."

Laura nodded. "Again, quite commendable, but we're fine." She immediately regretted the 'we.'

The man didn't register the plural, he just nodded. "I'd say so. Looks like you have a nice setup here. Is that a generator I hear running?"

"Just a small one. We, that is my husband and I, run it a few hours a day to keep the fridge cool and the freezer in the barn from defrosting. We don't have enough fuel for more than that."

"Well, might be we can help you out with the fuel. I'll check it out when we get back to the office and see if there's some allotment to spare. In the meantime, I guess we'll be going." He turned as if to leave, but the second deputy looked confused. Then the first deputy turned back.

"Actually, there is one thing you could do for us if it ain't too much trouble," he said.

"Yes?"

The man flashed a sheepish grin. "I hate to ask, but bein' as how y'all got a working fridge and all, do you think we could have a couple of glasses of ice water. Cold water's been pretty scarce since the power went out, and we're parched from riding around in that car all day. A cool drink would be welcome."

She hesitated. "Of course. Wait right here and I'll bring it out."

"Thank you kindly," the deputy said, and Laura nodded and turned to go back to the kitchen.

As soon as she was out of their sight, she raced to the kitchen pantry and retrieved the Glock 19, racking the slide to chamber a round before stuffing it into the back of her shorts. She'd considered closing and locking the front door on the pair, but knew they'd break through the latched screen door and the old wooden front door in seconds anyway, and decided not to alert them in order to buy a little time. She left the pantry and raced down the hall to the spare bedroom. The twins looked up in surprise.

"Okay," Laura whispered, "I don't have time to explain. There are some very bad men at the front door. I want you to slip out the back door and hide in the barn until I come get you. The gun safe in the garage is open, so stop on the way and get Dad's shotgun and the .30-30. Be quiet and be careful not to be seen. Do NOT come back to the house until I come to get you, no matter what happens. Do you understand?"

They both started to speak at once, but Julie got her protest out first. "But, Mom—"

"QUIET!" Laura hissed. "No buts. Just do it and do it now!"

"Wh-what if you don't come?" Jana asked. "Wh-what if the men come?"

Laura's face hardened. "Then shoot them. They're dressed like deputies, but they're fakes, so don't hesitate or believe anything they might say to lure you out of hiding. When they… go away… or you shoot them, take the truck and get to the Smiths' house as soon as possible."

"What… what about you?" Julie asked, almost sobbing now.

"Don't worry about me," Laura said, struggling to keep the emotion from her voice. "Now GO!"

Both girls nodded and then wrapped Laura in a fierce group hug. She hugged them back and then broke away, pushing them towards the door, emotion robbing her of the power of speech. In the hall, she watched them move quietly toward the back door, then turned back toward the kitchen, the Glock at the small of her back a cold comfort.

***

Jukes licked his lips as he watched the woman's ass through the screen door as she disappeared around a corner. He tried the screen door and found it latched.

"What we gonna do?" asked Morgan.

"Nothing," Jukes said, "she ain't gotta clue. When she comes back, she'll open the screen door. We'll grab her and have a little party. Easy as pie."

"Why don't we just bust in and grab her now?"

Jukes shook his head. "'Cause this is our new place, dumb ass. There ain't no need to be destructive."

Morgan looked around nervously. "What about her husband?"

"I swear, Morgan, sometimes I think you're dumber than a day-old turd! There ain't no husband, leastwise not close, or he'd of answered the door, now wouldn't he? And if he drives up, we'll hear his tires on the gravel and we give him a nice warm welcome. Maybe we can even let him watch us do his old lady before we kill him. Now you got any other stupid questions?"

Morgan glared at Jukes and fell silent, nursing his resentment.

"How long does it take to pour two glasses of water?" Morgan said.

Jukes looked pissed. "Not this long," he said, and pulled a switchblade from his pocket to pop the blade and slice the screen adjacent to the hook. He pocketed the knife and stuck his hand through the opening. The screen door opened with the shriek of dry hinges.

***

Laura heard the plaintive squeak of the screen door followed by hurried footsteps, and was reaching for the Glock just as the men entered the kitchen, guns drawn. Outmatched, she moved her hand away from the concealed weapon and decided to play for time.

"What is it? What's wrong? I was just getting your water, but I wanted to check the pantry. I think we have a little coffee left, and I thought you might like some."

The lead deputy holstered his sidearm, motioning his partner to do the same.

"Well, that's right nice of you, ma'am," he said, "and sorry to bust in, but we were concerned something might be wrong. Can't be too careful these days, ya know."

Laura nodded and moved toward the fridge. "I'll get that water now."

The big man moved closer—already too close, she realized. He closed the distance between them and pinned her arms to her side in a tight hug.

Laura felt the hard bulk of his body pressing against her, along with evidence of his aroused state. He stank of stale sweat, and his breath confirmed dental hygiene was not a priority. She felt rough stubble scratching her face as he bent and nuzzled her neck. She fought down revulsion and willed herself not to resist. She pressed her body back against him.

He lifted his lips from her neck and drew back to look at her, smiling.

"Well, well, well. Now ain't this a nice little surprise," he said.

Laura managed a smile of her own and shrugged in his grasp. "I'm not stupid. I know you're going to take what you want, so I don't see any need to get hurt in the process."

The man relaxed his grip. "Now that there is a good attitude, and I think we're gonna get along just fine." He spoke back over his shoulder. "What'd I tell you, Morgan. This is gonna work out perfect—"

Laura had worked her right hand to the small of her back, and though still in the loose embrace of her attacker, she whipped the Glock between them and pressed it to the man's crotch.

He looked back at her, anger clouding his face as he squeezed her tighter, which only managed to dig the Glock more forcefully into his crotch.

"That's a nine millimeter with hollow points. I've already used about half the trigger pull, and it's only going to take a twitch to discharge it," Laura said, "so unless you want to start singing soprano, I suggest you let me go and tell your friend over there to put his gun on the kitchen island and lay down on his stomach."

Her attacker dropped his hands to his sides and spoke over his shoulder again, to where his partner had his pistol out, pointed at Laura in a two-handed grip.

"You heard her, Morgan. Do what she says."

"Screw that," said the second man. "I got her dead to rights. I can drop her right now."

"And she twitches and blows my junk away, you idiot. NOW PUT THE GUN DOWN!"

Laura watched the one called Morgan's face as indecision warred with the need to comply. He started to lower his gun to the kitchen island when the sound of a floorboard squeaking came through the door to the hallway. He whirled towards the hallway door, gun still in hand.

"There's somebody else here," he said.

The girls, thought Laura, and as Morgan moved toward the hall doorway with his gun raised, her only instinct was protecting her children. She whipped the Glock from her attacker's crotch toward Morgan.

But freed from the imminent threat of emasculation, her attacker was too fast for her. As she brought the gun up, he hammered her wrist with his left hand before she got a shot off, and the Glock clattered on the floor. Simultaneously, a powerful right fist to her gut doubled her over. She dropped like a rock and lay gasping, her own attacker all but forgotten as she focused on Morgan framed in the hallway door with his gun drawn. Then there was a deafening blast and the back of Morgan's shirt erupted in a red mist as he sailed backwards to land on the kitchen floor, a lifeless lump.

"MOM?" she heard, followed by running footsteps, and her blood ran cold as she whipped her head toward the remaining attacker. He had his own gun out, ignoring her to focus on the immediate threat. He dropped behind the cover of the kitchen island, only his right knee visible to her as he crouched, waiting for his target to appear in the hallway door.

The footsteps were coming closer, but her attempts to call out a warning yielded a barely audible croak. She spotted her Glock halfway to the fridge and clawed her way toward it, forcing her oxygen-starved body to move, reaching the gun a scant second before her daughters burst into the kitchen. She flopped over on her back and sent a round into her attacker's exposed knee.

The man screamed in pain as he collapsed on the floor, his body in full sight now as he brought his own gun to bear. But Laura was faster and put shot after shot center mass, not stopping until the slide locked open and her hand started shaking so badly the gun fell from her hand and clattered on the floor beside her.

And then her daughters were beside her, and she hugged them tight with trembling arms and sobbed great racking sobs, and vowed come what may in this strange new world, no one would harm her children while there was life in her body.

**

They were big men, with the heavy musculature of bodybuilders, and it took improvisation to get the bodies into the trunk of the police car. Laura backed the cruiser up to the front porch and she and her daughters dragged the bodies most of the way on a plastic shower curtain before spanning the distance between the open trunk and the elevated porch with planks from the barn. Even at that, it was over an hour after they started when they rolled the second body in and closed the trunk.

"Okay," Laura said, "I'm going to park this out of sight in the barn until we're ready to leave. Y'all get cleaned up and make sure you get all the blood off. I'll do the same when I get back, but I don't want to take too long. I want to be rid of them before anyone comes looking."

The girls gave subdued nods, and Laura's heart went out to them. She'd have done anything to spare them the grisly task, but it was simply beyond her physical capability to do it alone.

"What are we going to do with them?" Julie asked quietly.

"I'm gonna drive their car to the Boyd's Bayou crossing down the road. You girls will follow me in the truck, and when we get there, we'll push their car into the bayou. We've had a lot of rain, so the water should be deep enough to cover it."

"But we can't drive," Jana said. "We don't even have our learner permits yet."

Laura shook her head. "But you both know HOW to drive. Dad's been letting you drive the truck around the pasture for two years."

"But what if the police... oh yeah. I guess that's not really a big deal," Jana said.

Laura nodded, longing for a time when a ticket for driving without a license was the worst thing they had to worry about.

"All right, go get cleaned up. I'll be right back," she said.

Half an hour later, Laura was behind the wheel of the cruiser as she turned on to the county road, hoping against hope they didn't encounter any other traffic. She looked in the rearview mirror and confirmed the girls were following at a safe distance, then looked back to the road ahead, second-guessing her hastily devised plan. The bayou was about fifty feet wide and varied from four to eight feet in depth, depending on the season. They'd had a fair amount of rain over the last few weeks, but the bottom of the canal was irregular. What if there wasn't enough water near the bridge to cover the car? She willed herself to stop worrying and focus on the task at hand. She didn't have a better plan. This one had to work.

After the longest four miles she'd ever driven, she spotted the bridge, a low, unimposing concrete span raised a few feet higher than the road to accommodate the bayou at full flood, approached by a gradual ramp on either end and fitted with steel guardrails on each side. She slowed, coasting to a stop near the top of the slight incline just before entering the bridge proper. She put the cruiser in park and rolled down all four windows, then cut the wheels to the right and left them there. She got out just as the girls stopped behind her, and motioned them out of the truck.

"Okay, I'm gonna get in the truck and pull it up against the back bumper of the cop car so it doesn't roll backward. I want one of you to get in the cop car and put it in neutral, then get out and shut the door and get well out of the way. Got it?"

Both girls nodded. "I'll do it," Julie said, moving to the cop car as Laura climbed behind the wheel of the truck.

When Julie completed the task and both girls were safely on the other side of the narrow road, Laura pressed the accelerator. As soon as the cop car started to move, she mashed down hard, sending both vehicles surging forward twenty feet before she stomped the brakes, stopping the truck as the police car shot off the road and bounced down the slight embankment toward the bayou. It hit the water with a grand splash and plowed forward, sending a bow wave to bounce off the opposite bank. It sank steadily, the weight of the engine pulling the front end deeper, until water began to pour into the open windows and the car plunged under the water.

Almost.

The car came to rest with a narrow strip of the trunk lid showing, reading SHERIFF in bright green letters against a white background. Laura watched it with a lump in her stomach and willed it to sink. It didn't.

"What are we going to do, Mom?"

She turned to find Jana and Julie beside her, looking down at the still-visible evidence of their deed.

"Not much we can do, except maybe pray for rain. Get in, girls, we need to get out of here before anyone sees us."

CHAPTER SIXTEEN

FEMA
EMERGENCY OPERATIONS CENTER
MOUNT WEATHER
NEAR BLUEMONT, VA

DAY 17, 5:00 A.M.

Congressman Simon Tremble sipped the coffee, his appreciation of the improvement in rations since he'd 'joined the team' tempered by the knowledge of widespread privation outside the privileged bubble of Mount Weather. He set the mug on the coffee table and picked up the bound notes for the 'briefing' he was scheduled to deliver over the FEMA National Radio System. He shook his head and tossed the offensive document across the room.

It was little more than a scripted cheerleading session, full of lies about 'help being on the way,' and assurances 'things will be improving soon.' He had difficulty reading it without flying into a rage, and he knew he could never speak those words into a microphone without betraying all he held dear. He stood and paced the living area of the small apartment he shared with his son, then stopped to look out the window at the lush foliage just becoming visible in the growing light of predawn. Sunlight and scenery was one advantage at least, of being 'special guests' of the President.

The massive underground complex at Weather Mountain teemed with bureaucrats and their lackeys, and it would be all but impossible to sequester anyone there confidentially. But spread over more than four hundred acres of mountaintop, the sprawling surface facility over the underground complex was impressive in its own right, and separate buildings lined roads winding through strips of untouched woodland. Tremble and his son were on the third floor of just such a building, at the far end of an access road with no internal traffic.

The whereabouts and involuntary nature of the residence of the former Speaker of the House of Representatives was on a need-to-know basis. The windows were sealed and there was a twenty-four-hour guard, always one of the same three men on rotating eight-hour shifts, with the guard who came on at six a.m. every morning providing their daily rations.

The guards were stone-faced, communicating by gestures and curt commands, obviously instructed to limit interaction. Tremble gently chided them at every opportunity, carrying on unfailingly pleasant, if one-sided conversations, telling jokes and doing anything he could to provoke a reaction. None wore name tags, but he'd named them all, and called them by their fictitious names. Come what may, it wouldn't hurt if their keepers viewed him and Keith as people, rather than assignments. He had no doubt these same guards might one day be given other, harsher orders, and if he built some rapport, no matter how tenuous, the guards' actions or facial expressions might telegraph the change.

He'd made most headway with the guard he'd named Sam, the morning man who brought the daily food ration. In recent days Tremble had even seen a suppressed smile tugging at the corners of Sam's mouth from time to time as he delivered the punchline of a particularly funny joke. Not much, but it was there. Sam, or whatever his real name was, acted a bit less guarded when he came into the apartment with the rations or when he stuck his head in for the head count every two hours.

Tremble picked up on other things as well. The guards did periodic visual checks during the day and entered the apartment to check on their sleeping forms at night, which told him electronic surveillance was unlikely. That made sense given the 'ad hoc' nature of their confinement in a totally isolated and secure facility like Mount Weather. Apparently neither the President nor the Secretary of Homeland Security felt there were any conversations between Tremble and his teenage son that warranted eavesdropping. If only the bastards knew.

His thoughts returned to Keith, the center of his universe for the ten years since cancer had taken Jane. He'd do anything to keep his son safe, but he knew Keith would never be safe under Gleason and Crawford's control. Tremble had no doubt as soon as he'd served his purpose, both he and Keith were loose ends. His worry was tempered with pride at Keith's response when he'd explained the situation to him yesterday, just laying out the facts without attempting to influence his son's opinion. Keith had fallen silent while he weighed the options.

"Do you really think President Gleason is setting himself up to be some sort of dictator?" Keith asked.

"A month ago, I'd have laughed at the suggestion," Tremble replied, "but after meeting him face to face, I have no doubt. As the saying goes, power corrupts and absolute power corrupts absolutely. If he has his way, we may get limited electrical power restored to serve the needs of those he's deemed worthy of saving, but we'll have paid for it with the complete loss of democracy."

"Then there are no options, Dad. You can't do what they want, and I'm sure not becoming one of their thugs. They might as well kill us both now. We know they're probably going to sooner or later anyway. On the other hand, as soon as you resist, they may separate us to increase the leverage, so I'd say pretend to go along and then we take a shot at getting out of here. Right now they need you, so they'll be hesitant to kill you, and if they kill me, they know you won't cooperate. That means if we try and fail, we're not any worse off than we are now."

From the mouths of babes, Tremble recalled thinking, then revised the thought—at eighteen, his son was a powerfully built young man and mature beyond his years. When did that happen? he wondered, a wistful smile on his face. Keith's bedroom door opened and his son walked into the living area, fully clothed.

"Fresh coffee in the pot," Tremble said, nodding toward the small kitchenette.

Keith returned his nod. "Might as well enjoy it while we can." He moved toward the kitchen, returning a moment later with cup in hand to sprawl on one end of the small sofa.

"You been up all night?"

"Since about two," Tremble replied, "I woke up and couldn't go back to sleep. I was just about to come in and wake you."

Keith shook his head. "I've been awake an hour or so myself. Nerves, I guess."

Tremble nodded. "Same here. You sure you're okay with this, son? Maybe I can play them a little while longer and form a better plan?"

"But what if they separate us? Then we're screwed. We're on borrowed time as it is, Dad."

Tremble nodded again and fished something out of the back pocket of his slacks before sitting down on the couch beside Keith and handing him the flattened ziplock bag. Inside was a document, folded small.

"What's this?"

"You've read it," Tremble said. "It's my official copy of Secretary Crawford's memo to the President detailing the 'recovery plan.' I got a copy because I was Speaker, and since we were already 'sequestered,' no one bothered to take it back. I put it in one of the ziplock bags from our food ration to protect it. I want you to take it."

"But why? You should keep it to prove—"

Tremble cut him off. "We have to get word out about what's going on. If we both make it, I'll take it back and get copies spread around. But if... if I don't make it, nobody is likely to take the word of an eighteen-year-old kid. I'm sorry, that's a fact. However, some documentation gives you at least a fighting chance to be heard. And if... if..."

"If I don't make it," Keith finished for him. "You're Speaker of the House, so people are much more likely to take your word without any backup documentation. Okay, Dad, I got it. Makes sense."

Tremble nodded and glanced at his watch. "Sam should be bringing the food soon. Let's go over the plan again.

'Sam' was right on time, and forty-five minutes later Tremble and his son were sitting on the sofa when they heard the low murmur of conversation outside the door, signaling the change of shift. Tremble nodded to Keith and pretended to turn his attention to the briefing script while his son quickly retreated to the small bathroom. There was a tap on the door before it opened to reveal the more genial of their keepers, who closed the door behind himself and moved toward the kitchenette with a plastic grocery bag, looking around as he did so, as was his routine.

"Good morning, Sam," Tremble said, "and what wonderful treats did you bring us today?"

The man scowled as he set the bag on the small counter separating the living area and kitchenette. "Where's the kid? I gotta see you both for shift change. You know that."

Tremble inclined his head toward the bathroom door. "Answering the call of nature, I'm afraid. I'm sure he'll be out any time." Tremble rose and walked toward the kitchenette. "There's fresh coffee, want a cup?"

The man shook his head as Tremble moved past him into the kitchen to refill his empty cup and returned to lean with his butt against the counter. He held the coffee in his left hand and studied the guard standing a few feet away, glaring at the bathroom door.

"KEITH! HURRY UP AND GET OUT HERE. SAM'S WAITING," Tremble yelled. The door to the bathroom opened, right on cue.

Keith came out muttering apologies, then stumbled and went down on one knee, drawing Sam's full attention. Tremble threw scalding coffee into the guard's face, and the man closed his eyes reflexively and stepped back, groping blindly for his sidearm. Tremble connected with a rising punch starting from his waist and landing on the point of the guard's chin, snapping the man's mouth shut and dropping him like a rock. Tremble was on top of the unconscious man immediately, stripping him of sidearm and stun gun, and handing Keith the man's handcuffs as his son reached his side.

"Hurry. Turn him on his stomach and cuff his hands behind his back in case he comes to," Tremble whispered. "Pete will be outside waiting for Sam to take over the shift so he can leave."

No sooner had Tremble spoken than the doorknob began to turn, and he crossed the small living area in four long strides and stepped behind the opening door. 'Pete' rounded the door to find a nine millimeter an inch away from his forehead.

"Just come on in, Pete. Lock your fingers behind your head, and don't make any sudden moves. I don't want to kill you, but I will if you make me." Tremble's tone left no doubt he meant it.

'Pete' nodded, his eyes wide, and did as instructed as Tremble closed the door with his foot, then pressed his back against it until the latch clicked, never once losing focus on the man in front of him. He instructed his captive to face the wall, then used his free hand to remove the guard's sidearm.

"Now keep looking at the wall and strip, very slowly," Tremble said. "One wrong move and you're dead."

The guard complied, and as soon as he was down to his underwear, Tremble instructed him to lay on this stomach and held the gun on him while Keith cuffed the man with his own handcuffs, bound his feet, and gagged him with strips torn from a bed sheet. Together, they then uncuffed and undressed 'Sam,' who was regaining consciousness but showing no signs of fight. When they finished, they put the cuffs back on and bound his feet and gagged him before stripping their own clothes to don the uniforms.

Keith finished first and sat down on the couch with one of the pairs of boots. He looked inside the shoe and quickly pulled his face back. "Whew! Sam here could use some odor-eaters, that's one rank pair of boots. Anyway, they're elevens. That'll work for me. How are yours."

Tremble sat down beside his son and checked the other guard's boots. "They're twelves, I'm good."

Moments later they stood side by side at a wall mirror.

"What do you think, Dad?"

"Close enough," Tremble said. "If we pull the caps low, we can definitely pass at a distance, at least until they raise the alarm."

"What now?" Keith asked.

Tremble held up the keys he'd fished out of 'Pete's' pocket. "I didn't see any security cameras on the buildings here. My guess is the bulk of the security effort is concentrated on the perimeter fences. So we get in their car and just try to drive out. Best I can tell from listening through the door, they report in randomly, but Pete here was due off shift, so we don't know if his failure to show up or log out someplace might set off an alarm. We'll keep his radio, so maybe we'll know if anyone starts getting suspicious."

"All right. Let's do it," Keith said, but his father hesitated, casting a pointed look at Keith's sidearm.

"You okay with that?"

"I've used it at the range, I'm good," Keith said.

"Trust me, shooting at another human being who's shooting back at you is quite a bit different. Don't hesitate to use it if you have to, but understand up front it's not nearly as easy as you think. You need to get your mind around that, because it could save your life."

Keith swallowed and nodded, and Tremble pulled him into an embrace. "I love you, son."

"I love you too, Dad."

Tremble fought down his own emotion and patted his son on the back.

Two minutes later, caps pulled low, they were in a black SUV moving at the posted speed limit along a well-paved road winding uphill through the western half of the complex. There were only a few people moving around the many buildings they passed, and Tremble heaved a relieved sigh. The early hour was working in their favor.

"How much further?" Keith asked.

"A mile or so on this road because of all the switchbacks," Tremble said, "then we'll pass over Blue Ridge Mountain Road. That's a state highway that cuts the camp in two. They couldn't close it, so they put high fences on either side and then built an overpass on this road to connect the east and west halves of the surface facility. The overpass is just around the next bend. After the overpass, we pass the back side of the main gate security building one street over and go down about two hundred yards to make a one-eighty back toward the gate. Then it might get hairy."

"So we just drive through the gate? No one's gonna stop us?"

"Not hardly, that's why it gets hairy, but the security is set up to keep people out and we've got that going for us. That and human nature."

"I don't follow," Keith said.

"There are steel barrier posts at the gate which hydraulically retract into the pavement to let vehicles pass. They're kept deployed on the entrance side of the gate and have to be lowered every time to admit a vehicle. The same thing is SUPPOSED to be true on the exit side, but it takes a minute or so to raise and lower the posts and is a bit of a pain in the ass. The bigger concern has always been people coming in rather than going out, and I noticed the few times I've been here the barrier posts on the exit gate were kept down in favor of using the secondary, and fairly flimsy, bar gate. We're pretty remote here, without much in the way of external threats, so I'm hoping they haven't changed their ways. We can crash the lift bar."

"What happens if the posts are up on the exit gate?"

Tremble's jaw tightened. "Then we're screwed."

They made the sweeping turn in silence and were moving across the overpass when the radio sprang to life.

"Unit Twelve, this is Control. Do you copy? Over."

Keith looked at Tremble. "So are we Unit Twelve?"

"Not a clue, but I'm guessing yes," Tremble said.

"Should we answer?"

"No. We don't know their communications protocol and risk alerting them if we say the wrong thing. If we're silent, they might get antsy, but they'll still be unsure. We're only a couple of minutes from the gate, and that's his first call. He'll probably try at least a couple of times before sounding an alarm. The cat's out of the bag when we crash the gate anyway, but maybe we can get there before anyone picks up the problem."

Keith nodded. They rode in silence, the back of the main gate security building visible one road over on the left. The radio squawked again.

"Unit Twelve, what is your status? Respond immediately. Over."

"Sounds like he's at the antsy stage," Keith said as his father slowed to make the U-turn back toward the main gate.

"All we need is a bit more time, and then it won't make any difference," Tremble said as he turned the SUV. As the exit lane became visible, he let out a relieved sigh. "Thank God, the posts are down!"

He increased speed, the gate now only a hundred yards away. The next transmission dampened his elation.

"All stations, repeat, all stations. This is Control. We have a non-responding unit. Initiate Protocol Alpha. Repeat, initiate Protocol Alpha."

"Hang on!" Tremble said as he saw the guard in the glass booth look down and press something on the console in front of him. He stomped the accelerator and held it there as the tops of the barrier posts began to peek from the pavement ahead.

"Air bags!" thought Tremble, much too late, as the SUV blew by the startled guard and hit the bar gate, smashing both front headlights. The heavy vehicle brushed the lift bar out of the way without slowing or bumper contact and the air bags didn't deploy. A fraction of a second later, the front tires contacted the rising barrier posts, now ten inches above the ground, and the vehicle leaped airborne, throwing both occupants forward against their straining shoulder belts, inducing a brief feeling of weightlessness before the vehicle crashed down. Again their luck held as the posts were below bumper level and the deceleration alone was insufficient to trigger the air bags.

The SUV careened down the road, tires shrieking, as Tremble fought for control. For three long, heart-stopping seconds, the issue was in doubt. Then he regained control and once again floored it, rushing toward the intersection ahead. Barely slowing, he turned north on Blue Ridge Mountain Road, roaring onto the two-lane blacktop in a controlled skid, then stomping the accelerator once again. He glanced to his right to see his son ashen-faced, knuckles white as he gripped the grab rail. Slowly Keith's face split into a wide grin.

"You did it, Dad! Where we going now?"

"Away from here," Tremble said, "but we won't have long. They'll be after us in a heartbeat and we have to—"

There was a loud bang and the SUV lurched to the right, once again testing Tremble as he fought the car to a stop on the shoulder. They both jumped out and looked down at the shredded right front tire.

"Damn it!" Tremble said. "I guess the damn posts got us after all. Must have weakened the tire."

"Let's change it," Keith said, starting for the rear.

"No time. Get back in. Driving on a flat's still faster than we can move on foot. We'll drive as fast and as far as we can, and abandon it on some side road out of sight. We were going to have to ditch it anyway, but if we can delay them finding it, the more time we'll have to get away.

PRESIDENTIAL QUARTERS
CAMP DAVID, MARYLAND

DAY 17, 6:25 A.M.

Gleason opened his eyes at the low buzz, groggy as he peered through the gloom at the glowing face of the alarm clock. Why the hell was the alarm going off? He groped for the button to kill the noise, then cursed as he overturned a glass of water on the bedside table. Fully awake now, he sat up as he realized the low trilling was not the alarm but the phone.

"What?" he barked into the receiver.

"Mr. President, I'm sorry to disturb you —"

"Then why the hell did you? What was so important it couldn't wait an hour or so?"

"Mr. President, I have Secretary Crawford on the secure link from Weather Mountain. I tried to take a message, but he insisted —"

"All right, all right. Just put him through."

"Yes sir," the operator said, and Crawford's voice came on the line.

"Good morning, Mr. President —"

"No, Ollie, it's not good morning. It will be a good morning in an hour or so when I've had my coffee. Now what's so damned important it couldn't wait until then?"

"It's Tremble, Mr. President. I'm afraid there's been a problem."

"Look, we've been over this. If he's not cooperating, squeeze the kid. He'll come around."

"I'm afraid Tremble… Tremble isn't here any longer."

"What the hell are you talking about? What do you mean 'not here'? Where the hell else would he be? Did you move him someplace?"

"I'm afraid he's… he's escaped, Mr. President."

Gleason struggled to contain himself. When he spoke, his voice was full of quiet menace. "And how did that happen, Ollie?"

"He and his son overpowered their guards, stole their uniforms, and escaped in their vehicle."

"So you're telling me a paunchy fifty-year-old politician and his pimply-faced teenage son overpowered two of your overpaid FEMA troopers and escaped from what is supposed to be one of the most secure facilities in North America. Is that what you're telling me?"

"Tremble is far from a sedentary politician and you know it. He was an airborne officer and served in both Iraq and Afghanistan. In fact, he still holds a commission in the North Carolina —"

"OF COURSE I KNOW THAT, YOU FRIGGIN' IDIOT! AND SO DO YOU! SO WHY THE HELL WEREN'T YOU WATCHING HIM MORE CLOSELY?"

Silence grew on the line in the wake of Gleason's outburst, broken by a sigh.

"All right, when did they escape and what are you doing to recapture them?"

"Less than ten minutes ago. A two-man chase team is leaving now and we're mobilizing a larger effort and preflighting the chopper in case we need it. The good news is there aren't many roads they can take, and the better news is all the facility vehicles have trackers. We know right where they are. Right now, they're headed north on Blue Mountain Road, at about thirty miles an hour, so we figure their car must be damaged. I'm confident we'll have them surrounded in less than an hour, but that's really not the reason I awakened you, Mr. President."

"Then what?"

"They're armed, and I doubt they'll surrender willingly so…"

"So you want permission to take them out, is that it?"

"I don't see any reason to risk good men —"

"Well, let me give you one. You screwed things up with Senator Leddy completely. First you killed his wife in front of him—"

"With respect, Mr. President, how was I to know she had a heart condition? It wasn't in the medical record."

"All right, all right. It's a damned waste, but the PR broadcasts will likely only buy us a few more weeks of calm compliance in limited areas anyway. So the preference is to take Tremble and his son alive, but take them out if you must. However, make those knuckleheads of yours understand that's not plan A. In fact, I don't want them taken out unless you PERSONALLY determine it's necessary. Is that clear?"

"Yes, Mr. President," Crawford said.

"And Ollie?"

"Yes, Mr. President?"

"It goes without saying anyone our fugitives make contact with may learn more than is good for them — or us. You take my meaning?"

"Absolutely, Mr. President. There will be no witnesses."

VIRGINIA STATE ROAD 601
AKA BLUE RIDGE MOUNTAIN ROAD
NEAR BLUEMONT, VIRGINIA

DAY 17, 6:39 A.M.

The SUV leaned right. Tremble nursed it along at thirty-five miles an hour, right side tires in the grassy verge. Of course 'tires' was a bit of a stretch, because the remains of the right front tire left them some miles back, its remnants spread all over the pavement behind them. The bare rim on pavement had been deafening, but worse than the noise was the incriminating evidence. Tremble had glanced in the mirror to see a line chewed in the pavement by the battered steel rim, leaving a trail a blind man could follow.

His attempts to compensate were only partially successful. Running with the right wheels off the pavement lessened the noise and left a much less obvious track, but they were still leaving a visible trail. And the steel rim digging into the dirt of the verge made the vehicle increasingly difficult to steer. Even with power steering, he was fighting the wheel constantly, his forearms aching from the effort.

"This is no good, Keith," he said. "We need to ditch the car. We're going too slow and our tracks will lead them right to us."

"There's a turnoff just up ahead on the left, you think it's a through road?"

Tremble shook his head. "I doubt there are any before we get to Highway 7, but we'll take it as far as it goes. We knew we'd have to take our chances on foot anyway. These woods are thick and we'll find a place to hide."

Keith nodded and Tremble horsed the wheel to the left, grimacing as the bare rim clanked and chewed its way across the pavement, leaving the equivalent of a flashing neon sign pointing in the direction of their flight.

BEAR'S DEN HOSTEL
18393 BLUE RIDGE MOUNTAIN ROAD
NEAR BLUEMONT, VIRGINIA

DAY 17, 6:40 A.M.

"That feels a LOT better," Bill Wiggins said as he walked around the lounge area, alternating between walking and raising himself on tiptoe. "It still hurts, but not nearly as bad."

Tex shook her head. "Better than nothing, that's for sure."

Necessity was the mother of invention, and they'd cut up the ample supply of washcloths in the hostel bathroom to pad the overly spacious toes of their work boots. It wasn't perfect, but it would cushion their toes somewhat going downhill.

Bill laughed. "Now if we could just figure out a way to get a couple of these mattresses in our packs, we'd have it made. That was the best sleep I ever had last night, bugs and all."

Tex nodded. "Me too. You ready to head out?"

"Ready as I'll ever be, I guess…" He stopped. "Hear that?"

She cocked an ear. "Something heading this way, but making too much racket to be a car. What do you think it is?"

"I don't know," Wiggins said, hefting his pack, "but no one we've met so far has been friendly, so I don't think we should be here when whoever it is arrives. Let's get into the woods. We can watch from there and just haul ass after we check it out."

Tex shouldered her pack to follow Wiggins out the door.

They jogged the well-worn path across the clearing to the AT access point, then darted off the path at the tree line, hiding behind adjacent tree trunks. As they waited, the sound of a laboring engine grew louder, accompanied by another sound neither could identify. The vehicle lurched into view, leaning to the right, and the mystery was solved. The tireless rim of the right front wheel slung gravel into the wheel well, producing a roar that almost drowned out the engine noise. The car stopped abruptly and disgorged two uniformed men, sidearms visible even at a distance.

"What do you make of that?" Tex asked quietly.

"Nothing good. Let's get the hell out of here," Wiggins said. They melted back into the woods and started downhill toward the AT, aching toes momentarily forgotten in the adrenaline rush to put this latest threat behind them.

***

Tremble got out of the car and looked around as Keith moved by his side. Their heads jerked in unison at the sound of an engine heard faintly through the dense woods.

"Damn! Already? I figured we'd have more time."

Keith pointed to the path worn through the clearing and they both started down it at a run.

"We'll follow this and get as deep in the woods as we can. If we hear them following, then we find a place to ambush them. We have to break contact or we don't stand a chance," shouted Tremble as they ran. Keith nodded his understanding.

***

Bill Wiggins turned back on to the AT and continued down the steep incline at a breakneck pace, his heavy pack adding to his downward momentum as he struggled to keep his feet on the rock-strewn path. His heart was pounding and he could hear Tex's labored breathing. Well behind them, he heard the faint sound of others crashing down the same path. They'd never outrun anyone, encumbered as they were with the heavy packs. He spotted a row of saplings lining the trail, and changed course slightly to grab the trunk of the first as he passed, clutching it momentarily to check his speed before releasing it to grab the next, bringing himself to a halt while remaining upright. Behind him, Tex followed suit, stumbling to a halt beside him. The sound of pursuit was unmistakable now.

"Why the hell are they chasing us?"

"I don't think they are," Wiggins said between labored breaths. "They can't even know we're here, and I'd like to keep it that way. I say we go off the trail and hide. After they get well ahead, we'll get back on the trail. If they double back, we should hear them before they see us, and we'll just reverse the process."

Wiggins nodded and they moved off the trail into the woods to once again hide behind tree trunks. Less than two minutes later the men flashed by, unencumbered by backpacks and racing downhill as if the devil were on their heels. They looked to be policemen of some sort, but why they were here was a total mystery. Not my problem, thought Wiggins, just stay the hell away from us.

The sound faded quickly, and Wiggins waited a couple of minutes before he turned to Tex.

"What do you think?"

"The guidebook shows it as steep downhill for another mile or so, through Snicker's Gap and across State Route 7. At the rate they're moving, I'd say we can maintain a good walking pace without too much fear of running into them."

Wiggins nodded and they moved back toward the trail. They were almost there when he felt something wrong. "Damn!" he said, staring down at his foot. "My lace broke."

"Can you tie it back together?"

"It'll probably just break again. Levi put some paracord in our packs, I'll just use some of that." Wiggins shucked off his pack and sat on a fallen log.

"I'll wait for you on the trail," Tex said. "I've given the ticks enough opportunity to crawl aboard, brushing through all this foliage."

Wiggins nodded absently, digging through the pack in search of the paracord, as Tex moved back on to the trail. He was pulling his improvised lace tight when a sharp command pierced the foliage.

"Freeze! And keep your hands where I can see them."

He dropped off the log onto his knees and crawled toward the trail, slowly separating foliage with his hand. Tex was facing one of the uniformed men and staring into the muzzle of an M4. Where the hell did that assault rifle come from and how'd they get back up the hill without us hearing? he wondered.

"Very slowly, turn and then drop the pack, put your hands on the back of your head, and get down on your knees," the man said.

Tex moved to comply. As the pack slid down her back and to the side, it tugged her shirttail over, exposing the Glock.

"Gun!" screamed the man, rushing forward with his M4 trained on Tex to kick her hard in the back, driving her face down on the path. He squatted and thrust his gun to the side of her head. Rage boiled up in Wiggins as another man rushed into sight, his own rifle slung, and quickly tossed Tex's Glock to the side. Wiggins heard Tex gasping for breath as the second man patted her down none too gently.

"Clean," said the second uniform, and the first man nodded. They dragged Tex to her feet.

"We're looking for two men dressed like us. Have you seen them?" the first uniform asked.

Tex nodded, unable to speak.

"When?"

"A… a few minutes… they ran by…"

"What did they say to you?"

Tex shook her head. "No… nothing… I… I hid in the woods."

"Why are you armed?"

"Pr… protection," Tex gasped.

The first uniform ran out of questions.

"What the hell we gonna do with her?" the second man asked. The man's face was heavily bruised, as if he'd been beaten.

"She saw them, you know the orders."

"Yeah, I know the orders, but I'm not doing it on the strength of a verbal."

The first man seemed ready to explode. "Look, asshole, it's your fault we're on the shit list for letting Tremble and the kid escape, so don't get us in even deeper by questioning orders! I had to do some fast talking to get them to let us head out first, and if we don't get 'em back, we'll probably both be in a 'fugee camp this time tomorrow."

"All right, then call it in for confirmation, and we can update Control at the same time. If they stay on the AT, they have to cross Highway 7. They can chopper a team there and we'll drive them right into their arms."

The first uniform shook his head. "You just don't get it, do you, Anderson? We do it that way and we'll get no credit at all. If we make the collar ourselves, it'll wipe out our screwup and we have a chance of redeeming ourselves and maybe hanging around a while—"

"But—"

"STOW IT! Cuff her arms around that tree over there and let's get on with it. We'll deal with her later."

Wiggins crept backwards and eased the little survival rifle out of his pack, moving soundlessly as he assembled it. He didn't like his chances, but he sure as hell wasn't letting them harm Tex without a fight. He slipped a magazine into the rifle and crept back through the foliage just as the two uniforms set off down the trail. He let them get out of sight then crossed the trail.

"Are you okay?" he whispered.

"Just peachy, except for being kicked in the middle of the back by a two-hundred-pound asshole. How are you at picking handcuff locks?"

"Not in my skill set, I'm afraid. But we'll figure out something. Did they take your gun?"

She shook her head. "I think they threw it over there where they put my pack."

Wiggins walked over and found the Glock. He shoved it in his waistband, then came back and studied the handcuffs.

"There's a wire saw in the pack, maybe I could cut through the tree," he said.

"This damn tree is almost a foot thick, Bill. It'll take you forever, and besides, even if you do my hands are still cuffed together."

"But we can find a place to hide and figure out a way to get them off. Besides, from what I overheard, it didn't sound like having seen those mystery guys was very healthy. You can't be here when those assholes get back."

Tex nodded, but Wiggins was already in the woods fishing in his pack for the wire saw. He shook it out of the little Altoids tin Levi stored it in and uncoiled it to cut a length of a one-inch-diameter branch from a nearby tree, then bent the branch and used paracord to secure the wire saw to both ends, improvising a bow saw.

"Sit on the ground and straddle the trunk," he said. "If I can cut it low, maybe when I weaken it enough I can push against it and snap it off."

Tex did as instructed, and Wiggins began sawing about six inches above the top of her head. The little saw ripped into the bark and the first inch of the tree as sawdust drifted down on Tex. Each stroke widened the cut and friction increased. Progress slowed exponentially.

Sweat dripped from Wiggins' forehead and his arm was already burning, but he gritted his teeth and pressed on.

"This might take a while," he said between labored breaths.

"It's not like I'm going anywhere," Tex replied.

***

In the end, their ambush site was chosen for them. Keith hurtled down the trail and landed on a loose rock, twisting his ankle to tumble head over heels down the steep slope. His father was several yards back, hard-pressed to keep up with Keith's youthful athleticism. He pulled up, trying to halt his own headlong rush, and managed a controlled fall back on his ass in preference to a face-plant down the hill. His forward progress stopped, he scrambled over to where his son sprawled on the trail, shaken and moaning.

"Keith, are you all right?"

"I twisted my right ankle. It hurts like hell."

Tremble raised the boy's pant leg and pulled down his sock, eliciting a soft moan. The ankle was starting to discolor and swell, but everything looked to be lined up correctly.

"I don't think it's broken, but you won't be running on that," Tremble said.

"I'm sorry, Dad. I screwed up big time."

Tremble forced a smile and patted his son's good leg. "No problem. We needed to set up an ambush anyway, and I guess this is as good a site as any." He pointed to large boulders on either side of the trail. "We've got good cover. If we take them down fast, we can still get away."

Keith shook his head. "You know even if we do, there'll be others, and we can't move fast enough to lose them now. It's better if I hold them off so you can build up a lead and get away. You have to let people know what's going on."

"Not happening, son. If I escape, you're just a liability. I doubt they'd even bother to take you back to Mount Weather."

"But, Dad—"

"No buts. Give me your hand and I'll get you set up behind one of these boulders. I don't know how many of them there are, but I'll take the left side and you take the right. Don't fire until I do, okay?"

"Yes, sir," Keith said and gave his father his hand.

***

Tremble was beginning to hope their pursuers had somehow missed the trail, when he heard muffled grunts of exertion uphill through the foliage. Keith nodded—he'd heard it as well. Tremble's heart sank when he caught glimpses of their adversaries through the foliage; both were wearing body armor and carrying long guns. That meant head shots, hard enough with a rifle, much less a handgun. He took in a deep breath and exhaled, then steadied himself, his pistol in a two-handed grip, arms resting on the flat top of the boulder—and waited.

Both men came into view and Tremble aimed at the man in the lead, firing as soon as he had a shot. He was gratified to see the man fall as Keith opened up beside him, sending a fusillade uphill and driving the second man to cover.

"Easy, son," Tremble called softly. "Conserve your ammo."

"You got one!" Keith whispered back, an elation in his voice Tremble didn't feel, knowing the fight was far from over.

***

'Sam' crawled through the foliage to where 'Pete' was kneeling behind a large rock, blood dripping from his right ear.

"You're hit!"

"The asshole took off a piece of my earlobe. I'll live."

"What are we gonna do?"

"I'm gonna stay here and keep their attention. You go into the woods on the right and work your way downhill off the trail. When you get in position below them with a good field of fire, fire a warning shot to let them know you can take them out at any time. If they don't surrender, shoot them both in the legs. Got it?"

Sam nodded and slipped quietly away through the foliage as his partner yelled downhill.

"IT'S ALL OVER, TREMBLE. YOU AND THE BOY LAY DOWN YOUR GUNS AND COME OUT WITH YOUR HANDS WHERE I CAN SEE THEM."

"THAT YOU, PETE? HOW'S SAM? SORRY I HAD TO HIT HIM."

"YEAH, IT'S ME. AND YOU CAN ASK HIM YOURSELF AS SOON AS YOU SURRENDER, BUT HE'S NOT TALKING TOO GOOD NOW ON ACCOUNT OF HOW YOU ALMOST BROKE HIS JAW. NOW DO AS I SAY AND NO ONE WILL GET HURT."

"WHY WOULD I DO THAT?"

"OH, I DON'T KNOW. MAYBE BECAUSE YOU'RE CUT OFF AND ANOTHER TEAM IS COMING UP THE TRAIL ON YOUR SIX EVEN AS WE SPEAK. ALSO BECAUSE OUR ORDERS ARE TO TAKE YOU ALIVE IF POSSIBLE BUT NOT TO RISK CASUALTIES DOING IT, BUT SINCE YOU'VE ALREADY SHOT AT US, WE CAN KILL YOU RIGHT NOW, NO QUESTIONS ASKED. YOU'RE NOT GETTING AWAY, SO THE ONLY QUESTION IS WHETHER YOU AND SONNY BOY LEAVE THESE WOODS ON YOUR OWN TWO FEET OR IN BODY BAGS. YOUR CALL, TREMBLE. I'M GOOD EITHER WAY."

"WELL, LET ME JUST THINK ABOUT THAT, PETE."

"SURE, TAKE YOUR TIME, ANYTIME WITHIN THE NEXT TEN SECONDS WILL BE FINE."

There was no response for several minutes and the man's impatience grew. Then there was the crack of a gunshot followed by the whine of a ricocheting round. The man smiled.

"AND THAT WOULD BE THE FIRE TEAM I TOLD YOU ABOUT, TREMBLE. THAT WAS A WARNING SHOT. YOU HAVE THREE SECONDS TO THROW OUT YOUR WEAPONS AND SURRENDER OR THEIR ORDERS ARE SHOOT TO KILL. ONE… TWO…"

The man's smile widened as he saw two pistols fly over the boulders and clatter on the rocks of the trail, followed by Tremble rising with his hands in the air.

"DON'T SHOOT! WE SURRENDER! KEITH CAN'T STAND BECAUSE HE HAS A SPRAINED ANKLE."

***

Tremble stood motionless, hands in the air as the two men converged on him from opposite directions. He nodded at Sam and got a glare in return. He wasn't surprised the 'fire team' turned out to be only Sam — it was the obvious maneuver and what he'd have done in a similar situation. He'd known their position was untenable from the moment Keith went down, but harbored the slim hope they might take down their pursuers on first contact. The outcome of the fight was a forgone conclusion when their first rounds failed to take out their opponents.

Pete held them at gunpoint while Sam frisked them. He also examined Keith, and Tremble clinched his teeth at his son's stifled moans.

"It's sprained all right, maybe even broken," Sam said. "He's definitely not making it back uphill without help."

"Then the friggin' hero here can carry him," Pete said.

"He's a big boy," Tremble said. "I'll need help."

"Not happening," Pete said. "You carry him, or we leave him here with a bullet in the head."

"I can make it, Dad," Keith said, "and you don't have to carry me. Just let me lean on you."

Tremble nodded and began to help his son to his feet under Sam's watchful gaze as Pete reached for his radio and raised it to his lips.

"Central, this is Unit Twelve, do you copy? Over."

He repeated the call with no response. "Crappy reception down in this holler. I'll try again closer to the top," he said to Sam.

His partner nodded, and they began the uphill trek, prodding their struggling captives before them.

***

Wiggins redoubled his efforts at the sound of the distant gunfire, his arm numb. He was a third of the way through the tree, and Tex sat below him, a pile of sawdust covering her head and shoulders. She stared at the ground to keep the sawdust out of her eyes.

"How much longer?"

"We're getting close," Wiggins said.

"You friggin' liar, how close really?"

Wiggins sighed. "A little over a third of the way. When I get halfway, I'll try to push it over."

"What do you make of the gunfire?"

"I'm worried it stopped. As long as they're shooting at each other, they can't be headed back. Now, who knows?"

"I agree… wait! Stop sawing a second!"

Wiggins did; then he heard it too. Sounds from downhill. He pulled the saw from the notch and set it down. Tex looked up and gave him a frightened nod, the action dislodging sawdust from her hair and causing her to squeeze her eyes shut again. He moved downhill and squatted behind a thick tree trunk to study the trail.

A minute passed and the sounds grew louder, low conversation punctuated by muffled groans. Then the tops of heads came into view followed by torsos. It was the two fugitives they'd seen earlier. He could see now one was considerably older and there was no mistaking the family resemblance. The older man was half carrying a man who could only be his son. The older guy looked familiar, and the memory of the earlier overheard exchange came flooding back. '… let Tremble and his son escape…'

Wiggins' blood ran cold. He had no idea what was going on, but knew without a doubt any witnesses had a very limited lifespan. He crouched, immobilized by fear as Tex's captors came into view behind their prisoners. Tremble stumbled and almost fell, and Wiggins could see he was struggling with the weight of his son.

"All right, take a break," called one of the captors, the one with a bloody ear. The captives moved to sit on a nearby boulder while their captors moved up even with them to stand in the middle of the trail.

Bloody Ear turned to his partner. "We're closer to the ridge now. I'll try Central."

The man turned his head to speak into a mike clipped to his shoulder.

"Central, this is Unit Twelve, do you copy? Over."

"Twelve, this is Central. We copy and request immediate sitrep. Over."

Bloody Ear grinned at his partner.

"Central, this is Unit Twelve. We have the subjects in custody. Repeat. We have the subjects in custody. Over."

"Copy that, Unit Twelve. We confirm you have subjects in custody. We have units about to deploy. What is your location and we will send assistance. Over."

"Central, we are on foot near Bear's Den but do not require assistance. We are returning to base ETA thirty minutes. Repeat. We are RTB in thirty mikes. Stand down assistance. Over."

"Negative, Twelve. We are sending assistance to your vehicle location. Over."

"Central, I say again we do not require assistance and believe presence of additional assets will attract unnecessary attention to the operation. Your call. Over."

There was no response for a moment and the other cop spoke to Bloody Ear.

"Maybe we should let them send—"

"Screw that. We need all the credit we can get on this to make up for your screwup. I'm not sharing this collar with anyone."

"Unit Twelve, this is Central. Very well, we confirm you are RTB in thirty mikes and we are standing down assistance. Please confirm you completed mission without complications. Over."

"Central, we have one loose end. Repeat. We have one loose end. Please advise preferred action. Over."

Again there was a long pause before the response.

"Unit Twelve, be advised loose end is best handled on site if local conditions permit. Please advise. Over."

"Central, we copy. We will tie up loose end on site. See you in thirty minutes. Unit Twelve out."

Any hesitation Wiggins harbored was laid to rest by the radio exchange. He pulled out the Glock and looked at it. The men wore body armor, and by the time they got close enough for him to get off a head shot, they'd be too close for comfort. That left the little rifle. They were well within range, and since he had to take head shots anyway, he liked his chances with the popgun a lot better. He stuffed the Glock in his waistband and raised the little Henry.

"All right," Bloody Ear said, "the break is over. Let's get a move—"

Wiggins pulled the trigger. He heard a muffled pop without even the slight recoil he expected from the little rifle. Bloody Ear stood unmoving and then slowly collapsed, but Wiggins was already targeting the second man. He aimed and tried to fire again, but the trigger wouldn't pull. Realization hit him between the eyes like a sledgehammer. He'd loaded the friggin' quiet rounds, without even enough recoil to cycle the bolt. In a panic he jerked at the bolt to chamber another round, his hands slipping on the small knob.

The second man seemed confused, unsure of the source of the attack until Wiggins' frantic movement caught his eye. He crouched to present a smaller target, and Wiggins' second round went high. Wiggins was attempting to chamber a third round when his target lifted the M4. The older man launched himself off the rock and struck the shooter hard in the side, sending his shot wild as the two men collapsed in a heap. Wiggins dropped the Henry and pulled the Glock to race downhill to where the men struggled for the M4. He jammed the Glock between the second man's eyes.

"Drop it!"

The man tensed for a moment; then the fight left him. He released the M4 to slump back on the ground, defeated. The older man struggled up and pointed the rifle at his recent captor, nodding to Wiggins as he did so.

"Keep him covered," Wiggins said. "I'm gonna check the other one."

The other man was dead, Wiggins' shot having taken out his left eye. There was no exit wound, indicating the low-powered round had ricocheted inside the man's skull, making multiple passes through his brain. He searched the man then took off uphill with the handcuff key.

***

Two minutes later the surviving FEMA man was cuffed to a tree some distance away, hasty introductions had been made, and Tremble gave Wiggins and Tex the short version of the State of the Union.

"We're screwed," Wiggins said to Tremble. "Even if we separate, they'll scoop up anyone in the vicinity who might have seen anything." He nodded toward their captive. "And then there's our friend here. Unless we dispose of him, he'll link us together anyway."

"I'm sorry," Tremble said, "we had no intention of endangering anyone else. I think you know that."

"Of course we do, Congressman," Tex said, "but—"

Tremble flashed a wan smile. "Considering the likely end of our short acquaintance, I think we're all on a first-name basis. Call me Simon."

Tex nodded. "All right, Simon. I was saying it doesn't matter how it happened, we have to deal with it. And given the fact you've been dealing with it a bit longer than we have, do you have any ideas?"

"We can't get far," Tremble said. "We're due back at Mount Weather in a bit more than twenty-five minutes. When we don't show up, they'll come looking. They already have a fair idea where we are, so they'll move to contain us. We need to get across State Highway 7 before that happens."

Tex and Wiggins nodded. "That makes sense," Tex said. "The highway is less than half a mile down this hill and there is a lot more woodland to search and fewer roads to access it north of the highway." She looked at Keith. "But we can't move very fast."

"Bill and I can probably carry Keith and still make pretty good time," Tremble said, "but you'll have to ditch some of your gear. After we cross the highway, we'll leave the trail and find a hiding place."

"What about him?" Wiggins nodded again toward their prisoner.

"I haven't figured that out yet," Tremble said. "Why don't y'all check what you can jettison and I'll go talk to our friend."

Tex and Wiggins nodded again, and Tremble got up off his rock and moved towards the captive.

***

"You present quite a dilemma, Sam," Tremble said. "I don't want to kill you in cold blood, but that seems the only logical choice."

The man surprised Tremble by shrugging. "It's George, not Sam. George Anderson. I reckon if you're gonna kill me, you might as well know my name."

"Very well, George. I have to say you seem remarkably calm about it."

George shrugged again. "You kill me or they kill me, so what's the difference? I've screwed up twice big time, and I've been around these people long enough to know that's not gonna go over well. I was thinking it would get me exiled to a 'fugee camp, but then I realized I know too damn much. They're not gonna just demote me or kick me out. They'll kill me, same as they'll kill you. So like I say, what's the difference? Y'all aren't gonna make it out alive and I'm never makin' it home to the Georgia backwoods. That's for sure. I wish now I'd never left."

Something clicked in Tremble's mind and a plan began to form.

"Why are you so sure we won't make it? These woods are pretty thick."

"And when we don't show up at Mount Weather, the search teams will be just as thick. They had four teams outfitting with more on the way when we left, along with a chopper with IR search gear. We stood them down, but they'll come back on line and be deployed in an hour, two at most. You can't get very far in that time, especially with the gimpy kid, and you can't hide your body heat from the IR, no matter how thick the cover is. You don't stand a chance."

"Assuming we do get past the infrared and the search teams, is there anything else we have to worry about. Tracking dogs maybe?"

George thought a moment, then shook his head. "Probably not. Mostly FEMA called on local sources when they needed tracking dogs, and you may have noticed things are a bit strained with the local folks these days."

Tremble rubbed his chin. "How'd you like a fighting chance at making it home to the Georgia backwoods?"

"I'm listening," George said.

***

Tremble walked back to the group with George in tow, without cuffs. Wiggins looked up and began clawing the Glock from his waistband.

168

"Easy, Bill," Tremble said. "There's been a change of plan. Our new friend George here has agreed to buy us some time."

"You gotta be nuts! You can't trust him. Why would you —"

"Because if we don't, we're toast. Don't trust him, trust me. Now are you with me?"

Wiggins hesitated. "Yes," Tex said; then Wiggins nodded.

"All right, pick a spot a bit off the trail to hide everything you're leaving and show George here where it is."

Wiggins looked skeptical and stalked off into the woods. He returned a moment later and motioned George and Tremble over, but Tremble noted he left his hand resting on the Glock in his waistband. He pointed through the foliage.

"See that big fallen tree, about seventy feet downhill?"

George squatted and peered through the trees. "Just barely," he said.

"We'll cache everything we leave behind it and cover it with leaves. We don't have time to bury it, but it'll be out of sight," Wiggins said.

George nodded, and Tremble motioned them back to where Tex was sorting out the contents of both backpacks. They looked down at the items spread out on the ground, and picked up a few things.

"These look like duplicates," Tremble said.

"Yeah, but two is one and one is none," Wiggins said. "We'll need —"

"We won't need anything if we're dead," Tremble said, ignoring Wiggins' glare as he slipped the items in his pocket. He looked at his watch.

"All right, we have twelve minutes before we'll be MIA. George, pick up your former colleague and start back south. Bill, you and Tex get everything repacked and see if you can maybe cut a couple of saplings and rig up a stretcher for Keith. We'll be able to move faster if you and I carry him that way, and maybe we can take more of the other stuff if we put your pack on the stretcher with him. Tex can carry what's left in her pack and scout ahead to make sure we're not ambushed. I'll be back as soon as I can. Y'all be ready to move."

"But where are you going?" Tex asked.

"To buy us some time, but I don't have time to explain," Tremble said as he scooped up the radio from where it rested on a rock and fell in behind George, who had his dead colleague in a fireman's carry.

"Wait a minute," Wiggins said, and ran over to George. "I might be able to use these." He unlaced the dead man's boots and tugged them off his feet, then stepped aside.

Tremble nodded and took the lead, his exhaustion forgotten as he set a grueling pace back uphill to the access cutoff to Bear's Den, then continued past it down the steep slope back toward a stream at the bottom of the hill as George labored behind him. He stopped at the stream.

"Okay, put him down," Tremble said, and George dumped his former partner on the trail.

"We'll make better time in the streambed," Tremble said, glancing at his watch as he splashed into the stream and away from the trail, George on his heels. They moved down the winding stream as quickly as conditions allowed, ever mindful of the time. The AT disappeared behind them in the foliage.

"Okay, this should be far enough off the trail," Tremble said, just as the radio crackled.

"Unit Twelve, this is Central. We request immediate sitrep. Do you copy? Over."

"Showtime," Tremble said, pulling the radio from his belt and handing it to George as he simultaneously drew his pistol. "And just on the off chance you haven't been straight up with me, if I sense the slightest hint of a double cross, you'll be the first to die. Got it?"

George nodded and took the radio.

"Central, this is Unit Twelve. We copy. Repeat your last. Over."

"Unit Twelve, our telemetry indicates your vehicle has not moved. What is your situation? Over."

"Central be advised the housekeeping task required more time than estimated, but it is now complete. However, we just arrived at our vehicle location to find a flat tire. We are changing now and will RTB in due course and will keep you advised of our progress. Over."

"Unit Twelve, we copy. Advise estimated departure from your current position. Over."

"Central, we estimate twenty to thirty mikes. Over."

"Unit Twelve, we copy. Advise when you begin RTB. Central out."

Tremble held out his free hand for the radio, keeping George covered with the pistol. George looked confused, but he handed the radio over, and Tremble slipped it on his uniform belt and then extracted the handcuffs he'd taken from the dead guard's belt. He tossed them to George.

"Now cuff your hands around that tree over there," Tremble said.

"Hey! What the hell are you talking about? That wasn't the deal!"

"I'll honor the deal, but I'm not quite that trusting, so move it. I don't have all day."

George glared and cuffed his arms around the tree trunk. Tremble holstered the pistol before unbuckling the gun belt and placing it out of reach. He moved toward George, pulling a length of paracord from his pocket as he did so.

"I'm going to tie your wrists with paracord, and when I'm sure they're secure, I'll take the cuffs off. Then I'm gagging you so you can't call out. I'll leave the gun and extra ammo hidden over there under some rocks. I'll also leave a wire saw and a lighter there." He held up a large folding pocketknife. "This I'm leaving on the ground under some leaves just beyond your reach. I figure a smart guy like you can get untied or think of a way to drag the knife close enough to use. You know where the others are discarding the extra gear, and you might or might not be able to get back to it."

"That's not the deal," George repeated. "I got no time to find a cave or other hiding place. When they put the chopper up, they'll spot me with the IR, sure as hell."

"Which means you better start working on getting loose as soon as I leave," Tremble said, "and heading south down the AT toward your Georgia backwoods. Just to be clear, I never promised you anything but a chance, and this is a chance. Or you can just stay here tied up, and when they find you, tell them I held a gun at your head to make you file the false report. I'm hiding the stuff I'm leaving so that won't give you away if you decide to just wait it out. Your call."

"Thanks for nothing, asshole."

"You're welcome," Tremble said, then pulled George's uniform shirt out of his belt and cut a piece off the tail to gag him before tying his hands with the paracord and removing the cuffs. He hid the other items as promised and dropped the knife just out of George's reach before starting back up the stream to the AT. The mostly uphill jog back to the others was grueling, but he had no time to spare. He reached them, gasping for breath, and bent over at the waist, hands on his knees as he sucked in long ragged breaths.

"I… I put the dead guard on the southbound trail… so… so maybe they'll look that way first… we got maybe fifteen minutes before we're expected back at Mount Weather, and that might stretch a bit. I think we got an hour or two at most to get across Highway 7 and find a hiding place. Are… are you ready?"

"What'd you do with the other one?" Wiggins asked.

"No time. Tell you later," Tremble gasped.

Wiggins nodded and walked to where Keith lay on a crude stretcher, holding Wiggins' pack and looking uncomfortable and embarrassed at his own helplessness. Tex grunted and shouldered her pack and Tremble moved to the other end of the stretcher.

"Let's lift on three," he said, and counted down. The load was well balanced and not as bad as he'd anticipated, but he knew negotiating the steep downhill path would likely make him rethink that soon.

"Take the lead and let's get the hell out of here, Tex," he said.

DOWNTOWN RIVERWALK
WILMINGTON, NORTH CAROLINA

DAY 17, 7:25 A.M.

Jerome Singletary stood on the dock, watching Jermain Ware loading extra ammunition aboard and feeling perverse pride in his little two-boat armada, thankful it hadn't been nearly as difficult to put together as he'd anticipated. Flat-bottom aluminum fishing boats were apparently not high on the 'things to be looted' list. He'd found several stacked in the back at the local outlet of a major chain store, with electric trolling motors and batteries at the same source. Charging the batteries had been a bit more of a challenge, but with Kwintell Banks' grudging approval, he'd used the generator at the "UBN Provisional HQ."

Best of all, he'd managed to pull it off without revealing he didn't have a clue what he was doing. He'd been equally fortunate to find a booklet of river charts in the third boat searched. He'd pored over it, hoping for a clue as to the whereabouts of Levi's hideout. He knew from eavesdropping it was on the Black River, a tributary of the Cape Fear, and two to four hours from the Wilmington terminal. His major problem was he didn't know the speed upon which that travel time was based. He did know it couldn't be too fast, because Levi's boat had only the small outboard and the electric trolling motor. He'd also heard them talk about weeping willow trees, which he hoped could help identify it if he could just get close.

Though truth be known, the location of Levi's camp was a matter of monumental indifference to him. He had no intention of leading Banks' men to it if he could at all avoid it. He doubted Levi would surrender easily. Bullets would be flying and Jerome Singletary had no desire to be in the middle of a gunfight. Rather, he planned to guide their boats ashore somewhere along the river with the stated intention of scouting Levi's camp from the landward side, then slipping away from his captors in the woods. It was a long shot, but pretty much the only shot he had.

He felt vibration through his feet and looked up to see Kwintell Banks striding down the dock from the riverwalk, his entourage in tow.

"You ready, Singletary?" Banks asked.

Singletary bobbed his head. "Just about. We're waitin' for the powerboat to come around. We'll put one man to drive the powerboat and tow the electric boats up the Cape Fear to the Black, that way we save the batteries. Then he'll anchor the powerboat in the river and get in with us. That'll give us three men in each boat and we go the rest of the way quiet like." Singletary paused. "Should be more than enough, seeing as how we're sneaking up on 'em. There aren't any men there except Levi and the old man. The rest are just women and kids."

Banks looked over at his lieutenant for confirmation. "How 'bout it Jermain? Y'all ready?"

Jermain Ware nodded. "Like he said, everything is ready soon as the rest of the boys get here with the powerboat."

"All right," Banks said, "remember you in charge. This shithead's just the guide, so don't trust him none."

Jermain nodded again and Banks smiled and motioned one of his entourage forward. Singletary noted for the first time the man was carrying a bag. From the looks of it, a heavy bag.

"Matter of fact," Banks said, "I got a little present for you, Singletary."

Singletary watched, horror stricken, as the minion set the bag down and extracted what looked like a cannonball attached to a leg shackle via a thick steel chain.

Banks laughed, enjoying Singletary's reaction. "Found this in one of the local museums. All sorts of interesting stuff in museums. Practical too." His smile faded. "Lift your pants leg."

"Just a minute! That wasn't the deal—"

Banks drew his gun and pointed it at Singletary's head. "Lift your pants leg. One. Two…"

Singletary stooped to lift his right pants leg and Banks' grinning minion hurried over to shackle the steel ball to Singletary's leg.

"I'll drown if I fall overboard!"

Banks shrugged. "Then don't fall overboard. Did you actually think I was dumb enough to let you out on the river where you could escape? No, you gonna be on the front of the first boat in, just in case it's an ambush or something. And in case you feel stupid enough to maybe try to cap some of my boys and unlock yourself" — he held up a padlock key — "ain't but one key and it's in my pocket, and I'm stayin' right here."

Banks looked over at Jermain. "He give you any trouble, or if it looks like he's bullshittin' us, or you take this Levi's camp and it ain't got the gold and silver and grenades and everything he promised, you just throw his punk ass out of the boat in the middle of the river. Don't be bringing his sorry ass back. You understand?"

Jermain grinned. "Straight up, boss."

Levi Jenkins' Fishing Camp
Black River, North Carolina

Day 17, 8:30 a.m.

Anthony McCoy watched his grandchildren climb in the flat-bottom boat, almost vibrating with excitement at the prospect of 'going to town.' He suppressed his smile and addressed them in a stern voice.

"Y'all settle down now, and put them life jackets on. Bein' on the river is serious business and y'all can't be poppin' around like jumping beans, ya hear?"

"Yes, Grampa," said the children in unison, marginally curbing their exuberance as they donned life jackets.

Anthony heard footsteps on the small dock and looked up to see Levi approaching with Celia and Jo, the two women looking almost as excited as the children. He held the boat while the women climbed in and got the children settled, then stood and nodded at Levi.

"Y'all should be there in two hours, now that we feel comfortable running in daylight. When is the Coastie patrol boat gonna be here?"

Levi shook his head. "He's not coming up this far. I agreed with Chief Butler on the radio to just meet 'em at the Brunswick River intersection. Nothing much to worry about on the upper part of the river and that saves them some time. Besides, Butler can't make it, so I don't want anyone else knowing our exact location. And though he didn't say it, I also know taking the time to escort us is a strain on resources. Everybody's got enough on their plate as it is these days. I appreciate the escort service and I don't want to abuse it."

Anthony's face clouded. "Why am I just hearin' about this now?"

"'Cause I knew you'd get your bowels in an uproar, that's why. It's only an hour's run to the intersection with the outboard, and I'm well-armed. We'll be fine until we meet up with the Coasties."

Anthony looked unconvinced. "I don't know, Levi, maybe you should postpone the trip until dark and run with the NV goggles and electric motors, just to be safe. Or maybe not go at all until we can work something better out."

Levi cocked an eyebrow. "Maybe you'd like to explain that to Celia and Jo and the kids," he said softly. "They been here three weeks and they're pretty much starved for some socializing. I didn't really realize how bad it was impacting them until I saw how they perked up when Wiggins and Tex were here. They're really looking forward to this trip and I don't want to be the one to tell 'em it's not happening. Fort Box is all we got that passes for a town nowadays. So if you want 'em to stay here, you go right ahead and tell 'em."

Levi looked at Anthony, one eyebrow cocked in a silent question.

Anthony sighed and shook his head. "All right, all right. But you call me on the radio the first thing when you get to Fort Box."

"I will. But why don't you come with us? We can set out extra feed for the animals to tide them over a day or so. I'm more concerned with leaving you here alone than I am with our trip."

Anthony shook his head again. "I'll be fine, and somebody needs to stay here just in case. You never know if you'll get delayed for some reason, and we can't risk the livestock. Besides, you'll need the room if you can talk Jimmy into coming back with you."

Levi nodded, but didn't move, reluctant to leave on a note of discord. Anthony sensed his hesitation and smiled. "Y'all go on now. Don't keep the Coasties waiting, else they might not be so accommodating next time."

Levi hugged Anthony and got in the boat.

GIBSON FARM
ON THE BLACK RIVER
WEST OF CURRIE, NC

DAY 17, 8:00 A.M.

Luke sat in the bow, watching as Vern Gibson deftly maneuvered the boat away from the riverbank. He had Long and Washington with him, and they were all clad in work clothes provided by the Gibson men. They were all long overdue haircuts and had several days' beard growth, so the only thing marking them as military was their M4s and the casual competence with which they handled them.

They'd decided one boat could be passed off as a scouting trip while two might look like an assault, and left the remainder of the group at the Gibson farm. Over Donny Gibson's strong objection, his father had exercised parental prerogative and assumed the role of local guide. The older Gibson had pointed out, leave periods aside, Donny had been away for several years and was no longer a familiar face to the neighbors along the river. Given the times, a boatload of armed strangers was apt to draw fire first and questions later, but having a neighbor at the helm should at least result in discussion before hostilities commenced.

Luke smiled at the recollection of the discussion. Donny had been inclined to debate the point until his mother had entered the fray, forbidding his participation on pain of unspecified but apparently feared consequences for both Donny and his father. Donny had flushed with embarrassment at the dressing-down, but grudgingly accepted his father's argument as correct. He stood on the bank as the boat pulled away, his hand raised in a wave of farewell, returned by his three colleagues.

"Gibson don't look too happy, LT," Washington said, "but I reckon he'd be a lot more unhappy if he crossed his momma. That is one tough lady." He looked back, suddenly self-conscious. He saw Vern Gibson smile.

"No offense, sir," Washington added lamely.

"None taken," Vern said. "Virginia's the toughest woman I know. It's one of the reasons I love her. And she's had her share of heartache. When Richard lost his arm, it was nip and tuck for a while, and we almost lost him too. Then Donny up and enlisted. She didn't say nothing and she was proud, but it damn near drove her crazy with worry. Since the power went out and things started gettin' crazy, she's been praying for his safe return at least three times a day. We all have, truth be known. So she's gonna keep him close a while, and he just has to live with it. She's earned a little peace of mind, and then some."

The other men just nodded, unsure what to say, the silence broken only by the growl of the outboard.

"How long to Wilmington?" Luke asked at last.

"Hard to say, three or four hours, give or take," Vern replied. "The main channel is the Black River until we get down to the junction with the Cape Fear River around Roan Island, then the combined stream is designated the Cape Fear. Then we'll keep going a ways to the junction with the Brunswick, and we'll take that south and keep Eagle Island between us and Wilmington. The Brunswick rejoins the Cape Fear less than a mile south of the container terminal. My neighbor said the Coast Guard boat was docked at the terminal."

Luke nodded and turned his attention back to the river. The banks were heavily wooded, but occasionally an opening through the trees revealed an expanse of open field or a farmhouse set well back from the river. At one point they rounded a bend and saw a row of large homes along the shore, set on expansive lots and served by floating docks in the river. Most were deserted, but figures stood exposed on one or two of the docks, their postures telegraphing unease at being caught in the open, even at a distance. As the boat passed them and Vern raised his hand in greeting, Luke saw the people relax. He wondered how many rifle scopes had been pointed at them thus far in their journey and considered for the first time whether foregoing their body armor to look 'less military' had been such a good idea.

M/V PECOS TRADER
SUN LOWER ANCHORAGE
NECHES RIVER
NEAR NEDERLAND, TEXAS

DAY 17, 8:00 A.M.

Hughes stood at the rail with Kinsey and Dan Gowan, watching Georgia Howell's deck gang lowering the Coast Guard boat over the side.

"Any sign of our fake deputies?" Gowan asked.

Hughes shook his head. "No, and we're fairly well out of sight here. There's nothing much but marsh and mosquitoes on this riverbank, and we're far enough up in the inlet we can't be seen from the opposite bank except by someone actually standing on the dock at the Sun Terminal. Same from the river; I had enough water depth to get well out of the main channel. A boat needs to get dead even with the mouth of the inlet to see us." He paused. "Besides, it's not like we have a choice; this is the only place we'll fit."

Gowan nodded. "Let's just hope those dipshit deputies don't figure that out."

Matt Kinsey laughed. "I'd say we're safe. Those boys didn't look like the sharpest tacks in the box. But we'll keep a good watch anyway. I suspect a few well-placed bursts with the fifty will discourage them pretty quickly."

Hughes smiled. "*Semper Paratus .*"

"Absolutely," Kinsey said. They turned back to the ongoing operation just as the Coast Guard boat gently kissed the surface of the water.

"Looks like you're about ready to go, Cap" Gowan said.

Hughes nodded. "Any hard feelings from the crew?"

Gowan shrugged. "Not that I've heard. I guess they all pretty much feel like I do. Everyone knows we can't all leave the ship at the same time. Someone's got to be first and you've got as much right as anyone. More, actually. None of us would even be here if you hadn't decided to move the ship. Go get Laura and the girls and bring 'em back, then send someone else." The engineer shook his head. "Besides, going first might not be such a benefit, since you don't know what's out there. Personally, I'm thinking second or third looks pretty good."

"Yeah, that hadn't escaped me either," Hughes said.

"How many you think we should take?" Kinsey asked.

"Take? I figured y'all would just drop me off with some gas. I can't ask anyone else to do this; it's my family."

"You're not asking, I'm volunteering, as have all the others. You don't know what you'll find, and my guys are the only ones with any weapons training. I figure I'll take two guys and leave four here for security. Your folks can supplement them with the extra weapons if need be."

"That's very generous, Chief Kinsey," Hughes said. "I don't know what to say. I just sort of figured when we got here... well, actually, I don't know what the hell I thought was going to happen. I don't even know what we're going to do with folks when we bring them on board. We sure don't have room for everyone."

"We'll play it by ear, Captain. And I want to get over to Louisiana as soon as I can, and I'll definitely be bringing my family back if I can get them to come. My guys all feel the same way, but their folks are scattered up and down the coast from here to Corpus Christi. As far as what's gonna happen, all I know is *Pecos Trader* is the lifeboat with all the provisions and we're in a shit storm. None of us really want to stray too far. Now what do you say? Is four enough?"

Hughes shrugged. "I'd say it has to be. We have to get wheels, and we have to have room to bring Laura and the girls back."

"You're the local, so where do we get a ride?"

"Anything we find abandoned is unlikely to have keys, so unless we have someone who can hot-wire a car, that's a nonstarter. I figure a car dealership or auto repair shop is our best bet; some place we're likely to find both vehicles and keys. The closest are along the main drag in Nederland. Maybe three or four miles from the river through mostly good residential neighborhoods. The boat can drop us off across the river at the refinery dock, just downstream."

"So we grab a couple of cans of gas and hump it to the main drag on foot and go car shopping?" Kinsey nodded. "Sounds doable."

"We might not have to hoof it," Hughes said. "They keep bikes for the dock workers to use when they're working a ship. When the lights went out, everybody probably just went home, just like Wilmington. I can't see anyone coming back down to the river to scavenge a bunch of old bicycles. I'm betting they're still there, and they all have big deep carrying baskets for tools, so we can each carry a gas can."

Kinsey grinned. "Sounds good to me. If I was fond of walking, I'd have joined the infantry."

***

Fifteen minutes later, Hughes and his little shore party were headed downriver in the patrol boat, a Coastie at the helm and another manning the bow machine gun. Nothing moved on the river and the refinery dock came into view as soon as the boat cleared the inlet. Kinsey directed the helmsman to the middle of the river, and they were running abreast of the dock five minutes later, checking it out. There was an empty tank barge riding high at the extreme downstream end of the dock, but no signs of activity. Hughes pointed out a vertical ladder midway down the tall dock, and they moved toward it.

Kinsey motioned to one of his men, who scampered up the ladder, his M4 slung beside him. The man disappeared and moments later he returned to sound an all clear. The other three men scurried up after him. Hughes brought up the rear, a coil of rope over his shoulder, which he shrugged off when he gained the solid footing of the dock. He tossed one end of the rope back down to the waiting boat, where one of the remaining Coasties tied it to the first of the red plastic gas containers so Hughes could haul it up. They repeated the process and all four gas cans were lined up on the dock when Kinsey returned, a grin on his face.

"Bunch of bikes parked next to the dock office, just like you said. Ready?"

"Almost," Hughes said as he tossed the end of the rope back over the side. Minutes later he dragged it up, and a crow bar and a large pair of bolt cutters hit the concrete dock with metallic clangs.

"Can't forget the precision instruments," Hughes said.

Kinsey nodded, then leaned over the side and ordered the boat back to the ship.

"Think we should do a comms check?" Kinsey asked.

"Negative," Hughes replied. "We don't know who's listening. The ship's walkie-talkies have limited range anyway, so I think we should limit transmissions to calling the boat back when we get within range inbound."

"Agreed," Kinsey said, just as the other two Coasties appeared, each guiding a bike with either hand.

"Let's get loaded up and find us a ride," Kinsey said.

The bolt cutters made short work of the lock on the dock gate, and they pedaled two abreast down the cracked asphalt of the long road between the refinery and the tank farm. The Texas heat and humidity was already oppressive despite the early hour. The total lack of traffic combined with the eerie silence of the abandoned industrial area created a pervasive air of unreality.

"This is friggin' spooky," said one of the Coasties. "Not a soul in sight."

"Count your blessings, Jones," Kinsey said over his shoulder. "There are a lot worse things than spooky."

"Yeah, like friggin' hot! I'll be glad to get in a vehicle and crank up the AC!"

They emerged from the tank farm to cross Twin City Highway and took Canal Avenue south, running through residential areas showing the beginnings of decay, with what were once obviously manicured lawns now overgrown. Far from opposition, the people they saw on the streets took one look at their guns and uniforms and disappeared behind locked doors.

"Something's not right," Kinsey said. "I mean, I expected things to be screwed up, but these people act terrified."

Hughes nodded and picked up the pace, thinking of his family.

They had their pick of places on US 69, and Hughes turned directly off Canal Avenue into the lot of a Ford dealership. They rolled to a stop in a lot half full of new cars, with gaps in the rows indicating someone might have had the same idea. There was an equally large stretch of 'pre-owned' vehicles beyond that, with fewer vacant spaces.

"Looks like someone got here first," Kinsey said.

Hughes nodded. "I suspect anything left has had the gas siphoned out. Pickings are probably better over in the used-car section. Y'all go pick out a likely vehicle, maybe a big SUV," Hughes said. "I'll bust in to the building and see if I can find keys, providing previous shoppers left the keys for what they didn't take."

"How far is your place?" Kinsey asked.

"About twenty-five miles. Say sixty or eighty miles round trip by the time we get back to the refinery dock, depending on detours. Why?"

"We have twenty gallons of gas, so I'm for taking a car and a backup. Two is one, and one is none, as they say. If we somehow get disabled or break down near your place, it's a long hike back to the river. "

"Good point. Pick 'em out and get the VIN numbers while I try to rustle up the keys." He started for the dealership showroom, the crowbar over his shoulder.

He found the double glass doors ajar, and the showroom itself looked like a storm had hit it. The tile floor was carpeted with slick four-color sales brochures and all the drawers in the desk in the reception area were standing open. Hughes started down a long hallway, open doors on either side revealing Spartan cubicles where salesmen haggled with customers in better times. The further he got from the glass-windowed showroom, the darker it became, until finally he fished a small flashlight from his pocket.

At the end of the hallway in a larger office he found what he was looking for, a large key cabinet, the door torn off and hanging by one hinge. A glance inside and his hopes plummeted at the sight of empty hooks. He sighed and turned away but something crunched underfoot, and he smiled as his light illuminated a litter of discarded keys. Moving quickly, he dumped the contents of a nearby wastebasket and began scooping the keys into it. Five minutes later, he and Kinsey stood at the reception desk, searching for VIN numbers on the key tags in the better light of the glass-walled showroom.

"Here's the SUV," Kinsey said.

"Go get it gassed up while I keep looking for the pickup keys," Hughes said.

"All right," Kinsey headed for the door. "When you find it, throw the rest of those keys back in the trash can and let's take them with us. No telling when we might have to come car shopping again."

Hughes nodded absently and kept looking.

Ten minutes later, Hughes was at the wheel of a big Ford Expedition with Kinsey riding shotgun as they turned south on the access road for US 69. The two other Coasties trailed them in a full-size Ford pickup.

There were scattered cars on the road, mostly on the shoulder, and Hughes passed them without slowing. He braked as they approached a deserted mall and swung right on Highway 365 as it passed under US 69.

"It's all rural roads from here," Hughes said as he accelerated, "and this wouldn't have been a road to attract refugees. We should make good time." He pushed the Expedition up to eighty-five and glanced in his mirror. The Coasties were right with him, eight or ten car lengths back. He accelerated to ninety-five and stared at the road ahead, running flat and straight through the coastal pastureland. His mind wandered as the SUV ate up the miles. With his myriad responsibilities, he'd compartmentalized worry about his family, because to do otherwise would have rendered him unable to function. But scant miles from home with an open road in front of him, all of his worries and fears came crashing down as he blasted down the blacktop, both eager and terrified of what might await him.

"You won't do your family any good if you hit a pothole at a hundred and ten and wrap us around a telephone pole. Besides, you're losing the pickup."

A quick glance in the mirror revealed the pickup some distance back. Hughes eased off the gas.

"Sorry," he said.

Kinsey shrugged. "Understandable. Are we making better time than you figured?"

"Yeah, but we're about to lose some. If I stay on this road, we'll pick up Texas 124 in Fannett, but that more or less parallels I-10 and I'd like to avoid it. I also want to miss Fannett and Hamshire, so we'll be taking to the back roads in a few miles."

"This isn't a back road?"

Hughes laughed. "Not by a long shot."

True to his word, a few minutes later he pulled off the highway on to a narrow path that ran due south through pastureland along a barbed-wire fence, little more than two graveled wheel tracks with weeds a foot tall growing between them.

"Doesn't look like anyone has used this lately, which is a good thing. We have maybe fifteen miles of this, and I'll have to do a lot of zigzagging and backtracking, but it will keep us off the public roads. We'll come up to the house from the back side, across the pastures. We should be pulling up behind our barn in half an hour. Be ready with those bolt cutters, we might have to 'unlock' a few gates along the way."

***

Laura Hughes stood partially concealed behind the white wood fence and studied the approaching dust plume.

"They're in a hell of a hurry, whoever they are," she said softly, then louder, "What do you see, Jana?"

Jana Hughes stood beside her twin sister, wrists braced on the top rail of the fence to steady the binoculars.

"There are four of them, Mom, and they're wearing some sort of uniforms. Not like the deputies, these are blue, but it looks like they've all got on that black army stuff. You know, like vests. And there aren't any markings on either the car or the truck."

Laura considered the possibilities. Given their recent encounter, the fact the approaching men wore uniforms was alarming, and the lack of any markings on the vehicles further supported the idea they were some sort of rogue element. Only by chance had they been working in the garden and spotted the approaching dust cloud across the wide expanse of the mostly treeless pasture. An armed group approaching across private property was obviously intent on avoiding detection. Nothing about the situation spelled anything but trouble, and if she waited to find out what they were about, Laura had no doubt she and the girls would be easily overpowered. That wasn't happening.

"Well, whoever they are, they shouldn't be on our property. And there's no way I'm letting 'em get close enough to hurt us."

She looked over at her daughters. "We've only got the .30-.30 and the .308 that are effective at this range. I'll take the .30-.30. Julie, you're the best shot of the three of us, so I want you to take the .308. I'm going to try to stop them and I want you to take them after they've stopped, either through the windows or as they get out of their cars." She paused. "Can you do this, honey?"

Julie swallowed hard and bobbed her head once in response.

Laura fought down an urge to sweep both her daughters into her arms and run to the house and hide, but hiding and waiting for the authorities was no longer an option. She brought the .30-.30 up and steadied it on the fence rail, wishing for the hundredth time Jordan had gotten around to fitting the scopes still in their boxes in the gun safe. She crouched a bit and took aim through the iron sights. The SUV turned slightly and she couldn't see in for the glare, but she focused on the windshield where she knew the driver's body would be.

"Okay, Julie," Laura said, her rifle still on the approaching target. "Take a deep breath and calm down. Take your time and let me know when you're ready."

She heard what sounded like a deep sigh, then, "Okay, Mom, I'm ready."

"All right, I'm going to take out the driver of the SUV. Don't fire until you hear me shoot, but when I do, the pickup may slow or stop. You try to get that driver first. After that, we both just fire at whatever targets we've got. Clear?"

"Yes, ma'am."

Laura refocused, then took a deep breath and exhaled as her target made a slight change of direction and the glare off the windshield dissipated. She took another breath and held it as she slowly squeezed the trigger.

Beside her, Jana screamed, "MOM! DON'T—"

She felt the recoil of the unpadded stock into her shoulder as the gunshot echoed across the pasture.

"IT'S DAD!"

Even at a distance, she heard the crack as her bullet shattered the windshield, and watched horror-stricken as the SUV veered off the dirt track to come to rest in the field. Then tears flooded her eyes and nearly blinded her as she dropped the rifle and fought back great racking sobs, to rush across the pasture, screaming her husband's name.

WARDEN'S OFFICE
FEDERAL CORRECTIONAL COMPLEX
BEAUMONT, TEXAS

DAY 17, 9:00 A.M.

"Missing? What the hell do you mean missing?" Spike McComb glared at Snaggle as the smaller man squirmed in the chair.

"Missing, that's all. They went out in their cruiser yesterday and they didn't come back, and they ain't answering the radio," Snaggle said.

"Who was it again?"

"Willard Jukes and Kyle Morgan."

"Wait a minute? Ain't those the two assholes doing all the bitching?"

Snaggle nodded. "The same."

"You don't think they did a jackrabbit, or maybe decided to go into business for themselves?"

"Well, maybe, but it don't seem likely. They'd have to know we'd find out, and then they'd be dead either way. Besides, I think they're both from around here somewhere, so I can't see no place for 'em to jackrabbit to. I think it's more likely they ran into trouble," Snaggle said.

McComb shook his head. "It don't matter. Only two things could have happened. Either somebody took 'em out, or they took off on their own, and we gotta deal with it either way. If someone took 'em out, we gotta find 'em and deal with it publicly so everyone knows not to mess with my PO-lice. And if they really did jackrabbit, especially after running their motormouths, we DEFINITELY have to bring 'em back and make an example of 'em. We can't have the rest of these assholes gettin' ideas." McComb paused. "Where was they working?"

"Last radio transmission said they was headed west toward the county line."

"All right, knock half the boys off whatever they're doin' and cover that area like a blanket. Find those assholes! And if they turn up dead, make sure people nearby know it ain't nice to piss off the PO-lice, but leave enough alive to spread the word."

"What if someone took 'em out and we can't figure out who did it?"

McComb released an exasperated sigh and shook his head.

"Jesus H. Christ, Snaggle! Do I have to do all the thinkin' around here? It don't MATTER who did it. You think we're gonna have a trial or something. Besides, why should I care who iced those ungrateful shitheads. This is damage control. Just pick a few people nearby, SAY they did it, and kill 'em as an example. Got it?"

Snaggle nodded and rose from his chair.

"Wait a minute. You found that ship yet?"

"Not yet. The boys been having trouble getting the boat started, but last report I had said they should be on the river this morning. They'll find it. It's kind of hard to hide a ship."

CHAPTER SEVENTEEN

CAPE FEAR RIVER
WEST OF WILMINGTON, NC

DAY 17, 9:00 A.M.

Singletary studied the chart intently, anxious to mask the fact he didn't have a clue where they were going. It backfired.

"For a guide, you sure got your nose buried in that map. You know where you going?" Jermain Ware asked.

"It's a chart, not a map, and around this next bend is the intersection with the Brunswick. We pass it by and stay right in this channel and go under the railroad bridge," Singletary said, hoping he was reading the damn chart right. He was on pins and needles as the boat turned left and it was all he could do to contain a relieved sigh as the railroad bridge and intersection came into view. Instead, he fixed Jermain with a superior look.

"What was that you was sayin'?"

Jermain grunted and guided the powerboat toward the railroad bridge, towing the other two boats, each with two men aboard. Once they were under the railroad bridge and around a bend, Singletary pointed ahead to the right.

"See that break in the bank over there?"

"Yeah, what about it?" Jermain asked.

"That's a little channel that runs alongside the river. We'll hide the powerboat there and go the rest of the way on the electrics."

"They damn slow! How far we got to go?"

"As far as I say, and they may be slow, but they're quiet. So unless you want to let everyone on the river know we're comin', why don't you do like I say?"

Jermain glared and turned toward the cut. Ten minutes later they had the powerboat anchored out of sight in the side channel and were shifting personnel between boats. Jermain took control of one of the electric-powered boats and indicated Singletary should join him. Singletary nodded and stood, his balance precarious as he held the iron ball.

"Look here," he said to Jermain and the other gangbanger in his boat. "One of y'all hold this damn steel ball for me so I can get over there."

Jermain smirked. "Hold it yourself, Mister High and Mighty River Guide."

"If I drown before y'all even get where y'all going because you gotta play the fool, just how pissed off you reckon Kwintell's gonna be?"

Jermain stared at Singletary for a long moment, then motioned the other man to take the steel ball. Unencumbered, Singletary transferred vessels easily and took his place at the front of the boat. He motioned Jermain to take off then immediately stopped him with a low cry.

"Hear that?" Singletary asked softly.

Jermain cocked an ear. "Sounds like another outboard coming downriver."

Singletary nodded. "Move the boat near the mouth, but keep it back out of sight. We'll be able to see 'em from behind after they pass. They won't see us unless they look back, so y'all stay quiet. We don't need no trouble now."

Jermain did as instructed, and the sound of the outboard increased. It was relatively quiet as outboards go, but still quite audible on the still river. The boat passed and Singletary could hardly believe his eyes. Levi was driving the boat with two women and two kids aboard, looking ahead and to both sides, but not back the way the boat had passed.

"Well, my, my, my," Singletary said softly, "don't that beat all. There goes Levi and his whole damn family. That only leaves the old man."

"Let's git 'em," Jermain said and turned the boat downstream.

"NO, FOOL!" Singletary hissed, terrified at the thought of getting into a running gunfight on the river with thirty pounds of iron shackled to his leg. He immediately regretted his choice of words as Jermain's hand flew to his sidearm.

"I mean that's not a good idea," Singletary said. "We can't catch 'em on the electrics, and if we switch over to the powerboat, we can't sneak up on 'em 'cause they'll hear the motor. It will take a while to catch 'em, and all that time, Levi can be layin' into us with that rifle, and it ain't like we'll have any cover."

Jermain seemed to be unsure, and Singletary pressed the point.

"Besides, they likely got a radio and they might call the Coasties or alert the old man back at their camp, and that would screw everything up. But this is perfect. Let 'em go about their business, and we just sashay on up the river quiet like and take the old man by surprise and clean out their camp. Then we leave a couple of boys there to wait for them to get back and surprise them and take whatever they bring back from Wilmington. I say we stay right here and let 'em get well out of sight around the bend, then head upriver just like we planned."

Jermain scowled and reached for their own radio. "I'm gonna call Kwintell and see what we should do."

Singletary shook his head. "That's exactly the wrong thing to do. You'd have to spell it all out in plain English for him to understand, and what do you want to bet them Coasties don't have a scanner, listenin' to radio traffic? They hear, they'll call Levi or the old man at his camp for sure, then we lost the surprise."

Jermain hesitated, obviously resistant to taking direction from Singletary but unable to deny the logic of his observations. Finally he nodded.

"All right," he said, and they sat there watching and waiting as Levi's boat disappeared around the bend. They waited a few minutes longer for the sound of the outboard to fade, then turned upriver, the powerful little trolling motors pushing the boats at a moderate but steady pace.

Singletary's mind raced. He'd racked his brain for a plan B ever since the ball was clamped on his leg, but now he saw a light at the end of the tunnel. Finding Levi's camp now offered his very best chance to survive, come what may. He had no doubt Jermain and the rest of the bangers would make short work of the old man, and then pitch in to loot the camp. At that point, he'd be on dry land and out of immediate danger, but the ball would preclude his participation in the looting. He might be able to slip away when they were focused on their task, or failing that, talk Jermain into leaving him as part of the crew to await Levi's return.

He liked his chances if left alone with only one of the others, who would now be more inclined to trust him, and there would likely be tools about the place he might use to free himself and escape. And even supposing none of those opportunities presented themselves, his success in delivering on his promise would prove his worth to Kwintell. He'd petition to join the gang and look for opportunities to escape when he wasn't being watched so closely. One way or another, he'd survive.

He bent his head to the chart. From what he'd overheard, he knew the camp was on the Black River, which joined the Cape Fear River some distance upstream. From the chart, the Black would be the larger right branch of the fork, some distance ahead. It didn't look like he could miss it, but after the fork things got tricky. All he could do was start looking for a stand of willow trees on the bank and hope he could spot it. His task was complicated by his urban roots — he had only a vague idea what a willow tree looked like, though he was pretty sure from the description it was droopy looking. He hoped like hell there weren't a lot of droopy-looking trees.

"How much farther?" Jermaine asked.

"It's a ways. We'll go right at the fork of the Cape Fear and the Black," Singletary said, with a confidence he didn't feel.

Time dragged as the little trolling motors powered them upstream at a steady clip, and Singletary began to worry they might run out of battery before they reached their destination. Then he relaxed as they swept around a long bend to the right and came upon the fork in the rivers.

"This is it. Keep to the right," he said.

"How far after that?" Jermain asked.

"A ways," Singletary said. "I only been there once, but I'll recognize it when I see it."

"Which side of the river?"

Fear shot through Singletary at the unanticipated but obvious question.

"The east bank," he said, glancing back at Jermain.

He suppressed a smile at the look of confusion on Jermain's face, and hoped pride would preclude any follow-up questions. Sure enough, the man's fear of appearing ignorant overcame his curiosity as to which side of the river they were searching, and he just nodded, as if satisfied with the answer. Singletary went back to scanning both sides of the river for droopy-looking trees.

Only belatedly did he realize Jermain's question presented another problem—he had to pick the right spot, or at least the correct side of the river—the first time. If they inspected an area on the right bank and it wasn't the entrance, he might be able to pass it off as a mistake and keep on looking. However, he couldn't then inspect a place on the left bank without revealing he was clueless. Jermain was ignorant, not stupid.

Tension built as they glided upstream, and a likely looking stand of trees grew close to the left bank, but they didn't quite fit Singletary's mental image. His forbearance was rewarded moments later as they rounded a bend and he spotted a much more likely prospect on the right bank—a stand of trees right on the water's edge, long limbs drooping over the river and trailing whiplike tendrils down to brush the water, shrouding the riverbank like a curtain. He hedged his bets with Jermain a bit.

"I believe this is it," he said quietly to Jermain. "Just nose the boat through them limbs hangin' down and let's make sure there's an inlet. A lot of these places look alike on the river, but it's either this one or the next."

Jermain reduced speed, barely moving as he nosed the boat up to the willow curtain at a right angle to the bank. The second gangbanger joined Singletary in the bow and they parted the thick willow curtain with their arms as the boat nudged through it. Sure enough, after working their way through a ten-foot thickness of trailing willow tendrils, the bow of the boat broke into a clear area, and they found themselves floating in a twenty-foot-wide channel, running inland at a right angle to the river between the trunks of two massive willow trees. It was dark and cool beneath the trees and Singletary could see the channel was obscured further on by a similar willow curtain.

He nodded up the little inlet. "You go through that and Levi's camp is just beyond."

"How far?"

Singletary had anticipated the question and dropped the last bit of info he'd gleaned from overheard conversation.

"A ways. There's a little dock, but you can't see it from the house."

Jermain nodded and moved to start the trolling motor.

"Wait a minute!" Singletary hissed. "What's the plan?"

Jermain shrugged. "One old man? I figure we just tie up at this dock and go up quiet like and surprise him. He gives us any trouble, we cap his ass. Why we need a plan?"

"What about me?"

"You stay in the boat. We'll come back and take care... we'll come back and get you later."

Jermain nudged the boat forward to make room for the second boat to move into the clearing near the tree trunks, and it suddenly occurred to Singletary he hadn't been the only one with a plan. Jermain wasn't likely to share credit with anyone for a successful raid.

After a hushed exchange with his men in the other boat, Jermain started through the second willow curtain as Singletary began to rapidly recalculate his own odds for survival. His mental exercise was interrupted by an event that changed those odds significantly, and not for the better.

The thick, heavy snake landed across Singletary's shoulders with a dull thud, surprising the snake perhaps almost as much as Singletary. As Singletary's terrified scream pierced the air, the equally frightened snake responded in kind, striking Singletary's right bicep. Singletary leaped to his feet, fighting the willow limbs and shaking his arm in an attempt to sling the snake off. He managed to break free of the snake's bite, but success was overshadowed as he lost his balance and plunged backward out of the boat, dragging his steel ball with him as five feet of pissed-off snake flew around the bottom of the boat.

Jermain and the other banger were on their feet now, screaming as well as they tried to avoid the snake. Then terror overcame common sense and their response was as dumb as it was inevitable. They drew their weapons and five seconds and twenty rounds later, the bottom of the aluminum boat was like Swiss cheese. As the boat sank, the snake swam away unharmed, perhaps the only participant satisfied with the results of the encounter.

The water was only six feet deep, and Singletary bobbed up and down off the bottom, dragging his leg ball through the mud until he could grab a protruding tree root and pull himself to the bank.

"HE BIT ME!" Singletary wailed. "I NEED A DOCTOR."

"If you don't shut up, I'm gonna cap you right here," Jermain said, hanging onto the side of the second boat.

"What we gonna do, Jermain?" the driver of the second boat asked.

"Pull us aboard and let's get to that dock. We need to take care of the old man, but it ain't gonna be no surprise now."

"What about him," the driver asked, nodding toward Singletary.

"Leave the fool here. We'll worry about him later."

* * *

Anthony McCoy's head jerked at the sound of the screams. He dumped the chicken feed on the ground and tossed the bowl aside to wade through the flocking chickens to his shotgun leaning against the house. The sound of rapid gunfire removed any thoughts of rescuing someone in distress. That much firepower this close to the camp could only mean trouble.

The disturbance came from the river, and he headed down the now well-worn path, but quickly thought better of it. He moved into the woods, paralleling the path and out of sight until he understood the situation. Staking out a position in the woods near the dock, he'd hardly settled in to his hideout when a boat pushed through the willow curtain with five heavily armed men aboard.

His first thought was of his family. Had they been caught on the river and attacked? Unlikely. Even if they'd been attacked and succumbed, Levi would have had time to get off a warning, and besides, sound travels far over water and he'd heard no gunfire. No, the camp was clearly the target, and he was both outnumbered and outgunned, and if they spread out, it would be difficult to defend against them. It was best to even the odds a bit while they were all together in the boat, but the shotgun presented problems of range and accuracy. The dock was at least fifty yards away and they were some distance farther.

He cursed himself for a stubborn old fool and wished he'd followed Levi's advice and started to carry the AR, or better yet, one of the M4s they'd gotten from the Coasties. Then he willed himself calm. His daddy had given him the Winchester Model 12 when he was ten years old, and the old twelve gauge had put a lot of meat on the table over the years—and even 'discouraged' a bunch of wannabee Klansmen one dark night years ago. He reckoned he could handle a bunch of bangers. Besides, his vision was none too good anymore, and it was comforting to know he just had to get in the vicinity.

He let the boat draw close and opened fire just before it reached the dock. His first load spread to punch into the boat driver's chest in a half-dozen places, and the man slumped as the boat veered away from the dock to push bow first into the opposite bank of the narrow inlet. Anthony ejected the shell before the man had even toppled over, and pumped four more loads of double-ought buckshot at the boat in quick succession. At least one more of the attackers was down, and all were showing signs of being hit, but two recovered quickly and began firing in his direction, wildly and without focus. He melted back into the woods to contemplate his next move.

**

Jermain rolled the dead driver out of the boat and took his place at the tiller of the trolling motor. Buckshot from one of the shotgun blasts had hit right at the waterline, and water leaked through the aluminum hull in half a dozen places to slosh around his feet. He cursed as he backed off the bank and swung the boat back over to the little dock. He'd lost one man killed outright and another seemed to be seriously wounded, and the rest of them suffered multiple non-life-threatening wounds in arms or legs. He was pissed.

He looked over to his least injured men leaning over a figure slumped in the bottom of the boat.

"How's Tyrone?" he asked.

"Gut shot — it's bad, man. He ain't gonna make it."

He cursed as he struggled out of the boat, nursing a leg wound, and tied off to the little dock.

"Leave him," he said to the man caring for Tyrone. "Y'all come on, but get the radio off Tyrone. I need to call Kwintell behind this shit."

The man shook his head and held up the radio. "Radio's busted. Looks like it took a bullet."

"Shit! All right, y'all come on. We gotta get that old fart."

One of the survivors shook his head. "I took one in the shoulder and can't move my right arm. I can't handle the AK."

Jermain removed his sidearm and held it out. "Then use this and shoot left-handed."

The man shook his head again. "But I can't hit nothin' with no pistol in my left —"

"TAKE THE GUN, GET YOUR SORRY ASS OUTA THAT BOAT, AND DO WHAT I TELL YOU OR I'LL CAP YOUR ASS RIGHT HERE! YOU UNDERSTAND?"

Cowed, the man nodded, and Jermain turned to his other soldier. "How 'bout you?"

"I took one in the leg, but I'm okay," the man said.

"All right. We goin' after him, but he's likely layin' up somewhere to ambush us again. We need to spread out so he can't target us all at one time. I'll go into the woods fifty feet or so, you" — he pointed to the man with the shoulder wound — "stay in the edge of the woods near the path, and you" — he nodded at the last man — "stay halfway between us. Then we all move together toward the house. He'll likely try to take one of you two, and when he does, I want the other one to open up on him, full auto. Force him down and keep his head down, to give me a chance to close on him fast. He likely won't hear me over the gunfire, and we can take him out fast. Any questions?"

The pair nodded, their expressions leaving no doubt about their lack of enthusiasm for the plan, but neither was willing to trade the 'possibility' of death for the certainty of it if they crossed Jermaine. They took their assigned positions and began moving through the trees.

**

Anthony knew one was down for sure, and possibly a second, and he wanted to take out at least one or maybe two more on his 'fighting retreat.' They'd undoubtedly split up now to hit him from different angles, but if he struck again quickly, they wouldn't have a chance to get too spread out. The more he evened the odds now, the easier it would be later. He picked a likely spot twenty yards or so off the path and crouched behind the thick trunk of a white oak and waited for his next target. He didn't have to wait long.

The man was approaching from his left, just off the path in the tree line, and Anthony heard him long before he began to catch brief glimpses through the relatively thin cover near the path. The banger was obviously injured; his right arm hung useless at his side and blood ran off his fingertips, staining the ground. He held an automatic pistol awkwardly in a left-handed grip. Anthony could tell by looking the man wasn't a lefty. The shotgun would win that gunfight hands down, long before the man got close enough to hit him.

He heard another man approaching to his right, some distance away, but the cover was thicker there, and he couldn't see his attacker. He surmised they were coming in a line, with any others perhaps too far to his right to be heard, and began to worry about being flanked if he got pinned down. He definitely had to fall back, but needed to cut down the odds a bit first.

The injured man with the pistol was the logical target, but also the lesser threat, and taking down the still-invisible man to his right would definitely do more to even the odds. He decided to try for a double, figuring even if he missed the second man, he'd instill caution and buy time to get to his next hide.

He swung the shotgun toward the man with the pistol, waiting for him to step into a gap between the trees, then fired. A tight pattern of buckshot riddled his target's midsection, and Anthony ejected the shell and swung the gun before the man even hit the ground. He pumped four loads of buckshot through the foliage in the direction of his unseen stalker, and turned to run, moving as fast as his old legs allowed. He stuck to the path now, knowing he'd make better time, and confident the surviving attackers were in the thick woods to the west.

His breath was coming in gasps and he was halfway to the cabin when a man stepped from behind a big tree and slammed the butt of an assault rifle into his gut.

***

Jermain moved through the thick woods at a hobbling run, as fast as his injured leg would allow, his noisy passage masked by distance. He figured the old man would set up another ambush closer to the path; that was the logical thing to do. His reluctantly advancing underlings would trigger that trap, spurred on by the thought Jermain was at the far end of their short line of advance, ready to deal with them if they faltered. But unknown to them, he'd already rushed ahead, moving fast and circling wide in an attempt to take the old man from behind.

There were only two possible outcomes: his men would pin the old man down or the old man would win the fight and fall back looking for a new ambush site, and Jermain was prepared for either eventuality. If his men survived the ambush and pinned the old bastard down, he'd creep up from behind and back shoot him. But if the old man sprang his trap successfully and then retreated, Jermain would become the ambusher. Either way, the old man was going down.

He ran on, adrenaline masking the pain in his leg, and when he thought he'd gone far enough, angled right, moving to intersect the path. The woods began to thin a bit, and he was brought up short by the sound of gunfire—a single shotgun blast followed by four more in rapid succession—with no return fire. His men were either down or cowering, and either way he expected the old man to fall back in his direction. He took a position near the path behind a thick tree trunk and was rewarded moments later by the sound of boots pounding the packed earth and labored breathing. He steadied his AK against the tree, sighting up the path. The old man came into sight, running hell-bent for leather with his eyes on the path immediately ahead of him, oblivious to the threat farther down the path. Jermain aimed—and then thought better of it.

What if they had the good stuff hidden? The old man would be the only one who knew where it was. He couldn't call for reinforcements to search the place because the radio was shot up, and he sure as hell didn't want to be here by himself when that Levi asshole got back. And showing up empty-handed after losing his whole crew to one old man and then trying to explain to Kwintell didn't bear thinking about. He knew his odds of survival would be infinitely improved with a few cases of grenades or the gold and silver that fool

Singletary was always babbling about. No way round it, he had to take the old man alive. Of course, he didn't have to be gentle.

He dodged back behind the tree and reversed his grip on the rifle, waiting for the old man to approach. He sprang from hiding to slam the rifle butt into his quarry's gut, sending the shotgun flying and dropping the old man flat on his back. Jermain flipped the old man onto his stomach and flex-cuffed his hands behind him with an electrical tie, then dragged him to his feet and pushed him down the trail toward the camp.

* * *

The thug heaved the rope a final time, and Anthony came almost off the ground, forced on tiptoe to relieve the racking pain in his arms and shoulders. He was suspended by his wrists from a crossbeam of the outdoor kitchen, and the sharp pain in his gut from the rifle butt was quickly palling compared to this latest abuse of his aging body. He stifled a moan and glared at the banger as the man tied the end of the rope to one of the support poles. He took satisfaction from the blood staining the leg of the man's jeans and his awkward movement, and regretted he'd failed to make every shotgun blast accurate. The man pulled the knot tight and limped back toward him.

"Now, old man, we gonna have us a little talk." The thug smiled. "You a pretty tough old bastard, I'll give you that. I looked around a little and y'all got a good setup here too. Thing is, I couldn't find the really good stuff, so you gonna tell me where you got it hid."

"What the hell are you talking about? We don't have anything hidden. It's ALL hidden here in the woods, so why would we need to hide anything from each other?"

"Don't play stupid! You know what I'm talkin' about. Where are the grenades, and the gold and silver?"

"Grenades? Gold? Silver? You been smokin' crack? Why would we have any of that stuff? We sure couldn't eat it."

"Don't act dumb. I know you got grenades from them soldiers at Wilmington, and Singletary told us about the gold and silver—"

Anthony scoffed. "SINGLETARY! So that's why you're here? Anybody stupid enough to listen to that fool is dumber than a box of—"

The blow was unexpected, driving into Anthony's midsection in the same place the rifle butt landed. The result was involuntary and equally unexpected, as the contents of his stomach erupted from his mouth, spraying into the thug's face. The man jumped back, then stood stock-still for a long moment, Anthony's vomit dripping from his chin. The rage seemed to build almost visibly until the thug trembled with rage, and he dipped a hand into his pocket to fish out a switchblade. The knife sprang open with an audible click.

"We still got some talkin' to do, old man, but you don't need your balls for that. Fact is, I figure an old man like you don't need 'em no way, so I'm gonna do you a favor and take 'em off."

Less belligerent now, Anthony closed his eyes and steeled himself as he felt the thug tugging at his belt, then something warm and wet splashed his face—followed a fraction of a second later by the unmistakable crack of a gunshot.

* * *

Anthony lay on the ground and braced himself as the big man probed his tender belly, looking over the man's broad back at the men standing behind him.

"I'm obliged, Vernon," Anthony said. "If y'all showed up a few minutes later, I reckon I'd have been changin' rows in the church choir."

Vern Gibson laughed. "Glad to help another river rat, Anthony, though I didn't know you were one. I figured you'd be at your place in Currie. When did y'all move here to the river?"

"Soon as the power went out. Levi figured it wasn't coming back anytime soon, and we were way too exposed on the county road."

186

Vern nodded. "That's a fact, though it looks like you're attracting a fair amount of trouble here too. Held your own right well too — taking down five out of six ain't bad."

"Five? I only got four that I know of."

"I was giving you credit for the snake-bit one we found in the willows," Vern said.

"Well, I'll be damned," Anthony said, "so THAT was the ruckus, then. Hadn't been for that snake, they'd have caught me flat-footed for sure. Guess they serve a purpose after all. Anyway, I'm obliged to you."

Vern nodded to the big man examining Anthony. "Then you ought to thank Sergeant Washington here. He took out the banger."

The big man finished his examination of Anthony and rocked back on his knees and flashed an embarrassed smile.

"And I do thank you, Sergeant," Anthony said.

"Not necessary, Mr. Jenkins," Washington said, "all in a day's work."

"How's it look, Washington?" said a young man who looked somehow familiar.

Washington shook his head. "I'm not a medic, Lieutenant Kinsey, but I think he's gonna be okay. He really needs to see a doctor, though."

"Kinsey," Anthony said. "I knew that face looked familiar. Your daddy in the Coast Guard?"

"Yes, sir," the man replied. "Is he here? I'm looking for him."

Anthony shook his head. "He took off a week ago on a ship headed to Texas. But I reckon they're checking in with the folks at Wilmington. We got a radio here, but their antenna is much taller. They can pass a message to him for sure."

The young man let out a relieved sigh. "Well, that's about the best news I've heard in a while. At least I know he's okay."

"Is there a doctor in Wilmington?" Vern Gibson asked.

"There was a medic with the National Guard unit," Anthony said, "and they were going to try to find medical personnel among the refugees, but I don't know if they did. But y'all don't worry about me. I'm fine right here."

"We're not leaving you," Vern said, "even if we got to tie you up. You need to get checked out."

"Somebody's got to stay here and feed the animals," Anthony protested.

"I reckon rabbits and chickens can get by on their own a few days," Vern Gibson said, "but even if they can't, we can cover it." He looked at Luke Kinsey. "You got 'em fed for today, and we'll likely overnight in Wilmington and head back up to our place tomorrow, so we'll stop in and check on them. Then we'll come down every day until y'all get back. How's that?"

"You don't have —"

"I know I don't HAVE to do it, but it's what neighbors do, and things bein' like they are, we're all gonna need good neighbors, Anthony."

Anthony grew quiet, then nodded. "I expect I can't argue with that. All right, have it your way. I'm all right, but I'll go get checked out if it makes you feel better. I gotta tell Levi and the others what happened anyway and I don't want to go into it over the radio. No tellin' what that puke Singletary told those bangers. I don't know how he found us to start with, but if they know we're here, I expect this isn't the end of our problems."

APPALACHIAN TRAIL
MILE 998.6 NORTHBOUND
JUST SOUTH OF BEAR'S DEN

DAY 17, 8:45 A.M.

George Anderson gasped as he sprinted up the hill, back toward Bear's Den, the gun belt on and the other items Tremble left in his pockets. He'd worked his way out of the paracord in less than ten minutes, but knew that was by design. He might be a country boy, but he knew a setup when he saw one, and he sure as hell didn't intend to be Tremble's diversion. Not that he didn't intend to bolt—he had no doubt he was on borrowed time as far as FEMA was concerned, and hauling ass was his last chance. However, he also knew his chances of outrunning pursuit were somewhere between slim and none, and the first thing they'd do when he didn't respond was deploy the chopper to check things out. They'd likely start with the known position of the car and work outward with IR scans. Ground teams were sure to follow, and quickly, but they'd take at least a half hour to get here, and the first priority was getting invisible to the chopper and fast.

He glanced at his watch as he broke into the clearing around Bear's Den and dashed toward the hostel. Their car sat right where they'd left it, and he changed course slightly, ripping open the door to grab the two half-full bottles of lukewarm water from the cup holders, stuffing one in each pocket before slamming the door and racing for the hikers' entrance at the back of the hostel. He moved inside, confident the thick stone walls of the building would mask his body heat, leaving only the task of finding a hiding place to wait out the ground search. Anderson liked his chances. The ground around the hostel and the various trails were now a confused welter of tracks, and four of the people making them were wearing standard-issue FEMA boots. With his partner's body likely to draw the search to the AT, the building itself was the last place they'd look, so he started a search for a hiding place.

He found it quickly—a deep narrow storage closet off the hikers' bunk area, almost empty. He grabbed a mattress off one of the bunks and maneuvered it through the closet door. Standing on end, it spanned the closet from side to side almost exactly. Perfect, he thought, and leaned the mattress out of the way against the long wall of the closet and went to the bathroom, hoping to drain a little water from the pipes to augment his meager supply. He was elated when water gushed from the faucet. Better and better, he thought, as he filled his bottles. He grabbed a small plastic trash can, in case nature called, and carried his amenities into the far end of the narrow closet and set them on the floor before returning for an armload of towels. The floor might get pretty hard over time and a little padding couldn't hurt.

In final preparation, he pulled three more mattresses off the bunks, standing them on end and leaning them in a row along the inside wall of the deep closet. He then maneuvered the mattress nearest the door across the width of the closet as he backed deeper inside the closet dragging it behind him. When he got to the next mattress, he let the top of the one he was dragging lean toward him a bit, then tossed it away from him and quickly flipped the next mattress across the closet in front of it before the first fell back against it. He repeated the process with the remaining two mattresses, dragging each back a foot or so each time. The top of the last one came to rest against the back wall of the closet, forming a nice little triangular cave near the floor of the closet, his shelter from prying eyes. All anyone looking in would see was a haphazard stack of mattresses in storage, filling the closet.

Anderson settled in to wait and thought about Tremble. *Two can play this game, Congressman, and I'm not gonna be your damned decoy. In fact, maybe you'll be mine.*

APPALACHIAN TRAIL
MILE 1002.3 NORTHBOUND
VIRGINIA/WEST VIRGINIA BORDER

DAY 17, 9:35 A.M.

Tremble's arms and shoulders burned as he grasped his end of the stretcher and struggled up the steep hill behind Wiggins, straining to keep up with a man two decades his junior. Then he heard the distant thump of chopper blades to the south.

"TEX!" he called ahead. "I HEAR A CHOPPER. FIND US A SPOT OFF THE TRAIL AND GET THE SHELTER RIGGED FAST. WE DON'T HAVE MUCH TIME."

Tex raised her arm in acknowledgment and darted off the trail to her right. Without urging, Wiggins picked up the pace until he reached the point Tex left the trail and followed her path. They found her a hundred feet off the trail where the steep hillside shelved a bit, tightening a length of paracord between two trees. She finished as they set the stretcher down, and began throwing one of their two 'space blankets' over the taut cord.

She tossed some small plastic tent stakes in Wiggins' direction.

"We've only got enough stakes to do the corners. Find a rock and help me pound these in," she said, then turned to Simon. "It will probably be easier if you help Keith crawl under while we set it up. We're going to have to lay on top of each other to fit anyway."

Simon nodded and helped Keith hobble over to crawl under one side of the emerging pup tent before it was staked down.

"I'll stack all our other gear on the stretcher and spread the other blanket over it to shield any residual body heat," Tremble said, and the others only nodded as they worked feverishly, driven by the increasing volume of the approaching chopper.

Tremble finished and crawled into the end of the makeshift tent next to Keith as Tex and Wiggins finished pounding in the stakes.

"Remember to bring those rocks in with you. They may have residual heat from your hands," Tremble called and got grunts of affirmation moments before Tremble was grunting himself as Wiggins crawled through the opening to lie on top of him.

"Damn, Wiggins, you're a heavy bastard, and watch where you put your hands." Keith stifled a laugh in spite of the circumstances and then grunted himself as Tex crawled on top of him.

"I think I got the better deal, Dad," Keith said.

"Yeah, well, don't get excited, Romeo, or you'll find my knee in your balls," Tex said.

They lay sweating under the thermal blanket as the chopper drew nearer.

"You really think this is gonna work, Simon?" Tex asked.

"No clue," Tremble said, "but it was the only thing I could think of. The foliage is too thick for them to get a visual and it's pretty hot out, so there shouldn't be much of a temperature differential. With the blanket masking most of our thermal signature, I think we at least have a shot."

They fell silent as they willed the chopper to pass, and heaved a collective sigh as it continued north without slowing. They lay there another twenty minutes as the chopper reached the northernmost limit of its search pattern and flew back south, some distance away. Only when the thump of the blades had completely faded did they crawl from their improvised shelter.

"That bought us a little more time, at least," Tremble said as they folded their shelter. "But when they come back, they'll be searching on foot as well, and we can't hope to outrun them. We need to open up the lead and find a place well off the trail to hide a while."

"Why didn't we hear anything on the radio?" Tex asked.

Tremble shook his head. "We didn't hear anything on ours either after they realized we likely had one, so they must have changed frequencies. That's pretty much standard procedure if comms are compromised.

And they probably suspected something after George's last transmission. At this point the radio's dead weight. I'll bury it here before we leave."

"You said hide 'a while.' How long is a while? I need to get home to my family," Wiggins said.

"Which won't happen if these guys find you," Tremble said. "We have to lay low several days at least."

"How long do you think we have to find a place to hole up?" Tex asked.

"I'd say that depends on whether our friend George is able to lead them on a merry chase in the opposite direction," Tremble said.

PRESIDENTIAL QUARTERS
CAMP DAVID, MARYLAND

DAY 17, 9:40 A.M.

Gleason saw the number on the caller ID and snatched up the buzzing phone.

"It's about damn time, Crawford. You were supposed to call me hours ago, so you better have good news."

Crawford's hesitation told him all that needed saying.

"DON'T FRIGGIN' TELL ME HE GOT AWAY!"

"It… it's only a temporary setback, Mr. President. We have teams on them and—"

"You had a team on them at the butt crack of dawn! What the hell happened?"

"The first team did apprehend them and were bringing them in. With them in custody, we stood down the rest of the search, figuring it was best to try to keep the operation as low key as possible—"

"So how did we get from 'in custody' to 'we don't have them'?"

"I'm afraid the Trembles are proving more… resourceful than we'd anticipated. They managed to kill one of the team members and the other is missing—"

"Missing? What the hell do you mean missing? So Tremble is a friggin' magician now?"

"I mean neither he nor his body are anywhere to be found. We're beginning to suspect he may be in league with Tremble and—"

Gleason erupted, heaping obscenities and abuse on Crawford for a full minute, only stopping when he ran out of bile and began to repeat himself. The silence grew until Gleason himself broke it, calmer now.

"All right, what are you doing to recapture them?"

"We have a chopper up with infrared telemetry, searching likely areas, as well as search teams working both north and south on the Appalachian Trail. They don't have a vehicle—"

"That you know of," Gleason said.

"That's correct, Mr. President, but there are few roads in the area and less vehicle traffic due to the fuel shortage. I'm confident they're still afoot, and if they break the cover of the woods, we'll be on them in a heartbeat. We've already contained them by putting up roadblocks on the few roads into and out of the search area. It is a bit of a needle in a haystack, but they most assuredly are trapped in the haystack."

"All right, that's something anyway. Tremble can wander around the woods like Moses in the damned wilderness for all I care, as long as he doesn't get a chance to communicate what he knows. Thank God he hasn't been in contact with anyone else."

Silence.

"He HASN'T been in contact with anyone else HAS he?"

"There is… some evidence he may have been in contact with an unidentified hiker—"

"Christ on a crutch, Crawford—"

"But we're handling it, Mr. President. We're treating anyone we find in or exiting the search area as a potential witness."

Gleason sighed. "All right. That sounds like all we can do at the moment, but prioritize the search. Keep your roadblocks and containment efforts in place until we recapture or terminate them, but focus your search to the south. They'll be trying to get home to North Carolina, where Tremble has family and a network of personal contacts. And he may not be a spring chicken, but he has had all that snake-eater evasion and escape training, so his best shot is probably staying in the woods anyway. I want you covering the trails south like a blanket, is that understood?"

"Yes, Mr. President. I won't fail you."

"You've already failed me, Crawford, and if you do it again, you're going to get to enjoy the 'fugee camp experience, up close and personal. We might even let your new neighbors know you're the architect of their lavish lifestyle."

Gleason hung up before Crawford could respond.

HUGHES' RESIDENCE
PECAN GROVE
OLEANDER, TEXAS

DAY 17, 1:00 P.M.

Laura Hughes sat at the dining room table, struggling to deal with the flood of emotions washing over her as she clutched her husband's hand: relief, unbridled joy—and anger. He sat beside her, dealing with emotions of his own, as their twin daughters crowded round, standing at each shoulder with the whole family touching as if to assure themselves they were indeed, all together and safe once again.

"Jordan Hughes, whatever were you thinking, roaring up through the pasture like that? I almost killed you." She could hear the tremor in her own voice and knew she was near an emotional breakdown.

Jordan reached over and pulled her to him in a fierce hug. "But you didn't and that's all that matters. And I was thinking we needed to stay off the roads, but in hindsight we should have stopped well out and sounded the horn and gotten out. I'm sorry, sweetheart, but I was so concerned about getting home to you and the girls I never gave a thought to how roaring up unannounced and unexpected would look from your side." He flashed the lopsided grin she loved. "Besides, I'm still learning the finer points of this 'end of the world' stuff."

She hugged him back then pulled away and wiped her eyes with the back of her hand.

"Well, you're home now, so it's all good." She looked over to where Kinsey and his two men stood, staying politely out of the way while the family reconnected. "And where are my manners? Chief Kinsey, it's past lunchtime and I expect you and your men could do with something to eat. We normally just have a cold lunch in this heat, if that's okay. The girls and I will put together some sandwiches, and we've all the iced tea you can drink."

"That sounds great, ma'am," Kinsey said, "but don't go to any trouble."

"It's the least I can do for y'all helping Jordan get home. We have plenty of food AND room, so y'all are free to stay as long as you like. As a matter of fact, given how things are, having some more men about would be reassuring."

Kinsey said nothing but shot a knowing look at Hughes. Laura followed the silent exchange then focused on her husband.

"What was that look about?"

"Ah, Laura, I can't stay. I've got *Pecos Trader* anchored in the river with a lot of folk on board I'm responsible for—"

"What do you mean you can't stay, Jordan! You can't leave us—"

"I have absolutely no intention of leaving you, honey. We came to get you and the girls and take you back to the ship. We have plenty of stores there, and it will be a safe place to stay until we figure out what we're going to do."

"What do you mean, what we're going to do? We're going to stay here, of course. We have plenty here, and with the garden and the generator keeping the freezer going and the pantry, we can just stay here until they get the power restored and things get back to normal."

Hughes fell silent and exchanged another look with Kinsey.

"That's just it, Laura, the power's not coming back on, at least for a long, long time—years, not months. And things... things might never get back to normal, at least what we used to think of as normal."

Laura shook her head. "We've been without power longer than this after hurricanes. It's just going to take a while, that's all."

"No, babe," Hughes said gently, "it's not like that, because the power's down everywhere, and there are no spares to fix the problem. I don't fully understand it all myself, but I've seen enough to know we're not recovering from this anytime soon. Have you seen any linemen working anywhere or picked up any television signal at all when you have the power on?"

"No, but that doesn't mean—"

"Yes, I'm afraid it does. And it's only been three weeks, so things are going to get a whole lot worse. We probably can't imagine how bad it's going to get. I need to know you and the girls are safe, or at least as safe as I can make you."

Laura's face hardened. "Jordan Hughes, counting the girls, my family has lived at Pecan Grove for six generations, and I'll be damned if I'm abandoning it to let it be overrun by a bunch of looters! I'm staying right here!"

"Ah, Captain, I think me and the boys are going outside to do a security check on the perimeter while you folks discuss this," Kinsey said, then exited the room when Hughes nodded.

Hughes turned back to his wife and gave an exasperated sigh before running his hands through his hair. "Honey, even if I could justify abandoning the ship and the people on it—"

"It's a JOB, Jordan, it's not some holy mission. And your family should come first!"

"You DO come first, which is why y'all need to come back to the ship. It's safer there, and this place is practically impossible to defend, even if I stay—"

Laura glared at him. "We've done okay so far."

Both the twins nodded emphatically. "Mom's right, Dad," Jana said. "When the fake cops came—"

"What fake cops? What are you talking about?"

Laura suddenly looked less sure of herself. "We... we had some trouble yesterday. Some men came, dressed like sheriff's deputies, but I'm pretty sure they were convicts. They had a lot of tattoos."

Shaken, Hughes dragged the story out of her, including the less than successful attempt at sinking the car.

When she finished, he sat shaking his head, stunned at how close his family had come to tragedy.

"That clinches it, Laura, we HAVE to leave now. If those guys radioed in your location before they rolled in here, or if any of their buddies knew where they were headed and come looking for them, this is the first place they'll look. The pecan grove rising out of this flat pastureland draws in people like a magnet and you know it. If you won't think of yourself, at least think of the girls."

"Maybe that was just an isolated thing," she said, uncertainty in her voice.

"No way," Hughes responded. "We ran into fake cops in Port Arthur on our way in, also with skinhead tattoos—two times isn't a coincidence. If they're riding around unmolested in police uniforms and cruisers, I'm guessing it means there's no one left to challenge them. They'll be here sooner or later. You can count on it, and we can't be here when they come."

"But what about the food and supplies, and the garden, and the horses... someone has to feed the horses."

"We have plenty of food and supplies on the ship, at least for now. We'll gather up all the long-life supplies and make a hidden cache somewhere, just in case we ever have to leave the ship. We'll shut down the generator and hide it as well, and take anything frozen or refrigerated to the ship. And we can turn the horses out in the pasture, there's plenty of grazing here, and they can drink from the pond."

Laura looked around the room, no doubt grieving for over a century of pictures and family heirlooms she would have to abandon. Finally she seemed to steel herself and nod.

"You're right. Things can be replaced, but family can't. All we need to survive is each other, because if we don't have that, nothing else matters anyway. When do you want to leave?"

Hughes looked at his watch. "Sunset's around eight, and I'd like to be back on board before full dark. I figure to leave an hour and a half travel time, just in case we run into trouble. That gives us five hours to pack and get out of here. Can you make that?"

Laura stood. "We can do anything we have to do, but we won't be serving lunch. I'll throw some cold cuts and fresh baked bread on the kitchen counter and people can help themselves when they take a break. Come on, girls, I want to get up in the attic and start dumping out some of the plastic storage tubs we have up there. We can use them to cache the nonperishable stuff. And if we have time, I want to hide family pictures and other stuff up there in the attic. If we take the rope off the pull-down stairway and pin it closed with a dozen wood screws, it might discourage looters, the lazy ones, anyway."

"Good idea," Hughes said, "I'll go get the Coasties to help us."

✧ ✧ ✧

Four hours later, Hughes stood in the barn, surveying the large circular hay bales stacked against one wall. There was a carefully constructed gap in the stack, a bit over three feet wide and bridged over by an inch-thick sheet of plywood resting on top of the first tier of hay bales, a quickly constructed hiding place for not only their generator, but stacks of plastic tubs containing all their nonperishable food.

"Whadda ya think?" he asked.

Laura examined the hastily improvised cache with a critical eye, then nodded.

"I think it will work, and it's a lot better than burying the stuff. Wet as the ground can get around here, I'd worry about the seal on the tubs anyway, and fresh dirt would probably be a dead giveaway. Those round bales weigh a thousand pounds each, and when you bury our cache under a couple of more rows of those, no one's getting at it."

"I agree, "Kinsey said, "though playing the devil's advocate, what if someone just cranks up the tractor and starts moving bales. I know it's unlikely, but still..."

Hughes stroked his chin, then nodded. "Good point. When I finish stacking the bales, I'll pull all the tractor spark plugs and fuses and hide them under the loose hay up in the hay loft. I'd just as soon not make it easy for someone to steal the tractor anyway. And since that's going to add a few minutes, I'd better get moving. Is everything else all ready, hon?"

"Just about," Laura said. "We have a few more things to load; then I'll feed the horses for the last time and turn them out to pasture. Maybe half an hour or forty-five minutes."

Hughes nodded and crawled on the tractor, to run the hay spear into a big circular hay bale to begin covering their cache.

BOYD'S BAYOU BRIDGE
NEAR PECAN GROVE
OLEANDER, TEXAS

6:00 P.M.

"It's their car all right, Snag," said the man into the radio.

"Did the idiots just run off the road, or does it look like they got hit? Over."

"Well, how the hell should I know? All we can see is the damned trunk lid. Over."

"Are there skid marks? Is the guardrail busted? Does it look like they tried to stop? USE YOUR GODDAMNED EYES! Over."

The man raised the radio again. "Ahh… none of that. Looks like it just rolled into the water. But like I said, we can't see nothin' but the trunk lid. If you want us to check it out better, we need a wrecker to pull the car out of the water. Over."

"I ain't wastin' time and gas to send a wrecker out there. We're losin' daylight, and if we don't get to the bottom of this quick, Spike's gonna be pissed. Now one of y'all strip down and drag the bodies out. And do it fast. Do you copy? Over."

The man cursed under his breath before responding. "We copy, Snag. This is Unit Seven, out," he said, then turned to his partner. "You heard him. Strip down and go check out the car."

"He was talkin' to you, not me. I ain't going in there, it's probably full of snakes and gators."

"He told me, and now I'm telling you, strip down!"

"You're not the boss just 'cause you're running the radio, Bolton. I say we flip for it, and if you don't like that, you can just kiss my ass and do it yourself."

Bolton considered for a moment, then reached for his door handle. "All right, let's get out and flip. I'd rather take my chances with a snake than get Spike and Snag pissed at us."

Five minutes later, Bolton's head broke the murky water of the bayou, and he moved toward the bank, sputtering and cursing. "Ain't a damn thing in the car, front or back."

"Well, they gotta be somewhere. They couldn't just fly off," his partner called down from the bridge.

"Yeah, smartass, well, unless they're in the trunk…" He paused as the logic of that possibility sank in. "Get the crowbar out of the back of the cruiser."

The man did as requested and then scurried down the bank to the edge of the bayou to pass Bolton the crowbar. Bolton waded back over to the car and stood in waist-deep water, trying unsuccessfully to pry the trunk open before moving away to point at the trunk.

"Blow the hell out of the lock and latch area — empty your magazine — that should weaken it."

His partner complied, and when the shooting stopped, Bolton waded back over with the crow bar and easily pried the trunk up to reveal the blood-soaked bodies of their former colleagues.

"Snag and Spike ain't gonna like this," Bolton said as he waded out of the water and started up the incline to their car, his partner close behind.

"This is Unit Seven to Central Dispatch, do you copy? Over," he said into the mike.

"Seven, this is Dispatch. We copy. Over," came Snag's distinctive voice.

"Snag, we found Morgan's and Juke's bodies in the trunk of the cruiser. Somebody definitely took 'em out. Over," Bolton said.

A burst of obscenity came through the radio, followed by silence. Snag returned to the air a moment later.

"All right, we already got units working that way. We'll have 'em rally on you and start combing the area. I want to show them local yokels what happens when you mess with the law. Where are you exactly?"

Bolton looked at his partner and shrugged. "I don't know exactly. The last good-size road we turned off of was Texas 124, but we been wandering around the back roads and they ain't got no signs. I reckon we're a good three or four miles off 124 now."

"What's a landmark on 124 where we could rally?"

Bolton thought a minute. "There's some kind of old chemical plant or refinery. Looks like it was probably closed even before the blackout, but if you come down 124 from Beaumont, you can't miss it. It's on the right."

"All right, I'll have everyone rally there, work your way back there, but check out houses along the way. Somebody had to do them two in, and I'm bettin' they ain't far away. You turn anything up on the way to the rally point, sing out on the radio and we'll figure out how to get to you. Understood? Over."

"Understood. We'll git 'er done. This is Seven, out."

HUGHES' RESIDENCE
PECAN GROVE
OLEANDER, TEXAS

DAY 17, 6:15 P.M.

"That it?" Kinsey asked, and both Jordan and Laura Hughes nodded.

"How you want to do this, Chief Kinsey?" Hughes asked.

"I think it's best if you take your family in the SUV," Kinsey said. "Then me and the boys will ride in the pickup, me driving and two in the bed with M4s. There's still enough room to move around in the bed of the truck, and they can bring the M4s into play much more easily if we need 'em. I figure the pickup can either run interference in front and they can shoot over the top of the cab, or they can be a rearguard and shoot behind us, depending on the situation."

"Sounds good," Hughes said, turning to his wife. "Hon, let's get the girls in…"

Everyone looked up at the sound of an approaching car, and watched as a Beaumont PD cruiser cleared the edge of the pecan grove and started up the long drive. Then the driver apparently saw them and skidded to a stop, both occupants of the cop car staring at them in disbelief.

"More fake cops!" Hughes said. "Honey, get the girls and y'all get down behind the SUV, NOW!"

Laura moved to comply, and Kinsey turned to face the cop car, M4 raised. His men followed suit.

"How do you know for sure they're fakes," he asked over his shoulder. "These are city cops and the others were sheriff's deputies."

"'Cause they're at least twenty miles outside their jurisdiction," Hughes said, standing beside Kinsey with the .308 trained on the cop car. "A county sheriff's deputy MIGHT stray a bit, but no city cops are driving twenty miles outside the city limits by mistake."

***

"Shit, Bolton, whadda we gonna do? Those look like navy guys or somethin'! Look at those M4s."

Bolton grabbed the bullhorn and pulled open the door. "If they was gonna shoot us, they would have opened up as soon as they saw us. Let's see if I can bluff 'em," he said, stepping out of the car.

"THIS IS THE BEAUMONT PO-LICE! DROP YOUR WEAPONS AND LIE FACE DOWN ON THE GROUND! NOW!"

"I DON'T THINK SO. JUST GET BACK IN YOUR CAR AND DRIVE AWAY AND NO ONE HAS TO GET HURT."

Bolton got back in the car and reached for the radio.

"Central Dispatch, this is Unit Seven. Do you copy? Over."

"We copy, Seven. What is your ETA at rally point? Over."

"We have a problem. I think we found who offed our guys, but they look like navy or something and they all have assault rifles. We are outgunned. Over."

"What do you mean navy?"

"Some of 'em have on blue coveralls and caps and they all got on body armor. Definitely look like military. Over."

"How many is 'all'? Over."

"Four shooters and some women. Over."

"All right, hold 'em there if you can, but if you have to move back, stay in contact so we know where they are. I'll send everybody in the area your way. Can you give me any better directions? Over."

"South of Texas 124 a couple of miles. If you get in the area, look for a clump of tall trees—sticks out like a sore thumb. Ya can't miss it if you're close. Over."

"We copy. Central Dispatch out."

Bolton nodded. "I guess we just sit and watch and wait."

"How the hell we gonna 'hold 'em' here if they decide to leave?"

Bolton shrugged. "I reckon we just sit here and block the drive. They'll likely fire warning shots if they get ready to leave, and we'll just back out of the driveway and down the road a ways and follow 'em. Like as not they'll run right into the other boys comin' in. It ain't like there's a lot of roads to choose from."

***

"You think they're just gonna sit there?" Hughes asked.

"Looks like he was talking on the radio, so yeah, I think they're gonna sit there and wait for backup," Kinsey answered.

Hughes nodded. "That's my thinking too, and we need to break contact and be long gone when they arrive. I'll get the girls into the SUV and take off and y'all provide the rearguard like you planned. But if they try to follow, we have to leave them sitting right here; otherwise they'll keep bringing the others down on us."

"I'm way ahead of you, Cap," Kinsey said. "We'll keep 'em covered and then move out after you."

Hughes nodded and lowered his rifle as he backed away. Seconds later Kinsey heard car doors slamming and the SUV's engine cranking.

"All right," Kinsey called to his men, "I'll keep 'em covered while you two set up in the bed of the pickup. Let me know when you got 'em covered again and I'll get behind the wheel."

"Roger that, Chief," Jones said, and Kinsey heard the two men scrambling into the back of the truck.

"Ready, Chief. We got 'em covered," Jones said, and Kinsey lowered his M4 and jumped behind the wheel, giving a tap of the horn to let Hughes know he was ready. Hughes waved his arm out the window in acknowledgment and started past the barn and toward the pasture. Kinsey followed, glancing in his rearview mirror at the cop car in the driveway. Don't do it, he thought, then shook his head as the car started to move.

***

"Where the hell they goin'? That ain't nothin' but a cow pasture."

"Must come out on a road somewhere," Bolton said, starting the car, "and we gotta stay with 'em, else we'll be in deep shit."

The cop car had barely started moving when the M4s in the truck ahead of them spoke in unison, and two separate three-round bursts shredded both front tires, followed by half a dozen rounds in the radiator. Bolton braked and the car thumped and bucked to a stop on the ruined tires and steam began to billow out from under the hood. He beat the steering wheel with the palms of his hands.

196

"SHIT! SHIT! SHIT! We're gonna catch hell from Snag and Spike on this one."

He sighed and reached for the radio. "Better let 'em know quick, or it'll be worse."

FEDERAL CORRECTIONAL COMPLEX
BEAUMONT, TEXAS

"GODDAMN IT!" yelled Spike McComb, flinging a chair across his newly established 'central dispatch' office for emphasis. Snaggle flinched as the metal chair smashed against the wall with loud bang, and the other cons fidgeted in their own chairs, glancing at the door as if they might take flight to avoid McComb's rage.

"We'll get 'em, Spike, don't worry," Snaggle said.

"I ain't worried, you moron, I'm PISSED! Those ain't navy guys, it's them damn Coast Guard pukes you dumb assholes let git away. You know, the ones you can't seem to find on a GIGANTIC GODDAMNED SHIP! And imagine that, here they are not even a day later causing trouble. Who would have guessed?"

"The boat's working now," Snaggle said, "and I got 'em on the river—"

"Never mind the damn boat, one problem at a time. And I'll start runnin' the show since you can't seem to find your ass with both hands. Bring me a damn map. NOW!"

Snaggle hurried to rummage through a desk drawer and produced a road map, which he spread on the desk in front of Spike.

"All right, where are those idiots who just got their car shot up?"

Snaggle pointed at an area on the map. "Round about here, best I can tell."

McComb rubbed his chin as he looked at the map. "If these assholes came from this ghost ship, then it stands to reason they're headed back to it, and it's got to be somewhere on the damn river, even if you assholes can't find it. That means they gotta be heading back east, toward the river—and us." He looked a little closer at the map and pointed to a blue line. "What's this creek here?"

Snaggle squinted. "Looks like Taylor's Bayou and then it branches off and becomes Hillebrandt Bayou…" He trailed off as the implications became obvious.

McComb nodded. "That's right, they gotta cross it and there ain't that many bridges. We just set up at each crossing and we'll pick 'em up at one of 'em for sure."

Snaggle ran his finger up the blue line. "Looks like bridges on 73, 365, 124, and I-10, but I doubt they'd use I-10, it's pretty much a parking lot."

"I agree," McComb said. "Get those other bridges covered right away."

"We'll have roadblocks up in—"

"Not roadblocks, you idiot! Cover 'em out of sight; then when we pick 'em up, we'll let 'em lead us back to the ship. When we know where they hit the river, we can take 'em out. The ship's gotta be somewhere nearby."

TEXAS HIGHWAY 365
DUE EAST OF FANNETT, TEXAS

Hughes pulled out of the pasture and through the shallow drainage ditch, stopping the SUV on the slight incline and motioning out the window with his left hand for Kinsey to pull abreast of him. The Coastie rolled up beside him as requested and powered down his passenger window to speak to Hughes across the empty cab of the pickup.

"We've made good time," Hughes said. "This is 365, the road we came out on. It's a straight shot due east back to Nederland."

Kinsey nodded and Hughes continued. "My only concern is the bridge. If they moved fast, it could be blocked, and if they blocked this one, chances are the other two are blocked as well and we're screwed. We have to hope they didn't and haul ass east as fast as we can."

"You want us to take point?"

"I figure that's probably best. If we encounter resistance, you might be able to brush them aside, or if the opposition is too strong, we can reverse course and you'll be in position to be the rearguard," Hughes said.

"Sounds good. I got no problem until we get back to Nederland, but once we get there, it would be better if you resume the lead if we have to bob and weave, because you know the local streets."

Hughes nodded and Kinsey powered up his window and swung on to the blacktop, leading the way east, and Hughes and the SUV brought up the rear. It was Hughes' turn to keep up now as Kinsey floored the pickup in an attempt to get across the bridge before they were cut off. He roared down the road after the pickup flat out for fifteen minutes, gratified when the bridge came into view with no sign of a roadblock.

He would have been less pleased had he noticed the police cruiser a hundred yards off the paved road along a gravel track, hidden from view by a small clump of squat Chinese tallow trees.

FEDERAL CORRECTIONAL COMPLEX
BEAUMONT, TEXAS

"We got 'em," chortled Snaggle as the radio transmission faded and he high-fived the con next to him.

"Don't be counting your chickens just yet," Spike growled. "You morons could still screw this up. Now, get back on the radio and tell the unit that spotted 'em to get on their tail, but stay back a ways so they can't be sure it's a cop car. Then tell the rest of the units to converge along their path but to stay at least a block or two away from 365. I'm thinking they'll head straight for the river, and most of those roads down to the river run through or between the refineries without many crossroads. After they turn down one of them, they're committed, and we'll know where they're headed. We just pile in behind them."

Snaggle nodded and raised the mike to issue the new orders.

TEXAS HIGHWAY 365
EASTBOUND
APPROACHING CENTRAL MALL

Hughes divided his attention between the pickup truck ahead of him and studying the faint dot in his rearview mirror. There was definitely a vehicle down the long straight road far behind them, but it was so far back he couldn't be sure what it was.

"Girls, put your young eyes to use and see if you can tell anything about that car back behind us," he said over his shoulder. He heard abrupt movement as the girls swiveled in their seats.

"I... I think it's a police car," Jana said, "at least there looks like there's something on top of it."

"She's right," Julie agreed, "definitely something on top."

Hughes blew out his cheeks. "Damn," he said, reaching for the handheld radio in the console between the seats.

"I thought you didn't want to use the radio in case they might intercept your transmissions," Laura said.

Hughes shook his head. "If they're following us, they already know where we are, and Kinsey needs to know."

Hughes keyed the mike. "Salty Dog One, this is Salty Dog Actual. Do you copy? Over."

"This is One. Go, Dog. Over."

"We have company on our six, so I will pass you and lead to the extraction point. Be aware it might get messy. Over."

"Dog, we copy. Take the lead and I will chat with the home folks. Over."

Hughes acknowledged and swung into the left lane, passing the pickup as it slowed almost imperceptibly. As he flashed by, he jerked his thumb behind him and the two Coasties in the truck bed nodded, and one turned his attention to the rear as the second shooter continued to look ahead. Kinsey gave him a short toot of the horn and a tight smile. As Hughes settled into the lead, he heard the radio crackle to life on the console beside him as Kinsey transmitted.

"This is Salty Dog One to Magician. Do you copy? Over."

Hughes heard Torres' slight Hispanic accent. "This is Magician. I copy. Over."

"Magician, be advised we may be coming in hot. ETA at extraction point in fifteen mikes. Over."

"One, we copy. Advise any change in ETA. Magician out."

They roared past Central Mall on their right, slowing only slightly to dodge the occasional car in the road, as Hughes considered the options. Best to stay on the wider main roads if possible, because there was always the possibility a smaller road might be somehow blocked. Decision made, he kept the pedal to the floor until the approach to Twin City Highway came into view, then flicked his right turn signal briefly to alert Kinsey before taking the turn entirely too fast. The SUV fishtailed and swung on to the access road to flash by a strip center and a huge HEB supermarket.

Seconds later he was turning left on to Twin City Highway, with Kinsey right on his tail. Time seemed to drag after that, despite his heavy foot, and they moved northwest up Twin City Highway, slaloming around many more abandoned cars than they'd encountered to date. Finally, he spotted the interchange with Texas 366 ahead, and exited left to take the long swooping curve that put him on 366, headed east now, with his landmark just ahead. He veered left onto a narrow paved road between a tank farm and the Nederland Little League complex and roared toward the river and the refinery docks, glancing in his rearview mirror to assure himself Kinsey was still with him—two miles to go.

FEDERAL CORRECTIONAL COMPLEX
BEAUMONT, TEXAS

"They made the turn toward the river by the Little League fields. I doubt there are any turnoffs that'll take 'em anyplace but the river. We got 'em, Spike!" Snaggle said.

McComb nodded. "All right, have the chase car plug the hole and close on them, then put as many units down that road after 'em as you can. How many units are close?"

"We got two units nearby and I'll have 'em running up the chase car's tailpipe, with three more behind them inside of two minutes and several more on the way. We can have at least six cars and twelve men on 'em by the time they hit the river. And the boat's just a ways downstream. Running flat out, I can probably have her up to that section of the river in maybe five minutes. They ain't gettin' away."

"About damn time something went right," McComb said. "Do it!"

Snaggle nodded and started issuing orders over the radio.

REFINERY DOCK ACCESS ROAD
NEDERLAND, TEXAS

Hughes sped down the access road, the high chain-link fence marking refinery property on his right and the tracks of the railroad spur serving the refining complex and tank farms on his left, confining him in the narrow corridor that ran straight to the river. The fence posts on the right flew by in a blur as he worked to avoid the frequent potholes in a road that saw more than of its fair share of heavy truck traffic. The SUV hit a particularly bad pothole and he fought the wheel to maintain control, then looked in his rearview mirror.

"Damn! That was a bad one. We're all buckled in, but I hope Kinsey doesn't bounce his guys out of the back of the truck," Hughes said.

"It seems longer than I remember. How much farther?" Laura asked.

"The main refinery gate's coming up," Hughes said, nodding ahead. "That's about the halfway spot. The road forks to the left just before the main gate and runs through a fenced corridor between the refinery and the Sun tank farm next door, straight down to the dock gate. Maybe a mile, give or take." He glanced over at her. "Don't worry, babe, we're almost there."

As if to emphasize his words, he began slowing the SUV and then veered left just before the main gate.

"Hang on," he cried, just before the SUV bumped violently over the railroad tracks and onto the road between the fences, down to the refinery docks.

He straightened and accelerated just as he heard the sound of gunfire and glanced in his rearview mirror to see the pickup come into view. It bounced across the tracks, its occupants hanging on for dear life as the pickup leaned to one side. The gunfire was steady now.

"Salty Dog One to Salty Dog Actual. Do you copy? Over."

Hughes snatched up the radio. "Go ahead, One."

"There's at least three cruisers behind us and closing fast. They got one of my rear tires with a lucky shot. We can't outrun them and we're bouncing around so bad my guys can't shoot. We'll make a stand here and hold 'em off while you get your family to the boat. Over."

"Negative One! Repeat. Negative your last! I'll slow and let you close on me; then I'll stop and let y'all hop in and we'll get to the river."

"That won't work. They're too close and they'll take us while we try to transfer. Get your family to the boat, Cap, then worry about us later. Salty Dog One out."

Hughes started to protest but could only watch in the mirror as Kinsey braked the truck and swung it across the road. The three Coasties leaped out and took defensive positions behind the pickup turned barricade just as three police cruisers bumped across the railroad tracks in rapid succession. Subject to the now accurate fire from the Coasties, the fake cops braked and moved their own cars across the road to form a barricade, and Hughes turned his full attention to the road ahead and accelerated.

A minute later he roared through the dock gate and slowed as he drove up the ramp onto the refinery dock, blowing out a relieved sigh when he saw the Coast Guard boat in the middle of the river. Both the helmsman and gunner were watching the dock and returned his wave as he rolled toward the nearest vertical ladder down to the water. He stopped by the ladder and opened his door, pausing to listen to the distant gunfire. Gunfire was good, because if it stopped, they were all in trouble.

"Okay, Laura, leave everything and let's get you and the girls safe on the ship," Hughes said, and his wife nodded and motioned the twins out of the car. They reached the top of the ladder just as the Coast Guard boat settled against it.

"We've got company, and a lot of it," Hughes called down. "Kinsey's holding them off, but you need to get my family to the ship and then get back here ASAP."

The helmsman nodded. "Torres is —"

He jerked his head up at the sound of powerful outboards approaching at full throttle, echoing around a bend in the river downstream.

"Christ! What now?" Hughes said.

"I doubt it's the cavalry. What do you think, Captain?" the helmsman asked.

"I think we don't have time for this crap, but it's coming whether we have time or not." He paused, thinking. "Okay, they haven't seen us yet and we can't be sure who it is. Y'all pull out of sight over behind that barge downstream until we find out. That way, you can surprise them if need be."

The helmsman considered a brief moment then nodded, easing the boat further downstream to shelter behind the barge, out of the sight of anyone approaching from downriver.

Hughes turned to Laura. "Honey, get the girls behind the car and lie flat on the dock. Anyone in a boat on the river won't be able to see up here on top of the dock."

"What are you going to do?" Laura asked.

"I'm gonna stand at the edge of the dock. That way they'll focus on me and likely won't even notice the patrol boat when they pass it."

"Jordan Hughes, you'll do no such thing! What if they just shoot you? You come with us, right now."

The gunfire increased in intensity, and Hughes shot a worried look back the way they'd come. "Honey, we HAVE to suck them in and deal with them quickly so I can get back and pick up Kinsey." The outboards were louder now and Hughes glanced downstream to see a boat rounding the bend. "They're coming. Now get down out of sight."

Laura wrapped him in a fierce hug and whispered in his ear, "If we survive this, I may very well kill you myself."

Hughes hugged her back, then smiled down at her.

"You may have to get in line. Now quick, you and the girls get down."

She moved to comply and Hughes looked downstream. He could see the boat clearly now. It was similar to the Coast Guard boat except the flotation collar was blue instead of orange and JEFFERSON COUNTY SHERIFF was written on the side. Hughes moved to the edge of the dock and waved his arms to attract attention, and the pitch of the outboards changed abruptly as the occupants of the boat saw Hughes and slowed, moving in his direction.

The boat had two occupants, both in sheriff's department uniforms. As hoped, both focused on him and didn't spare a backwards glance as they passed the barge where the Coasties were hiding. The boat stopped twenty feet from the dock and one of the men stepped out of the aluminum cabin with an AR-15 and pointed it up at Hughes.

"Put your hands up, then come down that ladder, nice and slow like."

Hughes raised his hands. "You do realize I can't do both of those things at once?"

"You know what I meant, smartass, so git your ass down that ladder or I'll drop you where you stand."

"Actually, maybe you should put YOUR hands up unless you'd like a fifty-caliber enema," Hughes said, inclining his head downstream.

The fake deputy glanced aft and found himself looking down the barrel of the machine gun in the Coast Guard boat, not fifty feet away. But rather than laying down his gun, he acted on instinct—a bad one, as it turned out. His attempt to raise the AR to his shoulder was answered by a short burst from the machine gun, shredding his chest and spraying blood through the open cabin door on the helmsman. The helmsman also acted on instinct, jamming the throttles forward in an attempt to escape upriver. The boat had traveled perhaps twenty-five feet when the fifty caliber spoke again, sending rounds through the thin aluminum walls of the cabin like they were tissue paper, three of them catching the helmsman in the back. He slid to the deck, never to rise again, as the boat roared upstream at an angle, to run aground on the opposite bank of the river, the outboards still straining in a futile attempt to push the boat through the riverbank.

Hughes was moving as soon as the boat was no longer a threat, waving the Coasties back to the ladder before turning back to the dock.

"Come on, ladies, your boat's waiting," he called as Laura and the twins appeared from behind the SUV.

Less than a minute later, his family was aboard the boat, moving upstream toward the *Pecos Trader* and safety, and Hughes jumped back in the driver's seat of the SUV and did a three-point turn to head back to Kinsey's side.

REFINERY DOCK ACCESS ROAD
NEDERLAND, TEXAS

"There's too damn many of them, Chief," Jones said, from where he sheltered beside Kinsey behind the engine block. Kinsey nodded and looked down the length of the pickup to where Bollinger sheltered behind the rear wheel and axle, the left shoulder of his blue coveralls ripped and the cloth around the tear stained darker by blood.

"How's the shoulder, Bollinger?" Kinsey asked.

"It's just a graze," the man replied. "Hurts like hell, but it's stopped bleeding. I'm okay, Chief."

His statement was punctuated by gunfire as Jones lifted his M4 above the hood of the truck and fired a three-round burst in the general direction of their attackers, without exposing his head or shoulders. His burst was answered with a sustained fusillade and the body of the pickup rocked as it was hit with round after round.

Jones shook his head. "We must have taken out at least a half dozen of the bastards, but they just keep multiplying. None of 'em can shoot worth a damn, but if they keep throwing lead at us, they're bound to get lucky sooner or later. Just throwing three-round bursts in their general direction isn't likely to work much longer either."

"I know that, Jones," Kinsey said, "but what do you suggest? You may have noticed we're in a flat straight strip of ground between two tall fences. There isn't crap for cover here, so we can't fall back. The second we move out from behind this truck, we're dead meat—"

His response was broken by another sustained round of firing, impacting the entire length of the truck.

"What the hell…" Kinsey dropped flat on the ground and peered under the truck. He saw four men coming toward them at a run, only the lower halves of their bodies visible from under the truck.

"Damn, they're trying to keep our heads down while they charge. Shoot under the truck—take out their legs."

He started firing immediately and was joined on the ground by his teammates. They dropped their attackers in seconds, leaving them screaming on the asphalt.

"That should hold 'em for a—"

Kinsey flinched as a bullet ricocheted off the asphalt in front of him and whined by his right ear.

"Damn! Back behind your cover," he yelled, and the trio scrambled back behind the more substantial cover of the engine block and the rear suspension, just as the area under the truck erupted with ricochets, some bouncing up to strike the undercarriage of the truck while others whined off into the distance behind them.

"Well, I guess THAT defensive move isn't going to work again," Kinsey said.

"This ain't looking too good, Chief," Bollinger yelled, just as an even more furious round of firing began rocking the truck.

Much more of this, and the damn truck will just be shot apart, thought Kinsey, just as the smell hit him.

"Oh, great, just what we need, gasoline! They must have punctured the gas tank with one of those ricochets," Jones said. "Instead of being shot, we get to be barbecued."

Kinsey's mind raced, and he stuck his finger in his mouth then held the wet finger up. He dropped it and duckwalked back to the door of the truck to reach up and rip the door open. Keeping low, he grabbed one of their discarded plastic water bottles from the floorboard and then fished the roadside emergency kit from the pocket on the open door. He slammed the door just as the movement drew the attention of their attackers, who sent a hail of bullets ricocheting under the truck in his general vicinity. One clipped the heel of his boot and knocked him on his butt, but he got to his knees and scrambled behind the front wheel and engine block before any more connected.

"Bollinger, can you see where the gas is coming out?" Kinsey asked.

Bollinger leaned down and looked around the rear wheel and under the truck.

"Yeah, it's about a pencil-size stream. I'm gonna be in the puddle pretty soon, by the way," Bollinger said.

"Can you reach the leak?"

"I guess so, but why?"

Kinsey held up the plastic water bottle. "'Cause I want you to catch this, then fill it up with gas and toss it back to me. Got it?"

"Ahh… I don't think plastic bottles work for Molotov cocktails, Chief, and none of us has a good enough arm to hit those assholes anyway," Jones offered.

"SHUT UP!" Kinsey said. "And make yourself useful. Dig the flares out of that emergency kit."

Kinsey turned back to Bollinger, who nodded and held out his hand to receive the toss of the empty water bottle. A minute later he tossed it back to Kinsey, capped and three-quarters full.

"Sorry, Chief, the leak was slowing down, so I guess the tank level has dropped down even with the puncture. That's all I could get."

"Should be enough," Kinsey said.

"Enough for WHAT?" Jones asked.

"Enough to get the supplies burning in the bed of the truck and make a smoke screen. There isn't much wind, but it's blowing in their direction. Maybe it'll give us enough cover to haul ass."

"Will that stuff even burn?" Bollinger asked.

Kinsey shrugged. "Who the hell knows, but I don't have any better ideas." He looked at Jones. "How many flares do we have?"

"Four."

"All right. I'm gonna reach up through the busted-out window and sprinkle a little of this gas on the upholstery in the cab; then I'm gonna go back and slosh the rest of it on the supplies in the bed, and hope the bastards don't see me and take my hand off or shoot my feet out from under me. Jones, toss a couple of those flares back to Bollinger. When I'm done with the gas, I want you guys to strike the flares and toss them into the truck; Jones' go in the cab and, Bollinger, I want yours in the supplies. Then we wait a bit for the smoke screen and run like hell for the river."

"Sooo… what if there isn't a smoke screen?" Jones asked.

Kinsey sighed. "Then we have to run like hell anyway, because when things get to burning and heat up that half-full gas tank, this thing's gonna blow."

Jones and Bollinger both nodded and watched Kinsey duckwalk down the length of the vehicle between them, reaching up one-handed to splash gas through the shot-out passenger window and over the side of the truck into the bed. When the gas was gone, he tossed the empty plastic bottle into the truck bed and nodded, signaling them to strike and deploy their flares.

The synthetic fabric of the upholstery caught first and filled the air with the vile smell of gasoline and burning plastic as a satisfying plume of smoke billowed from the cab to float across the road, obscuring but not totally blocking the view of their attackers. The fire in the bed produced less smoke, but did contribute somewhat to the haze.

"I think that's about as good as it's going to get, boys," Kinsey said. "We gotta haul ass, but don't bunch up or run in a straight line. Got it?"

The two men nodded.

"We all raise up and unload on them through the haze to get their heads down, then you two take off while I stay back and lay down cover fire. Then I'll run past you and you return the favor, shooting over the truck and through the haze from some distance back. Then we'll leapfrog again. If we're lucky, we might be able to open up the distance before they figure out what we're doing—then we all run like hell."

The plan almost worked. The wind shifted to blow at right angles across the road just as Kinsey finished laying down covering fire, sweeping the road clear. Left with no smoke screen, Kinsey had no option but to drop back down behind the now blazing pickup while his men in the open survived solely due to the timely arrival of Hughes, who pulled the SUV across the road to form a defensive position. Forced back by the heat of the now blazing pickup, Kinsey bolted for the cover of the SUV as rounds ricocheted off the asphalt around him.

He ran for all he was worth, expecting a hammer blow between his shoulder blades at any moment. Then he heard the familiar and authoritative bark of a Barrett fifty-caliber sniper rifle, speaking three times in quick succession. By the time he'd reached the shelter of the SUV scant seconds later, incoming fire had all but ceased as the big gun continued to speak. Kinsey turned to watch in amazement as the huge rounds penetrated the cop cars like they were cardboard, and screams of maimed and dying adversaries filled the air. In moments, the few remaining ambulatory survivors leaped into a partially intact cop car behind the barricade and fled back the way they'd come.

Kinsey keyed his mike. "That you, Magician?"

Torres' distinctive voice came through the speaker. "Abra-fucking-cadabra, boss. Sorry I'm late. I had to find a good spot."

Kinsey looked around. "Where the hell are you?"

"Look up and to your right."

Kinsey did and spotted Torres waving at him from the catwalk high atop a massive storage tank three hundred yards away in the neighboring tank farm.

"Outstanding job. Now pack up and get down here. We need to get back to the ship."

CHAPTER EIGHTEEN

M/V Pecos Trader
Sun Lower Anchorage
Neches River
Near Nederland, Texas

Day 18, 9:00 a.m.

Hughes set his coffee cup down and leaned back on the sofa, reaching for Laura's hand as he did so. She gave his fingers a reassuring squeeze and settled back beside him as he looked at the group gathered around the coffee table in his office sitting area. His gaze rested on Kinsey.

"I can't thank you and your folks enough for helping me get my family here, Matt," Hughes said.

Kinsey shook his head. "You'd have done the same, and none of us would be here if it wasn't for you. My only regret is I didn't think to grab one of those bastards still breathing. We could sure use the intel. I know we're all frantic to bring the rest of the families in, but we have to know what we're up against before we leave *Pecos Trader* shorthanded defense-wise."

"Well, that sheriff's boat increases our mobility a bit, anyway," Gowan said, flashing a smile at Georgia Howell. "Fast thinking, Mate!"

Monitoring the radio traffic the previous evening and hearing of the disabled police boat, Howell set out with a few volunteers and retrieved the vessel from the bank. It would be a welcome addition to their boat fleet.

Howell flushed at the praise. "Have you had a chance to check it out?"

Gowan nodded. "The First and I went over it this morning. Other than busted windows and bullet holes in the aluminum superstructure, she's fine. None of the controls were hit at all."

"Definitely a plus," Kinsey said. "I planned on taking the patrol boat to Baton Rouge to look for my family anyway, but I was really worried about leaving you here without some cover. Now we can mount the second M240 on the police boat and leave a couple of my guys here to run it and train some of your folks. I'll feel a lot more secure knowing you have adequate protection."

Hughes was about to speak when the phone on his desk rang. He excused himself and walked over to his desk.

"Captain speaking."

"Captain," said the second mate, "I've got Wilmington on the radio and they have a message for Chief Kinsey."

"What is it? I'll pass it along," Hughes said.

"Ahh... they're still on. I think Chief Kinsey may want to take this one personally."

"Okay, we'll be right up."

Moments later, Hughes followed a puzzled Kinsey across the bridge and over to the radio station.

"Fort Box, this is *Pecos Trader* . I'm putting Chief Kinsey on. Over," the second mate said, handing Kinsey the mike.

"We copy, *Pecos Trader* . Wait one. Over."

Hughes raised his eyebrows. "Fort Box?"

The second mate shrugged. "Yeah, that's what they've started calling it because—"

"*Pecos Trader* , this is Fort Box for Chief Kinsey. Over."

"This is Kinsey. Go ahead Fort Box. Over," Kinsey said.

There was a pause and then, "Dad? This is Luke. Over."

Kinsey looked shocked; then his face split into a wide grin and his eyes glistened before he turned away from the others and wiped them with the back of his hand, momentarily speechless as emotion washed over him.

"Dad? Do you copy? Over."

Kinsey spoke into the mike. "Yes, Luke, I'm here. It's great to hear your voice, son. How did you get there? Over."

"It's a long story, Dad. I'll tell you when I see you. What about Kelly and Aunt Connie's family? Are they okay? Over."

"I don't know," Kinsey said, "but I'm going there as soon as I can. It may take a few days. We have a lot of issues here. Over."

"Yeah, here too, but I'll try to get to you all as quick as I can. Meanwhile they don't want us talking too long, so I need to sign off. Over."

"Okay. I'll let you know about the family as soon as I know myself. And work hard on getting here." Kinsey looked around, a bit embarrassed. "I love you, son. Over."

"I love you too, Dad. Be careful. This is Fort Box, out."

Kinsey handed the mike to the second mate and turned to Hughes, still smiling.

"That's the best news I've had in over three weeks," Kinsey said.

Hughes nodded, returning Kinsey's smile. "Maybe this will all work out after all, Chief."

SUN OIL DOCK
NECHES RIVER
NEAR NEDERLAND, TEXAS

DAY 18, 9:00 A.M.

Spike McComb stood behind the huge loading arms and looked straight across the river into the anchorage inlet. He glared at the massive ship floating in the distance, with the Coast Guard boat and HIS patrol boat moored to its side. The longer he watched, the madder he got. He exploded at the most convenient target. Snaggle saw it coming and steeled himself before McComb even opened his mouth.

"TWELVE MEN AND MY NEW PATROL BOAT! CAN'T YOU IDIOTS DO ANYTHING RIGHT?"

Snaggle hesitated, unsure of the proper response. He tried positive spin.

"But we know where they are now, right? And they likely can't get away. That ship ain't goin' nowhere fast."

McComb grabbed Snaggle by the shirt and threw him against a vertical pipe so hard his head bounced off it. "SO WHAT, YOU MORON? THEY GOT OUR BOAT! And did you see that machine gun? They obviously got radar too, so we're not likely to be able to sneak up on 'em, and they'll cut us to pieces crossing open water, even if we get another boat."

McComb released Snaggle so abruptly the small man banged his head on the pipe a second painful time. McComb turned to glare at the ship once again.

"But I'll figure out something. 'Cause this is MY county now, and nobody comes in here and messes with me. I'm gonna have that ship and everybody on it, and you can take that to the friggin' bank!"

FORT BOX
WILMINGTON CONTAINER TERMINAL
WILMINGTON, NORTH CAROLINA

DAY 18, 9:30 A.M.

Luke Kinsey stood in the radio room, smiling like an idiot in the wake of his conversation with his father. He'd put the various possibilities out of his mind over the last few stressful weeks, dreading the worst. Confirming his father was alive and safe impacted him more profoundly than he would have thought possible. Now if his sister and Aunt Connie's family could only be brought to safety, the family group would be complete.

He felt a hand on his shoulder and turned to see the smiling face of Major Hunnicutt.

"I imagine there's a happy man in Texas about now."

Luke nodded. "No happier than the one right here, Major."

"So you're planning on joining your father in Texas? How you gonna get there?"

Luke shrugged. "Not a clue at the moment. Everything happened so fast I haven't had time to give it any thought."

"Well, we can provide supplies. That's the least we can do since y'all rescued Anthony, but beyond that we can't do much for you." He hesitated. "Of course, if you change your mind, you're always welcome here. We can always use more good folks."

"I appreciate that, but —"

"But family comes first," Hunnicutt said. "I get that. However, while you ARE here, I'd like to include you in our daily progress meetings so you can get a feel for what we're trying to accomplish. I'm figuring your dad and Captain Hughes are gonna set something up in Texas, and the more we share info, the better chances we all have to get through this. We're a long ways apart, but we'll face similar challenges. And I'd also like you to share what you told me about this Special Reaction Force."

"Sure, I'd like that. But what's the setup? I mean, who's in charge? Is it military or civilian or what?"

Hunnicutt grinned. "We're sort of making it up as we go along. I'm senior military, but both Sergeant Wright and Chief Butler have a lot of experience and some damn good ideas. And Levi Jenkins isn't military at all, but he's got a better handle on this whole situation than all of us put together, so he's welcome to the meetings anytime he's here. Then together we pick other folks to attend the meetings if we have any need for their particular skill set. We actually kind of do things by consensus. I've never been a big fan of 'committees,' but damned if it doesn't seem to be working for the moment, mainly because we don't seem to have any dumb asses involved." He frowned. "I suspect that won't last, but we'll cross that bridge when we come to it."

"Okay. I'm in. Just let me know when," Luke said.

"That would be now," Hunnicutt said. He led Luke down a hallway.

The group was already gathered when they entered the small conference room. Sergeant Josh Wright and Chief Mike Butler were there as expected, along with both Levi and Anthony. The older man got a clean bill of health from the resident medic, though he was still moving a bit slowly after his beating. Despite his pain, Anthony smiled and nodded when Luke entered the room, obviously pleased to see him at the meeting. The last attendee was a bit of a surprise; Vern Gibson sat at the conference table beside Levi Jenkins.

Hunnicutt motioned Luke to an empty chair and took his own seat at the head of the table.

"Okay, folks, I know we're all busy, so let's get right to it. Josh, please give us a quick overview on the defensive wall and the aide station?"

Josh Wright nodded. "The perimeter wall around Fort Box is finished, at least until we decide to expand it. We have clear fields of fire between the new wall and the original razor-wire-topped fence around the original perimeter of the terminal, and protected firing positions for the M2s at regular intervals. We're good to go there. As far as the aide station, we've picked out a level spot in the middle of one of the golf courses at the Pine Valley Country Club. We'll start moving empty containers there today, and should have a basic defensive position built by sundown. I figure we're two to three days from having the defensive outpost, storage area, and field kitchen completed. I think we can get the mess tents up the next day and be able to start feeding folks the day after that." He paused. "Of course, we'll try to shorten that if possible."

There were nods around the table.

"Good work, and stay on it," Hunnicutt said. "There are a lot of hungry people out there so this is Job One. Any intel on the bangers?"

"Just the usual," Wright said. "Except for their ill-advised run at Levi's place, they're concentrating on low-hanging fruit. They've grabbed all available resources for themselves, and are using food and water to control the local population. They're definitely steering clear of us, but that's liable to change when we move out from the fort and start helping the general population."

Hunnicutt nodded. "We'll just have to deal with that when it happens. But speaking of threats, I'm getting a little nervous about our government friends. I'm sure you've all seen the choppers flying over these last few days and all know we've been in intermittent radio contact with FEMA. They seem very interested in our level of stores, supposedly so they can 'supplement' our local relief efforts. Like the rest of you, I'm skeptical."

He nodded toward Luke. "Luke here was 'recruited' for the FEMA Special Reaction Force, and he's provided the first hard intel regarding what FEMA is actually up to. I've asked him to share his experiences."

Luke acknowledged Hunnicutt's nod and then related everything he'd observed from his short service with FEMA. By the time he'd finished, there were clenched teeth and balled fists around the table.

"In light of what we now know," Hunnicutt said, "we have to decide how best to respond to FEMA—"

"Fuck 'em," Chief Mike Butler said, a sentiment met with cries of agreement.

"I'd say that's pretty much unanimous, then," Hunnicutt continued, "but I doubt that's going to go down well. We have to add them to our list of potential threats, probably near the top of the list. Again, something we'll have to address if and when the time comes.

"But moving on and on a more positive note," Hunnicutt said, "our list of allies has grown as well. You've all met Vern Gibson, who has a farm upriver. At Levi and Anthony's suggestion, I invited him here. Levi, would one of you gentlemen like to tell us what you have in mind."

The three looked back and forth, each waiting for the other to speak. When no one did, Levi sighed and broke the silence.

"Just this, Major. There's a lot of stuff in these containers and the grain ships, but when it's gone, it's gone. For a community to survive, you need farms, and farms along the river are the best bet. Vern here says he and his neighbors are already trading among themselves, but with a little more labor and fuel, they can produce much more than they need. Likewise, we probably got stuff in these containers they need, and if we can get a stable community going here, at least it will be a place to trade. However, that's gonna take a little help from Fort Box here."

"I'm listening."

"The bangers and other marauder types aren't stupid. Sooner or later they're gonna start raiding the countryside, just like they tried to hit us yesterday," Levi said. "Fact is, I suspect they may already be doing that along the main roads. But between the Guard and the Coasties, y'all have fast boats and generally outgun the marauder types, at least for now. We're thinking you can maintain the safety of the river and we can distribute radios to the river farms that don't have them, kind of like a 911 to call a quick reaction force on one of those fast boats. In time, as you recruit more people out of the refugee population, maybe we can set up manned security stations up and down the river — I'm sure the farmers will donate the land and the labor to build small stations and docks."

There were general murmurs of agreement as Levi finished.

Hunnicutt nodded. "Sounds like a damn good idea to me. I take it from the comments everyone else likes it too?"

Everyone voiced approval and Hunnicutt nodded again. "We'll do it, then, but I don't know about the stations. We're stretched on manpower at the moment, so I don't know how long before we'll be in a position to staff those."

"Only need one at the moment," Anthony offered, "at the junction of the Brunswick and the Cape Fear. That way you could bottle up any bangers coming up the Cape Fear from Wilmington, and keep the Brunswick open so we can all come and go safely to Fort Box. I'm thinkin' two or three guys with one of them machine guns would do nicely, hidden in that nice little wooded knoll by the railroad bridge. They could see anybody comin' round the bend from Wilmington at least three hundred yards away. Hell, we'll even donate a pair of night-vision goggles to the effort."

Hunnicutt smiled. "And that would also solve your immediate worries about a re-visitation from your banger friends?"

Anthony shrugged. "It's all about back scratchin', Major."

Hunnicutt laughed. "That it is." He turned to Josh Wright and Mike Butler. "How about it? Can we spare the manpower to support this?"

Both men nodded, without hesitation. "We're stretched, but we can make it work," Butler said, "because they're right. Those river farms are likely to be our lifeline, at least in the long run. We need to start bringing them into the fold as soon as possible."

Hunnicutt nodded. "Okay, folks. That's it for this morning unless anyone has any other business. And for what it's worth, I think we're making real progress here. Let's all hit the bricks and see if we can save some folks.

FEMA
Emergency Operations Center
Mount Weather
Near Bluemont, VA

Day 19, 8:00 a.m.

The Honorable J. Oliver Crawford, Secretary of the Department of Homeland Security, glared at the man standing across from his desk.

"What the hell you mean you've got nothing? There's at least three people out there. Maybe four since we don't know about this 'loose end' those morons reported before they screwed the pooch. They can't have just friggin' disappeared."

"Agreed, sir, but I don't know what more we can do. We've sealed off all roads that touch the trail within a hundred miles, and I've put men searching the trail on foot in both directions; fifteen miles in either direction from Bear's Den." The officer shook his head. "We found nothing. It's hard to believe, but they either got past us, or they're holing up somewhere."

"What about the choppers?"

"We've had two up in rotation constantly, covering the trail from Bear's Den south for two hundred miles, just as you ordered. Every inch of that section of the trail is being scanned at least every two hours, but the foliage is too thick to see anything this time of year, and the IR isn't infallible either. It's possible to screen your body heat if you know what you're doing, especially in summer, and it picks up deer, bears, wolves too, all with body temps very close to humans—"

"GODDAMN IT! I DON'T WANT A BUNCH OF MEALYMOUTHED EXCUSES! YOU BETTER START PRODUCING RESULTS OR YOU AND THIS BUNCH OF ASS CLOWNS ARE GETTING A ONE-WAY TICKET TO 'FUGEEVILLE, ALONG WITH YOUR FAMILIES! IS THAT CLEAR?"

"Ye-yes, sir."

Crawford took a deep breath and tried to regain his composure. "What about dogs? Why aren't you using them?"

"Ahh… that's a bit of a problem. We use contract handlers and… well, let's just say the local guy isn't being real cooperative. These are mountain folk and they're not real fond of the federal government, less so since the power went out. His place is pretty remote and he's forted up. Made us state our business standing in the middle of the road, then told us to leave. When we weren't doing it fast enough, he shot the side mirror off one of the cars."

Crawford started staring again, visibly struggling to control his rage. "And why did you let him get away with that, may I ask?"

"The rules of engagement say to bypass resistance, and I didn't think it was worth the distraction now that—"

"I DON'T GIVE TWO SHITS WHAT YOU THINK! YOU'RE NOT ALLOWED TO THINK, AND I'LL BE DAMNED IF I'M GOING TO STAND BY AND LET SOME TOOTHLESS HILLBILLY THUMB HIS NOSE AT THE UNITED STATES GOVERNMENT. NOW YOU TAKE WHATEVER RESOURCES YOU NEED AND GET THIS REDNECK AND HIS MUTTS WORKING THAT TRAIL! IS THAT CLEAR?"

The man nodded, fearful any other response might provoke another tirade.

"All right," Crawford said, "now get out. And you better not screw this up!"

BEAR'S DEN HOSTEL
APPALACHIAN TRAIL
MILE 999.1 NORTHBOUND
NEAR BLUEMONT, VIRGINIA

DAY 19, 8:00 A.M.

George Anderson stood in the kitchen of the hostel, gulping water in an attempt to fill an empty stomach and assuage his hunger. It had been two full days since his former FEMA colleagues descended on Bear's Den in force. From the sounds he overheard from his dark hiding place, he figured they'd used the grounds as a staging area for searching the closest section of the trail. That activity seemed to last forever, but he steeled himself to wait and didn't emerge from hiding, hungry and thirsty, until things had been quiet a full twenty-four hours.

He set the empty water bottle down on the counter and contemplated his next move as he heard the chopper blades thump by overhead and then move away to the south. The chopper was routine now, crossing over Bear's Den at intervals varying from ninety minutes to two hours, from sunrise to sunset. The repetition told him they were doing scans, and the fact Bear's Den seemed to now be the northern terminus of the search pattern told him his hope of Tremble becoming a decoy was a dead issue. For whatever reason, the search was to the south, and directly in his path. He'd just have to live with it.

No longer pressed for time, Anderson began a detailed search of the hostel. A kitchen drawer produced a double handful of condiment packets as well as small packets of salt and pepper and some plastic picnic cutlery. He tore open packet after packet of ketchup, mayonnaise, and mustard to suck them down greedily, then washed them down with yet another bottle of water. Enough to dull the ache in his gut for now at least, and he continued his search.

The kitchen trash yielded empty water bottles, and in a nearby storage closet he found a discarded nylon backpack with a broken strap. Another closet produced a small quilt like those used for padding furniture when moving. Frayed at the edges, it smelled of mold and mildew. Perhaps best of all, the guest laundry trash produced a discarded jug of chlorine bleach, with a bit left in the bottom — enough to purify several gallons of water. He drained the jug into one of the empty water bottles and capped it tight.

The shelves of the small hikers' store on the main floor were empty, but he hit pay dirt in one of the cabinets — a small paperback booklet titled "The AT Guide" and bearing a publication date of several years before — probably the reason it was still there — he smiled as he flipped through it. Far back in a dust-covered cabinet he found another treasure, a full carton of a dozen protein bars. The faded ink on the carton was a testament to its age, and a gnawed corner and liberal sprinkling of mouse droppings bore evidence as to why it had been abandoned.

Anderson shook the mouse turds off and opened the box, extracting a bar and ripping the wrapper off. The bar was dry and hard, the embedded chocolate chips grayish white with age. He bit off a piece with difficulty and chewed half a dozen times before swallowing and taking another bite. It was the best thing he'd ever tasted. He finished the bar and, dry-mouthed, hauled his booty downstairs to the kitchen, where he ate two more mice-gnawed bars, washing them down with more water.

Hunger appeased, he glanced at his watch. He had well over an hour before the chopper returned. He grabbed the damaged backpack and was out the door, heading for the spot Tremble's group had cached their surplus gear. The path was all downhill, and he made it to the cache in less than fifteen minutes. He was disappointed but not surprised to find it contained no food — or little else. It looked like they'd only dumped nonfood items for which they had duplicates: a large Victor rat trap, several heavy-duty black plastic contractor trash bags tightly rolled, another small hank of paracord, a half-roll of duct tape, and a ziplock bag full of fire starters. Slim pickings perhaps, but better than he expected.

Anderson had piled the stuff into his ragged backpack and slung it over his shoulder by the one good strap when he noticed another pile of leaves. He brushed them away to find a pair of well-worn leather work boots, and he recalled the guy stripping the boots off his dead partner. After a moment's hesitation, he knotted the laces together and hung the boots around his neck, then took off for the hostel.

By the time the chopper thumped over again, he was ready. He'd used some of the paracord to repair the broken pack strap, then filled the pack with his meager supplies. He'd then cut the boots to pieces with the knife Tremble left him, bundling the soles and leather together, wrapped with one of the boot laces before it went into the pack. You never knew when leather might come in handy. He kept out one soft leather boot tongue and combined it with the other boot lace to fashion a sling, which he tested just outside the hostel door, using pebbles as projectiles. It was awkward, but with practice, he might take a rabbit or squirrel. The packing quilt was rolled tight and secured to the pack with more paracord, and four plastic water bottles were full and stowed in side pockets on the pack, where he could get to them. As an afterthought, he flushed the plastic bleach jug well and filled it with water. It just fit in the main compartment of the pack, adding eight pounds, but you could never have enough water.

He drank his fill from the kitchen faucet one last time, then rechecked the guidebook. He had an hour and a half to two hours before the chopper returned and almost four miles to cover over up-and-down terrain to reach a good-size stream. He could make that standing on his head.

An hour and twenty minutes later, struggling up a steep slope and still over a mile from his destination, Anderson heard the chopper approaching from the south and realized his error. He'd timed the chopper at the extreme northern end of its run, but once in the search area, it would fly over twice on each circuit, north and south bound, likely scanning on each run. Knowing he'd never reach the stream in time to soak the quilt as he'd intended, he slipped off his pack and fumbled with the knots holding the quilt, the sound of the chopper growing louder. Panicked at the unyielding knots, he slashed the paracord with his knife and threw the quilt on the ground in a heap before soaking it with the water from the bleach jug.

The chopper was almost on him now and he tossed the empty jug to one side and collapsed on the ground beside his backpack, pulling the sodden quilt over both himself and his gear. The chopper thumped overhead, hidden by foliage and without slowing. When it returned a few minutes later, he feared it had picked him up, but it passed again with no hesitation, now on the southbound leg. He gave a relieved sigh and rolled from under the quilt, then squeezed it as dry as possible before rerolling it. He tied it up with a carrying handle this time, so the wet quilt wasn't in constant contact with his pack.

It was a learning experience—the weight of the pack and steepness of the terrain slowed him more than he'd figured, and the extra water provided an unexpected benefit. He no longer had to adjust his speed to be near streams during flyovers as long as water sources afforded an opportunity to top up his big jug. The little AT guidebook showed multiple water sources along his route.

More confident now, he endured three more round-trip flyovers and made another eight miles before he started looking for a place to stop for the night. Three hundred yards off the trail he found a steep bluff and walked along the bottom of the near vertical rock face until he found what he was looking for. An undercut formed a shallow cave perhaps four feet tall and twenty feet deep, his bedroom for the night. He stowed his gear at the back and took the knife to cut some evergreen boughs to make a bed. He had two protein bars and a bottle of water for supper, then spent the remaining daylight hours practicing with his sling.

The final overflight of the day drove him into his hiding place, where the sun-heated rocks and substantial overhang masked all trace of his presence. With his pack as a pillow and exhausted by the unfamiliar exertion, sleep came with the fading sun.

***

George awoke stiff and sore at first light. He counted his dwindling supply of protein bars and restricted his breakfast to half a bar, washed down with a full bottle of water. He decided to try to make the highway crossing before the first chopper flight.

He was roughly two miles from crossing US 50 at Ashby Gap, a four-lane highway with a wide grassy median strip and a right of way cleared on either side. It was a logical place to intercept travelers on the Appalachian Trail, and his first major challenge. He'd driven the road countless times during his daily commute, back before everyone moved onto the base at Mount Weather. However, he'd never looked at it from the perspective of someone attempting to sneak across it in 'stealth' mode.

A half mile from the crossing, the first chopper flight of the day forced him under the wet quilt and he lay there until the return southbound flight a few minutes later. He was up and on his way again before the sound of the chopper faded. The trees thinned and he slowed, moving from trunk to trunk until he had a good view of the highway crossing in front of him left to right, fifty feet down a gradual slope. It looked clear, but he'd be totally exposed for a distance of at least two hundred feet. He was weighing the risk when a black SUV turned on to US 50 from Blue Ridge Mountain Road. He watched the car move in front of him and go west a few hundred yards before pulling to the shoulder in the shadow of some trees, right next to another black SUV he'd missed. Anderson looked at his watch—six a.m. straight up—shift change.

Sure enough, the men in the two cars spoke through their open windows; then the car being relieved started up and drove down Highway 50 to turn on to Blue Ridge Mountain Road, no doubt headed back to Mount Weather. This was not good, and Anderson considered his alternatives. There were one or two places nearby where streams ran under the highway, but he couldn't recall exactly where they were. That had never been important when he drove the road, and distances at sixty miles an hour and on foot were two completely different things.

He sighed. It was what it was. He'd have to stay in the woods north of the highway and head west until he found a stream, then follow it south and wade through the culvert beneath the highway. Once across, he'd find his way back to the trail. More importantly, in getting to the culvert he'd have to stay well back from the farmhouses along the highway and hope he didn't have to cross too many open fields. He cursed under his breath and faded back into the trees before he shouldered his pack to pick his way west through the dense undergrowth.

That's when he heard the dogs in the far distance, baying wildly as they came down the Appalachian Trail.

CHAPTER NINETEEN

DAY 20, 5:35 A.M.

Bill Wiggins and Simon Tremble made their way toward the plaintive squeals, moving carefully in the predawn light. Wiggins grimaced as they reached the source of the sound. The rabbit had almost escaped the snare; rather than breaking its neck as intended, the loop had caught a hind leg and the sapling jerked the animal skyward, to twist and squeal. Wiggins moved quickly, snapping the animal's neck before removing it from the snare and adding the now lifeless body to the plastic grocery bag they were using as a game sack.

"I hate when we don't get a clean kill," Wiggins said. "He could've been hanging here for hours. And it's not like it's always quiet. Shooting him might have made less commotion and been a lot more humane."

Tremble shook his head. "He'd have been squealing if he was being killed by a wolf or a fox, but a gunshot's an unnatural sound. Even that little popgun of yours has a sound signature that'll carry a ways. We all need some protein and we can't eat up what little jerky you and Tex have; you'll need it going north, and besides, it wouldn't last long anyway."

Wiggins sighed and inclined his head toward the snare. "Yeah, I know. Should I reset it?"

Tremble shook his head. "Between the rabbit and the squirrels we took out of the deadfalls, we have enough for today. We're not burning many calories hunkered down, and the meat won't keep anyway, so no point taking more than we can use. Let's step off into the woods a ways and skin and gut these. I want to keep the offal away from the cave; no point in drawing up predators."

They made short work of dressing their game, then started back through the woods toward their hideaway. They stepped over a small stream and set their guns and game on nearby rocks before turning back to the flowing water. Wiggins fished a small plastic bottle of soap from his pocket, another resource provided by Levi, and squeezed a dab into his palm before passing the bottle to Tremble. Both men lathered the blood off their hands, then squatted to rinse them.

"We haven't seen anybody since we dodged the chopper and search team the first day," Wiggins said. "You think they gave up? I mean, it's been three days, and I figured they'd be all over us like a blanket."

Tremble snorted. "They may not be looking here, but I can guarantee they're looking somewhere. Maybe Anderson drew them off, or they've just set up a perimeter and are waiting for us to cross it, but no, they haven't given up. Gleason won't want anyone to know his intentions, so Keith and I are probably now Public Enemies Number One and Two."

Wiggins stood up straight and slung water off his hands before patting them dry on his pants. He stood unmoving a moment and Tremble cocked an eye at him from where he still squatted at the stream. Then the older man rose and smiled, shaking the water from his own hands.

"You look like a man trying very hard to say something but unsure where to start, Bill," Tremble said. "Try the beginning."

"It's just… well, Tex and I've been talking, and we really appreciate the things you've taught us in the last couple of days, I mean the snares and deadfalls, and the Dakota fire hole and all that other survival stuff…" He trailed off.

Tremble smiled again. "Your tax dollars at work, and here I thought the army's attempt to kill me during SERE training was just an exercise. Now I'm using it to escape the government. Go figure."

"Well, that's kind of it. I mean, we wish you well, but I don't really know what we can do and…"

Tremble held up a hand. "And if y'all get caught with us, it won't go well for you, and your families need you. I understand. This is my problem, not yours and Tex's. I get that, and you have absolutely nothing to feel bad about. We're toxic, and in your position I'd stay as far away as possible. It's me that's sorry I dragged y'all into this and I'm grateful for your help. If you hadn't come along when you did, Keith and I would likely be dead by now. We owe you, not the other way around." He paused. "When you taking off?"

"We figure maybe tomorrow, if we don't see any more activity today."

"Are you up to it? How about your feet? We pushed pretty hard to get here, and you were in rough shape to start with," Tremble said.

Wiggins nodded. "It's a problem, and that's a fact, but mine are much better since I took that guy's boots, and Tex's feet weren't as bad as mine. She's had a couple of days off of them to rest up, but we still have to find her some better footwear—gotta be near some sort of population center to do that, though."

Tremble shook his head. "I don't know, maybe we should just separate and hide a while longer, just in different places. I can't help but think they'll be watching road crossings and such—"

"But not for a man and woman traveling together," Wiggins said.

"I think they'll be looking hard at ANYONE off this section of the trail that might have had contact with me or Keith. They might just take you out on the CHANCE you've come in contact with us."

Wiggins shook his head. "I know things are crazy, but for all that, I have difficulty believing the federal government has reached the point they're murdering people on the off chance they MIGHT have talked to you. And even if they are, we have our families to think about and we have to give it a shot. We can't just sit here forever."

"Your call," Tremble said as he walked over to pick up his gun and part of the game, "and I understand your urgency, because the most important member of my family is here with me, but I wish you'd wait a few more days."

Wiggins said nothing but fell in beside Tremble as they moved up the hill toward the cave.

***

Two hours later, Tremble sat on a rock under a tree thirty feet downhill from the cave, watching Tex grill the meat and listening for the sound of approaching choppers while keeping a sharp eye on the minimal smoke given off by the Dakota fire hole. It was a simple but effective arrangement, two holes about eight inches in diameter and a foot deep, dug a foot apart with the bottoms of each dug out so they connected underground.

A fire at the bottom of one hole drew oxygen from the second with the heat from the underground blaze in the 'fire hole' concentrated upward, where it cooked the meat on a grill of green sticks laid across the hole. The fire showed no light unless one peered directly into the hole, and burned hot and efficiently, so it could be fired with twigs and sticks broken by hand. Efficient combustion produced minimal smoke, and positioning the arrangement near a tall tree meant any smoke produced wafted upward along the tree trunk to be dissipated in the thick foliage overhead. An adjacent pile of excavated earth could be pushed in to smother the fire in less than two seconds and large flat rocks on the opposite side of the arrangement but far enough away from the fire to maintain their ambient temperature would cap both the holes a second after that.

The rocks would heat up in time, but it would take a while and look nothing like a human to the IR telemetry during a quick flyover. Detection was unlikely if they covered the fire and fled to the cave at the distant first sound of a chopper. Besides, not only did he not want to deplete Bill and Tex's stores, he got sick of jerky pretty quickly, and Bill and Tex's ultralight hiking stove was okay to boil water and pasta, but the fuel was limited, and it was a nonstarter for cooking much else. His mouth watered at the smell of the roasting meat.

"Damn! That smells good," he heard, and looked up to see Keith coming down the incline from the cave, picking his way carefully and supporting his weight on a crutch improvised from a tree limb.

"I made that crutch so you could get back and forth to do your business with a little privacy," Tremble said, "not so you could hobble around camp for the hell of it. You need to stay off that ankle if you expect it to heal."

"Hey, lighten up, Dad," Keith responded. "It sucks lying around in that cave all day, and I'm not helping at all. I thought I might come down and see if I could at least help with the cooking."

Tex looked up. "Got it covered, Romeo. All done. So sit your butt on that rock and give me your knife and I'll bring you some."

Tremble suppressed a smile as Keith flushed. Tex had nicknamed Keith 'Romeo' ever since the chopper scare and continued to tease him. Tremble sensed his son was more than a little smitten. Well, why not? Tex was likely only six or seven years older than his son, obviously smart and competent, and pretty in a very natural, no-makeup-required sort of way. He suspected she was also more than capable of taking care of herself.

"Uhh… thanks," Keith mumbled and unfolded the knife he'd found in the pocket of the uniform and handed it to Tex.

Tex accepted the knife and returned to the fire to spear a piece of meat and brought it to Keith. "Okay, you two," she said over her shoulder, "I'm only serving guys on crutches, so you're on your own. And that big piece of rabbit I put over to the side is mine."

Tremble laughed and took out his own knife to spear half of one of the squirrels. He saw Wiggins hesitate before doing the same. If you plan to make it all the way to Maine, my friend, you're probably going to have to eat things a lot worse than squirrel, he thought.

They ate in companionable silence, holding the hot meat on their knives to nibble while it cooled, then attacking in earnest when they could handle it, grease running down their chins. They ate until it was gone, leaving it to Tex to parcel the meat out fairly. When they'd dumped the bones in the fire hole and killed the fire, each was feeling pleasantly full. Tremble broke the silence.

"First light?"

Wiggins looked at Tex and nodded.

"Want to take one of the M4s?" Tremble asked.

"Negative," Tex said quickly. "Those are military-issue full auto. We could never explain them if we got caught, and they'd tie us right back to those FEMA guys. Besides, there's not much ammo anyway. Thanks for the offer, Simon, but it's not worth it."

Wiggins was nodding. "Tex is right, but we'll take one of those Sigs, though, and a little of the ammo. They're fairly common, so it shouldn't necessarily raise any questions if we're detained, and it's a nine millimeter like Tex's Glock so we can share ammo. That'll give us both a pistol along with the survival rifle. If we need more than that, we're probably screwed anyway. Our best defense is staying out of sight." He paused. "But what about you? We don't want to leave you with nothing. We'll split what we have."

It was Tremble's turn to decline. "You've got a long way to go, and y'all will need every bit of the food you've got and more. Dividing the food won't make much difference and there's plenty of game, so Keith and I can live off the land. But if you could spare a bit off that spool of wire I saw, some paracord for snares and such, and maybe a couple of those heavy garbage bags to carry stuff in, that would be great."

Wiggins looked at Tex, and she nodded. "Done," he said. "And I'll throw in a lighter. Levi gave us a half dozen and I didn't dump 'em 'cause they're light. But what about water? You got nothing to carry it in, nor anything to boil it in to sterilize it either."

Tremble shrugged. "There's a lot of water around, and as long as we can catch a spring where it surfaces and the water hasn't been contaminated with animal droppings, we should be all right. As far as carrying water goes, it is what it is, and we'll make do. I'm pretty sure if we hit one of the access points with a parking lot, we can slip down at night and raid a trash can for plastic water bottles."

Tex got a strange look on her face. "Just a minute," she said, and scrambled uphill toward the cave. She returned a moment later and handed two small packages to Keith and then stepped over and tossed two more in Tremble's lap. Keith was blushing, and Tex burst out laughing.

"Don't get any ideas, Romeo," she said, and Tremble looked down at the condoms in his hand.

"I found those in the side pocket of the pack and was starting to feel a bit negative toward Levi until I just figured out what they're for, besides the obvious, I mean. You can use 'em to carry water, and we can put a little of the bleach we're carrying in one of them as well, that way you can sterilize water if you have to," she said.

"So that's what those are for," Wiggins said. "I have some too, but we left Levi's place in a bit of a rush, and we didn't cover possible uses for those. When I found them, I was just a bit embarrassed to bring it up. We can let you have a few more, if you think you can use them." He laughed and shook his head. "That Levi's pretty resourceful."

Tremble looked at the condoms. "I think I'd like to meet this guy someday."

* * *

The four stood in the dim morning light, the leave-taking difficult despite their short friendship.

"Well, I guess this is it," Wiggins said, extending his hand.

Tremble nodded and grasped the outstretched hand, but didn't release it immediately. "You two take care of yourselves," he said, "and when you get home, if you have access to a radio, please spread the news about what's really going on to those folks in Wilmington and everywhere else you can. Whether we make it out or not, I feel better knowing that at least there's a chance Gleason's plans can be made public."

"You can count on it, Simon," Wiggins said, giving Simon's hand a firm squeeze before releasing it to offer his hand to Keith.

As Keith and Wiggins shook hands, Tremble turned to Tex and offered his hand. Even in the dim light he saw her eyes glisten with moisture, and she knocked his hand aside to wrap him in a hug.

"You take care, Simon," she whispered in his ear as he squeezed her back.

Tremble released her and she turned to hug Keith as well, quickly and fiercely before stepping back and wiping her eyes with the back of her hand and forcing a grin. "And you watch out for the old-timer, Romeo, and watch where you're stepping."

Keith merely bobbed his head in acknowledgment, as if not trusting his voice.

"I guess this is it," Wiggins said a second time, then shouldered his pack as Tex did the same.

They all stood for an awkward moment until Wiggins nodded a final time. "Take care," he said, and turned to walk into the woods. Tex stayed a moment longer then bobbed her head and turned to move after Wiggins. A moment later they were both out of sight, leaving Tremble and Keith staring at the spot where they'd disappeared into the thick woods.

"I hope they make it," Keith said quietly.

"Me too, son. Me too," Tremble replied.

They stood there quietly for a few minutes, each lost in their own thoughts. Finally Keith spoke.

"So what now?"

"We give them an hour to get on their way and then we pack up and move," Tremble said.

"What? Why?"

"Because as much as I hope they make it, their chances aren't good, and if they get caught, they know where we are."

"What do you mean! Tex and Bill would never rat us out —"

Tremble held up a calming hand. "No, not voluntarily," he said calmly, "but trust me. If they're caught, they'll be made to talk, because no one can resist forever."

Keith looked away, struggling to control his emotions. He swallowed several times before he could speak.

"So where are we going?"

"There's another cave about a mile south. I found it day before yesterday when I went out alone to set the snares. It's not quite as big as this one, but there's a little spring running out of it, so we'll have plenty of water."

"You planned on this? How did you know?" Keith asked.

"Family ties are strong motivators. Actually, I'm surprised they stayed as long as they did, and I really hope they make it back to their folks."

Keith nodded. "But what about us? We just hide in these woods for the rest of our lives? That means Gleason wins, doesn't it?"

"Nope, but we do hole up until that ankle of yours is a hundred percent, then we head south. It sounds like these folks in Wilmington are trying to put together a real recovery effort, and I'd like to be part of it."

EPILOGUE

DAY 25, 4:00 A.M.

Admiral Sam Wright reached for his coffee mug, wincing as the now stone cold and bitter brew shook him from his reverie. He shuddered and lifted his eyes from the memo to the large wall map on his office wall, festooned with colored pushpins representing the return of American military and diplomatic assets from across the globe. And they were all coming by ship — his ships, and already starting to clog the wharfs and anchorages of every naval waterfront facility, major and minor, from Kittery, Maine, to Bremerton, Washington, and all points in between.

And in the finest tradition of 'mission creep,' or perhaps 'mission gallop,' he was rapidly learning there was no coherent plan for dealing with the mass of humanity he'd been charged with 'bringing home to safety.' Ships arrived short on food, water, and fuel, and laden with people, to be shuttled to anchorages and ignored as the rapidly accruing liabilities overwhelmed the few remaining assets. He turned his eyes back to the memo.

25 April 2020
From: Chief - Naval Operations (CNO)
To: US Fleet Force Command (USFLTFORCOM)
Subject: Acquisition of Resources

As you are aware, recovery efforts are ongoing, focused on restoration of electrical-generating capacity at limited locations and the repair and build out of the electrical-transmission grid from those restored production facilities. Our national efforts must focus on this mission, if necessary to the exclusion of all else.
Pursuant to this goal, the President (POTUS), in consultation with the surviving members of congress now assembled at FEMA Command in Mount Weather, Virginia, has determined the most efficient course of action is a merger of the Department of Defense with the Department of Homeland Security, under the new title Department of Defense and Security (DEFSEC) to be led by Secretary Crawford, the present Secretary of Homeland Security (DHS). Secretary Tidwell will continue in a role similar to his current tasking as Secretary of Defense, but his new title will be Assistant Secretary of Defense and Security (ASECDEFSEC) and he will be reporting to Secretary Crawford (SECDEFSEC).
Secretary of the Navy (SECNAV) Murray has informed me, and I in turn inform you, that henceforth we will be taking direction from SECDEFSEC and cooperating more closely with FEMA forces, specifically the newly formed Special Reaction Force, the lead organization tasked with identifying areas where our acquisition efforts might best be focused.
The assets under your command will act primarily as support for Special Reaction Force (SRF) operations and be subordinate to them. While I understand there may be resistance to

this change, I remind you of our obligation to conform to our oaths and responsibility to follow the orders of our lawfully elected leaders, regardless of any differing personal views, and know I can count on you to lead by example. Your full cooperation is both expected and appreciated.

SRF operations have already pacified areas around several nuclear power facilities, and recruitment efforts for both the nuclear infrastructure and farm labor programs are well under way. The biggest need at the moment is food, fuel, and other necessities, and the emphasis going forward is to concentrate on parts of the national logistical supply chain that were beyond the reach or technical ability of rioters and looters and that still hold a sufficient volume of resources. A preliminary list of those locations is appended, prioritized in order of probable execution. Please review it and stand ready to support SRF operations as and when needed.

Richard W. Whiteley
Chief of Naval Operations (CNO)

Wright flipped the page and stared at the long list of targets, focusing on the top name. He shook his head wearily and rose to cross to the chart table occupying a corner of his spacious office, then stared down at the chart of the Cape Fear River and the Port of Wilmington. Home sweet home, he thought, wondering for the hundredth time how he could keep the SRF thugs out of his hometown.

The End - *Under a Tell-Tale Sky* - Book 1 of *The Disruption Trilogy*

PUSH
BACK

CHAPTER ONE

APPALACHIAN TRAIL
MILE 1199.7 SOUTHBOUND
JUST NORTH OF US 50/17

DAY 20, 6:15 A.M.

Briers ripped George Anderson's clothes, and small branches lashed his face as he crashed downhill, leaving a trail through the dense undergrowth a blind man could follow. The dogs' excited baying in the distance left no doubt they were closing, and the outcome of the chase was a foregone conclusion unless he could think of something, and fast.

The brush thinned abruptly, and his right foot met thin air, plunging him on hands and knees into a small fast-moving stream. He cursed as his knees smashed into the hard slate of the creek bed and he barely managed to avoid sprawling face-first in the water. Then hope rose anew — would water confuse the dogs? He ignored aching knees and bolted downstream through calf-deep water in a limping run. He slipped and slid on the slick bottom, barely managing to stay upright, his pulse pounding and his breath coming in loud, ragged gasps.

He moved faster in the creek and even imagined the barking was fading, but minutes later a change in the timbre and volume of the baying told him the dogs had reached the stream. He held his breath to quiet his breathing in the desperate hope he'd hear some sign the water had defeated the dogs. The triumphant baying of the lead hound dashed that hope — the chase was on again.

Anderson pushed even harder, oblivious to the treacherous footing as he splashed downstream. He had even increased his lead a bit, when his left foot plunged into a shallow depression in the creek bed. He went down face-first, striking his head on a large rock.

He struggled to a sitting position, stunned, his vision obscured. Water swirled around him, tugging insistently, and when he wiped his eyes, his hand came away bloody. He bent his face to the creek and shoveled water over his head with his cupped hands until his vision cleared. The baying of the hounds grew louder. His left knee throbbed. Time for plan B, whatever the hell that was.

He'd read somewhere dogs followed scent through the air, and the failure of the stream to confuse them supported that theory. Could he use that?

He limped to the stream's edge to strip off his ragged backpack and shirt, setting them both on the bank to peel off his sweat-soaked tee shirt. The sodden fabric clung to him, the sour odor of stale sweat intense as he tugged it over his head. He grimaced as he held the tee in his teeth and rummaged in the backpack for his water jug, a gallon Clorox bottle. He dumped the water and recapped the bottle, then wrapped the stinking tee shirt tightly around it, securing it with a length of twine from his pocket. Satisfied, he tossed the reeking float in the middle of the creek and watched it zip downstream faster than any human — or leashed tracking dog — was ever likely to move. "Please don't hang up anywhere," Anderson murmured.

"Okay, Anderson, stay calm," he told himself as he slipped into his outer shirt without bothering to button it. "There's plenty of time, so don't screw this up." The baying was closer.

He fumbled in the pack again for an old plastic garbage bag then transferred the meager contents of the pack to the bag before tossing the empty backpack into the stream near the bank. It tumbled downstream, half-submerged in the rushing water, to fetch up on a tree limb dangling into the edge of the creek. Anderson nodded—it looked natural, not staged—but his self-congratulations were short-lived as something ran into his eyes and he looked down at a blood-soaked shirt front and blood spots dotting the rocks around him. Still bleeding!

The dogs were close now, their yelps increasingly excited and mixed with human shouts. Panic rising, he tore his shirttail into a makeshift bandage—then stopped. *Stay cool, Anderson, stay cool—lemonade from lemons.*

He limped into the creek and bent at the waist, his hand cupped to his head wound to collect the blood. When he had enough, he slung the collected blood downstream, dotting the rocks along the creek's edge before he tied the makeshift bandage around his head, praying it would staunch the blood flow long enough.

Heart pounding, he dunked bloody hands in the creek, then waded out, splashing the bank thoroughly as he came, both to wash away the blood drops and hide his wet footprints as he exited. On the bank, he pulled one last tool from his 'garbage bag of tricks,' his homemade water decontamination system, a half-liter plastic water bottle containing an inch of chlorine bleach. He slipped the bottle in his hip pocket, grabbed the garbage bag and moved away from the bank carefully, fighting an urge to crash through the brush.

Panic barely contained, he entered the thick brush carefully, gently bending tall grass and shrubs aside and stopping to disentangle himself from briers and thorns rather than bulling through, then making the extra effort of rearranging the foliage behind him as he backed into the brush. Every few feet he sprinkled bleach to mask his scent, careful not to leave enough for the humans to smell, but hopefully enough to irritate sensitive canine noses and divert the dogs to the far more interesting scent trail planted downstream. Thirty feet into the brush, he could clearly hear voices with the dogs. He eased to the ground.

He'd barely quieted his breathing when his pursuers arrived, two of the three breathing so hard noise from his own breathing was no longer a concern. The third man, probably the dog handler, wasn't winded at all. Anderson recognized two voices—Cooney and Maloney—it would be those assholes. The dogs' baying changed to confused and plaintive yelps.

"What the hell's wrong? Why are they running around in circles and yelping?" Cooney asked.

"He stopped here," the tracker said. "There must be a lot of scent and it'll take 'em a minute to process it before they pick up the trail. He might have —"

"Pick up the trail?" Maloney scoffed. "The 'trail' is about twenty feet wide and has water flowing through it. Look! What's that? Get those mutts over there!"

Anderson heard splashing.

"He's tiring and shedding gear. And look, there's blood. He must be hurt," Cooney said. "We got him now! Let's get downstream."

Anderson heard Maloney laugh. "No hurry. I'll radio ahead to Renfro and Herndon and tell 'em to move up US 50 from the trail crossing to this hollow. The road's straight a mile in either direction from the bridge where this creek passes under the road. If they're on the bridge, they'll see him coming down the creek. Even if he gets out of the creek before the bridge, they'll spot him crossing the highway. We'll herd Tremble right to them."

"One thing bothers me, though," Cooney said. "If this is Tremble, where's his kid?"

"Who cares? That's a problem for our more 'specialized' co-workers back at Mount Weather. Our job is just to bring him in." Maloney spoke to the dog handler. "Get those mutts moving. If we keep him looking over his shoulder, he'll pay less attention to where he's going."

Their voices faded downstream. Son of a bitch! That bastard Tremble managed to use him as a diversion after all. He and the kid were laying up somewhere north, hoping Anderson would draw off pursuit—and he was. But why were the dogs following HIS scent? Surely they'd been given something of Tremble's to track?

Then it hit him. As Tremble's guard, he was constantly in and out of their apartment. His scent must be all over that place. And Simon Tremble escaped in Anderson's stolen uniform and his patrol vehicle, so depending on what FEMA gave the tracker, Anderson's scent was well mixed with Tremble's. The dogs were just following the best trail they found. Unfortunately that was his.

He briefly considered giving up, then dismissed the idea. He allowed Tremble to escape not once but twice and 'aided and abetted' the last time, even if it had been at gunpoint. That meant, at best, relocation to some squalid ''fugee' camp, but more likely a bullet in the head and a shallow grave.

The good news was this search wasn't about him. They probably thought Tremble left him in the woods somewhere with a bullet between the eyes. So if he DID get away, he was home free — assuming he kept his mouth shut and maintained a low profile.

Anderson considered his next move. The Appalachian Trail crossing at US 50/17 was now unguarded, at least for the moment, and he was sure his stinky decoy would sail under the highway long before Renfro and Herndon made it to the bridge. When his pursuers reunited at the bridge, they'd likely all conclude he'd just been faster than they figured, and start downstream after him.

He rummaged in his garbage bag for the dog-eared copy of *The AT Guide* he'd found at Bear's Den and flipped pages. The trail followed the ridgetop while the stream diverged at almost a right angle. He smiled as he traced the blue line to the Shenandoah River at Berry's Ferry — five miles west as the crow flew, but four or five times that via the stream's twisting route through rugged terrain. With luck a waterfall or two along the way might slow them down; it would be the better part of a day before they reached the Shenandoah, wondering where the hell he was. He'd bought precious time, now to spend it wisely.

They'd come back to the AT to pick up his trail — there was no help for that. But the roads were undoubtedly thick with FEMA agents, so the AT was still his only real option. He studied the trail guide. They'd watch trail crossings for sure. The pair Maloney so obligingly pulled off the nearest crossing was the primary containment, but Anderson had no doubt there was a second team where I-66 and Virginia 55 paralleled each other to the south at Manassas Gap. Would they set the net wider? Unlikely, for a fugitive on foot. If he could get south of I-66 undetected while they were looking the other way, he had a chance. He prayed the team at I-66 was listening to the radio traffic from the 'chase' now underway and had their guard down.

Another thought occurred to him. The average hiker under pack made twenty miles a day or less in this terrain. But the average hiker didn't have the motivation of a large group of heavily armed people trying to kill him. What if he made thirty or even thirty-five miles today, then rose at first light tomorrow to duplicate the effort? If he could just slip past I-66, chances were they would think he was hiding and focus the search — and the chopper coverage — where he'd BEEN instead of where he was.

Anderson fastened a better head bandage to avoid a blood trail, stuffed his meager belongings back into the garbage bag, and eased out of the brush, careful to leave no trail. He moved into the creek and glanced regretfully downstream — he had to leave the backpack undisturbed, as much as he wanted to reclaim it. Let them keep guessing as to when and how he eluded them.

He limped upstream in the creek, careful of his footing this time, to the point they'd all entered the water. The walk back uphill was easier in some regards, since his bull-like passage and that of his pursuers had blazed a trail. It was much more difficult in other ways, and his left knee throbbed as he walked uphill backward to avoid leaving a tell-tale footprint in the wrong direction.

At the point he'd originally left the AT, he diluted the remaining bleach with the contents of one of his smaller half-liter water bottles. The mixture wasn't strong, but there was more of it, and it would still be overpowering to the dogs' sensitive noses. He sprinkled the mixture behind him as he started south toward the US 50/17 crossing at a limping run, cursing the day he'd met Simon Tremble.

1 MILE OFF THE APPALACHIAN TRAIL
NEAR VIRGINIA-WEST VIRGINIA BORDER

DAY 24, 8:25 A.M.

Congressman Simon Tremble (NC), Speaker of the House of Representatives, looked down at his filthy stolen FEMA uniform and grubby hands and wished not for the first time they had managed to steal some soap during their escape. He sighed. Beggars can't be choosers, and he'd managed to get Keith to at least relative safety. Despite the circumstances, he smiled as he watched his eighteen-year-old move through the woods ahead of him, without the crutch now, but still with a noticeable limp.

"We got one!" cried Keith as he hurried forward in a limping run.

Tremble stifled a rebuke. They were in a densely wooded hollow and hadn't heard a chopper in days. He'd allow the boy what simple pleasures remained in this upside-down world, at least here in the deep woods. It would get a lot tougher when they left their sanctuary.

He followed carefully, head on a swivel and fully 'situationally aware,' employing all the skills learned as a US Army Ranger. He arrived at the snare to find Keith was already skinning the rabbit. His son grinned.

"That's two. We'll eat our fill today."

Tremble nodded. "More than we need. If there's anything in the last two snares, we'll smoke the meat. We won't have time to trap every day when we head south, not if we want to make any progress."

"When ARE we going? I'm sick of hiding."

"When you're ready, which isn't now. You've only been off the crutch two days, and it's not that tough to get around in this hollow, but it's a steep climb almost a mile just to get back up to the main trail."

"But, Dad, that asshole Gleason is lying to everyone and murdering people to cover it up and we're the only ones with proof. We HAVE to do something—"

"And it's BECAUSE we're the only ones with proof we have the responsibility to be cautious; if WE fail, there's no one else. We'll head south when we can, but that ankle's not near healed. We've got food, water, and shelter here and, most importantly, total invisibility. If they spot us when we start moving, we'll have to run for it, and you know what happened last time. If Wiggins and Tex hadn't come along, we'd both be dead. Have you forgotten that, or do you honestly feel you're up to running for it?"

Keith sighed and shook his head.

His father continued. "We have to give ourselves the best shot at success, and that's not starting across rugged terrain with you barely able to walk. Besides, we have to consider supplies."

"All right then," Keith said, "you're always telling me I need to have a plan. What's your plan for getting to Wilmington?"

Tremble nodded. "Now that you're off the crutch, you'll do exercises to strengthen your ankle. At the same time, we set as many snares and deadfalls as possible and dry or smoke jerky for provisions and gather up whatever else we can find—nuts, mushrooms, edible plants, whatever. I figure a week, but we'll reassess as we go along. When I think you're ready, I'll pick a steep slope on the side of the hollow as a dry run, and when you prove you can get up and down it without reinjuring your ankle, we're good to go. How's that sound?"

"Like it will take forever," Keith said.

"Take it or leave it," Tremble said. "I'm not putting you at risk without a fighting chance. Old and crafty trumps young and foolish, I'm afraid."

Keith sighed. "I'll take it." Then he muttered, "Like I have a choice."

Tremble suppressed a smile as his son turned back to the rabbit. *We'll all have to relearn old skills to survive*, thought Tremble as Keith finished and dropped the rabbit into the plastic garbage bag.

"Ready?" Keith asked, and Tremble nodded.

They walked through the woods, content in each other's company until Keith broke the silence.

"You think Tex and Wiggins will make it, Dad?"

"I hope so, son. I sure hope so."

SOUTH OF HARPERS FERRY, WEST VIRGINIA
INTERSECTION OF APPALACHIAN TRAIL AND CHESTNUT HILL ROAD

ONE DAY EARLIER
DAY 23, 9:35 A.M.

"You sure about this, Tex?" Bill Wiggins stared at the treeless gap where Chestnut Hill Road slashed through the woods in front of them. "I feel exposed anytime we come out of the trees now."

"So do I, but this is the best bet according to Levi's map," said Shyla 'Tex' Texeira. "It's less than a mile to a utility right-of-way that runs due east to US 340 and the bridge over the Potomac. Both this road and the right-of-way run through thick woods. We'll just walk the tree line and duck into cover if we hear anyone coming."

"How far before we get back on the AT?"

"Just on the other side of the bridge."

Wiggins sighed. "I'm not looking forward to that friggin' crossing."

Tex shrugged. "It's the best option. If we stay on the AT, we have to cross the Shenandoah bridge into Harpers Ferry and then cross the Potomac on the pedestrian walkway of the railroad bridge. It's ten miles longer and two bridges instead of one.

"Besides," she continued, "if those FEMA assholes are watching the southern approach from the AT, that's where they'll be looking. This way, if we're stopped on the eastern bridge, we say we're coming up 671. There's no way to connect us with the Trembles, and crossing via the eastern bridge fits our cover story. But no one walking north up 671 would go through Harpers Ferry unless that was their destination. Who the hell walks miles out of their way for no reason?"

"I know, I know. I'd just like to avoid bridges altogether."

Tex shook her head. "There are rapids and a lot of rocks, so even if we could find a boat, we might end up miles downstream. Or worse."

Wiggins sighed. "Yeah, I get that. Just wishful thinking. How are your feet?"

"They've been better, but I'll survive."

"When we get across this bridge, we need to find a secluded place to hole up and scout around the outskirts of Harpers Ferry to find you some better boots. You can't go much farther in those."

Tex nodded and looked up at the sky. "Then we need to get moving. It's two hours to the bridge, and we need to be across and well off the main roads before nightfall."

Wiggins nodded and started into the clearing.

SANDY HOOK BRIDGE—US 340
THREE MILES EAST OF HARPERS FERRY, WEST VIRGINIA
SOUTH BANK OF POTOMAC RIVER

SAME DAY, 11:55 A.M.

They crouched in the woods beside the highway and studied the bridge. "Not a soul moving," Tex said.

Wiggins nodded. "I'm not liking this. This is a main road; I expected at least local traffic. I was actually hoping we could mix in so we didn't stand out."

"I don't like it either," Tex said, "but maybe it's like Front Royal. Could be the locals banded together and barricaded the main roads further out. Loudoun Heights is due south, and there are other farming communities north of the river. Maybe they set up roadblocks to keep from being overrun? They wouldn't have blocked the AT, so we bypassed them."

"Or maybe those FEMA assholes did the same thing to make it easier to spot northbound AT traffic."

Tex shrugged. "Even if they did, what choice do we have? Besides, there are tons of secondary roads, so even with barricades, there'll be other people who make it this far. We're just two more lost souls trying to get home. They have no reason to detain us."

"We're armed. How will that go down?"

"How would I know?" Tex replied, temper flaring. "We just have to DO IT, all right? It's either that or turn back, and I'm going to get to my folks or die trying."

Silence grew between them until Tex spoke again.

"Look, I'm sorry I snapped, but my feet are killing me, and I don't see an option. If you do, I'm all ears."

Wiggins shook his head. "No, you're right. This is it. We'll play the hand we've been dealt." He gave her a nervous smile. "Let's cross the Potomac, partner."

Tex nodded at the Henry survival rifle. "Maybe you should break that down and stow it and move your Sig to the small of your back under your shirttail like my Glock. No point in showing our hand."

"Good point," Wiggins said as he shrugged off his pack and began to disassemble the little rifle. A minute later it was all stowed in the hollow plastic stock and he slipped it in his pack. He jammed the Sig into his belt at the small of his back and dropped his shirttail over it. He shouldered his pack and nodded at Tex, and they started across the weed-choked verge toward the highway.

"This is spooky as hell," Wiggins said as they stepped onto the long bridge.

"Tell me about it." Tex unconsciously moved closer.

"Uh, maybe we should separate," Wiggins said. "You know, just so they can't get us at the same time."

Tex grinned. "You want to run a zigzag pattern too? Anything else to make us look suspicious?"

Wiggins flushed. "Okay, dumb idea," he said, but they drifted a few feet farther apart anyway.

They walked in tense silence, eyes watering in the bright noonday sun reflecting off the water, and sweating profusely in the heat radiating from the hard pavement underfoot. It was an unwelcome change from the soft paths and comforting shade of the deep woods.

"I'll be glad to get back in the woods," Tex said, halfway across. "I feel like a bug waiting for a flyswatter."

"More like bugs on a friggin' griddle —"

He was interrupted by squealing tires as a black SUV swerved onto the bridge and roared toward them.

"FEMA!" Wiggins looked over his shoulder longingly at the sanctuary of the distant tree-lined south bank. "What are we gonna do?"

"Nod and smile a lot," Tex said out of the side of her mouth. The car swerved to a halt, blocking the bridge a hundred feet ahead of them. Two FEMA cops got out, male and female; both had their guns drawn but pointed down.

"Stop and place both hands on the top of your heads, NOW!" the man shouted.

"Doesn't look promising," Wiggins whispered as they complied.

"Walk forward slowly. Don't make any sudden moves," the man ordered.

They complied and he halted them twenty feet away. Both cops studied their faces as the man did the talking.

"Who are you and what's your business?" he asked.

"My name's Bill Wiggins, and this is Shyla Texeira. We're seamen who got stuck down south, trying to make it home to our families. We had a car until we ran out of gas. We've been afoot ever since."

"How'd you get past the south roadblock?"

Wiggins shrugged. "Didn't see it, but that's not surprising. There are bad people on the road, and we've been staying to the fields and woods as much as possible. We're only on the road now to get across the river."

The story seemed to be working, on the man anyway. His body language relaxed a bit and his gun moved a fraction lower. The woman was more wary. Tex saw her eyes narrow and followed the woman's gaze to Wiggin's boots. The boots he'd taken off the FEMA cop he'd killed to save the Trembles. Boots exactly like the two FEMA cops were wearing.

"FREEZE!" the woman yelled as she focused on Wiggins and raised her sidearm, but Tex's right hand was already going to the small of her back.

At over six feet and solidly built, Wiggins was the obvious threat, but appearances were deceiving. Tex aimed for center mass, but her shot went high and hit the woman in the throat. Too late, the man turned as Tex unloaded on him, hitting him twice center mass and multiple times in the legs. It was over in seconds, and Wiggins ran forward to kick the guns away from the fallen cops.

"Jesus, Tex! I think—"

He turned to find her trembling, staring at the female cop. The woman was face up, blood gushing from her throat as she made strangling sounds like a fish dying on a dock. Tex bent and vomited on the road.

The woman was beyond help, so Wiggins turned to the barely conscious man lying in a rapidly expanding pool of blood. A concealed vest caught Tex's rounds center mass, but from the blood pool, a round to his lower body struck a major artery. Wiggins knelt, fumbling with the man's belt. He tugged it free to make a tourniquet and twisted it tight, managing to slow but not stop the bleeding. He grabbed the man's hand and put it on the twisted belt.

"Hold this and you might have a chance. Do you understand?"

The cop nodded, unable to speak. Wiggins rose to find Tex still staring at the woman, now clearly dead.

"Tex! We have to go! Get in the car and start looking through your maps for a way out of here."

"I... I... killed cops—"

"Who would have killed us. Think about it later. We have to go!" Wiggins led her to the SUV and helped her out of her pack. He unzipped it and pulled the packet of maps out then tossed her pack in the backseat before shrugging out of his own pack and tossing it in behind hers.

"I'm okay. Give me the maps," Tex said as he slammed the back door.

He handed her the maps and she got in the passenger seat.

"Bill, the keys aren't here," Tex said.

"All right, I'll check the cops. You just concentrate on the maps."

The keys were in the dead woman's pocket. As an afterthought, he took the woman's boots and tossed them in the back of the SUV. He got behind the wheel to find Tex focused on *The AT Guide* and a local map.

"There are sure to be roadblocks on the main roads."

Wiggins nodded. "We can't be caught in this thing anyway. If we break contact, we'll have a shot at playing innocent if they catch us. There are two five-gallon gas cans in the back; let's find an empty car, gas it up, and get off road. With any luck we can find a four-wheel drive. Try to find us a nice secluded logging road that might keep us near the AT."

Tex nodded as Wiggins swung the car north and accelerated off the bridge. He floored it, and the trees flashed by on either side.

"How long do you think we have before someone comes looking?" asked Tex, eyes still on the map.

Wiggins shrugged. "Who knows? A half hour maybe?"

The radio squawked, "Unit 17, what is status of reported contact? Request immediate SITREP. Over."

"Or not," Tex said. "Should we try to fake it?"

Wiggins shook his head. "They didn't say anything about us moving, so either they aren't tracking this thing, or all the GPS birds are finally down. If we answer and they don't buy it, we're blown, but no response might just be a comms problem. That might buy us a few minutes of indecision. But there will be cars or a chopper coming our way soon, maybe both."

"So what's the plan?"

"We'll stick out like a sore thumb to a chopper no matter which way we run, so we have to ditch this thing and fast. Find a place to bury this beast in the woods." He sighed. "It was nice while it lasted, but we're afoot again."

Tex nodded and turned back to the map.

"Slow down," she said.

"SLOW DOWN? Are you serious? We have to get a little farther than this before we ditch—"

"Just slow down! I've got an idea, but I need a minute and I don't want to overshoot our turn," Tex said, turning back to the map.

Wiggins slowed and glanced over with a concerned look. "I sure hope you know what you're—"

"There! Right on Keep Tryst Road ahead."

Tires squealed as Wiggins powered the SUV around a long sweeping curve onto Keep Tryst Road and started to accelerate.

"SLOW DOWN," Tex said, "and get ready to turn onto Sandy Hook Road. It's a very sharp right just ahead."

Wiggins nodded and skidded around the turn onto Sandy Hook Road.

"Tex, this is taking us back—"

"Trust me. Watch for a dirt road to the left."

Wiggins' concern grew as they powered down the narrow road southwest, then swung due west and he saw US 340, the highway they'd just exited, loom above them in the near distance.

"WHERE THE HELL ARE YOU TAKING US, TEX?"

"There," she said, pointing to the left, "turn there. And put this sucker in low."

"WHERE?" Wiggins demanded; then he saw it, a dirt track through the trees. He braked hard to make the turn and dropped the SUV in low gear. He powered down the narrow track, dodging trees and mowing down scattered saplings as thick as his finger until they broke out of the trees and he slammed to a stop before a steep gravel-covered embankment rising across their path.

"What the hell—"

"Get us up on the railroad tracks," Tex said.

"What? Which way?"

"Either. We won't be there long," she said.

Wiggins cursed and started up the embankment at an angle, his heart in his mouth as the tires slipped in the loose gravel and the SUV rocked on its suspension, threatening to roll at any moment. He gained the top and they bounced due east along the tracks; Tex focused on the tree line down the embankment to their right.

"When do we get off this damn thing?" Wiggins asked, fighting the wheel, his speech unsteady as the vehicle slammed across the track ties at twenty miles an hour. "We may blow a tire any minute at this rate."

"As soon as I see a break in those trees," Tex replied, eyes glued on the tree line. "THERE!"

Wiggins whipped the wheel to the right, bouncing down the steep embankment toward a barely visible gap.

They lost the right-side mirror going in, and Wiggins was forced to a crawl, dodging larger trees and bulling his way over and through smaller saplings and brush.

"I give up," Wiggins said through clenched teeth as he held the wheel in a white-knuckled grip. "Where are you taking us?"

"In about fifty yards, we'll come to the old towpath for the Chesapeake and Ohio Canal, which runs concurrent with the AT here. Turn right and run due west along the river back to the bridge; then we'll hide in this same strip of woods that runs under the bridge. I figure the last place they'll look is the place we ran from. The woods should shield us from view, and the bridge will hide us from choppers. We don't have a chance of outrunning them, so we have to outsmart them."

They broke out of the trees as she finished, and a smile spread across Wiggins' face as he whipped the battered car right on to the towpath. "I'll be damned! Pretty smart, Tex."

She rolled down her window. "Save your admiration and step on it. I hear a chopper."

The chopper got louder as they raced for the bridge, but it was north of them, invisible below the tree line. They nosed their way into the wooded strip beneath the bridge with just seconds to spare. They heard the chopper circling as they cut brush and piled it around and on top of the SUV; it landed just as they crawled into their new hide.

"And now we wait," Wiggins said.

Tex nodded. "And hope like hell no one puts two and two together. We're sitting ducks if they figure this out."

CHAPTER TWO

DAY 24, 10:15 A.M.

The Honorable Theodore M. Gleason, President of the United States of America, glared at the two men seated across the desk, a study in contrast. One was balding and of late middle age, his receding chin clean-shaved. He wore an obviously expensive suit and sported a Mont Blanc pen in the pocket of his freshly pressed snow white shirt. A gold Rolex peeked from beneath the edge of a monogrammed sleeve bearing the initials OAC. Even given the man's current unease, he wore the uniform of the Washington power broker naturally, despite, or perhaps because of, the fact the world was going to Hell. But even wearing the external trappings of wealth and power, Secretary of Homeland Security Oliver Armstrong Crawford, or 'Ollie' to those who pretended to be his friends, was visibly uncomfortable. He was doing all he could to keep from squirming under the President's gaze.

The second man was the polar opposite. In his late thirties and the picture of composure, he wore the black uniform of the newly formed FEMA Special Reaction Force, with a tape above his breast pocket bearing the name RORKE, and a single star on each shoulder. His sandy hair was neatly trimmed, as was his goatee, and an otherwise handsome face was marred by a thin, ropelike welt of scar tissue emanating from the corner of his eye and running down his left cheek. In an odd way it seemed to enhance rather than detract from his appearance, and he looked for all the world like a movie version of a pirate or perhaps a Viking. Brigadier General Rorke returned Gleason's gaze evenly and without the slightest indication of concern.

Gleason focused his wrath where it was having the most impact. His voice was calm, but quiet menace dripped from every syllable.

"Four days, Ollie? Tremble gave you the slip four days ago and you're just now getting around to telling me?"

Crawford shifted uncomfortably in his chair. "Actually, Mr. President, it was a single fugitive, so it's unclear if it was really Tremble. I was attempting to ascertain —"

"Cut the crap, Ollie! Who the hell do you think you're talking to, some brain-dead group of congressmen on a fact-finding mission? The frigging dogs were following Tremble's scent, weren't they? The fact is, Tremble managed to give you the slip AGAIN, and you've been stalling for time trying to pick up his trail. You're in here now hat in hand because you've failed and you can't stall any longer. Tell me I'm wrong."

"We know which way he's headed, Mr. President, and we have a new strategy. it's only a matter of time before —"

Gleason pounded his fist on the desk. "ENOUGH BULLSHIT! Find the bastard. And if you can't pinpoint him, I want you sweeping up anyone moving in those woods along his path. Get him one way or another. Is that clear?"

"Yes, Mr. President," Crawford said.

"If I may, sir." Rorke spoke for the first time. "It's not quite as bad as it may seem. To date we've been pursuing Tremble and attempting to block his path and 'drive him into a net' so to speak. However, he's no fool and obviously can anticipate where we might have barriers and figure out a way to bypass them. In response, we've just implemented a two-prong strategy, keeping pressure up on his rear while simultaneously starting well south and sending search teams north up every even remotely viable route. Rather than stationary barriers and pursuit, he now faces active pursuit closing from all directions and must react to our actions rather than vice versa. As the Secretary said, it's only a matter of time, Mr. President."

Gleason stared at him a moment. "How far south?"

"Tremble is an ex-Ranger and stays in good shape," Rorke said, "but for all that, he's still in his fifties. He can't have much in the way of supplies either, so he's likely protein deprived. I doubt he can maintain twenty miles a day in that terrain at the outside, but we figured twenty-five to be on the safe side. This morning we started a unit north from Loft Mountain Campground, which is a hundred miles south of our last sighting. We're quite sure we're in front of him. We also put units in by chopper to start north on the few side trails in the area. We'll get him, Mr. President. You can count on it."

Gleason nodded, mollified. "Sounds sensible." He turned his gaze to Crawford. "And about damn time. Why didn't you think of that, Ollie?"

"With respect, Mr. President," Rorke lied, "this was Secretary Crawford's idea. He just hadn't had an… opportunity to inform you."

Crawford shot Rorke a grateful look and nodded.

Gleason nodded again. "All right, but catch the bastard. He's a loose end we can't afford, especially with this homegrown alternative to the Emergency Broadcast System. Now what are you doing to contain these damned HAMs? The information they're sharing about our FEMA operations is a direct contradiction to what we're putting out on the EBS."

"We got the HAM license database from the FCC, and General Rorke is preparing a coordinated operation to take all the operators and their families into custody and to destroy all of the equipment," Crawford said. "Our main concern is non-licensed operators, so we're waiting a few days to try to locate as many as possible via triangulation. Almost everyone is transmitting in the clear now, but as soon as we crack down, word will spread and any we miss will likely start evasive techniques. The more effective we can make the first raid, the more likely we are to stamp this out quickly."

"Okay, but don't take too long. And have your public affairs people gin up some sort of misinformation to cast doubt on the HAM operators. Say they're foreign infiltrators trying to spread discord and soften us up for an invasion at our time of weakness or something like that." Gleason paused. "Why didn't I think of that before? Let's run with that 'foreign invasion' thing. I can see all sorts of applications beyond smearing the HAMs."

"But, Mr. President," Crawford said, "we've already broadcast the situation is global and told people there wasn't an external threat. It was part of our strategy to keep the public calm. We can't —"

"We can do any frigging thing we want, Ollie, supposing you do your job and get those HAMs neutralized. We control the only means of mass communication and we'll employ it in the public good. See that it happens. Anything else?"

"Ahhh… there is one other thing, Mr. President. I'm having a problem out west. The Vice President inserted himself in the loop and countermanded some of my orders to the military there." Crawford paused. "I even have intelligence he's planning on leaving Cheyenne Mountain and returning to his home in Sacramento to, in his words, 'oversee recovery efforts.' I just heard about it this morning."

"That friggin' moron. He wouldn't even BE veep if I hadn't needed the support of all his moonbeam and granola Hollywood asshole buddies. When is this happening?" Gleason demanded.

"According to my sources, within the next few days," Crawford said. "Do you want me to —"

"I'll handle it," Gleason said, his tone leaving no doubt the topic was closed. "Now if that's all, you boys have work to do, so…"

"Yes, Mr. President," Crawford said. Rorke followed his lead and both men rose.

"And, General Rorke," Gleason added, stopping Rorke before he turned for the door.

"Yes, Mr. President?"

"I bumped you up on Crawford's suggestion, because you're one of the bright spots to date in his little shit show. A month ago you were a captain and now you're wearing a star. I don't think I need to remind you that sort of meteoric rise is unprecedented, so don't disappoint."

"It's appreciated, Mr. President," Rorke said, "but with respect, it's not totally unprecedented. Captain George Armstrong Custer was promoted directly from captain to brigadier general of the volunteers on the eve of the Battle of Gettysburg. He was only twenty-three at the time."

"I stand corrected, 'General,' but bear in mind what happened to him. Just don't start believing your own bullshit."

FEMA
EMERGENCY OPERATIONS CENTER
MOUNT WEATHER
NEAR BLUEMONT, VIRGINIA

SAME DAY, 2:20 P.M.

Ollie Crawford sat on his office sofa and sipped his ever-present bottle of water. He desperately wanted a drink, but knew the end of that road. He owed twenty years of sobriety solely to force of will. No twelve-step programs and, 'Hi, I'm Ollie and I'm an alcoholic,' for him. Power was his drug of choice now, and he mainlined it. The rush was almost sexual—better than sex, actually. Despite having to eat Gleason's crap, being the second most powerful man in the country was worth it—and he might not always be second.

He was relieved to be away from Camp David and back in his own luxurious office at Mount Weather, where he was the unquestioned king. He glanced at Rorke sitting across from him. He regretted his underling had witnessed this morning's humiliation, but it couldn't be helped. Gleason had insisted on a face-to-face with his newest 'general.'

"You did well," Crawford said to Rorke. "I didn't need your intercession. POTUS explodes at regular intervals, a bit like Old Faithful. But like Old Faithful, he can be anticipated and thus managed. He would have calmed down and listened eventually. However, I appreciate your effort, especially passing up credit for the strategy change. I value loyalty."

Rorke shrugged. "I succeed when you succeed. I figure it's my job to make the boss look good. But I thought you were going to bring up Harpers Ferry?"

Crawford snorted. "Yeah, well, given how spun up he got over Tremble, I didn't think an admission we also had a perimeter breach northbound was particularly relevant, especially since it appears unrelated. Did we get any more out of the wounded agent?"

Rorke shook his head. "I got a message a few minutes ago. He died without regaining consciousness. All he said to the guys on the chopper before he lost consciousness was something garbled about a woman shooter and shoes. The dead female agent was missing hers, so that fits. Nothing even remotely ties it to the Trembles."

"All right," Crawford said, "given the strong contact southbound, I think maintaining the northbound perimeter is a waste of manpower. Let's pull everyone off there and use them southbound."

"I'll see to it," Rorke said. "And speaking of manpower, we're still stretched. Any chance of more recruits from regular forces?"

Crawford shook his head. "I downplayed it with POTUS, but in truth those friggin' HAMs are having a bigger impact than I admitted. Some of your SRF deserters have spread the word about our ops, and the

HAMs picked it up. The main source seems to be that group in Wilmington, but wherever it's coming from, word is reaching the regular forces, especially the fact that a 'temporary' transfer to SRF is actually a one-way trip. We haven't picked up a recruit in the last week."

Rorke sighed. "All right. I'll accelerate the timetable and put more teams on triangulation. We'll spot as many HAMs as we can and sweep up all we can identify within the next week, but that still leaves this Wilmington bunch and scattered groups like them. They have radios too, and they're forted up well. It's not like we can just waltz in and take over, at least without a fight."

Crawford was about to take a drink and he stared at Rorke over his water bottle. "Isn't that the point of the Special Reaction Force?"

Rorke shook his head. "With all due respect, sir, seriously? These mercenaries are occupation and intimidation troops. They're okay for attacks on soft targets or limited hit-and-run firefights, but I haven't had time to turn them into a fighting force. Hitting an enemy entrenched in a prepared defensive position with crew-served weapons is a nonstarter. If word spreads we're even considering that, at least half these guys will melt into the landscape."

"Your confidence in your troops is inspiring, General, but I expected a bit more of a can-do attitude," Crawford said, menace creeping into his voice.

Rorke shrugged. "I've been handling trash like this since I became a contractor, and it never pays to deceive yourself about the capabilities of your forces. It's far better to recognize their limitations and plan around them."

"So what's your plan?" Crawford asked. "We've been picking the low-hanging fruit and consolidating our position ever since the blackout, but you know the Brunswick Nuclear Plant is next on our short list. We can't afford to have this 'Fort Box' thumbing their nose at us just miles away, especially if they're linking up with other uncontrolled groups—defiance is contagious. Besides, they're sitting on a huge load of supplies and starting to waste them on the refugee population. We have to get a handle on this if we're ever going to get the lights back on."

Rorke stroked his goatee absently. "And there's absolutely no chance the regular military will take them out for us?"

Crawford shook his head. "Only as a last resort. I convinced POTUS to put the military under my command by executive order, but my interactions with the command structure so far haven't been exactly cordial. Frankly, I view them more as a potential threat than an asset. A growing threat actually, since there are more of them arriving from overseas daily. They're a wild card and I'd like to keep them out of the game as long as possible."

"Just how do you plan to do that?"

"By not poking the bear, at least for now," Crawford said. "POTUS's order and ingrained respect for civilian command authority will contain them a while. If we maintain isolation and don't force a choice between harming civilians or disobeying orders, they'll stay in line and execute whatever support tasks we assign. If we force a choice, we might not like the one they make."

"And longer term?"

Crawford sighed. "A work in progress, I'm afraid. Any thoughts?"

Rorke stared into space and lapsed into a long silence.

"Controlled decay," Rorke said at last, looking back at Crawford.

"What the hell do you mean by that?" Crawford asked.

"I mean the regular military is going to fall apart, that's inevitable. We can benefit if we manage the process."

Crawford looked skeptical. "Go on."

"Look, by orders they're concentrating at major bases with families and dependents. They have what, maybe another two months of resources?"

"If that," Crawford confirmed.

"And ships are arriving from overseas with MORE military and dependents, MORE government employees and families, and any expats who made it to foreign departure ports. What's going to happen to them? Is the military going to force them into the countryside at bayonet point?"

"Of course not," Crawford said, "they'll take them in…"

Rorke smiled. "That's right. They'll take them in, further straining resources. Our friends in uniform are going to have their own little private humanitarian aid crisis. They'll be well distracted."

"So. How does that help us?"

"Because you, kindhearted guy that you are, order them to focus on that humanitarian mission while we defang them. We'll sacrifice some of the provisions we strip out of the countryside to keeping them fed, and in return we gradually but steadily draw down their ammunition stocks. Not completely, mind you, but enough so they're no longer a threat. It will seem like a fair trade, since the SRF is now on the pointy end of the spear and needs ammo to keep order. I'm betting they'll just focus on their own problems and be glad not to have to deal with the civilians as a whole."

Crawford nodded. "I like it, Rorke."

Rorke's smile widened. "And when they're no longer a threat, we cut off the food. Not openly, mind you, we just never get around to delivering. Their operations will fall apart and start leaking people, and we'll scoop up those useful to us. Hunger is a great recruitment tool; you'd be amazed how quickly it erases moral qualms. I used it all the time in Africa."

Crawford shot Rorke an appraising look. "Why do I think you didn't just think of that?"

Rorke grinned and put his briefcase on the coffee table. He extracted a map of the Wilmington area and spread it before Crawford, pointing to a spot near the mouth of the Cape Fear River.

"Because I didn't, at least not the part about the ammunition," Rorke said. "I've been worried about ammo for a while. Until we can restore manufacturing, the only stocks available are those presently in hand or in storage, and the largest stocks in the country are right here."

Crawford followed Rorke's finger and nodded. "The Military Ocean Terminal at Sunny Point. Okay, that's not a secret, but so what? It's an Army facility, we'll just draw it down too."

"That's just it, I doubt we need to, and even if we did, we're talking a LOT of ammunition, much more than we'd be able to transport or store elsewhere. And the terminal is RUN by the Army, but there are less than half a dozen regular Army personnel in supervisory positions; everyone else, including security, is a civilian contractor. The place is run much more like a civilian terminal than a military installation, and I'm betting they used regular commercial means like phone and the Internet for comms, which means they're cut off. I suspect none of the civilians showed up for work, and any of the Army guys who tried have likely given up and melted away by now. You just give the order transferring the terminal to SRF command, and we'll control well over half the military ammo left in the country, maybe more. When we draw down the stocks elsewhere, we should have a lock on the remaining ammunition supply."

Crawford scowled. "Why didn't you say something earlier? It's probably been looted—"

Rorke was shaking his head. "Not a problem, Mr. Secretary, at least not a major one. It would probably take a thousand men with a hundred pickups a month to make a dent in this stockpile, even working full time and presuming they had gasoline for the trucks. The majority of it has to still be there, just because there's too much of it to move."

Crawford nodded. "All right. I'll issue the order. Get men there ASAP."

"I'm already on it," Rorke said. "The terminal is close to the Brunswick Nuclear Plant and I have a force going there in the morning. I'd anticipated your approval and have an advance team ready to deploy from there into the Military Ocean Terminal at the same time. We just need a small force to establish security and patrol the perimeter."

"Good," Crawford said, "but this puts us back where we started. We can't have opposition sitting a stone's throw from TWO key assets. We HAVE to neutralize those assholes in Wilmington. They're too close for comfort and they're getting stronger by the day."

"I've been thinking about that too. Maybe it's time to steal a page from the Special Forces playbook and utilize 'indigenous forces.'"

UNITED BLOOD NATIONS HQ
(FORMERLY NEW HANOVER COUNTY
DEPARTMENT OF SOCIAL SERVICES)
1650 GREENFIELD STREET
WILMINGTON, NORTH CAROLINA

DAY 26, 2:35 P.M.

Kwintell Banks, first superior of the SMM (Sex, Money, Murder) 'set' of the United Blood Nation, glared down the long conference table at Darren Mosley, his Minister of Information.

"And y'all just stood by and let one of these punk-ass soldier boys off a UBN brother and disrespect us without firin' a shot back, is that what I'm hearin'?" Banks demanded. "When did this happen, and how come I'm just hearin' 'bout it?"

Mosley shifted uncomfortably in his seat. "Late yesterday, but straight up, Kwintell, nobody could do nothin'. They was in one o' them tank things with a machine gun and—"

"How many soldiers were there?"

"I... I don't know. Four, maybe five, I guess. But the machine gun—"

"And how many UBN soldiers watched this? One? Two? Twenty?"

"I... I don't know for sure." Mosley slumped further in his chair in a posture of defeat. "A lot, I guess."

"So let's just guess and say a dozen," Banks said. "A dozen UBN soldiers stood by with their fingers up they asses, watching a brother get capped like they was being schooled." He turned his gaze to Keyshaun Jackson. "And this was some of your crew? How'd this happen? I thought I told y'all to just stay away from the soldier boys?"

"Straight up, Kwintell, wasn't nothin' they could do. We got intel some nigga was holdin' food in his crib, so we went to check it out and found him sittin' on a bunch of stuff. He tried to fight back, so they beat him down and held him so he could watch the boys having a little fun with his shorty in the front yard—you know, to make an example so the whole hood could see. Then the soldier boys showed up, sudden like. They held that big machine gun on the whole crew; then one of the soldiers got out the tank thing and capped the brother bangin' the shorty. Then they took the tom and his shorty off in the tank. I expect they took 'em to that camp they set up over by the golf course."

"What the hell they doin' in the hood?" Banks asked. "They been leavin' us alone long as we leave them alone."

"This was right off one of the streets they use to go back and forth to the new camp," Keyshaun said. "I figure they must have heard the ho screamin' and come to look."

Banks shook his head. "This ain't good. We can't have our brothers bein' disrespected. Else we gonna start having all sorts of shit."

"It... it's only happened once," Mosley ventured, "so I don't think—"

"You ain't supposed to think. I be doin' the thinkin' around here," Banks said. "But if you wanna think, think about this. First we had this nigga holdin' out food, and this ain't the first time. Ever since those soldier boys come out of their little box fort on the river and set up that feedin' station, we been seein' more disrespect. This the way it starts. We on top now and control most of the city and we spreadin' into the farms. I figured long as the soldier boys stayed near the river, that's cool. But they spreadin' out too, and that means trouble. First, we lost the crew we sent out with that fool Singletary and the soldiers set up that machine-gun base on the river. Didn't matter much 'cause we got the rest of the countryside, so we can let 'em have the river for now. But now they got this feedin' station with a little fort in it. It won't be long before the little fort is a bigger fort. Then they likely gonna set up ANOTHER feedin' station that turns into ANOTHER fort that pushes us out of more territory." Banks shook his head. "This can't stand. We gotta do something."

"But, Kwintell," Keyshaun protested, "they got—"

"SHUT UP, FOOL! I'm tired of all this 'they got this' and 'they got that' bullshit, you hear! They got OUR TERRITORY is what they got. Now be quiet, all of you. I gotta think about this a minute—"

He was interrupted by a knock on the door, followed by the squeak of neglected hinges as the door opened and one of his soldiers stuck his head in.

"Sorry, Kwintell, but there's some creepy-ass cracker in the parking lot with a white flag sayin' he want to talk to you."

"Tell him to make an appointment," Banks snarled.

"Ah, Desmond tol' me to tell you he think you wanna see this guy. He a general or somethin' like dat."

***

Banks stood in the doorway of his building and squinted out across the sunbaked parking lot at a sight he could scarcely credit. In the middle of the lot stood an armored Humvee with a white flag flying from a whip radio antenna. A machine gun graced a turret manned by a large man in a black uniform with full body armor. There were five other similarly clad and armored men, one visible through the windshield in the driver's seat and one standing at each corner of the vehicle, holding M4 assault rifles pointed down but obviously ready to use at a moment's notice. All six of the armored soldiers were African-American, but despite that, they eyed the mob of armed gangbangers surrounding them warily, obviously ready to engage at a moment's notice.

But Banks focused on the last man clad in the same black uniform but without a weapon, armor or helmet, leaning back nonchalantly against the front of the vehicle with his arms crossed over his chest and his legs crossed at the ankles. He had thick sandy hair and a matching goatee, the stub of a cigar clamped in his teeth, and an air of unconcern completely at odds with the tense posture of his escort. When he saw Banks, he flicked the cigar stub away and smiled, then uncrossed his ankles and stood, obviously intent on stepping away from the vehicle. Beside him, one of his men voiced a protest, but the leader motioned his underling to silence and strode purposefully toward Banks. He halved the distance between them, then stood still and erect, looking at Banks with an expectant smile.

Despite being on home ground, a chill ran down Bank's spine. *That cracker look like a pirate*, he thought, *and a mean one at that*. He really, really didn't want to walk across the parking lot, but knew failing to do so would lead to an irreparable loss of face. If you want to lead the badasses, you gotta be a badass, and a badass don't back down from no creepy-ass cracker, pirate or not. Banks assumed his most menacing look and swaggered across to meet the pirate, feigning a confidence he in no way felt.

The pirate's smile widened as Banks approached and stopped three feet away. "Mr. Banks, I presume?" the man asked, in a voice loud enough to be heard by the mob of gangbangers, who were keeping their distance.

"Who wanna know, fool?"

"General Quentin Rorke, FEMA Special Reaction Force, at your service."

"You one of them fools from the box fort?" Banks demanded loudly, determined not to be cowed before his followers.

The pirate's smile never wavered, but the look in his eyes made Banks' blood run cold.

"No, Mr. Banks," he said, his voice still carrying, "I'm not from Wilmington. However, I did come to discuss the operation there, and I believe we may have a common interest." He lost his smile and lowered his voice so only Banks could hear. "And now you've established your courage for the benefit of your troops, but before you go further than I'm prepared to tolerate, you should understand that there are three snipers with fifty-caliber Barrett sniper rifles aimed at your chest as we speak."

Banks glanced up at the surrounding buildings, but hid his terror. He lowered his voice to match Rorke's. "Anybody can say that, fool. You bluffin'."

"Be so kind as to glance down at your chest, Mr. Banks," Rorke said before touching his throat to activate a microphone. "Light him up. One second."

Banks struggled to keep his composure as three red dots flashed briefly on his chest.

"Now, Mr. Banks, we have business to discuss. I came to you in this manner as a show of respect so you didn't lose the respect of your men. However, I advise you once again not to try my patience. I'm going to summon a chopper and you and I are going for a little ride. You will come voluntarily and tell your followers you'll return shortly. You will also inform them to take no action against my men in the Humvee as they withdraw. Is that clear?"

"I ain't comin' with you, foo… Rorke. What if you just cap my ass?"

"If I wanted to 'cap your ass,' as you put it, I could have done so at any time in the past." Rorke paused for emphasis. "OR the future. As proof, I ask you to consider just how easily I got three trained snipers focused on your chest. I can take you out any time I please, Banks, but I don't really want to. You see, we can help each other. Now, tell your subordinates a chopper is inbound and you're coming with me."

"And if I don't?"

Rorke shrugged. "Then fifty-caliber rounds will shred you into hamburger, my man on the machine gun will open up on your surprised and disoriented followers while the rest of us get back to the safety of the Humvee, and chopper gunships will be over us in a heartbeat to shred anyone else who even remotely looks like one of your people. You die; we leave. Any more questions?"

Bank's mouth went dry. He said nothing for a long moment, then nodded, and Rorke touched his throat again to order in the chopper.

"Keyshaun," Banks yelled over his shoulder, "a chopper comin' in, and me and the general here gonna take a little ride. You let the rest of these soldier boys here leave when they want. You got dat?"

"But, Kwintell, you need security —"

"DO IT!" Banks yelled, the thump of chopper blades already growing in the distance.

***

Ten minutes later, Banks was aloft, apprehension over his abduction completely overcome by the novelty of his first ever ride in a helicopter. They circled above the Wilmington Container Terminal at a respectful distance, and Banks stared down at a beehive of activity, movement on the ground broken here and there as the tiny ant-like figures stopped to stare and point upward.

"There's a lot more of them than I thought," Banks said into his helmet microphone.

"More every day," came Rorke's reply in his ear. "Our intel is they're recruiting people with needed skills out of the refugee population."

"So why you wanna be helpin' us?" Banks asked as he looked over at Rorke. "Look like they doin' the same thing FEMA supposed to be doing, right?"

Rorke smiled. "There's an old saying, Mr. Banks. The enemy of my enemy is my friend. Or to speak in the vernacular, let's just say the folks in 'Fort Box,' as they call it, are getting a bit too 'uppity.'"

Banks had no idea what the hell 'vernacular' was, but he recognized a gang war when he saw one. "So why you need us?" he asked. "You got machine guns and Humvees. You even got choppers. Why not just cap the mofos yourself?"

"Because I'd prefer not to be seen as the force that wipes them out. They're in contact with other groups, and if it becomes known FEMA took action against them, it will be more difficult to deal with the others later."

"So lemme get this straight. You gonna give us Humvees and machine guns and stuff, so long as we finish these soldier boys off?"

Rorke laughed. "Not quite. I'm not fool enough to release control of weapons you might later decide to use against me, nor do I intend to provide vehicles which can be traced back to FEMA. I'm going to LOAN you certain weapons along with advisers to help you plan and execute an attack on Fort Box. We'll put together 'technicals,' mounting the automatic weapons on pickups and other regular vehicles, and my advisers will operate them. No one will know of our involvement."

"Better just let us have the stuff. These 'advisers' ain't gonna fool nobody. They gonna stick out."

"My men come in all colors, Mr. Banks. I'm confident we can assemble an adviser corps who will fit in well with your organization. Let's let me worry about that, shall we?"

Banks reflected a moment. "What about after?"

"After, Mr. Banks?"

"After we cap these mofos for you, what then? I ain't stupid. We get our asses shot up cappin' this bunch of soldier boys, then we be weak and you take us out, easy like. That why you want to use us, 'ight?"

Rorke shrugged. "The group in Fort Box has training, crew-served weapons, and undoubtedly, some sort of air defense strategy in place, perhaps with RPGs. They may expect an attack from us, but a sudden and massive assault from your group will be a complete surprise. It's simple logic. And as far as taking you out, don't flatter yourself. You're already weak, and we could take you out in an afternoon with chopper gunships and little risk; unlike Fort Box, you have no defense against an aerial assault.

"So you see, Mr. Banks," Rorke continued, "in this new world, no one can be neutral. There are only enemies and allies, and as long as you're a good and helpful ally, I have no reason to take you out. But if you're not, well, in that case, we'll crush you like bugs when it suits our purposes. Unlike our friends in Fort Box, you're not in radio contact with distant allies who might get upset when we take you out, nor are you sitting on nearly as large a stockpile of looted stores I don't want to see damaged." Rorke smiled. "So in your case, I have absolutely no problem burning down the house to kill all the rats, and I'm not the least concerned about collateral damage. Your very best option is to join my command as unacknowledged irregular forces, but of course, the choice is yours. However, you must decide now. If you accept, we'll return to my base and begin planning the op. If you refuse, I'll just take you back to your headquarters and drop you off."

Banks glanced around the chopper as his mind raced, parsing the options. No way he was gonna be this cracker's bitch. There was a pilot and copilot in the front of the chopper, and two more soldiers in the back with him and Rorke. Maybe when they landed, he could order his men to open up on the chopper as soon as he got clear. If they massed firepower, they could bring it down and he could cap this creepy cracker. With the head cut off, the snake would just flop around a while and let him come up with a plan to deal with this unexpected development. He looked at Rorke and nodded.

"Okay, that sound all right. I call the shots, but I gotta go back and consult my council, you know, just to be cool with the brothers. I have you an answer in maybe fifteen minutes after we land."

Rorke gave him a look of obviously feigned surprise. "Land, Mr. Banks? I just said we'd drop you off, I never said anything about landing."

Banks said nothing for almost a minute. "So when your people comin' with the machine guns?" he asked at last.

CHAPTER THREE

Fort Box
Wilmington Container Terminal
Wilmington, North Carolina

Day 26, 3:15 p.m.

Luke Kinsey, formerly first lieutenant, US Army; formerly captain (and currently deserter from), FEMA Special Reaction Force; and most recently major, Wilmington Defense Force, squinted into the bright afternoon sun and shaded his eyes with his hand as he stared up at the chopper circling Fort Box.

"Looks like they takin' a good long look, LT—I mean Major," said Joel Washington.

Luke looked at his former sergeant and nodded. "That they are, Lieutenant Washington. Let's just hope they see enough of our teeth to decide to leave us alone." He couldn't suppress a grin at the big man's obvious discomfort at being addressed by his new title.

"What's the problem, Washington? Overwhelmed by the awesome responsibilities of your new rank?"

Washington shook his head. "It's okay for you, L—Major, but I never wanted to be no officer. I'll do any job needin' doing, you know that, but sergeant suited me just fine, and I see no reason I had to change."

"Hunnicutt is right about that. We're growing fast, and folks with leadership experience are in short supply. We have to have some sort of defined structure and hierarchy, both military and civilian, but we can't necessarily be guided by the old rules. People get the tasks and responsibilities, and the rank to go with them, they can handle. New folks coming in are going to have a tough enough time adjusting without trying to figure out why a sergeant seems to have more authority than say a junior officer…" Luke trailed off as the look of skepticism on Washington's face morphed into a poorly concealed smirk.

"Seriously, Major?"

"Okay, bad example," Luke conceded, "but you know what I mean. Fact is, I'm having some qualms myself. One of the senior noncoms should have been promoted over me. I should have stayed a captain and Wright or Butler should have been bumped up to major; both have more experience."

"Not real combat experience," Washington said. "They're good people, but Wright is, or was, a National Guard sergeant, and Butler was a Coastie chief petty officer. They'll both get things done, but the only ones who have any real combat time are you and those of us you brought in with you, and I gotta feeling we're gonna need all the combat experience we can find." He sighed. "Anyway, Wright and Butler don't like bein' officers any more than I do, and none of us think it's really necessary. Folks always figure out who to turn to when they need something. Always have, always will."

"You might be right, but you're still a lieutenant, Lieutenant."

The look of dismay on Washington's face was so comical Luke had all he could do to keep a straight face. "And my orders, Lieutenant, are to set up a twenty-four-hour sky watch. That's the third chopper overflight in the last two days and I don't like it. Make sure they have NV and IR gear at night. Even if the choppers come in dark, we'll focus on the blade noise and know where to point the gear."

Washington nodded, his forlorn look fading as he contemplated his new task. "Yes, sir," he said. "I'll get right on it. Anything else?"

"Not at the moment," Luke said, "but I'm headed to the council meeting. Catch up with me in a couple of hours and I'll brief you on what we discuss."

"Better you than me, sir. I'll see you in two hours." He was grinning now. "Unless of course the council meeting runs long, but I'm sure that won't happen."

"Anyone ever mention you're a wiseass, Washington?"

Washington's grin widened. "Regularly, sir. Now if that will be all…"

Luke shook his head. "Go."

Washington moved away across the concrete, still smiling, and Luke turned back toward his original destination. The former terminal building was a squat, three-story structure of utilitarian appearance, now the headquarters for 'Fort Box,' a name initially used as a joke referencing their improvised defensive wall of empty shipping containers, but which quickly became a point of pride as their little community grew.

Luke stopped at the door to the terminal building and looked back over what had previously been the container yard, amazed by what his new comrades had accomplished in such a short time. The change was remarkable, even since he'd brought his little band of deserters into the walls of Fort Box a scant week earlier.

A stout defensive wall of steel shipping containers stacked two high formed three walls of the fort, topped with a barbed wire barrier along the outer edge and with fortified firing positions at regular intervals. Machine guns were mounted on armored platforms at each corner, extending outward to allow them to sweep the length of the wall in any direction. All of the firing points were connected with a three-foot-wide wooden scaffold hung below the inside edge of the top container and running the length of the wall, allowing defenders to quickly move from point to point without exposing themselves to enemy fire. The new walls were set well back from the original terminal fence, and the area between had been cleared of containers. No one could approach the walls now except by crossing fifty yards of asphalt or concrete, all under the guns of the defenders.

The fourth side of Fort Box was formed by the container berths on the river, currently occupied by a collection of container and grain ships. The ships were moored bow to stern, their high steel sides forming a fourth wall, also protected by machine-gun emplacements at both ends with fields of fire sweeping the river approaches. The river side was perhaps the least secure perimeter due to irregular-shaped gaps between the ships, which were impossible to seal, but the river was a strong ally. The open water offered much wider fields of fire than the land sides, and a coordinated waterborne attack was considered unlikely.

But it was the progress inside the walls that was most remarkable; a collection of travel trailers and RVs mixed with military tents were lined up in a bizarre but strangely orderly looking series of newly created 'streets' radiating like the spokes of a wheel from the terminal-building-turned-HQ. In the central area next to the HQ stood a series of large army tents serving as central kitchen, mess hall, and clinic, while on the dock next to one of the ships was a collection of covered aboveground swimming pools known as 'Wright's Waterworks' in honor of the man who'd solved their water storage problem. And everywhere there were containers, stacks and stacks of containers: large brightly colored steel boxes crammed with a cornucopia of canned food, packaged generators, and other goods, the full scope of which was still undetermined.

Luke marveled at the controlled chaos as men and women scurried in all directions. The faint smell of diesel exhaust filled the air, and the sounds of generators and heavy equipment assaulted his ears as the fortunate inhabitants of Fort Box labored to secure their future. Luke nodded and entered the building, smiling as cool air washed over him. Air-conditioning and ice were two things that made Southern summers bearable, and he was glad he'd have a little of both, at least as long as he stayed.

He glanced at his watch. He was five minutes early, but he'd quickly learned Major, now Colonel, Hunnicutt considered ten minutes early as 'on time.' By that standard he was five minutes late. He hurried down the hall toward the conference room and the sound of raised voices.

"I don't give a damn, Lieutenant Wright. You know—" Colonel Hunnicutt looked up as Luke entered. "Well, nice of you to join us, Major. I do hope it wasn't an inconvenience."

"Sorry, sir," Luke said, slipping into an unoccupied seat and nodding at the dozen people seated around the conference table. Hunnicutt gave him a curt nod and turned back to Wright.

"As I was saying, Lieutenant, you know the protocol and so should your men. We CANNOT police areas outside of our tasking and still hope to provide any relief to the bulk of the refugees. These criminals piss me off too, believe me, but we just don't have the manpower and resources to be diverted by a conflict with the gangs at this point. I thought I made that clear?"

"You did, sir. And I've reprimanded Corporal Miles for disobeying orders, but honestly, I don't believe he did so intentionally. Our mission is providing relief to the civilians, so when they heard a woman screaming for help, he used his own initiative. I can't fault him for that. So what exactly was he supposed to do when his patrol stumbled on a gang rape, say 'carry on' and drive away?"

Hunnicutt heaved a sigh and fell silent. "I suppose not," he said at last. "Where is the woman now?"

"Miles' patrol took her and her husband to the refugee camp. They didn't much want to go, but he couldn't leave them there," Wright said.

"And the bangers?"

Wright shrugged. "Too many to do anything with, even if we had facilities. They just told them to scatter, all except for the one they caught," he hesitated, "you know…"

"I get the picture," Hunnicutt said. "What did they do with him?"

Wright hesitated. "He was killed resisting arrest."

The room grew deadly quiet as the meeting participants awaited Hunnicutt's reaction.

"Boo fucking hoo," Hunnicutt said, and the room erupted in laughter.

"But seriously, folks," he said, "we can't afford to get entangled with these bastards. We just have too much to do. Any expectations this will escalate, Lieutenant Wright?"

Wright shook his head. "We have them outgunned and they know it. If anything, they might try to lure a patrol into an ambush as payback."

Hunnicutt nodded. "My thoughts exactly. Make sure not to answer ANY calls for distress, and double both the size and frequency of the patrols between here and the relief station until we're sure this isn't going to escalate."

"Already done, sir," Wright replied.

"All right," Hunnicutt said, "let's move on. Chief… I mean Lieutenant Butler, can you give us a quick SITREP on the facilities?"

Mike Butler, formerly chief boatswain's mate, USCG, now first lieutenant, Wilmington Defense Force, nodded. "Our defensive perimeter is complete, though I'd still like to improve on the gate arrangement. Our snipes, along with the engineers from the merchant ships, have nearly solved our water problem. Between all the ships, we have multiple water distillers, and they rigged up a way to triple process the river water and basically heat the hell out of it to kill any bugs." He looked over at Lieutenant Josh Wright and grinned. "They tell me by this time tomorrow, they'll be producing enough water to keep Wright's Waterworks topped up for the foreseeable future."

"Great news," Hunnicutt said, "but how'd they manage that?"

Butler shrugged. "They didn't say and I sure as hell didn't ask, sir. Else I'd have had to listen to a two-hour lecture explaining the process in great detail." He paused to let the laughter die down before continuing. "But it gets better. They plan to use Wright's swimming pools as reserve water storage for excess production, but they seem confident they can tie the shore facilities into the potable water system from *Maersk Tangier* and use her water pumps to pressurize it all. Her tanks are more than adequate to supply our needs on a day-to-day basis. They'll have to dig up and disconnect the old supply from the city system, but after that, we'll have running water in the terminal again. They said two or three days max."

"That's good news. We've been wasting a lot of manpower hauling water, and I for one will gladly give up the joy of flushing with a bucket." Hunnicutt grimaced. "As long as the sewage lines aren't plugged up, anyway."

"Actually, there's good news on that front, too," Butler said. "The treatment plant's only a mile or so downriver, and the snipes figure if we're the only ones with running water to flush, it will take a while before we top out the storage capacity, even if the plant's not running. And if we can get a generator and some fuel down there, they figure they might be able to restore the plant to at least limited operation. They think it will be more than enough to meet our needs."

Across the table from Butler, a petite, dark-haired woman sat up straighter in her chair. "So does that mean if we can get water restored at the country club, we can establish some basic sanitation for the refugee camp? It's horrific there. The port-a-potties you brought in were overflowing by the second day, and people are back to doing their business behind any bush. The stench is overpowering and it's only going to get worse."

The request caught Butler by surprise. "Maybe, Doc," he replied, "but I don't think there's any way we can get water pressure back there and—"

"We could use the toilets in the clubhouse and swimming club. I think there are even some toilets over by the tennis courts. You told me yourself you've got a container full of portable generators from China, and we could pump the flushing water out of the small lake there. It's fed by that little creek, so we should have plenty of water and—"

Butler held up both his hands in a stop gesture. "Whoa! Doc, slow down. I know you want to get things done, but you've been here less than a week, so I don't think you fully appreciate how stretched we are. We can't do everything at once and—"

The woman's eyes flashed. "And I don't think you fully appreciate what those people are going through, Lieutenant Butler. But I was in that hell for three weeks and I can't forget. Just because I was fortunate enough to be offered shelter here, I'm not going to turn my back—"

"We're not turning our backs on anyone, Dr. Jennings," Hunnicutt said, "and we recruited you from among the refugee population not only because we needed a doctor here, but to form a medical team to help the refugees as much as we can. But Butler's right. We have to use what resources we have wisely, or else we won't be able to help anyone." He turned back to Butler. "But the Doc's right too, Butler. The camp's already turning into a cesspool; can we get sewage service reestablished, and if so, how long?"

Butler rubbed his chin. "I expect the country club area is served by the same treatment plant since it's on this side of town, but I don't know how long it will support us here and thousands of refugees. The engineers figure there's probably enough room in the facility's holding ponds to last a while before we have to get the treatment plant running. But they weren't considering several thousand folks from the refugee camp. If we dump that output into the system, I think the plan goes out the window; they'll have to get the plant running sooner rather than later." He sighed. "And they have their hands full now. They were hoping to hold off on addressing the treatment plant for a couple of weeks."

Hunnicutt nodded. "Okay, let's think about this. If we flush everything in the system and don't get the plant running, the holding ponds overflow and things get nasty, am I right?"

Butler shrugged. "I guess so, sir. I hadn't really thought about it, to be honest."

"So that means if they CAN'T get the plant going in time, we have a stinking mess a mile or so downstream of us in the middle of an industrial area. It seems to me a stinking mess there where no one is around is much better than a disease-producing mess in the middle of several thousand refugees, wouldn't you agree?" Hunnicutt asked.

Butler nodded, and Jennings beamed as Hunnicutt continued, "Okay then, let's get the good doctor her flushing toilets, and tell the engineers to do the best they can on getting the treatment plant running, but not to let it override other priorities. This situation is going to throw new challenges at us every day, folks, and we just have to be flexible."

"Yes, sir," Butler said, and made a note on the pad in front of him.

"Thank you, Colonel," Jennings said, "but it's still going to be tough. We have toilets in the club house and the swimming club—"

Luke cleared his throat loudly, earning him a glare from Jennings. "I don't think we should allow the 'fugees—"

"DON'T CALL THEM THAT!" Jenning snapped.

Luke colored and nodded. "You're right, Doctor, I apologize. But as I was saying, I don't think we should allow the REFugees uncontrolled access to the swimming club facilities. We set up our container wall around the swimming club so we could clean the pool and cover it to use it as drinking water storage, and that whole facility is now our forward base and defensive strong point. We have absolutely no way to vet the refugees, and if we allow them free access in and out of our fortified area, we don't really know who might come in." He paused. "From a security standpoint, it's a very bad idea."

"Agreed," the colonel said, turning to Jennings. "You'll get your sewage system, Doctor, but the swim club facility remains off-limits to all but authorized personnel."

"But there are ten toilets there! Maybe we could reposition the wall between the clubhouse and the pool—"

"Jesus Christ," Butler muttered, unable to contain his irritation, and Jennings whirled on him, obviously intent on dressing him down.

"ENOUGH!" Hunnicutt said. "The issue is settled. Flushing water will be restored to all country club facilities, but the swimming club is off-limits to all but authorized personnel. We'll look at the possibility of finding portable toilets that can be tied into the fixed system. Now, next issue." He looked down at his notepad. "Mr. Van Horn, how are we coming with getting food to the refugees?"

A slender man with wire-rim glasses looked over at Hunnicutt and shrugged. "We're starting to provide some calories, Colonel, but I can't call it more than that."

Terry Van Horn, ex-chief steward on the *Maersk Tangier*, had been appointed 'food czar' by acclamation and over his own strong objections. When Hunnicutt scoured the skills inventory of his small but growing group within the confines of Fort Box, he hadn't neglected either the American or foreign merchant ships. Between the 'culinary specialists' (aka cooks) of his own National Guard unit and the steward's departments of the various ships, he had no shortage of people who could cook for large groups, with a 'large group' defined as twenty to a hundred or so. Feeding thousands of refugees was a different matter entirely, and when it came out that Van Horn had regularly volunteered for various Third World famine relief efforts, putting him in charge was a no-brainer.

Van Horn continued. "That many folks, all I can hope to do is get some calories down 'em. I pulled one cook and a couple of stewards from each of the ships to work with me, along with most of your culinary people. We stripped the ships of every big stew pot we could find, and we been using your field kitchen to boil corn from one of the grain ships into a gruel and throwing in some of the canned seafood and meat from the containers for protein. I got no seasonings to speak of, especially not for the volume of food we have to put out. Even at that and workin' almost round the clock, we can only manage to get out one meal a day. As more people come in, I'm not even sure we'll be able to maintain that." He shook his head. "It'll keep 'em alive, but quite frankly, it looks like crap and tastes the same. I'd be ashamed to serve it if it wasn't the best we could produce in bulk."

"We know it's tough and we appreciate the job you and your people are doing," Hunnicutt said, to nods around the table.

Van Horn shook his head. "Thank you, Colonel, but the truth is, this isn't gonna work much longer. We got plenty of grain, but as the population grows, we don't have the manpower, equipment, or time to cook it fast enough. Yesterday we started running low, but one of my guys spotted it in time, so they started cutting down on the portion size and just made it to the end of the line. The day the food runs out before the line runs out is the day we're likely to have a food riot. I've seen it before and it ain't pretty." He paused and said softly, "Never thought I'd see it here though."

The room grew quiet a long moment as the others considered the possibility.

Wright broke the silence. "This sucks! We have so much grain in the ships and grain terminal it's likely to rot before we can get it distributed, and we'll be starving people we likely won't be able to feed for lack of resources."

"We need more manpower," Hunnicutt agreed. "How's recruitment coming?"

"No shortage of people who want to join us," Butler said, "but vetting them to make sure they have the skills they claim is a full-time job. I mean, they're desperate, boss. Ask for crane operators and everyone raises their hand. Same with mechanics or forklift drivers. I doubt it would be any different if we asked for nuclear physicists."

Jennings sighed. "That's true, I'm afraid. Of the five 'nurses' we took in yesterday, I doubt half of them had so much as ever emptied a bedpan. They're all willing workers, but not knowing who I can trust makes it hard. Fortunately, we got two more docs yesterday, but—"

"Then there's your answer," Hunnicutt said. "If you didn't have the docs before, they're a bonus and won't be missed, so re-task one. Put him or her in charge of vetting all the incoming medical personnel. Either that or spread vetting duty over your qualified medical staff as it grows. Butler, you do the same in the other areas. If you need crane operators, put a crane operator in charge of finding them. The people doing the job are the most qualified to decide if the new recruits are blowing smoke, AND they'll be the most motivated to resist bringing in screwups, since they'll be working closely with the new folks."

Everyone nodded and Hunnicutt looked over at Van Horn. "And perhaps you could find some cooks to help you from among the refugees, Mr. Van Horn."

"What we're doing isn't exactly cooking, Colonel, so warm bodies to help shouldn't be a problem. But manpower isn't my real problem. What I need is big-ass pots and burners to put 'em on," Van Horn said.

Hunnicutt turned toward Butler, but the man was already scribbling on his notepad. "I'll have someone search the bills of lading to see if there's anything of use in the containers, and ask the engineers if they can figure out some way to expand your kitchen facilities," Butler said to Van Horn, who nodded his thanks.

Hunnicutt glanced at his watch and down at his notepad. "Anything else?"

When everyone shook their heads, he nodded. "Okay, folks, let's get back to work."

People started filing from the room, but Hunnicutt motioned for Luke, Wright, and Butler to keep their seats. Jennings was halfway to the door when she noticed the men still sitting and turned to Hunnicutt, her eyebrows raised.

"A private meeting, Colonel?" she asked.

"Security issues, Doctor. I'm sure they'd be a waste of your valuable time and bore you to tears besides. Would you please close the door on your way out?"

Her look communicated her disapproval more eloquently than any words, and when she left, the closing of the door was just short of a slam.

"I think you pissed the good doctor off," Butler said.

"So it appears, and I truly regret that. She's good people, and she'll make a big difference. She IS making a difference," Hunnicutt corrected himself, then shook his head. "The problem is she thinks we can save everyone, and we all know that's impossible."

The others nodded as Hunnicutt turned to Luke. "Was that a chopper I heard, Major?"

"Yes, sir. It's what held me up. That's the third overflight in as many days, so it appears the FEMA folks are taking an increasing interest. I had Lieutenant Washington set a round-the-clock sky watch," Luke said.

"Good," Hunnicutt said. "Given your recent 'association' with our FEMA friends, do you have any insights into how much of a threat they might be?"

Luke shook his head. "Just very generally. We were only with the Special Reaction Force a couple of weeks, but my gut feeling is they won't have the stomach for a stand-up fight. Intimidation and bullying the defenseless seems to be more their MO. They may make a lot of noise, but as long as we show our teeth, I think we can hold them at bay."

"Let's hope you're right, Major. We sure as hell don't need to add a combat mission to everything else we've got on our plates." Hunnicutt turned to Wright. "But if that comes to pass, how do we stand on readiness, Lieutenant?"

"Just over eighty combat effectives, sir, counting the Coasties and the men that came in with Major Kinsey here. I can up that a bit as we place civilian recruits in some of the support roles, like cooks, mechanics and so forth. They aren't line troops, but they've all had at least basic weapons training and we can put them on the wall with a rifle if we have to. But we'll max out at a hundred shooters." Wright paused. "That's as many as we can arm anyway, and ammo is a concern, especially for the crew-served weapons. They're key to our defense, and if we have to hold off a sustained attack, those machine guns will burn through ammo like a house afire."

"We might be able to get some ammo from the Military Ocean Terminal downriver," Butler said. "The Coast Guard used to help them enforce an 'exclusion zone' around their wharfs, and I'm familiar with their facility, the part of it closest to the river, anyway. I was also pretty tight with a couple of NCOs that helped run the place."

Hunnicutt looked skeptical. "That's an Army facility, and I have no clue how the regular military is leaning. However, I doubt they're just going to hand out ammunition because we ask nicely."

"Maybe, maybe not, sir," Butler said. "It was actually kind of a hybrid operation and mostly civilian. The place is huge, much bigger than most people realize, and they used a lot of technology-based security to guard the place—CCTV, motion-detector-based alarms, stuff like that. None of that will be working now, and given how everything has gone to hell, we might just be able to slip in and grab some ammo at a five-fingered discount. With your permission, I'd like to do some recon and check it out."

Hunnicutt hesitated, then nodded. "Okay, go have a look, and JUST a look. We'll decide what to do based on what you find. And be careful, making an enemy of the Army is the last thing we need at this point. Put together a small team and go when you're ready."

"Yes, sir," Butler said and shot Luke a 'let's talk later' look.

"Now," Hunnicutt said, looking back and forth between Wright and Butler, "and before you two get your noses out of joint, you should know that I asked Major Kinsey here to have a look at our defenses. Given his much more recent deployment in the Sandbox, he's the only one with recent experience in setting up forward bases in hostile areas, and I figured we can benefit from a fresh set of eyes."

Wright grunted. "No problem here. I'd much prefer to be alive than admired for my work."

"Same here," Butler said, "I was a life saver, not a fort builder."

"Good," Hunnicutt said, nodding toward Luke. "You have the floor, Major."

"Okay," Luke said, "first let me say I'm blown away by what you guys have accomplished in such a short time. No one could have done a better job of establishing a defensive position with the materials at hand. I wouldn't have done a single thing differently as far as the defensive walls go. Establishing clear fields of fire between the walls and the original terminal fence was an especially good move. I only have one suggestion."

"Which is?" Hunnicutt asked.

"I think we have to take preemptive measures to keep the refugee population further away from the walls. You've set the relief station at the country club some distance away, which is a good thing, but it's still relatively close to us here. Despite your best efforts, the population will expand in this direction. They're desperate people, and they'll quickly figure out we're the source of the food and water, and they'll all want in. If we allow a lot of them to concentrate here, it could get ugly."

"So how exactly can we prevent that?" Wright asked.

"We need to set a perimeter much further out, as far out as we can without running into the gangbangers. We barricade all the roads in but Shipyard Boulevard with a container across the road, and put No Entry signage all around the perimeter to create an exclusion zone. We then enforce it with roving vehicle patrols on a random schedule so the bangers can't figure out a routine and try to ambush us."

Wright was shaking his head. "We can't possibly hope to stop people. That barrier will be porous as hell. They'll just walk around it."

"You're not expected to stop everyone," Luke said, "just discourage them from getting too near the fort. The signs and barriers will deter most of them, and a certain percentage of those who do slip through will be rounded up and politely but firmly returned to the camp. If we have repeat offenders, we can figure out some way to deal with them at the time."

"Extra patrols is extra manpower we don't have," Butler pointed out.

"Not extra," Luke said, "just task every third or fourth regular patrol headed out to patrol the route between here and the refugee camp with swinging through a portion of the exclusion zone. When we turn back a few people and return them to the camp, word will get out."

The room grew quiet as they considered Luke's plan.

"Worth a try," Wright said.

"Agreed," Butler added.

"That makes it unanimous. Set it up, gentlemen," Hunnicutt said, glancing down at his notepad again. "Which brings me to the last item on my agenda, the census; where do we stand, Lieutenant Butler."

Butler nodded. "As of this morning, counting military and dependents, the other civilians we brought in with us, all the merchant ship crews and the terminal personnel, and other folks we've recruited so far" — he glanced down at his pad — "eleven hundred and sixty-three, sir."

"And what's our capacity within the walls, best guess?" Hunnicutt asked.

"If we max out the living quarters we have now and start converting some of the empty containers to housing, we can probably shelter another two thousand people, maybe twenty-five hundred," Butler said. "We can push out the walls and accommodate more, but space isn't really the problem at that point, it's water. The engineers tell me they can probably make enough water to support three thousand total, at least until the diesel in their fuel tanks and the terminal starts to go off-spec in a year to two years. They're working on some solar-powered options for the longer term, but no way those will produce near enough water for that many folks. They're thinking maybe a stable long-term permanent population of fifteen hundred, with a bit of reserve for short-term increases."

"So we can survive here long term, but with a limited population, and in the short term we can accommodate extra people but have to find them some place to relocate, is that about the size of it?"

"Yes, sir, basically," Butler said.

"I've spoken to Levi Jenkins and Vern Gibson," Wright said, "they have pretty much all the farmers and landowners along the river out fifteen or twenty miles sold on the idea of a mutual protection network. I'm thinking we could build on that concept and turn the manned security stations we'd planned to establish along the river into small towns, each anchored around a fortified base. They could be mutually supporting and—"

"Whoa!" Hunnicutt said. "Towns and bases are a hell of a lot more intrusive than the security stations we were talking about, with much bigger footprints. How are the farmers going to feel about that?"

"I think they'll go for it, under the circumstances. We're talking fortified towns of up to two hundred people every mile or so on alternating sides of the river, each with maybe ten or twenty acres of land. A hell of a lot of that riverfront is undeveloped woodland anyway, sir, so it's not like they'd lose productive farmland," Wright said.

"So you figure everyone in these towns is going to live inside the fortified base." Hunnicutt shook his head. "That'll be a bit tight."

"Not nearly as tight as it will be here, sir."

Hunnicutt nodded. "Point taken. You think the farmers will go for it?"

"What's not to like," Wright said. "They'll have an employable labor pool without having to actually house folks on their own places. Each town can have a militia unit, and they can all be mutually supportive. We can house mechanics, medical facilities, and other needed services in the different towns, all accessible by water. We can—"

Hunnicutt held up his hands. "Okay, okay, I think I get the picture. Get with Levi and Vern and see if you can sell them on the plan, and if so, ask them to start scouting sites and working with their friends and neighbors to get buy in. Then I want you and Butler, in your spare time, of course, to start figuring out what skill sets we're going to need to start these towns from scratch. Grab anyone you need to help plan that, but make sure to include Levi and Vern. If we expect people along the river to buy in to us redesigning their world, it's only polite to get their input."

The pair nodded, and Hunnicutt muttered, almost to himself, "Then we just have to play God and decide which of these people get offered tickets to a decent existence and which ones we leave in Hell."

"It's going to be a tough call, sir," Luke said, sympathy in his voice.

"That it is, Major, that it is. Which brings me to contingency planning," Hunnicutt said. "We're hoping for the best, but we sure as hell need to be realistic and plan for the worst. I'm sure it hasn't escaped anyone's attention the odds are stacked against us."

Everyone nodded, and Hunnicutt continued.

"We're doing the best we can feeding and sheltering our growing refugee population, but we have to face facts. They're living in squalor in cardboard and canvas shacks, with minimal sanitation. We're essentially feeding them slop and providing them drinking water, and we'll do our best to improve that, but chances are pretty good that every advance we make is going to be offset by a population increase. And it's summer now; God knows how we'll cope when it gets cold."

Butler shrugged. "But what more can we do, sir? We're trying—"

"That's just the point," Hunnicutt said. "We're all flat out and working sixteen- and eighteen-hour days, seven days a week, and we're still falling behind. But I'm sure there's not a single person in that refugee camp who thinks we're doing enough. We wouldn't feel any different if we were there, because that's human nature. To those folks, we're the privileged ones with guns who eat good food, crap in real toilets, sleep in real beds out of the elements, and even get to take the occasional shower. Major Kinsey's suggestion to establish an exclusion zone, necessary though it is, will add to that resentment. I believe anyone in that camp who doesn't hate us already probably will within a week, or a month max."

Wright nodded. "Actually, you can already feel the resentment when you ride through the camp. But what can we do about it?"

Hunnicutt sighed. "There's nothing we can do except continue to do our best. But we can't ignore it either. That camp is becoming a powder keg of simmering resentment, subject to blowing up at any time. We need a contingency plan for rapid withdrawal of all our folks, including our civilian recruits like Dr. Jennings." He paused. "And we have to be prepared for the possibility safe withdrawal may require use of deadly force. I want you to pick out your most trustworthy NCOs and come up with rules of engagement if we have to activate the withdrawal plan. I want that strictly need to know, and God help anyone who lets any mention of the plan slip to ANYONE."

Wright hesitated. "Ah... what about the folks we have to evacuate? I mean Dr. Jennings—"

"Especially don't tell Jennings," Hunnicutt said. "She'll be appalled at the very idea, and advance notice won't make extracting her any easier. It will also likely mean endless arguments with her and guarantee everyone will know about the plan. If it comes to an emergency evacuation, just plan to hog-tie her and bring her along. In fact, make forced extraction of our civilians part of the plan if necessary. If things go to hell, we're not going to have a debate. After they're safely inside Fort Box, they can leave if they want, but at least they'll have an option at that point."

Hunnicutt's subordinates nodded in unison.

"Understood, sir," Wright said. "We'll get on it."

"Thank you, gentlemen," Hunnicutt said. "If there's nothing else, I think we're done."

The three nodded and began to rise.

"Oh, Major," Hunnicutt said to Luke, "a word, if you don't mind."

Luke settled back into his chair with a quizzical look and waited for the other two to file out. Hunnicutt waited for the door to close before speaking.

"Thank you, Luke. Have you given any more thought to your longer term plans?"

Luke shook his head. "I appreciate your confidence and the promotion, Colonel, and I'm not going to leave you while things are obviously as critical as they are, but I've always been up front with you. I want to join my dad and the rest of the family, which means they either come back here or I go down to Texas. Since there's only one of me, it makes more sense for me to go there. It would be near impossible for my dad to make it back up here with my sister and my aunt's family."

"You know my hope with the promotion was to make you second-in-command—"

"Yes, sir, and you know I declined. I'll stick around awhile and do anything you need me to do, but when the time comes, I'm leaving. That would be a great deal more difficult if I was in a leadership position." He paused and looked Hunnicutt in the eye. "And I think you know that, sir."

Hunnicutt smiled ruefully. "Busted. Okay then, any idea when that time will be?"

Luke hesitated. "I can give you six months, with the understanding if my dad needs me before then, I'm going."

Hunnicutt nodded. "Fair enough. I'll take what I can get. Thank you, Luke."

"You're welcome, sir. Now if that's all, I suspect Lieutenant Butler may want to talk to me about a little recon trip down to the Military Ocean Terminal."

CHAPTER FOUR

M/V Pecos Trader
Sun Lower Anchorage
Neches River
Near Nederland, Texas

Day 26, 6:35 a.m.

Captain Jordan Hughes felt the heat of the rising sun on his neck as he stood bent at the waist, his forearms resting on the ship's rail, studying the curious operation unfolding on the water below. Some distance down the deck, Chief Mate Georgia Howell was also at the rail, her eyes glued on the river's surface and her right hand raised, signaling the bosun in the cab of the hose-handling crane as he lowered a strange-looking contraption to the water.

Hughes heard a slap and a curse and looked around to see Matt Kinsey, formerly chief petty officer, USCG, staring at a large blood spot in his open palm, a dark blob in the middle of it.

"I don't know whether this is a mosquito or a frigging bat," Kinsey said. "I may need a transfusion."

Hughes laughed. "Well, they'll be worse in bayou country. But I anticipated you." He reached in his pants pocket and pulled out a small bottle and held it out to Kinsey. "Polak has some insect repellent squirreled away somewhere, consider it our contribution to the mission."

Kinsey grinned. "Outstanding! Thank you, Captain," he said as he slipped the bottle in his pocket and stepped closer to the rail. His grin widened as he looked down.

"But not the only contribution. That chief engineer of yours is a pretty smart cookie. I'd been driving myself crazy trying to figure out how to get the boat around those locks. This is terrific!"

Hughes nodded. "Well, maybe. Presuming it doesn't fall apart on the way there. It's not exactly the sleekest craft in the fleet." He watched as Georgia Howell lowered the subject of their discussion the last few feet to settle on the river's surface. It was a sturdily built aluminum boat trailer outfitted on either side with two large and ungainly-looking pontoons, each constructed of four fifty-five-gallon oil drums held in rigid alignment by a skeletal structure of lightweight angle iron. A sheet metal cone was fitted at what was apparently the 'bow' of each pontoon.

Kinsey watched the makeshift craft bob on the water. "It floats well enough," Kinsey said, "and I watched Gowan and the boys put those pontoons together. They'll hold up just fine. I figured we had no more use for that trailer. It was a stroke of genius to make it water-mobile."

"Think it'll work?"

"Well, we won't know that until we try. If we're lucky, Calcasieu Lock at least will be open. It's only a salt water control gate to keep tidal water out of the agricultural area. There's no water height difference across the lock and they keep it open much of the time. If we luck out there, we won't have to use the trailer until the Bayou Sorrel Lock."

"How fast can you tow that thing?" Hughes asked.

Kinsey shrugged. "No clue. Those sheet metal fairwaters will help, but it'll still slow us way down. I'll start slow and see how she tows. I hope to tow her at ten or fifteen knots, but even at ten we'll make Calcasieu

Lock before noon. God knows what we'll have to deal with there, but I'm hoping we can get clear of the lock and be well up the Intracoastal by nightfall."

Hughes nodded as he watched the Coast Guard patrol boat edging in to put a towing bridle on their new seagoing trailer. "I still don't like you going off shorthanded. Sure you don't want to find a car? It might take you a couple of days by boat, especially towing that thing. You could make it there in three or four hours by car, and we could send more people—"

Kinsey shook his head. "Pinch points are not our friend, Cap. We'd have to worry about the bridge at Lake Charles, to say nothing of twenty-plus miles of the Atchafalaya Basin Causeway with nowhere to run and nowhere to hide. And even if those places aren't compromised, I can almost guarantee you someone is sitting on the Mississippi River bridge into Baton Rouge. We couldn't send enough people to force a crossing in any of those places if someone is holding them, and if they decide to come after us, we likely couldn't outrun them long enough to break contact either." He nodded down at the Coast Guard boat. "But with that baby, we can outrun anyone on the water. We'll lose the tow if we have to."

Kinsey continued. "Besides, I don't want to leave YOU shorthanded. For sure those cons will be looking for some payback after the beat down we gave them last week. My family, my problem. Bollinger and I will be just fine."

"And my family was my problem, but y'all helped me get them on board. C'mon, Kinsey, at least take more of your own men. I know every one of them volunteered."

"They did, and I appreciate it," Kinsey said, "but everyone except Bollinger has dependents aboard, and I'm not going to let them leave their own families in possible danger to save mine. It was different when we went after your family; they were close by and we didn't fully appreciate how big a threat the escaped convicts were. Now we do, and we have to figure that into the equation."

Kinsey continued before Hughes could protest further. "Besides, as you may have noticed, our boat's on the small side. I have to pick up my daughter and my sister-in-law's family plus God knows who else." He sighed. "My wife has extended family all over Baton Rouge, and knowing Connie, they probably all went to her house. Which brings up another question, Captain Noah. Are you okay with me bringing everyone I find back to your rapidly filling ark?"

Hughes sighed. "How can I not be okay with it? We wouldn't be here if it wasn't for you and your guys. It's your ark as much as mine, so of course I'm okay with it. We'll make it work somehow." He hesitated. "I just hope... I just hope your trip is successful."

Kinsey cocked his head. "I hear a 'but' in there, Cap. If you have a concern, now is the time to voice it."

"Just thinking of the longer term. Everyone we take in has to pull their weight one way or another. We can't very well turn away immediate family members, but—"

"But we can't take in everyone without thinking how they can contribute to the survival of the group. Believe me, I get it." Kinsey grinned. "I figure having a small boat will be an advantage. I can be selective as to the passenger list."

Hughes nodded. "Good. We're on the same page, then. Now, about equipment. You sure you have everything you need?"

"Pretty much, but I'm still not sure about taking two sets of night-vision gear; you guys might need it. We can get by with one. I mainly figured to use it to run the canal in the dark if need be," Kinsey said.

"You might need it for more than that, and we'll still have two sets here, and some of the rifles have NV scopes. We'll be fine. And I wish you'd reconsider about taking one of the machine guns—"

"We've been all over that, Cap. If things DO go tits up, I'm not handing one of our three machine guns to the bad guys. The other boat can shadow us until we get to the Intracoastal. By the time the cons figure out what's up, we'll be well away from them. I'll try to contact you by VHF when we're inbound, and you can send out the other boat to escort us in."

Hughes sighed. "All right, but I don't like it."

"I'm not wild about it myself, but you know it makes the most sense." Kinsey waited for Hughes' reluctant nod, then continued. "Okay, Torres is in charge of my guys, but he's clear he's to take orders from you. That said, I'm figuring you'll defer to his opinion when it comes to defense and security issues."

"Absolutely," Hughes said.

"READY TO SHOVE OFF, CHIEF?" came a shout from below. Both men looked down to see Bollinger standing in the patrol boat as it idled at the bottom of the accommodation ladder, the floating trailer secured to a towing bridle behind it. Kinsey raised his hand in acknowledgment, turned to Hughes, and offered his hand.

Hughes shook Kinsey's hand. "Don't worry about us, Matt. Just get to Baton Rouge and bring your family back. And try checking in from the Calcasieu Lock. Your antenna's not very high, so you may be beyond VHF range, but call if you can."

"Thank you, Jordan," Kinsey said. "I'll be back as soon as I can. Take good care of the Ark for us while we're gone."

Hughes nodded and Kinsey released his hand to rush down the accommodation ladder to the waiting boat.

WARDEN'S OFFICE
FEDERAL CORRECTION COMPLEX
BEAUMONT, TEXAS

DAY 26, 10:45 A.M.

Darren 'Spike' McComb, formerly federal inmate number 26852-278, formerly recipient of a triple life sentence and currently captain of the Aryan Brotherhood of Texas, glared across the desk.

"So those idiots just let them cruise down the river liked they owned it? Is that what you're telling me, Snaggle?"

Across from McComb, Owen Fairchild, aka 'Snaggle' for his dental issues, squirmed in his seat. "They reported in soon as they saw it," he whined, "but you said no radios in case the ship had our frequency and was listening, and by the time they got word back here down the various lookout points along the river, the boats had already passed."

"And nobody thought it might be a good idea to, you know, SHOOT THE BASTARDS!"

"They had that damned machine gun, Spike. Can't blame the boys for not wantin' to tangle with that. Besides—"

"All right, all right," McComb said, "you say they split up?"

Snaggle nodded. "I had a couple of the boys on top of the big bridge. They said the Coast Guard boat with two guys on it turned up the canal toward Louisiana and our... the other boat with the machine gun hung around at the canal entrance for a while, like it was trying to make sure nobody followed the Coast Guard boat. Then they ran back to the ship at top speed."

McComb bit back his wrath at the mention of the Sheriff's Department patrol boat he'd lost in last week's fight with the ship's crew. He pondered the possibilities as the silence grew.

"Ahh... Spike?"

"Yeah, just thinking," McComb said. "So they put a machine gun on our boat, but what happened to the one on the Coast Guard boat?"

Snaggle shrugged. "The boys said it didn't have one. I guess that must be the one on our boat. Looks like they switched it over."

McComb rubbed his chin. "Which likely means they ain't got that many of them, maybe only the one. That's all we seen, anyway."

Snaggle shook his head. "I reckon one's enough when they got open water or marsh all around. Ain't no way to sneak up on 'em."

"You just let me worry about that, genius," McComb said. "Now what about this thing the Coast Guard boat was towing. What was it?"

"The boys said it looked like some sort of raft made out of oil drums. They never seen nothing like it."

"Well, whatever it is," McComb said, "I doubt it's a problem for us, and a boat and two shooters out of the way cuts down the odds a bit anyway. What sort of intel you been able to develop on that ship?"

"I been keepin' a lookout hidden at the terminal across the river, just like you said. Based on the uniforms and coveralls, we make it to be about a half dozen of those Coast Guard assholes, give or take counting the two that just left, and maybe twenty ship's crew. They also have a bunch of women and kids. Hard to tell for sure, we can only see who comes outside on deck, but for sure less than fifty all told."

"Shooters?" McComb asked.

Snaggle shrugged. "Best guess, I'd say max around twenty-five. We know the Coasties have M4s from our previous run-in, but we got no idea if the others are armed, and if so, how well. But it don't really matter, Spike. With all that open water and that machine gun—"

McComb silenced him with a look. "I swear, Snaggle, if you don't shut the hell up about that, I'm gonna cap your ass myself. It's hard enough to get these morons all movin' in the right direction without you wringing your hands like a pussy and moanin' about how tough it is. Keep it up and you WILL regret it. We clear on that?"

"S-sorry, Spike. It's just that—"

"How many troops we got?"

"Almost a thousand now," Snaggle said, "but that don't mean—"

"And how many shooters they got again? Maybe two dozen, if that? Now doesn't that seem like the situation is leaning our way pretty heavily? Maybe they shot the hell out of us when we weren't expecting it, but now we know the score, and we'll crush 'em like bugs."

"But that's just it, Spike. They're cut off on that ship, so they can't bother us. Why don't we just ignore 'em?"

"Because shit brain, they ain't a problem now, but they likely will be. They got guns, and they'll likely be lookin' to grow, 'cause they can't stay on that ship forever. Sooner or later, they'll be a problem, and I'd rather take 'em out while they're weak. They kicked our asses last week 'cause we didn't know who they were or understand what was happenin', but round two ain't gonna go like that at all." McComb paused. "I'll figure out some way to take 'em out. Leave that to me. Now, how's everything else going?"

"Damn good, actually. With the National Guard units tied up in Houston and Dallas and those FEMA assholes all clustered around the nuke plant in Bay City, we're golden. And pretending to be cops is the icing on the cake. The nigger and beaner gangs have been runnin' wild, and everybody was happy to see uniforms." He smiled. "At first anyway. Course, they feel a bit different after we mostly cleaned out the bangers and started collectin' taxes. But there's still a lot of guns out there, and people are startin' to get pissed, but we can handle it 'cause we're the only ones with any organization."

"Which is just my point. We don't want this friggin' ship to become the center of any organized push back. We need to take care of them now."

M/V Pecos Trader
Sun Lower Anchorage
Neches River
Near Nederland, Texas

Day 26, 1:35 p.m.

Hughes stood on the flying bridge, struggling to hide his skepticism as he watched the two engineers put the finishing touches on what he'd secretly christened 'Gowan's Folly." He cleared his throat loudly, and Dan Gowan, the chief engineer, turned from what he was doing, his irritation obvious, if unstated.

"You need something, Cap?"

"Uhh… are you sure this is completely safe, Dan. I mean, the starting air pressure is, what, three hundred pounds?"

"Four hundred and fifty pounds," Gowan corrected, nodding to the first engineer who was working beside him, "but Rich used extra-heavy pipe for it all and ran the new line straight up from the starting air tanks in the engine room. We hydrostatically tested it to over seven hundred pounds; she's safe. Whether it works is another question."

Hughes studied the arrangement. It was simple enough, a two-inch pipe running up the outside of the deckhouse and terminating in a high-pressure ball valve mounted on the top handrail at the edge of the flying bridge. The valve was connected via a short section of hydraulic hose to the closed end of a six-foot-long section of three-inch pipe, with the open end of the pipe pointed at the riverbank in the distance. The three-inch pipe was fastened to the top handrail via a ball joint that allowed the 'muzzle' of the little makeshift cannon to be pointed in any direction, and the flexible hydraulic hose accommodated that freedom of movement. Two handles welded on the back end of the pipe could be grasped like a steering wheel and used to aim the crude device.

"We'll need some sort of sight, but before we invest time in that, I figure we need to see if it even works. Ready, Rich?" Gowan asked the first engineer.

"Ready as I'll ever be, I guess," Rich Martin replied. He reached over and swiveled the muzzle of the cannon inboard, then dipped into a canvas bag at his feet and pulled out a Coke can. He held it with a rag and smeared it with a thick coating of grease from an open pail on the deck, then eased the greasy mess into the muzzle of the makeshift gun. It was a snug fit and the muscles in Martin's arms flexed as he pushed the can down the pipe with a broomstick handle.

Martin looked puzzled, then glanced over at Gowan. "It's getting harder. We forgot to open the vent, Chief."

Gowan nodded and opened a small vent valve at the rear of the crude cannon, rewarded by a hiss as trapped air escaped and Martin pushed the can all the way down the pipe with ease. Gowan grinned and closed the valve.

"Now that's a tight fit," he said.

Hughes gasped. "We're shooting COKES!"

"Just the cans," Gowan said. "Polak had a bunch of empties and I stopped him before he crushed 'em so we could use them as molds. We cut the top off and filled 'em with Quikrete. But this is just an experiment; we should be able to shoot anything that's a relatively snug fit. We're smearing grease all over 'em to make a tighter seal and speed the exit. Also if we have to point it down at something close, there's a vacuum behind the can now, which will keep the round from sliding out the barrel. That was Rich's idea."

Hughes was shaking his head in disbelief, but beside him, Manuel Torres, formerly petty officer first class, United States Coast Guard, was grinning. "First class, Chief," he said to Gowan. "So what's the range?"

Gowan shrugged. "We're about to find out." He turned to Martin. "You want to aim or work the valve, Rich?"

"The honor's all yours, Chief. You take the shot and I'll work the valve. What's your target?"

"I'm just gonna aim her up over the refinery docks so we see how far she'll throw a round."

"Sounds like a plan," Martin said, moving to the valve. "Just say when."

Gowan grabbed the handles with both hands and turned the pipe toward the refinery docks on the far bank, elevating the muzzle at approximately forty-five degrees.

"Ready. Aim. Fire!"

Hughes flinched as Rich Martin moved the valve handle a quarter of a turn and back, cycling the valve open and closed, and a roar momentarily filled the air. Then Torres shouted, "There," and Hughes followed his pointing finger to be rewarded by a flash of bright red as the sun reflected off the can already across the river and high above the refinery docks. It flew out of sight, and scant seconds later, a loud metallic CLANG was heard in the distance.

Rich Martin grinned over at Gowan. "Sounds like you killed a tank in the tank farm, Chief."

Gowan's grin was equally wide. "Well, I'll be damned. It actually worked."

Hughes was grinning too now, but he looked over to see Torres staring at the Sun Terminal docks across the river.

"What's up, Mr. Torres?" he asked.

"Watch the docks over there a minute. You'll see it."

Hughes turned his attention to the far terminal, and soon he did see it, the flash of sun reflecting off a binoculars' lenses.

"Dan, do you see—"

"I got it," Gowan said. "Right below the loading arms."

"Well, you got your range test," Hughes said. "You want to try for accuracy?"

Gowan grinned at Hughes. "Why the hell not. Let's see if we can treat our curious friend to a Coke, Rich."

Martin reloaded, and Gowan pointed directly at the target, but the shot splashed into the river just short of the terminal dock. They reloaded again and Gowan elevated the muzzle a bit, and the shot flew over the top of the loading arms to land out of sight in the open field behind the terminal. On the next reload, Gowan aimed lower and was rewarded by the ringing sound of a rock on steel as the fourth shot slammed into the top of the loading arms.

"Movement on the dock," Torres said, binoculars clamped to his eyes. Moments later they heard the roar of a distant engine and saw a plume of dust rising from the gravel road hidden from their view by the terminal dock.

"I do believe our peeping tom decided to leave," Hughes said, and the others laughed.

Hughes grew serious. "This is great, Dan. Can you rig up any more?"

Gowan stroked his chin. "I think we can probably scrounge up enough material to rig up a few more. But it needs work. We need to come up with a better sight for close shots and some sort of graduated angle marker so we can make sure we get it back on target after each reload when we have the muzzle elevated. Then we need to—"

Hughes held up both hands, palms outward. "Spare me the details. Let's just say you're going to improve it, right?"

"Well, of course," Gowan said.

Hughes' grin returned. "Good, because your new title is chief of engineering and artillery."

Gowan was about to protest when they heard the ring of footsteps on steel treads and turned in time to see Georgia Howell at the top of the stairway to the flying bridge.

"Captain," she said, "Matt Kinsey's on the VHF. They made it to Calcasieu Lock and he wants to talk to you."

CHAPTER FIVE

Day 26, 11:55 a.m.

Kinsey shook his head as he returned the VHF handset to its rack. "Nothing. I guess we're out of range. I figured it might be a stretch."

"Too bad," Bollinger said as he steered the boat toward the sharp bend in the river. "I gotta admit, knowing the cavalry was on the other end of the radio was reassuring. But we knew it wouldn't last."

"Yeah, but it sure makes it all real, doesn't it," Kinsey said, adding, "And I thank you for coming along, Bollinger. You know you didn't have to."

"Wouldn't have it any other way, boss. Besides—" Bollinger grinned "—Torres said it was my turn to watch you."

Kinsey chuckled, and Bollinger focused on the river ahead.

"Crap!" Bollinger said as he eased the boat around the bend in the short section where the Intracoastal Waterway followed the existing river channel. "I guess that settles whether or not the lock's open, Chief."

Ahead in the distance, where the Intracoastal left the winding river to continue southeast as a man-made gash through the marsh, both sides of the entrance to Calcasieu Lock were lined with push boats, their barges grounded in the soft mud of the banks to hold them in place. Like the rest of the idle tows they'd seen so far, there were no signs of life. Anyone aboard was either staying out of sight or the crews had abandoned the boats to strike off for their homes.

"Half a dozen tows," Bollinger said. "Actually, I'd have expected more with the lock closed all this time."

"Me too, now that you mention it." Kinsey stifled a curse. "I'd hoped we wouldn't have to try the trailer until the locks further on. And I hadn't figured on all these tows jamming access to the bank. I'm not sure we can get close enough to pull her out."

"What are we going to do?" Bollinger asked.

Kinsey turned the VHF selector to channel 14. "Well, I doubt it does any good, but I guess I'll hail the lock and see if anyone's still there."

He keyed the mic. "Calcasieu Locks, Calcasieu Locks. This is the US Coast Guard. Do you copy? Over."

He repeated the call with no response. He was about to hail a third time when his radio crackled.

"'Bout time y'all showed up, Coast Guard. Ain't nobody home at the lock. Y'all come on over and have some coffee."

Movement caught Kinsey's eye and he saw a man waving from the wheelhouse door of one of the towboats.

"That you waving at me?" Kinsey asked into the mic.

"That would be me," came the reply.

"Take us alongside, Bollinger," Kinsey said. "But lay off a ways until we get a better feel for the situation."

Bollinger nodded, then glanced back to see how their own tow was riding before edging alongside the towboat. Kinsey studied the vessel as they approached. It was an older boat, but well maintained. Even under the present conditions, the blue and white paint looked fresh, the brass was bright, and the decks were clean, obviously freshly washed. The name JUDY ANN was neatly lettered across her stern and on a name board attached to the pilothouse. Under her name on the stern was her hailing port, Greenville, Mississippi.

Kinsey's study of the boat was interrupted as someone came out of the deckhouse to stand at the rail. He recognized the man who'd waved to him and let Bollinger bring their boat to within twenty feet of the towboat.

"Hold her right here, Bollinger. And be ready to jet if I give you the word."

"Got it, Chief," Bollinger replied. Kinsey exited the small cabin, his hand resting casually on his sidearm.

"Mornin'," he called across the gap.

The man's smile faded as he noticed Kinsey's hand. He nodded. "Mornin' back. You plannin' on shootin' somebody?"

Kinsey flashed an uneasy smile. "You can't be too careful these days."

The man nodded. "That's a fact. So why don't you take that hand away from your gun nice and slow."

"And why would I do that?" Kinsey asked.

"Because there's a feller in that boat just ahead of us who has your head in the crosshairs of a thirty ought six, and another one with a bead on your boat driver there. One signal from me and you're both dead meat."

Crap, Kinsey thought, *how could I be so friggin' dumb?* He started to glance back toward Bollinger.

"I wouldn't do it," the man said. "I don't want to blow y'all away, but I will, you force my hand. Now do us both a favor and take your hand away from your gun, slow like."

Kinsey hesitated, wondering whether the guy was bluffing, then did as ordered.

"Look," he said, "You don't want to —"

"Now," the man said, "unzip them coveralls and drop them to your waist. I want to see your arms."

"What the hell —"

"I'm lookin' for tattoos. Just do what I say and don't make a move for that gun, and everything will be fine," the man said.

Suddenly, Kinsey understood. He shucked his Coast Guard coveralls to his waist, exposing his tee-shirt-clad upper body and bare arms. On his right upper arm, a small tattoo read US Coast Guard and, below that in script, *Semper Paratus.*

The man smiled. "Now that there's about the most welcome sight I've seen in almost a month."

"A youthful mistake," Kinsey said, 'but one I'm glad I made now. Can I pull my coveralls back up?"

"Oh yeah, sorry," the man said, "but like you said, you can't be too careful these days."

Kinsey nodded and struggled back into his coveralls. "I understand," he said, glancing at the boat ahead. "Now about those rifles…"

The man grinned again. "You might say that was a little creative exaggeration."

Kinsey felt a flash of irritation, but it passed quickly. Things had worked out well, considering the alternatives. He returned the man's grin. "Play much poker?"

"Now and again," the man replied. "By the way, I'm Lucius Wellesley. The *Judy Ann* is my boat." There was obvious pride in his voice when he mentioned the boat.

"Matt Kinsey," Kinsey replied as he zipped his coveralls and nodded toward the small cabin of his own boat. "And that's Dave Bollinger at the wheel. So you were looking for prison tattoos, right? How'd you know about that?"

"It's a long story," Wellesley replied. "Why don't y'all come aboard and I'll tell you all about it. And the offer of the coffee stands. I just made a fresh pot."

Kinsey nodded and instructed Bollinger to bring them alongside the *Judy Ann*, then moved to pass lines to Wellesley. Minutes later with their own boat secure alongside, the Coasties boarded the push boat and followed Wellesley into the mess room, where other men waited. Wellesley made introductions, going down the line of men, who each nodded as they were introduced.

"This here's Dave Hitchcock, captain of the *Rambling Ace* tied up just ahead of us. Then we got Jerry Arnold, Sam Davis, Bud Spencer, and Tom Winfield; they're all from boats that left." Wellesley grinned. "And that greasy-looking customer on the end is Jimmy Kahla, chief engineer of the *Judy Ann*."

Kinsey introduced himself and Bollinger, and Wellesley waved them to a table as the other men took other available seats in the galley and Wellesley excused himself and moved into the small galley. He returned with three steaming white china mugs of coffee on a tray and set it down on the table before them.

"The rest of you jokers can serve yourselves," Wellesley said, "I'm only waitin' on the guests." There was good-natured laughter as the others got up and headed into the galley. "There's sugar and creamer there on the table if you need it," Wellesley said to Kinsey and Bollinger.

The Coasties nodded and took a cup, both preferring it black. Kinsey sipped his and set it down on the table as the other men drifted back into the mess room to take seats.

"So, back to my original question, Captain Welles—"

"Call me Lucius," Wellesley said. "You mean about the tattoos?"

Kinsey nodded, and Wellesley continued. "Well, some of the boys that left ran into some trouble west of here—"

"The boys that left?" Kinsey asked, obviously confused.

Wellesley sighed. "It would probably be better if I just started at the beginning."

Kinsey nodded.

"Well, there were already tows stacked up on either side of the lock, waiting transit, when the lights went out. We was all just sitting here the night before, watching all the pretty lights in the sky; then come daylight, the power went down ashore. At first we just thought it was some sort of routine problem, and we didn't hear much else because VHF reception was horrible and nobody had cell reception. Then after a couple of days, more tows were stacking up, and nobody showed up to work on the lock. VHF reception started to gradually improve, and we started hearing bits and pieces of news from Lake Charles all about this solar storm thing. There wasn't much we could do but sit here, because even when the radios started working better, cell reception was out, and none of the boats could call their company offices to find out what we were supposed to do. What we were hearing on the radio didn't sound too good, and of course, everyone started worrying about their families."

"Understandable," Kinsey said. "What happened?"

Wellesley smiled wanly. "You might say we had a little imbalance. Most everyone on the stranded tows lives somewhere along the waterway system, but way more of 'em live east of here, either along the coast near the Intracoastal or up the Mississippi system. Thing is, it's not divided evenly by boat; most crews are a mixed bag with crewmen from all over. Well, naturally, everyone wanted to head home, or at least in the general direction, and based on what we were hearing on the VHF, we all figured sticking to the water was way safer. Headin' home in the boats seemed the natural choice, but the problem was, only the tows on this side had anywhere to go."

Kinsey nodded. "The locks."

"That's right," Wellesley said. "All the boats on the east side are trapped between locks. They can't get north to the Mississippi from Morgan City because of the locks at Bayou Sorrel and Port Allen. And likewise, they can't get east to New Orleans because the Bayou Boeuf Lock is closed at Morgan City, and even if they could, they couldn't lock up into the Mississippi, 'cause both the Harvey and Algiers locks are abandoned, just like everything else." He shook his head. "Not that anybody in their right mind would head for New Orleans. It's a war zone, last we heard."

"You have contact?"

"Had. Just a VHF relay passin' news from boats spread along the waterway as far east as New Orleans and north to Memphis. But we ain't heard nothin' from those guys for a week now. It appears like anyone who could leave the cities did, and the gangs are running wild. From what we hear, those FEMA assholes ain't doin' nothing to help the situation. They seem more focused on looting the civilians."

Kinsey stiffened. "Baton Rouge?"

"Not quite as bad, I hear. The governor and the state government are there, so I imagine they kept some National Guard troops there to try to keep a lid on it." Wellesley sneered. "Politicians are right good at lookin' out for number one."

Kinsey gave a relieved nod, then refocused on the topic at hand. "You said something about an imbalance…?"

"Oh yeah. Like I said, the crews were mostly a mixture, so we all congregated up there on the lock wall to try to hash it out. As you can probably imagine, there was a lot of arguing back and forth. Finally, everybody who lived on the west side of the lock, which means this part of Louisiana and Texas down as far as the Mexican border, came over to boats on this side. The problem was, there weren't near enough people left on this side to crew all the boats, so there was a lot more arguing. They finally decided on six boats, and each one of them took a barge of diesel and loaded up on groceries and water from the abandoned boats and headed west. That's how we knew about convicts pretending to be the law."

"They warned you?" Kinsey asked.

"Not directly," Wellesley said. "They separated and one of 'em stopped in Port Arthur to let some guys look for their families, and had a run-in with the fake cops. They were at the edge of VHF range and breaking up pretty bad, but we heard 'em warning the other westbound boats about the cons on the radio; then we lost 'em. They mentioned prison tattoos. That's why when you showed up from that direction, I wasn't sure if you were legit or not. I didn't know what to do, which is why I bluffed you into the little striptease."

Kinsey laughed. "And quite well, I have to admit. But what about the boats on the other side of the lock?"

"Still there, of course," Wellesley said. "The tows anyway. Lots of the guys took the towboats' aluminum skiffs and took off to see how far they could get, and a few lit out up the road, luggin' gas cans and hopin' to find an abandoned car. There are a lot of single guys in this life, though; those of us with no close family figured with everything going to hell, this didn't seem to be a bad place to ride things out. We're at the dead end of a road in the middle of nowhere with marsh and river all around us, so I doubt we'll attract much unwanted attention. The boats that left loaded up supplies, but that still left plenty of groceries on the abandoned boats. We got power and showers and air-conditioning. Our biggest worry is fresh water, but between the tanks on the abandoned boats and the few of us, we'll be okay until things get better." He paused. "Which I think makes it your turn to share. I'm hoping the US Coast Guard showing up means things ARE getting better."

Kinsey shook his head. "I'm afraid I have to disappoint you there, Cap—Lucius. I'm actually trying to get to Baton Rouge to find my own family. This isn't in any way an official Coast Guard operation."

"So is the government doing anything?"

"Nothing I want to be a part of," Kinsey said, and beside him Bollinger nodded.

Wellesley's face fell; then he looked resigned. "Yeah, actually that's kind of what I'd figured from the VHF traffic. It's kind of a shock to hear it 'official like' though."

"How many of you are left?" Kinsey asked.

"Seven on this side, and around thirty on the other side of the lock, grouped together on four boats. Staying close to where the stores are made more sense than trying to drag everything to a few boats." He grinned. "Besides, I kind of like being on this side where I can take off if the need arises."

"So thirty-seven all told?"

He shrugged. "Last time I heard. We don't keep a muster or anything. Could be some of those boys took off. Why?" Wellesley asked, suspicion rising in his voice.

"Just curious," Kinsey said.

Wellesley gave him a long look, then nodded. "All right, but like I said, it's your turn to share. How exactly do you plan on getting to Baton Rouge? Small boat or not, you're not getting through that lock or the ones after that."

"We brought a trailer and we figured—"

"Is that what you're towin'?"

"Yeah," Kinsey said. "We got a winch we can mount on the front of the trailer, and long leads to run from the winch to an extra battery in the boat. I figure if we can find someplace with a reasonable slope, we can hook on to something ashore and drag the boat out of the water on the trailer, then push it around the locks by hand and relaunch on the other side of each lock."

Wellesley looked skeptical. "You better have a look at the canal bank before you go settin' your hopes on that."

"Excuse me, Chief," Bollinger said, "but if the *Judy Ann*'s higher antennas give her VHF coverage as far as Port Arthur, we could probably give Captain Hughes an update."

Kinsey looked at Wellesley, who shrugged. "Help yourself. If there's friendly folks within VHF range, I'd like to connect with them anyway."

Kinsey nodded. "We'll take you up on that, but first I think we ought to have a look at the situation so we can let our people know what we plan to do."

Wellesley nodded. "Leave your rig tied off to us. The boys will keep an eye on it, and I'll run you up to the lock wall in our skiff. That'll be a lot easier than crawling across all these tows. Matter of fact, I probably need to go on over with you, just so the boys on the other side don't get antsy."

***

Fifteen minutes later, Kinsey and Bollinger stood beside Wellesley on the steel and concrete bulkhead leading into the lock, staring across a narrow backwater at the canal bank. Kinsey studied the sloping bank covered with a jumble of rough-cut granite blocks the size of washing machines.

"See what I mean?" Wellesley asked.

Kinsey nodded. "Even if we can get you to shuffle the barges so we can access the bank, that riprap stone is pretty rough. I don't see us dragging the boat and trailer over that."

"I was hoping there might be a boat launch ramp, but I guess that was wishful thinking," Bollinger said.

"Nothing solid to hook the winch cable to either, and no way we'll be able to manhandle her out of the water without a mechanical assist." Kinsey sighed. "All right. Let's look the whole situation over and start working on a plan B."

Bollinger nodded and the Coasties followed Wellesley along the top of the narrow bulkhead until they got to the wall of the lock proper and walked across a grassy verge to step into a large square asphalt parking lot flanked by a metal storage building. Across the expansive square the asphalt narrowed to a road running the length of the lock, with what were obviously the administrative offices and workshops at the far end.

Bollinger cast an appraising eye down the long straight road. "This is good surface. It shouldn't be too hard to roll her past the lock, presuming we can just figure a way to get her up the bank to start with."

"Let's go see what we're up against on the other side," Kinsey said, and they started walking down the quarter-mile length of the lock.

"Whoa. Slow down there," Wellesley said, and led them around the storage building to a bicycle rack holding a dozen battered bicycles. "No use walking when we can ride. The lock workers used these to get back and forth. There's another rack at the opposite end of the lock."

Kinsey grinned. "No argument here, Lucius."

They pedaled to the opposite end of the lock, only to find more problems. Even more tows jammed both banks of the canal. The bank sloped steeply to the water's edge, and the jumbled riprap stones protecting the bank from erosion were even larger here, sharp corners pointing skyward at odd angles. Kinsey's heart sank at the sight of it.

"Even if we manage to get the boat out, there's no way we're getting the trailer back down over that crap, even with the planks," Bollinger said. "What are we gonna do, Chief?"

Kinsey said nothing for a long moment. The access road ran straight and true beside the canal another quarter mile, then turned sharply to the left, away from the water. A tall bridge loomed over the waterway in the near distance.

"Okay," he said. "This whole area is marsh, with inlets and bayous all over the place. We only draw three feet or so of water, so we can likely get up most of them. We just need to find one that gets us close enough to the canal on the east side of the lock for us to use the trailer to get the boat across and back into the canal."

"But how, Chief? There's probably a dozen inlets like that, and the marsh grass and cane is six or eight feet high. It'll be like a maze. We won't know which one to go into, and even if we get close to the canal, we likely won't know it. We can't see anything from water level."

"Which is why we're gonna have a look from up there." Kinsey said, pointing to the top of the highway bridge arching high above the canal and the flat land it ran through.

Wellesley cleared his throat, and Kinsey turned his attention from the bridge to one of the boats about halfway down the road. A group of men was starting to form at the rail of one of them, obviously in expectation of a visit.

"I figure y'all are eager to have a look at that bridge," Wellesley said, "so let's ride down together. I'll stop and fill the boys in and y'all can head on up the bridge. These fellas haven't had anyone new to talk to in a while. Stop now and I doubt y'all will get away before nightfall."

***

Accessing the bridge proved easy. The lock road turned left and intersected State Route 384 a half mile north of the bridge; then it was a straight shot back south. They ate up the distance quickly, and minutes later they hopped off to push their bikes up the bridge, the old single-gear, fat-tire conveyances no match for the steep incline. Soon they stood atop the bridge, surveying the flat land spread before them, the sun glistening off channels crisscrossing the half-submerged terrain.

"I'll be damned," Bollinger said.

A wide channel roughly paralleled the south bank of the canal, punctuated at intervals with side channels that extended northward toward the canal like crooked, arthritic fingers. One of those fingers ended at the southern abutment of the bridge they stood on, the 'fingertip' separated from the canal itself by a narrow strip of land. At the bridge abutment there was a gravel parking lot, and Kinsey grinned as he pointed down at it.

"You see what I see, Bollinger?"

"Well, I'll be double-damned. A boat ramp!"

Kinsey nodded. "That takes care of the hard part, and there's not any riprap on the canal side down this far, so we should be able to get her back in without any problem."

"And getting there's a piece of cake," Bollinger said. "We just go back out into the river and turn into the first wide channel south of the lock."

Kinsey grinned. "Well, let's get to it. If we can talk the towboat guys into helping, we may be able to get around the lock and well down the canal before dark. But first, we need to have a long talk with our new friends. I've got an idea."

***

Matt Kinsey stood on the lock wall in front of the assembled group, glancing at his watch. This was taking far longer than he'd anticipated and he was eager to get away. He'd had Wellesley assemble the towboat men so he could present them with his proposal, but it had ignited a much more spirited debate than expected. Finally, Kinsey put two fingers in his mouth and whistled loudly. When he had the group's attention, he held up both his hands in a stop gesture and raised his voice.

"Okay, fellas, I understand this is a big decision, but I can't give you any more time. I have to call *Pecos Trader* and put the proposal to Captain Hughes, and I'm not even sure he'll go for it himself. But first I need to know how many of you are in. It's entirely your call, and not everyone has to agree. But if you'd like to give it a shot, I need to know now, because Bollinger and I need to get out of here."

No one said anything for a long moment; then Lucius Wellesley shook his head. "I don't know, Kinsey. We've got a pretty good setup here, and it sounds like those folks over in Texas have already attracted some unwanted attention. I mean, I sympathize, but I'm not sure puttin' ourselves in the middle of that is very smart. I think it might be best if we just stay here and lie low until things get back to normal."

Some of the others nodded their agreement.

Kinsey sighed. "You might be right, Lucius, assuming things do get back to normal, but from the way I understand it, the time frame for that happening, if ever, is years not months. How long you figure you can stay here?"

"We've got food and water for maybe six months, a bit longer if we ration it," Wellesley said, "and enough diesel, gasoline, and lube oil in all these barges for years. I figure when push comes to shove, we can trade for what we need."

"And trading means letting people know you're here with fuel to trade," Kinsey said, "so you'll be sitting on a goldmine with no means to defend it. Just how long you think that's going to last before either gangs out of Lake Charles or FEMA shows up to take your boats and cargo? You got what, three or four handguns between you all?"

Wellesley said nothing for a long moment, then glanced at the other towboat men before turning back to Kinsey. "Would you and Bollinger mind taking a walk down to the other end of the lock for a bit. I'm not the king here, and I don't speak for these other fellas. We really need to discuss this among ourselves in private."

"Understood," Kinsey said as he and Bollinger walked toward the far end of the lock. When they were well away from the group, Bollinger shot Kinsey a questioning look.

"Ah, you sure about this, boss? How do you think Captain Hughes is going to feel about us 'recruiting' extra people? Shouldn't we have checked with him first?"

Kinsey shook his head. "I thought about it, but I figure Wellesley's gonna be standing right beside us when we use the VHF, so I didn't figure he should hear my idea for the first time while we're on the radio. And we don't have time to engage in a lengthy debate and negotiation. They either want to go or they don't. As far as Hughes goes, he can always say no, but I don't think he will. If even a few of them take the deal, it will add guys with needed skills, and from the looks of 'em, I'm thinking at least half of them have some military service, and I'm betting the others are probably at least hunters. We start increasing our dependent population, we're gonna need more shooters to protect them. Besides, that's not the only thing they bring to the table, there's also—"

Kinsey turned at a shout from down the lock wall, to see Wellesley waving them back. They turned and walked back to the group.

"Well," Wellesley said when they reached the group, "it appears we should get on the VHF to your Captain Hughes."

"How many?" Kinsey asked.

"All of us," Wellesley said.

Crap, thought Kinsey.

CHAPTER SIX

M/V Judy Ann
Intracoastal Waterway
West End of Calcasieu Lock
Lake Charles, Louisiana

Day 26, 2:40 p.m.

The relief in Hughes' voice changed to irritation when he learned of Kinsey's freelance recruitment efforts.

"You did what? Thirty-seven guys? Dammit, Matt! You know —"

"They've got their own food, at least for six months or so. Water too. And they're bringing their own housing with them. Over," Kinsey said. Beside him, Wellesley nodded, suddenly concerned Hughes might reject the deal.

But news the recruits wouldn't strain existing resources mollified Hughes to some extent, and as Kinsey presented the merits of his case a bit more fully, he sensed Hughes' resistance weakening. Kinsey sealed the deal.

"Is the chief engineer with you, Captain Hughes? Over," Kinsey asked.

"Yes, Dan's standing right beside me. Over," Hughes replied.

"Well, ask him how he'd like a couple of twenty-thousand-barrel barges full of lube oil of various grades. It seems like I recall hearing him moaning about how hard it was going to be to find any. Over," Kinsey said.

There was a long pause until the radio crackled again. "This may be the only time I've ever seen Dan Gowan speechless," Hughes said. "He's nodding his head so hard I'm afraid it might fly off his shoulders." Kinsey heard Hughes sigh into the radio. "Put Captain Wellesley on and we'll work out the details. If he gives me an ETA at the Neches intersection, we'll send the patrol boat out to escort his little convoy in and keep the cons off him. And, Matt," Hughes added, "this will likely be the last we hear from you before you return, so Godspeed in finding your family. Over."

"Thanks, Cap," Kinsey replied. "Here's Captain Wellesley. Over."

***

Kinsey and Bollinger sat at a table in the galley of the *Lacy J*, one of the towboats trapped east of the lock. They had a chart booklet open on the table between them, and Wellesley was hunched over them, studying a chart.

"We appreciate this, Lucius," Kinsey said. "Obviously, *Pecos Trader* didn't carry inland charts."

Wellesley laughed. "Well, it ain't like these boats are likely to need them anytime soon."

"Still, we appreciate it," Kinsey said. "I knew the route, but operating with a Louisiana road map and a general idea leaves a lot to be desired."

Wellesley waved away their thanks. "No problem. Y'all about ready to shove off?"

"Yeah," Bollinger said, "thanks again to you fellas."

As hoped, their new shipmates had readily agreed to help get the Coasties' boat over the narrow strip of land and back into the canal. If many hands hadn't made 'light work,' they had at least made it much faster and possible without necessitating the use of the electric winch.

A dozen towboat men had taken their flat-bottom aluminum skiffs and motored over to come ashore by the bridge abutment and meet the Coasties at the boat ramp they'd discovered earlier. The patrol boat nosed into the ramp and Kinsey untied the trailer tow rope and tossed it to the men ashore before Bollinger backed the boat back out into the bayou. Their new helpers pulled the trailer toward shore until the wheels engaged the sloping concrete ramp and then held it there until Bollinger drove the boat onto the trailer, and Kinsey splashed down to hook the securing cable into the pad eye on the front of the boat and used the hand winch to pull the boat the rest of the way on to the trailer. Bollinger hopped out of the boat as well, and the mass of men clustered around the trailer, straining and grunting, to roll it up the boat ramp.

Even with a dozen extra men, the task had been difficult, with the combined weight of the boat and trailer increased by Dan Gowan's improvised flotation pontoons. They worked the trailer up the ramp in increments, all of them heaving on a count of three. It took two dozen heaves to get the trailer to level ground, but after that, rolling it over to the canal had been relatively easy.

They reversed the process to relaunch the boat into the canal, the challenge here being the muddy slope of the canal bank. They countered that with wide wooden planks the Coasties had brought along, lashed to the trailer in anticipation of just such a situation. They laid the planks end to end behind each wheel, providing a firm path for the trailer to roll into the water until the boat and trailer were both afloat. The boat had separated from the trailer easily and was now tied alongside the *Lacy J*, the floating trailer in tow behind her, with the planks lashed down securely.

"About that," Wellesley said. "That was a bear even with a bunch of folks to help. And I ain't so sure you're gonna find convenient shortcuts at the Bayou Sorrel and Port Allen locks. I'm thinkin' you and Bollinger here are gonna have a tough time gettin' around those locks. I mean, you really think that electric winch is gonna work?"

Kinsey's nod was less than confident. "I think it will if we can find some sort of reasonable slope to pull the trailer up and something heavy and stationary to hook the winch cable to. For that matter, we got plenty of spare gas in the boat; if we can find an abandoned car or truck, we can use that. Don't worry, Lucius. We'll make it work."

Wellesley nodded and held out his hand. "All right then. I best get to work before the rest of the fellas think I'm goofin' off. Y'all have a safe trip, and I hope to be meetin' that family of yours one of these days before long."

Kinsey stood and took the outstretched hand as Bollinger rose to follow suit.

"Thank you, Lucius," Kinsey said. "When are you leaving for Beaumont?"

"It'll be a few days, at least. We got enough folks to take all six tows on the west side of the lock. I mean, I can't see leavin' all that fuel here. Even if we can't use it, it'll sure come in handy for trading. And besides, the boats will give us some extra beds when we get to Texas. Likewise, we're stripping all the tows on this side right down to parade rest. Not just the food, but mooring lines, spare parts, basically everything." He smiled. "I got a feeling we ain't gonna be sendin' in any purchase orders any time soon."

"That's a fact," Kinsey said. "Sounds like you have your work cut out for you."

"You know, it feels good for a change. We been sittin' on our asses for weeks, gettin' on each other's last nerve, but now we got a plan and it just feels good to have a purpose." He smiled again. "Even if we don't really know what the hell we're doing." He grew serious. "But the problem is gettin' it all to the other boats. Some of that stuff is heavy and gettin' it up on the lock, all the way down to the other end, and back down on to the boats is gonna take some time."

"Something tells me you'll make it work," Kinsey said.

"You can count on it," Wellesley said.

M/V *Pecos Trader*
Sun Lower Anchorage
Neches River
Near Nederland, Texas

Day 26, 6:45 p.m.

"So how long before these towboats get here?" Gowan asked.

Hughes grinned across the coffee table. "You mean how long before you get your hands on that lube oil, don't you?"

Gowan shrugged. "I can't deny it was welcome news. We got diesel coming out of our ears, but lubes are gonna be hard to come by, especially in the quantities we need. It's not like we can raid an AutoZone for a thousand gallons of lube oil. Two barges full is about a gazillion times overkill, but it means we'll have enough for anything we do in the future, to say nothing about its trade value. Everyone's worried about fuel, but machinery won't run very long without lubrication."

Hughes nodded and looked at the group assembled in the sitting area of his office, his ad hoc advisory council, for want of a better term. There was no doubt he was in charge (whether he wanted to be or not), but it wasn't the military, and the situation on the 'Ark,' as everyone had begun to jokingly refer to *Pecos Trader*, was outside anyone's experience. He needed all the help he could get and had no problem whatsoever listening to the advice of subordinates.

His three senior officers sat across the low coffee table from him on the sofa, Dan Gowan in the center flanked on either side by Georgia Howell and Rich Martin. Torres sat to his right in an armchair, filling in for the absent Kinsey as security chief. But perhaps the most surprising member of the informal advisory council sat beside him on the love seat. He glanced at his wife and silently marveled at how quickly she'd adapted over the last week.

Laura Hughes had rebounded quickly from the harrowing ordeal of her family's rescue. With their twin daughters safely aboard *Pecos Trader* and with neither the obligations of the farm at Pecan Grove nor her large animal veterinary practice to occupy her, she'd quickly become bored. She first attempted to 'help' in the galley, where her suggestions to make things 'more efficient' did nothing to endear her to Chief Cook Jake 'Polak' Kadowski. Rebuffed there, she'd found a perfect outlet in seeing to the needs of the Coast Guard dependents who'd joined *Pecos Trader* in Wilmington.

Essentially passengers, the five Coast Guard wives made themselves as unobtrusive as possible and tried to keep their nine kids out of the way. The officers and crew of *Pecos Trader* were kind, but there were neither facilities nor activities for dependents on a working ship, and no one really knew what to do with the non-sailors. For their part, the women never complained, as they understood they represented a disruption to the normal rhythm of shipboard life, but they were nearing their wits' ends. As one woman confided to Laura soon after she arrived, they were all going 'totally frigging Loony Tunes.'

But if the Coastie wives had been hesitant to address the situation with the captain, Laura was anything but. He wasn't the 'captain' to her, but 'Jordan,' and she quickly pointed out that unless accommodation was made for the children and if the women weren't somehow blended into shipboard life, things would go downhill in a hurry, especially since they expected even more passengers as the families of other crewmen were rescued.

Hughes had conceded the point and placed her in charge of organizing the dependents. Delighted to have a representative with 'the captain's ear,' the wives responded enthusiastically, and Laura was presently engaged in planning classes for the children as well as learning as much as she could about shipboard routine to see where the women's skill sets might be most useful.

As a veterinarian, she was also the closest thing they had to a doctor and was already treating minor injuries, earning her the nickname of 'Doc' from both the Coasties and the *Pecos Trader* crewmen. Hughes was proud of Laura, but a bit uneasy. This was a dynamic they'd never before experienced in their twenty years of marriage, and he wasn't completely sure he liked it.

He turned his attention back to the group and cleared his throat.

"I talked with Captain Wellesley on the VHF a couple of hours ago," Hughes said. "They're stripping all the trapped tows of everything that might possibly be of use. He figures three days minimum before they head this way. He's gonna check in with us every day with a progress report."

"Which gives us some time to try to gather in some of our folks," Gowan said. "The crew is getting restless, Cap." Both Howell and Martin nodded agreement.

Hughes sighed and sat back in his chair. Things had been tense since the rescue of his own family and the unexpected skirmish with the escaped convicts ashore. They'd all been on high alert since then, as well as helping Kinsey prepare for his mission to Baton Rouge. He knew his crew was anxious about their own families, and rightfully so, but he just couldn't figure out how to send out shore parties and protect the ship simultaneously.

"The problem is intel," Torres said. "They got it; we don't. We got no idea how many people they have and how they're spread out, but they can watch us easy enough. We scared 'em away this morning with the air cannon, but they're probably back by now, and there's a hundred places to hide across the river. They'll just be more careful."

"That's my concern," Hughes said. "They already saw Kinsey leave, so they know we're down a boat and two shooters. If they see the police boat leave, loaded with a shore party, I'm afraid they might be tempted to hit us when we're the weakest."

"Well, we can't just SIT here," Gowan said. "Most everyone's got family out there, and with these assholes pretending to be the law, who knows what's happening."

Hughes started to respond, but Torres spoke first. "Maybe we can send out a party without them seeing it."

"How?" Hughes asked. "At night? Y'all have night-vision glasses, so what makes you think the cons haven't looted police and sheriff's armories. They might have it too."

Torres shook his head. "Nope. I'm talking broad daylight. We're anchored with the bow upstream, so they can't see the starboard side from the opposite bank. What if we launch the starboard lifeboat and go around the island, keeping the ship between the shore party and any observers on the opposite side of the river? If we're slick enough, they won't even know anyone left."

Hughes stroked his chin. They were anchored in what was known locally as the Sun Lower Anchorage, directly across from the Sun Oil Company docks. An inlet off the main channel of the river, the secondary 'oxbow' channel continued inland perhaps a mile and then made a U-turn, rejoining the main channel of the Neches about a half mile upstream of their present location. The mouth of the downstream inlet had been dredged to the same depth as the main river channel, both to give loaded tankers a place to turn around in the narrow river and to anchor when fogbound or awaiting a berth. Nestled between the hairpin turn of the secondary channel and the main channel was a low marshy island and, at the slightly higher third of the island nearest the main channel, a thick stand of Chinese tallow trees and brush.

Hughes shook his head. "They'll hear the engine and see the boat when it comes out the upper inlet. It's only a half mile away and the boat's bright orange, for God's sake."

"It's bright orange now," Torres said, "but it doesn't HAVE to be. And as far as the noise, I think we can mask the noise of the lifeboat engine as well as giving any peeping toms something to worry about. With any luck, they won't even know anyone left."

"That might work once," Georgia Howell said, "but we have over a dozen crewmen with families in the area. No way we're gonna find everyone and get them back with one shore party, so how are we going to handle that?"

"How about a collection point?" Gowan suggested. "We take enough food and water to feed people a few days, then head upstream and find a place to hole up. That way we can just leave a few guys up there to find and collect folks, then bring 'em back as a group, or maybe groups. In fact, we could probably use the yacht club just north of the I-10 bridge. It might take a couple of trips, but that's better and a whole lot less obvious than sending out parties every day."

Hughes nodded. "Might work. In fact, it sounds like our best bet."

"I'll do it," Gowan said. "Me and—"

"No way," Hughes said, "we need you here."

Gowan reddened. "Dammit, Jordan, it was my idea."

"And it's a good one, but you and Rich have a hundred things working no one else can handle, at least easily. I'm sending Georgia and whoever she wants along, along with some of the Coasties for security." Hughes turned to Torres. "That is, if you agree."

Torres shrugged. "It's not perfect, but it's probably the best option. We'll make it work, but I sure wouldn't send less than two."

"I still think I should go. I know where the yacht club is," Gowan said lamely.

Georgia Howell grinned. "Let's see. It's on the river just upstream of the I-10 bridge. I think I can find it, Dan. I did pass the navigation part of my license exam you know."

"I know you're worried about Trixie, Dan," Hughes said, "but sending Georgia is the right choice. It's not like we're standing navigation watches or handling cargo. The second mate and I can handle any deck-related stuff in her absence, but I need you here to help me figure out how we're going to make a ship built to accommodate twenty-five people house four times that many."

Gowan nodded sullen acceptance, and Hughes looked around. "Well, if that's it, let's make it happen."

Howell was the first to stand. "I'll head down to the paint locker and see what we have to redecorate the lifeboat."

M/V Pecos Trader
Sun Lower Anchorage
Neches River
Near Nederland, Texas

Day 28, 5:45 p.m.

Chief Mate Georgia Howell looked at the starboard lifeboat and raised her voice to be heard over the racket of the power saw. "That looks like crap."

Beside her, Hughes nodded agreement. "That it does, but Torres is right. It will be much harder to spot."

The previously bright orange enclosed lifeboat was now a collage of dull greens, grays, and browns of differing shades, some original from the can, and others mixed to yield over a dozen different hues. The paint was applied randomly in irregular splotches to help break up the outline of the boat. In the middle of the river, it would still be quite visibly a boat, but if Howell hugged the far bank, the boat would be considerably harder to spot against the brush, marsh grass, and mud flats bordering the riverbank in this area.

"You all set?" Hughes asked.

"We are from my side. We're just waiting on Dan."

She nodded to the boat, where the end of a reciprocating saw blade poked out of the fiberglass canopy, doing a jittering dance in time to the raucous roar as a cut line appeared behind it. They watched as the line traced a narrow rectangle, then the noise stopped and the saw blade disappeared back inside the canopy. There was a dull thud as something struck the inside of the canopy and the rectangle of fiberglass popped out and landed on the deck at their feet. A neat hole framed Gowan's sweaty face.

"Whadda ya think, Georgia?" Gowan asked. "Maybe four firing ports like this on each side?"

Howell nodded. "That should do it, just so we're not completely blind."

"Rich is down in the engine room, cutting up some steel plate," Gowan said. "We'll manhandle it through the lifeboat door in sections and rig it to the inside of the canopy. We can do the same around the conning position. It might not stop everything, but it should offer considerably more protection than fiberglass."

"Thanks, Dan," Howell said.

"Think nothing of it." Gowan grinned. "Besides we don't have time to train a new mate." He laughed as she grinned back and shot him the finger.

"How long, Dan?" Hughes asked.

"An hour, two max," Gowan said.

Hughes nodded and turned back to Georgia Howell. "You and Torres all squared away?"

"Yeah. Twilight's at 8:20, and he'll start raising hell at eight. That'll cover our engine noise and give us twenty minutes to get around the island and ready to scoot out the upstream mouth of the inlet. He'll lay it on heavy again right at 8:20 and we'll make our run for it then. Between him distracting any watchers, fading light, and our new paint job, I don't think we'll have any problem. We'll slip around the bend into the McFadden Cutoff and hide among the reserve fleet ships overnight, then head upriver at first light. At that point, even if our engine noise carries, it'll be coming from well upriver and they won't connect it with *Pecos Trader*."

Hughes nodded again. It was the best plan possible under the circumstances, allowing the boat the chance of escaping unnoticed while there was still enough light to make it to a safe haven for the night. He marveled again at just how dark a moonless night was in this new blacked-out world. There would be absolutely no references for Howell to use to navigate through the darkness, and if her own boat tried to use a searchlight, it would be a beacon to any watchers. He said a silent prayer of thanks that the mothballed ships of the US Maritime Administration Ready Reserve Fleet were clustered together at anchor just around a bend in the river.

"I wish we had enough night-vision equipment to give you a set," Hughes said.

Howell shrugged. "Me too, but we don't, and you'll need it more here if you're attacked, because you know they may come at night. They're likely terrified of those machine guns. Anyway, it's like Torres said, our best protection is invisibility. If we have to fight it out with anyone, we're screwed, and if they have a boat, it's not like we can outrun them in a six-knot lifeboat."

Hughes hesitated. "Maybe we should rethink this. We could delay a day and set up the collection point with the fast rescue boat and then send the lifeboat to pick up people after you've rounded them up."

"You know that won't work, Cap. The rescue boat can't carry enough supplies, and besides, the cons have seen it. If it disappears, they'll put two and two together and start looking for it. You made the right decision."

"It's hard to know what the right decision is when all of the options suck and any one of them might get people killed," Hughes said, almost to himself, then louder, "But be that as it may, we have to get it done. You need anything else we CAN provide?"

"I don't think so. The boat's loaded with food and water, and I'm all set crew wise. Everybody volunteered, so I had 'em draw straws. I'm taking Jimmy and Pete, and I have a list of addresses and directions for all the families within a twenty-mile radius and a map with the locations marked. That's seven families, including Jimmy's and Pete's."

"Any heartburn about that?"

"Some, but everyone understands we're doing the best we can. Truthfully, I'm not quite sure how successful we're going to be with the twenty-mile radius, but I figure we'll play that by ear. I'm bringing as much gasoline as we can find containers for and figure we'll have to find transportation ashore. I'll hit the closest families first. If they have wheels, we'll give 'em some gas and let 'em make their own way to the collection point while we continue to the other addresses. And if they have more than one set of wheels and someone willing to help, we'll enlist them to help spread the word and contact as many crew families as possible." She shrugged. "So I guess we're as ready as we can be."

Hughes nodded. "Good plan. Did Dan talk to you?"

Howell made a face. "Yeah, Trixie's on the list, though I didn't really count her as one of the families. I mean, I thought the divorce was final." She shook her head. "Though with Trixie, I guess that didn't make much difference one way or another. How a smart guy like Dan can be so stupid about a woman, God only knows."

Hughes shrugged. "Like they say, love is blind. And listen, bring her along if you find her and she wants to come. We owe that to Dan, but if she's not right where she's supposed to be—"

Howell snorted. "Not something you have to worry about, Cap. And if we don't find her, it's on me, not you. I know you and Dan go back a long way."

"Fifteen years, give or take," Hughes said, then changed the subject. "How about the Coasties?"

"I'm taking Jones and Alvarez. They volunteered, and Jones at least has some experience with the cons from when you rescued Laura and the girls." She added, "And Torres says Alvarez is a good shot."

"High praise, coming from Torres," Hughes said.

Howell laughed. "Actually, what he said was 'Alvarez is almost as good as me.'"

***

Hughes stood at the rail on the starboard side of the deckhouse, staring down to where the newly camouflaged lifeboat floated beside the ship. Behind him on the port side of the ship, he heard the roar of powerful outboards as Torres sped away from the ship at full throttle, in full view of any possible watchers. Georgia Howell heard it as well, and she looked up and waved to Hughes before stepping through the door in the rear of the enclosed lifeboat. He heard the growl of the starter then the more subdued sputter of the lifeboat engine, and watched Howell move the boat away from the ship and up the inlet, hugging the grassy shore and keeping the bulk of *Pecos Trader* between her boat and any watchers on the far bank. He murmured a prayer for his crew's safety and moved across the ship to watch Torres' show.

Hughes got to the port side to find the former sheriff's patrol boat in midstream, blasting upriver at full throttle, already a quarter mile away. As he watched in the fading light, the boat turned toward the opposite bank and then downstream before throttling back to idle noisily along the far bank, as if in search of something. He smiled as the Coastie manning the M240 sent a short burst of automatic fire into the opposite bank.

***

Bolton lay prone on the concrete dock, peeping upriver over the twelve-inch-square creosoted timber that bordered the dock's edge. "What the hell is he doin'?"

"Lookin' for us, I suspect," his partner said, then laughed. "But it looks like he ain't got a clue."

Both men flinched and ducked down behind the timber as the heavy machine gun fired.

"Looks like he's just shootin' at any place he thinks we might be," Bolton said.

The other man was pressing himself into the concrete so hard his cheek was turning red. "Should we haul ass?"

Bolton shook his head. "He ain't that far away, and this is a long dock. If he sees us and cranks that boat up, he'd be even with us before we could get away, and that machine gun will chew us up. He's just guessin' where to shoot, so our best bet is to keep our heads down until he leaves."

***

Hughes watched as Torres cruised down the far riverbank, punctuating his progress with bursts of machine-gun fire at random targets. At 8:20 p.m. on the dot, he reversed course and roared full throttle back to where he'd started, then retraced his previous route downriver, his gunner firing sustained bursts at more regular intervals. *That should keep their heads down if anything will,* Hughes thought.

Light was fading fast, and in ten minutes, the opposite bank was almost invisible. Hughes heard the engine noise increase and grow nearer, then decrease as Torres throttled back and edged up to the boat's mooring point at the bottom of *Pecos Trader's* port accommodation ladder. Hughes watched the Coasties secure the boat and scramble up the ladder to the main deck.

"Hear anything from Georgia yet?" Torres asked.

"Not yet," Hughes said. "It may take a while to—"

His radio crackled. "Mate to Captain Hughes. Do you copy? Over."

Hughes keyed the mic. "Go ahead, Mate. I copy."

"Captain, I'm on the bow and I checked the anchor chain like you asked. Everything is fine," Howell said, using the prearranged code to let Hughes know they were safely sheltered behind a cluster of mothballed vessels and tied off to one of the big ships' anchor chains.

"Thank you, Mate. Now get some rest. You have a busy day tomorrow. Over," Hughes said.

"Roger that. Mate out."

CHAPTER SEVEN

Day 26, 4:25 p.m.

Kinsey flipped a page in the chart booklet and nodded to himself before speaking to Bollinger over the muted roar of the twin outboards.

"Shut her down a minute, Bollinger. We need to strategize a bit."

Bollinger pulled back on the throttles, careful not to cut speed too fast so the trailer didn't plow into them. As they drifted in mid-channel, the outboards idling, Kinsey laid the chart booklet on the console.

"That channel we just intersected goes north to Calumet and south straight to the Gulf, so I figure we're here," he pointed at the chart, "less than ten miles west of Morgan City, way ahead of schedule. I think we need to adjust our plan. We're getting into a more populated area, and the natives we've seen so far didn't look too friendly. I'd just as soon not run into a large group of them."

Bollinger nodded. They'd encountered three boats since they left Calcasieu Lock; the first two fled up side channels as soon as they spotted the Coasties' boat. The third they'd met less than an hour before, coming toward them westbound, a large center console boat carrying four armed men. That boat cut speed and hugged the north bank, not fleeing but obviously intent on keeping their distance. When Kinsey and Bollinger motored past, the occupants glared at the Coasties and held their guns at the ready, not returning or even acknowledging the Coasties' waves. A far cry from the friendly greetings almost universally directed at Coasties in times past.

"It won't be full dark for at least four hours," Kinsey said, "and we're going right through the middle of Morgan City. We need to find a place to hole up a while, then travel at night with the NV goggles, at least through the populated areas. It'll slow us down, but I'd like to be as low profile as possible."

"Roger that, boss," Bollinger said. "I didn't like the way those guys were looking at us either."

"All right," Kinsey said. "Pull into the next side channel. The grass is high enough we should be able to get out of sight in the marsh while we're waiting."

"Maybe I can find one with a shade tree," Bollinger joked. "Damn, I thought it was hot when we were moving, but stopped with no breeze blowing through the windows, this friggin' cabin is like an oven."

Kinsey looked out over the featureless marsh. "Well, good luck finding a shade tree."

Bollinger grinned. "A guy can dream, boss." He pushed the throttles forward and the boat roared to life.

A mile east, they rounded a slight curve in the channel and spotted an inlet entering the south bank at a sharp angle, an empty tank barge, riding high, grounded in the inlet mouth.

"Let's check that out," Kinsey said, but Bollinger was already changing course.

They moved into the inlet slowly, eyes on the depth finder to ensure they had enough water as they maneuvered around the stern of the barge and into the narrow width of the inlet not occupied by the barge. Bollinger grinned.

"Well, my, my. There's our shade tree," he said, staring down the length of the barge.

Kinsey nodded. It was late afternoon, and the high-sided barge cast a shadow over the narrow sliver of water next to it, a shady oasis in the flat, sunbaked marsh.

"We can slip right up in that shady spot. And what's even better," Bollinger said, swiveling his head to look behind him, "if it's deep enough to pull up a bit, we'll be completely out of sight from the main channel."

"But then we can't see the channel either."

Bollinger shrugged. "I doubt anyone is going to sneak up on us in a canoe, especially since they won't even know we're here, and we can hear an outboard or engine a mile away. This looks like a winner to me, boss."

Kinsey thought a minute. "Okay, but we have to get far enough behind the barge to hide the trailer, and I don't want to pull in bow first with the trailer behind us. I want to be pointed out in case we have to leave in a hurry. Take us back out into the channel a bit. I'll untie the trailer and you circle around and nose up to it. I'll get in the bow and hold it and you push it up behind the barge. When it's in place, we'll back out, turn around and back into the gap. Then we can make up the tow again."

"Roger that," Bollinger said, and eased the boat back into the main channel.

Fifteen minutes later, the maneuver complete, Kinsey was reattaching the tow rope. Bollinger killed the outboards and stepped out of the oven-like little cabin just as a faint breeze stirred the tops of the nearby marsh grass and moved through their shady hiding spot.

"Feels better already... DAMN!" Bollinger slapped a mosquito on his forearm.

Kinsey laughed and dug the bottle of repellent from his pants pocket and tossed it to Bollinger. "I suggest a liberal application. Now that we're stationary, I expect every mosquito in ten miles will be looking for a meal."

Bollinger began rubbing the clear liquid over his exposed skin. "What now, boss?" he asked as he rubbed.

"We'll be up all night, so let's get some sleep. I'll take first watch and wake you in a couple of hours."

Bollinger nodded and tossed the bottle back to Kinsey, then stretched out full length on the deck in the narrow walkway beside the little cabin. Kinsey checked his watch and sat down on the deck forward of the cabin, his back against the side of the hull. Soon Bollinger was snoring softly and Kinsey rechecked his watch. Five minutes. Not bad.

The untroubled sleep of a man with only himself to worry about, Kinsey thought, with a transient flash of envy. Worry had been his constant companion since this whole mess started, first for his men and their families, the focus on that immediate problem masking the deeper concern for his own family. Worry came with the title of parent, no matter how old your kids were. A 'good night's sleep' for Kinsey these days was two to three fitful hours, punctuated by the occasional period of five or six hours when exhaustion led him to the edge of collapse. Only on *Pecos Trader* at sea had he felt a temporary respite, and that was over a week ago.

He was running on adrenaline and, thanks to several cups of strong coffee on the *Judy Ann*, caffeine. He thought about the thermos Wellesley had pressed on them and considered having another cup now, then dismissed the idea. They'd be up all night; better to save it until he really needed it. Besides, if he chugged coffee now, he'd have no chance of even a catnap when it was his turn.

He knew he should probably stand and pace, but the cramped confines of the boat allowed little room for movement without disturbing Bollinger. So he sat, parsing the possible outcomes of the coming mission, but focused on the positive. Things were looking up, really. His son, Luke, was safe in North Carolina. With any luck, by tomorrow he'd be with his daughter, Kelly, and his extended family, preparing to return to *Pecos Trader*. He smiled as he imagined their reunion and let his thoughts drift to happier times.

***

Kinsey awoke with a start, heart pounding, confused and disoriented until he saw Bollinger snoring away. He silently cursed himself for falling asleep and checked his watch. An hour. But what woke him? He listened. No noise coming from the main channel. A voice above him chilled him to the bone.

"Bonne après-midi."

He looked up into the barrel of a shotgun ten feet above him. Three shotguns, actually, in the hands of decidedly hostile-looking bearded men staring down from the deck of the tank barge.

"Now," the man in the middle said, his Cajun accent distinct, "wake up your friend. I could do it, but he might react badly and we would have to shoot him. It would be a shame if a slug went through him and damaged the nice boat you have been so kind to bring us, eh?"

Kinsey looked over to see Bollinger on his side, still snoring with his hands folded beneath his head. His snoring eased and he began restless movements indicating he was on the edge of wakefulness. Kinsey's eyes darted to his own M4. The man above him spoke again.

"And do not move anything but your lips," he said, "because if you try for that gun beside you, you will soon have a large hole in your chest, even if it means damaging my new boat. *Comprenez vous?*"

Kinsey nodded. "BOLLINGER! BOLLINGER, WAKE UP," he called.

Bollinger's eyes fluttered open and he lay unmoving for a moment before raising his head and giving Kinsey a sheepish grin. "I was having a dynamite dream—"

"Don't move, Bollinger. We've got company and they have the drop on us."

Bollinger followed Kinsey's gaze to the three men standing above them.

"Motherfucker," Bollinger said.

The spokesman shrugged. "It is possible. Did your mother hang around the honky-tonks in Lafayette thirty or thirty-five years ago?"

The other two men chuckled, but when their leader spoke again, his voice was hard. "Now both of you turn—"

"You're making a big mistake here, friend," Kinsey said. "We're US Coast Guard and we're—"

"First, I am not your *ami*, and a blind man could tell you are Coast Guard, or at least pretending to be Coast Guard." He shrugged. "For me it makes no difference. And the mistake was not mine, but yours."

"Look, we mean you no harm. We're just—"

"Let me guess, eh? You're from the government and you're here to help? And how do you intend to help, eh? Perhaps by shooting my son, raping my daughter-in-law and killing my wife? Well, you are too late, as we already got that 'help' from your government friends. *Mais*, it is nice of you to come back. I thought I would have to leave the bayou to start killing you bastards." He smiled, but there was no humor in it. "But now me and the boys gonna pass a good time, eh?"

Kinsey's blood ran cold. "Look, I don't know who you think we are, but shooting us won't—"

"Shoot you? Only if you make me. *Mais*, I think in a few days you gonna be begging me to put a bullet in your head."

APPALACHIAN TRAIL
MILE 1379.9 SOUTHBOUND
10 MILES EAST OF BUENA VISTA, VIRGINIA

DAY 29, 11:20 P.M.

Anderson staggered the last few steps up to the crest of Bald Knob and stared out over the sea of green spread before him in all directions. A few miles away, a break in the treetops formed a line roughly north to south, indicating a road through the woodland—Lexington Turnpike according to his battered trail guide. Another highway to cross, another chance to be killed or captured.

He was almost beyond caring, a hunted animal driven by survival instinct. His initial goal of making thirty-five miles a day proved far too ambitious, but the effort had been sufficient, barely. He made over a hundred miles in four days and had just passed Loft Mountain Campground when he'd heard the choppers. Terror mounted as they set down at the campground three miles behind him to the north, followed by a relief bordering on elation as the sounds faded. They were searching back to the north. He'd cleared their cordon and bought more time, but how much?

He lived on adrenaline the next five days, using every moment of daylight to force himself over rugged terrain. He made another twenty-five miles the first day after escaping the cordon, then twenty-two the next, but rapidly reached the limits of his endurance as fatigue and hunger took their toll.

His stale protein bars gone, he stopped before dark on the third day to hunt. Supper was a handful of darting minnows chased through a shallow creek and flipped out on the bank with one of the plastic bags from his makeshift pack. Two crawfish supplemented his catch, and afraid to start a fire, he wolfed it all down raw then filled his still-near-empty stomach with water from a nearby spring. His bleach was long gone, used to kill his scent, and he hoped like hell the water didn't give him the runs.

He was burning through calories at an insane rate, and the fourth day 'post-cordon' he made barely fifteen miles as his malnourished body rebelled. He stopped early again near another spring, where he managed to kill a fat squirrel with his homemade slingshot. Unable to stomach it raw, he risked a small fire. He seasoned the animal with the salt and pepper he'd scrounged from Bear's Den, then smeared it with the contents of his last two ketchup packets. It was charred on the outside and semi-cooked on the inside. It was delicious.

But that was yesterday, and hunger pains once again competed with blistered feet and his left knee, now swollen to almost twice normal size. The injury from the spill in the creek hadn't benefited from nine days of pounding, and Anderson knew he couldn't go on. He needed food, real food, and a place to rest for at least a day or two.

He looked out over the green canopy again and spotted the faintest wisp of smoke rising above the trees in a place where no road or habitation should be, well off the beaten track. Would they be hospitable? Yeah, right. Who was hospitable these days? He laid his hand on the Glock. *Well, like it or not, folks, you're about to have a houseguest.*

Anderson started the steep descent down Bald Knob, pain shooting through his left knee at every jarring step.

***

He sat on the slope behind a large oak, well back in the trees as he watched the house in the little clearing. He'd left the trail a quarter mile from the Lexington Turnpike crossing and made his way carefully down the steep wooded slope, clinging to saplings to keep his balance. He'd have missed the old logging road if he hadn't been looking for it. It was an overgrown slash through the trees, probably originating down on the turnpike and disappearing north into the thick woods to his right. He followed it deeper into the woods in the direction he'd seen the wisp of smoke.

The house was over a mile up the rough track, set on a level shelf about a half-acre wide at the base of Bald Knob. As soon as he'd spotted it, he moved back in the woods and circled around, struggling back up the steep slope with difficulty to his current vantage point. It was more a glorified garden shed than a house, like the largest models of the kit-built storage buildings found at Lowe's or Home Depot. For all that, it was neatly built. No smoke came from the metal stovepipe now; he'd probably spotted them cooking a meal.

A white PVC pipe led down the slope beside him and disappeared into the house; from a spring, he figured. There were both front and back doors and windows on both sides of the house, and a lean-to-like back porch with a small generator, silent at the moment. There was what appeared to be a side-by-side UTV under a black cover in the front of the house and a small structure in the rear; a chicken coop, he realized, as he spotted a few rust-colored birds pecking at the ground in the shade under the house. He salivated at a sudden vision of golden fried chicken.

A wire stretched from under the eaves of the house just below the center ridge of the roof and up through the branches of a large oak tree nearby. A friggin' antenna, probably for a HAM set. So much for being isolated. Maybe he should move on.

He was cursing his luck when the back door opened. A man moved across the small porch and down into the dirt patch that served as a backyard. He was short, with close-cropped dark hair, and appeared to be solidly built. He wore jeans and a white tee shirt and he had a tin can in his hand.

"Here, chick! Here, chick, chick, chick!" the man called, spreading the contents of the can on the ground. A dozen chickens exploded from under the house to peck the ground furiously at the man's feet. Thoughts of a chicken dinner rose unbidden once again, and Anderson contemplated taking a couple of those chickens with him, even if he did move on. They'd roost for the night in the chicken coop. If he waited until the people in the house were asleep, he could grab a couple and take off. He could likely make it down the old logging road and across Lexington Turnpike with his small flashlight. It was only a couple of miles, maybe three miles tops, and it would be better to cross the road under cover of darkness anyway.

He was laying his plans when the back screen door opened again and a woman stepped out, also in jeans and a tee shirt, though she filled it out considerably more attractively. She was petite, a bit over five feet, he guessed, and looked to be in her thirties. She had dark hair like the man's, but hers was pulled back in a ponytail.

"Jeremy, please bring in some wood when you finish there, and then get on your homework. This is the third time I've reminded you and I'm not going to do it again. Just because things aren't normal doesn't mean you get to ditch your lessons. No homework, no dessert tonight."

"What does it matter now, Mom? I know everything I need to know to keep up the place. Ain't nobody else going to school anyway."

"No one else is going to school," she corrected, "not 'ain't nobody.' And it matters to me. You've got a year of home schooling left and you're gonna finish it, even if I have to stand over you eight hours a day. Is that clear?"

"Yes, ma'am," the man answered with a put-upon sigh as old as the concept of homework itself.

Anderson reevaluated. The man-boy's age was indeterminate. Though physically mature, perhaps in his late teens or early twenties, his deference to his mother and mannerisms seemed much younger. His round face was animated and expressive, but seemed somehow innocent. Down syndrome. Anderson shook his head; this brave new world was tough enough without being handed that challenge. He sighed. Maybe he wouldn't steal their chickens.

His head snapped up at the growl of an engine, and he edged further behind the tree trunk. The boy heard it too and turned, then moved toward the logging road.

"Jeremy! Come in the house, now," the woman called from the porch.

Excited, the boy ignored her. "Maybe it's Uncle Tony! We haven't—"

The woman cursed and flew down the steps toward the boy. "Jeremy! Get inside—"

A Humvee burst into the clearing, a black-clad figure manning the machine gun on top, and a loudspeaker blaring.

"GET ON YOUR KNEES NOW, AND PLACE YOUR HANDS ON YOUR HEAD. COMPLY IMMEDIATELY OR WE WILL SHOOT!"

Anderson ducked completely behind the tree trunk. Special Reaction Force! He didn't think much of his former colleagues in the regular FEMA police, but these SRF thugs were in a class by themselves. But how did the assholes find him? Guilt washed over him at the thought of having drawn the bastards down on these people. He shook it off. If he could escape, they'd be all right; he'd had no interaction with them. That should be obvious to even these SRF morons. He glanced uphill, searching for a large tree he could fall back behind.

But despite himself, he couldn't ignore the drama playing out below him. "Is there anyone in the house?" he heard and peeked around the tree trunk.

There were three troopers, all in the black uniforms of the SRF and in tactical vests but wearing boonie hats instead of helmets—obviously they weren't anticipating much resistance, he thought. They were all out of the vehicle now and holding the boy and the woman at gunpoint. The pair were on their knees in the dirt about ten feet apart, both with their hands on their heads.

"N-no. There's just us," the woman said.

"If you're lying, you're dying," the SRF trooper said.

"It's the truth. I swear," she said.

"Carr, check it out," the spokesman said, and one of the men trotted to the house, his gun up and ready as he mounted the back porch and burst through the back door.

He emerged. "Clear, Sarge," he called. "It's all one big room and a bathroom. And I found the radio."

The sergeant waved his man back then turned to the woman. "You're both under arrest for unlawful possession of a radio transmitting device, spreading false information prejudicial to public order, treason, and sedition."

"But I didn't mean any harm. J-just take the radio if you want—"

"No need. It'll be destroyed when we burn down the house." The sergeant smiled. "After we take anything of use, of course. A traitor's property is subject to forfeiture."

All the men were laughing now.

Anderson looked back at the Humvee. There had been rumors of an operation to take out the HAMs when he was at Mount Weather, but this didn't look anything like he'd have expected. They would certainly hit targets simultaneously, but where were the transport vans? Unless they didn't intend to transport anyone.

"Can I have her second, Sarge?" the man called Carr asked. "Dwyer got seconds yesterday."

The third trooper bristled. "Screw you, Carr—"

"Flip a frigging coin," the sergeant said, stepping over to grab the woman by her wrist and pull her to her feet. She tried to twist away and, when unable to, spit in his face. He twisted her arm behind her back savagely. She screamed.

The boy was on his feet in a single motion, surprising them all with his speed. He buried his shoulder in the sergeant's gut, driving the bigger man to the ground. He was clawing his way on top of the surprised mercenary when Dwyer clubbed him down with a vicious rifle butt stroke to the side of the head.

"Jeremy!" the woman screamed, starting toward the fallen boy, but Carr slapped her to the ground just as the sergeant regained his feet.

The sergeant leveled his gun at the fallen boy's head. "YOU FRIGGING LITTLE RETARD. I'LL SHOW—"

"STOP! D-don't hurt him. I-I'll do whatever you want. Just please don't hurt him," the woman said.

The sergeant leered at the woman, renewed lust replacing anger. A slow smile spread across his face. "Well, that's more like it. Let's me and you head on into the cabin and get to know each other a little better."

He looked down at the boy lying still with blood flowing from a two-inch gash in the side of his head. "Carr," he said, "you and Dwyer zip-tie the retard."

As Anderson watched, the sergeant stepped over the boy and dragged the woman to her feet by her ponytail, then shoved her toward the cabin.

Not your fault, Anderson, he told himself. *It was the radio, nothing to do with you. This is happening a hundred times a day out here, and there's nothing you can do about it. NOTHING! Not your problem. Just slip away while the assholes are preoccupied. You're outnumbered and outgunned, and getting yourself killed or captured won't help anyone. Walk away, Anderson. Walk. Away.*

He eased back up the slope, then moved to his left slowly to a large maple tree. When he was totally out of sight of the clearing, he moved more quickly, reaching the logging road in less than three minutes. He started toward Lexington Turnpike and walked twenty feet before he stopped.

He looked back north at the road disappearing through the woods toward the cabin. He shook his head and turned back south. He walked ten feet this time before he stopped again.

"You're a damn fool, Anderson," he said to himself. He unholstered his Glock and turned back toward the house.

CHAPTER EIGHT

THE CABIN
9 MILES EAST OF BUENA VISTA, VIRGINIA

DAY 29, 12:45 P.M.

Anderson stayed off the road and crept to the edge of the woods. Sun washed over the little clearing and the house, but the Humvee was parked just beyond the tree line, still in the shadows. The boy lay facedown in the sun, his wrists and ankles zip-tied, but there was no sign of his captors. Anderson panicked, then calmed when he heard voices on the far side of the vehicle. Of course. They were staying out of the sun.

He eased his makeshift pack to the ground and stooped. He looked under the vehicle and spotted both pairs of feet. The men were leaning back against the other side of the Humvee, facing the house. He belly-crawled to the vehicle, keeping their feet in sight.

Anderson lay on the ground and considered his options. He could shoot them both in the ankles then finish them when they hit the ground. But what then? The other bastard would hear the shots and hold the woman hostage — or just kill her. He had to take them silently, and he was no commando.

"It ain't right, even if you won the toss," a voice said. "You got seconds last time, and you bastards take so long I won't have any time at all. We got two more places to hit before we head back, and when Sarge finishes, he's gonna be in a lather to finish these two off and head out."

Laughter. "Tough shit, Carr. Luck of the draw, dude. Besides, take it up with Sarge. He's the one who strings it out, especially when we get a hot one. I guarantee he's in there making her put on a little show. He's into that."

"Whatever. I'm hungry. What did you do with that chili we got from the last place?" Carr asked.

"It's in the back, but Sarge will be pissed if you get into that stuff before he's had his pick," Dwyer said.

"Well, screw him. Anyway, he's kind of busy right now and he won't know unless you open your big mouth, now will he? Want some?"

"No. I gotta piss," Dwyer said.

"Well, move off a ways, you lazy turd!" Carr said. "You're always doin' that; then everybody gets your piss on their boots and it starts stinkin'."

"Maybe I'll go piss on the retard," Dwyer said.

"You're a sick bastard. You know that?"

Laughter. "Ain't we all?" Dwyer said.

Panic shot through Anderson as the boots moved out of view, and indecision cost him his shot. He scrambled to his feet and crouched behind the vehicle. He stuffed the Glock in his waistband for quick access and pulled a large knife from his pocket and unfolded it as he stayed low and moved to the back of the vehicle.

Anderson peeked around the back of the Humvee to see Dwyer with his back to him, walking toward the boy. He crept further around to find Carr standing in the open rear door of the vehicle, oblivious as he rummaged in a cardboard box, looking at cans. Anderson covered the distance to Carr in three steps. The man sensed his presence and turned, no doubt expecting to see Dwyer. His surprised cry never reached his lips as the blade penetrated his throat to the hilt, ravaging his vocal cords then severing his carotid artery as Anderson sawed sideways with the sharp edge of the blade as he withdrew it. Bright red arterial spray soaked the front of Anderson's shirt as he held Carr upright until he was sure the fight was out of him, then lowered him to the ground. The seconds seemed like hours.

He spun to find Dwyer oblivious, standing over the boy perhaps fifty feet away, intent on unzipping. Anderson drew his Glock and closed the distance, adrenaline erasing all pain from his battered knee. He was within ten feet before Dwyer realized he was there, and five by the time the man turned, right hand holding his penis. Anderson had the Glock pointed between the man's eyes, his hand steady as a rock.

"Put both hands on the top of your head, turn toward the house, then get on your knees," Anderson said.

"You're screwed, friend," Dwyer said.

"Do it!"

"Can I put my dick back—"

"NO! Do it!" Anderson said.

Dwyer grinned. "So what if I don't? You shoot me and you'll have company."

"And you'll be dead and the odds are even. I can handle that as a worst-case scenario."

"But you don't have a hostage."

Anderson laughed. "Who cares about them. I'm after your gear. Soon as I got you out of the way, I'll give your buddy a chance to give up. If he doesn't, I'll just shred the house with the Ma Deuce on your Hummer and haul ass. Collateral damage, dude. I'm sure you're familiar with the concept. Cooperate and I'll leave you alive for your buddies to find. Or I can waste you. Your call."

Dwyer looked at Anderson's blood-soaked FEMA uniform and his smile faded.

"Now! Turn. Around," Anderson repeated. "I'm not gonna tell you again."

Dwyer complied, dropping to his knees as he did so.

"Zip ties?" Anderson asked.

"The left side pocket of my vest." Anderson bent down behind Dwyer and fished out several with his left hand as he pressed the Glock to the back of the man's head with his right.

He straightened and considered the situation. Dwyer was a head taller than him and powerfully built. If he put down the Glock to zip-tie him, the man might jump him. Anderson quietly backed up two steps then sprang forward, planting his right foot in the middle of Dwyer's back and driving him face-first into the stony dirt, all his weight behind the blow. Air rushed from Dwyer's lungs with an audible WHUMP as his chest hit the ground. Anderson stuffed the Glock in his waistband and jerked the stunned man's hands behind his back. He had Dwyer bound wrist and ankle before the man could manage even a strangled gasp. He gagged him with his own boonie hat, using the drawstring to secure it behind his neck, then took Dwyer's sidearm and shoved it in his pants pocket before relieving him of the two spare M4 magazines in the tactical vest. The M4 itself was leaning up against the Hummer with Carr's, and on the way back to collect one of them, Anderson knelt and checked the boy.

He was still unconscious and covered in blood, though the bleeding had stopped. He seemed to be breathing all right, and Anderson felt his neck and found his pulse strong. Possible concussion, but no time to deal with it now. He glanced at his watch and started across the clearing, scarcely crediting it had been only seven minutes since he left his hiding place up the steep slope.

He circled wide to approach the house from a windowless end wall, then stayed pressed up against the house as he moved around to the back wall and climbed up over the porch railing, hoping against hope none of the porch boards creaked. Pain shot through his swollen left knee as he knelt on the rough boards, spiking with each contact as he crawled awkwardly along the porch with his side pressed to the wall of the house, trying to keep the M4 from rattling over the boards. He was almost under the window when he froze.

"You can do better than that! Dance, you bitch! Make me want you! Or do you want me to bring the retard in and let him watch?" The words were followed by a muffled sob some distance away from the speaker.

The man was close to the open window. Very close, maybe just on the other side of the screen. Anderson carefully laid the M4 on the porch and eased out the Glock. He'd determine the man's position, then shoot him through the screen. Chances were the asshole wasn't looking out the window. He eased forward.

SQUEEEEAK!

Anderson froze at the sound of cursing on the other side of the screen.

"Dwyer, you friggin' pervert, get the hell out of here. I'll call you when it's your turn."

Anderson kept stock-still for a long moment, then began to ease back.

SQUEEEEAK!

"All right, that does it! I'm comin' out there to kick your ass!" There was the sound of squeaking bedsprings and heavy footsteps.

Well, how about that? Anderson thought as he braced himself against the cabin wall and leveled his Glock at the back door. The man charged onto the porch naked and turned toward the open window, stopping short at the sight of Anderson. His face registered surprise, then understanding, seconds before two nine-millimeter hollow points penetrated the center of his chest.

Anderson deflated like a balloon as the adrenaline ebbed. His hands were shaking and his left knee hurt so badly he wanted to cut the thing off. He leaned against the cabin wall and struggled to get his shakes under control, then attempted to stand up; it took three tries. No time for this. He had to come up with plan B. He scooped up the M4. He'd help the woman and kid as much as possible and get the hell out of here.

"IT'S ALL RIGHT! YOU'RE SAFE NOW," he called as he opened the screen door and moved into the house.

The woman was nowhere to be seen. He took another step into the room.

"I'M A FRIEND—"

BLAM! A two-inch-diameter section of the door jamb exploded at head height just behind him, driving splinters into the back of his neck as he dove for cover. He heard the racking sound of a pump shotgun.

"DON'T SHOOT! I'M A—"

BLAM! The back of the recliner he was hiding behind exploded in a shower of Naugahyde fragments and furniture stuffing. A buckshot pellet stung the top of his right ear.

Well, this obviously wasn't working. Anderson played his ace.

"LOOK, JEREMY'S HURT BADLY, AND WE CAN'T HELP HIM IF WE'RE SHOOTING AT ONE ANOTHER."

Silence.

"H-he's still alive?" Quieter now. "I figured…" She trailed off, unable to finish the question. It was replaced by another—a demand. "How do you know his name?"

"I… ah… I was watching you from the woods when these guys showed up. I heard you talking to him."

"Well, that's not too creepy, is it? Watching us why?"

He hesitated. "I'm starving, okay? I was gonna steal some chickens?"

More silence. The woman's voice hardened. "I know that uniform. You're FEMA, just like these other assholes. Why should I trust you?"

"I'm not. I mean I WAS with FEMA, but I was a cop. Never like these guys." Or not quite anyway, Anderson thought. "Besides, you don't exactly have a lot of options here, lady. Or much time."

"So you just grew a conscience and decided to leave FEMA? Yeah, right." He heard uncertainty in her voice despite the dismissive words.

"It's a long story, but let's just say I'm not very popular with FEMA these days. They're doing their best to kill me." He paused. "Look, how about this? We lower our weapons; then we both stand up nice and slow and try not to shoot each other."

A long pause. "All right. You first."

Anderson cursed under his breath. Why the hell hadn't he just kept going? He sighed. In for a penny, in for a pound; if they didn't get moving soon, he was likely dead anyway. He rose slowly, half-expecting a blast of double-ought buckshot to rip into his chest.

He stood there a long moment until the woman rose from behind a center island near the kitchen sink, her shotgun held tightly, but with the muzzle pointed toward the floor. She was stark naked, with the tight, sculpted body of a dancer. She seemed totally unselfconscious and in control, a far cry from the sobbing woman he'd seen dragged into the cabin. She saw him ogling her body and sneered.

"So much for 'I'm not like the others.' Go ahead, get an eyeful, pig," she said.

"Ahh... sorry," Anderson said. "Uhh... you wanna get some clothes on?"

"So you can get the drop on me while I do? No, thanks, I'm good," the woman said. She walked backward as she spoke, feeling around on the floor with her feet. She found a pair of well-worn moccasins and slipped her feet into them, her eyes never leaving Anderson.

"I'm George."

She sneered again. "Great. Nice to meet you. I'm none-of-your-damn-business. You can call me 'none' for short. Now grab that first-aid kit off the shelf behind you and let's go look at Jeremy. You first."

Anderson did as ordered and led the way outside and down the short steps. When the woman saw her son on the ground, concern overcame control and she rushed across the bare clearing. Dwyer had recovered somewhat and was sitting up, the boonie hat protruding from his mouth looking almost comical. His eyes widened at the sight of the naked woman. She ignored him to squat beside her son and place her left hand to his neck, keeping a firm grip on the shotgun with her right.

"I think he might have a concussion," Anderson said as he walked up.

The woman bobbed her head in agreement, then looked momentarily pensive, as if making a decision. She laid down the shotgun and held out her hand.

"Give me the first-aid kit. I suppose if you meant to kill us, we'd already be dead," she said.

He handed her the kit. "Yeah, well, thanks for the vote of trust, None."

"It's Cindy," she said as she opened the kit and extracted a small bottle of alcohol and some sterile gauze pads.

Anderson nodded and then squatted beside her and watched silently as she gently but expertly cleaned the blood off her son. The boy groaned and stirred. The woman laid a hand on his cheek.

"Jeremy? Are you all right, honey?" she asked softly.

His eyes fluttered open and he immediately squeezed them shut. "My head hurts, and why is the light so bright?"

"You'll be fine, honey. Just keep your eyes closed if it hurts. I'm going to bandage the cut on your head; then we'll get you into bed. Okay?"

The boy groaned and nodded. Cindy looked over at Anderson, the hard set of her features replaced by a mother's concern. "We need to get him into the house. I'll have to watch him for at least —"

"Negative," Anderson said. "We can't stay here. We're bound to have company sooner or later. Probably sooner."

"He needs to rest!"

"Agreed," he said, "but not here."

"Then where? If these assholes are coming after us, we sure as hell can't outrun them."

WE can't, but I sure as hell can, Anderson thought. *I've been doing it for nine days now.* He looked wistfully at the logging road, and the woman followed his gaze. Her face hardened.

"Go ahead and take off," she said. "Thanks for your help, but I got this now."

Anderson looked back at the pair on the ground, shook his head and sighed. In for a penny, in for a pound. "It's too late for that now. I'm in this up to my neck whether I want to be or not. I've given them the slip twice, but if they pick up my trail again, I won't escape them a third time. And if they catch y'all, they'll figure out —"

"We won't give you up, if that's what you're thinking —"

He laughed mirthlessly. "Oh yeah you will, regardless of what you think now. When they start cutting pieces off Jeremy here, you'll sing like a bird. That's just the way it is, and we both know it." Anderson nodded toward Dwyer. "And then there's Mr. Loose End over there."

She looked at Dwyer and narrowed her eyes. "That the asshole that hit Jeremy?"

Anderson nodded and she stared at the man. He was ogling her naked body despite his circumstances. She broke eye contact with Dwyer and turned back to Anderson.

"All right. I know a place that might work. I'll finish dressing Jeremy's wound while you pull their vehicle over here to give him some shade. We'll make him as comfortable as possible while we work things out. Then maybe you can have a little chat with our friend over there to see if you can figure out how much time we have, while I go put some clothes on."

Anderson nodded. "I have to admit the view is a bit distracting."

"Yeah well, that was the idea. I figured if you were watching my ass, it would be a lot easier to get the drop on you."

***

"He says they were supposed to hit two more places and return to their base, which is in Buena Vista," Anderson said. "And I'd say their radio protocol is pretty lax, else someone would have been calling on the Hummer radio by now."

"You trust him?" Cindy asked, now fully clothed in jeans and a tee shirt.

"Hell no," Anderson said, "but that concurs with what I overheard him and the other one say when they didn't know I was listening, so I think he's telling the truth. We may have two or three hours. Maybe more if we can create a diversion. How far did you say this cave was?"

"Six or seven miles, but rough miles. We can follow a creek bed maybe five miles in the UTV, but the last leg is too steep for the vehicle. I'm worried about bouncing Jeremy around on the ride up, so we need to go slow, and I have no clue how long it will take us to get him up to the cave. We'll need all the time we can get."

Anderson looked down at the boy. He'd started opening his eyes for short periods and made a halfhearted attempt to sit up a bit earlier, but his mother chided him and pushed him back down gently but firmly.

"Looks like he may be feeling a bit better," Anderson said.

"I hope so, but we still need that time. What's your diversion?"

"This Hummer will have a GPS tracking device on it. I don't know if the satellites are still working, but if they are and FEMA pings the Hummer, they'll know it's sitting right here. I doubt they will as long as these guys don't call in any problems. However, I'm sure they check in at least sporadically, and if someone at their base can't raise them, they'll start pinging the tracker to locate the Hummer. When they do, we don't want them to send the cavalry here. Is there a gorge or steep drop-off near here on the turnpike?"

"Take your pick," she said. "There are a dozen places on the turnpike within a mile in either direction."

Anderson nodded. "The nearest one to the south then, since that's the direction of the assholes' next stop."

She shot him a questioning look and he told her his plan.

***

Anderson had just finished stripping the Humvee when Cindy drove up in the UTV. She looked at the pile and the two five-gallon fuel cans sitting beside it.

"That's diesel, right? What good will it do us?"

"We'll need a couple of cans here, for... you know."

Cindy sighed. "You sure we have to?"

He nodded. "Yeah. I'm sure. That seems to be their standard operating procedure. Otherwise they may start searching for us."

"All right." She glanced at the bound Dwyer and let out a slow, ragged breath. "I... I'll take care of him then help you load the bodies."

"I got the bodies. I'm already covered with blood anyway." He paused. "You sure you don't want me to take care of this asshole?"

She shook her head. "It was Jeremy and me he was going to murder. If we had a trial, I have no doubt how it would turn out. It's just quicker now is all. Besides, you said it yourself, leaving him alive guarantees they'll be on us. He has to die. You did your share taking out the other two. This one's on me."

Anderson nodded, then changed the subject. "What about Jeremy?"

"I think he'll be okay here. We shouldn't be gone over twenty minutes tops, and I'd just as soon bounce him around as little as possible."

Anderson nodded, then reached down to lift Carr's body and wrestle it into the Hummer. He finished and drove the short distance to the house and dragged the sergeant's naked body off the back porch. He noticed the man was his size and had conveniently left his uniform in the house. He filed that for future notice. He'd just heaved the body into the Hummer when he heard the Glock bark twice. He looked back toward the logging road and saw Cindy standing over Dwyer's body, the gun in her hand. *That's one tough woman*, he thought.

***

Fifteen minutes later, the Humvee was burning at the bottom of a steep embankment half a mile south of the logging road intersection with Lexington Turnpike. They drove the UTV back to the cabin to find Jeremy as they left him, no better, but no worse. Anderson went into the cabin and stripped off his bloody clothes to put on the dead sergeant's uniform, but the rank stench of his own unwashed body overwhelmed him. He looked longingly toward the small bathroom. Screw it! He finished stripping and stepped into the small bathroom to wash.

He emerged from the cabin feeling ill at ease in the SPF uniform, but almost human after cleaning up. The woman was loading the UTV.

"Sorry, I took some time to clean up," he said.

She nodded. "And we're all glad you did. No offense, but you smelled like a dead skunk rotting in the sun. I wasn't looking forward to being cooped up in a cave with you."

"Hey, it wasn't that bad."

"Oh yeah, it was." She sniffed the air. "But it's much better now."

Anderson looked at the rig. It was a Kawasaki Mule, the big crew cab model. She had the rear seat folded down to extend the bed, and a small trailer attached behind.

"Where did the trailer come from?" he asked.

"Behind the chicken coop. I'm not sure it will make it, but if we have to ditch it, we'll at least have a cache closer to the cave."

He looked skeptically at the piles of gear beside the Mule. "Are you leaving ANYTHING here?"

"Not if I can help it. If it won't all fit, we'll toss it back in the house and torch it, but I can't see leaving it for those assholes. And like I said, if we can't get it to the cave, we'll cache it somewhere in the woods."

He nodded. "Point taken. How can I help?"

"I want to check on Jeremy. You keep loading."

Anderson nodded and set to work as Cindy moved to where Jeremy still lay on the ground, a pillow from the cabin under his head. He focused on the task at hand and looked up twenty minutes later when Cindy returned leading a slow-moving and still befuddled Jeremy by the arm. She guided her son gently to a seat on the front steps of the cabin and turned to Anderson.

"Wow. That's progress," she said, looking at the Mule and trailer.

"I think we'll be able to load it all," he said. "Assuming you don't have another pile somewhere."

"Just the chickens."

"Seriously? How the hell we gonna carry chickens?"

"We tie them in pairs by their feet and throw them over the crossbar above the seats. And you'll be happy to have them if we have to hole up in that cave. Chickens and eggs are protein we don't have to hunt."

Anderson shook his head and looked at his watch. "All right, but we've burned almost an hour of our grace period. We have to get out of here soon."

***

Thirty minutes later, Cindy pulled the fully loaded and chicken-festooned Mule well away from the cabin. She left Jeremy resting comfortably on top of a pile of softer items in the bed of the UTV and walked back to where Anderson stood in front of the cabin. He looked up as she approached.

"I spread the diesel from the Humvee all over the place inside and spread piles of easily flammable stuff like curtains and books around. It should go up fairly quickly."

Tears glistened in Cindy's eyes. She nodded.

"You okay?" Anderson asked.

"Yeah. It's just hard. Jeremy and I built this place ourselves from one of those kits, then insulated it and turned it into a real little house. It might not look like much to you, but we were happy here. It… it's just hard, that's all."

Anderson nodded. "It looks fine. Better than fine the way things are now, but we have to do it. They'll find the burned house and think the SRF thugs torched it with you inside. Then hopefully, they'll figure the patrol left the scene and was ambushed by forces unknown." He paused. "It's the only way, Cindy."

Her face hardened. "Okay. Do it, and let's get the hell out of here."

***

They pulled out of the clearing five minutes later, Anderson at the wheel, and Cindy riding in the bed with Jeremy's head on a pillow in her lap. The cabin blazed behind them as they headed north, deeper into the woods.

"How far to the creek?" Anderson asked.

"About a quarter of a mile," Cindy said. "Then just turn right up the creek bed and we'll go as far as we can."

Anderson did as instructed, and soon they were bumping north in four-wheel drive along the slate-bottomed creek. He drove up the middle of the shallow creek, leaving no tire tracks on the hard rock of the creek bed. He drove slowly, trying to minimize the jarring, but the creek descended the slope in terraced steps, and it was like driving up a staircase in places. He kept glancing back to see Cindy riding tight-lipped, holding on to a crossbar above her with one hand while she steadied Jeremy's head with the other.

The fast-running water was only an inch or two deep in most places, though it collected in scattered tranquil pools. He rolled through each with a silent prayer none hid a hole deep enough to swallow a tire or break an axle. At spots the stair-stepped slate bottom was covered with slick green slime, and the wheels slipped as the Mule slid from side to side. He powered through each spot, voicing apologies over his right shoulder for the rougher ride, and with a nagging worry they were leaving tracks in the slime.

The creek bed followed a meandering path, almost doubling back on itself in places. He found it all but impossible to judge how far they'd come. When they'd been traveling a little over an hour, he shot a worried glance up at a darkening sky and the steep, rocky sides of the stream. The creek was narrowing and the banks were getting even steeper as the creek disappeared around a bend. He stopped the Mule and set the brake before he turned back to Cindy.

"How's he doing?" he asked.

Cindy shrugged. "Okay, I think. Why are we stopping?"

"The banks are getting really steep. We couldn't get the Mule out here if we tried, and it looks like this thing is turning into a gorge. Are we going to be able to get out when we get where we're going? And how much farther is it anyhow?"

"Another mile, more or less. Look for three big oak trees on the left bank. And the creek does narrow between high rock walls for most of the way, but then the banks drop down again. We should be able to drive out just past Three Oaks, if not before."

"SHOULD? Aren't you sure —"

"Look, I've never been here in the Mule, so I'm not SURE of anything, all right? Except my kid's hurt and I just killed someone and burned down my friggin' house and —"

Anderson was raising his hand in a 'calm down' gesture when he heard something over the Mule's engine. He reached down and switched it off.

Cindy stopped mid-rant. "Why did you —"

She was silenced by a low distant rumble echoing down the little hollow.

"Thunder," Anderson said, "and this is absolutely the last place we want to be in a thunderstorm. It looks like this creek drains the whole hollow."

He swiveled all the way around and looked back downstream. He had no room to turn around without unhitching the trailer, and even then, it would be blocking the way downstream. He contemplated trying to back the trailer down the windy, bumpy stream bed until he could find a place to get out of the creek. How far? A half-mile at least with a dozen hairpin turns to back around. He envisioned missing a turn and the Mule and trailer jamming between the steep banks of the creek.

"Crap!"

He faced back upstream and felt a freshening breeze and the smell of ozone as the sky got darker. He started the Mule and released the brake.

"I'm sorry, but this is gonna be bumpy. We have to try to make it through that gorge before the creek floods. Hang on!"

"DO IT!" she shouted over the engine and a sudden crash of thunder.

CHAPTER NINE

UP A CREEK
12 MILES NORTHEAST OF BUENA VISTA, VIRGINIA

DAY 29, 4:45 P.M.

Anderson picked up speed, and the Mule bounced over the rough creek bed, the hitch shrieking as the trailer bounced over its own rocks out of sync with the Mule. Fat raindrops exploded against the Plexiglas windshield, mixing with the film of dust and running down in muddy streams. It hardly mattered—within two minutes the rain was hitting them in sheets and the windshield was both washed clean and totally opaque as the rain washed over it in buckets. Anderson hung his head out to the left around the windshield, squinting as the driving rain lashed his face. The chickens, quiet up to now, all began to cluck plaintively.

He was driving by guess, using the left bank as reference and hoping like hell he didn't hit anything on the right. But hope failed him regularly, and both the Mule and the trailer sideswiped the right bank frequently as he swerved around blind turns. On a particularly sharp turn to the left, a protruding tree root lashed his shoulder, narrowly missing his head. He cried out in pain and surprise, jerking the wheel and almost running the Mule directly into the right bank before he recovered.

They were well into the gorge, the sheer stone of the banks towering fifteen or twenty feet on both sides, the water rising higher as it rushed beneath them. He leaned out and looked—six inches up the front tire and beginning to offer resistance. He mashed the accelerator harder in an effort to maintain headway and risked a glance back over his shoulder. His passengers were wet to the skin, with Cindy hunched over Jeremy, holding him tight. The boy was fully awake now, his eyes wide with terror.

Anderson turned back just in time to dodge another tree root protruding from the rock wall, then leaned out again. It was almost dark as night now, and he turned on the Mule's headlights, which did little but illuminate the driving rain. He had no idea how far they'd come, but it seemed like miles, and still the banks towered above them, sheer and unforgiving. The water was rising insanely fast. It was over halfway up the wheels now, the wake from the front tires rebounding off the creek sides and sloshing into the Mule. He had the accelerator to the floor, but he could feel the Mule slow with each passing second.

He hunched over the wheel, the water sloshing up to the headlights now and the motor straining to inch them forward. He was desperately searching for plan B when he noticed the left bank was not nearly as high, barely above the top of the Mule. Three vertical shapes flashed white in the headlights—Three Oaks!

"ALMOST THERE!" he yelled back over his shoulder and mashed the accelerator so hard his foot hurt, even though he'd floored it long ago.

The Mule was almost stopped, and he willed it forward. The rain was slackening a bit, the sky slightly lighter, and he felt a rush of adrenaline as he saw the left bank ahead was fairly steep but climbable. Inch by inch, the Mule gained ground and he felt the front end rising out of the water; then the wheels started spinning, and forward progress halted. He set the brake and turned to Cindy.

"WE'RE TOO HEAVY TO GET UP THE BANK. I'M GONNA TRY TO RUN THE WINCH CABLE UP AROUND ONE OF THOSE TREES TO HELP GET US OUT. I NEED YOU AT THE WHEEL IN CASE WE START SLIDING BACK!"

Cindy wiped a wet strand of hair out of her face and nodded. She gently disentangled herself from her frightened son and splashed down in the creek on the driver's side and slid into the driver's seat as soon as Anderson exited.

"WE COULD SLIDE BACK AT ANY TIME. KEEP A CLOSE EYE ON IT AND FLOOR IT THEN RELEASE THE BRAKE IF IT LOOKS LIKE YOU'RE LOSING IT. IF I CAN GET THE CABLE AROUND ONE OF THOSE TREES, I THINK WE'LL BE OKAY."

She nodded as he moved to the front of the Mule and hit the cable release on the winch; then she watched as, hook in hand, Anderson pulled out the cable and scrambled and limped up the slippery slope. He hooked the cable around one of the big oaks and started back down, almost falling several times.

"HIT THE WINCH AND TRY TO DRIVE OUT! I'LL STAY OUT TO TAKE THE WEIGHT OFF."

She nodded again, and Anderson stepped back and gave her a thumbs-up. She hit the gas and the winch simultaneously, and the Mule shuddered and began an agonizingly slow crawl up the steep bank. Anderson grinned like an idiot; a bit prematurely, as it turned out. The Mule ground to a halt and Cindy yelled over the pounding rain and roaring creek, the Mule, and the shrieking chickens.

"IT'S STILL TOO HEAVY. MAYBE IF WE HELP JEREMY OUT—"

Anderson looked back at the fast-rising creek, well up his calves even close to the bank. He shook his head.

"I DON'T THINK THAT'LL BE ENOUGH, AND WE'VE ONLY GOT ONE SHOT AT THIS. IT'S THE TRAILER. IT'S JUST TOO HEAVY. WE HAVE TO DITCH IT NOW, OR WE LOSE EVERYTHING."

Cindy gave a hesitant nod, and the chickens shrieked agreement as Anderson splashed to the back of the Mule. He felt for the hitch in the dim light, operating as much by touch as sight. The safety retainer clip came off easily, and he popped up the lever on the coupler, but there progress stopped. The overloaded trailer was sitting cockeyed, with one wheel halfway up one of the stair-step ledges in the slate creek bottom, with all of the weight pulling backward on the ball of the trailer hitch. No amount of lifting or bouncing would free it. And the water was rising.

Anderson's panic was rising as fast as the water and he forced himself calm. If he couldn't unhitch the trailer, then he'd unhitch the hitch. He'd pull the receiver tube retaining pin and let the ball mount go with the trailer. He squatted and felt for the receiver tube then pulled the cotter key on the retainer pin, cursing when it slipped from his hand into the water. He tugged at the retainer pin. CRAP! Jammed in place just like the ball hitch by the weight of the trailer. But it was a straight pin, and he might be able to knock it out from the opposite side. Desperate, he patted the creek bottom for a rock, then rose and stepped over the trailer tongue to squat on the opposite side, waist deep in the rushing water. It was up to the trailer hitch now, boiling over the pin and obstructing his already poor view. He adjusted his squat, gripped the back of the Mule with one hand for balance and hammered blindly at the pin with the other. Hindered by the rising water and unable to see his target, he smashed his knuckles on the steel, but held on to the rock and bit down the pain. It took a dozen blows before he connected solidly enough to free the pin, and the result was both immediate and unexpected.

Free from constraint, the trailer tongue whipped to the right as the trailer sought equilibrium and rushed backward into the torrent. A glancing blow from the swinging tongue knocked Anderson back. He shot upright and took a step backward in a futile attempt to maintain his balance, but stepped into a shallow depression in the creek bottom, unbalancing him further. He stretched out full length in the raging water, sucking water up his nose as his head went under. The flood rolled him along the creek bottom underwater, strangling and gasping for air, as he clawed for something, anything, to keep from being swept away. His hand closed on a tree root and his legs swung downstream. He felt his hand slipping and scrambled futilely to get a purchase with his feet so he could stand.

He felt something snag the back of his collar, then a tug under his armpit, strong hands helping him to his feet. His head broke the water and he gasped and coughed before wiping the water from his eyes to see— Jeremy. The boy was hip-deep in the edge of the flood, his lower body braced against a thicker section of the same tree root that saved Anderson. The fear in the boy's eyes was mixed with something else — determination.

"JEREMY!"

Cindy was in the creek, splashing toward them.

"STAY THERE," Anderson shouted. "WE'RE OKAY."

She did as ordered, though with visible reluctance, and Anderson surveyed the left bank. There were scattered handholds, and with Jeremy's help, Anderson pulled himself to the edge of the creek and made his way upstream to the nearest one, then reached back and gave Jeremy a hand forward. They alternated, leap-frogging back to the half-submerged Mule. Water was over all four tires now and running over the floorboard. Steam rose from the rear of the Mule where the water was flashing against the hot muffler. They had minutes to get the Mule up the bank.

"GET IN AND DRIVE. JUST LIKE BEFORE. ENGINE AND WINCH TOGETHER. JEREMY AND I WILL PUSH."

Cindy nodded and jumped behind the wheel, and Anderson turned, putting his back against the tailgate and then squatting to push with his legs. Jeremy copied him and they both pushed for all they were worth when the engine pitch changed and the Mule began to move. It was slow at first and then faster, and they walked backward, pushing as they went. Then the Mule was free of the water and it raced away from them up the bank, dumping them both on their butts on the sodden creek bank.

Anderson looked over at Jeremy as they lay in the mud, soaked to the skin with hair plastered to his scalp framing his mud-spattered face. "YOU OKAY, JEREMY?"

The boy nodded, wide-eyed and serious. "Did I do good?" he asked, barely audible above the ambient noise.

"YOU DID GREAT, BUDDY! YOU SAVED MY LIFE," Anderson said.

The smile that split Jeremy's face was like the sun itself.

NEAR THE CAVE
15 MILES NORTHEAST OF BUENA VISTA, VIRGINIA

DAY 30, 6:15 A.M.

The rain didn't stop until well after midnight, continuing to swell the creek. They spent the night well up the rocky creek bank, huddled together under the shelter of a tarp pulled from the back of the Mule. At some point, exhaustion had overcome him, and Anderson fell asleep. He awoke stiff and sore from his night on the hard ground, his multiple injuries competing for his attention. Jeremy snored softly beside him, but Cindy was already up, inventorying the contents of the Mule. He slipped from beneath the tarp and walked stiffly over to the UTV.

"How's it looking?" he asked.

Cindy shook her head. "Most of the food was in the trailer. That's gonna be a problem."

"After we get settled in the cave, maybe I can scout downstream. I might be able to find some of the stuff."

She looked skeptical. "You might want to check out the route up to the cave before you volunteer for that. It's a pretty tough climb and I saw you favoring that leg."

Anderson shrugged. "It is what it is. But I suspect you're right, and if it's as steep as you say, the rain won't have helped. You think we'll be able to get up there today?"

"Shouldn't be a problem," she said. "Most of the path is rocky, and it looks like it's going to be a sunny day. Any patches of mud will dry quickly. We'll start as soon as we break this gear up into loads."

At the mention of the upcoming climb, hunger won the competition as Anderson's most pressing problem. "Ahh, I know we don't have much food, but is there anything at all for breakfast? I'm freaking starving."

Cindy reached in the back of the Mule and tossed him a gallon-size Ziploc bag stuffed with something nasty looking. "Venison jerky. Knock yourself out. You'll need the calories, trust me."

He ripped the bag open and stuffed his mouth full, chewing happily.

Cindy laughed. "I never saw anyone quite so enthusiastic about that stuff. You better take it easy, or you're gonna choke."

Anderson nodded and swallowed a half-chewed lump. "I told you. I haven't had anything to eat in two days." He looked over to where the chickens were hanging quietly. Here and there one stared at him, but most were unmoving. "And I'm looking forward to a chicken dinner. How many of them bought it?"

"You're out of luck there, I'm afraid. They're all hale and hearty, so no fried chicken. However, we might have eggs in a day or two, provided they weren't too traumatized."

She smiled at his crestfallen look. "I'm going to wake Jeremy up. We need to get this show on the road."

***

With Jeremy's apparent full recovery and their reduced inventory of supplies, load distribution proved less difficult than anticipated. Cindy had backpacks for herself and Jeremy, and they jury-rigged one for Anderson out of a small tarp. Cindy divided the loads efficiently and equally, snorting at Anderson's not-so-subtle inference she was making her own pack too heavy for 'a person her size,' and suggesting she divide the heavier ammo between his pack and Jeremy's.

"You mean a 'woman' my size?" she asked, looking pointedly at his swollen left knee. He shut up.

Other than a few days' supply of food, Anderson's bag of scrounged and improvised equipment, and an assortment of gear and tools, there were, of course, the chickens. They each tied four clucking birds to their packs, Cindy watching Anderson carefully to ensure he didn't 'accidentally' kill one.

Cindy carried her shotgun, and Anderson took one of the M4s, giving a second to Jeremy and hiding the third in the Mule. They pulled the UTV into a thick stand of trees and piled brush around it, then set out for the cave. Cindy led up the steep slope with Anderson bringing up the rear, his left knee already throbbing with every tortured step. Jeremy was in the middle, visibly proud of being trusted with the M4.

The trail was as challenging as Cindy said, and sweat poured off Anderson as he struggled upward. They walked with their long guns slung, leaving both hands to grab brush and saplings as they scrambled up the slope. At particularly steep points, Jeremy gripped a sapling with one hand and extended his free hand back to Anderson. The first time Anderson was annoyed, but quickly got over himself. So this was the kid they were worried about helping up the slope?

Anderson's knee throbbed, and Cindy was a hard taskmaster. Despite her diminutive frame, she handled the heavy pack with ease, and she was obviously no stranger to hard physical effort. Each time he noticed her looking, judging how he was doing, he nodded and motioned her onward. The quicker they got to this cave, the quicker he could get off his knee.

Well over an hour later, he limped over the lip of a rocky ledge to stand by Cindy and Jeremy as they stared into the cave. He was bitterly disappointed.

It was big all right, maybe fifty feet wide and twenty feet high. But it was just a shallow depression in the rock face no more than twenty feet deep, with the low morning sun shining all the way to the back of the 'cave.' It was little more than an overhang really, something to keep the rain off if the wind wasn't blowing, nothing he would dignify with the term cave.

Cindy looked at him expectantly. "So what do you think?"

"Ahh... it's great," he said.

Jeremy was grinning, and Cindy managed a straight face for only a second before she too burst out laughing.

"Follow me," she said, walking toward the back of the depression.

Anderson limped after her, Jeremy at his side. The boy burst out laughing again, and Anderson looked over at him, then turned back to Cindy. She was... gone.

Then he saw it, a vertical fissure in the back wall of the cave, just a fine line from his present vantage point. As he approached, he saw it cut into the rock face at an angle and was perhaps eight feet high and two feet wide, running straight back, a black vertical gash in the rock face, narrowing to a point at the top. Cindy's pack with her clucking chickens lay on the ground by the opening, and a bright light flashed out of the blackness.

"Just drop your pack and come on in," Cindy said, and he did as ordered, turning sideways and ducking slightly to squeeze in, with Jeremy close behind.

In twenty feet the passageway widened, and soon he could neither touch nor sense the walls. She ordered him to stop, and he complied as she bent down, her flashlight illuminating a stack of what looked like sticks on the rock floor. There was the snap of a butane lighter and flame flared. She was lighting a torch, and as it caught, the growing circle of light illuminated only the single wall next to them with blackness on the other sides. She handed him the burning torch then reached down and picked up two more, keeping one and handing the other to Jeremy.

"Might as well save batteries," she said as they lit their torches off Anderson's. His eyes widened as the circle of light grew. Even with all three torches going, he couldn't see any other walls.

"How big is this thing?"

Cindy shrugged. "Don't know. We've only explored this part. This room is about a hundred feet wide by two hundred feet long, but after that it gets dangerous. The floor drops straight off into a hole. You can't see the bottom even with a real strong flashlight, but there's water. If you throw a rock in, it takes a long time to fall and then you hear a splash."

"This is amazing," Anderson said.

"That's not all," Cindy said. "Watch the smoke from the torches."

Anderson did, unsure what he was supposed to see. Then he noticed it, the smoke was moving away from them toward the back of the cave.

"We figure there's some sort of crack all the way to the surface further up on the mountain. It must make a kind of natural chimney. We've had some pretty good size fires in here and never had to worry about the smoke."

Anderson laughed. "Next you're going to tell me you have running water and a bathroom."

"Not quite. But there are a couple of springs in the back of the cave. Just trickles running into the hole I was talking about, but it's good water."

"How the hell did you find this place?" Anderson asked.

"We didn't, our grandpa did. Or maybe his father, I was never quite sure about that. This all used to be Grissom land, back before they had to sell to the timber companies during the Depression."

"Grissom land?"

"That's our last name, Grissom," Cindy said. "But we can talk later. You need to get off that knee, and Jeremy and I need to get in some firewood and more torch material."

***

Anderson sat by the fire, perched on a short, round log Cindy had rolled from somewhere in the back of the cave and upended as a stool for him. His left leg was stretched out in front of him, the knee pain dulled by the Extra-Strength Tylenol Cindy had dug from her pack. At the edge of the flickering circle of light, Jeremy snored softly on a bed of evergreen boughs brought in to cushion the hard rock. Across from him, Cindy sat on an identical makeshift stool and poked the fire with a stick.

Dinner had been more venison jerky, chopped fine and boiled with most of their remaining noodles in a battered, blackened, and disreputable-looking iron pot also fetched from somewhere in the cave. He figured boiling water killed any pathogens, and the salty jerky flavored the noodles. It was surprisingly good.

"This is a pretty good setup," Anderson said. "Y'all been using it a long time?"

Cindy looked up. "Not lately, but we used to come all the time with my grandpa."

"You and Jeremy?"

She shook her head. "No. I meant my brother, Tony, and I when we were kids. Then things got... complicated. Anyway, Jeremy's only been here once, but he's always bugging me to come back." She looked over at her snoring son, her face softening. "I expect he'll get his fill of the place now."

"He's a good kid. How old is he? He seems pretty capable."

Cindy's head snapped around. She scowled. "For a 'retard' you mean?"

"Whoa! Time out! I didn't mean it that way."

She sighed. "Yeah, you did, whether you realize it or not. But I'm probably a bit hypersensitive too. Anyway, he'll be twenty-one next month."

"You don't look old enough."

She laughed. "Thanks, I think. I started early. I was fifteen when I had him. Same sad old story, I guess, local teen gets knocked up by older boyfriend. He was seventeen."

Anderson just nodded. It was none of his business, really, but Cindy looked over to make sure Jeremy was fast asleep and lowered her voice.

"Our parents were super religious, and we got married and moved in with my folks. I'd embarrassed them terribly, and despite being outwardly supportive, it was pretty obvious they considered Jeremy 'God's punishment.' They made excuses not to be with me in public, and I soon understood without them saying it that it might be better if I didn't take Jeremy out at all."

"How about your husband and your in-laws? Were they supportive?"

She laughed mirthlessly. "Not hardly. Jimmy's dad was a deacon in our church and even more ashamed than mine. And Jimmy? Well, Jimmy was a hotshot high school jock not at all thrilled with marriage, much less having a Down syndrome son. On graduation day he joined the navy and never came back. It took several years, but we divorced, yet another cause for family embarrassment."

"So how did y'all end up in the cabin in the woods?" Anderson asked.

She sighed. "That's a long story."

Anderson shrugged in the flickering light. "I got nothing but time."

"I didn't go back to high school after Jeremy was born. I just studied at home and got my GED. Then I got a job as a nurse's aide in the local nursing home. There aren't that many jobs available in a small town. I knew that wasn't going to work. Jeremy had no chance for any sort of life unless I got him out of the house where he was considered a burden. I left him with my folks and took the bus to Richmond to find a better job."

Anderson looked puzzled. "But how was that better? Even if you got a job that paid more than minimum wage, you would've still had living expenses. And Jeremy was with your folks, so how did that get him out of the house?"

Cindy didn't say anything for a long moment. "Because I had no intention of looking for a minimum-wage job. I... I took a job dancing in a club. The tips were good and it was all cash. It was the only way I knew for Jeremy and me to be independent. I told my folks I was in business college on a government grant and came home once a week to see Jeremy. It didn't take long to save enough to get a decent apartment and afford a babysitter for Jeremy. We only came home for the holidays, and things actually improved with my folks. At least until they found out."

"But how —"

"I'd been dancing about three years. I stayed away from drugs and resisted the considerable pressure to do… other things, and I was saving a lot of money. My folks believed I was working as an administrative assistant. Then one day one of the local good old boys from Buena Vista came into the club and recognized me. I suspect he couldn't get home fast enough to spread the news, and needless to say, my folks didn't take it very well. In fact, the entire family disowned me except for Tony, and he took a lot of crap from everyone for still talking to me."

She sighed. "So then I pretty much had to make it work, because I sure wasn't getting any help from anyone else. Dancing isn't the sort of thing you can do forever, and besides, when Jeremy got older, I didn't want him asking what I did for a living. So I danced five more years, socking money away and learning about investments. When my grandparents died, Tony inherited some of this land. As the disowned family slut, I wasn't in the will, but when the dust settled, Tony quietly gave me half of what he'd inherited. That's the ten acres our cabin is… was on. By that time I had enough investment income to live modestly, presuming we kept our expenses minimal. Jeremy loves the woods, so I decided to build a cabin and live a simple lifestyle. So that's my whole sad story."

Anderson nodded in sudden realization. "The dancing. That's why you weren't self-conscious back at the cabin. When —"

Her face hardened, and she nodded. "You learn to make yourself numb and ignore being stared at like a piece of meat. If you're smart, you even learn how to use it. I had a plan even before you made your grand entrance. The shotgun was under the bed and there was a knife along with it. I knew they were going to kill us regardless of what I did. I planned to take out the sergeant with the knife and just play it by ear with the other two."

She'd tensed visibly at the mention of the previous day's ordeal, and Anderson tried to change the subject.

"Tony sounds like a stand-up guy," Anderson said.

Cindy grew very quiet, but no less tense. "He is," she said at last. Her eyes glistened in the flickering firelight and she wiped them with the back of her hand.

"What's the matter?"

She glanced over to confirm Jeremy was still sleeping. "Tony and his family live in Staunton. We've been talking on the HAM set every day since the blackout, and there was a lot of FEMA activity in his area lately. I haven't been able to raise him in two days, and given what happened to us yesterday, I figure FEMA probably hit them too. Otherwise I would've heard from him."

He nodded and they drifted into silence again. After a long pause, Cindy changed the subject.

"Okay, I spilled my guts, so what's your story?"

Anderson smiled. "Not nearly as interesting as yours, I'm afraid. I graduated from high school, tried college, but it didn't work out, then ended up in the Army just in time to be sent to the Sandbox and shot at. I got out and was a deputy sheriff for a while down in Georgia; then I got on with FEMA as a law enforcement officer —"

"And FEMA is now trying to kill you. That sounds fairly interesting."

He shook his head. "It's probably better for both you and Jeremy if you don't know about that. Sometimes knowledge is a liability."

Cindy looked skeptical. "Aren't you the frigging man of mystery," she said. "All right then, what about family. Married?"

"Once. Quite happily," he said. "But now divorced."

"Care to elaborate?" she asked.

"Infidelity," Anderson said.

"Yours or hers?"

"Mine," Anderson conceded.

"I thought you were happily married?"

Anderson grinned. "Well, I wasn't a fanatic about it."

She shook her head. "Pigs. You're all pigs."

"Hey, at least I'm an honest pig," Anderson said.

Cindy laughed. "Yeah, I guess you are at that."

CHAPTER TEN

Delaware River Viaduct (Abandoned)
South Bank of Delaware River
Mount Bethel, Pennsylvania

Day 30, 5:55 a.m.

Shyla Texeira stared across the weed-choked length of the abandoned bridge to the New Jersey shore beyond and thought of home, less than twenty miles away. A few minutes' drive in normal times, but times were anything but normal. Still she shouldn't bitch. They'd made much better time than she dreamed possible when they sat trapped under the bridge at Harpers Ferry a scant week before.

Their elation at having eluded their pursuers by ducking under the bridge was short-lived when they realized escape was near impossible. They heard traffic overhead on the bridge regularly and choppers beat the air at all hours as the search for them intensified. They had a ringside seat to the search, because through negligence or indifference, FEMA failed to change radio frequencies. They pieced together what was happening from reports on the radio in the stolen SUV.

It was hot in the car, but the shade of the bridge overhead helped. There was the added discovery of a supply of both bottled water and MREs in the vehicle, allowing conservation of their own meager supplies, along with two M4s and ammunition. Activity on the bridge above and radio traffic was frantic that first day and most of the next, but the third day brought a reprieve. They could hardly believe it when radio calls went out for all units to stand down. The 'suspects' had been spotted southbound, and all resources were being reallocated in that direction.

They assumed the suspects were Simon and Keith and felt a twinge of guilt their deliverance resulted from the Trembles' misfortune, but they could neither help that nor afford to dwell on it. They focused instead on their big decision: whether or not to use the stolen car. It had almost a full tank of gas and two extra five-gallon jerry cans in the rear. Tex and Wiggins were already exhausted, and both nursed badly blistered feet. The temptation to ride proved to be too great. At first light on the fourth day they dragged the brush from the vehicle and drove east on the AT where it ran concurrent with the Chesapeake and Ohio Canal towpath.

They had no illusion as to the danger. Having observed radio traffic and FEMA activity seemed lightest during early mornings, they started each day at first light and drove no longer than two or three hours before finding a hiding place. Firm believers in Levi's plan now, they stayed as close as possible to the Appalachian Trail and always knew the direction and distance to the nearest access. They used secondary roads, logging roads and power line right-of-ways—any route the SUV could handle that kept them close to the AT and away from people. It was a disciplined progress, darting between hiding places for forty or fifty miles at a stretch, resisting the siren song of the open road, which might get them home—or dead—in a matter of hours. It was agonizingly slow, but orders of magnitude faster than traveling by foot.

The challenges were the rivers and streams: the Delaware and the Lehigh, the Schuylkill and the Susquehanna, and a half dozen major creeks in between. They planned each crossing like a military campaign, poring over their inventory of local maps for the least traveled bridge, and saying a silent thanks to Levi Jenkins each time they did so. At times they went miles out of their way to access seldom used and hopefully unguarded crossings. They bumped across rivers on railroad bridges, and twice crossed creeks on pedestrian bridges barely wide enough to accommodate the SUV, holding their breath and gambling the bridge would take the weight.

Twice they were fired on by civilians who no doubt mistook them for FEMA, but they escaped both encounters with only a bullet hole in the SUV. At one point they rolled into a concealed checkpoint when they attempted to cross a little-used bridge across the Lehigh River. Fortunately the new toll-keeper was a semi-honest former sheriff's deputy now in business for himself. Negotiation rather than gunfire ensued, and three MREs turned out to be the toll. A man had to feed his family, after all.

And now they were here, the last bridge between Tex and home.

"What the hell is this?" Wiggins asked. "I never saw a bridge with bushes and trees growing on it."

Tex laughed. "It's structurally unsound. They condemned it years ago, but never tore it down because some group or another was always coming up with a plan to fix it. After a while, it turned into kind of a local landmark. The kids crawl around up underneath it and inside it and paint all sorts of graffiti; some of it's actually pretty good. And it's sort of an unofficial walking path too. There's... well, there used to be... a really good ice cream place here on the Pennsylvania side. We'd come here when I was a kid and walk across to get ice cream."

"Well, they sure as hell don't want anybody driving on it," Wiggins said. "I didn't think I was going to make it around that barrier. And for that matter, I don't know if I WANT to drive on this thing. Are you sure it's not gonna fall down?"

Tex shrugged. "No, but I think it will be all right. Besides, it's a minor risk given what we been facing lately."

"Yeah, you got that right," Wiggins said. "How far to your folks' place?"

"Twenty miles more or less. How's the gas?"

Wiggins shook his head. "Running on fumes, but I'll try to get us there, or as close as I can, anyway."

***

Reynoldsville, New Jersey, looked like a typical American town. Or more accurately it looked like it at one time HAD been a typical American town. As Wiggins followed Tex's directions through the deserted streets, he saw the flash of a face in a window or a curtain quickly drop back in place. In the small-business district, two fast-food restaurants stood empty, their windows smashed, and trash blew through the empty parking lot of the looted supermarket.

Wiggins glanced over at Tex. She was visibly upset, and he tried to take her mind off what she was seeing.

"So how's a Portuguese girl end up in western Jersey?"

She glanced over. "Make that Portuguese-American. My folks came here from Newark, where there's a very big Portuguese community. My dad is actually kind of a big deal here. He and Mom came here first, long before I was born. They liked it, and Dad saw an opportunity. Land was relatively cheap, and he was a contractor. A lot of people in Newark were really sick of the inner-city blight and many had the money to move. The only thing holding them back was reluctance to leave the established Portuguese community. Dad figured if they were able to move in groups, they might be willing, so he got a loan and built six houses and marketed them in Newark. He sold them right away and plowed the profits back into twelve more houses. In a few years, Reynoldsville had the biggest Portuguese population in New Jersey outside of Newark, and Dad became sort of the unofficial patriarch."

Wiggins grinned. "So does that make you, like, first daughter?"

Tex laughed. "Maybe first daughter to run away to sea."

"Yeah, so how did that go over —"

"Turn here." Tex pointed. Wiggins turned right, and they moved down the tree-lined street into an upscale area of nice homes. Very nice homes.

"So you really are a princess," Wiggins joked, but Tex ignored him, intent on studying the silent street ahead.

"It's the third house on the left, just past the next cross street," Tex said. "But where the hell is everyone? I expected at least a little activity."

Wiggins had no answer, so he just followed Tex's instructions and turned into the driveway of an impressive stone house. It looked abandoned, curtains fluttering in the wind from an open upstairs window. They got out and Tex ran to the door. It hung open on one hinge, the door frame around the deadbolt splintered.

***

Tex stopped and stared as Wiggins moved up beside her. Wiggins drew his Sig. "Uh… Tex, maybe I should go first."

She shook her head and moved through the open door, Wiggins close behind her. The overpowering stench stopped them.

"Stay here," Wiggins said, and slipped past Tex with his Sig in a two-handed grip.

Even breathing through his mouth, he had difficulty forcing himself forward. Had it not been for Tex, he had little doubt he would've turned and left. He found them in the living room and, from the state of decomposition, figured they'd been lying in the heat quite a while. They were facedown on the floor, a pool of long-dried and stinking blood spread around them on the hardwood floor. He disturbed a cloud of flies, who buzzed their annoyance before settling back down to their meal. Both the corpses had their hands zip-tied behind their backs.

Wiggins heard a strangled sob behind him and turned to find Tex staring down at the bodies. He took her arm and gently led her back outside, into the yard and away from the house. He took a deep breath, but the fetid stench of death clung to him like it had soaked into his clothes. Tex was almost catatonic.

"Was it—"

She nodded. "I… I recognize Dad's slippers, and that was Mom's favorite housedress."

The silence grew, and after a long moment, Tex spoke. "We… we have to bury them."

Wiggins shook his head. "Not you. Me. That… that's just too much to expect anyone to deal with."

Tex looked as if she was going to object, then closed her mouth and nodded.

***

Tex seemed still in shock, and Wiggins rethought things. His grisly task was going to take a while and she needed something to keep her mind occupied. They found two shovels in the garage and he gave her one and suggested she find an appropriate resting place in the expansive backyard. Tex nodded and disappeared out the back garage door with the shovels while Wiggins mentally steeled himself. This was easily the most difficult thing he had ever done.

He protected himself as well as possible, donning a pair of coveralls and some rubber gloves he found in the house; but he could do nothing about the smell but breathe through his mouth. He found heavy-duty black garbage bags in the garage and made his way reluctantly into the living room. Over an hour later he stepped back and surveyed his work critically, looking at two bundles neatly wrapped in colorful quilts he found in the upstairs bedrooms, the blankets held tight by duct tape. He nodded, satisfied. He hadn't wanted Tex to have a final memory of her parents wrapped in the black bags like so much garbage; no trace of the black plastic was visible.

One by one he carried the bodies out and laid them on the large patio, then walked to the back of the yard where Tex was working. She'd gone back into the garage and gotten a pickax, the better to break the ground, and she was working with a will, slamming the heavy implement into the ground with a ferocity bordering on savagery. He watched as, oblivious to his presence, she buried the blade so deep it took all of her strength to pry it free. She punished the ground as if it were the murderer, and tears streamed down her cheeks. Wiggins cleared his throat and spoke.

"Tex?"

She looked up. "Oh. Sorry," she said, climbing out of the hole.

She looked over and saw the bodies and her chin began to quiver. "Those were Mom's favorite quilts."

Oh no, thought Wiggins. "Tex, I'm so sorry—"

She shook her head. "No, it's all right. Actually it's perfect. She would have loved that. Thank you, Bill."

Wiggins nodded, relieved, and picked up one of the shovels to begin removing loosened dirt from the grave.

They buried them in a common grave, together in death as they had been in life. Tex and Wiggins worked wordlessly, as if idle chatter would profane the task. It took two hours, and when they finished, Tex dropped to one knee and bowed her head over the graves and Wiggins followed suit respectfully. Her lips moved in a silent prayer; then she crossed herself and rose, wiping a tear from her eye.

She looked over at Wiggins as he stood. "What now?"

Wiggins reached over and squeezed her arm. "We'll figure it out, Tex."

***

Wiggins had covered the spot on the living room floor with plastic, then covered that with blankets. The stench still lingered in the house, but it was far less pervasive. They found the motive for murder in the walk-in closet in the master bedroom. The large floor safe was open and empty.

"They got what they wanted. Why did they have to kill them?"

"Because some people are just murdering scum," Wiggins said. "And with no law enforcement around, those assholes all crawl out from under their rocks."

Tex nodded. "I saw other broken doors up and down the street as we rolled in. I'm betting whoever did this probably hit the entire neighborhood. Maybe even the whole town. That's why there's no one on the streets. They've likely run away, or they're dead or in hiding."

Wiggins nodded. "So what do you want to do, Tex? You want to stay here?"

She shook her head. "Definitely not here. Not after what... what happened."

"How about other family? Anyone nearby?"

She shook her head again. "We weren't the stereotypical big Portuguese family. Mom had a tough time getting pregnant, and I'm an only child. They had me late in life, and all of my grandparents died when I was a kid. I've got a lot of relatives in Newark, but no way in hell I'm going into a city right now."

"Well then," Wiggins said, "I guess you're going to Maine."

"You... you don't mind?" Tex asked.

"Mind? Like I WANTED to travel all that way alone? You think I'm nuts?"

Tex smiled wanly. "Well, now that you mention it—"

"Very funny. Ha-ha," Wiggins said. "Do you want to stay here until morning? Is there anything we can use?"

She considered it. "The place is ransacked, but I doubt they hit the attic. There may be some camping gear and other stuff up there we might be able to use, and it didn't look like they hit the garden shed either; there might be something there." She shook her head. "But I don't want to stay in here. Not... not in the house anyway. Let's just pull the SUV into the garage and close the door."

"Understood. Let's see what we can find, then make a plan," Wiggins said.

***

The attic yielded a pair of old but serviceable hiking boots Tex had put away years before, and they found a pair of Tex's dad's boots that fit Wiggins well. They threw those in the SUV to replace their own rapidly deteriorating footwear. There were also a few odds and ends of camping gear. But the real find was in the garden shed, a nearly full five-gallon can of gasoline for the riding lawn mower, with another half-gallon or so in the mower itself. Wiggins drained the gas from the mower into the can and was about to pour it all into the near-empty SUV when he stopped.

"We should change cars," he said. "We've been hiding way off the beaten path most of the time, but surely we can find another ride here. If we get stopped, a stolen FEMA vehicle previously driven by two dead people might be kind of tough to explain."

Tex nodded. "Gas is more valuable than cars these days. I'm thinking we need to scour all the garden sheds and garages anyway to scavenge as much overlooked gas as we can find, so we might as well look for a car while we're at it."

They found one several houses down the street, a ten- or twelve-year-old Honda SUV sitting in a driveway. The hood was down, but not latched, and Wiggins opened it to find the battery gone.

"It figures," he said, "but I can just swap the battery out of our car. I'm sure the gas has been siphoned as well. I guess we need to see if we can find the keys."

Tex pointed to where the front door of the house stood open, and they started in that direction. A now familiar smell washed over them as soon as they stepped inside, and Tex's face turned white.

Wiggins gently led her outside. "Stay here."

He ignored the smell and moved through the house, hoping to find the keys before he found the source of the smell. He found a high-end kitchen, all natural wood and granite and stainless steel. A door led to a spacious mudroom and what he presumed was the garage beyond. On the wall by the garage door was a keyboard with multiple hooks, but only one set of keys. He confirmed they were Honda keys and then grabbed them and fled the house. Tex was still where he left her, staring at the open door.

He held up the keys. "Got 'em."

Tex nodded and turned, almost running in her haste to get away from the open door.

They moved their car over, and Tex transferred gear while Wiggins swapped the battery. He sloshed a little gas into the Honda to confirm it started and ran, then grinned at Tex and dumped the rest of their newly discovered fuel into the tank.

Wiggins drove the Honda back to Tex's house and parked it in the garage; then they grabbed the empty gas can and siphon hose and went scavenging. They pilfered garden sheds and garages and found enough gasoline in dribs and drabs to almost fill the tank of the Honda. Toward sundown they celebrated their good fortune by sharing the last of their MREs and leaned the front seats of the Honda back to settle in for the night. But sleep wouldn't come, and they talked until well after sundown.

"How far back to the AT?" Tex asked.

"About twenty-five miles if we head due west," Wiggins said. "But I still think heading north and angling back toward it is a better idea. We'll pick up a full day at least, and this whole side of New Jersey seems pretty rural."

Tex put her hand on Wiggin's forearm. "And it will also put us a hard day's walk from the trail and exposed, with no exit strategy for a full three days if we have to abandon the car and run for it. I know you want to get home, Bill, but there are still plenty of bad guys around. Levi was right; we need to stick close to the trail, even if it is longer."

Wiggins sighed and nodded in the growing gloom. Nine hundred more friggin' miles at fifty miles a day. He did the mental calculation and stifled a curse.

BRUNSWICK NUCLEAR POWER PLANT
CAPE FEAR RIVER
NEAR WILMINGTON, NORTH CAROLINA

TWO DAYS EARLIER
DAY 28, 10:00 A.M.

Rorke sat behind the plant manager's desk and looked around the spacious office. It was a far cry from his luxurious new office at Mount Weather, but it would do for those occasions when he had to be 'in the field.' The uniformed man across the desk from him shifted nervously in his chair, focusing Rorke once again on the task at hand.

"We need to get this plant up and running as soon as possible, Saunders. Give me a SITREP, just the high spots," Rorke said.

The man nodded. "Everything is going according to plan, sir. We've got the area fenced off for the family residence camp, and the communal tents are going up today. The barracks tents for the workers are already finished. We should have everyone at work in two days, four at the outside."

"How did they take the separation?"

The man shook his head. "About like you'd expect, sir. But a few beat downs and a little armed intimidation took care of it."

"They'll fall in line," Rorke said. "Allow them all daily family visits at first until they get used to it. Then we'll make the standard weekly visits as long as they're on good behavior. Daily visits will be conditioned upon how much progress we make getting the lights back on. Make it quite clear to them those visits must be earned, and their families' well-being depends upon their full and enthusiastic cooperation."

"Yes, sir…" The man looked hesitant. "But about the single guys—"

"What about them?"

"A few of them are getting mouthy. You know, making noises about this 'not being what they signed up for.' That kind of stuff. And they have no families we can use as leverage. Should I pick one or two and make examples of them?" the man asked.

Rorke fell silent, considering the problem. He shook his head. "Only as a last resort. There aren't that many of them, so let's try a more positive approach. Let them know in no uncertain terms their behavior won't be tolerated, but couple that with inducements. Better food perhaps, and set up a few small 'recreation tents' and round up some local women to staff them." Rorke smiled. "Food and sex are the best inducements we have in our brave new world."

The underling nodded, and Rorke changed the subject. "What about the terminal, is everything in hand?"

"Yes, sir. I sent a ten-man force in by chopper yesterday, carrying a copy of secretary Crawford's order. There were only three guys there, a major and two sergeants. The major gave our boys some lip, so I had them arrest him and one of the sergeants. We're holding them here, but we had to leave one of them back at the terminal to show us around."

"How about security? Can we spare ten men?" Rorke asked.

"Possibly, sir, but we can always use them elsewhere, and truthfully, it's a waste of manpower. The place is huge, and we couldn't guard the perimeter adequately with a hundred men. They relied heavily on electronic surveillance, which obviously isn't working now. Realistically, I think we should leave a small force in radio contact, just to establish our control and begin an inventory. That's all we really need at present. The terminal's only a couple of miles away, and we can have additional boots on the ground there in less than five minutes by chopper. I took the liberty of establishing a four-man force there and pulling everyone else back here. Subject to your approval, of course."

Rorke nodded, satisfied. He sensed an unasked question. "Something else, Saunders?"

"What about those people upriver, sir?"

The general smiled. "Oh, I don't think we'll have to worry about them much longer. Our friends at Fort Box will soon have their hands full."

CHAPTER ELEVEN

DAY 29, 1:35 P.M.

Mike Butler stood at the wheel and idled the Coast Guard patrol boat in the current, just north of the Military Ocean Terminal Sunny Point, the world's largest military terminal. Luke Kinsey stood beside him in the cabin, and Washington, Long, and Abrams from Luke's old unit stood on the small deck outside. With possible hostile contact in the offing, Butler and Luke agreed the mission should be long on combat experience. Like Butler, they all wore Coast Guard overalls. If they encountered Special Reaction Force troops, there was no point advertising they were SRF deserters.

Butler studied the empty wharf through the windshield. "About what I figured," he said. "Deserted. Most of the workforce is civilian. I figured if anyone came to work to start with, they would have stopped coming by now. There may be a few Army types around, but even that's doubtful."

Luke looked skeptical. "So we just tie up and look around?"

Butler shrugged. "What the hell else are we gonna do? The place is huge. I guess we could come up an inlet and approach from the far side, but to be honest, I wouldn't have a clue where we were. We'd just end up tramping around in the woods."

Luke sighed. "I guess you're right, but it still feels hinky."

Butler chuckled and eased the throttle forward, moving their boat down the length of the northernmost of three long concrete wharves. At the downstream end of the high wharf, a ramp led down to a floating dock that accommodated a number of service boats. Butler eased up to an unoccupied stretch of dock, and Long and Abrams jumped out to tie up. Butler studied the little marina, eyes resting on a pair of small patrol boats.

"Hmmm. A lot of good stealin' material here," he said. "We might go home with more than we figured."

Luke nodded absently, eyes on the wharf looming above them. "Tell me again how this is gonna work?"

"We're just the US Coast Guard come to visit to see if there's any interest in mutual assistance. If we run into the Army, we won't have a problem. And if we run into those SRF assholes, I don't think they'll shoot on sight and we can play it by ear."

"I wish I was as sure about that 'won't be a problem' part as you seem to be," Luke said as they climbed out of the boat onto the floating dock.

"I'm not sure about it." Butler grunted. "I just think it's our only real option."

They climbed the ramp to the towering wharf then spread out as they walked toward shore on the concrete pathway. The wharf accommodated a two-lane road, and train tracks ran down the left side for the length of the structure. Luke turned and looked back down the wharf. Any structure built to bear the weight of a fully loaded freight train was one stout piece of work. There were three of them spread down the riverbank at regular intervals.

Butler took point, with Luke on his right some distance back, and the others spread out behind at intervals. They reached shore, and a paved road ran right and left through a thick stand of trees, paralleling the riverbank. The railroad tracks continued straight ahead, down one of the many rail sidings spread throughout the terminal.

"The road to the left will take us to the terminal offices," Butler said over his shoulder, turning in that direction through the trees.

They were a quarter mile down the road when it happened.

"HALT!" barked a voice from the trees. "GROUND YOUR WEAPONS, AND PLACE YOUR HANDS ON YOUR HEADS! COMPLY IMMEDIATELY, OR WE WILL FIRE."

Butler looked at Luke and shrugged before following the order. Luke turned to his men and nodded before following suit. When all their weapons were on the pavement, the voice rang out again.

"YOU MEN IN THE REAR, CLOSE RANKS. I WANT YOU ALL TOGETHER. THEN I WANT YOU ALL TO FACE THE RIVER AND DROP TO YOUR KNEES. KEEP YOUR HANDS ON YOUR HEADS."

They did as ordered, and soon heard movement behind them. A black-clad figure came into view, his M4 trained on the group. He wore a black uniform and was trailed by another man, an Army sergeant, who appeared to be unarmed. The frigging SRF.

"Don't even think about moving, or my friend behind you will light you up in a heartbeat," the SRF thug said.

"Hello, Hill," Butler said.

"Hi, Butler. It's been a while," the Army sergeant replied.

The SRF thug looked back and forth between Butler and the sergeant. "You girls know each other?"

"It's like I told you before," the sergeant said, "they're just Coast Guard. They come here all the time to help us with riverside security. It's just routine."

The black-clad SRF man seemed to relax slightly. "Yeah, well, we'll see about that. We'll take them back to the terminal building and call it in."

Sergeant Hill shrugged. "Suit yourself."

The man was about to respond when Hill looked down the road away from the terminal. "What the hell is that?"

The man turned, obviously puzzled, and Hill stepped close and smashed the man's face with a left elbow strike, pulling the man's sidearm from its holster with his right hand as he stepped back. He brought the gun around in one fluid sweep, transitioning into a two-handed grip and firing over the heads of the kneeling men. Luke heard a gasp behind them, and the clatter of a weapon on the pavement, but kept his eyes on the scene before him. Hill already had the first SRF man on his knees, his own gun pressed to the man's temple as blood gushed out his nose.

"Y'all can get up now, Butler," the sergeant called. "And I hope like hell there are more of you wherever you came from."

* * *

Two minutes later they had the SRF men hidden in the woods; the live one zip-tied hand and foot, and mouth duct-taped. Hill motioned them away so they could speak in private.

"How many more?" Butler asked.

"Only two here," Hill said. "They're over in the main terminal complex. But there seem to be a bunch of the bastards over at the nuke plant. I've been seeing chopper traffic in and out of there all day."

"The two in the terminal building will have heard your shot," Luke said. "They'll call in backup for sure."

Hill was shaking his head. "I doubt it. It's almost a mile, with thick trees all the way. That's a long way to hear a pistol shot. There's also a generator running, powering a window AC unit. A very noisy window unit. And these boys ain't what I'd call the most situationally aware troops, if you get my drift."

"What's going on, Hill? How long have these goons been here, and where is everyone else?" Butler asked.

"Everybody else in this case was me, the major, and Sergeant Brothers. The others either took off or never showed up in the first place. As far as these assholes," Hill said, "two chopper loads of them hit us day before yesterday. They showed up with some sort of bogus order we were to turn the terminal over to them. The major refused until he could clear it with our chain of command. That basically meant never, because we haven't had comms since the power went down. Anyway, they beat the major down, and when Brothers tried to intervene, he got a beat down for his trouble too. By that time they had a nine millimeter to my forehead, and I had no doubt whatsoever they'd use it."

"So they're holding the others in the terminal building?" Butler asked.

Hill shook his head. "They took 'em out by chopper. Maybe over to the nuke plant or maybe someplace else. I don't really know. They kept me here because they needed someone who knew the layout. They been dragging me all over the place, making me show them what's where. They're up to no good, for sure, and I had no illusions when they knew what I knew, I was toast. When I saw y'all and recognized Butler, I figured my best bet was to throw in with you folks."

Hill looked back toward the terminal. "And right about now, I'd say, would be a good time to get out of here."

"Negative," Luke said. "If the two left pick up on something wrong, a chopper could intercept us long before we got back upriver."

Butler nodded agreement. "We'd be sitting ducks on open water. What's their routine?"

Hill shrugged. "Well, they haven't been here that long, but so far they seem to change shifts by chopper every twelve hours at noon and midnight. A couple of 'em scour the hard copy bills of lading, tryin' to get a handle on how much there is here, while the other two drag me around to show them where things are. They swap off and argue about it a lot, since they all want the 'let's sit on our butts in the air-conditioning' duty. We were goin' down to check one of the rail sidings when we heard y'all's boat. They just pulled the vehicle off the road into the woods and waited."

"So they didn't come out specifically in response to our arrival or radio back to the others when they heard the boat?" Luke asked.

Hill shook his head. "Nope. Like I said, not the sharpest tools in the shed."

Luke looked at his watch. "So if they follow routine, we've got ten hours, more or less, before the next shift change."

"About that," Hill said, "presuming you think two days' experience qualifies as routine."

"How about weapons?" Butler asked.

"Just what you saw. M4s and sidearms," Hill said.

"No, I mean weapons here in the terminal? Is there anything easily accessible we can grab now?" Butler asked.

"Well, we got, or had I should say, our own security force, so there's an armory in the terminal police station. That's still under lock and key. And there are weapons in inventory, a lot of them, but they're a bit harder to get to."

Luke nodded and looked at Butler. "Okay, at a minimum I say we take out the two in the terminal building, alive if possible, then load out all available weapons and ammo. We sure as hell can use the firepower, and prisoners will give us some much-needed intel." They both looked at Hill.

He shrugged. "I'm in as long as it buys me a boat ride out of here."

***

Hill wasn't exaggerating the SRF men's lack of situational awareness. Long and Abrams donned the black uniforms of the two neutralized thugs and followed Hill as he walked nonchalantly into the small air-conditioned office in the main terminal complex. The waiting men looked confused, but not unduly alarmed, no doubt assuming the pair were new faces from the larger SRF contingent at the nuke power plant. They both had guns to their foreheads before they discovered their mistake.

With the new prisoners trussed up beside their first captive in the back of a commandeered terminal pickup, they walked across the parking lot to the terminal police station. Hill used a ring of keys retrieved from the pocket of one of the SRF men to unlock the police station and armory.

Butler and Luke entered the armory behind Hill, their eyes as wide as kids in a candy store. There were multiple rows of M4s standing at vertical attention, with cartons of ammo stacked on shelves behind them. Butler pointed at several boxes labeled night-vision gear, and racks of tactical gear, including body armor. Another shelf held cases of flash bang grenades. Luke shook his head in disbelief.

"Were you expecting a war?" he asked.

Hill grunted. "Your tax dollars at work. I never thought they needed all this crap, but nobody asked me. That's what happens in a government organization when you get a budget—spend it all or lose it next year."

Butler grinned. "Well, I can assure you, Sergeant Hill, that we'll put this material to the very best of use."

"You got that right," Luke said. "We need to get this stuff back to Fort Box ASAP, but I've been thinking, we need to know what the hell is happening over at that nuke plant too."

Butler shook his head. "Sounds like mission creep."

"You know I'm right," Luke said. "As soon as they know we've been here and gone, they're going to put more troops into this place. And for sure there will probably be more chopper overflights. If we're gonna find out what's going on next door, now is the time."

"All right. I can see that, but what do you have in mind? We have to get this stuff back to Fort Box."

"Maybe we can do both." Luke looked at Hill. "Are those patrol boats we saw tied up down at the wharf operational?"

"Absolutely," Hill said. "And both have full tanks of gas. That's standard operating procedure. Not that we had anybody to run them."

Luke nodded and turned back to Butler. "All right then. I think Long, Abrams, and Sergeant Hill here should load all of this gear and our three prisoners in those two boats and return to base. The rest of us will recon the nuke plant."

"I should go with y'all. I know the area," Hill said.

Luke shook his head. "Negative. I'd love to have you, but you're far too valuable. I think we'll be making some more trips to the terminal, and having someone who knows it inside and out will be a tremendous advantage. We can't risk you on a recon like this."

Hill scowled, then grinned. "Well, what do you know? For the first time in my military career, I'm too valuable to be expendable."

Everyone grinned, then Butler spoke. "Actually, there's a small tributary of the river that runs by the north side of the power plant. There are homes along that stretch with boat docks. That's how I know about it; I've towed a few disabled boaters back to their home docks. We can get pretty close. My only concern is the engine noise."

Hill shook his head. "I don't think you have to worry about that, at least during the day. A lot of folks on this end of the river have been using their boats for transportation. We been hearing boat motors for some time. Less, of course, since gasoline started running low, but we still hear one now and again. I doubt these boys will come looking for you even if they hear the motor."

"I hope you're right," Luke said.

CAPE FEAR RIVER (TRIBUTARY)
NEAR BRUNSWICK NUCLEAR PLANT

SAME DAY, 5:35 P.M.

Butler eased the boat along, running dead slow on only one of the two engines and oversteering to compensate for the slight uneven thrust. They crept through the ever-narrowing tributary, looking across the marsh bordering the stream to the tree line and solid ground beyond. Ahead of them in the distance, high-voltage wires stretched through the air from left to right.

Butler pointed at the power lines. "We're almost to the power plant now. We should probably nose her in somewhere along here."

"Try to find a place where the channel gets as close as possible to the tree line," Luke said. "That marsh looks like cottonmouth central, and I'd like to minimize the amount of muck and marsh we have to wade through."

Beside him in the open door of the little cabin, Washington visibly shuddered. "Amen to that, brother. I do hate snakes."

"I'll do my best," Butler said, "but we don't have a lot of options here. I pretty much have to go where —"

"There!" They rounded a bend, and Luke pointed out a narrow inlet, barely wider than the boat, running through the thick marsh grass toward the tree line marking firmer ground.

Butler stopped the boat and studied the inlet. "Okay. I'll try it, but I'm gonna back her in. If we have to leave in a hurry, I sure as hell don't want to be backing out."

His companions nodded and watched as he turned the boat expertly and maneuvered stern first up the narrow inlet. The inlet dead-ended at the tree line, but Butler killed the engine thirty feet short.

"We'll paddle her back the rest of the way," he said. "I don't want to take a chance on damaging the propeller on a submerged stump."

Three minutes later, and to Washington's obvious relief, they only had to walk a few steps through mud and muck to solid ground.

"What now, LT… I mean Major?" Washington asked.

Luke shrugged. "We play it by ear, I guess. We'll work our way through the woods to the power plant, then take it from there depending on what we see."

The others nodded and followed Luke through the woods, maintaining their intervals. As the trees thinned, they moved more carefully from tree to tree until the power plant came into view.

"Son of a bitch," Luke said. He glanced over his shoulder as Butler and Washington moved up beside him. "What's that look like to you?"

They stared past him at a large area in the middle of an open field, surrounded by a tall chain-link fence with coils of razor wire running along its top. The area was rectangular, and each corner was topped with a tower, complete with the searchlight and machine gun. They could make out two figures standing in the nearest tower.

Inside the fence were row on row of large tents, obviously communal shelters. They heard shouts of children playing and saw an open area at the far end of the enclosure. People moved listlessly from tent to tent.

"It's a frigging concentration camp," Washington said as Butler nodded agreement.

"So much for a volunteer effort," Luke said.

He pulled a monocular from his pocket and looked beyond the fenced area toward the plant itself. There was a long row of tents outside the fenced area, and here and there civilians moved among them. He judged the SRF presence to be at least company strength, if not greater. Several choppers sat in the asphalt parking lot, and on the far side of the parking lot, tents were arranged in the orderly rows of an advance military base.

Luke passed the monocular to Butler, who looked, nodded, and gave the instrument to Washington.

"Looks like some civilians in the concentration camp and more in the tents outside. What do you make of that?" Butler asked.

Luke shrugged. "I don't know, but my guess is anyone outside the wire is cooperating with them, and those inside are less enthusiastic."

Butler nodded. "Makes sense."

"Yeah, and it looks like they plan to stay a while," Washington said.

Butler nodded again. "And between here and the military terminal next door, I expect there will soon be a whole lot more of them. Which makes the likelihood of them leaving us alone —"

"Somewhere between slim and none," Luke finished.

Washington looked thoughtful. "Maybe it ain't a bad thing, if they get the power back on, I mean."

"I got no problem with that," Luke said. "My problem is the way they're doing it, and what they intend to do with it after they restore it. They seem much more inclined to take things for themselves and toward consolidating control than helping others. Somehow I get the feeling if they get the power back, it's not going to help anyone but them."

"But what are they really up to?" Washington asked. "I mean, all we can tell is they're holding a bunch of prisoners."

"We got the three prisoners. Maybe we can get some intel out of them," Butler said. "I'm thinkin' we shouldn't push our luck."

Washington shook his head. "We're not going to learn too much from those SRF fools. Maybe how many troops and where they're from, things like that. But they're not likely to have a clue what's going on inside the power plant. They're not exactly geniuses."

Luke nodded. "Washington's right. If we want good intel, we're going to have to talk to one of those civilian 'volunteers.'"

"And how the hell we gonna do that?" Butler asked.

Luke checked his watch. "It'll be midnight or maybe a bit later before they change shifts at the terminal and figure out anything is wrong. We've got the night-vision gear we kept from the armory, so I say we wait until after dark and grab one of the civilians. It won't be full dark until nine or a little after, but if we grab him at ten, we can be almost back to Fort Box by midnight."

"Kidnap him? Are you nuts, Kinsey?" Butler asked.

"Think about it. It's probably our only shot at finding out what they're up to. I mean, do those people behind the wire look happy to you?"

Butler shook his head. "No. Of course not. But if we go around friggin' kidnapping people, how does that make us any better?"

Luke grinned. "Because we're the good guys." Washington grinned too and Luke continued. "Look, we keep him blindfolded until we get to Fort Box and make sure he doesn't see anything while he's there. We question him, learn what we can learn, and give him the choice of staying or coming back here. If he wants to come back, we just blindfold him and bring him partway down the river, then put him in a small boat and let him make his own way back here. No harm. No foul."

Butler shook his head. "All right. I guess it will work. But how did an honest Coastie end up running around with a couple of criminals like you."

"Just lucky, I guess," Luke said, and Washington grinned.

* * *

The sun set around eight, and thirty minutes later they heard the whine of an electric starter as a generator rumbled to life somewhere on the other side of the concentration camp. The reason became apparent as the searchlights on all four corner guard towers winked to life. Luke felt a momentary concern until it became clear the lights were focused on the camp, sweeping over the tents and playing over the fence lines. One by one, lights came on inside the tents, glowing through the fabric and setting shadows dancing on the tent walls. Individual lights bobbed through the gathering darkness here and there as people walked with flashlights, but there was no general outside lighting. Better and better, Luke thought.

They passed the time talking quietly, waiting for ten o'clock. Like the tents in the concentration camp, the tents outside the wire seemed to be shared facilities, which meant they had to catch a civilian alone, outside the tents.

Their 'collection point' was obvious, a row of portable toilets serving, but set some distance away from, the row of civilian tents.

At nine o'clock, lights began to wink off inside the tents, and Luke's concern grew. What if the bastards all went to sleep before ten? They couldn't hang around indefinitely, waiting for someone to wake up and come out to make a piss call. Fewer and fewer flashlights were bobbing between the tents or back and forth between the portable toilets. Then all the tents were dark except two. Then one.

Luke glanced up at the sky still dimly lit on the far western horizon. Close enough.

"Come on," he said, folding down his night-vision goggles as his two companions followed suit.

He led them in a crouching run over the open field to the row of toilets a hundred yards away. Since they couldn't know which toilet their quarry would choose, the plan was to wait until the man selected his toilet, then creep up behind the unit and grab him as he exited.

Washington was by far the strongest of the three, and by consensus, he was to grab the victim and clamp a hand over his mouth while Luke shoved a gun in the man's face to convince him not to struggle. Butler was to quickly duct-tape his mouth and zip-tie his hands before they hustled their captive back to the tree line and the boat beyond. It was going to go like clockwork.

Except it didn't.

They waited impatiently, staring at the last lighted tent, willing someone to come out and come their way. They heard voices through the still air, audible in the distance.

"Dempsey, will you put that book away and turn off the friggin' light! You know what time we have to get up in the morning."

"All right, all right. Keep your shirt on, Goodman. I'm gonna go take a piss and then I'll turn the light out."

Relieved, Luke saw the beam of the flashlight bobbing toward them. The first hint of trouble came when the bobbing flashlight got halfway to them, then stopped.

What the hell? Luke watched in his night-vision goggles as their mark shoved the flashlight under his arm and fumbled with his fly. He wasn't coming to the toilets. He was just going to take a leak on the ground.

Plan B. Luke got up and started running, circling wide off the gravel path so the grass muffled his footsteps as he approached the man from the rear. Twenty feet from the man, he had to step back on the path, and gravel crunched underfoot. Startled, the man whirled, and Luke's world went supernova as the piercing beam of the halogen flashlight hit him full in the night-vision goggles. Too late, he flipped up the goggles and closed his eyes.

He heard gravel crunch as the man backed away from him. "What the hell—"

The question was cut off with an emphatic *oomph*, and Luke felt a strong hand on his upper arm and heard Butler whispering in his ear.

"Washington cold-cocked him. Looks like he's down for the count, but be quiet. His buddy's moving around in the tent. I can see the shadows on the tent wall."

"Dempsey? What the hell you doing out there, talking to yourself? Come on, man. Get a frigging move on. I want to go to bed," came the voice from the tent.

They all kept their positions frozen in place, unsure what to do.

"Dempsey, God dammit! Answer me, you turd."

Butler whispered in Luke's ear again. "Get ready to run if this doesn't work out. I'll hold your arm to keep you from running into anything. Just follow my lead and run like hell."

Luke whispered back, confused, "If what doesn't —"

Butler called toward the tent, "Gotta take a dump. You can turn out the light. I got my flashlight."

"You catching a cold, Dempsey? You sound like hell. And you better not give it to me, you asshole."

"Screw you, Goodman," Butler called.

There was a muffled curse, and the light blinked off in the tent. Luke's sight was mostly recovered, and he flipped down his night-vision goggles to find Washington zip-tying their victim's hands. The man was out cold, and there was already duct tape across his mouth. *I hope like hell he's still alive,* Luke thought.

Luke helped Butler, and they split up Washington's gear so the big man could carry the prisoner. Washington reached down and picked up their prisoner effortlessly, throwing him over his shoulder as they all set off for the boat.

CHAPTER TWELVE

Intracoastal Waterway/Calcasieu River
East End of Calcasieu Lock
Lake Charles, Louisiana

One Day Earlier
Day 28, 2:45 p.m.

"That's a lotta gear, Lucius," Dave Hitchcock said, staring at the massive pile of boxes and assorted loose gear heaped on the deck of the *Miss Martha*.

Lucius Wellesley nodded. "And there's a pile that big or bigger on every one of the boats on this side. It's gonna be a bear to ferry it all to the lock wall in the skiffs then haul it all the way to the other end of the dock, then down the other end of the lock wall and back into more skiffs to spread it out among our boats." He sighed. "But I can't bring myself to leave it. We ain't likely to see any more spares or supplies from now on. We're gonna NEED this stuff, sooner or later."

Hitchcock nodded soberly, overwhelmed by the task in front of them. Then he smiled. "Why don't we do what those Coast Guard guys did?"

Wellesley cocked an eye. "What do you mean?"

"We could load the stuff into the skiffs on this side," Hitchcock said, "then move the loaded skiffs to shore at that narrow place the Coasties brought their boat over. They needed the boat ramp to pull out, but there's a much narrower place where it can't be more than twelve or fifteen feet across. After we nose the loaded skiffs into the bank, we set up like a bucket brigade to pass the stuff across that narrow neck of land to skiffs from the other boats. That would save us a lot of handling, to say nothing of hauling it up and down the lock wall."

Wellesley stroked his chin. "That's a good idea, Dave. And I think it may have given me a better one."

***

Wellesley eased the blunt nose of the *Miss Martha* into the massive concrete piling of the highway bridge. He touched it lightly, then slowly worked the boat's stern around until the towboat fit snugly in the narrow channel between the bridge piling and the slender neck of land separating the Intracoastal Waterway and the Calcasieu River. He looked up as Hitchcock stepped to the open door of the wheelhouse.

"How we lookin'?" Wellesley asked.

Hitchcock nodded. "The stern's about twenty feet off the bank, and we're dead on perpendicular, so we couldn't ask for a better setup." Hitchcock hesitated. "But you sure we should be doing this, Lucius?"

Wellesley shrugged. "I can't see as it's gonna make much difference. The only reason for the lock in the first place is to keep saltwater out of supposedly agricultural land, and depending on conditions, it's wide open more than half the time anyway. And the way things are going, I don't see anybody planting that land anytime soon, if they ever did in the first place. I been runnin' this stretch goin' on twenty years and never saw nothin' but swamp. Besides, it'll be a little hole, and if they want to fill it in later, it won't take more than a few truckloads of dirt."

"Well, if you say so. I guess you might as well let 'er rip," Hitchcock said.

Wellesley eased the twin throttles forward, and the *Miss Martha* pushed against the concrete piling holding her immobile. A powerful wash jetted aft from her flailing twin propellers, striking the canal bank and sending a boiling mass of muddy water over the narrow neck of dirt and marsh grass into the waters of the inlet beyond. The volume of water slowly increased as Wellesley went to full throttle, and the powerful prop wash from twenty feet away made short work of the dirt bank, opening a shallow channel in less than a minute. But he kept at it, and when he shut the engines down fifteen minutes later, there was a clear passage through the dirt bank almost as wide as the *Miss Martha*.

Wellesley maneuvered the big towboat out of the slot and brought her around expertly to lay against the bank some distance away to watch the proceedings. One of the flat-bottom aluminum skiffs all the towboats carried as tenders was making its way toward the newly opened hole, heavily loaded and deep in the water.

Sam Davis was operating the outboard, and Bud Spencer stood in the bow, with a long pole. Wellesley watched as Davis slowed and conned his skiff tentatively through the new channel as Spencer probed the bottom with his pole, checking the depth.

Then Davis was through, and Spencer dropped the measuring pole into the skiff and cupped his hands around his mouth.

"FOUR FEET OR MORE ALL THE WAY THROUGH, CAP!" he yelled, then lowered his hands to reveal a wide grin as he flashed Wellesley a thumbs-up.

Sam Davis grinned and waved as well before increasing speed and disappearing down the channel, around the lock to the *Judy Ann* waiting on the far side.

"I think this is gonna work just fine," Wellesley said.

"Damned if it ain't," Hitchcock said.

FORT BOX
WILMINGTON CONTAINER TERMINAL
WILMINGTON, NORTH CAROLINA

DAY 30, 7:35 A.M.

Levi Jenkins enjoyed the wind on his face as the boat glided across the glistening surface of the river toward Fort Box in the distance. Even this early in the morning the sun was formidable; it was going to be another hot one.

"You think this new plan is workable?" asked Anthony McCoy.

Levi looked over at his father-in-law and shrugged. "I don't know enough to say. Wright couldn't go into detail on the radio. It sounded like it might have possibilities as long as they don't try to ram it down our throats."

"Amen to that," said Vern Gibson, from behind them at the outboard. "We could all use some new neighbors as long as they're good, hardworking folks. But how do we know before they're our neighbors; that's my problem."

"Well, I guess we'll see, won't we? These guys are practical, so I'm sure they probably thought of that. Let's just keep an open mind and hear what they have to say."

They lapsed into silence, each with his own thoughts, as the boat covered the remaining distance to the Fort Box waterfront. They arrived under the watchful eyes of armed guards manning the rails of the container ships tied up to the wharfs. More guards than usual, it seemed to Levi. He mentally filed that away as Vern Gibson deftly maneuvered the little craft to the vertical ladder.

Levi fended the boat off the wharf pilings and tied up at the bottom of the ladder. The trio scrambled up to the dock.

"About time you river rats made it to town," said a voice just as Levi's head cleared the top of the ladder. He looked up to see Josh Wright's grinning face and outstretched hand, and grabbed the hand for an assist up the last few rungs.

Levi returned the grin. "Good to see you too, Sergeant... I mean Lieutenant Wright."

"All right, rub it in, why doncha?" said Wright, with a sheepish grin.

Levi laughed. "Every chance I get."

Wright greeted each of the other two men cordially as they cleared the ladder, then turned and led them toward the headquarters building. He started off at a brisk pace, but slowed to accommodate his guests, who looked around wide-eyed as they walked.

Vern Gibson shook his head. "Dang if it don't look different every time I come. I was just here ten days back, and there's a lot of changes. And a whole lot more people."

Wright nodded. "That's the point of this meeting. We're hoping to put some programs in place that will be beneficial to everyone."

His guests nodded noncommittally, and they walked in silence to the headquarters building. Wright led them into the former break room, now known as 'Conference Room A,' and nodded toward a pot of coffee on the sideboard.

"Fresh pot. I started it when we saw y'all on the river."

The three men grinned in unison. "Now that's what I call hospitality," Gibson said. "I don't suppose you might have any of that coffee we could take home, do you?"

Wright grinned back. "Just a full forty-foot container. Ask and you shall receive."

Vern Gibson laughed. "Well, this meeting is gettin' off to a good start. I can't be bought, but I can be rented. Especially if there's coffee involved."

They were still chuckling when the others arrived, with warm greetings and handshakes all around before they settled around the conference table, each with a steaming mug. Colonel Hunnicutt wasted no time fleshing out the proposed concept, with Wright, Butler, and Luke Kinsey adding details as appropriate. The three visitors listened silently but attentively. When Hunnicutt finished, the men from the river looked back and forth at each other, each waiting for the other to speak. Finally Levi broke the silence.

"How many of these fortified towns you figure again?"

"We were thinking twenty," Wright said. "One every mile or so up the river, alternating sides where we could. But that's the ideal, in practice we'll place them wherever the local folks will go along with it, as long as they're reasonably spread out."

"And you want to build them all at once?" asked Vern Gibson, his doubts obvious.

"Yes, or at least as many as we can. Besides the advantages the colonel outlined, our census here is increasing rapidly." He sighed. "So to be honest, we also have a lot of desperate people that need new homes."

No one responded, and the room lapsed into an uncomfortable silence. Finally Hunnicutt spoke. "I'd hoped for a bit more enthusiastic response."

"It's not that we don't like the concept, Colonel, but I think it's the 'desperate people' part that's giving us all a little trouble," said Anthony McCoy. "I'm sure we all like the part about towns and fortified positions and militias and all that. But you're basically talkin' about dumping strangers among us just because they're desperate and need a place to go. We're sympathetic, but I think we can all see the potential for this turning out to be a real bad idea."

Hunnicutt nodded. "Point taken. But if you like the basic concept, we're open to suggestions. How would you improve it? If you'll each give us your comments and criticisms, maybe we can still get to yes. Would you like to start, Anthony?"

Anthony nodded. "Okay, for starters, I sure wouldn't try building 'em all at once. I'd say start with one or two, maybe halfway out from here and the one furthest away. Say twenty miles out. It'll be a lot easier to get folks on the river enthusiastic about two towns than twenty. Just make those two towns bigger than you planned, then stick to the security stations everybody's already agreed to in between. If the towns turn out to be workable, and everybody likes them, we can always build more by expanding the security stations. But if not, we haven't wasted a whole lot of effort for nothing."

Hunnicutt nodded, encouraged by Anthony's use of 'we.'

"And another thing, we'll need assurances y'all don't use the river towns as dumping grounds for misfits. There are gonna be a lot of 'recruits' and you're not going to be dead right on every one of them. Some of them are going to fool you, and when you end up with fools like that Singletary, we don't want 'em on the river. We got enough homegrown fools without importing any," Anthony said.

Everyone laughed, and Hunnicutt nodded. "Agreed."

The laughter died, and Vern Gibson spoke. "We're all laughing now, but this is serious, Colonel. It's not just us three you gotta convince. I don't think the majority of folks up and down the river will buy it unless they have some say-so about their new neighbors. That's especially true if you're plannin' on asking them to donate the land for these towns." Gibson cocked his head and fixed Hunnicutt with a knowing look. "Which I suppose you are."

Hunnicutt nodded and was about to speak when Wright interrupted. "If I may, sir? I have an idea about that."

Hunnicutt made a go-ahead gesture.

"What if," Wright asked, "we set up a vetting committee? It could include mostly folks from the river farms, with maybe one or two advisers from Fort Box they trusted, who've had an opportunity to observe the potential recruits more closely and offer opinions. The committee could interview and approve anyone who applied to move to the river."

Vern Gibson nodded slowly, as did Levi and Anthony. "Might work," Gibson said.

Hunnicutt beamed. "Excellent! We're making progress. How about you, Levi? Do you have any suggestions or concerns?"

Levi laughed. "So many, I don't know where to start. But I think the plan is workable. However, I think we all know no matter what we decide here or what we plan, it's all going to fall to pieces at some point. We need to be prepared to be true to the CONCEPT while maintaining some flexibility."

The others nodded, and Levi continued. "But like Vern said, folks on the river have to buy into the concept."

Hunnicutt nodded and turned back to Gibson. "How do you like our chances, best guess?"

Gibson shrugged. "I'm thinkin' maybe sixty percent will go along after they think about it a bit, another twenty-five or thirty percent can be convinced, and ten percent will be dead set against it, just because they're dead set against everything."

"I'll take those odds. Can we ask you gentlemen to take the lead in discussing this with your neighbors?" Hunnicutt asked.

Vern Gibson sighed. "I'm not what you'd call real eager, but I guess I can do that. Assuming these other two jokers agree. I'm sure not doing it by myself."

Levi and Anthony nodded, and Hunnicutt's face was creased by a relieved smile. "Thank you, gentlemen. We really appreciate it."

His smile faded. "But now that we've settled that, I'm afraid I have less welcome news. It may not impact you immediately, but I thought you should know about it." He nodded at Luke. "Major Kinsey?"

"Yes, sir," Luke said, and turned toward their visitors. "Yesterday, we did a reconnaissance of the Military Ocean Terminal at Sunny Point and also the Brunswick Nuclear Station. The FEMA Special Reaction Force is occupying both facilities. We managed to take prisoners, and what we've learned from them is concerning."

"Ahh… isn't taking prisoners kind of like poking the bear?" Levi asked. "Maybe we ought to just leave those folks alone. Live and let live."

"Based on what we know, they don't intend to live and let live," Luke said. "They plan to build both of those facilities up as major SRF bases, and it's unlikely they will tolerate an armed presence nearby they don't control. In fact, under interrogation, the prisoners revealed they believe an attack against us is imminent."

"They're going to attack Fort Box?" Anthony asked.

Luke shook his head. "Not them, but someone. They had no hard intel, just rumors in their ranks. So the reliability is suspect, but we can't discount it. Rumors are a lot more accurate than people realize."

"If not them, then who?" Anthony asked. "The regular Army?"

Beside Luke, Hunnicutt shook his head. "They seem to think it would be a surprise attack, and I can't see the regular military attacking us without at least engaging us first and demanding our surrender. We're no match for the regular military, and they know it. Besides, they just don't operate like that, especially against fellow Americans. They would talk first and only attack as a last resort. Nonetheless, we're taking the threat seriously. We've been on increased alert since we heard about it."

Levi nodded. "I noticed extra guards."

"We've doubled up security everywhere," Hunnicutt said. "But it's stretching us thin. Which is another thing we wanted to talk to you about."

Levi looked confused. "But what can WE do…" He trailed off as he understood.

"Major Kinsey's force managed to capture almost a hundred M4s and a substantial amount of ammunition. We now have rifles without riflemen. We don't have time to vet and recruit people out of the refugee population. It's one thing to recruit a forklift driver or a cook, but we'd have to trust a recruit completely before we turned them loose inside Fort Box with a weapon. There just isn't time."

"You want volunteers from the river," Gibson said.

"Only until the threat passes," Luke said. "I'm sure Donny and Richard…"

Vern Gibson visibly bristled at the mention of his sons, then calmed and nodded. "Donny thinks highly of you, Major. I reckon if he knew you needed help, he'd be here in a heartbeat. Richard too, for that matter." He smiled ruefully. "Thing is, you ain't the one who's got to explain it to their mama."

"We know we're asking a lot, Mr. Gibson," Hunnicutt said. "And we wouldn't ask at all if we weren't desperate. But if Fort Box falls, I think it's only a matter of time before the FEMA thugs start moving upriver."

"Maybe, maybe not," Gibson said. "There's some who think we're too little to mess with. Out of sight, out of mind. Personally, I'm not of that school of thought, but I can't speak for my neighbors." He shook his head. "It's one thing to ask folks to buy off on settin' up these towns, but it's another to ask 'em to maybe stop a bullet."

"Agreed," Hunnicutt said. "We can only ask."

The room fell silent again as the river men mulled the request.

Luke broke it. "How many veterans do you estimate are on the river, Mr. Gibson?"

Gibson shrugged. "Countin' old Vietnam-era dinosaurs like me, more than a hundred I'd say, but I can't rightly be sure." He sighed. "I can't speak for anybody else, but I'll tell my boys and they can make their own decisions. And if they decide to come, I'm sure they'd be willing to go up and down the river and ask other folks."

"That's more than generous, Mr. Gibson. Thank you," Hunnicutt said.

"I'm in," said Levi quietly.

"Me too," said Anthony.

"Hell, Anthony," Gibson said. "What war are you a veteran of, the Spanish-American?" He turned to Hunnicutt. "If you're takin' old coots like Anthony here, I guess I'll sign up too."

"He's not taking Anthony," Levi said, glaring at his father-in-law. "One of us has to stay home and protect the family."

Hunnicutt held up his hand. "Gentlemen, I appreciate your willingness to help us, but Levi is right. We don't want to leave any family defenseless, so please make that clear to any of your neighbors who might be willing to help us."

***

After more discussion, the three civilians took their leave with promises to consult their neighbors on the 'town plan,' as it had come to be known, and the much more pressing issue of volunteers. Hunnicutt and Luke Kinsey saw them off at the waterfront, sending them on their way with five pounds of coffee apiece.

"Think we'll get any volunteers?" Hunnicutt asked.

"I think a few at least," Luke said. "Whether it will be enough is anyone's guess."

Hunnicutt nodded. "How's your exclusion zone plan coming?"

"We have all the signs posted and about half the barriers in place. And Wright started random patrols two days ago. They rousted a few refugee families that were squatting inside the zone and drove them back to the country club camp." Luke sighed. "But your prediction was accurate. It wasn't popular, and it's increasing resentment in the camp. Maybe it wasn't a good idea."

Hunnicutt sighed. "Resentment was inevitable anyway, if not about this, then about something else. It may as well be over something that actually enhances security."

UNITED BLOOD NATIONS HQ
(FORMERLY NEW HANOVER COUNTY
DEPARTMENT OF SOCIAL SERVICES)
1650 GREENFIELD STREET
WILMINGTON, NORTH CAROLINA

DAY 30, 11:35 A.M.

"So how many they roust all together?" asked Kwintell Banks.

"'Bout twenty, mostly from over around Newkirk Avenue," Darren Mosley replied. "But yesterday it was Wellington, and they puttin' those Exclusion Zone signs all along Seventeenth Street. Look like that the closest they want anybody to get to their fort."

"Who they rousting, black or white?"

Mosley shook his head. "Don't seem to matter. You squattin' in that exclusion zone, they gonna roust you."

Banks stroked his chin, considering this latest development and how he might use it to advantage. "How dat goin' down in the camp? What our spies there say?"

"All the 'fugees be seriously pissed, no matter the color. Thing is, about half the squatters they brought back to the camp was never there in the first place. And a lot of them had gathered a lot of stuff in the crib they was squatting in, and the soldiers only let them bring what they could carry. So those be double pissed," Mosley said.

Banks nodded, a plan forming in his mind. "When the next soldier patrol?"

Mosley shook his head. "They ain't regular now. They mix it up."

"All right then. We just gotta be ready for them whenever they come. I want you to have our guys in the camp get them 'fugees all riled up. Spread a rumor the soldiers run over a kid that was just asking for food or something like that. The worst the better. Get a crowd gathered around the camp entrance, so whenever the soldiers get there, they gotta run through it. Then block the road so they CAN'T get through, and start throwing rocks and bottles. The rest of the crowd will pitch in, guaranteed. You follow me so far?"

Mosley nodded, and Banks continued. "The soldiers likely won't shoot, at least right away, so the crowd will get bolder. When they good and excited, just have our guys slip away. If we lucky, at some point the soldiers will panic and shoot at the 'fugees or at least over their heads."

Mosley nodded again, then asked, "But what if they don't? Shoot, I mean."

"Then we do it for them. Have some of our boys hid nearby, and you give them the signal to shoot," Banks said.

"At the soldiers?"

Banks exploded. "NO, FOOL! THE 'FUGEES!"

Mosley nodded his head vigorously. "Oh yeah. I get it now. That smart, Kwintell. Real smart."

Banks sighed. "All right. Get your ass outta here and go take care of it."

Mosley bobbed his head again and scurried out of the conference room.

"Real crack team, Banks," scoffed a low voice from the end of the table.

Banks' heart raced. He swallowed the lump in his throat and did his best to hide his fear. "He all right. He just need supervision sometime. You know what I mean."

The man stared unblinking. He stood six feet six, and even sitting at the conference table he towered over Banks. His African DNA was clearly undiluted, and he was the blackest black man Banks had ever seen. It was almost impossible to tell where the black tee shirt stretched over his massive chest stopped and his bulging biceps started. His shaved head bore many scars, and there was a small gold ring in one earlobe. His only earlobe actually, the other was cut off in a straight line. If Rorke was pirate scary, this guy was insane-serial-killer-under-the-bed scary. Banks had difficulty keeping his composure in the man's presence. Rorke called him Reaper.

Reaper snorted. "Yeah, I know exactly what you mean. He's a frigging idiot."

Banks changed the subject. "This is all good. All the 'fugees bein' pissed at the soldiers, I mean. That can help us out a lot, we play it right. We got lucky on that one."

Reaper snorted again. "Only fools need luck. You do what I told you?"

"Yeah, but what you need—"

"I hope you're not about to ask me a question. You know I hate questions. As a matter of fact…" Reaper smiled and produced a Fairbairn-Sykes fighting knife seemingly out of thin air and buried the point in the wooden conference table. He released it, and as it stood quivering, upright in the table, Reaper pointed at the leather-wrapped grip. "Know what kind of leather that is, Banks?"

Banks looked at the knife handle and shook his head.

"It's the nut sack of the last fool to ask me a question without my permission," Reaper said. "I ask the questions. You give the answers. We clear on that, fool?"

Banks nodded, cowed, as he had been since Reaper and his small contingent had arrived the morning before. Like Banks and his gang, all the newcomers were African-American, but there the similarity stopped. The SRF troopers were hard men and openly disdainful of the gangbangers posturing as badasses. They arrived in Humvees laden with crates, which disgorged their cargoes then disappeared. The newcomers set to work immediately, confiscating pickup trucks from the UBN thugs or nearby parking lots. They brought an ample supply of gasoline in jerry cans, and by nightfall they had converted over a dozen pickups into 'tacticals' with the addition of machine guns and improvised armor. Banks had seen rocket-propelled grenades among the gear, and he was eager to know when his men would get access. Now he was afraid to ask.

"How many of these fools you got?" Reaper asked.

"Almost fifteen hundred, if you count the baby ganstas —"

"I'm not wasting an M4 on a third grader," Reaper said. "How many man-sized fools you have smart enough to tie their own shoes?"

Banks ignored the insult. "'Bout a thousand, give or take."

Reaper nodded. "I got four hundred M4s. Pick out your four hundred best men, and divide them into groups of twenty. One of my men will be in charge of each group, to teach them how to use —"

Banks bristled, terror momentarily forgotten at this affront to his authority. "These my men. I'm in charge. And the M4s just like the ARs, ain't they? We know —"

Reaper glared and looked pointedly at the knife still upright in the table.

"Course, we can always use some pointers," Banks finished lamely.

"You can use more than pointers. 'Cause every one of you fools is gonna be blasting away on full auto if I don't nip that in the bud. We gonna teach you to fire single shots or three-round bursts, no more. I see one fool firing on full auto, I'm gonna waste him myself. You got that, Banks?"

Banks nodded.

"We can't actually shoot; otherwise they'll hear it inside the fort. We're just going to have to do weapons familiarization by dry firing and hope these idiots of yours learn enough to keep from shooting each other when it's for real. As I said, each twenty-man group will be under one of my men, and the rest of us will man the tacticals and carry the RPGs. I want all fifteen hundred of your men on the front line with whatever they've got, and the four hundred men with the M4s will be evenly spread among them. The tacticals will be spread in the line along the front behind them, out of sight until they're needed and then coming out to provide suppressing fire against the crew-served weapons on the wall. Is that clear?"

Banks nodded again.

"Good," Reaper said. "You may now ask a question if you have one."

"Ahh… where you want me?"

"With me, of course. You're a fool, but you're not completely stupid. Riling up the 'fugees wasn't a bad idea, and it's going to make things a whole lot easier."

WILMINGTON REFUGEE CAMP
(FORMERLY PINE VALLEY COUNTRY CLUB)
PINE VALLEY DRIVE
WILMINGTON, NORTH CAROLINA

SAME DAY, 1:45 P.M.

Corporal Jerry Miles looked at the road ahead and cursed. Why did this crap always seem to happen on his patrols? First they stumbled across the gang rape, and Lieutenant Wright chewed his butt to hamburger even though he'd done the right thing, and now this. Three cars were across the road ahead, blocking the western entrance to the camp. They were surrounded by what looked like a far from friendly mob of refugees.

Miles sighed. "Slow down," he said to the driver. "We don't want to be in the middle of that."

"How we gonna get into the camp?" asked the driver.

"Well, not through there, that's for sure," Miles said. "This is shaping up to be a shit show, and we're not playing. Stop the vehicle."

The driver did as told, stopping well back from the crowd. But not far enough. The angry mob surged forward and encircled the Humvee. Curses filled the air and angry faces pressed against the windows. Miles reach for the radio.

"Box Base, this is Rover One. Do you copy? Over."

"Rover One, this is Box Base. We copy. Over."

"Box Base, be advised we have a situation. Our vehicle is surrounded by hostile civilians. Repeat. We are at the west entrance to the refugee camp, and our vehicle is surrounded by hostile civilians. Please advise. Over."

"Rover One, we copy. Stand by. Over."

Miles cursed under his breath again and looked out at the crowd, noise rising as they began to beat on the vehicle with their fists. The driver flinched as a large black man with gang tattoos hammered at his window with a fist-sized rock.

"We can't stand by too long," the driver said, wide-eyed.

The radio squawked. "Rover One, this is Box Base. Can you disengage without casualties? Repeat, can you disengage without casualties? Over."

"Box Base, unknown. Repeat, unknown."

There was a long pause before the radio squawked again. "Rover One, we copy. Do your best. You are clear for RTB. Repeat. You are clear for return to base. Advise when you have disengaged from civilians. Do you copy? Over."

"Box Base, we copy. Rover One out."

Miles snorted. "Yeah, assholes. I copy just fine. I just don't have a clue how to 'disengage without casualties,'" he muttered and turned to the driver.

"All right, back her out of here slow before they get the bright idea to start trying to rock the vehicle, and we have to hurt 'em to get loose. When we start backing up, hopefully the ones behind us will get out of the way and stack up around the other three sides of the Hummer. Keep gradually increasing speed backwards until you have a clear opening; then floor it, and get us the hell out of here."

The driver nodded, and the crowd behaved as Miles anticipated. At the first sight of an opening to the rear, the driver gunned it and they shot backwards, free from the mob. They barely cleared the crowd when the interior of the Humvee began to ring with clangs and bangs as the thwarted mob showered the vehicle with rocks and bottles.

"Don't stop!" Miles yelled as he glanced at the open street behind them. Then he jerked around at the sound of gunfire. In the space they'd just vacated, civilians at the front of the mob jerked in a macabre dance as bullets impacted them, and the crowd evaporated almost instantaneously, leaving a dozen bloody bodies on the street.

"I think we're about to have a very bad day," Miles said.

FORT BOX
WILMINGTON CONTAINER TERMINAL
WILMINGTON, NORTH CAROLINA

SAME DAY, SAME TIME

"Does he have a clue what's going on?" Hunnicutt asked.

Luke shook his head. "No, sir. Washington hit him pretty hard; then we duct-taped his mouth and eyes and flex-cuffed him. He didn't start moving around until we were well up the river on the way back, and we were careful not to say anything he could overhear. He's been blindfolded and restrained ever since. I had Dr. Jennings check his vital signs last night, but I didn't allow her to talk to him —"

"As well I know, Major," Hunnicutt said, "because immediately thereafter I got the good doctor's 'I won't be party to barbarism' speech, so thank you. I don't suppose you could have just grabbed one of the nurses instead?"

"I tried, sir. Dr. Jennings caught me and demanded to know what was going on. I figured it would be worse if I didn't tell her," Luke said.

Hunnicutt nodded, and Luke continued.

"Anyway, we've kept him disoriented, and I want to try to learn as much as I can from him without giving up anything. That way we can let him go without being too concerned he might leave with any usable intel."

"And you're sure he's voluntarily working for them?"

Luke shrugged. "He wasn't behind the wire in the concentration camp and he seemed to have the run of the place. So yeah, I'd say he was cooperating."

Luke gestured down to his SRF uniform. "He has no clue where he is or why he's here. He saw me for less than five seconds last night, but it was dark and I was in Coastie coveralls with night-vision gear hiding my face, so I doubt he recognizes me. I'm going to go in there in this uniform with food and water, and we'll just see what he says."

Hunnicutt sighed. "Do the best you can, Major. What we got from the SRF prisoners was vague at best; maybe understanding exactly what their plan is for the power plant will shed some light on things."

Luke nodded and glanced over at Hunnicutt's weary face. The man had aged visibly in just the short time Luke had known him. He stood now, a look of dejection on his face as he studied the floor.

"Problem, sir?" Luke asked.

Hunnicutt shook his head. "Nothing new, Major. I was just thinking how different our lives have become in a few short weeks. We were all just going our own merry ways, and now we're worried about 'enemy forces' and 'collaborators' and who the hell knows what else we never even thought about except maybe when watching an old war movie. Now it's all happening right in my hometown. It just all seems so unreal."

Luke said nothing for a long moment. "What did you do in civilian life, sir? If I might ask."

Hunnicutt smiled wanly. "Well, you might say I wasn't without combat experience. I was a high school principal."

Luke chuckled. "I didn't see that one coming."

"Well, we all have our stories, Major." Hunnicutt nodded at the door. "And right now, I'd say you need to see how much of Mr. Dempsey's you can pry out of him."

"Yes, sir," Luke said, and Hunnicutt nodded and set off down the hall.

Luke opened the door quietly and slipped into the room. It was formerly a large storeroom, a windowless cube in the middle of the building, recently turned into a makeshift isolation cell. There was a small table with two metal chairs, and a single bare light bulb. The prisoner lay on a cot on the opposite wall, zip-tied hand and foot, with duct tape over his mouth and eyes.

Luke set a paper bag and a bottle of water on the table, and the prisoner raised his head at the sound. Luke walked over to the cot.

"I'm going to slip a knife blade under the duct tape around your eyes and mouth to cut the tape, but I'm not going to hurt you. Nod if you understand."

The man nodded, and Luke cut the tape. As he tried to remove it, it was obvious the hair was going to be a problem.

"I'm sorry," Luke said, "but it's stuck in your hair pretty good, so I'm just going to jerk it off fast. This might hurt a bit."

The man nodded again, then flinched as Luke snatched the tape off first his eyes, then his mouth. He blinked at the light, then squeezed his eyes shut as Luke cut the plastic flex cuffs off his wrists and ankles and helped him sit up on the cot.

"I have some water, and there's a sandwich in the bag on the table, Mr. Dempsey," Luke said.

"Wh-where am I?"

Luke ignored the question and gently tugged the man to his feet and helped him walk unsteadily across the short distance to the table and sit. The man twisted the top off the bottle and chugged the water. Luke pulled another bottle from the leg pocket of his pants, and the man nodded gratefully before downing half of the second bottle, then pulled the sandwich from the bag and began to eat, barely chewing before swallowing.

The guy's half-starved, thought Luke as Dempsey attacked the sandwich. He was in his late thirties or early forties, with the red hair and fair skin of his Irish heritage. Half his face was covered by a purple and yellow bruise from Washington's fist. To Luke's relief, the man finished both the sandwich and the water without choking.

"Better?" Luke asked.

Dempsey nodded. "Wh-why am I here?"

"I think you know," Luke said.

The man shook his head vehemently. "I don't, really. I've been cooperating, ask anyone. I... wait, if it's about the start-up sequence, I can explain."

Luke merely nodded. "Please do."

"Look, I know you want the plant on line ASAP," Dempsey said. "I get that, we all do. But there are certain safety procedures we have to... I mean need to... follow. I'll take all the shortcuts we possibly can, but some things we just can't ignore."

The man was obviously terrified, almost at the point of babbling. What could induce such fear?

Luke shrugged. "You know the price of failure, Mr. Dempsey."

All color drained from the man's face, and the hideous bruise stood out in even greater contrast. "Please," he whispered, "please don't hurt my family. I... I'll do it any way you want me to."

Luke kept his face a mask. "And when did you last see your family, Mr. Dempsey?"

Dempsey looked confused. "Yesterday, the same as everyone else, when you let us all inside the wire for visiting hours." He paused. "But wait. If you're SRF, why didn't you know—"

There was a soft knock at the door.

"Excuse me, Mr. Dempsey," Luke said, rising and moving to the door.

He cracked the door to see Washington standing in the hallway, beckoning. He stepped into the hallway and closed the door behind him.

"What is it?" Luke asked.

"There's been some sort of problem at the camp," Washington said. "The colonel wants you up on the wall if you can break away."

Luke sighed and shook his head.

"What is it, Major? You don't look so good."

"We screwed up, Washington. Dempsey isn't a collaborator; they're holding his family hostage in the camp. That's how they're 'encouraging' all the people who are 'cooperating.'"

Washington looked puzzled, then a look of concern crossed his broad face. "You're worried those FEMA bastards are gonna think he took off and harm his family."

Luke nodded. "Maybe we got this guy's family killed."

Washington shook his head. "Probably not. Remember we grabbed the three SRF guys at the same time, and chances are, they found where our boat was pulled up in the mud. They'll likely just figure it for what it was."

"I hope you're right," Luke said. "But what's so important that can't wait?"

"I'm not sure. All I heard was trouble at the refugee camp; then the colonel asked me to come get you."

"All right, just let me tell Dempsey I'll be back later and then lock up here."

CHAPTER THIRTEEN

Luke hurried up the ladder to the top of the wall, to find Hunnicutt standing with Wright, staring in the direction of the refugee camp. He could hear gunfire in the distance.

"… and Miles' patrol was attacked by the mob, and someone opened fire on the crowd," Wright said. "There are fatalities and injuries, extent unknown."

"Dammit! I thought we told them—"

"Miles swears the fire came from a neighboring house, sir. He thinks it was bangers trying to stir things up."

Hunnicutt took off his helmet and ran a hand through his thinning hair as he muttered a curse. He glanced up as Luke arrived and turned back to Wright. "Major Kinsey is here, Lieutenant Wright, so go over the SITREP again, please."

Wright nodded toward Luke. "The refugees are rioting, but our folks are safe for the moment inside the swimming club perimeter, but it's going south in a hurry. I ordered the extraction protocol on my own initiative."

Hunnicutt nodded. "Good call. Status?"

"It'll be close, sir, but we should be okay," Wright said. "They have six up-armored Hummers and two school buses for the noncombatants. They'll exfiltrate from the country club east entrance on Pine Valley Drive in five minutes. Lieutenant Butler is organizing a relief column to roll out to support them if necessary. I turned Corporal Miles' patrol around with orders to hold the intersection of College Road and Pine Valley Drive, in case this is part of some larger attack we don't yet understand."

"Very good," Hunnicutt said. "Get our people out ASAP. Delay for nothing. Take only our people, our weapons, and vehicles. If anyone else objects, don't waste time arguing. Bring them out by force if necessary."

Wright nodded, then hesitated. "Confirm rules of engagement, sir?"

Luke saw Hunnicutt's jaw tighten. When he replied, it was slow and deliberate. "Scatter them with warning shots if possible. But you are weapons free at shooters' discretion. Don't take chances. All of our people are coming home alive."

FORT BOX
WILMINGTON CONTAINER TERMINAL
WILMINGTON, NORTH CAROLINA

SAME DAY, 3:10 P.M.

"Prior Planning Prevents Piss Poor Performance," Hunnicutt said with a satisfied nod as he stood on the wall an hour later and watched the little convoy roll through the gates of Fort Box. "SITREP, Wright?"

"No casualties, sir. Unless you count Dr. Jennings' pleasant disposition," Wright said. "She's madder than a wet hen and demanding to speak to you."

Hunnicutt sighed. "Which I'll do, sooner or later. But please hold her at bay until we get this mess sorted out."

Wright nodded. "Then I best go meet the convoy and give her a target. Though I'd rather trade fire with the bangers."

Hunnicutt chuckled and nodded his thanks, and Wright headed for the ladder down. Hunnicutt turned east and raised his binoculars. Smoke rose in towering columns from around the refugee camp. He shook his head.

He lowered the glasses. "What's it look like, Major?"

Luke shook his head. "Not good, sir. Washington and his team have eyes on the camp, or what's left of it. I sent them out with the relief column with orders to set up an overwatch. The rioting is general and aimless for now. They're burning everything in sight in and around the camp, but I think we can count on them heading this way. There's a lot of anger there, seeking a target."

Hunnicutt nodded and turned to Butler. "What was the camp census, Lieutenant Butler?"

"We stopped trying to estimate several days ago, sir," Butler said. "Given all the squatters in the surrounding neighborhoods, it was a near impossible task, but our best guess four days ago was at least thirty thousand."

Hunnicutt raised the binoculars again. "And they'll all be heading this way," he said softly as sporadic gunfire sounded in the distance.

WILMINGTON REFUGEE CAMP
(FORMERLY PINE VALLEY COUNTRY CLUB)
PINE VALLEY DRIVE
WILMINGTON, NORTH CAROLINA

SAME DAY, 5:40 P.M.

Kwintell Banks stood with Reaper by their technical, watching the mob on the golf course. All around the perimeter of the former country club, homes and businesses joined the club structures burning in the afternoon sun. Towering columns of smoke rolled skyward in the still air, and the acrid smell wafted across the now unkempt green expanse of the golf course.

Banks watched Darren Mosley at work. For all his shortcomings, Banks thought, nobody worked a crowd quite like Mosley. With Banks' permission, Mosley had dipped into the UBN provisions and handed out food and drink liberally, including cases of beer and whiskey. He was well on his way to convincing the mob he had all the answers.

It was a mixed crowd he addressed, black, white, and Hispanic refugees of all ages, some formerly middle class and others impoverished. They were all the same now: desperate people clinging to a miserable existence in squalor, surviving on inadequate rations of horrible food, all looking for someone to blame. Mosley was serving them up a target on a platter.

"… and that ain't all," Banks heard Mosley yell. "I was a soldier in there. North Carolina National Guard. Yes, I was. But I couldn't take it no more, couldn't live with myself. It's disgusting what they got inside, hidin' it away, not sharing with folks. Man, they got whole containers full of canned hams and shrimp and salmon. All kinds of shit. And what they feeding you? Crappy-ass boiled corn come off one of them skanky old foreign ships, probably full a rat turds, and not even American rat turds. Foreign rat turds. Chinese rat turds."

There were cries of agreement and outrage, scattered at first, then general as Mosley fired up the crowd.

"But you know what they ain't got? And what they want you to think they got a lot of? Ammunition. Oh, they got enough to make a show, but if we decide to go in there and take what we got coming, they can't stop us. They probably just gonna load up their boats and run away, just like they did here today."

Mosley paused and drank from the long-neck beer bottle in his hand. Refreshed, he redoubled his efforts, striding back and forth in the pickup bed, gesturing wildly to the crowd around him.

"You done this here today," he yelled, taking in the entire crowd with a sweeping gesture. "It was YOU who made them fool soldiers run. It's YOU they afraid of. I say we march right down to that dumb-ass little fort they built and DEMAND they give us the food they STOLE so we can share it out equal for everybody."

Mosley shot a look to Banks, who nodded, and Mosley turned back to the mob.

"WHAT DO YOU SAY? ARE YOU WITH ME?" Mosley screamed.

"YES!" the mob screamed in unison.

"ARE YOU READY TO GET SOME GOOD FOOD?"

"YES!" the mob screamed again.

"THEN GET YOUR ASSES IN GEAR, AND LET'S GO GET WHAT'S RIGHTFULLY OURS!"

With that, Mosley beat his fist on the top of the pickup, and the driver set out across the golf course, driving slowly as the crowd parted and fell in behind Mosley's truck like he was the Pied Piper, headed for Shipyard Boulevard and Fort Box beyond.

Banks looked over at Reaper. "What you think of my boys now?"

Reaper shrugged. "Any fool can talk big. We'll see how they do when bullets start flying, but this is a good diversion. We need to keep the guys with M4s and the technicals well back out of sight until we're ready to use 'em."

FORT BOX
WILMINGTON CONTAINER TERMINAL
WILMINGTON, NORTH CAROLINA

SAME DAY, 6:10 P.M.

Luke raced up the ladder. Hunnicutt stood on the wall with Wright and Butler.

"Lieutenant Washington says they're on the move, sir. Pretty much the entire mob as far as he can tell, with a few gangbangers mixed in," Luke said. "Things are about to get real, so I ordered Washington and his men to RTB."

Hunnicutt nodded. "Agreed. Please tell Lieutenant Washington I said well done."

He turned to Butler. "How many M2s do we still have along the river?"

"Two each on both the larger boats and one on the smaller boat. Plus a couple set up on the outboard side of the ships, placed to sweep the river in both directions." Butler hesitated. "Why, sir? You want to reposition them?"

"Some of them, yes," Hunnicutt said. "An attack from the river looks less likely, at least in the immediate future. What can you spare?"

Butler rubbed his chin. "We can take all four off the larger boats. The smaller boat is more mobile anyway, and between that gun and the two on the ship sides, we should be able to handle any threats from the river. At least long enough to reposition guns if necessary."

"Do it," Hunnicutt said. "Work with Lieutenant Wright here to reposition them. Space them evenly along the top of the wall to supplement the guns at each corner."

Wright spoke up. "We'll have to improvise, sir. We won't have time to armor them like the corner gun emplacements or the other firing positions."

Hunnicutt nodded. "I understand; use sand bags or whatever you can find. I doubt they'll be taking fire anyway. My hope is seeing them stretched along the wall will serve as an intimidation factor. The best battle is one you don't have to fight, gentlemen."

"Amen to that, sir," Butler said, moving toward the ladder to carry out his orders, with Wright close behind.

"You really think they'll attack, sir?" Luke asked.

"Hunger and desperation make people do extreme things," Hunnicutt said. "But I hope staring up at the wrong end of a row of M2s, with maybe a burst or two fired above their heads, will bring them to their senses. But if it doesn't… well, we'll just have to be prepared to deal with that."

Luke shook his head. "Even the dumbest of them should understand they're no match for armed soldiers in prepared positions with crew-served weapons."

Hunnicutt turned and looked to the east. "You would think so," he said. "But there are thousands of them, and as Stalin once said, quantity has a quality all its own."

***

The leading edge of the mob came into view twenty minutes later, surging up Shipyard Boulevard. Hunnicutt ordered the gate in the outer perimeter fence closed and locked, and reinforced it by having two of the container transporters block the gate completely with several containers pre-staged nearby for that purpose. The big machines completed the task and moved back inside the stout defensive walls of Fort Box itself, where they duplicated their efforts and barricaded the more substantial gate there as well. The defenders were as ready as they could be.

As the mob reached the fence, Hunnicutt got his first inkling of trouble. Rather than massing at the gate as anticipated, the mob spread down the fence line in both directions at the exhortations of a man in the back of a pickup and his minions. Fighting a rising unease, Hunnicutt adapted and ordered defenders spread more evenly along the threatened walls, in between the newly repositioned machine guns.

Beside Hunnicutt, Luke watched the mob flow down the fence line. "I'm not liking this. This looks way too coordinated for a rioting mob."

"Agreed, but we'll handle whatever they throw at us. Hopefully without a wholesale slaughter," Hunnicutt said.

Luke looked due west at the sun nearing the horizon. "I'm not sure the intimidation factor is going to work, sir. The sun's directly in their eyes now. They probably can't see the machine guns that well. Should we fire a burst over their heads to give them a clue?"

Hunnicutt looked west then glanced at his watch. "Let's not waste the show. We'll wait till they all have a ringside seat and light 'em up. How many are loaded with tracer?"

"Every other gun," Luke said, and Hunnicutt nodded.

They stood in silence and watched the mass of humanity flow against the chain-link fence, screaming and shaking fists and improvised weapons.

LOUISIANA STREET
2 BLOCKS FROM THE PERIMETER FENCE

SAME DAY, 6:50 P.M.

Banks stood in the street next to the technical, listening to the radio squawk and reduced to observer status as Reaper directed the operation. The technicals were spread evenly along the perimeter fence, one to two blocks back and out of sight from the fort walls. His own men, weapons concealed, were spread evenly at the back of the mob along the fence. They were anonymous faces in the crowd, with the bulk of the milling mass of screaming refugees between them and the guns of Fort Box.

All except for the baby gangstas. Fifty preteens were spread across the front of the mob near the fence, all volunteers eager to prove their worth to the UBN. The single qualification for their current task was sufficient strength to operate the bolt cutters they kept concealed in plastic garbage bags. They would strike at the first gunfire either from Fort Box, or if that was not forthcoming, from their brothers at the back of the mob. Their task was simple: cut the fence to ribbons along its entire length.

Banks glanced over at Reaper. "I don't like this. We shoulda made the signal something else. Them soldiers can shoot any time; what if we ain't ready?"

"What's important is that the fence gets cut. Exactly when makes no difference. If we made the signal something else, half those little morons would miss it. This way, all they have to remember is 'hear guns, cut the fence.' Even they can remember that," Reaper said. He narrowed his eyes. "And you let me worry about things like that. You're starting to get on my nerves again."

Banks fell silent, and Reaper looked down the street and grinned. A pickup approached, and Banks saw people in the bed. They were all women and children, refugees in ragged clothes with haggard faces. Their wrists were zip-tied, and terrified eyes showed over duct-taped mouths.

"Put them in the bed of the technical," Reaper yelled to the driver of the arriving pickup. "Zip-tie 'em to the rack, standing up, and make sure they can be seen."

Banks stared. "What the hell you doin', Reaper?"

Reaper grinned. "That's an unauthorized question, fool. But I'll give you a pass, seein' as how I'm in a good mood. That's 'enhanced armor.' When it hits the fan, the technicals are gonna be priority targets, so I'm givin' our heroes over there in Fort Box a little extra to think about before they pull the trigger."

Reaper's smile faded. "Now you ridin' with me. So get your ass up in the bed of that truck before I put you in a dress and mount you as a hood ornament."

FORT BOX
WILMINGTON CONTAINER TERMINAL

"GIVE US OUR FOOD! GIVE US OUR FOOD!" the mob chanted in unison, those nearest the fence shaking the chain link in time to the chant. Luke looked on with growing concern as Hunnicutt swept the fence with his binoculars, then dropped them to hang on his chest by the strap.

Hunnicutt sighed. "I guess it's time to offer a bit of discouragement, Major."

"Yes, sir," Luke said, raising the radio mic. "All tracer-loaded guns, repeat, all tracer-loaded guns, fire a short burst over the heads of the hostiles on my signal. Confirm. Over."

He listened as each gun confirmed promptly; then he gave the order. "All tracer-loaded guns, execute. Repeat, execute."

All along the wall, the guns barked, and fiery tracers shot out hot and straight, well over the heads of the screaming refugees. The chanting stopped at once, silenced by the fifty-caliber snarl. When the guns stopped scant seconds later, a deathly quiet fell over the fort and mob alike.

Like a hysterical person slapped back to sanity, the mob was shocked, and on the wall, soldiers held their breath, hoping this would end it. Hunnicutt raised the glasses again, scanning the faces pressed up against the fence, encouraged by what he saw. Maybe it would be this easy after all.

And then he saw an African-American boy perhaps twelve years old, perhaps younger, resolutely cutting through the chain-link fence with a pair of bolt cutters almost as big as he was. The cut was already two feet from the bottom of the fence and growing. Oh God, please not this, he thought, a lump in his throat. It took three tries to get the next order past his lips.

"Corporal Miles," he said to the rifleman kneeling to his right, "there is a perimeter breach directly in front of us. Take him out. Now."

Miles raised his M4, searching, then looked up at the colonel. "Sir, it's… it's a kid. I… I can't shoot a kid."

Hunnicutt's voice was shaking, "That's an order, Miles."

"But, sir —"

"PERIMETER BREACH!" came a scream from down the wall, followed by a second, then a third.

Things seem to go in slow motion for Hunnicutt, and he felt a steely calm run through him. He put a hand down on Miles' shoulder. "Take the shot, son," he said softly. "This is on me, not you."

The young soldier looked up with glistening eyes, bobbed his head once, and raised his rifle. The sound of the shot seemed to tear through Hunnicutt's own heart. He shook it off and turned to Luke.

"Pass the order, Major. Weapons free. Repeat, weapons free. Anyone inside the fence is a legitimate target."

The fence was fully breached in two dozen places before they got the situation neutralized. The mob reacted like a living thing, recoiling from the fence in panic, none even attempting to enter the newly opened breaks now blocked by dead children's bodies. Hunnicutt ordered a cease-fire and crossed his fingers.

But it was not to be. He heard sustained gunfire behind the mob, and like a blind and wounded beast, the massed humanity surged back toward the fence and Fort Box beyond, charging without thought, reacting to the immediate pain. It crashed into the fence with a horrific scream, those refugees nearest the fence unable to prevent themselves from being pinned against it. Some, the lucky ones, were forced through the multiple breaches. Free from the crush of the mob, they looked fearfully towards the fort walls, raised their hands in surrender, and huddled near the groaning fence, unable to retreat and terrified of going forward. Hunnicutt ordered his men to hold their fire.

But it was only a matter of time. Gunfire continued to come from the back of the mob, though the exact source was impossible to ascertain. The fence was leaning along its entire length with the press of thirty thousand refugees. Blood dripped from the chain link as faces and hands and arms and legs were mashed into the wire, far beyond the limits mere flesh could endure.

And then it happened. At places the mesh separated from the poles, and in others the poles themselves toppled over, concrete foundations breaking free of the ground like uprooted trees in a windstorm. Whatever their pattern, the failures occurred in quick succession, and in seconds the perimeter fence ceased to exist. The mob flowed toward the defenders like a fast-rising tide.

And on the tide came sharks. The shooters drove the mob forward at gunpoint, more visible now, but always careful to stay close enough to use the mob as cover. As they cleared the battered remnants of the fence, the shooters ran forward, mixing in the terrified and milling crowd to turn their fire toward Fort Box.

What they lacked in accuracy, they made up in volume. Hunnicutt heard a grunt, and he looked down to see Miles down, blood flowing from a shoulder wound.

"IT'S BANGERS. THERE MUST BE A THOUSAND OF THEM!" Luke shouted.

"TARGET THE SHOOTERS," Hunnicutt yelled.

Along the wall the defenders fired sporadically, coping with the near impossible task of differentiating between armed bangers and their human shields. The horrific roar of the battle increased, augmented by the sound of roaring engines and stuttering machine guns as the technicals burst from hiding and roared forward.

It was all about survival now, and every defender knew it without the need for orders or commands. The fire increased without regard to collateral damage as defenders began to fall. A machine gun fell silent, victim of sustained fire from two of the technicals. Another ceased to exist, hit by an RPG. The attackers' strategy was obvious, and by unspoken agreement, the defenders turned their fire on the technicals.

And paused. There was a perceptible lull in defensive fire as the defenders saw the technicals' ghastly human armor. But in the end, it could make no difference. Tracers streaked toward the technicals from the M2s and drew fire and RPGs in return. Riflemen pulled triggers again and again, tears rolling down their cheeks as their rounds tore through innocents to impact the monsters behind them. Each defender became an emotional island, the revulsion and shame at their own action fusing into a white-hot hatred of the bastards who forced them to it.

It lasted fifteen minutes — and forever. Here and there, a banger reached the wall with a grappling hook on a rope, but such penetrations were few and easily dealt with. In the end, the human shield strategy proved to be the attackers' undoing. The mass of refugees was packed so tightly against the walls, the bangers behind them couldn't reach the wall in any significant numbers. They found themselves a readily identifiable fringe at the back edge of the packed mob, and easy targets for the defenders. They fell in increasing numbers, and the more intelligent among them hid or dropped their weapons and burrowed into the safety and anonymity of the crowd.

When the attack stalled, the technicals changed tactics. Oblivious to the huddled refugees, they targeted their remaining RPGs at one small area at the base of the wall, hoping to force a breach. A half dozen explosions rocked the sidewall of a single container and opened a gaping hole. But the inside wall of the container held, and the surviving technicals fled the field. By dusk, it was over.

And the worst was just beginning.

CHAPTER FOURTEEN

FORT BOX
WILMINGTON CONTAINER TERMINAL
WILMINGTON, NORTH CAROLINA

SAME DAY, 10:30 P.M.

The guns fell silent in the gloaming, replaced by the heartrending cries of the dying and wounded. Hunnicutt forced himself to ignore it and concentrate on the tasks at hand. He ordered all available night-vision equipment spread along the wall and posted an overwatch. Anyone approaching the wall was labeled a threat and terminated. Anyone fleeing the huddled mass of refugees along the wall was allowed to leave unmolested unless they were armed, in which case they were to be terminated.

Those defenders without night-vision glasses worked by flashlight, assisting wounded comrades and carrying down the dead. They moved silently, on wooden limbs, and spoke in quiet monosyllables when they spoke at all, barely audible above the piteous cries outside the walls. More than one defender broke down and sobbed, and Hunnicutt had cotton balls brought up from the dispensary. They stuffed their ears and kept working.

***

Hunnicutt heard approaching footsteps and turned to see a flashlight bobbing toward him along the top of the wall. "That you, Luke?"

"Yes, sir," came Luke's voice.

"How bad?"

"Twenty-three, sir. Seventeen wounded and... and six KIA."

Hunnicutt didn't speak for a long moment. When he did, his voice had a detached, almost philosophical tone. "It sounds better somehow, doesn't it? KIA, I mean. Somehow less final than dead. Noble somehow."

Luke didn't respond, and Hunnicutt shook himself out of his funk. "Sorry, Major. How about the wounded? Are any of them..."

"Three are critical, sir. Dr. Jennings doesn't think one will survive the night, but she's optimistic about the other two."

Hunnicutt nodded, then realized Luke couldn't see him in the dark. "Very well. Continue to rotate personnel on the night-vision glasses every two hours. Everyone not on watch should get some sleep. I have a feeling we're going to need all the rest we can get."

"Yes sir," Luke said, but he didn't move away. "What about... out there?"

The moans and cries of the wounded outside the walls had subsided into background noise, punctuated by sporadic shrieks of pain and the crack of M4s as armed bangers attempted to leave the scene.

Hunnicutt shook his head. "We can't send anyone out there to help them until morning when we can reestablish a perimeter. We don't know how many hostiles are still in the mob, and there are at least a half dozen technicals still out there somewhere. Anyone outside the walls would be sitting ducks. You know that."

Luke sighed. "Agreed, sir. But with respect, I don't think you should be standing here dwelling on it either. You need rest too."

"I'll be down directly, Major, but thank you for your concern."

***

Despite his promise, Hunnicutt paced the wall all night, listening as the moans outside the fort faded. As if by agreement, his subordinates left him with his own demons. As the sky lightened in the east, Hunnicutt confronted the sight he'd been dreading. The carnage was even worse than he remembered. He sank down cross-legged on the hard steel of the container, buried his face in his hands, and wept.

After a while, he felt the warmth of the sun on top of his bowed head, then looked up, wiped his eyes with the back of his hand, and rose. There was work to be done.

***

Relief washed over Luke as Hunnicutt descended the ladder and started toward him with a determined step.

"SITREP, Major Kinsey," Hunnicutt said.

"We're maintaining overwatch, sir. There don't appear to be any more armed hostiles in the crowd. At some point during the night, they must have figured it out and begun to leave unarmed. Nor is there any sign of the technicals, but Lieutenant Wright is preparing a reconnaissance using the up-armored Hummers. Lieutenant Butler is seeing to the disposition of forces along the wall, and Dr. Jennings reports that two of the critically wounded are out of the woods. She expects them to make full recoveries. But I'm sorry to say the third casualty didn't make it, sir."

Hunnicutt's jaw tightened. "Who?"

"One of your folks, sir. Corporal Susan Phelps. She was—"

Hunnicutt nodded. "A driver in the transport group. She's from Hankins Corner. Engaged to be married next month; her boyfriend's name is… was Byron." He sighed. "Who else?"

"Corporal Miles—"

"I saw Miles get hit. It didn't look like a mortal injury, and I saw him being attended to—"

"He returned to the firing line and was hit a second time manning an M2."

"A good man," Hunnicutt said softly. "Who else?"

"Another guardsman, sir. I'm sorry, but I can't recall his name offhand. And two of the guys who came in with me, Corley and Abrams, former jarheads. And the Coasties lost Wilson and Fontaine. All the units lost someone."

"We're all one unit, Luke," Hunnicutt said.

"Well, if we weren't, we are now," Luke said.

Hunnicutt nodded, then looked toward the waterfront. Luke followed his gaze to see Levi Jenkins and both the Gibson brothers approaching, long guns slung and followed by a group of armed men.

"What's going on?" Hunnicutt asked.

"I took the liberty of radioing Levi to bring him up to speed and expedite the call for volunteers. We have no clue what we're up against."

Hunnicutt gave an approving nod just as the group reached them.

"Sorry we couldn't get here any sooner," Levi said. "We didn't have enough boats to move this many people at once without leaving the folks on the river short on transportation. Some of them just ferried us down and went back for the others. Can you top them up with fuel for the trip home?"

"Absolutely," Hunnicutt said, extending his hand. "Thank you for coming."

The three men nodded as Luke studied the group, trying to count heads.

"There's a lot more of you than I expected," he said. "How many?"

"This isn't all of us," Levi said. "We got about thirty here, but there are a hundred and fourteen all told."

"Outstanding. Thank you," Luke said.

Levi nodded toward the Gibson brothers. "Don't thank me, thank them. Turns out they're natural born recruiters. Where you want us?"

Luke glanced toward Hunnicutt. "I was thinking they could relieve our folks on the wall. As soon as we can get a new perimeter established, we have a lot to do."

Hunnicutt nodded grimly. "Let's get it done, Major."

**

Wright led his up-armored Humvees in a sweep through the nearby neighborhood. Finding it all clear, he ordered them back into a protective ring around Fort Box at the point formerly marked by the perimeter fence, and positioned them facing outward in mutually supporting positions. Only then did Hunnicutt allow Dr. Jennings and a team of volunteers to treat the still living among the fallen refugees.

If Hunnicutt had expected recriminations from Jennings, he got none, for even she recognized the impossible situation in which he found himself. Instead she combed through the shattered specimens of humanity, seeking signs of life. She found almost a hundred, including a dozen who were clearly bangers and four in the wreckage of the technicals who appeared to be something else entirely.

It was only at that point Hunnicutt and Jennings clashed, with the colonel insistent the former combatants be physically restrained and treated in a tent outside the walls of the fort. After a halfhearted and somewhat obligatory protest, Jennings let it go. Beyond her Hippocratic oath, she had no sympathy for the savages who caused this carnage.

After attending to the living, they turned to the dead, a task made more urgent by the weather and the southern sun. Their own honored dead were buried as they had fallen, together, a twenty-foot container their shared coffin.

Flags were no problem; the ever-resourceful Wright discovered a container containing two pallet loads of American flags among its mixed cargo, made in China, of course. He found folding cots from the same source, which they mounted permanently in the container turned sarcophagus, to hold the flag-draped remains of their fallen comrades. They welded the vents and doors shut while a backhoe made short work of the asphalt in a secluded corner of Fort Box and dug a perfectly rectangular hole to receive the container.

They left six inches of the container protruding from the ground as both a headstone and monument. The best welder in the group inscribed the names of each of the fallen in weld bead on top of the container. The improvised sarcophagus was lowered into the hole slowly and reverently, with full military honors.

Then Hunnicutt dismissed the company, and they set about the altogether more grisly task of dealing with the refugees. There were hundreds of bodies clustered near the walls or spread across the asphalt in a macabre tableau of violent death, and over a hundred more dead bangers facedown near the remains of the perimeter fence, weapons on the asphalt beside them.

Hunnicutt asked for volunteers and set the example by being the first volunteer himself, despite his rank. When almost everyone followed his lead, he divided them into five teams to finish the task as quickly as possible. They turned once again to their store of empty containers and positioned five twenty-footers on the asphalt as group coffins.

They handled the bodies as respectfully as possible, but the sheer volume of the task and the need to get the corpses sealed inside the containers before decomposition began mandated they work as quickly as possible. They reserved four of the containers for the refugees, and used the fifth for the bangers. It didn't seem fitting to bury the sheep with the wolves.

The work went mercifully quickly, and by noon it was complete. Hunnicutt left instructions for the disposition of the containers and went to his quarters to stand under the blasting hot shower for long minutes, his guilt at wasting precious water overcome by the need to feel clean. But he felt dirty to his soul and doubted he'd ever really feel clean again.

He'd just changed into a fresh uniform when he heard a tentative tap at his door. "Come," he said. The door opened and Luke stood in the threshold.

"We're ready, sir," Luke said.

Hunnicutt nodded. "Thank you, Major. It will take me a moment to collect my thoughts. Please have the garrison assembled in thirty minutes."

Luke nodded and started to leave, then turned back to Hunnicutt. "What can you say after something like this, sir? Words just seem so… so inadequate, somehow."

Hunnicutt smiled sadly. "My thoughts as well, but I have to give them something, some… I don't know, some closure somehow. They've just been through a horrific ordeal. If they can't put it behind them, it'll eat at us like a cancer."

Luke shook his head. "But how?"

Hunnicutt hesitated, thinking. "Ever heard of the 'conscience round,' Luke?"

"You mean like the blank they loaded at random in a firing squads' rifles, so no one was sure whether or not they fired the killing shot?"

Hunnicutt nodded. "We'll have to do some difficult things to survive, but some things — things like we did yesterday, if we have to do those things too often, our humanity won't survive."

"But it's done, Colonel. And it can't be undone. So how can you —"

Hunnicutt held up his hand. "I don't know, Luke. But hopefully it will come to me in the next half hour."

* * *

Thirty minutes later, Hunnicutt stepped out of the HQ building into the afternoon heat and strode across the asphalt to their newly designated cemetery. As ordered, the garrison was formed up in ranks in front of four neatly excavated holes in the asphalt. The coffin containers were lined up neatly to one side, one of the half doors slightly ajar on each container, as Hunnicutt had ordered. He glanced toward the walls of the fort and saw the river volunteers standing at attention, facing inward toward the cemetery, except every third man, who faced outward to maintain a watch. *Good folks, those river people*, Hunnicutt thought.

He spotted Luke at the head of the garrison and motioned him over to hand him four sealed Ziploc bags and a roll of duct tape.

"Major, please see that one of these bags is taped securely to the inside door of each container, then have them sealed and prepared for burial."

"Yes, sir," Luke said, and went about the task as ordered.

Hunnicutt watched Luke in whispered conversation with the senior noncom before returning to his place at the head of the garrison. Five minutes later the task was complete, and Hunnicutt heard the screech of the locking bars as the containers were sealed for the last time. He waited until everyone returned to ranks, then extracted a folded paper from his pocket. He took a deep breath and began to speak.

"We gathered earlier today to perform the sad and solemn task of honoring our fallen comrades. We come together now to pay our respects to those who, through no fault of their own, fell before our guns. These were not evil people, but victims. Not our victims, but victims of those who would use and manipulate them. They were driven not by hatred, but by fear and desperation, and taken advantage of by evil men. Though they died by our hands, it was not by our intention, and I know there is no one among us who does not wish with all their heart and soul this tragic outcome could've been avoided."

Hunnicutt unfolded the piece of paper.

"I've prepared a statement and placed a copy in each of the coffin containers. I did so in anticipation of some future time when normalcy is restored. I would like to read it to you now."

There was a murmur in the ranks, which Hunnicutt ignored.

"In these containers lie the remains of eight hundred and fifty-two souls, known only to God, who died by my hand and on my orders on the thirtieth day of April, 2020. I accept full and sole responsibility for these deaths and am prepared to provide a full accounting of my actions at such time as a legitimate government is established to hear my account.

"At no time or in no way did any of the officers or troops serving under my command act except at my direct orders. Collectively and individually, they behaved properly and honorably and maintained the highest standards of the American soldier.

"We lay these souls to rest, on this, the first day of May, 2020. May God have mercy upon their souls, and upon mine.

"Colonel Douglas David Hunnicutt, Commanding

"Wilmington Defense Force

"Fort Box

"Wilmington, North Carolina"

Hunnicutt folded the paper and slipped it back into his pocket.

"And on a personal note," Hunnicutt said, "let me say that I have never had the honor of commanding or serving with a finer group of people."

There was no loud cheer or shouted response, nor did he expect one. Rather there were scattered nods and a glistening eye here and there. They knew what he was doing, and whether it mitigated their collective guilt or not, they loved him for it. The feeling grew into an almost palpable thing, and the healing began.

"Major Kinsey," Hunnicutt said, "please proceed with the interment."

Luke nodded and motioned to the heavy equipment operators, who mounted their machines and began to lower the containers to their final resting places. Throughout the garrison, people bowed their heads or murmured prayers or placed their hands over their hearts. Halfway through the interment, the clear sweet notes of 'Amazing Grace' rang out across the Fort, and the group turned to see Donny Gibson on the wall, singing a cappella. One by one, the river men on the wall joined him, as did the garrison. The last note sounded as the final container was laid to rest in the mass grave.

The lump in Hunnicutt's throat made it difficult to dismiss the formation.

MUNICIPAL WASTEWATER TREATMENT PLANT
RIVER ROAD
WILMINGTON, NORTH CAROLINA

DAY 31, 3:20 P.M.

Luke rode in the lead vehicle as the little convoy wound its way down River Road. There were five vehicles in all: two Humvees front and back, with the container transporter riding in the middle. The technicals were still unaccounted for, which necessitated any trip outside the immediate area of the fort to be of sufficient strength to repel an attack.

If the burial of their comrades and the refugees was an emotional task, no such positive or respectful feelings were attached to the disposal of the remains of their attackers. This was simply taking out the trash, and Wright's suggestion of a suitable disposal site won quick and universal acceptance. Luke nodded to the driver and they made a right turn into the sewage treatment plant.

It didn't take long to find the holding pond. They stopped alongside and Luke got out of the Hummer. He motioned for the transporter to drop the container as far as possible up the sloping berm surrounding the pond. The driver did as ordered, managing to leave it teetering on top of the berm at a crazy angle. The transporter moved away, and one of the Humvees nosed up to the end of the container, and tires spinning and engine roaring, tipped the container the rest of the way over the berm, into the fetid waters of the pond.

Luke and his men watched as the container drifted to the middle of the pond, slowly sinking as water rushed in the holes they'd drilled in the bottom.

"Ashes to ashes, shit to shit. May you all burn in Hell," Luke said.

"Hallelujah, amen," one of his men added, with a derisive snort.

"You reckon they might pollute the pond?" another asked, to general laughter.

"Let's saddle up and get out of here," Luke said, and they all moved back to their vehicles.

OVER FORT BOX
WILMINGTON CONTAINER TERMINAL
WILMINGTON, NORTH CAROLINA

DAY 32, 7:10 A.M.

Rorke heard the muted thump of the chopper blades muffled through his headphones as they circled high above the fort. Far below, heavy equipment was moving new containers in to replace those damaged during the attack.

"They're rebounding pretty fast," Rorke said into his mic. "And it looks like they have a lot more people on the wall, and some of them aren't in uniform."

Beside him, Reaper shrugged. "I don't think it makes much difference, General. Bodies alone won't make much difference, and they have to be low on ammo now. A Guard unit in peacetime wouldn't have had a very big ammo load out to start with, and they can't have much left. We ain't gonna sword fight them; another attack like the last one and they're finished."

"You got anybody left to attack them WITH, especially after what happened?"

Reaper laughed. "Funny how it happens, isn't it? The bangers are mostly shot to hell and useless. We might get a little more mileage out of them somewhere, but I seriously doubt we'll get them to throw themselves at that wall again. They're dumb, but they're not completely stupid. But the refugees, that's a different story. Most of them are cowed, right enough, but some are white-hot mad at the fort for killing their friends and relatives. They're so pissed they don't seem to connect with the fact it was us that threw them under the bus, and those that have a clue blame the bangers, not us. We play our cards right and spread some of those MREs around, I think I can recruit us 'Indigenous Force Act Two.' It will just take a little patience, that's all."

"How much patience?" Rorke asked.

Reaper shrugged again. "Two, three weeks tops."

"You have two, and another fifty advisers. But at two weeks and one day, I want possession of that fort and all of their supplies. Is that clear?"

"Crystal, General," Reaper replied.

Rorke nodded and looked down at the fort. "Well, it wasn't the success I'd hoped for, but we've hurt them badly at little cost. As you say, they must be low on ammunition and are undoubtedly demoralized at having slaughtered the very people they were trying to save." He smiled. "They may even disintegrate on their own. Anyway, they're much less of a threat than they were two days ago, and they're no longer squandering my supplies on the refugee rabble. We'll just let them sit there until we're ready to take them out for good."

FORT BOX
WILMINGTON CONTAINER TERMINAL
WILMINGTON, NORTH CAROLINA

DAY 32, 8:15 A.M.

"You're sure?" Hunnicutt asked, looking around the table at what he'd come to think of as his war council. Luke Kinsey and Joel Washington were there, as was Josh Wright and Mike Butler. As a courtesy, Levi Jenkins and the Gibson brothers were now sitting in, representing the river volunteers.

Washington nodded. "Absolutely, sir. They're SRF, and the mercenary scum, not the recruits from regular forces like us." He looked toward Luke for support.

"Washington's right, sir," Luke said. "I recognize them too. Two of them were in Jacksonville when we were."

Hunnicutt grunted. "Well, too bad none of the wounded ones made it. I'd have loved to get some intel out of those bastards."

Across the table, Mike Butler shrugged. "Well, a half dozen of the bangers did survive, and they seem pretty pissed at their 'advisers.' Every one of them identifies these SRF thugs as being from 'the pirate in the chopper.' I think that's pretty definitive."

"It's Rorke, all right," Luke said. "They all describe him to a T."

"Pretty smart, actually," Wright said. "I mean, they risk a few of their own guys and throw the bangers out as cannon fodder. It's quite a force multiplier. If they win, they bought a cheap victory, and if they lose, they haven't lost much."

Hunnicutt sighed. "And when we won, we didn't really win anything, except staying alive to fight another day. How do we stand?"

Butler glanced at his legal pad. "We picked up almost two hundred M4s from the fallen bangers and scavenged six M240s from the disabled technicals, along with some ammo for each. But that's our Achilles' heel. We burned through ammo like a house afire." He shook his head. "No way we could survive another attack like that, even if the mob is carrying clubs."

Hunnicutt nodded. "You think your friend Sergeant Hill would guide a little trip to the Military Ocean Terminal?"

"Absolutely, sir," Butler said. "But I'm pretty sure SRF will have more forces guarding the place now, especially after our previous trip. It will be tough to sneak in and out with enough ammo for our entire force."

Hunnicutt shook his head. "That's not exactly what I had in mind." He turned to Luke Kinsey. "How's Dempsey doing?"

Luke shook his head. "I almost wish I hadn't told him. When he finally accepted we'd snatched him and his family was still back behind the wire, he's been going crazy."

"Understandable, but we need to get him calmed down, because I think we're going to need him," Hunnicutt said.

"I'm a bit confused, sir," Butler said. "What's the Duke Power guy got to do with any of this, and if we're not going to slip in and steal ammo, what's the plan?"

Hunnicutt smiled enigmatically. "Gentlemen, in another life, I was a history teacher, and despite my love of my home state, I've always harbored a deep and abiding admiration for Joshua Lawrence Chamberlain and the Twentieth Maine. Are you all familiar with Colonel Chamberlain's defense of Little Round Top during the Battle of Gettysburg?"

A few heads nodded, some more confidently than others.

"Chamberlain was in a somewhat similar situation," Hunnicutt said. "Out of ammunition and besieged by a larger, seemingly more capable force, it appeared his only option was surrender. But he —"

"Ordered his men to fix bayonets and charged, breaking the back of the attack and saving the day for the Union," Josh Wright finished.

"Exactly, Lieutenant Wright. Exactly." Hunnicutt's face hardened. "I'll be damned if I'll sit here waiting for this man Rorke to crush us like a bug. He's about to find out some bugs have a deadly sting."

CHAPTER FIFTEEN

Six Days Earlier
Day 26, 7:20 p.m.

Matt Kinsey shifted uncomfortably against the hard bottom of the boat and leaned forward to relieve the pressure on his aching arms. His hands were behind him, bound at the wrists with duct tape, and the edge of the seat he'd been forced to lean against for the past two hours had restricted circulation. He was losing feeling in his fingers.

The Cajuns had separated them, placing Bollinger in the Coast Guard boat with the two underlings while Kinsey rode in the Cajuns' boat with the older man who'd done all of the talking. They backtracked up the channel north to Calumet and from there into the Atchafalaya River, only to leave the main channel of the river an hour later to wind their way through a maze of twisting, narrow bayous beneath towering cypress trees. Kinsey was facing backwards, and he watched the Cajun at the outboard deftly maneuver the boat through the narrow channel, the electric trolling motor up and out of use at his side.

"I can't feel my hands," Kinsey said. "You think you could adjust these bindings?"

The Cajun glared at him and spat over the side.

Kinsey tried a different approach. "What's with the trolling motor?"

"You writing a book, *couyon*."

Kinsey shrugged. "Just curious."

The Cajun said nothing for a long moment then shrugged himself. "When we leave the bayou, we like to be quiet."

"How'd you find us?" Kinsey asked. "I know you couldn't see us."

The Cajun smiled. "Just lucky, *couyon*. We drain diesel from the barges. All those tank barges have pump engines, and the engines have fuel tanks, *non*? Even if the barge is empty, there's fifty or sixty gallons of fuel there, and the tanks are nice and high — easy to drain into the cans in our boat."

Kinsey tried to keep the conversation going. "You know we had nothing to do with what happened to your family. We're not even here on an official mission. I'm just trying to find my family in Baton Rouge."

The Cajun's face hardened. "So when you try to scare me, you're Coast Guard, but when you're caught and tied up, you're just a simple man trying to find his family. Very convenient, *couyon*. But a fancy boat, M4 rifles, and night-vision equipment, they tell a different story, eh? Besides, you ain't from Baton Rouge or anywhere around here. You're a Yankee, for sure. There's no family in Baton Rouge."

"I'm from Wisconsin originally," Kinsey said, "but my wife's maiden name was Melancon, and my daughter goes to LSU. She's on the soccer team."

"And your wife, she is in Baton Rouge?"

Kinsey shook his head. "She passed some years back, and I haven't heard from my daughter since this all started. I hope she's with my sister-in-law's family in Baton Rouge."

The Cajun said nothing, suddenly intent on something ahead. Kinsey twisted at the waist, straining to see. In his peripheral vision, he could just make out the stern of the Coast Guard boat rounding a huge cypress tree, the trailer close behind, into an even narrower channel. The Cajun reduced speed, and seconds later followed the Coast Guard boat into the smaller bayou.

"Where are we going?" Kinsey asked.

The man ignored him, and fifteen minutes later the boat bumped against a low wooden dock where several men waited. There was a hurried exchange in a combination of French and heavily accented English, and Kinsey and Bollinger were dragged from the boats and hustled down a path through the cypress swamp to a clearing with a dozen houses on an island of high ground in the wetland, the term 'high' being relative. All the houses were constructed of rough-cut cypress planks, gray with age, but there the similarity ended. Some were small, little more than sheds, but others were large and sprawling and looked as if they'd been added on to willy-nilly. They'd all been there awhile, that was obvious.

Kinsey's appraisal was cut short as he and Bollinger were marched up the rickety wooden stairs of one of the smaller buildings and forced to the floor. Their captors bound their ankles together with duct tape and left without saying a word, closing the door behind them. A padlock rattled in a hasp and then silence.

"What are we gonna do now, boss?" Bollinger asked.

Kinsey shook his head. "Damned if I know. Looks like the only way in and out of this place is by boat. Do you think you can find your way out if we stole one?"

Bollinger looked skeptical. "Lots of twists and turns, and all this swamp looks alike. We must have passed a couple of dozen little interconnecting channels. Even if we can steal a boat, I doubt anyone could get in and out of here without knowing the landmarks. I'm thinking that's why they didn't bother to blindfold us."

"Either that, or they don't figure on leaving us alive long enough to try to escape," Kinsey said.

***

Andrew Cormier peeked into the darkened room. His daughter-in-law sat at the bedside in a straight-backed chair, silently reading a Bible in the light of a kerosene lamp. A floorboard creaked as he shifted his weight, and Lisa looked up and put a finger to her lips. She rose quietly to join him, softly closing the bedroom door behind her.

"How is he?" Cormier asked.

"He's been in and out of consciousness since we got the bullet out. But he's in a lot of pain, so I think it's better when he's unconscious. He has a fever, so I'm afraid the wound is infected. I only wish we had a real doctor and antibiotics and better pain medication and..." The woman shook her head, unable to continue.

Cormier nodded sadly then shrugged. "We have what we have, *cher*. And my son is a strong man." He pulled the woman into his embrace and whispered in her ear, "And besides, it takes more than one bullet to kill a Cormier, *eh*."

She nodded and her body moved in what could have been a laugh or sob or both, and he put his hands on her shoulders and held her at arm's length. She looked gaunt and hollow eyed, with the pain of a lifetime written prematurely across her young face.

"But, *cher*? Maybe you should be resting—"

The woman shook her head and gave him a wan smile before gently disengaging his hands. "I'm a Cormier now too, Pop." Her face hardened. "And I won't shrink into a shell because of... because of what they did to me."

Cormier could only nod, not trusting himself to speak. After a long moment, he found his voice.

"We caught two of the bastards this afternoon."

She stared at him, blood in her eye. "FEMA?"

He shrugged. "They dressed like Coast Guard and claim they're looking for family, but who knows? And even if they are, it doesn't mean they're any better than the FEMA bastards. The world has gone crazy, *cher*, and we're safer here with the old ways. We trust no one who isn't from the bayou. We'll survive here like our ancestors did, and any *fils putain* stupid enough to come in after us will be gator food."

Andrew Cormier had been a gentle man, a good father and husband, quick with a joke and equally quick to laugh at one. All that changed two horrible weeks ago in a once well-kept suburb of Lafayette. He'd been away from the house at the time, out with his neighbors on bicycles, scavenging for food. He'd returned to find his home ransacked, his wife murdered and his son near death, and his daughter-in-law naked and tied spread-eagled to a bed in the back of the house. He'd cared for his son and daughter-in-law as well as he could, buried his wife in the backyard, and then loaded his family in his truck and, bass boat trailing behind, used their small hidden store of gasoline to get to the only refuge he could think of, the bayou. He was tortured daily by thoughts he should have made the move the day the lights went out.

For many modern-day Cajuns, 'the bayou' was a place shrouded in myth, but not for Andrew Cormier. His father left the twisting waterways and Cypress swamps as a young man and settled in nearby New Iberia, but Andrew spent each summer on the bayou with *grandpere* and *grandmere*, speaking the blunt, archaic and unadorned peasant French of the Cajuns and learning the old ways. His grandparents died within a month of each other, just two months before he graduated from vocational school. He'd never returned to the bayou, but neither had he forgotten what he learned.

He began life in 'the real world,' as he called it, as an air-conditioning technician, guaranteed steady employment in Louisiana, and eventually started his own business. He hadn't wanted to move to Lafayette, but his wife was from there, and the larger population offered good business opportunities. Opportunities that fueled a lifestyle he'd been far too reluctant to abandon, even with the writing on the wall.

Others joined him daily in reclaiming the scattered and weathered little communities hidden among the Cypress swamps of the Atchafalaya. Men and women like himself, not far removed from life on the bayou, who instinctively shed the now useless trappings of modern life. They were a people whose peasant ancestors had marched as foot soldiers under William the Conqueror and later swore curses instead of allegiance to George the Third. A people who prospered in the bitter winters of the Canadian Maritimes and the steamy swamps of Louisiana. A people with survival in their genes and, when crossed, blood in their eyes.

"What are you going to do with them?" she asked.

"Don't worry, Lisa. The boys and I will take care of it."

"But what if they're… you know. Not like the FEMA thugs. What if they're what they say they are?"

"They got a radio, so I figure they have to know what the government is doing. The way I look at it, anyone still running around pretending to be part of the government likely IS part of the government or at least close to it. The only difference is this time we got them before they got us. And we ain't the only ones who lost people. All the people here want some payback, *cher*."

"I want payback too," she said, "but aren't you at least going to talk to them or have a trial or something?"

"I have talked to one of them. Says he's going to Baton Rouge lookin' for family and his wife's maiden name was Melancon. Which proves exactly nothing. How many Melancons you figure are in Baton Rouge?"

"I don't know. A lot, I guess. But is that all he said? What's HIS name?"

Cormier shrugged. "Didn't ask, don't care. But he did say he has a daughter who plays soccer at LSU."

The woman looked thoughtful. "Tim and I went to a game last year. Maybe if we know the name, I might be able to remember if there was a player by that name. At least we'd know if he was telling the truth about that."

"Even if he is, so what? He's still —"

Lisa put a hand on his arm and looked into his eyes. "Pop, I know you're hurting about Mom and you haven't had a chance to process it because you've been too busy taking care of us. But this isn't you. You can't just cut up two men who may be innocent just because of what they're wearing."

He returned her gaze. "Yes, I can," he said, then paused. "But maybe you're right. We talk a bit more first."

***

Kinsey and Bollinger sat up as the rickety steps squeaked and they heard the padlock rattling in the hasp. The door swung open with a plaintive squeal and they squeezed their eyes shut as a bright flashlight painted their faces.

"Okay, *couyon*, question time," said a familiar voice. "What are your names?"

"I… I'm Matt Kinsey, and this is Dave Bollinger."

"Tell me about your daughter. The soccer player."

"What do you want to know?"

"Her name, for starters."

"Kelly. Kelly Kinsey. Her friends call her KK for short."

Kinsey heard murmurs and realized there were at least two people behind the light. He heard a woman whisper.

"What position does she play?"

"Goalie. But why the hell do you want to know —"

The light retreated abruptly and the door closed, but he didn't hear the padlock.

"What the hell was that about?" Bollinger asked.

"I don't know," Kinsey said, "but maybe I shouldn't have said anything. If something happens to Kelly —"

He was interrupted by heavy footfalls on the stairs outside, several men this time. The door flew open again and four men burst in with flashlights. He and Bollinger were hoisted to their feet by hands under their armpits and dragged outside and across to a larger building, the toes of their bound feet digging furrows in the dirt. Soft lantern light spilled from the windows of the building, casting another set of wooden steps in a soft glow. Not that they needed the light. Their captors half dragged, half carried them up the steps and through the front door to dump them unceremoniously into straight-back chairs in the center of a large sparsely furnished room, across from the head man.

"Now, Coast Guard," the man said, looking at his watch, "you have exactly five minutes to convince me I shouldn't cut you up for gator bait."

***

It took closer to thirty, but Kinsey started liking their chances a lot better when the allotted five minutes passed with none of the Cajuns unsheathing a knife. Their captor insisted on a blow-by-blow account of everything that had happened to them from the time of the blackout, jumping on anything that seemed the slightest far-fetched and demanding more in-depth answers.

Finally, Kinsey finished, and there was a long silence punctuated only by the breathing of the people collected in the room. Their captor rose to unsheathe a large hunting knife, and Kinsey's heart fell. *I guess I wasn't that convincing after all,* Kinsey thought as he watched the man approach slowly, his step deliberate.

He stopped in front of Kinsey's chair, just out of range of a two-footed kick, and squatted to look Kinsey straight in the eye.

"I got a good ear for BS, and I don't think anyone could make up a story like that," the Cajun said.

Kinsey heaved a relieved sigh as the man reached down and sliced the duct tape binding his ankles, then motioned for Kinsey to rise and turn so he could cut the tape from his hands. Kinsey rubbed his wrists and rolled aching shoulders as the man freed Bollinger.

"Andrew Cormier," the man said, turning from Bollinger to sheath the knife and extend his hand to Kinsey.

Kinsey took the man's hand. "Matt Kinsey," he said.

The Cajun grinned. "Yeah, I think we been over that."

"So we have," Kinsey said. "So what now?"

"I suggest y'all get settled down in the bayou. You gonna be here a while."

Kinsey shook his head. "Negative. I have to get to Baton Rouge."

"That may be a problem," Cormier said.

SOMEWHERE IN THE ATCHAFALAYA RIVER BASIN
NORTH OF MORGAN CITY, LOUISIANA

DAY 27, 9:20 A.M.

Cormier shook his head. "It won't work. I mean, your floating trailer's a good idea, but I still don't think you'll be able to get around the locks at Bayou Sorrell and Port Allen. Plus there's a lot of people up and down that stretch. The good people gonna take a shot at you for being feds, and the bad people gonna shoot you to take your stuff. It won't work, Kinsey. I doubt you make it halfway."

"We have to make it work," Kinsey said, tapping a point on the chart spread out on the table between them. "Port Allen Lock is directly across the Mississippi from LSU, and my sister-in-law's house is just southeast of there. It can't be much more than a mile from the river. I figure that's the most direct and quickest way in and out."

Cormier shrugged. "Figure all you want, *couyon*. Y'all go that way and you're dead meat."

Kinsey blew out an exasperated sigh. "Look, Andrew. I have to get there—"

"I didn't say you couldn't get there. I said you can't get there that way." Cormier put his own finger down to the chart and traced a line. "You need to go up the Atchafalaya. It's mostly farmland and woods on either side, and when you get to the Mississippi, there's a couple of different places you can cross over the levee without an audience, eh."

Kinsey followed Cormier's pointing finger, his doubt obvious. "But that's twice as far, and when we reach the Mississippi, we'll be over fifty miles upriver from Baton Rouge, maybe twice that with all the river bends."

"And you'll be alive," Cormier said. "You can't do your family much good if you're dead."

Kinsey fell silent, then gave a reluctant nod and studied the proposed route. "There's a few towns along the way, do you think we'll have any problems there?"

Cormier shook his head. "They're small places, and the river is plenty wide. You can stay to the far side of the river and blow right by before anyone can think about it."

Kinsey shook his head. "You're forgetting something, aren't you? We still have to tow the trailer to get over the levee into the Mississippi. I don't think we'll be 'blowing by' anybody with that thing in tow."

"We ain't takin' the trailer," Cormier said.

"What do you mean we're not taking the trailer…" Kinsey trailed off and stared at Cormier.

"And what do you mean WE?" Kinsey asked.

Cormier nodded. "I figured me and a couple of the boys will take a little boat ride with you. We'll take aluminum boats. If we tie off to yours, you got enough power to take us all up the river pretty fast. And the aluminum boats are light enough that we can manhandle them over the levee. We leave your Coast Guard boat on the Atchafalaya side."

Kinsey was speechless. "But why? I mean we appreciate it, but why are you helping us?"

Cormier shrugged. "A lot of reasons. Maybe because every time there's a hurricane, it was always the Coast Guard we see with helicopters, pulling folks off rooftops. Getting the job done while everybody else seems to be running around with their finger up their ass. Maybe because I've been thinking about this ship of yours over in Texas, and think maybe having some friends outside the Bayou might be a good thing. We're self-sufficient in everything but gasoline, and you tell me they got plenty of that." Then Cormier smiled, but there was no humor in it. "And maybe because my only son is lying in the next room near death. He is in God's hands, and there is nothing I can do here. But maybe while we're out, we catch a few of these FEMA bastards to bring home and pass a good time, eh? Everybody was a little disappointed we didn't get to chop you two up for gator bait."

Kinsey chuckled politely, not altogether sure Cormier was joking. "Whatever your reasons, I appreciate it," he said. "When can we leave?"

"We'll get everything ready and leave at first light tomorrow," Cormier said.

"It's still morning; we could get out of here today."

"'Cause there's planning to do," Cormier said, putting his finger on the map again to indicate a bend in the river. "There are a lot of things we have to think about, and this is a big one right here. There aren't so many places to run into trouble going this way, but there could be a lot of trouble in one place, *eh?*"

Cormier removed his finger, and Kinsey looked at the point indicated, the Louisiana State Penitentiary at Angola, bounded on three sides by the wide Mississippi.

"There are a lot of bad, bad people there," Cormier said. "And I'm bettin' by now they're out and maybe on the river, and —"

"And we gotta get by them," Kinsey said.

CHAPTER SIXTEEN

Day 28, 11:15 a.m.

The Atchafalaya River flows south, though much more directly than the Mississippi, its sinuous cousin to the east. Bollinger was at the wheel, guiding their strange little convoy over the sluggish brown surface of the river at twenty-five knots. They ran three abreast, a sixteen-foot aluminum boat lashed tight and unmanned to either side of the Coast Guard boat. Cormier and two of his men rode in the Coast Guard boat with them.

As Cormier promised, they left the Cajun village at first light and wound their way through a maze of bayous for a good hour before reaching the main river. Kinsey attempted to memorize the path, but was hopelessly lost by the sixth turn in the first fifteen minutes. The only thing he was sure about was that they were leaving by a different path from the one they used coming in. Cormier watched him scrutinizing the banks closely and laughed.

"Good luck remembering the way, *couyon*. The bayou, she is changing all the time. Tomorrow she will look very different, *non*? You have to know the things that do not change, and for that you will need a lifetime or a teacher. And I think no Cajun is going to be schooling outsiders anytime soon. We will be friends, I think. But we will come visit you when we want to talk, not the other way around."

Kinsey shrugged and grinned back. "Fair enough, I suppose. If I had a secure place, I wouldn't be too eager to share it with anyone either."

They'd ridden upriver mostly in silence as they made their way through cypress swamp and pine forest, passing the occasional ramshackle tin-roof shack five to six feet off the ground on pilings, with an almost obligatory tumbledown dock jutting a few feet into the river. But no people. At one point Kinsey commented on the deserted feel of the place, and Cormier just smiled.

"Oh, there are people there, *mon ami*, and we are in their gun sights. Trust me on that," Cormier said, then pointed ahead at a bridge looming in the distance.

"We're makin' good time," Cormier said. "That's the I-10 causeway, so we're halfway to the Mississippi. We'll reach the levee in time to get the boats over in daylight, and we want to go downstream in the dark anyway."

Kinsey nodded and watched the top of the bridge, looking for threats but finding none. Bollinger kept the boats to the center of the river as they motored beneath the double concrete span, and Kinsey noticed an opening in the trees ahead on the right bank. As they drew abreast of the small clearing, he glimpsed flashes of white between the trunks of the pine trees and after a moment made out the familiar shapes of recreational vehicles. A dozen people lined the bank, mostly men, but here and there a woman or a child. They stared at the passing boats in sullen apathy.

"An RV park?" he asked Cormier.

Cormier shook his head. "Not a park, I think a squat. Likely they were running from Baton Rouge in their RVs and made it here before they ran out of gas. Luckier than some, I suppose. They have shelter and they can fish from the river, and they're hidden from I-10 by the trees. But by now, I suspect they are as desperate as everyone else."

Kinsey nodded and turned his gaze back upriver. There were more than enough desperate people in this cruel new world; right now the only ones who mattered to him were his family.

"We'll be coming up on Krotz Springs in an hour or so, and after that there are four small river towns scattered between there and the Mississippi levee. How much faster can we go?" Cormier asked.

Kinsey moved to the door of the little cabin and looked into where Bollinger stood at the wheel, then glanced down at the throttle lever. He moved back to where Cormier stood astern of the cabin. "We have a bit of throttle left. Your boats are dragging us down, but I think Bollinger can get another ten knots out of her if need be. Why? Do you expect trouble?"

Cormier shrugged. "These days, I always expect trouble. Then I can be happy if it doesn't happen. I just want to know what our options are if we run into it."

Despite Cormier's worries, they made it by Krotz Springs and the other villages upriver without incident. They stayed to the opposite bank, as far from the towns as possible, and accelerated past at full speed. The sun was well on its way toward the western horizon when Cormier pointed to a channel to the right.

"That's the channel to the Lower Old River lock. I think that'll be the easiest place to cross."

Kinsey nodded and moved into the little cabin with Cormier close behind. Space was tight, so Cormier stood just outside, where he could talk to both Coasties. Kinsey ordered Bollinger into the side channel, and they all stood silent as he negotiated a bend and came to a split in the smaller channel.

"The right fork goes to the lock. Take the larger fork to the left," Cormier said. "That's the old riverbed, and it dead-ends at the Mississippi levee."

Bollinger did as ordered, and they approached the dead end, a narrow sandy beach. Beyond it, a grassy slope rose like a great wall, filling their vision from left to right.

"That thing must be a hundred feet high," Bollinger said.

Cormier shook his head. "More like fifty or so," he said. "But it will seem like a hundred when we're trying to carry a three-hundred-fifty-pound boat. That's why I picked this spot. There's grass on both sides, so we can drag the boats up and slide them down the other side."

Kinsey looked up at the towering levee. "You sure this is gonna work?"

"No," Cormier said. "But I'm sure five of us have a better chance of getting aluminum boats over the levee than you two had of getting your Coast Guard boat weighing many times as much around those locks, trailer or no trailer."

"Point taken," Kinsey said.

It went surprisingly well. They stripped everything from the first boat to lighten the load, and Cormier produced wide web strapping they slipped under the floating boat in two places as lifting straps. Grunting and straining, they walked the boat out of the water and across the little beach, two men on either side, with the fifth man lifting the stern.

They set the boat down at the foot of the levee, and Cormier ordered one of his men up the slope with one end of a long rope. While the man climbed, Cormier tied the other end of the rope to the bow ring of the boat and then waited for his man to reach the top and take up the slack. By prearrangement, the others positioned themselves around the boat, and on the count of three, pushed and pulled for all they were worth, sliding the boat up the slope through the long grass as far as possible. The man with the rope gathered in the slack as the boat advanced to a stop, then braced himself, the friction of the boat on the slope sufficient to help him keep it from sliding back. In a dozen heaves they had it resting on the crest of the levee and started back down for the second boat.

More confident now, they loaded both outboards, trolling motors, and other gear in the second boat after first positioning it at the base of the levee. It made the boat heavier, but it would be faster and easier than carrying the heavy gear up the steep slope piecemeal. Twenty minutes later, the second boat rested beside its twin on the levee.

Gravity was their friend now, but the big concern was the boats might slide down too fast and damage their thin aluminum hulls on a hidden rock. They sent them down the slope bow first, with the rope tied off to the transoms now, and two men holding back on the rope. Two others guided the boat down the slope, while the fifth walked in front, checking for any obstacles that might damage the boat. They had the boats in the water and fully outfitted just as the sun reached the horizon.

Kinsey turned to Cormier. "Who you gonna leave with our boat?"

Cormier nodded to one of his men. "I'm leaving Breaux. I told him to move it into the little inlet up in the trees to the right of the beach. You see it?"

"I was going to suggest it," Kinsey said. "When should we take off?"

Cormier looked west, then turned back to Kinsey. "This channel puts us in the Mississippi directly across from the prison farm, but a wooded island in the middle of the river will screen us from sight. And I doubt anybody is in the fields of the prison farm at night, or maybe at all now. I say we wait until full dark, maybe two hours, then take off. We lash the boats together, so we don't lose each other in the dark, and go on the trolling motors, using y'all's night-vision goggles. We'll hug the west bank until we get well past the prison; then we can stay close to whichever side is least inhabited."

"The trolling motors are gonna be slow," Kinsey said.

"They also going to be pretty quiet," Cormier said, "and we're gonna have a strong current behind us. But we do need to save the batteries, because we definitely need quiet when we go through Baton Rouge. We switch to the outboards when we're safely past the prison, then go back to the trolling motors to go through the city."

Kinsey nodded, and they took advantage of the waning light to eat a meal. Then they said their goodbyes to a forlorn Breaux, the man obviously irritated he'd drawn the short straw and boat-sitting detail, and watched him scramble up over the levee and out of sight.

The minutes dragged for Kinsey. Being this close to his family and unable to fly downriver grated on his nerves. But ever so slowly the sky darkened until finally they were wrapped in the inky blackness of a post-event night. After whispered conversation with Cormier, they cast off and moved down the short channel and into the stream of the mighty Mississippi.

They moved on a single trolling motor, propelling both of the lashed boats, and Kinsey was amazed how quickly the bank slipped by in his nightvision goggles. Cormier had been right about the current.

By mutual agreement, Cormier's man, Bertrand, was at the helm, wearing one of the Coasties' pairs of NV goggles. Kinsey and Bollinger were alternating overwatch duties, trading off the other pair of NV goggles every half hour to keep their eyes fresh.

It was near the end of Kinsey's first watch when the channel turned almost due south. He glanced over to where Cormier sat, staring into the dark.

"We're turning due south," Kinsey said softly. "We're past the prison, right?"

Cormier nodded in the green-tinted world.

"That wasn't too bad," Kinsey said.

"It ain't going downstream I was worried about," Cormier said. "It's clawing back against this current with the outboards blastin'. We won't be exactly hard to spot."

"They might hear us," Kinsey said. "But it will be night, and we have the NV equipment."

"They might have it too. You ever think of that?"

"Yeah, but I've been trying not to," Kinsey said.

MISSISSIPPI RIVER
SOUTHBOUND
JUST NORTH OF BATON ROUGE

DAY 29, 1:25 A.M.

Their approach to Baton Rouge was signaled by increasingly large fleets of idle river barges tied up along both banks and glowing green in Kinsey's night-vision goggles. They made a sharp bend to the right, and a bridge loomed across the river in the near distance.

"That's the 190 bridge," Bertrand said softly. "Should I kill the outboard?"

"*Oui*," Cormier replied, and the rumble died abruptly as Bertrand switched back to the trolling motor.

The quiet was eerie, but short-lived. As they moved closer to the city, Kinsey heard sporadic gunfire, and here and there distant fires flared green in his glasses.

"You sure you can recognize this place, Kinsey?" Cormier asked.

"I'm not sure of anything," Kinsey said, "But the place I saw on the chart was just south of the I-10 bridge and almost directly across from the Port Allen Lock. If we start hugging the east bank at the bridge, we should be able to spot it. Besides, any dock in the area should work. We'll be close to LSU and I know the way from there. We just cut across the campus to Connie's neighborhood."

When Cormier spoke again, there was doubt in his voice. "Just how much do you know about Baton Rouge?"

"Not a lot," Kinsey said. "We visited Connie fairly often, but my brother-in-law always did the driving around town. Why?"

"Because not every neighborhood around LSU is a good one, and it sounds like we're headed right into the projects," Cormier said. "The locals say to stay off streets named after presidents if you don't want to end up dead. And that's when things were normal; I can't imagine how it is now."

"Okay, what's the alternative? Beyond this short stretch, there are no other good landing spots for at least four miles. That would make it a long hike to Connie's house, to say nothing of getting back to the boats. Besides, I know my way from the LSU campus, but we get too far away and we're gonna be groping around in the dark with no clue where we are."

Kinsey heard Cormier sigh. "No, you're probably right. We'll just have to slip past the projects. It's the middle of the night, and if we don't show a light, we should be okay. The LSU veterinary school is right near the river. We can use that as a landmark."

"I-10 bridge coming up," Bertrand called softly from the stern. "What y'all want me to do?"

"Hug the east bank," Cormier said. "Let's see if we can find Kinsey his dock."

Bertrand did as ordered, and the bank grew more distinct in the green glow of Kinsey's NV goggles. They passed a dock almost immediately under the I-10 bridge. Kinsey shook his head and waved Bertrand forward. The riverbank was lined with large blocks of empty and idle barges now, and Kinsey was beginning to worry the dock he was looking for would be blocked. Then he saw it through an opening in the blocks of barges, a floating dock with a crane in place, tethered to shore by a movable ramp designed to accommodate the changing level of the river.

"That's it," Kinsey said. "Take us in."

Bertrand reversed the trolling motor to slow the boats, but momentum and the current behind them were strong. The boats slowed ever so slowly as the little electric motor strained. It was obvious the motor could not counter the powerful current, and for a long, terrifying moment, Kinsey was afraid they'd be swept past the dock. But the Cajun handled the joined boats expertly, maneuvering them so they bumped along beside the dock at much reduced speed, allowing Kinsey to grab one of the ropes hanging down from the dock, no doubt placed there for that very purpose. Kinsey held them alongside in the current as Bertrand killed the trolling motor and rushed to tie them up securely to the dock. Only then did Kinsey release his grip on the catch rope.

"I think we should be safe using the headlamps here as long as we keep them in low-intensity red-light mode," Cormier said. "Anyone who spots us from across the river can't get to us, and we're well below the levee, so we don't have to worry about anyone spotting us from this side."

"Agreed," Kinsey said. "But first Bollinger and I should take the NV glasses and sweep the area to make sure we're alone. We can't stumble ashore lit up like Christmas trees."

"Okay," Cormier said. "But hurry, eh? We need to do this fast. This place ain't gonna be too healthy in daylight."

Kinsey murmured agreement, and Bertrand passed his NV goggles to Bollinger. Moments later, the Coasties were moving up the sloping ramp toward solid land, night vision in place and M4s at the ready. The ramp terminated in the well-worn gravel parking lot of what had previously been McElroy Fleet Services, empty except for a battered flatbed truck of indeterminate but ancient vintage.

The offices were in a utilitarian metal building, the windows smashed and front door standing open. They entered to find the large one-room structure ransacked. Metal desks and filing cabinets were overturned, no doubt savaged by looters frustrated at the lack of anything of value. They exited the building and made their way around the periphery of the parking lot, examining the open shops and work areas. All were vacant and vandalized. Satisfied the area was secure, Kinsey signaled Bollinger, and they started toward the dock.

"I wonder if that heap runs," Bollinger said as they neared the old truck. "A ride sure would be sweet."

Kinsey stopped and opened the truck door, grimacing as it squeaked. "Not locked, but good luck finding any keys."

"Not a problem, boss," Bollinger said. "I wasn't always the model citizen you know and love. I have a few skills from my misspent youth."

Kinsey grunted and raised the hood. "Surprise, surprise. No battery. It's probably the only thing of value the looters found. I doubt anyone wanted this old beater, but you're right, it's worth a shot. Let's go get the others."

Cormier looked in their general direction as they moved across the dock in the darkness, obviously locating them by sound. "That you, Kinsey?"

"It is," Kinsey replied. "And we found—"

"We got a problem," Bertrand blurted. "I clicked on my light to check the lines, and the stern line is already chafing. We can't leave the boats tied up like this and bouncing around on this current; if one line breaks, the other will go quick. And what if we don't make it back before daylight? We can't just leave the boats here in plain sight. We gotta find a hiding place out of this current."

Kinsey cursed and turned his NV goggles toward the riverbank. He was scrutinizing a block of empty barges lashed together and moored to the tree-lined shore downstream when Bollinger spoke.

"Maybe we can take them around the downstream end of these barges into the backwater between the barges and the bank," Bollinger said. "Nobody will be able to see them from either the dock or the river, and the trees will screen them from the bank. There can't be much surface current there."

Kinsey nodded. "Looks like our best shot, but first let's get our gear ashore." Kinsey turned to Cormier. "Andrew, we're done with the trolling motors, right?"

"*Mais* yeah," Cormier replied. "They ain't gonna do no good against the current. We go back upstream on the outboards. Why?"

"Because I want one of the batteries." Kinsey told them about the old truck.

They got their gear ashore, including a battery and a five-gallon can of gas, working in the soft warm glow of their red headlights. Given his claimed expertise, Kinsey left Bollinger working on the truck with Bertrand's assistance while he and Cormier hid the boats. As hoped, they found a protected backwater between the barges and the riverbank and tied the boats up securely to a tree. By the time they'd slogged up the muddy riverbank and through the trees to the parking lot, their two companions were ready to try the truck.

"Ready when you are, boss," Bollinger said from the driver's seat.

Kinsey nodded, then grimaced as Bollinger touched two wires together under the steering column and the starter ground loudly, followed immediately by the roar of an unmuffled exhaust as the engine caught.

"Shut it down!" Kinsey hissed, and Bollinger complied.

"We can't drive around in that," Kinsey said. "We may as well take out an ad."

But Bollinger was already out of the truck and on his back in the gravel, inching under the truck with his headlight. He emerged with a diagnosis. "The exhaust system is Swiss cheese, but I saw some sheet metal scraps in one of the shops. I can patch it, at least temporarily."

Cormier looked at his watch. "It's two thirty. We don't have much time."

Bollinger ignored the Cajun and fixed his gaze on Kinsey. "Five minutes now can save us an hour later. It's worth a shot, boss."

Kinsey looked from Bollinger to Cormier. "Okay. Five minutes. No more."

Bollinger was moving before Kinsey finished speaking, and emerged from the nearest shop moments later with a handful of sheet metal scraps of various sizes. He tossed them on the ground, then rummaged in his pack for a roll of duct tape. He motioned for Bertrand to assist, and dove under the truck again. Kinsey and Cormier watched as Bollinger periodically asked for a piece of sheet metal and Bertrand passed it under the truck. Kinsey kept glancing at his watch.

"Time's up, Bollinger," Kinsey said. "Get out of there and let's —"

"Almost done, boss. One more minute, two max."

And so it went for ten. Kinsey was about to drag Bollinger out feet first when the man scrambled out, grinning. "Done!"

"And how long is friggin' duct tape gonna last?" Kinsey asked.

Bollinger shrugged. "Ten or twenty minutes or until we catch fire, whichever comes first. I figure it'll keep us quiet enough to get past the projects and to your family's house, and that's all we need, right?"

"Let's hope so," Kinsey said. "Give it a try, but shut it down if it's too loud."

Bollinger slid into the driver's seat, and Kinsey cringed again as the starter ground. But this time the engine was much quieter; still not exactly a whisper, but not a roar.

"All right, I'll drive. Bollinger, get in back with night vision and an M4. Andrew, you guys ride front or back, whichever you want," Kinsey said.

"Back," Cormier said. "Even if we can't see nothin', if Bollinger starts shooting we can shoot in the same direction. Maybe we get lucky, eh?"

"Fair enough," Kinsey said, sliding behind the wheel as Bollinger got out.

"Just a minute, boss," Bollinger said, and disappeared around the back of the truck. Kinsey heard several loud whacks and the sound of something breaking.

"Dammit, Bollinger!" he hissed. "Can you make any more noise —"

"Sorry, boss," Bollinger said softly. "Just takin' out the brake lights."

"Okay, okay. Let's go," Kinsey said.

He settled behind the wheel of the idling truck, and moments later, Bollinger knocked on the cab, signaling everyone was ready. Kinsey put the truck in first gear and crept out of the parking lot and up the steep incline to the top of the levee. He turned right, down the road on the levee crest rather than descending to the mean streets below. The higher vantage point would make it easier to avoid an ambush and give Bollinger a clear field of fire.

Any pretensions to stealth quickly evaporated when he shifted into second gear and the raucous sound of mechanical mayhem rose from the ancient transmission. He cursed and shifted back to first, and the transmission quieted. He built up sufficient speed to shift directly into third, hoping it wasn't gone as well, and heaved a relieved sigh as the truck slid smoothly into higher gear. The old beater moved quietly along the crest of the levee, 'quiet' being a relative term. In less than a mile he spotted a large office complex to his left at the foot of the levee: the vet school. He slowed, looking for a way down, and spotted a wide sidewalk angling down the side of the levee to the street below.

He stuck his left hand through his open window and pointed at the sidewalk. Bollinger knocked quietly on the top of the truck cab in acknowledgment and Kinsey started down. All went well until he bumped across a high curb and into the street, and cursed at the loud, grating sound of the truck dragging bottom. The impact was followed immediately by a rumbling roar, announcing he'd just undone Bollinger's makeshift repairs to the exhaust system.

***

Kinsey gritted his teeth and cursed himself for not vetoing the use of the truck immediately. But it was too late now. If anyone was around, they'd already heard, and since that was the case, the truck would minimize the time to Connie's house. He muttered another curse and rumbled east on the first street he came to.

He was unfamiliar with the campus this near the river and drove six or seven blocks before he saw Tiger Stadium looming in the glow of his NV goggles. Reassured, he accelerated and the old truck rumbled through the dark.

Stadium Drive took him to Highland Road, where he made a sharp right. Connie's house was less than a mile away, and for the first time since they left Texas, Kinsey felt optimistic. He fantasized about getting his loved ones back to the safety of *Pecos Trader*, but his daydream was interrupted by frantic knocking on the truck cab.

"WHAT?" Kinsey yelled out the open window, the roaring exhaust system negating any need for silence now.

"I THINK THE DUCT TAPE IS ON FIRE! THERE ARE FLAMES SHOOTING OUT FROM UNDER THE TRUCK!" Bollinger yelled.

"WE'RE ALMOST THERE," Kinsey yelled. "HOW BAD IS IT?"

"WHO THE HELL KNOWS? JUST KEEP GOING," Bollinger replied.

Kinsey mashed the gas, trying to coax a bit more speed out of the old beater. He almost missed the turn to Connie's subdivision, but he braked hard, managing to negotiate the left turn on to Sunrise Drive with his passengers still aboard. Then he slowed, remembering the numerous speed bumps along the quiet tree-lined street, a point of some irritation and frequent complaints from his brother-in-law. Flickering light illuminated the trees beside the truck as they passed, evidence of the growing fire under the truck.

He drove as fast as the speed bumps would allow, and bits and pieces of the exhaust system clattered to the pavement as they lurched over each bump. But whatever was falling off didn't seem to have duct tape attached, because the flames continued to grow beneath the vehicle. *How much of that crap did he use?* Kinsey wondered as the truck moved forward. The engine noise was deafening now, precluding even shouted conversations.

Kinsey spotted the entrance to the gated community ahead. The ornamental wrought-iron gate was closed, and he wondered if the old truck would hold together long enough to force it open. There was a sharp crack as a bullet shattered the windshield a foot to the right of him, and he slammed on the brakes just as the front wheels were starting over yet another speed bump. The combined assault transmitted through the steering system and jerked the wheel from Kinsey's hands and the truck veered into the trunk of a massive oak tree. Only the relatively slow speed prevented the collision from being worse.

He pushed himself back from the steering wheel, thankful his tactical vest had spread the force of the impact. He'd be bruised, but there were no broken ribs. But his self-congratulations were brief as the smell of gasoline from a broken fuel line drove him from the cab. Bollinger and the two Cajuns were still on the truck bed, disentangling themselves from a heap against the back of the cab. Another round ricocheted off the street near Kinsey and whined into the distance.

"Get the hell off there and away from the truck!" he yelled at the others. "There's a gas leak somewhere and this heap is liable to blow, and the fire is silhouetting us for the shooters."

Kinsey was dragging a groggy Bertrand off the flatbed as he spoke, and Cormier and Bollinger were gathering their weapons and gear. They were on the ground in seconds, moving away from the burning truck into the shadows and safety of the massive oaks on the opposite side of the street. They barely reached cover when the air was split by a thunderous explosion and the night flashed bright for a brief instant as the gas tank exploded.

The truck continued to burn; no need for night vision now. Kinsey flipped up his goggles and peeked around the tree trunk to see something he'd missed earlier. The guardhouse by the gate, occupied in better times by a lethargic and geriatric rent-a-cop, was now sandbagged. He could just make out heads popping up over the sandbags for a quick look: two or possibly three men. A shout rang out across the distance.

"YOU ARE SURROUNDED! DROP YOUR WEAPONS AND STEP INTO THE LIGHT WITH YOUR HANDS ON YOUR HEADS."

Kinsey was contemplating his response, when Cormier made it for him.

"MAYBE YOU SHOULD DROP YOUR WEAPONS, *COUYON*, BEFORE I THROW A GRENADE IN YOUR LITTLE HOUSE, *EH?*"

"I REPEAT," the man at the gate yelled, "DROP YOUR WEAPONS AND STEP INTO THE LIGHT WITH YOUR HANDS ON YOUR HEADS."

Something about that voice? Relief washed over Kinsey as he shouted a reply. "ZACH! ZACH DUHON! IS THAT YOU?"

There was a long silence. "WHO WANTS TO KNOW?" the voice replied.

"MATT. MATT KINSEY."

More silence. "IF YOU'RE MATT, STEP INTO THE LIGHT AND WALK TOWARD US AND KEEP YOUR HANDS WHERE I CAN SEE THEM."

Kinsey stepped out from behind the tree, hands on the top of his head, and walked toward the gatehouse. When he was halfway there, a tall man moved from behind the sandbag barricade and rushed to meet him. They embraced in the area in front of the gatehouse, then stepped back, both embarrassed by the gesture.

"Man, it's good to see you," Zach said. "We thought you were —"

"Is Kelly okay?"

"She's fine," Zach said. "And she'll be more than fine when she sees you."

Zach looked toward the trees in the shadows. "Is Luke with you?"

Kinsey shook his head. "No, but he's safe. He's in North Carolina."

"I'm relieved to hear it," Zach said, and grinned. "You want to bring the rest of your folks in. I promise we won't shoot them."

Kinsey turned and motioned the others forward. When they arrived, he made quick introductions all around, and they all turned toward the gate. Zach's fellow guards were a bit less welcoming, holding their weapons pointing downward, but leaving no doubt they were prepared to raise them at the slightest provocation.

"They're okay," Zach said. "This is my brother-in-law and he vouches for the others."

One of the guards shook his head. "You know the rules, Duhon. We're not supposed to let anyone in without approval from the council."

"I don't think that applies to family," Zach said. "But if you want to go wake up Fat-Ass Fontenot at three in the morning, be my guest. Meanwhile, I'm taking these boys to my house. You know where to find us if anybody has a problem with that."

The two men held their ground for a few seconds, as if contemplating pressing the point, but seemed to think better of it. They both stepped back to let Zach pass. Zach clicked on a headlamp to light their way and started down the middle of the street. Kinsey and his comrades turned on their own headlamps and fell in beside Zach. Kinsey held his tongue until they were well away from the gate.

"I get the impression there's no love lost there?"

Zach shrugged. "They're all right, but the longer this drags on, the more strained things get. We were doing okay for the first two or three weeks. There was rioting and looting after the first few days, but the governor called out the guard and they were able to contain a lot of it. Then as it got worse, most of the guardsmen just left and went home to protect their own families, and those that were left were tasked with defending the governor's mansion."

"Have you had any trouble?" Kinsey asked.

Zach nodded. "Yeah, at first the looters were running all over the place. But we've only got the one way in and out, so me and a few of my neighbors set up a guard on the gate. The wall around the community isn't much of an obstacle, but between that and guys with guns at the gate and a roving neighborhood patrol, it was enough to encourage the bad guys to look elsewhere. There were a lot more vulnerable places around."

"So what happened?"

"Fat Ass Fontenot happened, that's what. He's retired, but he was some sort of corporate bigwig. He ran for city council a couple of times but always lost, but for all that he has a pretty good line." Zach shrugged. "With things like they are, some people aren't thinking straight, if they ever thought straight to start with. They want someone to tell them what to do, so Fontenot took it upon himself to start beating the drum for a 'community council.' A lot of us just figured he was a blowhard and ignored him, but that turned out to be a mistake. More than half the residents went along with it, and the next thing we know we got the council, and surprise, surprise, the council elected Fat Ass as president. He didn't do much for the first week, but then he started trying to control things, and it's gone from bad to worse."

"Worse how?"

"Like now everybody is supposed to pool their food and supplies for the COUNCIL to distribute. Except the people on the council, and most of the people who voted for it, don't have anything to contribute. Hell, we can't even get most of them to take a turn at guard duty, but they want to run things." He shook his head. "Most of us have resisted, but they're getting more aggressive, and like I said, things are getting tense."

"Actually I'm relieved to see you in such good shape," Kinsey said.

"You can thank Connie for most of that," Zach said. "You know how she loves her garden. She wouldn't even let me put in a pool because she didn't want to give up the garden space, and she took up over half the storage room in the garage for the stuff she canned out of the garden."

Kinsey grinned. "You can take the girl out of the country, but you can't take the country out of the girl."

Zach snorted. "You got that right. Anyway she had another idea. We had two freezers in the garage full of fish and game, and our neighbors on either side had pretty much the same. And between the three households we had a couple of little Honda generators, so we moved the generators around and ran the freezers three or four hours a day to preserve the food. Then we pooled our propane bottles, and Connie and the other ladies used the gas grills and camp stoves to can as much of the meat as possible. And when they ran out of propane, we started pruning our trees real hard and finished the job on wood fires in the backyard. When they ran out of canning jars, we started eating the frozen stuff and consolidating the rest in one freezer. We didn't lose any of it at all; we either ate it or canned it."

"Pretty smart," Kinsey said. "What about water?"

"We had a rain barrel, and I helped the neighbors rig tarps for rainwater. We treat it with a few drops of Clorox for drinking. One of our neighbors has a pool, and we've been using buckets for washing and flushing toilets. The pool's half-empty now and it's gettin' kind of green, but it's better than nothing." Zach shrugged. "It sucks, but it's doable."

Kinsey nodded, and Zach shot a worried sidelong look at his companions and lowered his voice. "Ah... about that, Matt. We don't have much left, maybe a week for the folks we're supporting. I don't think—"

"Relax, Zach," Kinsey said. "I've got a safe place in Texas, and I came to get you all. It's not without its challenges, but there are plenty of supplies for at least the immediate future."

Zach's relief was visible, even in the peripheral light of the headlamps; then he looked concerned again.

"What's the problem?" Kinsey asked.

"It's not just us," Zach said. "Reba and George are here with their two kids, and so are my folks. And we've always been tight with our neighbors; they're like family, especially now. We can't just leave them here to fend for themselves. I wouldn't feel right about it, and I know Connie won't leave them."

Kinsey was quiet a long moment. "How many?"

Zach was quiet, mentally counting. "Seventeen."

Crap, thought Kinsey.

CHAPTER SEVENTEEN

DAY 29, 7:25 A.M.

Kelly Kinsey sat on the couch beside her father, a hand slightly resting on his forearm. She'd hardly let him out of her sight since they woke her. For all her nineteen years, she was very much a little girl again, unwilling to be separated from her dad for even a moment. Kinsey gave her hand a reassuring pat and turned his attention back to the group. He sighed. Nothing was easy.

After a joyous and emotional reunion, his plan derailed almost immediately. The quick race upriver under the cover of darkness never happened, and he sat now in a group meeting in Zach and Connie Duhon's living room, discussing 'options.'

"We appreciate you coming, Matt," Connie Duhon said, "but I don't see how this ship is an improvement on our situation. We all have gardens planted and enough supplies to last until they start producing, if we're careful. We get plenty of rain, so drinking water isn't a problem, and we're already rigging more tarps to replenish the wash water in the swimming pool." She shook her head. "It's not perfect here, but I doubt any of us want to go to some strange ship. And what about these convicts you mentioned? It sounds like we're safer here."

Around the room there were nods and murmurs of agreement. Kinsey nodded as well, suppressing a surge of secret, guilty relief as his life just got a hell of a lot less complicated. Still, they were family, and his own conscience wouldn't allow him to leave it at that.

"It's not without its dangers," he said. "I've been up front about that. But in the long run, it's the better option. You've done great here, but you've got no reserves. When you get right down to it, you're one failed garden crop away from starvation in increasingly hostile territory. But if you don't want to come, that's your call. I came here mainly for Kelly, so the rest of you can make up your own minds."

Connie hesitated. "Aren't you forgetting something? Kelly is an adult now. She has a say in the matter."

Kinsey was dumbstruck. He'd been so focused on getting here and so relieved at finding Kelly well, it never even occurred to him she might not agree to his plan. He turned and saw the indecision on her face.

"Kelly, honey, what DO you want to do?"

"I want you to stay here. Why can't you do that?"

"Because I have obligations there too," Kinsey said. "A lot of people are depending on me, and I really think it's the best option in the long run. You're scared; we all are, but I need you to trust me on this."

Kelly shot a look at her aunt Connie, who almost imperceptibly and perhaps unconsciously shook her head. Kelly looked conflicted, then turned back to her father.

"If... if you think it's best, Dad, I'll come."

Kinsey reached over and folded his daughter in a hug as he fought down a lump in his throat.

"Okay," he said, releasing her, "that's that. We'll leave as soon as it's good and dark. I'm sorry the rest of you —"

"Just a minute, Matt," Zach Duhon said, then turned toward his wife. "Connie, let's not be hasty." He glanced across the room to two men standing on either side of the door into the dining room. "Things are getting a lot worse with the council." He hesitated. "I'm not so sure how long it's going to be safe here."

"What do you mean, Zach Duhon? You've been telling me Fat Ass Fontenot was just a big blowhard and nothing to worry about."

"He is, but he's managed to control the council, and three days ago they started taking food and supplies by force, for the 'community store.' The only reason they haven't messed with us is they know we have six men and we're all armed. But we're one of the few places neighbors have banded together, and Fat Ass's group is getting stronger all the time. Even folks who should know better are going along for self-preservation. When they finish all the easy marks, I think we're next."

"And you're just telling me this NOW?"

Zach shook his head. "And why would I tell you before? So y'all could all go crazy worrying about it too? I haven't had a decent night's sleep since it all started." He nodded to the men standing near the door. "Me, George, and Jerry have been trying to come up with a plan, but I think maybe Matt's offer is the best answer."

Kinsey listened, conflicted and thinking of his earlier conversation with Hughes. Seventeen people was considerably more than Hughes was expecting.

His thoughts were interrupted by a loud knock.

"DUHON! GET YOUR ASS OUT HERE!" yelled a voice from the front porch.

Zach rose and walked to the door as Kinsey gently disengaged himself from Kelly's hand and rose to follow. The others in the room followed suit.

Zach opened the front door to face a man standing at the glass storm door. He was in his sixties, red-faced, and agitated. Overweight despite the times, the man was dressed casually but expensively, as if about to play eighteen holes. However, his clothing was rumpled and dirty, and he had graying stubble on his cheeks. He looked like a fat, homeless golf pro.

Zach pushed the storm door open and stepped onto the porch, forcing the older man back. The man's eyes widened as Kinsey and the others crowded out behind Zach, filling the small porch. It was almost comical to watch him scamper down the two steps to stand on the sidewalk, just out of reach. As Redface stood there trying to recover his dignity, Kinsey looked beyond him into the front yard. There were six armed men there, and two more stood on either side of a pickup backed into the driveway.

"What do you want, Fontenot?" Zach asked.

The man ignored the question. "You've crossed the line this time, Duhon. You know it's against the rules to let outsiders inside the perimeter. Who are these people?"

Duhon started to reply, but Kinsey touched his arm. "I'm Chief Petty Officer Matthew Kinsey, US Coast Guard," he said. "And who might you be?"

The man puffed up. "I'm Ronald Fontenot, president of the Community Council."

Kinsey nodded. "Congratulations."

He suppressed a smile as the older man turned redder still, but the others on the porch were less diplomatic and laughed out loud. Fontenot turned back to Zach Duhon.

"Folks around here are sick and tired of you acting like the rules don't apply to you, Duhon. First you hoard food and supplies, and now you're harboring outsiders. By order of the council, these men are to leave the community immediately, and you are further ordered to turn over all your food and supplies. They'll go to the community store, and you will receive your fair daily distribution, just like everyone else." He inclined his head toward the pickup truck. "Now start loading it into the truck. If you refuse, I am authorized by the council to arrest every person in the household eighteen years old or older. Is that clear?"

Kinsey saw Zach tense, and he put his hand on his own sidearm. He was about to respond when a voice rang out from the side of the house beside the garage.

"What is clear, *couyon*," Cormier yelled, "is that you don't know what the hell you're doing. 'Cause, you see, I got me five shells fulla double-ought buck in this old Model 12, and I can take out all your men standing there all grouped together. And I mean right now."

Fontenot stared at the corner of the garage, where only the barrel of Cormier's shotgun was visible. "You're bluffing."

"No, he's not, and neither am I," came Bollinger's voice, and Kinsey looked to the right to see the barrel of an M4 protruding from the opposite corner of the house.

"Me neither, *Gros Tcheu*," called a voice from above, and there were titters of laughter from the porch at the use of the Cajun for 'fat ass.'

Kinsey smiled. Bertrand! He must be in an upstairs window.

Fontenot made a strangling sound of impotent rage, and his men, never too enthusiastic to begin with, were decidedly less so when faced with armed resistance. They all took obvious care to keep their hands away from their weapons, and one actually had his hands raised.

"This isn't over, Duhon," Fontenot finally managed.

"Oh, I think it is," Zach said. "Now get the hell off my property, Fat Ass."

Fontenot stalked to the truck and motioned his men to follow. He got in the passenger side as his men piled into the bed, and the truck sped away.

"He's right about one thing," Kinsey said. "I don't think it's over."

Zach nodded. "I know. Let's go talk some more about your ship."

***

"But we can't leave tonight," Connie Duhon said. "We have to pack all the stuff, and most of the food is in jars, so we have to pack well to keep them from breaking."

Kinsey shook his head. "No way, Connie. I'm not even sure we can get all the PEOPLE up the river, much less supplies. Everyone gets one small bag, a change of clothes, toothbrush, stuff like that, along with enough food for three days. Each person will carry their own bag, except for the kids, who carry as much as they can. We'll divide the rest of the kids' food among the adults."

Andrew Cormier stood in the dining room doorway, his arms crossed as he leaned against the door jamb and watched the confused back and forth of the meeting. He broke his silence.

"Y'all need to take every gun and bit of ammunition you have. It don't spoil, and if you don't need it, you can trade it."

Kinsey nodded. "Good idea." He turned to Zach. "How you fixed for gas? We brought enough for our own small outboards plus a bit extra, but some of that went up with our truck. I'm not sure we have enough fuel left for that gas-hog boat of yours."

Zach shrugged. "There's most of a tank in the boat plus what we have left around here. We stopped making scavenging runs when the gangbangers ran wild, so all the cars have at least a little left. We can siphon it and leave just enough in a couple of cars to get to the river. The problem is, other than a few gas cans for our lawn mowers, we got nothing to put it in. And speaking of the boat, how the hell we gonna get it in the river? There aren't any boat ramps near where y'all are tied up."

"Just make sure it's loose on the trailer and back it down the bank," Cormier said. "We'll keep a rope on it to make sure it don't get away from us in the current."

"But the bank is mud. How will I get the car… oh yeah, I don't guess it matters, does it?" Zach said.

Cormier grinned. "It'll be a one-way trip. And I'd have all the windows down and my seat belt off if I was you, just in case the car slips in the mud and keeps going. We don't have time to chase nobody downriver on the current. Not that we could find 'em in the dark anyway."

"I really love that car," Zach mumbled.

"If we can't take all the food," Connie said, "I'm not leaving it for Fat Ass. I'm going to give it to the Wilsons and the Trahans on the next street over. They—"

"No, you're not," said Kinsey and Cormier in unison.

"Why not?" she demanded.

"Because word will spread we're leaving, and Fat Ass would likely try to shake us down for the gas or make some problem," Zach said.

"Why would he care? He'll be happy to see us go."

"Only if he can make a big show of kicking us out," Zach said. "We don't have time for his drama."

"Agreed," Kinsey said. "We'll leave at ten. I'd like to leave later, but we have to make it past the prison while it's still dark. We can't afford any delays." He looked pointedly at Connie.

She bristled. "You don't worry about me. And if we have to leave food anyway, as soon as we get packed and ready, I'm feedin' us all until we pop," she said.

SAME DAY, 9:15 P.M.

Kinsey stifled a yawn as he walked into the kitchen and accepted a cup of strong black coffee from Zach. Gathering the supplies for the trip had been finished before noon, and true to her word, Connie had set about preparing a feast. No longer constrained by the need to conserve, the Duhons and their neighbors pitched in with a vengeance, and cook fires topped by cast-iron cookware had sprouted across the privacy-fenced backyard. By midafternoon the dining room table groaned with the weight of a sumptuous buffet of the rich Cajun food Kinsey had grown to love since marrying into the Melancon clan.

Full from the meal, almost two days without sleep had caught up with him, and his eyelids grew increasingly heavy. When it became obvious the rest of his team was in the same shape, Connie and Zach had insisted they sleep while the rest of the group finished departure preparations. Kinsey had agreed, not without reservations.

"The others up?" Kinsey asked.

His brother-in-law nodded in the light of the lantern. "About a half hour. They're out checking the cars now." Zach smiled. "Makin' sure we didn't screw anything up."

Kinsey ignored the dig. "Everything go okay?"

"Yeah, we decided to put all the gear and supplies in the boat, that way we can get on our way in a hurry. Since the boats will be lashed together for stability, we can redistribute the load among the three boats en route," Zach said.

Kinsey nodded and took another sip of coffee. He looked down at the cup. "This stuff could resuscitate the dead."

Zach laughed. "Yeah, well, the way you were snoring, I figured you needed to be resuscitated."

Kinsey chuckled and turned toward the door to the garage, cup in hand. Zach followed him out.

The garage was also lantern lit, and the far bay held a large center console fishing boat with an equally large outboard motor. The Duhon's SUV was backed up to the open garage door and hitched to the trailer. Kinsey reached up and turned on his headlamp so he could see better, then walked over and looked in the boat. He sighed.

"I see Connie's fine hand here," Kinsey said. "What part of one small bag per person didn't she understand?"

Zach shrugged. "You know Connie, she's kind of like a force of nature. Besides, there is one bag per person, there's just a little extra, that's all."

Kinsey played his light over a collection of boxes and bags, then shook his head. "Zach, we have to hump all this stuff over a fifty-foot-high levee, and even if we get it to Cormier's place, there's no way we'll get it all to Texas. I haven't even figured out how I'm going to get all the PEOPLE there."

He played his light over boxes as he spoke, stopping on one with distinctive markings. "What the hell is this?"

Zach looked embarrassed, but he quickly recovered. "What does it look like? It's a case of Jack Daniel's."

"Dammit, Zach—"

"Trade goods," Zach said. "I'm figuring it will be valuable, and I'd rather give up booze than ammo."

Kinsey let out a resigned sigh. "Okay, I'll grant you that, but here's the deal. One, if you folks want this stuff over the levee, YOU hump it, not me or any of my guys. Two, you do that AFTER you help us get the aluminum boats over. And three and most important, if at any point it slows us down or we can't find a reasonable way to carry it, we're dumping it, and I won't tolerate any bitching about it. Are we clear?"

Zach nodded his head. "Absolutely."

"Okay," Kinsey said. "What about life jackets?"

"We got regular life vests for the four kids, but after that it's a bit of a hodgepodge. Between the three houses we've got a mismatched collection of life jackets, ski vests, and ski belts. I think we'll have enough for everyone to have some sort of flotation, with maybe a few old ski belts extra," Zach said.

"Bring 'em," Kinsey said. "They're light, and you never know when they'll come in handy. How about glow sticks, got any?"

Zach glanced at the pile of supplies in the boat and grinned. "I suspect we do, why?"

"Break some out and tie one to each flotation device. If anyone goes overboard, they can activate it. Otherwise we don't have a chance of recovering anyone in the dark in that current."

Zach nodded just as Bollinger walked in, flanked by Cormier and Bertrand. Bollinger nodded toward the boat and shot Kinsey a questioning look. Kinsey shook his head, then shrugged, and Bollinger grinned. "Looks like you lost that one, boss," he said.

Kinsey ignored the remark. "How's everything else look?"

"Pretty good," Bollinger said. "They found a bunch of empty gallon milk jugs to collect the gasoline. They're out by the driveway, but we'll load them in the boat before we take off."

Kinsey nodded, suppressing a mental picture of the overloaded boat and trailer rolling backwards down the riverbank and straight to the bottom of the river. "What about a route?"

Cormier spoke up and nodded at Zach. "I showed Duhon here where the boats are on a street map. We should let the locals get us there. If we run into trouble, they'll have a better idea how to bypass it."

"You okay driving with the NV gear, Zach?" Kinsey asked.

"Do we HAVE to go dark?" Zach asked. "I mean, if everything goes well, we'll just reverse the route you came in on until we hit River Road and head north beside the levee. Running fast with lights, we can get to that intersection in five minutes tops. We keep a shooter with the NV stuff in each car, and if we run into trouble we can't avoid, we stop and kill the lights until the shooters take care of it. But I honestly think we'll be okay; I mean, if anybody sees or hears us, we'll likely blow past them before they can react. Even if someone decides to chase us, it'll take 'em a minute or two to get organized, and by then we'll be at River Road and dark again. We have to go dark the last half-mile stretch anyway to sneak past the projects and over the levee, and you guys wearing the NV gear can take over driving for that. We just stop, switch drivers, and haul ass, quick and quiet."

Kinsey nodded. "Well, even with the lights on, I guess we can't possibly be more obvious than we were coming in."

Cormier laughed, and Bollinger looked indignant until Kinsey grinned to take the sting out of his jibe. Only Zach seemed unamused.

"Problem, Zach?" Kinsey asked.

Zach shook his head. "That last half mile worries me big time. Y'all tied up next to some of the worst projects in Baton Rouge. If we attract the wrong kind of attention, we gotta get over that levee and upriver fast."

CHAPTER EIGHTEEN

SAME DAY, 10:00 P.M.

Their plans aside, they did go dark for the first very short leg of the journey. They stuffed both SUVs full to capacity and beyond, every seat occupied, with wives on their husband's laps and, in places, children perched on top of parents. Kinsey and Bollinger wore the NV gear and eased the vehicles through the subdivision to a side street a block from the entrance gate.

Taking out the guards was child's play; they weren't expecting an approach from the rear. Both surrendered without heroics when they felt the M4 muzzles touching the backs of their necks. The Coasties bound the guards' hands behind them with duct tape and eased them to the floor to wrap their ankles as well. Then they whistled for Zach.

"Gene, Pete," Zach said as he entered the little guardhouse. The pair squinted in the harsh light of his headlamp, glaring at him over duct-taped mouths. "We're leaving now," Zach said, "and we won't be back. I checked the schedule and see Bill and Dan are set to relieve y'all in two hours. You're all good people, despite how Fat Ass has your heads twisted up, so I'm gonna give you a little present."

The glares turned to looks of interest.

"We left all the food and supplies we couldn't carry in our garages. When Bill and Dan let y'all go, you can go get it and split it four ways. Fat Ass has no idea what we had, so he'll think we took it all. Nobody but y'all will know when we left, so if you leave Bill and Dan tied up until morning, you got all night to move and hide it and nobody will be the wiser. I don't care one way or another, but I'd rather y'all have the stuff than Fat Ass. 'Cause make no mistake, anything that goes into his 'community store' is gonna end up where HE decides, not the community."

The men exchanged a glance, then shrugged and nodded to Zach. He nodded back and exited the guardhouse.

"Feelin' better?" Kinsey asked.

"I am," Zach said. "The thought of leaving anything for that bastard was irritating the hell out of me. It was like he won somehow."

***

As Zach predicted, the run to River Road was uneventful. They raced through deserted streets, headlights blazing, with the unencumbered vehicle in the lead and the SUV towing the boat following. They pulled up in front of the veterinary school scarcely three minutes after leaving their subdivision. They killed the lights on the cars, and Kinsey and Bollinger flipped down their NV goggles and changed places with the drivers to head north up River Road. The vehicles swapped places, with Bollinger in the lead, towing the boat. He was to cross the levee first and head immediately to the riverbank while Kinsey followed behind. As soon as they crested the levee and dropped down toward the river and out of sight from town, Kinsey would use the chase car's headlights to light up the riverbank to aid launching and departure preparations.

All went well until Bollinger approached the road up the levee and slowed to make what was almost a U-turn. Kinsey was almost blinded as red lights flared.

"I thought we took the bulbs out of the brake lights?"

"It's the trailer," Zach said. "Someone must have plugged in the lights out of habit. It was in back before, so nobody noticed, and with the lights off, nothing showed until Bollinger braked."

Kinsey shot a look to his right, into the heart of the projects.

"Maybe nobody saw it," Zach said.

"Maybe not yet," Kinsey said, "but Bollinger doesn't even know he's doing it, and you can be sure he'll hit the brakes again at the top of the levee before he heads down. That's gonna be a great big flashing red sign fifty feet in the air. As dark as things are, it'll be visible for miles, and it might as well read VICTIMS HERE."

"What are we going to do?"

Kinsey shook his head. "Improvise."

In the short time it took Kinsey to make the tight turn to follow Bollinger up the levy, he had a plan.

"All right," he said to Zach, "I'll bail out on the crest and take up a defensive position. Take the wheel and turn on the lights; the cat's out of the bag now anyway, so it won't make any difference. Use whatever light you need to get the boat launched and everything ready to take off, but send Cormier or Bertrand back up here with the other set of NV gear. We'll hold off any visitors, and when you're ready to go, sound the car horn and we'll come running."

"Got it," Zach said as Kinsey bumped over the crest of the levee and skidded to a stop. Both doors flew open, and Zach jumped behind the wheel as Kinsey settled into the grass on top of the levee, eyes focused on the mean streets below.

Kinsey was studying the mob forming at the foot of the levee when Bertrand plopped down beside him five minutes later, puffing from his run up the steep slope.

"What you got, Coast Guard?" Bertrand asked.

"Twenty or thirty bangers, best I can tell. So far they're just milling around, but they keep looking up this way. We'll have company sooner or later," Kinsey said.

Bertrand was studying them now, and he grunted agreement. "Maybe we ought to discourage them."

"We will, but let's wait until they actually start up the levee. I'd like to drag this out as long as possible to give the others time to get the boats ready. I doubt these bangers are military geniuses, but they have a lot of cover down there if they decide to use it, and they'll shoot back at our muzzle flashes. Don't let them fix your position. Shoot, pull back behind the crest, then pop up someplace else; shoot and move, shoot and move. Got it?"

"This ain't my first rodeo, Coast Guard," Bertrand said.

"Army?"

"Travel to exotic places, meet interesting people, and kill them," Bertrand said. "I'm a sucker for a catchy motto."

Kinsey chuckled. "Okay, I'll shut up now."

"So much for waiting," Bertrand said. "Here they come. I'll take the fat guy on the left."

Kinsey sighed. "I'll take the tall one in the middle."

No sooner had Kinsey spoken than Bertrand's rifle barked, and the fat banger stumbled and fell. Kinsey fired a three-round burst, and the tall banger joined his fallen comrade. Both defenders dropped back below the levee's crest, and when they rose again in different positions several yards apart, the situation at the foot of the levee had changed dramatically. The bodies of the men they'd shot lay unmoving at the foot of the grassy slope, but the others had scattered, no doubt to positions in and around the houses lining the opposite side of River Road.

"THEY CAPPED FAT DOG AND T-BOY!" someone shouted.

"YO, WHOEVER Y'ALL ARE UP THERE, WE GONNA MESS YOU UP! AIN'T NOBODY DISRESPECTIN' US IN OUR OWN HOOD."

"Is it just me, or are they pissed?" Bertrand asked.

"Just as long as they stay pissed off down there, it doesn't matter."

Kinsey had hardly finished speaking when his position atop the levee allowed him to glimpse the flash of headlights several blocks away. Then there was another, and within seconds, he could see a steady stream of vehicles pouring out of the surrounding neighborhoods and heading in their direction.

"I'd say they have radios," Kinsey said. "It looks like we've stirred 'em up."

"Not good." Bertrand shook his head. "With enough shooters, they can keep raking the top of the levee to keep our heads down while the rest climb right up in our laps."

"Ya think?" Kinsey asked, then flipped up his NV glasses and looked back down the levee toward the river. There was a pool of light at the riverbank, and he could see moving figures. "What's taking them so long?"

"Uh-oh," Bertrand said. "Look toward the vet school."

Kinsey heard the distant throaty snarl of motorcycles and, a half mile south, saw headlights bouncing up the slope of the levee at an angle.

"They get up top, and we're flanked," Bertrand said. "And the boats are lit up like Christmas trees down there. They'll be sitting ducks."

"Let's go!" Kinsey said, and he started down toward the river at a run, Bertrand hot on his heels.

The scene below reminded Kinsey of some surreal tableau from the tragic past. The boats were lashed three abreast, floating in the shallow water near the riverbank, with the larger fishing boat in the center and a smaller aluminum hull on either side. They rode low in the water, and the huddled mass of passengers and heaps of supplies were cast in sharp relief by the harsh glare of the car headlights. Kinsey saw Zach removing the cowling of the big outboard on the fishing boat. He ran to douse the headlights of the nearest car while Bertrand scrambled and slid through the mud of the riverbank to the second vehicle. In seconds everything was plunged into darkness, and a howl of protest rose from the boats.

"Dammit!" yelled Zach through the darkness. "Who turned off those lights? I can't see what I'm doing."

Multiple flashlights flashed toward Kinsey.

"Shield those lights and get ready to get out of here," Kinsey said. "Every banger in Baton Rouge is about to come over that levee."

"The outboard keeps dying. I can't—"

He was interrupted by the roar of approaching motorcycle engines, and headlights popped over the crest of the levee and raced down toward them.

"Better do something quick," Kinsey said. "These guys are just the scouts and there are a whole lot more where they came from."

He turned and braced his M4 on the hood of the car and opened fire on the approaching cycles. He heard Bertrand do the same from the other car. Their first rounds hit the lead cycle almost simultaneously, and it dropped sideways in front of two bikes following closely behind. All three bikes went down in a tangled mass of steel and flesh, the riders' screams echoing above the sound of the crash. Two bikes trailing the leaders managed to swerve around the wreck, but Kinsey and Bertrand took them out. But there was no time to celebrate victory; the headlights of more bikes and cars began pouring over the levee.

"READY OR NOT, HERE WE COME!" Kinsey yelled as he and Bertrand stumbled and slid down the muddy riverbank and splashed into the water.

They were waist deep when they reached the boats, and willing hands reached out to drag them aboard. Kinsey heard the muttering pop of the smaller outboards, but nothing from the fishing boat motor.

"It's no use," he heard Zach say. "I can't get it going."

"Bollinger?" Kinsey said into the dark.

"Here." Kinsey turned and was relieved to see Bollinger sitting at the small outboard, glowing green in the NV goggles. He wormed his way down the boat, stepping over people sitting terrified in the darkness, until he was within arm's reach of Bollinger.

"Put your hand out. I'm going to hand you the NV gear. Put it on and get us the hell out of here. Where's Cormier?"

"Here," called Cormier. "I'm at the other outboard."

"The same for you, but just keep your motor straight ahead and let Bollinger do the steering," Kinsey said.

"Do you want me to pass Cormier my glasses?" Bertrand asked.

"Negative," Kinsey said. "We might need you to shoot somebody."

He looked back toward the levee, a hundred yards away, and watched headlights stream down the slope into the parking lot. With no light to attract the bangers' attention, and the roar of the bangers' own cars and motorcycles drowning out the outboards, they had a bit of time. However, it wouldn't take the bangers long to find the cars on the riverbank and figure out where they should be looking. When that happened, the sound of their outboards would give them away; they needed to get out of range upriver as soon as possible.

He felt the boat buffeted by ever stronger currents as they moved into the river, and watched impotently as headlights and powerful flashlights cut the night ashore. Then he heard raised voices ashore over the low conversation of his fellow passengers, and the lights began to converge on the riverbank near the cars. The bangers' vehicles began to die one by one, and he knew it wouldn't be long before they heard the outboards, if they didn't already.

"Can't you and Cormier get any more juice out of those sewing machines?" Kinsey asked quietly.

"They're having all they can do to make any headway at all," Bollinger responded. "They're not exactly designed for this."

Kinsey said nothing as powerful beams of light began to stab out from shore, motorcycle headlights and handheld spotlights no doubt, dancing across the water in search of what the bangers could hear but not yet pinpoint. One seemed more aggressive than the rest, the beam sweeping toward them.

"See it, Bertrand?"

"I got him," Bertrand replied, and his M4 barked. The beam of light veered off at a crazy angle.

"Kill those outboards," Kinsey said abruptly.

"But what —"

"DO IT!" Kinsey said, and the two men complied.

"Let's hope they didn't see the muzzle flash," Bertrand said softly.

"On the contrary, let's hope they did. Now everyone be absolutely quiet," Kinsey said.

No longer fighting the powerful current, the odd little convoy floated free on the powerful flood, streaking downstream in the dark past the bangers on the riverbank. Kinsey held his breath as they floated by barely fifty yards from the bank and said a silent prayer they wouldn't be captured by a probing beam. But with no sound to guide them, the bangers were momentarily confused and concentrated their search in the direction they had last heard the sound and seen the flash. Kinsey had no doubt the bangers would eventually put it together, but all he really needed was five minutes on the swift current to put them beyond the range of the bangers' lights and guns.

He gave it ten.

"Okay, boys," Kinsey said. "Crank up the outboards and let's find a place on the far bank to get this mess straightened out."

Mississippi River
West Bank
One Mile South of Port Allen Lock

Same Day, 11:20 p.m.

Their temporary refuge was another backwater between a wooded stretch of the west bank and a string of abandoned barges. They pulled into the gap, the empty barges hiding them from Baton Rouge across the river.

"Okay," Kinsey said. "Bertrand, get up on that barge and keep watch. The rest of you, get some lights on and get this squared away. We've already lost too much time. Bollinger, you're our mechanical genius, give Zach a hand with his engine."

"No genius required," Bollinger said. "I already told him he's got bad fuel."

Kinsey looked at his brother-in-law. "How old is the gas in your boat, Zach?"

"We haven't use the boat since last summer, but I added fuel stabilizer… anyway I THINK I added stabilizer." He shook his head. "To be honest, I don't really remember."

Kinsey sighed and bit back a rebuke. "All right. Bollinger, help me out here. What are we lookin' at?"

"I got no clue until I get into it, boss. At a minimum we have to dump the tank and put in new gas. After that, it depends on what we're dealin' with." Bollinger turned to Zach. "You got a spare fuel filter?"

Zach shook his head.

"Tools?" Bollinger asked.

Zach reached in his pocket and produced a small adjustable wrench and a couple of screwdrivers.

"Friggin' lovely," Bollinger muttered.

"I got a toolbox," Cormier volunteered. "It ain't much, but it's better than that."

Bollinger thanked Cormier and moved over to accept the toolbox the Cajun produced from underneath a seat. He took it and moved back to the big outboard.

Kinsey worked his way back to where Bollinger and Zach were about to tear into the engine. He spoke softly. "Will we have enough gas to make it now?" he asked Bollinger.

Bollinger shrugged. "No way of knowing, but it'll be close, that's for sure."

"Okay," Kinsey said. "You and Zach do the best you can. I need to talk to Cormier."

Bollinger nodded and Kinsey worked his way across the crowded vessels closer to Cormier. "What are your thoughts on our little flotilla?"

Cormier shook his head. "We're unbalanced and too heavy. We didn't have time to rearrange anything before the bangers showed up, but we need to spread stuff out." Cormier glanced at Connie Duhon. "And get rid of some of it. And we need to think about the outboards. We're gonna have to run them all now to make any speed against the current with this load, and we can't have three people steering. We should just tie the tillers of the small boats so the outboards are pushing straight ahead, then steer with the motor on the big boat in the center."

"Makes sense," Kinsey agreed, then looked back at the pair working on the motor and lowered his voice even more. "What if they can't get the motor going? You think we can make it in the smaller boats?"

Cormier looked at Kinsey as if he were insane. "Even with just the people we'd be dangerously overloaded. We planned on bringin' back four or five people, not seventeen. No way we'd make it in less than a full day, if we made it at all. You saw how they was strainin' against the current. I doubt they could go over five or six miles an hour by themselves, not to mention being unstable like hell in this river. But you know that, I think."

Kinsey nodded. "Yeah, I do, but I was hoping you might see something I missed." He sighed. "Oh well, can you take care of setting up the smaller outboards and getting the gear redistributed?"

Cormier nodded. "Mais oui."

Kinsey turned to his sister-in-law, "Okay, Connie, you can see for yourself we're overloaded. I'll let you choose, but I want you to lose at least half of it; then you and the others help Cormier redistribute it between the boats evenly. Are we clear?"

"Yes, Matt. And I'm sorry."

"Not a problem, let's just get this done."

"Don't throw away them glow sticks," Cormier said. "I'm gonna need some of them."

"What for?" Kinsey asked.

"Just an idea," Cormier said. "It's easier if I show you than tell you."

***

The others finished their respective tasks long before the engine was ready, and as they waited, Kinsey watched Cormier implement his idea and smiled as the Cajun explained it to him.

That was the bright spot; things were going much worse with the engine repair. Kinsey checked the time repeatedly as Bollinger tore into the outboard with Zach's help. It was over two hours later before they got the motor off to a sputtering start. Bollinger wiped his hands on a greasy rag and looked over at Kinsey and shook his head.

"I cleaned everything that's cleanable with the tools at hand. I'm hoping it smooths out when we run it under load. But I doubt she can develop full power." Bollinger shrugged. "She'll get better or she won't, and it's even money either way. I'm sorry, boss. I did the best I could."

"I know you did, Bollinger. We'll just give it a shot and hope for the best." Kinsey shot another worried glance at his watch and called Bertrand down from the barge.

They put the kids and nonswimmers in the fishing boat, along with most of Connie's much-diminished load of supplies. Adult swimmers were in the aluminum boats on either side. The Coasties took full control of the NV gear again, though Bertrand returned his set with obvious reluctance. Bollinger took the wheel of the larger fishing boat, and Kinsey provided overwatch with his M4 as they moved upriver.

The big engine sputtered and popped, but overall performed better than expected. But it was almost two in the morning, and they had to cover seventy miles against the current before daylight, a bit over three hours away.

Presuming they made it at all; the noise from the outboards was significant and if they couldn't be seen, they could certainly be heard. They still had to get past the bangers and God knew who else.

"What you think, Kinsey? Time for my toy?" Cormier asked.

"Do it," Kinsey said, and Cormier squatted at the back of the fishing boat, working on the two surplus ski belts now festooned with chemical glow sticks. He bent the sticks one by one, his face illuminated by the eerie green glow as they activated; then he stood and tossed the ski belts out the back of the moving boat. The boat raced onward, leaving the glowing ski belts in its wake and with Cormier paying out the line attached to them and coiled at his feet with the end secured to a cleat near the boat's stern. The line finished paying out and went taut, towing the glowing ski belts in line twenty feet apart, racing along a hundred feet behind the boat.

"What the hell?" asked Zach Duhon.

"We killed some of those bangers and they're pissed off," Cormier said, "and Kinsey thinks they got radios. So who knows what we're going to run into. For sure, we ain't gonna sneak by with these outboards, and if they shoot at the sound, they might even hit somebody, especially if there's a bunch of 'em. I figure we give 'em something to shoot at that ain't us, far enough away that even if they're lousy shots, they won't hit us."

"Think it'll work?" Zach asked.

"Don't know," Cormier said. "But sound is hard to pinpoint in the dark, and if you heard an outboard in a general direction and saw something speedin' through the water, what would you shoot at?"

They hugged the west bank, keeping well out of range of the bangers from the LSU area until they passed under the I-10 bridge and moved back to the center of the river. Suddenly, the bridge erupted in gunfire, with muzzle flashes visible along half its length. Kinsey grinned as the surface of the water near their glowing decoys was peppered with splashes that looked like green pinpricks in his NV glasses.

"Looks like it's working, Andrew," Kinsey said.

"Let's just hope we can get through Baton Rouge before they figure it out," Cormier replied.

But their luck held. They were fired on three more times, each time with the same result. When they finally passed under the US 190 bridge, Kinsey heaved a sigh of relief and focused on their real enemy, the clock.

An hour later, the clock gained an ally.

"We're sucking fuel like there's no tomorrow," Bollinger whispered, worry in his voice.

"Will we have enough?" Kinsey asked, equally quiet.

Bollinger shrugged. "No way to tell. The motor's running flat out. It's settled down a little, but still not running anywhere near normal efficiency. Throw in the extra resistance of the current on this lash-up we're pushing, and fuel efficiency is in the toilet anyway."

"Suggestions?"

"Not really," Bollinger said. "If I slow down to conserve fuel, it'll take longer to get there and pretty much guarantee we're limping past the prison in daylight."

"Should we lighten the load more?"

Bollinger shook his head. "I don't think it matters unless you're planning on throwing people overboard. Nothing else is heavy enough to make much difference, and we're pretty well-balanced now; changing things might even make it worse. Avoiding the strongest currents will help. We got nothing but farmland on either side now, so I'll hug the banks and take every bend on the inside radius. Whether it helps enough is anyone's guess."

"Do what you can," Kinsey said.

So they clawed their way upriver through the darkness. Around them the others rode in quiet uncertainty, wives leaning against husbands' shoulders, and kids sleeping in mothers' laps. Two hours later, they swept around a long bend and began to head due west as the sky lightened in the east.

Kinsey glanced back east. "How far you think?" he asked Bollinger softly.

He almost jumped out of his skin when a voice answered out of the darkness from the seat in front of him. "Let me have the glasses, and I'll tell you."

"Geez! You scared the crap out of me," Kinsey said.

Cormier chuckled. "Nervous, Coast Guard?"

"Hell yes," Kinsey said, taking off the NV glasses and reaching over to press them against Cormier's chest so he could accept them by feel.

The big Cajun put the glasses on and studied the riverbanks. "We're about five miles from Angola Landing, I think. We ain't gonna make it past the prison in the dark. Keep to the left bank from now on. The channel to the levee is about two miles beyond the prison landing."

They rode in silence under a lightening sky, and Kinsey imagined the outboard was getting louder with the rising sun. People were starting to stir on their seats, and Cormier and Bollinger took off the NV glasses.

Kinsey strained to see the far bank of the river. "You think there'll be anybody at the landing, Andrew?"

Cormier shrugged. "Who knows? I'm hoping all the cons like their beauty sleep. Even if they see us, we're out of range, so they'll have to chase us. If they don't have a boat ready, we might get a big enough lead to slip behind the island and up the channel to the levee without them seeing which way we go."

"Your lips to God's ears," Kinsey said.

The landing was clearly visible across the river now, and Kinsey saw boats tied to the dock. He saw no movement and said a silent prayer the cons were all asleep and there was no one to hear the roar of the outboard.

They were in the swiftest part of the current now, forced to the outside of a sweeping river bend to maintain their distance from the prison landing. Their progress slowed perceptibly, and Kinsey realized the big outboard WAS louder as it strained against the increased load. Just two more miles and they'd be home free. Kinsey turned his attention from the prison dock and stared upriver, willing them forward.

They'd covered a half mile when Bertrand spoke.

"Trouble," he said, and Kinsey turned and followed the man's pointing finger. Behind them, a boat was leaving the prison dock. Kinsey watched as it cut across the river diagonally to fall into their wake, growing larger with each passing minute.

"They're gaining on us," he said.

Bertrand raised his rifle, but Kinsey reached up and pushed it down, nodding toward the passengers. "Let's not start a gunfight just yet. We're a much bigger target and have a lot to lose."

Bertrand nodded, and Kinsey turned to Cormier. "Think we can lose them behind the island, Andrew?"

Cormier shook his head. "Doubtful. They're already too close and gaining. They'll be right on our butt when we turn up the channel."

Kinsey muttered a curse. "All right," he said. "It probably won't help, but let's start lightening the load." He tossed one of Connie's remaining boxes over the side.

There was some hesitation; then the others began to toss things over as well.

"How we looking on fuel?" Kinsey asked Bollinger.

"Running on fumes," Bollinger replied. "But I think we'll make it."

The words had hardly left his mouth when the big outboard sputtered, coughed three times, and fell silent.

"Or not," Bollinger said as their speed dropped dramatically, and the pitch of the two smaller motors changed as they coped with the suddenly increased load.

"We're screwed," Bollinger said.

CHAPTER NINETEEN

DAY 30, 5:50 A.M.

Kinsey looked back. He could make out five convicts in the boat, and he saw one of them point to a jettisoned box as they flashed by it. The con shouted something to the others, and Kinsey saw them all laugh. They knew they had won the race and were enjoying the victory.

Then it hit him.

"ZACH! Put that down."

Zach looked confused, but set the case of Jack Daniel's he'd been about to jettison on the deck. Kinsey pushed past the others to get to him at the stern.

"Take your ski belt off, and buckle it around the booze. Make sure not to cover the markings on the box."

"What are you —"

"DO IT!" Kinsey screamed, and Zach hastened to do as ordered. Kinsey reached over and began to untie the tow rope for Cormier's decoy, which still trailed the boat. Zach finished buckling the whiskey in the ski belt, and Kinsey pulled ten feet of the tow rope in and handed it to Zach, letting the loose end trail on the deck at their feet.

"Don't let this go," Kinsey said as he dropped to his knees and began tying the end of the rope to the ski belt encircling the case of whiskey. When he was done, he gave it a tug to make sure it was secure, then ordered Zach to toss the slack back over the side.

"Cormier and Bertrand," Kinsey said, "get to the small outboards. Slow down to just hold us in place against the current, but DON'T stop. Then be ready to haul balls when I give the order."

"We ain't haulin' anything with this rig, but we'll do what we can," Cormier replied as he and Bertrand maneuvered through the crowded boats to take control of the two functioning outboards.

Kinsey looked astern, judging the distance to the oncoming boat, as he waited for the Cajuns to get into place. When they were there, he said, "Cut speed now."

He heard muttered curses from the passengers as the speed dropped further, and he slipped the whiskey over the stern and let it go, watching briefly as it fell behind in the boat's wake. He stood and faced the others.

"You're going to have to trust me on this, folks," Kinsey said. "I want everybody to turn and face the oncoming boat, with your hands over your heads."

"Are you nuts?" Zach asked.

"Do it," Connie said as she raised her hands as ordered.

One by one, the others followed Connie's lead. Kinsey turned back to face the oncoming boat himself and raised his own hands.

He heard the motor on the convicts' boat change pitch as, unsure what was happening, they cut their own speed. They closed the gap steadily, but not as rapidly as before. The whiskey floated between the two boats, moving ever closer to the cons. When he thought they were close enough to hear him, Kinsey shouted across the gap.

"WE SURRENDER."

Kinsey heard angry muttering behind him; then after a moment's hesitation, a cheer went up from the convicts' boat. About that time, one of the cons shouted and pointed at the whiskey, and the boat veered toward it and circled it, preparing to pull it aboard.

Kinsey held his breath as the cons' boat passed over the semi-submerged towline, then smiled as the plaintive sound of mechanical mayhem announced the rope had wrapped in the propeller and jammed it tight. As soon as he heard the cons' motor stop, Kinsey reached for his M4 and began to shout.

"GO! GO! GO! EVERYBODY DOWN. EVERYBODY DOWN."

He steadied himself against the slight rocking of the boat on the current and began firing at the cons, dropping one immediately and sending the rest diving for cover. He heard firing beside him and glanced over to see Bollinger, M4 at his shoulder.

"Hold your fire," Kinsey said, "so we're not both changing mags at the same time. We don't have to take them out, but one of us has to keep their heads down until we're out of range."

Bollinger grunted his understanding and his gun fell silent as Kinsey continued to fire well-placed single shots anytime one of the cons showed himself. The distance between the boats widened as the disabled craft bobbed downstream on the swift current, and Kinsey's overloaded and lashed-together boats clawed their way slowly upstream on the small straining outboards.

When they were out of range, Kinsey lowered his rifle and swiveled to look upriver.

"How much farther?" he called to Cormier.

"A bit over a mile, I'd say," Cormier replied. "But we're barely moving and the big boat's nothing but drag now. We gotta lose it or it will take us more than a half hour to get there, and for sure we ain't got that much gas."

Kinsey nodded. "Bollinger, you and Zach go through our empty gas cans and those milk jugs and drain every last drop that's left. Split it between the gas tanks on the smaller boats while I divide everyone between the two smaller boats. Then we'll figure out how to separate."

Bollinger's task didn't take long, as 'every last drop' from the various gas containers amounted to less than a cup, which he and Zach dutifully split between the two boats. Dividing the people was more difficult, as Kinsey had to move them one at a time so as not to destabilize the delicate equilibrium of the overloaded boats. It took five long minutes with Kinsey making on-the-fly assessments of each passenger's weight before he had both boats loaded more or less equally, with him in the bow of Cormier's boat and Bollinger in the bow of Bertrand's.

"Okay, folks," Kinsey said, "we're really overloaded, so please keep as close to the centerline of the boats as you can, and don't move around. We're going to separate from the center boat, then bring the two boats back together and tether them side by side as we move upstream. That way, if one of our motors runs out of gas, we should still have enough power to at least maneuver both boats to the west bank. Everyone ready?"

There were murmurs and fearful nods, and after he confirmed Cormier and Bertrand were ready, Kinsey loosened the bow lashing on his own boat and held it wrapped around the cleat, ready to be thrown off at a moment's notice. Bollinger duplicated his actions in the other boat as Kinsey called back and had men untie the stern lashings completely.

"Okay, Bollinger," Kinsey yelled, "we separate on the count of three. Are you ready?"

"Affirmative," Bollinger replied.

"ONE, TWO, THREE!" Kinsey yelled and threw the line off the cleat as Bollinger did the same, and Zach's fishing boat slipped from between the two boats and fell astern. No longer encumbered by the dead weight of the larger boat or tied together, the smaller boats surged forward at different speeds and separated.

"CORMIER," Kinsey yelled, "HOLD YOUR COURSE AND SPEED. BERTRAND, BRING YOUR BOAT ALONGSIDE, BUT CAREFULLY! THE BOW WAVES WILL FORCE US APART, SO DON'T PUSH IT. JUST GET CLOSE ENOUGH FOR US TO PASS LINES."

The Cajuns handled the boats deftly, and soon the boats were running side by side, just feet apart and tethered together bow and stern. The rest of the short trip was uneventful, and they'd just turned out of the current and into the still backwater of the Lower Old River when Bertrand's outboard sputtered to a stop and his boat bumped back alongside of Cormier's.

"Pull in the slack and lash them side by side," Kinsey ordered, then looked back at Cormier. "Think we have enough gas to make the levee, Andrew?" he asked.

Cormier shrugged. "Maybe, maybe not, but we can paddle from here if we have to."

Kinsey nodded, relief written on his face.

Cormier grinned. "Relax, Coast Guard. The hard part's over. Now we just gotta get back to the bayou."

SOMEWHERE IN THE ATCHAFALAYA RIVER BASIN
NORTH OF MORGAN CITY, LOUISIANA

DAY 30, 4:20 P.M.

As Cormier predicted, the trip back to his bayou stronghold was uneventful. The extra manpower made getting the aluminum boats and gear over the levee easier, and the addition of more armed men discouraged any who might have considered challenging them on their return trip down the Atchafalaya. They arrived in the late afternoon, and Kinsey saw Cormier's daughter-in-law, Lisa, standing on the little dock.

"How'd she know we were coming?" Kinsey asked.

Cormier scoffed. "Seriously, Coast Guard? You don't understand by now nothing moves on the bayou we don't know about?"

"Okay, dumb question." Kinsey nodded to where Lisa stood, smiling. "But she does look happy to see you."

Cormier nodded, and as they neared the dock, Lisa called across the gap, "Tim's much better, Pop. The fever broke last night, and he demanded breakfast this morning. I think he's gonna be all right."

Kinsey saw Cormier swallow hard, then blink away sudden tears before he looked skyward and crossed himself. He laid a hand on the big Cajun's shoulder and the man turned to him, grinning from ear to ear, but he could only bob his head, as if he were incapable of speech.

Cormier stepped across the gap between the boat and the dock without waiting for the boat to be secured, and raced away with Lisa, eager to see his son.

***

Cormier seemed like a new man when he came back down to the dock twenty minutes later to find Bollinger and Kinsey still on the Coast Guard boat.

"Where's everybody else?" he asked.

"Some of your folks are showing them where to bed down for the night," Kinsey said. "Bollinger and I figured we'd stay here to plan our trip to Texas. We appreciate the help, but we don't want to abuse your hospitality."

Cormier shrugged. "We'll take anyone who wants to stay, as long as they pull their weight. They're Cajuns too." He paused and looked from Kinsey to Bollinger. "You too, Coast Guard, if you want."

The offer took Kinsey by surprise. "Thank you, Andrew. That's very generous, but I have to say I'm surprised."

"It's no mystery. They were doing okay in Baton Rouge, so I think they'll be willing to work. The bayou and our gardens will provide our food, and it rains enough here that freshwater is no problem. Finally, we can use the extra manpower, both for survival and defense," Cormier said.

Kinsey thought about it a moment, then nodded. "I'll put it to them. I suspect some of them will accept."

"What about you two?" Cormier asked.

"I'll be going back to the ship," Bollinger said quickly. "I appreciate the offer, but I'd feel like I was deserting my friends when they need me."

Kinsey was nodding. "Same here."

Cormier nodded. "*Je comprends.*"

They lapsed into silence a moment before Kinsey spoke. "It may be crowded, but if we reduce the number going back, maybe we can fit them all into our boat."

"Too bad we can't get word to Wellesley to wait for us," Bollinger said. "He should be taking off any time, but our rescue took a lot less time than we figured, thanks to Andrew. If we can get to the lock before he leaves, we can put some of the folks in one of the push boats and all go back to Texas together. I don't really look forward to having a boatload of noncombatants if we get into another gunfight."

Cormier shrugged. "Why not call him on your radio?"

Kinsey shook his head. "Even if he's still at the lock, that's over a hundred miles from here. The VHF won't reach that far."

Cormier rubbed his bearded chin. "I know a lot of people between here and there. Some worked on crew boats, and others own shrimp boats. We could probably set up a relay to pass word to him, if you want to try."

Kinsey nodded enthusiastically and reached for the VHF handset, but Cormier stopped him with a raised hand and shook his head.

"No transmitting here. We have to go on the river, and I want to be moving while we transmit. I don't want to take the chance on anyone locating us from your transmission." Cormier looked at the sky. "It'll be dark in a couple of hours. We take your boat on the river with your NV glasses, almost down to Morgan City."

SAME DAY, 10:20 P.M.

They went south almost to Morgan City before Cormier felt comfortable transmitting. Bollinger killed the engine and Kinsey nodded at Cormier. The big Cajun picked up the handset and began speaking French.

"What's with the French?" Bollinger asked.

Cormier shrugged as they waited for a response. "I figure if any FEMA assholes are listening, they're probably less likely to speak Cajun than English."

Kinsey nodded. "Good point."

Cormier called several times before he raised anyone, but when he got a response, he explained he was attempting to relay a message to the push boat *Judy Ann*. The message was simple, consisting of only 'Kinsey coming. Please wait.'

After almost an hour and three relays, the message was apparently delivered, with the last relay link switching to English for Lucius Wellesley's benefit. The radio squawked in Cajun, and Cormier bobbed his head at the two Coasties. He acknowledged the transmission then lowered the mic and looked at Kinsey quizzically.

"What is it?" Kinsey asked.

"There was a reply," Cormier said. "Wellesley said, 'Trouble in Texas. We are holding here.'"

Kinsey felt a chill run down his spine. He thought about the reply a moment.

"Pass the word for Wellesley to try to find a French speaker among his guys. We need to discuss this a bit more."

CHAPTER TWENTY

The Previous Day
Day 29, 5:10 a.m.

Chief Mate Georgia Howell eased open the aft door of the enclosed lifeboat, struggling to do it quietly with one hand. She stepped out onto the almost nonexistent rear deck, set the bucket down on the two-foot-wide shelf, and used both hands to close the door for privacy. That is, if pissing outside in a bucket, floating in the middle of a river between the massive hulls of two gigantic, but empty and unmanned, ships could be considered private. Lifeboats didn't have toilets, and they certainly weren't designed for coeducational occupancy. *Here's hoping I don't fall overboard*, she thought as she dropped her pants and squatted over the bucket. Just another thing women had to worry about that guys didn't, pissing in an enclosed lifeboat during the apocalypse.

She finished and pulled up her pants, then emptied the bucket overboard and dropped to her knees, leaning down to rinse the bucket in the river. The sky was lightening in the east now, and she'd be able to see well enough to navigate in fifteen or twenty minutes; she was considerably less quiet when she opened the door.

"Up and at 'em, guys. It's almost daylight and we'll be taking off in a few minutes. I'm leaving the bucket just inside the door. Do whatever you need to do and get something to eat and drink. This is likely to be a long day." She heard sleepy acknowledgments, then closed the door and leaned back against the cabin to watch the eastern sky.

She wanted an early start, her theory being miscreants were unlikely to be early risers. It was nine miles to the boat club, and she figured they could make it in three hours max, even against the current in the lumbering lifeboat, but they had to pass some pretty crappy sections of town. Her 'boat of many colors,' as she came to think of it, might blend in well with the natural riverbank in the dusk, but it would still stick out like a sore thumb in broad daylight in an industrial area. She wanted to be safely docked at the boat club before the lowlifes woke up.

The lifeboat door cracked open tentatively, and she shifted to make room as it opened wider and Juan Alvarez stepped out and emptied the bucket over the stern. Then he dropped to one knee and repeated the ritual she just performed, though his longer arms made it much easier to reach the water's surface. Alvarez finished the task, rose and leaned through the open door to pass the empty bucket to one of the others inside before turning back to Georgia.

"So what's the drill, ma'am?" he asked.

"We'll head upriver as soon as we can see," Howell said. "It's mostly vacant land or industrial areas on both sides of the river, but if we have any problems, I expect they'll be from the west bank, probably closer to downtown. I want you and Jones watching that side, with Jimmy and Pete on the other. If we have any problems, I suspect it'll be near Riverfront Park. Other than that, we play it by ear."

Alvarez nodded. "Yes, ma'am. Rules of engagement?"

"I'm not second-guessing anyone," Howell said. "If it looks like we're in danger, fire at your own discretion. But remember, there are just five of us, so if we draw the wrong kind of attention, we're toast. The plan is to get in and out as quietly as possible."

"Copy that, ma'am. We'll be ready when you are."

* * *

They were moving ten minutes later. The east bank of the river was mostly undeveloped almost all the way to downtown Beaumont, and their camouflage paint job in the dim light of early morning still afforded some protection. *Use it while you got it,* Howell thought as she steered to starboard and hugged the east bank.

Despite the plodding pace of the underpowered lifeboat, they passed the Exxon-Mobil refinery on the west bank and were approaching Harbor Island Terminal in just under two hours. It was full light now, and the boat was readily visible. A railroad bridge spanned the river ahead and she steered as close as she dared to the right bank and called softly to the others. "Look sharp. Riverfront Park coming up on the left bank, just after the railroad bridge."

There were murmured acknowledgments, and Howell put her hand on the throttle, unconsciously trying to press it forward, even though the lumbering boat was topped out. But the park was deserted, the area devoid of activity in the early morning hours. Minutes later she heaved a relieved sigh when she negotiated a sharp right turn and left the downtown area behind her to pass the old shipyard on her left.

"Almost there," Howell said. "Fifteen or twenty minutes max."

They rounded another turn to the left, and through the viewing port at the conning station, she saw the I-10 bridge looming across the river just ahead. The tops of abandoned cars were visible above the guardrail the length of the bridge.

"Alvarez," Howell said, "can you see the bridge from the gun ports? We'll be sitting ducks for anyone on the bridge, and we don't have any armor on the top of the canopy."

"Negative. It's too high. We best move outside."

"Do it," Howell confirmed, but the two Coasties were already moving toward the back door and front entry port of the lifeboat. In seconds, they were standing on the bow and stern, M4s pointed up toward the bridge ahead.

"Have you given any thought to live-aboards, ma'am?" Alvarez asked Howell through the open rear door of the lifeboat, never taking his eyes off the bridge. "Some of the boats in this yacht club likely have generators and what have you. If I owned one, that's where I'd be."

"Agreed," Howell said, hands on the wheel and her own eyes fixed up at the bridge as they approached. "But I also figure the last place I'd stay is in an urban marina when I could duck out of sight into a wooded inlet upriver where nobody could get to me by road." She hesitated. "But you're right, it's better safe than sorry."

Howell cut speed abruptly as they moved under the bridge, steering hard left toward the strip of wooded land lining the western riverbank under the bridge.

"What are you doing?" Alvarez asked.

"We're only a hundred yards from the yacht club channel," Howell said. "It's to the left, just past these trees. We'll go ashore here under the bridge and do a little recon from the safety of the trees. The boat will be directly under the bridge, so no one can spot it from above."

"Good idea," Alvarez said. "Jones and I will —"

"Negative," Howell said. "I need to see it myself. It'll be me and you while the other guys watch the boat."

WEST END OF I-10 BRIDGE
BEAUMONT, TEXAS

The police cruiser was parked at right angles across the highway in the westbound lanes, barring nonexistent traffic. The windows were open and its occupants sat in a lethargic daze. They were unkempt and unshaven, and a successive series of circular sweat stains emanating from the armpits of their rumpled shirts tracked the number of days since their last uniform change as surely as rings marked the age of a tree.

One of them stirred. "This sucks! The sun ain't hardly up, and you can already fry an egg on the road. Turn on the AC."

The driver shook his head. "You know the orders; fifteen minutes of AC every hour after eight. We got a while yet, and if Spike catches us wasting gas, we're dead meat. So quit bein' a whiny pussy; you're gettin' on my nerves."

"Come on, who's gonna know? There ain't nobody around but us, and I don't even know why we're here. Nobody's traveling the interstate anymore. We ain't pulled any pussy or plunder off the bridge in a week."

"Everybody's gonna know when you get drunk again and start running your mouth. These orders came straight from Spike. Have you forgotten what he did to Miller last week when he screwed up?" The driver shuddered. "He is one mean dude, and I ain't gonna cross him. And if Spike wants us here, we're here. That's all there is to it, so quit your bitchin—"

The driver cocked his head. "Hear that?"

"I don't hear nothing—"

"It's a boat. Not an outboard, something else," the driver said.

His partner shrugged. "Still don't hear nothing."

"That's 'cause it's stopped now, numb nuts," the driver said, reaching for the radio mike. "I'll call it in; you go see if you can spot it."

"Up yours," his partner said, motioning to the bridge jammed solid with abandoned cars. "We can't drive, and I ain't walking all the way up there in this heat to see some boat that ain't even there. If you're so damned anxious to see what it is, YOU go, and I'LL call it in. Maybe I'll turn on a little AC while I'm at it."

The driver glared. "Am I going to have to kick your ass, Cecil? You do remember the last time, right?"

Cecil cursed under his breath. "All right, dammit, but you come with me. If I have to tromp around in this heat, I want company. And besides, we shouldn't call it in unless we really see something; otherwise they'll have us chasing our tails all over the place."

The driver considered, then nodded. They got out, the driver grimacing when Cecil slammed his door. "Think you can make any more noise, asshole?"

Cecil snorted. "Like it matters. Let's get this done. And when we get back, we WILL be turning on the AC."

It was nearly a half mile walk from the foot of the bridge to the center of the river, and the two cons arrived sweat-soaked and irritable.

"We're here, genius," Cecil said. "So where's your boat."

"Keep it up, Cecil, and your ass is going in the river." The driver looked over the guardrail. "Don't worry, it's not much of a fall; but, oh yeah, you can't swim, can you?"

Cecil stepped back from the guardrail and changed the subject. "What about that marina down there? Reckon the teams hit it yet?"

The driver shrugged. "Probably not. There's a lot of low-hanging fruit out there, and plenty of stuff in mid-county. I doubt they've had time to get this far north."

"Wonder what's in all them covered docks? I can't see nothin' but roof from up here."

The driver glanced at his watch. "Not our problem. Let's head back. By the time we get to the car, we can run the AC."

***

"That was close," Howell whispered to Alvarez as the men above them moved away, their voices fading. "It was a good thing we heard the car door."

Alvarez nodded and whispered back, "Sound carries a long way when it doesn't have to compete with a thousand other sounds. It's like being in a library twenty-four seven."

"I don't hear them anymore. You think they're gone?"

Alvarez glanced at his watch. "Let's give them five more minutes, just to be sure."

Howell nodded, and they waited in silence until Alvarez nodded and moved silently from beneath the bridge. She followed through the scrub brush and trees. They reached the bank in minutes, and Alvarez parted the brush to reveal covered docks across the man-made access channel. What had been invisible to the cons on the bridge above was all too visible at water level. The berths were largely unoccupied, validating Howell's theory of the likely behavior of any boat owners lucky enough to have reached their boats.

"What do you think, ma'am?" Alvarez asked.

"Looks like only about a third of the berths are occupied, and I don't see any activity, so I'm guessing the boat owners aren't around. There's plenty of room for us under cover, but I'm concerned about the noise, especially since our arrival drew a look."

Alvarez nodded. "I was thinking the same. That enclosed boat won't paddle worth a damn, but we can walk it around to this point on a rope. We'll be less than a hundred feet across to the docks, with no current up in this side channel. We should be able to paddle it that far without any problem, right up into one of those covered berths." He shook his head. "But it's not getting in I worry about, it's leaving."

"We'll worry about that when the time comes."

***

They pulled into an empty berth between two large cabin cruisers, and the Coasties worked in tandem to check and clear the abandoned boats in the covered berths. When they confirmed all the boats were unoccupied, they turned their attention to the yacht club grounds while the *Pecos Trader* crewmen checked the boats more closely. Alvarez and Jones returned a short time later, both grinning.

"What's the deal?" Howell asked.

"All clear, ma'am," Alvarez said. "And we're grinning because all the boat owners who bugged out left their vehicles here—"

"And left hidden keys," Howell finished his sentence.

Alvarez's grin widened as he held up three magnetic key holders.

"There's almost forty cars out there," he said. "It stood to reason some folks would suffer from lack of imagination as far as hiding places go. We got wheels, and the marina has aboveground tanks for both gas and diesel. The departing boat owners hit 'em hard, but there's some left. We can drain out enough to supplement the fuel we brought."

"Terrific," Howell said. "We're looking good all around. Six boats are big enough to accommodate folks, all with generators and toilets and at least some fuel. We won't risk running the generators and we'll flush with buckets, but at least we'll be able to house people while we gather them up. And maybe we can take some of these boats with us. It's cramped on the ship now and likely to get a whole lot worse."

The next decision was how to deploy. After mulling it over, Howell decided not to leave a guard on the lifeboat. Jimmy and Pete knew the way to most of the other crewmen's homes, and she needed both of the Coasties for security. If cons or gangbangers found the boat, the only thing an outgunned defender could do was die. They came together, and they would stay together.

The storage buildings housing trailered boats yielded enough gas cans to drain the club's tank. They loaded their newfound bounty and several of the cans they brought into the three 'borrowed' vehicles, and

Howell held her breath as they tried the engines. Each started smoothly and ran quietly, much quieter than their boat engine. *Maybe this will work after all*, she thought from the passenger seat as Jimmy Gillespie drove through the yacht club gate and turned north on Marina Street.

716 WILLIAMS ROAD
BEAUMONT, TEXAS

SAME DAY, 10:40 A.M.

Jimmy's parents' house was closest, and he figured his family would congregate there in an emergency. Howell was also hoping for a read on the situation ashore and figured it was better to stay together until they had one. They worked their way to the far north edge of town through older, less traveled neighborhoods, some blighted and run-down, others neatly maintained and resistant to the march of urban decay. All the while, they were ever vigilant for 'cons turned cop' or any other threats.

The deserted streets were eerily quiet, as if the populace had fled at the sound of their engines. Here and there the flash of a face at a window or movement of a curtain told them they were being watched, but not welcomed. The houses got more and more run-down and farther apart, and many seemed deserted as they moved north on potholed streets.

"Mom and Pop have both lived up here since they were kids," Jimmy said. "My brothers and I tried to get them to move, but they wouldn't hear of it. We finally just left them alone."

Here and there, the run-down homes were separated by vacant lots, and Howell glanced woodland through the openings.

"Are we still in the city?" she asked.

Jimmy snorted. "Barely, but it depends on who you ask. If you asked the property tax people, the answer is yes. But if you're looking to get a pothole fixed, the answer is no."

They rode on in silence for another few minutes before pulling to the curb across from a modest but neat frame dwelling. Alvarez pulled up in the center of the deserted street, abreast of them, to form a sheltered area between the two vehicles. Jimmy got out between the cars and Howell joined him.

Jimmy stared at the house.

"What is it, Jimmy?" Howell asked.

Jimmy swallowed. "I've been thinking of nothin' else for a month, and now I'm scared. What if... what if they're..."

She put her hand on his arm. "I'm sure they're fine, Jimmy," she said, then paused. "But—"

"But if they're not, I gotta know that too," Jimmy said, and moved from between the cars to start across the overgrown lawn.

He was halfway to the door when it burst open and a slim red-haired woman darted across the porch and over the lawn into his arms. She was sobbing and laughing at the same time, clinging to Jimmy like she'd never let go. Seconds later, two small boys, twins by the looks of them, ran out of the house and wrapped their arms around their parents' legs. Jimmy separated himself from his wife with difficulty and scooped up a boy in each arm, whereupon his wife wrapped all three of them in a hug. The boys' facial resemblance to Jimmy and flaming red hair left no doubt as to their parentage.

Howell smiled. At least something was working out.

More people emerged—men, women, and a few kids. All the men and some of the women were armed, and they were all smiling, some less confidently than others as they studied Howell and her group and shot nervous glances up and down the street.

An older woman, obviously Jimmy's mother, separated herself from the group and rushed toward him, a man close behind her. Jimmy's wife gave ground grudgingly and let the older woman hug her son.

"Dang, boy," said the older man, "Y'all scared us to death rolling up like that and sittin' there. We almost shot you."

Jimmy grinned. "That would've been a fine homecoming, Pop."

The two other men in the group bore a strong family resemblance; brothers, Howell concluded. One of them shot a worried glance up and down the street and spoke.

"We best get those vehicles out of sight," he said.

The second brother nodded and ran to open a wooden gate beside the house, revealing a narrow passage into the fenced backyard. Jimmy turned to Howell, but she was already moving to their vehicle and ordering the others to do the same. Seconds later, she rolled through the narrow opening into a surprisingly spacious backyard.

The lot was narrow and deep, well over an acre, she guessed, and hidden from street view by the bulk of the modest house. It was screened on both sides by a tall wooden privacy fence, which ran well back into the yard before it was replaced by an even taller, impenetrable-looking hedge around the remaining border of the large lot. Behind the hedge at the back of the lot, she could see the towering trees of thick woodland; no neighbors there.

On closer inspection, the 'modest' house was a bit less so, with a substantial extension on its back side. Fruit trees ran down either side of the long yard, and she could see a large garden to the rear, with the green splash of growing plants. There was a three-bay garage, with what looked like an attached shop, and a small aboveground swimming pool. Half a dozen vehicles of various types were parked around the garage, including a boxy delivery truck with Lone Star Marine printed on the side in large letters, underneath an even larger stylized logo of a ship painted like the Texas state flag.

She parked her SUV next to the other cars and got out as Alvarez and Pete Brown followed suit. The others followed the cars through the gate, and one of his brothers closed and barred it as Jimmy's father separated from the group and walked over, his hand extended.

"Earl Gillespie," he said as Howell shook his hand. "We sure appreciate y'all gettin' Jimmy home."

Howell smiled. "He more or less got himself home. We just came along for the ride. I'm just glad we found you folks all okay. It's been pretty rough all over."

Earl Gillespie nodded. "It has that. We been blessed with not having to get out much since all the meanness started. We catch rainwater for drinking and cooking, and we cut a hole in the back hedge and dug us a latrine in the woods. There's enough deadfall back there so we got plenty of firewood for cooking and such, and plenty of wash water from the swimming pool. It ain't exactly what we're used to, but we been gettin' by — better than most folks, I reckon."

"It sounds like it," Howell said. "What about food?"

"We still had stuff in the pantry and things we put up from the garden last year —" he nodded toward the Lone Star Marine truck "— but mostly we been eatin' outa Mike's truck."

Howell looked confused.

"That would be me, Mike Gillespie," one of Jimmy's brothers said. "I drive... or drove, I guess, for a local ship chandler. When we have a real early morning delivery, we load up the night before and the driver takes the truck home. That way we can go straight to the ship in the morning. Except when the power went out and all the traffic lights were down, everything was all screwed up, so I tried to wait it out. When we finally figured out what was going on, I brought the truck over here. It wasn't a real big order, mostly canned goods and noodles and stuff, but we've been able to stretch it."

Earl Gillespie shook his head. "We're blessed to have it, but we been eatin' some weird stuff."

Mike Gillespie grinned. "It was for a Korean ship, so you might say some of the canned stuff is a little 'exotic.'

Earl shuddered. "Eyeballs and assholes is what it is."

"EARL GILLESPIE, mind your language," Mrs. Gillespie said.

"The truth is the truth, Dorothy," he said.

Howell suppressed a grin and changed the subject. "What's up with the fake cops, Mr. Gillespie?"

He shook his head. "Call me Earl. And it ain't good. After the first week or so, the gangs and no-goods were running wild, and the cops couldn't seem to keep a handle on 'em. Then the cops changed and started putting 'em down hard, just shoot first and no questions, no Miranda rights, none of that stuff. Just bang, you're dead. At first folks thought that was okay until they realized the cops were cons and they were only killing the bangers to keep all the loot for themselves."

"Did anyone do anything?" Howell asked.

Earl shrugged. "Like what? All the cops are dead, and from what we hear on the radio, the National Guard seems to be tied up in Houston and Dallas and San Antonio, places like that. And from the rumors about FEMA, we sure as hell don't want them here, so who's left?"

"I just figured people would fight back," Howell said.

"We are. They come around here, and they'll get ventilated and they pretty much know that," Earl said. "They don't seem real eager to take up anything resembling a fair fight. After they put down the bangers, they seem more than happy to stick to folks who can't fight back. If you have a few armed men and you're minding your own business, they'll like as not leave you be unless you're sittin' on a big load of goodies they know about. That's why we been real cagey about the truck. The only other time they seem to strike hard is if they think someone's trying to get resistance organized. I guess they figure that's a threat."

Howell nodded, silently processing the information. Earl cleared his throat and looked pointedly at Pete Brown and Alvarez.

"One other thing you should know," Earl said. "If you ain't white, they'll pretty much shoot you on sight, no questions asked."

Howell saw both men stiffen. She turned her attention back to Earl. "Do you know how many of them there are or where they are?"

"There's a bunch of them, for sure," Earl said. "But we been seeing less of them in the last few days. I'm figuring they're low on gas, so they're not moving around as much. The boys say they're sticking to the major intersections and roads in and out of town."

"That's right," Mike Gillespie confirmed. "We know other people through the town who are scraping by. One of us goes out a couple of times a week on a bicycle to connect with them and share news. The rumors are the cons control mainly Jefferson County, but like Pop says, lately they're keeping to major streets and intersections in the more populated areas. That makes sense if gas is an issue."

"Well, that's something, anyway," Howell said. "We may be able to bring in our folks without drawing undue attention."

"Bring 'em in where?" Earl Gillespie asked.

"To the ship, Pop," Jimmy said. "*Pecos Trader* is anchored in the river down near the reserve fleet. We came ashore to get everybody and take them to the ship. We got plenty of food and water—"

"You mean you're not staying here? You can't leave, Jimmy! You just got home," his wife said.

Jimmy turned to his wife. "I'm not going back by myself. I want y'all to come with us—"

"This is my home. Our home," Earl Gillespie said. "It might not look like much to some folks, but I'll be damned if I let a bunch of convict trash run me off. Besides, we're way off the radar here, and I'm thinkin' a ship in the river's gonna stick out like a sore thumb."

Howell nodded. "You're right, Mr. Gillespie. Earl. In fact, we've already had some run-ins with the convicts, so we're very much on their radar, and coming with us might be more dangerous in the short run.

But even if you stay here, you can't be invisible forever. And when the cons get strong enough, I think you can expect a visit."

Earl Gillespie shook his head. "I can't say I like livin' like a scared rabbit in a hole, but this is pretty sudden. We need to think on it."

The rest of the family all started talking at once, and Howell raised her hands. "I know it's a big decision, folks, and I'm sorry I can't give you more time, but we're burning daylight and I need a decision one way or another. However, we will give y'all some privacy. We'll wait in one of the cars while you folks talk it out."

Earl shook his head. "It'll be hot in the car. Y'all wait out here in the shade and we'll go in the house to talk."

There were murmurs and nods of agreement, and the family followed their parents up across the deck and to the back door of the house, Jimmy in the rear. He gave Howell an apologetic shrug.

"Ten minutes, Jimmy. No more," she whispered.

***

At twenty minutes, Howell glanced at her watch and was about to start across the deck just as the back door opened and Earl emerged, followed by the rest of his clan. He approached slowly, a solemn look on his face. She prepared herself for bad news.

Then he grinned. "So tell me, y'all got anything to eat on this ship besides noodles and assholes?"

CHAPTER TWENTY-ONE

Day 29, 4:35 p.m.

Howell bit back a curse as a small boy ran past her down the enclosed dock, squealing as he was chased by a second. She grabbed the second kid's arm and pulled him up short.

"Get back to your boat, NOW!" she hissed, and the boy's eyes went wide in his dark face, and his lip started trembling.

Howell immediately regretted her action and softened her tone. "I know it's tough," she said, "but there are very bad people close by, and if they hear you, they might find us. Do you understand?"

The boy nodded solemnly and glanced over at his brother, subdued since Howell had captured his sibling.

"I didn't mean to be loud, ma'am. Me and Clarence was just playing chase, that's all," the boy said.

"I know you didn't," Howell said, "but you have to be real quiet, and you have to tell your friends, okay?"

"Yes'm," the boy said and motioned his brother to follow and turned down the dock. They were running again inside of ten steps, but no longer screaming. *That's something, at least,* thought Howell.

"Not exactly a low-profile operation," said Alvarez. "I didn't figure on so many."

Howell shook her head. "Neither did I. I guess success has its downside. How many so far?"

"Over fifty, with more sure to come," Alvarez said. "Way too many to keep under wraps for long, especially if the cons have men stationed up at the foot of the bridge."

"Did you get 'em all fed?"

"Jones and I passed out food," Alvarez said. "Since it looks like we're headed back tomorrow anyway, I gave 'em all they wanted. Some of 'em were near starving."

Howell nodded absently. "Good."

"What's the problem, ma'am?" Alvarez asked.

"Just wondering how pissed the captain's going to be at the number of new mouths to feed," she said.

Alvarez grinned. "Well look at the bright side. If we need help getting out of here, we have a lot more shooters. Everyone that's come in so far has been well armed."

Howell laughed. "God bless Texas."

Alvarez chuckled as well and Howell turned her attention back to the line of rapidly filling boats.

After convincing the Gillespies to join them, she'd been faced with a decision. All three of the Gillespie men volunteered to help, and Jimmy argued persuasively that with the extra vehicles and manpower, it made more sense for Howell and the Coasties to go back to the yacht club to protect the families and get them settled in as they arrived. Unable to fault the logic, Howell had reluctantly conceded the point.

They were three for five so far, with Jimmy and Pete having safely collected their own families and one other. More than 'families' actually, as groups of survivors generally included extended family, friends, and neighbors grouped together for protection. Thus a significant portion of the people she'd collected had no connection to the ship, and she was worried about Hughes' reaction.

Of the missing families, one was gone without a trace, their home abandoned. The second were apparent victims of the cons 'ethnic cleansing,' and the weeks-old crime scene was beyond grisly. Jimmy could only describe it in general terms as 'horrible,' and Pete wouldn't speak of it at all, shaking his head with jaw clenched and rage in his eyes. Given the condition of the remains and their lack of tools, burying multiple bodies was impossible. After an impromptu prayer in the front yard, the late arriving 'rescue party' burned the house to the ground; a crematorium of sorts and the best they could do for a shipmate's family.

Howell shook her head to clear the tragic image from her imagination and turned at the sound of tires on gravel outside.

"I hope they got the other families all right," she said.

Alvarez nodded as the door to the enclosure swung open and Jimmy and one of his brothers ushered in a group of new arrivals.

"Where you want them, ma'am?" Jimmy asked.

"Wherever they can find room on one of the boats, Jimmy. They're all pretty full." She looked toward the door. "Any more?"

Jimmy shook his head. "No, ma'am. The other house was… we had to burn it."

Howell felt a lump in her throat. Unable to speak, she nodded, and Jimmy hurried his charges down the dock just as Pete came in.

"I… I'm really sorry, Pete," she said.

Pete nodded but didn't speak.

"How's the gas in Mr. Gillespie's truck?" she asked.

"About half a tank. Why?" Pete asked.

"Because I have one last job to do."

Pete nodded. "The chief's wife?"

"Ex-wife," Howell corrected.

"We'll come with you," Pete said.

Howell nodded, and Pete walked down the dock to where the new arrivals were wrangling with the occupants of the largest cabin cruiser while Jimmy tried to keep things under control. Howell ignored the altercation, happy to let Jimmy and Pete handle it.

"How you want to do this?" Alvarez asked.

"I'll take you, Pete, and Jimmy," she said. "We'll leave Jones in charge, with the Gillespies to help. They all seem pretty capable, Earl in particular. Let's put them to trying to organize our getaway while we're gone. If they can keep these folks undercover and busy, the less chance they'll do something stupid to call attention to themselves."

"Works for me," Alvarez said. "You think there's enough daylight to get to this woman's house and back?"

Howell nodded. "She lives in town, and if she's not there, we just come straight back. Trust me, I'm not gonna waste time on this bitch."

***

They made good time, using a technique Jimmy and Pete perfected during earlier forays, avoiding main streets to parallel them in residential areas. When they couldn't avoid a major intersection, Jimmy scouted ahead, silent on the bicycle they carried in the truck bed. A double-click on his radio signaled all clear.

They stayed north of I-10 and crossed under US 96 on Delaware Street, a route scouted earlier. They ducked south off Delaware as soon as possible and made their way westward on secondary streets before Howell stopped a block from their destination. It was an upscale area of large homes set on larger lots, with privacy fences hiding backyard swimming pools.

"According to Dan, it's the next left," Howell said. "1616 Windsor Court at the end of the cul-de-sac."

"This Trixie's done all right for herself," Jimmy said, looking around. "These are some nice little shacks."

Howell grimaced. "Dan paid for it. He signed it over as part of the divorce settlement. According to Captain Hughes, he didn't even fight it. He said it meant nothing to him if he had to live in it alone." She shook her head. "Even after he caught her…" Howell trailed off. There were few secrets on a ship, and the whole crew knew of the well-liked but socially awkward chief engineer's short-lived marriage, at least in a general way. But as angry as she was at her friend's situation, discussing a fellow officer's private life with crewmen was straying out of bounds.

Jimmy nodded. "It's strange how a man can be so smart about everything else and so dumb about women. I reckon the chief was just thinking with the wrong head."

She ignored the remark. "Take the bike and check it out. I don't want any unpleasant surprises."

Jimmy nodded, unloaded the bike, and pedaled away.

Howell waited tensely for the double-click, impatient to complete an unpleasant task and secretly hoping they'd find another vacant house. She was fairly sure 'rescuing' Trixie was a mistake, but she'd promised to make the effort, and a promise was a promise.

Ahead, Jimmy rounded the corner at full speed and skidded to a stop beside her open window.

"There… there's a police cruiser," he said, breathless.

"Where?" she asked.

"In the friggin' driveway."

They all got out of the truck.

"We obviously can't just roll in beside them," Alvarez said. "Let's check it out on foot."

Howell nodded, looking around. She spotted a long driveway across the street, which turned to disappear behind a large home.

"We need someplace to stash the truck. Alvarez, you and Pete check out that house. Give me two clicks on the radio if it's vacant."

Alvarez took the radio from Jimmy and the men took off as Jimmy threw his bike into the truck bed. Minutes later, she heard the all clear and pulled into the driveway to hide the truck behind the house.

They moved down the cul-de-sac cautiously, to positions overlooking Trixie's driveway; Alvarez and Jimmy on one side behind a parked car, with Howell and Pete opposite, hidden behind a hedge.

Howell shook her head. "We need to figure out what's going on here. I don't want to go in blind."

She'd hardly finished speaking when the front door opened and two uniformed men came out, trailed by a blonde with an obviously enhanced anatomy, wearing sandals and a see-through negligée. The woman had her arm around the shoulders of a similarly clad girl of perhaps fifteen. The girl's body language telegraphed fear and shame.

Howell swallowed her rage. Trixie. She had no use for the bitch, but she'd thought her better than this.

"She's just learning," Trixie said. "She'll be better next time."

"She better be," one of the cons said, "and a helluva lot more enthusiastic. You got a good setup, Trixie, and if you expect to keep eatin', you best make sure these little bitches get trained up right."

Trixie laughed and fondled the con's crotch. "Don't worry about that, big boy. Besides, I made up for it by taking care of you both, didn't I? Was I enthusiastic enough?" She draped herself over the con and stuck her tongue in his ear, then jumped back playfully as he grabbed at her.

Pete whispered, "Murderin' bastards."

"Yeah, and obviously Trixie doesn't need rescuing," Howell whispered back, still watching the driveway. "We'll wait until they go and then get the hell out of —"

BLAM!

Blood and brains splashed Trixie as the con beside her dropped like a rock, and Trixie started screaming. The second con stumbled back toward the patrol car, looking in all directions and clawing at his holster.

Howell whirled to see Pete standing, his dark face a mask of hatred, the M4 at his shoulder.

"DAMN IT, PETE!"

BLAM! BLAM!

The second deputy dropped, dead before he hit the ground.

Howell cursed and rounded the end of the hedge, running toward the screaming woman. "Trixie! Shut the hell up!"

Trixie stopped, confused. "Who the hell are —"

The other three were in the driveway now, and Howell pointed to the dead cons.

"Drag them into the garage and pull the car in after them," Howell said, glaring at Pete. "We're gonna be real lucky if those shots don't draw a crowd."

"You ain't seen what we seen, Mate," Pete said. "All these sons of bitches need killing."

Beside Pete, Jimmy nodded agreement.

"Sure they do," Howell said. "But we still have to get the families back to —"

"Hey! You're that bitch from Danny's ship," Trixie said. "You're going to be sorry you ever —"

Howell turned. "Get inside. You got some explaining to do."

"I don't have to explain a thing to —"

Howell backhanded her, and Trixie stumbled back, catching her sandal on the edge of the sidewalk to sprawl on the overgrown lawn.

"That was my backhand," Howell said. "If you'd like to feel my rifle butt, keep it up. Now get inside."

Trixie scrambled up and fled into the house. Howell looked at the frightened girl and motioned her after Trixie with a nod.

Trixie tried a different tack in the living room. "I'm gonna tell Danny how you treated me. Then we'll see who has the last laugh, bitch."

Howell pushed her down on a sofa. "Sit. And shut up. If you open your mouth again except to answer a question, you're gonna lose some teeth."

The woman glared and Howell turned to the girl. Her look softened. "What's your name, honey?"

"L-Lana," the girl said.

"That's a pretty name," Howell said softly. "We're not going to hurt you, Lana. But I need your help. Is there anyone else here?"

The girl nodded. "J-just the others. L-like me —"

"MATE?" yelled a voice from the kitchen.

"IN HERE," Howell yelled back, and Jimmy Gillespie rushed in.

"You need to see this," he said. "The garage."

Howell nodded. "Watch Trixie. If she tries to get up, shoot her."

"My pleasure," Jimmy said.

Howell was unprepared for what she found in the three-bay garage. The two corpses sprawled in one bay, and the middle bay held the police car, but in the third was a wire cage perhaps ten feet square. The door stood open, and cowering in the far corner were three naked girls, all in their early teens. Alvarez stood at the cage door with his back to her, but he turned at her approach, a look of helplessness on his face.

"They won't come out, and I didn't want to scare them anymore. I thought maybe a woman…"

Howell nodded. "Go find something for cover, blankets, bedspreads, anything. Bring it out, then y'all stay in the house."

Alvarez nodded and turned to go.

"Oh. And get the kid in the living room something too, and ask her to come out here."

TRIXIE'S HOUSE
1616 WINDSOR COURT
BEAUMONT, TEXAS

"What the hell did you expect me to do?" Trixie asked. "They caught me right after the blackout and put me in a horrible cell in that prison." Her lower lip began to tremble. "And they… they raped me."

Howell looked down. "Cry me a river, bitch. That 'wounded victim act' might work on Dan, but I see through you like glass."

Trixie sneered. "Screw you. A girl's gotta get by."

"And let's welcome back the real Trixie," Howell said. "You know, I could almost buy it; the whole 'surviving by your feminine charms' thing, I mean. It's the training these children to be sex slaves I have a little trouble with."

Trixie shrugged. "Get real. This is a win-win. They were already sex slaves and they had it a hell of a lot worse in the cells with the cons having twenty-four access. This way I got to have my own place, we all got better food, and the cons have to travel to us, which really cuts down on the visits. I'm teaching them to be survivors."

"No, you're raping them just like the cons."

Trixie glared, and Howell walked over to where Alvarez sat at a built-in bar, watching the interrogation.

"Real friggin' humanitarian, ain't she?" Alvarez said. "The question is what the hell we gonna do with her?"

Howell shook her head. "I'd like to shoot her right between the eyes, but I guess we have to take her back to the ship."

The color drained from Trixie's face at the mention of going to the ship, and Howell laughed.

"What's the matter, Trixie? You worried Dan is finally gonna find out just what a bitch you are?"

"I… I just don't want to disappoint him, that's all," Trixie said.

Howell snorted and turned back to Alvarez. "How are the girls?"

Alvarez shrugged. "Better since we let them into her closet to find clothes. Jimmy and Pete found some food for them in the pantry. They're packing it down like there's no tomorrow, so I don't think Trixie was sharing much of that 'better food' she mentioned."

Howell looked concerned and moved toward the kitchen. "We shouldn't let them gorge themselves. They could get really sick."

"I have to pee," Trixie said from the couch.

Alvarez looked at Howell, who nodded agreement and continued to the kitchen. Once there, she found Jimmy and Pete way ahead of her, trying to withdraw some of the food they'd initially set out. But the girls' pleading was heartbreaking, and she could see indecision on the men's faces. Howell interceded and firmly but kindly moved the food out of sight into a cabinet, then turned to the now agitated girls. She had just calmed them when Alvarez came in.

"Uhh… we've got a problem, ma'am. The bitch went out the bathroom window. You want us to go find her?"

"Good riddance, I say," Jimmy said, and Pete nodded.

Howell shrugged. "Solves a problem, actually. I guess she didn't want to go to the ship."

At the mention of the ship, the girl Lana flinched and started shaking her head.

"Lana, honey, what's the matter?" Howell asked.

The girl was on the verge of tears. "Don't… don't take us to the ship. The convicts will get us again."

Howell wrapped her in a hug. "There are no convicts on our ship, and I won't let anybody take you. Okay?"

Lana shook her head vehemently and pulled free of Howell's embrace. "You… you don't understand. He was bragging he had almost two thousand men… and… and he's gonna kill all the men on the ship and make whores of all the women and take—"

"Who, Lana? Who's going to do this and when?" Howell asked.

"The one they call Snag; today or tomorrow, I think… I… I'm not sure. He was drunk last night so I couldn't understand everything he said, but I know it's soon. He was bragging about it to Trixie."

Howell suppressed her rage. That bitch! "Who's Snag?"

"He's one of the boss convicts. He's skinny and real mean, with bad teeth and stinky breath. When he's drunk, he brags a lot and… and he likes to hurt us."

Howell pulled the girl back into a hug and held her until she calmed. "No one's going to hurt you now, honey. Not when I'm around."

She straightened and released Lana to dig in her pocket for the truck keys and toss them to Alvarez.

"Alvarez, bring the truck around. Jimmy, you and Pete find some trash bags and collect anything of use. We're rolling in five."

CHAPTER TWENTY-TWO

Trixie's House
1616 Windsor Court
Beaumont, Texas

Same Day, 5:40 p.m.

Howell rolled out of the driveway in the cop car, with Lana sitting beside her and the other girls in the backseat. The cop car was Alvarez's suggestion, and a good one. If they were attacked, she could get the girls to safety while the men in the truck fought a rearguard action. As an added bonus, the cop car radio might give them an early warning if the cons were onto them.

There was no picking their way cautiously down side streets now. They had to warn the ship, and the sooner the better, but she had the families to think about too, and they had no hope if they were cut off on land. Her best bet was to get on the river southbound as soon as possible, then break radio silence to warn the *Pecos Trader*.

She raced east on Delaware, with the truck close behind. Their plan was simple. If they encountered cons, she was counting on the cop car to confuse them, at least momentarily, and she would swerve around them as Alvarez and Pete popped up from the truck bed and unloaded on the cons in full auto. Even if they survived, the cons would be reluctant to give chase. All she really needed was a little breathing room.

She flew under US 96 and across North 11th Street at ninety miles an hour and scant minutes later made a sharp right south on Magnolia, tires squealing. She glanced at her rearview mirror to confirm the truck was still with her, and let out a relieved sigh when she saw it negotiate the turn. They were going to make it with no problems, as far as the yacht club, anyway. The radio crackled.

"Unit 18 to base. Repeat, unit 18 to base. Over."

"This is base. Go ahead 18."

"Base, Trixie flagged us down in Rogers Park. She claims a bunch of people off that ship killed Red and Leon at her house and tried to kidnap her. She wants to talk to Snag. Over."

"Wait one, 18. I'll try to confirm. Over."

There was a brief lull, then the radio squawked again. "Unit 7, this is base. What is your situation? Over."

The call was repeated three more times as Howell raced south on Magnolia. It changed when she made the left onto Elm Avenue.

"Unit 7, please respond. Damn it, Red, talk to me. Over."

She'd just made the final turn onto Marina Street when the dispatcher gave up and switched back to Unit 18.

"Unit 18, this is base. Proceed to Trixie's house and confirm. Over."

"Base, we're rolling into the driveway now, and there's a big puddle of blood. I think you better call Snag. Over."

"He's already on the way. Did Trixie say anything else? Over."

"Yeah. She overheard one of 'em say something about the yacht club by the I-10 bridge. She thinks that's where they're headed. Over."

"Roger that, Unit 18. Confirm the situation at Trixie's, then check back in for orders. Base out."

Howell's blood ran cold as she heard the dispatcher begin routing units to the yacht club and sending others to various places south along the river. *They're probing*, she thought, *and when they get a fix on us, we're screwed.*

She slowed as she approached the entrance to the club and stuck her arm out the window to wave the truck past. Running up unannounced on the Gillespie clan in a police cruiser wasn't likely to produce a happy ending.

She followed the truck in and skidded to a stop in front of the enclosed dock, confused by the scene before her. People, mostly women, were digging in the narrow grassy strip immediately next to the dock, shielded from view from the bridge above by the dock house itself. They were shoveling the dirt into black plastic bags held open by children. Here and there men were disappearing into the dock house with the half-filled bags while elsewhere along the back of the long dock building, men were removing sections of corrugated sheet metal.

What the hell?

Howell ordered the girls out of the car just as Alvarez and the others joined her. She asked Pete to find one of the families to look after the girls, and as he hustled away, Howell turned to Alvarez.

"They're onto us and headed this way and also setting up a gauntlet all along the west bank of the river between here and the *Pecos Trader*. I don't know what the hell is going on here, but we need to load up and leave, and now. I'm thinking we jam everyone in three or four of the fastest boats and run for it. Any suggestions?" Howell asked.

Alvarez grimaced and shook his head. "It doesn't matter how fast the boats are, ma'am. If they're already setting up south of us, they'll be in place when we pass, and those boats are only wood and fiberglass. They might not sink us, but they'll chew the hell out of the boats and anyone in them. We've got a better shot in the lifeboat, at least we can shield some of them."

Howell cursed. "But it can't hold everyone, and even with the current we won't make over five or six knots downstream and it's twelve miles back to the ship. That's a long time to be under their guns, and I'm not sure our makeshift armor will stand up to that either."

"We're almost ready," said someone behind her.

Howell turned to see Earl Gillespie, dirt on his hands and his shirt soaked with sweat.

"Earl, stop whatever you're doing. We need to get out of here," Howell said.

Earl nodded. "We just gotta finish the sandbags."

Howell looked confused. "Sandbags?"

"Well, dirt bags, actually. We found a couple of boxes of heavy contractor bags in the club office and some shovels in the maintenance shed. I figured if we piled dirt bags behind that sheet metal… hell, just come look."

Howell followed Earl into the enclosed dock and shook her head in admiration. The bridge level of the closest cabin cruiser was obscured by a length of the corrugated sheet metal, as was the open deck near the stern.

"I figured anybody shooting at us will be on our right side, so we only rigged up that side of the boats to save time," Earl said. "We tied a triple thickness of that sheet metal to the rail, then piled up dirt bags about two foot thick behind 'em. I don't know if it'll stop everything, but I figured it's a hell of a lot better than nothing. We protected the boat drivers and made a covered shooting position on each boat. We can put the young'uns and anyone who ain't drivin' or shootin' in that lifeboat of yours, where there's already protection. Then we run these other boats as a screen on the right side, between the lifeboat and the bank."

Howell was speechless.

"Something wrong?" Earl asked.

"Hell no," Howell said. "How did you get this done so quickly without attracting attention?"

Earl shrugged. "I've found when you put folks to work, hard work anyway, they usually quiet right down. It's hard to run your mouth when you need all your air to breathe. And givin' young'uns something to do and makin' 'em feel important tends to keep 'em from runnin' around like wild injuns. The hard part was gettin' the sheet metal loose without making too much noise."

"Great job, Earl. We just need to get everyone situated—"

"In progress," Earl said. "Five or ten minutes max."

Howell saw Alvarez glance south, even though he couldn't see the bridge on the other side of the dock house. "We still don't have any protection on top," he said. "If they get shooters on the bridge before we get under it, we're toast."

Howell nodded. "Those guys from the foot of the bridge are probably already there. Think you can take them out?"

Alvarez shrugged. "Piece of cake if they're dumb enough to stand at the guardrail and give me a shot. But I'll need Jones. If there are multiple targets, we need to take them down fast. If any get to cover, it will become a standoff, and that means we lose."

"Do it," Howell said. "And take a radio, but use it sparingly."

"Copy that. I'll go find Jones." Alvarez jogged away.

Beside her, Earl looked at the boats and sighed. "They're all leanin' more than I like. I wish we had time to load some weight on the other side to compensate."

Howell shook her head. "You did just fine, Earl. If we make it through this, it will be thanks to you and your boys. And I'm sorry I got you into this. I guess y'all would have been safer where you were."

Earl shrugged. "Maybe in the short run, but like you said, they'd have come for us sooner or later. Anyway, it ain't me I'm worried about, it's the young'uns."

BEAUMONT YACHT CLUB
560 MARINA STREET
BEAUMONT, TEXAS

DAY 29, 6:05 P.M.

Alvarez peeked around the thick trunk of the tree next to the clubhouse and cursed. The con standing at the guardrail was an easy shot, but he could see the guy talking to someone behind him, out of sight farther back on the high bridge. His radio double-clicked; Howell requesting an all clear.

"What the hell are we supposed to do?" he hissed. "If I give her an all clear and we can't take them all out, she's screwed."

"Maybe not," whispered Jones from the next tree. "When those boats crank up, I'm betting it'll draw all those turkeys to the rail. Then we can have a turkey shoot. We either take 'em down fast, or we don't, and if we still have an active shooter, you can warn her in plain language before they back out of the docks." Jones paused. "It is what it is, bro. I don't think you have much choice."

Alvarez sighed and keyed the transmit button on the radio twice, and from up the channel to their right, multiple powerful engines rumbled. Alvarez smiled. Just as Jones predicted, the turkeys came to the turkey shoot. There were four of them lining the guardrail.

"I got the two on the left," Jones said.

"I got the two on the right," Alvarez confirmed. "On three. ONE. TWO. THREE."

The M4s barked four times in quick succession, and three of the cons tumbled over the guardrail to splash into the river below. The fourth man, Jones' second shot, grabbed his left shoulder and hesitated a split second too long before attempting to drop down behind the cover of the guardrail. The Coasties' guns barked as one, and the con joined his brothers.

Alvarez double-clicked the radio and got an answering signal from Howell before breaking cover to run across the yacht club lawn to the bulkhead at the edge of the channel. Earl Gillespie pulled alongside in the leading screen boat just as they arrived, his boat listing to starboard from the weight of the improvised armor. He barely slowed as the Coasties leaped across the narrow gap and scrambled behind the improvised shooting position.

"Welcome aboard, boys," Earl yelled. "I hope y'all brought plenty of ammo, because I don't think there's gonna be a shortage of targets."

***

Howell hugged the left bank as she ran downstream at a blistering seven knots behind the screening vessels. As they cleared the bridge, she raised her radio.

"*Pecos Trader, Pecos Trader,* this is Howell. Do you copy? Over."

Jordan Hughes' voice answered immediately. "We copy loud and clear, Georgia. Over."

"*Pecos Trader,* we're at the I-10 bridge southbound, with sixty-seven survivors. We are coming in hot. Repeat, coming in hot. Over."

"We copy, Georgia. The cavalry is on the way. Repeat. The cavalry is on the way. Over." She heard the stress in his voice.

"NEGATIVE! Repeat, NEGATIVE! We have intel an attack on your position is imminent. Repeat, attack on your position imminent. You may need all your resources. Over."

There was a long pause; then the radio squawked again.

"We copy. Do you have details of attack? Over."

"Negative. Repeat. Negative. Nothing but a possible, repeat, possible time of today or tomorrow. Over."

The river narrowed ahead and took a sweeping bend to the right, forcing the little convoy closer together and uncomfortably close to the old shipyard in the inner radius. The radio continued to squawk, but Howell ignored it as she conned the lifeboat through the turn.

Earl Gillespie's lead screening boat had just drawn abreast of the shipyard when all hell broke loose. There was a shooter behind every piece of abandoned equipment and junk pile, all pounding the screening vessels at point-blank range. The radio squawked again, and Howell raised it to her mouth without taking her eyes off the river.

"We're kind of busy now, Cap. I'll check in if… when we get clear. Howell out."

The screening vessels were being pounded, but Earl's makeshift armor was doing the job, due in part to their attackers' weaponry. Most cons were diverted from patrol, armed with handguns and tactical shotguns. Accuracy was spotty at best, and though they could easily hit the screening vessels at close range, stopping them was a different story. The engines were low in the boats, and it would take a fantastic stroke of luck to hit the control cables. The boats were hit repeatedly above the waterline, but the operators crouched behind protection and drove on.

After the initial terrifying onslaught, the tables turned. The defenders loosed a deadly accurate fire from M4s and ARs and a variety of long guns far more accurate than the weapons of their attackers. Convicts fell and began to lose their appetite for the fight.

The boats swept around the tight shipyard bend, guns blazing, and the river widened to allow them to move out of the effective range of their attackers' weapons while maintaining their own accurate fire. Then the river bent left and narrowed again, once more exposing them to fire from convicts scattered along the shore in Riverfront Park. But here too, superior accuracy carried the fight and soon scattered their attackers.

The children were frightened into silence by the violence of the onslaught, but rather than calming their fears, the slackening fire fueled them, and the children all began to cry.

Howell flinched at a loud crack and saw a hole in the fiberglass canopy in front of her just as another round penetrated six inches to the left of the first, missing her completely. All of the kids were screaming now, and several women were praying. She keyed the radio, shouting over the noise.

"Alvarez, do you copy? Over."

The speaker clicked twice.

"Sniper on the railroad bridge ahead. Over."

The speaker clicked twice, followed a few heartbeats later by the distinctive sound of multiple three-round bursts from the screening vessel ahead of her.

Alvarez's voice came over the radio. "Clear."

They crept under the railroad bridge and past the city docks at their glacial pace, giving better than they got. The river widened a bit more as they neared the Exxon-Mobil refinery, and she hugged the undeveloped east bank as closely as she dared to put as much distance as possible between her little fleet and any shooters.

Then the firing slackened before stopping completely. She could see nothing from behind her screen and she keyed the radio.

"Alvarez, what's happening? Over."

"I'm not sure. They seem to be leaving. Over."

"Roger that. Keep your eyes open. Howell out."

They were a good ten miles from the *Pecos Trader*; almost two hours at this speed. It seemed unlikely the cons would abandon the attack, especially given what she'd heard on the cop car radio. What the hell were they doing?

Spike McComb stood on the small observation deck near the top of the courthouse, fuming as the little convoy crept from under the railroad bridge and made its way downstream. He lowered the binoculars and turned to glare at Snag, who was fidgeting nervously.

"I told you this was gonna happen. These assholes are doing whatever they want right here in our territory. And now they go makin' a recruiting trip right under your frigging nose, Snag."

Snag began to protest, but Spike cut him off. "And then, they fall in your lap, and this is the best you can do?"

"Spike, we only had a half hour, and we still got—"

"You got shit for brains, is what you got, Snag," Spike said. "Now get on the radio and move everybody south, and get some of those boats you been roundin' up on the water. But call the armory first and make sure they get their butts over to the launching ramps with long guns and ammo."

"But, Spike, we're gonna need those boats for the attack—"

Spike's eyes narrowed as he glared, and Snag shut up. "As I was saying, pick your best marksmen and put a couple in each boat. I want two or three more guys with shotguns in each boat. The riflemen will keep the shooters' heads down so the boats can get within point-blank shotgun range; then I want the shotguns to unload on the boats right at the waterline. They ain't nothing but fiberglass, and we can sink 'em right from under 'em."

"I dunno, Spike, we're gonna have to get pretty close. Are you sure it's worth maybe gettin' a bunch of the boys shot up before —"

"I swear sometimes, Snag, I don't think there's one of you sumbitches who can think beyond the end of your dicks. Now just why do you figure the people on the ship would come ashore to gather up MORE people? And they came for Trixie, and she says her ex is on the ship. So just think about that. I mean, they can only carry so much food, and they only got so much room, so why get more crowded and share your food with somebody unless those somebodies are..."

Spike waited expectantly for Snag to make the obvious connection and fill in the blank. Snag screwed his face up a moment, followed by a smile of understanding.

"Pussy?"

Spike's face purpled. "FAMILIES, YOU MORON! The crew's families must be on those boats. And if we got the families, we won't NEED to attack; we'll have 'em eatin' out of our hands. Now get going, and have some boats standin' by to pull survivors out of the river. They won't do us much good if they're dead."

Snag turned and raced for the stairway, but Spike called after him.

"On second thought, maybe we can use the dead ones. Make sure to collect any bodies too, especially kids. We'll pile 'em in a boat and send 'em to the ship with one of the survivors, just so they get the point about what's gonna happen to the rest of them if they keep messin' with us." Spike grinned. "Ain't nothin' says surrender like a buncha dead kids."

CHAPTER TWENTY-THREE

Neches River
Approaching Hawkins Slip
Beaumont, Texas

Same Day, 7:05 p.m.

"I knew it was too good to last. We got company," Alvarez said to Jones.

He turned and was about to yell up to Earl, but saw him already waving to the other boats and moving to tighten the cordon around the lifeboat. Alvarez's radio squawked.

"Talk to me, Alvarez. What's up?" Howell asked.

"Six boats of shooters coming out of the slip ahead," Alvarez said. "Hug the left bank as close as you can, and we'll pull in tight around you in a semicircle and try to keep them away. Over."

"Roger that," Howell said, and Alvarez watched her inch the lifeboat even closer to the east bank.

Jones raised his M4. "Here they come—CRAP!"

Jones ducked behind their sandbags and Alvarez instinctively followed suit as a dozen rounds splatted into their improvised armor. Jones was clutching his right ear; blood flowed between his fingers.

"Son of a bitch got me in the ear," Jones said. "I think this bunch is a little bit better equipped, and they can sure shoot straighter."

Alvarez nodded and took off his booney hat to raise it above the sandbags on the muzzle of his rifle. It immediately drew heavy fire, and he pulled it down and stuck his finger through a neat hole.

"They're serious about keeping us down," he said, "but we can still screen the lifeboat, so I don't get it."

The roar of the outboards on the approaching boats grew louder, almost deafening, but not loud enough to mask the blasts of automatic shotguns seemingly only a few feet away. Their attackers sped by in line, now intent on savaging the second boat in the screen. As they came into view astern, Alvarez and Jones opened fire at the last attack boat in line as it sped away. Two men fell in the boat, including the driver, and the boat veered off to the left at a crazy angle, uncontrolled and out of the fight.

"They ripped us a new one just below the waterline," Earl yelled down. Alvarez turned back forward to see Earl out from behind his sandbags and leaning over the starboard side, peering down at the hull.

"How bad is it?" Alvarez yelled.

"It ain't good," Earl yelled back. "We was already leanin' right from all these sandbags, so any water coming in is gonna stay on that side, and we're just going to lean more and more. Like as not we'll sink, if we don't flip over first."

"How long?" Alvarez asked.

"How the hell should I know? I ain't no sailor. I was in the Army."

Alvarez watched the remaining attack boats speed upriver and execute a long arcing U-turn to roar back downriver, hugging the far bank. He had no doubt they'd repeat the maneuver downstream and come roaring back on another strafing run. He turned back to Jones.

"How are the other boats?"

Jones shook his head. "We got it worst, but they all took hits. None of them will take much more of this."

Alvarez nodded. Their own boat was listing noticeably more to starboard now, and moving sluggishly. He looked downriver as their attackers completed the turn.

"Earl, cut speed and fall back against the next boat," Alvarez yelled. "If we can tie off to her, at least we can protect her hull. They can't shoot her through us."

Earl nodded and cut speed, and in seconds they were bumping along the starboard side of the second boat in the screen. They barely had time to get tied off and back behind their sandbags before their attackers returned.

They could do nothing but absorb the blow, then fire on their retreating attackers. Three more screening vessels were badly damaged, one so badly it sank almost immediately, and its three occupants scrambled aboard the next screening vessel in line. The remaining damaged vessels had enough reserve buoyancy to stay afloat, with the more severely damaged quickly roped together and towed as a screen for their two less damaged sisters.

With surprise no longer a factor, the outcome of the third attack was a bit different. The defenders were a compact mass now, much more difficult to suppress, and no longer engaging their attackers piecemeal. When the line of attack boats roared toward them the third time, they met the concentrated fire of a dozen rifles and broke off the attack long before they were in shotgun range. They sped out of range downriver to circle and wait, like hyenas waiting for a wounded gazelle to bleed out.

That was the good news. The bad news was that the gazelle WAS bleeding out. The more severely damaged boats rode ever lower in the water, and they lost a second when they were five miles from *Pecos Trader*, cut loose to sink as they rearranged their makeshift screen.

"You thinking what I'm thinking?" Alvarez asked.

"If you're thinking we're going to be screwed when the river opens up to that big anchorage where all those old reserve fleet ships are, I guess I am," Jones said.

Alvarez nodded. "That's two miles of open water where we can't hug the bank. We can try screening the lifeboat on both sides, presuming we have at least two screening boats still floating, but all the sandbags are on the starboard sides…"

Alvarez and Jones both looked up at the distant roar of outboards UPRIVER. A lot of outboards. "Or maybe not," Alvarez said. "Sounds like our friends have called in reinforcements."

"What the hell are we gonna do?" Jones asked.

Alvarez didn't hesitate. "Put Pete, Jimmy and the rest of the Gillespie brothers in the lifeboat. Keep all the noncombatants low in the boat and a shooter at every gun port. Maybe they can keep those hyenas downstream off the lifeboat long enough for Howell to get it to the ship. You and I and everybody left will cut loose from the sinkers and take the two good boats back upstream to engage the bunch coming downriver. We'll try to slow these bastards down long enough for Howell to get the families to the ship."

"You know that's at least a half hour, maybe more, right?" Jones asked.

Alvarez merely nodded.

"And you know your plan sucks, right?"

Alvarez nodded again.

"Just checking," Jones said. "For the record, if we don't survive this, I'll be seriously pissed off at you."

NECHES RIVER
NEAR OLD MANSFIELD FERRY ROAD
SOUTH OF BEAUMONT, TEXAS

Earl Gillespie drove back upstream toward the island they'd passed just a few minutes before in their downstream flight. The island split the river evenly, with the deeper, dredged shipping channel on its west side and an equally wide but shallower channel to the east.

As they neared the island, Earl slowed the boat, and fifty feet away, his counterpart in the other boat did the same. The sound of multiple powerful outboards could still be heard in the distance upstream, just around a bend.

"Which side of the island you reckon they'll come down?" Earl Gillespie asked. "I mean, I DO figure you mean to set an ambush, seeing as how we have two slow, sluggish boats with bellies full of water, against God knows how many faster, maneuverable ones. Thing is, sounds like we gotta set it fast, and if we pick the wrong side of the island, they'll just cruise on past."

Alvarez was already nodding and pointing to the west channel. "There, those empty barges moored against the island. We'll leave some bait to draw them into this channel then ambush them from the barges. Get us to the upstream end of the island, quick."

Earl turned into the west channel, and the second boat fell in behind. When they reached the north end of the little island where the channel split, Alvarez ordered Earl to stop a hundred yards inside the entrance to the west channel and put them alongside the second boat. He shouted over to the man at the wheel.

"Drop your anchor, then cut power and come aboard our boat. We'll leave your boat as bait, and when they stop to check it out, we'll open up on 'em from those barges," Alvarez said.

"The anchor will drag in this current," the man replied.

"It doesn't matter. It only has to slow the boat enough so it's still visible when they come around that bend," Alvarez said. "Which may be any minute, so move it."

The man was moving before Alvarez finished speaking, putting out the anchor as the others switched boats. Less than a minute later, Alvarez glanced nervously upriver and pointed Earl toward the first in a line of empty barges moored against the shore of the little island. He shouted instructions as they moved toward the barge.

"Okay. We'll split up. Jones, pick four men and we'll land you on this first barge." Jones nodded, and Alvarez continued. "Does anyone else have combat experience; before today, I mean?"

One man raised his hand.

"All right, you pick four men and we'll drop you at the second barge. That will leave Earl, me, and two men here on the boat. We'll pull out of sight downstream behind the third barge and engage targets of opportunity or any boats that make it downstream past you. Clear?"

There were hesitant nods, and Alvarez continued, looking at Jones and the other newly created squad leader.

"Spread out on the barges, and find something solid for cover. I don't know how many boats to expect, but it sounds like a bunch. If you get overwhelmed, do the best you can. If you have to retreat, jump into the mud and water on the shore side of the barges and crawl into the brush cover on the island. We'll reform on the opposite side of the island if it comes to that."

"When do we engage?" Jones asked.

"You'll be in the best position to see what's going on, so you decide when to fire, and when YOU open up, everyone else will fire at will. Got it?" Alvarez looked around the group. They were all nodding now, a bit more confidently.

"One last thing," Alvarez said. "A still target's a lot easier to hit than a moving one, so target the boat drivers. That should slow down their response as well."

He finished just as Earl pulled alongside the first barge. One by one, the men stood on the bridge rail and crawled up aboard the tall barge. He left Jones deploying his group and moved on to the second barge to repeat the operation. Two minutes later, Earl nosed the boat in behind the third barge, and Alvarez boosted himself up and moved across the barge to crouch at its edge, where he had a better view upstream.

He smiled as the first few boats rounded the bend at high speed, then slowed and made for the west channel and the bait boat. His smile faded quickly.

"Sweet Mother of God," he whispered to himself as he watched boat after boat turn into the west channel. They were powerboats of all types, no doubt looted from dealerships and private garages. He stopped counting at fifty, and the only thing they all had in common was they were all faster and more maneuverable than his own waterlogged vessel. He turned and moved rapidly back across the barge to yell down at the boat.

"Plan B, Earl. Pull the boat completely out of sight between the barge and the bank, and everyone climb up here and spread out. There's no way we could survive engaging this force on the water. We'll have to add our guns to the fight from this barge," Alvarez said.

Alvarez barely had his men positioned when Jones opened fire, prompting a fusillade from the second barge as well. It went as planned, and a dozen boat drivers dropped.

Except the plan hadn't included so many boats. Though the first strike was deadly, it wasn't disabling, and the other boats started moving again immediately. They'd stirred up a hornet's nest, and the hornets were pretty pissed.

Even though the distance was greater, Alvarez ordered his group to open fire, in hopes it would spread the cons out and draw some of the hellacious fire away from the first two barges.

Alvarez crouched behind the block of a pump engine, firing in disciplined three-round bursts, while the others fired from their own spots of cover.

"Hey, Alvarez," called Earl, from behind a hatch coaming.

"What?" Alvarez replied.

Earl flashed Alvarez a nervous grin. "Jones was right. Your plan sucks."

NECHES RIVER
JUST NORTH OF MCFADDEN BEND

Howell started to pull the lifeboat door closed after the last of the men had come aboard, but Jimmy Gillespie stopped her.

"I'm thinking we should keep a shooter here," Jimmy said. "And the same for the forward access hatch. Between that and a shooter at the gun ports on either side, we won't have any blind spots."

Howell nodded. "Makes sense. They'll probably start circling us like a pack of wolves anyway. We can at least try to hold them at bay until we get to the ship."

Jimmy nodded to Pete, who picked his way to the forward access hatch through the women and children seated on the deck. Jimmy's two brothers did the same, taking positions at the improvised gun ports on opposite sides of the lifeboat. Movement was difficult, with the boat full to over twice its rated capacity. Howell had ordered all the passengers to get as low as possible, and they were taking up almost every square inch of real estate the bottom of the lifeboat had to offer, in many cases on top of each other.

Howell headed downriver as fast as the lumbering lifeboat would go, wondering how long it would be before their attackers engaged. She didn't have to wonder long.

"Here they come," Pete said from the front hatch.

"They may not realize we have teeth," Howell yelled. "Make the first shots count. You only get to surprise them once."

"They're forming two lines to run down both sides," Pete yelled. "I'll take the lead boat on the left."

"I got the right," Jimmy yelled from behind her. She glanced back through the open door and only then realized he had used the closing dogs on the open door as footholds to boost himself up so he could steady his rifle on the top of the fiberglass canopy and shoot over it.

She watched through her viewing port as the attacking boats separated, two in line to her left, and three to her right. They grew larger as they raced toward her, and she had all she could do to keep from screaming SHOOT! SHOOT!

But she needn't have worried. She heard Pete's M4 in the front of the boat, and the driver of the lead boat slumped at the outboard, and the boat veered off at a crazy angle. Then Jimmy's gun barked, and like Pete, he had targeted the driver, striking the man in the arm.

The driver jerked, sending his boat smashing into the now driverless boat from the left column, capsizing both. The following boats only narrowly avoided the wreck and spread out wide to either side of the lifeboat, guns blazing.

Howell heard the strange double THWACK of bullets passing high, through and through the fiberglass canopy, punctuated with the altogether more terrifying sound of rounds striking the steel plates protecting her position. But most of the fire was directed at the front hatch, below which Pete now crouched, out of sight.

So intent were they on the front hatch, the cons roared past on either side oblivious to the side gun ports. The Gillespie brothers rewarded their inattention by shooting two cons out of their boats, one on each side.

The attackers roared past out of sight. Howell willed the lifeboat downriver as she heard Jimmy in the open doorway behind her, blazing away at the boats as they raced away upstream.

"GOT ONE OF THE BASTARDS!" she heard him yell, followed by, "THEY'RE COMING BACK!"

Jimmy's gun was their only defense now, as he was the only one who could see the attacking boats. She heard repeated three-round bursts as he fired, punctuated by lulls and muttered curses as he changed magazines.

"GET DOWN, MATE!" Jimmy yelled as he backed down the short steps into the lifeboat and fired aft through the open door.

Howell rolled out of the coxswain's chair to drop on top of him just as bullets shredded the unprotected fiberglass at the back of the canopy and tore through the coxswain's chair where she'd been sitting seconds before.

"Sorry, Jimmy," she said. "And thanks."

Jimmy only nodded. "This ain't good, ma'am. They stay back here on our ass, and we can't steer. Plus we only got one shooting position, and they'll have five or six guns on it. All they have to do is creep up close and start laying into us with those shotguns."

No sooner had Jimmy spoken than the back fiberglass bulkhead behind the coxswain's seat exploded as it was shredded by multiple loads of buckshot. Round after round tore through the bulkhead until all that was left was a ragged spiderweb of glass fibers. The coxswain's chair was destroyed, and the steering wheel hung at a crazy angle. All the children were screaming and crying out, and she had to yell to be heard above the bedlam.

"It doesn't matter now," Howell said. "Nobody's gonna be steering. But the engine is still running, so I hope —"

Another fusillade destroyed what was left of the fiberglass bulkhead, and debris rained down on their heads. When Howell looked up again, the throttle control was hanging by a single wire as the engine sputtered to a halt. Behind them, she heard the outboards cut back to a guttural rumble. They were there waiting, no doubt with all their guns trained on the lifeboat.

"Y'ALL THROW YOUR GUNS OVERBOARD AND WE'LL GO EASY ON YOU. BUT IF ANY MORE OF US GET HURT, Y'ALL ARE GONNA REGRET IT. THAT'S A PROMISE."

"What we gonna do, ma'am?" Jimmy asked.

Howell thought a moment. "As long as we stay low below the steel plates, I think we're safe enough. And they can shoot as many holes in us as they want, but they're not likely to sink us with all the extra buoyancy there is in a lifeboat. I don't think they're too eager to come charging in and get shot either, so it's a standoff as long as we're still armed."

"So what we gonna do?" Jimmy asked again.

Howell shrugged. "Stall and wait."

"Wait for what?"

"The cavalry," Howell said, reaching for the radio. "The ship's less than three miles away now. They can send the patrol boat out for a quick punch in the face, then rush back to cover the ship—"

But Hughes had apparently anticipated the situation. She lowered the radio as a new sound penetrated the bedlam of the screaming children and praying women—twin outboards, and big ones. She'd hardly processed the sound when it was blotted out by the sweet tune of a large-caliber automatic weapon. They raised their heads in unison just in time to see the cons' boats, and the cons in them, shredded by machine-gun fire. It was hard to watch, even though she had no doubts the men dying would have done the same to her, or worse.

She was still staring when the radio squawked.

"Mate? Georgia? Are y'all okay?" She recognized Torres' voice.

"That you, Magician?"

"That's me," came the reply. "First you see 'em, then they're dead. Any casualties? On our side, I mean?"

"We're okay here," Howell said, "but there are more cons coming downriver. A lot of them. Alvarez and Jones took some guys up to try to cover our escape. You have to help them."

"Roger that," Torres said. "Captain Hughes gave me fifteen minutes to bring y'all in, and I have ten left. Can you get back to the ship?"

"Don't worry about us, Magician. The current is with us and we'll paddle if we have to. Go help Alvarez, and hurry!"

* * *

Torres raced upriver at forty knots toward the sound of distant gunfire. It was measured at first, the intermittent three-round bursts of disciplined fire, but that soon dissolved into a continuous roar—fully automatic weapons or a whole lot of undisciplined shooters with semiautomatics. He had no doubt it was the latter.

The man beside him shook his head. "Sounds like a war."

Torres nodded. "And as long as it keeps up, we know our guys are in the fight."

He held that thought, an ear cocked to the sound of battle, straining to hear who might be carrying the day. But the disciplined fire was slacking, and the battle began to sound one-sided. Finally the firing stopped completely, a lull followed by separate individual shots. Torres' blood ran cold. Executions?

The building roar of powerful engines replaced gunfire, growing louder as his boat flew upriver. Ahead, the river divided into two channels around an island, and racing toward him out of the left channel was an armada of small craft, perhaps twenty or thirty boats. He saw the muzzle flashes and heard a bullet whiz by his ear before he heard the shot itself.

"Let 'em have it," he called to the bow gunner and was answered by the roar of the machine gun.

Heavy rounds tore into the approaching boats as if they'd hit a brick wall. The first wave stopped dead in the water, blasted to bits, and the following boats ran over the debris, either capsizing at speed or fouling their propellers.

It was over in seconds, with a few boats in the extreme rear turning to escape upstream while Torres circled what was left of the convict armada, his machine gunner blasting anything that moved. He saw a head surface to gulp air then submerge. He stopped, and as the boat drifted, the gunner turned back to him, his eyebrows raised in a question.

"We need intel," Torres said. "I want a prisoner."

The gunner nodded, and they floated silently, drifting down the river with the mass of debris. When the head didn't reappear, Torres surveyed the debris field and pointed toward the hull of a flat-bottom aluminum boat floating upside down.

"Put a burst through the far end of that hull over there," Torres said.

The gunner complied.

"WE'RE GONNA UNLOAD ON THAT HULL IF YOU DON'T COME OUT IN FIVE SECONDS. FIVE. FOUR. THREE…"

A head bobbed up beside the overturned boat. "Don't shoot. I'm unarmed," the man said.

"Swim over here, and don't try anything funny or we'll shred you. Got it?" Torres said.

The con swam over, and Torres ordered him to place his hands on the edge of the boat so the gunner could flex-cuff his wrists. Only then did they drag him into the boat and flex-cuff his ankles as well. They dumped him facedown in the bottom of the boat.

Torres started up the left channel around the island.

"Damn!" the gunner said. "Would you look at that?"

Drifting toward them on the current were scores of boats, many with bullet holes above the waterline, with dead cons sprawled in more than a few. Here and there along the west bank were more boats, obviously run aground by dying cons unable to control them.

The gunner shook his head. "Ain't this something. But where the hell are Alvarez and Jones?"

Torres shrugged and crept up the channel, finding no sign of the Coasties or their companions. At the north end of the island, he turned back downstream via the eastern channel. As he neared the southern end of the little island, a man in Coast Guard overalls stepped out of the brush and waved. Relief washed over Torres as he nosed the patrol boat into the little beach.

The relief faded when he saw the look on Alvarez's face.

"How bad?" Torres asked.

Alvarez took a deep breath. "Bad enough. Jones lost part of his ear and took another one in the shoulder, but I think he'll be all right. Two other walking wounded, both arm wounds. But we… I… lost one. His body's up on the barge."

"Who?" Torres asked.

Alvarez looked away, gazing downriver. When he turned back, his eyes were glistening. "A really good guy," he said. "Jimmy's dad, Earl Gillespie."

She released him and busied herself with her own boots as he dashed out the door and up the steps to the bridge. He joined Howell at the radar and heard hurried footsteps clang on the metal stairs to the flying bridge—Torres and Alvarez moving into position with sniper rifles.

"What ya got, Georgia?" he asked.

"Looks like a push boat and multiple barge tow," Howell said. "We won't have a visual until she makes the next bend; then we should be able to see her across the marsh with the binoculars. But something else bothers me." She pointed at the screen. "What do you make of that?"

Following close behind the towboat was a large, amorphous, flickering ghost of a target. Hughes looked at it and shook his head. "I'd say it was a whole lot of fiberglass and wood pleasure boats running close together."

Howell nodded. "That was my take."

"How long before we have a visual?" Hughes asked.

"Five minutes, maybe ten. Then another ten before it gets here."

Hughes nodded and walked over to kill the clanging general alarm. "We have a lot of nervous folks out there; I better give them an update." He picked up the PA system mic, and his voice boomed through the deckhouse and across the open deck.

"We have a target on radar approaching from downriver, with an approximate ETA of twenty minutes. We are assuming it's hostile until we know otherwise. We will have visual contact in five to ten minutes and I will update you at that time. Please stay vigilant and watch upstream as well as down. If you see anything suspicious, please pass the word to the bridge. Thank you."

Hughes hung up the mic and gazed down at the main deck. He watched Laura move to her position on the port side near the center of the defensive line, with their twin daughters Jana and Julie in tow, and silently cursed them all for their stubbornness. Laura had seen through his plan to station her in the infirmary to await casualties and quietly but firmly informed him she would do more good on the firing line. Then she had to reap what she'd sown when their twins insisted on joining her.

In the end, it had been fifteen-year-old Julie's logic that carried the argument. "So let me get this straight," she'd asked innocently. "We'll be LESS likely to get hurt if the convicts actually DO get aboard?" Even in the stress of the moment, the memory brought a smile. She was destined to be a lawyer, that one, except there weren't any more lawyers.

There were fine folks falling in all along that defensive line as he looked down on the main deck. Two Coasties manned the machine gun aft while Jones, despite his injuries, had insisted on handling the gun on the bow. He was assisted by Pete Brown, who hadn't recovered from finding the massacred families. Gone was Pete's quick smile and easy laugh, replaced by the weight of perpetual sorrow and suppressed fury even the presence of his family failed to lift. He only seemed comfortable with Jimmy Gillespie, Jones, and the other members of the earlier rescue mission, as if the shared experience had bonded them more closely than family.

The rest of their new Coastie shipmates not otherwise assigned and those survivors and crewmen with military experience were spread along the firing line to support the inexperienced. Hughes sighed. They were as ready as they'd ever be. He turned back toward the radar, but Howell was gone. He found her on the port bridge wing, peering through binoculars across the flat marsh toward the distant river bend.

"A little early, aren't you?"

She lowered the binoculars and turned to him with a sheepish grin. "Patience isn't one of my virtues."

Hughes laughed. "Believe me, after four years I've figured that out."

Her smile faded. "Are you as scared as I am, Captain?" she asked quietly.

"Frigging terrified," Hughes said. "And if I could move us all out of harm's way, I'd do it in a heartbeat, but this isn't exactly a speedboat we're on."

Howell nodded and raised her binoculars again to stare downstream.

"What do you make of that?" she asked.

Hughes raised his own glasses.

He muttered a curse, then called to the Coasties on top of the wheelhouse. "HEY TORRES! DOES THAT DEFENSIVE PLAN OF YOURS HAVE AN OPTION B?"

***

Torres stood on the bridge wing and lowered the binoculars. "They're shields all right," he said. "But I doubt they're armor plate, and I don't know how thick they are. We might be able to punch through them, but the problem is we don't know what the target is on the other side. That's an awful big area just to shoot and hope. We might do better with the wheelhouse on the tugboat. It's armored too, but I'd say that's our best shot to keep 'em away."

Hughes nodded and looked downstream at the approaching tow. The boat was made fast to the opposite side of the barges, using the bulk of the barges themselves plus the shields atop them to screen the boat. Only the top of the towboat's wheelhouse peeked over the bulk of the barges, and it was shielded as well. He rubbed his chin, wondering how they intended to push the barges up to the ship without seeing it, then realized they didn't have to. *Pecos Trader* was a stationary target; all they had to do was move into position using landmarks on the opposite riverbank, then push the barges straight across the river and up against the ship.

"Well, we have to try something," Hughes said. "Can you hit the wheelhouse from here?"

Torres looked at Hughes as if he found the question insulting and yelled up to the flying bridge. "ALVAREZ! PUT THREE ROUNDS INTO THE WHEELHOUSE ON THAT BOAT."

Alvarez responded by firing three shots at short intervals. All produced loud clangs which echoed across the water, but nothing more. The barges continued toward them as if nothing had happened.

"Well, that sucked," Georgia Howell said.

There were nods from the small group on the bridge wing, which now included Dan Gowan.

"How about the RPG?" Hughes asked.

Torres shook his head. "Maybe if we could hit the boat, but she's way out of effective range for an RPG, and nothing else we have will work. We might have a shot with concentrated rifle fire if we could see the rest of the boat, but it's hidden behind the barges. We need a friggin' mortar."

Gowan nodded and started toward the wheelhouse door. "Be right back," he said.

M/V *TILLY*
NECHES RIVER
APPROACHING *PECOS TRADER*

SAME DAY, 5:19 A.M.

Snag almost lost control of his bladder when the first round slammed into the wheelhouse shield. He was cowering on the deck with the ashen-faced towboat captain when the next two rounds impacted scant seconds later. He pulled his Glock and shoved the muzzle against the captain's head.

"Get back up there and drive this boat," Snag said. "Or it ain't bullets from outside you'll need to worry about."

Trembling, the man did as ordered, and Snag scrambled to his feet as well, thankful none of his underlings had witnessed his momentary weakness. He looked at the shielding and smiled. He'd had a feeling Spike was gonna send him on the boat, and he'd tripled protection here just to be on the safe side. He hadn't survived as long as he had by being dumb.

"Then you better make sure we get across the river sooner rather than later," Snag said.

The man nodded and rammed the throttles further forward in hopes of coaxing a tiny bit more speed out of his ungainly tow.

Snag looked aft from the wheelhouse at the flock of boats sheltering around them in the shadow of the barges. Close-packed and hard-pressed to maneuver in the tight space, they nonetheless managed; none of them wanted to become easy targets for a machine gun.

The boats held the second wave: five hundred hard-core members of the Aryan Brotherhood of Texas. But on the edges of the swarm were boats full of sacrificial meth heads, armed to the teeth and outfitted with boarding ladders and grappling hooks. To this group Snag had also promised the pick of the women captives to the first man who boarded *Pecos Trader*. He smiled. Dumb asses, all of them. It never seemed to occur to the meth heads the man or men capturing the machine gun AND the first man aboard from the small boats couldn't ALL have first pick of the captives. Not that it mattered. Presuming they lived, all they were getting was more meth.

Snag watched the west bank recede as the boat maneuvered the barges across the river toward the ship, the boats clustered in the shadow of the barges following like so many mechanical ducklings.

∗∗∗

Hughes stood on the bridge wing as the burning barges crept toward them in a line parallel to the ship. He saw gaps near the tops of the burning shields, each perhaps four to five feet wide. Through the gaps he glimpsed platforms and what he took to be handrails, and then he understood; they'd built shielded stairways up from the decks of the barges to allow the cons to rush aboard the main deck of the *Pecos Trader* from a dozen sally ports. Hughes looked over to where Torres stood at the rail, well aft of him on the bridge deck, with their single Cuban RPG on his shoulder.

"Ahh... he's getting pretty close, Mr. Torres," Hughes called, just as flame shot out the rear of the tube on Torres' shoulder, and the grenade flew across the gap toward the shielded wheelhouse of the approaching push boat.

Things seemed to move in slow motion as the projectile moved straight toward its target, then veered sharply at the last moment to miss the boat by a foot and explode harmlessly in the river two hundred feet beyond the approaching threat. Hughes muttered a curse and looked back to where Torres was lowering the tube from his shoulder, a scowl on his face.

∗∗∗

Snag flinched as the grenade flew past the wheelhouse of the push boat and exploded in the river beyond. A rocket! They had frigging rockets!

He jammed his gun into the captain's cheek again.

"How much longer, damn you?" he demanded.

"T-ten minutes! Ma-maybe less," the terrified man stammered.

Snag glanced nervously at his watch. "If it's eleven, you're a friggin' dead man."

∗∗∗

"Can we pull our people back and set up one of the machine guns to sweep the port side as they try to board?" Hughes asked.

Torres shook his head. "I'm betting they're going to try to shoot the gaps on either end of the ship with the small boats and hit us on the starboard side too. We need the machine guns to plug those holes. Besides" — Torres nodded down the deck — "if we hit those shields at an angle, any ricochets might take out the opposite machine gun. There's just too much of a likelihood of friendly fire."

412

Hughes looked at the barges again and gave a nervous nod. "I guess this is the 'no plan survives first contact with the enemy' part, right?"

Torres nodded. "But we should pull back from the rail to the centerline like you suggested and divide our shooters into groups, each to concentrate fire into one of the barge sally ports. And half of each group should be ready to switch fire to the starboard side as needed. We'll use the Cuban machine gun as planned to target any boats that make it to the starboard side of the ship, and Alvarez and I will stay up top as overwatch to help deal with anyone who makes it aboard."

Hughes nodded, moving toward the stairs. "I'll get them organized—"

Georgia Howell moved to cut him off. "That's my job, Captain."

"Negative, Mate. Stay here and warn us if something is developing, and be ready to sound the signal if it looks like we're about to be overrun—"

"No, sir! You're commanding. You need to see—"

"And I'm commanding from the front and telling YOU to follow orders. Are we clear?"

"But, Captain... Jordan..."

"My family's down there, Georgia. I won't stand up here and watch them being shot at. It's just... it's just too hard. Are we clear?" The question was softer this time.

"Clear," Howell said softly.

Hughes turned toward the door, then hesitated. "What about the kids and noncombatants? That all squared away?"

Howell nodded. "Forted up in the steering gear room. Polak and one of his guys are down there with twelve gauges. They'll shoot anybody coming in who's not us."

Hughes nodded and moved to the central staircase. He glanced to port as soon as he reached the open deck. The barges were less than fifty yards away now, and he could see movement through the gaps of the sally ports. He moved along the defensive line, pulling his people back to the centerline of the vessel to find cover as best they could, and formed them into groups charged with defending the section of railing across from each barge sally point.

Task done, he found cover behind a pipe support in view not only of his designated sally port, but Laura and the girls in the next group further aft. If they retreated back to the deckhouse, he'd make sure his family didn't get left behind in the confusion. The barges were ten feet away now, inching closer.

"I never expected to be here doing this."

He turned to see Dan Gowan standing beside him, facing the approaching barges with a Winchester .30-30 in his hand. His cheek bulged from a huge wad of chewing tobacco.

Hughes nodded and turned back toward the barges. "Me neither. But don't let me catch you spitting that nasty—"

His voice was drowned in a maelstrom of noise as the machine guns opened up on the bow and stern, and a savage war cry sounded from hundreds of crazed meth heads on the barges.

CHAPTER TWENTY-SIX

M/V *TILLY*

SAME DAY, 5:40 A.M.

Snag stood in the wheelhouse window of the towboat and gave the hand signal. Engines roared, and boats peeled off the outside of the swarm into two roughly equal groups to jet at full speed around opposite ends of the barges, bound for the narrow gaps at either end of the ship. He heard the machine guns and seconds later felt a shuddering thud through his feet as the barges impacted the ship's side.

"Now you better well hold them there, if you know what's good for you," he said to the towboat captain.

The man looked relieved. "Nothing to it now. As long as I keep the engines going ahead and don't touch the steering, we'll stick here like glue."

"You don't have to do anything else?" Snag asked.

"No. That's it…"

The man realized his mistake a split second before Snag shot him in the forehead.

"Good," Snag muttered. "I got things to do, and I was worried about leaving you alone.

Snag moved down the inside stairway and found the young deckhand cowering in the main deck passageway. The boy put up his hands. "Don't kill me, mister, please! I'll do anything you want."

Snag smiled. "Relax, son. I won't shoot you as long as you're straight with me. Now what's the best way for us to get off the boat?"

"Starboard side's burning like hell, but the port side is all right. I can show you," the boy said.

"No need," Snag said, then shot the boy in the head and moved toward the port side. He exited the deckhouse and waved one of the boats over. He was about to jump aboard when he glanced toward the barges and saw the still figures of meth heads at the back of the mob. That wasn't right; they should all be pressing forward.

He motioned for the boat driver to wait, then ran forward to climb the ladder on the port push knee at the front of the towboat. When his head was above the barge deck, he yelled at the milling mob.

"THE TOWBOAT IS ON FIRE AND SINKING!" He pointed to the burning shields on the barges. "AND THESE BARGES ARE FULL OF GASOLINE! Y'ALL NEED TO TAKE THAT SHIP AND TAKE IT NOW SO YOU CAN GET OFF THESE BARGES AND WE CAN MOVE THEM AWAY! AND DON'T TRY TO JUMP IN THE WATER, IT'LL SOON BE COVERED WITH BURNING GASOLINE. PASS THE WORD!"

Word spread through the back of the mob like fire through the nonexistent gasoline. The pressure from the back of the mob would likely counter any developing lack of enthusiasm at the front. Snag smiled. Sometimes you just had to know how to motivate people.

***

Hughes braced his rifle against the vertical stanchion, firing economically. Their impromptu plan was working better than he'd dared hope. Though sheltered behind their shields, the screaming cons were fully exposed when they topped the improvised stairways to drop over the rail on to the ship's deck, and the defenders' massed fire into each sally port was keeping the corks in all the bottles. Moreover, the growing piles of dead and wounded at the top of each stairway seemed to be noticeably diminishing the enthusiasm of those attackers still behind the shields.

The success of the main deck defenders left Torres and Alvarez little to do on the port side, but as the machine guns fell silent, Hughes heard the sporadic boom of the sniper rifles engaging targets to starboard. He keyed his radio.

"Captain to bridge. Request SITREP. Over."

"The boats swarmed the gaps. The machine guns took some of them out, but there were just too many and too close. Estimate thirty to forty boats made it to starboard. Repeat. Estimate thirty to forty boats made it to the starboard side. Snipers and bridge machine gun are trying to engage, but most of the boats are sheltering close to the hull where they can't be seen well without our guys exposing themselves to massed return fire. Do you copy? Over."

"I copy. Can we re-task the lower machine guns to starboard? Over."

"Negative. There are still a lot of boats behind the barges. If we change the guns, it will only get worse. We need to—"

Loud clangs from behind him on the starboard side diverted Hughes from the situation in his immediate front.

The PA system boomed. "GRAPPLING HOOKS AND BOARDING LADDERS SIGHTED STARBOARD SIDE. STAND BY TO REPEL BOARDERS STARBOARD. REPEAT. STAND BY TO REPEL BOARDERS STARBOARD SIDE."

Hughes glanced up and down the line as the designated defenders responded, then turned himself and walked a few steps to starboard to crouch behind another pipe support. Gowan was there, focused on the rail where the top end of a boarding ladder appeared.

"Isn't this some John Paul Jones shit?" Gowan asked.

Hughes was about to answer when a would-be boarder scampered up a boarding ladder and reached for the handrail. Hughes raised his rifle, but inexplicably, the attacker lost his grip and screamed as he fell from sight. Elsewhere down the starboard side, other boarders were falling, without a shot being fired.

"What the…"

"Damned if it didn't work," Gowan said.

"Damned if WHAT didn't work?" Hughes asked.

"Rich and I greased up all the handrails last night." Gowan glanced over with a lump-jawed grin. "I didn't want to bother you with it, seeing as how particular you are about keeping the main deck clean and all." He turned back toward the starboard rail and shot a stream of tobacco juice on the deck, then turned back to Hughes and grinned even wider, the picture of satisfied innocence.

"How is it you can piss me off even when you're doing something good?" Hughes asked.

Gowan shrugged. "Just a knack, I guess."

But Gowan's smile faded at the clang of grapples and boarding ladders in two dozen more places along the side. Then an attacker was up and over, ignoring the rail and diving over it to roll on the deck. The man scrambled for the cover of a set of mooring bitts, but was shot several times before he got there. Incursions increased, each ending with a dead boarder. They were containing the assault, but using half their defensive firepower to do it. The gunfire increased in intensity behind them, and Hughes glanced nervously back over his shoulder.

Something had changed. The attackers were no longer probing tentatively from the sally ports, but vomiting out of them as if pushed from behind. Most were shot down at the rail, but the sheer volume and speed of their advance ensured a few made it to the ship's deck. Some, but not all of those, fell to the guns of the overwatch; Torres and Alvarez were split now, port and starboard, and the surviving attackers found cover on board and began to return fire.

Hughes flinched as a bullet ricocheted off a pipe beside his head — from the wrong direction.

"DAN," he shouted, "PASS THE WORD! EVERY OTHER SHOOTER TO STARBOARD SHOULD SWITCH BACK TO THE PORT SIDE!"

"I'M ON IT," Gowan yelled back.

Hughes nodded and moved back a few steps to port in a crouching run. He glanced aft, relieved to see Laura and his twin daughters unharmed, firing steadily. But here and there along the line, he saw defenders down. He swallowed his panic and sighted down his rifle to take out an attacker.

"It's like they're friggin' crazy or something," said Jimmy Gillespie beside him. "I swear the last two bastards I shot were grinnin' like idiots."

Hughes' radio squawked.

"Bridge to captain. Over."

Hughes keyed his mic. "Go, Georgia."

"They've broken out forward, just aft of the forecastle. We've lost control of the forward sally port and they're pouring aboard." Hughes heard the stress in her voice and glanced forward to see the backs of defenders falling back toward him, running backwards from one place of concealment to the next, firing as they fell back.

"It's time, sir," said Howell over the radio.

"What about the guys on the bow?" Hughes asked.

"Cut off," Howell said. "The boarders are all the way across the deck and have hooked up with the attackers to starboard. The guys on the bow can't turn the machine gun on them without risking that any misses will hit your position. There . . . . there's nothing we can do for them."

Hughes felt a hundred years old. Lose two good men . . . or risk everyone? He swallowed. "Sound the signal."

The air was split with the mournful sound of the ship's whistle and the raucous clanging of the general alarm, competing with but not blocking out the gunfire. Up and down the line, designated shooters held their positions as the rest fell back toward the deckhouse, establishing new positions to cover the retreat of the others. They leapfrogged aft, carrying their casualties with them, with Hughes always in the rear. He'd leave no one else behind.

The deck behind them filled with attackers spilling through the now undefended sally ports. With strength in numbers and the tide of the battle going in their favor, they grew increasingly bold and aggressive, and Hughes was only twenty feet ahead of the surge when two seamen slammed the watertight door of the deckhouse behind him and dogged it down tight. He gave an approving nod as they lashed the dog handles so it couldn't be opened; then he started up the stairs for the bridge.

They were secure for the moment. As a precautionary measure before the attack, Georgia Howell had supervised the unbolting and removal of all the external stairways and ladders for the first two levels of the deckhouse and machinery casing. They'd hoisted them to the top of the machinery casing with chain falls, where they now rested in a jumbled heap, out of reach and of no use to the attackers. They'd also closed and secured all the steel doors anywhere on the deckhouse below the bridge and fitted heavy sheet-metal covers on the insides of the thick glass of the non-opening windows. No one was getting at them easily, but neither was anyone inside getting out.

When he got to the bridge, he found Howell on the radio, confirming all possible entrances were locked down tight. He walked out to the port bridge wing, where Torres had his Barrett sniper rifle resting on the wind dodger, peering forward through the scope. Hughes heard a noise above him and looked up to see the Coasties from the stern setting up a second machine gun on the flying bridge. He glanced toward the bow and his blood ran cold.

"Good Lord," Hughes muttered.

Beside him Torres nodded. "As soon as y'all got inside, most of the cons started for the bow. Looks like they're real interested in that machine gun."

Hughes glanced at the bow again and then back up at the flying bridge. Torres followed his gaze.

"Can we—"

"Not a chance," Torres said. "Jones and Brown have shifted to deal with the threat, and we can't tell exactly where they are in that mob. If we open up with the machine gun, we're as likely to hit them as the bad guys. Alvarez and I have the same problem. It takes a lot to stop these fifty-caliber rounds. I could shoot through a tango and take out Jones or Brown without knowing it."

***

"To your right!" shouted Pete Brown, and Jones whirled to drop a charging attacker with his Glock before ducking back behind the cover of the anchor windlass.

"We're screwed," Jones said. "We can't open up with the machine gun, and we can't hold out long with just my Glock and your AR."

"Why not use the machine gun? We're shooting aft anyway." Pete snapped off a shot to the left.

"Too risky," Jones said. "Even if we hit the cons, it will keep on going right through 'em and maybe hit our folks as well. Even if they all made it back to the deckhouse, it's only thin steel. That gun will open it up like Swiss cheese. Besides—"

"Y'ALL SURRENDER AND WE'LL GO EASY ON YOU. BUT IF YOU MAKE IT HARD ON US, IT'LL GO TEN TIMES HARDER ON YOU. GIVE UP AND GIVE US THE MACHINE GUN AND WE'LL PUT YOU ASHORE AND LET YOU WALK AWAY," yelled a voice from aft.

"Sounds like they really want this gun," Pete said.

Jones nodded. "And they'll get it, one way or another, if we don't do something. Then our guys in the deckhouse don't stand a chance."

"Got any ideas?" Pete asked.

Jones snorted. "You know as well as I do there's only one. We gotta ditch it, but we can't reach the rail from here. We gotta get closer."

Jones surveyed the situation. "It's thirty or thirty-five feet to the rail on either side, and maybe fifty straight forward to the bow," Jones said. "The bow is farther, but I'll still have the anchor windlass between me and most of the shooters, at least partway."

"We should draw straws or something," Pete said.

Jones just looked at him. "Like it matters. Shoot me now or shoot me later. Besides, I got the gimpy arm and just the Glock. You can provide much better cover fire with the AR."

Pete nodded. "When?"

"No time like the present," Jones said. "Get ready to empty a mag at 'em, and as soon as you start shooting, I'm off. With any luck I'll have it over the side before they figure out what's going on. On three?"

Pete nodded, and Jones picked up the M240 with his good arm, took a deep breath, and began to count. When Pete leaped up to fire, Jones was off like a shot. He'd covered two-thirds of the distance when two rounds slammed into his back simultaneously. He heaved the machine gun as he fell, hoping against hope it would clear the rail.

***

Pete was changing mags when he heard the M240 clatter to the deck. He looked back to see Jones face down and unmoving, with the machine gun on the deck beyond him, ten feet from the bow. Pete slapped the fresh magazine home and rose without hesitation, running backwards as he fired.

A round slammed into his left shoulder, and he sprawled across Jones' body as a dozen more rounds pierced the space he'd occupied a scant second before. His left arm useless, he clawed at the deck with his good hand and pushed with his feet to move forward on his belly as bullets ricocheted off the deck all around him. He reached the twenty-five-pound gun and rolled over on his back to grab it with his good right hand and sling it toward the bow in an awkward toss, then rolled over again and crawled after it, oblivious to the whine of bullets off the deck around him. One struck him in the shin, but still he crawled as he heard boots pounding towards him.

He reached the gun and looked up at the solid steel of the bulwark, towering four feet above him. It might as well be forty.

Then he spotted the bull nose chock penetrating the bulwark and crawled toward it, summoning the strength to lift the butt of the gun and rest it in the opening. He used his good leg to push himself forward a bit more and grabbed the barrel of the gun with his good hand and heaved, gratified when it slipped through the chock.

And hung up at the tripod.

He reached to free it as a shadow loomed over him.

"DON'T TOUCH THAT GUN, NIGGER!"

He looked up to see a big man approaching, not ten feet away, gun at his shoulder. With a speed Pete didn't know he possessed, his right hand shot out and freed the tripod, and the machine gun disappeared to splash into the river below.

Pete Brown smiled. "Bite me, cracker."

He felt the first round penetrate his gut; then his attacker's head exploded.

***

"You got the bastard!" Hughes said, lowering the binoculars. "Keep the rest of them off him!"

Beside him, Torres squeezed off another shot, and Hughes heard Alvarez's gun bark from the other bridge wing as well.

"We'll try," Torres said, his eye still glued to the scope, "but it looks like he's already wounded and it's only a matter of… wait. It looks like they're losing interest."

Hughes raised his binoculars. With the treasured prize no longer on offer, the mob was turning back toward the deckhouse. They moved down the deck in a wave, screaming like injured and enraged animals. Hughes lowered the glasses.

With an icy calm he didn't quite understand, he turned to Torres. "Mr. Torres."

"Yes, sir," Torres replied, equally formally.

"Let's kill as many of these bastards as we possibly can, shall we?"

Torres responded, his jaw clenched, "It'll be our pleasure, sir."

Torres yelled up to his men on the machine gun, and they opened fire, driving the attackers to cover as Torres and Alvarez pitched in with the Barretts. Elsewhere from the flying bridge and along the bridge wings, other shooters joined the line, eager to avenge their shipmates. Hughes walked to the telephone.

"Engine room, Chief," Dan Gowan answered.

"You ready, Dan?"

"Just waitin' on the word."

"Do it," Hughes said.

"One nasty surprise, comin' right up," Gowan said, and hung up.

Hughes went back to the bridge window and waited. Their attackers were spread out over the main deck now, taking advantage of the ample opportunities for cover there to move on the deckhouse, despite the defenders' fire. He spotted the old fire hose, visible in places as it snaked under the deck piping toward the bow, multiple lengths joined together and lashed at intervals to the stanchions supporting the centerline pipe rack. The after end of the hose was connected via a jury-rigged fitting and some Gowanesque chicanery Hughes didn't want to know about to the engine room waste oil pump.

The hose was mostly obscured by deck piping, but Hughes picked out a visible section and waited. Soon it pulsated and a long black puddle formed along the centerline of the ship as used lube oil flowed from the perforations cut every three or four feet along the full length of the hose. It spread like a giant inkblot, covering the deck to run down the slight slope of the deck to each edge. In a nod toward pollution prevention, they'd plugged all the scuppers and deck drains, so the oil pooled at the edges of the deck and ran aft to run down each side of the deckhouse toward the stern.

Frantic cries rose from the main deck as startled attackers scrambled to escape the spreading oil, to no avail. In less than a minute, the previously pristine deck of *Pecos Trader* became one gigantic oil slick, and Hughes' grimace morphed to a smile as attackers attempted to move on the deck below and slid from behind their cover. Rifles barked along the wind dodger as the defenders dispatched the newly exposed attackers.

Hughes walked to the console and dialed the phone.

"Cargo control room, Chief Mate."

"All right, Georgia," Hughes said. "The deck's fully coated. Use all the ballast pumps and let's get her off the bottom and put as much starboard list on her as you can. When you get all the ballast shifted, transfer cargo to help out if you have any slack tanks."

"I'm on it," Howell said, and hung up.

Hughes nodded at the familiar sound of the hydraulic deep well pumps coming up to speed.

SUN OIL DOCK
NECHES RIVER
NEAR NEDERLAND, TEXAS

Spike McComb cursed before lowering the binoculars to grab his radio. "What the hell is going on, Snag? Over," he snarled into the radio.

There was a long pause before Snag's tentative reply. "Uhh… we got a problem, Spike."

"I CAN SEE THAT, SHIT BRAIN! WHAT IS IT?" Spike demanded.

"I can't see from where I am, but I sent some of the boys around in a boat. It looks like the bastards pumped oil all over the deck to make it slippery, then started tilting the ship. The meth heads are all sliding to the low side against the rail, and there ain't no cover. They're gettin' the hell shot out of themselves and they're all starting to jump in the water. We fished a few of them out, and they say there's no way in hell anybody can cross that deck." Snag hesitated. "Uhh… what do you want me to do, Spike? Uhh… over," he added as an afterthought.

Spike controlled his urge to scream while he thought through the situation. "All right. The meth heads ain't much of a loss anyway. I wanted to capture those damn sailors, but it ain't worth getting our hard-core guys shot up. We'll have to settle for just killing 'em all. How many of your boats got flare pistols?"

"I don't know," Snag said. "A lot of them, I guess."

"Okay, listen up."

M/V PECOS TRADER
STARBOARD BRIDGE WING

Hughes nodded as the last few living attackers clawed their way over the piles of bodies to fling themselves into the river. Below him the surface of the water was black with oil leaking over the side, and here and there an oil-coated head bobbed as their would-be attackers swam for shore. The boats previously attacking the starboard side had long since fled back to the safe cover of the barges.

He heard a cargo pump wind up to speed and remembered in the excitement, he'd forgotten to let Georgia Howell know they had enough list. Along the centerline of the ship, liquid sprayed from a pipeline in countless places and the pungent smell of gasoline assailed Hughes' nostrils. He cursed and raced into the wheelhouse and up the canted deck, hamstrings straining, to reach the console phone and dial the chief mate.

"Cargo control room, Chief Mate speak—"

"SHUT DOWN! THE CARGO PIPING IS SHOT FULL OF HOLES!" Hughes yelled.

"On it," Howell said, and Hughes heard the pump winding down almost before she finished speaking.

"Secure the pump. Close all the remote valves," Hughes said.

"Roger that," Howell said.

Hughes hung up as a red-faced Dan Gowan appeared in the door from the central stairway. "Damn! Getting up those stairs with this list is a bear. It's enough to give you a heart—"

Gowan was interrupted by the strident buzz of an alarm from the inert gas panel. Both men made their way to the panel across the tilted deck, but Gowan arrived first and silenced the alarm.

"What the hell? We're losing inert gas pressure on the cargo tanks. I'll go below and check out the system." He turned to go, but Hughes shook his head.

"It's not the system. I bet the IG main is shot up, just like the cargo piping," Hughes said. "The cons were using all the deck piping for cover, and we were unloading on them with everything we have. That piping is all mild steel, not armor plate. For that matter, we likely have holes in the main deck into cargo tanks as well. We're probably losing the inert gas blanket to a hundred leaks."

Gowan looked back at the panel. "We still have at least some positive pressure, but it's falling fast, and we can't patch the leaks until these assholes leave." Gowan shrugged. "All we can do is keep the system running and hope for the best."

Hughes nodded. "And everything on deck's been sprayed with gasoline. Let's get the fire pump going and wash down the deck with a fire hose from up here, at least as far as the stream will reach."

Gowan nodded and started back down to the engine room while Hughes eased back down the sloping deck to the console to inform Georgia Howell of the plan. Before he called, he hesitated and looked out over the chaos of what had just a few hours before been the pristine deck of his ship. *God help us if they get men up on deck now*, he thought. A single muzzle flash could ignite a firestorm that didn't bear thinking about.

CHAPTER TWENTY-SEVEN

M/V TILLY

Snag looked the abandoned towboat over carefully before motioning his own boat back alongside. The starboard side of the towboat was still burning, but the fire hadn't yet engulfed the little deckhouse or spread to the port side of the boat. A pile of moisture-laden mooring lines smoldered on the stern, the water trapped in the fibers producing a loud hiss as the moisture flashed to steam and mixed with smoke from drier sections of the line now burning. The steam-smoke combination boiled from the pile to wreath the entire boat in a thick cloud of noxious and foul-smelling mist. The lines securing the boat to the barges were burned through, but as the late towboat captain predicted, they were no longer needed. The towboat's propellers still churned the water, pinning the barges against the side of *Pecos Trader* as surely as if the captain was still at the helm.

Snag's boat bumped against the port side of the towboat, and he and his henchmen scrambled aboard. A half dozen more boats awaited to disembark their convicts in turn as Snag barked orders.

"You two"—Snag pointed to two men—"y'all go to the engine room and the galley and round up anything glass or breakable with a screw top. It don't matter what it is, just empty it out and bring the containers up on the barge."

The men eyed the burning towboat unenthusiastically before giving reluctant nods and disappearing inside. Snag turned to the other men filing aboard, most lugging gas cans taken from other boats in their little flotilla. One carried a case of beer bottles.

"The rest of y'all haul those gas cans up the push knee and get on the barges. Spread out even behind the shields and start fillin' those bottles," Snag said.

The man with the bottles muttered something under his breath, and Snag moved across the deck in two strides and got in the man's face. "You got something to say, Murphy?"

"I said I don't see why we had to dump the beer. Fightin' is thirsty work. That's why I brung it. Besides, how do you know this is even going to work? That's a big steel boat, and last I heard, steel don't burn too good."

"It's a big steel boat fulla gasoline," Snag said. "And if we can make a big enough fire, it'll catch, one way or another. Now you gonna stand there and give me lip, or do what I told you? Or maybe you want me to get Spike on the radio and you can tell HIM it's a dumb idea. I'm sure he'd love to hear it, seeing as how it's his idea after all."

Cowed, Murphy stared at the deck and shook his head. Snag shoved him forward and motioned for the other convicts to follow, then fell in behind them.

Hughes stood on the port bridge wing with Gowan, holding on to the wind dodger to steady themselves against the slope of the deck as they cast nervous glances toward the barges beside them. The napalm had burned itself out, but smoke still rose from the edges of the shields as the plywood behind them continued to smolder. More smoke rising from behind the barges indicated something on the towboat was still burning as well.

"At least we don't have any more open flames close to us," Gowan said.

"Thank God for that," Hughes said. "A fire is about the last thing—"

"Ready, Captain," said Georgia Howell, from near the wheelhouse door.

Hughes looked over to where Howell stood beside two seamen, holding a fire hose pointed over the top of the wind dodger and aimed at the main deck below. He nodded, and one of the seamen opened the combination nozzle, sending a powerful stream of water downward to smash violently against the steel deck. At Howell's direction the men played the stream across the deck immediately in front of the deckhouse, starting on the high port side and sweeping the stream to starboard, flushing the accumulation of gasoline and used lube oil across the deck and over the side.

Howell turned back to Hughes. "I'm not sure how far we'll be able to reach—"

They all looked forward as something clanged loudly on the deck, and a fireball bloomed near the port cargo manifold.

"What the hell..." Hughes turned back to Howell. "Georgia, get some water on that—"

A dozen more projectiles flew over the smoldering shields on the barge and smashed on the main deck. In seconds, the deck was a raging inferno as the Molotov cocktails ignited not only their own fuel but the gasoline not yet flushed away. Hughes hadn't fully absorbed what was happening when fireworks erupted from the gaps between the barge shields into the labyrinth of piping along the centerline of the ship. Fiery projectiles ricocheted crazily in the complex maze before falling to the deck to continue to burn brightly, setting off even more gasoline fires, which raced across the ship to the starboard side.

"Flares!" Gowan said. "What's next?"

His question was answered immediately as even more Molotov cocktails flew aboard, and another volley of flares danced their crazy dance in the piping. In less than fifteen seconds, the entire main deck of the *Pecos Trader* was a raging inferno. Hughes glanced up to the flying bridge and saw Torres and Alvarez with their sniper rifles, scanning for targets on the barge.

"CAN YOU TAKE THEM OUT?" Hughes called.

Torres shook his head. "THE SMOKE FROM THE SHIELDS IS TOO THICK. WE CAN'T EVEN SEE THE SALLY PORTS."

Hughes turned back to see Georgia Howell pointing, directing the fire hose at various targets, but it was too little, too late. Hughes held on to the rail behind the wind dodger and made his way down the sloping deck.

"It's no use, Georgia. Just concentrate on keeping the fire off of us. Get as many hoses as you can on the front of the deckhouse. Set them on spray, and tie them off to the rail up on the flying bridge to make a water curtain on the front of the house—"

Howell was shaking her head. "It's better not to tie them off. If we keep people handling the hoses, they can make sure no hot spots develop."

Hughes shook his head in turn. "Unless I miss my guess, our convict friends don't have any intention of letting us stand in the open and fight the fire. There are still a lot of them out there in boats, and I suspect any minute they're going to swarm and mass fire on the deckhouse to keep us all inside while it burns down around us. Rig the hoses to keep water on the front of the house unattended so nobody has to stand out here exposed."

Howell nodded and started shouting orders as Hughes turned back to Dan Gowan.

"If you have anything left in your bag of tricks, now would be a good time to trot it out."

Gowan shook his head. "I'm afraid the bag's empty, Cap."

***

Snag kept his boat under the overhang of the ship's bow, where he could see down the starboard side without exposing himself. He motioned the boats with his lieutenants closer and went over the plan again. You couldn't say things enough with this collection of morons.

"All right, Drake," Snag said. "You got fifty guns. Y'all's job is to shut down them machine gun and sniper rifles. Nothing else. Take 'em out if you can, but if you can't, it don't really matter. Mainly y'all just have to keep them off the rest of us. Keep your boats spread out so they can't target you easy. You got that?"

Drake nodded, and Snag turned to the next boat.

"Hopkins, you and your boys shoot up their boats. Spike's pissed, and he don't want nobody coming off now, even if they decide to surrender. They're all going to burn up right on that ship. Any questions?"

Hopkins shook his head, and Snag turned to the last boat.

"Nolan, you and your boys just shoot at anything that moves. Take out any other shooters and especially anybody who looks like they're fighting the fire. Hopkins and his guys will join y'all after they take care of the boats." Snag smiled. "Then we can all back off and wait for the bastards to fry. There ain't need for anybody to be a hero here."

M/V Pecos Trader
Bridge

Hughes squatted with the others on the deck of the wheelhouse, well back from the doors and windows, trying to find a solution when he knew there wasn't one. They lost three people before being driven back into the wheelhouse, and anyone so much as showing themselves in a window became a target for a dozen guns. He looked at Georgia Howell.

"The boats?" he asked, raising his voice to be heard over the roar of the high-velocity tank vent valves on the flaming deck outside.

She shook her head. "Both the lifeboats and the fast rescue boat were chewed up resting in their davits. It doesn't take much concentrated fire to put a fiberglass boat out of business. We loaded the patrol boat on the stern, so it's not as easy a target. It might be okay, but we're sure not going to evacuate all these people with one boat and a couple of hundred convicts shooting at us."

Hughes looked at Gowan. "How much time you think we have?"

Gowan shook his head. "The deck's hotter than a firecracker, and the gas blanket on top of the cargo is expanding; that's what's poppin' the vent valves. At this point, the pressure in the cargo tanks is so high the fans can't push inert gas in, even if the IG main wasn't shot full of holes. That's the bad news. The good news is the inert gas is being replaced with expanding gasoline vapor but no oxygen, so the mixture in the tanks is probably too rich to support combustion. I think what's burning is the vapor shooting out of all the bullet holes in the deck and piping."

"How long, Dan?"

Gowan heaved a sigh. "Until the deck starts to fail and the pressure equalizes. Then oxygen will rush in and we'll likely have the first in a series of explosions or at best an unstoppable fire. I'm thinking an hour, maybe less."

Hughes nodded and was about to speak when the VHF squawked.

"*Pecos Trader, Pecos Trader*, this is Kinsey. How do you copy? Over."

SUN OIL DOCK
NECHES RIVER
NEAR NEDERLAND, TEXAS

Spike McComb watched the flames and smoke boiling up from the deck of the *Pecos Trader* and smiled; it was about friggin' time those morons did something right. He'd wanted to capture the ship, with all their stores and supplies, but that was an unknown payoff. He didn't mind risking the meth heads, but his power was based on force, and he couldn't afford to risk good soldiers. At least the troublemakers would be out of his hair now.

As he lowered the binoculars, something caught his eye downriver: a towboat pushing a couple of empty barges. What the hell? He raised the glasses again and saw not one towboat but two, both pushing empty barges and running side by side, as if racing. The name of the nearest was *Judy Ann*.

Spike watched, puzzled. The mystery was solved a heartbeat later when the Coast Guard patrol boat roared out from between the barges, followed by an armada of small craft bristling with armed men, all headed for the gap between the stern of the burning ship and the bank.

Spike cursed and reached for his radio.

BESIDE THE M/V *JUDY ANN*
NECHES RIVER
APPROACHING *PECOS TRADER*

Andrew Cormier sat in the driver's seat of the big airboat and looked over at Bertrand, who occupied the driver's seat of a slightly smaller model running next to him. They'd 'liberated' the airboats from a swamp tour operation Bertrand knew about near Lake Charles, and there was plenty of gasoline available in the barges abandoned at the Calcasieu Lock.

Bertrand nodded. Cormier returned the nod and turned to look back over what Kinsey had jokingly called the 'Cajun Navy.' Over two dozen boats of various types moved along, hidden from sight between the barges. They were all very fast and carried heavily armed men, and a few women, from both the cypress swamps of the Atchafalya and the ranks of Lucius Wellesley's towboat crews. People who made loyal friends and very bad enemies, and who in just one short day had come to view the term Cajun Navy with more than a little pride.

Cormier faced forward in time to see Kinsey's hand signal from the Coast Guard boat. He nodded his understanding, then stood up in full view of the other boats and wound his right hand above his head in a circular motion, then pointed forward at the Coast Guard patrol boat.

"ALLONS!" Cormier shouted, his voice booming above the muted rumble of the outboards creeping along in their moving hideaway.

The Coast Guard boat rocketed from between the barges toward the gap between the stern of the *Pecos Trader* and the shore. Bollinger was at the helm, and Kinsey and a half dozen armed Cajuns literally rode shotgun. The airboats followed, running side by side and close together fifty yards back, with the rest of the little armada following at the agreed interval.

The Coasties were first through the gap, hugging the bank and shooting past the stationary convicts, firing as they passed, not so much a threat as a distraction as they roared past the convicts and raced away up the oxbow channel. The cons were all still tracking the Coast Guard boat when the airboats roared through moments later, side by side. Bertrand glanced over at Cormier, who nodded. As the boats began to separate, a man in Cormier's boat fed a half-inch-diameter cable into the water between them. The boats diverged quickly, and when they were fifty feet apart, the wire shackled securely to the heavy fan frames of each boat leaped out of the water, stretched taut between the boats, a scythe running two feet above the surface at sixty miles an hour.

The other Cajuns in the airboats blazed away at the confused convicts while Cormier lined up on a half dozen boats in a rough line and roared toward them with Bertrand at his side. They bracketed the convict boats, and their improvised scythe put twenty men in the water in seconds, not all of them in one piece. It was as effective as it was bloody and barbaric, and terrified convicts began to flee toward the gap near the bow of the *Pecos Trader*.

The Coast Guard boat executed a tight turn and raced back toward the convicts, guns blazing, just as the remainder of the Cajun Navy burst through the gap and fell on the fleeing convicts from the rear. Though outnumbered five to one, the Cajuns attacked with a ferocity and confidence that totally unnerved the convicts. The rout was complete.

The first few boatloads of convicts fled through the gap under the bow, but a collision soon blocked the only escape route. Boats jammed together in a confused knot, unable to flee the tightening ring of approaching Cajuns, who poured fire into the convicts as they came. Some convicts fought back while others raised their hands. All of them died.

M/V PECOS TRADER
BRIDGE

Hughes reached for the radio as the gunfire died. "Kinsey, this is *Pecos Trader*. Request SITREP. Over."

"We're good here. Can you contain the fire? Over," Matt Kinsey replied.

"Unknown. We'll try, but please get all the boats you can spare to our stern so we can start evacuating our nonessential folks in case we can't. Over," Hughes said.

"Roger that. Do you need manpower? Over."

Hughes looked over at Howell and Gowan, who shook their heads in unison.

"Negative your last. Please just concentrate on getting our families off. Over."

Kinsey acknowledged, and Hughes hung up the mic and turned to the others. "All right. Let's break out the fireman suits and see if we can get some foam—"

Gowan reached over and put his hand on Hughes' shoulder. "She's gone, Jordan. If the cargo piping was shot up, the firefighting systems were as well. And even if they weren't, everything on deck has been engulfed in flames, and if it's not melted, it's red hot or close to it. We go pumping cold water into it, it will crack wide open." Gowan paused. "I don't want to write her off either, Cap, but the only thing we're likely to do if we try to fight this fire is get more people killed. That's the bottom line."

Hughes looked away and stared out the bridge window, his view of the raging fire distorted by the water gushing over the glass from the hoses rigged on the flying bridge. He could feel the heat, despite the water curtain, and he knew Dan Gowan was right. He blew out a sigh.

"You're right, but we might be saving these people just to starve to death. Most of our extra supplies were in the containers on deck, and they're toast. And even if we get everyone ashore, there's no way we're going to have time to even save what we have here in the deckhouse."

Gowan rubbed his chin. "We might be able to do something. Let me and Georgia work on that while you figure out where the hell 'ashore' is. I expect there's still plenty of pissed-off convicts on the other side of the river, and there's nothing over here but marsh and mosquitoes."

**

Thirty minutes later Hughes stood at the stern rail, alternating between casting worried glances forward at the raging fire and watching his crew help the families over the stern rail and down the rigid aluminum ladder to the deck of the barge below. He'd been relieved when Lucius Wellesley pushed the empty tank barge up against the stern and held it there with the *Judy Ann*. It was a much shorter drop and allowed them to use one of the aluminum extension ladders they had on board rather than subject everyone to the terror of the swaying rope ladder dangling over a small boat.

It also freed up Kinsey and the Cajuns. They transferred a machine gun back down to the Coast Guard patrol boat, and Hughes nodded as he watched the well-armed patrol boat providing security for the evacuation. On the other side of the ship, Cormier and his Cajun Navy were moving among the convicts' boats, scavenging weapons, ammunition, and the boats themselves if they weren't too badly shot up. Hughes looked over as Georgia Howell joined him at the rail.

"All done," she said as the rest of the crew filed out of the deckhouse and took their place in line to descend to the barge. "We formed a human chain and passed things hand to hand down to the engine room. All the storerooms are cleaned out, but we just had to stack it wherever we found room down there. God only knows if we'll ever be able to find anything, but if the deckhouse goes, the stuff should be all right until we can come for it." She looked back toward the fire. "Whenever that is. How long you think it'll take her to burn herself out?"

Hughes shrugged. "Until the cargo's gone, I guess. God knows she won't sink; we're only a foot or two off the bottom."

Hughes heard the muffled wail of the CO2 sirens and looked up as Dan Gowan and Rich Martin rounded the corner of the machinery casing, both red-faced and sweating.

"We got the engine room closed up tight, and we're flooding the space with CO2," Gowan said. "Kind of strange, actually, using something designed to fight an engine room fire to prevent it from happening to begin with. But whatever works, right?"

"Whatever works," Hughes agreed. "That it, then?"

Gowan nodded. "I'm leaving the emergency fire pump running to keep the water curtain on the deckhouse as long as possible. It might not help, but it can't hurt."

"Then let's get out of here while we still can," Hughes said, and the group took their place at the back of the now short line waiting at the ladder. Hughes was the last one down and took a last long look at *Pecos Trader* as she died a fiery death. It was almost like losing a family member, and he swallowed a lump in his throat and climbed over the rail and onto the ladder.

But his real family waited on the barge, and he gave Laura and the girls a hug as crewmen lowered and stowed the ladder and the *Judy Ann* pulled the barge away from the ship. He left his family and made his way down the length of the barge to climb down one of the push knees to the short foredeck of the *Judy Ann*. From there he made his way up to the wheelhouse.

"Captain Wellesley?" Hughes asked as he stepped into the compact wheelhouse.

Lucius Wellesley extended his hand. "Call me Lucius."

Hughes took Wellesley's hand. "Only if you agree to call me Jordan."

Wellesley smiled. "Deal," he said. "And it's nice to meet you face-to-face, Jordan."

"I expect it was nicer for me," Hughes said. "Y'all saved our asses."

Wesley shrugged. "That was those other fellas. I'm just the bus driver."

"It was a bit more than that, and you know it. But I'll say I'm grateful and leave it at that," Hughes said. "You know where we're going?"

Wellesley nodded. "I've been up the Neches a time or two."

The men fell silent as the *Judy Ann* pushed the barge upriver under Wellesley's expert hand. In less than five minutes, the river widened dramatically into the expanse of the McFadden Bend Cutoff, home to the US Maritime Administration's Reserve Fleet. Clusters of empty, unmanned ships, most far beyond their useful economic life, floated moored together in groups, held in reserve against a far different, and now unlikely, type of national emergency.

Wellesley nodded to starboard. "Which one?"

Hughes pointed. "We may as well check out the biggest group."

Wellesley nodded and steered toward a group of ten ships of various types and sizes moored side by side near the center of the wide expanse of water. He moved in slowly, looking for the best place to put the barge alongside.

Hughes studied the aging ships as they approached, his seaman's eye focusing laser-like on spots of bleeding rust and other signs of indifferent maintenance. He shook his head and sighed.

"Welcome to home, sweet home," he said under his breath.

CHAPTER TWENTY-EIGHT

BEAR MOUNTAIN BRIDGE
HUDSON RIVER — WEST BANK
APPALACHIAN TRAIL
MILE 1400 NORTHBOUND

ONE DAY EARLIER
DAY 32, 6:35 P.M.

Wiggins moved the last few feet through the thick woods and stopped at the six-foot-high wooden fence, Tex at his side. They'd left the Honda hidden in the woods almost a mile away while they checked out the bridge approach.

Wiggins grasped the top of the fence and pulled himself up a few inches to peek over the top, holding himself there a few moments to study the approach before lowering himself back down to stand beside Tex.

"Well?" Tex said.

"It's manned all right," Wiggins said. "But I'd have been amazed if it wasn't."

"FEMA?"

Wiggins shook his head. "I don't think so. It's more like an ambush setup. There are cars parked haphazardly, like they stalled, with a zigzag gap through them about a car-width wide. It looks passable, but you'd have to take it dead slow. Whoever is manning the roadblock is staying out of sight between the pillars of the tollbooth. I spotted an elbow sticking out from behind one and what looked like cigarette smoke drifting up from behind another, so there's at least two of them. I'm thinking freelance. FEMA will likely get around to it sooner or later, but they're probably concentrating on the interstate crossings up- and downstream. This is about the most remote crossing we're likely to find."

"Maybe we can buy our way across," Tex said.

Wiggins shook his head. "More likely they'll kill us and take everything we have. And I doubt there's only two of them. On a positive note, if this end is blocked, the other side is probably open. We need to watch a while before we figure out what to do. Let's pile some deadfall and rocks against the fence to stand on."

Tex nodded, and they set to work. Ten minutes later, they had a serviceable if somewhat rickety platform, which allowed them both to peer over the fence at the tollbooth fifty yards away. They didn't have to wait long.

Three bicyclists approached from the west: a middle-aged couple and a teenage girl of perhaps sixteen. All had bulging packs on the handlebars of their bikes, and all looked dirty and road weary. The man and woman wore sidearms.

The man held out his hand and stopped in the road, eying the blocked tollbooth warily. There was conversation, and the woman pointed to the gap between the cars. The man nodded, then drew his pistol and started forward alone, steering with his left hand.

As he neared the tollbooth, there was a sharp crack, and his head exploded in a geyser of blood. He dropped the pistol and rolled forward a few feet before death overcame inertia and the bike toppled over.

Two rough-looking men in camo leaped from behind the tollbooth pillars, both bearing ARs pointed towards the woman and the girl.

"RUN, CARLY," the woman screamed, clawing at her holster, obviously intent upon covering her daughter's escape.

"She does, she's gonna have a big hole in her," said a voice behind the woman.

She spun, leveling her gun at a third man ten yards behind them, with a shotgun leveled at her daughter.

"Drop that shotgun and get out of the way, or I'll kill you," the woman said.

The bearded man laughed. "Maybe you will, but the question is, can you put me down before I pull the trigger and blow a great big hole in Carly here? And even if you do, don't you figure my friends are gonna kill you? And they'll be pissed you killed me. Too bad there won't be anybody but Carly here to take it out on. So go ahead and shoot, bitch."

Wiggins watched the woman's shoulders slump; then she slowly lowered the gun. The man was on her in a heartbeat, backhanding her so violently the gun flew from her grasp and she went down in a tangle with the bike between her legs. The girl screamed and scrambled off her bike to help her mother, but the men from the toll booth dragged her away to duct-tape her hands behind her as the third man knelt and did the same to the fallen woman.

Wiggins heard footsteps on the pavement to his right and saw four men running toward the action from a stately stone building across a narrow parking lot.

"Well, what have we got here?" said the first to arrive. "A little feminine company for the night."

"YOU ain't got shit, Atwood," said one of the men from the tollbooth. "You know the deal. Whichever watch takes spoils gets first dibs. And that ain't you."

"Don't be an asshole, Hollingsworth. You guys all have the watch until midnight. We'll just warm these ladies up for you. How about that?"

"How about you go catch your own pussy," Hollingsworth said. "'Cause these bitches are stayin' tied up in one of the cars until we get off watch. You guys can have sloppy seconds tomorrow afternoon."

"All right, if you're going to be like that about it. They have any other good stuff?"

"We ain't exactly had time to look, now have we?" Hollingsworth said. "They got a couple of pistols for sure. We'll sort through the packs together at change of watch, just like always."

Wiggins saw Atwood nod, and as the excitement of the encounter faded, so did the volume of the conversation. He heard no more. He touched Tex's arm, and they lowered their heads slowly to avoid attracting attention, cautious despite the distance and their cover. When they were fully concealed behind the fence, Tex spoke first.

"We won't be negotiating with these assholes," she said.

Wiggins nodded. "We have to take them out. One good thing is at least we know how many of them there are. I'm thinking they must be holed up in that stone building over there, and that they all turned out at the sound of gunfire. Four guys came from the building, so I figure two watches of four guys each. The fourth guy on each watch is probably —"

"Hiding in a car on the bridge," Tex finished his sentence, "so he can cut off the escape of anyone coming across the bridge who has second thoughts when they suspect an ambush at the tollbooths. Just like the guy that sneaked up behind the two women on this side."

Wiggins smiled briefly. "Great minds."

Same Day, 11:55 p.m.

Wiggins knelt behind a rock in the dark, trying to ignore his stiff muscles. He'd moved into position hours before, and kneeling motionless was taking its toll. The fence had covered his move away from the tollbooth to the west end of the bridge approach, but then things got dicey. Without the fence for cover, he'd waited for the partial darkness of dusk to work his way back through the scattered foliage into a position behind where the backup man hid in the strip of wooded verge bordering the highway. He'd moved cautiously, torn between rushing to take advantage of the fading light, yet terrified a snapped twig or stumble might betray him.

An unnecessary worry, as it turned out. He'd heard the faint sounds of a heavy rock beat as he got close to his target's position and realized the man was listening to music turned up loud enough to leak around his headphones. Wiggins had breathed a relieved sigh and settled in to wait.

They'd decided to strike after the midnight shift change, on the theory they were all at an equal disadvantage in the dark, and if they were able to get past the toll booth, the man on the bridge would be unsure what was happening until they roared past him. That was the theory, anyhow.

Wiggins tensed as he heard someone approaching from the road, then ducked further behind his rock as he saw a flashlight bobbing closer.

"Who's there?" asked a voice.

"It's Baker, numb nut. Were you expecting the friggin' Easter Bunny? Besides, don't tell me you broke the night-vision glasses."

"I didn't break 'em. The battery is low, that's all."

"Didn't you bring a spare?" Baker asked.

"I forgot it. Don't you have one?"

"Yeah, I got one," Baker said. "Just like YOU'RE supposed to —"

"Give it a rest, Baker. Squattin' out here in the bushes sucks, and I'm not in the mood to take any crap. Just once I'd like to get the bridge side and sit in a nice soft car seat. Who's got the bridge end for your shift, as if I didn't know."

Baker snorted. "Atwood, who else? Rank has its privileges."

"Yeah, well, I'm getting a little sick of that too. But whatever, I'm hauling ass. I don't want the party to start without me. You have a great night."

"Yeah, screw you too, Hardy," Baker said.

Hardy laughed, and Wiggins heard him moving back toward the road. He flinched, startled, as Baker turned on the red night light of a headlamp and sat on a nearby rock. The man sat facing away from Wiggins with his head bent, apparently changing the battery in the night-vision goggles.

Wiggins fingered the thick, two-foot section of rebar he'd found on the roadside and hesitated only a split second before rising and closing the gap separating him from Baker. He raised the club as he came, and it struck the man's skull with a crunch of sickening finality. Baker toppled over soundlessly, and Wiggins stood staring down, his heart pounding.

Slowly his heart rate dropped, and Wiggins glanced at the luminous dial of his watch. It was just after midnight, and Tex was due in less than thirty minutes, but their opponents' night-vision capability changed everything. They'd assumed the sentry on the bridge was out of the equation until they'd taken out the men on the toll booth and started across the bridge. However, if the bridge sentry clearly saw what was happening at the toll booth and engaged too soon, not only could he pin them down, the firing would alert the others off watch. Game over.

Wiggins looked down at the dead man and cursed. He'd seen the opportunity and reacted without thinking it through, but he should have waited. Maybe he could have faded back and cut through the woods to intercept Tex on the road, and they could make a new plan that accounted for their enemy's NV capabilities. But what if he missed her? She'd be heading into a trap without a clue things weren't going according to plan.

He muttered another curse. It was too late for second-guessing anyway. If they pulled back now, the dead man would put the marauders on high alert, and he and Tex would have zero chance of surprising them. No, he had to make it work. He'd just have to take out the bridge sentry first, quickly and quietly, then run back to support Tex.

Wiggins stooped and pulled the still-glowing headlamp from Baker's head and put it on, ignoring the wet stickiness, then scooped up the fallen NV goggles and examined them in the red glow of the headlamp, relieved to find the battery compartment closed. The man had made the battery swap, so Wiggins didn't have to hunt through the weeds for an errant battery. He doused the headlight and powered up the night-vision goggles. The night became like an eerie green day, almost like an old video game.

He stuck the rebar in his belt and turned to go, then stopped. The dead man was about his size. Wiggins swallowed his distaste and wrestled the camo shirt off the corpse and pulled it on over his own. After a stop at his hiding place to scoop up one of the M4s they'd taken from the FEMA SUV, Wiggins trotted back the way he'd come; he didn't have time to waste.

The privacy fence shielded him until just past the tollbooths. From the end of the fence, it was a dash across a half-empty parking lot to the pedestrian walkway along the side of the bridge, separated from the roadway by a waist-high concrete wall. If he could make it to the wall without being spotted, he could stay below it and crawl onto the bridge without being spotted.

He peeked around the fence toward the tollbooth and said a silent prayer of thanks for the NV gear. Unlike the daytime operation, the night guards seemed unconcerned about being seen at a distance and leaned side by side against the stone wall of the tollbooth, chatting and smoking. He nodded to himself and planned his route to the shelter of the pedestrian walkway.

He took a zigzag course, from car to scattered car, and five minutes later huddled against the low wall of the walkway, the guards less than thirty feet away on the opposite side. He could hear them plainly and was terrified they might hear his labored breathing.

He checked his watch: fifteen minutes until Tex arrived, and the long crawl coupled with the need to do it silently was going to take time. He set out, the rough antislip coating of the walkway biting into his hands and knees. As he passed the stone building, he heard muffled music through the thick walls, punctuated by what sounded like a scream. He ignored it and crawled. Terrible things were happening in the world, and he couldn't fix them all.

The next challenge was location; Wiggins had no idea how far out the bridge sentry was or whether he was facing back over the bridge or toward the tollbooth. In the end, Wiggins decided the man wouldn't be too far out, so he'd crawl until he was sure he was past, then count on Tex's approach to draw the man's attention toward the tollbooth.

The plan was for Tex to come in slowly with only her parking lights on, as if she were using the minimal lights necessary to see. She'd quickly kill the lights when she saw the situation at the tollbooth, then stop like she was surprised and evaluating the situation. At that point, she was to play it by ear, doing whatever was necessary to hold the tollbooth guards' attention while Wiggins took them from the rear. They figured the bridge sentry would know something was going on, but counted on him not being able to see enough to matter until it was too late. They'd been wrong there, but Wiggins now planned to use Tex's arrival as a distraction.

He crawled cautiously, gauging progress by the vertical stanchions of the handrail to his right. He'd just passed a hundred and fifty feet when he caught a whiff of cigarette smoke from over the low wall. Thank God for bad habits.

He moved another thirty feet to make sure he was past the sentry, then risked a peek over the wall, moving very slowly to keep from attracting attention. He saw the glowing end of a cigarette in the drivers' side window of an SUV forty feet back toward the tollbooth. He could see the tollbooth guards clearly as well, and a chill shot through him as he realized if either of them took a few steps to the side and looked in his direction, they now had an angle to see him clearly as well. He slowly sank back behind the wall and hoped Tex arrived before one of the guards decided to stretch his legs.

The clock now slowed to a crawl, and Wiggins hugged the low wall and sweated until he saw the dim parking lights of the Honda turn into the entrance ramp. Across the wall and back toward the roadblock, he heard the squeak of an opening car door and pulled himself up cautiously to peep over the wall.

The bridge sentry was standing behind the open door of a late model SUV, watching the toll booth. Wiggins crawled over the waist-high wall silently and moved forward, pulling the rebar from his belt as he approached. He'd closed half the distance when he kicked a pebble. It skittered along the roadway as the bridge sentry turned.

Wiggins dropped the rebar down beside his leg and sped up. He needed to disorient the man before he yelled or got a shot off.

"Atwood! It's me, Baker," Wiggins said as the man completed his turn, facing Wiggins ten feet away, looking insect-like in the green glow of Wiggins' NV goggles. Wiggins knew his NV gear made him look the same to the man and hoped Baker's voice wasn't distinctive.

"Baker! What the hell? What are you doing out here? You're supposed to…"

Atwood connected the dots far too quickly and reached for his sidearm when Wiggins was still five feet away. Wiggins leaped the last few feet, bringing the rebar up as he charged, driving the end into Atwood's throat with all his weight behind it. The rough rod tore through the carotid artery and punched out the back of the man's neck. Atwood's cry died on his lips, and blood sprayed on Wiggins' stolen camo shirt. The man clutched the open car door and sank to the pavement.

Wiggins disarmed him and threw his pistol over the side of the bridge, then dragged the still-gasping man well away from the vehicle. He looked back toward the tollbooth. Tex had stopped as agreed with her lights off, but the two guards had moved only a short distance toward her and stood staring at the Honda.

He looked back down. Atwood wasn't dead, but he soon would be and was no longer a threat. Wiggins started for the tollbooth, then thought better of it and came back to collect the rebar. He grasped the end firmly and put a foot on Atwood's chest, trying to ignore the pitiful sounds as he reclaimed his most effective silent weapon.

BEAR MOUNTAIN BRIDGE
TOLL BOOTH

"What do you make of that?" Stanfield asked.

"I think Baker's screwing off," Hargraves replied. "He should have that shotgun stuck in the driver's face by now. I bet the son of a bitch is sacked out again."

"What should we do?"

"How the hell should I know what we should—"

He was interrupted by the sound of an opening car door as the driver exited the vehicle, followed by a seductive feminine voice.

"Evening, boys. I just want to cross without any trouble. I'm sure I can make it worth your while."

"You alone?" Stanfield yelled.

"Yep. Just a poor girl trying to get home the best way she can."

"Step away from the car with your hands in the air, then turn in a full circle, real slow," Stanfield said.

The men watched as the woman complied.

"She's a looker, even in these NV glasses. I like the little ones. What do you think, Stanfield?" Hargraves asked quietly.

"I think she seems willing, and we can have a nice little party through the night takin' turns in one of the cars. Atwood won't care if we let him go first. We won't even have to tie her up until she figures out we're not gonna let her leave."

"What if it's a trap or something?"

Stanfield snorted. "Look at her. She's maybe five feet tall and weighs a hundred and nothing. She's got no visible weapons, and we won't let her go back to the car to get any. I say we put her in one of those cars and have ourselves a party. I'm going to go search her. You stay back and keep your eyes open and cover me. Then you keep an eye on the girl and I'll holler at that dumb ass Baker to get his butt out here and help me make sure there aren't any unpleasant surprises in the car."

"Roger that," Hargrave said, and Stanfield started toward the woman, pistol in hand.

***

Wiggins' heart pounded as he crouched behind the tollbooth pillar and watched the scene unfold. He'd heard Tex's shouted inducement and watched as the two men discussed it, too low for him to hear what they were saying. They were only partially turned away from him, and he didn't think he could close on them before one of them saw him.

He could challenge them with his Sig or the M4, but what if they called his bluff? They were much more likely to do so at a distance than they were at point-blank range. He needed them both to focus fully on Tex so he could get closer. His heart sank as they separated.

One of the men started toward Tex, pistol drawn, and the other stayed behind, both with their backs to him now. He covered the distance to the closest in long silent strides and raised the rebar to deliver a crushing blow to the back of the man's head. Wiggins was inured to the violence now. It would haunt him later, but not now, not with Tex's life on the line.

Wiggins grabbed the man as he fell, almost toppling from the weight before stabilizing himself and easing the man to the ground. The second man continued towards Tex, oblivious to the action behind him. Wiggins had almost overtaken him when the man heard him and spun, pistol leveled.

"Don't shoot! It's Baker," Wiggins tried for a repeat.

But the dead man lying on the pavement behind Wiggins gave lie to the claim, and the guard fired without hesitation, but missed. Wiggins flung the rebar underhand with all his might, knocking the man's NV goggles askew as Wiggins jogged left.

Sightless now, the man fired repeatedly at where Wiggins had been, until Wiggins drew his own Sig and shot the man three times, center mass. The man fell, and Wiggins stood trembling, his heart pounding.

"Bill?"

"Here, Tex," Wiggins said. A flashlight came on.

"TURN THAT OFF!" Wiggins said.

Tex complied. "But how —"

"Wait there," Wiggins said, stooping to strip the NV gear off the dead guard. He pulled his own glasses off and looked through the guard's. Dead. Optics didn't like being smacked by rebar. He dropped the damaged gear and hurried to the first guard he'd dropped, to find his NV gear working. He hurried back to Tex with it.

"NV gear. Put it on and grab one of these guys' M4s. We'll divide their extra mags. The guys in the house will likely be out here any minute."

"Let's just crash the bridge," Tex said. "The guy further out is probably confused. We can get past them if you drive and I lay down suppressing fire."

"The guy on the bridge isn't a problem," Wiggins said. "Creeping through that obstacle course they've set up is. We'll never make it through in time, and if they catch us in transit, they'll just hunker down behind the concrete wall of the pedestrian walkway and shoot us to pieces at point-blank range. It'll be a friggin' shooting gallery."

"Speak of the devil," Tex said, pointing toward the stone house, where flashlights bobbed. "They're coming."

Wiggins studied the bobbing flashlights. "They traded off the NV gear during the watch change, and they wouldn't be using flashlights if they had any more. Now we have it and they don't."

Shouts now accompanied the bobbing flashlights.

"Uhh… I think maybe we should curb their enthusiasm while we figure this out," Tex said.

"All right. Grab a gun and let's separate a bit and both fire a short burst toward the lights to send them to cover, then move in case they return fire at the muzzle flashes. On three?" Wiggins asked.

Tex stooped to pick up the fallen guard's rifle and nodded, and she walked away a few paces. Wiggins counted down, and they both fired a three-round burst, then scrambled thirty feet to the right. Sure enough, the pavement where they'd been standing erupted in sparks.

"What now?" Wiggins asked.

Tex shrugged. "You've been right so far about what they'd do, so why not turn this into OUR shooting gallery."

BEAR MOUNTAIN BRIDGE
PEDESTRIAN WALKWAY NEAR TOLL BOOTH

"Who the hell's out there, and where are our guys?" Saunders asked.

"How should I know?" Hollingsworth said. "The chickenshits likely ran off. I never did trust that Atwood."

"What are we gonna do?"

"I can tell you what we AIN'T gonna do. We ain't gonna move from behind this wall until we know what we're facing," Hollingsworth said.

An engine started to their left, somewhere along the entrance ramp to the toll plaza. It seemed to move toward them as they listened.

"Now that's more like it. The dumb ass is gonna try to shoot through our little obstacle course." Hollingsworth grinned. "We'll chew him up. Lay those three big flashlights on the wall, pointing toward the obstacle course, but everybody pick out a firing position at least ten feet away from the lights in case they draw fire. When I hear him stuck in the obstacle course, I'll give the word to light him up; then you guys turn on your lights and jump back to your firing positions. After that, it's just a turkey shoot."

* * *

Tex stared at the backs of the four men lined up along the wall, oblivious to her presence. Gaining her present advantageous position had been no more difficult than walking through the pitch-black night down the middle of the paved driveway to the parking lot.

She thought about what she was about to do. It was murder, really. Or was it? No, murder was what was done to her parents and many good people like them by scumbags like the four in front of her. This was an execution, and a just one. Wiggins had volunteered, but someone needed to create a diversion to keep all of their opponents focused on the same place, and Bill had done more than his share of killing.

Tex felt a flash of remorse at what they'd become. Mild-mannered Bill Wiggins, well liked on the ship for his quick smile and even temper, a man who seldom raised his voice much less his hand to anyone. A man who just killed four human beings without hesitation. They weren't the same people they were just a few short weeks ago; their 'old selves' couldn't survive in this new world. And she would survive. Tex pushed her misgivings to the back of her mind and studied the men in front of her.

She heard the Honda and watched the men prepare their trap. She could hear them clearly, and their laughter and apparent enthusiasm for the task erased any lingering doubts. It was over in four three-round bursts, and she walked over and pointed one of the large flashlights skyward so as not to blind Wiggins. She flashed a signal in the air and watched through the NV glasses as the SUV approached the roadblock and zigzagged through the obstacle course.

She turned and looked east, over the bridge. They were lucky this time, again. She wondered where their luck would run out.

CHAPTER TWENTY-NINE

Day 33, 00:55 a.m.

They found the women locked in a storeroom, beaten and thoroughly traumatized. Tex comforted them as Wiggins checked out the stone building, originally some sort of local museum.

One room was crammed with guns and ammunition of all types, and another held canned goods, MREs, and other nonperishables—all undoubtedly looted from refugees. A carport held the greatest treasure, two rows of red plastic gas cans of various sizes, all full. Here was the fuel to get home—all the way home.

He returned to find Tex sitting with the women in the glow of a Coleman lantern, drinking instant coffee she'd found and prepared on a nearby camp stove. Wiggins shot her a questioning look. She gave a hesitant nod and he moved to a couch across from the women.

"Bill, this is Fran and her daughter, Carly," Tex said.

Wiggins nodded. "Nice to meet you ladies."

Fran nodded, but Carly just stared at the floor. The silence grew.

"I... uh... I'm sorry about your husband," Bill said.

The woman shook her head. "We only met John three weeks ago, at our hotel in Scranton. We all live near here and he was helping us get home. He's a... I mean he was a good man. Did you find... I mean is his..." She trailed off, unable to finish.

Wiggins shook his head. "I'm sorry. His body's not there. They probably dragged it into the woods, and I'm afraid we don't have time to search. We need to be far away when the sun comes up. More bad guys might turn up at any time."

The girl whimpered and moved into her mother's arms. Tex glared at Wiggins and he gave a helpless shrug.

"We can't ride the bikes in the dark," Fran said. "But we live near Lake Carmel—only about twenty-five miles. Tex said... I mean I thought maybe... can you take us there?" Her plea was heartbreaking.

Except Wiggins couldn't afford a broken heart. He shook his head. "No, but there's plenty of gas, and I'm sure I can get one of the cars in the parking lot running for you. We'll gas it up, give you food and guns for protection, and you can go on your own."

"But Tex said you were following the Appalachian Trail," Fran said, "and it crosses Route 52 not three miles from our house. So it's not really out of your way. And you could rest at our house a bit and sleep in real beds. And—"

Wiggins raised his hand to cut the woman off and glared at Tex. "See you outside a minute, Tex?"

He started for the door without waiting. Tex found him pacing in the dark, ready to explode.

She didn't give him a chance. "Look, Bill. Those women have been through a lot. I thought we could—"

"YOU thought. No, actually, you DIDN'T think. She doesn't just want a ride, she wants us for protection against the unknown, can't you see that? What happens if their house is burned down or full of gangbangers or subject to any one of a hundred horrible, screwed-up conditions now common in our new *Mad Max* world. What then? Do we just say 'see ya' and drop them in the bad guys' laps? Do we take them with us? Or do we get guilt-tripped into taking them to a friend or relative's house, which will further delay us?"

Wiggins blew out an exasperated sigh. "Look, Tex. I'm glad we saved them, but we can't keep saving them. I'm worried about my OWN family. If they can't make it twenty-five miles on their own with guns, a car, and a full tank of gas, they sure won't be able to cope with whatever disaster they find when they get there. I can't be responsible for that. I WON'T be responsible for that. My family comes first. Sorry, but that's just the way it is."

Silence grew. Finally Tex nodded.

"I didn't think it through," she said. "It's just they're so traumatized, I wanted to offer comfort. I let my heart overrule my brain, and in this world, that's a recipe for disaster." She paused. "That said, it's done and we are going in the same direction. I think we can help them without getting further entangled."

Wiggins sighed. "Okay, then how do you see that playing out? I damn sure don't want to be a houseguest or guilted into taking them to Aunt Suzy's."

"We figure our closest point of approach to their house. If they're right, it's a few miles at most. How much food and gas is there?"

"More than we can possibly carry in two cars," Wiggins said.

"Okay. We load up the Honda and another car with as much as we can carry. We'll go heavy on gasoline in our car, but they just need enough gas to get home. We'll give them all the food and water they can carry and whatever weapons they think they can handle. How many sets of NV gear do we have?"

"Three, if the set of the guy on the bridge wasn't damaged. Why?" he asked.

"Are you going to give them a set?"

"No way. We'll be able to drive at night now, with one of us driving and the other as security. I'm not giving that up. Presuming the third set's working, we'll keep it for a spare. It's like Levi says, 'two is one and one is none.'"

"All right. I'll drive them in the second car, using the NV glasses and following you. Even going a roundabout way to stay close to the AT, it shouldn't take more than an hour to reach the point we part company. We find them a side road to hide on and leave them there. They drive the few miles home at first light. By then, we'll be far away. I hope everything goes well with them, but whether it does or not, it's no longer our concern. What do you think?"

"Works for me," Wiggins said. "Let's get on it. You bring them up to speed and start trying to find a working car. I'm going to look around for a charger for the NV batteries. If we're lucky, there'll be a solar-powered one."

"I'm on it," Tex said.

I-84 AND MOUNTAIN TOP ROAD
NEAR STORMVILLE, NEW YORK

DAY 33, 3:40 A.M.

They dropped the women off at the intersection of State Route 52 and Mountain Top Road and proceeded on their way after making sure the women's car was well concealed in the wooded verge. It was clear Fran wanted them to accompany her home, but Wiggins was resolute. They parted company stiffly with a curt nod from Fran and no word of thanks.

Thirty minutes later they sat in the Honda, stopped on the narrow ribbon of blacktop called Mountain Top Road. Wiggins studied the bridge ahead over the broad lanes of I-84, alert for any signs of a trap.

"What do you think?" he asked.

Tex shrugged. "It's pitch black, with no lights on the interstate or background light at all, and the bridge looks clear. If anyone was using so much as a flashlight down on the interstate or in the woods, the NV would probably show it. I think it's clear, Bill."

"Agreed." Wiggins took his foot off the brake and drove forward. "Let's see how much mileage we can make by our usual stopping time. I'm starting to feel good about this."

***

Wiggins' good feelings soured just across the New York border. River crossings were their greatest challenge, and as the Appalachian Trail wound its way northward through Connecticut, it hopped back and forth across the meandering Housatonic with frustrating regularity. They decided to take the last bridge the trail crossed, north across the Connecticut border in Massachusetts. They stayed to the west of the river, roughly paralleling the trail as it wound from one side of the river to the other.

Wiggins gripped the wheel tightly and peered at the green landscape ahead, the twisting back roads and range of the NV glasses limiting his speed. But as irritating as it was, he reminded himself they were making miles under cover of darkness they couldn't have made before.

He was driving north on a one-lane gravel track when he noticed his vision improving due to increasing ambient light from the sky in the east. He increased speed.

"It'll be light soon. How far is the crossing?"

"Less than two miles," Tex said.

"Think we'll have any trouble? There seem to be a lot of freelance toll collectors these days."

"The river's narrow here, with a lot of crossings," Tex said. "There are half a dozen just between here and Great Barrington, a few miles north, and they're all in more built-up areas. There's not much on either side of the Kellogg Road bridge we'll be using, so I think anyone going into the toll-collecting business would pick a busier bridge."

Wiggins sighed. "Let's hope so. I've had about all the conflict I want for a while."

"Me too. Turn right ahead on Lime Kiln Road. We follow that half a mile, then turn right on US 7—"

"Whoa! US 7 sounds like a major road."

"Well, 'major' for around here maybe," Tex said. "But relax, we'll only be on it a few hundred yards before turning on to Kellogg Road anyway. The river looks to be a hundred yards from the last turn, max."

Five minutes later, Wiggins turned right onto US 7 and went less than fifty feet before stopping. There were two sawhorses in the middle of the road, supporting a sheet of plywood with a hand-painted sign.

"Keep out or face the Lord's wrath," Tex read aloud.

"Crap! What now?"

"I'd say the Lord doesn't want visitors," Tex said.

"What about the crossings to the north?"

She shook her head. "There are three communities before the first bridge, and we'd have to stay on US 7 the whole way, somewhere between five and ten miles. On the other hand, we're less than a quarter of a mile from the Kellogg Road bridge. Choose your poison, I guess."

"Well, it's still dark, so let's hope the Lord's sleeping in." Wiggins pulled the SUV around the roadblock.

They'd gone less than a hundred yards when Tex pointed. "That's it on the left ahead."

A paved side road led left from US 7, turning immediately in front of a large frame building with a sign reading Believers Tabernacle. Wiggins powered through the turn, anxious to get past the area and over the bridge. The road curved sharply back to the right through a cluster of homes, and he had to slow.

"So far, so good," he said. "But I wouldn't want to try this in daylight—"

A handheld air horn blasted behind them.

"What is it, Tex? Can you see?"

"Two guys just ran into the road behind us. Both armed, but it doesn't look like they have NV, so I think we're all right."

The road veered sharply to the left, and Wiggins cursed and braked hard. A shot rang out, and the driver side mirror disintegrated.

"Unless, of course, you show them our brake lights," Tex said as Wiggins accelerated.

The bridge appeared around the bend, a short distance ahead. There was an obstruction in the road, and Wiggins realized it was one of the sawhorse and plywood barricades, no doubt to warn off anyone approaching the community via the bridge. There was no room to swerve, and he punched the accelerator, intent on knocking the barricade aside.

An armed man stepped from the wooded verge beside the road, peering in their direction, hearing the engine but unable to see the vehicle. They were almost upon him when he fired. There was a loud metallic *whack* at the front of the SUV, and then they were past, smashing through the flimsy roadblock and across the short bridge to race away down Kellogg Road at sixty miles an hour.

"You think he damaged anything?" Tex asked.

"No way of telling, but we need to put some distance between us and them before we stop to check. What's my next turn?"

"This road dead-ends into another one. You'll be making a left," Tex said.

Wiggins made the turn and got two miles up the road before the temperature gauge and the sun began to rise at the same time.

"We have to pull over," Wiggins said. "Start looking for a hiding spot."

JUST OFF EAST SHEFFIELD ROAD
NEAR GREAT BARRINGTON, MASSACHUSETTS

DAY 33, 6:10 A.M.

A dirt track across a farmer's field led to a secluded strip of woods well off the road and bordering the river. In happier times it might well have been someone's favorite picnic spot; now it was Wiggins' impromptu repair shop.

Tex watched as he squatted at the front of the car and peered through the grill. Steam rose from under the open hood, and the distinctive and unpleasant smell of engine coolant wafted up from the engine compartment.

"It's the radiator all right," Wiggins said.

"Can you fix it?"

Wiggins shrugged. "We don't have much in the way of tools, but I may be able to patch it. It won't be pretty, but it will at least get us somewhere to find a ride. No way this baby's making it to Maine."

Wiggins sighed and stood up. "Give me a hand unloading the back so I can get at the tire tool."

"Anything else I can do?" Tex asked a moment later as Wiggins started toward the front of the car with the tire tool.

He stopped and nodded. "Yeah. Find that bag where we dumped all the unused condiment packets from the MREs and pull out those little packages of black pepper. Then go through all that food we just got at the bridge and pull out all the pepper you can find."

"Pepper? What are we going to do with pepper?"

"Plug the leak, if we can find enough. I'll explain later. For now just see how much you can round up," Wiggins said.

Tex looked puzzled, but she nodded and set about the task as Wiggins moved to the front of the Honda. He shoved the chisel-like end of the tire tool into the plastic grill and pried down sharply. The thin plastic of the grill broke with a series of sharp pops, and he moved the tool and repeated the process before reversing the tire tool to hammer at the broken pieces. He examined his work critically then set about enlarging the hole until he could reach the front of the damaged radiator with both hands. He'd just finished when Tex came around the car, holding up a paper bag.

"One pepper plug, as ordered," she said. "What else?"

"Fill up a bunch of those empty plastic water bottles with the river water, if you will," Wiggins said. "We need to replace the missing coolant, and I don't want to waste our drinking water."

Tex collected the bottles and started for the river as Wiggins went around to their pile of gear and fished the multitool out of the backpack Levi Jenkins had prepared. He folded out the needle-nose pliers and returned to the front of the car.

Working through the hole in the grill to mash the damaged tubes of the radiator flat was difficult. He had to first use the chisel end of the tire tool to flatten the cooling fins before he even had room to get the pliers in around the tubes. Then it took both hands locked around the small pliers and all his strength to mash the damaged tubes flat for two inches on either side of the bullet damage.

By the time Tex returned with an armload of water, Wiggins' forearms were bleeding from repeated scrapes against the sharp broken plastic of the grill, and his shirt was soaked in sweat. But the damaged tubes were crimped, or at least as close as he could make them.

Minutes later, the ground in front of the SUV was littered with empty water bottles, and the engine was running as Wiggins and Tex tore open packet after packet and dumped pepper directly into the radiator.

"Is this really gonna work, Bill?" Tex asked.

Wiggins shrugged. "Beats me. I read about it once, but I've never had to do it before."

"You READ about it? Who reads about stuff like this?"

Wiggins grinned. "I'm an engineer, remember?"

Tex laughed. "And I'm glad you are. What next?"

"When we get all the pepper in, we put the radiator cap back on and let the pressure build up. The radiator is still seeping, and the pepper grains will all be sucked to the leak. The difference in pressure will force the pepper into the leak and it will clog up and solidify. That's the theory anyway. If it works, there won't be any water dripping off the bottom of the radiator."

"And if it doesn't?" Tex asked.

"Even if it doesn't work completely, it should slow the leak," Wiggins said. "We'll fill all our empty bottles with river water, and if the engine temp starts to rise, we pull over and let it cool then top off the radiator. Not perfect but it beats walking."

CHAPTER THIRTY

DAY 33, 5:20 P.M.

The plug was holding, at least for the moment. They decided to celebrate by pigging out with a big meal from their now ample supply of food, only to discover to their disappointment there wasn't really anything in their stores tempting enough to warrant overindulgence.

They slept in shifts, Wiggins first for a few fitful hours while Tex stood watch. He relieved her around noon, the growing heat and his own anxieties banishing any hope for further rest. He had a map spread out on the hood of the Honda when she awoke in the late afternoon, with the now battered *AT Guide* open beside it.

The Honda rocked a bit as she crawled out of the back. Wiggins looked up and smiled.

"Sleep well?" he asked.

Tex yawned. "Better than you, I think. It's still hours before dark, would you like to try again?"

Wiggins shook his head. "Nah. I'm good."

She nodded toward the map. "Finding a better route?"

"Well, I don't know if it's better, but I've definitely come to a conclusion," he said.

"Which is?"

"Which is, it doesn't make much sense to stick close to the AT any longer." He pointed to the map. "The terrain is getting rougher and the roads follow the valleys. Just look at this stretch through the White Mountains; sure, a road parallels the trail five miles away, but the terrain in between is impassable. It might as well be five hundred miles away, and half the trail between here and Maine is like that. There's no point in sticking close to a trail we can't possibly access. Access and escape is the whole point, right?"

Tex looked doubtful. "Maybe, but Levi's plan has worked so far, and I don't—"

"But Levi said himself this was all theoretical, and he's not from New England. I know this area, Tex, look at the elevation changes in the guide if you don't believe me."

"Of course I believe you. It's just that every time we come into a populated area, we court trouble, that's all I'm saying."

"And I'm saying we have no choice," Wiggins said. "There are four major river crossings between here and Maine, and they put the bridges where the people are. Those are our points of greatest risk, and there's nothing we can do to avoid them, so I can't see wasting time in between. We can run the back roads at night now, with no lights, and that's an advantage Levi never even considered when he made his plan. We can cover the distance between the rivers in an hour or two at most, then hide the car and scout the crossing on foot during the day. If it looks too dangerous, we can wait until dark and go upriver to the next crossing, and keep checking them out until we find a place to cross."

Tex sighed. "It sounds reasonable. I just doubt we're going to find unguarded crossings. It seems to be getting worse the further north we go."

"It is what it is," Wiggins said. "One thing for sure, though, we have to get a reliable ride. The plug is holding, but if we have to run for it, it may leave us afoot at the worst possible time."

Tex snorted. "Reliable ride. At this point I long for a Greyhound or even Amtrak."

Wiggins smiled wanly. "Yeah, well, I doubt that's happening anytime soon…"

He stopped mid-sentence and glanced down at the map a moment, then traced a line with his finger. He looked up, his smile genuine now.

"I have an idea," he said.

SAME DAY, 9:10 P.M.

With great difficulty, Wiggins forced himself to wait until full dark before they started out. They found what they were looking for less than two miles down the road and pulled in to a weed-choked gravel parking lot. They sat for a minute examining the modest frame building. A large sign on the front read The Yogurt Hut and another slightly smaller sign proclaimed Frozen Treats.

"You think this place was even in business before the blackout?" Tex asked. "It looks pretty run-down."

"Well, if it was, I figure the frozen treats melted long ago," Wiggins said. "But as long as they have a phone book, I couldn't care less."

He pulled the Honda behind the building. The back door had a cheap padlock rather indifferently attached to the wooden door frame. It yielded to the tire tool easily.

Wiggins hopes fell when they entered, and it was obvious the Yogurt Hut hadn't been a going concern in some time. Hope was restored when Tex found a stack of dusty phone books in a cabinet.

"What's that thickest one?" Wiggins asked.

Tex shined her light at the cover. "Springfield."

Wiggins grabbed the book and opened it to the yellow pages, then began flipping pages.

"Track Services, Inc., in Westfield," he said triumphantly.

"If it's still there," Tex said. "That phone book is ten years old."

Wiggins was carefully tearing the page out of the book. "We'll find out when we get there, won't we?"

***

As it turned out, their frustrations weren't over. Westfield was on the east bank of the Westfield River, a minor tributary of the Connecticut. Their original route paralleling the AT took them west of its headwaters, but going directly to Westfield meant they had to cross the river or travel almost two hundred miles around, not an option given the jury-rigged repair.

There were bridges in the city of Westfield itself and on the Mass Turnpike west of the city: main crossings likely to be controlled by someone, either government or freelance toll collectors. Their maps showed two crossings upstream, one in the center of a tiny hamlet named Woronoco and a second just upstream of the town.

"What do you think?" Tex asked.

"The one upstream from town might work," Wiggins said. "I've been thinking about our problem back at that last bridge. They probably weren't trying to block the bridge as much as protect the borders of their community." He pointed at the map. "There's nothing much on either side of this bridge upstream, and the road bypasses the town, so the good folks in Woronoco might care less."

It was a bit over sixty miles to Westfield via Woronoco, all on state roads, with no back road alternatives shown on their maps. The unknowns, besides the Woronoco bridge, were what they would find in the more populated areas they had to transit. With little choice, they could only trust darkness to shield them. They left at eleven, shooting for a midnight arrival at the bridge.

Things went smoothly until they rounded a curve approaching the town of Blandford and Wiggins saw two police cars across the road ahead. He stopped in the middle of the road and stared at the roadblock glowing green in his NV glasses.

"Is there a way around this, Tex?"

"Negative. The only road south dead-ends at a reservoir, and there are no roads to the north until a ways further into town. What are we going to do?"

"They look like legitimate cops instead of freelancers. It's probably something like we ran into at Front Royal, but maybe we can talk our way through. We really don't have a choice." Wiggins pondered it a moment. "Take off your glasses and put them under the seat."

Tex complied as Wiggins put the Honda in reverse and backed around the curve they'd just transited. When he was sure they couldn't be seen from the roadblock, he stopped the car and put his own glasses out of sight.

"Practice looking innocent," he said, and turned on the headlights.

He drove around the curve and toward the roadblock. When his headlights illuminated it, he stopped suddenly, as if he were seeing it for the first time. The Honda had barely come to a stop when he was blinded by a powerful spotlight, and an amplified voice boomed from the roadblock.

"KILL YOUR LIGHTS AND DRIVE FORWARD SLOWLY. BE PREPARED TO STOP ON MY COMMAND."

Wiggins held a hand up to shield his eyes and did as ordered. He'd crept a hundred feet when he was ordered to stop, kill his engine, and to keep both hands visible on the wheel. Tex was ordered to raise her hands as well. Totally blinded by the light, Wiggins was regretting his decision when more bright lights probed into the car, one through the driver's side window and the second through the passenger window. The light on the driver's side played over first Wiggins, then Tex, then the gear in the back of the Honda. The light on the passenger side held steady, continuing to blind them both.

"Are you armed?" asked the cop on the driver's side.

Wiggins cursed himself for a fool.

"Seriously, officer? Do you run across anyone traveling these days who ISN'T armed?" Wiggins asked.

"I take it that's a yes?"

"Yes, we're armed," Wiggins said.

"Very well, sir. I would like you both to keep your hands in plain sight. We will open your doors and then you will exit the vehicle, keeping your hands in plain sight at all times. Is that clear?"

"Really, officer. Is this necessary —"

"IS THAT CLEAR, SIR?"

"Yes, officer. It's clear," Wiggins said.

The car doors squeaked open, and Wiggins and Tex stepped out, holding their hands up. They were ordered to put their hands on the top of the car and then patted down.

"Nothing here, Chief," called the cop across the roof of the car.

"Where are your weapons?" the cop behind Wiggins asked.

"On the car seat," Wiggins said. "It's not real comfortable driving with them stuck in your belt or the small of your back."

The cop shined his light into the car and spotted the Sig and the Glock on the seat. He called across to his partner to bring Tex around to the driver's side, and when she was standing beside Wiggins where he could keep an eye on her, told his partner to collect the guns from the car.

Wiggins started to protest but thought better of it. Losing the handguns was acceptable if that was the end of it. They had plenty more hardware under blankets in the back. Best just to smile and get the hell out of here as soon as possible.

"Where are you going, and what's your business?" the chief asked.

"We're merchant seamen. We got stranded down south by the blackout, and we're just trying to get home to Maine."

"Where in Maine?"

"Just outside of Lewiston," Wiggins said.

"IDs?"

"In my back pocket, if you'll let me get it," Wiggins said.

"Go ahead," the chief said, and Wiggins fished his wallet out of his hip pocket, overcoming a sudden impulse to laugh hysterically at just how ludicrous it was that he was still carrying a wallet full of useless cash and even more useless credit cards. Old habits die hard.

Wiggins opened his wallet and removed his Maine driver's license and, as an afterthought, his Transportation Worker Identification and held them both out. The cop took them and backed away, holding the documents in front of the light so he could see both the IDs and Wiggins and Tex at the same time. He stepped closer and handed them back to Wiggins.

"Thank you, Mr. Wiggins. How about you, ma'am?"

"My IDs are in my backpack," Tex said. "Do you want me to get them?"

The cop considered that a moment. "No. I guess it doesn't matter."

"Look, officer," Wiggins said. "We don't want any trouble. We'd go around your town if we could, but the only way we can get where we're going is through town. But I promise —"

The chief was shaking his head, the action casting outsize dancing shadows in the harsh spotlights from the roadblock. "Be that as it may," he said, "I have to ask you folks to turn around and go back the way you came. Nobody's coming into Blandford from any direction, not even to pass through. No exceptions, by order of the town council."

The cop's voice softened. "I wish you luck, but you can't come through here. We'll unload your guns and leave 'em in the car. Then you have to turn around and leave. Is that clear?"

Wiggins nodded, relieved it wasn't worse.

"Warren," the chief said to the other cop, "unload the weapons and toss them and the loose rounds in the backseat. These folks can stop and reload when they get down the road a piece." The cop glanced at Wiggins. "No offense, but you can't be too careful these days."

"None taken," Wiggins said.

The second cop unloaded the weapons quickly and expertly, then tossed the guns and ammo in the back window. The chief nodded at Wiggins and Tex to get back in the car. Wiggins complied and was about to start the car when the chief spoke again, hesitantly.

"My kid brother's at sea. He's on one of the government ships in Diego Garcia. This is probably a stupid question, but I ... I don't suppose you heard anything on your ship ..."

"Is he on the *Lopez*?" Wiggins asked.

The cop looked surprised. "How did you know?"

"Just a lucky guess. There aren't that many ships at Diego Garcia, and I did a few rotations on the *Lopez* a few years ago. But I'm sorry, we don't know anything about her. Our communications went down right along with everyone else's."

The chief nodded. "Well, thanks anyway. He ... he was almost due home on vacation when the blackout hit."

"Then he's lucky he wasn't en route when it happened," Wiggins said. "And if it's any consolation, he's probably better off than any of us here. Those pre-positioned ships have tons of supplies. And no gangbangers."

"Yeah, that's what I've been telling Mom, but it's tough on his wife and kids."

Wiggins nodded, sensing an opening. "So tell me, Chief, if your kid brother was trying to make it home to his family, wouldn't you want someone to help him out?"

The man didn't speak for a long moment, then smiled wanly. "I walked into that one, didn't I? And to answer your question, of course I want to help you out, but I take my orders from the town council."

"So what if it's not helping me out, but making a trade to substantially improve security? I mean, it's the middle of the night, and I doubt the town council wants to be awakened, but neither would they want to miss a great opportunity," Wiggins said.

"And what opportunity would that be?"

Wiggins reached under his seat for the NV goggles and held them out the window.

"Are those what I think they are?" the chief asked.

"State of the art," Wiggins said, sensing the cop wavering. "And for an escort through town I'll let you have these and sweeten the deal with two M4s and a hundred rounds of ammo. Hell, make it two hundred."

The cop examined the NV glasses. "How do you know I won't just arrest you both and take these and everything else you have?"

"First, because if you were going to shake us down, you'd have done so by now, and second, because I think you're still a decent guy trying to make the best of a truly screwed-up situation, and this is the decent thing to do," Wiggins said. "But mostly because you've got a kid brother who's in exactly our situation who will be trying to make it home sooner or later, and if he doesn't, you'll always wonder if it was because there was some guy somewhere who could have helped him but didn't. Karma's a bitch."

The chief shook his head and chuckled, then extended his hand through the open car window. "You missed your calling, Wiggins, you should have had a mind-reading act. You've got yourself a deal. I'm Jesse Walters."

Relief washed over Wiggins as he took the cop's hand. "Bill Wiggins," he said, "but you knew that. This is Shyla Texeira, Tex for short."

The exchange was completed quickly, and as promised, Walters escorted them through Blandford then pulled into the parking lot of an animal hospital at the edge of town. He got out of his patrol car and came over to Wiggins' window.

"State Route 23 parallels the Mass Turnpike," Walters said. "It's only a couple of hundred yards away through the trees. There are all sorts of refugees camped along the turnpike with nowhere else to go. Some are good people and some bad, but all of them are desperate. That's what our roadblock's all about. You're going to be running with your night vision, so you probably won't have a problem, but don't stop for anyone for any reason. There have been a lot of ambushes, and they often use women or children as bait, so trust nothing you see."

Wiggins nodded, and Walters continued.

"In about ten miles, Route 23 crosses the turnpike via a bridge. Hit the bridge at speed and don't slow down. The woods are close to the road, and the ambushers' sometimes throw rocks to distract drivers and make them run off the bridge approach and crash down the bank onto the turnpike. Be warned."

Wiggins shook his head. "Wow! That's hardcore. Thanks for the warning."

Walters reached into his shirt pocket and extracted a folded paper and handed it to Wiggins.

"At the intersection of 23 and 20, you'll hit another roadblock. There'll be a deputy sheriff in charge named Jimmy Jacobs. He's my cousin, and that note should get you through the roadblock and an escort over the bridge."

Walters grinned. "Of course, I suspect one of your 'extra' M4s and some ammo might get you an escort almost into Westfield, especially if you offer to replace the gas they use."

Wiggins grinned back and extended his hand out the window. "I expect that can be arranged. Thank you, Jesse."

Walters took Wiggins' hand and shook it firmly.

"Thank YOU, for what you said about my brother's ship. It might not seem like much to you, but it will mean a lot to my family. It's getting harder to keep hope alive nowadays," Walters said.

He released Wiggins' hand and nodded across the car. "Tex, Bill, Godspeed. I hope you make it home and find your families safe and well when you get there."

Wiggins glanced over at Tex and saw her quickly suppressed flash of pain.

"Thank you, Jesse," Tex said. "I hope your brother makes it home too."

Wiggins nodded his agreement, then flipped down his NV glasses and put the SUV in gear.

TRACK SERVICES, INC.
LOCKHOUSE ROAD
WESTFIELD, MASSACHUSETTS

DAY 34, 2:50 A.M.

Despite Walters' warning, the anonymity of traveling without lights allowed them to reach the next roadblock without difficulty. Once there, Walters' note and a little horse trading got them an escort not only into Westfield, but to the very gates of Track Services, Inc.

The company was located in an industrial area along a railroad spur. The gate to the tall chain-link fence hung open, and the building looked abandoned. The asphalt parking lot was full of equipment the use of which could only be guessed at, but most appeared intact.

Wiggins handed over an M4 and ammo, along with a five-gallon can of precious gasoline. The escort was worth it, and if his plan worked, they had more than enough gasoline. If not, they'd be looking for a plan B anyway. The deputies wished Wiggins and Tex well and left.

They hadn't disclosed the existence of the NV gear to the deputies at the second roadblock, as they no longer had an extra set to barter and were concerned the deputies might not be willing to settle for just guns and ammo if they knew about the NV. That meant running into Westfield with lights, which they extinguished as soon as the deputies' car pulled out of sight. They donned their goggles and moved the Honda out of sight from the road between two large pieces of equipment.

They found what they were looking for at the back of the lot. Backed against the fence were three Ford crew cab pickups. They had customized beds, with toolboxes mounted on each side, but of most interest were the odd units mounted at the front and rear bumpers of each truck. A pair of rail car wheels at each end of the trucks were fitted to a hydraulic power unit to raise and lower them.

"Bingo!" Wiggins said.

"I'm surprised they're still here," Tex said.

"I'd have been surprised if they weren't. I mean, think about it, no one's likely to want one except to ride the rails long distance, and they have to have the gas to do it."

"Presuming they even think about it," Tex said. "This never occurred to me."

Wiggins nodded. "Necessity might be the mother of invention, but desperation is its favorite aunt. I gotta get home, Tex."

"Well, we have a better chance now."

Wiggins nodded at the open hoods. "This place hasn't escaped notice completely; it looks like someone's taken the batteries. I'm betting all the gas tanks have been siphoned dry as well. We'll have to swap the battery out of the Honda."

He moved to the driver's side of the nearest truck and glanced in. "No keys. We'll hot-wire one if we have to, but let's look in the building. We might get lucky."

The building had several large roller doors, with a regular man door to one side. The man door was open, obviously forced. They entered cautiously, guns drawn. The pitch-black interior yielded no ambient light for their NV gear to intensify. They listened, but heard only dead silence.

"We'll need flashlights," Wiggins said softly as he raised his NV glasses out of the way.

When he was sure Tex had done the same, he switched on his flashlight. It illuminated a cavernous maintenance garage served by the large roller doors. To the right was a large office, overturned desks and chairs visible through the open door.

"Let's try the office," he said.

He found a key cabinet on the far wall, standing open with empty hooks, keys scattered on the floor beneath it. Wiggins piled keys on a nearby desk to sort through them. He'd found several Ford keys when Tex spoke.

"Well, well, well. What have we here?"

Wiggins looked up and his face split into a grin. Tex was ten feet away, playing her light over a large route map of New England rail lines, thumbtacked to the wall.

"Great find, Tex. We'll be taking that."

Tex was already removing it.

Wiggins jammed a handful of Ford keys into his pocket. "I'm going to try these keys. If one of them works, I'll start swapping the battery over and gas up."

"Okay," Tex said. "I'll poke around a bit more to see if I can find anything of use."

Wiggins grunted his agreement and headed for the door. The keys were marked, but the system wasn't immediately obvious, but there weren't that many keys, so Wiggins just climbed into the first truck and tried them one by one. He hit pay dirt on his fifth try and hurried across the parking lot to move the Honda over to transfer the battery.

With the new battery, the pickup turned over smoothly, and Wiggins was filling their new ride with gas when Tex showed up and dumped the folded railroad map and a small plastic bag in the front seat of their new truck.

"Find anything of use?" Wiggins asked.

"The map's the prize," Tex said. "But I did find a portable air horn and refill cartridges. If we're gonna ride the rails in the dark, we might want to sound like a train at some point."

Wiggins laughed, his mood much improved. "Well, you never know. I'll finish fueling, then siphon the gas from the SUV into one of the empty cans. Would you start transferring everything else over?"

"On it," Tex said.

***

Half an hour later they were ready to roll, but hadn't quite decided the best direction to roll in. They grabbed the rail map and went back inside where their lights would be shielded. Wiggins spread the map out on a desk and studied it under his flashlight.

"It's almost four," Tex said. "If anyone saw us come in here lit up like Christmas trees, they might come nosing around come daylight. We need to be well away from here and out of town before sunup. What do you think, maybe an hour or so to get out of town, then another hour to get off the rails and find some place to hide?"

"Agreed." Wiggins traced a line on the map with his finger. "We don't have to plan the whole route now, but if we head north to Greenfield, we can pick up this line running east, which looks like it connects with northbound lines well outside Boston. We'll fine-tune the route when we stop for the day. For now let's just get the hell out of here."

***

Unfortunately, getting the truck lined up on the rails proved to be a matter of trial and error and not nearly as easy as Wiggins anticipated. They used a nearby street crossing with Wiggins driving and Tex giving hand signals, and it took them almost an hour before the truck was centered on the rails with the guide wheels locked in place. Wiggins cast a worried look at the lightening eastern sky as Tex climbed into the passenger seat.

"Let's hope we get better with practice," she said.

"Let's hope we don't have to use it long enough to need much practice," Wiggins said.

Despite the inauspicious beginning, the truck moved smoothly on the rails. Though, Wiggins' dreams of speeding home were dampened by the large safety notice on the dashboard, limiting the top speed on straight track to forty-five miles per hour and dropping that to thirty for curves, and warning of the near certainty of derailment if those limits were exceeded.

They'd just made a sweeping turn to the left under the Mass Turnpike when Wiggins nodded at the sign. "For sure we won't be outrunning any bad guys."

"Which is why we're running in the dark. Speaking of which, it will be full light in a half hour or so," Tex said, her NV glasses flipped up as she studied the map with a flashlight. "The delay is going to cost us. If we follow our original plan, we'll be in a populated area come sunup."

"Plan B?" Wiggins asked.

"We're in it," Tex said. "We're in a heavily wooded area for the next few miles, with no roads or buildings for at least a half a mile on either side of the tracks. Stopping on the track along here is probably the safest option."

"Okay," Wiggins said, tapping the brakes.

CHAPTER THIRTY-ONE

DAY 34, 4:25 P.M.

They decided one of them would keep watch in the driver's seat in case they had to run. Wiggins volunteered for the first watch, and Tex stretched out in the backseat of the crew cab and was dead to the world in minutes.

Wiggins was poring over the map for the tenth time when he heard Tex stirring. He looked back over the seat and smiled.

"Lazarus awakes."

There was a red ridge down Tex's cheek from a seam in the upholstery, and her hair was flattened on the side of her head. She looked about groggily, then glanced at her watch.

"You let me sleep all day, Bill!"

Wiggins shrugged. "You needed it, and I'm too excited to sleep anyway." He grinned again. "Even at thirty miles an hour, I'll make it home by morning, Tex."

"All the more reason to sleep. You can't drive all night —"

"Oh yes I can, and I'm going to," Wiggins said.

"Okay, but don't forget the river crossings, even on the railroads. There are at least four major —"

"Twenty-nine," Wiggins said.

"What?"

"There are twenty-nine major rail bridges on our route. We'll cross the Nashua River five times, and some big creek I never heard of six times, and several of the rivers twice or three times each." Wiggins grinned.

"Then why are you so happy?"

"Because ninety-five percent of the crossings are out in the boonies without a road nearby, much less anyone likely to contest our crossing, AND I confirmed we can give Boston a wide berth. We still have to transit some smaller cities, but I don't think we should have a problem on the rails in the dark."

"Still, we need to be cautious. For sure some of those railroad bridges are going to be blocked or guarded," Tex said.

"Yeah, but it's like we were talking about before. People guarding the major highway bridges pull cars across the road or make other strong barriers because they EXPECT cars might try to crash the roadblock," Wiggins said. "But where we've seen railroad bridges guarded, have we ever once seen one with a substantial barrier?"

"No, I'll grant you that. But that doesn't mean —"

"That's exactly what it means, Tex. Anybody guarding a railroad bridge is expecting to stop pedestrian traffic or maybe bikes or motorcycles, or at the very most, a car bumping along at slow speed. Nobody will expect a rail vehicle to take a bridge at speed, and it's such an unlikely event they're not likely to waste time constructing a barrier against it."

"I agree, this is our best option by far," Tex said. "I just don't want to see you get your hopes up too high. We're bound to have to go through some rail yards, and we don't know how all the rail switches are set. Or the blackout might have left a train on the track somewhere, blocking our way, or any one of a dozen things—"

"In which case we raise the guide wheels, get off the track, drive around the problem, and get back on," Wiggins said.

"Which we found out last night is not quite as easy as it sounds," Tex said.

"Well, maybe," Wiggins said, his enthusiasm not noticeably dampened.

***

Wiggins' patience was tested almost immediately when he suggested leaving as soon as it was full dark. Tex pointed out they had to transit Holyoke to reach open track, including a section of track running down the center of a city street for a half mile. Wiggins grudgingly conceded the point, and they delayed their departure until eleven.

Once clear of Holyoke and running north at full speed, a new variable surfaced; they were much noisier than anticipated. The guide wheels rode the tracks with a metallic hum and shrieked a piercing lament as they rounded curves. Likewise, there was a clunk at each rail joint, not unlike the clackety-clack of a freight train, but with a different cadence due to the short length of their vehicle and the odd spacing of the guide wheels and the truck tires.

"So much for stealth," Wiggins said. "I'm sure we can be heard for miles."

"That might be a good thing," Tex said. "Nobody's likely to try to stop a train, and by the time they figure out we're NOT a train, we'll be long gone."

Despite Wiggins' determination, he soon realized his goal was unrealistic. Braking of the rubber tires on the smooth steel rails was touchy at best, and every time they came to a rail yard, they slowed to a crawl, fearful they might find themselves switched to a siding and hurtling toward a stationary string of freight cars.

Likewise, the sound they produced at full speed gave far too much advance notice to anyone who might be waiting at a rail bridge. After some discussion, they decided to slow down well in advance of all bridges and creep forward in the dark until they could use their NV gear to see what awaited them.

It was an expenditure of time made all the more grudgingly because Wiggins had been right about most of the bridges. However, on two occasions their caution paid off, and they spotted guards ahead. The first time, they crept close enough in the dark to dash across and escape down the track before the sleepy guard knew what was happening.

On the second occasion, the guard was more alert and raised a powerful flashlight as they barreled toward the bridge. But Wiggins and Tex were prepared. They'd raised their NV glasses, and Wiggins hit the high beams just as Tex blasted the portable air horn in the guard's direction. The terrified guard leaped to one side, and the pickup rushed past. By the time the guard recovered, Wiggins killed the lights, and the pickup sped away in the darkness.

They were through Lowell by three o'clock, and halfway through Lawrence when Wiggins let out a resigned sigh. "We're obviously not going to make it tonight. We need to start thinking about a hiding place. We'll push across the Merrimack at Haverhill and out of the city. The track runs through rural areas north of there."

"The Merrimack is a pretty substantial river," Tex said.

"Definitely not one of the ninety-five percent. It's a major crossing in an urban area, so I expect it's guarded." Wiggins laughed nervously. "I guess we'll see how valid my 'no barricade' theory is, now won't we?"

Tex studied the map. "There's another problem, I'm afraid. There's a commuter train station to the left, then a long sweeping curve. We won't be able to see a thing until we're practically on top of the bridge, and if we take that curve at anything but a crawl, those metal wheels will squeal a warning. Anyone there will know about us before we know about them."

"What're you thinking?"

"I'm thinking we should stop before we round the curve and check it out on foot," Tex said.

***

Wiggins began slowing as soon as he saw the commuter rail station, and they rolled to a silent stop just as the tracks began to curve left. They started down the track on foot, carrying their M4s and moving cautiously.

They reached a viaduct, which carried the tracks over a city street. Tex touched Wiggins' arm and pointed; the street passing below them ran the short distance to the river and onto a car bridge. Wiggins followed Tex's pointing finger to see a roadblock across the bridge entrance, glowing green in his goggles. Three cars blocked the bridge. He could make out people seated in each of the cars, and one man leaning against the hood of one, holding an assault rifle.

"Well, there are definitely toll collectors on the car bridge, so there's probably someone on the rail bridge, since they're side by side," Wiggins whispered.

Tex nodded, and they started across the viaduct, being careful not to miss a step and plunge between the ties. They were halfway across when Wiggins spotted it.

"Well, so much for that theory," he muttered softly, then pointed to a car parked across the tracks a hundred feet away.

Tex studied the scene for a moment before responding. "It looks like there's some sort of little parking lot there, so all they had to do was back across the tracks." She paused. "I see one guy at the wheel zonked out. You see anyone else?" she whispered.

"Negative," Wiggins whispered back. "Stay and watch the roadblock while I take care of the guy in the car and roll it out of the way. If those guys down there hear us, be ready to discourage them from charging to the rescue too quickly."

Tex nodded and Wiggins moved forward. He circled around to the driver's side of the car and studied the man through the open window. His head lolled back against the headrest and he was snoring softly; drool dribbled from the corner of his open mouth. Wiggins put the muzzle of the M4 against the man's head.

"Make a move and you're dead," Wiggins said quietly.

The man's eyes flew open, puzzled at first, then terrified.

"Put both your hands on the wheel where I can see —"

Wiggins saw the movement in his peripheral vision and reacted instinctively, stepping back several steps as the man who'd been sleeping unseen in the backseat raised a pistol. Wiggins silenced him with a three-round burst, then turned back to the driver, who was now bringing up a pistol as well. Wiggins fired a three-round burst through the thin sheet metal of the car door, and the man jerked and fell forward on the wheel. The blare of a car horn split the night air.

Wiggins looked helplessly at Tex, who shook her head in insect-like astonishment. He jerked open the car door and dragged the dead man out, relieved the horn stopped at least. He laid his M4 down and jumped behind the wheel to pull the car off the tracks, then was out and scooping up his weapon to run back towards Tex. He found her crouched behind the short steel wall of the viaduct, watching the men at the roadblock.

They were all awake now, and Wiggins counted seven. All were well armed, but he could see no NV gear at all.

"I think we're all right," Tex said. "They don't know what the hell is going on, and they can't cut us off unless they crawl up that steep slope to the tracks, and it's pretty overgrown with brush. The only other way up here passes under this viaduct, and we have the advantage. I'll hold them off while you bring up the truck."

"I'll stay. You go get the truck," Wiggins said.

"Knock off the Sir Galahad crap, Bill. You know I'm a better shot. Just go get the truck. And hurry, before those clowns get organized."

Wiggins hesitated, then set off down the tracks at a run. He'd just reached the truck and started it when he heard all hell break loose. He could easily distinguish Tex's disciplined three-round bursts from the roar of full-automatic fire from the street below. He mashed the accelerator and sent up a silent prayer for Tex. He had no doubt she was giving better than she got, but the goons on the street below were throwing out a lot of rounds, and they might get lucky.

He rounded the curve and was relieved to see Tex on the opposite side of the viaduct, firing and moving, taking advantage of the fact her opponents could only see her muzzle flash, and making sure she immediately vacated the place they'd last seen it. With the truck on the rails, Wiggins had no need to steer it, so he shouldered his M4 and stuck it through the open window. He smiled when their opponents came into view. Far from advancing, they'd all taken cover behind the three-car barricade, popping up to spray rounds in their general direction then dropping down again. He added his own fire to Tex's as the truck rolled across the viaduct, then belatedly remembered the rather limited stopping power of the rubber tires on the slick rails and slammed on the brakes.

Tex glanced over her shoulder as the pickup flashed past, tires squealing, and she turned and raced after it. It was still moving when she managed to throw open the door and leap inside.

"GO, GO, GO," she yelled.

Wiggins transferred his foot to the gas and they were off, racing over the Merrimack.

HAVERHILL, MASSACHUSETTS
SAME DAY, 4:55 A.M.

They rode in tense silence through the dark city, expecting to be fired upon any moment. Slowly the tension ebbed, and Tex started chuckling.

"What?" Wiggins said.

"The next time the task requires silence, I'm doing it," Tex said. "Seriously? The frigging horn?"

"It's not like I planned it," Wiggins said.

"Obviously," Tex said, and laughed harder.

Her laughter was infectious, and soon Wiggins was laughing along with her, but a glance at the lightening sky to the east killed his good humor.

"We have to find a hiding place, and soon," he said.

Tex looked at a highway bridge towering above the track ahead, then glanced at the map.

"That's gotta be I-495. The area ahead looks to be a mix of rural land and subdivisions. There's a crossing about five miles ahead. We should be able to get off and on there with no problem."

A few minutes later Wiggins started slowing, and as Tex had predicted, the road crossing proved a perfect place to exit the tracks. He pulled into the crossing and raised the guide wheels, allowing him to steer off the tracks and onto the pavement.

"Which way?" he asked.

"Left," Tex said. "But go slow, and let's see if we can find an opening in the woods to the right."

Wiggins had driven no more than fifty feet when Tex yelled and pointed to a dirt track.

"This isn't the SUV, Tex," Wiggins said. "I doubt the off-road capabilities are close to the same."

Tex nodded and opened her door.

"What are you doing?" Wiggins asked.

"I'll walk in front to check things out. I'll walk a bit, then motion you forward. If we run into problems, we can always back out."

She closed the door without waiting for a response and walked forward. She went fifty feet and motioned him forward, then repeated the process. They'd gone about two hundred feet when he emerged on the now neglected green expanse of a golf course. Tex came over, grinning.

"I saw it on the map," she said. "I figure not too many people are playing golf these days, so hiding in the woods off the eighteenth hole should be fairly secure."

GRANITE FIELDS GOLF COURSE
KINGSTON, NEW HAMPSHIRE

DAY 35, 7:25 P.M.

Wiggins didn't argue when Tex insisted on taking the first watch. He collapsed across the backseat of the crew cab and was snoring soundly before the sun was fully up. He awoke in the early afternoon, rested but sweaty, and relieved Tex. She woke near sundown to find Wiggins standing in the fading light, the railroad map spread out before him on the hood of the truck. She went into the woods to relieve herself and came back to stand by Wiggins' side.

"Problem?" she asked.

He shook his head. "I was just going over the route again to see if there were any more blind approaches like that curve back there."

"And?"

He shook his head again. "There aren't any, but I've had second thoughts about our route. Riding the rails all the way to Lewiston means transiting Portland and two long bridges we don't really need to cross. I don't think it's worth the risk, BUT"—Wiggins put his finger on the map—"there's a spur here in Biddeford with its own bridge across the Saco River. It dead-ends in an industrial park less than forty miles from home. I'll feel a lot more comfortable maneuvering on back roads I know well and with a night-vision advantage instead of being stuck on rails in a city."

"Sounds reasonable," Tex said.

They were close now, and as much as he wanted to rush, Wiggins forced himself to be patient. They decided to wait until after midnight to increase the odds the people in the towns they transited would be asleep. They ate MREs and passed the time talking about their lives. Wiggins hadn't spoken much of his home and family, suppressing his worry to concentrate on the all-important task of getting home. Now that goal was in reach, and he felt a need to verbalize his fears. Tex offered quiet encouragement, silent most of the time but asking questions when appropriate.

He smiled when he talked of his wife, Karen, and their three-year-old, Billy, and his own parents who lived nearby. Then he turned somber.

"Karen's folks were killed in a car wreck when she was in college, but my folks love her as much as I do. She had a real hard time when Billy was born, and my folks were right there with her." His face clouded. "But I wasn't and I've never really forgiven myself."

"Why? What happened?"

"Billy came early and Karen had to have a C-section. I planned to work until a couple of weeks before delivery so I could be there and still have most of my vacation left to help out, but I was a day out of port

453

when she went into labor. I practically rode the gangway down when we made port, but by the time I got home, it was all over. Luckily it turned out okay, but this time I was determined to be there."

He shook his head. "Look how well that turned out."

"When is she due?" Tex asked softly.

Wiggins didn't respond. "Five days ago," he said at last. "And she was likely going to need another C-section. But now…" He trailed off, unable to complete the thought.

"I'm sure she's fine, Bill," Tex said, but it sounded lame even to her.

"She has to be," Wiggins said, his face a mask of grim determination.

They lapsed into silence, checking the luminous faces of their watches as the minutes dragged. Finally at eleven, Wiggins could take it no more.

"Screw it," he said, and donned his NV glasses and started the truck.

CHAPTER THIRTY-TWO

RIDING THE RAILS
NORTHBOUND
NEAR BIDDEFORD, MAINE

DAY 36, 2:25 A.M.

They got off to a good start, managing to get the pickup lined up on the rails and the guide wheels locked on the second try. Wiggins started down the track and they were soon at the prescribed safe speed limit and then five miles over it. Tex said nothing as Wiggins stared ahead grimly.

They rolled through Exeter and Newmarket without difficulty and barely slowed through the University of New Hampshire campus at Durham. Movement seemed to lighten Wiggins' mood, and he began to make small talk once again. They slowed for the Cocheco River bridge at Dover but found it clear, but only five miles further down the line, they spotted a self-appointed toll collector at the Salmon Falls River bridge at Rollinsford.

They surprised him with their high beams and air horn technique and were almost across the bridge before the man recovered and fired at them, or rather their sound, somewhat perfunctorily.

Wiggins let out a relieved sigh as they rolled off the bridge on the far side.

"We're in Maine, Tex! That was the border!" he said.

"How far to Biddeford?" Tex asked.

"Thirty miles to the switch for the spur," Wiggins said.

"Do you have any idea how we're going to manage that? Don't they have padlocks or something?"

"We'll figure it out," Wiggins said.

Tex raised her NV goggles and studied the map. "Maybe we don't have to. After the lines diverge, they cross Main Street about three blocks apart. We can follow this line to Main Street, get off and drive three blocks, and get back on the spur at the crossing. That should be a lot faster than messing around with a switch when we don't know what we're doing."

"Agreed. Good thinking."

Tex smiled. "That's why I'm the navigator."

The miles clacked by beneath the truck's multiple sets of wheels. As they entered Biddeford, the track curved to the right, and Wiggins was forced to slow so the screeching wheels didn't announce their presence as they made their brief foray on the city streets. The transfer to the spur was uneventful, and the rail bridge was unguarded. Wiggins picked up speed again, rushing through dark residential areas before plunging again into heavy woods.

Tex looked at the map. "Take it easy, Bill. There's a sharp turn to the left coming up."

Wiggins slowed, but not enough, and the metal guide wheels screeched a piercing lament as the truck rounded the curve at speed, barely managing to stay on the track.

"Oops! Sorry, Tex," Wiggins said, slowing the truck even more. "I guess I need to keep it together. "Any more curves I need to worry about?"

She looked at the map again. "There's a slight jog to the right around some sort of big facility ahead on the left. Then a bit farther there's a sharp turn to the right under the interstate and maybe a quarter of a mile to the dead end."

Wiggins sighed. "Almost there."

He increased speed again as they hurtled through the thick woods, but mindful of the slight curve ahead, he kept the speed well below the prescribed limit. They rounded the curve, and the trees thinned enough for him to catch fleeting glimpses of a huge industrial building through the trees to his left. He saw movement on the track ahead and glanced back toward a large sign on the building. Uh-oh!

The movement resolved itself into two figures standing astride the track, both in full combat gear with helmets and NV gear. Wiggins watched in mute surprise as one raised his hand in a stop gesture.

"Who the hell are those guys, and what are they doing in the middle of the woods?" Tex asked.

"Army, National Guard, or FEMA I'd say," Wiggins replied. "That building is the General Dynamics Weapons facility. It was a big employer here, but I forgot all about it. They make machine guns and ammunition, so no doubt any number of groups want to control it. They probably heard us screech around that curve and sent guys to check the track."

"What are we going to do?"

"Well, I'm NOT letting them stop us this close to home. At a minimum they'll be suspicious about all the guns and how we happen to be riding the rails. Nothing good can come of dealing with them. Get ready to sound that horn and dive for the floorboard."

The men were both raising their assault rifles now, and Wiggins braked, the rubber tires squealing on the slick rails. He saw their body language relax slightly, and one stepped to the side, obviously intent on questioning them, while the other remained in place on the track. They held their rifles ready, but pointed down. The truck was fifty feet away and coasting to a stop when Wiggins raised his NV goggles and told Tex to do the same.

"NOW!" he hissed, and stomped the accelerator as he hit his high beams.

Tex blasted the horn at the now blinded men as the truck tires squealed and spun on the rails. Wiggins realized his mistake and eased off the accelerator, allowing the tires to bite, and the truck shot forward. They brushed aside the man blocking their way, who barely managed to get off the track in time, and a hundred feet away they heard gunfire. A round slapped into the truck, and Wiggins belatedly killed the lights to make them a more difficult target.

"You all right?" Wiggins asked.

"I think so. You think they'll chase us?"

"No clue, but we need to disappear as soon as possible," Wiggins said.

He pushed the truck as fast as track conditions would allow, and less than five minutes later they rolled under the interstate and into the industrial park. There were multiple places to exit the rails where entrance drives crossed the track. Wiggins overshot the first one, but got the truck stopped at the second.

He raised the front guide wheels, freeing the front tires from the rails, but when he hit the control for the rear guide wheels, there was no response. He cursed and they both got out. Oily hydraulic fluid dripped off the back bumper, and a quick inspection found a bullet hole near the bottom of the hydraulic tank for the rear unit.

Wiggins cursed. "We can't raise the wheels without hydraulic fluid."

***

"What are we going to do?" Tex asked, but Wiggins already had the back door open and was pulling out empty water bottles.

"Drain oil out of the front unit and transfer it to the rear. We only have to get enough in to cycle the rear wheels once."

"But the hole —"

Wiggins started toward the front of the truck with an armload of water bottles. "One problem at a time. Grab a bunch of those bottles and give me a hand."

He squatted down and located the drain plug for the front unit and loosened it with the multitool.

"Okay, Tex. There's no valve on this thing, and when I pull that plug, it will be slick as hell. I doubt I can screw it back in without dropping it, especially with hydraulic fluid gushing out. We've only got one shot at this, and if we don't catch enough, we're screwed."

"What can I do?"

"I'm gonna have a bottle in each hand and swap them out one after another. I need you to take the full ones, set them out of the way, and feed me empties. You ready?"

Tex nodded, and Wiggins pulled the plug. Fluid gushed over his fingers and ran down his elbow as he jammed the narrow neck of the plastic bottle under the stream. It filled in seconds and he swapped bottles, trying and failing to capture every drop. They ran out of bottles before they ran out of fluid, and though he tried to get the plug back in, most of the remaining hydraulic fluid ran onto the pavement before he managed to do so.

"Well, let's just hope we have enough," Wiggins said and started toward the back of the truck with an armload of bottles. Tex did the same.

"What about the hole?" Tex asked as Wiggins opened up the fill cap for the rear unit.

"Let's find a plug. It's only got to hold long enough to fill the lines and cycle the wheels once," Wiggins said.

Tex jammed her index finger in the hole.

"Seriously?" Wiggins asked.

"Got a better idea? We're sort of in a hurry here, right?"

"I can't argue with that," Wiggins said, and started pouring hydraulic fluid into the tank.

He finished quickly and moved around to the driver's side. "Let's just hope there's not too much air in the system, because bleeding the lines could take forever," he said as he got behind the wheel.

He hit the switch and was rewarded with the expected whine, followed a long moment later by a clunk as the rear guide wheels locked into their stowed position. He called to Tex, and she crawled in the passenger side, wiping greasy hands on her clothes.

"I feel like a damned engineer," Tex muttered, and Wiggins laughed despite the situation.

"Intelligent?"

Tex smiled. "No, greasy and irritable."

***

There was no need for maps now, and Wiggins pressed the pickup through the inky darkness with a confidence born of familiarity. They took two-lane blacktops and one-lane gravel roads through farm land and forest and across country bridges. At one point they pulled onto a dirt track, and Tex gasped as Wiggins plunged across a wide dark stream of unknown depth. Or unknown to her, anyway, for Wiggins seemed to have no doubts.

They were speeding down a county road through thick forest when Wiggins began to slow. Tex saw two mailboxes beside a driveway, and Wiggins turned up the gravel track and followed it a hundred yards through the trees. He spoke for the first time since they'd left Biddeford.

"My folks have a hundred acres, but they gave half of it to Karen and me. We built our house two years ago, or I guess I should say we started building it. We're doing most of it ourselves, and my mom says you never really finish building a house," Wiggins said.

They'd come to a large clearing in the woods, and the gravel driveway diverged into two separate lanes, each serving a tidy, rustic home built of logs and native stone. They had an honest look about them, and Tex thought they looked like homes Wiggins might build: neat, sturdy, practical buildings.

Wiggins stopped at the split between the driveways.

"What's the matter, Bill?"

Wiggins didn't answer right away, and when he did, there was a catch in his voice. "I'm scared, Tex. For over a month I've been telling myself everything was gonna be okay, but now I have to find out. What if it's not okay? I . . . I think I just want to sit here a bit." He nodded toward the lightening sky. "It'll be daylight soon anyway. No need to wake everybody up just yet."

* * *

They sat there silently for almost an hour as the gloom turned to gray. A light flared in a window of the house on the right, the flickering of a flame lighting a lantern. It seemed to be what Wiggins was waiting for.

"That will be Dad," Wiggins said. "He's always the first one up."

He started the truck and turned toward his parents' house. They got out in the driveway, Tex suddenly unsure what to do. She hung back as Wiggins climbed the short steps to the porch and knocked on the storm door. There was the sound of footfalls inside the house.

"Who is it?" asked a cautious voice.

"It's Bill, Dad," Wiggins said.

There was the sound of locks being turned; then the inner door opened and an older man burst through the storm door and enveloped Wiggins in a hug. Then he saw Tex and flushed red, obviously embarrassed by his display of emotion. He straightened and released his son.

"It's sure good to have you home, son." The man looked at Tex. "And who is this —"

"Dad, is Karen here or at our house?"

The joy on the elder Wiggins' face morphed to anguish, and Tex had no doubt as to the cause.

THE WIGGINS PROPERTY
NEAR LEWISTON, MAINE

The lights had been out almost two weeks when Karen Wiggins went into labor early, the same day Tex and Bill Wiggins had left North Carolina. By that time, the Central Maine Medical Center in Lewiston had closed their doors for good, having exhausted not only the fuel for their emergency generator, but all medicine and supplies.

Ray and Nancy Wiggins used the last of their gasoline and braved the chaos of the city to get their daughter-in-law to the hospital, where they'd found the doors shuttered. Desperate, they'd returned to their home ten miles out of town and done the best they could. It had been a breech presentation, and neither mother nor child had survived.

Ray Wiggins told the story in a flat monotone, as if hoping his unemotional presentation could wring the anguish from the tale. Bill's mother, Nancy, sat beside her son and held his hand, mixing her tears with his own on the kitchen table. Tex, feeling very much an outsider, took it upon herself to entertain three-year-old Billy in the living room.

The days took on a sameness after that. The Wiggins' homes were well off the beaten track, and they'd had no problems with marauders as of yet. Tex was made welcome, and the supplies they brought meant no immediate hardship.

458

The Wiggins were both avid gardeners and home canners, and Ray and Bill were hunters, so they were generally self-sufficient in the way of rural people. They had no electricity for the well pump, but a spring in the woods behind the homes and a few drops of chlorine bleach provided their drinking water. Tex volunteered for water-hauling chores, eager to pull her own weight.

Bill Wiggins became lethargic almost to the point of catatonia and went about his chores with a listlessness that was heartbreaking to anyone who had known him even two months earlier. Ray and Nancy had buried Karen and the infant on a gentle slope overlooking the two homes, and Bill moved a picnic bench from their patio up to the graveside. He was spending more and more time there, sitting alone by the graves and thinking thoughts to which only he was privy.

The elder Wigginses grew equally morose, their joy at Bill's homecoming sapped by the enormity of their son's loss, and their own guilt they'd been unable to prevent it. The only bright spot in the house was little Billy, who viewed life with the wonder and irrepressible optimism of a three-year-old. He took an immediate liking to Tex, and she to him, and he followed her everywhere.

Her chores done for the day, Tex was playing hide-and-seek with Billy in the backyard late one afternoon. She flushed him from his hiding spot and chased him squealing across the backyard before picking him up and tickling him. She set him down on the picnic table and was about to resume her tickling when a solemn look crossed his face.

"Will Daddy always be sad?" Billy asked.

Tex turned to follow Billy's gaze and saw Bill sitting at the top of the knoll on the picnic bench, staring down at the twin crosses.

"He just misses your mom and your baby sister, that's all," Tex said.

"But he never met the baby, and she and Mommy are happy in Heaven and that's a good place. Nana told me so," Billy said. "Doesn't he want them to be happy?"

"Sure he does, honey, but when someone you love goes away, you miss them a lot."

"But we're here." Billy's lip started trembling. "Doesn't... doesn't he love us?"

Tex felt as if her heart would break. She blinked back a tear and folded Billy in a fierce hug. "Sure he does, baby. He just needs a little time, that's all."

"You're smushin' me," Billy said.

Tex laughed. "Sorry," she said, releasing him and holding him at arm's length. "What say we go in and see if your nana might have a little snack for you?"

***

Bill looked up as Tex sat down on the bench.

"Like some company?" she asked.

He shrugged, and they sat in silence.

"What's up, Tex?" Bill asked at last.

Tex took a deep breath. "You have to move on, Bill. Karen and the baby died, and that is truly heartrending and tragic, but there's nothing you can do about it, and there are three people in that house who love you and need you very much."

Bill Wiggins bristled. "You don't get to tell me when it's time to move on. You don't understand —"

"You're right I don't understand. MY family is gone, and yours is right here in front of you, being dragged along to your pity party whether they like it or not. If my folks were still alive or if I was blessed with a great kid like Billy, I sure as hell would be counting my blessings instead of my losses. Do you honestly think KAREN would want this? Do you know Billy thinks you don't love him?"

"You leave Karen out of —" Wiggins stopped mid-sentence. "What do you mean Billy thinks I don't love him?"

Tex took another deep breath and told Wiggins about her exchange with Billy. When she finished, he turned his head away, but not before she saw a tear leak down his cheek. She reached over and took his hand.

"Bill, this is tough. I know that, but you were there for me, and I'm here for you. We all are."

Wiggins squeezed her hand. "I. . . I just don't know what to do, Tex? Everything is so screwed up."

Tex shrugged. "We do what people have always done. We live, and if we're lucky, we love and laugh a little. Fundamentally, the world hasn't changed that much as far as the basics go, except nobody is hooking up with total strangers on an iPhone or getting their panties in a bunch because someone dissed them on Facebook."

Wiggins laughed and wiped his eyes with the back of his free hand. Then he stood and pulled Tex to her feet and wrapped her in a hug.

"So are you going to hang around to kick my butt when it needs kicking?" he asked softly into her ear.

"I sort of have to," she whispered back. "You got my choo-choo train shot up."

Wiggins threw his head back and laughed again; then he and Tex walked down the hill hand in hand.

CHAPTER THIRTY-THREE

Anderson sat on his makeshift log stool in his skivvies, pants around his ankles, examining his left knee in the flickering light of the torch. A few days' rest had done wonders; the swelling was down, and it hardly hurt at all now, at least if he was careful how he put weight on it.

The last days seemed like paradise compared to the ordeal of his escape and flight. Concerns about food eased somewhat on the second day when the chickens made themselves at home in a corner of the cave and began laying again. Likewise, both Cindy and, under her instruction, Jeremy had proved surprisingly proficient at woodcraft. By the third day, their snares and deadfalls were producing at least one meal a day, the protein supplemented by edible greens Cindy foraged from the forest. Between nature's bounty and the water source at the back of the cave, they wouldn't starve or die of thirst anytime soon.

In fact, Anderson's only real complaint was boredom. Cindy insisted he stay off his knee, a prohibition enforced with the rigidity of a drill sergeant. The result was days of boredom, stretched out on his mattress of evergreen boughs or sitting in the sun in front of the cave, waiting for Cindy and Jeremy to return from checking their traps or gathering firewood. His only pastime was digging insects out of cracks in the rock face, which he tossed to an appreciative audience of chickens.

The evenings were better, sitting around the fire. Jeremy inevitably began to nod and retired to his mattress to snore until sunup, but Cindy, like Anderson, was by nature a night owl. They talked long into the night about everything, and nothing. The more he learned, the more he admired her; and she was definitely easy on the eyes.

"How's it looking?"

Anderson jumped. Cindy stood in the flickering torchlight with an armload of firewood, which she bent to add to the nearby pile without waiting for his answer.

"How do you do that?" he asked.

She straightened. "Do what?"

"Move so quietly," Anderson said. "You're like a cat."

Cindy shrugged. "You have to be light on your feet to dance, and moving quietly over rock isn't very challenging."

Anderson nodded and began to stand to pull up his pants. Cindy waved him back down.

"Leave it," she said. "I want to look at that knee."

"It's fine."

"I'll be the judge of that. Now sit your butt back down," Cindy said.

Anderson sighed and sat back down on the upended log. "Yes, mother."

Cindy squatted and peered at his knee. "Looks like the swelling's gone. Is it giving you any pain?"

Anderson shook his head and was about to say no when Cindy reached out with both hands and began to gently probe his knee. Her touch was electric and totally unanticipated. The fly of his boxers gapped open as his erection rose unbidden.

"Oh geez! I'm sorry, Cindy. I didn't mean —"

Her laughter resonated into the darkness of the cave, and she reached out and wrapped her hand around him.

"Jeremy's checking the deadfalls. We've got at least twenty minutes," she said.

***

As it turned out, they had a bit over thirty, and it was easily the best half hour of Anderson's life in recent memory. Correction, pretty much everything in recent memory sucked, so he amended that to the best half hour ever.

Afterward, he hardly felt the evergreen needles of his sleeping pallet scratching his bare back as he enjoyed the pleasant weight of Cindy's naked body on top of his. He began to stir again, and she lifted her cheek from his chest and grinned.

"There's nothing I'd like more, Romeo," she said. "But I'll have to take a rain check. Jeremy will be back soon."

"So there's going to be a next time?"

She studied his face. "Do you want there to be?"

"Absolutely," Anderson said. "Though I have to admit it took me by surprise."

She laughed. "That was sort of obvious."

"No, I mean that you would... that you wanted..."

Cindy silenced him, her fingers on his lips. "You do realize you're working pretty hard to spoil the moment, don't you?"

Anderson was totally confused.

"You're a decent guy, George. You risked your neck for us when you didn't have to, and let's just say facing death with someone is a pretty intense bonding experience. Add that to the fact we're both single and horny as hell, and the sex was pretty much inevitable," Cindy said.

"Sooo..."

She bent down and kissed him tenderly. "So let's just play it by ear, and see where it goes. But now we better get up and get dressed before Jeremy comes in and decides he needs to shoot you."

***

They'd just gotten dressed and moved back outside when Jeremy's head appeared over the lip of the ledge, followed in short order by the rest of his body. He beamed when he saw them and held up two gutted rabbits.

"Lunch," Jeremy said.

"Good job!" Anderson said while Cindy just returned Jeremy's wide smile.

With no refrigeration, they normally cooked and ate small game as soon as it was killed, and two rabbits made for a bountiful early lunch. Anderson finished his third piece of rabbit, licked the juice from his fingers, and heaved a contented sigh.

"That was really good. In fact, the only thing that could have improved it is a little seasoning," he said.

"I had all my seasonings and spices in big Ziploc bags in the trailer," Cindy said. "Maybe they're still there."

"You thinking we should go look?" Anderson asked.

Cindy nodded. "If anyone was looking for us, I think we would have heard or seen them by now. I think it's safe."

"The current may have smashed and scattered it from here to who knows where," Anderson said.

"And the trailer could be sitting high and dry on the creek bank a half mile downstream," Cindy said. "One thing is for sure; if it's there, it will be in or near the creek bed. We'll just follow it a ways; if we don't find it in a reasonable distance, we turn around and come back."

Jeremy was excited at the prospect. "Let's go today!"

Cindy shook her head. "We should leave at first light tomorrow to give us as much daylight as possible. We don't know what we're going to run into, and we don't want to make the steep climb up to the cave in the dark."

***

They all turned in early for a change. As usual, Jeremy's soft snores were drifting across the dying embers of the fire in minutes. The sleep of the innocent, Anderson thought as he rolled on his side. He was almost asleep himself when Cindy crawled in beside him and kissed the back of his neck.

"Rain check," she whispered. "Presuming you can be quieter than you were earlier."

Anderson smiled in the dark and shifted in place to face her, his smile widening when he discovered she was naked. "Me?" he whispered back. "I seem to remember you might need to take your own advice."

Day 36, 5:40 a.m.

They rose early to a breakfast of leftover rabbit and eggs and left as soon as there was enough light to navigate the steep slope down to the creek. They traveled light, carrying only water, some hard-boiled eggs for lunch, and their weapons. Anderson and Jeremy both carried M4s, but Cindy stuck to her tried and true shotgun.

The steep climb down put Anderson's knee to the test. There were twinges of pain, and he mentally put his recovery at ninety percent. He caught Cindy watching him, and smiled and gave her a thumbs-up. She gave him a skeptical nod and continued to watch during the rest of the descent. They had their first disagreement when they got to where the Mule was hidden.

"This is premature," Cindy said. "You're still favoring the leg, and this is a good way to reinjure it."

"It's fine. I'll let you know if it starts bothering me, and I'll stop and rest it."

"It's already bothering you; I can tell by the way you're walking. We'll take the Mule," Cindy said.

Anderson shook his head. "Too noisy."

"We're at least ten miles from the nearest house or road," Cindy said. "Unless someone's in the woods—"

"Exactly," Anderson said. "We've got as near to a perfect hideaway as we're likely to find, and we should keep a low profile. If someone hears the Mule in the woods, who tells someone else, who then tells someone else, before long a whole lot of someones know there are people back here. Sooner or later FEMA might get nosy. Besides, we don't even know if we're going to FIND the trailer, in which case, we've made a lot of noise for nothing."

Cindy looked unconvinced. "But if we DO find the trailer, that's a lot of gear to hump uphill to the cave. It's going to be hard enough getting it up this far, without being exhausted by the time we even start."

They argued for five minutes, finally agreeing to make the initial search on foot. If they found anything worth salvaging, they'd assess the most efficient way to get it back to the cave at that time. Anderson considered that a win, though he didn't press the point. From the look on Cindy's face, she was less than thrilled at the 'compromise.'

Descending the creek proved to be much less of an ordeal than reaching it. It was back down to its normal flow, only an inch or two deep in most places, and the stair-step breaks in the slate bottom, which had made the Mule's ascent difficult, had the opposite effect when traveling by foot. Their biggest concern was slipping on the slimy bottom or losing their footing on a loose rock.

They moved down the creek almost as fast as the heavily laden Mule and trailer had crawled up it and, after two hours, reached the spot they'd entered the creek days before. *Was it only a few days?* Anderson thought. It seemed like a lifetime. He stood at the crossing and peered downstream.

"It gets a lot steeper," he said.

Cindy nodded. "The creek runs directly downhill with a considerable drop over just a few hundred yards, then starts winding again with a more gradual incline. If it's down there, it'll be a bitch to get stuff back up this hill."

"What do you want to do?" Anderson asked.

Cindy shrugged. "It's not even midmorning. Let's look a bit further, but if we don't find it soon, it's a lost cause."

Anderson nodded and started downhill. They hadn't gone far when Jeremy let out an excited whoop.

"Mom! I see it!"

They followed Jeremy's pointing finger to where the trailer rested on the creek bank, bridging the gap between two large trees growing in a line perpendicular to the stream. They scrambled down.

The trailer had hit the trees sideways, borne on the raging floodwaters. Its short tongue rested against the upstream side of the tree closest to the creek bed, and the rear end of the trailer was jammed against the other tree. Debris and trash was mounded on the upstream side of the trailer, and as Anderson got closer, he could see the force of the partially dammed water against the side of the trailer had bent the tongue at a significant angle.

"There'll be no towing that even if we managed to get it out of here," he said.

Cindy nodded in agreement. "But everything is still lashed down. It's a miracle it didn't roll over. Now we just have to get the stuff back up to the cave."

She gave Anderson a withering look. "Which would be a lot easier if we had the MULE with us."

"All right, all right," Anderson said. "You made your point. I'll go back and bring it down."

Cindy shook her head. "I can get back up faster than either one of you two, and we're not getting the Mule down this last slope anyway. I'll go get the Mule while you two hump this stuff up to the crossing."

Anderson sighed, then nodded.

"And one more thing," Cindy said. "It's going to be a three- or four-hour round-trip to bring the Mule back, so take your time and don't overdo it on that knee. Remember, we still have to hump all this stuff up to the cave. Jeremy?"

"Yes, ma'am?"

"Keep an eye on George. If it looks like his knee is hurting, I want you to remind him to rest. Can you do that?"

"Yes, ma'am," Jeremy said.

***

Jeremy took his instructions seriously and badgered Anderson the entire time they humped supplies up the hill. But truth be told, the young man also carried far more than his fair share up the steep slope, and Anderson was happy to let him. They finished in a little over three hours.

"How long until Mom gets back?" Jeremy asked.

Anderson shrugged. "I'd say another hour."

Jeremy began to nod, then stopped and grinned. "You're wrong, George. I hear her coming now."

Anderson heard it too, but it was wrong somehow. It wasn't the throaty rumble of the Mule, and it came from the clearing where the cabin once stood, a quarter of a mile away. He put his finger to his lips to caution Jeremy and stood listening. The sound stopped, and Anderson heard the sound of two car doors slamming.

"Someone's at your cabin site, Jeremy. You stay here while I check it out."

Jeremy nodded. "I'll go too. You may need help."

What I don't need is worrying about you getting shot, Anderson thought, but he didn't say that.

"Negative. You need to get up the creek and warn your mom. Okay? If whoever it is hears the Mule, they'll get curious, and we don't want them looking for us."

Jeremy looked scared. "Is it the bad guys?"

"I don't know, Jeremy, but I don't want to take any chances. Now go warn your mom."

CHAPTER THIRTY-FOUR

Jeremy nodded and splashed up the creek at a run. Anderson waited for him to move out of sight, then started for the clearing, moving through the woods parallel to the trail. He slowed as he approached the clearing, then dropped to one knee and slowly parted the foliage.

He suppressed a curse. Cindy and Jeremy's cabin was still standing, though the walls were black and the roof was caved in at one corner. The rain! The same torrential downpour that claimed the trailer had doused the fire they started in the cabin.

A FEMA Special Reaction Force Hummer stood in front of the blackened cabin, and Anderson could make out voices coming from the inside. After a long moment, two black-clad SRF troopers emerged from the cabin, one of them dragging a small black tarp. He threw the tarp on the ground and spread it out. Anderson's heart sank.

"It's a UTV cover all right, for a big unit, probably one of those multi-seat side by sides." The man scanned the ground around the cabin and pointed. "And look at that! Those ain't hummer tracks; there was a UTV here for sure."

The second trooper seemed unimpressed. "UTV, BFD. Who cares, Carr? All I know is we're supposed to be patrolling this section of the Lexington Turnpike, and this wild-goose chase is going to get all of our asses in a crack."

"Yeah, well, you'd feel a bit different if it was YOUR brother that got capped. This never felt right to me. If the patrol visited here first, then got ambushed on the road later, why ain't there any bodies in the cabin?"

The second trooper shrugged. "All right, I'll admit it's strange, but what exactly do you plan on doing about it? We ain't even supposed to be here, and I sure as hell ain't joining no posse to chase ghost UTVs through the woods."

Carr bent and started rolling up the UTV cover. "We take this as evidence. That and the fact you and I both saw there ain't any bodies in the house and there's old UTV tracks all around should convince the captain. I mean, somebody out there murdered three SRF troopers, and we can't let that stand. I'm sure I can convince him to mount a search and destroy mission. And if he won't, I'm gonna round up volunteers and do it myself in my off time. Nobody murders my brother and gets away with it."

Anderson crouched, parsing the possibilities. They were leaving now, but it sounded like they'd be back. He felt his dreams of living the idyllic life of a cave dweller fading. He was debating his next move when the one called Carr looked in his direction and shouted, "STAND DOWN!"

Anderson heard a sound behind him to the left and swiveled in that direction, unable to stifle a groan as an unexpected pain knifed through his left knee. He brought his M4 up, but knew it was too late even before the butt reached his shoulder.

"FREEZE!"

He stared into the muzzle of an M4 less than twenty feet away.

"Ground your weapon very slowly. Then drop to your knees and put your hands on top of your head and face away from me. Do it now," the man ordered.

Anderson did as instructed.

"HEY, CARR. WE GOT A VISITOR. AND HE'S WEARING ONE OF OUR UNIFORMS."

***

Assumptions can get you killed, and they probably already had, Anderson thought as he lay facedown in the grass, wrists tied behind him. Two slamming car doors did not necessarily mean two people. In this case, it meant four, with two on overwatch at the clearing perimeter. It was a bonehead mistake, and he probably had this coming.

The initial beat down had been almost perfunctory. They'd flex-cuffed his wrists and ankles, and two of them held him upright while a third worked him over with fists and feet. The one called Carr had just stood back and watched, a smile on his face, until the men grew tired of the sport and threw him facedown in the dirt and chicken droppings.

Anderson figured he was dead already, and the only question now was whether he could deflect attention from Cindy and Jeremy. If these guys thought he'd taken out their friends alone, they'd take him back to HQ to make an example of him. With the shooter eliminated, the SRF no longer had any reason to be poking around in these woods.

He contemplated the best way to play it. The uniform would help sell his story, but if he confessed too quickly, they might put two and two together and figure he was protecting someone. On the other hand, Cindy was sure to come looking, and if he was still here and alive, she might do something stupid.

He didn't really know how much time had passed, but he grew increasingly desperate for them to either take him away or deal with him quickly, before Cindy arrived. He might have to provoke them.

That was still a half-formed thought when he was jerked to his feet and held erect by a strong hand in each armpit. His eyes had barely focused when the rifle butt struck him in the stomach and doubled him over. The men on either side jerked him back upright, and suddenly Carr was in his face, the man's pockmarked visage mere inches away as his fetid breath washed over Anderson.

"That was just another little love tap, asshole," Carr snarled. "We were gonna take you back to base, but I thought about it and decided we can have more fun here. I'm gonna skin you alive and make it real, real slow. But I'm a fair guy. You seemed real interested in us, so I'll let you have the first question. What would you like to know?"

Anderson smiled through the pain. "I'll take personal for five hundred, Alex. Didn't your mommy teach you to brush your friggin' teeth? Your breath smells like a skunk crapped in a sweaty jockstrap."

Carr flushed and delivered three hard rights into Anderson's gut in the general vicinity of the rifle butt strike, then stepped back with a malevolent smile.

Anderson gasped, and only the men on either side of him kept him from collapsing.

"What was that, tough guy?" Carr asked. "I don't think I heard you."

"I said you hit like a girl, and your mother blows sailors in bus station bathrooms."

Carr reddened again, but this time he pulled a knife from a sheath on his calf and came toward Anderson with blood in his eyes. *I guess I hit a nerve with that one,* Anderson thought as he closed his eyes.

Something warm splashed his face a split second before he heard the crack of a rifle shot. He opened his eyes to see Carr sinking in front of him, his face distorted and bloody. The men supporting Anderson released him to reach for their own guns, and rubber-legged, he did a strategic face-plant in the dirt. There was a protracted roar of gunfire that seemed to go on forever, and in the midst of it, a body landed on top of him. He heard the man curse and attempt to rise, then felt him jerk before the man's entire dead weight crushed him into the ground.

And then it was quiet.

He heard the whisper of rapid footsteps through grass, then the welcome sound of Cindy's voice.

"Cover them with the shotgun, Jeremy. If any of them move, shoot them."

467

Then he heard her grunt, and felt relief as she rolled the dead man off his back. He rolled over to find her staring down at him, her face a mask of fear.

"Are you hit?"

Anderson shook his head. "This isn't my blood."

He sat up and looked around in amazement. The four sprawled around him, all dead from head shots. Cindy ignored them and grabbed the knife Carr dropped and cut the flex cuffs off Anderson's wrists and ankles. He sat there a moment, rubbing his wrists.

"Where the hell did you learn to shoot?"

Cindy shrugged. "Right here. Tony used to bring his AR out every weekend. Jeremy and I both got pretty good with it."

Anderson shook his head. "That's an understatement."

She shrugged again. "The dumb asses were standing in a tight group fifty feet from the nearest cover. My biggest worry was the body armor and whether I could take them all down before they got there."

"Still, head shots…"

"Only the first one, really. He was about to gut you and I had no choice. I shot the legs out from under the others and finished them when they couldn't move around."

Anderson just stared. She'd said it matter-of-factly, as if she were discussing taking out the trash.

"And you devised this plan on the fly?"

Cindy flushed. "Not completely. I'm a single mom living in the middle of friggin' nowhere, and I couldn't exactly expect to call 911. So yeah, I had a pretty good idea of what I'd do in different situations and just modified one of my imaginary scenarios to fit. The only reason I didn't have an AR yet was because I couldn't afford one, but I was saving up. And you're welcome, by the way."

It was Anderson's turn to flush. "Thank you."

Cindy nodded as Anderson crawled to his feet, unable to suppress a groan as a sharp pain gripped his midsection.

"Are you all right?"

"Nothing serious. He worked me over pretty good, so I'll probably be sore for a few days. But there's no time to worry about that now; we've got to decide what to do."

CHAPTER THIRTY-FIVE

It was obvious they couldn't stay. Elimination of a second patrol in the same area in less than a week was sure to bring a massive response, including dogs and thermal imaging sweeps by chopper. As much as they loathed the idea, they'd have to leave their comfortable cave and flee.

A big unknown was the length of their escape window. The unauthorized nature of Carr's visit would help, but they had no clue whether the patrol was outbound from nearby Buena Vista or returning to the FEMA base there. Sooner or later they would be missed, and it was only prudent to assume it would be sooner.

They couldn't afford the long round-trip to the cave, so they abandoned Cindy's and Jeremy's sleeping bags and left the chickens to their own devices. Cindy and Jeremy went to get the Mule from where Cindy left it upstream while Anderson set about salvaging things from the Hummer.

Forty-five minutes later, Anderson heaved the last of the bodies into the back of the vehicle and closed the door. He then climbed into the driver's seat and locked the differential just as Cindy and Jeremy emerged from the woods in the now-loaded Mule in time to see the Hummer back across the clearing and settle its rear bumper against the cabin.

Anderson floored the accelerator, and the house shook and began to move, then toppled off its cinder-block piers in a cloud of dust to settle upright on the ground. He pulled the Hummer away from the cabin, then threw it in reverse to crash backwards through the cabin wall. He emerged from the ragged hole only seconds later, coughing into his fist from the billowing dust.

Cindy stopped beside the cabin and leaped out. "Are you nuts? What are you doing?"

Anderson shook his head as he finished his coughing spasm. "Buying... a little time," he said at last.

"How?" Cindy asked.

"They seem pretty lax about tracking their patrols; otherwise I don't think Carr would have taken the chance on his unofficial side trip. So even if the Hummer has a working tracking device, I don't think they'll monitor it until the patrol is overdue. And since I'm not real sure where to find and disconnect a tracking device, or if there might be more than one, I figure we just burn up the whole car. That should destroy any trackers."

Cindy grinned. "Pretty smart."

Anderson nodded. "Even if they track it to this clearing as the last known location, they still won't know what's going on. All they'll find is a raging cabin fire, and it'll be too hot to poke around in the ashes for at least twenty-four hours."

"Think it will stay lit this time?" she asked.

Anderson looked up. "It doesn't look like rain, and the cabin is mostly charred now and pretty dry. I've got ten gallons of diesel from the back of the Hummer to help it along," Anderson said, then nodded to a pile some distance away. "Come look at what I salvaged. You guys can load up while I start the fire."

Cindy shook her head as she followed Anderson. "We stopped and loaded the stuff from the trailer, so there isn't much room left, and when we run out of gas, we're afoot."

"How much gas do we have?" he asked.

"I topped up with gas from the trailer, so we've got a full tank plus part of a five-gallon can. Why?"

Anderson grinned as they reached the pile and he pointed to two red plastic containers. "Because now we have ten more gallons. I guess our friends were doing a little scavenging. There's also a box of MREs, several jugs of water, and a couple of boxes of canned goods."

Cindy's initial smile faded.

"I thought you'd be pleased," Anderson said.

"If they have gas and boxes of canned goods, it means they've already BEEN scavenging. Which likely means they were headed back to base, which means for sure they'll be missed sooner rather than later," Cindy said.

"Point taken. I'll get that fire started."

***

Despite Cindy's misgivings, she was able to cram everything into the back of the Mule. They left the clearing twenty minutes later, all jammed in the front bench seat, with the remains of the cabin burning brightly behind them. Cindy was at the wheel, and she cast a worried glance over her shoulder at the rising smoke.

"I didn't think about the smoke," she said.

Anderson shrugged. "I doubt anyone is manning the fire towers these days."

Cindy nodded and turned her attention to the road. Their only real option for going off road and making any time was the Appalachian Trail. However, the Mule left tracks, and they didn't want those tracks leading from the burning cabin to the soft dirt of the AT on the opposite side of Lexington Turnpike. They had to run on the hard pavement a while, a long while preferably, so it wouldn't be obvious they'd taken the AT.

Cindy was familiar with both the Appalachian Trail and the back roads and knew a circuitous route to intersect the AT over ten miles away. The bad news was a two-mile run on Lexington Turnpike, north towards Buena Vista. The good news was the guys tasked with patrolling that road were all now well on their way to well done in the remains of the cabin, presuming no one came looking for them early.

They turned right on Lexington Turnpike, the Mule straining immediately as they crawled up a hill. Anderson looked ahead nervously.

"Is this as fast as this thing will go?"

"It's got a governor. Top speed is twenty-five," Cindy said. "But that's not the problem. We're going uphill with three adults and twice as much cargo weight as we're supposed to carry."

"Is it uphill all the way to the turnoff?"

"No, just this stretch," Cindy said. "Relax, George. We'll be off the highway in ten minutes or so."

"Won't be soon enough for me," Anderson muttered.

It took seven minutes, and Anderson breathed an audible sigh when Cindy turned left on a gravel track and they disappeared into a dark green tunnel of woodland. It was a twisting odyssey she apparently knew by heart, never hesitating at the numerous intersections or forks in the path. They moved slowly but steadily, occasionally climbing hills requiring her to stop and lock the differential before she engaged four-wheel drive to crawl up a steep slope at a snail's pace.

"How far did you say it was?" Anderson asked. "Seems like we've been traveling forever."

"It's eight or ten miles as the crow flies." Cindy looked over at Anderson and smiled. "But obviously we're not crows. We'll hit the AT in twenty minutes or so."

Her prediction was accurate, and twenty minutes later, the gravel track they were on intersected a slightly better state road. She darted across the state road to a footpath through the woods.

"We're on the AT," Cindy said.

Anderson nodded, then noticed a paved road through the trees to the right. "Uhh… what's that road?"

"The Blue Ridge Parkway," Cindy said. "We'll cross it just ahead; then the trail moves away from it. But I think they weave south together for quite a ways. I don't know for sure because I've only been as far as the James River."

"I think that's right," Anderson said. "I remember that from the trail guide…"

He cursed.

"What's the problem?" Cindy asked.

"The trail guide. It's back in the cave."

Cindy shrugged. "We didn't have time to go back for it anyway, so it doesn't matter."

Anderson gave an unenthusiastic nod of agreement just as Cindy emerged from the woods to scoot across the Blue Ridge Parkway. She drove several hundred feet into the woods and stopped.

"It might get a bit hairy here. We're going up Punchbowl Mountain, and I have no idea if the Mule will make it on this trail," Cindy said.

"Do we really have a choice?" Anderson asked.

"No good ones. If we can't make it, we either abandon the Mule and proceed on foot or back down the mountain and try our luck on the Blue Ridge Parkway," she said.

"Then let's hope we make it," Anderson said.

Cindy nodded, locked the differential, and put the Mule in four-wheel drive.

The trail got ever steeper and rockier as the Mule inched up the incline. Halfway up, they had a series of switchbacks, and the mule tipped and swayed precariously as they crawled through them. At one point, the UTV teetered at the very edge of overturning before settling back on its springs.

"Why don't I drive while you and Jeremy go ahead and check out the trail?" Anderson said. "That will take some of the load off the Mule."

Cindy shook her head. "Good idea. But I already know what's ahead and I'm considerably lighter than either of you two, so y'all get out to lighten the load."

Anderson hesitated.

"Go on and get out," Cindy said, "because I'm not stopping. It'll be a bitch to get this thing moving uphill again from a standing stop."

Anderson shook his head and grabbed the overhead handhold to swing out of the slow-moving vehicle, with Jeremy close behind. The Mule was going so slow they passed it in a dozen long strenuous uphill strides, all of which Anderson felt in his knee. Once ahead of it, and unburdened by packs, they easily maintained their interval.

"It's making a difference," Cindy called. "She's not laboring as bad, and the engine temp stopped rising."

They reached the summit fifteen minutes later, and Anderson and Jeremy climbed back in to ride another mile and a half along the ridgeline to Saddle Gap. Cindy said the trail rose another four hundred feet to a second peak before starting an equally steep descent. They decided to stop for the night, both to allow the Mule to cool down and because, if something happened, they didn't want to find themselves on the equally steep descent in the dark.

SADDLE GAP
APPALACHIAN TRAIL
MILE 1398.2 SOUTHBOUND

DAY 36, 8:50 P.M.

The ridge between the peaks was relatively narrow, but they managed to find a wide enough stretch of level ground to allow them to pull the Mule into the trees well off the trail. Anderson and Jeremy cut brush and low-hanging tree limbs to camouflage the Mule in the unlikely event of unexpected company. Cindy got evergreen boughs and piled them behind the Mule before covering them with the camouflage tarp to make a communal mattress.

They decided against a fire and had a dinner of MREs warmed by the chemical heaters included with the meals. Jeremy, as usual, had gone down with the sun, and Anderson and Cindy sat on the ground nearby, sipping MRE coffee as they leaned back against a large fallen log.

Anderson looked over to where Jeremy snored on the makeshift mattress and smiled as he shook his head in the dim light. "I envy him his ability—deep sleep in five minutes flat, every time."

Cindy smiled. "The sleep of innocence. Some folks pity me, but every challenge has its silver lining. Jeremy is a truly good human being, and I doubt he's had a mean or evil thought in his life. How many mothers can say that?"

"Very few, I expect. But I think it may be the sleep of the secure as well. Jeremy knows you're in his corner. Not a lot of people have that either, especially these days."

"Yeah, well, I'm afraid I'm not doing too well in that department lately. Which brings me to the elephant in the room; where the hell are we going, George?" Cindy asked.

Anderson sipped his coffee. "God, this is foul crap!"

"You'll kill for it when there's no coffee at all," Cindy said. "But quit stalling. What are we gonna do?"

"Honestly? Not a clue," he said. "All I really know is what we CAN'T do."

"Which is?" she asked.

"Live out here in the woods, at least when it starts turning cold. It would've been a stretch even in the cave, and there we had a shelter with an even year-round temperature and a protected source of fresh water. All we really had to do there was make sure we got in an ample supply of firewood and that we smoked meat or made jerky from the game we trapped. Out here, we have no durable, weather-tight shelter unless we managed to stumble on an abandoned cabin, and I put that chance somewhere between slim and none."

"I'll take my chances out here before I go to one of those hellhole FEMA camps." There was steel in her voice.

"Well, if you stick with me, that's not an option anyway. I doubt I'd be welcome in a FEMA camp, for obvious reasons," Anderson said.

"Actually, they're not—obvious, I mean. But what IS obvious is that we ARE going to stick together. I think it's time for you to tell me what you're running from."

"It's like I told you, it's better for you if you don't—"

"Would you give me a frigging break? In the last week, I've shot five SRF thugs. I'm pretty sure that qualifies me for a place on FEMA's hit list all by myself. And we're traveling together, for God's sake. Do you honestly think if we get caught, they're going to believe I don't know anything about whatever it is you did before we met? So since we're at risk anyway, I'd at least like to know why."

Anderson hesitated a long moment, then told her the whole story of how he ended up guarding Simon Tremble, Speaker of the House of Representatives, and how that duty caused him to be a wanted fugitive.

"But how did you end up in FEMA to start with? You're not like those other assholes."

Anderson shrugged. "Decent pay, health insurance, and benefits. Look, I went to work for them like five years ago, and it was just a pretty good law enforcement gig. It's not like there were posters of Darth Vader saying things like, 'Welcome to the Evil Empire.' In fact, a lot of the FEMA people are decent folks, or were anyway. It was a job, that's all, and I was pretty good at it. I got transferred to Mount Weather, which was a plum assignment." He shook his head. "Then came the blackout and everything went to hell fast. I didn't particularly like what was going on, but like a lot of people there, I figured I didn't know the whole story, and I certainly didn't want to quit and end up out in the chaos. Then I ended up guarding the Trembles, and I didn't feel right about that at all, but what exactly was I supposed to do? In the end, the decision was made for me, and as tough as it's been, I'd rather be here than there."

Cindy reached over and squeezed his hand. "So they never caught the Trembles?"

"I'd say no, since the guys chasing me thought they were chasing him." Anderson shook his head again and chuckled. "Simon's a crafty bastard, I'll give him that." She heard the admiration in his voice.

"So you're one of the few people who actually knows Tremble is still alive, and who is a firsthand witness to the President's illegal actions?"

Anderson shrugged again. "I guess so. At least one of the few people that's not actively involved with it. But so what? All that's likely to get me is a bullet in the head and a shallow grave. Why? What're you thinking?"

"Wilmington."

"Delaware or North Carolina?"

"North Carolina. Just before those FEMA goons swooped in to confiscate radios, there was a lot of chatter on the ham networks, and Wilmington was the source. They have some defectors from the SRF who were putting out word about what FEMA was actually up to. It sounded like they were doing okay down there, all things considered, and beginning to offer an alternative to FEMA," Cindy said.

"I still don't see what that's got to do with me, or us."

"Don't you think they'd like to have an eyewitness to illegal government actions? They'd probably welcome you with open arms," Cindy said.

"I doubt it makes any difference, and you may not have noticed, but I'm not really hero material. I just want to find a place where everyone will leave me the hell alone, and I'll do likewise. Is that too much to ask?"

Cindy studied him through the gloom. He could barely make out her face. "Yeah, George," she said, "in this screwed-up world, it probably is. I mean, we tried that and it didn't work out. People kept showing up trying to kill us. The way I look at it, our choices are to hide in the woods, hunting and scrounging food and becoming less human every day, or using what resources we have to get to Wilmington, where we can join people trying to make a difference."

"Who you THINK are there trying to make a difference. We haven't had any information in over a week," Anderson said.

"Granted," Cindy said. "Have a better option?"

Anderson shook his head. "So how do we get to Wilmington?"

"Not a clue," Cindy said. "But we're sure not going down I-95. We have to steal a map."

EPILOGUE

Congressman Simon Tremble (NC), Speaker of the House of Representatives, suppressed a grunt as he grabbed a sapling to pull himself up the steep slope. Fifty feet ahead of him, he watched his son, Keith, top the hill and turn to look back at him with a wide grin.

"Come on, old-timer, you're almost there," Keith taunted.

Tremble laughed and closed the distance with ease, though it took more of his reserves than he'd ever let on. Things had started getting a bit more challenging after he hit fifty, but he was too stubborn to acknowledge it.

He grinned at his son. "Just hanging back in case I had to carry you."

"Hah! That'll be the day. So did I pass?"

Tremble frowned. "I'm sorry, I can only give you fifty percent."

Keith's face fell.

"You don't get the other fifty until you get back to the bottom without reinjuring that ankle," Tremble said.

"You're on," Keith said, starting down the steep slope.

***

Tremble stood in front of the cave, inspecting their gear. He'd lashed together pack frames from pliable green limbs, essentially wicker baskets to hold the black garbage bags they'd mooched from Wiggins and Tex. The pants of their FEMA uniforms were now secured with paracord drawstrings, and the web belts had become pack straps. Their homemade packs each held a supply of squirrel and rabbit jerky, wild onions, and dried mushrooms. Bulging water bladders improvised from a double thickness of condoms rode in the wicker packs but outside the garbage bag liners, in case the condoms burst or leaked.

The one thing that wasn't improvised was their weaponry. They both carried M4s taken from the FEMA cops, and each had a 9 millimeter Sig and ammo for both in their packs.

"How long will it take us, Dad?" Keith asked.

"How long, I can't say, only how far. Wiggins and Tex picked up the AT at Black Horse Gap, but they were paralleling it in a car. By the trail that's a little over two hundred and fifty miles. Then they used the Blue Ridge Parkway and rural roads from this guy Levi's house, they said about five hundred miles, all told. I don't know quite how far his house is outside of Wilmington, but evidently he has a place on the Black River. I'm thinking if we can find a way to get to the Black, we might be able to float down into friendly territory and right into Wilmington."

Keith shook his head. "That's gotta be like twice as far than if we just stayed off the interstates and just took back roads! I still think we should go as direct as possible."

Tremble nodded. "We might not have a choice. They ran into problems northbound at Front Royal, and I doubt things have improved. We'll just have to play it by ear. But that won't be a choice we have to make for a few days yet."

Tremble reached down and shouldered his pack, and Keith did the same.

"Ready?" Tremble asked.

"I've been ready," Keith said. "I just keep thinking about the look on that bastard Gleason's face when we get to Wilmington and you start broadcasting the truth."

Tremble nodded and smiled as they set off up the hill, though he felt far from confident. His mood improved as they plodded up the hill back to the Appalachian Trail. Perhaps Keith's youthful optimism was contagious, or maybe it was just the effect of setting out with a purpose at last, surrounded by the beauty of nature.

That sense of purpose grew with each step, and as they reached the ridgeline and moved onto the trail, Tremble felt the doubts and fears slip away, replaced by grim determination. *I'm coming you bastards. I'm coming at last.* And at that moment, the Honorable Simon J. Tremble of North Carolina, Speaker of the House of Representatives of the United States of America, promised himself as long as there was breath in his body, he'd never stop fighting to put things right — or at least as right as he could make them.

There was a new spring in his step, and Keith looked over and grinned as he matched his father's faster pace. "You gonna run all the way to Wilmington, Dad?"

Tremble grinned back. "I just might at that, so try to keep up. We have promises to keep."

The End - *Push Back* - Book 2 of *The Disruption Trilogy*

PROMISES TO KEEP

CHAPTER ONE

Appalachian Trail
Mile 1209.5 Southbound
Just north of I-66 Underpass
Near Front Royal, VA

Day 33
May 3, 2020 - 9:15 a.m.

Simon Tremble stopped his descent down the steep wooded slope and motioned for his son, Keith, to do the same. Keith complied, his eyebrows arched in a question.

"I think we're getting close to the I-66 crossing near Front Royal," Tremble said. "That's where Tex and Wiggins had trouble and I don't want to just stumble through there blindly. Let's check out the trail guide and map."

Keith nodded and slipped off his pack and lowered it to the sloping ground of the trail. 'Pack' was a bit of an overstatement, as it was actually a crude basket woven from slender green branches, with straps made from his web belt. A length of paracord had replaced his belt, and he hitched up his pants for what seemed like the tenth time that day before he bent down and untied the loose knot securing the 'liner' for his makeshift pack — a common black plastic garbage bag. He fished out a thick bundle of paper, all folded and held together by rubber bands, and handed it to his father.

Tremble marveled once more at the forethought of this Levi Jenkins guy, as he shucked the rubber bands off the bundle. There were state road maps, city and county maps, US Forest Service maps, tourist brochures; anything that might provide information on the route they were traveling. Perhaps most valuable were the loose-leaf pages torn from an Appalachian Trail Guide. He sorted through the thick bundle until he found what he wanted, then squatted and spread the map on the ground. He looked back and forth between the map and a loose AT Guide page he held in his hand.

"It was nice of Tex and Wiggins to share their maps and stuff with us," Keith said.

His father shrugged. "They were going north and we were going south, so it made sense to share what they didn't need. Info on where they'd already been was basically dead weight for them anyway." Simon Tremble looked up at his son. "But I am glad Tex thought of it. She's a sharp young lady."

"That she is," Keith said.

Tremble grinned. "Cute too."

Keith blushed and changed the subject. "How far to the crossing?"

Tremble looked back at the map. "A mile, more or less. It looks like the trail runs concurrent with a road called Tucker Lane for a couple of hundred yards, then it crosses state Route 55 and goes back into the woods. With luck, there'll be tree cover along the road so we can stay out of sight until this Tucker Lane dead-ends into 55. Then we'll just have to make sure no one's in sight in either direction and dash across the road."

"You think we'll have trouble?"

Tremble shook his head. "Not really. With luck, we'll only be exposed crossing the road. Tex and Wiggins attracted the unwanted attention because they were driving out in the open. We'll be staying in the woods and bypassing Front Royal completely. Invisibility is our best defense."

Keith scowled. "I guess there has to be SOME benefit to moving like snails."

"Hey, we made twenty miles yesterday and over six today so far. You want to pick up the pace?"

"You know what I mean, Dad. We need wheels. We'll get to Wilmington a lot sooner."

"More likely dead or captured a lot sooner." Tremble refolded the map and loose guidebook pages and bundled everything together with the rubber bands. He rose and handed the bundle to Keith, who returned it to his makeshift pack.

"Now let's check out this Tucker Lane. And be extra quiet; there may be houses nearby until we get well back into the woods on the other side of I-66," Tremble said.

Keith nodded, and both men shouldered their packs and set off down the steep hill. They'd gone a hundred yards and just rounded a sharp bend in the trail when they both stopped in their tracks.

"Holy moly," Keith said. "What's that doing on the trail?"

Tremble shook his head in disbelief. In the middle of the path ahead was an older Toyota Highlander, much the worse for wear. Cracks spider-webbed the windshield, emanating from two very obvious bullet holes. There were also multiple bullet holes in the front bumper, grille, and hood, and both the side mirrors were gone, long scratches down both sides of the vehicle indicating they'd been knocked off as the car plowed up the narrow trail.

They spread out and approached cautiously, their M4s held ready. As they got closer, Tremble could see the back window was completely gone as well. The car was obviously abandoned, and from the vines starting to grow up one side, it had been for some time. He signaled Keith to stop and processed what he was seeing. Then it hit him.

"This must be Tex and Wiggin's car," Tremble said. "They said they abandoned it and made a run for the trail. I just assumed they left it on the road."

Keith looked toward his father. "That means it's been here almost a month. Do you think maybe . . ."

"Only one way to find out," Tremble said, and both men slung their weapons and rushed toward opposite sides of the car.

Keith got there first and ripped open the passenger-side rear door to rummage in a cardboard box and emerged grinning from ear to ear, holding up a can of chili.

"Outstanding! I'm really sick of squirrel and rabbit jerky!" Keith said.

Tremble returned his grin. "Me too, son. Me too."

***

The SUV was a cornucopia of supplies. Much of the back of the vehicle was taken up with five-gallon jerry cans of gasoline, but there were also boxes full of food and supplies of all types. Suddenly nervous someone might stumble upon them and rob them of their newfound wealth, the Trembles spent a frantic half hour ferrying everything but the gasoline to a small clearing well off the trail.

"I can't believe it," Keith said.

Tremble shrugged. "It's not that surprising when you think about it. I guess this section of the trail hasn't seen any traffic since the solar storm."

"They left a lot of stuff."

"Not by choice, I'm sure. They had to leave in a hurry with just what they could carry. The gas and the canned goods and bottled water were all assuming they would make it home in the car." Tremble hesitated. "And you know we can't carry all this stuff either."

"About that," Keith said. "There have to be a lot of abandoned cars on I-66, and now we have all this gasoline just sitting here for the taking. So I'm thinking—"

"Well, you can just STOP thinking, because we're staying on the trail and that's that. As long as we're armed and can melt into the woods, we have a fighting chance, but we'd be both visible and vulnerable on the open road."

Keith sighed. "All right, all right. What ARE we going to do, then?"

His father grinned. "The first thing we're going to do is have a damn good meal. Then we'll figure out what we CAN carry, and re-stow our packs. We can probably manage enough to allow us a full week of solid hiking without having to stop to hunt or set snares."

Appalachian Trail
Mile 1326.3 Southbound
Just north of I-64 Overpass
Rockfish Gap, VA

Day 40
May 10, 2020 - 7:35 a.m.

Tremble steadied the monocular against the tree trunk and gazed at the scene below him, saying a silent prayer of thanks he'd searched the abandoned car thoroughly. He'd found the monocular under the driver's seat. It was a cheap model, little more than a child's toy, really, but orders of magnitude better than the naked eye.

They'd crossed under I-66 without incident six days earlier, the same day they found the abandoned car. From their hiding place, they'd seen I-66 above them lined with abandoned cars, but had managed to stay out of sight in the strip of woods paralleling Tucker Lane. Likewise, they'd seen motorcycles pass on state Route 55, and from the looks of the riders, assumed they were part of the group that attacked Tex and Wiggins. They'd crept to the edge of the concealing woods and darted across the highway only when they were sure no one was in sight in either direction.

Their 'dash' was made difficult by bulging packs, as a full inventory of the abandoned supplies proved even more encouraging than first thought. A case of water in half-liter bottles had allowed them not only to drink their fill, but the reusable empties provided a more secure way of carrying water, allowing them to abandon their fragile 'condom water bladders.' They'd added a half-dozen bottles to their packs and also filled one of the empties from a half-gallon bottle of bleach they found in the back of the SUV; they had no more worries about water purification.

Besides canned goods, they'd found a dozen dehydrated camping meals in foil bags and three separate gallon-size Ziploc bags containing mixed nuts, pasta crushed to minimize air pockets, and beef jerky. Rounding out the lightweight food stores, another Ziploc held individual packets of salt, pepper, sugar, and various condiments. Another box held duct tape, a small cooking pot, plastic cutlery, a flashlight and batteries, paracord, a wire saw, a first aid kit, two bars of soap, and perhaps best of all, a flattened roll of toilet paper in a Ziploc bag.

They had gladly ditched dried rabbit and squirrel meat to make room for a maximum load of more palatable food and new gear. Then they'd gorged on the heavier canned food and put the rest back in the SUV with the gasoline. The food would do them no good, but it might help some future traveler in difficult circumstances.

Invigorated, and with ample calories in a more palatable form, they'd made good progress. Tremble thought under other circumstances he would've even enjoyed the experience. They encountered no one, nor did they hear the ominous thump of chopper blades in the distance. The only times of tension were those points where the trail crossed a road, including over two dozen crossings of scenic Skyline Drive, as that road meandered through the mountains. Those were minor crossings of two-lane thoroughfares, dashes measured in feet and seconds of exposure. Until now.

Tremble squinted through the spyglass, down the two-lane road to the attractive and rustic rock-faced bridge carrying Skyline Drive over both I-64 and the Rockfish Gap Turnpike, the point where Skyline Drive became the Blue Ridge Parkway. The Appalachian Trail ran concurrent with the road here, traversing both major highways via the bridge—a full quarter mile of exposure, with nowhere to run and a thirty-foot drop on either side.

But that wasn't the problem. Standing in the middle of the bridge were two men dressed in camo, hunting rifles slung on their shoulders. Smoke rose from cigarettes as they chatted, their eyes turned toward I-64 running below them.

"Why would anyone block Skyline Drive?"

Tremble lowered the monocular and shook his head. "I'd say they're watching I-64. They've got binoculars and I'm betting they have radios as well. They're probably spotters or lookouts." He sighed. "Whoever they are, we can't get over that bridge with them there."

"What are we going to do?" Keith asked.

"Slip back into the woods and parallel Skyline Drive north until it curves enough that I can cross it without being seen. Then I'll slip through the woods and see if I can see what's down below the bridge at the interchange. Maybe we can descend the slope here north of the interstate and cross under it unseen by walking alongside Rockfish Gap Turnpike. That will depend on how much tree cover there is beside the turnpike and the situation below the bridge."

Keith nodded. "Let's go—"

Tremble shook his head. "I'm trained for this and you're not. Besides, if something happens to me, you have to get the information to Wilmington."

Keith looked as if he were about to argue, then swallowed and bobbed his head. "Okay, but what CAN I do?"

Tremble considered that a moment. "Look through the maps while I'm gone. I saw some local county maps and tourist brochures mixed in with the other stuff. If we can't get by here, we'll have to circle way around somehow; see if you can find us an alternate route."

Keith nodded again and followed his father through the woods, paralleling Skyline Drive as it curved north. When they'd gone far enough that they could no longer see, or be seen from the bridge, Tremble stopped, shucked his pack off his back, and set it on the ground. He laid his M4 across it and turned to face his son.

"I'm only taking the pistol; I'll be staying undercover and the M4 won't be necessary. I'll be gone an hour, maybe two max, but if I'm not back by dark, spend the night here and take off on your own first thing in the morning. Understood?"

"But—"

"No buts, son. Understood?"

"Yes, sir," Keith managed, his voice near cracking.

Tremble wrapped Keith in a fierce hug, which his son returned.

"Don't worry, son," Tremble said into Keith's ear. "Smarter people than these bastards have tried to kill me, and I'm still here."

Keith nodded, unable to speak, and Tremble broke the embrace and moved toward the road.

"Dad?"

Tremble turned. "Yes, son?"

"Be careful, okay?"

Tremble smiled. "Always. Now get to work and see if you can find us a way around these guys."

***

Tremble dashed across Skyline Drive, intending to move well into the woods on the opposite side before turning south toward the bridge. That proved unnecessary, because the ground sloped so steeply Tremble had to hang on to trees to keep from plunging down the slope. Fifty feet from the road, he knew he was well below the line of sight of the men on the bridge unless they stepped to the edge and looked down. Satisfied, he worked his way south along the steep slope.

He smelled it before he saw it—the putrid smell of too many humans living in close quarters without basic sanitation. He moved farther along the slope until the abutment for the Skyline Drive bridge was visible between the tree trunks to his left and I-64 stretched out below him left to right, a parking lot of abandoned cars.

He had no difficulty imagining how it came to pass. People desperate to escape the rapid societal collapse of the cities fled to the countryside, only to find their rural neighbors had neither the resources nor, in many cases, the inclination to entertain uninvited guests. The refugees had crawled along bumper to bumper until they'd run out of gas and then either stayed by their cars or walked until they ran out of food or water or both. Eventually the strongest and more opportunistic among them realized they could remain civilized or they could survive; most decided to survive.

Tremble studied the cars from his perch well above them. Though likely not apparent when approached from ground level, there was an obvious pattern to the arrangement of the 'stalled' cars. In one area, the cars were halfway into the road on either side, seemingly at random but leaving only a narrow passable lane down the center of the road. There were spaces between the cars, giving the appearance of openness, but in fact the open spaces were less than a car length, effectively walling off each side of the interstate. A few car lengths from either end of the makeshift corridor, a car was parked at a right angle to the road, and near both such cars, armed men sat in the overgrown verge, as if waiting for something.

A trap, Tremble realized. The lookouts on the bridge would alert the men below, who would hide until the passing car slowed to transit the narrow passage, and then emerge to roll the 'gate' cars across the road, behind and in front of their target. The prey would be unable to escape and surrounded. He had little doubt as to what happened next.

He raised the monocular and studied the area farther south of the interstate, and the source of the foul smell became apparent. A tent city filled the little valley around the highway interchange, marching up the slope to the south to an unattractive boxlike building that could only be a motel from the last century. Just uphill from the motel was a very large cylindrical tank, and as he watched, Tremble saw a man in camo walk across the parking lot and enter a small shed near the tank. There was a puff of smoke from an exhaust pipe on the shed, followed by the distant dull roar of what sounded like a lawn mower. Tremble nodded to himself; a good well with a gasoline-powered pump and massive water storage might explain the presence of the tent city.

That, and the fact he figured the city of Waynesboro three miles to the west had likely barricaded I-64 on both sides of town. The major interstates ran past some towns like Front Royal on I-66 to the north, where Tex and Wiggins had encountered problems. In such places, the locals barricaded the accesses to town and 'encouraged' the refugees to keep moving, but I-64 ran right through the middle of Waynesboro. If the locals let the refugees in, there would be no way to care for them or contain them when things got desperate. The thought of Americans turning on each other both saddened and angered him, even as he was forced to admit he'd have likely done the same to protect his family and community.

He studied the run-down motel. The parking lot was cracked and potholed and he could see multiple broken windows and graffiti. The precious water tank was almost uniform rust red, except for scattered splotches of white where the original paint was intact. But rusty or not, it contained wealth beyond measure; clean water was life in the current circumstances.

Tremble saw what he took to be working vehicles in the motel parking lot, including a dozen large motorcycles parked in a row. The 'power elite' of this new community obviously preferred to protect the source of the wealth. It made sense, really; as shabby and run-down as it was, the old motel had a roof and gravity-fed running water.

Three men exited the building, two wearing denim jackets with some sort of identical red and yellow logo on the back, which Tremble couldn't quite make out, and the third wearing camo. They were all big men with, like everyone now, full beards. Even at a distance, Tremble could tell by the body language the man in camo was deferential toward the two bikers.

The trio moved to the bike at the end of the row and the two bikers got into an animated discussion. One of them turned and spoke to the man in camo, who bobbed his head and ran back to the building to return moments later with a small red toolbox. Yep, the camo guys are definitely the lackeys in this operation, Tremble thought, and moved his spyglass over the rest of the camp.

Downhill from the first motel was a building with the distinctive architecture and bright orange roof of a Howard Johnson's restaurant, though there was no sign and it didn't look like it had been a HoJos for a while. The windows were boarded up, but it was obviously occupied, as a roof of any description beat no roof, hands down. Sharing the potholed parking lot with the ex-HoJos was a cluster of buildings that appeared to be another run-down and previously abandoned lodging establishment. There were two structures, one of which had obviously suffered fire damage at some time in the distant past. People of both genders and various ages were moving around the buildings, but none were wearing either camo or denim jackets. *Worker bees*, Tremble thought.

The rest of the camp was a confused jumble of tents and shelters fashioned from blue tarps, plywood, and cardboard. There was no discipline to the layout, and Tremble spotted several hand-dug latrines, their placement ad hoc. There were perhaps as many as a thousand people in the camp, and the stench was overpowering even at a distance. He supposed the residents had become accustomed to it, as impossible as that seemed.

Tremble suppressed a sigh. One thing was certain; they couldn't afford even casual contact with these people. They had to get by them and do it quietly. But how? Even if they could get across the Skyline Drive bridge, the Appalachian Trail ran along the ridgeline not more than four or five hundred feet uphill from what he'd mentally dubbed the Biker Motel. He turned and started back the way he'd come, holding on to trees to keep from sliding down the steep slope.

His hamstrings and glutes burned as he struggled back up the slope to Skyline Drive, thankful there were trees for handholds. Had the slope been bare, he doubted he could have made the short ascent. He was winded when he reached the top, and stopped a minute to catch his breath before dashing back across Skyline Drive.

Tremble moved through the woods to where he'd left Keith to find — nothing.

"Keith?" he called, his voice barely above a whisper.

Keith stepped from behind the trunk of a big oak tree, his M4 in hand and a relieved look on his face.

"I wasn't sure it was you," he said.

Tremble gave him an approving nod. "Good situational awareness. That was exactly the right thing to do."

Keith flashed a brief smile at the praise and then grew serious. "What does it look like below? Can we get by them?"

Tremble shook his head. "I don't think so, at least not from what I can see. What about the maps? Could you come up with any way around them?"

Keith grinned. "Not exactly AROUND them, but would you settle for UNDER them?"

Tremble looked puzzled as Keith leaned his M4 against a tree trunk and reached into his pack to extract a map and unfold it on the ground. He squatted over it and motioned for his father to join him, then traced a line on the map with his finger.

"See this line with the cross marks on it? That's a railroad, right?" Keith asked.

"Yes, but what—"

"And see here, where it changes from cross marks to a dotted line? That dotted line runs right through where we're standing. See any railroad tracks?" Keith asked with a grin.

"I'll be damned. A tunnel," Tremble said, smiling himself now.

Keith nodded. "Right smack through the mountain below us. It looks to be a mile long. From the map, I'd say the west entrance is about half a mile northeast of us, back towards Waynesboro," Keith said. "The eastern outlet is about the same distance to the southeast, on the far side of both I-64 and Rockfish Gap Turnpike. When we come out on the southeast end, we'll only be seven or eight hundred feet downhill from the Appalachian Trail."

"Good job, son," Tremble said. "Let's go find that tunnel."

CHAPTER TWO

Appalachian Trail
Mile 1326.3 Southbound
Just north of I-64 Overpass
Rockfish Gap, VA

Ten Minutes Later

The Trembles dashed across Skyline Drive and started their descent down the heavily wooded slope to US 250, known locally as Rockfish Gap Turnpike. The slope was even steeper here, forcing them to move down the slope at an angle northward, both to ease their descent and put more distance between themselves and the tent city around the Biker Motel. When they glimpsed asphalt through the trees, Keith slowed.

"So what's the plan, Dad?"

"We need to get at least a mile north on 250 before we head west through the woods. Then we'll be sure we're north of the entrance, and when we hit the tracks, we just follow them to the tunnel."

Keith nodded. "Sounds good."

"Our biggest challenge is the unknown. We sure don't want to be in the open this near that camp, but clinging to this slope like a damn mountain goat will make it tough to judge distance. Between the slope and the pack, it feels like we've already gone several miles, but I doubt it's more than two hundred yards." Tremble sighed. "But I guess we best get to it. I'll lead for a while."

Keith fell in behind his father and they started north again. They hadn't gone far when Tremble squatted and peered through the trees.

"The road has narrowed to two lanes. Do you see that metal guardrail starting on the opposite side?" he called softly.

"Yeah, what about it?"

"That probably means there's a drop-off, and if the ground is sloping away from the road on that side, we'll be much less visible below the road level. We have to cross somewhere anyway, so this is as good a spot as any," Tremble said.

Keith nodded and followed his dad to the edge of the woods, approximately twenty feet above the road, with a good view in either direction.

"Looks clear," Keith said.

"Yeah, and look at that," Tremble said, pointing to the opposite side of the road. "There's our landmark."

Keith followed his father's pointing finger to the large sign. A huge red arrow read MOTEL, and in smaller letters, COLONY HOUSE MOTEL, FREE INTERNET, OUTDOOR POOL, 1 MILE ON RIGHT.

Keith laughed. "Yeah, we probably can't miss that."

Tremble looked both ways before descending the grassy slope and dashing across the road with Keith close behind. They rounded the guardrail and plunged into the woods. As anticipated, the ground sloped steeply away from the road, but to their delight, a narrow ledge paralleled the road about ten feet down the slope. It made for easier walking, and better yet, they were completely out of sight.

Fifteen minutes later Tremble held up his hand. "Better have a look. The farther we go north, the farther we'll have to backtrack to the tunnel. Let's not overdo it."

"I'll go." Keith shucked off his pack and leaned his rifle against it.

Tremble watched his son scramble up the bank with the strength and agility of youth, then nodded in silent approval as Keith hesitated as he neared the top, then raised his head cautiously to peek beneath the guardrail without exposing himself.

"Bingo!" Keith called softly. "The motel entrance is just ahead."

Tremble started to respond when Keith looked back in the direction of the biker camp and stiffened.

"Dad," he hissed, "you need to see this."

Tremble shed his pack and scrambled up the slope, his rifle slung. When he stretched out beside Keith, he could hardly believe his eyes. Rounding a bend in the road were two children, a boy of perhaps ten and a much younger girl. The boy gripped the girl's hand and tugged her along, the girl stumbling in the zigzag gait of total fatigue. She managed only a few more steps before collapsing to sit upright in the road, staring ahead blankly.

The kids were in bad shape. Their clothes were filthy rags, and they both had the gaunt, hollowed-cheeked look of hunger. The boy tugged insistently at the girl's arm, obviously trying to get her to stand. His verbal entreaties were unintelligible at the distance but growing in volume. Then he jerked his head up and stared back the way they'd come. Tremble heard it a fraction of a second later—from out of sight around the bend came the growing roar of approaching motorcycles.

The boy became frantic, his body language telegraphing his fear more eloquently than any words. He swiveled his head in all directions, obviously in search of a hiding place—a shelter, any shelter, from the approaching danger. Finding none, he pulled harder at the girl's arm, his panicked pleading audible now.

"COME ON, MOLLY! THEY'RE COMING! WE HAVE TO RUN!"

But the girl merely stared ahead, refusing to rise.

"Dad, we have to do something," Keith hissed.

"That something doesn't include exposing ourselves before we fully understand the situation," Tremble said, fighting to remain calm as he rolled to one side and unslung his M4. "We don't know who's coming around that bend or how they're armed. Getting ourselves killed won't help anyone. Now slide down and get your rifle; looks like we may need it."

He heard Keith crashing down the slope as he kept his eyes fixed on the scene and readied his rifle. The boy stopped tugging at the girl's arm to slip a book bag from his shoulders and rummage in it. He rose with something in his hand and moved between the girl and the roar of the approaching motorcycles.

Tremble tried to process what he was seeing. What the hell—

The kid faced the threat, squared his shoulders, and raised a handgun.

Tremble's heart sank. *No kid! Put it down and hide! Get out of my line of fire!*

He'd hardly finished his thought when two bikers burst around the curve and braked hard at the sight of the gun, but the kid didn't fire. He lowered the gun and fumbled frantically, obviously trying to chamber a round, as one of the men leaped off his bike and closed the short distance. The biker drove his fist into the side of the boy's head with a blow that would've felled a grown man, and the kid collapsed, the pistol clattering on the asphalt.

Tremble bit back his anger as he heard Keith settle on the ground beside him. The other biker dismounted and pointed a handgun at the two children. Tremble held his fire and cursed under his breath: if he started a firefight now, the kids would be in the middle and who knew what the result would be?

The first biker glared down at the boy and dug in the pocket of his filthy jeans to pull out a large folding pocketknife and open it.

"What ya gonna do, Rooster?" the second biker asked.

"I'm gonna take care of this little pissant, that's what, just like I did his bitch of a mother. Ain't nobody coldcocks me, then points a gun at me and lives to talk about it; don't matter if he is a kid."

"Dad!" Keith whispered, urgency in his voice.

"Don't shoot! You might hit the kids," Tremble whispered back.

Then Tremble saw the flash of a knife as Rooster bent toward the boy, and he knew he could wait no longer. His M4 barked twice, the rounds hitting the biker in the face and throat and driving him backward. He swung the rifle toward the second biker, who was sweeping his pistol around wildly, unsure of his target. Tremble fired again, hitting the biker center mass, and the man jerked and fired his pistol reflexively, the round whining off the asphalt. He stumbled backward three steps and collapsed against his motorcycle.

Tremble clawed his way to his feet, but Keith was over the guardrail before him, rushing toward the children.

"KEITH!" Tremble called as he climbed over the guardrail.

Keith stopped and turned, obviously frantic to get to the kids.

"Always check your enemy first to make sure they're dead. A lot of good men have been killed by dead enemies," Tremble said.

Keith nodded and resumed his run, Tremble only steps behind them.

Tremble's heart sank when he found the little girl in a pool of blood. He dropped to one knee and was relieved to find her breathing and her pulse strong. She opened her eyes and Tremble saw a flash of terror, followed by a blank stare. She neither helped nor resisted as he checked her out.

"How is she?" Keith asked as he returned from checking the bikers and dropped down beside the boy.

"His round hit her calf, probably a ricochet. It went all the way through and doesn't look like it hit anything major and the bleeding isn't too bad. I think she's gonna be okay. Physically, anyway," Tremble said. He glanced over to see Keith checking out the boy. "How is he?"

Keith was feeling for a pulse and didn't respond for a moment. Then he nodded. "He's breathing and has a strong pulse, but that guy really clocked him. His face is already black and blue. I'll be amazed if he doesn't have a concussion."

Keith's face contorted in rage. "Who does this to kids?"

For a moment Tremble was afraid his son was going to lose it, but Keith shook his head as if physically resetting his emotions. "What now, Dad?"

"We have to get them off the road, and soon; there's no telling when we might have more company. We'll reassess down on the ledge. Can you carry him?"

Keith nodded and worked his hands under the boy's body. "He's not exactly a heavyweight."

Tremble turned to the girl, who was sitting up now. "Okay, Molly, honey," he said softly. "We're going to get off the road and then I'll take care of that leg, okay?"

She didn't respond.

Tremble considered wrapping her leg, but he had nothing that wasn't filthy. She had on shorts, so no bacteria-laden clothing fragments were carried into the wound, and he didn't want to risk contaminating it. He considered retrieving the first aid kit from his pack, but decided carrying her to the kit was faster. Besides, they HAD to get off the road.

He slung his rifle and began to pick her up, when his eyes fell on the book bag and boy's Sig 1911 lying in the road. He rose and picked up the gun, ejected the magazine and checked the chamber, and then dropped both the Sig and the magazine in the bag and slung it over his shoulder before returning to the girl.

The short trip down the steep slope was difficult, and when he arrived at the ledge, he saw eighteen-year-old Keith appeared to be winded as well. Things didn't look good for plan B, whatever the hell it turned out to be.

He sat Molly down against a tree and put his rifle and the book bag down to rummage in his pack. He fished out a bar of soap, a bottle of water, a roll of duct tape, and the first aid kit, and then turned back to Molly and sank down on his knees beside her.

"How's the boy?" he asked over his shoulder.

"No change. He's still out," Keith replied.

"There's nothing more you can do," Tremble said. "Come give me a hand."

Keith came to squat by his father, who handed him the water bottle.

"Pour a bit on my hands, just enough to wet them," Tremble said.

Keith complied, and Tremble took the bar of soap and worked up a good lather, scrubbing his hands thoroughly before holding them out for Keith to rinse. Then he worked up a fresh lather.

Tremble looked down at the girl. "Molly, honey, we're going to be working on your leg and it might hurt, but we're trying to make it better. Okay?"

There was no reaction, and Tremble nodded at Keith. "Wet her leg a few inches above and below the wound."

Keith did as instructed, and Tremble began to lather Molly's leg all the way around the wound area, as gently as possible, relieved the girl was not fighting him. He finished and rocked back on his knees, nodding to Keith, who rinsed the soap off to leave a six-inch band of clean skin around Molly's leg.

"Damn," said Keith as Tremble looked through the little first aid kit, "I thought some of that was tan, but I guess not."

"We have to keep it clean," Tremble said. "The wound will heal on its own if we can keep it from getting infected. Under these conditions, that's a pretty big if."

He fished a small bottle of alcohol from the first aid kit and soaked a sterile gauze pad to wipe down the area around the wound again. He then reached for a tube of antiseptic cream, which he squirted liberally into both the entry and exit wounds before taping clean gauze squares over both with adhesive tape. He finished off with a wrapping of duct tape around her leg to cover the entire area.

All the while, Molly hadn't reacted at all.

Tremble rocked back on his knees and sighed. "That's not much, but it's the best we can do. I'm hoping the duct tape will protect it and keep it dry."

Keith looked down at the kids.

"What are we gonna do, Dad? They can't walk, either of them, and we can't carry all our gear down that slope and them too. Heck, we might have to hang on to trees to get down ourselves. And for sure they heard the shots back in the biker camp. I'm just surprised no one has shown up yet."

Tremble nodded. "Which means we HAVE to carry them. Break out the wire saw and let's take down a couple of small saplings. We can run paracord between them and make a stretcher to carry both kids at once." Tremble glanced down the steep slope. "It won't be easy, but it's the only thing that comes to mind."

They worked fast and had just finished the stretcher when they heard an approaching vehicle. Tremble checked his watch.

"Just under twenty minutes; that's longer than I thought we'd have. That's definitely not a motorcycle. What do you think? One vehicle or more?"

Keith listened, almost visibly straining to parse the sound.

"One, I think. Why?"

"Because it means either the car is unconnected with the biker camp, or the camp is only mildly concerned and only sent one car out to check it out."

"So what?" Keith asked.

"If they're unconnected, they'll hurry by, not wanting to be involved. But if they're from the camp, they'll radio it in and wait. If they start poking around and either hear us or look over the guardrail and spot us through the trees, we're screwed. We can't carry these kids under fire, and if we hunker down and return fire, we'll be pinned in place until all their friends show up. Then it's game over."

"So what can we do?"

"Buy some time," Tremble said. "We'll set up at the guardrail out of sight, and if it's the bad guys, we take them out. Whether or not we get them before they report, the gunfire will draw a response, likely in force. However, if the responders don't know what they're driving into, they'll be more cautious and thus slower. By the time they get here, we'll have broken contact. They won't know where to look and will likely assume we continued north on the road."

"You think that will work?" Keith asked.

"I hope so. It's the only plan I have."

Tremble grabbed his rifle and started up the slope, Keith right behind him. They'd barely settled in when they peered beneath the guardrail to see a jacked-up truck roar around the bend and skid to a stop at the sight of the dead bikers. The camo-clad men in the truck stared at the scene in stunned disbelief.

"Are they with the bikers? How do we tell?" Keith asked.

"Target the passenger and shoot if I tell you," Tremble said as he drew a bead on the driver.

"Drive on by. Please, just drive on by," Tremble murmured under his breath.

The whisper had hardly left his lips when the driver raised a radio to his mouth.

"SHOOT, KEITH," Tremble yelled as he loosed a three-round burst at the driver.

His son's rounds shattered the windshield less than a second after his own, and both men in the truck died instantly.

"Let's go." Tremble started down the slope, but turned when he realized his son wasn't with him. Keith was still on the ground, staring under the guardrail.

"Come on, son," Tremble said gently. "We just bought some time, but we have to move fast."

Keith rose, his face ashen. He started down the short slope and Tremble turned to continue his own descent. He stopped at the bottom and looked back to see his son grab a sapling for support and bend at the waist to empty his stomach on the hillside. Tremble dug a water bottle out of his pack and handed it to Keith as the boy stumbled the rest of the way down to the little ledge.

"Rinse out your mouth; you'll feel better."

Keith did as instructed and turned back to his father. "I . . . I'm sorry, Dad—"

Tremble put his hand on his son's shoulder. "I'm the one that's sorry you had to experience that, and I would have done anything to prevent it, but that's not the world we're living in. Taking a life should never be easy, regardless of the circumstances. The first time I had to do it, I puked too. As a matter of fact, my first time under fire, I messed my pants, so I figure you're doing fifty percent better than me."

"You? No way!"

"Believe it." Tremble smiled. "But if you ever tell anyone, also remember I'm still not too old to kick your butt. Now let's get these kids down that hill."

Keith nodded, anxious to move past his anxiety to something positive.

They laid the kids side by side on the stretcher, and there was enough room to put their packs on the other end. As an afterthought, Tremble dug into the boy's bag and extracted the Sig 1911, inserted the magazine and stuffed it in his own backpack.

"More weight?" Keith asked as he moved to one end of the stretcher.

"More firepower," Tremble said. "Now let's get out of here."

***

The stretcher idea was better in concept than application. Even moving down the slope at an angle proved difficult. The load was unwieldy, and to keep the children from rolling off, Keith had to hold the front of the stretcher high while Tremble in back was at times almost bent at the waist. After struggling fifty yards, they lowered the stretcher.

"This is obviously a bust," Tremble said. "Any ideas?"

Keith turned, red-faced and sweating, to cast an appraising eye at the hillside. "What if we both stay on the downhill side and each grab one of the poles? Then we can drag it, you know, like a travois. The uphill side will be a lot lower, and the whole stretcher will be closer to level," Keith said. "And we'll each have one hand free to grab handholds so we can go straight down the slope."

His father was already moving to his side. "Damn good idea; let's do it."

The new method worked, and they were halfway down the slope when Tremble glanced back to see the flaw. He signaled Keith to stop, and then studied the hillside in their wake. Drag marks through the disturbed detritus of the forest floor marked their path as clearly as a neon sign.

"If they DO come down the hill, our escape route won't exactly be a mystery," Tremble said.

"Should we try to cover our tracks?" Keith asked.

Tremble shook his head. "I doubt we could. Those poles left deep marks in places; besides, we don't have the time. Our best bet is to find that tunnel and get through it as quick as we can."

They started down the slope with renewed urgency.

"Dad," asked Keith between labored breaths, "what if the bikers know about the tunnel? They could just wait for us on the other end."

"I doubt they're locals, so there's no reason why they should know about it." Tremble stopped talking a moment to catch his breath as they continued. "And if they do, there's not a damn thing we can do about it."

They reached the bottom and the welcome sight of rusty rails. They lowered the stretcher and Tremble checked his watch.

"Over ten minutes since last contact. We need to keep moving."

"Should we keep the packs on the stretcher and just carry everything together? It will be much easier walking along the tracks," Keith said.

Tremble nodded. "Yeah, I think—"

He stopped mid-sentence as he heard the growing throaty roar of multiple motorcycles above them. The sound crested and then died out as the engines stopped one by one. The engine noise was replaced by angry shouts, loud enough that they could make out the words.

"It sounds like our biker friends aren't too pleased," Tremble said softly.

"They sound close," Keith whispered.

"It's not as far down that hill as it seems. But we're okay. I'm betting they'll search along the road first. They'll eventually find our trail through the woods but hopefully after we're long gone. Now go."

They each grabbed the stretcher and turned left, southeast down the tracks. Tremble was at the rear, and as they moved, he studied the unconscious children on the stretcher. He didn't like to jostle the boy, but they had no choice. His real concern was the continued unconsciousness; the boy had been out just over thirty minutes, and if he didn't come to soon, his injury was likely more than a simple concussion. Tremble suppressed a sigh; the kids were a huge complication, and he had absolutely no clue how they were going to cope with this latest challenge.

He shifted his gaze to little Molly and was pleased to see her eyes were closed and her chest rose and fell in even breaths. He had no idea what lay beneath the vacant stare she wore as a shield, but he felt instinctively that sleeping through this latest round of stress was probably better for her. However, as he watched, her little face contorted, and she began to squirm on the stretcher and shake her head violently. Suddenly she sat bolt upright, her eyes wide, and stared as if seeing him for the first time. Apparently she didn't like what she saw.

Her bloodcurdling scream was likely heard in the next county. She rolled off the stretcher and tried to run, but her injured leg collapsed and she went down hard on the gravel ballast of the railroad track. Undeterred, she leaped to her feet and moved toward the tree line in a limping walk-run.

Tremble flinched at the scream and cursed under his breath as the girl rolled off the stretcher. "Keith, put down—"

But Keith was already lowering his end as Tremble grounded his own end and raced after the girl. He overtook her at the edge of the woods, and she fought and screamed even louder until he clamped a hand over her mouth and wrapped his free arm around her frail body, pinning her to him in a bear hug.

"Bring the duct tape," he hissed, and held the struggling girl, trying unsuccessfully to calm her until Keith was at his side with the tape.

"We don't have time to calm her, even if we could," Tremble said. "Tape her mouth, then her wrists and ankles. Tape her eyes too. Maybe she'll struggle less if she can't see. I hate to do it, but we can't deal with this now."

Keith nodded and taped the girl's eyes and mouth. Once sightless, she became less agitated, and he taped her wrists as Tremble held her and then gently lowered her to the ground. As Keith bent to tape her ankles, Tremble saw movement out of the corner of his eye.

"DUCK!" he yelled, and shot out his hand just in time to deflect a fist-sized rock held in a small hand, the blow aimed at the back of Keith's head.

"LEAVE MY SISTER ALONE!" The boy's bruised face was contorted in rage, and he reached for another rock.

Tremble grabbed the boy roughly and pinned his arms in a hug.

"No time for this," he said. "Tape him the same way, Keith, and fast."

Keith did as ordered, and a minute later they were running southeast along the tracks with the bound children on the stretcher between them. Tremble heard men crashing through the brush, far up the hill.

After fifty yards, he called softly to Keith, "This won't work. They'll be on us before we can get away, and as soon as they hit the tracks, all they have to do is shoot us in the back. We have to ambush those in front to make the rest of them less enthusiastic about getting close. Remember, they don't know our numbers or who we are. We can use that to our advantage."

"So what do we do?" Keith said over his shoulder.

"See that big tree in the edge of the woods up on your left? Stop behind that."

Keith made a beeline for the tree and they stopped behind it.

"Okay, let's move the kids into the woods and out of the line of fire. Then you hunker down behind this tree, and I'll find a spot in the edge of the woods on the other side of the track, but where we can see each other. These guys aren't exactly SEAL Team Six, so I'm betting when they hit the tracks and don't see us, they'll figure we're out of sight around the bend ahead and come after us along the track where the walking is easier. When I start firing, join in, and we put them down hard and fast. If they spread out, I'll target guys on your side of the track and you target guys on mine. That gives us both better firing angles. Got it?"

"Got it." Keith hesitated and then added, "What then?"

"What then? You do realize I'm making this up as we go along, right, son?"

Keith flushed. "Ah … yeah, sorry, Dad."

"No problem, but let's do it. They'll be here any minute."

As it turned out, it was two or three minutes, and they not only had time to get ready, but a minute or so for Tremble to consider the options. By the time the three camo-clad men emerged from the woods well behind them and began examining the right-of-way in both directions, Tremble had the beginnings of a plan. He saw the man closest to them squat and examine the ground where they'd scuffled with the children, then look down the track in their direction before calling the others. As he anticipated, they chose the easier path along the tracks rather than the slower but safer option of keeping to the cover of the woods. Tremble's plan became considerably more viable when he heard a radio squawk.

"Renfro, you copy?"

The largest of the three men raised a radio. "Yeah, Spider, I copy."

"You dumb asses picked up the trail yet?"

The three men exchanged pissed-off looks and Renfro spoke into the radio again. "Yeah, we followed it downhill to a set of railroad tracks. We just got here. It looks like they headed southeast. What do you want us to do? Uh … Over."

"I want y'all to FOLLOW THEM, DUMB ASS. What do you think?"

"Uhh … Just us? They already took out four guys, and we don't even know how many there are. Maybe some of y'all need to come down the hill and help us out," Renfro said into the radio.

"We ride; we don't crawl through the woods. That's why we keep y'all around, so stop being pussies and earn your keep or we'll replace you with someone else. You got it?"

"Okay, but you said you wanted at least one of 'em alive as an example, and I ain't promising nothing with just three guys, especially when I don't even know for sure what we're facing. YOU copy? Over."

There was silence for a long moment before the radio squawked again.

"All right, but we ain't stomping through the damn brambles and briers and gettin' covered with ticks. I remember seeing a railroad crossing farther up 250 toward Waynesboro, about a mile before the barricade those friggin' townies set up. It's gotta be the same tracks. We'll ride down to the crossing and then ride up the track right-of-way to meet you. Meanwhile, y'all make contact with our runners and hold them in place 'til we get there. You copy, Renfro?"

"I copy. How many you bringin'?"

"We're all here, so I reckon everybody can use a little fun. Presuming, of course, you pussies get off your asses and make contact. 'Cause I swear, Renfro, if you let them get away, it'll be you we make the example of. Spider out."

The three men stared at each other in silence as the sound of motorcycles firing up reverberated from the road above.

"That Spider is an asshole," one of them said.

"They're all assholes," Renfro said. "But they're mean and dangerous, and they all have each other's backs, so we best not cross 'em. Now, come on. Let's get down the tracks and find these bastards, whoever they are."

Tremble raised his M4 and looked over at Keith, who gave him a nervous nod and did the same. Tremble studied the men in his sights; they were walking bunched up in the center of the tracks. He almost felt sorry for them. Almost.

He shot Renfro center mass and immediately targeted the man next to him and took him down. The third man was already falling to Keith's shot. Tremble bolted from cover and ran toward the downed men. None could be allowed to live, and if any were breathing, he wanted to take care of it quickly and spare Keith the task.

Keith's man was still alive, though he'd likely bleed out quickly. It was time they didn't have, and Tremble shot him in the head. He grabbed the radio from Renfro's vest pocket then turned to motion Keith forward.

As Keith reached him, Tremble nodded at the bodies. "Two of these guys have ARs, so we can use their ammo. We'll scavenge it all and check their pockets for spare mags and loose rounds. As soon as we're done, we'll drag the bodies into the woods. Go."

Keith bent to comply just as the radio squawked.

"Renfro, what's happening? You copy?"

Tremble shook his head. "Damn. I was hoping they wouldn't hear the shots over the noise of their bikes."

"Ignore it?" Keith asked.

Tremble considered his son's suggestion and then shook his head. "It's a hard call. No response and they'll be wary, but if I DO respond and they figure out it's not Renfro, they'll be on full alert. My plan relies on surprise."

"So we have a plan now? Since when?"

"Since about two minutes ago," Tremble said. "And my plan says fortune favors the bold. Now keep working, I got this."

He raised the radio to his mouth. "We made contact. Everything is fine," Tremble said, alternately pressing and releasing the mic button so that his transmission would seem garbled and hopefully make voice identification more difficult.

"Renfro, you made contact? Say again. You're breaking up. Over."

Tremble repeated his transmission, using the same ruse. Then when Spider asked him to repeat it again, Tremble transmitted the same 'you're breaking up' message back to Spider, again pressing the mic button intermittently. Then he stopped transmitting and ignored the subsequent and increasingly irate requests from Spider as he turned to the task of helping Keith collect ammo.

"He's getting pissed," Keith said as Spider's rants echoed from the radio. "Should you answer him?"

Tremble shook his head. "If I give him too many chances, he may figure out I'm not Renfro. Now, he just thinks the radios are screwed up. And besides, angry people don't think clearly, and right now we need him reacting, not thinking."

As they dragged the bodies into the woods, Tremble told Keith his plan. When they dropped the last body, Keith turned back toward the stretcher.

"Wait a minute," Tremble said, pulling out a pocketknife.

Keith watched in confusion as his father brushed aside the detritus of the forest floor and punched the knife into the ground repeatedly, loosening the earth.

"Fill your pockets with dirt," Tremble ordered.

"What? Why—"

"Just do it, son. I'll explain later."

Moments later they picked up the stretcher and started for the tunnel again, exhaustion offset by adrenaline. They rounded the nearby bend in the track and saw the black hole of the tunnel mouth in the distance. By unspoken mutual agreement, they began to jog, and the black spot got larger, ever so slowly. They were almost there when the radio squawked.

"Renfro, do you copy? Over."

The call was repeated three times, followed by, "Okay. If you can hear me, we found the rail crossing and we're headed your way. We'll probably be there in a few minutes, and God help you if you let them get away."

In the distance, Tremble could hear the faint sound of the bikes as he and Keith plunged into the tunnel, a small white dot of light marking the exit on the far end, a distant mile away. Moving from the bright sunlight into the tunnel's gloom rendered them almost blind, and they stopped and lowered the stretcher as their eyes adjusted. Tremble fished out a small flashlight and moved up beside Keith.

"You can't hold the light and carry the stretcher at the same time. We'll each grab a side with one hand and drag it like we did coming down. Let's get the kids well into the tunnel and out of harm's way," Tremble said.

Keith nodded and they set off, dragging the stretcher along to one side of the tracks to keep it from bouncing over the cross ties. They completed their task and returned to the better light of the tunnel mouth at a run. The bikes were clearly audible now.

"You really think we got a shot, Dad?" Keith said, gasping for breath.

Tremble pulled a water bottle from his pocket. "With luck. You got the dirt?"

Keith plunged his hands into his pockets and came out with a double handful of dirt. He held it in cupped hands as Tremble poured water over it, then returned the bottle to his hip pocket and reached into the bowl formed by Keith's hands to knead the mass into black mud. When it was the right consistency, Tremble scooped half out for his own use and began to smear the black mixture over any exposed skin. Keith nodded, understanding now and copying his father's actions. They checked each other out and touched up any missed areas, then wiped the remaining mud on their clothes in irregular dark blotches.

The bikes were getting louder. Keith was trembling and unable to hide it.

"We'll be fine, son. Remember what I told you. We can't let any escape. If they didn't know about this tunnel before, any survivors will know now. So even if we get away, they'll find the exit and put two and two together. Then they'll hunt us down on the Appalachian Trail. This HAS to end here. Understood?"

Keith nodded solemnly.

"Okay. Go back and set up where I showed you."

"Aren't you coming?"

Tremble held up the radio. "I'm not sure the radio will work inside, and I need to let them know about the tunnel so they're expecting it and don't stop to think about it too much when they see it." He grinned, feigning a calmness he didn't feel. "Maybe I can stir them up a little bit in the process. Now go on, I'll be right behind you. Here, take the flashlight."

Keith declined. "I can go slow and find my way. You'll need the light more when you come. You'll be in a hurry."

Tremble murmured agreement and looked back down the tracks as Keith retreated into the blackness of the tunnel.

The roar of the bikes was louder now, just around the curve in the near distance. Tremble would have to risk speaking a bit more clearly, counting on the roar of the bikes and Spider's agitated state to mask any differences from Renfro's voice.

"Spider, you copy?"

The response was immediate, Spider's voice almost drowned out by the roar of the bikes.

"Dammit, Renfro, where are you? You better not have lost 'em."

Tremble responded, "... other side of the tunnel. Hurry! They're gettin' away."

"What tunnel? What the hell are you talkin' about?" Spider responded.

"Hurry," Tremble said into the mic. "Gettin' away."

Tremble ignored the stream of abuse that followed and pocketed the radio to move farther back into the shadows where he knew he couldn't be seen. He pulled out the little monocular and focused on the bend in the track, waiting for the bikers to appear.

They rounded the curve in less than a minute, and what he saw filled him with relief. There were two columns of five bikers each, riding on either side of the tracks to avoid the bumpy ride across the wooden ties. He'd seen twelve bikes in the camp, so counting the two bikers he'd taken down earlier, it looked like the gang was all here. Any remaining 'camo guys' were still a threat, but taking out the bikers would leave a power vacuum, likely accompanied by infighting and confusion. Tracking down whoever killed their biker overlords would be the last thing on the camo guys' minds. Besides, anyone badass enough to take down the bikers was probably not someone they were too eager to find.

Presuming, of course, he and Keith COULD take down the bikers.

He pocketed the monocular and folded his hand over the lens of the flashlight before switching it on, so only enough light leaked out to help him make his way back to where Keith waited, a hundred yards into the tunnel. He stopped before he got there.

"Close your eyes and keep them closed," Tremble called out as he approached Keith. Only after his son had acknowledged his order did Tremble close the distance.

"Okay, they're coming, and they're pissed. Now here's the hard part. We have to draw them far enough into the tunnel so none of them can turn and make it back to the entrance before we have a chance to take them out. We have no cover here, and they'll light us up with their headlights when they come in. We have to hide in plain sight, so stand perfectly still and hug the tunnel walls while they're coming, and count on blending in. They're moving from bright sunlight to near darkness, so their vision will be compromised, and most of them are wearing sunglasses besides. They're not expecting anything, so if we're still, we won't register as a threat, at least not until it's too late."

I hope, thought Tremble.

"Now this is very important. Keep both eyes shut tight until I yell GO, understand? I've been keeping one eye closed to establish and preserve what night vision I could and I'll keep it closed and target their headlights with my open eye. When I've taken out the headlights, I'll yell and you get in the game. At that point, anyone still moving should be trying to escape. My night vision in my sighting eye will be screwed, but I'll be able to see them silhouetted against the tunnel opening. I'm relying on you to take out anyone in the shadows." He paused. "Are your spare mags where you can get to them quickly?"

Keith patted his hip pocket. "Yes, sir."

Tremble patted Keith's shoulder. "Good man," he said, and moved across the tunnel to his own position and switched off the light.

CHAPTER THREE

Approaching New Blue Ridge Rail Tunnel
3.5 Miles Southeast of Waynesboro, VA

Jeff 'Spider' Harris, president of the Satan's Seed Motorcycle Club, stared at the rapidly enlarging black hole of the tunnel entrance and cursed. If Renfro let the shooters get away, he'd castrate the moron personally, right out in the parking lot with everyone watching.

But that wasn't going to happen, they were going through this tunnel to nail these guys, whoever they were. Nobody took down HIS boys and lived to tell about it. That notwithstanding, he had an uneasy feeling about this, a touch of the 'Spidey sense' that earned him his nickname. And now that he thought about it, charging into a black hole didn't seem like the smartest idea, even if that moron Renfro had cleared it first. In fact, leading the charge suddenly struck Spider as a particularly dumb idea, and he hadn't lived this long and gotten to the top by being dumb.

On the other hand, if he crept through the tunnel like an old lady or some kid afraid of the dark, and the shooters got away, he'd lose credibility with his boys — likewise if he didn't lead them through personally. The tunnel mouth was getting larger by the second, and his mind raced, trying to figure out some way to get out of this position without looking like a pussy. Then it hit him.

Spider slipped his thumb over and flipped the bootleg toggle switch he'd installed on his handlebars to kill his headlight. He sounded his horn, and Roadkill, leading the column to the left of the tracks, glanced over. Spider pointed down toward his own headlight, then motioned his second-in-command forward. Roadkill pulled ahead a bit to get a better look at Spider's headlight and then shook his head. Spider made a show of flipping the toggle switch several times (without actually touching it) and shot Roadkill another questioning look. Roadkill shook his head again, and Spider feigned irritation followed by a resigned shrug.

Now that it was obvious Spider's headlight was out, he moved to the right and waved the four riders behind him forward, then dropped into last place in the right column. An unnecessary precaution perhaps, but better safe than sorry.

***

Tremble watched the riders in one of the approaching columns shuffle positions, unsure what that meant. However, they were close now and he had no time to worry about it. The bikers slowed at the tunnel entrance and spaced themselves out a bit, but as he'd hoped, they didn't stop.

When they were fifty yards inside the tunnel, Tremble's first shot took out the headlight of the lead bike of the left column. Startled, the biker swerved in the close confines of the tunnel and glanced off the wall to veer back into the path of the rider behind him. Both went down in a heap, setting off a chain reaction behind them.

The tunnel flashed red as the bikers braked at once, and Tremble's second shot took out the headlight of the lead bike on the right. Silhouetted in the lights behind him, the rider was an equally easy target; he fell to a shot center mass.

It was instantaneous bedlam as the roar of the bikes and shouts and screams of their riders were punctuated by the thunderous bark of the rifle, echoing in the confined space. Tremble had a fleeting thought he should have plugged his ears, as he took out four more headlights in rapid succession. He got a fifth light, but the flash of taillights revealed that two riders had managed to turn their bikes. With the headlights pointed the other way, it was time to call up reinforcements.

"KEITH! GO! GO! GO!"

Keith's rifle sounded beside him immediately, and Tremble drew a bead on one of the escaping bikers, both of whom were silhouetted against the light of the tunnel entrance. He dropped them both before they cleared the tunnel. Here and there, the surviving bikers crouched behind their downed bikes and returned fire, but the advantage was still with the Trembles. For the moment.

"How's your vision?" Tremble yelled to Keith over the noise.

"Not great with the muzzle flashes, but I can still see movement in the shadows," Keith yelled back.

"In the land of the blind, the one-eyed man is king," Tremble said. "Unload on anything you see moving. I'll target the muzzle flashes."

The firefight continued and then crested as the surprised bikers fell victim to the Trembles' deadly accurate fire and quickly surmised a muzzle flash invited instant death. The tunnel grew quiet, and Tremble's eardrums rang with the assault on his senses, compromising his hearing. There were an unknown number of bikers left, lying prone behind their downed bikes. Not good, Tremble thought as he pondered a way to break the stalemate.

***

Spider was lagging behind the right column when they were ambushed, and that was all that saved him from the chain-reaction pileup. He'd started to run for it, but again his 'Spidey sense' was tingling, and he pulled close to the tunnel wall and stayed still, no headlight to reveal his location as he assessed the situation. His caution was justified when the two runners were gunned down, and he realized the shooter spotted them by their taillights and waited for them to be silhouetted in the tunnel opening. Moving slowly in the dark to avoid attracting attention, he got off the bike and smashed his own taillight with the butt of his handgun. He'd just gotten the bike turned around when a round ricocheted nearby, and he killed his bike and dropped out of sight between the bike and the tunnel wall.

The massacre had taken only seconds. Three of his boys were still returning fire, but the outcome was a foregone conclusion. Spider looked toward the tunnel mouth and weighed his options. The two runners had been dumb asses, hugging the track near the center of the tunnel, no doubt concerned about grazing the tunnel wall in the dark. But staying on a straight path near the center of the tunnel also made them much easier targets for the shooter, who was damned good. If Spider was going to escape, he'd have to veer back and forth across the tunnel erratically. Bumping back and forth over the tracks would slow him down, but he had to make himself as difficult a target as possible. If he got that far; he knew as soon as he even got on the bike he was likely to draw fire. What he really needed was a diversion. He called softly through the dark to the nearest biker.

"This is Spider. Who's there, and are you wounded?"

"Flathead. And no, I ain't wounded, but I'm near out of ammo," came the reply.

"Who else is there, are they wounded, and can you call to them without those shooters hearing?" Spider asked.

"Monk and Cricket. Monk's okay, but I think Cricket took one in the left arm. And yeah, they can hear me. Why?" Flathead asked.

"'Cause the only way any of us are getting out of here is if we all haul ass at once. Can you get to your bikes?"

"They're screwed. The ones that ain't tangled up are shot to hell by now. We might get three working, but not with these bastards shooting at us," Flathead said.

Spider cursed softly. "All right, then you'll have to run for it."

"You mean, like, on foot?" Flathead asked.

"Of course on foot, dickhead. How else are y'all gonna get out of here?"

Silence.

"And y'all can't run in a straight line 'cause it makes you easy to target. When I give the word, I want everyone on their feet, running for the entrance. Everyone runs along the walls, then zigzags across the tunnel to the opposite wall—back and forth, back and forth—got it? And DO NOT BUNCH UP. Y'all need to keep 'em confused; otherwise you're dead meat. Now pass the word to Monk and Cricket and tell me when everyone's ready. Got it?" Spider asked.

"Yeah, I got it," Flathead replied, far from enthusiastically.

A moment later, Flathead confirmed the men were ready.

"GO!" Spider yelled, sitting still until his men's movements began to draw fire. Then he fired up his bike and started a zigzag course for the tunnel entrance.

***

Tremble stood in the dark, listening to the surviving bikers talk among themselves, but unable to make out what they were saying. He was pondering how to end the stalemate when he heard a shout followed by the sound of movement. One of the men was outlined briefly against the tunnel entrance before disappearing once more into the shadows.

"They're running," Tremble shouted across to Keith, hardly able to hear his own voice. "We can't let them get away—"

The sound of the bike starting was a distinctive snarl, even to his battered ears, and it grew louder as the bike accelerated.

"FORGET THE RUNNERS! TARGET THE BIKE!" Tremble yelled as he opened fire on the bike roaring past the men on foot, zigzagging across the tunnel and bouncing over the tracks with each transit.

Keith scored the first hit, shredding the rear tire just as the bike exited the tunnel. The biker was fighting for control, struggling to keep the machine upright, when Tremble sent a round into the man's right shoulder. The bike went down hard in the gravel ballast of the track, but the rider rose with a long gun and darted to the right, out of the opening framed by the tunnel entrance.

"HE'S GETTING AWAY!" Keith yelled.

"Nothing we can do," Tremble said. "We have to get the others."

Panicked at their leader abandoning them, the three remaining bikers stopped zigzagging and ran straight for the exit; they fell like ducks in a shooting gallery.

Tremble dug the flashlight from his pocket and handed it to Keith.

"We have to assess the situation, but we're not leaving anybody alive to back shoot us after we pass. Shine the light on each body as we pass, and I'll make sure they're dead," Tremble said.

"Yes, sir," Keith said, and they started out of the tunnel.

"All these guys have ARs on their bikes," Keith said as they picked their way through the carnage. "Why not use them?"

Tremble kept his eyes on the bodies, alert to any signs of life. Only when he was sure there were none did he respond.

"If they had time to think, they would have, which is why we didn't give them any. The guys firing back were separated from their bikes and used the guns on their hips because they had no other options. And the guys still on their bikes just wanted to escape," Tremble said.

As they neared the entrance, he held up his hand.

"And speaking of long guns, the guy outside managed to get his out before he ran off. I know I hit him, but like as not, he's sitting up in the woods, waiting for us to step out," Tremble said. "So we're not going to do that unless we have to."

Keith looked confused. "Then why did we come back to the entrance?"

Tremble pulled out the radio.

"Because we have to figure out where the other radio is. It's either somewhere back there in that mess in the tunnel, on that bike outside, or with the guy that got away, and that determines our next move," Tremble said.

He keyed the mic. "Test, test, test."

His words echoed back from outside the tunnel.

"It's on the bike," Keith said. "I see a pouch hanging off the handlebars. I bet it's in there."

Tremble nodded as he raised his M4. "Let's test that theory."

He put three rounds in the pouch, then tried another test transmission and heard nothing. He nodded to Keith. "Looks like you were right. Let's both empty a mag into that bike to make damn sure it's not going anywhere."

Tremble punctuated his statement by opening fire on the bike, concentrating on the engine and tires, and Keith followed suit. When they lowered their rifles, Keith turned to his father.

"What about the guy outside? Do we go after him?"

"Negative. He's got the advantage now. He knows where we are and we have no clue as to his position. He'd get one of us for sure. I actually hope he IS sitting out there waiting; we need all the time we can get. But even if he does decide to go back to the camp, he has to make it up a thousand feet of steep brush-covered hill and then hike two miles, and he's wounded to boot. We probably have twenty or thirty minutes at least, so let's make the best of them."

Tremble nodded toward the nearest bikes, the ones ridden by the two bikers who tried to escape.

"Go over those bikes and see if they're operational. I don't think I hit these two, but all the rest took quite a few rounds."

Keith grinned. "You mean it?"

"We've got no choice now. With a survivor who knows our whereabouts, if we leave on foot, it can only mean we're on the Appalachian Trail, so they might hunt us down. And we sure can't get very far carrying these kids, so we pretty much have to take the bikes." Tremble gave Keith a pointed look. "But it's still a riskier means of travel, so don't get your hopes up. We're going back on the trail when I'm sure we're clear of these guys. Now get busy. I'm gonna check the bodies and the other bikes for ammo, food, or anything else we might be able to use. You have enough light here to see what you're doing?"

Keith nodded and handed his father the flashlight.

"Come give me a hand when you're done," Tremble said, and started back deeper into the tunnel.

As Tremble approached the site of the ambush, the pungent smell of gasoline assaulted his nose. The firefight had been brief but furious, with the bikers sheltering behind the downed bikes, so he doubted even one of the remaining bikes had an intact gas tank. He ignored the smell and began the grisly task of stripping the dead.

Most of the bikers had ARs on their bikes, with no shortage of usable ammunition. There was no food in the saddlebags, but he found a few bottles of water and several working flashlights. As he began to stack the loot against the tunnel wall, he heard Keith fire up first one bike, then another. Shortly Keith rode toward him, the bike's headlight a beacon in the darkness.

"They're both good; a half tank of gas in each. Maybe we could ..." Keith wrinkled his nose. "I guess not. All the gas is on the ground, right?"

"Mostly," Tremble said. "And we've got no siphon hose anyway."

"What if I took one of the empty water bottles and caught the gas draining out of the bullet holes? There's probably a little left in each tank and if I rocked each bike, I could collect it. It might be enough to top up the two tanks."

Tremble looked skeptical, but handed Keith one of the newly acquired flashlights. "All right, but don't take too long. I'm done scavenging and we need to leave in ten minutes max. While you're doing that, I'm going to grab the maps and figure the best way out of here. Then we throw everything on the bikes, load up the kids, and leave. Got it?"

Keith nodded, and Tremble walked over to retrieve a map from Keith's pack and spread it on the tunnel floor. Determining their escape route took less time than he thought, because there weren't a lot of choices—roads through the mountains were few and far between. He went over the route a second time to fix it in his memory, then folded the map and slipped it in his back pocket for easy access.

He looked over as Keith brought up the second bike and began pouring gasoline into the tank from a half-liter water bottle.

"How's it going?" Tremble asked.

"This is it," Keith said, tossing the bottle aside and twisting the cap back on the gas tank. "Not as much as I'd hoped, but I got maybe an extra gallon in both bikes. Let's start loading up."

They tied their makeshift packs in front of the handlebars and stowed their newfound wealth of ammo and water in the saddlebags. After double-checking to make sure everything was secure, they started the bikes and rode down the tunnel.

"Wait a minute," Tremble said as he circled back to stop several feet from the tangle of bikes and dead bikers. "I'll be damned if I want any of these guys salvaging firearms or bike parts."

He dug in his pocket for a box of matches, courtesy of Levi Jenkins, struck one, and tossed it at the jumble of bikes and bodies. The gasoline ignited with a whoosh, almost singeing his eyebrows, and bathing the interior of the tunnel in an eerie, flickering light. He turned his bike and they rode down the tunnel to where the bound children lay on the tunnel floor.

"Ahh … How you want to do this, Dad?" Keith asked.

Tremble sighed. "We can't untie them yet. This is going to take some explaining, and now isn't the time. Molly's beyond understanding anyway, and all the boy knows is that some biker bashed him in the face, and when he woke up, two strangers were tying up his sister. I say we free their ankles and put them astride the bikes in front of us, where we can hold on to them if necessary. Otherwise, we have to free their hands so they can hold on, and I don't think that's a good idea just yet."

"I agree," Keith said, dismounting. "You stay there. I'll put them on the bikes."

Neither of the children struggled, and soon they were in place. Keith remounted his bike behind the boy and looked over at his dad. "So where to?"

"Directly away from the trail to start, to throw any followers off our track. We follow the tracks east into Afton, then take Afton Mountain Road south to Rockfish Valley Highway. At Beech Grove Road, we'll cut back due west to the intersection of the Appalachian Trail and the Blue Ridge Parkway at Reeds Gap. We'll end up back on the trail twenty miles south of the biker camp and then reassess the situation," Tremble said, but there was hesitancy in his voice.

"You don't sound too sure, Dad."

"I'm not; it's just our only viable option. There are several intersections along the way, so even if the bikers somehow pick up our trail, it will grow cold pretty quickly. But I'm more worried about the unknown. It's a short run, but the roads are like corkscrews and rural, but populated. There are several small communities and plenty of houses along the route, as well as a few vineyards and other small businesses. I'm thinking there'll be plenty of self-reliant and well-armed country folks, and we could just as easily be shot by good guys as bad guys."

"At least we won't be exposed long. It'll be a half hour at most," Keith said.

Tremble snorted. "Right. A half-hour dash through Second Amendment country on outlaw bikers' motorcycles, wearing FEMA uniforms and carrying two bound and gagged children. What could possibly go wrong?"

Appalachian Trail
Maupin Field Shelter
Mile 1348.3 Southbound
South of Reeds Gap, VA

Same Day - 12:20 p.m.

Tremble's fears notwithstanding, they made the short run to Reeds Gap without incident. They met no vehicles, and though armed people stared at them at a distance from near homes and outbuildings, their body language telegraphing both anger at the sight of the bound children and indecision at the prospect of interfering in something that might end up jeopardizing their own families, no one attempted to stop them. He had no doubt things might have been different if they hadn't flashed by quickly, and he constantly checked his mirror until they pulled off the paved road at Reeds Gap and were swallowed once again by the thick woods on either side of the trail.

The Appalachian Trail wasn't particularly challenging at this point, and the heavy road bikes negotiated it easily. Tremble took the lead as they rode south on the trail to the first field shelter. It was a primitive structure, three-sided and open in the front, just sufficient to give hikers a place to sleep out of the elements. He rolled to a stop and Keith pulled up beside him.

"We're a good two miles from any road," Tremble said. "This is as good a place to stop as any, and we need to take care of the kids and figure out what we're going to do. We'll camp in the woods, well off the trail."

Keith nodded, and Tremble led the way into the woods behind the shelter, creeping along slowly so he'd be able to stop the bike if necessary. Fifty yards off the trail, he judged they were out of sight, stopped, and dismounted.

"Let's sit the kids over by that tree; then you make a fire hole and get some water boiling while I go back and cover our tracks," Tremble said.

Keith moved to comply, and when both children were sitting with their backs against a big oak tree, Tremble started through the woods on foot, back the way they'd come. When he reached the main trail, he started backing toward the campsite, carefully scanning the ground and brush for signs of their passage. The forest floor was thick with years of dead and decaying leaves supporting a variety of low-lying ground cover, mashed flat here and there by the heavy bikes' passage. Tremble picked up a dead branch and broke off a four-foot length with a forked end and used it to tease the mashed ground cover back into place. When he was done, he retraced his route again to examine the result, careful where he stepped to avoid leaving footprints. His efforts were unlikely to deceive an experienced tracker, but they would serve to shield their location from the eyes of a casual passerby. He judged it sufficient.

The task took him longer than he anticipated, and when he returned, Keith was checking the contents of a small pot balanced over a Dakota fire hole near the base of a tree. Tremble squatted beside him.

"Almost boiling," Keith said. "What's the plan?"

"I thought we'd feed them first," Tremble said softly. "They don't look like they've been eating regularly, and we have to do something to gain their trust. How we fixed for food?"

"We have two freeze-dried meals left, both chicken and biscuits. Besides that, we have about half the bag of pasta, about half the nuts, and maybe a third of the beef jerky. I thought we might stretch it out to four days, but with the kids it will be less," Keith said, following his father's lead and keeping his voice down so the kids couldn't hear.

Tremble shrugged. "Then we'll have to stop to set snares anyway, so we may as well enjoy a good meal now. Fix both the backpacker meals and add some of the crushed pasta to stretch them; then we'll split it four ways. Let's get it cooked before we untie them. Maybe the smell of the food will distract them."

Twenty minutes later, the Trembles squatted beside the children, and Simon Tremble opened one of the resealable foil food pouches. The pleasant odor of cooking food rolled out of the pouch, eliciting a definite response from the boy, but none from Molly. Tremble nodded, and Keith set his still-sealed pouch on the ground. They had decided it would be better if Molly weren't blindfolded and gagged when the boy first saw her again, so Keith went to work removing the tape. After a moment's hesitation, he ripped it away quickly, but the girl still showed no reaction.

"Okay, kid," Tremble said to the boy, "it's time to eat, so I'm going to untape your mouth and eyes. I'll do it quick, but it may hurt and there's nothing I can do about that. Do you understand?"

The boy hesitated, his body tense and telegraphing nonverbal defiance, but in the end the smell of the food trumped his anger. He nodded, and Tremble ripped away the tape. The boy blinked in the bright daylight, squeezed his eyes shut, then opened them to mere slits until he became accustomed to the light. His relief at the sight of his sister was palpable, and Tremble realized with a flash of guilt the youngster had had no way of knowing whether or not his sister was still with him.

"Are you hungry?" Tremble asked.

The boy looked at Tremble, anger not gratitude in his eyes, but hunger prevailed. He nodded and Tremble stuck a plastic spoon into the foil pouch and took a small bite to confirm it wasn't too hot to eat. Satisfied, he dipped out a spoonful and held it to the boy's mouth.

The boy started to take a bite and then stopped. "Let Molly eat first. I'll eat when she's done."

Tremble nodded towards Keith. "There's plenty. Keith here is going to feed Molly."

On cue, Keith opened his pouch and held a spoonful to Molly's mouth. Though nonreactive in most regards, the smell of the food apparently triggered a more primal response, and Molly opened her mouth immediately and accepted the food. The boy watched her swallow several more spoonfuls, then opened his own mouth and let Tremble feed him. After a few spoonfuls, Tremble set the pouch and spoon down and fished out his pocketknife. The boy stiffened

"Relax, kid," Tremble said. "You and Molly aren't prisoners. While you were unconscious, we rescued you from the bikers, but you were fighting us and making a lot of noise, so we had to tape you up so we could all escape. I'm going to cut your hands free now so you can feed yourself, but first I want your promise you won't do anything stupid. After you've eaten, you can decide whether you want to stay with us or go off on your own. Deal?"

Keith shot his father a questioning look at the mention the children might go off on their own. Tremble ignored it and stared at the boy, who nodded slowly. Tremble sliced through the duct tape and freed the boy's wrists and ankles before handing him the pouch and spoon.

Tremble immediately had second thoughts about his decision as the boy began shoveling the food into his mouth.

"Easy, easy. You're going to choke yourself. Here, have some water." Tremble handed the boy a half-full bottle of water, which he downed in three gulps and went back to shoveling in the food.

The boy finished the entire pouch in record time, licked the spoon clean, then turned the pouch inside out and licked the inside clean as well. Only then did he look over to where Keith was feeding his sister.

"I can feed Molly," he said. "And why is she still taped up?"

"Because we didn't know how she'd react and we don't have time to chase her if she runs," Tremble said.

"She'll stay with me," the boy said, moving to his sister's side.

Tremble hesitated and shot Keith a warning look. Keith set the food packet on the ground and moved to Tremble's side as Tremble made a show of taking out his pocketknife and handing it to the boy.

"Here," Tremble said, "why don't you cut her loose before you feed her?"

The boy took the open knife and stared at it, as if debating whether to cut his sister free or attack his recent captors. With a visible effort, he turned to his sister and gently sliced through the tape binding her wrists and ankles, closed the knife, and handed it back to Tremble.

Wordlessly, the boy turned back to his sister and began to feed her.

"Looks like it's a jerky and nuts dinner for us," Keith whispered to his father, who smiled wanly and nodded.

***

The boy's name was Jamie Mills and his family had been hijacked two weeks earlier as they attempted to make it to his grandparents' farm in Tennessee. His father was murdered and then 'more bad stuff happened.' Jamie didn't go into detail at first, nor did Tremble ask; he had no trouble imagining what the family endured. He turned the conversation to Molly.

"Does Molly talk at all?"

Jamie shook his head. "She mostly stopped talking when they killed Daddy. She cried a lot and they told Mom they'd kill Molly too if she couldn't make her shut up. Mom got Molly to stop crying, but she hardly talked at all after that. They kept us all locked in a room up in that crummy motel and didn't give us any food, but there was water from the bathroom faucets. We found an old soda bottle in the room, one of the big ones, and we filled it from the bathtub faucet and took turns drinking from it. We were really hungry, and then after a couple of days, one of them came in with a can of soup and started whispering something to Mom. She shook her head, but he kept talking and looking over at us and he must have been talking about us, because Mom looked real scared, and finally she nodded. She was crying and came over to us and told us to go sit in the closet and close the door and not to come out until she came for us."

Jamie stopped, obviously having difficulty talking about it, and Tremble didn't press him. Just when he thought the boy would say no more, he continued.

"There was a lot of funny noise for a while and then the biker guy laughed and the room door slammed. Then I heard Mom in the bathroom and it sounded like she was throwing up. When she opened the closet door, she was standing there trying to smile and holding up the soup can, but I could tell she'd been crying. She sat us on the bed and opened the can and had Molly and I each eat half the soup," Jamie said.

"After that," he continued, "guys started coming to the door all the time and Mom would tell us to get in the closet. Sometimes there was food when they left, but mostly they just said they'd hurt Molly and me if Mom didn't do what they wanted. When there was food, Mom almost never ate any and made us eat her share. I . . . I tried to get her to eat some, but she said I needed it to stay strong so I could take care of Molly."

Jaimie lapsed into silence and Tremble could only nod, his rage robbing him of the power of speech. Keith's young face was twisted into a scowl, as he shared his father's outrage at the ordeal inflicted upon this young family.

After a long moment, Tremble composed himself enough to speak. "How did you get away, son?"

"Last night one of them came to the door and said they were having a party in the bar and that Mom had to come. She didn't want to go, but the biker pulled out his gun and pointed it at me, so she said yes. Then she tried to take us, but he made her leave us in the room. She was gone a long time and it was really dark because they didn't let us have any candles or anything. We stayed there a long time until it was just starting to get light outside. Th-that's when it happened," Jamie said.

"What happened?" Tremble asked.

"Th-the one they called Rooster came into the room. He was really drunk and he smelled bad. He threw Molly on the bed, and when I tried to fight him, he grabbed me by the throat and said if I didn't shut up and get in the closet, he'd kill Molly. So . . . so I did it."

Jamie paused and swallowed, his lower lip trembling as if he was about to burst into tears. Tremble laid a comforting hand on the boy's shoulder.

"Molly started screaming and Rooster was yelling at her to shut up if she knew what was good for her. I didn't know what to do; then I heard the door open and Mom was screaming at Rooster. I heard them start fighting and then it sounded like Mom was strangling. I opened the closet door and Rooster was on top of Mom on the bed, choking her with both hands, with his face right down in her face, screaming at her. I grabbed the soda bottle from the closet. It was almost full and pretty heavy and I ran over and hit Rooster on the back of the head as hard as I could. He fell across Mom and I tried to roll him off, but he was too heavy. I was crying then and really scared and I was shaking Mom to wake up and help me, but she wouldn't and then I figured out sh-she was dead. I thought Rooster was dead too and I was glad, because he'd not only killed Mom, but he was the one who killed Dad. Molly was curled up in the corner with her eyes closed and shaking, and I knew we had to get out of there. Rooster stole my dad's gun, so I took it from his belt and put it and the water bottle in my book bag and then got Molly and left. The sun was just coming up and it was hard because I had to drag Molly from one hiding spot to another until we got clear of the camp. It took a long time and I think the only reason we got away was because most of them were still drunk and sleeping after their party. I didn't really know where I was going, I was just running. That's all I remember until I saw Rooster again and he hit me."

"You're a pretty brave guy," Tremble said.

Jamie shook his head, slowly at first, then more emphatically as his face dissolved into an anguished mask. His lower lip began to quiver again.

"It … it's my fault," he croaked. "Wh-when Dad went on business trips, he always said I was the man of the house and to look out for Mom and Molly. And … and now Mom's dead and Molly's … like she is, and it's all my fault."

The boy burst into tears and Tremble pulled him into his lap, hugging him and patting his back until the tears subsided. When Jamie calmed, Tremble sat him back down on the ground and put a hand on each of the boy's shoulders. Jamie was downcast, unwilling to meet Tremble's eye.

"Jamie, look at me," Tremble said softly.

Reluctantly, the boy raised his head.

"This is NOT your fault. You've been incredibly brave and resourceful, and your sister wouldn't be alive now if not for you. If you were my son, I'd be proud of you, and I can guarantee your mom and dad are looking down from heaven and they're proud of you too. Not many grown men would have the courage to do what you did. I want you to remember that."

"You … you really think so?" Jamie asked.

"I know so," Tremble said, "so just put any idea it's your fault out of your head, okay?"

Jamie sniffed and wiped his nose with the back of his hand. "Okay."

Tremble released the boy's shoulders. "Now, you have to decide what you want to do. I can give you back your dad's gun and half the food, and you and Molly can go your own way, or you can come to Wilmington with us."

"I guess I need to get Molly to Tennessee. Is Wilmington on the way?"

"It's in the opposite direction, I'm afraid, but you could come with us and rest up in Wilmington and plan your trip to Tennessee. Where do your grandparents live?"

The boy looked surprised as if something just occurred to him. "I … I guess I don't really know for sure. They have a farm near Nashville, but I'm not sure exactly where. I never thought I'd have to get there on my own."

Tremble stroked his chin and nodded. "Well, that could be a problem. Why don't y'all come to Wilmington with us and then we'll try to figure it out from there." He looked over at Keith. "We could use another good man on the trip, don't you think, Keith?"

Keith nodded. "Absolutely."

Jamie looked relieved. "I guess we can do that."

His little face hardened. "But when Molly's safe, I'm gonna come back here and kill that Rooster."

Tremble said nothing for a long moment, shocked by the ferocity of the boy's sudden anger.

"You won't have to," Tremble said. "I killed him right after he knocked you out. Most of the other bikers are dead too."

The boy considered that for a moment, then nodded. "Thank you."

Tremble returned the nod, inwardly saddened at the thought this was the 'new normal,' a world where monsters could inflict such pain, and a ten-year-old boy could casually thank you for killing them.

***

The children were exhausted and it was obvious they couldn't continue. The Trembles made a mattress of evergreen boughs and with full stomachs and feeling secure for the first time in days, the kids were soon snoring softly, dead to the world.

Keith looked over at them and nodded. "They've been through hell. It's good to see them sleeping peacefully."

"That it is," Tremble agreed.

"So, Dad," Keith asked, "you weren't seriously going to let them go off on their own, were you?"

Tremble shook his head. "Of course not, but I thought things would go a lot better if Jamie made the decision on his own. He hasn't had much control over his life and he needs that, to say nothing of what a pain in the ass it would be if he thought we were forcing him to do something. This is going to be tough enough without worrying about them trying to sneak off."

"So what is the plan?" Keith asked.

Tremble studied the map spread out before him and sighed.

"I don't see we have much choice. We can't make much progress with the kids, even if Molly didn't have the bum leg. We have to stick with the bikes at least as far as the gas will carry us," Tremble said.

Keith grinned. "Finally! We can make some progress."

Tremble shook his head. "Don't get too excited, because we're not blasting down the highway in the open. These are road bikes, not trail bikes, but we can use them on sections of the Appalachian Trail where the terrain isn't too challenging. We have about another hundred miles of the Blue Ridge Parkway, and the trail cuts back and forth and intersects the parkway in over a dozen places. I figure we'll study the AT guidebook and figure out the terrain for each stretch of trail. If it looks like we can get over it with the bikes, we'll take the trail to the next intersection. If the trail appears to be too tough, we'll take the parkway, get off the road, and assess the next section. The intersections are twenty miles apart or less, so we should be on the open parkway for less than a half hour at a time."

Keith nodded, still grinning, his exuberance undiminished by his father's caution. "When do we leave?"

Tremble looked over at the sleeping children. "We're back to living off the land, so we have to gather some food anyway. We'll let them rest today and all of tomorrow while we set snares and deadfalls and see what we can gather as far as mushrooms and berries. We'll check our traps tomorrow morning then spend the rest of the day processing and drying the meat." He sighed. "It looks like rabbit and squirrel jerky are back on the menu."

Keith made a face. "Yum."

"Look at the bright side," Tremble said. "At least we have salt and pepper now."

CHAPTER FOUR

Saddle Gap
Appalachian Trail
Mile 1398.2 Southbound
50 Miles South of the Trembles' Position

Same Day - 5 a.m.
(Ten Hours Earlier)

George Anderson sat with his back against a fallen tree, sipping the horrible instant coffee from the MRE. He could just make out Cindy's form in the early morning light as she knelt beside Jeremy a few feet away on his makeshift mattress of evergreen boughs. She rose and walked over to sink down beside Anderson, then switched on her headlamp to study the fever thermometer in her hand. She nodded to herself and switched off the light.

"What is it?" Anderson asked.

"One hundred point two," Cindy said. "It's coming down. The antibiotics are working, thank God. He should be fine by tomorrow or the next day."

"Sounds like the voice of experience," Anderson said.

She sighed, and he saw her nod in the growing light of the new day. "Yes, unfortunately. Down Syndrome kids have a lot of related medical issues; Jeremy's prone to bladder and urinary tract infections. That's why I'm always nagging him to drink water and stay hydrated. It's usually not bad if I catch it and start the antibiotics in time, but I don't know what we'll do when they run out. I kept a pretty good supply at the cabin because we were so remote, but they all have a shelf life."

Cindy lapsed into silence, and Anderson could think of nothing to say. She was right; the future wasn't bright for those with chronic medical problems.

"I'm sorry we're slowing you down, but I appreciate your patience. I know it must be hard to just sit here and stare at the trees for days," she said.

Anderson chuckled softly, put his arm around her and pulled her close.

"Slowing ME down," he said. "It seems like I recall you're the one all fired up to get to Wilmington. Besides, I'm sure the apocalypse isn't going anywhere."

Cindy sighed. "Unfortunately."

Anderson changed the subject. "I'm still concerned about crossing the James. How far do you think we are from the river? Five miles?"

"About that, maybe six at the outside. I've never actually been this far south on the trail. Why?"

"Because if we're going to have problems, I think it'll be there. If there aren't feds sitting on the crossing, there may be freelance toll collectors," Anderson said.

"I know there's a footbridge for trail traffic, but like I said, I've never been this far south. But a footbridge would be low priority for the feds, right? And there's no traffic on the trail, so any freelancers probably gave up on it long ago," Cindy said.

Anderson looked unconvinced, but he smiled and pulled her close. "Well, like they say, we'll just have to cross that bridge when we come to it."

Presidential Quarters
Camp David Complex
Maryland

Same Day - 9 a.m.

Oliver Armstrong Crawford, Secretary of Homeland Security, finished his briefing and then waited anxiously for what he assumed would be an outburst. To his surprise, the Honorable Theodore M. Gleason, President of the United States of America, set his coffee cup down on the low table separating them and leaned back into his easy chair, nodding.

"Lemons to lemonade, Ollie. Lemons to lemonade. We've been waiting for a good time to announce Daniel's death, and there's no time like the present. We can roll that into the continued report of this latest atrocity in Wilmington. The more crimes we can lay at Fort Box's doorstep, the more we can discredit them."

Crawford returned Gleason's nod and sipped his now cold coffee as he considered the possibilities. Vice President Cyrus Daniel's helicopter had crashed ten days earlier en route from his emergency shelter at Cheyenne Mountain to his home in Sacramento, California, where he was going (against a direct presidential order) to 'oversee recovery efforts.' The chopper went down under 'mysterious circumstances' with no survivors and the deaths had yet to be broadcast to the public over the Emergency Alert System. Crawford looked up to see Gleason glaring at him, his brief temperate mood broken by Crawford's failure to voice immediate and enthusiastic agreement for his last proposal.

"You disagree, Ollie?" There was quiet menace in Gleason's voice.

"No, Mr. President," Crawford said quickly, "but perhaps you should let the cabinet know of the Vice President's death before you go public on the EAS."

Gleason gave a dismissive wave. "They're irrelevant. None of them have the balls for what we have to do, that's why I put you in charge."

Gleason's eyes narrowed. "And it's also why I had the bunch of them moved down to Mount Weather so you could ride herd on them. Are you telling me you can't handle that?"

"I can handle it fine, Mr. President," Crawford said. "But each of the remaining cabinet members still have scattered connections, and if I'm to control them while still maintaining the fiction of 'business as usual,' I do need you to put in an appearance from time to time to remind them who's in charge. My thoughts are the announcement of the Vice President's death might present a perfect opportunity to do so while simultaneously sending a not-so-subtle message as to the penalty for disloyalty. I feel the news would be much more effective coming directly from you, sir."

Gleason stroked his chin. "You might be right." He nodded. "Okay, set up a video link."

Crawford hesitated, he hoped convincingly. "I'm sorry, sir, but the video link between here and Mount Weather is down. The technical people tell me it will be at least a week before they can have it working again."

"Well, I'm not waiting a damn week to make the announcement. Get them up here for a briefing, then," Gleason said.

"With respect, sir, I was hoping you'd be willing to make a quick chopper trip down to Mount Weather, not only to brief the cabinet but perhaps to make a short inspection tour? You're isolated here, and I think at least the upper echelon of the rank and file should see you occasionally. An appearance will be good for morale, sir, especially given our recent setbacks."

Gleason said nothing for a while, and Crawford held his breath, fearing an outburst, but finally Gleason sighed and nodded.

"All right, goddamn it, but not in some damn tunnel. You know that place gives me the creeps. I want to stay above ground."

"Not a problem, Mr. President." Crawford looked at his watch. "I can be back in Mount Weather in a half hour and arrange things for early afternoon if that's convenient."

"All right, all right," Gleason said.

Crawford rose. "Thank you, Mr. President. If that will be all, I'll get things rolling."

"See that you do," Gleason said, "and Ollie?"

"Yes, Mr. President?"

"We'll try to turn this Wilmington situation to our advantage, but you'd better get that cleaned up, and soon. We have the upper hand as far as communications go, but there are still too damn many ham sets out there and unrest is spreading in Texas and a dozen other places. If you can't handle this, I'll find someone who can. Is that clear?"

"Crystal, Mr. President. I won't let you down," Crawford said.

Gleason snorted. "Too late there, I'm afraid. Just make damn sure you get this Wilmington situation laid to rest if you know what's good for you."

Helipad M-4
FEMA Emergency Operations Center
Mount Weather
Near Bluemont, VA

Same Day - 9:45 a.m.

Ollie Crawford exited the chopper and rushed across the tarmac to the waiting SUV and climbed into the front passenger seat.

"So he took the bait?" asked Brigadier General Quentin Rorke, commander of the FEMA Special Reaction Force (SRF), as he pulled the SUV off the tarmac and headed toward the office complex.

"Hook, line, and sinker. So everything better be ready on your end," Crawford said.

Rorke nodded, his eyes on the road. "I've had an Apache staged at the Charlottesville airport since yesterday, and I mobilized them as soon as you radioed me the code word. They'll be landing at M-7 within the hour."

"Weapons load out?"

"We trucked the munitions up from the Military Ocean Terminal at Wilmington to Charlottesville, four Hellfires on either side, and a full twelve hundred rounds for the chain gun." Rorke smiled. "I think that should be more than adequate."

"It better be. I don't need to tell you what happens if we fail. You sure everything is ready?" Crawford asked.

Rorke shrugged. "As sure as I can be. You know the deal."

Crawford did indeed 'know the deal.' The 1-130th Attack Reconnaissance Battalion (ARB) of the North Carolina Army National Guard was headquartered at the Morrisville Army Aviation War Fighting Center at

Raleigh-Durham International Airport, with twenty-four AH-64D Apache Longbow choppers and a reserve force of pilots and maintenance technicians. Strictly offensive weapons used primarily against armor and in close support of ground-combat forces, the 'tech-heavy' and high-maintenance Apaches were of little use for the type of missions required in the post-apocalyptic world. Consequently, though the 1-130th ARB was originally activated in the national emergency, it soon became clear they had no role to play, and one by one, the guardsmen had drifted home to protect their own families until the few who remained locked their facility and left, leaving their war birds lined up forlornly on the tarmac.

Rorke had been enthusiastic when he found the abandoned resources, though his enthusiasm waned when he discovered none of his mostly mercenary FEMA pilots and technicians possessed the skill sets to handle the Apaches. However, when the current situation arose, he'd done a 'workaround' to get at least one of the war birds aloft, if briefly. Scouring the duty roster of the abandoned ARB facility yielded the names and home addresses of two of the Apache pilots and a handful of maintenance techs, all of whom had been induced to 'volunteer' for his mission.

"Any more problems with the pilots or ground crew?" Crawford asked.

Rorke shook his head. "Given what's been going down, I really didn't have much difficulty convincing them of Gleason's continuing evil intentions. Portraying Homeland Security and the Special Reaction Force as 'unwilling pawns' was a harder sell, but in the end, what choice did they have? We have their families and we've made it clear what happens if they fail to cooperate. They accepted my story, if for no other reason than to convince themselves they're doing the right thing."

Crawford nodded, his anxiety easing a bit.

"And none too soon," Rorke continued. "This is actually coming together faster than I'd anticipated. I figured POTUS might need more convincing."

Crawford snorted. "The whole 'addressing the troops' thing appealed to his vanity, as I knew it would, and I've known about his claustrophobia and aversion to being underground for some time. Everything else is set up to make it look like we're bending over backward to avoid inconveniencing him. We'll have him land at M-1 and use the conference room in the unused operations building immediately adjacent. It's big enough to accommodate what's left of the cabinet and not staffed, so we won't have to worry about collateral damage to our own people." Crawford looked nervous again. "You sure these pilots know the target?"

"Relax, Mr. Secretary. We've done everything but paint a bull's-eye on it. They won't miss." Rorke grinned. "Not that it matters."

"Of course it matters," Crawford snapped. "This has to look like the real deal. Now humor me and go over it again."

Rorke suppressed an urge to roll his eyes.

"The Apache will be standing by at M-7 to pop up when you signal you're clear, and they'll launch as soon as they have eyes on the ops building. The elevation of Helipad M-7 is about two hundred feet lower down the mountain from the target, so they'll need about ten seconds to reach visual. Are you sure POTUS will only have the two choppers?"

Crawford nodded. "Fuel's short. We've scaled back to a single decoy for Marine One, flying over-watch during takeoffs and landings. Having a friendly pop up directly under him will come as a surprise, and all he has to do is hesitate long enough for the Apache to get off a Hellfire; then you can detonate our little surprise. Whether or not the Hellfire takes out the building, there's enough C-4 inside to vaporize it. But it has to LOOK like the Apache did the deed."

Rorke nodded. "Count on it. What about the advance team?"

Crawford shook his head. "They'll be here in an hour, but Gleason suffers with allergies from hell and refuses to let the dogs be used anywhere within twenty-four hours of his arrival, and they'll never spot the explosives without them. Besides, it's Mount Weather; the advance team will just be going through the motions."

Rorke nodded again as Crawford considered his actions for what seemed the thousandth time. The President was becoming increasingly ruthless, and after the murder of the Vice President, Crawford felt his own position was tenuous at best. He had no qualms about killing Gleason, but like any gamble, it came with its own unique set of risks. As Secretary of Homeland Security, he was dead last in the order of succession, and he enjoyed his current position as 'second in command' only by virtue of Gleason's patronage and direct intervention. With Gleason dead, every one of the six surviving cabinet secretaries legally outranked him.

"You said they'll have eight Hellfires?" Crawford asked.

Rorke nodded. "Yes. One should do the job, with a second for good measure, but I want to save the rest of the missiles for the Marine choppers and to have plenty of backup in case we have a problem."

"Use more. At least four on the building," Crawford said.

"Mr. Secretary?"

"I said use more Hellfires."

"But we don't need—"

"I SAID USE MORE, RORKE! CLEAR!"

Rorke bit off a reply. "Yes, Mr. Secretary."

Crawford calmed. "Look, Rorke, we have to think about how this is going to play out with the regular military. Gleason put them under my command already, but you know they haven't been particularly receptive. I don't want them to have any grounds to question my legal authority, so not only do I need everyone in that building dead, there can be no doubt the act was committed by a 'rogue element' of the North Carolina National Guard. The more explosions, the more confusion, the better. We'll have some challenges explaining how the Apache got on base to start with, but nothing we can't handle. The Marine pilots might be a problem, depending on how realistic our takedown is, so we can't screw this up. I want nothing left of that building but a smoking hole in the ground."

"I understand," Rorke said. "The crew of Marine One on the ground will be the closest witnesses, but they'll be sitting ducks for a Hellfire. I'm not sure about the over-watch. The Apache should be able to take it down, but they're reservists, and Marine One pilots are the best of the Marine Corps. If the airborne chopper makes a run for it, our National Guard guys might have their hands full."

Crawford stroked his chin. "That might not be a bad thing, presuming it looks like the Apache took out the building. If the Marine pilots are engaged by the Apache and escape, they'll be the perfect witnesses."

"So you want me to order the Apache pilots to fake an attack?"

Crawford shook his head. "No, have them go at it for real. If the Marines survive, it will be more convincing, and if they don't—" he shrugged "—then there are just more unfortunate casualties. The last thing we need is for the Marines to escape with the suspicion they were being played. Now what about the other loose ends?"

"All tied up," Rorke said. "There's a little surprise package hidden on the Apache, on an altimeter switch set to arm it when they reach seven hundred feet and then to detonate it when they fall below seven hundred feet again. We're at seventeen hundred feet here at Mount Weather, and the airport at Charlottesville is at five hundred ninety-four. The pilots won't make it to the ground in one piece, and the ground crew and all the families will disappear as soon as the Apache's mission is complete here. In a few hours, you'll be the constitutionally designated successor to the presidency with no witnesses around to shed light on how that transpired."

Helipad M-1
FEMA Emergency Operations Center
Mount Weather
Near Bluemont, VA

Same Day - 2:35 p.m.

Ollie Crawford sat at the wheel of a golf cart at the edge of Helipad M-1, watching Marine One settle to the ground. Four Secret Service men sat in pairs in golf carts on either side of him, their heads on swivels, watching the area as the President's chopper landed. Crawford suppressed a smile. They were one of the smaller advance teams, used for sweeps of 'secure' facilities like Mount Weather and other government installations. They'd spent almost four hours inspecting the now seldom-used operations building adjacent to the helipad, but Rorke's people were good; without the dogs, the advance team had little chance of finding the explosives.

Marine One settled gently to the tarmac and the door opened. Four Secret Service agents exited the chopper and deployed in a defensive semicircle around it. Crawford saw the Secret Service agent driving the golf cart next to his look toward the chopper and speak, obviously talking into his throat mike. The lead agent at the chopper motioned the golf carts forward, and they all drove towards Marine One, Crawford's golf cart sandwiched between the two Secret Service carts.

Crawford pulled up near Marine One and got out just as Gleason exited the chopper and crossed the short distance to the golf carts.

"Welcome to Mount Weather, Mr. President," Crawford said.

Gleason grunted and climbed into the passenger seat of the cart. "Cut the crap, Ollie. Let's just get this over with, shall we?"

"Absolutely, Mr. President," Crawford responded and climbed behind the wheel of the golf cart.

They made the short ride across the tarmac in silence and reached the operations building in less than sixty seconds. One of the Secret Service agents leaped out of the lead cart and hurried to hold the door open for Gleason and Crawford.

"This way to the conference room, Mr. President," Crawford said. "And I'll apologize in advance for the rather spartan surroundings, but I know you're busy and I thought using the old ops building beside the helipad would minimize your time on the ground."

Gleason nodded and followed Crawford's lead down the long hall.

None of the surviving functionaries felt it healthy to miss 'face time' with the President, especially under the current circumstances. Besides the six cabinet secretaries, their aides and support staff raised the number of attendees to an even two dozen. Crawford marveled inwardly as Gleason morphed into 'politician mode' as they entered the room, a broad smile on his face as all the attendees rose and he extended his hand to the nearest cabinet secretary. The man accepted Gleason's offered hand.

"Welcome, Mr. President," the man said.

"Great to be here, and great to see you again, John." The President beamed, making eye contact as he placed his left hand on the man's forearm, holding the 'two-handed shake' for a moment. "I can't tell you how much your support means to me, to our nation, in these troubled times."

Perfect, Crawford thought, realizing Gleason was going to work the room before he gave his little pep talk and laid down the law. Crawford suppressed a smile as he leaned forward and whispered in the President's ear, "Excuse me a moment, Mr. President; I'm going down the hall to the men's room."

Gleason nodded absently and turned toward the next cabinet member. Crawford made for the door and hurried back down the hall towards the men's room, then right past it to the main entrance. The Secret Service agent at the door turned at his approach.

"Can I help you, Mr. Secretary?" the agent asked.

Crawford smiled ruefully as he held up a small radio. "I wish you could, but I just got a call; another one of these damn things that crop up a dozen times a day. POTUS is all over this one, so I have to attend to it personally. And I have to hurry, as he wants me back here in a half hour."

The agent nodded and held the door open. Crawford rushed outside and took the wheel of the golf cart and raced along the downhill road toward the main campus. At the first switchback on the steep road he raised the radio to his lips and uttered a single word.

"Clear."

Approximately 1 Mile Away
Helipad M-7
FEMA Emergency Operations Center
Mount Weather
Near Bluemont, VA

Fifteen Minutes Earlier

Rorke stood under the makeshift canopy he'd had rigged to screen the Apache from above. Helipad M-7 was at the far western edge of the Mount Weather campus, but he was nothing if not cautious. After Gleason was on the ground and in the building, things would happen too fast for the 'opposition' to do anything, but the pilot of Marine One would undoubtedly circle and do a threat assessment before he set down, even at a secure government facility. An Apache sitting nearby in plain sight might seem out of place.

He turned to the two Apache pilots standing next to him.

"My people will pull the canopy as soon as I give them the word; then I want you in the air. Is that clear?" Rorke said.

The two men nodded sullenly.

"And I don't want any screwups. Repeat your orders."

The senior man glanced at his partner then glared at Rorke before speaking. "Climb as fast as we can. As soon as we get eyes on the target, we put one Hellfire into the edge of the building at the south end, count to three, then three more Hellfires into the building."

Rorke nodded. He believed in redundancy in all things, and he had no intention of relying on the Apaches to finish the job. The C-4 they'd hidden in the building was deployed to do maximum damage, and he didn't want to take a chance the first Hellfire might damage the detonators. The Hellfires would probably detonate the C-4 anyway, but the stuff was terrifically stable. The three follow-up missiles would just be icing on the cake.

"What next?" Rorke asked.

"We take out the chopper on the ground with a Hellfire, then engage the over-watch chopper still in the air," the pilot said.

"Right," Rorke said. "But remember, these are the best pilots in the Marine Corps and they'll have every electronic and physical countermeasure available. They won't have any offensive weapons, but if you don't take them out quick, they may well outfly you and escape. However, they are Jarheads, so they likely won't abort their mission or abandon their comrades on the ground until they're absolutely sure they're beyond hope. Use that. Engage them aggressively from the start, before they run for it."

There was silence, broken finally by the second pilot who had not yet spoken. "What if they DO outfly us? What about our families?"

Rorke fixed both pilots with an icy stare. "Don't let them escape and it won't matter, now will it?"

The silence grew, broken by a single word from Rorke's radio.

"Inbound," said a voice.

Rorke motioned the pilots toward their chopper. "All right, here they come. Get in your bird and get ready to go on my order."

***

It went like clockwork—up to a point.

Rorke sat in his car near the Apache until he got the signal from Crawford, whereupon his underlings manhandled the canopy off the Apache. Faithful to their orders, the Apache crew lifted off and put the first Hellfire into the ops building in less than eight seconds. Rorke triggered the C-4 immediately after the first explosion, and the Apache sent three more Hellfires into the inferno. There were no survivors.

As predicted, Marine One on the ground was a sitting duck, dispatched with a single Hellfire, but then things got tricky. The pilot flying cover stubbornly refused to abandon his stricken comrades, but the Apache's next two Hellfires were defeated by the Marine chopper's countermeasures. However, by that time the crew of the sole surviving chopper had apparently determined no one could have possibly survived the inferno on the ground, and Rorke watched them dive to the deck and out of sight with the Apache in hot pursuit. That was five minutes ago.

Rorke keyed the mic on his radio, transmitting on the closed frequency he'd assigned to the Apache. "Sitrep, now."

He waited impatiently and was about to repeat his request when his radio squawked.

"We ... we missed them with the last Hellfire. They ... they got away. Over," the voice said.

Rorke sighed, but the result wasn't unexpected, and the surviving Marines' testimony might actually work in their favor.

"Very well," he replied. "Do you have enough fuel to return to your base? Over."

The pilot ignored the question. "What about our families?"

Rorke smiled and delayed answering, enjoying his power over the man.

"Consider this your lucky day," Rorke said at last. "Your mission was an overall success, so your families are unharmed and will remain that way. Now, I ask again, do you have enough fuel to RTB?"

The relief in the man's voice came through the speaker. "Affirmative, if we start back now."

"Very well. Your families will be waiting in Charlottesville and you will debrief there. Maintain radio silence. Out," Rorke said, switching to another frequency immediately, leaving the Apache pilot no chance to respond.

"Reaper, do you copy? Over," Rorke said into the radio.

"I copy. Over," came the reply.

"Take care of all the loose ends, and when the Apache goes down, I want you to get a visual on the crash site to confirm there are no survivors," Rorke said.

FEMA Emergency Operations Center
Mount Weather
Near Bluemont, VA

Same Day - 4:15 p.m.

Crawford stared hungrily across the coffee table at the drink in Rorke's hand, mesmerized by the tinkle of ice cubes as his underling casually swirled the amber fluid in the squat glass tumbler, oblivious to its effect on his boss. Crawford struggled with the notion of a celebratory drink; just one wouldn't hurt, right?

He shook his head slightly as if to drive the demon away, just as Rorke raised his glass in a toast, the man's wide smile emphasizing the jagged scar that ran down the side of his otherwise handsome face.

"Here's to you, Mr. President," Rorke said. "Long may you rule!"

Crawford raised his own glass then sipped his water before returning Rorke's smile. "President Crawford does have a nice ring to it, doesn't it?"

"Absolutely," Rorke responded.

They'd wasted no time after the attack. The surviving legislators sheltering at Mount Weather had by now become accustomed to their roles as pawns. Crawford, under Gleason's direction, had eliminated any 'obstructionists' weeks earlier, and the men and women who remained were entirely dependent upon Crawford for food, shelter, and protection for their families. Compliance was made even easier since there was literally no choice; as far as anyone knew, Crawford was the only one left in the legitimate order of succession. He was approved by acclamation within an hour of the attack and immediately sworn in by the single surviving Supreme Court justice.

Crawford's smile faded as he contemplated the tasks still before him. "What about the crew of the other chopper? Any problems there?"

Rorke shook his head. "You radioing the news of the assassinations ahead to Camp David and saying the returning crew was to be 'detained for questioning' was just the right touch. They became suspects before they even touched down. As soon as you were named president, I had them returned here, and I don't think we'll have any difficulty convincing them to support our story. All we need is an explanation for how the Apache got here in the first place, and I've already picked out a few lower level people here to take the fall for that. With that little detail out of the way, our story looks plausible from their perspective. Trust me; they'll WANT to believe it, to clear their own names if for no other reason. Besides, even if they DON'T believe it, you're POTUS, what can they do?"

Crawford nodded. "Get them in line sooner rather than later. If any of them seem particularly convincing, we can use them in the broadcast. We have to play up this whole 'nest of traitors led by dissident elements of the North Carolina National Guard' thing. Between the assassinations linked to a Guard chopper and spinning that whole fiasco down in Wilmington as the unprovoked slaughter of helpless civilians, we should be able to craft a compelling narrative. Even if people only believe half of it, it should seriously erode support for these pockets of resistance, particularly any sympathy from the regular military. We have to keep them on the sidelines until we either have them under control or we've weakened them to the point of ineffectiveness. How's that coming, by the way?"

Rorke hesitated. "It's a limited success. They reluctantly accepted our argument the SRF is doing all of the general 'security tasks,' so trading any surplus ammo for rations to feed the growing civilian populations of their bases seems justifiable. However, as their stocks are depleted, they're increasingly reluctant to part with ammunition." Rorke shrugged. "I never figured we'd manage to strip them completely anyway; my goal was to slowly reduce stocks enough to eliminate them as a potential offensive threat."

"And have you done that?"

Rorke shrugged again. "There's really no way of knowing, but it's early yet. Besides, it's not just ammo, but food, and that's probably more important in the long run. We have free rein to loot whatever food supplies we can find. Conversely, the regular military is unlikely to move against civilians without a direct order to do so, and maybe not even then. As their food stocks dwindle, they're more than happy to stay on their bases in a defensive posture and accept food from us without asking questions. Even if the 'food for ammo' thing winds down, as I anticipate, we'll slowly reduce food shipments, always promising more. When they can't provide for their families, troops will start slipping away. The regular military will cease to be a cohesive force, and its less squeamish former members can be recruited into the SRF. We're playing the long game, Mr. President."

Crawford snorted. "Yeah? Well, we're playing it on an increasingly short field, Rorke. We need to keep a lid on things if we expect to buy enough time for that plan to play out. What's the status at Wilmington?"

"We'll strike within the next few days. With your radio address publicizing their slaughter of innocent civilians and now linking them to this massive assassination plot, we'll effectively paint them as villains. The regular military will stay out of it, and as you just said yourself, if only half the population buys that, it will be enough to sow doubt and slow down the growth of active resistance elsewhere," Rorke said.

"I know what I said, Rorke, and I also know what YOU said ten days ago. The attack we're struggling to spin as an unprovoked slaughter was supposed to have solved the problem of our troublesome 'Fort Box' once and for all, yet here we sit, discussing another plan to eliminate them. Make sure your plan WORKS this time. Is that clear?"

Rorke nodded before draining his drink and setting the empty glass on the coffee table. "Absolutely, Mr. President," he said as he started to stand. "So if there's nothing else at the moment, I'll go double-check details to make sure everything goes as planned."

Crawford waved him back to his seat. "Of course there's something else. Have you forgotten about Tremble? How do we stand there?"

"No change," Rorke said, sinking back into his seat. "We've had no contact since that fiasco three weeks ago, and as you know, testing on the discarded backpack proved that wasn't Tremble, or at least his DNA wasn't on it."

"So have we figured out whose DNA WAS on the damn thing?"

Rorke shook his head. "The match databases aren't accessible and our computer and lab resources are extremely limited. However, we WERE able to run a very broad sample based on DNA sources from the Trembles' apartment. In short, we have sufficient resources to prove who it's NOT, but we can't determine exactly who it IS. But some genetic markers were an absolute mismatch, and the lab guys are confident whoever slipped through was neither of the Trembles." He paused. "I view that as good news. Tremble is probably dead in a gorge somewhere."

Crawford glared. "Well, I view it as a loose end, one that could totally destroy us. Note that I say US, Rorke. What are you doing about it?"

"He's not a threat unless he surfaces," Rorke said. "And when he does, we'll be all over him. His most likely destination is somewhere in North Carolina, maybe even Wilmington. We're maintaining checkpoints at all major river crossings and pinch points south of his last known location. We have complete control of the airspace and nothing is flying without our approval, so unless he sprouts wings, he's basically contained. We'll get him eventually, Mr. President, presuming he's even still alive."

"Major crossings, Rorke? Has Tremble done anything so far to make you think he's dumb enough to try a 'major' crossing?" Crawford's face turned red. "I want you to cover every back-road bridge, railroad trestle, footbridge, and cow ford, and I want it done yesterday. If Tremble IS out there, I want him caught. Is that clear?"

"But, Mr. President, that will severely strain our resources. I think—"

"I don't care what you think, Rorke," Crawford said. "What I do care about is stopping Tremble if he's out there and putting an end to all this troublesome resistance. Is that clear?"

Crawford watched as Rorke visibly struggled to swallow his anger.

"Yes, Mr. President," Rorke said at last.

"Good," Crawford said. "Now what about the bigger picture? What's the status of the resistance, in general?"

"All of the pockets developing any sort of organization are isolated, and when we take out Wilmington, I suspect everyone else will fall into line. Based on radio traffic, the group with the closest ties to Wilmington is down in Southeast Texas," Rorke said. He added, "But they don't seem to be much of a threat for now."

"You assume. Just like you underestimated the Wilmington group. Take a closer look, and if this Texas group shows the slightest indication of organization, take them out before they become a threat."

Rorke shook his head. "We're thin on the ground there and concentrating on harvesting resources from the Houston area and getting the nuke plant at Bay City up and running." He stroked his bearded chin. "But our intel is that escaped convicts control the Beaumont area, and they've already clashed with this Texas group and chewed them up pretty badly. If the survivors still appear to be a threat, I'd suggest using the cons as a force multiplier just like we used the bangers in Wilmington." He shrugged. "What do we have to lose? They kill each other and we'll just step in and squash whoever is left."

Crawford nodded. "Do whatever you think best, but don't let this get out of hand. I want an immediate evaluation of the Texas situation, and then base your action on whatever you find."

CHAPTER FIVE

Captain's Quarters
S/S *Cape Mendocino*
National Defense Reserve Fleet
Neches River
Beaumont, Texas

Day 40
May 10, 2020 - 8:25 a.m.

Captain Jordan Hughes stood at the wall of windows, looking out across the waters of the McFadden Bend Cutoff at the tanker dock on the opposite riverbank.

"I can't believe these quarters," said his wife, Laura, from her place on the settee.

Hughes glanced around the expansive space and nodded. "Yeah, things are a bit shopworn now, but this old girl must have been something in her day. They don't make them like her anymore. Come to think of it, they didn't make many in the first place."

The S/S *Cape Mendocino* started life almost fifty years earlier as the S/S *Doctor Lykes*, the first of a series of 'SeaBee' barge carriers whose innovative cargo system design proved considerably more workable in theory than practice. After several years of trouble-plagued operations, the owners realized their dream for the costly miscalculation it was and managed to sell the three ships to the government as military sea lift vessels.

Originally intended to be the "jewels" of the company fleet, the SeaBees' designers had lamented the ships' lack of space for sufficiently impressive public areas in which to entertain visiting dignitaries and port officials. They solved the problem by expanding the captain's quarters into a three-room suite occupying the entire deck just beneath the navigation bridge. In addition to a spacious bedroom and an equally large office, the suite featured an expansive and well-appointed lounge for entertaining visitors, all fitted with huge windows offering a panoramic view of the ship's bow and the sea beyond. Right now, that included a half-mile view of the brown water of the anchorage area, ending at a rather nondescript and unoccupied tanker dock on the west bank of the Neches.

Hughes shook his head. "I still don't feel right staying here with everyone else crammed into tighter quarters."

"You know it's only until Dan can get power going on a few of the other ships." Laura smiled. "Besides, he didn't seem inclined to take no for an answer."

Her husband grunted. "He can be a stubborn cuss when he wants to be, but he was right about that."

When the survivors of the *Pecos Trader* fled their burning ship to the relative safety of the 'island' of ten old reserve ships moored side by side, Chief Engineer Dan Gowan had been adamant that they set up housekeeping on one of the steamships in the little fleet, quickly settling on the *Cape Mendocino* as the most centrally located. Hughes couldn't fault Gowan's logic; with diesel fuel now in finite supply and no refineries operating, it was only a matter of time until the fuel on hand degraded to the point it was unusable in the engines. However, even degraded and off-spec fuel could be burned in a boiler, so the steamships offered a much more reliable power source theoretically capable of burning just about whatever they could scrounge up for fuel, within reason of course.

"Speaking of Dan, where is he?" Laura asked.

Hughes smiled. "God knows. He and Rich have been running all over the ships, looking for spares and things to scavenge. I asked him to come up here at two." His smile faded. "Georgia should be back from ... you know."

M/V *Judy Ann*
Sun Lower Anchorage
Neches River

Chief Mate Georgia Howell stood on the bow of the barge and quickly brushed away a tear as the *Judy Ann* edged closer to the charred remains of the *Pecos Trader*. The ship's keel rested in the mud now, and she was a blackened and almost unrecognizable hulk, her steel deck distorted and buckled from the heat. Only the deckhouse offered any clue as to the proud ship she had once been, the water curtain they'd left running having held the fire partially at bay until the emergency generator ran out of fuel. Howell swallowed a lump in her throat and concentrated on the grim task before her.

They'd watched for a full five days as *Pecos Trader* died an agonizing death in the distance. Her burning cargo contained on all sides with oxygen only reaching the top of the cargo tanks, the fire had settled into a steady blaze, almost burning out at times then flaring anew; it took a long time to burn forty thousand tons of fuel. They sent the patrol boat to have a look as soon as the fire appeared to be out, but *Pecos Trader* was still too hot to even consider boarding. River water splashed up on the blackened hull sizzled and flashed to steam, and it had taken two full days for the hull to cool enough to allow anyone to touch the warped and buckled steel. That had been yesterday at dusk, and with Hughes' concurrence, Howell had immediately organized this morning's mission.

An acrid burned smell assaulted Howell's nose as Lucius Wellesley expertly maneuvered the *Judy Ann* to push the empty tank barge toward the remains of *Pecos Trader*, and Howell turned away from the wreck to stare at a reminder of even more tragic remains. On the deck of the barge were five rough coffins fashioned from wood Gowan had scavenged from the stores of the old ships of the reserve fleet. She'd come to lay her shipmates to rest.

Howell turned to the bosun. "Kenny, you and Jimmy get the ladder ready."

Kenny Nunez nodded, and Howell raised her radio and turned to look back down the length of the barge to the wheelhouse of the *Judy Ann*.

"Just push us up against the hull and hold us there if you will, Captain Wellesley. We'll try to make this as quick as we can," she said into the radio.

"Y'all take your time and do whatever needs doin.' I'll hold her here as long as need be," came the reply.

Howell nodded her thanks and saw the towboat skipper's answering nod through the wide window. She turned back to the group on the barge. "Mr. Torres, I'll take my guys up to retrieve the ... the remains. I'd appreciate it if you and your Coasties would handle things on this end, with a couple of you keeping a lookout and the other four handling the bodies as we lower them to you."

"Roger that, Mate," Torres replied, then hesitated. "Would you rather we—"

Howell was already shaking her head. "They're our shipmates, but I may need help on the bow to identify Jones. With the fire, I don't know if ..." She trailed off.

The Coastie nodded, his face grim. "Affirmative. There'll be a lot of bodies there and we don't want anyone confusing Jonesy with one of those scumbag cons. Besides, I saw where Pete fell and I'm betting Jonesy is right beside him."

*** *** ***

Driven from the ship by the fire, they'd been unable to take the bodies of their three shipmates who died during the siege of the deckhouse. Forced by circumstances to abandon the bodies in the crew lounge, now they were returning to give their friends a proper burial. Howell led her crew through the dark interior, their flashlights illuminating bubbled paint and charred walls, a testament to the terrific heat inside the deckhouse during the fire.

"Looks like it all baked pretty good, but didn't catch fire," said Kenny Nunez just as Howell reached the door to the crew lounge.

Howell nodded as she reached for the door handle. "I guess there's something to all those fire-retardant requirements after all … damn. The door's jammed."

She stepped back and motioned Nunez forward with one of the long crowbars she'd had them bring, anticipating the ship's twisting and settling would result in at least some jammed doors.

The door yielded with a shriek of steel on steel, and they found their fallen shipmates where they'd left them, their bodies damaged by the heat but recognizable. Howell blinked back a tear and left Kenny Nunez to supervise strapping them into the Stokes baskets they'd salvaged from the reserve ships, while she completed her secondary but equally important mission. She tapped Jimmy Gillespie on the shoulder and he followed her, crowbar in hand, farther down the passageway to the engine room entrance.

The engine room fire door was jammed even tighter, and it took both of them on the crowbar to force it open. Howell flashed her light into the cavernous interior; there was heat damage at this level, but it was definitely less severe inside the engine room. She held her breath against the CO_2 the engineers had used to flood the space and took a few steps inside along the elevated catwalk until she could play the beam of her powerful light over the rail, down to the engine room below the waterline where it would have been much cooler. The precious pile of stores they'd frantically transferred to the engine room flashed under her light far below, the cardboard boxes looked undamaged.

Bless you, Dan Gowan, she thought as she hurried back out of the engine room.

*** *** ***

The blackened expanse of what was once the main deck was punctuated by holes in places and bulges in others, where the deformed steel had either sunken into the cargo tanks or been blown upwards by a dozen localized explosions. The melted and deformed deck piping drooped all across the charred deck at anywhere from knee to shoulder height, its steel support stanchions distorted and collapsed from the intense heat. The whole deck was covered with a thick layer of black, greasy soot. One look convinced Howell it would be impossible to get to the bow across that hellish expanse, and she ordered her crew off the ship.

Lucius Wellesley repositioned the barge against the bow, and they repeated their climb up to the ship, Torres with them this time to help identify Jones. As she'd anticipated, the bow was thick with charred remains from where Jones and Pete Brown had made their heroic last stand. But 'remains' was a relative term, as all the fallen were mere piles of ash from which bits of unburned bone protruded, recognizable only vaguely as human.

Torres squatted near the bullnose chock and poked tentatively in a pile of remains to fish out a blackened lump.

"This is Jonesy's harmonica. He never went anywhere without it." Torres smiled a sad smile. "Couldn't play the friggin' thing worth a damn. He was the world's worst harmonica player and I swear he just carried this thing around to irritate me."

"That … that looks like Pete's pocketknife, or what's left of it, right there in that pile … right there beside Jones," Jimmy Gillespie said.

Howell nodded. "They must have crawled together to try to help each other before they died," she said softly.

"Uh ... ma'am?" Jimmy asked softly, "they're all mixed together and there ain't much left. How we gonna separate them?"

Howell considered it and then looked at Torres. "Bury them together?"

Torres nodded slowly. "They died protecting each other. Yeah, I'm okay with that; I think Jonesy would be too."

"How we gonna get 'em down to the barge?" Jimmy asked.

Howell stared down at the remains and then over at Torres, the solution obvious. "I hate to do it," Howell began, "but—"

Torres glared at Howell. "I'm not putting Jonesy in a garbage bag, if that's what you're thinking. That's final."

Howell started to argue and then thought better of it. "You're right, Mr. Torres. I apologize for even considering it. Let me get on the radio to Captain Wellesley to see what he might have aboard *Judy Ann*."

***

"Satisfied, Mr. Torres?" Howell asked a few minutes later as she and Torres stood looking down as one of *Judy Ann*'s deckhands hurried toward them along the deck of the barge, carrying a large white beer cooler.

Torres smiled. "Absolutely. Actually it's kinda fitting if you knew Jonesy."

Howell smiled back. "Well, Pete was no slouch in the beer-drinking department either, from what I hear."

Anticipating the need, Wellesley had the foresight to send two whisk brooms and a dustpan, all brand new, along with the cooler. Thus supplied, the team went to work, taking turns gently and respectfully transferring the combined remains of Able Bodied Seaman Pete Brown and Petty Officer Third Class David Jones (aka Jonesy) United States Coast Guard into the cooler.

Once back down on the barge, they placed the cooler inside one of the wooden coffins, then transferred the coffins ashore for burial beside the first of their fallen, Jimmy Gillespie's father, Earl. It was a chore to dig the graves by hand, but the crew of the *Judy Ann* pitched in and the work went quickly. Howell said a short prayer, then closed with the promise they would do better by their fallen when circumstances allowed. The Coasties formed up and fired a ceremonial salute.

I hope we don't need this cemetery again anytime soon, thought Howell as the group moved toward the aluminum skiff that would ferry them back to the *Judy Ann*.

S/S *Cape Mendocino*
National Defense Reserve Fleet
Neches River
Beaumont, Texas

Same Day - 2:15 p.m.

"So the stores looked okay?" asked Jordan Hughes.

"Best I could tell, Captain," Georgia Howell replied, "but we'll have to clear the CO2 out of the engine room before we can check for sure, and the sooner the better."

Hughes heaved a relieved sigh and looked around the lounge at the gathering of what was rapidly becoming his informal 'advisory council.' In addition to Georgia Howell, both the senior engineering officers were there, as was former Chief Petty Officer Matt Kinsey, representing the Coast Guard contingent. Jimmy Gillespie was there, not as a crewman but because Hughes sensed that he knew many of the people they'd recently rescued and might have a better sense for what skills they possessed. Lucius Wellesley represented the towboat contingent, and Laura was there both as their medical adviser and, well, he thought, just levelheaded Laura.

"Well, you're right about that." Hughes nodded toward Wellesley. "Captain Wellesley and the rest of the towboat guys have been keeping us going, but we can't keep drawing down their stores. We need to salvage what we can as soon as possible." He sighed. "It's gonna be a chore to carry that stuff all the way up on main deck by hand and then lower it to the barge one box at a time." He turned to Gowan. "How soon do you think you can get the CO2 cleared, Chief?"

"We're already on it," Gowan said. "Rich scrounged up a couple of cutting torches and some oxygen and acetylene. I figure we'll just cut a bunch of holes in the hull, right above the waterline. The CO2 is heavier than air, so most of it will just drain out like water from a bucket with a hole. Whatever is left below the waterline we'll blow out. We found some portable blowers if we can run them with power from the towboats." Gowan looked at Wellesley.

"Not a problem, Chief. Whatever you need," Wellesley confirmed.

"And y'all won't have to haul the stores up to the main deck," Gowan said to Howell. "I figure we'll just cut another big hole in the hull even with the deck of the barge and just pass the stuff out from the engine room. In fact, now that I think about it, we might not need the blowers at all. We'll just cut some big holes all along both sides of the engine room and get some natural cross ventilation going." He heaved a sad sigh. "It's not like we can hurt the old girl at this point."

"Best be careful not to fall in when you're working over the side," Lucius Wellesley said. "I must have seen two dozen big gators during our little trip, and I didn't see any dead convicts to speak of. I'm thinking humans are back on the menu."

Laura shuddered. "Gators give me the creeps."

"I reckon we'll be seein' a lot more of 'em without much boat traffic to disturb 'em, and they'll likely become more aggressive," Wellesley said. "Given how bad things are and with a city upstream, there'll be more bodies in the river for sure. From the gators' point of view, folks are starting to look less like a threat to avoid and more like lunch."

Laura shuddered again. "Wonderful."

Wellesley shrugged. "Maybe that's not all bad. Gators are a good source of protein."

"I'm with Laura on that," Georgia Howell said. "I'd rather eat a snake."

"Well, you might just have to at some point," Wellesley said.

Hughes looked at his wife. "And that brings us to the next thing on the agenda, which is how long our stores will last. How's Polak? He's the only one with any experience feeding large groups."

Laura sighed. "I'm a vet and horses don't have heart attacks, so I honestly don't know. The aspirin seemed to help and I'm keeping him on a low dose, but all I can really do is try to make him take it easy for at least a few weeks, and you know how damned excitable he is."

Hughes did indeed know. Back in the day, baiting the excitable chief steward was a popular pastime among the unlicensed crew. 'Getting Polak spun up' had evolved into almost an art form for some of the sailors before the blackout. However, despite the irascible steward's rough edges, he was well-liked by the crew.

"Well, keep him in bed, whatever it takes," Hughes said.

"I'm way ahead of you," Laura said. "And apparently that means becoming his 'assistant' with updates several times a day. With one hundred forty-three survivors, counting the towboat guys, he figures the undamaged stores left on the *Pecos Trader* will last a month or six weeks max. Throwing in what the towboat guys have will double that, to maybe three months." Laura looked at Wellesley. "That's assuming Captain Wellesley and his friends are willing to share."

"No question there," Wellesley said. "We figure our odds of surviving are better in the group. If the price of admission is sharing, we're okay with that."

"Thank you, Lucius," Hughes said, then added, "So three months."

"That's assuming the convicts and everyone else leaves us alone," said Matt Kinsey, speaking for the first time, "and what happens AFTER three months? We're relatively safe here in the middle of the river, but I don't see how we can sustain ourselves long-term."

"He's right about that," Jimmy Gillespie said. "We gotta have some dirt and put in a crop of some kind. The thing is though, if we get off these ships and try to start a settlement ashore, we'll be sitting ducks."

"I feel like we're back in the Dark Ages. This is medieval," Georgia Howell said.

"Yeah, where's a castle with a moat when you need one?" Gowan asked.

Hughes smiled. "Maybe not as far away as you think, Chief."

The group exchanged puzzled looks as Hughes rose and walked into the adjoining office. He returned carrying a rolled nautical chart, which he spread on the coffee table. Curious, everyone gathered to stare down at the old chart.

"I scrounged this off the bridge," Hughes said. "It's out of date, but it'll do in a pinch." He pointed down at the chart. "Clark Island."

No one spoke until Jimmy Gillespie broke the silence. "That's the island where Dad … where Dad and Alvarez held off the cons," Jimmy Gillespie said softly.

"That's right," Hughes said. "How big do you think it is?"

Again there was silence as everyone studied the chart. Lucius Wellesley leaned down and measured with his fingers from the latitude scale on the side of the chart and did a rough mental calculation.

"Ninety or a hundred acres, I'd say. But I know that place. It's low as hell and floods all the time, especially when a hurricane sends a storm surge up the river. I can't see that being a fit place for a farm OR a settlement. Anything we build will be swept away with the first storm," Wellesley said.

"And it's a long way from easily defensible, even with water all the way around it. That's a lot of open perimeter to defend," Matt Kinsey added.

"Bear with me," Hughes said. "Look at the water depth on either side."

Wellesley shrugged. "Okay, the island splits the channel, so you got deep water all the way around the island, so what? I still can't see … " Wellesley trailed off, a slow smile spreading over his face. He looked up at Hughes. "We got enough ships to cover the island?"

Hughes nodded. "I make it just over eight thousand feet of shoreline. We have ten ships in our group here and there are four tankers rafted together upstream and two more ships at the MARAD dock—sixteen in all. I'm not sure exactly, but that's gotta be over ten thousand feet of ship if you put them end to end. So yeah, I think we have enough ships and then some. The question is, can your push boats position them around the island?"

Wellesley shrugged. "Not a problem, especially if we don't have to worry if we bang 'em up a bit. If you can get 'em busted loose from the anchorage, we can shoehorn 'em in tight together, bow to stern, and ring that island—"

"Would someone PLEASE explain to me what you're talking about," Laura said.

"Sorry," Hughes said. "My idea is to take the ships from here in the reserve fleet and position them end to end all around the island. We'll ballast them down to put them aground as close to the island as possible; then we'll lash them together with wire rope and the anchor chains. We'll have to come up with some way to fortify the gaps between the ships, but the high ship sides will act like a fort, with a protected land area in the middle."

"But, Captain Hughes, Captain Wellesley was right. Even if we protect that island, it's not good for anything; it's about one step up from swamp," Jimmy Gillespie said.

"It is now," Hughes acknowledged, "but I'm hoping that among the folks we rescued there are some dozer and heavy equipment operators, or at least people with related experience, and I'm betting there's some heavy equipment sitting idle we can get at on the east side of the river without going through

Beaumont, say in Vidor or Orangefield. We lost all the fuel in *Pecos Trader*, but we still have plenty in the barges Captain Wellesley brought with him. Put all that together and I figure we can build up the island, at least a few feet, and then top it off with some good topsoil."

Across the table, Dan Gowan nodded, warming to the idea. "Actually, Cap, we won't even need to build up the whole island; we can just fill in the gap next to the ships' hulls and then build an eight- or ten-foot berm around the perimeter, packed tight against the hulls of the ships to stabilize it. That'll help stabilize the ships in place too. Even if the river comes up five or six feet, the berm will hold the water out."

Jimmy Gillespie nodded tentatively. "My brother Bobby used to drive a dozer and I know some others who were equipment operators or dump truck drivers …" He trailed off and began to shake his head. "But so what, Captain Hughes? I mean there are plenty of places to get dirt on the east bank, but how do you plan to get the heavy equipment and dirt to the island? If we move it by barge, it will take about a million years."

"Not a problem, we'll drive," Gowan said before Hughes could respond. "There must be thirty or more cargo lighters aboard this ship, and God knows steel isn't a problem; Rich and I can just cut it out of noncritical areas on the ships. Presuming I can get the stern elevator on this ship working, we can offload the cargo lighters as floats and build a pontoon bridge to the east bank."

The group fell silent, each considering the bold plan.

Matt Kinsey shook his head, his skepticism obvious. "I don't know, Jordan. That's pretty ambitious. Do you really think we can get this done before our stores run out and still have a crop ready to harvest too? If not, we'll still be short of food."

For a brief moment, Hughes looked defeated, the crushing weight of the responsibilities thrust upon him showing on his face. He sighed and ran his hands through his hair and looked down at the deck, as if gathering strength. When he lifted his head, his face was hard, his doubts banished, or at least concealed. "I don't know either, Matt. But I do know if we just sit on our asses and don't do anything, we won't survive. I think this is our best option."

Kinsey nodded, and here and there in the group, others nodded as well.

"Okay, folks," Hughes said, "you all have the general idea. Now we need to survey our people and see what skills we have available; even the regular *Pecos Trader* crew all led separate lives ashore and they might well have skills we're unaware of. Georgia, I'd like you and Dan to poll the crew to see how each feels they can best contribute. Jimmy, I want you to talk to all our new arrivals to do the same, and don't leave anyone out. Same goes for you, Lucius," Hughes said to Wellesley. "Your towboat crews will be busy positioning the ships for the first few days, but after that, we'll need all the help we can get with the larger effort."

"What about us?" Kinsey asked.

"I was coming to that," Hughes said. "We're going to be strung out like hell until we can get the ships consolidated around the island, and we'll be sitting ducks if the remaining cons decide to attack us before we're ready, so we need to get the ships circled up around the island as soon as possible. Until that happens, I'd like you and your Coasties to provide security. We can keep some guys both near Clark Island and with the ships being moved and use the two patrol boats to police the river in between. We can also arrange a series of air horn signals so if we're attacked at any point, the patrol boats can bring their machine guns to the party."

Matt Kinsey nodded. "We're really low on ammo, especially for the Cuban gun. Almost nothing left there."

Hughes shrugged. "Well, the convicts don't know that, and at least the guns look threatening. We'll just have to do the best we can."

Kinsey nodded again and Hughes looked over the group.

"Okay, folks. Let's get busy. We have three months to build our castle with a moat."

S/S *Cape Mendocino*
Clark Island
Neches River
Beaumont, Texas

Day 41
May 11, 2020 - 5:35 p.m.

Jordan Hughes stood on the bridge wing of the S/S *Cape Mendocino* and watched as the *Judy Ann* and *Rambling Ace* nudged his vessel tightly into place just ahead of the already positioned and grounded USNS *Paul Buck*, nodding in appreciation of the skill of the towboat skippers. They'd likely get only the first group of three ships in place before sundown, but it was better than he'd expected, and it should go much faster the following day now that they had a feel for the process.

Their first obstacle had been dealing with the anchors and chains with no power. They'd solved that problem by breaking each chain at the first available detachable link and allowing the short section of massive chain on deck to rattle down the hawse pipe, abandoning the anchors on the river bottom. After all, a ship about to be put aground had little need for an anchor. Dealing with the anchor chains and heavy mooring wires without power to the deck machinery was difficult and dangerous work, but led by Georgia Howell, the crew set to it with chain falls, ingenuity, and a will to succeed; one by one, the old ships were separated from the group. With an early start and a strong push, they might be able to finish the repositioning by sundown the following day, and he'd rest easier with the more dangerous work behind them and with all his people in one place, not spread out up and down the river, inviting attack.

Despite his confidence in the concept for the 'fort,' he'd been unsure as to the details and was thus relieved when Dan Gowan waded in to organize the effort. The first order of business had been a more accurate measurement of the island shoreline from the chart, as well as a much more time-consuming visit to all the ships to verify vessel lengths on the general arrangement drawings wall-mounted on each vessel. That had consumed the remainder of the previous day.

As it turned out, they only had room for a dozen ships and had argued long into the night as to the most useful mix to form the 'walls' of their new fortress. However, they'd hit technical challenges immediately, and in the end, the final selection had been governed largely by circumstance, with Gowan's views prevailing.

The small diesel-powered emergency generators on the old steamships making up the majority of the reserve fleet were adequate for lights and emergency services, but not up to the task of powering the main ballast pumps needed to 'ground' the ships around the island.

Likewise, though the old steamships would be vital in the long term when fuel quality and availability became a problem, in the near term Gowan lacked the time and manpower to get the more labor-intensive steamships running. Only the four motor ships in the reserve fleet could be quickly and easily 'ballasted down' under their own power as envisioned by Hughes' initial plan.

Gowan proposed solving the problem by positioning each of the four motor ships equidistant around the perimeter of the island, flanked by a steamship on either end. The motor ship of each three-ship group would be positioned first and ballasted down under its own power. Once firmly aground, the generator on the motor ship could be left to run unattended while the push boats moved the steam vessels in place on either end of the motor ship and held them there. Then the engineers could run temporary power from the centrally located motor ship to the main pumps of each of the steamships long enough to ballast the steamships firmly aground. It would be a matter of 'rinse and repeat' with each group of three.

Beyond 'steam versus motor,' there had been other discussions of the best ship types, with Gowan's views prevailing there as well. There were two tankers because 'you never knew when those extra tanks will come in handy,' and the two old 'crane ships' were to be positioned on opposite sides of the new 'fort' because Gowan figured he might eventually be able to get the cranes working to lift things inside the fort if need be. Last on the chief engineer's shopping list had been an old training ship, long in the tooth but equipped with ample, if spartan, quarters against the potential expansion of their group.

"I got enough to do without worrying about building more quarters if we fill up what we've got," Gowan had said, daring anyone to disagree with him.

Dan's like a force of nature, Hughes thought as he watched the chief engineer on the deck of the already ballasted down *Paul Buck*, Rich Martin at his side as the two engineers dragged a heavy electrical cable down the deck toward the *Cape Mendocino*.

Hughes' radio squawked, interrupting his thoughts.

"Jordan? You there?" Laura asked.

He grimaced. For all her intelligence and ability, his wife seemed to find proper radio procedure a complete mystery. Or more likely, he thought, she just thought it was unnecessary bullshit given the current situation.

"I copy, Laura. Go ahead. Over." He emphasized the *over*, hoping she'd get the hint without him bringing it up again.

"You best get down here," she said, ignoring his hint. "There's something you'll want to hear. And bring Matt Kinsey if he's aboard."

"As soon as I can. Over," Hughes said, looking over the ship's side at the operation in progress. In truth he was a passenger in the shifting operation. The ship had no power, and Lucius Wellesley and the other push boat skippers had the operation well in hand. He radioed Wellesley to tell him he was leaving the bridge and then called Matt Kinsey and told him to meet him in the captain's lounge as soon as possible.

***

Matt Kinsey walked through the door of the lounge right behind Hughes.

"What's up, Cap?" he asked.

Hughes shook his head and looked at Laura. His wife sat on the couch with a small NOAA Weather Radio receiver on the coffee table before her. They'd found the receiver on board, and because they'd not yet been able to get the regular radio equipment on the old ship operational, they'd activated it to pick up any official broadcasts. Though more than skeptical of government-supplied information, Hughes figured it was best to know what was being put out via the Emergency Alert System, and the EAS messages were still broadcast on the now unused National Weather Service frequencies. They kept the little radio in silent mode with the alarm feature set.

"The radio alarmed a few minutes ago, so I turned it up," Laura said. "President Gleason is dead, and so are Cyrus Daniel and most of the rest of the remaining cabinet members. Oliver Crawford is the only surviving cabinet member and he's now the president. And—"

"What? How? How is that possible—"

"That's not the worst part," Laura continued. "They're blaming Wilmington and talking about an attack—"

"Who's blaming Wilmington? What attack?" Matt Kinsey said, his concern for his son in Wilmington obvious.

Laura shook her head. "They're repeating the message every fifteen minutes. I called you down so you could hear it for yourself."

She'd hardly finished speaking when the alarm on the radio shrieked its annoying, attention-getting tone for what seemed like five minutes but in reality was only a few seconds, followed immediately by an announcement.

ATTENTION! This is an Emergency Alert System broadcast. The President of the United States will address you shortly. REPEAT! This is an Emergency Alert System broadcast. The President of the United States will address you shortly.

There was a short pause, followed by a new voice.

My fellow Americans, this is Oliver Crawford, formerly Secretary of Homeland Security, and I come to you today with both a heavy heart and tragic news. I regret to inform you that Vice President Daniels was killed some days ago when his helicopter crashed under what we thought at the time were suspicious circumstances. President Gleason and I, by mutual agreement, withheld this information while we investigated.

However, two days ago the assassins struck again, murdering not only President Gleason, but most of the remaining members of his cabinet in a cowardly attack that will live forever in infamy. I was injured as well and barely escaped with my life. As the sole surviving person on the official succession list, I reluctantly accepted the responsibility and was sworn in as your president immediately after the attack. We all face a challenging future, but I pray God gives me strength to rise to those challenges. That will be a daunting task without the superb leadership of the late President Gleason and the aid of my old friends and colleagues in the cabinet, but I pledge myself to my duty to both our nation and each American, and I ask for your prayers in this difficult undertaking.

To that end, the first order of business is justice, both for our late president and the common citizens who've fallen victim to evil forces. It is no secret our nation is reeling, nor that evil people will always try to turn disorder to their own advantage. We have incontrovertible proof that these assassinations and other recent crimes were the work of just such a criminal network centered in Wilmington, North Carolina, who call themselves the Wilmington Defense Force.

This group includes criminals, military deserters, rogue elements of the North Carolina National Guard, and opportunists of every stripe, who banded together to seize the Wilmington Container Terminal and the bounty of supplies it contains for their own selfish ends. Ten days ago, apparently feeling threatened by the existence of a nearby FEMA feeding operation, these criminals lured the defenseless refugees close with promises of food and shelter then slaughtered them by the thousands, including women and children. They then attempted to cover up this wholesale slaughter under the claim they were attacked by street gangs in league with the government.

This group's attempt to subvert the orderly restoration of electrical power and rule of law doesn't stop in Wilmington. Their influence is growing. An allied element of the North Carolina Air Guard carried out the recent assassinations, and based on radio intercepts, we have good intelligence the group has allies in Southeast Texas and elsewhere. They recruit by spreading misinformation, principally outlandish tales of government misdeeds, helped in this effort by naive members of the ham radio community.

We will deal with this threat firmly and decisively, but in the interim, I ask for the help of ALL Americans. Do not listen to lies being spread by these criminals or pass them along to others. Instead, rest assured your government is struggling mightily not only to restore power, but to ensure fair distribution of our limited resources.

Desperate times call for desperate measures, and our response to these murderers will be swift and without mercy. Know also that anyone helping these so-called dissidents, either actively or through spreading their lies, will be considered a criminal and an enemy of the nation and treated accordingly.

I close with the fervent prayer that God protects our nation in these trying times, my pledge to do my utmost to see our country through this crisis, and my vow that our country will return to greatness once again.

God bless America.

There was a short pause, followed by an announcement the message would be repeated every fifteen minutes for the rest of the day. Hughes and the others sat stunned.

"We have to know what's really going on in Wilmington," Kinsey said at last. "Is the main radio working yet?"

Hughes shook his head. "You know no one's had time to look at it. The best we can manage is relaying messages via the towboats' VHF and the ham network, but Wellesley hasn't been able to raise any of the hams since we got our last message to Wilmington about abandoning *Pecos Trader*." Hughes hesitated. "Besides ..."

"Besides what?" Kinsey asked.

"What can Luke really tell you if we DO make contact? From Crawford's broadcast, it's clear everything we pass in the open is monitored, so he sure as hell can't tell you anything meaningful."

Kinsey nodded, worry still written on his face. "You're right. I wasn't thinking clearly. It's just ..."

Laura put her hand on Kinsey's arm. "They're pretty resourceful folks from what I hear," she said. "I'm sure they'll be all right."

Kinsey sighed. "Your lips to God's ears."

Hughes nodded sympathetic agreement, but his own thoughts were elsewhere. Based on Crawford's reference to 'allies in Southeast Texas,' he figured they had a whole new set of problems themselves.

"What's that?" Laura asked, at the growing sound of a repetitive low thump.

Kinsey listened a moment. "That's a chopper, for sure."

1500 Feet Above Clark Island
Neches River
Beaumont, Texas

Major Jake Gerard, FEMA Special Reaction Force, stared down at the ships moored next to the island. From the tugs against two of the vessels, it looked like he'd happened upon some sort of operation in progress, but he wasn't sure exactly what. What he was sure of was that he didn't have time for this; looting the Houston area while simultaneously trying to get the Bay City nuclear plant back on line was already straining his limited resources. That said, all of East Texas was in his area of operations, and as much as he didn't need a third task, Rorke hadn't really been inclined to argue the point when he radioed this morning.

The Beaumont area wasn't a high priority for him, and when he got word last week via radio intercept the fake cops were openly at war with some newly arrived ship-based group, his initial reaction was relief. If the two groups killed each other, all the better. It would be just that much less resistance for him to deal with when he finally got around to 'pacifying' the area.

He motioned his pilot to make a wider circuit over the area. The burned-out hulk south of the current activity looked like a total loss. He'd be amazed if anyone had survived that fire.

Here and there on the ships and towboats beside the island, people gazed up at the chopper. Their body language wasn't friendly, nor did anyone wave. His pilot pointed and Gerard saw activity on the ships of the reserve fleet as well. Then he understood; they were moving the old ships to the island. But why?

Not that it mattered. His orders were to take them out if they showed any signs of organization, and you had to be fairly organized to move a bunch of ships. He considered making contact and demanding their immediate surrender, but he knew that was a nonstarter; any group surviving this long with the cons on the loose was unlikely to be intimidated. Besides, if he gave them an ultimatum now, they'd probably ignore it and then be even more wary of a coming attack. Better to keep them guessing, at least to some degree.

"Drop a little lower and circle the island," he ordered the pilot.

The pilot threw Gerard a doubtful look before complying, and Gerard turned to the troopers next to him.

"Slide open the side doors, and smile and wave when they look up," he said.

His men did as ordered, receiving no response from the people on the ships below.

"All right, let's take a quick look at the prison complex then head back to base," Gerard said to the pilot.

Less than five minutes later, the chopper hovered high above the former Federal Correctional Complex and Gerard peered down at the facility, now an anthill of activity no doubt caused by the chopper's presence. Men rushed about in the complex, looking skyward, their body language telegraphing tension, even at a distance.

Good, thought Gerard. No doubt their recent run-in with the shipboard group had left the cons a bit less confident. He wasn't dumb enough to set down in the prison complex now, with just one chopper at his back, but when he returned leading an overwhelming ground force complete with air cover, the cons shouldn't be too hard to intimidate. After he'd 'recruited' them, he'd rearm them with a few automatic weapons and set them against the river people again, while his own men went back to their work near Houston. He'd comply with Rorke's orders to a tee, but he'd be damned if he'd tie up resources if he didn't have to. Even if the cons proved inadequate to the task, they could soften up the target a bit at the very least.

Gerard ordered the pilot to return to base, and then smiled. Maybe this wouldn't be too time-consuming after all, and if the cons wiped out the river people, he could take credit.

S/S *Cape Mendocino*
Clark Island
Neches River
Beaumont, Texas

Hughes, Laura, and Kinsey stood on the bridge wing, watching the chopper recede into the distance, the distinctive *whump, whump* of its blades growing increasingly softer.

"What do you make of that?" Kinsey asked.

"I think maybe the feds are sizing us up in preparation of making good on their threat," Hughes said.

"It looked like they circled the prison complex too," Laura said. "Maybe it was just a general inspection of the area."

"Maybe," Hughes replied, "but they never seemed interested enough to send out a chopper before. One showing up on the heels of Crawford's speech is a bit too coincidental, don't you think?"

"I agree," Kinsey said, and then sighed. "So now we have to worry about a possible air strike. I'll keep either Torres or Alvarez on watch at all times with one of the Barrett 50 calibers. If they come at us by air and we drop a chopper or two at long distance, I think we can convince them to keep their distance, at least for a while."

"How much ammo do you have?" Hughes asked.

"Not enough," Kinsey replied. "But like you said before, they don't know that."

Hughes nodded and looked at the sun moving toward the western horizon. "I'm gonna raise Lucius on the VHF and see if his boys are willing to work through the night with their searchlights. I know everyone's beat, but the injuns are just over the hill and we need to get the wagons circled up."

CHAPTER SIX

Fort Box
Wilmington Container Terminal
Wilmington, North Carolina

Day 41
May 11, 2020 - 3:25 p.m.

Colonel Doug Hunnicutt looked at his 'council' gathered around the conference table, all talking at once, and sighed. He could hardly blame them; news of the assassinations of almost the entire Gleason administration and the rise of Oliver Crawford was sobering enough, but to be wrongly accused of those crimes by the new President was a shock beyond imagining. He held up his hands to quiet the meeting.

"All right, people, let's settle down," Hunnicutt said, continuing when he'd restored some semblance of order. "It's a pretty standard disinformation campaign. The problem is Crawford's dominance of the airwaves via the Emergency Alert System makes it tough to counter, especially since he managed to take out so many ham operators." He glanced at Lieutenant Mike Butler. "Any idea how many are left, Mike?"

Butler shrugged. "Best guess, maybe twenty or thirty percent, but they have to be a lot more careful now to keep their transmissions short and change locations regularly so the SRF can't triangulate them. That's not so easy. They're trying to get the truth out, but remember, people aren't listening to ham transmissions directly. The operators pass word among themselves, and then it's spread by word of mouth from each individual ham operator; it takes time."

Dr. Sarah Jennings was unable to contain herself. "But who would believe these lies in the first place? That we'd slaughter unarmed refugees is ludicrous enough, but that we'd somehow be able to assassinate practically the entire administration is preposterous!"

Lieutenant Joel Washington shook his head. "Folks will believe a lot of stuff when they're hungry and scared, Doc. You were in that refugee camp, you know how it is."

Jennings grew quiet and nodded slowly.

"What I don't understand is why," Major Luke Kinsey said. "They clearly have the upper hand, so why bother trying to smear us now?"

"Because by defying them and establishing contact with others in similar positions, we're a threat," Hunnicutt said. "They tried to take us out using surrogates and that didn't work, so they'll move against us openly now. But first they want to demonize us in the minds of as many people as possible, and especially the regular military. Crawford is playing to multiple audiences, and he has to make it appear, at least to a significant number of people, that he's crushing criminals; otherwise they'll make us all martyrs."

"Well, I agree with him on that part, at least," Lieutenant Josh Wright drawled. "I can't say I'm too eager to be a martyr."

The remark broke the tension somewhat, and there were chuckles around the table. Even Hunnicutt managed a wan smile before once again turning serious.

"I'm sure we all share that sentiment, Lieutenant Wright," Hunnicutt said, "but I think we can count on direct action against us, probably sooner rather than later. How do we stand?"

Wright shook his head. "Not good, sir. We've been scrounging every last round, but we're critically low on ammo, especially for the crew-served weapons. If they come at us in force like they did last time, we'll likely burn through our ammo in fifteen, maybe twenty minutes, max. And that's just assuming a frontal assault against the walls. If they coordinate that with an air assault . . ." He trailed off. "I think you get the picture."

Hunnicutt looked grim. "I do indeed." He turned to Butler. "How's the intel looking?"

"The SRF thugs have taken over our old base in what's left of the refugee camp," he said. "We managed to get a couple of guys in pretending to be 'fugees—" Butler stopped as he saw Dr. Sarah Jennings tense at his word choice "—I mean refugees. According to them, the SRF is now all sweetness and light, passing out MREs and recruiting people for what they're calling the 'civilian militia.' They're arming them and giving them rudimentary training. They're not exactly a crack military force, but they'll likely be more capable than what they threw at us last time."

Dr. Jennings was aghast. "But surely no one willingly sides with the SRF after what they've done!"

"That's just it, Doc," Butler replied. "They ran that first assault with their own guys disguised as gangbangers, so the surviving refugees don't even know the SRF was involved. What they do know is that a lot of their friends and family died at our hands, and the ones still alive are hungry. Now these uniformed SRF thugs show up, being sympathetic and providing food, so they look a lot like the good guys to the folks in that camp. Throw in the added inducement of revenge, and they have people lining up to join this 'civilian militia.' These people are being played big time, but you'll never convince them of that."

"How soon?" Hunnicutt asked.

Butler shrugged. "Pretty much whenever they want, I'd say. SRF started recruiting right after the last attack. They've got at least three or four thousand 'militia' by now, with the number growing daily, and my guys say the rumor is an attack is imminent."

Hunnicutt stifled a curse and turned to Luke Kinsey. "We need resupply and need it badly. How's Operation Little Round Top coming, Major?"

Luke shook his head. "Four days at the absolute soonest, Colonel. There are a lot of moving parts, and if this goes south—"

Hunnicutt held up his hand. "I understand. Go over it again and get back to me. I need you to reduce that time, Luke."

"Yes, sir," Luke said.

Hunnicutt turned back to the others. "Very well. Until we're ready to move ourselves, we have to be prepared for an attack. Based on what we know, the most likely threat is from the city, so I want all the crew-served weapons except one placed along the eastern perimeter wall, facing the city. Put the remaining machine gun on one of the small patrol boats to provide a mobile defense of the river-side approaches. If we're attacked from the river side, it should be able to hold the attackers off until we can move our reserves. And speaking of reserves, how many of the river volunteers are still with us?"

"All of 'em, well over a hundred last count," Josh Wright said, then added, "They're not folks to run from a fight."

Hunnicutt allowed himself a smile. "That they're not. Please ask the Gibson brothers to hold the river volunteers to act as a rapid reserve force to reinforce the perimeter as needed."

"Yes, sir," Wright replied.

The room fell silent.

"Uh . . . sir?" Luke asked. "What about aerial assault? If they attack us openly, they're bound to use those choppers, and with most of our firepower facing the city approaches, we'll be wide open to an attack from across the river. The patrol boat might be able to hold a waterborne attack at bay for a while, but an airborne attack coming in low and fast could get on the ships along the dock before we could react." Luke paused. "If they gain a toehold on the decks of those ships, they'll be able to shoot down into the entire fort and shoot the defenders on the east wall in the back. We'll be toast."

Hunnicutt sighed and ran his hands through his hair. "Point taken, Major. Change of plan; we'll spread half the river volunteers along the decks of those ships and reduce the size of our reserve force. They'll just have to hold until reinforced if it comes to that; we can't ignore a known threat to defend against a hypothetical one, no matter how probable."

Luke nodded, and the room fell silent.

"All right, folks," Hunnicutt said, "let's get back to work. There are plenty—"

Mike Butler raised his hand tentatively, and Hunnicutt nodded at him.

"What is it, Lieutenant?" Hunnicutt asked.

"I … uh … I have kind of a crazy idea about a chopper defense," Butler said. "It might not work, but I thought maybe—"

"Let's hear it, Mike," Hunnicutt said. "Crazy is the name of the game these days."

M/V *Maersk Tangier*
Fort Box
Wilmington Container Terminal
Wilmington, North Carolina

Same Day - 7:50 p.m.

Luke Kinsey stood slightly bent over, his forearms on the ship's rail as he gazed at the yellow ball of the sun hanging on the western horizon. It was calming, the gentle flow of the river in the waning light a timeless constant, indifferent to whatever strife might have impacted human kind.

He heard steps on the main deck behind him and straightened and turned to see Doug Hunnicutt.

"Sorry, Luke," Hunnicutt said. "I didn't know you were here. I don't want to disturb you."

Luke smiled. "No problem, Colonel. I come here and watch the sunset when I can. We moved around a lot when I was a kid, but Dad being in the Coast Guard, it was always somewhere near the water. I really miss it when I'm not around it. It sort of helps me keep things in perspective."

Hunnicutt nodded and looked out over the river. "The natural elements are a constant, regardless of what happens to us." He glanced up at the stack of containers towering behind them and the container cranes far above and sighed. "Unfortunately, we're forced to occupy our thoughts with more stressful things these days."

Luke followed Hunnicutt's gaze. "Do you think Butler's idea will work?"

Hunnicutt shrugged. "It might, and no one has a better one, so I guess we'll see."

Luke said nothing, and Hunnicutt filled the silence.

"You've been distracted lately. Are you worried about your family?"

"Yes, sir," Luke replied. "My dad mostly. Kelly and the others are safe in Louisiana, but things seem a lot less stable in Texas, and communications have been pretty spotty since they had to abandon the ship."

Hunnicutt put a comforting hand on Luke's shoulder. "He'll be all right, Luke. Your dad and the guys he took with him are pretty resourceful, as is Jordan Hughes and his crew. They'll make it if anyone can."

"That's what I'm worried about, sir. The 'if anyone can' part."

CHAPTER SEVEN

Blue Ridge Parkway
Mile Marker 40
Southbound

Day 42
May 12, 2020 - 8:15 a.m.

Jeff 'Spider' Harris, president and sole surviving member of the Satan's Seed Motorcycle Club, suppressed a curse as the pickup rounded a curve and centrifugal force pressed his injured shoulder into the truck door.

"Slow down, dickhead! This ain't a race," he growled at the driver.

The man blanched. "Sorry, Spider."

Spider merely grunted and looked through the rear window into the bed of the truck, where two armed men rode. Two more trucks followed. He'd have liked more, but gas was in short supply and the trucks burned far more than their bikes, now all blasted or burned to wreckage. These militia idiots were a poor substitute for his brothers in the club, but they were all he had. Fortunately, they were all still terrified of him, even though he was wounded and now alone. He suppressed a smile despite his pain. He'd been right to give the militiamen the impression he was the president of the 'Richmond chapter' of Satan's Seed and that the far larger 'national chapter' was headquartered in Raleigh-Durham. The 'national' existed only in Spider's tall tale, but the thought alone of hundreds of affiliated bikers relatively nearby was enough to keep the militia idiots in line.

He cursed again as he thought of the ambush. He'd hoped his attackers would come out of the tunnel so he could take them out with his AR, but when he'd heard the bikes crank up, he knew that wasn't happening. It had taken him three hours to claw his way up the steep brush-covered slope to the road and stagger back to camp.

The wound was a through and through, with no permanent damage, but it hurt like hell. Fortunately, the club had been hoarding a looted supply of oxy, and he popped the painkillers like candy. He'd led a group back to the tunnel the next morning, where he stood speechless and enraged at the sight of his brothers' charred bodies among the smoldering wreckage of the bikes.

He was even more enraged when he did the math. From the signs, they'd come down the steep hill to the railroad tracks on foot, and they'd left the site of the massacre on two stolen bikes. That meant no more than four shooters, probably less since, from the scream they'd heard, his ambushers had the two kids as well. His best guess was two shooters; two men had murdered his entire motorcycle club. Well, they'd live to regret the day they didn't finish him off as well. It had taken a full day to organize these militia idiots, but they'd finally set off at first light this morning.

Spider figured the attackers had come down the Appalachian Trail on foot southbound; otherwise they wouldn't have needed the tunnel to get past the biker camp. A single road led south from the railroad depot at Afton, and they got lucky at the first occupied house they saw. Armed men confronted them from behind a barricade thrown across the long drive up to the farmhouse, and Spider had no doubts more guns were trained on them from undisclosed locations. He'd exited the truck slowly, his bandaged right shoulder clearly visible, with his good left hand held high above his head.

"Hello the barricade! We mean you no harm!" he yelled.

"Then you best get back in your truck and go on back where y'all came from. We ain't got nothin' to share but lead, but some of that will be comin' y'all's way if you're still standin' there in thirty seconds," came the reply.

"No need to be hostile, friend. We're just lookin' for a little information. Did you see some guys on motorcycles pass this way yesterday, maybe with a couple of kids?"

There was a long silence before the man from the barricade spoke again.

"You mean them two FEMA scumbags? Yeah, they hauled ass past here around midday yesterday. Had them poor children tied up and gagged, and they was past before we could think to do anything about it, and we didn't have the gas to chase 'em." A note of sympathy crept into the man's voice. "They your kids?"

Spider nodded solemnly. "My brother's. They killed him and my sister-in-law and stole the children. I'm obliged for the information. We'll be leavin' now."

"Hope you catch the sorry bastards," the voice said. Spider waved with his good hand and got back in the truck.

Things were easier after that. They met wary defenders at every stop, but the passage of the bikes hadn't gone unnoticed and their new cover story about being a posse out to recover stolen children fell on sympathetic ears. It was slow work, and they had to stop at each intersection and check each habitation to confirm which route the bikes had taken, but by mid-morning they'd tracked the bikes to the intersection of the Blue Ridge Parkway, Reeds Gap Road, and the Appalachian Trail. When queries at the next houses along Reeds Gap Road indicated no bikes had passed, Spider knew his quarry had gone south either along the Blue Ridge Parkway or, more likely, moved into the cover of the woods southbound on the trail. He was pretty sure he knew which.

* * *

Spider cursed again as he was thrown against the door during a tight turn.

"Damn you, Lindhurst, slow down! You do that again and I swear to God I'm gonna kill you," Spider said.

"So-sorry Spider," the driver said. "But ain't we trying to catch 'em?"

Spider sighed. "No, shit brain, we're trying to get ahead of them."

Lindhurst looked even more confused and Spider blew out an exasperated sigh.

"Look, I figure they're a couple of renegade FEMA cops and they probably want to keep as low a profile as possible. They were likely on the run from FEMA and the feds to start with, else they wouldn't have been on the trail. Now they're on loud motorcycles with a couple of tied-up kids. They might as well be wearing a 'look at me' sign; I mean look how easily we tracked them. So," Spider said, "I figure they'll try to make some distance south by stayin' out of sight on the Appalachian Trail, at least until they finish doing whatever it is they plan to do with the kids and dump the bodies."

Lindhurst looked troubled. "You figure they're doin' something funny with the kids?"

Spider scoffed. "What the hell do you think, dumb ass? You think a couple of rogue FEMA cops grabbed those kids out of the goodness of their hearts? Frankly, I don't give a shit as long as it slows them down and makes them easier to track."

"But, Spider, if they're on the AT, shouldn't we be chasing them on the trail?"

"How, on foot? These trucks won't make it up the trail. Hell, I'm not even sure the bikes can make it. Anyway, suppose we did chase them? Presuming we even get close to them, all they have to do is set another ambush and let us walk right into it."

Spider held up a tattered park service map of the Blue Ridge Parkway. "But two can play that game. The trail zigzags back and forth across the parkway, and we just have to get far enough ahead of them to set up our OWN ambush at one of those intersections. There's one up ahead near milepost 52 that will do nicely." He grinned. "Then we'll see who has the last laugh."

Robinson Gap Road
Intersection with Appalachian Trail
100 Yards East of the Blue Ridge Parkway

Same Day - 12:15 p.m.

Spider crouched in the concealing foliage, confident his ambush would go undetected until it was sprung. The setup was perfect; the dirt and gravel Robinson Gap Road roughly paralleled the more substantial Blue Ridge Parkway to the west, sometimes nearer and sometimes farther away, as they both wound south through the mountains. He'd selected a point where the Appalachian Trail crossed both roads at a right angle, and the roads were only a hundred yards apart. He set the trap on the less traveled road to the east on the theory his prey might be at least somewhat wary at crossings, but probably less so on the minor dirt track.

He and seven of his men were hidden around the ambush site, with overlapping fields of fire. On the off chance one of his prey escaped the death trap, they wouldn't get very far. He'd placed a pickup out of sight around the nearest bends in the dirt road in each direction, both drivers with orders to shoot anyone fleeing toward them. He'd left the third truck and driver back on the Blue Ridge Parkway in case he was wrong and his quarry had somehow gotten back on the main road somewhere farther north. Given his recent experience, Spider wasn't about to underestimate this pair.

He concealed the last man three hundred yards east on the AT, in the direction of the expected arrival. He couldn't be sure his targets were still on their bikes, and the concealed forward observer was to pass word of their approach and then let them pass unmolested. As the quarry walked, or rode, into the trap, the advance observer would then serve to 'close the back door' should the men try to flee back the way they came.

In the event something went wrong, all the four outlying men really had to do was delay the quarry's retreat until Spider and the rest of his men could fall on the targets and overwhelm them. The hardest part was waiting.

***

Lindhurst slapped a mosquito and stifled a curse, regretting he'd used the last of his insect repellent two days earlier. He shifted in his hiding spot, trying unsuccessfully to lessen his discomfort, and wondered how many ticks he was now hosting. Spider had it in for him, that was for sure, but the friggin' guy was insane, so he sure as hell wasn't going to argue with him.

He fished a crumpled cigarette package out of his shirt pocket and peered inside. One left, just like the last three times he'd looked. He considered smoking it yet again. He figured Spider wouldn't like it, but he hadn't actually said not to. Besides, no one else in the group had any smokes left at all, and if he lit up around them, every swinging dick in the group was gonna be buggin' him for a drag. If he was stuck out here by himself, he might as well get the benefit of having his last smoke in peace.

He put the cigarette under his nose and inhaled deeply, savoring the aroma of the tobacco. He exhaled deeply. *Screw it*, he thought, then put the cigarette to his lips and lit it, drawing the smoke deep into his lungs.

Appalachian Trail
Mile 1392.8 Southbound
One Half Mile East of Robinson Gap Road

Tremble drove in the lead, maneuvering the heavy street bike along the narrow trail, grateful they were nearing the Blue Ridge Parkway. Despite what was shown on the pages of the trail guide, the last thirty miles had been hell. The AT was definitely a hiking trail, not a biking trail. They'd have to avoid the next section; he knew they couldn't handle Punchbowl and Bluff Mountains. Alone, he and Keith might try it, but it was just too risky with the kids aboard.

He drove partially distracted, his mind turning over their options, when a familiar, almost forgotten smell filled his nostrils, invoking a sudden intense yearning. He stopped, and Keith rolled up beside him, his forehead furrowed in a question.

"Smell that?" Tremble asked, just loud enough to be heard over the bikes.

Keith wrinkled his nose. "Cigarette smoke," he said, reaching to kill the bike.

Tremble shook his head and caught Keith's hand before he hit the kill switch.

"That means people, and if we smell their cigarette, they hear our engines. It's best not to let them know we've smelled them until we know who they are."

Keith peered around into the thick woods, then leaned closer to his father and spoke. "They have to be damn close if we can smell their cigarette smoke."

Tremble shook his head. "Maybe not as close as you think. We've just spent a month in the woods away from any unnatural scents, so I suspect we can smell better. Did you notice how strong the gas smelled when you topped up the tanks?"

Keith nodded. "Now that you mention it, I thought I was going to pass out." He looked up the trail. "So what are we gonna do, Dad?"

Tremble rubbed his bearded chin. "It could be nothing, but I'll have to go check it out, and if it is trouble, we can't let them know we're onto them. I'll leave my bike here idling to add to the noise a bit, and I want you to drive up and down the same fifty feet so it sounds like we're still moving. We need to hide the kids in the woods just in case." Tremble hesitated. "Give Jamie the pistol."

Leaving Keith to attend to the kids, Tremble grabbed his M4 and melted into the woods to the south, moving quietly and effortlessly through the thick forest. The smell of smoke grew stronger to his right and he slowed, creeping back towards the trail from the south. He heard the sound of the engines behind him change as Keith began his ruse. Tremble melted against a tree and raised the monocular to his eye, panning along the trail slowly.

***

Lindhurst jerked at the sound of the engines and stubbed out his cigarette on a tree trunk, hastily returning the unsmoked butt to the package for later. Then the noise changed; maybe they were stopping, but he couldn't be sure. He was supposed to click the radio three times when he heard them, but what if they'd stopped? Spider didn't say anything about that. He decided to wait until he was sure.

It seemed like a long time, and he desperately wanted to finish his smoke. Then the noise changed; they were definitely moving, but it sounded like they were getting closer and then farther away. What if he signaled that they were coming and they were actually going the other way?

Hesitantly, he raised the radio to his mouth and keyed the mike. "Spider, I hear them, but—"

"GET OFF THE RADIO, YOU FRIGGING IDIOT!"

***

Tremble almost jumped out of his skin when, no more than thirty feet away on the opposite side of the trail, the man spoke. He said a silent prayer of thanks the battery had died on their own stolen radio the day before.

It would appear Spider had survived and that he'd learned from the last encounter. This would be the advance scout, with the ambush site farther up the trail. Tremble had spent hours studying the possible routes and he visualized them now. If he were planning an ambush, he'd set up at Robinson Gap Road, and he had no doubt that was where Spider was.

He glanced at his watch and considered options. Keith's little charade wouldn't fool them for long, and no matter how many men Spider had, he and Keith couldn't hope to win a gunfight without surprise on their side. The only option was to run.

He briefly considered retreating back down the AT, but dismissed the idea. Spider had apparently been smart enough to figure out they were using the trail, and he'd heard them now. All he had to do was leave a blocking force at this intersection and then send another group to the next trail intersection to the east. Spider and his men obviously still had transportation, and they could probably travel faster on the National Forest Service roads than the Trembles could on the much more rugged trail. If that happened, he and Keith would be like a player caught in a baseball rundown, and their only hope would be if one of the blocking groups 'dropped the ball.' If that was going to be the inevitable situation anyway, they had a much greater chance of breaking out before Spider and his gang were prepared for the breakout. Forcing himself to go slow, Tremble melted back away from the trail and into the full concealment of the woods.

Robinson Gap Road actually ran east and west almost paralleling the Appalachian Trail for approximately half a mile before it returned to its meandering southern course beside the Blue Ridge Parkway. From his present position, the road was only two hundred yards away through the woods. He struck out for it and, when he glimpsed it through the trees, paralleled it until he reached the first bend. He knew there might be a stopping force here, a group placed down the road to cut off escape from the ambush.

When he saw the 'stopping force,' he almost smiled. A single pickup was parked across the road, with one man standing behind it, his AR laid across the hood of the truck, pointing in the direction of the assumed ambush site. It made sense; any fugitives from the ambush would come screaming around the curve and right into the sights of the shooter. *We can work with that,* he thought and listened for the sound of Keith's bike so he could cut directly through the woods back to it.

He moved quickly now, less concerned with noise as he moved away from their pursuers. Thirty yards into the woods, he pulled out his pocketknife and blazed trees as he went along. They wouldn't have time to be groping when they came back. He burst out onto the trail fifty feet in front of Keith and his son braked to a stop beside him.

"Leave your bike running on the kickstand. You go get the kids while I cram everything from the saddlebags into the packs. Then come back and help me with the bike. Hurry!" Tremble said.

"But—"

"Just do it, Keith! I'll explain later."

∗∗

Spider made his way down the trail to Lindhurst's hiding spot, listening to the distant sounds of the motorcycles. He cursed as he smelled the cigarette smoke, but filed that away for later. Capping these bastards was what mattered now.

"Damn you, Lindhurst! If you've warned them—"

"I didn't do nothin' Spider, I swear. It's just goofy, that's all. First I heard 'em comin', then it sounded like they was stopped, then they started comin' toward me again and then it sounded like they was goin' away. Like that, over and over. Then just before you got here, it sounded like they were stopped again."

Spider stood looking down the trail, trying to figure out what was going on. As he stood there, the engine once again changed pitch, much louder now.

"Sounds like they're comin' this way again, much louder now," Lindhurst said.

"All right. Keep out of sight and let 'em pass, just like we planned. I'm going back to warn the others." Lindhurst nodded and Spider dashed back up the trail.

* * *

Tremble squatted beside the idling bike and looked up at his son standing on the opposite side, gripping the handlebars.

"Lean it a bit more toward you, Keith. Maybe an inch," Tremble said.

Keith grunted and leaned into the handlebars, pivoting the heavy weight of the bike on the kickstand so the back wheel lifted farther off the ground. Tremble jammed the short log in under the bike.

"That's it! Ease it down and make sure it's steady before you let go," Tremble said.

Keith did as ordered and the bike came to rest canted at a slight angle, but relatively steady with the rear wheel an inch off the ground.

Tremble rose, put the bike in gear, and revved the throttle. The engine roared and the back wheel spun in the air. He nodded to Keith, who grabbed the roll of duct tape off the bike seat and wrapped the throttle and secured it to the handlebars.

"Think it'll fool 'em?" Keith asked.

"Not forever, but I hope for long enough," Tremble said. "Now let's grab the kids and get out of here. We don't have much time."

* * *

His foresight in blazing the trail paid off, as they moved through the woods swiftly, carrying the children as well as all their gear. When they neared the road, Tremble motioned Keith to stop, then looked at Jamie and put his finger to his lips. The boy nodded, wide-eyed, sensing the tension as Tremble lowered him to the ground.

"Okay, Jamie," Tremble whispered, "Keith and I have to take care of something. We're going to leave you guys here for a little while. I want you to protect Molly and all of our gear. Can you do that?"

The boy nodded solemnly.

"Good man! I knew I could count on you," Tremble said, then stripped off all his gear except his weapons and motioned for Keith to do the same. When Keith was ready, Tremble started for the road, Keith close behind.

At the edge of the road, Tremble carefully parted the bushes and pointed. Keith followed Tremble's finger to where a camo-clad man stood fifty feet away, his back to them as he leaned across the hood of the pickup, his AR pointed toward the bend in the road.

"How we gonna do this?" Keith whispered.

"As quietly as possible," Tremble whispered back, looking around on the ground. He stooped and picked up a hefty rock, perhaps twice as big as his fist.

"I figured you knew some ninja stuff or something," Keith said.

"I guess I slept through that part of the course. Besides, I think that's mostly movie bullshit anyway; it's pretty tough to kill a man quietly. I'm going with a rock to the noggin."

"What if he hears you and turns before you get there? You won't have time to go for your gun. You'll be a sitting duck," Keith said.

"That's where you come in. I'm gonna go wide to the left, so you'll have a clear shot at him right up to the point I'm within striking distance. But if you have to shoot him, the cat's out of the bag, so don't wait around. Go grab the kids and bring them to the road. Leave the gear if you have to, but get back out here. I'll be checking him for the keys and getting the truck turned around. I figure we got maybe a minute after a shot is fired and then they'll be coming around that bend in force," Tremble said.

"Got it," Keith whispered, and Tremble rose cautiously and started toward his target, rock in hand.

***

Spider crouched in his hiding spot, his apprehension growing. The roar of the bikes wasn't getting any closer and they should have been here by now. And there was something else, something he couldn't quite put his finger on at first; then it hit him. He was hearing one bike and the drone was steady, as if it were tooling down the open highway, not negotiating the twists and turns of a forest trail, rougher in some spots than others. The sound should be rising and falling to the variable load on the engine.

He looked around nervously. This had decoy written all over it, and if they weren't coming from the expected direction, where were they? Were they trying to slip by? He needed to give his outposts a heads-up.

Spider looked down at his radio, undecided. The units had crappy battery life, so chances were the stolen radio was now useless unless the fugitives also had a solar charger. Besides, if they WERE trying to slip by, it meant they'd figured out the ambush anyway. Spider raised the radio.

***

Tremble was halfway to his target when the radio squawked. He froze.

"Bailey, do you copy?"

Tremble's intended target rose from where he was sprawled over the pickup hood, still facing away as he fumbled a radio from a belt holster and spoke into it.

"Bailey here. I copy, Spider. What's up?"

"Somethin' ain't right," Spider said over the radio. "Have a look around your position, especially in the woods in the direction of the sound of those bikes. Tell me what you see. Over."

"I'm on it," the man said, turning as he spoke.

Tremble was already lowering the rock to reach for his pistol, but Keith was quicker. His son put a three-round burst center mass as soon as the man turned, and Bailey sank to the ground twenty feet from Tremble.

So much for plan A, Tremble thought as he turned toward Keith, but his son was already disappearing into the woods to grab the kids. Tremble rushed to the truck, hoping to spot the key in the ignition. *Of course not. That would have been too easy*. He turned and dropped to one knee, his apprehension rising as he rifled the dead man's pockets without success. Frantic, he returned to the truck cab and relief washed over him when he spotted the keys in a cup holder.

He was about to climb into the truck and turn it around when the roar of an engine just around the curve told him he was too late. He moved back to a defensive position behind the truck just as Keith burst from the woods with the kids.

"PUT THE KIDS BEHIND THE WHEELS AND GET READY!" Tremble yelled. "WE'RE ABOUT TO HAVE COMPANY."

***

Spider was moving as soon as he heard the shots. If they got one of his trucks, they might get away.

"THOMPSON! GET THAT TRUCK TO MY POSITION NOW!" he screamed into the radio, calling the truck parked just up Robinson Gap Road to the north.

He briefly considered bringing the last truck over from the Blue Ridge Parkway, but he doubted it could make it through the strip of thick woods separating the parkway from his present position. He'd had to bring the two trucks he was using for the ambush onto Robinson Gap Road at an intersection two miles to the north, but there was no time for the truck he' left on the parkway to backtrack in time to join them. It was just out of play for the moment.

The truck from the northern outpost appeared and Spider jumped into the passenger seat, motioning four more men into the bed of the pickup.

"Haul ass, Thompson," Spider said, and the driver floored it.

***

But the lesson Spider learned in the railroad tunnel was forgotten in the heat of the moment. He was so accustomed to terrorizing people it never occurred to him running wasn't necessarily his intended victims' default reaction. However, the Trembles had no intention of 'getting away,' at least not immediately.

Tremble heard the engine roar increase around the curve and knew their attackers would come into view any second. He marveled at the fact that Spider had been smart enough to set up this secondary ambush point yet was apparently dumb enough to rush into it himself.

"Target the vehicle first," he called to Keith. "I'll take the engine and radiator; you try to shred the tires. We can't drag this out, because if we get pinned down, their numbers will tell. Our best bet is to disable their vehicle fast and break contact."

Keith raised his M4, targeting the bend in the road fifty yards away.

The truck burst into view seconds later, and as soon as it rounded the curve, both Trembles opened up to devastating effect. Simon punched multiple holes in the radiator, but Keith's fusillade had the most immediate impact, shredding both front tires. The truck swerved out of control, the terrified driver compounding the problem by practically standing on the brakes, sending the truck skidding into the woods, glancing off a tree trunk en route. The truck piled into a hedge of wild blackberry vines and lurched to a stop, throwing the shooters into the dense brambles.

"If anyone's still feeling frisky, I'll keep their heads down," Tremble said, his M4 still at his shoulder. "You get the kids in the cab and get behind the wheel. When you're ready to roll, I'll stay in the back to play defense if need be."

"Sounds good," Keith said, keeping his rifle trained toward their attackers. "But you've been studying the maps more. You should drive and let me ride in back. That makes more sense."

Tremble hesitated, reluctant to put his son in the most exposed position.

"I'll be fine, Dad. And we don't have time to argue. Besides, you know it makes sense," Keith said softly.

Tremble gave a curt nod and lowered his rifle. "Jamie, let's get you and Molly in the truck and get out of here."

***

Spider shoved on the truck door again and again, battering it against the mass of brambles. He finally succeeded in forcing a big enough opening to squeeze through, thorns ripping his bare arms as he clawed his way around the cab and into the bed of the truck. His nose hurt like hell from where the airbag had bashed him in the face.

He looked through the rear window at Thompson slumped over the wheel, dead or unconscious, and Spider didn't really care which. If the dipshit was a better driver, they wouldn't have crashed.

One of the men thrown from the truck bed had hit a tree and was obviously dead. The rest, without benefit of airbags, were injured to varying degrees, mostly broken bones or sprains. Spider left them tending their wounds and limped back up the road toward their original site.

He arrived to find Lindhurst coming off the trail from his hide.

"Wh-what happened, Spider?" Lindhurst asked.

"What does it look like, dumb ass? We just got our asses kicked, that's what, and if I figure out you're to blame, your ass is toast," Spider snarled.

Lindhurst blanched and Spider motioned for him to join the three men he'd left behind because there hadn't been room in the truck.

"You four follow me. We're going back to the truck on the parkway; I ain't done yet."

The men followed him down the trail to the Blue Ridge Parkway and the waiting truck. Spider climbed into the passenger seat without a word to the driver and began to rummage in the glove compartment. He found a map and spread it on the dashboard.

"Robinson Gap Road has about a gillion side roads, but they're all dead ends." He pointed at the map. "The only outlet is down this old logging road and back to the Blue Ridge Parkway right here."

The driver leaned over and looked at the map. "Three or four miles maybe on the parkway, and that way is shorter for them — and they got a head start."

"And we got a better road. Now get off your ass and get this thing movin'. We got some payback to deliver," Spider said.

CHAPTER EIGHT

Logging Road
Robinson Gap Road
Southbound

Tremble pushed the battered truck down the old logging road as fast as he dared, a dust plume behind him as he bounced through rutted stretches and fishtailed around hairpin turns in a spray of rocks and dried leaves, silently praying a blown tire wouldn't send them over a precipice. He glanced in the rearview mirror to see a grim-faced Keith hanging on for dear life. Keith met his gaze in the mirror and managed a smile and a thumbs-up, the gesture short-lived as they bounced through another rut and Keith grabbed the side of the truck with both hands to keep from being thrown out.

Tremble slowed; there was no point in escaping Spider to die in a truck crash.

He glanced over at the kids. The dilapidated old truck had no working seat belts, and Jamie was holding Molly tight with one arm while he clung to the armrest with the other hand, doing his best to keep them in the threadbare seat. Molly was staring ahead with a vacant unseeing look, perhaps seeing a scene she found preferable to reality.

The road curved out of sight to the right just ahead, and as they rounded the curve, the road, such as it was, transited a shallow creek. Tremble stopped and studied the creek, envisioning the map he'd studied so thoroughly; this had to be Brown's Creek, with the Blue Ridge Parkway intersection just ahead. He stepped on the gas and they splashed across the shallow creek and back onto the logging road to reach the parkway — and disappointment — minutes later.

Tremble got out of the truck and stared up at the parkway in dismay. The map was accurate: the Blue Ridge Parkway and the old road did indeed intersect, but there was no interchange. The logging road passed under the parkway via an underpass. Tremble was studying the wooded slope when he heard Keith move up beside him.

"Can we make it up?" Keith asked.

Tremble turned from the slope and looked back at the old truck.

"I doubt it, but it's our only shot. According to the map, the logging road dead-ends in about a mile, so we either try to make it up on the parkway or go back the way we came, and I don't think that would be too wise," Tremble said.

Tremble sighed. "Between winding through the trees and that slope, I figure the odds of rolling the truck over are fifty-fifty. Take the kids and gear up on foot. I'll try to get the truck up."

"Leave it," Keith said. "We've lost them and we can make it back to the trail on foot if we have to."

Tremble shook his head. "Not with the kids, and we don't know for sure Spider's out of action. If he isn't, he's already proved he can read a map, so he'll find the truck and be back tight on our trail. Besides, if I roll the truck, there are so many trees I won't roll far." He paused and looked at his son. "I'll be all right, son, and it's our best shot. Now get the kids up the slope so we can get out of here."

Keith nodded and did as instructed, and Tremble got back behind the wheel. He backed up a ways and sat a moment, staring at the wooded slope, trying to plan the best route through the trees. Then he dropped it into first gear and charged, hoping his chosen path worked.

He hit the slope at an angle, the old truck leaning left as it clawed its way upward, tires spinning through the detritus of the forest floor. He shot between two trees, the opening barely wide enough for the truck. *Or maybe not*, he thought as the tree on the left sheared off the side mirror. It was all a blur from there, an intense exercise in turning the wheel incrementally to avoid trees without reducing momentum. There were jolts and scrapes and the moaning sound of tortured steel, and at one point he felt a momentary sense of weightlessness, sure he was going over, but then the truck bounced onto the parkway, side mirrors gone, and sides battered, but drivable.

"GET IN," Tremble yelled, but Keith was already shoving the kids into the cab, and seconds later vaulted into the bed himself, beating on the top of the cab to let his father know he was ready.

Tremble only planned to go a mile or so on the parkway, presuming the road he was looking for actually HAD a connection with the larger road, something he was now unsure of given their recent experience. He checked the odometer and hit the gas; the good news was, of course, they still had wheels.

The good news ended five seconds later when the back window of the cab shattered and the bullet whizzed by his right ear to spider-web the windshield. A frantic look in the mirror showed a truck visible in the distance behind them, and Keith preparing to return fire.

***

"FASTER!" Spider screamed at the driver as rifles cracked above their heads, the shooters in the bed firing over the cab.

"I'm goin' as fast as I can on this road, Spider," the driver said. "If I go any faster, I'll throw the guys out on the curves."

"I DON'T GIVE A SHIT!" Spider yelled, beating the dashboard. "CATCH THOSE BASTARDS!"

The driver swallowed and increased speed, praying they didn't end up wrapped around a tree.

***

Tremble looked down at the speedometer, checking both his speed and the odometer as the trees flew past. The truck was gaining on him, but he dared not go faster for fear of throwing his son out of the back on the twisting road. The one advantage he had was that the frequent curves gave shooters from neither vehicle time to accurately target the other. The pursuers' first effort had been luck, assisted by the fact it had occurred on one of the rare straight sections of the Blue Ridge Parkway and that Tremble hadn't been moving very fast at the time.

The cat-and-mouse game continued as they dashed south, alternately visible to each other and then hidden from view. The odometer clicked over one mile and Tremble nodded as he saw the road curve to the right ahead. As he recalled, Route 812 was on the right, just after a long sweeping curve. It was a 'secondary road,' which probably meant a gravel track, but at least it was assigned a number, so maybe it actually connected with the parkway. He braked hard and swung around the curve, tires squealing, as he prayed Keith was hanging on tight.

He would have missed it if he hadn't been alert. There was an asphalt apron to the right; a small tongue of blacktop leading off the main road and about the width of a narrow driveway, running to the tree line a scant thirty feet away. Tremble plunged into the woods, the 'road' immediately transitioning to a gravel track running through a tunnel of green barely wider than the truck.

He rounded a sharp curve and felt a surge of hope; if they'd gotten off the parkway before their pursuers rounded the last curve, they might escape unseen. That hope died quickly as he heard the squealing tires of a truck braking followed by engine sounds on the track behind them.

Route 812 twisted through the thick forest, their pursuers invisible now, sensed only by the sound of a straining engine. In places the road almost doubled back on itself and he had the disconcerting sensation of running to rather than from their tormentors, passing perhaps fifty feet apart but separated by dense forest.

It was impossible to tell if they were gaining or losing ground, and Tremble racked his brain for a solution. If he could get a long enough lead, they might be able to stop and set an ambush, but that was problematic because their pursuers would hear the engine stop. Twice burned, Spider would be unlikely to rush into a third ambush.

He was still pondering the possibilities when the road opened up. It still ran through endless walls of green, but it was all downhill now, wider with longer straight stretches and it was more well-maintained. Tremble screamed for Keith to hang on and stomped the gas, driving like a wild man to open up his lead and expand their options.

He alternated between studying the increasingly straight sections of road ahead and watching the mirror for signs of their pursuers. On one long stretch they appeared a quarter mile back. He'd opened the lead, but knew that would be short-lived now that their pursuers had better road themselves. He needed to do something, and fast, but all he could do was mash the already floorboarded accelerator even harder, willing the truck to go faster.

Their luck ran out when they bounced through a pothole; the right rear tire finally had all the torture it could take. It blew with the sound of a gunshot, and Tremble fought the wheel for all he was worth, twisting it first one way and then the other to keep the truck both on the road and upright, praying that Keith could hold on.

He skidded to a stop across the road and leaped out, relief washing over him at the sight of Keith on his back in the truck bed, white-faced.

"Are you all right, son?" he asked.

Keith nodded, sitting up just as a round slammed into the side of the truck.

"GRAB THE KIDS AND LET'S GET IN THE WOODS," Tremble yelled as Keith leaped from the truck.

Their weapons slung and the children in their arms, they ran for the nearby tree line.

"THERE," Tremble shouted, pointing to a break in the forest, next to a tree with a white blaze on the trunk.

Johns Hollow Shelter
Appalachian Trail
Mile 1402.8 Southbound

Ten Minutes Earlier

George Anderson was sweating as they rolled past the crude hikers' shelter. Cindy looked over at him and smiled.

"There's a privy over there if you need to clean out your pants," she said.

Anderson returned the smile somewhat sheepishly.

"That was a pretty hairy descent. I thought I was gonna fall out of the Mule in a couple of places," he said.

She laughed. "Not likely. I figure your fingerprints are permanently etched in that hand grab. What's the matter? Don't you trust my driving?"

"Your driving is fine; it's the near vertical descents I have a little problem with."

"Well, that part's over at least. Now we just have to figure out how to get across the damn river," Cindy said.

Anderson nodded. Jeremy's fever had broken two days earlier, but they'd waited an extra day to be sure, and it felt good to be moving again. They hadn't gotten quite as early a start as he'd planned, but they were back on the trail at last.

He motioned to the primitive hut. "If there's a shelter, there may be a spring nearby. Maybe we should stop and top off our water?"

Cindy nodded and braked, stopping the Mule and turning it off.

"There probably is one. They usually locate the shelters near a good water source if possible. Let's have a look. Jeremy," she said over her shoulder, "would you please collect the empty water bottles?"

"Yes, ma'am," Jeremy said, climbing off his perch on top of the gear.

They found a piped spring near the shelter and were filling their water bottles when Anderson jerked his head up.

"What?" Cindy asked.

"Just listen," he said.

Muffled by the trees and just audible was the distant sound of a straining engine. The volume increased as they listened.

"Are we near a road?" Anderson asked.

"Maybe. How should I know? I told you I've never been this far south on the trail," Cindy said.

"It sounds close. I think we should stay right here until it passes," Anderson said.

He'd barely finished speaking when there was a loud pop.

"Gunshot?" Cindy asked, concern in her voice.

Anderson shook his head. "Or blowout. It's hard to tell. But we're staying put until we don't hear anything for a good long time. If it's a blowout, we need to give whoever it is time to change it and be on their way—"

A second, more distinctive pop echoed through the forest, followed almost simultaneously with the sound of metal striking metal. In seconds, more guns joined the fusillade with a flurry of furious firing followed by sudden silence.

"That would be gunfire, three or four shooters at least. And their target is either dead or undercover; otherwise they wouldn't have stopped," Anderson said. "We're definitely staying right here."

"Maybe we should go back up the trail," Cindy said.

Anderson shook his head again. "If we start the Mule now, someone might hear the engine. Our best bet is just to lie low here and let trouble pass us by."

The words were hardly out of his mouth when they heard the sound of running footsteps through the trees, coming down the trail toward them.

"Or not," Anderson said. "Get the guns."

They separated, Cindy and Anderson on opposite sides of the trail, with Cindy keeping Jeremy close to her where she could watch him. They were reacting rather than acting and had no plan. Anderson had a slightly better angle down the trail, so he'd likely take the first shot, but beyond that, they were winging it.

He figured they'd stumbled into the middle of a turf war, and just being here was unhealthy, regardless of which side won. At a minimum the winners were likely to have designs on the Mule and all their gear. *Not happening*, he thought. They had to put this group down hard and fast and hope they could handle whoever was chasing them.

***

Tremble's breath came in ragged gasps as he clutched Molly to his chest and struggled to keep up with his young son's man-killing pace along the trail. The girl clung to him like a second skin, her arms wrapped around his neck and her face pressed tightly to his chest. Jamie was similarly glued to Keith as they flew up the trail.

Tremble knew they had to find some sort of defensible position before Spider closed on them, but he hadn't seen anything yet. Then he saw it ahead through the trees, glimpses of a wooden building. A hikers' shelter! Maybe they might find a defensible position there.

***

Anderson started seeing glimpses through the trees. There looked to be two of them, running hard. *Good. They're intent on escaping the threat behind them and not expecting an ambush.* He'd wait for a clear shot and take them both down before they could react. Whoever was chasing them would hear the gunfire and be alerted, but that couldn't be helped. If he could take care of these two quickly enough, maybe they could get down the trail and ambush the pursuers just as they entered the woods.

The forms slowly began to resolve as he got incrementally longer glimpses; they were wearing dirty uniforms. They looked like … FEMA cops, men clad in the same uniform he'd worn for many years. They were disheveled with full beards and were wearing some sort of bulky body armor or chest packs in addition to the M4s they carried. His initial fears were confirmed; FEMA cops, rogue or not, were unlikely to be potential allies. He'd take them down with a clear conscience. He braced his M4 against a tree and sighted in on the spot where they'd appear around a bend in the trail, his only concern whether the body armor would necessitate a head shot.

The first man burst into view and Anderson studied him in his sights. What he'd taken for body armor during his brief glimpses was actually a pale blue, obviously a chest rig of some sort and likely nothing that would stop a round. Anderson's lips twisted in a grim smile and he aimed center mass, concentrating on the shot. He heard a sudden noise to his left and the target looked in his direction, alerted and slowing to a stop. Anderson cursed and pulled the trigger.

***

"Go! Go! Go!" Spider yelled as he leaped out of the truck and screamed at the shooters in the truck bed. "Get after them and keep the pressure on before they get a chance to hunker down and fight back!"

The men jumped down to follow Spider into the woods, but a single shot, followed by a three-round burst, brought them up short.

"What's up, Spider? Maybe they decided to shoot each other and save us the bother," one of the militia men said.

Spider backhanded the man. "Shut the hell up! If I want your opinion, I'll ask for it. Now shut up, all of you, and let me think."

Chastened, the men stood silent while Spider considered the possibilities. The seconds stretched to minutes as he racked his brain to figure out what the hell was going on. A single shot could have been an accidental discharge, but not when followed closely by a three-round burst. Someone was exchanging fire, which meant he might have a potential ally. He shook his head. No, more likely it meant there would be a three-way fight. He considered withdrawing, but figured he really had nothing to lose. The militia men were expendable, and he'd be damned if he'd let the murderers of his entire gang escape. He made up his mind.

"Lindhurst," he said, "take these four guys and head up the trail, leapfrog style. Two of you advance while the other two cover you from behind trees; then you swap. I'll bring up the rear to make sure no one slips up on us from behind."

Lindhurst looked puzzled. "But how they gonna do that, Spider? There ain't but two of them, an if—"

Spider's vicious slap rocked Lindhurst's head back. "I swear to God, Lindhurst, if you don't shut the hell up right now, I'm gonna put a bullet between your eyes myself. Now do what I told you to do. Is that clear?"

Cowed, Lindhurst nodded and led the others toward the woods.

546

Near Johns Hollow Shelter
Two minutes earlier

Someone crashed into Anderson, and a hand drove the barrel of his M4 skyward just as he pulled the trigger.

"They're kids, George. They're carrying kids," Cindy said.

Almost immediately, a three-round burst of fire forced Anderson to drop behind a nearby boulder, pulling Cindy with him.

"Maybe," he hissed, "but that's not a kid shooting at us, now is it?"

"You shot at them first. And it doesn't matter," Cindy said. "I'm not shooting kids. Are you?"

Anderson cursed. "No, of course not, but what the hell are we going to —"

"WE MEAN YOU NO HARM, BUT THE PEOPLE CHASING US ARE A THREAT TO US ALL. LET'S TALK," came a voice from the trail.

Anderson sat stock-still, processing what he'd just heard, and the familiar voice that said it.

***

Tremble was jogging behind Keith, rounding a turn and looking past his son when he saw the movement—a small figure darted across the trail and collided with a large man in the black uniform of the Special Reaction Force a split second before a shot tore through the foliage high above his head.

"DOWN, KEITH," he screamed, stepping to one side and raising his M4 one-handed to fire a three-round burst past his son and toward the shooter. He had the satisfaction of seeing both figures dive out of sight before he took cover himself, Molly beginning to sob against his chest.

"Dad? What are we gonna do?" Keith asked from where he was crouched in the foliage beside Tremble.

"I don't know, son; I'm thinking," Tremble replied.

Not that there was much to think about. Spider and his men would kill them both and God knows what they'd do with the kids. The future was equally dismal if they turned themselves in to what was apparently an SRF force ahead of them. There was literally no place else to run—or was there?

"Okay," Tremble said. "I'll try to stall these guys in front of us while you take the kids and quietly sneak off at right angles to the trail. Get as far away as you possibly can, then cut back through the woods to the road we came from. I'll keep stalling until I hear Spider's guys closing in, and then I'll drop down and start shooting in both directions. With any luck, the two groups will each think the other is firing on them and get in a firefight. While they're all shooting at each other, I'll belly-crawl out of here and follow you to the road. We'll figure out what to do after that."

Keith nodded and gently pulled Molly away from Tremble. "And, son," Tremble said, and Keith looked at his father.

"Check the time when you get to the road. If I'm not out in ten minutes, it means I'm not coming. Take the kids and do the best you can. I'm counting on you," Tremble said.

Keith looked as if he were about to protest, then nodded. He swallowed hard, pulled his father into a fierce, quick hug then released him to begin to speak softly to the kids.

Tremble gave himself a second to get his own emotions under control and then whispered to his son, "Wait until I have these guys' full attention before you crawl away."

Keith nodded again and Tremble called out down the trail, "WE MEAN YOU NO HARM, BUT THE PEOPLE CHASING US ARE A THREAT TO US ALL. LET'S TALK."

There was a long pause, and Tremble was beginning to think his plan wouldn't work when the answer came back down the trail.

"THAT YOU, TREMBLE?"

What the hell?

"WHO'S ASKING?" Tremble yelled back.

"GEORGE. GEORGE ANDERSON."

Tremble sat, momentarily confused. Then he smiled.

"SAM? SO YOU MADE IT!" Tremble yelled.

"THAT'S GEORGE. AND YEAH, I MADE IT, IF 'MADE IT' MEANS THEY HAVEN'T CAUGHT ME YET, AND NO THANKS TO YOU, I MIGHT ADD. BUT IF YOU WANT TO CONTINUE THIS CONVERSATION, SHOW YOURSELF AND KEEP BOTH HANDS WHERE I CAN SEE THEM."

CHAPTER NINE

FEMA Special Reaction Force
Regional HQ
Brunswick Nuclear Power Plant
Cape Fear River
Near Wilmington, North Carolina

Same Day - Same Time

Reaper glared at Rorke over the map and shook his head. "You told me I had two weeks. This is too soon."

Rorke shrugged. "Things change. Crawford's calling the shots now and he's nervous about Fort Box. And he's right; we have to deal with this problem before it gets any further out of hand. Besides, quit bitching, you've got the easy part now. Do you think I'm HAPPY about sending SRF regulars in? We're bound to take casualties, and it's hard enough to keep this collection of scum together without tasking them with anything approaching a fair fight. The longer we delay, the better prepared the defenders are likely to be. We go tomorrow, just before sunset, and that's final."

"But we're not ready. You said—"

"I KNOW WHAT I SAID. NOW I'M SAYING TOMORROW AT SUNSET. DO. YOU. UNDERSTAND?" Rorke glared at his underling.

Reaper swallowed hard and nodded.

"Good," Rorke said. "As I said, we'll attack out of the setting sun and use that to our advantage."

He pointed down at the crude representation of Fort Box he'd drawn on the map. "Their firepower is concentrated on the eastern wall, facing your people in the old 'fugee camp. That's the most obvious threat, and I think they're counting on the open river on the western side to give them time to shift forces in the event of an assault from the river."

Rorke smiled and moved his finger farther west on the map. "We're going to make that a fatal assumption. We'll assemble the SRF assault force at the intersection of 17 and 140 near Grayson Park during the day tomorrow. We'll fly our choppers one at a time 'nap of the earth' to the assembly point. They likely won't spot us, and even if they do, they'll likely take it as a single chopper. We'll pop up right before sundown and attack out of the setting sun from five or six miles away. We'll be on them before they can react or reposition. Do you know your role?"

Reaper nodded glumly. "Before you assault, I'm supposed to take the 'fugee militia and attack the east wall in force to keep most of the defenders tied up. But we're gonna get massacred—"

Rorke cut him off with an impatient wave. "No, you're NOT supposed to attack in force! You're supposed to send a sacrificial assault force across to FAKE a full assault but open fire with the bulk of your force from protected positions. Use the automatic weapons, RPGs, or whatever the hell you can find. Keep the defenders' heads down and make as much noise as possible, both to provide a distraction and cover the sound of the approaching choppers when they come from the west. Is that clear?"

Understanding—and relief—showed on Reaper's dark face. "So just a demonstration, then?"

"Correct," Rorke said. "The chopper assault should be over in minutes, and after our troops control the main decks of the ships, they can fire down into the fort and take the defenders on the east wall from behind. Any surviving defenders will have to abandon the wall and retreat into the buildings. When we have the ships and have forced the defenders to retreat from the east wall, I'll give you the signal to launch the REAL attack on the east wall. We'll keep the SRF troops on the ships and let your 'fugee militia pour over the wall and dig any survivors out of the buildings. The 'fugees are all seeking revenge on the Fort Box defenders anyway, so we'll let them do all the hard work. The more of them the defenders kill, the more their blood will be up. Let them have any survivors, and when their bloodlust is spent, we'll step back in and get them under control."

Reaper nodded, smiling now. "Brilliant."

"Yeah, well, just make sure you hold up your end," Rorke said. "Crawford's status with the regular military is still shaky, and we have to squash all this resistance now. I'm pulling in every chopper within range for this assault so we can get as many boots as possible on those ships in minutes. By this time tomorrow, there will be no Fort Box."

Johns Hollow Shelter
Appalachian Trail
Mile 1402.8 Southbound

Day 42
May 12, 2020 - 1:05 p.m.

Anderson glared at Simon Tremble across the ten feet that separated them, his admiration for the man tinged with suspicion.

"So how do I know this isn't another setup, Tremble? Just some way for you to get us to take the fall while you and sonny boy slip out the back door? It's not like you haven't done it before," Anderson said.

Tremble nodded. "Fair enough. You've a right to be suspicious, but you also know I didn't have a choice. Besides, we escaped from you twice, so you were likely toast with FEMA anyway; leaving you as a decoy didn't really worsen your situation."

Anderson snorted. "Really nice of you to decide that for me —"

Cindy shot a nervous glance down the trail. "This is really fascinating, but can we discuss the immediate problem, like who's coming down that trail?"

Tremble nodded. "Between four and six shooters. Militia types mostly. No real training that I can tell or at least not top tier."

Anderson raised an eyebrow. "Mostly?"

"They're led by a biker type named Spider," Tremble said. "He'll be in a denim jacket. I'm not sure about his training, but he's got some natural instincts. I figure they'd be here by now except that he heard the gunfire and is being cautious."

Anderson nodded. "All right then, let's get set up to give them a warm —"

Tremble shook his head. "We've ambushed him twice in as many days. After he heard the shots, he's not likely to charge in here. Unless we can set up some way to entice him, he'll probe until he makes contact, and then we'll settle into a long stalemate. Not only is that much more likely to get one of us killed, a prolonged firefight this close to the river and main roads might attract unwanted attention."

"All right, then what do you suggest?" Anderson asked.

Tremble looked over at the Mule. "Does that thing run?"

"Of course it runs!" Jeremy said, sensing Anderson's ambivalence toward Tremble.

Tremble looked at Jeremy for the first time, a brief but noticeable flicker of surprise crossing his face as he picked up on the young man's handicap.

"Can you drive it, son?" Tremble asked, smiling to cover his lapse.

"I'm not your son, and course I can drive it," Jeremy replied.

Cindy laid a calming hand on her son's arm and looked evenly at Tremble. "Jeremy is quite capable. Why do you ask?"

"I thought we might put the kids in the Mule and have him drive them back up the trail out of harm's way. Meanwhile the rest of us can spread along the trail in mutually supporting positions and hope Spider's men focus on the sound of the Mule up ahead. We can take them out—"

Anderson interrupted. "If you want to end this fast, we'll need every gun. You haven't seen Jeremy shoot."

Jeremy straightened under the implied praise.

"Okay, then perhaps the young lady can drive the Mule—"

Anderson laughed out loud. "Cindy's a better shot than anyone here."

"I can do it. I can drive the Mule," Jamie said, and all eyes turned to the boy.

"It's just like my grandpa's and he lets me drive it all the time. I have to stand up to reach the gas pedal, but I can do it."

Anderson looked at Tremble, who shrugged. "Tough times mean we all have to rise to the occasion, I guess." He squatted beside Jamie.

"Are you sure, Jamie? Can you drive the Mule away to keep Molly safe while we deal with the bad guys?" Tremble asked.

Jamie nodded solemnly, and Tremble looked at Anderson, who led the way to the Mule, Jamie walking and Keith carrying Molly. Keith placed Molly in the passenger seat while Jamie climbed into the driver's side, standing with his butt against the edge of the seat and leaning back so he could get behind the wheel. He gripped the wheel with both hands, staring through it rather than over it. He started the Mule and deftly released the hand brake.

"Okay, Jamie," Anderson said, "in about a quarter mile you'll come to a little clearing and the trail starts uphill. It gets steep real fast with no place to turn around until you get all the way to the top of the mountain, so just drive around in circles in the clearing to make noise. Got it?"

Jamie nodded and Anderson continued. "If you hear someone and you're not sure it's one of us, stop the Mule and leave it running; then you and your sister hide in the woods fast. Okay?"

Jamie nodded again. Forehead wrinkled in concentration, he put the Mule in low gear and drove off around a bend in the trail.

Anderson turned to Tremble. "What now?"

"Four of us spread out down one side of the trail with overlapping fields of fire, but well back so we can see but can't be seen. The fifth shooter needs to be set up farther up the trail in the direction of the Mule," Tremble said.

"I thought you wanted to take them down at once," Cindy said.

Tremble nodded. "I do, but they may not cooperate. I'm betting Spider's in the rear, and if they're too spread out, we may need to let some of them pass until we see him. Then we take down everyone we can in one go, but if some get by us, we'll need someone at the back door to drive them to cover and pin them down until we can close behind them and mop them up. It's a contingency, really, but better safe than sorry."

Cindy nodded, both impressed with the logic, and seeing an opportunity to place her son in a less exposed position. "Jeremy honey, you heard the man. Go on down the trail a good long way and find a place to set up."

"But, Mom, I want to stay here. I'm a good shot and—"

"I know you are, honey, that's why I want you holding the rear. It's important," Cindy said.

"Seriously, big man," Anderson added. "If the bad guys get past us, you'll be the only one between them and those kids. If anyone makes it as far as you, we need you to take them down. We're counting on you."

Jeremy considered that for a moment then nodded and set off down the trail, his rifle slung.

"All right," Tremble said. "I'll deploy farthest down the trail toward the road, with Keith behind me and you two next in whatever order you prefer. Be tracking your targets, but everyone holds their fire until I take down Spider. My shot will be your signal it's open season."

***

Tremble squatted behind a massive oak and surveyed the trail. He could hear the Mule clearly, though the sound was muted by distance. He hoped the noise duped their attackers into believing they were still far from first contact.

He was beginning to think the assault wasn't coming when he saw a flicker of movement, followed by another. The men were advancing far more skillfully than he'd anticipated, with the lead man rushing forward a short distance to cover, no doubt while other unseen rifles waited to provide cover fire if needed. This newfound caution might complicate his 'quick takedown' plan, as the attackers weren't all exposed simultaneously. *No plan survives first contact with the enemy,* he thought.

Five camo-clad militiamen passed him one by one, the last disappearing with still no trace of Spider. Tremble cursed his failure to have a plan B and rose to work his way through the woods toward the road. If he didn't find Spider and take him out fast, he'd have to fire a shot in the air just to initiate the attack— assuming his shooters were still in position. This plan was going south fast.

***

Anderson knelt behind a tree at the edge of the shelter clearing, watching unseen as the third attacker rushed across the clearing and plunged back into the woods in Jeremy's direction. He glanced to where Cindy squatted some distance away, visible from his position but not from the trail. He could see tension in her posture as she glanced from the trail to the clearing. *What the hell is Tremble waiting for?*

A single shot rang out from Jeremy's direction, and then all hell broke loose.

***

Tremble watched, trying to get a clear shot as Spider sprinted from tree to tree, working his way up the trail well behind his expendable minions. Spider was halfway between trees when the distant shot rang out, followed by the sound of a multi-gun firefight. Spider stopped mid-stride, barely hesitating before turning to run. Tremble rose and put a three-round burst into the Satan's Seed logo on the back of the denim jacket. Spider was dead before he hit the ground, and Tremble didn't bother to confirm the kill, but turned to crash through the woods toward the sound of the gunfire.

"FRIEND," he shouted as he neared Keith's position, but his son wasn't there.

He made the clearing at a dead run and found two dead militiamen there, their wounds in the back indicating they'd been caught unaware. The gunfire stopped and he plunged into the woods, moving from tree to tree as he advanced. He rounded a bend and found Keith and Anderson behind trees on opposite sides of the trail. Both whirled at his approach, the look of relief on Keith's face was obvious. Tremble moved up beside his son.

"What's happening?" he asked.

"When you didn't shoot, they just kept coming," Keith said. "Three of them made it by us and across the clearing before the first one ran into Jeremy. Looks like Jeremy took two of them down, but he got hurt and the last one managed to capture him. Cindy's—"

"AIN'T NO NEED FOR MORE SHOOTIN'! LET'S TALK," came a voice from down the trail.

Anderson looked at Tremble. "I got this," he said, and Tremble nodded.

"ALL RIGHT," Anderson yelled back. "LET'S START WITH YOU LETTING OUR YOUNG FRIEND GO! HE NEEDS MEDICAL ATTENTION."

"HE AIN'T HURT BAD. A ROUND JUST GRAZED HIM ABOVE THE EAR. KNOCKED HIM OUT IS ALL, BUT HE'S COMIN' AROUND. HE'LL BE GOOD AS NEW IN NO TIME. THAT IS PROVIDIN' YOU FOLKS ARE COOPERATIVE.'

"GO ON," Anderson yelled.

"Y'ALL GET ME THAT VEHICLE I HEAR AND LEAVE IT RUNNIN' ON THE TRAIL THEN BACK OFF. I'LL HAUL THE BOY TO THE ROAD AND LEAVE HIM THERE AND THEN TAKE OFF. DEAL?"

"AND IF WE DON'T AGREE?" Anderson asked.

"THEN I KILL THE BOY. I FIGURE IF YOU DON'T LET ME GO, YOU AIN'T GONNA KEEP ME AROUND AS A MOUTH TO FEED, SO I'M FINISHED EITHER WAY. I MIGHT AS WELL MAKE IT COST YOU."

"HOW DO WE EVEN KNOW HE'S ALIVE? LET US TALK TO HIM," Anderson said.

"HE'S JUST COMIN' AROUND AND HE AIN'T WHAT YOU CALL REAL TALKATIVE RIGHT NOW. BUT HE'LL BE FINE. I SEEN PLENTY HURT WORSE."

"THEN YOU GOTTA LET ONE OF US COME OVER AND CHECK HIM SO WE CAN MAKE SURE," Anderson said.

"SO YOU CAN JUMP ME? I'LL PASS, THANKS."

"NO DEAL WITHOUT PROOF OF LIFE. IF HE CAN'T TALK AND WE CAN'T COME THERE, THEN GET HIM ON HIS FEET AND MOVE HIM OUT IN THE OPEN WHERE WE CAN SEE HIM. YOU CAN USE HIM AS A SHIELD IF YOU HAVE TO, BUT UNTIL WE CAN CONFIRM HE'S ALIVE, THIS DEAL'S NOT HAPPENING," Anderson said.

There was a long pause until finally the man spoke again.

"ALL RIGHT, BUT AT THE FIRST SIGN OF ANYTHING FUNNY, I'M BLOWIN' HIS HEAD OFF. YOU GOT THAT?"

"LOUD AND CLEAR," Anderson yelled back.

Tremble watched as Jeremy stumbled out of the woods onto the trail, a man's arm around his neck and a pistol pointed at his head. His captor stayed behind him, only one eye and the side of his face visible.

"OKAY, I KEPT MY PART OF THE BARGAIN —"

Blood sprayed over Jeremy as his captor's head exploded, followed a millisecond later by the crack of a rifle. Jeremy stumbled forward, confused, as Tremble and the others raced toward him. Before they got there, Cindy burst out of the woods to their left, where she'd circled to flank her son's captor.

She wrapped her son in a hug. "Are you hurt, Jeremy?"

"My head hurts, Mom. Did we get all the bad guys? Did I do good?"

Tears rolled down Cindy's cheeks as she hugged Jeremy. "Yes, son," she said. "You did great."

Appalachian Trail
Mile 1403.4 Southbound
Intersection with VA Route 812

Two Hours Later

Tremble carried the two five-gallon gas cans over to the Mule and set them down, then wiped the sweat from his forehead with the back of his hand. A short distance down the trail he could see Cindy fussing over Jeremy and checking his eyes with a small penlight, alert to any sign of possible concussion.

"Cindy's quite a mom," Tremble said. "I expect a momma bear could take lessons from her. How did you hook up anyway? And what's with that SRF uniform you're wearing."

Anderson looked up from where he was sorting through a stack of gear next to the Mule and grunted. "Let's just say it was the only available clothing, and it's all a long story."

"I'd like to hear it sometime," Tremble said.

"Maybe when, or if, we get where we're going." Anderson shook his head as he looked at the reconfigured Mule and the pile of gear still to be loaded. "Which is looking less likely unless we bite the bullet and ditch some of this stuff."

Tremble looked at the Mule and nodded. They'd unloaded the cargo to allow them to raise the rear seat and transform the vehicle into the 'crew cab' configuration, with two bench seats. Unfortunately, that meant reducing the size of the bed by half. To make matters more challenging, the pile of gear was growing, augmented both by the Trembles' meager stores and the much larger bounty they'd stripped from the militiamen and their trucks.

"We need to prioritize," Tremble said. "For sure we take all the gasoline and ammo. We have bleach to purify water, so we only haul enough water to get us from one source to the next. We can shoot or trap for protein, so we should only take whatever lightweight carbs you have, along with whatever medical supplies—"

"If you're almost finished, Professor Obvious, you might notice that's pretty much how I have it separated out. But the ammo and gas weigh the most, and with seven people and all this gear . . ." Anderson trailed off, shaking his head.

"You're thinking the Mule won't make it very far before it packs up," Tremble said.

Anderson nodded and looked back toward the road, where Keith approached with two more gas cans.

"Keith and I could just take our own gear and go on foot," Tremble said. "Y'all don't have to wait for us and—"

"And leave us with the kids and without the benefits of two more adults and their rifles? Nice try, but I don't think so," Anderson said.

Tremble flushed. "I wasn't trying to dump the kids on you and bug out. But the truth is it's probably not too healthy to be around us. We're targets."

"Yeah, well, we're not exactly on the government's Christmas card list either," Anderson said. "Besides, our whole point in going to Wilmington is to throw in with people who're trying to make a difference, and as ex-FEMA, I'm not likely to be welcome. I hoped telling them about you might convince them I was on the level, but that was a crap shoot at best. Having you along seals the deal." He grinned. "Besides, having two more adults to push on the hills will help, and we're gonna need all the help we can get. We'll run the Mule until it won't run anymore; then we'll play it by ear. Now help me get this gear loaded."

* * *

Thirty minutes later, Anderson stood and admired their handiwork. Gear was stacked high in the cargo bed, prevented from tipping only by secure lashings to the roll cage of the Mule. Additionally, they'd fashioned a roof rack of branches and lashed it to the top of the roll cage to accept even more gear, and packs and miscellaneous bags hung from the vertical bars of the roof supports. It had taken every bit of paracord they had between them to get everything secured.

"What do you think?" Anderson asked.

Tremble shook his head and chuckled. "I think we're going to look like the Beverly Hillbillies of the Apocalypse."

"I'll second that," Cindy said. "Just call me Ellie May."

"Molly's the youngest, so that makes her Ellie May. You have to be Granny," Anderson said, ducking away as Cindy tried to punch him.

Keith looked up from the trail guide page he was studying. "Who are Ellie May and Granny?"

"Different times, son. How far are we from the river?" Tremble asked.

"About a mile as the crow flies, and one point three miles along the trail. That's to the footbridge," Keith said.

"Does it describe the footbridge?" Tremble asked. "Can we cross it in the Mule?"

Keith shook his head. "It doesn't say anything but 'footbridge,' but there's a railroad bridge right beside it, so we should be able to get across one way or another."

Tremble looked at Anderson and Cindy. "If there IS anyone guarding the crossing, they'll hear us coming. I think we should stop partway and recon on foot. The question is how far away are they likely to hear the Mule?"

Anderson shrugged. "The foliage will partially muffle the sound. I'd guess the distance between the clearing where Jamie was driving and the shelter was a quarter of a mile and we could hear the Mule on the trail maybe half again that distance, say three-eighths of a mile. I'd say we're probably safe up to half a mile."

"Even then," Cindy said, "anyone on the bridges would probably start looking for a vehicle on the road before they thought about the woods."

Tremble nodded. "That's it, then. We'll stop in the woods a half mile from the bridges and recon on foot."

***

It was a short ride to their stopping point, and despite level terrain, the overloaded Mule labored and rocked on its chassis. No one spoke, but it was obvious the long-term reliability of their transport vehicle was doubtful. As they reached the half-mile point, the thick woods opened, as the trail intersected a hundred-foot-wide slash through the forest where massive steel pylons ran from horizon to horizon, carrying now dead electrical wires.

"Power line right-of-way," Tremble said. "This is as good a spot as any, I guess. Cindy, pull off into the woods on the other side."

Cindy nodded and did as requested, and Tremble and Anderson got out and continued down the trail on foot.

There'd been no debate as to who would be the little group's 'recon force.' As the only two with military training, that task had naturally fallen to the older men, and Tremble was assuming leadership almost naturally. Anderson seemed relieved by the development more than anything and, despite their history, found himself following Tremble's lead both willingly and somewhat gratefully.

They moved quietly and quickly, Tremble in the lead and Anderson following fifty feet back and slightly to one side. The trail began to parallel a small stream on their left, and a few hundred yards later the trail curved left and they crossed the creek on a small footbridge. Tremble stopped and eyed the bridge doubtfully as he fished the trail guide page from his pocket. Anderson moved up beside him.

"This would be Rocky Row Run," Tremble said softly. "We'll cross back to the other side in another couple of hundred yards. The guide doesn't mention footbridges, but if we come this way, we'll have to find a way through the woods to keep the Mule on the west bank. There's no way in hell these bridges are wide enough for the Mule."

Anderson nodded and Tremble moved ahead. Sure enough, they crossed back across Rocky Row Run as indicated, and on an equally narrow footbridge. A hundred yards beyond the bridge, Tremble stopped and motioned Anderson forward to join him again, at the edge of a gravel road. Fifty feet south, the gravel track intersected a paved two-lane road, and a crude sign indicated the trail continued on the far side of the highway.

Tremble fished a map from his pocket and squatted to spread it on the ground.

"The gravel road is Route 812, where Spider was chasing us, and the paved road must be US 501; the river is just beyond that guardrail and the fringe of trees," Tremble said, pointing at the map. "The trail goes along the road at this point and leads to the footbridge and the rail bridge. The problem is we'd be walking right into anyone guarding the bridges and visible as soon as we round the curve."

Anderson nodded and looked back the way they'd come, and then back at Tremble.

"You thinkin' what I'm thinkin'?" Anderson asked.

Tremble nodded. "Rocky Row Run has to flow into the river, which means it has to pass under the road. If we get under the road and into the fringe of trees along the river, we can get a look at the bridge entrances without being seen."

"Exactly. Now let's just hope the road crossing is a bridge and not some rusty, snake-infested culvert," Anderson said.

Tremble grimaced, pocketing the map as he rose, and led Anderson back down the trail to the last footbridge. They moved downstream along the shallow creek, hugging the right bank. To their mutual relief, the highway crossed the creek via a fairly substantial bridge. They stepped into the swift-flowing creek, and cold water surged around their legs knee-deep as they moved under the bridge and into the trees lining the riverbank beyond.

The James spread out before them, flowing wide and strong, with the bridge spans dominating their view. The rail bridge was closer, with the footbridge visible beyond it upstream, both spanning the river at an angle. It was an odd arrangement, with both bridges starting at nearly the same point on their side of the river, but diverging from each other at a significant angle so they landed on the far bank perhaps three hundred feet apart, with the railroad bridge being almost twice as long as the footbridge.

Tremble studied the bridges briefly, then nodded to Anderson and started upstream through thick undergrowth. They were silent now, communicating by hand signs in what Tremble thought was the increasingly likely event the bridges were guarded.

Five hundred feet later, they reached the abutment of the railroad bridge and crossed under it to get their first good look at the footbridge. Tremble gazed up the bank at the entrance and stifled a curse.

Steps!

The pedestrian footbridge was a raised affair, accessed by a short staircase, and while the footbridge itself looked strong and wide enough for the Mule, the steps were easily two feet narrower. There was no way they'd get the Mule onto the bridge. He looked up at the railroad bridge and shook his head. That was doubtful too. There were no side rails and the railroad bridge crossed the river on a diagonal, making it easily twice as long as the pedestrian bridge, and the spacing between the cross ties didn't appear to be much closer than the diameter of the Mule's tires. It would be a rough ride, if they could use it at all.

He turned to Anderson and found him looking at the footbridge and shaking his head. Anderson pointed up at the railroad bridge and made a back and forth seesaw motion with his hand, then pointed two fingers at his own eyes before pointing up at the railroad bridge again. *Looks doubtful, but we should check it out,* he signed.

Tremble nodded and started to move from under the bridge and up the bank when the squawk of a radio above froze him in place.

"Troll One, this is Troll Actual. Do you copy? Over."

There was no immediate response and the call was repeated, followed by the sound of movement and muffled cursing before someone spoke above him.

"Troll Actual, this is Troll One. We copy. Over."

"Troll One, you are five minutes overdue for comms check. Initiate protocol alpha. Repeat, initiate protocol alpha. Over."

There was more muffled cursing followed by footsteps, and Tremble and Anderson squatted in the undergrowth and tried to make themselves small against the stone wall of the abutment as someone scrambled out onto the railroad bridge above them. They looked up to see a black-clad figure moving over the cross ties and prayed the man didn't look down. The man stopped right above them, looked downriver and waved.

"Troll One, I have a visual. Confirm status. Over," the radio squawked.

The man above them raised the radio to his mouth. "Teacup. Repeat, teacup. Over."

"Troll One, your status is confirmed. Over." Then the voice changed.

"Troll One, I agreed to let you put up a weather canopy and alternate on the bridge, but be advised if you screw up again, I will personally drive over there and kick your asses. Then you will BOTH find yourselves standing out in the sun all day. DO YOU COPY? Over."

"Uh … I copy, Sarge. It won't happen again. Troll One out."

There were hurried footsteps overhead as a second figure moved onto the bridge.

"What the hell, man? You were off post and missed the check-in! Now Sergeant Garrity has a hard-on for us," the first man said.

"Sorry, man," the new arrival said. "That chili mac MRE I had for lunch gave me the runs. I yelled at you when I went by the canopy, but I couldn't rouse you and I couldn't wait. I'll take over … oh shit!" The man turned and ran from the bridge, hunched over and holding his stomach.

"Wonderful! Just frigging wonderful!" the man above them said as he started to pace back and forth on the bridge.

Tremble looked at Anderson, who was shaking his head. They could only hope the guard didn't look down between the ties and spot them, but the bigger problem was escape; in his present position the guard would see them clearly if they tried to retrace their path back to the creek. Only luck and the other guard's stomach problems had prevented them from being spotted coming in.

Tremble pointed to his watch and then to the sun in the western sky. Their only hope was waiting until nightfall and hoping neither of the guards looked down in the meantime.

***

They got their break just at dusk, when they heard an engine approaching on the highway. The vehicle stopped and they heard the sound of two car doors slamming, followed by banter. Through the dim light, Tremble saw the guard on the bridge walk back toward the bank, obviously eager to be relieved.

Tremble touched Anderson's shoulder and pointed toward the creek, and Anderson nodded emphatically, obviously having the same thought. Tremble's muscles ached from the strain of remaining motionless and he stifled a groan as he followed Anderson through the woods. There was just enough light for them to see a few feet in front of themselves, and they moved quickly, hoping the banter of shift change would keep anyone off the bridge for the few minutes it would take them to get under cover.

It was darker under the small bridge over the creek and in the thicker woods surrounding it, and they stayed in the creek, unwilling to show a light and groping toward the first footbridge in the dark.

Tremble heard a thump, followed by a muttered curse.

"What's wrong?" he hissed.

"I found the friggin' bridge with my head," Anderson whispered back. "You think we're deep enough in the woods to use a little light? Otherwise we're gonna be bouncin' off trees."

Tremble thought a moment. "Yes, but keep it pointed at the ground with your hand cupped around the lens and only show enough light to see where you're going."

"Like I wouldn't do that anyway," Anderson muttered, and Tremble saw a light switch on, the illumination leaking between Anderson's fingers casting an eerie glow on the creek bank.

He covered his own light and switched it on to light his way out of the creek. On the open trail with enough light to see where they were going, they made good time. They were nearing the Mule when Cindy's voice came out of the darkness.

"Stop right there and identify yourselves."

"That you, Granny?" Anderson asked.

"Keep it up, George, and I'll shoot you yet. And what the hell took you so long? We've been going nuts here. I've had all I could do to keep Keith from charging down the trail after y'all," Cindy said.

"We ran into a few complications," Tremble said. "Long story short, we're not getting across the river this way."

***

They shielded their light with a tarp rigged to the side of the Mule as a lean-to, and the adults gathered around Tremble and the map. The kids were snoring softly, each stretched out on a bench seat of the Mule, where Cindy had placed them hours before, and dead to the world. Tremble spoke softly to keep from waking the children.

"The steps make the James River Foot Bridge a nonstarter for the Mule, even if we could find a way to bypass the small footbridges over Rocky Row Run. Likewise, even if we took out the guards and tried the rail bridge, we can't be sure the tires will span the gaps between the cross ties, and for sure it will be a rough, slow ride, presuming they do," Tremble said.

"And a noisy one," Anderson added. "The guard waved at someone downstream, so at least part of the bridge is visible from the next checkpoint. No way we'd escape notice."

"So what's left? Upstream?" Cindy asked.

Tremble shook his head and pointed to the map. "There are a couple of crossings at the ten- and twenty-mile points upstream, but here at Glasgow, the Maury River comes in from the north, and we'd have to cross THAT before we can even get to the bridges across the James. Our options for crossing the Maury are pretty much the same as here, a railroad bridge or a highway crossing right in the middle of town. Our best, probably our only, options for getting across the James are somewhere between here and Lynchburg twenty miles downstream."

"You don't sound too optimistic," Anderson said.

"I'm not. There are half a dozen road or rail crossings between here and Lynchburg, and about an equal number of low-water dams. I'm betting the crossings are all guarded, but maybe, just maybe, one of the dams might have a walkway wide enough to accommodate the Mule. The bigger problem is that to get to ANY of them, we'll have to use the roads at some point," Tremble said.

"What other choice do we have?" Cindy asked.

"None, really," Tremble said, then sighed. "Okay, let's take this one step at a time. The next crossing is US 501 just south of the rail bridge. That has to be the location of 'Troll Actual' our friend on the rail bridge was waving to, because with the bends in the river, that's the only spot downstream the rail bridge would still be visible. No matter what we do, we have to get past that checkpoint even to keep going downstream on this side of the river. We obviously can't just roll down the road past them, so we'll have to try this power line right-of-way. It's not marked on any of the maps, but I'm betting it parallels the river." He looked around in the dim light. "Any suggestions, objections, or better ideas?"

No one spoke.

"Okay. Let's all try to get some sleep and we'll leave at first light," Tremble said.

CHAPTER TEN

Day 43
May 13, 2020 - Sunrise

Tremble slept fitfully, as did the other adults. By the time the sky began to lighten in the east, they were all leaning on the Mule, sharing the contents of MREs Cindy warmed with the heat packs. The children stirred and were fed soon after, and the group set off as soon as it was light enough to see.

To say the right-of-way was 'cleared' was a relative term; annual maintenance was overdue, and spring growth carpeted the width of the slash through the forest with knee- to waist-high grass, and near head-high saplings were beginning to leaf out. Visibility was limited, and the overloaded Mule trundled through the foliage, leaving a trail a blind man could follow. He could only hope there were no choppers around.

The terrain near the river was level to rolling, and they made steady progress for the first few minutes until the undergrowth thickened and the ground began to slope downhill.

"Hold up, Cindy," Tremble said. "Let's check this out before we roll into it blind."

Cindy nodded and stopped the Mule as Tremble and Keith got out and pushed forward through the thickening brush, Keith in the lead. The slope steepened as they moved forward.

"I hear running water," Keith said. "There must be a creek —"

He dropped out of sight and Tremble heard a splash and curses.

"KEITH! ARE YOU OKAY?" Tremble said.

"Yeah, I'm fine. Just wet and maybe a little bruised. Watch it, there's a drop-off."

Tremble moved cautiously through the brush to look down on his son standing ankle deep in a swiftly moving creek perhaps a dozen feet wide, contained on both sides by vertical banks between three and four feet high. He stifled his own curse.

Keith looked up and down the little creek and shook his head.

"This thing must carry a lot of water in big rains. The banks are eroded vertical as far as I can see; it's even worse upstream than it is here. There's no way we'll get the Mule across this. Heck, we couldn't get it across even if it wasn't overloaded," Keith said.

"Any chance of digging out the banks and making ramps on either side?" Tremble asked.

Keith studied the bank a moment then shook his head. "No way, Dad. It looks to be mainly really big rocks mixed with dirt. We'd need a backhoe to make a dent in this stuff."

"All right. I guess that's it, then. Here, grab my hand and I'll help you up," Tremble said, gripping a sapling for support with his left hand and extending his right over the bank down to his son.

Keith gripped his father's hand and scrambled up the bank, and then both men made their way back to the Mule to break the bad news.

**

"It might not make much difference anyway," Anderson said, pointing ahead to where the power line towers began to curve to the right. "Unless I miss my guess, the right-of-way is turning to cross the river. From the looks of it, I doubt we could have used it to get past the checkpoint."

Tremble followed Anderson's pointing finger and realized he was right.

"All right, time for some tough decisions," Tremble said. "This looks like the end of the line for the Mule."

They argued for fifteen minutes, Cindy adamant they needed the Mule for carrying their supplies, and Tremble equally convinced it was turning from an asset to a liability.

"Okay, suppose we ditch the Mule, then how do we get back to the AT after we finally cross the James," Cindy demanded.

"We're not even sure we'll be able to get back to the AT," Tremble countered, "and traveling along regular roads in the Mule makes us bigger targets. It's noisy and sure as hell can't outrun anything. If we have to abandon it quickly to take to the woods, all our provisions will be lost with it. If we're traveling on foot with everyone carrying a share, we can melt into the woods if we hear a vehicle coming and they'll pass by oblivious. On the contrary, if they find an abandoned Mule with a hot engine, we can count on some company."

"We can't carry near all this stuff," Cindy said. "And what about Molly, she can't walk well enough to keep up."

"Much of the Mule's load is gasoline. We can carry most or probably all of the food, and we have bleach to purify water as we need it. We'll just top off the loads with as much ammo as possible and hope for the best. We just have to prioritize and take only the absolutely necessary stuff and leave the rest. As far as Molly—"

"We're not leaving my sister," said a small voice. "I can carry her."

Tremble squatted next to Jamie, who was trembling but defiant. "No one's going to leave Molly, Jamie. Don't worry about that."

"But you said—"

"I meant things, Jamie. Not people," Tremble said. "

"I can carry Molly," Jeremy said, and Jamie's tension eased.

"All right then," Tremble said. "You all know what I think. Who else is for leaving the Mule?"

Keith raised a finger, and Tremble turned to Anderson. Anderson shot a sheepish glance at Cindy.

"Sorry, Cindy. I have to go with Tremble on this one. I'm not a fan of walking either, but the Mule's outlived its usefulness. Even if we get back to the Appalachian Trail with it, I'm pretty sure we're going to find more and more places it can't transit."

Jeremy supported his mom, but looked conflicted about it, and the kids didn't get a vote, but Molly was still mostly nonresponsive and it was clear Jamie would do anything Tremble wanted. They stood at an impasse for a long moment, and then Cindy heaved a defeated sigh and nodded.

"All right. I hate to leave it, but you've made your point. Let's start sorting through the gear and dividing it up," she said.

**

An hour later they set out, Keith in the lead. They helped each other across the steep-banked creek and through more thick undergrowth before the right-of-way returned to the same state of waist-high grass they'd previously encountered. They walked single file through the tall grass and scattered saplings. The trees began to thin on their right and there was a solid wall of green ahead in the distance. After a few more steps Keith stopped and pointed up to the pylon looming in front of them. The electrical wires stretched away from the top of the huge steel tower at a sharp angle to the right. In the far distance they could just barely make out the top of the next pylon.

"That's got to be across the river," Keith said. "It looks like this is the end of the trail—"

"DOWN!" hissed Tremble, and after the slightest hesitation they all dropped to their hands and knees, invisible in the tall grass.

They heard a vehicle pass in front of them from right to left, quite close. The sound continued briefly and then the engine noise changed briefly to an idle and then stopped altogether, followed by the sound of slamming car doors. There were men's voices but too far away to make out the words.

"Anderson! You're with me. The rest of you stay put, stay quiet, and stay down," Tremble whispered.

Tremble crawled forward through the grass, Anderson behind him.

They were less than fifty feet from the road, and only luck had prevented them from attracting the attention of the passing vehicle. Tremble parted the long grass carefully and peeked through, down the road to the left where they'd heard the vehicle stop. Perhaps fifty yards down the road there was a side road to the right. No vehicles were visible, but Tremble could hear an occasional raised voice.

"I'm thinking that's the entrance to the next bridge and the checkpoint we were hoping to bypass by using the right-of-way," Tremble whispered.

"Agreed," Anderson replied softly. "But without the Mule, the right-of-way's not an issue. We'll just fade back into the woods and parallel the river downstream until we find an unguarded crossing."

Tremble nodded and faded back into the grass, with Anderson close behind. When they reached the others, he led them on a crawl well away from the road before they rose and dashed for the concealing safety of the tree line. Once there he spread the map on the ground and the others gathered round. Tremble pointed at the map.

"If they're guarding the foot and railroad bridges and this crossing at 501, for sure they've got the Blue Ridge Parkway crossing just downstream covered. The next road crossing goes from this side across to the Georgia Pacific paper mill at Big Island. That seems to serve a network of rural roads on this side, probably just to bring pulpwood into the mill. They can't have unlimited manpower, so they may not have that covered," Tremble said.

Cindy shook her head. "They can read maps as well as we can, and they're covering a footbridge and rail bridge; what are the chances they've left a drivable bridge uncovered?"

"Not good, I'll admit," Tremble said. "But if that's covered, it's only a few miles farther until we start hitting the dams—"

"Which may or may not have walkways. And even the bridge at the paper mill is ten miles away." Cindy gestured around at the undergrowth, a snarl of saplings, berry vines, and briars. "Ten miles, or more likely fifteen, on foot through this stuff with no road or even a trail, to find a crossing which may or may not exist, all in a direction away from the Appalachian Trail. And suppose we get across? We'll be in the Lynchburg suburbs by then, with more people, and where we have no clue about local roads or trails." She shook her head. "I'll admit I was fixated about the Mule, but I can't really see this as a better option."

"All right, then what do you suggest," Tremble said.

"I think we at least have to consider trying to force a crossing at this bridge," Cindy said.

Tremble glanced at the kids.

"Too dangerous," he said. "Besides, even if we get across here, we can't backtrack upstream to pick up the trail; it's too close. Even if the guys guarding the upstream crossing don't see us, they might still put dogs on our scent later and figure out we're using the AT, and if they KNOW we're on the AT, they'll know where to ambush us. Forcing a crossing puts them on alert and the only way that works is if we can immediately break contact and get far enough, fast enough, so we don't leave a trail they can follow back to the AT."

Cindy shrugged. "All our options suck. We just have to pick the one that sucks the least. We need to at least LOOK at that bridge."

The silence grew.

"She's not wrong, Tremble," Anderson said. "Making our way down this side of the river isn't a great option. We should look at the bridge before we decide."

* * *

The terrain rose a bit, so as they made their way through the woods to a point directly across from the bridge entrance, they were thirty feet or so higher than the level of the road, with a good vantage point to look straight across the bridge. Tremble parted the undergrowth and raised the monocular to his eye.

The entrance to the right lane of the narrow two-lane bridge was blocked by a concrete Jersey barrier, behind which a large portable canopy was set up, obviously as a rain shelter and sunscreen. Two men in black SRF uniforms were playing dominoes at a folding card table at the front of the open-air shelter, and a number of folding cots were set up in the back, two of them occupied. There were three vehicles parked along the guardrail next to the bridge entrance, one of the black SUVs favored by the SRF and two civilian vehicles, a crew cab pickup truck and a smaller SUV, both likely commandeered. Tremble took it all in, then passed the monocular to Anderson, who studied the scene a while before passing the glass to Cindy, who had accompanied them over Tremble's objection they needed to limit the size of the recon group.

Cindy took a long look, then nodded and handed the monocular back to Tremble before they moved deeper into the cover of the woods. They said nothing until they reached the others; then Tremble spoke first.

"I don't like it. This is obviously a central location they're using to staff the crossing at the rail bridge and probably the one downstream at the Blue Ridge Parkway as well. That's likely why they have three vehicles; they keep one chase vehicle at each crossing; then the relief guys drive out in the cars they keep here and they swap. The footbridge/rail bridge checkpoint and the Blue Ridge Parkway crossing are both close, and we know they're in radio contact. They're more than likely in contact with Lynchburg as well. I see no way in hell we can get across there without setting off all kind of alarms, and they'll be on our tails fast," Tremble said.

"We can do it," Cindy said.

Tremble blew out an exasperated sigh. "Cindy, haven't you been listening? So we surprise them and force a crossing, just how do you expect to escape?"

"Get out that map," Cindy said.

Tremble shot her a look but did as she asked.

"See the railroad line running along the far side of the river?" she asked.

"Yes, but what of it —"

"Did you see it when we looked at the bridge?"

Tremble shook his head. "No, there must be a fringe of woods separating it —"

He stopped mid-sentence and studied the map, then gave a grudging nod. "All right, suppose that works. We have to take them down first and preferably quietly, and they have the river at their back and a whole lot of open ground in front of them. How do you propose to get close enough to do that without attracting their attention?"

Cindy snorted. "Trust me, Simon. Their full attention is exactly what I want."

Approach to James River Bridge
State Route 501/130

One Hour Later

Anderson parted the tall grass and looked both ways before he slipped out on the road and beckoned to Cindy. She emerged, holding Jeremy's hand, and Anderson had to avert his eyes to keep from staring. She had on a pair of jeans hacked into the briefest of cutoffs, worn low on her hips and cut so high a significant portion of her well-toned dancer's butt was visible. A skimpy sports bra and hiking boots completed the ensemble, the boots looking oddly out of place; but no one was likely to be looking at her feet.

"You sure you're okay with this?" Anderson asked.

She gave him a grim smile. "Trust me; I've worn less for worse reasons."

She glanced at Jeremy. "But Jeremy should stay here. I still don't like —"

"I can do it, Mom. Besides, everybody said it was a good idea. Right, George?"

Cindy glared at Anderson.

"You have to admit it makes the story more believable, and it WAS Jeremy's idea," Anderson said.

Cindy sighed, then nodded and set off down the road, leading Jeremy by the hand, with Anderson walking a bit apart and to one side, his M4 at the ready as if he were guarding the pair. Jeremy had assumed a somewhat unsteady gait, and his mouth was open with his tongue protruding slightly. As Anderson watched, a stream of drool dripped from the corner of the man/boy's mouth.

Jeez, Jeremy. Don't overplay it, Anderson thought.

***

"HELLO THE BRIDGE!"

Garrity looked up from his dominoes.

"What the hell?" he said, upsetting his folding lawn chair in his haste to grab his rifle and move to the front of the Jersey barrier, Tanner right behind him.

"What do you make of that, Sarge?" Tanner asked.

Fifty yards away stood a bearded man in the same black SRF utilities they wore, though his obviously hadn't been changed in a while. He was holding his M4 casually on a scantily clad woman who was leading a man, a boy really, by the hand.

"I make it to be one fine piece of ass," Garrity said. "Other than that, I'm not too sure."

"Ain't we supposed to call in a contact?" Tanner asked.

Garrity eyed the woman hungrily. "Not just yet. Let's check things out first."

"But the orders are —"

Garrity silenced Tanner with a stony glare and turned back to their visitors just as the man started walking toward them. Garrity and Tanner raised their rifles.

"That's close enough, friend. Now why don't you set that M4 on the ground, real slow like, then put your hands up. The woman and the boy too," Garrity said.

The man did as ordered, and the woman let go of the boy's hand and spoke to him quietly. He looked confused but followed the woman's lead and raised his hands.

"Very good," Garrity said. "Now who might you be?"

"George. George Cooper," the man said. "I got wounded and separated from my unit a month or so back. By the time I was able to make it back to base, they'd moved. I'm just trying to join up again."

"Separated, you say? Now how did that happen, exactly?"

"That's a long story," the man said.

Garrity snorted. "Yeah, I'll bet. Why don't we start with your lady friend here?"

"This is Cindy. I found her and the boy in an abandoned house." The man grinned. "You might say she's been a real comfort to me."

Garrity grinned. "Cindy's in the 'comfort business,' is she?"

"Not really a business, but she'll do anything you want if you slap the kid around a bit. And I do mean ANYTHING. She's sensitive like that," the man said.

Garrity nodded and tore his eyes off the woman a moment. "Getting 'separated from your unit' has a strong smell of bullshit, Cooper. So how do you see this playing out?"

The man shrugged. "Yeah, you might say me and my former comrades didn't exactly see eye to eye on things, which is why I tried it alone awhile. The thing is, it's tough out here without someone to watch your back, so I want to come back, just to a different unit. Call it a little 'do it yourself' transfer. You make that happen for me and the woman is yours. I'm tired of her anyway."

"What makes you think we just won't shoot you and take the woman anyway?"

The man grinned. "Because I figure you're smart enough to know I wouldn't just waltz in here with all my trade goods in hand. I got plenty of other stuff squirreled away; play ball with me and it'll be a good deal for both of us." The man shrugged. "Shoot me and it's your loss as much as mine."

Garrity thought about it for a moment. "All right. You stay just where you are with your hands up, but send the woman forward. I want to check her out."

The man spoke to the woman, who lowered her hands and took the boy's hand before she walked toward Garrity.

"JUST THE WOMAN!" Garrity said.

Cooper let out a theatrical sigh. "I'm afraid it don't work like that. The boy goes everywhere with her unless you're bangin' her, but then he has to be close by but out of sight. Trust me when I tell you tryin' to change that is WAY more trouble than it's worth."

Garrity hesitated, and then nodded. "All right." He started forward to meet the woman but whispered to Tanner before he left, "Keep an eye on the guy. If he so much as twitches, shoot him."

"Will do, Sarge," Tanner said, glancing at the woman. "Can I have seconds on the bitch?"

"We'll see," Garrity said, and moved to meet the woman and the boy.

She had her eyes down as he approached. He liked that. She obviously knew her place. He drew near and reached out and lifted her chin, then looked from her face down her scantily clad body. She was a looker alright.

He looked over at the boy, and his lip curled in a sneer. This was a bit of a complication, but as long as she kept the boy in line, he supposed it was worth it. Unlike some of his comrades, he didn't really like women to resist; he much preferred their enthusiastic cooperation. If that cooperation had to be coerced by slapping this subhuman around a bit, this piece of ass was probably worth it — for a while anyway.

Garrity dropped his hand down and fondled the woman's breast through the bra. He felt her stiffen and he smiled as the subhuman whined and moved closer to the woman's side. Garrity leaned in closer.

"You're upsetting your little retard. You probably need to be a little friendlier if you don't want me to shoot the dummy here in some non-vital area, say the kneecap," Garrity whispered.

***

Despite her resolve, Cindy stiffened as the black-clad thug fondled her breast, and as he leaned in to whisper his threat, she had all she could do to keep from vomiting as his fetid breath washed over her.

She felt Jeremy's hand moving to the holster at the small of her back, and then felt it lighten as he removed the Glock. The thug's eyes went wide as Jeremy shoved the muzzle of the handgun under the man's chin, pointing directly up at his brain, the action masked from his companion by the bulk of the thug's body. Despite the tension of the situation, she had to suppress a smile as Jeremy whispered to the man, "Who's the dummy now, butt wipe?"

"Jeremy here will be more than happy to blow your brains out," Cindy whispered. "So if you want to keep that from happening, I suggest you play it cool and tell your friend back there to put his gun on the ground."

She saw indecision in the man's eyes for the slightest moment, and then he called back over his shoulder, "Ground your weapon, Tanner."

Over the man's shoulder she saw the one called Tanner hesitate, a confused look on his face. He started to lower his weapon then seemed to think better of it and raised it again, keeping it trained on Anderson. "What the fuck, Sarge?" he said.

Then it all went south.

Jeremy had been watching Tanner as well, and seeing the boy's momentary inattention, the thug wrested the Glock from him in one deft motion and jumped back several steps, raising the pistol as he did.

"WASTE 'EM!" the thug screamed over his shoulder just before a three-round burst from the tree line dropped him and a similar burst silenced Tanner. Anderson was already charging toward the canopy and Cindy grabbed one of the fallen men's M4s and raced behind Anderson.

The sleeping men were on their feet, confused but with weapons in hand, no doubt roused initially by the voices. Anderson and Cindy fired one burst each and the men died in their underwear. Cindy left Anderson to check the bodies and went back to check on Jeremy. She found him holding the Glock on the man who'd groped her, as the man sat on the pavement, holding his right shoulder above a blood-soaked sleeve.

"This one's still alive, Mom," Jeremy said.

The man glared up at her, hatred in his eyes, just as the radio squawked from under the canopy.

"Troll Actual, this is Troll One. What's going on down there? Over," said the voice on the radio.

The man smiled. "You're about to be in a world of hurt, bitch."

***

Tremble tried to calm his racing pulse as he held the black-clad trooper in his sights. He'd targeted the man standing farther back, assuming that Cindy and Jeremy would be able to neutralize the first man and that the 'backup' was the greater immediate threat. Keith was back-stopping Cindy and Jeremy, and Tremble obsessed again whether that decision was a correct one.

So far things had gone as Cindy predicted, and Tremble held a faint hope they'd be able to take out the checkpoint quickly and silently. That hope died as the SRF thug next to Cindy and Jeremy jumped back with a pistol in his hand, yelling as he raised it. Tremble loosed a three-round burst and heard Keith do the same. When his own target fell, Tremble targeted the other man but found him down as well, felled by Keith's fire. The man was still moving and he started to put another round in him, but Jeremy scrambled for the fallen Glock and then stood directly in Tremble's line of fire. Tremble cursed and looked back to Cindy and Anderson charging the sleeping canopy, then turned to Keith.

"Let's grab the kids and get down there fast. We don't have much time."

Keith nodded and stood, slinging his rifle and jogging the short distance to where the kids were hidden. He scooped up Molly as Jamie ran towards Tremble. Tremble bent to pick up Jamie, but the boy ran past him, half-running, half-falling down the steep slope, breaking his descent by grabbing tree trunks. Tremble could hardly keep up.

They arrived at the bridge just as the radio squawked and he heard the surviving SRF trooper sneer at Cindy, "You're about to be in a world of hurt, bitch."

Tremble had a flash of inspiration.

"Get the radio and bring it here," he said to Cindy. "Our friend here is going to call off the dogs."

"Well, if it ain't Simon Tremble, not dead after all," the SRF trooper said.

"So you were expecting me?" Tremble asked.

The SRF man started to shrug and then grimaced at the pain in his shoulder. "Not really, but every checkpoint has your picture with shoot-to-kill orders. You'll be dead soon enough."

The radio squawked again, this time an inquiry from 'Troll Two,' which Tremble figured was the downstream checkpoint.

"Well, I don't plan on dying today," Tremble said, holding up the radio Cindy had just handed him. "Because you're gonna get on the radio and smooth this over."

The man sneered again. "Screw you. Why would I do that—"

Tremble shot him in the right elbow. The man howled.

"What the fuck! Are you nuts?"

"Maybe," Tremble said. "But that right side of yours is getting pretty sketchy. They might even have to amputate. I hope you'll enjoy spending the rest of your life wiping your ass left-handed. Then again …"

Tremble made a show of slapping a full magazine into his M4, moving the selector to full auto, and lowering the muzzle to six inches away from the man's crotch.

"Then again maybe you'll enjoy singing soprano in the SRF glee club. You've got two seconds to make up your mind before I shred your junk," Tremble said.

"Okay. Okay. Give me the radio," the man said.

"Sure thing," Tremble said. "But first you should know we know all about your little code word system. You know, 'teacup' and the rest of them. So if you signal anyone in any way, your genitals are hamburger. Copy that?"

The man swallowed hard, and all resistance left his eyes. He nodded and Tremble handed him the radio. The man keyed the mic.

"This is Troll Actual to all Troll units. Be advised we had an attempted incursion by armed locals, who we terminated with extreme prejudice. Watch your fronts in case there may be coordinated attacks. Teacup. Repeat. Teacup. Acknowledge. Over."

"This is Troll One. Acknowledge your last, Troll Actual. Over," said a voice over the radio.

"This is Troll Two. We copy, Troll Actual. Over," came a second transmission.

"This is Troll Actual, Out," the SRF trooper said, then passed the radio back to Tremble.

"What are we gonna do with him?" Anderson asked, glaring down at their prisoner. "If this is just a random event, the feds might not chase us too hard, but if they know for sure it WAS you who crossed here, all sorts of resources are gonna be back on our asses."

Tremble sighed, hearing the unasked question. He shook his head and looked down at the prisoner. "Y'all have medical supplies?"

The man nodded. "There's a kit in the back of the black SUV."

Tremble motioned to Cindy and Anderson. "Slap bandages on his wounds and restrain him. We'll take him with us and deal with him later."

Cindy glared at Tremble. "Why bother? He'd cut our throats without blinking."

"Because I haven't reached the point of executing prisoners yet, and he might prove useful later. We've got no clue what's been going on and he does."

Mollified by the second part of the answer at least, Cindy nodded and headed toward the SUV.

"Keith," Tremble said, "let's organize transport. We'll take the big pickup. You and Jeremy slash the tires on the other vehicles, then load every bit of gas, MREs, guns, ammo, and anything else you can find in the pickup."

Keith looked confused. "But why? If we're going back on foot, we can't possibly carry all that."

"Because if this was a random raid by locals, do you think they'd leave anything? If WE leave it, it might get them to thinking," Tremble said. "Now get a move on, we're rolling in five minutes —" Tremble stopped mid-sentence as a thought occurred to him. He walked over to the edge of the road and looked down the steep bank to the surface of the river.

"Cancel that. After you get the supplies loaded in the truck, load the bodies into the other two vehicles and we'll roll them into the river. When they find the checkpoint empty, they won't know what the hell happened, but they might think these guys deserted. The more options we can present them, the more confused they'll be, and that might buy us a bit more time," Tremble said.

Keith nodded and he and Jeremy set about the tasks.

Ten minutes later, Tremble watched the top of the second of the two vehicles sink out of sight in the swift river. The brush near the river's edge was mashed flat by the vehicles' passing, but it was starting to spring back, and there were no tire tracks in the hard, rocky ground. Tremble sighed. They might see it if they thought to look, but it was the best that could be done on the fly.

He crossed the dozen steps and got in the front passenger side of the crew cab and nodded at Anderson behind the wheel. They crossed the bridge and swung off the road, picking their way through the woods and down onto the roadbed of the rail line. They ran south, a straight shot through the trees, with the woods shielding them from sight from either the river to their east or the Lee-Jackson Highway to the west. They drove at a steady twenty miles an hour, the truck canted at an angle as they ran beside the tracks, and covered the three miles to the Blue Ridge Parkway in a tense ten minutes, the last bit made even more tense as the woods on their right thinned and they rode in full sight of the Lee Jackson Highway.

In the front passenger seat, Tremble saw the Blue Ridge Parkway crossing looming over the tracks ahead and checked the map.

"Slow down. We need to be as quiet as possible," Tremble said. "Troll Two is probably on the east end of the parkway bridge, but let's not give them any reason to look in this direction. Right after you cross under the parkway, turn right and pick your way through the median and up on the Lee Jackson Highway. From there the access ramp onto the Blue Ridge Parkway will put us on it well beyond the first curve; we won't be visible to anyone on the bridge."

Anderson nodded and did as instructed, edging through the vegetation of the shallow ditch that separated the tracks from the highway and then moving up the Blue Ridge Parkway access ramp at a quiet ten miles an hour. Five minutes later they were on the parkway, southbound.

"What now?" Anderson asked as Tremble studied the map.

"We're eleven twisting miles to the next intersection with the Appalachian Trail. Get us there as quick as you can and let's hope that's before they figure out what happened and get choppers up. We'll get into the trees and decide what to do next," Tremble said.

Anderson nodded and reached down to reset the trip odometer.

***

"That's eleven miles," Anderson said twenty minutes later, and he slowed to a crawl, "but I don't see any trail."

"There." Tremble pointed to a blaze of white paint on a tree, with a barely visible trail disappearing into the woods between two large trees.

"We're not getting this vehicle in there," Anderson said.

"Just creep along until you spot a place where we can drive into the woods a ways. We need to get under cover," Tremble said.

They found a spot a bit farther down the parkway, and Anderson managed to pull the truck about fifty feet off the road, winding between trees and leaving a path of mashed vegetation in its wake. They all got out of the spacious cab and Tremble spoke to Keith and Jeremy, who rode in the back of the truck with the prisoner.

"Keith, you and Jeremy bend that foliage back into place and cover our tracks," Tremble said.

The two moved to comply and Tremble looked down at their prisoner, who lay bound in the truck bed, duct tape across his mouth and fear in his eyes.

"Now let's see what our friend here can tell us," Tremble said, but Anderson was already dropping the tailgate.

***

"So you've only been in place two days? Where else are they looking, Garrity?" Tremble asked.

Like most bullies when their advantage is taken away, the man's defiance faded quickly. He seemed eager to ingratiate himself with his captors.

"Pretty much every crossing of the James, no matter how minor," Garrity said. "We were first looking for you on the Appalachian Trail, but when you managed to give us the slip there and didn't show up at any of the road crossings, everybody figured you were likely dead, and the search kind of died down until a couple of days ago. Then word came down directly from General Rorke to set up along the James. We were to shoot you and anyone with you on sight and cover the bodies, and they only used guys on the detail who'd already been involved in the search." He paused. "Kinda like they wanted you to disappear without a trace."

Beside Tremble, Anderson snorted. "What do you bet as soon as you disappeared, the SRF unit that bagged you was going to disappear as well?"

Their captive looked startled, as if realizing for the first time he'd been as much at risk as his quarry.

"But what changed? Why pick up the search after they'd written us off?" Tremble wondered aloud.

"Rumor is it came down right from the top," Garrity said.

"The President? Why would Gleason suddenly change —"

"Not Gleason, Crawford's president now."

"How the hell did Crawford get to be POTUS? He's way down the —"

"'Cause Gleason and the VP and all the other high-ups got killed. Crawford was the only one left," Garrity said.

They stood in stunned silence for a moment, and then Anderson turned to Tremble. "Except you."

Tremble nodded. "That explains the renewed focus on my possible existence. It's even more important that we get to Wilmington now."

Garrity shook his head forcefully. "We need to stay clear of Wilmington. Crawford blamed all the assassinations on them, and word is he plans to wipe them out."

Tremble noted Garrity's use of 'we.' Apparently the realization his life was now forfeit because of his knowledge of Tremble's existence made the man think he was one of the team.

"When?" Tremble asked.

"I don't know for sure, but soon if not already. Rorke started pulling in all available choppers about the same time we deployed along the river. That's probably why there aren't any on our ass by now. I just know Wilmington isn't a healthy place to be right now."

Tremble looked at Anderson, jerked his head to the side, and walked away. Anderson nodded and followed Tremble. Cindy joined them, having been observing the interrogation.

"This changes everything," Tremble said quietly. "Going to Wilmington won't help; at best we'd add a few more rifles to the resistance and my presence there would make Crawford even more determined to isolate them and wipe them out. We have to figure out another way to help them."

"Okay. Do you have a plan?" Anderson asked.

"Not yet, but I'm working on it," Tremble said.

Cindy nodded toward their prisoner. "What about him?"

Tremble sighed. "I'm working on that too."

CHAPTER ELEVEN

Fort Box
Wilmington Container Terminal
Wilmington, North Carolina

Day 43
May 13, 2020 - 7:15 p.m.

Colonel Doug Hunnicutt stood on the east wall, staring across fifty yards of asphalt at the newly repaired barrier fence, the setting sun at his back throwing a long shadow in front of him. He had no expectation the patched-together fence would hold for even a fraction as long as the original, but it was one more thing to slow down an attack, an attack that seemed imminent. He raised his binoculars and watched flickers of movement between the houses of tree-lined Louisiana Street in the distance.

"We should have burned down those houses and razed the neighborhood," he said aloud. "We left them a protected place to mass."

Luke Kinsey shook his head. "It's hard to destroy a neighborhood, even if we had the resources, sir. And it won't make much of a difference anyway; we don't have enough ammo to engage until they hit the perimeter fence." He paused. "You're doing fine, sir. No one could have done better."

Hunnicutt lowered the glasses and glanced at Kinsey with a sheepish grin. "Is my insecurity that obvious, Luke?"

"We're all making it up as we go along, sir, and you're doing a better job than most. I don't think of it as insecurity but concern, and I'D be concerned if you weren't showing a little," Luke said.

Hunnicutt nodded. "Did all our scouts get in?"

"The last one came through the gate an hour ago. He puts the refugee militia at eight to ten thousand strong, but only about a third with firearms. The rest have clubs or edged weapons of some sort, and they're all massing in that residential neighborhood. He figures they'll attack at any time," Luke said.

"With those numbers, they can overwhelm us with their bare hands when our ammo runs out," Hunnicutt said. "How about the SRF?"

"Maybe fifty manning a dozen crew-served automatic weapons and some RPGs. He figures they'll provide supporting fire and let the refugees do the dying, just like last time."

Hunnicutt nodded again, absently this time. After a long moment he spoke again. "So tell me, Luke; if you were on the other side, what would you do?"

"I wouldn't attack now," Luke said. "They have to know they vastly outnumber us, and just threatening us means we have to keep the wall fully manned, or nearly so. Conversely, they can take potshots at us and use part of their force to keep us in place all night, or even for days, and then hit us at a time of their choosing after we're exhausted and strung out from the waiting. I'd wait until I thought we were at the end of our endurance and then attack at just after sunup, with the sun at my back."

"My thoughts exactly," Hunnicutt said. "So I guess we'll just have to wait and see how long—"

A round clanged into the container wall just below Hunnicutt as the entire length of tree-lined Louisiana Street erupted in gunfire. In seconds, the enemy's crew-served weapons joined the fusillade, and Hunnicutt and Luke dived behind cover.

Hunnicutt looked at Luke. "Now why would ..." He trailed off and turned to look at the blazing ball of the sun just above the western horizon.

"Get on the radio and tell Butler to expect a chopper attack out of the setting sun, NOW!" Hunnicutt said to Luke as he gazed west nervously.

I guess we'll find out just how well Butler's crazy idea works, he thought, then whispered a quiet prayer to St. Jude, the patron saint of lost causes.

Intersection of US 17 & State Route 140
Near Grayson Park, North Carolina

Rorke spoke into the radio as his chopper rose, signaling Reaper to commence the feint on the eastern wall. On his orders, the pilot kept the chopper low, moving north a half mile to allow the rest of his force to ascend and hover, forming for the attack.

Rorke was no gambler. He always stacked the odds, and this was no exception. He'd gathered every chopper and every available SRF trooper with air assault training. They'd sweep in low and out of the sun, overwhelming the defenders in moments and planting an unstoppable force on the decks of the ships forming the western wall of Fort Box.

He'd kept six choppers for support, fitted as gunships with crew-served fifty-caliber machine guns in their open doors. They'd stand off and suppress any fire from the ships so a dozen more choppers could sweep in unopposed with SRF troopers to rappel down on the defenders. The battle would be over before it started, and he intended to stay well back and enjoy it from his vantage point aloft.

Fort Box
Western Defenses
Wilmington Container Terminal
Wilmington, North Carolina

Lieutenant Mike Butler looked down from his position high atop the boom of the downstream container crane and nodded to himself; they were as ready as they'd ever be. The seven massive container cranes were positioned equidistant along the line of ships that formed their defensive wall, the crane booms deployed and stretching over the tops of the ships like skinny fingers. Each boom was manned, bristling with a collection of ex-Coasties, merchant seamen, terminal workers, and river volunteers. Butler glanced up to the maintenance platforms on the very tops of the crane towers, where what he hoped was an even deadlier surprise waited.

As one of two sniper-qualified former Coasties in the fort, he'd taken the far downstream position for himself, while Finnegan manned the crane at the upstream end of their defensive line. Butler glanced down at his Barrett fifty caliber, then at Donny Gibson farther back on the crane boom. Gibson saw Butler looking over the preparations and gave him a nod. Butler managed a grim smile and nodded back. Someone was about to get a very unwelcome surprise, and Butler could only hope it wasn't him. He stiffened and fought down his fear as he heard the distinctive thump of chopper blades in the distance. He raised his radio.

"Get ready, folks," was all he said.

A dozen choppers came in fast and low out of the sun, then popped up to hover high over the river and directly overhead, making straight-up shots difficult. Before Butler could engage, all hell broke loose below as automatic fire into the steel of the ships and containers below him produced a cacophonous roar. He squinted into the sun, where gunships stood off what they no doubt thought was a safe distance and raked the decks of the ships with their machine guns. Butler raised his weapon, intent on schooling his adversaries in the true meaning of 'safe distance' as defined by Mr. Ronnie G. Barrett of Murfreesboro, Tennessee.

The Barrett sniper rifle barked once and an Mk211 round tore through a gunship, eviscerating the pilot and killing the machine gunner behind him. The chopper spun out of control and plunged down on barren Eagle Island across the river. Butler targeted another, but it spun out of control and plunged into the river before he could pull the trigger, undoubtedly the work of Finnegan at the far end of the line. A chill of fear shot down Butler's spine as the stream of tracer rounds from the remaining gunships walked upwards toward the cranes, his enemies having too soon identified the general location of the threat.

He hesitated, knowing the muzzle flash from his next shot might make it his last, as it confirmed his position for the chopper gunners. He swallowed hard and targeted another chopper when Lieutenant Josh Wright's voice came over the radio.

"All units open fire. Repeat. All units open fire. Let's buy our snipers some time. Open fire NOW!"

Wright had hardly finished speaking when all along the tops of the cranes and from the decks of the ships below, men and women with conventional weapons opened fire, the distance impossibly long and their fire ineffective, except to provide a 'target rich' environment of muzzle flashes to mask the positions of their snipers. As his comrades invited fifty-caliber death from above, Butler clenched his jaw and vowed to make the most of their sacrifice as he steadied on his next target.

The engagement was as brief as it was savage. Neither the defenders perched on the cranes nor those squatting behind the thin steel of the ships' bulwarks had any protection against the lethal machine-gun fire. They fired with grim determination, offering themselves as targets to buy their snipers precious time.

In the intervening seconds, Butler took down another gunship, as did Finnegan, but their respite was short-lived as the distinctive muzzle flash of the Barretts soon resolved their enemies' confusion. The two remaining gunships ignored Butler to concentrate on Finnegan, as Butler targeted them in support of his comrade. Another gunship fell, but too late to save Finnegan, as his gun fell silent as well. The two-minute battle culminated in a duel between Butler and the remaining gunship, as the chopper gunner found his range, and Butler died thinking he'd lost the fight. But the valiant Coastie had been more successful than he knew. His copilot dead, his gunner wounded, and smoke billowing from the chopper's tail rotor, the SRF pilot turned his wounded bird west and fled into the setting sun.

SRF Command Helicopter
Two Miles West

Rorke watched the engagement, enraged by the loss of his gunships. Seeing the last gunship disengage and start back toward him provided a focus for that rage. He grabbed the radio mic.

"Hammer Five, this is Thunderbolt Actual. What is your intention? Over."

There was no response and Rorke was about to repeat the inquiry when the reply came.

"Thunderbolt Actual, this is Hammer Five. We've taken fire and are ineffective, repeat ineffective. My copilot is dead, my gunner is wounded, and we have damage to our tail rotor. Request permission to RTB. Repeat, request permission to return to base. Over."

"Hammer Five, state nature of damage. Over," Rorke said into the mic.

"Thunderbolt Actual, exact nature of damage unknown. Half my friggin' instrumentation is out and forced landing may be imminent. We are declaring an emergency and RTB. Over," the pilot said.

Rorke's rage spiked at the pilot's insolence, no longer requesting permission to withdraw but stating it as his intention.

"Hammer Five, negative your last. Repeat. Negative your last. Your mission is to provide support. Return to the fight. That is an order. Acknowledge. Over," Rorke said.

Another hesitation. The choppers were only two hundred yards apart now and Rorke could clearly see the damaged chopper, shattered Plexiglas, and black smoke billowing from the tail rotor.

Rorke keyed his throat mike and spoke to his door gunner on the internal comms. "Get ready to take him down on my order," he said.

"Sir?" came the confused reply.

Unable to contain himself, Rorke screamed into the mic. "YOU HEARD ME! GET READY TO SHOOT THEM DOWN! UNDERSTOOD?"

"Yes, sir," the gunner replied.

Rorke's external radio squawked again. "Thunderbolt Actual, this is Hammer Five. I regret I cannot comply with your order as —"

"Take him down," Rorke ordered, rewarded immediately with the rattle of the machine gun behind him. All the rounds went into what was left of the Plexiglas bubble and the gunship immediately veered off at a crazy angle and plummeted downward to crash into a subdivision below.

Rorke considered his options. Of the remaining choppers, only his was equipped with a machine gun; all the rest were configured as troop carriers. He had no intention of providing close support, but his machine gun would serve another important function. He keyed the mic again.

"This is Thunderbolt Actual to all units. Attack will commence at once, in two waves of six birds each, as planned. Any Thunderbolt units attempting to withdraw without first landing troops will be shot down. Repeat. Any units attempting to withdraw without first landing troops will be shot down. Now execute. Repeat, execute."

***

Lieutenant Josh Wright watched from the main deck, at first in elation as the gunship fled, then in confusion as it was apparently shot down by friendly fire. He tried to raise Butler on the radio, and his heart sank as Donny Gibson's voice responded.

"Butler's . . . he's gone. Finnegan too, I think," Gibson said.

Wright swallowed hard. "What else can you see up there?"

"From here it looks like we have six KIA. If that machine gun hit 'em, there was no surviving that. Orders?" Gibson asked.

"You time deployment of the defenses from up there. We'll handle any that make it down to the deck. Other than that, we'll play it by ear and hope the hell Butler was right. Good luck . . . uh-oh, HERE THEY COME!"

***

Donny Gibson tipped his head up and watched the choppers drop almost straight down toward the ships. They had to get low enough for troops to 'fast rope' down to the ships and that was what he was counting on.

He looked down to the ships below, where a cobbled-together arrangement of cargo nets, old mooring lines, old electrical wire, and anything else they'd been able to find and tie together lay draped unnoticed across the tops of the container stacks.

Six choppers were descending, probably all the enemy felt they could safely deploy at one time along the wall of ships. He watched the choppers targeting the open areas between the crane booms and waited until they went into a stationary hover and the coils of rope began to drop out of their open doors.

"STRETCH THE NETS! NOW!" All along the line of ships, seamen engaged the air motors of improvised hoisting arrangements, and the patched-together spiderweb of junk leaped from the tops of the container stacks and stretched taut between the booms of the container cranes.

Gibson's timing was near perfect and the rising nets met the first wave of fast-roping SRF troops, snarling them in the defensive netting at crane boom height as defenders on the crane booms savaged the hapless attackers with rifle fire from near point-blank range.

Gibson raised his radio again. "FOULING WIRES DEPLOY AT WILL. LET'S BRING 'EM DOWN, BOYS!" he ordered.

The choppers were actually slightly below the very tops of the massive cranes, and on the very uppermost maintenance platform of each crane, tarps were whipped away to reveal seven former Coasties, each armed with a shoulder-fired Bridger line-throwing gun. The Coasties all fired without hesitation, angling their shots slightly downward into the top of the whirling rotors, targets they were unlikely to miss at such a range. The eighteen inch long, half pound brass bolts from the line throwing guns slammed through the whirling rotors, to strike the blades and be deflected downward or batted up to fall in front of yet another blade. With minimal resistance, the tough nylon line attached to each projectile was not cut, but yielded, wrapping in the spinning blades in a heartbeat to drag with it a much more lethal load. The thin, braided, high-tensile wire secured to the end of each throwing line was light but strong, and it ripped off spools clamped to the handrails of the maintenance platforms, the spinning spools shrieking like the reel of a sport fisherman who'd inadvertently hooked a great white shark.

The exact method of failure varied. On some choppers, the wire snarled in their rotors was sufficient to doom them. On others, the process was hastened when sections of the brittle titanium corrosion sheathing on the leading edge of the blades detached, slung off by centrifugal force after being cracked by the heavy projectiles. On all, the result was the same. The pilots fought their controls, white-knuckled, to keep their wobbling birds in the air, but no amount of skill could defeat the laws of physics. With their rotors all severely out of dynamic balance, they went down. Two crashed down directly on the ships and the other four pitched sideways into the river, all leaking screaming, black-clad SRF men from their open doors

The assault of the first wave ended ten seconds after it began; its only survivors two badly injured SRF troopers hanging in the defensive netting. The defenders looked up at the choppers of the second wave and waited, unsure of the result of a continued assault now that they no longer had the advantage of surprise. The choppers hovered, uncertain, and then one by one turned and fled the way they'd come.

There was a moment of stunned disbelief, and then a great cheer rose from the defenders of the western wall, echoed by their comrades to the east, who'd watched the fight from afar.

SRF Command Helicopter
Two Miles West

Rorke was apoplectic as he watched his first wave savaged in seconds. When the second wave turned back toward him without attempting to engage, he flew into a towering rage.

"THUNDERBOLT TWO, YOU ARE ORDERED TO RESUME THE ATTACK. ACKNOWLEDGE. OVER!"

"With respect, General, it's impossible. Even if I went in myself, I doubt the others would follow me. Over," the squadron leader replied over the radio.

The choppers were returning in a ragged line, more or less in the order they'd decided to turn tail. The squadron leader was at least in the rear, being the last to run. Perhaps this could be salvaged yet; Rorke switched to internal comms.

"Gunner, shoot down that lead chopper," Rorke said.

The fifty-caliber hammered and the lead chopper pitched and veered to one side, then crashed.

"THUNDERBOLT TWO, I REPEAT, YOU ARE ORDERED TO RESUME THE ATTACK. ACKNOWLEDGE. OVER!"

There was a momentary hesitation and then the squadron leader's chopper turned, and one by one, the other four choppers turned as well, heading back toward Fort Box. Rorke nodded, but as he watched, all five choppers gained altitude, way too much altitude, as if they were trying to avoid any ground fire whatsoever.

He watched in disbelief as they flew past Fort Box and kept on going. His radio squawked.

"Thunderbolt Two to Thunderbolt Actual. Do you copy? Over."

"I copy. What the hell are you doing?" Rorke snarled.

"Saying goodbye and a big screw you, General. None of us signed up for this crazy shit. We'll leave the choppers where you can find them. This is Thunderbolt Two, out."

Rorke cursed and considered giving chase, but the deserters' choppers already had a substantial lead and all the birds had more or less the same top speed. Plus the deserters were likely to fly as far as their fuel would take them before they set down and abandoned the choppers, while he had to conserve enough fuel to return to base. He had to let them go for now, but God help them if he ever caught them.

He turned his attention back to the fort. Crawford was going to go bat-shit crazy when he found out they'd just lost eighteen choppers and a hundred and fifty troops, including many trained pilots. To suffer those losses and still not take the fort compounded the failure. Rorke HAD to put a silver lining on this, which meant taking the fort. He keyed the mic and ordered Reaper to start the attack on the east wall.

***

"We're holding, sir. For now at least. Over," Josh Wright said into the radio.

"Excellent, Lieutenant," Hunnicutt said. "Please congratulate Lieutenant Butler on his idea. Over."

There was a long pause.

"Mike ... Mike didn't make it, sir," Wright said.

Hunnicutt couldn't speak for a moment. *Had it been only weeks since he'd met the tall and competent Coastie who'd become so much a part of the success of Fort Box?* He pushed down his anger and sadness. He'd have to mourn later, if they were all still alive.

"How many other casualties, Lieutenant? Please accept my apologies. I should have asked that first. Over."

"Eight, sir. All KIA in the initial chopper assault. Over," Wright said.

Hunnicutt was about to ask for names when all hell broke loose, and Luke Kinsey ran up, ducking low to stay below the short firing wall.

"They're coming, sir. They're out of the residential neighborhood in force and the lead elements will be at the fence in thirty seconds or less. With your permission I'd like to give the guys 'weapons free' when the attackers reach the fence," Luke said.

Hunnicutt shook his head. "We have to conserve ammo, so let the attackers build up along the fence a bit to present a better target before you open fire, and emphasize again everyone is to make every shot count. If our intel is correct, we don't have enough bullets to shoot them all, and we can't afford to waste a single round. Take charge for the moment. I need to finish getting the sitrep on the western defenses from Wright."

"Roger that, sir," Luke said and headed down the line in a low crouch.

Hunnicutt picked up the radio. "Lieutenant Wright, we're about to have company. What's your assessment of your situation there? Over."

"I think we knocked their dicks in the dirt pretty badly, sir. I don't expect they'll be looking for a return engagement here today. Over."

Hunnicutt smiled at Wright's terminology. "Very well. Keep enough people there to hold until reinforced if necessary, then bring the rest of your folks and join us on the east wall. Do you have anyone … anyone left qualified on the Barretts? Over."

"Both the sniper-qualified Coasties are KIA, sir, but I think several more are familiar with the Barretts, and if not, I'm sure we can handle it."

"Good. Expedite transfer of the Barretts. We may need them," Hunnicutt said.

"They're on the way, sir. And we'll be right behind them. Wright out."

***

The assault began with a fusillade of RPGs fired by SRF 'support' troops from protected positions along Louisiana Street, but accuracy at the ranges involved was problematic. Targeting the defenders on the top of the wall resulted in the rockets flying high, soaring over the fort completely or impacting a container stack or the sides of the ships at the dock, where they did nothing to diminish the fort's defenses. Aiming lower produced a few hits to the container wall itself, but no breaches, and as the attacking force neared the wall, the RPGs were as likely to inflict 'friendly fire' casualties as damage the defenders. The RPGs stopped in minutes.

SRF machine-gun fire was more effective, since it could be accurately targeted at the top of the wall. However, the defenders had learned their lesson from the attack days before and had greatly reinforced the entire top of the wall with protected firing positions. When the Barrett sniper rifles came into the fight and took out three machine guns in as many shots, the SRF gunners quickly decided discretion was the better part of valor and ceased fire.

But the SRF 'support' had always been a sideshow, meant to encourage the 'Refugee Militia' more than anything. It soon became apparent no such encouragement was needed. The SRF propagandists and spin artists had done their jobs exceedingly well, and the vast horde of attackers was literally screaming for the defenders' blood. There were no children this time, and the scattered women seemed, if anything, more enraged than the men. There was no doubt as to the attackers' intentions and no ambivalence on the part of the defenders — these people were the enemy, no matter how they'd become that.

The men and women of Fort Box shot the attackers down dispassionately, expending their limited ammunition with an almost painful economy. They targeted individuals pushing at the fence first, and were often rewarded when two or more attackers fell as the full metal jacket rounds went through one and took out others.

Lady Luck was in their corner at the fence as well, for the patch job held longer than anyone anticipated. There was literally a berm of bodies along its length when it finally collapsed and enraged attackers clawed their way over their own dead to get at the defenders. Hunnicutt saved his machine guns until the attackers got past the fence, and then the gunners raked the fifty yards of asphalt with short bursts, mowing down attackers like ripe wheat. And still they came.

Some carried makeshift ladders and Hunnicutt calmly ordered every third defender to concentrate on ladder bearers. But in the end, it was like trying to keep back the incoming tide with a boat paddle, and that tide crashed against the wall of Fort Box in a hissing, screaming wave of hate-filled humanity. Bangers and the SRF thugs could be discouraged by death, but these poor bastards had literally nothing left to lose. Death in the pursuit of avenging their loved ones was for most their only remaining option.

The few ladders that made it through came up and were pushed over with poles deployed among the defenders for that very purpose. Undeterred, the attackers formed human pyramids, their close proximity to the wall making it impossible for the defenders to see or fire down on them without exposing themselves. Here and there, attackers reached the top and only the defenders' more stable positions allowed them to topple the attackers back into the seething crowd below using improvised poles and spears.

Hunnicutt stood transfixed for a long second, momentarily unable to process what he was seeing. *God! This is medieval! Two months ago these people could have been my neighbors or attended the same church.*

"It's time, sir. We can't hold them back much longer."

Hunnicutt looked over to find Luke Kinsey by his side, and he nodded, unable to speak.

Luke nodded back. "Sir, would you like me to ..."

Hunnicutt shook his head and managed a sad smile. "No, Luke, I've already got plenty to answer for. There's no use in both of us going to hell."

He walked to the edge of the wall and looked down into the fort, where men stood ready around a gasoline tank truck connected to a large portable pump.

"START THE PUMP," he yelled down.

The men below rushed to comply and Hunnicutt turned back to the wall. As he walked back toward Luke, he heard the pump start, and within seconds the air was filled with the pungent smell of gasoline as the liquid filled the slotted pipe bolted to the front edge of the fort's wall and sprayed down on the horde below. The howl from the mob hushed for a moment, then increased in intensity, now a mixture of rage and, as realization dawned, something more—fear, an animal's instinctive fear of fire.

"Execute, Major," Hunnicutt said, weariness in his voice.

Luke Kinsey spoke into the radio, and all along the wall, the defenders fell back to the inner edge, as far away from the front edge as possible. Here and there gasoline-soaked attackers appeared over the wall to be shot down with a dwindling supply of ammunition. All the defenders were clear in seconds, and Luke spoke into the radio again. At equal distances along the wall a dozen grenades flew from the defenders, soft underhand lobs that arced the instruments of death over the edge of the wall and into the gasoline-soaked mob below.

The attackers killed outright were the lucky ones, as the explosions ignited a firestorm along the length of the wall—a raging furnace fed by the continual supply of gasoline. The roar of the crowd morphed into one of fear and pain, and then rage again as those in the back of the horde were held at bay literally by a wall of their burning brethren.

The heat grew unbearable, and by prearrangement the defenders evacuated the wall in good order, rushing down to prepared positions inside the fort in the event the attackers somehow managed to breach the wall of flame. Hunnicutt and Luke followed the last of the defenders off the wall and then raced across the asphalt toward the three-story operations center and up the stairs to its flat roof. Hunnicutt hesitated a moment, casting a critical eye over a tall spindly-looking wooden tower, obviously newly built.

"You sure that thing will hold us both, Luke," he asked.

"Lieutenant Washington assures me it's solid as a rock, sir," Luke said.

"Well, let's hope he's right," Hunnicutt said, starting for the ladder.

From their vantage point atop the tower, they could see over the wall to the mob beyond, held back by the flaming barrier and screaming in impotent fury.

Hunnicutt sighed. "I'd hoped to avoid this, but they're still there and still outnumber us. Three or four to one, I'd say. We have to stop them now while they're in one place and within reach."

"Agreed, sir," Luke said.

"Tell Lieutenant Washington and Mr. Jenkins we're ready, Major."

***

Levi Jenkins looked down the line of a dozen wooden contraptions and went over his mental checklist again; they were as ready as he could make them and this harebrained idea was either going to work or it wasn't.

The short message they'd received recounting the loss of *Pecos Trader* had saddened him beyond measure, but he'd taken solace in the fact that most of his former shipmates and friends had survived.

Included in that brief message had been a cryptic message from his friend and old boss Dan Gowan. It read simply, 'Tell Levi gasoline plus Styrofoam equals napalm. It works.'

As the threat of another attack against the east wall loomed, and with ammunition in short supply, Levi had experimented and discovered he could indeed make napalm. Welcome news, since the full tanks of the adjacent terminal and hundreds of shipping containers left to unpack meant neither gasoline nor Styrofoam were in short supply. A review of bills of lading also turned up a shipping container with a consignment of 'glass jars—2160 ml—wide mouth—screw top,' which were, as it turned out, conveniently packed in Styrofoam. He looked to where those jars now rested in a huge stack, filled to the brim with homemade napalm and wrapped in gasoline-soaked cotton toweling secured tightly to the jars with zip ties.

For all the effort that pile of 'ammunition' represented, his biggest challenge had been devising a delivery system to get the napalm where it was needed fast enough and in sufficient quantities to make a difference. The idea for the trebuchets had actually been Joel Washington's, who was, it turned out, something of a medieval history buff. He'd described the device to Levi and the pair had worked together for two days to perfect a prototype. Then they'd disassembled the prototype and used the parts as templates to quickly mass produce a dozen more.

Their improvised devices sat now in a long line, jokingly referred to as the 'Washington Artillery,' facing the burning wall and the unseen enemy beyond. Hastily trained volunteers stood ready beside them.

Levi looked over at Washington, who appeared equally nervous. "You think this is gonna work, Washington?"

Washington nodded, pointing to a pile of sandbags beside the long row of trebuchets. "Only thing I'm worried about is the range, and we got 'em all weighted different and marked. Soon as Major Kinsey dials us in, we should be okay. I just hope—"

The radio squawked. "Slingshot, this is Eagle Eye. Do you copy? Over."

Washington raised his radio. "We copy loud and clear, Eagle Eye. Over."

"You may fire Unit One for effect, Slingshot. Good luck."

***

Luke Kinsey watched as the ball of flame soared over the burning wall to strike the asphalt and bloom into a twenty-foot circle of fire at the front of the mob. The impact was impressive, and flaming napalm splashed a dozen attackers, who screamed and beat at the flames in desperate attempts to extinguish them.

"Unit One, slightly short," Luke said into the radio. "Fire Unit Twelve for effect. Over."

The second shot from the most heavily weighted trebuchet was long, and Luke quickly reported that back to Washington. By the forth shot they'd determined the range of optimum firing weights and in less than two minutes, the 'Washington Artillery' began to rain fiery death down on their attackers.

The enraged roar increased as the first few impacts deterred only the victims of the strikes. Then the impacts became constant and widespread, accuracy irrelevant given the massive size of their target. The roar of the mob became hesitant, then fearful as more napalm-coated victims ran screaming mindlessly through the mob. In ten minutes half the field was burning and those yet unscathed turned and fled, terror finally overcoming their thirst for revenge. As the last of those still able to run fled the field, Luke raised his radio.

"Cease fire, Slingshot. Repeat. Cease fire. They're running."

SRF Command Helicopter
Two Miles West

Rorke raised his binoculars and watched in disbelief as the area east of the fort erupted into flames and the attackers fled.

Trebuchets? Frigging trebuchets! And where the hell did they get those sniper rifles?

His musings were interrupted by Reaper's voice on the radio.

"Tidal Wave to Thunderbolt Actual, do you copy? Over?"

Rorke stifled a snort. *Tidal Wave? More like a frigging ripple.*

"This is Thunderbolt Actual. I copy, Tidal Wave, and I have a visual on the east wall. What is your condition? Over," Rorke responded.

"Three KIA from those damned sniper rifles. Request orders. Over," Reaper replied.

Rorke fought down his rising rage to concentrate on the situation at hand. The 'refugee militia,' like the gangbangers before them, was obviously a spent force; there was nothing more his men were likely to accomplish there.

"RTB. Repeat. Return to Base. Acknowledge. Over," Rorke said into the mic.

"Acknowledge RTB. ETA at the nuke plant is one hour. Over."

"I copy, Tidal Wave. Thunderbolt Actual out," Rorke said, and racked the mic before giving the pilot instructions to return to the nuke plant. He had to figure out some way to salvage something out of this mess before Crawford got wind of it.

Fort Box HQ
Conference Room
Wilmington Container Terminal
Wilmington, North Carolina

Same Day - 9:45 p.m.

Sergeant Jerry Hill rose partway from his chair and reached across to tap the map spread on the conference table. "Based on what I overheard when I was their prisoner, I think they only have a garrison force at the nuke plant, maybe company strength—just enough to maintain plant security, guard their worker/prisoners, and provide security for the Military Ocean Terminal next door. I doubt they've had time to expand their overall operation at the nuke plant too much."

Luke Kinsey nodded and looked across the table at Hunnicutt. "That fits Rorke's MO and pretty much matches what we saw when we checked out the nuke plant, sir. SRF companies run small, just under a hundred and fifty, and based on the tents we saw, that looks about right."

"What do you mean it fit's Rorke's MO?" Lieutenant Josh Wright asked.

"Maximizing assets," Luke said. "The SRF is substantial, but the ground it has to cover is enormous, and as an occupation force, Rorke's spread really thin. He's using a technique he developed in Africa and that he shared with me back when he had illusions I might be his protégé. Basically he establishes strategically located bases strong enough to withstand an attack and close enough together so if any one is attacked, the others can send reinforcements. He can control a lot of territory that way and send out his looting teams over a wider area. He'll figure the nuke plant and MOT as one base, but I'm sure he has supporting troops nearby. The big questions are where and how many?"

Hunnicutt shook his head. "No, Major, those are important questions, but the crucial ones are how fast reinforcements will arrive and how long we can hold the MOT. Rorke will have set these bases up assuming

578

chopper support, and we've just knocked the hell out of his air assets. He'll likely bring in more choppers, but until he can, he'll have to bring in reinforcements by road, which will buy us some time." Hunnicutt turned to Josh Wright. "So the real question is, will it be enough time?"

Wright nodded toward Jerry Hill. "The terminal guys tell me they can move a lot of freight in eight hours, so if Sergeant Hill here can make sure we don't waste time finding what we need, I think we can get in and get out with all our ammunition needs taken care of for the foreseeable future. What we can't carry, we'll blow up as we leave."

"So can we hold for eight hours?" Hunnicutt asked.

There was silence around the table until Luke spoke up. "We'll do what we have to do, sir."

Hunnicutt nodded. "And the secondary objective? Are you sure you really want to add that to your plate, Major?"

"I feel we owe it to Dempsey, sir. We put his family in danger, so we at least have to try to rescue them and there'll never be a better time. And in the long run, presuming there is a long run, we'll need Dempsey and anyone else he can convince to join us. Besides, I'm betting as soon as word goes out the MOT is under attack, Rorke will strip the nuke plant first to try to retake the terminal. Without choppers they'll have to come around by road, and Lieutenant Washington won't engage at the nuke plant unless and until he likes his odds." Luke smiled. "If nothing else, it will confuse them, and a confused enemy is never a bad thing."

Hunnicutt nodded and stood, signaling the end of the meeting. "All right, gentlemen, see to any last minute preparations and try to get some rest. We'll shove off at oh one hundred, right after the moon sets."

There were surprised looks around the table, followed by nods and murmurs of assent as the men rose and filed out of the room. Luke Kinsey hung back and shut the door after the last man.

"WE'LL shove off, sir?"

Hunnicutt stiffened and fixed Luke with a stony glare. "That's right, Major. I'm coming with you."

Luke shook his head. "With respect, sir, that's a very bad idea."

Hunnicutt glared. "I was in command here last I looked, MAJOR."

"Indeed you are, sir, and again with respect, being in command means you have to do what's best for the mission and the command, not what you WANT to do. We still have the noncombatants here, many of them the families of the very men going with me; how do you think they'll feel if there's not someone they trust back here literally holding the fort?"

Hunnicutt glared again and then his face sagged and he blew out a sigh. "All right, all right. Point taken. Leave me a token force, one of the Barretts, and some of the folks who can run those trebuchets. You'll have to take most of the ammo we have left anyway. How much did you scrounge up?"

Luke shrugged. "Not much, but it will have to do. And if things go according to plan, we'll resupply at the Military Ocean Terminal. Besides, an attack right now is sure to be the LAST thing Rorke is expecting." He smiled. "Even if we did, as Wright put it, 'knock his dick in the dirt.'"

Hunnicutt chuckled and reached into his desk drawer to extract an almost empty bottle of bourbon and two semi-clean water glasses. He divided what was left of the whiskey between the two glasses and handed one to Luke. Then Hunnicutt raised his glass, the brief smile chased away by more somber thoughts.

"To Operation Little Round Top," he said.

"Operation Little Round Top," Luke repeated solemnly and clinked glasses.

CHAPTER TWELVE

S/S *Cape Mendocino*
Clark Island
Neches River
Beaumont, Texas

Day 43
May 13, 2020 - 5:45 a.m.

Jordan Hughes stood with the others on the bridge wing of the S/S *Cape Mendocino*, watching the first truckload of dirt creep across Gowan's pontoon bridge. His enthusiasm for that accomplishment was dulled only slightly by his pounding headache, a result of both lack of sleep and caffeine withdrawal.

Not that he was alone in that; no one had slept much in the last two days, but things were coming together at a pace far beyond his expectations. Lucius Wellesley and his towboat boys worked through that first night to circle all the ships around the island, and Gowan and Howell had driven their people mercilessly to get the old ships secured together and ballasted firmly aground. Then Gowan had faced the more difficult task of running temporary power to the massive barge elevator on the stern of the *Cape Mendocino* to launch the cargo lighters. The improvised pontoon bridge now stretching from the island to the east bank of the river was silent witness to the success of those efforts.

But the first barge down the elevator didn't become part of the bridge, but immediately turned into a car ferry. A ferry Lucius Wellesley and the *Judy Ann* used to retrieve the SUV Hughes had abandoned on the refinery dock when he'd rescued his family days before. Transferring the vehicle to the east bank gave them 'wheels,' and the Gillespie brothers had traveled the back roads to Vidor, Bridge City, Orangefield, and a dozen wide spots in the road in between, activating their 'good ole' boy network' and contacting friends, and friends of friends, and even old enemies, as long as they had a dozer or a backhoe or a dump truck or the necessary skills. The Gillespies were effective recruiters and the idea of 'an island fortress' was particularly compelling in these troubled times. Hughes found his workforce increased by a hundred skilled workers overnight, and more worryingly, his 'community' increased by not only those workers but their extended families. It seems the Gillespies' recruitment efforts had been a bit vague about the shortage of supplies.

Hughes turned from admiring Gowan's bridge to face two of the architects of his current dilemma.

"It'll work, Captain Hughes," Mike Gillespie said. Beside him, his brother Jimmy nodded emphatic agreement.

Hughes shook his head. "It's been six weeks since the blackout, Mike, and those places are in the middle of town. What makes you think they haven't all been stripped to the walls by now? It's not worth the risk."

"That's just it, I'm sure they haven't," Mike Gillespie countered. "Look, I drove for Lone Star Marine, and there weren't more than eight or ten people in the entire operation. Plus, and with all due respect, Captain, I don't think you really understand how these ship chandlers operate."

Hughes bristled. "I've been going to sea—"

Mike held up his hands in a calm-down gesture. "I don't mean it like it sounds. What I mean is, you guys on the ships see the chandler's trucks drive up all painted up nice and pretty with their logo and all, and you think what a slick operation. But it's not like that at all. There are four ship chandlers in Beaumont and I've worked for all of them at one time or another and they're all shoestring operations. Nobody, or no customer at least, ever sees their warehouse, and they all rent the cheapest places they can find and don't even put up signs. It's not like they sell to the public or need to advertise. I'm telling you people drive past those places every day without a clue what's inside. I'm bettin' no one has looted them because no one even knows they're there."

Hughes was unconvinced. "What about the people who worked there? If you've thought of it, so have they, likely several weeks ago."

Mike Gillespie nodded. "I'm sure they did, but that's like maybe six to ten people at each company. I figure they took some stuff, but I'm bettin' they left the rest of it right where it was so they could go back and get more. First because there's so much you NEED a warehouse to store it, and second because if you did manage to get it all to where you were living and someone raided you, you'd lose everything. So it would be much better to keep things hidden in plain sight and then resupply from that point when you needed it. Anyway that was MY plan for when we ran through the stuff in my truck, before y'all showed up, I mean."

Matt Kinsey broke his silence. "Maybe we should hear him out, Captain. I don't want to tangle with the cons again either, but this sounds like something we can't afford to pass up, especially with a growing population."

Mike Gillespie shot Kinsey a grateful look and dived back in before Hughes could object. "Look, Captain, my old company is the closest, less than two miles from here on Cardinal Drive. At least let us check it out. Then if the warehouse is stripped, I'll shut up. But if it's not …"

He left the tantalizing prospect of a huge cache of stores hanging in the air, and Hughes felt himself weakening, a vision of cases and cases of coffee in his mind.

"We could be low profile," Matt Kinsey said. "It's close enough to reach on foot and avoid the cons. I think it's worth the risk, Captain."

Hughes said nothing, weighing the risks. Finally he nodded. "All right, but let's get a plan together. If we're going to take the risk, let's be prepared to make it count if y'all find anything."

***

Hughes stood atop the 'ferry barge' with Gowan, sweat beaded on his forehead as he watched some of the newly recruited members of Gowan's work crew drag a raggedly cut steel plate across the deck with chain falls and prepare to weld it in place to reinforce the hatch cover.

Gowan nodded toward the work in progress. "Based on the dimensions Mike gave me, we can cram six trucks on in a pinch, but hauling one SUV is one thing, and a bunch of loaded trucks is another. I've got no idea whether the hatch covers will take the weight. All we can do is beef them up and hope for the best."

"Mike said there are only four or five trucks in the warehouse anyway. We should be able to spread them out to keep from concentrating the weight," Hughes said. "How's the reinforcement of the ramps coming?"

Gowan nodded farther down the barge where two men were welding angle iron supports on two long, narrow ramps slightly wider than the double width of dual-wheel truck tires.

"They're coming along, but this is engineering by approximation," Gowan said. "I have to make educated guesses as to how much the loaded trucks weigh, and if I get too conservative, the ramps will be so heavy the guys won't be able to manhandle them into place. On the other hand, if they're not strong enough, they'll collapse under the weight of the loaded trucks."

Hughes suppressed a grin, long used to Gowan's habit of listing all the challenges he faced in great detail before he successfully, and inevitably, solved the problem at hand. "Well, if anyone can do it, it's you, Dan," Hughes said, keeping a straight face.

"That's for sure," Matt Kinsey said as he walked up on the end of the conversation.

Sensing he was the recipient of 'management by ego massage,' Gowan looked at both men and snorted, then walked off without another word.

Smiling, Hughes turned to Kinsey. "Everything ready on your end, Matt?"

Kinsey nodded. "We'll leave from behind the island as soon as it's dark. With just the one small barge, Lucius figures he can run dark and maneuver on the radar alone as long as he avoids really tight quarters. It's less than a mile to the Union Canal inlet and the sulfur plant dock, and after we're inside the inlet and out of sight, we'll just hang there until it's light enough for him to see what he's doing. Then we'll find a place to get the barge to the bank and set up before we take off for the warehouse."

"Any second thoughts?"

Kinsey shook his head. "Should be a piece of cake, getting there on foot anyway. I had a closer look at that old street map we found in the SUV and it looks like we can cut through industrial properties and follow train tracks for a lot of the distance. If we stay off surface streets and near cover, we shouldn't run into any cons." He nodded toward Gowan farther down the barge, inspecting the work on the ramps. "All assuming Chief Gowan is ready by nightfall."

"Don't worry about Dan. If he says he'll be ready, you can take that to the bank," Hughes said.

M/V *Judy Ann*
Union Canal Inlet
Neches River
Beaumont, Texas

Day 44
May 14, 2020 - 5:50 a.m.

Captain Lucius Wellesley stood ashore, studying the end of the cargo lighter turned car ferry he'd grounded on the bank just a few minutes earlier. The boxy barge stretched a hundred feet back in the inlet to where the *Judy Ann* was made fast, her powerful diesels chugging softly. An extension ladder angled down steeply from the deck of the barge to the bank where he stood.

"What do you think, Lucius?" Matt Kinsey asked.

"The angle on the ramps will still be a mite steep, but we can get 'er done. I'll work on it while y'all are gone," Wellesley said.

"You need us to wait and help you?"

Wellesley looked over to where the rest of Kinsey's shore party was climbing down from the barge, hauling weapons and two five-gallon cans of gasoline. He shook his head. "You best be moving. I reckon the cons aren't early risers, so y'all should take advantage of that. Me and my boys will take care of things on this end."

Kinsey offered his hand. "Thank you, Lucius. And good luck."

Wellesley took the offered hand and smiled. "Good luck to you, Matt. You're more likely to need it than I will. I'm just the bus driver."

***

The shore party was bigger than Kinsey needed for a straight reconnaissance, but they'd decided that if they DID find stores, they'd bring them back to the island, or the 'fort,' as they were all beginning to think of it. Assuming they found the warehouse undisturbed, Mike Gillespie figured there would be trucks locked inside. That meant they needed multiple drivers, bodies to load the trucks, and perhaps gasoline to power them. The distance was short, so they wouldn't need much fuel for each vehicle, but they couldn't risk the trucks being empty.

Beyond Mike Gillespie as a guide, Kinsey had planned to fill the ranks of the team with his trusted Coasties, but when Jimmy Gillespie had insisted on coming, he could hardly say no. In the end, they decided on a team of five, Kinsey, Alvarez, and Baker, along with the Gillespie brothers. He'd considered bringing Torres instead of Baker, but in the end decided he shouldn't risk his two most capable marksmen in one mission. He left Torres on the ship with his trusty Barrett, just in case Hughes needed to, as Torres put it, 'reach out and touch someone' in the group's absence.

They were all armed, and the two gas cans were fitted with improvised shoulder straps to make them easier to carry. They intended to travel fast, and the intention was to stop regularly to swap out the gas cans so no single team member was worn out from lugging the forty-pound loads.

They moved up Sulfur Plant Road in the predawn, briefly exposed as they crossed beneath US 69, but soon reaching the parking lot of an industrial complex, its guard shack unattended. Kinsey didn't hesitate, but led them through the gate and angled across the massive lot to the chain-link fence in a tree-lined back corner. He motioned to Alvarez, who attacked the fence with a pair of bolt cutters they'd brought along for that very purpose, and in less than a minute they were concealed in trees.

They made their way west, avoiding streets to cross vacant lots and alleys, and used railroad tracks when possible. The flat terrain of southeast Texas provided little in the way of natural cover, but Kinsey made the best use of buildings, fences, and the scrub trees that grew in unkempt abundance next to railroad tracks. In places where gaps between cover made exposing themselves unavoidable, he studied the gap carefully for any signs of movement, then sent the team members sprinting across one at a time. More than once he whispered a silent prayer of thanks that the cons did indeed seem to be all still asleep.

When they got close, Mike Gillespie took the lead, and they moved through a residential neighborhood of modest homes scattered on one-acre tracts to approach the warehouse from the rear and across a vacant lot. They arrived at the rear of the parking lot and stared at the large nondescript warehouse through a chain-link fence spotted with rust. There were pickups and a couple of small vans with the Lone Star Marine logo on their sides scattered across the large lot, the hoods of some raised, undoubtedly stripped of their batteries by looters.

"We'll cut the fence and go in the back door. The building will screen us from the street. The delivery trucks are inside the warehouse, and presuming we find anything, we can load them inside, raise the roller doors, and get out of here. We can be back to the river in ten minutes, max," Mike Gillespie said quietly.

Kinsey was nodding his assent when Alvarez spoke.

"Uhh … it looks like we won't need to cut the fence. Someone's been here before us." He nodded at a place where the fence had been cut, the split now held closed by black twist ties, likely invisible at any distance beyond a few feet.

They all stared at the cut. Mike spoke first.

"Someone obviously paid a visit and then closed up the hole so they could use it again without the breach being visible." Gillespie pointed at trampled grass near the cut. "I'm thinking someone has been coming in on foot to resupply. Like I told the captain, I bet they've been using this place like their own secret supermarket."

Kinsey looked around nervously. "Well, I suspect whoever it is won't take kindly to us making off with the inventory."

Mike shook his head. "They'll come and go at night, especially if they have to travel any distance on foot. They wouldn't want to risk drawing attention to the place. I think we're good."

"Well, let's take precautions, all the same." He looked around and spotted a clump of Chinese tallow trees and some overgrown shrubbery.

"Alvarez, take the gas cans and hunker down over there in that bunch of trees. If you see anyone, give us three double-clicks on the radio. We want these groceries if they're here, but I don't want to get ambushed in the process," Kinsey said.

Alvarez nodded and started for the hiding place, his weapon slung and a gas can in each hand. Kinsey turned back to the others. "All right, folks, let's go see whether or not the cupboard is bare."

The fence opened easily and they secured it behind them with only one twist tie in case they needed to make a fast exit, and then dashed across the rear parking lot, Mike Gillespie in the lead. The regular door beside the huge roller door yielded to a key Mike produced from a chain around his neck, but Kinsey put out his hand before Mike could enter.

"Best let Baker and me clear the place first," Kinsey said quietly. "We can't have you getting shot. You know where everything is inside."

"Which is exactly why I should go in with you," Mike whispered back. "I know the layout and you don't."

Kinsey hesitated a moment. "Point taken. You go in with me, and Jimmy pairs up with Baker."

All three nodded, and Kinsey went through the open door, followed closely by Mike Gillespie. It was easily ten degrees warmer in the warehouse, even in the early morning, and dark as well. But it wasn't pitch black, as light leaked in through fiberglass skylights set into the corrugated metal roof high above. Kinsey could just make out the back of a large box truck, and he quickly crouched beneath it for cover to let his eyes adjust. He heard rather than saw Mike Gillespie beside him. There was a flash of light again as the door opened and closed, and rushed footsteps on the concrete as Jimmy Gillespie and Baker joined them under cover.

Kinsey crouched without speaking as his eyes adapted. Soon he could make out three more box trucks parked end to end in front of him down a wide center aisle. Then row upon row of shelves resolved from the darkness, marching down both sides of the center aisle. On the far end wall he could just make out a man door and the outline of two forklifts beside what appeared to be a row of pallet jacks.

"So what's the layout, Mike?" he asked softly.

"Pretty simple. The center aisle is the loading area, with rows of shelves opening off either side with wide aisles so the forklifts can maneuver. That door down at the end goes into the office area with the break room and the restrooms. The warehouse is huge, but there aren't a lot of places to hide." Mike hesitated, and when he spoke again, Kinsey heard an 'I told you so' in his voice. "And it looks like the shelves are still full."

"All right, you and I'll take this side and Jimmy and Baker will take the right side, making sure there's no one hiding down the side aisles. We'll meet up front and clear the office area, then see what we've got," Kinsey said.

They cleared the main warehouse quickly and moved into the office area, where no skylights and windowless interior offices meant they had to use their flashlights. They encountered no one, but did get a surprise.

"People have definitely been living here," Kinsey said, standing in the break room, one of the few rooms with an exterior window. Light leaked through the drawn shade. "All of the offices have bedding of one kind or another and dirty clothes. It looks like they left in a hurry."

The others nodded agreement and Jimmy Gillespie pointed to a camping stove connected to a large propane cylinder on the counter near the window. "I'd say they were using this as the eating and dining area. Where do you reckon they went?"

"I don't know and I don't care, but I don't want to be here when they get back," Kinsey said. "They're obviously coming and going through the back fence. We'll keep Alvarez watching our six while we load up and get the hell out of here. Let's get started."

Kinsey led the others back into the warehouse area, where they stopped in front of the nearest set of shelves, for the first time able to appreciate the magnitude of their find.

"I don't think we can take all this stuff, even in four trucks," Baker said.

"That's good, 'cause you won't be taking any of it," said a voice behind them, and they turned to find a black man pointing a shotgun at them. Before they could react, they were blinded by the beams of multiple powerful flashlights all around them.

Lone Star Marine Warehouse
West Cardinal Drive
Beaumont, Texas

"There are a bunch of guns leveled at you, so if you don't want to die where you stand, put your own guns on the floor slowly and carefully and get on your knees, facing the shelves with your hands on top of your heads."

"Darius? Is that you?" Mike Gillespie asked.

There was silence a long moment then the voice spoke again from behind the glare of the flashlights. "Yeah, it's me, Mike. Now do what I said and y'all won't get hurt."

"But, Darius, you know me. We don't —"

"I know you're comin' in here takin' our stuff, and I know white folks ain't exactly treated us too kindly since the lights went out. And I know we worked together, but so what; it's not exactly like we were fishin' buddies." Darius' voice hardened. "Now you best do what I say 'cause I'm not playin' around here. We got too much at stake to trust anyone, so DO IT!"

The silence stretched, tension mounting as Kinsey's mind raced for options and found none.

"Do as he says, folks," he said at last, turning to face the shelving as he sank to his knees with his hands on top of his head.

✱✱✱

Kinsey perched uncomfortably on the metal folding chair, his wrists duct-taped behind his back and feet taped at the ankles. In the growing light filtering through the drawn blinds of the break room, he could make out the rest of his team similarly restrained. He blinked as sweat stung his eyes. The sun rising in the Texas sky was beginning to pound the enclosed warehouse like a hammer, and with no power to the vent fans, the place was easily ten degrees hotter than when they'd entered less than an hour ago. The man called Darius sat on the edge of a table, facing the captives, he and his two armed comrades seemingly oblivious to the heat. *They must be used to it*, Kinsey thought.

"That was pretty smart, hiding on the very tops of the shelving units. How'd you get everyone up there?" Kinsey asked.

"There are hand and footholds at the far end of each unit, and we've been holding drills, just in case anything like this happened," Darius said, obviously pleased his ploy had worked.

"So y'all been here a month? How can you stand the heat?" Mike Gillespie asked.

Darius snorted. "You can stand just about anything if your other choice is dying. Besides, it's not like we had anyplace else to go, now is it? Not only was there no food, but the cons hit our neighborhood hard. They murdered a lot of good people. We fought back and killed some of 'em, but they had the firepower and we all had families to protect. I knew in the long run they'd either starve us out or burn us out, so I gathered up all my family and neighbors I could reach and brought 'em here to hide."

"But how have you been livin' here? I mean you got plenty of food, but what about water and, you know, sanitation?" Mike Gillespie asked.

"We do our business in buckets in the restrooms and every couple of days we bury the waste in the vacant lot out back. Water's a bit tougher and we have to ration it, but fortunately it rains a lot. When it does, we spread tarps in the back parking lot at night and catch the water in barrels; then we purify it with bleach. We got a couple of pallets full of Clorox, so we're not likely to run out soon." He nodded toward the propane stove. "Our biggest problem is propane; when that runs out, we won't have any way to cook. We scavenged everything we could find out of our old neighborhood, but we'll have to figure out something else soon."

"So you're basically just hiding and surviving," Mike Gillespie said. It was a statement and not a question.

"Pretty much," Darius said. "Everybody's goin' stir-crazy, but it's hardest on the kids. We tried takin' them out a few at a time to let 'em run around in the vacant lot right at dark, but it didn't work. How can a kid have any fun when they have to be dead quiet? It's kinda like that story of the Jewish girl and her family hiding from the Nazis. You know the one they made the TV movie about."

Kinsey nodded. "Anne Frank. How many of you are here?"

Darius glared at the Coastie. "What's it to you?"

"We're building a community on a protected island in the middle of the river. Let us go and we'll go try to convince the group to let you join, then come back and get you," Kinsey said.

Someone scoffed behind them. "Or more than likely come back with enough people to kill us and steal our stuff. THAT'S why you want to know our numbers, so you can figure how big a force you need."

Kinsey attempted to turn, but he could see the speaker only imperfectly from the corner of his eye. He turned back to Darius to find him nodding agreement.

"I wanted to know so I could figure out if we could accommodate your numbers, that's all," Kinsey said.

"And suppose we told you and the answer was no? Would you tell us, or just lie so we'd let you go?" Darius nodded toward the unseen man behind Kinsey. "Like Langston says, we didn't see any white folks stepping up to help us out when the cons were murderin' us."

Jimmy Gillespie spoke for the first time. "It's not like they were HELPIN' the cons either. EVERYBODY is just tryin' to save their own families. The cons are bad news for everyone."

"But they just happened to be singling out US for 'special attention,' and there seemed to be a whole lot of folks who were okay with that as long as it wasn't THEM," Langston said.

"Not 'okay' with it, but more than likely just terrified," Jimmy Gillespie countered. "Just because people are too scared to put their own families at risk by helping someone else, that doesn't make them bad guys—"

Langston exploded, obviously agitated as he moved into view and confronted Darius. "THIS IS BULLSHIT, DARIUS. You KNOW what we got to do; we can't let these people go. No matter what they say, they'll come back with more men and take our stuff, and those they don't kill in the process will starve to death anyway, presuming the cons don't get 'em. It won't make a damn bit of difference whether we're killed by 'good folks' or cons, we'll all be just as dead. This is about SURVIVAL, man, and we're gonna have to do some hard things to survive."

Darius blew out a sigh, looking suddenly as if the weight of the world were upon him. "So what you want me to do, Langston? Murder them? How's that make us any better than the damned cons? I'm not ready for that yet. Just ... just let me think a minute, okay."

The silence grew, broken by Kinsey's radio now sitting in the middle of the table with the rest of their gear. Six clicks in three groups of two came clearly from the speaker.

"What the hell was that?" Darius demanded.

Kinsey hesitated. If they faced an external threat, Alvarez's presence outside would soon be obvious anyway. "We've got company outside."

Darius' face hardened. "You left a lookout."

Kinsey shrugged. "It seemed prudent. But does it matter? The signal means someone is coming, who probably isn't on anyone's Christmas card list, so we need to—DON'T," Kinsey screamed, but he was too late.

The man nearest the window cracked the edge of the shade to peek out. His reward was a burst of rifle fire that tore through the window, smashing the glass and causing the shade to dance as a bullet took him in the forehead, killing him instantly.

Darius gaped, panic on his face.

"Free my hands!" Kinsey said, leaning sideways and bending at the waist to allow access to his wrists. "I have to talk to my guy on the radio."

Darius hesitated, then turned back to look at his friend on the floor in a growing puddle of blood.

"For God's sake, Darius! We're not the enemy here! Let us help you, or we're all dead," Mike Gillespie yelled.

Darius wavered only a second more before pulling out a pocketknife. He looked back at Langston and nodded toward Kinsey. "Langston, I'm gonna free this one's hands and give him the radio. You shoot him at the first sign of a double cross. You got it?"

Langston nodded and Darius cut the tape on Kinsey's wrists and offered him the radio. Kinsey snatched it without hesitation.

"What you got, Alvarez? Over," he said into the radio.

"Four cons behind two patrol cars in the front parking lot, all with long guns," Alvarez said.

Kinsey sighed and looked at the Gillespie brothers. "I guess we weren't quite as invisible as we thought."

"YOU LED THEM HERE?" Darius growled, menace in his voice.

"Obviously, but there's nothing we can do to change that now," Kinsey raised the radio but was interrupted by an amplified voice from outside.

"YOU IN THE BUILDING. COME OUT WITH YOUR HANDS UP AND YOU WILL NOT BE HARMED. REINFORCEMENTS ARE ON THE WAY, AND IF YOU DO NOT SURRENDER, WE WILL BURN THE BUILDING DOWN WITH YOU IN IT."

"Alvarez, can you flank them? Do you have a clear shot? Over," Kinsey said into the mic.

"Already there, boss. Over."

"Take 'em out. Over," Kinsey said.

He heard the bark of Alvarez's M4, short bursts in quick succession.

"Done, boss. Over."

"Get in one of the cruisers and monitor radio traffic, then stay off the radio until I come out and we can talk face-to-face. Over," Kinsey said.

"Roger that. Alvarez out."

Kinsey turned to find Darius and Langston glaring.

"We're all dead thanks to you," Langston said.

"Not quite yet. Let us go and we'll figure this out," Kinsey said.

"Why, so y'all can run off back to your island and leave us all facing the cons alone? For my money you just stay tied up right here so the cons can take care of you after they finish murderin' our folks. Then at least the ones that caused this will be—"

"WOULD YOU PUT A SOCK IN IT?" Kinsey yelled, and then turned to Darius. "Look, I understand you're pissed, but we truly don't have time for this. So decide right now; do you want to stand here and piss and moan until the cons show up to kill us all, or do you want to try to do something?"

Darius hesitated only the slightest second and then reached down to slice the tape from Kinsey's ankles as he gestured to Langston to free the others.

"All right, how many of you are there?" Kinsey asked.

"Fifty-seven ..." Darius looked at the dead man on the floor. "Fifty-six."

"Good. We'll cram them all in the back of one of the delivery trucks—"

Darius was shaking his head. "The trucks are all full. We got several orders late in the day before the blackout and loaded the trucks for deliveries the next day. Obviously, those deliveries never happened. When we moved in, we didn't bother with the trucks because there was plenty of stuff on the shelves easier to get at. Also, we planned to move the loaded trucks to different hiding spots so we wouldn't have all our eggs in one basket, so to speak, but we've been nervous about attracting attention." His face hardened. "But y'all took care of that for us, now didn't you? Anyway, we'd never get a truck unloaded in time. But what's the problem? You said it was only a couple of miles, and y'all came on foot, can't we go back the same way?"

"Not in time and not with over sixty people, including kids, and the cons on our ass. We need transport and we need it now, and just the two cop cars won't hack it. What about the vehicles in the parking lot?" Kinsey asked.

"All dead. Looters stripped the batteries and siphoned the gas before we even got here. They only missed the delivery trucks because no one bothered to look inside the locked warehouse. I mean, it's in an industrial area and most people think it's a machine shop or something like that. There are much more tempting targets around to loot."

"Maybe we can siphon gas out of the delivery trucks," Langston offered, beginning to warm to the idea.

"No need. We got the gas covered. How many company vehicles are out there?" Kinsey asked.

"Seven, I think," Darius replied.

"You got keys?"

"They're in the key cabinet in the operations office, but—"

Kinsey cut him off and turned to the Gillespie brothers. "You boys go find the keys, then get the gasoline we brought and divide it up. That should be more than a gallon for each car and we only have to go three miles."

The brothers set off and Baker shot Kinsey a questioning look. "What about me?"

"Hang here a minute until we get a bit more organized," Kinsey said, turning back to an increasingly confused Darius.

"But what good will gas do if we don't have batteries?" Darius asked.

"We'll start one of the cop cars," Kinsey said, "then leave it running and move the battery from car to car to get them all running—"

"The cars will run without batteries?" Darius asked.

Kinsey nodded. "It depends on their electrical systems, but some of 'em will run for at least a little while. We might eventually fry the systems from voltage spikes, but I'm gambling they make the two or three miles we need to go. Besides, you have a better idea?"

Darius didn't reply and was already moving toward a cabinet on the break room wall. He jerked open a drawer to extract a handful of wrenches, which he handed to Langston.

"Get someone started on the battery, and then start getting everyone ready to leave. Make sure they understand they can't carry anything that won't fit in their pockets besides weapons. There's not gonna be a lot of room," Darius said.

Langston nodded and then cast a look over at the body on the floor. "What should I tell Carol about Lamont?"

Darius hesitated and then shook his head. "Don't tell her nothin', and if she presses, make up some reason he's not around. You know, helpin' with the cars or something. Find someone who'll keep their mouth shut to help you and hide Lamont's body in one of the restroom stalls. I hate to do it, and Carol will be mad at us later, but we don't have time for a funeral and I can't have anybody goin' to pieces in the middle of this. It's gonna be hard enough already, and the best thing we can do for Lamont now is to get his family to safety."

Kinsey interrupted. "Baker can help with the body. That way none of your other folks will even know."

Baker nodded to Kinsey and looked toward Langston, who murmured a thanks and started toward the body. Darius and Kinsey watched the pair carry Lamont's body out, then Darius turned to Kinsey. "Seems like you got a plan."

"Let's see if Alvarez has us a timeline on the cons yet. Everything depends on that," Kinsey said.

Darius nodded and led him from the break room and out the main entrance to the front parking lot. A breeze dried the sweat on Kinsey's forehead, and despite the rising heat, it felt almost cool outside after the muggy confines of the warehouse. Alvarez sat in a police cruiser, listening intently to the radio and seemingly oblivious to the dead cons leaking blood on the pavement all around the cars. He saw them coming and got out, to nod to Kinsey and shoot a questioning glance at Darius. The black man hesitated a fraction of a second then extended his hand.

"Darius Green," he said.

Alvarez shook his hand. "Juan Alvarez."

A smile flickered across Kinsey's face. "Oh yeah. I guess we should have done this before." He extended his hand. "I'm Matt Kinsey."

Darius shook the outstretched hand and nodded, and then Kinsey turned back to Alvarez. "What's our timeline?"

"Not good, boss. From the radio traffic, there's a bunch of them down at that prison complex, gearing up. About the only good news is they figure it's us, and since we've already bitch-slapped 'em a few times, they're being cautious and putting together a good-size group; sounds like eight or ten carloads. My best guess is they'll be rolling out of the prison in ten minutes, max," Alvarez said.

Kinsey pulled out his map. "Shit, that's only five miles —"

"More like seven," Darius said, "and they'll be comin' straight up Port Arthur Road, which, assuming we head straight towards the river via Cardinal Drive, means if we don't move real fast, they'll cut us off."

Kinsey had the map open on the hood of the cop car and Darius tapped an intersection on the map and then pointed east. "See that overpass?"

Kinsey followed the pointing finger across the flat landscape to the top of a highway overpass sticking up a quarter mile away.

"That's the intersection of Cardinal Drive and Port Arthur Road. They'll cut us off right there if we're not past before they get here," Darius said.

"How long you figure?" Kinsey asked.

Darius nodded toward Alvarez. "If he's right about the ten minutes, you can add another five or six. I'd say fifteen or maybe twenty minutes at the absolute outside."

Kinsey glanced at the map again then raised his eyes to the overpass. "Port Arthur Road is straight as an arrow for miles, and that overpass is the highest thing around. Anybody on top should have a good defensive position."

Alvarez was already nodding.

"Alvarez, you and Baker take one of these cop cars and set up a firing position on that overpass. If they show up before we get past, you need to buy us some time. After we get past and head for the river, you'll fall in behind us as a rear guard; one guy driving, the other shooting. Got it?"

"Got it, boss," Alvarez said.

Kinsey dug in his vest and handed over his two extra M4 magazines. "You'll need these more than me, and if not, we're likely screwed anyway."

"We have a couple of vets with ARs and some ammo. Y'all want some help there?" Darius asked.

"Absolutely," Kinsey said.

CHAPTER THIRTEEN

Lone Star Marine Warehouse
West Cardinal Drive
Beaumont, Texas

Five minutes later the four-man cover force roared away from the warehouse in one of the police cruisers as the rest of the group raced the clock. Despite Kinsey's theories on automotive electrical systems, the remaining cop car shuddered to a stop as soon as they disconnected the battery, nor were they universally successful with the other vehicles; at the twelve-minute mark, only the three older pickups were running.

Kinsey, Darius at his side, raced over to where the Gillespie brothers and a frustrated Langston were trying to coax the last dead vehicle back to life.

"Leave it," Kinsey said. "There's no time. Darius, cram as many of your folks as possible into the cabs of the delivery trucks, but make sure the kids and anyone who isn't physically fit is among them. Divide the rest between these three running pickups. If one of those dies en route, the passengers may have to run for it."

Darius nodded. "Mike and I will drive two of the delivery trucks, and I have a couple of other experienced truck drivers. What about the rest?"

Kinsey thought a moment. "I'll ride in the lead car with Jimmy driving, since he's a local. You pick the drivers for the other two pickups, and we'll lead the convoy. The big trucks will come next and Alvarez's group will fall in as rear guard after we clear the intersection. If we take fire from the rear, the loaded trucks will at least offer some protection to the passengers in the cabs, and also provide some cover for the cars in front and—"

Gunshots echoed over the parking lot, the ragged sound of several single shots fired almost simultaneously, followed by the thunderous sound of a series of distant crashes and prolonged shrieks of metal on metal. There was a gap of seconds, and then the sound of steady but disciplined fire from multiple weapons.

Kinsey looked at Darius. "Our guests are a little early, it seems. Let's move it! Now!"

Cardinal Drive (US 69/96/287) at Port Arthur Road
Beaumont, Texas

Juan Alvarez raised the binoculars and studied the approaching threat, a dozen police cruisers with various markings, coming fast. They were running close up, almost nose to tail in an obvious rush and very likely counting on being safe until they got much closer to the warehouse. He continued to scan the route, selecting the best point to engage. He steadied the glasses and smiled. *Surprise, surprise.*

He handed the glasses to the man crouched next to him behind the police cruiser, one of Darius' men from the warehouse. "Take a look at that little bridge about two hundred yards out. What is that?"

The man raised the glasses. "One of the LNVA canals, I think. Never paid much attention to it, to tell you the truth."

"Is there another way across it nearby, like to the east?" Alvarez asked.

The man thought a moment and then gave an uncertain nod. "There must be, 'cause the next interchange is Highland Avenue and it's a through street paralleling Port Arthur Road."

"How far to the interchange?" Alvarez asked.

The man glanced east and shrugged. "Not far. Maybe a half mile. Maybe a bit more. Why?"

Alvarez smiled again. "Because if we plug the bridge here, they'll have to backtrack to get there, and they'll lose at least some time figuring that out, which means we might all get past it before they reach it."

A smile of understanding spread on the man's face.

Alvarez continued, addressing the group. "Okay, boys, I want everyone targeting the driver of the lead cruiser just as it starts over the bridge. Hopefully, he'll crash and set off a chain reaction. If we can stack them up here, we're golden. They can't flank us and they'll be sitting ducks. Everybody waits until I fire. And no 'spray and pray' crap; I want aimed single shots. Got it?"

There were nods and affirmative grunts, and Alvarez laid his M4 across the hood of the stolen police cruiser and sighted in, watching as the driver of the approaching car grew larger in his vision. He fired just as the car reached the bridge, his shot followed almost instantaneously by three more from the other shooters, killing the driver outright.

The driver's foot slipped off the gas, slowing the car abruptly from seventy miles an hour, with no brake light to warn the car tailgating him. To his credit, the driver of the second car was alert and almost managed to swerve into the left lane as he stood on the brakes, but 'almost' didn't cut it. He smashed into the left rear of the first car, driving its front right bumper into the guardrail and forcing the car sideways across the bridge in a maelstrom of shrieking metal and squealing tires.

Partially restrained on the right front and its momentum far from expended, the second car also skidded sideways but in the opposite direction, its rear bumper dragging against the left guardrail, the two cars forming an instant barricade across the bridge.

A barricade the much less attentive driver of the third car, who'd been lighting a cigarette at the time, T-boned at full speed.

In less than three seconds, 'the plug was in the bottle,' and the cars able to avoid the crash careened to abrupt halts at odd angles along the road south of the little bridge, squealing tires punctuated by the sounds of less serious collisions. The dazed survivors emerged from their vehicles, confused and unsure what had happened, as the sounds of the few well-placed shots had mixed with the mayhem of the multiple car crash and not been immediately recognizable.

Alvarez looked over at the others and grinned. "I love it when a plan actually works. Now let 'em have it, and make every round count."

***

Kinsey rode shotgun in the lead vehicle, a pickup with a brightly painted Lone Star Marine logo on the side. Jimmy Gillespie was at the wheel and their new acquaintance Langston Williams was jammed between them. Eight people rode in the truck bed, five men and three women, all adults and all carrying a mismatched collection of firearms.

The gunfire had been steady since they left the parking lot moments before, at first only the sounds of the steady disciplined fire of the M4s, but now mixed with the sound of increasingly heavy return fire. He saw the overpass in the distance and the cop car on top and spoke into his radio.

"Alvarez, do you copy? Over."

"Loud and clear, boss. Over," came the reply.

"We'll be passing you in two minutes. Give me a sitrep. Over."

"We're good, but there's a lot of lead flying for y'all to drive through. Give me three clicks when you start up the ramp and we'll lay down suppressing fire until y'all are past. Do you copy? Over," Alvarez said.

"Loud and clear. Out," Kinsey said.

Kinsey gripped the radio as the police cruiser grew larger in the windshield. When they started up the overpass ramp, he keyed the mic three times. Ahead, he saw the four men behind the police cruiser rise as one and begin firing furiously. *Good man, Alvarez*, he thought.

"Floor it, Jimmy. The quicker we clear the overpass, the quicker Alvarez and his guys can get out of there."

Jimmy nodded and stomped the gas as Kinsey keyed the mic again, hoping the cons hadn't yet figured out their frequency. "This is Kinsey to *Judy Ann* and home base. ETA to extraction point five minutes. We're coming in rolling and hot. Repeat. We're coming in rolling and hot."

West Port Arthur Road
South of Lower Neches Valley Authority (LNVA) Canal
Beaumont, Texas

Owen Fairchild, aka 'Snag' for his dental issues, squatted behind the police cruiser and cursed. Their snitch had reported only five of the ship people on foot, but apparently that had been enough to take out his advance scouting party. And now they had the balls to actually ATTACK a much larger force. They'd pay for that, and for all the other things they'd done.

He didn't know why they were here, but figured they must be after more family members. Well, when he caught 'em, he'd figure out just who those family members were and hunt them down; then they could watch their loved ones die very publicly and very slowly, right before they died themselves.

And catch them all he would. They might have given him a bloody nose here, but he had units converging from all over the area. Let's see how they fared without the protection of those patrol boats and machine guns. Besides, he HAD to catch them now; Spike was gonna be pissed he'd lost three, no make that five cars and over a dozen soldiers to an ambush. Again. But if he brought in prisoners, or at least their bodies, Spike would likely blow off their own losses. If anyone hated the damn ship people more than Snag, it was Spike. The prospect of torturing some of them to death would brighten everyone's day.

The firing from the overpass increased in ferocity; what had been measured and controlled fire was now intense. Snag duckwalked to the end of the car and peeked around the rear bumper, where his presence was less likely to draw fire. He peeked out just in time to see a line of pickups streak across the overpass behind the shooters, followed by four large panel trucks, all painted similarly and headed east. He watched until he was sure there were no more, and was about to pull back behind the car when the police car on the bridge began to slowly move east, three shooters moving with it and using it for cover as they moved out of sight behind a screen of distant trees.

Son of a bitch! The thieving bastards had come ashore to steal supplies, and it looked like they had four truckloads. They were headed for the river for sure, but there was no way they could get four truckloads of loot unloaded into boats quickly. They'd obviously hoped to get in and out unseen, that was why they'd come in on foot. Snag smiled. *We'll just see about that!*

The shooters no longer a threat, he rose and got into his car, reaching for the radio before he even settled into the seat.

"All units, this is Snag. I am at the intersection of Port Arthur Road and Cardinal Drive and just spotted a convoy of pickup and delivery trucks headed east toward the river. All units be on the lookout for the convoy and report sightings at once. Delay them if possible but priority is maintaining contact and reporting position. Repeat, priority is maintaining contact and reporting position so we don't lose them. Snag out."

He nodded to his driver, who was doing a K-turn in the road when the radio squawked.

"Unit Twelve to all units. We have the convoy turning south off Cardinal Drive onto Spur 380. We are in pursuit and maintaining contact — OH SHIT!"

M.L. King Jr. Parkway/Spur 380
Southbound
Beaumont, Texas

Alvarez clung to the seat of the cop car as they rounded the corner at high speed, centrifugal force pressing him against Baker, who knelt beside him on the rear bench seat. Both men were staring backward through the gaping hole where the rear window had been before they'd smashed it out to turn the rear seat into a shooting platform. By mutual agreement, the locals more familiar with the streets did the driving.

They were straightening out of the turn when Baker yelled, "Bogie at six o'clock."

Alvarez was already targeting the cop car a hundred yards back, just passing under the highway overpass.

"I got him. Save your ammo," Alvarez said, sighting down his M4 at the driver just as the passenger raised a microphone to his mouth and a voice echoed from the radio in their own car.

"Unit Twelve to all units. We have the convoy turning south off Cardinal Drive onto Spur 380. We are in pursuit—"

Damn! Too Late! His M4 barked and the windshield of the pursuing car shattered and the car veered into a utility pole, snapping it on impact. Alvarez watched as, almost in slow motion, the pole tumbled across the roof of a squat building painted garish purple and green, with signs proclaiming it to be Wizard Tattoo and Piercing.

"Tattoo that, asshole," Alvarez muttered as he scanned the road for more threats.

No sooner had the words left his mouth than news of more sightings came through the radio speakers. Another cop car pulled onto the road from a side street, well back behind them, and Baker bent his head to his rifle, but Alvarez laid a hand on his shoulder.

"Wait," he said quietly, then turned to address the two men riding in the front seat. "How much ammo y'all got left up there?"

"Maybe a mag and a half between us," the man in the front passenger seat replied. "Why?"

"'Cause Baker and I have less than a mag each, and seein' as how the cat's out of the bag, I'm thinking we're gonna need that to hold them off while everybody boards the boat," Alvarez said.

"Shoot 'em now, we won't have to deal with them then," Baker said.

"Maybe, maybe not," Alvarez countered. "We just heard half a dozen radio calls, but how many cars do you see? Just the one, right?"

Baker nodded.

"The rest are keeping their distance, but you can be sure they'll be in the fight when we're stationary. The main fight will be at the river, and we need to conserve our ammo," Alvarez said.

Sulphur Plant Road
Eastbound
Beaumont, Texas

Kinsey suppressed a curse as Jimmy Gillespie flew across the railroad crossing, buffeting the old pickup. Instinctively, he glanced behind him, relieved to see that the occupants of the truck bed were all still there, though they were all looking toward the cab and cursing the driver.

"Sorry, Chief. I didn't realize it was that rough," Jimmy said.

"I expect things are about to get a lot rougher," Kinsey said. "Just get us to the *Judy Ann*."

Jimmy Gillespie nodded, and Kinsey looked out the windshield and sighed. This was turning into a screw up of monumental proportions and he cursed the luck that had him leading the cons directly back to the *Judy Ann*. If he had only his small team, he'd have led their pursuers on a wild-goose chase until he could break contact and arrange an extraction. However, with over fifty people, including children, he had no choice. His only hope was getting them all aboard the towboat and onto the river before the cons could overwhelm them. This was 'mission creep' of the first order, but he'd heard what the cons had done to some of the families of the African-Americans among *Pecos Trader*'s crew, and had no doubt what awaited these people if they fell into the hands of the Aryan Brotherhood. Abandoning them to that fate was not a viable option in any world he wanted to live in.

He spotted the wheelhouse of the *Judy Ann* in the distance, rising over the bulk of the ferry barge. As they closed the distance, he could see Lucius Wellesley had indeed gotten the ramps in place, and the pugnacious towboat skipper was on the shore next to the ramps, an M4 slung over his shoulder and waving a welcome.

Fifty yards from the ferry barge, they drove through the gate of the tall chain-link fence that surrounded the gravel parking area and Kinsey spoke into his radio.

"Alvarez, do you copy? Over."

"Loud and clear, boss. Over," Alvarez replied.

"As soon as you pass the gate, close it, pull the cop car against it, and set up a defensive position. As we get folks unloaded, I'll send the pickups back to string along the fence and we'll try to get enough shooters in place to hold the cons off until we get all the families and noncombatants on the barge. Then when Lucius is ready to pull out, we'll separate into two groups and leapfrog each other back to the barge. You copy? Over," Kinsey said.

"I copy, boss. Anything else? Over," Alvarez asked.

"That's all for now. I'll be up there as soon as I can. Kinsey out," he said just as Jimmy skidded to a stop near the barge.

"Jimmy, I'm going back to the fence. As soon as everyone gets out, get with Captain Wellesley and relay the plan, just like we discussed coming over, then bring the pickup to the fence. Ask Wellesley to send every single person he can spare to join us on the firing line and tell them to bring all the ammo they've got. Langston, you and Darius get all your noncombatants started up on the barge, and then bring the other pickups and any shooters back to help at the barricade. It'll be tough to disengage, but much easier if we have more folks laying down covering fire," Kinsey said.

Both men nodded, but Kinsey was already out of the truck, running for the fence with his M4 in hand. He arrived to find the cop car already in place against the closed gate in the chain-link fence. A round whined off the hood and Kinsey ducked behind the front of the car, where Alvarez sheltered behind the protection of the engine block. He watched as Alvarez popped up and fired a round before dropping back under cover.

Alvarez grinned. "What kept you, boss? I was afraid I might have to shoot them all myself."

Kinsey grinned back. "Torres told me you were a glory hog, Alvarez, but I never believed it."

"Believe it," Alvarez said, popping up for another quick shot, then back down. "So what's the plan?"

Kinsey told him and Alvarez shot a pointed look at the delivery trucks.

"What about the groceries?" he asked.

"How much ammo do you have?" Kinsey countered.

Alvarez shrugged. "If they come at us in any strength, we'll be throwing rocks in about five minutes."

"Well, there's your answer," Kinsey said. "Wellesley's guys will bring us some more ammo, but I doubt it will be enough. It's gonna take time to work each of those trucks onto the ferry, and we can't do it without a lot of cover fire. It's time and ammo we don't have. We'll have to leave the trucks and just be happy getting these folks to safety."

Alvarez shot another look toward the loaded trucks. "Man, that stinks. I hate the thought of leaving it."

"No more than I do," Kinsey said. "Besides, you're not the one who has to tell Captain Hughes he now has over fifty more mouths to feed and no additional food to do it with."

Alvarez nodded. "It sucks to be you right now, boss."

Sulphur Plant Road
Beaumont, Texas

Snag's car roared down Sulphur Plant Road, leading the surviving cars from the ambush. Ahead he saw several police cars across the road, with men sheltered behind them firing toward a fence lined with a single police cruiser and three pickup trucks perhaps fifty yards away. There were defenders behind the fence, returning fire, and as Snag's car approached, a bullet shattered the center of the windshield.

"Shit!" Snag said as the driver lurched to a stop at the side of the road and they both jumped out, running bent over to the protection of the makeshift barricade ahead. The men in his now diminished convoy followed suit.

"What the hell is going on, Weaver?" Snag demanded as he reached the barricade and squatted behind it.

"They're loadin' a bunch of niggers on that barge, women and kids mostly," said the man he'd addressed. Then the man grinned. "Duke here winged one of the women, but it must have pissed 'em off 'cause they started unloadin' on us big time. It's worth your life to stick your head up. Anyway, they ain't started unloadin' the trucks and I reckon they can't be shootin' at us and unloadin' at the same time. Probably they'll just haul ass back to their boat without the loot, I figure."

"That's exactly what I DON'T want, you moron," Snag growled. "They came into our territory and made fools of us again, and we're gonna catch 'em and make 'em pay, them and their mud people pals. So we ain't gonna sit here with our thumbs up our asses and watch 'em git away, or git back into the river, where that machine gun can cut us up. Is that clear?"

The man nodded tentatively. "But wh … what we gonna do, Snag? We kinda got a standoff here."

Snag duckwalked over and ventured a peek between cars. The barge and towboat were pushed up into a narrow channel that ended in the gravel parking lot where the defenders were now arrayed against him. To his right, running parallel to the road and perhaps fifty feet away, was a line of huge tanks of some sort, rising high in the air, all with metal staircases spiraling around them to access the tops of the tanks. The line of tanks extended past both his own makeshift barricade and also the raiders' defensive position to end approximately even with the barge. The opposite bank of the little inlet was just a stretch of vacant, marshy land covered in weeds and head-high scrub brush. Snag nodded. This was workable.

"Okay, Weaver, I want you to pick your best six shots and back away down the road behind us until you can cut over behind that line of tanks to our right. Use 'em as a screen and move behind 'em to get as close to that boat as you can, then get up on top of the tanks. You should be able to shoot down on the guys behind the fence from up there, but I also want you to put two guys targeting that towboat and blow the hell out of anyone who tries to get into the wheelhouse. They ain't goin' nowhere. You got that?" Snag asked.

Weaver nodded tentatively. "But what if they see us? We'll be sittin' ducks goin' up those staircases until we get to the top of the tanks."

"That's where Duke here comes in," Snag said, nodding towards the other man. "He'll take six or eight guys and work his way back and then go into that brush on our left. That fence doesn't extend into the field, so once there, they can work their way through the brush until they're past the ship people's barricade then open fire on 'em from their flank. We'll let 'em have it from here at the same time, and they'll be so busy shootin' to their front and right, they won't have time to be watching the tanks to their own left. Weaver, y'all get in position at the bottom of the tanks then wait until you hear Duke open up before y'all start up the stairs."

Weaver looked relieved, but Duke was anything but. He looked at the terrain he was supposed to cross and shook his head.

"But, Snag, there's likely snakes in there, maybe even gators. And besides, there ain't nothing to hide behind once we open up on 'em. I mean, we can sneak up on 'em, but once they open up, we gotta go flat and lie low, 'cause if they see a muzzle flash, we're toast," Duke said.

Snag glared at Duke. "Quit bein' a pussy, Duke, or you'll have more to worry about than snakes and gators. Y'all just spread out in the brush and shoot and move; that way if they target the muzzle flashes, you'll be gone when they shoot. Besides, it ain't like y'all have to hit anything; you just have to keep 'em lookin' the other way while Weaver and his boys get in position. Now quit whinin' and do what you're told."

Duke gave a sullen nod and moved down the barricade in a crouch, rounding up men for his mission. Snag glared at Weaver, ready to squash any insubordination there as well, but Weaver merely bobbed his head and moved off to collect his own force.

In Front of the M/V *Judy Ann*
End of Sulphur Plant Road
Beaumont, Texas

Kinsey kept his head down, sheltering from the withering fire inundating the top of their defensive position. Wellesley had sent all four of his crewmen to the firing line, along with all available ammo, which they were sharing out evenly along the defensive line.

The attackers' fire increased in intensity, but Kinsey couldn't figure out why. Then it became clear as a volley of gunfire sounded from his right. *They were keeping our heads down so they could flank us*, he thought, and he spotted scattered muzzle flashes in the thick brush to their right, and one of Darius' men took a round in the shoulder.

"They've flanked us," Alvarez said as all along the line, defenders swung to their right and began to fire at the brush.

The fire from the brush subsided except for sporadic shots, but the withering fire from the other barricade continued, and Kinsey knew their current position was rapidly becoming untenable. Relief washed over him when he heard Wellesley's voice on the radio.

"*Judy Ann* to Kinsey. Do you copy? Over."

"Go ahead, *Judy Ann*. Over," he replied.

"All passengers safely in the crew mess. Withdraw to the barge. Repeat. Withdraw to the barge. I'm just going into the wheelhouse now and we'll be out of here in —"

BLAM! BLAM!

Kinsey jerked his head up as two shots rang out from the top of the tanks behind him and almost even with the ferry barge.

"*JUDY ANN!* DO YOU COPY? OVER. LUCIUS, ARE YOU OKAY?" Kinsey screamed into the radio as beside him Alvarez raised his M4 and fired at the shooter on top of the tank.

Kinsey continued to try to raise the *Judy Ann*. "LUCIUS, DO YOU COPY—"

The radio, along with the tip of his little finger, was torn from Kinsey's hand by a bullet. Other guns opened up, and one of Darius' people fell, a woman this time, with a leg wound. Then one of the towboat crewmen fell, the severity of his head wound leaving no doubt he was dead.

Alvarez screamed a warning and pointed upward, and the surprised, beleaguered, and now vulnerable defenders concentrated their fire at the top of the tall tanks right next to them. The opposing fire slowed, suppressed mainly by accurate fire from Alvarez and Baker, as the defenders burned through their limited ammo at a furious rate, and Kinsey scanned the gravel expanse, desperate for options.

The barge and towboat were too far away. He eyed the delivery trucks sitting to one side, halfway across the lot.

"JIMMY," Kinsey yelled, "WE'LL COVER YOU WHILE YOU AND MIKE GET EVERYONE UNDER THE DELIVERY TRUCKS; THEN YOU COVER US WHILE WE JOIN YOU."

The Gillespie brothers did as ordered while the Coasties covered them. Kinsey smiled as he saw an AR tumble over the tank edge, the con having fallen to a well-placed round from Alvarez. In what seemed like hours but was surely only seconds, Jimmy Gillespie's shouts pierced Kinsey's consciousness and the Coasties scrambled for the safety of the delivery trucks under the covering fire from the others.

Kinsey dropped and clawed his way under one of the trucks to lie on one side in the gravel, gasping from the sprint. His finger throbbed and blood covered his hand. He tried to wipe his hand clean on his pants and flinched as he hit the raw place where his fingertip used to be. *I'm way too old for this*, he thought as he held out his uninjured hand to Alvarez.

"Rad … radio," Kinsey said, and Alvarez passed him his radio.

Kinsey waited a moment to catch his breath then nodded to Alvarez.

"Alvarez, consolidate all our ammo and get a count. I'm gonna call the ship," Kinsey said. Alvarez nodded and Kinsey keyed the mic.

"*Cape Mendocino*, this is Kinsey. How do you copy? Over."

Hughes' voice came through the speaker. "We read you loud and clear. Be advised we're monitoring your situation and the gunboat is en route at full speed, ETA your position two minutes. Repeat. ETA your position two mikes. Also be advised—"

"Negative, Jordan. I say again, negative on the gunboat. They have snipers on the tall tanks near us and the gunboat will be a sitting duck coming up the inlet. I doubt the crew can easily elevate the machine gun high enough to target the snipers and they will be shot to pieces while they try. I say again ABORT GUNBOAT. Do you copy? Over."

There was a pause.

"I understand. We will stand down the gunboat. Be advised the *Rambling Ace* is also en route with reinforcements and ammunition. ETA your position ten minutes. Repeat. ETA your position ten mikes. Do you copy? Over."

"We copy, *Cape Mendocino*," Kinsey replied. "Advise you move the machine gun to the *Rambling Ace* and advise crew they need to improvise some sort of protected position and be prepared to fire high. Also advise Captain Hitchcock to rig protection in wheelhouse windows against sniper fire."

"We copy, Matt," Hughes replied. "Anything else? Over."

"Yeah. Ask them to kick it in the ass because I'm not sure we have ten minutes. Kinsey out."

CHAPTER FOURTEEN

Union Canal Inlet
End of Sulfur Plant Road
Beaumont, Texas

Kinsey slipped the radio into a pocket on his tactical vest and looked over to where Alvarez had a handkerchief spread on the gravel, staring at a depressingly small pile of ammunition piled on it, while Baker stared out from under the truck toward their former defensive line, his M4 at the ready.

"What's the verdict?" Kinsey asked.

Alvarez shook his head then nodded at Baker. "Counting the magazine Baker has in his weapon, we have fifty-eight rounds. Basically we're screwed. We can't move out from underneath these trucks without cover fire at those shooters on top of the tanks, and if we try that, the ammo we have left would last about ten seconds, not ten minutes. Which doesn't make much difference anyway, because as soon as the main group figures out how screwed we are and crosses the gap to take up firing positions on the opposite side of our pickups, they'll shoot us right out from under these trucks. We got no cover, boss, except the truck tires."

Kinsey blew out a sigh. "Well, they don't know we only have fifty-eight rounds, so we'll just have to bluff them until the cavalry arrives."

***

Snag crouched low, keeping the bulk of the abandoned pickup between him and the defenders as Duke cut through the chain-link fence with a pair of bolt cutters. He glanced down the fence line to see cons similarly engaged behind each of the abandoned pickups.

"Done," Duke said softly, and held the wire open for Snag to enter.

Snag glared at the big man and moved through the wire to peek over the truck at the gravel lot beyond. He supposed he shouldn't be too pissed. His plan had worked perfectly, even if Duke and that band of pussies HAD come streaming back behind the barricade, spooked out of the bush by the sight of a couple of cottonmouths. They'd provided enough of a diversion to get his men up on the tanks, and that was all that mattered. He allowed himself a satisfied smile. It was all over but the cryin' now.

That said, as he looked over the scene, he was unsure how to proceed. His prey had to be under the delivery trucks, but they must be spread out and lined up behind each set of tires, because he couldn't see them. He looked to his left and considered ordering Duke back into the brush where they'd have a better angle, but then he dropped the idea; they were piss-poor soldiers at best and they'd likely all be too worried about snakes to get the job done.

He looked at the situation again. The defenders were pinned down. They didn't dare move out from under the trucks or his guys on the tanks would obliterate them, and they couldn't easily move from tire to tire without his guys here on the pickup truck barricade blasting them.

Then on the other hand, he'd already lost more men than he could afford, especially given how badly they'd been hurt by previous run-ins. And the defenders had to know their situation was hopeless; maybe he could talk them out. He'd tell them he only wanted the supplies and promise to let them go — anything to get them out from under those trucks so he could kill or capture them.

Snag was about to call out when his radio squawked.

"Snag, this is Weaver. Do you copy? Over."

He keyed the mic. "I copy, Weaver. Go ahead. Over."

"There's a tugboat headed this way with a bunch of guys runnin' all over it. I can't tell for sure, but it looks like they're riggin' up a machine gun on top of the wheelhouse and they're all in a line passin' up boxes and stuff to build a bunker around it. I'd say they'll be here in ten minutes or so. Over."

"Well, shoot 'em, you moron. Over," Snag said.

"We'll try, but by the time they get in range, I expect they'll be under cover, and WE'LL be in range of that machine gun. If that machine gun gets in the fight, we ain't gonna be able to stay up here very long. Over."

Snag cursed then trembled at the thought of reporting yet another failure to Spike. He looked down the barricade and figured the odds. He outnumbered his opponents at least three, or maybe even four to one. He turned back to Duke. "Get the boys ready. We ain't leavin' here without prisoners and loot. On my signal I want everybody pouring fire into those truck tires, and then we'll charge 'em on my command. And pity the fool who hangs back because I'm gonna be right behind him to put a bullet in his head. Get 'em ready, NOW!"

***

Kinsey lay in the gravel next to Alvarez behind one set of the big dual rear wheels of a delivery truck, a handkerchief wound and knotted tight around his injured finger. Baker lay behind the next set of tires, and the rest of the outnumbered defenders were sheltering behind others.

Though 'defenders' was hardly applicable, as most now had no means to defend themselves. Kinsey divided their limited ammunition between Alvarez and Baker, the acknowledged marksmen in the group, and stationed the pair closest to the direction of the threat. The others could only make themselves small behind the scant shelter of the other tires and hope for the best. The outlook wasn't promising.

"You really think this is gonna work, boss?" Alvarez asked, his eyes on the pickup barricade that had so recently been their own defensive line.

"Actually, I'm hoping they screw the pooch until the *Rambling Ace* shows up to give us some cover fire. If they can keep those guys on the tanks occupied, we've got a chance at running for the water," Kinsey said.

Alvarez nodded but said nothing, his eyes still looking out. Kinsey could sense the unspoken reply; ten minutes might as well be ten days if the cons decided to press the attack. As it turned out, they didn't have to wait on the answer to that question.

The fusillade was both sudden and intense, and the defenders could do nothing but draw themselves back behind their makeshift defenses and hope for the best. As it turned out, the best was not bad at all. The inflated tires gave on impact, the thick, steel-reinforced rubber absorbing much of each bullet's force as it penetrated. Hollow-point rounds expanded on penetration, with the fragmented remains lacking the power to exit the tire, and full-metal-jacketed rounds fared no better. After penetrating the first tough barrier, the jacketed rounds tumbled as they struck the curved inside of the steel rims, to be deflected up or down and exit the tires at the top or bottom, away from those the tires sheltered.

The onslaught lasted thirty seconds—and forever. The tires vibrated from the impacts of hundreds of bullets and there was a strange muted roar as high-pressure air hissed from as many holes and some jetted into the gravel, raising a thick dust cloud. It took Kinsey a few seconds to realize the firing had stopped and he peeked around the rapidly deflating tires in front of him to squint through the dust. Cons were pouring around both ends of the pickup barrier, charging across the gravel toward them.

He raised his voice to be heard above the hissing tires. "GET READY! HERE THEY COME—"

His cry was cut short by Alvarez's shot, followed almost immediately by Baker's, and a con went down on either end of the advancing line. For a moment it looked like the defenders might carry the day as the two Coasties concentrated their fire on either end of the cons' line, their accuracy taking a deadly toll on the cons pouring around the ends of the line. Then Kinsey heard distant pistol shots behind the cons' line and even more men erupted from between the trucks, racing toward the beleaguered defenders as if pursued by the Devil himself.

Faced with attackers across a broad front, the Coasties did what they had to do, and Kinsey didn't admonish them when he heard first Alvarez and then Baker switch to full auto.

The rapid fire worked, at least momentarily. The advancing line wavered as cons fell across a wide front, and hope surged in Kinsey's chest. *Run, damn you,* he thought. *Break and run!*

And then the firing stopped as the last rounds were expended, and the bluff was called.

The cons looked from one to another in disbelief as understanding dawned, and they all began to yell and move forward. Kinsey swallowed hard and reached for his knife, his plan B already thought out. He had no intention of being taken alive; he'd play dead and hope to gut the first son of a bitch that came to check on him. If luck was with him, he'd grab the con's gun and put a few more of them in the ground before they took him out.

He moved the knife under his body to hide it, then closed his eyes and murmured a silent prayer. A prayer that was answered by a tremendous, and familiar, thunderclap. It was followed closely by a second, and both conjured up the image of a brown face and a cocky, impudent grin, as the man saluted him with two fingers and said, "Abra fucking cadabra, *jefe!*"

The Magician was in the fight!

* * *

Snag stood peering over the pickup barricade at the backs of his advancing men, screaming in frustration as they wavered in the face of the defenders' fire. He'd had to shoot a couple to get the attack moving, and now the pussies were blowing it. Well, they better damn well capture the boat people or he'd shoot every damn one of them — unless Spike shot him first, which was looking increasingly likely.

Suddenly the firing stopped, and near silence prevailed, broken only by the loud hissing sound coming from the truck tires. It took Snag a moment to understand, but when he did, his face split into a wide grin. *They're out of ammo!* He screamed encouragement, and all along his line, he could hear jubilant cries as his men started forward again.

A second later he heard an impact above him and looked up to see a body tumbling off the top of the farthest tank, followed a second after that by the thunderous boom of a large-caliber weapon in the distance. He watched in horror as his men on top of the tanks ran for the staircases. The man on the closest tank almost made it before he was disemboweled by a fifty-caliber round to the small of his back, the force of the impact and his own momentum carrying his body off the edge of the tank. The man cartwheeled through the air almost in slow motion, leaking entrails, to land in a wet, bloody pile right in the path of the advancing force.

The impact on morale was not positive.

The line of cons stopped and looked up just as another body came cartwheeling down, an arm missing and the terrified con still alive and screaming all the way to the ground. The line stopped, shaken, when a command rang out from beneath the trucks. They turned and ran.

* * *

Kinsey grimaced as the bodies hit the ground not more than thirty feet away. His heart stopped as the cons halted, disconcerted by the mangled remains of their comrades.

His mind raced. Wherever Torres and his Barrett were, he was likely only a threat to the men on the tanks, and having taken them out, there was little more he could really do. The carnage had disconcerted the cons on the ground, but they'd soon figure out they weren't in harm's way. Kinsey didn't intend to give them that chance.

600

He cupped his hands on either side of his mouth and screamed for all he was worth. "THE DUMB BASTARDS FELL INTO THE TRAP, BOYS! FIRE UP THE FLAMETHROWERS AND LET'S GET 'EM!"

He held his breath for a long second, praying the bluff would work, and then his face split into a grin as the cons turned and fled.

"Flamethrowers, huh? Nice touch."

Kinsey looked over to see Alvarez grinning at him. "Yeah, well, sometimes things just come to me . . ."

Kinsey trailed off, a strange look on his face.

Alvarez looked at him. "What is it, boss?"

Kinsey held up his hand in a 'wait a minute' gesture and reached for his radio. "This is Kinsey. Is that you, Magician? And where the hell are you? Over,' he said into the radio.

"None other, boss. And I'm on the flying bridge of the *Cape Mendocino*. Over," came Torres' voice over the radio.

"That's gotta be over a mile! Over," Kinsey replied, wonder in his voice.

"One point one miles to be exact. God bless Ronnie Barrett. Over," Torres replied.

Kinsey looked over at Alvarez. "What do you think is in all these tanks?"

Alvarez grinned, a look of understanding spreading across his face. "Something nasty and flammable more than likely."

Kinsey smiled back and raised the radio. "Do you think that Barrett has a bit more range in it, Magician? Over."

"Depends on the size of the target. Over."

"Oh, it'll be pretty big. Over," Kinsey said.

***

Snag was beside himself. The dumb asses hadn't stopped running until they got back to their initial position at the line of police cruisers across the road, and he'd had no choice but to run with them. He only stopped their further flight by shooting the first man to crawl behind the wheel of one of the police cars, with the obvious intention of fleeing. Now that the idiots were out of immediate danger from the ship people, their fear of Snag was once again a motivating force. He had them assembled behind the barricade of cop cars and had just finished giving them a verbal lashing.

"But, Snag," Duke said, "it was a trap. We can't go up against flamethrowers—"

He stopped at the sight of the bulging vein throbbing on his boss' forehead, as Snag held a Glock in a white-knuckled grip, trembling with the effort to keep from shooting his lieutenant between the eyes.

"There wasn't no trap and there ain't no flamethrowers. They ran a con on you dumb asses plain and simple, and every single one of you fell for it. Jesus wept, how did I get stuck with such a bunch of idiots?" Snag snarled.

"But the sniper—"

"Took out the guys on the tanks who were clearly visible targets at a distance, but he didn't shoot at us, which likely means he can't see us. I'm sure that tugboat and barge and maybe even those trucks are in his way. If he could see us, he'd be shootin' the hell out of us right now."

Snag stopped to let his words sink in, and was rewarded by nods as the group accepted his logic. He looked at his watch.

"Okay, we got maybe five minutes before that boat with the machine gun shows up, and those assholes are sitting down there waitin' with no ammo. We're gonna go kill everyone we can find and take those trucks. Flat tires or not, we can drive 'em on the rims as far as the main road and then set up a defensive position out of range of that machine gun or sniper rifle; then let them attack US for a change," Snag said.

He was relieved to hear growls of agreement, the cons' embarrassment at being duped morphing to anger.

"All right," he said. "Let's go back down there and—"

There was a loud clang of metal on metal and he looked up and behind their position to see a large gash two-thirds of the way up the last tank in the row, the one nearest the highway. The clang was followed immediately by a noise like a thunderclap as the report of the sniper rifle reached its target at the speed of sound, less than half the muzzle velocity of the bullet that preceded it. Snag watched, mesmerized, as liquid shot from the hole in the tank, gushing down on the road behind them. A pungent odor filled the air.

"Holy shit! Gasoline," Duke yelled as a flaming tracer round struck the tank.

A huge fireball erupted at the tank side and then subsided into a torrent of burning liquid pouring out behind them to block the road and turning the shallow drainage ditch beside it into a flaming river running directly toward the cons. There would be no traveling that road, with the supply trucks or anything else, and the fire was spreading out of the ditch to ignite the scrub brush in the adjacent field. Their only avenue of escape was the increasingly narrow width of the field not yet burning, but in minutes, they'd be completely cut off and caught between the advancing wall of fire and the unknown force arriving on the tugboat.

Snag stifled a curse and dashed through the ditch and across the field of scrub brush toward the rapidly shrinking gap in the wall of fire, his men on his heels, all their cars and equipment abandoned.

M/V *Judy Ann*
Union Canal Inlet

Minutes Later

Kinsey glanced over his shoulder at the approaching wall of fire, then back toward his men moving toward the barge. He did a double take; then his face split into a grin. Making his way unsteadily down the ladder from the barge was Lucius Wellesley, a mostly white tee shirt tied around his head, stained with blood.

"Lucius! Thank God! I thought you were—"

"Damn near was," Lucius replied. "He clipped me on the side of the head and knocked me out. I did wake up in time to see the sons of bitches running though."

Wellesley staggered a bit and Kinsey reached out to steady him, but Wellesley knocked the hand away and looked over at the trucks then at the approaching fire.

"I'm fine," Wellesley said. "Now we best get these groceries loaded."

Kinsey shook his head. "The tires are all flat and those loaded trucks are heavy as hell. They'd have had trouble making it up those steep ramps before, and they sure as hell won't make it now, not before that fire gets here."

"No step for a stepper. We came for groceries, and we're leaving with groceries," Wellesley said, looking over at the group who'd gathered round and spotting Mike Gillespie. "Mike, can y'all get those trucks started up the ramps, just the front tires, I mean?"

Mike Gillespie looked over at Darius Green, who nodded.

"Sure. We can start 'em up the ramps, but like the chief says, I don't think—"

Wellesley looked over at one of his men. "Willy, you and Dennis get up to the head of the boat and drag that tow wire on the forward winch to the front of the barge. We'll run it down and shackle it to the front bumpers. Between the trucks' power and the winch assist, we'll drag the trucks aboard one at a time."

The two men nodded and Wellesley shot a worried glance back at the approaching wall of fire, then turned back to his men.

"Well, don't just stand there bobbin' your damned heads, MOVE IT! We don't have a lot of time here," Wellesley said.

***

They managed it in the proverbial nick of time, as the loose gravel of the parking lot absorbed some of the gasoline and slowed the spread of the fire. Even so, the heat had been near unbearable, and it was a close thing. Kinsey stood on the bow of the ferry barge as they chugged across the river and looked at the scorched and bubbled paint on the rear roller door of the last truck they dragged aboard.

"That was damned close," said Darius Green, and Kinsey turned to the man and nodded.

A strange transformation had come over Green during their escape and especially since the *Judy Ann* had backed out of their makeshift slip. He seemed more animated and positive and had gone from reluctant participant to enthusiastic ally in well under an hour.

"That it was," Kinsey said, and then hesitated before continuing. "You feel better about your decision now?"

Darius Green snorted. "What decision would that be? Join us or die like rats in a trap? I can't say I liked having it shoved down my throat, but yeah, I think it will turn out for the better. I kept appearances up for everybody, but it was clear to me we didn't have a future in that warehouse; we were just hiding and buying time until the cons found us. Y'all have a means of defense and it sounds like you're planning for the future."

Darius looked at his group gathered some distance away on the ferry barge; all stood watching as the *Judy Ann* nosed the barge toward the ring of ships encircling the little island. He blew out a sigh. "We lost Lamont and got two wounded, but it could have been way worse. In fact, it WOULD have been way worse when the cons eventually found us. And truth be told, it will be kinda nice to have someone else doing the plottin' and plannin' for a change. Being responsible for whether or not a bunch of folks live or die isn't exactly a job I ever volunteered for."

Kinsey smiled wanly. "Trust me, I know the feeling."

They rode in silence a bit longer, but as they neared the *Cape Mendocino*, Kinsey saw a familiar figure at the ship's rail raise a radio to his mouth.

Kinsey's own radio squawked. "Hughes to Kinsey. Do you copy? Over."

Reluctantly, Kinsey raised the radio. "I copy, Captain. Over."

"Glad to see you back safe and sound, Matt, but who the HELL are all those people? Over." Hughes did not sound pleased.

"Ahh. It's a long story, Cap. I'll explain when we get aboard. Over," Kinsey replied.

"It better be damn good. Hughes out."

Kinsey lowered his own radio and blew out a sigh, the look on his face so forlorn it drew a smile from Darius Green.

"Guess who's coming to dinner?" Darius said.

603

CHAPTER FIFTEEN

Cape Fear River
Just North of
Military Ocean Terminal Sunny Point

Day 44
May 14, 2020 - 1:45 a.m.

On a sweltering late afternoon in early July 1863, on a rocky Pennsylvania hillside just south of Gettysburg known locally as Little Round Top, an unproven Union Colonel named Joshua Lawrence Chamberlain led the outnumbered men of the 20th Maine in an operation that would forever define the concept of initiative and valor against desperate odds.

Out of ammunition and ordered to 'hold the line at all costs,' Chamberlain ordered his men to fix bayonets, and met the fourth Confederate charge with a charge of his own. The forces clashed on the hillside, the momentum of the downhill charge and its unexpected nature carrying the day for the Union and preventing the Confederates from flanking and 'rolling up' the Union line.

Colonel Douglas David Hunnicutt's reverence for that amazing act stemmed not only from his former role as a history teacher, but also from the fact his three times great grandfather had been on the Confederate side of that charge. It was an act of such stunning audacity it gained Chamberlain the respect and admiration of even his adversaries, and by the war's end, he was almost as well respected in Confederate ranks as he was in the Union.

That Hunnicutt should choose to name his own Hail Mary after that iconic battle seemed to him only fit and proper.

**

All the occupants of Fort Box were now 'combat veterans' in the broader sense, but there was a big difference between the defense of a fortified position, however heroic, and taking the fight to the enemy. Luke Kinsey wanted only people with a certain skill set 'at the tip of the spear,' and fortunately he found them among the defenders of Fort Box.

Washington, Long, and both the Gibson brothers were a given, and Josh Wright had his own short list of combat vets from among the former members of the North Carolina National Guard. Fortunately military service was a long tradition among the rural folk of North Carolina, and there was no shortage of combat vets among the river volunteers either. In fact, the only limiting factor had been the availability of night-vision gear, and here too, the folks from upriver contributed more than their fair share, as many had arrived with their own night-vision equipment. In the end, Luke had been able to arm and equip two dozen shooters, which he divided into two twelve-man teams.

Luke led Team Alpha, supported by Sergeant Jerry Hill, previously assigned to the Military Ocean Terminal Sunny Point, and Joel Washington, over his own protests, led Team Bravo. Accompanying Team Bravo as a guide was Brian Dempsey, the former Duke Power employee who'd become an ally, his enthusiasm fueled by an opportunity to rescue his captive family.

Luke and the men who deserted from the SRF with him were wearing their old uniforms, and a few of the others donned the uniforms of the SRF soldiers captured in the previous raid on the terminal. They glided silently downstream in six large aluminum fishing boats outfitted with powerful outboards but pushed now by electric trolling motors. Trailing them with a trolling motor jury-rigged to its own stern was the smaller Coast Guard patrol boat.

A midstream island glowed green in Luke's NV goggles and he turned back to Donny Gibson at the helm.

"That's it, Donny. Keep right of the island, but hug its shoreline. We have to be able to spot our landmark," Luke said softly as he keyed the mic on his radio three times, followed by a pause and two more clicks. He heard a single click in acknowledgment. Across the water, he watched the glowing green ghost of the Coast Guard boat separate from the group to move out of sight behind the island, where it would move farther downstream and establish a lookout.

Not that it matters much, Luke thought. They were stretched so thin they had little recourse if they were attacked by boat from downriver, but at least a timely warning might afford some of them time to escape.

He pushed the negative thoughts from his mind and turned to study the shoreline of the little island to his left, searching for the small projection he'd identified on the river chart and used to plot a course to their intended landing point. He saw it almost immediately and watched it grow larger in his goggles.

"Okay, get ready to turn hard right on my mark. Five, four, three, two, one, MARK," he said, keeping his voice low.

The boat swung immediately to almost a right angle from their previous course as Luke flipped up his NV goggles and stared at the luminous dial of the compass in his hand.

"There. Hold her steady on that course," he called softly as they slipped silently across the river, the rest of the boats trailing like ducklings behind their mother.

Hill had chosen their landing spot well, the mouth of a small creek that dumped into the river midway between the two most upstream terminal docks. The docks were a thousand yards apart, which put the boats of the little assault force five hundred yards from either one, likely out of the range of night-vision equipment in the moonless night. Or at least Luke hoped they were out of range.

He focused on the compass intently, whispering course corrections to Gibson at the helm and relying on Hill in the bow of the boat to spot the creek. The minutes seemed like hours, and sweat soaked through Luke's tee shirt and began to dampen his black SRF utilities as he started second-guessing himself. *Did I correct enough for the current, or perhaps I corrected too much?*

"I got it," Hill whispered from the bow.

"I see it too," Donny Gibson whispered back.

Relief washed over Luke, and he snapped down his NV goggles to see the welcome site of a creek perhaps fifteen feet wide spilling into the river. Gibson nosed the boat into its mouth, winding his way up the creek between tall vegetation on either side, with the rest of the little fleet following behind.

They passed a nondescript metal pole set off to one side of the creek, and Hill pointed at it. "Motion sensor," he whispered to Luke. "There was no way we could afford to secure a place this massive with people. The entire perimeter has state-of-the-art instrumentation, none of which is working without power."

Luke nodded and turned back to the bow, where he saw a large culvert and road crossing ahead, blocking their way.

"That's the connector road between docks one and two," Hill said. "We'll leave the boats here and ..." Hill trailed off as they heard an engine in the distance.

"Pass the word," Hill hissed. "Everyone needs to be absolutely quiet."

Luke did as told and waited as the engine sound grew louder and things grew sharper in his NV goggles as the light from the approaching vehicle augmented the ambient light. He flipped his NV goggles up just before a pickup truck rolled slowly past on the road above. *Please don't let them spot us before we resupply,* he thought. *We can't afford to engage without more ammo.*

"Perfect," Hill whispered as the vehicle rolled past without stopping. "They can't have nearly enough people to guard this place, even if they brought over more after your last little visit. The primary threat is from the river, so I figure they're just patrolling the river approaches. He'll likely go to the end of this road and then turn back when the road turns inland."

"How far," Luke asked.

"Two miles to the end and two miles back. Figure he's going twenty or thirty miles an hour, that gives us at least ten minutes. But better than that, we can figure his schedule. Now let's get this show on the road," Hill whispered.

Luke nodded and passed the word, and Alpha team got out of the boats and followed him up the inclined creek bank to the road, followed by Washington and two men from Bravo team pushing a wheelbarrow.

At the road, Luke turned to Joel Washington. "Okay, you know the drill. As soon as you get your ammo, spread out among all six boats and take off for the nuke plant. Signal me on the radio when you're in place." He paused. "And remember, don't engage unless you're sure you can do this. Dead heroes are no help."

Washington gave a hesitant nod. "I still don't like leaving you here cut off. Let me at least leave you one of the boats."

Luke shook his head. "We've been over that. You don't know how many people you'll have to deal with and you may need all the boats. Besides, if this works, we'll soon have all the transport we need. And if it doesn't, it won't really matter."

Still Washington lingered. "It just doesn't feel right somehow. We've always had each other's backs."

"There's no choice," Luke said. "You know that. That creek system is a maze, and with Butler gone, you're the only one left from our original recon who knows the way to the 'back door' of the nuke plant. Dempsey was blindfolded when we came out, so he can't help. Our timetable is tight as it is, and we can't afford for Bravo to get lost or delayed."

Washington said nothing and Luke extended his hand. "We'll be fine, Joel. Now get going, and Godspeed."

The big man gripped Luke's hand, then turned and started down the creek bank toward the waiting boats.

* * *

Luke jogged beside Jerry Hill down the paved connector road. After a hundred yards or so, Hill veered right and led them onto a rough dirt track through the dense pines.

"This is an old plantation road," Hill said as he slowed his pace. "It's a shortcut, but it's not maintained, so we'll have to slow down a bit to keep from being slapped in the face with a tree limb."

"How far?" Luke asked.

"About a quarter mile to the nearest storage berm with small-arms ammo," Hill replied.

Luke murmured his understanding. The vast terminal sprawled over more than eight thousand acres, mostly heavy pine forest separating hundreds of short rail sidings and asphalt-paved storage areas, each surrounded by an earthen berm for safety. The idea was that an explosion at any single storage area would not become a chain reaction, igniting all the rest of the massive stockpile of ammunition. That was the theory anyway; it had never been tested in practice.

Luke slowed his pace to match Hill's and sent up a silent prayer of thanks for the good fortune that had brought Sergeant Jerry Hill into their ranks. There were huge stocks of weapons and ammunition in the terminal, but without Hill's experience to guide them, they would have had no way of knowing what was where.

They followed Hill through the trees to a railroad crossing, then through more trees to another paved road, where he once again picked up the pace. Six minutes later he led them around an earthen berm to where a dozen shipping containers sat on an asphalt rectangle. Hill didn't slow but raced to the nearest container, extracting a pair of large bolt cutters from his backpack as he ran. The bolt cutters made short work of the padlock on the container, and Hill threw open the double doors and stepped back.

"There you go, boys," Hill said, and Luke glanced down at his watch.

"That patrol should be passing the creek southbound about now," Luke said. "How long will it take them to run the southern leg?"

"It's over twice as far. It'll be at least a half hour before they're back," Hill said.

Luke turned to the group. "Okay, boys, you heard the man. Bravo Team, you two get that wheelbarrow loaded and back to Washington. Alpha Team, everyone else get a full ammo load out and take extra mags if you can. The clock is ticking."

Military Ocean Terminal Sunny Point
Dock Connector Road

Same Day - 3:10 a.m.

The waiting was the hardest part, followed closely by the uncertainty. They were literally making things up as they went along, operating more on assumptions than reliable intel, and with no real knowledge of how big an opposing force they might be facing. However, Luke knew that to have any hope of success, they had to strike by surprise out of the darkness when most of their enemies slept. The minutes dragged with no word from Bravo Team, and Luke fancied he saw the sky lightening in the east.

Finally he heard the two clicks on the radio, heaved a relieved sigh, and answered with one of his own.

"That's it. Bravo's in position," Luke said to Hill. "Drop it!"

Hill passed the word, and twenty feet away, a man began working a wire saw to chew through the remaining uncut portion of the trunk of a four-inch pine. The tall spindly tree began to sway and then toppled across the connector road, blocking it completely.

"You sure this won't alert them?" Luke asked, doubt in his voice.

"With thick tree cover right up to the edge of the road, it's a pretty regular occurrence," Hill said. "We kept chainsaws in the backs of the pickups as standard equipment. I'm thinking the SRF has been here long enough to have had to deal with a downed tree or two. It'll seem natural to them by now." He paused. "I hope."

"Yeah, me too," Luke said. "How long?"

Hill looked at his watch. "Less than five minutes. We better get ready."

Luke nodded and crossed the road, concealing himself in the dense pines on the opposite side. In all likelihood they were at least two miles from the main SRF force, but they didn't know that for sure and they couldn't afford to take the slightest chance they might alert the enemy. What they were about to do were executions plain and simple, and Luke and Hill had taken that disagreeable task on themselves.

Luke crouched, waiting long minutes until he heard the sound of the approaching pickup; then he flipped up his NV goggles. As expected, the vehicle slowed, then came to a stop perhaps thirty feet from the obstacle and only feet away from Luke, its headlights illuminating the bushy green barrier. Luke watched as the passenger got out the opposite side of the pickup and examined the fallen tree in the headlights.

"It ain't very big," the man called. "We can probably drag it out of the way without messin' with that damn chain saw."

Luke heard a muttered curse from the SUV; then the driver's door swung open as the man got out and started forward. Luke let him pass and then darted from cover and closed the distance in a half-dozen steps, bringing up the .22 pistol as he came. The man began to turn, but not fast enough, as the little pistol gave a barely audible *sphut* and the subsonic hollow point entered the back of the man's skull from less than a foot away. The man crumpled, dead before he hit the ground, and Luke looked up to see the second man illuminated in the glare of the headlights, turning his way and raising his M4, oblivious to Hill emerging from the woods just feet behind him. There was a second *sphut* and the SRF trooper crumpled to the pavement, dead.

The rest of the men boiled from the woods and began to drag the tree aside. Luke stopped two of them.

"Barnes, you and Davis strip the uniforms off these guys and then drag the bodies into the woods. You can change in the back of the truck while we're moving," Luke said, then turned to Hill.

"You're the local expert, what now?"

"If it was me and I had to try to secure this place with a limited force, I'd have a riverside patrol, which we just took out, and I'd defend the single access road in, so I'm bettin' there are people there. They'll have a central location where they're barracked, and likely there's a watch there to coordinate with the two patrols and the nuke plant by radio. We need to take them out first." Hill glanced over to where the rest of the men had just finished dragging the tree out of the way. "Everybody pile in. I'll drive."

The rest of the operation went far better than Luke dared hope. Hill got them to within a quarter mile of the administration complex and then they went the rest of the way on foot. The only building lighted was the base police headquarters, and the plate-glass windows revealed two less than alert SRF troopers on watch. They took them out merely by walking in the front door in their stolen uniforms and leveling pistols at the surprised SRF troopers at point-blank range.

Neither man was exactly hero material, especially when Hill explained in great detail the effects of a subsonic .22 hollow point on the human knee joint and offered to provide demonstrations. They competed with one another to offer details of the garrison, and the thirty SRF troopers sleeping in the adjoining building were soon awakened to guns in their faces then zip-tied hand and foot and locked in a storeroom. The two sentries on the main access road were equally surprised and soon joined their brethren in the storeroom.

The sky was beginning to lighten in the east when a relieved Luke Kinsey turned to Hill.

"Well, we've got it. Think we can hold it?"

Hill shook his head. "Long term, no way. But for a few hours, definitely. They'd kick our ass with air support, but without it they have to come at us overland, and there's only one access road with a choke point about half a mile before the main gate where it runs between a couple of small man-made lakes. It's probably not more than fifty yards wide. We can hold 'em off there quite a while."

"Your lips to God's ear," Luke said. "Let's get this show on the road. We'll set up at the choke point and you take one of the trucks and head back to the docks. Wright and his crew will need your expertise."

Hill nodded and Luke raised his radio and keyed the mic. "Shopping Cart, execute. Repeat. Shopping Cart, execute."

Task Force Shopping Cart
Cape Fear River
Three Miles Upstream

Lieutenant Josh Wright sat in one of the larger Coast Guard patrol boats and watched the lightening sky as he cursed the luck that placed him in what he saw as a support role. Then he sighed; he knew there was no help for it. With Mike Butler gone, he was the one officer left who'd been intimately involved in bringing the container terminal back to life, and who was most familiar with both the strengths and weaknesses of the civilian terminal workers recruited for the operation.

He suppressed a smile as he looked out at his little task force. 'Chosen' would be a better verb than recruited, because to a man, and woman, the workers of Fort Box had volunteered. Almost fifty of them swarmed the decks of the five flat-top construction barges he'd found upstream at the boatyard.

They had three harbor tugs crewed by some of the merchant seamen with tug experience. More importantly, he had Captain Randall Ewing running the marine end of things. Well supplied after trading his services as a harbor pilot to get ships waiting at anchor upriver to Fort Box, Ewing had felt secure in his secluded riverside home. However, when the occupation of the Brunswick Nuclear Plant put SRF troops less than a mile from his doorstep, he'd rethought his plan.

As luck would have it, Ewing had brought his family into what he thought was the relative safety of Fort Box just in time to endure the harrowing first attack. That experience and the following events had cemented his resolve to see the fort and its occupants survive. He'd volunteered for Task Force Shopping Cart, and having an experienced river pilot along eased Wright's mind considerably. Handling barges in the swift and often unpredictable currents of the Cape Fear River wasn't a task for the inexperienced, and there was little point in stealing ammo if you ran aground getting it home.

Wright could make out more details in the growing light: drums of diesel and gasoline, rows of fully charged spare batteries, toolboxes, and basically anything else they figured they might need to hit the ground running and bring the Military Ocean Terminal to life. Among his volunteers were a dozen people who'd previously worked in the MOT, and he'd made them section leaders, each with a specific assignment. They had no time to waste.

He jumped as his radio squawked and Luke Kinsey's voice came from the speaker. "Shopping Cart, execute. Repeat. Shopping Cart, execute."

Wright keyed the mic twice in response and stood up in the boat.

"Showtime, folks! Let's get this shopping cart filled," he yelled across the water as he started downstream, leading his task force.

Special Reaction Force Regional HQ
Brunswick Nuclear Plant
Southport, North Carolina

Same Day - 7:15 a.m.

Rorke roused, groggy from the brandy he'd consumed the evening before. Despite his efforts to spin his defeat as a temporary setback, Crawford had seen through the attempt and administered an ass-chewing of epic proportions. Rorke had sat up late into the night, alone with his thoughts and a bottle, but neither provided the solution to his current dilemma.

"Quinton! Quinton! Wake up! Someone's at the door."

He rolled over, knocked a hand away from his shoulder, and shot Maria Velasquez a baleful glance. She was getting to be a pain in the ass and less attractive by the day, especially in the morning without her makeup. Having abandoned her workout and diet regime, her formerly tight body was beginning to bulge in all the wrong places and she seemed to have the ludicrous notion her position was secure. He'd have to get rid of her soon, he thought. Then again, if he didn't do something soon to correct his own fall from favor, she'd probably leave on her own to attach herself to someone else in power. He had no illusions as to her loyalty.

"See who it is." Rorke rolled back over and pulled the pillow over his head.

"You do it. I have to pee." She was in the bathroom with the door closed before Rorke could protest.

He muttered a curse. *Yep, she is definitely history.* The knock became insistent. Still cursing, Rorke rolled out of bed and walked to the door, jerking it open without regard for his own nakedness.

"This better be good," he growled at Reaper.

"Sorry, boss, but the MOT missed both the oh six hundred and oh seven hundred radio checks and we can't raise them on any of the assigned frequencies. Something's up and it's not good," Reaper said.

"Well, send a patrol around to check it out! You need me to tell you that?" Rorke said.

"I did that after they missed the second check. Ten minutes ago the patrol radioed they were starting up the terminal access road; then the guards in the towers reported hearing automatic weapon fire from that direction and we've been unable to raise the patrol. We need an aerial recon and the only chopper we have left on station is yours. Can we use it?" Reaper asked.

Rorke stood stunned then let out a stream of obscenities. "All right," he said at last. "I better see this for myself. Give me five to get dressed."

* * *

He had his pilot go straight up from the nuke plant, painfully aware of the damage inflicted by the sniper rifles the previous day. His fifty-caliber machine gun was manned, but he had absolutely no intention of getting close enough to engage with those Barretts in the picture; the chopper would be a clear target and the sniper rifles would be firing from cover. He didn't like those odds.

The extent of his problems unfolded in his binoculars before they'd even reached altitude. The single narrow road to the MOT was barricaded by a line of cars and trucks stretching from tree line to tree line. He had no doubt the defensive line extended through the narrow strips of woods to the banks of the small lakes on either side of the road. It was a strong position, one he'd have chosen himself.

The nightmare became real when he panned over the terminal and focused on the upstream dock; he sat transfixed, unable to believe his eyes. The dock and the storage areas closest to it were beehives of activity, with barges and boats pulled alongside the dock and two of the massive diesel-powered container cranes in operation, lowering containers onto the barges. Farther inshore, a switch engine was pulling a long line of rail cars toward the dock.

Blood drained from Rorke's face; they were stealing his ammo! This was the final straw; if he didn't stop this, he doubted he'd survive the next twenty-four hours. On the other hand, they HAD to be using most of their resources for this, and for the first time he'd caught them outside the walls of that damned fort; maybe he could crush them once and for all. They'd hardly reached altitude when he signaled the pilot to return to base.

* * *

"Get on the radio to Myrtle Beach, Sumter, Florence, Fayetteville, and everyplace else within a hundred-mile radius," Rorke said. "Tell them to leave minimal garrisons in place and get everyone else on the road with full combat load out. I want 'em headed this way in ten minutes. Anyone not here in three hours will answer to me personally. Is that clear?"

Reaper bobbed his head, as if afraid to speak.

"How many troops is that?" Rorke asked.

"Probably over a thousand, not counting the two hundred we have here," Reaper said.

Rorke nodded. "All right, get that going, then pick half the men here, including anyone who knows anything about boats, and send them to me. I want ten machine guns and all the RPGs. You'll take the rest of the men and take out the force defending the MOT access road."

"What about the nuke plant?" Reaper asked. "We can't leave the prisoners unguarded."

Rorke hesitated. "All right. Leave a minimal security force—a dozen max. We need to clear that access road and retake the MOT."

Reaper nodded and left, and Rorke turned back to the chart spread on the coffee table before him. He had no illusions Reaper and his band of misfits would be very enthusiastic in assaulting a well-defended position, but that really wasn't the point. They just had to keep the pressure on and make it look real. Let the ammo thieves have all the time they wanted; in fact, the more time, the better. They could load their barges to near sinking for all he cared, because he was going to make sure they never got them back upriver.

This was a Hail Mary, pure and simple. As audacious as it was, it clearly telegraphed his opponents' desperation — Fort Box was out of ammo. When he'd wiped out this raiding party and received the necessary reinforcements, he'd finish off the troublesome fort once and for all.

Rorke looked down at the map and traced the ferry route to Fort Fisher with his finger. The ammo thieves would have a little surprise waiting for them upstream. He smiled. This was turning out to be a pretty good day after all.

Access Road
Military Ocean Terminal Sunny Point

Same Day - 9:05 a.m.

Luke scanned their position for what seemed like the hundredth time, looking for weak points; he found none. Without ammo, the machine guns at Fort Box were useless, and Hunnicutt had sent them along with Task Force Shopping Cart. Wright sent up two of the guns to Luke as soon as he arrived, along with a newly liberated supply of ammunition. Those guns now anchored either end of their defensive line with overlapping fields of fire.

Nor was that the only enhancement. The chain saws they'd found in the terminal had been an unexpected bonus, and they'd set to work immediately, dropping tall pines one on top of the other across the narrow strips of woodland on either side of their position. The result was near impenetrable jumbles of downed trees and interlocking limbs, stretching from the road to the shores of the small lakes on either side. The only access was now the road, currently blocked solid by a barricade of vehicles and equipment moved from the maintenance areas of the terminal.

It was a formidable and intimidating barrier, and apart from the initial SRF patrol who died before they had a clue what they were facing, the only other challenge had come a half hour before, when Luke's small force had handily beat back an assault by a much larger group of newly arrived SRF troops. Those troops now sat behind their own vehicle barricade farther down the access road, a respectful distance away.

"Those boys don't seem too eager to engage."

Luke looked over at a grinning Donny Gibson and nodded agreement. "I can't say I blame them," Luke said. "This is a strong position. I'd have doubts about a frontal assault without air support myself."

"Well, that's fine by me," Gibson said. "If we can buy Wright and his crew the time he needs without getting shot at, you won't hear me complaining."

Luke nodded, a new worry growing in the back of his mind. *What if they were TOO successful?*

CHAPTER SIXTEEN

Nancy's Creek
Just East of Brunswick Nuclear Plant
Southport, North Carolina

Lieutenant Joel Washington crept quietly through the undergrowth, Brian Dempsey following closely. He stopped just short of where the undergrowth ended and slowly parted the bushes. He had a clear view up the raised levee to the access road that ran atop it, and he pondered his course of action.

He'd had a bad moment an hour earlier, when the chopper ascended unexpectedly from the nuke plant. Fortunately, they'd pulled their boats far enough onto the bank of the tree-lined creek for their camouflage netting to be effective. That, and the fact the SRF was unlikely to look for anyone literally at their back door, had helped them escape detection, even when the chopper landed less than ten minutes after it took off.

Near pandemonium broke out as the chopper settled to earth with men running everywhere in obvious panic, confirmation Luke's little force had been spotted. Washington smiled to himself twenty minutes later when vehicles full of SRF troops poured out the gate in response to Luke's incursion. Washington checked his watch as the SRF troops departed, and sure enough, right about the time he figured they'd traveled the four road miles to the MOT, he heard a sharp, but brief, exchange of gunfire. The plan was definitely working.

Sort of.

Washington was racked with indecision. He still only had a dozen men and he was unsure what they faced in the nuke plant. Defending a prepared position was one thing; rescuing unprepared civilians without a real plan was quite another.

Beside him, Dempsey shifted. "I think that was—"

Washington raised a hand. "Shsss!" he hissed. "There are more coming."

They instinctively drew back into the brush a bit but could still make out twelve Humvees and SUVs passing, loaded with men. Washington's jaw tightened when he recognized Rorke in the last car. *Leading from the rear, as usual,* he thought.

As the little convoy sped out of sight, Washington turned to Dempsey. "You know the drill here; how many do you think are left?"

"I can't be sure, but that has to be most of them. I'd say not more than ten or fifteen are left, say twenty to be conservative. There will be one on a machine gun in each of the guard towers on the four corners of the prisoner compound. Normally the rest are spread out through the plant, watching us while we work. They don't ever leave us without supervision, but I'm not sure what they'll do with a reduced crew. There aren't enough of them left to keep an eye on everyone unless they put them all in one place," Dempsey said.

Washington nodded. "That's what I'm counting on," he said, and headed back through the woods toward the creek.

It was now or never.

***

Washington crouched fifty yards from the prisoner compound, in the edge of the broad strip of woods that lined Nancy's Creek. He watched nervously as Dempsey peered through the binoculars, studying the people behind the tall chain-link fence.

"There's McElroy, and that's Lynch," Dempsey said at last as he lowered the glasses. "There are fourteen nuke workers counting me, and I've spotted six of them. They don't normally let us behind the wire to see our families but once a week on Sunday, so I'm thinking they stuck all the workers in the compound for safekeeping while they respond to the attack on the MOT."

Washington nodded. *Thank you, Lord!* he thought.

The guard towers on the corners of the compound were open affairs with a roof to protect their single occupants from the sun and rain, designed solely to intimidate and control the captives. Unarmored and lacking protective sandbags, their machine guns pointed inward at the captives, not outward for defense. Each was essentially a target on a stick.

Washington had detailed three shooters for each tower, ordering them to move through the woods until they had clear shots at their designated targets. Operation Little Round Top had spread resources thin, and they were short of radios, so he was improvising. He gave his teams plenty of time to get into position, with orders to fire when they heard his team engage. He alerted the men on either side of him and raised his M4.

"FIRE," he said, targeting the guard in the nearest tower. His rifle barked and three-round bursts sounded on either side of him, followed in seconds by gunfire from the other teams. All four guards were dead before they knew what was happening.

Washington grabbed the whistle hanging around his neck and blew a long blast, and the piercing shriek echoed through the sudden stillness after the gunfire. His entire twelve-man team erupted from the woods and raced toward the compound.

But they were hard-pressed to keep up with Dempsey, who bounded for the compound gate like a man possessed, his only weapon a pair of bolt cutters. By the time Washington got to the gate, Dempsey had demolished the padlock and thrown open the gate to dash into the compound.

"DIANE! DIANE, WHERE ARE YOU?" Dempsey screamed, and Washington saw a woman with honey-blond hair come out of the terrified crowd and rush toward Dempsey, two small boys in her wake. Washington turned back to the task at hand.

"Flickinger and Bonsack! Man the two nearest towers and turn those fifties around. Blow the hell out of anything you see moving in the plant," Washington yelled, and then he pointed to the chopper sitting on the helipad fifty yards away.

"Johnson and Melendez! Get some thermite grenades in that chopper and make damn sure it's not flyable. We damn sure don't need that thing on our six getting out of here. The rest of you spread out and take cover behind those abandoned cars in the parking lot and anything else you can find. Keep them off us, but be ready to pull out back to the boats on my signal," Washington yelled.

Satisfied his orders were being carried out, Washington raced over to Dempsey, who was embracing his wife and children.

"We have to move it, Mr. Dempsey," Washington said. "I don't know how long we can —"

A big man pushed his way out of the crowd.

"Who the hell are these people, Dempsey? Are you trying to get us all killed?" said the man.

Dempsey turned to face the man. "This is Lieutenant Washington from the Wilmington Defense Force. They're here to —"

"The Wilmington Defense Force? You mean the traitors who murdered all those refugees?"

The crowd, previously cowed into silence, now erupted in chaos, some shouting abuse and others trying to ask questions, while Dempsey attempted to shout over the din. Washington pointed his M4 into the air and loosed a three-round burst.

"EVERYONE SHUT UP!" Washington yelled, continuing before the stunned crowd could react. "MR. DEMPSEY WILL EXPLAIN THE SITUATION, AND THEN YOU CAN COME WITH US OR STAY AS YOU PLEASE. NO ONE WILL FORCE YOU TO DO ANYTHING. BUT WE DON'T HAVE MUCH TIME AND WE WILL NOT DEBATE THE ISSUE. LISTEN TO MR. DEMPSEY AND MAKE YOUR DECISION."

Washington stopped and waited a moment to make sure the silence held, and then he nodded at Dempsey.

"I came here to get my family and anyone else who wishes to join us. The people in Fort Box aren't at all like they're being portrayed by the government broadcasts. They're just trying to survive and help others, but the government doesn't like anyone acting on their own. If you need any proof of that, just think about the way you've been treated here. There is plenty of food and water in Fort Box and they can defend themselves. There are risks, but I'd rather be there than here as a prisoner."

"What risks?" the angry man demanded.

"Big ones, Lynch. They've been attacked twice and likely will be again. They managed to beat back both attacks." Dempsey motioned at the fence surrounding them. "But even with the risks, the bottom line is I'd rather be with them than part of this."

"I don't like the way the feds are going about this either," Lynch said, "but they ARE trying to get the power back on and what we're doing here is important. And at least our families are being fed and safe."

Dempsey scoffed. "Safe? Really? What about Harnedy's wife, or Gentry's daughter? Just because these SRF thugs haven't gotten around to YOUR family doesn't mean they're 'safe.' And when we do get the power back on, who do you think it's going to benefit? You know as well as I do it will just be one more thing they use to control and manipulate us."

"So you expect us to just drop everything on your say-so and —"

"I don't expect you to do a damned thing, and I don't really care. I'm here for my family and anyone who cares to can come with us," Dempsey said. "If you want to wait here in your unlocked cage until your masters come home, that's fine by me, but —"

Lynch bristled. "Who the hell died and made you king —"

"ENOUGH," Washington bellowed, and all heads snapped in his direction. His shout was punctuated by the din of both machine guns in the guard towers opening up on some targets in the direction of the nuke plant. Washington cast a nervous glance over his shoulder.

"What Mr. Dempsey has explained is essentially the situation in a nutshell. Anyone is free to stay or go, but we're leaving here in five minutes with anyone who wants to come with us," Washington said.

Diane Dempsey spoke for the first time. "But ... but five minutes doesn't give us time to pack. We have —"

Washington was shaking his head. "There's no time to pack nor room in the boats for luggage. You'll be leaving with the clothes on your back and you have to decide now."

Diane Dempsey looked at her husband and pulled her two young sons close. "Brian, do you ... do you think going with these people is safer?"

"No place is safe, honey. But I think —"

Washington interrupted. "Just to be clear. No one has to stay with us. We'll take everyone back to Fort Box, and if you want to stay, you'll be welcome. However, if you want to leave, we'll give you food, water, and whatever weapons we can spare and send you on your way."

Washington's speech turned the tide. There were murmurs of approval from the crowd, and Diane Dempsey nodded. Washington turned to Brian Dempsey.

"Get your family headed toward the boats," Washington said.

Dempsey scooped up one of his sons while his wife lifted the other boy and followed her husband out the gate.

Washington turned back to the crowd. "Anyone who wants to come, follow Mr. Dempsey."

Despite the earlier murmurs of approval, indecision hung over the crowd like a cloud until a woman left the group and started for the gate, holding the hand of a little girl of six or eight. A man left the smaller group of workers and joined the woman, taking his daughter's other hand. Then came a third family and a fourth until only Lynch and a woman, obviously his wife, stood in the middle of the now-deserted compound. Lynch looked at his wife and she nodded, and the pair fell in behind the rest.

Washington looked back toward the nuke plant. Less than ten minutes had elapsed since they'd hit the guard towers, and they'd kept the surprised and confused garrison on the defensive. The chopper was burning brightly on its pad, but here and there from the plant he heard more sustained fire. They needed to disengage now; if the SRF troops closed on the banks of the creek before they were out of range, it would be a shooting gallery.

He lifted his whistle and gave three shrill blasts, and Flickinger and Bonsack scrambled out of the towers, dropping the last few feet to the ground in their haste. Then his other men came into view, leap-frogging backwards from their previous places of concealment and maintaining a withering fire to discourage pursuit.

When he had a full head count, he kept two men with him and ordered the others to fall back to the tree line while his rearguard covered them. When the retreating men reached the trees, they turned and returned the favor, as Washington and his two men zigzagged across the open ground, bobbing and weaving to present more difficult targets. A bullet whizzed by Washington's ear a fraction of an inch away just as another grazed his upper arm. Then he was in the trees.

"All right, boat drivers on me. The rest of you hold them back, but haul ass to the creek when you hear the signal," Washington said as he plunged deeper into the woods with five men close behind.

There was chaos at the creek. Dempsey had recruited others to strip the camo netting off the boats, but there was total confusion as the mass of over seventy terrified civilians vied for spots in the boats, with husbands unwilling to be separated from wives, or wives from children.

Washington looked at the boats, which suddenly looked very small.

"QUIET!" he roared, and a hush fell over the group.

"Now listen up," he said. "I don't have time to repeat this, and if you all don't follow my orders to the letter, you risk getting us all killed. You have to fit into five boats while my men stay here to stop any pursuit and give you time to escape. The boats will all be severely overloaded, so we need to distribute the weight as evenly as we can. That means some of you will be separated, but your loved ones will be in the next boat. We will try to keep children with at least one parent, but we don't have time for argument. One of my men will drive each boat, and you are to follow their orders immediately and without question. Understood?"

There were tentative nods throughout the frightened crowd.

"Good. Now follow directions and we'll have you safely away in no time."

Washington motioned his boat drivers forward, and they quickly took charge, adjusting people and family groups between boats based on load. Gunfire increased through the woods behind them, adding validity to Washington's words, and the escapees cooperated without complaint. Five minutes later Washington pushed the last boat of the little flotilla from the bank—and he saw an unanticipated flaw in his hastily contrived plan.

With sound no longer a concern, he'd envisioned speeding away on the powerful outboards, but he now saw traveling at such speeds would court disaster. The deeply loaded open boats were producing substantial bow and stern waves and appeared unstable in the extreme. The slightest bit of oversteering or a sudden decrease in speed could swamp a boat in seconds, and realizing that, his men were driving the boats not much faster than the electric trolling motors had pushed them initially.

A road ran through the trees paralleling Nancy's Creek for over a mile. If the SRF troops realized what was happening, they could break off from where they were engaged and race along the creek road in trucks, targeting the defenseless escapees.

Washington fingered the whistle hanging from his neck and looked from the slowly moving boats back through the woods toward the sounds of gunfire. The din was horrific and it was obvious the fire from the SRF troops was increasing. The plus side was the noise was masking the sounds of the outboards.

Change of plan—they'd have to keep the noise up a while longer to ensure the escapees were out of danger, and then hope their more lightly loaded boat could race past the danger zone before the SRF troops figured out what was going on. He started back through the woods toward his men. Halfway there he heard the unmistakable jackhammer sound of a fifty-caliber machine gun.

Oh shit! he thought and began to run.

Fort Fisher Ferry
Halfway Across Cape Fear River

Rorke sat in the Humvee, poring over the map, oblivious to the throb of the ferry's engine. Under threat of severe punishment, his men had managed to get the ferry operating in record time, and it was being piloted adequately but inexpertly by one of his men who'd spent some time as a helmsman in the navy.

Rorke lifted his head and gazed out at the hundred men of his strike force, glad he'd decided to come. He was much more comfortable directing things from his chopper, high above the fray, and he'd toyed with the idea of sending Reaper to run this end of the operation. However, there were a hundred things that could go wrong, and if you wanted something done right, you often DID have to do it yourself. He'd make sure everything was going to plan and then have the chopper fly out to pick him up.

From what he'd seen during his brief chopper recon, it should be a piece of cake. He figured his men must outnumber the total raiding party by at least two to one, and given that the bulk of the opposition appeared to be terminal workers, it was probably more like five or six to one if you just counted shooters. That advantage would be multiplied when he ambushed them on the open river. He looked at his watch; they were ten minutes from the Fort Fisher ferry landing.

His radio squawked. "Base to Thunderbolt, do you copy? Over."

"This is Thunderbolt Actual. Go ahead. Over," Rorke said.

"Sir, we are under attack. A large force came out of the woods behind the compound and took the prisoners. Over."

"What the hell do you mean they 'took the prisoners'? Over."

"They, uhh … they just charged out of the woods and killed the tower guards, then herded all the prisoners into the woods. Over," the man said.

Rorke cursed. "All right, what's the current situation? Over."

"I have five men KIA and one badly wounded, but the rest of us have them pinned down in the woods. I request reinforcements. Over."

Rorke turned the situation over in his mind, and despite his anger, he was impressed. Obviously it was an assault on multiple fronts to keep him off balance in the hope he would split his force and withdraw troops from the task of retaking the MOT.

He smiled. He was splitting his force right enough, just not like his enemy anticipated. His smile faded as another possibility crossed his mind; the last thing he needed was his overzealous troopers shooting up the nuke workers or their families. Those people's skill sets were hard to come by, and no one was making it back to Fort Box anyway; he'd let them go for now until he could personally supervise their recapture. He lifted the mic to his mouth.

"Thunderbolt Actual to Base. Negative reinforcements. Repeat, negative reinforcements. Keep the enemy engaged until they withdraw, but do not pursue. Repeat. Do not pursue. Send the chopper up to have it track the fugitives' movements and have it report directly to me. Confirm. Over," Rorke said.

There was a long pause.

"Uhh … about the chopper, sir. It's inoperable. The attackers hit the controls and engine with thermite grenades. Over." There was fear in the man's voice.

Rorke let out a stream of obscenities. Aerial reconnaissance gave him a huge advantage and now he felt blind. He'd stripped all nearby air assets, and more importantly, pilots, for his abortive attack on Fort Box. He had a few more choppers coming in from more distant (and less troublesome) regions, but the first wouldn't arrive until tomorrow at the earliest.

Decisions made in anger were bad decisions. He fought down his towering rage and focused on the problem at hand. This changed nothing, really. He had good aerial reconnaissance from less than two hours earlier, and he was en route to cut off his enemy's only line of retreat. Fort Box was out of ammo and therefore out of the equation. The escaped nuke workers were obviously joining the raiders and he was going to be in position to take out the raiders and recapture the nuke workers anyway.

When he was sure he was calm, he lifted the mic again.

"Thunderbolt Actual to Base. I copy, chopper is inoperable, and repeat my earlier orders. You will receive negative reinforcements. Repeat, negative reinforcements. You are to keep the enemy engaged until they withdraw, but do not pursue. Repeat. Do not pursue. Confirm. Over," Rorke said.

"We copy, Thunderbolt Actual. Do not pursue. Repeat. We copy, do not pursue. Over." The voice sounded both confused and relieved.

"Affirmative. And when I return to base, I look forward to your explanation of how you allowed them to steal all our workers and destroy my chopper. Thunderbolt Actual out." Rorke smiled as he hung up the mic, imagining the fear of the trooper at the other end of the exchange.

Life was short, so it was always best to take small pleasures where you could find them.

Mid-stream Island
Cape Fear River
1.5 Miles Downstream from
Military Ocean Terminal Sunny Point

The two Coasties lay prone in the sand, staring south, their patrol boat hidden by the tall grass on the north side of the island.

Petty Officer Third Class Maggie Sanders lowered the binoculars and passed them to the man next to her.

"What do you make of that?" she asked.

He grunted. "Looks like the ferry, and they're headed right for the Fort Fisher Terminal. What the hell is up with that?"

"I don't know," Sanders said, "but we better let Wright know. Something hinky is going on here."

Access Road
Military Ocean Terminal Sunny Point

Noon (Two Hours Later)

Luke glanced at his watch and then over their makeshift barricade. Intimidated by the strength of the defensive position, the SRF efforts had been desultory at best.

"Looks like we bought Wright his eight hours. It was way easier than I figured too," Donny Gibson said.

Luke nodded. "Way easier, which may be a problem. I figured we'd withdraw under fire to make 'em think they pushed us back. This has to look real if we're going to sell this thing—"

Wright's voice came over the radio. "Shopping Cart to Alpha. Do you copy? Over."

Luke picked up his radio. "Go ahead, Shopping Cart. Over."

"Bravo Team is back with some company. I put all the noncombatants up on the barges between the containers. As soon as they get settled, we'll be ready to check out. Our ETD is five minutes. Y'all better get a move on if you want a ride. Over," Wright said.

"Roger that, Shopping Cart. Alpha out."

Luke looked over at Donny Gibson. "Are those claymores set?"

Gibson nodded. "Daisy-chained together just like you ordered. They won't know what hit 'em." Gibson looked toward the enemy. "Providing they have the balls to chase us to begin with."

Luke smiled. "Well, maybe we can encourage them. Divide the men into two groups and we'll bug out in a couple of the terminal pickups. Let's be loud and obvious about it, but make sure no one shows themselves. No point in getting anyone shot at this point."

"Fine by me," Gibson said, and he moved to pass the word.

***

Luke and his men raced onto the upstream dock to find a vastly different situation than they'd left just hours before. A twelve-car freight train was pulled onto the rail siding atop the massive dock, half of the boxcar doors open to reveal case upon case of small-arms ammunition, with more ammunition stacked on the dock, awaiting transfer to the barges. One of the deck barges they'd brought was tied up next to the dock with more ammo boxes stacked on board, clear evidence of a cargo operation interrupted hastily mid-transfer.

Farther down the dock were the four remaining deck barges, each carrying four full-size containers stacked one high and arranged two to a side—sixteen containers in all. The three tugs waited nearby, their engines chugging softly with the boats secured to the dock with a single line, ready to get under way. Josh Wright, Joel Washington, and Captain Randall Ewing stood on the dock, waiting for them.

Luke's truck skidded to a stop and he jumped out, ordering his men to board the barges. As they leaped out of the back of the pickup, Luke walked over to Wright and the other officers standing on the dock. He could tell by the looks on their faces something was wrong.

"Everything ready?" Luke asked.

Wright nodded toward Washington. "Washington's group brought the folks from the nuke plant in an hour ago. I put them between the containers on one of the barges. But we may have a problem."

Luke raised his eyebrows and motioned for Wright to continue.

"Our Coasties downstream spotted the ferry headed in from Southport to the Fort Fisher Terminal across the river. It has to be an SRF operation of some kind," Wright said.

Luke nodded. "Okay, but what? If they were going to hit Fort Box again, it's faster to go up west of the river; why bother crossing the river on the ferry?"

Randall Ewing spoke up. "'Cause I don't think they're headed for Fort Box, they're looking to cut us off. There are a bunch of marinas upriver on the east bank, especially in the Pleasure Island and Sea Breeze areas. I'm thinking they mean to grab a bunch of boats and swarm us on the river in a surprise attack."

Luke cursed and rubbed the back of his neck. He turned to Washington. "I figured they'd send reinforcements when you hit the nuke plant. Did you see any evidence of that?"

Washington shook his head. "No, and they had plenty of time. The overloaded boats were a lot slower than we figured and the rear guard had to hold a full half hour longer than expected. But when we left, it was like they didn't care. There was no pursuit at all."

Luke nodded. "That's why they haven't been pressing harder, either here at the terminal or at the nuke plant; they're happy to let us take all the time we want here so they can set up between us and Fort Box."

"That's what I figure too," Captain Ewing said.

Luke sighed. "Well, it is what it is. Do we have a plan?"

"We're working on it," Wright said, then flinched as a violent explosion sounded ashore, followed by a dozen more in rapid succession as each daisy-chained claymore detonated and set off the mine farther down the chain.

"Think fast," Luke said. "The lead elements of the SRF just hit our tripwire, and the survivors aren't going to be in a very good mood. You'll be sitting ducks if they catch you at the dock or in the process of leaving, so I suggest you get the hell out of here now. Are the incendiaries set?"

Wright nodded. "Thirty-minute delays, but we had to jury-rig the timers, so I can't guarantee accuracy. With luck, they won't go off until the bastards have passed."

"Then you better shove off and work out your plan on the way upriver. Things are likely to get hot here really quick," Luke said.

Wright nodded and headed towards the tugs, with Ewing beside him. Luke turned to Washington. "You ready to do this, Lieutenant?"

"Wouldn't miss it for the world, sir," Washington said.

"Do you have us a fast boat?"

Washington nodded. "The Coasties loaned us the smaller patrol boat. It's the fastest thing on the river."

"Then let's get to it," Luke said.

Access Road
Military Ocean Terminal Sunny Point

Reaper stood at the breached barricade and cursed in the sudden silence following the explosion of the booby trap a hundred yards farther down the access road, glad he'd had the foresight to have the main force lag the advance element. Four SUVs full of SRF troops newly arrived from Myrtle Beach had been in the lead, and the claymores shredded both men and vehicles. He ignored the anguished cries from the wreckage and looked back over his growing command.

The troops from the outlying areas had begun to arrive thirty minutes earlier, and he now had over a thousand men under arms, with more arriving every few minutes. He belatedly deployed a squad of men on foot and ordered them to jog the half mile to the main gate in advance of the main force, looking for tripwires or other signs of a booby trap. Once they reached the main gate, he became less concerned with booby traps; there were many paths to the docks via the terminal's internal road system, and the opposition couldn't have the resources to booby-trap them all.

He divided his force among the various routes and headed cautiously for the docks, lagging well behind the lead element of his own contingent, just in case. His troops converged on the docks without incident to find them deserted, the cargo operation obviously interrupted in progress. A trainload of small-arms ammo sat on the rail siding and a barge with a harbor tug still attached was moored alongside the dock, a few cases of ammo stacked on the deck of the barge. Reaper stood on the dock and studied the scene, trying to make sense of it.

Rorke had said the container cranes were working, so why had they been transferring cased ammo by hand? Then it came to him; the thieves obviously had to deal with the situation as they found it. They no doubt prioritized the removal of the most accessible containers loaded with small-arms ammo, then started on the more labor-intensive task of stripping the ammo case by case from the boxcars.

It appeared as if they'd interrupted the latter operation in progress. Spooked by something, the raiders had abandoned the last barge and its attendant tug. He nodded. What was the old saying? *Pigs get fat, but hogs get slaughtered.* The raiders were no dummies; they'd grabbed all the ammo they could and hauled ass while the getting was good.

But how had they known overwhelming force was en route? Or had they somehow figured out Rorke planned to cut them off? Reaper shrugged; figuring that out was Rorke's job, not his. He was raising his radio to call Rorke when Monley spoke.

"Do you smell smoke?" he asked.

Reaper lowered the radio. He DID smell smoke, and then he saw it wafting through the pine forest adjacent to the dock. It thickened as he watched.

He turned to Monley. "Get patrols out on every road back to the main gate. I want to know where this fire is and—"

The explosion was of such magnitude it knocked Reaper to his knees, even though it was over two and a half miles away in one of the farthest storage areas. He struggled to his feet, only to be shaken again by a second distant explosion of equal magnitude as another storage bunker detonated. He stood stunned until clods of dirt and bits of metal began to rain down around him; then he leaped into his SUV and ordered Monley behind the wheel just as a three-foot square of metal clanged down on the concrete dock fifty feet away, the corrugations in the steel leaving no doubt it was a piece of a shipping container.

"GET US THE HELL OUT OF HERE!" Reaper yelled, and Monley barreled down the dock and onto the road back to the main gate.

Elsewhere along the dock, newly arrived SRF troops were having the same idea, jumping back in their vehicles and fanning out on the multiple roads back to the main gate.

With the same result.

Two to three miles up each road and a mile short of where the roads converged on the single escape route, they all encountered a wall of flame moving inexorably through the dry pine forest toward the river, its progress punctuated by periodic horrendous explosions as the contents of storage units overheated to the point of detonation. The men turned and fled back to the docks, the river their only escape.

The first to leave, Reaper was among the last back to the dock, where he found bedlam. The remaining barge was jammed with troops, but it couldn't accommodate even half their number. Other troops swarmed the tugboat, where men labored in vain to get the boat started.

As he arrived, the men unable to board the barge were coming to the inescapable conclusion they were being abandoned. It was obvious that even if the tugboat managed to pull the barge away from the dock, gunfire from those enraged at being left behind would mean the death of most of the men crowded onto the barge, jammed together so tightly they would be unable to take cover or return fire.

Reaper climbed up on the hood of his SUV and emptied the magazine of his M4 into the air on full auto. "ENOUGH!" he screamed when the startled mob turned to face him. "IF YOU ALL DON'T STOP ACTING LIKE A BUNCH OF SCARED PUSSIES, WE'RE ALL DEAD, SO LISTEN UP."

"WE'RE DEAD ANYWAY IF WE DON'T GET ON THAT BARGE," screamed a man just in front of the SUV.

Reaper pulled out his Glock and shot the man in the head.

"WE AIN'T HAVIN' A DEBATE. NOW I SAID LISTEN UP. WE'RE GONNA FIND SOMEONE TO RUN THAT TUGBOAT, AND THEY'RE GONNA TAKE AS MANY GUYS AS THE TUG WILL HOLD AND HAUL ASS DOWN TO THE SOUTHPORT MARINA. THEY'LL TAKE THE SPARE FUEL CANS OUT OF OUR VEHICLES AND GRAB EVERY BOAT THEY CAN FIND AND HEAD BACK HERE. IT'S ONLY A FEW MILES, SO IT SHOULDN'T TAKE LONG. THEN WE'LL USE THE BOATS THEY BRING BACK TO FERRY EVERYONE ACROSS TO THE ISLANDS IN THE RIVER AND OUT OF DANGER FROM THIS FRIGGIN' FIRE. WE'RE ALL GONNA GET OUT OF THIS, SO YOU PUSSIES CALM DOWN."

Here and there in the crowd, Reaper could see nods of approval, the men desperate to believe they would be saved.

"IF WE CAN GET THE TUGBOAT RUNNING, WHY CAN'T WE JUST USE THE BARGE TO FERRY PEOPLE TO THE ISLANDS? IT'S BIG ENOUGH THAT IT WOULD PROBABLY ONLY TAKE FOUR OR FIVE TRIPS," called a voice from the crowd.

"BECAUSE, SMART ASS, THE BARGE IS TOO BIG. I DOUBT THERE'S ANYBODY HERE WHO COULD HANDLE IT IN THE RIVER CURRENT EXCEPT GOIN' DOWNSTREAM. AND IT TAKES SIX OR EIGHT FEET OF WATER TO FLOAT IT, WHICH MEANS IT CAN'T GET CLOSE ENOUGH TO THE ISLANDS TO DROP YOU OFF WHERE THE WATER'S NOT OVER YOUR HEADS, AND THAT CURRENT IS REALLY STRONG. IF WE TRY TO USE THE BARGE, HALF YOU DUMB ASSES WILL DROWN. SO WHY DON'T YOU JUST SHUT THE HELL UP AND LEAVE THE THINKIN' TO THOSE OF US EQUIPPED FOR IT," Reaper yelled.

There were scattered cries of approval, and Reaper sensed he was getting the crowd under control. He desperately wanted to board the tugboat and sail away himself, with the promise he'd return with more boats. However, he knew the men in the mob before him weren't THAT dumb, or at least all of them weren't. Chances were high that if he even attempted to save himself, they'd open fire on him in a heartbeat.

He suppressed a sigh. He'd have to save them all to save himself, and he had to keep them occupied to have even the slightest chance of keeping them under control while the tugboat brought back rescue craft. He looked over at the open doors of the boxcars on the siding and had an inspiration.

"AND I'LL TELL YOU SOMETHING ELSE. THESE BASTARDS HAVE JUST SENT OUR ENTIRE AMMO RESERVE UP IN SMOKE AND I DON'T NEED TO TELL YOU HOW WELL WE MIGHT FARE WITHOUT AMMO. HOWEVER, WE CAUGHT 'EM BEFORE THEY UNLOADED THAT TRAIN BEHIND ME, SO WHILE WE WAIT FOR THE RESCUE BOATS, I WANT EVERY SWINGIN' DICK UNLOADIN' THOSE BOXCARS AND GETTING THE AMMO ON THIS BARGE. WE HAVE TO SAVE AS MUCH OF THIS AMMO AS WE CAN. NOW MOVE IT. GET OFF THAT BARGE."

No one on the barge moved, and Reaper raised his Glock and shot one of the men on the barge at random.

"THOSE OF YOU ON THE DOCK GET READY TO FIRE ON THE BARGE ON MY ORDER," he yelled.

One man on the barge hastily climbed back onto the dock, and then another, and soon it was a flood.

Reaper turned to Monley. "Monley, get the tugboat operation organized and pick the men to go. Make sure to let 'em know I'm passing their names to Rorke via radio. If they even think about haulin' ass or draggin' their feet and not comin' back here with the boats in time, their deaths are gonna make ours look easy."

Monley nodded and hurried away as Reaper raised his radio. Rorke wasn't going to like this.

CHAPTER SEVENTEEN

Keg Island
Cape Fear River
7 Miles Downstream from Fort Box

Rorke terminated the radio call and cursed. There was little he could do that Reaper hadn't already thought of, but that brought him no solace. The fire was unexpected, though he probably should have anticipated it. He didn't have the slightest doubt President Crawford would think so.

He shook it off to concentrate on the problem at hand. *What had spooked the raiders into bolting early? Did they know his plan? Was there a traitor in his command?* Nothing really made sense except perhaps they'd been spotted crossing the river, though he thought that unlikely; his lookouts on the ferry had seen nothing.

No matter, it was done. He looked over his little navy clustered in a hidden bend of a long shallow inlet extending into the island, further obscured from view by tall brush on either side. The marinas had proved to be fertile hunting grounds. Except for scattered 'liveaboards' who were no match for the SRF troopers, they'd had little trouble assembling a flotilla. They'd brought extra fuel and batteries with them, and he now had his hundred troopers spread among eighteen fast boats, ten hastily fitted with machine guns and the rest carrying RPGs.

Rorke frowned. The loss of the huge ammo stocks of the MOT was a major complication requiring a change to his original plan. Even if Reaper managed to salvage the trainload of ammo at the burning terminal, that was a two- or three-month supply at most. He now needed not only to take out the raiders, but to recapture the stolen ammunition. He couldn't afford to send an RPG into the side of a container loaded with precious ammo.

Then there were the nuke plant workers; he needed them too. He assumed they'd still be in the separate boats he could cut off and isolate, but if not, he'd have to be careful. People with nuke plant experience were hard to come by, and Crawford would have his ass if he lost them. *How had things gotten so damned complicated?*

There was only one answer, really. He didn't have to take out the barges; he only had to stop them from reaching the safety of Fort Box. If he took out the boats pushing the barges, the strong current would do the rest; he could watch at a safe distance as they drifted back downriver into his area of control. He could even have Reaper stretch a line across the river to snag them or drag them onto a sandbar, then wait them out. He doubted they'd brought much food and water on a raid, certainly not enough to feed the nuke plant escapees. They'd give up quickly enough, and then he'd use the vastly superior force he'd just assembled to take out a defenseless Fort Box once and for all.

He could make this work yet. Rorke motioned the other boats closer to give them instructions.

Cape Fear River
2 Miles Downstream of Keg Island

Lieutenant Josh Wright stood in the wheelhouse of the rear harbor tug, beside Captain Ewing, looking ahead through the narrow slot between the barges on either side of the boats.

The arrangement had been Ewing's idea and it was a good one, or the best they could come up with, anyway. They'd lashed the barges in pairs, end-to-end, and then made up the tow with the two tugboats sandwiched between the barge pairs, one near the front of the barges and one near the stern. The barges and the containers rising on either side shielded the boats, though a shield packed with potentially explosive material was hardly ideal. Wright tried to put the possible consequences out of his mind; he wasn't particularly worried about small-arms fire, but an RPG or something similar might prove disastrous.

Ewing was doing all the steering from the stern tug, with the rudder of the forward tug locked amidships. In fact, there was no one in the wheelhouse of the more exposed forward tug, and it was manned by a single engineer controlling the engine locally in the engine room, taking his orders by radio from Ewing. It was an awkward arrangement at best, but one that seemed to be working, at least for the moment.

Both the larger Coast Guard patrol boats were ranging ahead of them as escorts, their machine guns now amply supplied with ammunition. Between the escort and their barge shields, Wright felt good about their chances. As improbable as it seemed just a few short hours ago, it looked like they might actually pull this off.

Maybe.

He shook his head as he peered forward through the narrow slot between the barges, even that view partially obscured by the forward tug.

"I don't know how you do it. We can hardly see anything, much less any landmarks," Wright said.

Ewing adjusted their course a bit and smiled. "This is a tough one right enough, but I've run this river over thirty years, sometimes multiple times a day, so I pretty much know every island and rock and tree on the bank. Mostly in this case it's a matter of what I DON'T see. Don't worry, Lieutenant. I'll get us there."

"It's not you I'm worried about," Wright said. "If Rorke hits us with RPGs before —"

"Hill to Wright. Do you copy? Over."

Wright reached for the radio mic. "This is Wright. I copy. Have you got them? Over."

"Negative. They're buried pretty deep in the container and the containers are sitting too close together to get the doors fully open. This may take a while. Over," Hill replied.

"How long is 'a while'? Over," Wright asked.

"Hard to say. Maybe thirty minutes, maybe longer. We're working as fast as we can. Over," Hill replied.

Wright cast a worried look forward through the narrow slot between the barges, seeing only the brown water of the river and the wooded bank beyond. They were almost halfway home and Rorke was bound to hit them soon.

"Sooner would be good," Wright said into the mic. "Wright out."

Dock No. 1
Military Ocean Terminal Sunny Point

Reaper paced the dock, forcing thoughts of rescue boats from his mind to focus on the immediate problem. Once set to the task, his men had begun to unload the boxcars with unusual enthusiasm, to take their minds off the approaching fire, if for no other reason.

The smoke was thicker now, and the roar of the fire could be heard in the distance. That is, it would have been audible were they not all near deaf from the periodic blasts from exploding storage bunkers that rocked the dock. The good thing, if there could be said to BE a good thing in their current situation, was that the slightly nearer positions of the exploding bunkers meant the trajectory of the debris had changed; it was no longer falling on the dock but splashing down some distance out in the river.

They were working efficiently, using manpower as a substitute for machinery. They formed a dozen long lines from the door of each boxcar to pass the cased ammo hand over hand like a bucket brigade to be stacked on the edge of the dock. On the dock, more SRF troops with ropes were passing the stacked cases down to comrades on the barge, who were arranging it in neat and compact rows.

Reaper heard his name being called, and looked up to see one of the troopers near the door to a boxcar waving at him; he walked over.

"You want this stuff too?" the trooper asked, motioning to a wooden crate sitting in the door of the boxcar.

Curious, Reaper read the markings stenciled on the crate.

> Charge, Demolition
> Plastic, C-4, 1.25 LB
> Lot PCE05B08-09

"How much is there?" Reaper asked.

The man shrugged and pointed into the boxcar. "See for yourself. There was a lot of ammo stacked in the door and the rest of the car is full of this shit. So do you want to take the C-4 or just the ammo?"

Reaper hid his sudden concern.

"No, we'll take the C-4 too. You never know when it will come in handy," he said.

The man nodded and lifted the case and passed it to the next man in line before yelling to the men in the boxcar to keep the crates coming. Reaper nodded and walked to the next boxcar, observing a moment until his heart fell as the crew there too uncovered case upon case of C-4.

He knew he was looking at the mother of all booby traps. The question was what to do about it? Could they defuse it? Unlikely, as he had no trained demolition people, even if they could find the detonators undoubtedly hidden somewhere in the huge volume of cases. Moreover, the mere mention of his suspicions would send this rabble back into a panic, which would have them killing each other for a place on the barge.

The answer, of course, involved discretion. And saving his own ass.

Reaper casually instructed the troopers to keep unloading and walked back to the edge of the dock and looked down at the substantial stack of ammo on the barge. He hoped it was enough to satisfy Rorke.

He motioned Monley over. He couldn't save everyone, but he'd save his own company if he could; besides, he needed help.

"Round up all of our guys, and get them down on the barge, rearranging those crates and making room for more," Reaper said quietly.

Monley looked down at the barge, confused. "Why? There's plenty of room left. We don't need—"

"JUST DO IT!" Reaper hissed, keeping his voice low. "And be quiet about it. I don't want to make a big deal out of this."

Monley nodded and left to do as instructed, and five minutes later the confused men of Reaper's original company began climbing down the ladders onto the barge as Reaper quietly relayed his suspicions to Monley. There was some grouching among the troops as the men of Reaper's original company relieved the others and sent them up to join the lines on the dock. However, Reaper had managed to reestablish his authority and the troops were following his orders without question.

Ten minutes later, most of Reaper's men were on the barge, receiving and stacking cases of ammo. Monley stood on the upstream end of the barge, making a show of adjusting the mooring line there, while Reaper stood on the downstream end, also near the mooring line, ostensibly watching the loading operation.

When Reaper saw the first cases of C-4 coming down from the dock, he knew they had all the ammo they were going to get. It was time.

He glanced again at the fast-moving river behind him. The haze from the thickening smoke was beginning to cut visibility, and that would help. Between the haze and the current, he was counting on the river carrying them out of range quickly before the troops he was deserting understood what was happening and opened fire. If not, scattered throughout the troops on the barge were a dozen reliable men who'd received quiet orders; they were stacking cases with their M-4s close at hand. He was counting on them to suppress any fire from the dock until they were out of range.

Drifting free on the river was a risk, but a calculated one, and it was damn sure better than waiting here to be blown up or burned to death. As soon as they'd cleared the dock and were out of range, he'd hail the tugboat on the radio and get them to intercept the barge as it drifted downriver. The guy driving the tug wasn't great, but all they really needed to do was get a line on the barge and drag it aground somewhere. When they stopped, they could sort things out.

Monley looked in his direction and Reaper nodded. Without hesitation, Monley threw off the mooring line on the upstream end of the boxlike barge, and still secured to the dock at the downstream end, the barge began to swing away from the dock like a door on a hinge, increasing speed as more surface area was exposed to the force of the current. Surprised shouts rose from the dock above, but Reaper ignored them, intent on timing the release of his own mooring line until the barge was fully ninety degrees to the current so they would move away from the dock at maximum speed.

That was his mistake.

The tremendous weight of the barge on the single remaining mooring line jammed the figure-eight knot tight on the mooring bitt, and try as he might, Reaper couldn't release it. Above him, the surprised shouts turned to cries of understanding, understanding to anger, and anger turned to gunfire.

Cape Fear River
Island Midstream
1 Mile Away from MOT Sunny Point

Luke Kinsey lowered the binoculars.

"They took the bait," he said as he passed Washington the glasses. "They're all over it like ants on a sugar cube."

Washington peered through the binoculars at the dock in the distance and nodded. "But why did they send the tug downstream? To bring back more boats?"

"That's what I figure," Luke said. "The barge isn't near big enough to hold them all, even if they left the ammo. We hadn't figured on that."

"But where did they all come from? Given what we know about the nuke plant garrison and if Rorke's deploying upstream in any force, there should be a hundred there, or maybe two hundred at most. There's a helluva lot more than that."

"I'd say a thousand, easy," Luke said. His voice hardened. "But the more the merrier."

Luke had been intrigued when Sergeant Jerry Hill mentioned boxcars full of C-4 in the terminal, thinking the high explosive was the perfect tool to destroy the ammo they had to leave. However, at that point he still hadn't fully wrapped his mind around just how vast the MOT was and how much time and effort it would take to set charges throughout the massive complex. The fire had been the ever-practical Hill's idea and it was much more workable.

But Luke hadn't been able to forget the C-4 and he'd decided to leave the 'mother of all booby traps' as a kiss goodbye. Like most professional soldiers, Luke Kinsey was no fan of booby traps, but the memory of his short time in the SRF and their barbaric behavior mitigated any qualms; these weren't soldiers, they were thugs, rapists, and murderers.

Still, he hesitated. Leaving a booby trap was one thing, but pulling the trigger yourself was another, and it suddenly felt a lot more like mass murder than combat. Were they ALL thugs, or were some perhaps like he and Washington, recruited from the regular military under false pretenses and now trapped by horrendous circumstance? Was the driver he'd shot in the head only a few hours before a murderer or an honorable soldier? Could he be judge, jury, and executioner for a thousand men whose crimes he could only guess at? Luke squinted through the thickening haze and recalled a quote from Sun Tzu: *To know your enemy, you must become your enemy.* Was he becoming Rorke?

"The haze is getting worse," Washington said, still peering through the binoculars. "We better pull the trigger pretty soon … HOLY SHIT!" he said as he kept the binoculars clamped to his eyes and the sound of small-arms fire echoed across the river.

"The barge is coming loose from the dock," Washington said, "and they're shooting at each other—"

"DOWN!" Luke shouted as he pressed the button on the remote, sending a signal to detonators in scattered cases of C-4 buried in each boxcar. He dropped the remote and flattened himself facedown in the sand, hands clamped to his ears.

The effectiveness of their booby trap had been a matter of conjecture, specifically as to whether the multiple scattered explosions would be sufficient to detonate the rest of the C-4. But it was conjecture no longer as upwards of a thousand tons of high explosive detonated.

The shock wave crossed the mile separating them from the terminal in less than two seconds, pressing them into the sand and forcing the air from their lungs, leaving them stunned and gasping as the sound wave enveloped them three seconds later. It started as a low rumble, vibrating the very sand where they cowered with palms clamped tight over their ears, then progressed into a tooth-rattling crescendo that seemed to last forever before it tailed off.

Luke staggered to his feet. He saw Washington's mouth moving but could hear no sound, instead following the big man's pointing finger to the river, white with splashes as debris of all sizes fell from the sky. He flinched as the steel wheel from a rail car smashed down to half bury itself in the sand at the edge of their little island.

But the steel rain was short-lived, and Washington handed him the binoculars, pointing now toward the terminal dock—or rather where the dock had been.

In its place was—nothing. No trace of anything but a huge, blackened, smoking circle of bare dirt. The pine forest had been flattened for as far as he could see, and the raging forest fire snuffed out like a candle on a birthday cake, with white smoke drifting upward from the flat black jumble of downed trees.

Luke stood staring at the blackened shore as another phrase came to mind. *Kill 'em all and let God sort it out.* Whatever the guilt or innocence of the men he'd just dispatched, they'd faced the same choice he and Washington had, and made the wrong decision. He took one last look and pointed to the boat. They had to get upriver.

Keg Island
Cape Fear River

Even from over six miles away, the fireball was clearly visible as it rose into the sky. The shock wave followed seconds later, diminished by distance but still sufficient to sweep Rorke's little armada before it like a broom, pushing the boats together against the north shore of the narrow inlet and knocking several troopers over the side. Only the shallow water prevented their heavy body armor from becoming a death sentence.

The sound wave followed by a full thirty seconds, giving Rorke time to call a warning, and the men cowered in the boats with their hands over their ears. The wait seemed interminable, and when the sound wave hit, it was like nothing any of them had ever experienced and seemed to go on forever, a sound so powerful it seemed to physically pummel them.

When it subsided, Rorke was unsurprised he was unable to raise Reaper on the radio. He was nothing if not a realist, and he knew the MOT was gone; he only hoped some of his force had survived.

This latest unwelcome development meant his own operation was even more critical. He'd need the ammo more than ever now, and he was damned sure going to get it. He motioned his man to move his boat ashore and he got out and worked his way through the brush to where his lookout crouched peering downstream. The man looked up as Rorke settled beside him.

"I was just about to call you, General. Those Coast Guard pukes just came around the bend, so the rest of 'em probably aren't far behind," the man said.

Task Force Shopping Cart
Cape Fear River
Just Downstream of Keg Island

Josh Wright uncovered his ears and shook his head, still unsteady from the effects of the distant blast. Despite expecting it and briefing both their own troops and the freed captives on protecting themselves, the magnitude of the forces involved was beyond belief. He hoped the Coasties who'd just rounded the bend ahead of them had been prepared.

"I guess the major's booby trap worked," he said.

Randall Ewing shook his head, preoccupied as he peered through a forward wheelhouse window now spider-webbed with cracks and almost opaque. "If I'd known it was gonna be that big, I'd have busted out the windows ahead of time. I can't see."

"Let's see if we can improve that," Wright said, removing a fire extinguisher from its rack and moving forward to slam it against the cracked and weakened glass of the front window. The glass yielded and dropped out of the window in sheets onto the foredeck below.

"Good enough?" he asked when he'd cleared a sizable hole.

Ewing nodded. "Yeah. I can see as much as I'm gonna see stuck here between the barges. I just wish —"

Ewing was cut off mid-sentence as all hell broke loose just out of sight around the bend ahead.

Keg Island
Cape Fear River

Rorke smiled as he saw the Coast Guard boats, spread apart with one slightly ahead of the other. It was a good deployment, where each boat could support the other, but the channel was narrower here, which was why Rorke had chosen this spot. No matter how far the boats spread out, both must pass close to his hidden fleet. After he took out the Coasties, the barges and towboats became a much softer target.

His men were mercenaries accustomed to fighting in shit holes worldwide with the weapons at hand, which was why they favored the more familiar, if less accurate RPGs. But that didn't really matter; he planned to hit the Coasties so fast and with such an overwhelming force they stood no chance. He watched from the brush as the Coasties chugged forward, heads on swivels and scanning for threats—except behind them.

They were a hundred yards past the inlet when his boats glided silently out on electric trolling motors and lined up behind their slow-moving prey. They managed to close the distance significantly before one of the Coasties, a woman, looked back and raised the alarm. It was her death warrant.

Surprise was complete as Rorke's men opened up at near point-blank range, shredding the boats with machine-gun fire even before they hit them with multiple RPGs, blowing them to bits and throwing their now lifeless occupants into the fast-moving river, never to be seen again.

Rorke smiled at how efficiently they'd dealt with the primary threat. This was going to be even easier than he thought. He raced back to his boat and moved into the channel, waving his hand in a circle above his head and then pointing downriver, turning his force toward the approaching barges just as they rounded the distant bend.

His smile turned into a confused frown as he studied the approaching craft. He'd expected two boats pushing two barges each. Indeed, his greatest worry had been they might separate and go on either side of the island, forcing him to split his force.

His frown deepened as he closed the distance. The tow was made up with both tugboats sandwiched between the barges, no doubt limiting their own visibility but almost eliminating their target profiles. Rorke cursed. The tugs could only be attacked from straight ahead or straight astern, and he had absolutely no doubt the defenders had machine guns set up to protect those lanes of approach. He raised his radio.

"All boats, listen up. Machine-gun-equipped boats divide into two groups, five per side. Your job is to run at the enemy and lay down suppressing fire to allow the RPG-equipped boats to attack the tugs. RPG-equipped boats, I want you to target the lead tugboat between the barges, but DO NOT, REPEAT, DO NOT put an RPG into one of those containers. Keep your RPG shots low, near the waterline. We'll complete a run from ahead, then go past them and swing around using the same tactic from astern, this time targeting the rear boat. After we knock those tugs out, the river will do the rest. Acknowledge," Rorke said.

One by one, his boats acknowledged, and Rorke ordered his driver to slow and move closer to the riverbank as he raised his radio again. "Execute," he said into the mic, and watched his boats roar past before he retreated to the relative safety of the mouth of the inlet.

Task Force Shopping Cart
Cape Fear River
Abreast of Keg Island

Josh Wright lay prone on the top of the container, heat from the sunbaked steel burning his legs and stomach despite the layer of cardboard they'd scrounged from the tugboats. The rest of his riflemen were similarly positioned around the top of the containers, where they could fire down on the approaching boats and present less of a target. He'd positioned their four machine guns at the four corners of the tow; they were more exposed there, but it couldn't be helped, they had to defend the towboats at all costs.

Wright spoke into his radio. "Wright to Hill. How you coming? Over."

"Still working at it," came Hill's voice over the radio. "I can see the crates but can't get to 'em yet. Soon. Over."

NOW *would be good*, Wright thought, but he didn't voice it. He knew Hill was working as fast as he possibly could. He looked back forward to see the approaching boats fanning out, rooster tails of water rising in their wakes as they sped toward him. He spoke into his radio again.

"Get ready, boys and girls; here they come!"

***

Rorke's boats raced toward the raiders, machine guns rattling as the defenders returned fire. There were muzzle flashes all along the tops of the containers, which he realized were riflemen, and true to their orders, his troops targeted the container tops in an attempt to suppress that fire.

Covered by their comrades, the boats carrying the RPGs rushed straight down the center, intent on disabling the lead tug. They'd just come within range when machine guns on the barges opened up, alerting the attackers to their presence for the first time by riddling the lead boat before it managed to fire an RPG. The boat veered off full speed at a crazy angle, its crew dead.

Two of the remaining boats got off RPGs; one blew a massive hole in the front end of one of the barges right at the waterline, but the second hit the lead tug dead center, just below the wheelhouse. The crew of the successful boat paid with their lives as the machine guns on the corners of the barges cut them to pieces before they could get out of range.

Rorke smiled, not even upset the other RPG boats abandoned the attack to join the others to sweep downriver past the barges at high speed. He picked up his radio to order them to regroup and attack from astern.

Task Force Shopping Cart
Cape Fear River
Abreast of Keg Island

Randall Ewing winced as the RPGs hit the front of the tow, obliterating the upper superstructure of the tug M/V *Mighty Mite*. He reached for the mic.

"*Linda Lou* to *Mighty Mite*. You okay up there, Scott? Over."

"I am apart from havin' to clean out my pants. What the hell was that? Over," replied Scott McFarland, the engineer on the lead tug.

"Our friends from the SRF just gave you a haircut. I think that … hold one. Over," Ewing said and studied his compass.

The tow was swinging to starboard and he gave it left rudder to compensate. He felt the vessel shudder as the engines, already near their max with the cumbersome towing configuration, loaded up even more. The forward barge on the starboard side was settling lower, almost imperceptibly, but obvious to his seaman's eye.

The answer came to him quickly; the starboard barge was taking on water and likely a lot of it. If she was holed at the waterline, the forward motion of the tow would be scooping water into the hole even faster than if it were free-flooding. How far she would settle was anyone's guess, with no way to tell how many compartments had been breached. He keyed the mic again.

"*Linda Lou* to *Mighty Mite*. We're developing a major drag on the starboard side. I need you to lock your rudder to port to compensate. Can you do it? Over."

"I … I guess so. How much? Over."

Ewing looked down at his own rudder angle indicator. "Try ten degrees. Over."

There was a pause before the response. "That's gonna be like pushing a barn door against this current, Cap. Over."

"I understand, Scott. I need you to do it. Over," Ewing said.

"I'm on it," McFarland said.

***

Rorke raised his binoculars and watched his boats re-forming downstream, worried about their resolve. They'd gone in like gangbusters on the initial assault, but they'd lost two of the RPG-equipped boats and one of the machine-gun boats. He knew this rabble; the quite reasonable and acceptable losses of three out of eighteen boats would make them all much less enthusiastic.

He turned his binoculars back on the tow; it had slowed perceptibly. *Had they actually taken out the lead tug?* He didn't think so, as there was no decrease in the throb of the engine noise; if anything, the noise had increased, as if both tugs were working harder. Rorke studied the tow more closely, assessing the damage. The damaged barge was riding lower in the water, noticeable even at this distance. The area of impact was mostly below the water now, a ragged hole in the front of the barge, scooping up water as it was pushed forward.

Would it sink completely? Probably not if there were other tanks still intact, but as the front sank, the barge would become more difficult to push against this current. He smiled as he realized the implications. It didn't matter exactly what his RPGs hit, as long as it was at the waterline at the front of the tow. That was a much easier target, allowing his RPG boats to engage at a greater range without running the gauntlet of the raiders' machine guns. He raised his radio.

***

Josh Wright flinched as the machine-gun rounds tore through the steel of the container just below him. The SRF boats were hugging the riverbanks on either side, flying past the slow-moving tow at maximum distance, their machine guns blazing as they headed back upriver. Next to him Donny Gibson muttered a curse.

"What the hell are they doing?" Gibson asked. "I figured for sure they'd have a run at us from the back."

"I don't know," Wright said, "but I don't like the looks of it."

He shot a worried glance at the barge across the gap. The forward end was now riding at least two feet lower than the barge he was on, and the entire tow was moving much slower. Something was up for sure.

He switched his gaze back to the speeding SRF boats and watched, puzzled, as some of the boats from each group broke ranks to cut across the tow's course on converging diagonal courses, zigzagging to present more difficult targets for the machine gunners. Suddenly the boats launched a barrage of RPGs, seemingly not aimed at the *Mighty Mite*, but at the front of the tow in general. Explosions vibrated through the steel as fireballs and plumes of water erupted from the front of both barges.

What the hell?

"*Linda Lou* to Wright. Do you copy? Over."

Wright raised his radio. "I copy, *Linda Lou*. What's happening? Over."

"They're chewing the hell out of the front of the barges right at the waterline. We're taking on water badly, and our forward motion is just making us scoop up more. The heavier we get in front, the more water we take on. We've already lost over half our speed and this tow will soon be too heavy to push against this current. Over."

"Do the best you can, Captain. We'll try to get 'em off you. Over," Wright said.

"Soon would be good. *Linda Lou* out," Ewing said.

Wright keyed his mic. "Wright to Hill. We need those AT4s. Over."

When Hill answered, Wright could hear him panting from exertion. "Just got the first batch of 'em on deck. Send your shooters down to grab 'em and I'll wrestle some more out of the container. Over."

Wright looked over at Donny Gibson, who was already crawling across the top of the container to the inboard edge. Wright turned away from Gibson and barked an order into his radio, then turned back to watch as across the tops of the containers, others crawled to the inboard container edges, gripped the tops of the containers, then rolled over the sides, hanging by their fingers and extending their bodies full length before letting go and dropping the last foot or so to the deck of the barge below.

It was time to fight fire with fire.

CHAPTER EIGHTEEN

Task Force Shopping Cart
Cape Fear River
Abreast of Keg Island

When Colonel Hunnicutt had made up his 'shopping list' for the raid on the MOT, he was fully aware the recent victory provided only a temporary respite. He knew they might face choppers again, and that the success of their unconventional 'line-gun defense' had been a onetime event based on surprise and thus unlikely to be repeated.

Of course, the Barretts were formidable defensive weapons, but he really wanted more tools in his toolbox, and was pleased when Jerry Hill alerted him to a substantial number of *Rocket Launchers, M136 AT4, 84 mm, lightweight, self-contained, antiarmor,* or commonly called AT4s in the inventory of the MOT. Though developed as an infantry weapon to take out enemy armor, they'd proved to be a relatively effective anti-helicopter weapon as well, and Hunnicutt wanted some.

The problem was they were onetime use weapons and, in their shipping containers, took up the space of several cases of equally vital small-arms ammunition. He'd compromised at twenty AT4s, because as he said to Wright, if they faced a chopper assault that required the use of more than twenty rockets, it was probably all over anyway.

Now faced with the task of getting ANY of the 'liberated' stores safely back to Fort Box, Wright made a command decision. If the AT4s worked on tanks and choppers, he figured they'd work just fine against boats. He looked over the edge of the container to the deck of the barge below where, out of sight from the river, Hill was stacking the last of their meager store of AT4s, surrounded by the five men with the most AT4 experience. Beside them were two more men to help Hill pass the shooters more rockets as they needed them.

He hung his head over the container and called down to them, "All right, I want y'all to stay out of sight until they're committed and within range. We'll only be able to surprise them once, so don't hold back. When I give the word, pop out and pour it on. We need to take out as many as possible on the first pass. And spread out and be careful of the back blasts. I don't want y'all killing each other. Clear?"

There were nods and 'oorahs' from the group and Wright scooted on his belly back from the edge of the container and looked upriver. The boats were some distance away, circling and preparing for another run, seemingly with more confidence now that they could attack 'free form' and weren't restricted to a tight, and predictable, formation.

He looked back down at the barges and frowned. The tow was hardly moving now, and the forward ends of both barges were only a few feet above the surface of the river with a noticeable incline from the back of the barges to the front. Wright wondered briefly if they'd be able to get the tow to Fort Box even if they defeated their attackers.

This was it. If the SRF boats inflicted any more damage, the tow would be unable to continue, and from the looks of it, they were about to be subjected to another hard frontal assault. He made another decision and spoke into his radio.

"Wright to machine gunners aft, bring your guns forward on the double and set up with the other guns on the bows of the barges. All riflemen, deploy forward as well. The boats will be zigzagging and we don't have time for aimed shots. Stack all your spare mags by your side and I want everyone firing full-auto on my mark. Let's make sure they run into a wall of lead. Wright out."

He pushed his doubt down and focused his gaze laser-like at the enemy before him, hoping he'd read the situation correctly.

**

Rorke was elated. His stratagem had confused the defenders on the barge completely and all of his boats had survived the last run without casualties. More to the point, all six of the remaining RPG-equipped boats had launched their missiles and three had achieved hits. The fronts of both lead barges were now twisted masses of metal, rapidly sinking deeper in the water as the tow plowed ever more slowly upriver.

But this wasn't the time to slack off. One more run should finish her off. He raised his radio.

"Thunderbolt Actual to all boats. You've done a good job, but we need one more run at maximum effort. I want EVERY boat fully engaged, with the RPG boats staying in the fight until you've used every round you have. There will be bonuses for those of you who perform to expectations." Rorke paused. "And punishment for those who do not."

He waited a moment to let that sink in and then continued. "Hit them now. Hit them hard, and let's finish this!"

He smiled as he heard cheers sounding across the water, then saw rooster tails of water behind his boats as they accelerated toward their target, a confused mass of zigzagging boats, the RPG boats mixed with the ones carrying machine guns.

They were all idiots, of course, but at times like this he did feel a certain affection for them.

**

Wright watched the approaching boats with an almost surreal calm, compartmentalizing his fear and doubt, and turning his considerable intelligence to a detached analysis. There was a downside to being the defender; both the RPGs and the AT4s had roughly equal maximum effective ranges of three hundred yards and he had to risk letting the RPGs within that range before his own AT4s could take them out. Therefore he couldn't throw up his 'wall of lead' until the boats with the RPGs were fairly close. He was forced to hold his fire while, under no similar restraint, the attackers' boats were already well within machine-gun range and blazing away.

Fortunately without effect. Few rounds were even hitting the barges. As expected.

It had come to him earlier as he'd watched the boats zigzag; the same defensive tactic that made them truly difficult targets also greatly lessened the accuracy of their fire. Arranged in two lines running down both sides of the tow, the massed fire from ten machine guns HAD been somewhat effective, but it also meant their course was predictable, and allowed the barge gunners to take out one of the boats.

During the second attack, the boats carrying the machine guns adopted the zigzag tactic, but it wasn't that which resulted in success but the complete surprise they'd achieved by 're-attacking' the bow of the tow when all the defenders were anticipating an attack astern.

Believing their zigzag maneuver successful, the attackers were now using it on their final assault, and the boats were anything but stable gun platforms as they repeatedly bounced across each other's wakes at high speed. Nor was their fire as intense, being intermittent now rather than constant, repeatedly paused to avoid friendly fire as the boats crossed back and forth in front of each other.

Even the RPG-equipped boats were zigzagging, and Wright knew these guys were going to have to get MUCH closer than three hundred yards to fire their RPGs. All he had to do was let them.

He smiled. The SRF pukes in the boats probably thought the lack of return fire was a good thing. *Well, surprise, surprise!* he thought.

Conversely, the ponderous, slow-moving barges were not bouncing at all and were much more stable firing platforms. Both the RPGs and the AT4s were manually targeted weapons, relying on the skill of the operator, and Wright was intent on giving his guys every advantage. The biggest challenge was judging the optimal time to strike, and then staying still, out of sight, waiting for it as he listened to rounds clang against the steel with increasing frequency. The fire from the boats might be inaccurate, but there was still a LOT of it.

"Uh … Lieutenant? Shouldn't we, you know, shoot back?" the man beside him asked.

Wright ignored the man and peeked over the edge of the container. He judged the attackers to be a bit over three hundred yards away and forced himself to wait, counting to five slowly before raising his radio.

"Machine guns and riflemen, open fire. Repeat! Machine guns and riflemen, open fire! AT4s, hold your fire to the count of three, then let them have it!" Wright said into the radio.

Across the front of the barges, shooters fired from various places of concealment, four machine guns and almost forty M4s on full auto, sending Wright's 'wall of lead' toward the attackers. Fire from the SRF boats all but ceased just as the AT4 shooters stepped around the corner of a container and deployed themselves in a line, sending five rockets into the line of attackers, not waiting to distinguish which boats carried RPGs.

Two of the rockets were direct hits, while the other three were near misses, but still close enough for the resulting explosions to overturn the boats and dump their occupants into the fast-moving water, where their heavy body armor sealed their fates.

Momentum rather than courage carried the stunned attackers forward, increasing their rate of fire as almost a survival reflex. One of the machine guns to Wright's left fell silent as an SRF machine gunner stitched the position; then he too fell dead a second later as the man beside Wright shot him in the throat. Forgetting his instructions, an SRF trooper fired an RPG at the men wielding the AT4s, but it went high, soaring over their heads to explode far downriver.

The attack disintegrated as boats in front turned to flee and ran into boats piloted by less quick-thinking men behind them. Another salvo of five rockets tore into the center of the confused mass, obliterating three boats and overturning three more. The four remaining boats somehow worked their way free and turned to flee.

"Shred 'em," Wright said into his radio and the combined firepower on the barges targeted the fleeing boats.

One boat overturned as Donny Gibson targeted it at extreme range with an AT4, and two veered off at crazy angles, running toward the riverbanks at full speed with dead drivers slumped at the controls. The last boat sped away with only the driver still alive and was almost out of range when Wright heard a familiar throaty growl coming from downriver.

"Hold your fire," he said into his radio. "We got friendlies coming in."

"Alpha to Shopping Cart. I thought you might need a hand. Over," came Kinsey's voice over the radio.

"Alpha, you're just in time. We got a runner and I expect the colonel could use the intel. Think you can collect him for us? Over," Wright said.

"Consider it done. It looks like you're in pretty rough shape. Can you make it back to Fort Box? Over."

Before Wright could answer, Captain Randall Ewing's voice came over the radio. "Don't worry about us. We'll get her home. Over."

"See you there, then. Alpha out."

✳✳✳

Rorke watched from the inlet, elation turning to despair as the defenders on the barge annihilated his little flotilla. There was no choice now; he had to lie low and let them pass. He turned to his boat driver.

"Quick! Pull back into the inlet out of sight! Do it NOW!"

The driver did as ordered, and when they were well out of sight from the main channel, they tied up the boat. Rorke motioned for his man to follow and swiftly made his way through the brush to his earlier observation post. He parted the brush carefully to reveal a scene that sent him into a fresh rage. The sole survivor of his attack force was speeding upriver with a Coast Guard patrol boat in hot pursuit. The fleeing boat was obviously shot up and moving at less than full speed and the patrol boat was rapidly overtaking it.

He let out a stream of obscenities. "Take out the driver," he said to the man next to him.

"It's a long shot. Maybe I should wait until our guy leads them closer," the man said.

"OUR GUY is who I'm talking about, you idiot! He's leading them right to the inlet, and even if they catch him before he gets here, do you honestly think he's not going to give us up? Now DO IT!" Rorke said.

"But if I fire, they'll know we're here —"

"But not exactly where, and the fire will be coming from the shore. They'll hesitate offshore, trying to determine the source and the strength of the opposition. While they're trying to decide, we haul ass out of the inlet and around the north end of the island. We can head downstream, keeping the island between us and them," Rorke said.

"Won't they just follow us?"

Rorke shook his head. "Probably not. They need to get that ammo home and we're a single boat and no longer a threat. Faced with a chase, they'll probably break off. UNLESS they figure out right away we're only one boat and they have us bottled up in the inlet. Then they'll stay to finish the job and maybe call in help, especially if our friend running away out there tells them it's me."

The man nodded and raised his M4, and Rorke focused his binoculars on the fleeing boat just as the rifle barked beside him. He gave a satisfied grunt as the escaping man slumped at the wheel and the boat veered back toward the center of the channel. He swung the binoculars back toward the pursuing patrol boat to assess their reaction.

There were two men in the boat, both wearing the black utilities of the SRF. The man in the bow was Caucasian, with binoculars pressed to his eyes, studying the boat they were chasing. Through the window of the patrol boat's tiny wheelhouse, he could see the driver was a black mountain of a man. Rorke recognized them, even at a distance; Luke Kinsey and the ever-loyal Washington. A chill ran down Rorke's spine.

This changed everything.

It was personal now. Even without the fleeing survivor to identify him, if Kinsey and Washington saw a single boat fleeing, they'd likely put two and two together. If they thought they had the slightest chance to capture or kill him, mission notwithstanding, Rorke knew this pair would follow him to the ends of the earth. He didn't like the odds of fleeing downriver in an open boat with a faster boat and expert marksman on his tail.

Rorke kept the binoculars to his eyes, watching as Kinsey turned to scan the shoreline of the island with his own binoculars before turning to say something to Washington. The boat began to slow.

"Take out the men in the patrol boat," he said.

"They're out of range. Besides, I thought you said —"

Rorke let his binoculars fall and jerked the M4 out of his underling's grasp.

"Change of plan," he said as he raised the rifle to his shoulder. He'd take out the driver first to keep them from moving out of range.

***

Luke Kinsey saw the man slump at the wheel and heard the gunshot across the water, barely audible over the roar of the patrol boat's powerful outboards. He raised his binoculars and studied the fleeing boat as, driverless, it veered off toward the middle of the channel. He turned his glasses toward the island for a quick scan and saw nothing, then lowered them and turned back toward the little wheelhouse and called to Washington.

"Someone shot him from ashore. Stop the boat before we get too close and let's figure out what we're dealing with."

Washington nodded and pulled back the throttles, slowing the boat abruptly just as the wheelhouse window shattered with a loud crack and a heartbeat later the sound of a gunshot echoed across the water. Luke was ducking as he moved and thought he heard a bullet whine by his own ear as he dropped down behind the wheelhouse and crawled through the door.

He found Washington sprawled on the floor, dazed but conscious, his right shoulder bloody where a bullet had penetrated outside the area protected by his body armor. Blood spurted from the wound with each beat of the big man's heart.

Brachial artery, Luke thought.

Another round shattered a side window of the wheelhouse, followed quickly by a three-round burst that ripped through the fiberglass bulkhead of the little wheelhouse. The shooter was firing blind now, seemingly intent on just ripping the hell out of the wheelhouse, with the sure and certain knowledge he'd take out everyone inside it.

Luke grabbed Washington's left hand and put his fingertips on the wound. "Press there hard and hold it, Washington. Do you understand?"

He got a groggy nod from Washington and then forced himself to ignore his friend to focus on the problem at hand. He had to get them out of range or they were both dead anyway. He crawled over Washington to kneel beside the wheel, then reached up and pushed both the throttles forward without exposing himself, just as a three-round burst ripped through the fiberglass of the little cabin and stitched him across his chest. He gasped as the rounds impacted against the armor, transferring their energy to him like gut punches, as he turned the wheel to take the boat directly away from shore. As the boat picked up speed, Luke dropped to the deck, reaching up with one hand to hold the bottom of the wheel steady as more rounds tore through the wheelhouse bulkheads. He looked over to find Washington unconscious with blood pulsing from the shoulder wound.

It seemed like forever before the rounds quit shredding the wheelhouse and Luke released the wheel and pulled the throttles back. The little boat bobbed and wallowed as her stern wake overtook them, and Luke struggled to stay upright on his knees as he stripped off his armor and utilities, to rip his tee shirt off his body. Blood covered the wheelhouse deck now, and Washington's dark skin had faded to an ashen gray.

"Hang in there, Washington. You're gonna make it. That's an order by God," Luke said as he folded the sweaty tee shirt into a rough compress and clamped it on the wound with one hand while he took off his web belt with the other. He fastened the belt around Washington's arm but left enough slack to twist it, forcing the compress tight against the wound before he tied it off.

Satisfied he'd done all he could, Luke stood and keyed his radio.

"Kinsey to Shopping Cart and Base. Washington has been hit. Repeat. Washington has been hit. I'm returning to base. ETA ten minutes. Repeat. I'm RTB with ETA of ten mikes. He will need blood. Repeat. Washington will need blood. Please have Dr. Jennings standing by. Kinsey out," Luke said.

He rammed the throttle forward and spun the wheel to drive the patrol boat upriver as fast as he could, mumbling a prayer it would be fast enough.

His radio crackled and he heard Randall Ewing's voice, thick with emotion. "Godspeed, Luke."

Fort Box
Wilmington Container Terminal
Wilmington, North Carolina

Just Before Sunset (Six Hours Later)

Hunnicutt stood on the deck of the *Maersk Tangier*, gazing downstream at the approaching tow. It was in one sense a sorry sight. All the barges were riddled with bullet holes, and two were listing at odd angles, with ends that were masses of twisted and mangled steel. The wheelhouse of the *M/V Mighty Mite*, or rather where the wheelhouse had been, was nothing but blackened wreckage and the tug itself little more than a hull with an engine, an engine that was running nonetheless. The *M/V Linda Lou* was a bit more presentable, but there was no glass in her wheelhouse windows. The whole strange lash-up looked in danger of sinking at any minute.

And well it might have, had it not been for the skill of Randall Ewing. After the onslaught, he'd judged the tow too shot up to continue safely and pushed the whole thing into the bank to prevent the damaged barges from sinking farther. There he'd called for pumps and material from Fort Box, which had been sent immediately. He patched the worst of the holes with hydraulic cement, pumped some of the water out of the barges to lighten them, and then reversed the barges in the tow so the mangled ends were at the rear rather than acting as scoops to suck up more water.

Only then had he deemed the barges and their cargo of precious ammunition sufficiently seaworthy to complete the seven-mile journey to Fort Box. Hunnicutt smiled at the recollection of the most recent radio response from Ewing, after he'd tactfully suggested that perhaps the old seaman was being overly cautious.

"With all due respect, Colonel," Ewing had responded, "I haven't lost a vessel on this river in over thirty years of piloting and I'll be damned if I let one sink on me a few miles from the dock. We'll move when I think we're ready to move and not before."

And true to Ewing's word, the tow was in sight, and to a relieved Hunnicutt, it was a thing of beauty, almost stately as it moved slowly up the river in the fading light of day.

Hunnicutt heard footsteps behind him and turned to see Luke Kinsey approaching.

"How's the patient?" Hunnicutt asked.

Luke smiled. "Claiming he's hungry, so he must be on the mend. Dr. Jennings repaired the artery and says he'll be right as rain in no time. And thank you, sir. For the blood, I mean."

Hunnicutt laughed. "Five minutes after you radioed in, the word had spread and every person left in the fort volunteered to donate. I had to pull rank to put myself at the head of the shortlist of folks with type O."

His smile faded. "Seriously, Luke, I was concerned. We've lost so many, the folks in the first attack, then Mike Butler and the others in the chopper assault, the two Coastie boat crews and the machine gunner on your own mission . . ."

He trailed off, unable to continue for a moment. When he continued, there was resolve in his voice. "I damn sure wasn't going to lose Washington, especially not to a sucker punch when the fight was over."

Luke nodded. "My thoughts exactly, sir."

They fell silent, watching the tow approach. They could make out Wright and Hill standing side by side on the lead barge, casting long shadows in the fading light. Farther back, Randall Ewing's face was framed in the glassless wheelhouse window.

"Well, Major," Hunnicutt said softly, "you led the charge with near empty rifles, managed to engage and take out over twenty times your own number, and secured our ammunition stocks while denying the enemy his own. When I named this operation Little Round Top, it was based more on hope than expectations, but damned if you didn't live up to the name. I expect ole Joshua Lawrence Chamberlain would be proud. I sure as hell am. Well done, Luke."

CHAPTER NINETEEN

Presidential Office
Laurel Lodge
Camp David Complex
Maryland

Same Day - Same Time

President Oliver Armstrong Crawford glared at Rorke across the coffee table, struggling to contain his temper. The man had come directly from 'the fight,' as he called it, though from Crawford's perspective 'rout' was a more apt description. Rorke was still in his black utilities and smelled of rank sweat — and something else — fear perhaps? Crawford suppressed a smirk in spite of the circumstances. It was about time something took the cocky bastard down a peg, though it was unfortunate it took the loss of irreplaceable resources to do it.

But every event had an upside, and Oliver Armstrong Crawford was all about upsides. He'd built his career on spinning often disastrous circumstances into positive outcomes and this was no different. The forces at this so-called Fort Box had clearly crossed the line from simple defense to armed aggression against the government of the United States, which, ironically, made eliminating them considerably less complicated, at least politically.

He let Rorke stew a bit longer before he broke the tense silence.

"So let me get this straight, Rorke. Over two engagements you lost your entire force to enemy fire or desertion, against a cobbled-together bunch of misfits who were low on ammunition and using improvised weapons. Is that about the size of it?"

Rorke shifted uncomfortably in his chair. "Yeah, but —"

Crawford's eyes narrowed. "Yeah? Yeah, General? Why don't we try a 'Yes, Mr. President'?"

Rorke unconsciously straightened. "Yes, Mr. President. But I didn't anticipate either the sniper rifles or —"

Crawford let out a mirthless laugh. "Or anything frigging else from the looks of it. These guys played you like a fine violin. However, you have been consistently right about one thing, this is a job for the regular military, and I'm bringing them in on this now. We'll rid ourselves of this Fort Box once and for all."

"Will they go for it? Military action against US citizens, I mean. It's against both the law and tradition —"

Crawford shook his head. "The brass can't hide behind the Posse Comitatus Act any longer. This is no longer a matter of law enforcement. These people are clearly in armed rebellion against the lawful government of the United States. I'm on firm legal ground here and I'm also now Commander in Chief. It's no longer a matter of cajoling them or encouraging their cooperation. I'm the President; the military HAS to follow my orders on this now."

Rorke nodded. "All right. What do you want me to do?"

Crawford steepled his fingertips under his chin, feigning deep contemplation. He sighed somewhat theatrically and shook his head. "I'm afraid, General, that I no longer have need of your services —"

Rorke's transformation was immediate, no longer the groveling underling. "Now wait just a friggin' minute, Crawford! Remember, we're both in this together. You NEED me and the SRF."

Crawford's face hardened. "Once again, you forget yourself, General. And yes, I DID need the SRF, or at least I thought I did. But if you can't even safeguard your own established bases, then I'm afraid I'll have to take my chances with the regular military. Besides, I've sensed much less resistance and more respect from the regular military in just the short time since I assumed the office, and I already have some followers among—"

"I warned you the SRF mercenaries weren't attack troops, but you insisted on attacking anyway. You're equally responsible for this mess, Crawford."

Crawford took a deep breath and contained his temper, choosing to ignore Rorke's continued disrespect. "Be that as it may, General Rorke, as I said, I no longer have need of your services—"

"So that's it? You're just kicking me to the curb?"

Crawford could contain himself no longer. "You're damn right I'm kicking you loose. And after this last debacle, consider yourself lucky I don't make you disappear."

Rorke glared back at Crawford for a long moment and then leaned back in his chair, a smile on his lips. "Yeah, well, I'm afraid it's not quite that easy, *Mr. President.*" Rorke sneered as he said the title. "Are you forgetting I know, quite literally, where all the bodies are buried? I took the liberty of recording our recent chats regarding the unfortunate demise of the former president and cabinet members. Should anything happen to me, those recordings will be distributed as necessary."

Crawford scoffed. "Distributed how? Via the media? There IS no more media and I control the Emergency Alert System. What will you do, have the info sent to a few ham operators? Recordings are easy to fake, and half the ham operators are wacko conspiracy theorists anyway. They've been spreading those types of rumors, or worse, for months, so your posthumous 'great revelation' will just be more noise. At this point the public, what there is left of it, only cares about their own safety and getting enough to eat."

Rorke's smile lost none of its confidence. "Who said anything about the public? I was thinking more in terms of the Joint Chiefs and a dozen other high-ranking military officers. Even in their current rather reduced circumstances, I think they'll have sufficient resources to confirm the authenticity of the recordings. Just how long do you think they'll support a president who murdered his way into office?"

Crawford's face purpled. "Those recordings implicate you too."

Rorke laughed. "I'll be dead, remember? Do you actually think I care about my reputation?"

Rorke continued, but having made his point, he reverted to a more respectful tone. "But it doesn't have to come to that, Mr. President. Despite this latest setback, the SRF is still a potent force ready to serve you in many ways the regular military can't or won't. Use the military boys for the heavy lifting and me and my SRF as your private security force. You'll still need a force that knows all your secrets and is willing to back you anyway."

For a price, of course, Crawford thought as he contemplated the situation. Rorke had him, at least for the moment, and Crawford was smart enough to realize that without letting his ego get in the way. He nodded.

"All right. Point taken," he said. "I'll give you another shot, but I'm warning you, recordings or no recordings, don't screw up again."

Rorke smiled. "I live to serve, Mr. President."

Crawford ignored the sarcasm. "This Texas group appears to have the potential for being almost as big a thorn in our side as Wilmington. Unfortunately, they haven't accommodated us by attacking government forces, so we can't make a legitimate case for the military intervention. What's their status?"

"Gerard was looking at using escaped cons as surrogates, but I've been a bit preoccupied with Wilmington; I haven't had a recent update."

"Well, GET updated," Crawford said. "As a matter of fact, I'll arrange a plane. Fly down and take charge personally. I'll press the military boys to take out Wilmington ASAP, and let's wipe this Texas group out at the same time. If these two places fall in a one-two punch, I think the other organized groups will get the message."

"Our intel on this Texas group is a bit sketchy. They appear to have ties to Wilmington, but their main problems have been with the cons. They may surrender if we surround them with SRF troops and promise amnesty and protection from the cons," Rorke said.

Crawford shook his head. "That's the last thing we want. If they have ties with Wilmington, they may understand the real situation there. If they do, how do you think they'll react to their friends being wiped out? Even if they cooperate now, they'll likely change their minds. We've been too easy on these groups anyway. It made no difference in the beginning, but we have to make them understand that resistance will not be tolerated. If we have to crush a few to set an example, so be it. Is that clear, General?"

Rorke stood. "Absolutely, Mr. President. I'm on it. I'll leave for Texas right away."

Crawford pushed an intercom button on his desk.

"Yes, Mr. President," replied a female voice.

"Connie, please arrange General Rorke a plane to Houston, priority one," Crawford said into the intercom. "And when you've done that, come in, please."

"Right away, Mr. President," Connie said.

Crawford waved Rorke toward the door and, when he'd left, rose and walked to the window to gaze out over the grounds. He was still standing there, hands clasped behind his back, when he heard the door open softly behind him.

"You wanted to see me, Mr. President?" she said from the office door.

Crawford turned. "Have those morons got the video-conferencing setup working yet?"

"No, sir. I'm sorry, but it's still down. Would you like me to call for another update?"

"No, don't bother. Send word to Secretary Murray, Admirals Whiteley and Wright, and General Mitchell to get here ASAP. Arrange choppers as necessary with top priority. I want them all here in three hours, tops," Crawford said.

"At once, Mr. President. Will there be anything else, sir?"

Crawford shook his head and the woman left, closing the office door behind her. *And now,* thought Crawford, *we'll see just how much resistance I get from these brass hats.*

He turned back to the large office window with its picturesque view of the Camp David grounds. It was his favorite view, calming somehow. *President Crawford!* He smiled. The solar flares were a tragedy for many, but it was all about survival of the fittest, wasn't it? And for Oliver Armstrong Crawford, the ultimate survivor, the event was the opportunity of a lifetime.

President of the United States! He said it aloud and let it roll off his tongue. There would be ups and downs and challenges of course, but he'd paid his dues in full, and no one could control him now! He was the most powerful man in the world, or what was left of it anyway.

He felt a familiar thirst, long suppressed, and by reflex fought it down with an almost feral look at the ornate walnut sideboard against the office wall. Gleason had been a confirmed bourbon drinker, and there was a crystal decanter of the amber liquid sitting on the sideboard with a tray of squat, heavy glasses. Crawford left it there as proof it no longer had power over him, just as he'd kept whiskey in all his previous offices. He'd even played the good host and served his guests drinks from time to time, willing his hands not to shake as he poured the liquor and passed out the glasses, leaving his own untouched as others drank.

Nothing controlled Oliver Armstrong Crawford. He'd mastered not only his own urges but bent an entire nation to his will. As he stood there savoring victory, he had another thought. What could be more fitting to demonstrate his complete victory over all his foes than a demonstration of absolute power over his personal demon?

A congratulatory drink was in order. One drink and no more, to confirm to himself his iron will and make his victory complete over ALL things. He walked to the sideboard, and his hands didn't tremble as he poured two fingers of whiskey into the short glass. It went down smooth, like a conversation with an old friend, and he felt the warmth starting in the pit of his stomach and spreading up through his chest. He closed his eyes and savored it for a long moment before returning to the window, glass in hand. He smiled as he looked out. The good times were just beginning, at least for him.

Conference Room
Laurel Lodge
Camp David Complex
Maryland

Same Day - Three Hours Later

"What about one of those big bombs? The M something?" Crawford asked.

A single civilian and three men in uniform exchanged looks, clearly taken aback by the suggestion. No one spoke for a long moment until the civilian cleared his throat.

"Do you mean the MOAB, Mr. President?" asked the Secretary of the Navy, Brian Murray.

"That's it. The MOAB. That would take them out, right?" Crawford confirmed.

Murray shook his head. "Well, yes, but I hardly think—"

"A MOAB would kill everyone in the fort, including the women and children, and very likely a large percentage of the people left in the city of Wilmington as well, to say nothing of the possibility of igniting the petroleum terminal next door," interjected Admiral Sam Wright, Commander, US Fleet Forces.

The lone army man in the room spoke. "Mr. President, I know Doug Hunnicutt and despite what's happened, I believe he can be persuaded to lay down his arms. If we can just speak to—"

Crawford slapped the table and glared at the general as the sound reverberated off the walls. "ABSOLUTELY NOT! The time for talking is past. You are not to contact these people under any circumstances. Is that clear?"

"But surely, Mr. President," Admiral Wright said, "if they surrender—"

Crawford cut him off with a glare. "Is that the game you want to play, Admiral? We let traitors attack us, kill our people, kidnap our nuclear workers, and blow up our vital stocks of ammunition, then let them surrender and pat them on the head? Then what? Do we have a trial? Do we publicly execute them or lock them up, or what?"

"I ... I don't know, but—"

"Well, unfortunately," Crawford said, "I DO know. I know we'll have to set up a prison, tying up men and supplies vitally needed elsewhere. I know we'll have to feed these traitors while they await trial, all while we have starving citizens elsewhere. I know that disgruntled citizens will spread the news via the damned ham radio network that all you have to risk from challenging the government is a slap on the wrist. AND I KNOW WE CAN'T AFFORD THAT! This so-called Wilmington Free State and Fort Box must be utterly and completely crushed, without regard to any collateral damage. It's harsh, I know, but will prove kinder for all concerned in the long run."

A quiet fell over the room as the group sat looking down at the conference table. Finally, Murray spoke. "Your points are well taken, Mr. President. However, I cannot in good conscience participate in the dropping of a weapon of this type on US soil. My letter of resignation will be on your desk as soon as I can write it."

Crawford glared at the man, but Murray didn't flinch. Crawford sensed the others were about to join the secretary in his opposition. Trusting his gut, he relented a bit, buying time.

"Very well, Secretary Murray, then what do you suggest?"

Admiral Whiteley, the Chief of Naval Operations, answered instead. "If I may, Mr. President, perhaps we could use a bombardment of smaller, more controllable ordnance. We could keep the area of conflict within the confines of the fort. It would be less dramatic, granted, but the result would be the same. All of the fort's occupants would be —" he hesitated "— would be neutralized."

Crawford suppressed a smile at the bloodless euphemism. He'd never quite understood the modern military tendency to avoid words like *kill*, but if it made things work more smoothly, he'd play along. He had things going his way and he didn't want to jeopardize that by being overly blunt. "And you're absolutely sure you can neutralize them all that way?"

Whiteley looked at the others and they all nodded. "Quite sure, sir. But —"

"No buts," Crawford said. "I want this all done at a distance and don't want any of our fine military folks killed cleaning this mess up. Prepare your plan and strike without warning or mercy. And don't waste any time communicating with the traitors, even if they reach out to you. No communication whatever, and that's a direct order. And under no circumstances are you or anyone under your commands to accept the surrender of the fort. Is that clear?"

Whiteley looked at Murray and the others, who all nodded.

"Then get on with it, gentlemen," Crawford said.

CHAPTER TWENTY

I-10 Eastbound
At State Highway 73 Split
Winnie, Texas

Day 45
May 15 - 7:15 a.m.

Rorke rode in the front passenger seat of the SUV, the rising sun in his face as they sped due east on I-10. He was sweating, and the humid air blasting through the open windows was doing nothing to ease his discomfort. He hated the Gulf Coast, every inch of it. The weather reminded him of the African shit holes where he'd spent half his life as a mercenary, always looking for the big score that never quite came. Well, things were different now, and the whole planet was turning into one big Third World shit hole, and people with his skill set were going to prosper. He'd make his mark and take what he wanted, whatever it took; then he'd move someplace where he never had to worry about melting when it wasn't even summer yet.

The road forked, with the signs indicating interstate to the left, but Gerard stayed in the far right lane, passing under a large green sign for Texas State Highway 73 toward Port Arthur.

"I thought the prison complex is in Beaumont," Rorke said.

"About halfway between Beaumont and Port Arthur, actually, in an area they call 'mid-county.' It's faster this way though, and we have to transit fewer built-up areas where we might be ambushed," Gerard said.

Rorke leaned forward to look in the side mirror at the convoy of SUVs and Humvees behind them. Twenty black vehicles stretched out along the highway, the Humvees all sporting turrets with machine guns. It was a show of force meant to intimidate the cons, and Rorke had no doubts it would be equally intimidating to anyone they met en route. He leaned back in his seat.

"I doubt an ambush will be a problem," he said. "Christ, doesn't this damn thing have air-conditioning?"

Gerard glanced over at Rorke before turning his eyes back to the road. "Just following your standard order for saving fuel, General. No AC allowed."

"Raise those damn windows," Rorke said as he turned the AC on to maximum. He ignored the smile that flitted across Gerard's face and positioned the two vents to blast cold air directly at him.

"With their choice of places, why the hell did the cons base themselves at the prison?" Rorke asked.

Gerard shrugged. "It's pretty smart, if you think about it. The complex is huge and they have plenty of room, they have clear fields of fire all the way around it, and they can fall back into the maximum-security unit if they're ever attacked. It was designed to keep people in, but the high walls, razor wire, and gun towers work both ways. Looking at it from the air, it looks like it would make a pretty defensible fort in a pinch."

Rorke nodded and craned his neck to glance skyward. "And speaking of the air, where's our air cover? I don't want to roll up to their front door without someone watching our six."

Gerard looked at his watch. "Relax, General. It's under control. We're twenty minutes from the prison, and the choppers are en route. They'll be over us before we get there, easy."

"They better be," Rorke growled. "I have no intention of going in there without air support. I don't trust our potential new 'allies' any further than I can throw them."

"About that," Gerard said, "are you sure it's a good idea to let 'em have crew-served weapons? They might just as easily turn them on us."

"Which is why we only dole out enough ammo for them to attack their assigned objective," Rorke said. "We'll 'loan' them the machine guns but keep them on a short leash as far as ammunition goes."

Gerard grunted. "With the Wilmington stockpile gone, we'll likely all be on a short leash as far as ammo goes."

Rorke glared at his underling. "We'll deal with it down the road. You have any other concerns, Major?"

"Just one. Our troops aren't exactly Boy Scouts, but these cons are even worse. What do we do with them after they've served their purpose?"

Rorke shrugged. "We'll keep them around as long as we have need for them, but leave them no doubt of our ability to crush them in a heartbeat if they get out of line or try to double-cross us. Speaking of that, did you have any difficulty recruiting the 'volunteers' for our little mission today?"

Gerard laughed. "No, when I let it be known we were going to pay a visit to the Aryan Brotherhood and piss in their cornflakes, I had to turn guys away."

Aryan Brotherhood of Texas HQ
Formerly Federal Correctional Complex
Knauth Road
Beaumont, Texas

Darren aka 'Spike' McComb, formerly federal inmate number 26852-278, past and present captain in the Aryan Brotherhood of Texas, and currently self-appointed sheriff of Jefferson County, Texas, paced what had once been the warden's office.

"What the hell is keeping them? I expected them here by now," he said aloud.

"I got guys tucked away out of sight along all the approaches. They'll radio me directly when they pass. Don't worry, Spike, we got this covered," Snag said.

Spike stopped and glared. "Yeah, that's what has me worried. You said the same thing about the raiding party yesterday and you ended up losing two dozen soldiers and damn near as many vehicles. So excuse me if your assurance doesn't make me all warm and fuzzy."

"It ain't like it was a complete loss, Spike," Snag whined. "We got all the stuff left in that warehouse, and after I figured out this 'ship chandler' thing, we found those two other warehouses, so I think all in all —"

"All in all we got more shit and two dozen less guns to guard it, and what you can't defend, you can't keep. So don't break your damn arm patting yourself on the back, Snag. The fact you got lucky on those warehouses don't make up for losing over twenty men, and Brotherhood members too, not those damn throwaway meth heads."

Spike resumed pacing. "First these damn ship people and now the feds. If it ain't one thing, it's another."

"Well, it's good the feds wanna talk, right? I mean, they got those choppers and machine guns and they coulda just come in and shot the hell out of us, right?" Snag said.

"Maybe," Spike said, "but I still don't understand —"

"Unit Fourteen to Snag. Do you copy? Over," came a voice from Snag's radio.

Snag raised the radio to his mouth. "This is Snag. Go ahead. Over."

"They just passed me. Ten SUVs and ten Hummers with machine-gun mounts, and six choppers with machine guns flying support. I figure over a hundred shooters, not counting the air support. ETA your position in less than five minutes. Do you copy? Over," the voice said.

Spike shot Snag a nervous look. "Helluva lot of firepower if 'talking' is all they have in mind."

Snag nodded and raised his radio. "I copy, Unit Fourteen. Anything else? Over."

There was a long pause. "Well, yeah. I ain't likin' the looks of this. They're mostly niggers and beaners."

Spike looked at Snag. "Get everybody in the max-security unit and put shooters in the towers, NOW!"

Knauth Road
Approach to Aryan Brotherhood of Texas HQ
Formerly Federal Correctional Complex
Beaumont, Texas

Gerard leaned against the hood of the SUV and squinted through the binoculars. Then he lowered them and grinned as he handed them to Rorke.

"It looks like our little visit is having the desired effect. I only see movement around the maximum-security unit, so it seems we scared the rats back into their hole," Gerard said.

Rorke nodded as he raised the glasses. "I see shooters in the towers. Radio the choppers and tell 'em to get those machine guns in their faces. I don't want them to have any doubts as to what will happen if any of them are stupid enough to take a potshot at us. Then deploy the armed Hummers in a line facing the prison. We might as well make a good show of it."

Gerard nodded and moved to carry out the orders as Rorke raised his own radio and changed it to the agreed frequency.

"This is General Quentin Rorke of the FEMA Special Reaction Force calling the person in charge of the prison complex. Do you copy? Over."

There was a long pause, and then he got a response.

"This is Sheriff Darren McComb. What can I do for you, General? Over."

"To start with, you can get me out of the damned heat. I can hear a generator running, and I assume your main office complex has a working air conditioner? Over," Rorke said into the radio.

"It does," came the reply.

"Good. I'm going to drive there alone, and I want you to meet me, also alone. And you should know that if anything happens to me, my command has both the authority and capability to reduce your little sandbox here to rubble, and they will take no prisoners. Is that clear? Over."

Another pause. "Brave talk, General. Over."

"Just the facts, McComb. I'll meet you inside the main complex. Come alone, and don't keep me waiting. Rorke out."

Rorke turned off the radio and tossed it through the open door onto the passenger seat of the SUV before he nodded to Gerard and climbed behind the wheel.

***

He was disappointed and irritated when he walked into the lobby of the main office complex and felt no relief from the heat, but he swallowed his irritation and followed the signs to the warden's office. The outer office was as much a sweat box as the rest of the building, but when he opened the door to the warden's office itself, he was instantly enveloped in a cloud of chilled air. He breathed a relieved sigh and stepped into the dark cool office to find a window unit laboring away.

It was a spartan space by any standard, though it was obvious recent attempts had been made to 'decorate' it by someone of rather questionable taste. That notwithstanding, the temperature alone made it a paradise, and Rorke sank into the leather office chair behind the desk, helped himself to a cigar from the box on the credenza, then put his feet on the desk to wait.

He was amusing himself by blowing smoke rings when the office door opened five minutes later to reveal a burly man of perhaps thirty-five and medium height, dressed in a none-too-clean sheriff's uniform. The short-sleeve khaki shirt was pit-stained as if it had been worn several days — or perhaps longer. The man was muscular in a bodybuilder sort of way but running to fat — and his arms were covered in multicolored tattoos; Rorke spotted both a cross and a swastika.

The man's principal feature, however, was an angry scowl, no doubt occasioned by seeing Rorke sitting in HIS chair and smoking HIS cigar. Rorke fanned the flames by greeting the man with a sneer.

"Ah, *Sheriff* McComb, I presume. Please, take a seat," Rorke said, the sarcasm unmistakable as he waved the man to a chair.

Rorke saw the man start to react, then catch himself and smile instead as he moved to sit down across the desk from Rorke. "That's right, General. To what do I owe the honor?"

"Well, you might say I came to save your life," Rorke said.

McComb snorted. "Yeah, right. So how are you gonna do that?"

Rorke smiled. "Why, by not killing you, of course. Surely you understand I have enough firepower in the air alone to blast you and your band of miscreants straight to hell." Rorke took a drag of the cigar and blew another smoke ring. "I also have complete authority to do so."

McComb attempted to hide his concern but failed miserably. "Go on."

"But you see, I'd rather not do that. As loathsome as your actions have been, they actually cause the government less concern than do those of the group you've been fighting with for some time now. So I came to offer you a deal," Rorke said.

McComb's confusion was evident. "The ship people? What the hell do they have to do with this? What kind of deal? Why?"

"It's quite simple, really. The enemy of my enemy is my friend. We'd like you to make the 'ship people,' as you call them, go away, and we're prepared to — discreetly, mind you — offer assistance in achieving that goal. It will be a win for both of us," Rorke said.

"If you're so powerful, why don't you just wipe them out yourself? Why do you need us?" McComb asked.

"Excellent point. We can and will, as you say, 'wipe them out' if that becomes necessary. However, strictly speaking, they haven't done anything wrong, so politically it will be better if their demise is at the hands of someone other than the federal government." Rorke shrugged and put his feet back on the floor as if preparing to rise. "However, if you're not interested — "

"Just hold on a minute," McComb said. "I didn't say we're not interested, but what's in it for us?"

"Full presidential pardons for you and all your men for starters. Then when we start bringing this area back under our control, you and your men stay on in your current positions. To be honest, we don't give a damn about what happens in Beaumont. You keep a lid on things here, deliver votes and various other things when we ask for them, and the federal government will be more than willing to ignore any little 'minor' problems you might have here," Rorke said.

McComb nodded. "What else?"

Rorke fixed him with a withering stare until McComb broke eye contact. "That's the best offer you're likely to get today — or ever. Don't push your luck, McComb."

"Okay, what kind of help can you give us? They're chewing the hell out of us with their machine guns. Can you get us some of those?"

"That can be arranged, along with training," Rorke said. "Anything else?"

Obviously pleased with the way the conversation was going, McComb grew assertive again. "Yeah, just so you understand, we ain't taking training from or otherwise mixing with those mud people. Y'all seem to have a helluva lot of 'em. Frankly I expected better from white men, even the feds."

Rorke smiled. "Actually I brought those 'mud people,' as you call them, along to prove a point. You see, they're all chomping at the bit for a shot at you and your little cracker coalition, so if you refuse this deal, or accept it and then screw up, or otherwise get out of line in any way, I'm turning them loose on you with all the firepower they want. I can't imagine it will be very pleasant for you. Is that clear?"

Rorke saw McComb swallow hard, and could almost see the man turning the situation over in his mind, examining alternatives; but really there weren't any. Finally McComb swallowed again and nodded.

"How we gonna do it?" McComb asked.

"Leave that to us," Rorke said. "You boys don't seem to be particularly good at intel or planning, so Major Gerard and I will come up with the plan; you'll only be executing the mission."

S/S *Cape Mendocino*
Clark Island
Neches River
Beaumont, Texas

Day 46
May 16 - 2:45 p.m.

Hughes stood on the main deck, shaking his head in disbelief at what a concerted effort had accomplished in such a short time. Two bulldozers were at work in the area between the ships, and a steady stream of dump trucks was bringing fresh dirt across Gowan's pontoon bridge from the pits they were digging a half mile away on the east bank of the river.

The island between the ships was mostly level now, with dirt pushed right up against all the ships' sides. The dozers were presently in line, circling the perimeter of the island next to the ships, making sure the new 'land' was compressed as much as possible to make a solid foundation for the even more dirt they would pile against the ships as a protective berm.

The roar of the earthmoving equipment was deafening, and dust and dirt hung in the air like a cloud, settling on every horizontal surface. Hughes nodded to himself as he thought of Dan Gowan's constant harping about keeping all hull openings sealed tight to protect the machinery from airborne contamination. He smiled as he saw Gowan now, half-running across the expanse of raw dirt toward some unknown objective, like as not to chew someone a new one for not doing an assigned task or not doing it fast enough.

"Does that guy ever sleep?"

Hughes turned to see Matt Kinsey and shook his head. "Actually, since he got the floodlights working to light the work area at night, I doubt he has slept except a few minutes at a time," Hughes said. "He's frantic to get all the dirt into the center of the island so we can close the gap."

Kinsey nodded. From a defensive standpoint, their new fort had one glaring fault. The ships ringed most of the island, their high sides forming a very defensible steel wall, but the north end of the island facing upstream came to a point, and it was from this low-lying point that Gowan had extended his pontoon bridge to the east bank. To accommodate the bridge and the rapid movement of the dirt, they'd had to stop their 'ring of ships' short of completion, leaving a 'gap' approximately five hundred feet wide across the island, and it was through this gap the steady stream of dump trucks was moving.

The plan was to pile all the needed dirt into the center of the island, even if it couldn't be spread immediately, and then to close the gap with a retaining wall built from steel cut from non-vital areas of the various ships. They would then push up a berm against the inside of the retaining wall, and it would close the rough circle and present a defense against both attack and rising water. The rest of the interior berm could be completed as time allowed after they'd established the defensive perimeter.

"I can't say I won't be happy to see the gap closed," Kinsey said. "But still, most of the perimeter will be relatively easy to defend with limited manpower, and we got more shooters with the construction crews and Darius' group." He grimaced. "Truth be known, we have more shooters than ammo to shoot."

"How much?" Hughes asked.

"It's hard to say exactly because we've got a mishmash of civilian weapons and ammo that all the folks joining us brought in. As far as the military standard stuff goes, we don't have anything left for the old Cuban machine gun, and after Torres saved our asses, we only have a few rounds left for the Barretts. Add to that maybe two thousand rounds for the M4s, and about the same for the M240s; that sounds like a lot, but those babies really chew through the ammo." Kinsey shook his head. "We can likely give a good accounting of ourselves in a short, sharp fight, but we're toast if there's any sort of sustained action."

"Well, I doubt the cons are enthusiastic about attacking us again—"

He was interrupted by the growing throb of a chopper blade, and both men looked up to see an SRF chopper coming toward them from the west. They stood staring up as the chopper slowly circled their little island at high altitude. They could make out a black-clad figure in the open doorway with something in his hand. The chopper made several orbits of the island then flew back the way it came.

"There's another one. What the hell are they doing now?" Kinsey asked.

"It looked like he was holding a camera," Hughes said.

Kinsey gave him a pointed look. "As I was about to say, it's not really the cons I'm worried about at this point."

Hughes shook his head. "Seems to me if the feds were going to attack, they'd contact us first and demand our surrender or something. They haven't attempted contact or responded when we've called them, so I can't see them just attacking us out of the blue."

"They attacked Fort Box," Kinsey said.

"Yeah, but they have a couple of thousand containers of all kinds of stuff. We're barely scraping by; I doubt we're worth their time."

"Well, maybe," Kinsey said, obviously unconvinced, "but I'd feel a whole lot better about it without all these no-contact flybys. Something is going on here, and whatever it is, I doubt it's good for us."

Aryan Brotherhood of Texas HQ
Formerly Federal Correctional Complex
Knauth Road
Beaumont, Texas

Day 46
May 16 - 3:40 p.m.

Rorke stood at the conference table, Gerard at his side, and stared down at the aerial photos. Across the table, Spike McComb looked on, trying to see the photo upside down.

Rorke tapped the photo. "There," he said. "We have to move quickly and rush this gap before they get it closed up."

McComb craned his neck to see what Rorke was talking about then finally just moved around the table. He shook his head.

"We gotta cross open water and we can't sneak up on 'em, especially now they got those floodlights. Those machine guns will chew the hell out of us," he said.

Rorke looked up and smiled. "On the contrary, they just THINK we need to cross open water and we'll keep 'em thinking that way." He tapped the photo again. "Meanwhile we'll use this nice bridge they so kindly built for us."

CHAPTER TWENTY-ONE

Fort Box
Wilmington Container Terminal
Cape Fear River
Wilmington, North Carolina

Day 47
May 17 - 10:45 a.m.

Hunnicutt stood on the deck of the *Maersk Tangier*, gazing across the river at Eagle Island, a barren strip of land formerly used only as a dumping ground for the spoil dredged from the river to keep it accessible for ship passage. Now the grass-covered island was taking on a far different role, as big Chinook helicopters came and went, depositing troops and equipment on the far side of the island a thousand yards away. There was a rising cloud of dust as the new arrivals worked feverishly with small tracked excavators, building a defensive earthen berm that seemed to grow even as he watched it.

"Should we engage, sir? They'll be easy shots for the Barretts," Luke Kinsey asked.

Hunnicutt lowered the glasses and shook his head as he continued to stare toward the island. "They know we have Barretts, and they don't seem to care, so you can be damn sure they have snipers of their own. If I was a betting man, I'd bet they used the cover of darkness to put a dozen sniper teams in ghillie suits in the grass on the near side of the island and they'd like nothing better than for us to expose our own snipers; anyone opening up from here probably has a life expectancy of about three seconds. As a matter of fact," Hunnicutt said, "we may be in the crosshairs right now, so I suggest we move around behind the deckhouse."

Luke shot a nervous glance across the river and followed Hunnicutt to a less exposed position. "If they have snipers in place, why haven't they engaged? They could have picked off a lot of us by now."

"Probably for the same reason we haven't fired on them," Hunnicutt replied. "They're not SRF scum, they're soldiers like us. Hell, we've probably served with some of them and I'll bet any number of them are sympathetic to our situation." He shook his head. "I've taught history most of my life, but in many ways I never truly appreciated it. I guess this is how Robert E. Lee must have felt."

"With respect, sir, Bobby Lee had a little more room to maneuver. They're ringing us in tighter by the hour. There's a lot of chopper activity to the east in the city as well as the sound of heavy vehicles. It looks like they're preparing for a siege," Luke said.

Hunnicutt shook his head. "To what end, Major? They know we now have plenty of ammunition and the contents of all these containers make us self-sufficient for a very long time. The government hasn't exhibited that sort of patience so far, so I can't believe they've suddenly developed a long game. This looks more to me like containment; they're locking us in to make sure none of us escapes."

Luke nodded. "What are we going to do?"

Hunnicutt studied the deck at his feet in silence for several seconds and then raised his head. "Ask the council to gather in the conference room as soon as possible."

***

"Surrender?" Lieutenant Josh Wright said, disbelief in his voice. "But we just restocked with ammunition and lost people doing it, and now we're gonna surrender?"

"I understand your reluctance, Lieutenant, but that store of ammunition gave us more than just the means to defend ourselves; it also makes attacking us a clearly costly proposition and increases our leverage in negotiations," Hunnicutt said.

"Still, sir, I think I agree with Wright," Luke said. "Surrendering just doesn't seem right considering all we've gone through and the uncertainty we face."

"And taking on the regular military decreases that uncertainty how, Major? Do you think they're just going to go away? These aren't SRF thugs, they're regular troops, disciplined and more than likely well led. Even if we hold out for a prolonged period, which I'll grant you may be possible, in the end there will still be either a complete defeat and surrender or, at best, a negotiation. We haven't confronted the regular military yet, and I seriously doubt many of them will shed a tear for the SRF troops we killed. If we're going to negotiate, aren't we more likely to get a better outcome BEFORE there's a big body count and irreversible enmity on both sides?" Hunnicutt leaned back in his chair and looked from one face to another, challenging them to dispute his logic.

No one spoke for a long moment until Luke broke the silence. "I guess I can't argue the point, but what's the endgame. How are we any better off surrendering now than we would have been to start with?"

Hunnicutt sighed. "I honestly don't know that we will be, Major, but I'm much more willing to surrender to the regular military than I was to SRF troops. There are good people facing us now, and if we can make our case to them, I think it may be the best option in a very bad situation. You and Lieutenant Washington and others among us can testify firsthand to the crimes and barbaric actions of the SRF troops, and I believe that testimony will fall on receptive ears. Appealing to the regular military is our last, best hope of getting the truth out about our actions here, and I'd MUCH rather surrender these supplies to the military than to Rorke's thugs."

Across the table, Dr. Jennings cleared her throat. "But it won't be as easy as all that, will it, Colonel? The government's already spun our defensive actions as the mass murder of helpless refugees. There'll have to be scapegoats for that, now won't there?"

Hunnicutt gave her a sad smile. "Astute and to the point as always, Doctor. I expect you're correct; the government will want their pound of flesh. That's why I'll make that part of the negotiations—the nonnegotiable part. It will be *scapegoat* singular, and I will assume that role. Nothing else is acceptable to me."

There was stunned silence followed by chaos as everyone tried to speak at once. Hunnicutt held up his hands. "Okay, folks, just calm down. I appreciate the concern, but I think you all know it's best that—"

"With respect, sir, we DON'T know. We all participated in the defense, and I for one am not willing to let you accept sole responsibility," Luke said.

"Well, let's explore that, shall we," Hunnicutt said. "I was in command during what they have characterized as a massacre, so do you see any way whatsoever the authorities WON'T hold me responsible?"

"Well, no," Luke said somewhat sheepishly.

"So presuming they decide to hang me, what possible benefit can come of them also executing or imprisoning you and, say, Lieutenant Wright and Lieutenant Washington, or maybe even Dr. Jennings here as well? Let's face facts, Major; I'm toast eventually, whether we fight the good fight and then surrender, or whether we surrender now. The only difference if we surrender now is that there's less chance of any more of our folks being killed in the fighting and I'll have more of a chance to save some of you from punishment. And yes, that sucks, but it's the hand we've been dealt, so we have to play it. I can't really see any other logical choice, but I would like everyone's agreement before we proceed. Do I have it or not?"

Around the table there were reluctant nods and muttered assents, Luke's being the last.

"Good. Then we'll proceed," Hunnicutt said, with a wan smile and a pointed look at Luke. "And please remember if any of you are harboring ideas of playing out the 'I am Spartacus' scene when the time comes, that little bit of bravado got EVERYONE killed at the end of that movie. I'm working very hard to avoid that."

There was a ripple of laughter and Hunnicutt continued speaking to Luke. "So, Major, please radio the folks out there and tell them we wish to meet under a flag of truce."

"Yes, sir," Luke said, and rose from his seat.

Conference Room
One Hour Later

Hunnicutt shook his head, stunned as he realized the likely implications of what he'd just heard. "You're sure, Major?"

Luke nodded. "They're jamming every frequency. It's like they don't want to communicate with us, or want anyone else to either."

"Jamming isn't selective. Maybe they're just trying to isolate us from the remaining ham operators," Hunnicutt said. "It's much easier to spin a narrative if your account is unchallenged. Try approaching them physically. Send a boat over under a flag of truce."

"I already tried, sir. They fired a shot across the bow before it was halfway across. It's pretty clear they have no interest in anything we have to say," Luke said, then paused. "How can we surrender if they refuse to communicate with us? I don't understand why they're doing this. Do you, sir?"

Hunnicutt nodded. "They have no intention of letting us surrender. They plan to wipe us out as an example; it's the only thing that makes sense."

The color drained from Luke's face. "No witnesses?"

"That would be my guess," Hunnicutt said.

Luke stood, his face a mask of rage. "I'll go pass the word. If we're going down, we'll go down hard, by God."

Hunnicutt shook his head. "I'll see to that. I have a more important task for you. Get Lieutenant Wright and some of the terminal workers and put together a container bunker for Dr. Jennings' patients, the children, and all the rest of the families and noncombatants. Stack containers full of nonflammable supplies three deep around it for protection and slap bright white paint with red crosses all over it. Even acting on direct orders, I'm hoping our military isn't so far gone they'll attack a clearly marked hospital and murder noncombatants."

"I'll get right on it," Luke said, then turned to go.

Hunnicutt sat at the conference table, the crushing weight of responsibility bearing down on him like a boulder, an almost physical sensation pinning him in his chair. He took a deep, ragged breath, then folded his hands together below his chin and bowed his head in prayer.

Battleship Memorial Park
West Bank
Cape Fear River
Wilmington, North Carolina

Admiral Sam Wright stared out from the large tent. The sides were rolled up to take advantage of a nonexistent breeze, affording him a view of the gray hull of the venerable battleship permanently moored nearby. The grassy expanse next to the iconic landmark was a logical place for the operation headquarters, offering proximity to the objective and clear lines of sight for defensive purposes. He'd have preferred just about any assignment to this one, but that was why they called it duty, wasn't it; it wasn't optional.

Ironic, he thought as he looked out over the old battleship, *a North Carolinian leading an assault on fellow North Carolinians from a site dedicated to the memory of North Carolinians killed in battle.*

He turned back to the 'discussion' in progress.

"How the hell can we just ignore a flag of truce and attack a position we KNOW shelters women and children?"

Wright sighed. General Duncan Beasley was a 'Marine's Marine,' revered and respected by his men, but with a tendency toward speaking his mind that made it unlikely he'd ever be Commandant. *Probably the reason I like the bastard*, Wright thought as he returned the crusty Leatherneck's glare without blinking.

"The same way Curtis LeMay fire-bombed the hell out of Tokyo and we dropped the big ones on Nagasaki and Hiroshima, Duncan. By following the orders of our civilian leaders," Wright said.

Beasley snorted. "I suspect a reference to the Nazi buzz bombs over London would be more appropriate. These are our OWN people, Sam, or near enough anyway. I can't say if I were in Hunnicutt's place, I'd have done things any differently, and this whole 'murdering defenseless refugees thing' sounds like a fairy tale and you know it. Besides, nobody elected Crawford."

"He's the constitutionally designated successor. The Congress, what's left of it anyway, accepted him, as have the SECNAV and the CNO, Duncan. What the hell would you have me do? Tell all our superiors, 'Beasley and I disagree so we're not going to follow your orders'? No communication whatsoever was a clear and direct order, and we're following our orders to the letter," Wright said.

"Yeah, well, I'd feel a lot better if the guy ordering me to kill people hadn't been shit-faced at the time," Beasley said.

Wright had no reply. President Crawford had clearly been under the influence during their discussion. He'd had bourbon on his breath and was slurring his words badly. Now Wright regretted his momentary lapse in mentioning it to Beasley. He changed the subject.

"Are you all set?" he asked.

Beasley nodded. "Don't worry about our end."

Wright smiled to take the sting out of his words. "That's why they pay me the big bucks, General, to worry about everything. What about those Barretts? We need them neutralized before the Army guys go in; we can't be losing choppers."

"My Marines have enough mortars set up behind that berm on Eagle Island to cover every square inch of that 'fort.' Give me ten minutes and there won't be any worry about the Barretts. Hell, there likely won't even be anything for those airborne pukes to do. It'll be like it always is, the Marines get the job done and the Army shows up for the photo op," Beasley said.

Wright shook his head, wondering if the only things likely to survive the end of the world were interservice rivalries and cockroaches. "I doubt anyone will want any pictures of this op, Duncan," Wright said, then sighed. "How about the lights?"

"I've got choppers standing by to pop up and take out all the lights on the ships and throughout the terminal with machine-gun fire. Whatever night-vision equipment they have can't be anywhere near enough for all their shooters. Most everyone not neutralized by the initial barrage will be stumbling around in the dark. They'll be like fish in a barrel. Mitchell's airborne boys won't have a problem."

Wright nodded. "All right. Nautical twilight is at twenty-one hundred; let's give it an hour to get full dark and start the barrage at twenty-two hundred."

Beasley nodded and stood to go, then stopped. "You sure about this, Sam?"

"I'm sure I swore an oath to protect and defend the Constitution and the government of the United States from 'all enemies foreign and domestic,' and part of that oath was following the orders of the Commander in Chief, just like you did, Duncan. Unfortunately, there's nothing in that oath that gives us a pass if the Commander in Chief is a drunken scumbag who got there largely by circumstance. Our duty is clear, whether we like it or not," Wright said.

CHAPTER TWENTY-TWO

Approaching Cape Fear River Bridge
Avents Ferry Road
Near Brickhaven, North Carolina

Same Day - Same Time

Tremble leaned out the window, scanning the sky, still nervous about the possibility of being spotted by a chopper. He pulled his head in and glanced at the map in his lap.

"The bridge is just around this next curve. Slow down and let's find a place to hide the truck while we scout ahead," Tremble said.

Anderson pulled to the side of the road. "You sure this is the last one?" he asked as he crept along, studying the trees to the right of the road.

Tremble nodded. "Yes, and it should be a small bridge, the Cape Fear isn't very wide this far up. There!" He pointed to a break in the trees, and Anderson turned the truck toward it.

Despite his desire to get south, Tremble had forced himself to be patient. His plan was sketchy at best, and he could help no one in Wilmington if they were captured en route. They'd stayed hidden off the AT a full day to confirm no one was tracking them, but just as Garrity claimed, they'd seen no aerial surveillance or other signs of pursuit.

That was the good news. The bad news was as Tremble studied the increasingly tattered maps and other info he'd inherited from Tex and Wiggins, he found no straightforward way to get to their destination undiscovered. They had to avoid population centers like Roanoke and Lynchburg, and if forced to stay on 'drivable' roads, there were literally dozens of rivers, streams, and lakes in their path, all with bridges that were potential traps. To reduce the risk, he'd chosen the most isolated crossings, often detouring a hundred miles or more in the process.

Unable to travel at night when headlights might mark their position and invite unwelcome attention, their journey south had been a series of daytime darts from one hiding place to the next, each planned with precision. They bedded down each night in a cold camp, with no fires to betray them, alternating shifts at watch. Now, and finally, they were nearing their objective.

The pickup rolled to a stop in the woods and Tremble and Anderson got out, closing the doors softly. Cindy exited the backseat of the crew cab, whispering to Jamie to stay and keep an eye on Molly, who was fast asleep. Keith and Jeremy joined them from the truck bed, where they left Garrity, his wrists and ankles bound and a piece of duct tape over his mouth.

Tremble motioned them all away from the truck to keep from waking Molly.

"Okay, Keith and Jeremy, cover our trail and cut some brush to make sure we can't be seen from the road. Cindy, please keep an eye on our prisoner while Anderson and I scout the bridge. With any luck this will be the last time we have to do this," Tremble said.

"Dad," Keith said, keeping his voice low, "something is up with Garrity. For the last half hour he's been looking all around like he's nervous and he's sweating."

"I'm sweating too, son. It's hot," Tremble said.

"No, it's more than that. I can't really describe it, but it's like he recognized something or he's worried. Before he always wanted to ride sitting up with his back against the cab, but the last hour or so he's slipped down in the bed on his side, like he doesn't want to be seen." Keith looked at Jeremy. "Did you notice, Jeremy?"

Jeremy nodded and Tremble looked back toward the bed of the truck.

Tremble's loathing for the mercenary had only intensified during their short journey. On his turns at night sentry duty, he'd removed the duct-tape gag and engaged Garrity in conversation, not because he liked the scumbag, but to learn what had transpired while he and Keith were in hiding. To loosen the man's tongue, he'd pointed out repeatedly that Garrity's knowledge of the Trembles' survival made him as much a target as the rest of them, and he'd watched as Garrity turned it over in his mind and slowly became convinced they were on 'the same team.'

With that conversion, Garrity became something of a talker, eager for an audience, and some of his revelations of SRF ops shocked Tremble to silence. Garrity had taken the silence as rapt interest and gotten even more detailed. In his lurid accounts he was 'just following orders,' but the enthusiasm with which he described various horrific crimes left no doubt in Tremble's mind Garrity had been a willing participant.

Though managing to hide his disgust, Tremble became ever more determined to see Garrity tried for his crimes. In truth, he was often a hair's breath away from putting a bullet in the man himself. He forced himself to smile and walked back over to the bed of the truck, to lean in and rip the duct tape off Garrity's mouth.

"Damn!" Garrity said. "That hurt."

Tremble shrugged "Sorry, but better fast than slow, right?"

Garrity nodded. "Why are we stopping?"

"Just scouting a bridge. Why? You look a little nervous," Tremble said.

"Just cautious, that's all, and best you be too. There's marauders in this area. Me and the boys were running a pacification mission here until they reassigned us to the roadblock, looking for you. We hit 'em pretty hard, but we couldn't get a handle on the situation. They're not stationary like Wilmington, they're more like smoke; they would pop up anywhere. They stayed spread out too, so we couldn't get them all in one place. We found some of their hidden camps with IR from the choppers and were able to take prisoners, but they were mostly women and kids. And even when we managed to take one of the shooters alive, it was hard to squeeze any intel out of them, at first anyway." A smile flitted briefly across Garrity's face.

"What do you mean 'at first'?" Tremble asked.

"Well, everybody has a weak point, so I ... I mean our orders were to use the women and kids. If we captured one of the marauders alive, we'd put 'em in with the other prisoners and watch who they reacted to. Then we'd drag 'em all out and work on the woman or kids in front of 'em. The kids worked best, because then the guy's old lady was yelling at him too. Pretty soon the guy was singin' like a canary. We just about had the area pacified when we got called off."

Garrity shook his head. "Between us leavin' before we got the job done and no choppers to worry about, I'm thinkin' the weeds will grow back in the garden pretty quick. I expect there's plenty of those boys around here just waitin' to bushwhack anyone they see in a FEMA or SRF uniform."

Tremble held the edge of the truck bed in a white-knuckled grip and swallowed his rage. He smiled. "Good to know. Thanks," he said as he reached in and slapped the tape back over Garrity's mouth, none too gently, fighting an urge to pinch the man's nostrils together as well and watch him die a slow death of suffocation.

He turned his back on Garrity and his smile morphed to a grim frown as he motioned to Anderson and started through the woods toward the bridge.

***

The bridge was unguarded and an hour later Tremble and Anderson were back at the truck, pulling out of the woods and back onto the road south. They were on full alert crossing the bridge, despite their reconnaissance. Three miles past the bridge they all began to breathe easier, and Anderson broke the silence.

"How much longer you figure to Fort Bragg?" he asked.

"In normal times, less than an hour," Tremble said. "But hopping around from one back road and wagon track to the next, I'd say three. With any luck we should still make it well before sundown."

"How do you know they're not in on it? They might just lock us all up and make us disappear," Anderson said as he slowed to negotiate a sharp bend in the road.

"It's possible," Tremble conceded, "but if they do, we're likely screwed anyway. But I know some folks —"

"HANG ON!" Anderson cried as he stood on the brakes to avoid a downed tree across the road.

The truck shuddered to a stop, eliciting curses from Tremble and Cindy and startled cries from the children as they were all thrown forward.

Tremble was already reaching for his M4 when armed men boiled out of the woods that grew thick up to the road on either side. He almost had it pointing through the open window when Cindy yelled from the backseat.

"NO, SIMON! THE KIDS!"

A fleeting image of the children shredded by return gunfire flashed through Tremble's mind and he lowered his weapon, defeated, as a dozen men surrounded the truck, pointing a mismatched collection of rifles and shotguns in their direction. A rough-looking man with a full beard and a well-worn boonie hat stepped forward.

"Y'ALL GET YOUR HANDS UP WHERE WE CAN SEE 'EM AND DON'T TRY NOTHING FUNNY. MY BOYS WILL OPEN THE DOORS AND Y'ALL GET OUT NICE AND SLOW, THAT GOES FOR YOU IN THE BACK TOO. ONE FALSE MOVE AND WE OPEN FIRE. IS THAT CLEAR?"

"YES! DON'T SHOOT," Tremble yelled back, then got out of the truck when the door was opened.

They were prodded into the middle of the road in a group, well behind the truck, and guarded by four wary gunmen. Cindy carried Molly and held her close, and the girl screamed when one of the gunmen tried to take her away. Jamie attacked the man before Tremble could stop him.

"YOU LEAVE MY SISTER ALONE," Jamie screamed, his small fists smashing ineffectually into the gunman's midsection.

"Easy, sport," the man said, not unkindly, as he trapped the boy's wrists in one of his hands and held him helpless. "I ain't gonna hurt her. I just wanna get you kids separated from the grown-ups."

"Be careful. She can't walk well. She's been shot in the leg," Cindy said.

"Yes, ma'am, I'll be careful," the man said, then glanced down at Jamie. "I'm gonna take your sister and move off down the road a bit while my friends talk to the grown-ups. You can come along and make sure she's okay. How will that be? Now if I let you go, will you behave yourself?"

Jamie stood trapped and confused, his chin quivering.

"Do it, Jamie. We'll be all right. You look after Molly," Tremble said softly, and the boy nodded.

The man let Jamie go and peeled a distraught Molly off Cindy, to take the two children farther down the road out of earshot.

What the hell? thought Tremble. *Definitely not how I envisioned marauders.*

The positive vibes stopped a moment later when the spokesman glared at him.

"Well, this is a first now, ain't it?" the man said, looking from Tremble's and Keith's dirty FEMA police uniforms to Anderson's black SRF utilities. "I don't believe I've ever seen you FEMA types hooked up directly with this SRF scum — not that either of you are worth a shit. I ain't too sure about the little lady here either, but she seems pretty chummy with y'all and she was armed, so I'm guessing she ain't a hostage. I can hardly wait to hear this fairy tale—"

"DAVE," called a man from the truck, "YOU'RE GONNA WANNA SEE THIS! IT'S THAT BASTARD GARRITY!"

Tremble looked over to where two men were dragging an obviously terrified Garrity from the truck bed. They threw the prisoner facedown on the asphalt and both began kicking him savagely from opposite sides. The man named Dave left them and ran over to push the men apart.

"Easy, boys, easy," he said as he pushed them back. "He'll get what's comin' to him, but bein' beat to death by the side of the road is way too good for the likes of him. Now y'all back off, y'hear?"

The men complied with obvious reluctance, and Dave turned and grabbed one of Garrity's elbows and heaved him onto his back. He stood staring down at the man and a slow smile split his bearded face. "Well, damned if it AIN'T you, Sergeant Garrity. And here I'd quit believin' in Santa Claus and it ain't even near Christmas. We'll be takin' you back to camp for a little heart-to-heart, but you can consider that tune-up the boys just gave you a down payment." Dave launched a wad of spittle that hit Garrity square in the face, then turned on his heel and walked back toward Tremble and the others, still ringed by four gunmen.

"I don't know who the hell you are," Dave said, "but seein' as how you had that piece of crap tied up in the back of your truck and it's obvious you ain't exactly bass fishin' buddies, I'd say y'all earned yourselves the benefit of the doubt. Now start talkin', but before you do, you need to understand I gotta real good ear for bullshit, so I better not hear none."

"Fair enough. My name is Simon Tremble, and this is my son, Keith," Tremble said, nodding toward his son. "And this is George—"

"The hell you say!" Dave said as Tremble's name sank in. He drew closer, eyes narrowing as he squinted at Tremble. "Well, damned if you ain't. You're supposed to be dead, and I sure as hell didn't recognize you with the beard and in that uniform."

"It's a long story," Tremble said.

"You'd best get started, then. Congressman or not, that still don't explain away those uniforms," Dave said.

***

Ten minutes later, Tremble finished the much-abbreviated story of their journey and lapsed into silence, staring at Dave. The man said nothing for a long moment then slowly nodded. He stuck out his hand.

"Dave Tuttle," he said.

Tremble shook his hand, and Tuttle called to the men surrounding them.

"You boys can lower your guns. It appears Congressman Tremble here is still one of the good guys," he said.

Dave Tuttle followed Cindy's glance down the road toward where the children were.

"Randy," Tuttle called, "bring them kids back on over to these folks."

"Thank you," Tremble said.

"It's Randy you should be thankin', Congressman. We was all ready to shoot y'all straight to hell when he spotted the kids. We figured we'd rescue the kids and THEN kill y'all." Tuttle smiled. "Glad it turned out to be unnecessary."

Tremble laughed, the tension broken until he turned and saw them leading Garrity toward the woods. "What about Garrity?"

Tuttle's face hardened. "What about him?"

"I presume you're going to have some sort of trial?"

Tuttle said nothing for a long time and then nodded. "Yeah, we can do that. We'll make it real efficient and have it close to the tree."

Tremble thought a moment and then nodded back. "Glad to hear you're not wasting a bullet."

Tuttle smiled, but there was no humor in it. "Ammo is hard to come by these days. You run across any of the rest of his crew?"

"We left three dead a few days back," Tremble said.

Tuttle nodded. "We're obliged."

They lapsed into silence again, and after a moment Tremble nodded toward the fallen tree. "If y'all could help us get that tree clear, we'll be on our way. I figure we can still make Bragg before nightfall."

Tuttle shook his head. "You ain't gettin' near Bragg, at least not in daylight. There must be a half million or so 'fugees between here and there. The army boys cleared a quarter-mile strip around the place and keep it clear, but that's as close as you can get." He paused. "And even gettin' that close is worth your life. There's a lot of desperate folks there."

"The army set up a refugee camp?" Tremble asked.

"Not really. It just sorta grew up by itself. People from Fayetteville or off of I-95 mostly—city folks lookin' for a place to go. There's some good people no doubt, but a lotta bad ones too. They likely ALL figured the government was gonna help and Bragg was a logical place to turn. The problem was, Bragg wasn't set up to help them. We was talkin' to one of the army patrols in the first days, before these SRF scumbags showed up. The regular army guys said the rumor was President Gleason himself ordered no contact between the army and the civilians, and it must be they were right because that was the last time we seen a regular patrol. Right after that they cleared the strip around the perimeter and started reinforcing it with razor wire and concrete barriers and closed everything tight but the main gate."

"But the refugees kept coming?" Tremble asked.

Tuttle shrugged. "Like as not they didn't have nowhere else to go, and just 'cause Gleason said so, it didn't stop people from showing up. Then pretty soon things got desperate, and good folks turned into people trying to feed their families at all costs, and the bad ones was no-account to start with. Now there's pretty much a no-man's-land around the base. It's thickest from Cross Creek Mall to the main gate approach— must be three miles or more. When the military has to leave to go from post to post or whatever, they transit the 'fugee camp in convoys of armed Humvees; you won't stand a chance by yourselves in a pickup, day or night."

"I HAVE to get into Fort Bragg," Tremble said.

"Well, you ain't gettin' there in THAT," Tuttle said, nodding toward the pickup, "but we might be able to help."

"I'm listening."

"We can get within maybe five miles by vehicle, and then a few of us movin' at night on foot might get through. We got some NV gear we got off SRF patrols we ambushed. If we wait until most everybody is asleep, I think maybe me and one of the boys can guide you through the 'fugee camp and put you into the cleared approach to Bragg. After that, you'll be on your own," Tuttle said. "But I'll tell you right now, they ain't lettin' anyone close enough to that gate to even state your business. From what we hear, they're turning everyone away, no exceptions."

Approach to Main Gate
All American Expressway
Fort Bragg, North Carolina

Same Day - 11:45 p.m.
(Twelve Hours Later)

It took all of Tremble's considerable powers of persuasion to convince the others to stay behind in Dave Tuttle's hidden camp. With Cindy he'd emphasized the unnecessary risk to Jeremy and the children, and the very real point that they needed someone to look after them, come what may. Keith was even harder to convince, but in the end had yielded to the argument that he was plan B. Tremble had no idea what the situation was inside Fort Bragg or who was in charge, and if he lost the gamble, Keith alone would be the sole witness to Gleason's and Crawford's perfidy. The 'eyes only' memo Keith carried, folded and sealed in a ziplock bag, was proof to the world that what remained of the US government had been hijacked.

Tuttle and the big man Randy drove them within a half mile of the Cross Creek Mall on a side road and left their car parked out of sight behind an abandoned and looted convenience store. It was a moonless night and pitch black until they crept cautiously onto the wide expanse of the All American Expressway and they saw low fires across the road in the near distance, flaring green in their night-vision glasses.

"That's the mall, or what's left of it," Tuttle whispered. "Last I heard, some gangs had divided it up as headquarters. There's a bunch of folks camped out in the parking lot there too." He pointed down the wide multilane road toward Fort Bragg. "From here on out we'll hit the 'fugee camp on both sides of the road. The army keeps the road itself clear and won't let nobody set up in the median strip, so that's where we'll travel. I'll take point and Randy will watch our six. Y'all just keep quiet and move fast and we should be all right."

Tremble nodded and fell in behind Tuttle, with Anderson at his side, looking insect-like in his own NV glasses. As Tuttle indicated, the grassy center median was overgrown but clear, and they moved swiftly between the squalid camps crowding both sides of the road. There were abandoned vehicles and improvised shelters everywhere, with the luckier residents having tents or the occasional RV. Permeating it all was the putrid smell of too many humans in too little space without even the basics of sanitation; a miasma composed of equal parts of the scent of unwashed bodies and human waste hung over the road like an almost impenetrable cloud, and Tremble had all he could do to keep from throwing up. In places, sluggish streams passed under the road via culverts, likely the only sources of water for the occupants of this human hell.

He heard sounds of packed humanity, restless in the night—snoring, snatches of conversations, and here and there a crying child or a voice raised in anger or drunken laughter. The camp seemed to be a place to be pitied rather than feared, but he had no doubt the situation would look quite different in daylight.

He blocked out the camp and focused on Tuttle's back until they stopped under an overpass and could see the lights of the main gate in the near distance. Tuttle turned to Tremble.

"This is it," Tuttle said softly. "I got no idea what sort of ruckus will happen when y'all head down the access, so give us time to get mostly back through the camp before you head in. We'll take your NV gear back now, if you don't mind."

Tremble removed the NV glasses and handed them to Tuttle. In the dim shadows from the distant lighted gate, he saw Anderson doing the same.

"You sure about the guns?" Tuttle asked.

"We only need the Glock to sell the story, and if it doesn't work, there's no point in giving away the M4s," Tremble said.

"All right then. We'll take 'em and head back. Good luck, Congressman," Tuttle said, and Tremble felt rather than saw Tuttle reaching for his hand. He groped for Tuttle's hand and met his firm handshake.

"Thanks, Dave. And ... and if this doesn't work ..."

Tuttle squeezed his hand. "We'll take good care of your folks and do our best to make sure your boy gets to deliver that memo where it'll do some good."

Tremble returned the squeeze and then released Tuttle's hand. He and Anderson groped their way to one of the upright support pillars of the overpass and made themselves small against it in the gloom. Their two guides disappeared into the darkness the way they'd come, wraiths in the night.

***

Fifteen minutes later, Tremble and Anderson stared down the arrow-straight length of the All American Expressway toward the lights of the main gate. From what they could see, the road was completely clear of vegetation or obstructions on either side, as it bisected what Tuttle had described as a quarter-mile strip all the way around the perimeter of the base.

"Looks like they're serious about controlling access. You sure this is gonna work? Anderson asked.

"I haven't been sure about anything in a very long time, but I think this is our best shot," Tremble said.

"Well, at least with shorter hair and no beard, you look a bit more recognizable. I give it a fifty-fifty chance they don't just shoot us on sight and figure it out later," Anderson said.

Tremble had gone from seeking anonymity to desperately needing recognition for his plan to work. He'd replaced his stolen FEMA policeman's uniform with a pair of jeans and tee shirt that might have once been white, courtesy of Dave Tuttle. Tuttle also contributed a pair of scissors and what must have been the world's dullest disposable razor and a scrap of bar soap to work up a lather. Lava, as it turned out.

Tremble chuckled. "Yeah, I never knew shaving could be so painful."

"Well, let's hope it was worth it, and if your plan works out, please remember to try to stop them from putting a bullet in ME," Anderson said.

Tremble chuckled again. "I'll make it a priority," he said. "And speaking of that, I think it's time. Tuttle and Randy should be well away by now."

"Let's do it," Anderson said, and moved behind Tremble.

He fished a zip tie from his pocket and felt in the dark for Tremble's hands, binding them at the wrists by feel.

"Not too tight," Tremble said, "you'll cut off the circulation."

"All right, all right, but it has to look real, so it's not gonna be comfortable."

"Just don't overdo it," Tremble said.

Anderson just grunted and finished his task and patted Tremble on the back. "All done. Let's get out there."

They moved away from the pillar and started up the center of the access road toward the camp gate. Tremble walked ahead and to the right, with Anderson behind him, the Glock clearly visible and pointed at Tremble.

Tremble had visited the base many times, both in his role as a reserve officer and later as a congressman, and the changes to the approach were quite obvious. They had abandoned the multilane vehicle-access gate designed to speed traffic in and out of the busy base in normal times. A line of concrete Jersey barriers crossed the road, even with the old visitors' center, and was reinforced by a berm of sandbags and razor wire. There were machine-gun emplacements on either side of the visitors' center, which was now obviously the guardhouse, and only one lane open directly beside the building. There was no one visible, but Tremble had no doubt there were eyes on them as they walked into the broad circle of light thrown off by floodlights on the roof of the building. They were halfway to the gate when that assumption was confirmed.

"HALT! YOU ARE IN A RESTRICTED AREA. LEAVE IMMEDIATELY OR WE WILL FIRE!" came an amplified voice from behind the barricade.

"Showtime," whispered Anderson before he raised his voice and yelled at the gate, "I AM SERGEANT GEORGE ANDERSON OF THE SPECIAL REACTION FORCE COMING IN WITH A HIGH-VALUE PRISONER. I REQUEST PERMISSION TO APPROACH."

There was no apparent reaction. Seconds stretched into minutes.

"What the hell?" Anderson whispered. "Are they going to have us stand here until we die of old age?"

"A little patience, Anderson," Tremble whispered back. "You know the drill. The corporal is checking with the sergeant, who's checking with the lieutenant, who's clueless and racked with indecision, wondering whether to follow standing orders and send us away or to take a chance on waking up his immediate superior in the middle of the night. Either way he's evaluating the risk of an ass-chewing."

Tremble had hardly finished speaking before the amplified voice rang out again.

"BE ADVISED YOU ARE BEING COVERED BY MULTIPLE WEAPONS. IF YOU DO NOT FOLLOW MY INSTRUCTIONS TO THE LETTER OR ATTEMPT TO WITHDRAW, YOU WILL BE FIRED UPON. YOU IN THE BACK, GROUND YOUR WEAPON, NOW! AND DO IT SLOWLY."

"Well, that's encouraging. Sort of," Anderson whispered as he slowly bent at the waist and laid the Glock on the asphalt.

"NOW WALK FORWARD SLOWLY, AND BE PREPARED TO HALT ON MY COMMAND."

They were allowed to approach within fifty feet of the gate and then ordered to face away and get on their knees. A half-dozen soldiers boiled out of the gatehouse to verify Tremble's bonds and bind Anderson's hands behind him. Both men were frisked for more weapons or explosives and then pulled roughly to their feet and herded through the gate, to be stood before a lieutenant, a man quite obviously just awakened.

The man glared at Anderson, taking in his dirty SRF uniform and wrinkling his nose, perhaps unconsciously, at his two prisoners' body odor. When he spoke, it was obvious his distaste had as much to do with the SRF uniform as their lack of hygiene.

"Okay, 'Sergeant,' why don't you explain to me why I should give a damn about you and your prisoner here," the man said.

"Maybe I should take that," Tremble said. "I'm Congressman Simon Tremble and I urgently need to speak to the base commander."

The lieutenant scoffed. "Yeah, and I'm the tooth fairy. Tremble's dead . . ."

He stopped mid-sentence and studied Tremble's face. "Son of a bitch," he murmured, reaching for the phone.

***

Contacting the commanding general in the middle of the night is not something done casually in any military organization, and the request was routed through two more pay grades before Tremble and Anderson were loaded into a Humvee twenty minutes later, still zip-tied.

"Where are we going?" Tremble asked.

"The general's at the operations center," the lieutenant said.

The ride was a short one, and they were deposited in a conference room with a glass wall overlooking a room full of workstations, with large digital displays on the walls. Tremble's heart sank when he recognized a map of his hometown of Wilmington and realized all too clearly what the map symbols meant.

Hope rose a scant second later when he saw someone talking to a burly, red-faced man wearing general's stars, and pointing toward the conference room. The general followed the man's pointing finger, then nodded and moved toward the window with a grace that belied his large stature. He burst through the door of the conference room and looked first stunned, then confused.

"Simon? My God, I thought you were dead! How on earth did you …" The general trailed off, noticing the zip ties for the first time. He turned on the hapless lieutenant. "Goddammit, Neilson. Cut those restraints off the congressman right now!"

The lieutenant moved to comply as Tremble ignored him and addressed the general. "Joe, is that an operation against Wilmington I see in there?"

"What? Yes, it's a direct order from the President—"

"I don't have time to explain, but you need to stop it right now," Tremble said.

"Stop it? I couldn't even if I had the authority, Simon. We launched almost two hours ago; we're just mopping up now."

Fort Box
Wilmington Container Terminal
Cape Fear River
Wilmington, North Carolina

Two Hours Earlier

Hunnicutt had just left the 'hospital bunker' after checking that all the noncombatants were safe. Some of the families had already started to complain of the cramped conditions and demanded to know when they could leave. He'd passed the buck to Dr. Jennings and departed when all hell broke loose outside.

There was a wall of deafening noise as hundreds of mortar rounds were exploding across the compound and atop the defensive walls. Hunnicutt staggered and adjusted his senses to the assault, realizing that mixed with the explosive rounds were others with gas billowing from them. The fort was quickly enveloped in a thick cloud, and dimly through the choking smoke, Hunnicutt watched soldiers fall without firing a shot. He reached down under his utility jacket and pulled his rank tee shirt up over his nose and sprinted toward the safety of the headquarters building.

Gas!

He reached the door to the building just as, unseen, he heard the throaty snarl of multiple machine guns in the distance, and lights winked off across the compound, throwing him into darkness. He grabbed his NV glasses and wrestled them on, one of a dozen sets they had, distributed among the senior officers and noncoms.

He heard the dull thump of the blades of approaching choppers—a lot of them—and watched in the NV glasses as the choppers' downdrafts blew the gas in strange patterns, dissipating the cloud and revealing defenders in various stages of defeat, some on their knees, choking, and others stretched unmoving on the ground.

Ropes flashed down from the choppers, a forest of green lines dancing in his vision, followed seconds later by the assault troops hitting the ground and fanning out, unopposed. Despite his expectations of an attack, the surprise was complete and the assault overwhelming.

Hunnicutt raised his radio. "All units, this is Hunnicutt. We'll make our stand in the headquarters building. Repeat, rally in the headquarters building. Get here if you can. Hunnicutt out."

He took up a defensive position behind the corner of the building, ready to wave any defenders inside to begin organizing a defense as he held off their attackers. In moments, he was pinned down by a half-dozen airborne troops as he waited in vain for reinforcement. It was futile, and he knew it, but perhaps if he could get them to accept the fort's surrender, he could still save some of the others.

"DON'T SHOOT," he yelled. "THIS IS COLONEL HUNNICUTT. I SURRENDER THE FORT. I'M THROWING OUT MY WEAPON AND COMING OUT."

The shooting stopped and Hunnicutt felt a flash of hope.

"SHOW YOURSELF," came the reply.

He tossed his weapon out and stepped from behind the building, hands up. He'd barely stepped into the open when he took a round to the middle of his chest.

CHAPTER TWENTY-THREE

Old Mansfield Ferry Road
Vidor, Texas

Day 48
May 18 - 1:15 a.m.
(Three Hours Later)

Rorke stood beside Gerard and 'Sheriff McComb,' studying the glow to the southeast, five miles away as the crow flew, amazed at how clearly any light was visible in the new darkness of the post-apocalyptic nights. From the direction of the light he could hear the sound of engines and the clanking of heavy machinery.

"Sounds like they're working through the night," Gerard said.

Rorke nodded. "Good. They'll be tired when we hit them."

"Yeah, well, so will we," McComb said. "I still can't see why we have to sit on this goddamn road all night and get eat up by skeeters. And if that ain't bad enough, y'all won't even let us have a smoke. The boys are pretty pissed off, and I can't say as how I blame 'em."

Rorke stifled an urge to shoot McComb and stared into the night behind them, imagining the force of almost a thousand of McComb's 'deputies' spread out along the road in the darkness in the buses they'd modified.

"Because, McComb, if we can see their lights in the dark, they'd be able to see ours. That's why we came at dusk when we could still see without headlights. We're close enough now that we can be on them at first light. Even when they see us, they won't have time to react. We'll be coming almost directly out of the rising sun, so with luck they might not spot us at all until we're right on top of them, and I'm sure not going to compromise that tactical advantage by a couple of hundred cigarettes glowing in the dark," Rorke said.

"Y'all got night vision," McComb countered. "We could have just given it to the drivers and come in the morning before daylight."

"And risked a collision?" Gerard said. "If we can hear them, they can hear us. How do you think they'd react if they heard a crash over here?"

McComb sighed. "All right, I see your point. But the boys still ain't happy. That's all I'm saying."

"The happiness of your group of morons is a matter of complete indifference to me, McComb," Rorke said. "Besides, if they're pissed off, maybe they'll be in a fighting mood and able to get the job done for a change. From what I understand, your track record isn't too good in that department."

"You just make sure we got the bridge," McComb said, "then my boys will get the job done. I'm gonna go walk the line and see how they're doing."

"You do that, McComb," Rorke said, and listened as McComb's footsteps faded down the road.

"You think they're up to it," Gerard asked when McComb was out of earshot.

"We're hitting them with overwhelming force at a weak point," Rorke said. "I think even these clowns should be able to manage that. You all set up on your end?"

"Yeah, the scouts spotted two sentries about a hundred yards out from the bridge, both with NV. I sent a six-man team with two M240s through the marsh to an old equipment shed about a quarter mile away from the sentries. They'll hide there until we give them the go-ahead, then take out the sentries and rush forward to set up the machine guns to cover the pontoon bridge. They'll hold until McComb's boys arrive. How long you figure?"

Rorke shrugged. "A bit over five miles on a decent road? I'd say five minutes, ten max. Then make sure to pull our men back as soon as the cons take the bridge. We'll give these jokers some support to get them started, but if anyone has to stop bullets, I want it to be the cons who get shot up, not our troops."

"I've already issued orders. They'll fall back as soon as the cons are across," Gerard said. "When do we move?"

"The diversion force will deploy at sunup. We'll wait until they're fully engaged." Rorke smiled. "It's always easier to hit your enemy when he's looking the other way."

Sun Oil Docks
Near McFadden Bend Cutoff
Neches River
South of Beaumont, Texas

5:15 a.m. (Four Hours Later)

Snag looked out over his little fleet in the growing light, increasingly unsure whether being placed in charge of the diversion was such a plum assignment. Any job that kept him from being shot at as part of the main attack force was welcome, but it was only after they'd come up with the diversion plan that Spike and that spooky Rorke asshole had started talking about the diversion fleet engaging the ship people. Snag was pretty sure 'engaging' meant getting shot at, and he was none too happy at the prospect.

He fought down his panic at the thought. He had only two dozen men spread among the six boats, so he knew Spike couldn't expect too much; all he had to look like was, *what had Rorke called it? Oh yeah, a credible threat.*

Snag smiled as he looked over the boats; they were a 'credible threat' all right. They were duplicating their attack on the *Pecos Trader*, sort of. He'd rounded up six push boats of various sizes and found enough at least partially skilled people from their captives to run them. Each boat had an 'attack barge' tied off to its starboard side, shielding the boats themselves from gunfire, the same tactic they'd used during the *Pecos Trader* assault. However, there the similarity ended.

Instead of two inches of plywood sandwiched between a double thickness of three-quarter-inch steel plate, the shields on these diversion barges were shams. They were hastily thrown-up affairs constructed of a single thickness of half-inch plywood with sheet metal screwed on the outside, the whole thing spray-painted flat black. At a distance, they looked like the original versions with strong shields, no doubt sheltering an attack force of armed, bloodthirsty cons. At least, that was what they intended the ship people to think. In truth he only had four men on each vessel, one to keep a gun to the head of the boat driver and two to man the machine gun the SRF had given them for each barge. The fourth man was both a backup in case someone was killed or wounded, and also a decoy, to move about at random and fire from behind the fake shields; all to create the illusion the barges were fully manned.

Snag's orders were to move against the east and south sides of the island fortress, spreading the defenders thin and drawing them away from the real attack on the pontoon bridge on the north end of the island. He only had to occupy the defenders' attention long enough for Spike and the main assault force to capture the pontoon bridge and swarm the island, and then he could break contact. It couldn't be soon enough for him.

Snag saw the top of the sun begin to peek over the flat eastern horizon and let out a sigh. *Might as well get it over with*, he thought as he raised the radio to his lips to order his little fleet to get under way.

Officers Mess
S/S *Cape Mendocino*
Clark Island
Neches River
Beaumont, Texas

Same Day - Same Time

Jordan Hughes took a sip of his coffee and looked over the rim of his cup at Dan Gowan. The engineer looked haggard, with a streak of dirt on his forehead. His coveralls were stained with grease and dirt with damp circles emanating from the armpits.

"You look like crap, and you don't smell too good either," Hughes said.

Dan Gowan chuckled and set down his own coffee cup. "Jeez, Jordan, if you ever decide to try another line of work, I'd give motivational speaker a miss if I were you."

"Seriously, Dan, how long has it been since you had a shower and a nap? You can't go on at this pace," Hughes said.

"We're almost done," Gowan said, "at least temporarily. We've got a twenty-foot-high berm across the gap. The boys packed it down last night and we started cutting the outside slope into a vertical wall. We're about three-quarters of the way across. It's not perfect, but when we're done, anyone trying to get at us from there will be faced with a vertical wall of dirt. We'll have to leave a ramp for the last dozer to get inside over the wall, but a ten-foot-wide access at the top of a steep incline is a helluva lot more defensible than two hundred feet of open ground. When things calm down, we can look at putting in a proper and defensible gate, but given the time, it's the best we can do."

"Nobody could have done better, and they don't need you to finish. Get some rest, at least a couple of hours. That's an order," Hughes said.

"I'm okay, Cap. Besides," Gowan said, nodding toward Matt Kinsey, "the stores Matt brought in included soft drinks, so we have soda cans now, and I put Rich building more air cannons like we had on *Pecos Trader*. He got one up last night, but with this much perimeter to defend, we'll need a lot more. I need to help him—"

He stopped short at the distant but unmistakable sound of machine-gun fire.

Hughes' radio squawked. "Bridge to Captain Hughes. Do you copy? Over."

"Loud and clear, Georgia. What's up?" Over," Hughes responded.

"You better get up here right away, and bring Chief Kinsey if he's with you. Over," Georgia Howell said.

Hughes was out the door in seconds, with both Gowan and Kinsey in tow. They raced up the interior stairway to the bridge, to find Georgia Howell on the port bridge wing, a pair of binoculars clamped to her eyes as she stared downriver. She lowered the glasses at the sound of approaching footsteps and offered them to Hughes.

"What's up?" he asked as he raised the binoculars.

"Lucius picked up targets on *Judy Ann*'s radar, so he let me know and headed downriver to investigate. He was fired on just as he rounded the first bend and reports barges moving toward us," Howell said.

"Anyone hurt?" Hughes asked.

"Negative. He turned tail and managed to get back around the bend, and he can move a lot faster without a tow than the barges can," Howell said.

Hughes nodded as he adjusted the focus on the binoculars, and the *Judy Ann* came into focus, pushing a bow wave as she moved back toward the island at full speed. Behind her in the distance he could see an all too familiar shape coming into view around the bend.

"Holy shit," he said softly, then to Howell, "You said targets. Did Lucius get a count?"

Howell nodded. "Six."

The group stood in shocked silence for a moment.

"And they have machine guns this time. Where the hell did they get those?" Gowan said softly, almost to himself.

"If I had to guess, I'd say those SRF scumbags just found themselves some new best friends," Kinsey said.

Hughes nodded. "Well, however it happened, we have to deal with it. Georgia, sound the general alarm and let's get folks to their stations."

As Georgia Howell nodded and moved toward the general alarm switch, Hughes turned to Kinsey. "You're in charge of our defenses, Matt. What should we do?"

Kinsey held out his hand for the binoculars, and when Hughes passed them over, he stared into the distance at the approaching threat. Then he turned and looked north, focusing on the sentries on Old Mansfield Ferry Road. He raised his radio.

"Base to Sentry One. Do you copy? Over," he said into the radio just as the general alarm bell started its raucous clanging.

"This is Sentry One to Base. We copy. What was the shooting, and why's the general alarm bell ringing?" Over."

"We have visitors from downriver. Have you seen anything suspicious out that way? Over," Kinsey said.

"Negative, Base. All quiet here."

"Okay. Keep your eyes open and be ready to pull back. We'll let you know. Base out," Kinsey said.

"Acknowledge. Sentry One out."

Kinsey looked back downriver, assessing the situation. "I'd say we have about twenty minutes before they get here, but they'll be within machine-gun range within half that time. Those guns won't do them much good at close quarters, so I'd say they're meant to suppress our fire, particularly Gowan's little air cannon, to allow them to close. They know our best chance is to keep them at a distance, and if they close with us at six different spots in large enough numbers, we can't repel them all." Kinsey shook his head. "I'd say they learned some lessons from their previous attack."

"Shouldn't we cut the pontoon bridge loose from the bank and let the river current swing it in alongside the island?" Hughes asked.

Kinsey shook his head. "Let's wait a while. There are six barge loads of them and those machine guns may change the equation radically. I'm not sure we can hold them off, and if we CAN'T ..." He let the sentence hang in the air.

Hughes nodded. "And if we can't, moving the families and noncombatants across the pontoon bridge in the dump trucks is our only avenue of escape."

Kinsey nodded in return. "If it comes to that. Our shooters will have to fall in behind them on foot to fight a rearguard action if the cons come ashore after us."

Hughes blew out a sigh and ran his hands through his hair. "Well, let's hope that it DOESN'T come to that, but we'll leave the bridge open for now just in case. If we change our minds, Sentry One can fall back and cut the bridge loose from the bank as they cross. I'll pass the word and get folks ready to evacuate if necessary, but what are we going to do about those damn barges?"

"Change our plan. We can't spread riflemen evenly like we thought. Our perimeter defenses aren't beefed up enough; we can spot a few shooters where there's something substantial for cover, but everywhere else, those guns will just chew us up." Kinsey thought a minute and then turned to Howell. "Order everyone back out of sight and send someone to find Torres and Alvarez and get them up here."

***

"We've got exactly five rounds left. How do you want to split 'em?" Kinsey asked.

Alvarez nodded toward Torres. "Torres usually outshoots me on the range, barely. So three to him and I'll take the last two."

"What the hell you mean barely? I kick your butt every time," Torres said.

Alvarez opened his mouth to respond, but Kinsey silenced him with an impatient wave. "Okay, it's settled. Now remember, you likely won't be able to pinpoint the machine guns until they start shooting, so the Barrett's longer range is no advantage; by the time you spot them, they'll be able to reach you too, so don't linger to admire your kills. No more than one shot from a position. Shoot and move. Shoot and move. Is that clear?" Kinsey said.

Torres and Alvarez nodded.

"And for God's sake, stay well apart. Let us know when you're in position and we'll signal the others," Kinsey said, and the men nodded again, grim faced, and left.

Kinsey looked back toward the barges growing larger as they approached, then down on the main deck, where a dozen volunteers sheltered behind mooring winches or any other scattered equipment likely to stand up to the devastating firepower of the machine guns. Half the volunteers were new arrivals from Darius Green's group.

"I hate using them as decoys," Hughes said, following Kinsey's gaze.

"They know the risks, and it can't be helped. If we don't engage the barges first, they'll just cruise up alongside and swarm us without firing a shot," Kinsey said. "Now let's get out of sight. Things are gonna get hot pretty quickly."

M/V *Johnnie B Goode*
.5 Miles Downriver from Clark Island
Neches River
Beaumont, Texas

Same Day – Same Time

Snag jammed his Glock into the tug skipper's neck. "SLOW DOWN! WE NEED TO KEEP OUR INTERVAL."

As usual, he was leading from the rear; these damn ship people were slippery customers and he had no doubt those friggin' sniper rifles would get into the act. He was going to make damn sure the first boat they targeted wasn't his.

He was anticipating return fire, of course, and all the machine-gun emplacements were sandbagged, armored, and disguised to look like the rest of the shielding. However, nothing they could contrive was likely to stop a round designed to go through an engine block, and all the machine-gun crews had radios and were ordered to concentrate their own fire whenever a sniper was identified. Besides, a long-range gun battle would suit his purposes just fine, since he had no attack troops anyway. He just needed to string things out long enough to satisfy Spike. Hell, he didn't even care if the ship people hit them with that damned napalm again, because he fully intended to cut the barges loose and run after they'd served their purpose.

He got his wish, as rifle fire started from scattered locations along the deck of one of the ships and he heard the machine guns begin to return fire.

S/S *Cape Mendocino*

Torres lay prone on the starboard stack deck and peeked through the scope, amazed the dumb asses were using tracer rounds. The 'decoys' on deck had done their jobs well and prompted a withering return fire from the machine guns on the barges. He followed the tracers back to their source on the closest barge and centered the crosshairs on the machine gun and squeezed the trigger. The Barrett kicked and the target disintegrated in his scope, but Torres didn't linger. He crawled to the small hatch and down the steel ladder into the stack casing and hurried to his next position. As he entered the hatch and started down the ladder, he heard the report of the second Barrett and prayed Alvarez got his kill as well.

M/V *Johnnie B Goode*

Snag was apoplectic. The hasty training his men had received from their SRF benefactors had been quick and dirty, and no one thought to question the machine-gun ammo except to make sure there was plenty of it. In fact, the tracers made the marksmanship of his inexperienced gunners considerably more accurate, and none of the gunners had considered how clearly the tracers highlighted their own positions for the snipers.

Snag glanced at his watch and cursed. Five guns down in five shots, and barely three minutes into his 'attack.' Three friggin' minutes! Only the machine gun on his own barge was still in action and he expected it to be targeted at any moment. He considered retreating, then hastily dismissed the idea. He hadn't drawn the defenders' attention nearly long enough, and if he failed again, either Spike or that spooky ass 'general' would likely have him executed. He raised his radio and ordered the other boats to spread out and move slowly toward the island on a broad front. He had to buy more time.

The boats executed his orders on command, and he watched as they crept toward the island, surprised his own machine gun was still firing. A slow smile of realization spread across his ugly face; the snipers must be out of ammo. Even with one machine gun in operation, he could keep their attention for quite a while.

He changed frequencies on the radio and keyed the mic. "Snag to Spike. We are engaged and have their attention. Over."

Flying Bridge
S/S *Cape Mendocino*

Dan Gowan and Rich Martin crouched, peeking over the section of steel plate Martin had bolted to the rail.

"This plate might stand up to rifle rounds, but no way will it withstand a hammering by those machine guns. When they spot us, they'll cut us to pieces," Martin said, then added, "You sure this is gonna work? We've never fired this one before and that machine gun's a tough shot."

"Only one way to find out. Let's get ready," Gowan said as he reached up to swing the muzzle of the air cannon so Martin could reach it, and then raised his radio.

"Gowan to shooters. Execute," he said.

Stern Barge Elevator
S/S *Cape Mendocino*

Torres raised the M4, a toy compared to his beloved Barrett, and sighted at the single machine gun still spitting fiery tracers in their direction. Elsewhere at the opposite end of the ship, he knew Alvarez was doing the same. The idea was to concentrate fire at the machine gun from two widely separated locations, both of which were far away from Gowan and Martin on the air cannon, to hopefully give the cannoneers a shot or possibly two at the last remaining gun.

Torres sighted at the source of the tracer rounds, took a deep breath, let it out halfway, and then squeezed the trigger.

Flying Bridge
S/S *Cape Mendocino*

Gowan watched the stream of tracers swing toward the stern, almost in slow motion.

"Now, Rich!" he said, and Martin lit the improvised napalm round, pushed it into the muzzle of their air cannon with his broomstick ramrod, then closed the vent valve at the rear of the gun and nodded as he moved his hand to the quick-closing valve.

Gowan grabbed the twin handles on the rear of the cannon and swung the muzzle outboard, rising enough to sight down the barrel at the source of the tracers on the distant barge. "Three, two, one, FIRE!" he said, and Martin cycled the valve open and closed, expelling the round from the cannon and sending it flying toward their target.

Unable to help himself, Martin began to raise his head to watch the trajectory, and had to duck back down as Gowan swung the muzzle back toward him.

"MOVE IT," Gowan yelled. "We don't have friggin' time to admire our work."

Martin nodded apologetically and slammed another burning round down the muzzle. They got off the second shot when Gowan saw the tracer stream moving back toward them.

"DOWN! DOWN! DOWN!" Gowan screamed, throwing himself to the deck and crawling away from the air cannon, Martin by his side.

They moved thirty feet away from the air cannon and then flattened themselves on the deck as the machine-gun rounds vibrated the steel plate of their shield, penetrating it in places and making the steel rail to which it was bolted vibrate like a tuning fork. The fire was unrelenting for several seconds and then the deadly tracer stream stopped abruptly, the machine gunner apparently satisfied that he'd neutralized the threat.

Gowan and Martin raised their heads and looked at the still-approaching barges.

"Damn! Close but no cigar," Gowan said.

There was a circle of fire burning on the shields on either side of the machine-gun emplacement, but they'd missed the gun itself.

Rich Martin nodded then squinted and shook his head. "Something's up, Chief," he said. "Look how those shields are burning. I mean, the last time the napalm burned on top of them and they started smoking and smoldering, but those things look like a damn bonfire. The way those fires are spreading, they're gonna engulf that machine-gun emplacement anyway."

Gowan nodded. "Damned if you're not right, Rich."

Two minutes later the entire line of shields on their target was burning brightly and Gowan turned to Rich Martin.

"Let's go see if our gun is still operational. Maybe we can send a few more little gifts their way," Gowan said.

* * *

Hughes stood on the main deck, looking around the corner of the deckhouse, his binoculars raised. The barges had stopped their approach and the shields were blazing all along their lengths. *All right, Dan,* Hughes thought and lowered the glasses.

"Something's fishy," he said to Kinsey. "Even without the machine guns, maybe ESPECIALLY without the machine guns, I'd expect them to try to close fast to try to overwhelm us at widely separated points on the perimeter. Instead they stop, and those shields seem much more flammable than—"

He jerked his head right at the sound of guns. First rifle fire, then a machine gun. It came from the north. His radio blared.

"SENTRY ONE TO BASE! WE ARE UNDER ATTACK. JEFF IS DOWN. THEY POPPED UP OUT OF NOWHERE AND—"

Hughes' blood ran cold as the transmission ended to the sound of intense small-arms fire.

The barbarians were at the gate.

CHAPTER TWENTY-FOUR

Old Mansfield Ferry Road
Two Miles from Clark Island

Rorke's SUV roared down the road at the head of the assault column, Gerard at the wheel. Behind them was a line of twenty vehicles, a mixed bag of former city buses and school buses. The only thing they all had in common was armor plating and gun ports on their left sides.

As they rounded a turn and came out of a pine thicket, Rorke looked over a flat, marshy plain, areas of water glistening here and there in the tall grass. In the distance, Clark Island and its new ring of ships stood above the surrounding land.

"Pull over and let McComb's group pass. We can see from here with binoculars, and this is as far as we're going. I want to make damn sure we stay out of range of those sniper rifles," Rorke said.

Gerard did as directed and the buses roared past them just as the sound of automatic fire reached them from the river.

"Sounds like our machine guns are engaged at the pontoon bridge," Gerard said.

"Good," Rorke said. "Let's just hope they can keep it open for the two or three minutes it will take these morons to storm the island."

Clark Island
Neches River
Beaumont, Texas

Kinsey, Hughes by his side, rushed across the raw dirt expanse of their island fortress toward the unfinished north wall. All around them others ran for the wall, rifles in hand. Hughes saw Georgia Howell approaching, cutting across the black dirt at an angle, and he motioned Kinsey to stop.

Howell reached them and bent over, panting as she placed both hands on her knees and fought for breath.

"Okay," she said at last to Kinsey. "The barges seem to be pulling back, but I did like you said in case it's a trick. Dan and Rich are still in place at their air cannon and they'll let us know if we need to reinforce there. I sent everyone else to the north wall. What now?"

"We need to get that bridge cut loose from the east bank, but—"

They were interrupted by machine-gun fire from the direction of the north wall and they turned as one and resumed their run. They got there to find Jimmy Gillespie staring east, where two hundred yards away in the middle of the pontoon bridge, a body was sprawled in a growing circle of blood.

"What the hell happened?" Hughes asked.

Jimmy Gillespie shook his head. "It was Jeff Crowley, one of the new guys from Bridge City. He started across the pontoon bridge to throw off the lines on the other end and they hit him with machine-gun fire. I couldn't see where it came from, but they just raked him."

"Damn," Kinsey said. "We gotta know what we're facing."

He looked up at the bow of the *Cape Vincent*, the last ship in line on this side of the fort, her bow looming over both the river and the pontoon bridge.

"There," Kinsey said, pointing. "I should be able to see across the marsh from up there. Maybe I can figure out what we're up against."

Kinsey turned to Hughes. "Captain, if you and Georgia will stay here and get the defense organized, I'll go up to see what I can. If I can take out that machine gun, I'll radio you and you can send a team out to cut the bridge loose."

Hughes nodded and Kinsey ran for the gangway of the *Cape Vincent*.

Kinsey's thigh muscles burned as he sprinted up the steep gangway then ran toward the bow along the port side of the ship. He slowed and crouched when he reached the bow, staying out of sight below the steel bulwark until he reached the offshore side of the ship and slowly raised his head above the bulwark to study the flat terrain on the opposite side of the river.

He squinted into the sun, now a fiery ball halfway above the horizon, and shaded his eyes to let them adjust to the glare. In a few moments, he saw them, not one machine gun, but two, strategically positioned far enough back so as not to be visible from the earthen north wall of the fort, but able to rake the bridge from both sides.

Kinsey nodded in grudging respect. The gunners had chosen their ground well; they were well over five hundred yards out, maybe even six, and while well within the range of their own M240s, they were at the upper limit, or probably beyond, of any shoulder-fired weapons from the fort except a Barrett. *I've got a snowball's chance in Hell of taking them out with an M4 at this distance*, thought Kinsey, feeling the loss of the Barretts.

Maybe with enough shooters up here they could distract the gunners while Hughes dealt with severing the bridge. He was about to call Hughes with an update when he heard laboring engines and looked farther east. The sight that greeted him made his blood run cold. Rushing toward the bridge out of the rising sun was a long line of buses, and he had no doubt they were crammed full of cons. They were less than half a mile away.

"Kinsey to Hughes. We gotta string of buses inbound, ETA less than a minute. No way we can cut the bridge in time. Target everything you can bring to bear on the bridge. DO IT NOW! Kinsey out."

"We're on it," came Hughes' voice.

But even as Hughes acknowledged the order, Kinsey knew it was too late. The first bus closed the gap in less than a minute, then slowed as it picked its way onto the bridge, the driver tentative. All hell broke loose below as the combined firepower of the defenders raked the bus. To no avail.

The front and left sides of the bus were armored, with only a slit for the driver to see and with gun ports all along the side. The noise was deafening as rounds ricocheted off the bus trundling across the bridge, seemingly unconcerned. Kinsey saw now that all the other buses were armored as well. *They brought their own mobile forts.*

The bus continued across the narrow bridge, slowed by the driver's limited vision. It bounced over Jeff Crowley's body without stopping and then rolled ashore as three machine guns opened up from the gun ports to rake the top of the earthen wall of the fort.

The North Wall
Clark Island

Hughes cursed as their fire bounced off the bus. They were aiming at the openings in the armor, but the slits were tiny at this distance and moving targets. The bus made it ashore unscathed and raked the wall with machine-gun fire, driving the defenders to cover.

"What are we going to do, Captain?" Georgia Howell said.

Hughes shook his head. "Not a clue, but if they get many of those damn things in place, they can just keep our heads down until they position an attack force too close to the ramp for us to repel. We have to figure out—"

He jerked his head around at the sound of a powerful engine cranking behind him, and saw Bobby Gillespie in the seat of their largest bulldozer. Mike Gillespie was running to join his brother on the dozer, an M4 slung over his shoulder. He reached the dozer and climbed up and stood beside the seat. Bobby nodded and expertly spun the dozer toward the exit wall over the ramp. He'd just reached the ramp when Jimmy Gillespie ran over.

"Y'all aren't goin' without me," Jimmy yelled up at his older brothers.

The older Gillespies looked at each other and Mike nodded, extending a helping hand down to Jimmy. When Jimmy accepted the outstretched hand and climbed up on the tread, Mike waited until he was unbalanced then pushed him backward off the machine. Jimmy landed flat on his back in the soft dirt, the breath knocked out of him, and Bobby took off.

As they roared up the ramp to the top of the wall, Mike shouted back, "Sorry, little brother. We can't all go. Someone's got to look after Mom and our families. Bobby and I took a vote and you're elected."

"GODDAMN YOU, MIKE," Jimmy Gillespie yelled as he struggled to his feet and started up the ramp in a limping run, but his brothers were already gone, over the crest of the berm and down the ramp on the opposite side.

Hughes watched in stunned disbelief as the dozer charged down the ramp at full speed, its blade raised high as a shield. All the enemy attention focused on the dozer now, its blade ringing like a school bell as fire from multiple machine guns struck the thick steel of the upraised blade.

The cons had positioned the bus parallel to the wall and across from the ramp, obviously intent on bringing all their firepower to bear to support a charge up the only entrance. That also made the bus an easy target as the dozer charged straight down the ramp, the raised blade catching the bus dead center near the top and flipping it on its side.

With the gun ports pointed skyward and no longer a threat, Bobby backed up ten feet, lowered the blade, then crashed back into the underside of the bus, loose dirt flying from the spinning tracks as he drove the overturned bus toward the river at full speed and to the accompaniment of the screams of the cons trapped inside. He slowed at the riverbank to avoid following the bus in, and then eased it off the bank into the river. The bus tipped over completely as it slid into the water and drifted into the current, wheels up.

Hughes turned back toward the second bus about to roll off the bridge behind the Gillespie boys. His heart sank as he realized they'd likely be cut to pieces from behind before they could turn around and raise the blade as a shield.

***

"BOBBY! BEHIND US!" screamed Mike Gillespie as his brother backed the dozer away from the river.

His brother reacted immediately, but as Bobby spun the dozer around, Mike noticed something else. The bus was just rolling off the bridge and he could see all the cons clearly, and they were clearly confused.

"Bobby! This side isn't armored. They're only set up to shoot out the other side," Mike said.

"Take out the driver. Maybe we can block the bridge," Bobby yelled back to be heard over the roaring engine.

674

The words hardly left Bobby's mouth before Mike put two three-round bursts into the now exposed driver, and the slow-moving bus coasted to a stop thirty feet beyond the bridge. Mike continued firing, stitching the unarmored right-side windows of the bus with three-round bursts, sending the cons inside diving for safety. To his left, he could see a third bus moving on to the opposite end of the bridge.

"HERE COMES ANOTHER ONE!" Mike called over his shoulder as Bobby backed the dozer toward the center of the island at full speed.

When he'd lined up his approach, Bobby charged the stationary bus from straight ahead, blade down, striking it and driving it backward onto the bridge. He was unrelenting, pushing the skidding bus half the length of the bridge before a front wheel hit something and the bus turned slightly, sending a rear wheel off the downstream edge of the bridge. The bus tipped and rolled into the river, almost in slow motion, and as it turned on its side and sank, Mike saw Jeff Crowley's body jammed in the wheel well. *Well, you took a bunch of the scum with you, buddy. Good job!* Mike thought.

They were well onto the bridge now, facing the third bus stopped fifty feet away, its driver obviously confused. From the shorter distance and with both vehicles stationary, the driver's vision slit was an easier target, and Mike took out the driver with a single burst. Bobby accelerated into the front of the bus, driving it back until the rear wheels were on the bank, and then canting the dozer blade to push the front wheels off the bridge and leave the bus sitting nose down across the bridge entrance at a crazy angle, blocking it completely.

Mike kept his M4 on the bus and called over his shoulder, "We better get out of here while the gettin's good."

"Amen to that, brother," Bobby said, spinning the dozer in its own length on the narrow bridge and heading back toward the island at full speed.

Above them, Mike heard rifle fire and saw someone on the bow of the *Cape Vincent*, shooting toward the marsh behind them. The immediate response was machine-gun fire from somewhere in the marsh, driving the man to cover. Their defender popped up elsewhere and engaged the machine gun again, and the unequal duel continued as Bobby pushed the dozer for all it was worth. They'd just reached the island when the dozer was stitched with machine-gun fire, and something took Mike's right leg out from under him and he toppled backwards, retaining enough presence of mind to roll as he hit the moving tread. He landed hard, facedown in the dirt.

***

Matt Kinsey watched the Gillespie brothers' attack with a mixture of awe and hope. If the Gillespies could seal the bridge, they all had a chance. He cheered them on, but as they started back across the bridge, he realized the danger. The machine gunners to the east had no doubt been blocked by the buses, but when the dozer moved from behind the bus blocking the bridge, the gunners would have clear shots.

Kinsey gazed eastward at the machine-gun emplacements. *No way I can take those guys out at this distance*, thought Kinsey, *but maybe I can distract them for a few minutes.*

He steadied his M4 on the top of the bulwark, aimed at the nearest gun, took a deep breath and fired. The air still rang from the shots as he dropped down to belly crawl away from the position as fast as he could. The response was immediate as machine-gun fire riddled the thin steel of the bulwark where he'd been.

He took another deep breath and popped up, his shot more rushed now. He barely made it flat on the deck again before rounds tore through the bulwark where he'd been, and he belly crawled for all he was worth in the opposite direction to pop up and fire. It was a deadly game of Whack-a-Mole and he was doing his damnedest not to get whacked, varying the distance he crawled each time to avoid establishing a predictable pattern.

By his fourth shot, Kinsey was gasping for breath, but feeling more positive. It seemed like hours had passed; surely the Gillespies were safe back in the walls now. Then he heard one of the machine guns firing but not at him, and he realized it must be targeting the Gillespies. He popped up where he was, but the other gunner was waiting for him this time, and a round slammed into his shoulder, knocking him onto his back and whipping his head back hard against a set of mooring bits.

His vision blurred. He heard the distant machine-gun fire continuing and said a silent prayer the Gillespies had made it. His left shoulder was numb and it took all his strength to turn his head and look at it. All he saw was a blurry field of red. It didn't hurt exactly, but felt like it was happening to someone else. He reached for his radio and brought it to his mouth, pausing for a moment when he couldn't remember what he was doing. Oh yeah, calling in. He keyed the mic.

"This is … this is Kinsey. I've … I've been hit. I think … I think …"

The radio slipped from his hand and oblivion enveloped him.

**

Bobby Gillespie stopped the dozer and dove off to help Mike seconds before bullets shredded his now-empty seat. He found Mike conscious but bleeding badly and struggling to his feet. Bobby ducked down and pulled his wounded brother across his shoulders in a fireman's carry just as another burst of gunfire rattled off the dozer on the side he thought was safe, and he realized now there were two gunners.

With no shelter, he started for the ramp at a full run, bullets kicking up dirt around him and adrenaline giving him the strength to carry Mike as if he weighed nothing. He'd covered half the hundred yards when a round slammed into the small of his back, severing his spinal cord. He crashed to the ground, Mike's weight crushing his face into the dirt. Mike rolled off him to pull himself into a sitting position and roll Bobby onto his back. There was a lull as both gunners changed belts at once, the sudden quiet almost dreamlike. Bobby's breathing was labored, but his eyes blinked open and he looked up at Mike, strangely calm. A wan smile creased Bobby's dirt-streaked face.

"We kicked their asses, bro," he said weakly.

Mike smiled back. "Yeah, we did, man. You are one badass dozer jockey. Remind me never to —"

Mike jerked and fell back as two rounds caught him in the chest, and another slammed into Bobby's side. The angry gunners both had their range now, and the brothers' bodies jumped from the impact of multiple rounds as the gunners vented their rage at the defeated assault.

**

Hughes stood at the top of the wall with the other defenders, concealed from the machine gunners across the river by the angle, calling encouragement to Bobby Gillespie as he sprinted toward the ramp with his brother on his shoulders. His heart stopped when Bobby was shot down, and he jerked his head to the right at an anguished cry next to him.

"BOBBY! MIKE! GET UP!" Jimmy Gillespie screamed.

But Hughes knew there was no getting up in the offing, only more death. When Jimmy started for the ramp down, Hughes was after him in a heartbeat, tackling him from behind and bringing him to the ground before he'd run ten yards.

Hughes had twenty pounds and four inches on Jimmy Gillespie, but that was balanced by a twenty-year age difference and near hysteria. The wiry young seaman twisted in Hughes' grasp and hammered the top of his head with a rock-hard fist. Hughes saw stars, but hung on as Jimmy landed another blow, this time to his shoulder.

"LET ME GO, GODDAMN IT! THAT'S MY FAMILY OUT THERE!"

Hughes ducked his head and braced for another blow, which never came, and he heard Georgia Howell's voice raised over the renewed rattle of the machine guns.

"There's nothing you can do for them, Jimmy. They're gone. All you can do if you go down there is join them. Do you think they'd want you to die too?" Howell asked.

Hughes looked up to see Howell kneeling beside them, her hand on Jimmy's chest. A man knelt on either side of Jimmy, pinning him on his back with a firm hold on each arm.

Jimmy's face morphed from anger to pain and he began to cry, his whole body shaking with deep racking sobs. Howell nodded to the men holding his arms and they let go as Hughes unwrapped his own arms from around Jimmy's legs and stood. Jimmy sat up and covered his face with his hands, unable to control his grief but embarrassed by it.

"Why … why'd they have to be so goddamned dumb, going out there like that? What am I gonna tell Mom, and their wives and kids?"

"You won't have to tell them anything, Jimmy," Howell said softly. "I'll tell them if you like, and I'll say they were two of the bravest men I've ever known, and that they died saving the rest of us. But for now, we're still in the fight, and if you don't want what your brothers did to be for nothing, you have to shake it off. Not forget it, but put it in a place you think about tomorrow, or the day after, or a week from now."

Jimmy lowered his hands and nodded, visibly struggling to compose himself. He rose and turned back towards his brothers' remains, but Hughes stepped in front of him, blocking his view.

"It's not a memory you'll want," Hughes said. "We'll take care of them as soon as we can do something about those machine guns. Now why don't you—"

Hughes' radio squawked. "This is … this is Kinsey. I've … I've been hit. I think … I think …"

M/V *Cape Vincent*
Clark Island
Neches River
Beaumont, Texas

One Hour Later

Hughes crouched low behind the bulwark, peeking through the twelve-inch opening of a Panama chock at the force across the river and hoping not to attract unwanted attention. He counted seventeen buses arrayed in a line along the riverbank, their armored sides facing the island. There were at least a dozen machine guns, which opened up at the slightest indication of movement on the ship.

Hughes heard a noise behind him and pulled his head back from the opening, then turned and saw Howell and Gowan crawling toward him on deck, staying low and out of sight behind the bulkhead.

"How's Kinsey?" Hughes asked.

"His shoulder's torn up and will take a while to heal, and he took a nasty blow to the head and likely has a concussion, but Laura thinks he'll make it," Howell said, then added, "Presuming any of us do, that is. What's the plan, Captain?"

"Looks like we have a standoff," Hughes said. "They can't move the disabled bus and cross the bridge without taking heavy fire from our guys on the wall, and we can't dislodge them from their position across the river."

"Unless they reposition a machine gun a bit upriver to suppress our fire and send men over the bridge on foot," Howell said.

"Or bring up a dozer of their own to push the bus off the bridge and into the river," Gowan said.

Hughes sighed. "Yeah, well, nothing much we can do about that. They have all the flexibility; all we can do is react." He looked at Gowan. "How about downstream? We clear there?"

Gowan nodded. "The barges went back around the bend. Lucius says they're out of range of the *Judy Ann*'s radar. Rich is keeping lookout on the air cannon, and I sent everyone else to join Georgia's folks on

677

the north wall." He leaned over and peeked through the Panama chock, then shook his head as he turned back to Hughes. "I wish we'd had time to rig up more air cannons. We could've made it hot for them."

Hughes said nothing but lowered his head to look across the river again at the armored buses lining the riverbank, surrounded by acres of salt grass marsh. He pulled his head back and stuck his finger in his mouth to wet it, then held it up. After a moment he smiled.

"So, Dan, can your cannon on the *Cape Mendocino* hit our friends across the river?" Hughes asked.

Gowan looked irritated. "Don't you think I thought of that? They're at least a quarter of a mile out of range, maybe more. And we can't see them from the air cannon anyway."

"But you can land rounds on the opposite bank of the river?"

"Well, sure. That's only two or three hundred yards. Why?" Gowan asked.

Hughes smiled again. "'Cause we might just get a little help with that. Head back to the cannon and call me on the radio when you're ready to shoot."

***

Gowan called five minutes later. "Ready, Cap. Over."

"Okay," Hughes responded. "Target the buses, using your best guess, and fire one for effect. Over."

Hughes heard a dull thump to the south, and long moments later, there was a splash downstream, right along the edge of the east bank.

"You were in the water. Repeat, you were in the water. Shift a bit to your right. Over," Hughes said.

Moments later he heard the thump again and smiled as the round came down on land, well away from the riverbank. His smile faded as the fireball eruption he was expecting didn't occur. "It must have gone out," Hughes said to Howell as he raised his radio.

"You're on target, Chief. Let another one fly. Over," he said.

There was another thump and the third round landed near the second one, again with no fireball.

"What the hell is going on?" Hughes asked aloud.

"It must be the impact," Howell said. "When they smash into something hard, the can splits open and spreads the napalm, but it's all soft ground or even mud over there. I bet they're just burying themselves."

"Damn it!" Hughes said. "So much for that—"

"Cap, wait!" Howell said, peeking through the Panama chock toward the second round's landing spot, where a thin wisp of smoke rose skyward. It got thicker as they watched, then smoke began to rise from the area of the third round, drifting toward the buses upriver on a steady southerly breeze. In minutes the smoke thickened and they saw flashes of orange flame dancing through the salt grass.

Hughes smiled, nodding as he watched. "Dan said that stuff was practically impossible to extinguish; I guess it just takes a few seconds to melt the can and ignite the grass." He raised the radio.

"Hughes to Gowan. You're on target. Repeat. You're on target. Give 'em, say, ten rounds then shift your aim to the right a bit and give 'em ten more. Call me when you're done and we'll reassess. Over."

"Roger that. Gowan out," came the reply, followed almost immediately by another round arcing through the air.

But there was no need to reassess. In ten minutes a wall of flames was racing toward the armored buses, pushed by a freshening south wind and preceded by choking clouds of dense white smoke. Visibility across the river dropped to near zero, and Hughes heard the sound of engines starting over the dull crackling roar of the approaching fire.

Hughes looked over at Howell and grinned. "They're running."

CHAPTER TWENTY-FIVE

Old Mansfield Ferry Road
Two Miles from Clark Island

Rorke stood by the SUV and stared through the binoculars in frustration as a billowing cloud of thick white smoke rose in the distance and moved rapidly northward across his field of vision, obscuring most of the island and his forces attacking it. Frustration turned to rage as he heard laboring engines, and the armored buses burst out of the white wall of smoke and raced toward his position.

He muttered a string of obscenities as he lowered the glasses and looked across the hood of the SUV at Gerard.

"I'm sure that worthless McComb will be leading the retreat. Flag them down and get him over here. I may shoot him myself," Rorke said.

Gerard nodded and moved into the middle of the road and Rorke considered his dwindling options. He sure as hell couldn't report THIS to Crawford, not after Wilmington. No, if his next message to the new president wasn't to report a victory, he needed to start working on his own exit plan, which left him in a bind.

Word of this operation was bound to get out sooner or later. He'd wanted to avoid any obvious SRF involvement whatsoever, but that was now clearly impossible. He'd have to involve his own forces now, but maybe he could still spin them into the 'good guy' role of separating two 'warring criminal factions.' That was something he could work with.

He looked up as the buses began braking to a halt. Moments later Gerard walked up, a shame-faced Spike McComb in tow.

"Well, 'Sheriff,' that was a great success, wasn't it?" Rorke said.

McComb recovered some of his defiance. "It wasn't MY plan, Rorke."

"That's GENERAL Rorke and there was nothing wrong with the plan. You just didn't move fast enough—"

"Now listen, 'General.' SRF or not, I'm pretty sick of—"

Before McComb knew what was happening, the muzzle of Rorke's sidearm was pressed against his forehead.

"No, YOU listen, 'Sheriff,' because if one more word comes out of your piehole unless it's an answer—a respectful answer, mind you—to a direct question from me, I will blow you away. So SHUT. THE FUCK. UP. Got it?" Rorke asked.

McComb nodded.

"Good," Rorke said, holstering his weapon. "Now what the hell happened? I couldn't see everything from here. They didn't fall for the diversion?"

McComb shook his head, glancing at Rorke to make absolutely sure it was okay to talk. Rorke suppressed a smile and nodded.

"The diversion worked just fine as far as I could tell, but we didn't count on those crazy bastards on the dozer," McComb said. "If we go back—"

"WHEN you go back," Rorke corrected.

"When we go back," McComb said, "I think we need dozers of our own to clear the bridge."

Rorke looked at McComb like he was something he was trying to scrape off the bottom of his shoe. "Really, 'Sheriff? You think that friggin' bridge is gonna be there when the smoke clears?"

McComb turned red. "I … I guess not."

"Well, I KNOW not," Rorke said, "so get this collection of losers back over the I-10 bridge to Beaumont and start rounding up more boats or whatever you'll need. You screwed the pooch on doing it the easy way, so now we're back to a water assault."

"What about choppers?" McComb asked. "We'll need air support.'

Rorke shook his head. "I'm not risking choppers with those sniper rifles in play."

"That's just it, I don't think they are. Snag radioed me they didn't even have enough ammo to take out all the machine guns on the attack barges; they took out the last one with that fire cannon of theirs," McComb said.

Rorke said nothing for a moment. "I'll consider that. Now get this rabble back to Beaumont and start preparing for the assault." He looked at the morning sun still low on the eastern horizon. "And be quick about it. I expect that island to be captured or wiped out before sundown. And hear this. I want every single man you've got on this mission. Is that clear?"

McComb bobbed his head. "Yes, General, and if we get those choppers—"

Rorke glared and dropped his hand to his pistol. "You've got a short memory, Sheriff. I don't recall asking two questions."

Spike McComb blanched. "Sorry, General. I didn't mean nothin—"

"Just get the hell out of here and do what I told you to do," Rorke said, and McComb scurried back toward his bus.

"You think he's right? About the sniper rifles, I mean. A few choppers with machine guns could wind this up in a hurry," Gerard said.

Rorke shrugged. "Maybe, but I'm not inclined to rely on intel from these clowns."

Gerard nodded and Rorke mentally parsed the possibilities. The cons were mostly pathetic except as cannon fodder, but neither did he have illusions about the quality of the SRF troops. Cowardice is contagious, as he'd learned to his dismay during the Wilmington fiasco, and he had to avoid a repetition of that at all costs. His chopper pilots might even refuse to engage if they knew the opposition had the Barretts. On the other hand, he HAD to chalk one up in the win column, and chopper gunships were without doubt his best chance to cement a quick victory.

"Who else knows they have sniper rifles, I mean among our guys?" Rorke asked.

"I don't know, just me and you, I guess. I mean, we got the intel from the cons, and we're really the only ones in close contact other than the guys who trained them on the machine guns and the few SRF guys in the gun crews covering the pontoon bridge."

"All ground troops? None of the chopper jockeys know?" Rorke asked.

Gerard looked confused. "I doubt it. Why?"

"Just something I'm thinking about. I'll explain later," Rorke said.

He glanced over at the SUV. "Call in a chopper to pick us up, an armed one. Tell him to fly up I-10 until he hits Vidor and then to approach us from the north. If there IS any sniper ammo left on that island, I don't want 'em taking potshots at a chopper, not yet anyway," Rorke said. "How soon can it be here?"

"Maybe twenty minutes. What are we gonna do with the SUV?" Gerard asked.

"Have the gun crews drive it back," Rorke said.

Aryan Brotherhood of Texas HQ
Formerly Federal Correctional Complex
Knauth Road
Beaumont, Texas

One Hour Later

It took thirty minutes for the chopper to arrive and another thirty to brief the pilot and fly back to the prison. Too long in Rorke's opinion and he wasn't in a good mood as they set down in the parking lot of the administration building. The chopper settled on its skids and the pilot swiveled to look at Rorke in the rear seat.

Rorke keyed his mic. "Are you clear on your orders?"

The pilot nodded. "First we're to do a flyover threat assessment. If we see nothing of concern, we're to go in for short machine-gun runs as an intimidation exercise, first on a north-south axis, then on an east-west run."

"Correct," Rorke said. "There is no specific target, just hit targets of opportunity."

The pilot nodded again. "Ahh … may I ask what opposition we may expect, General?"

Rorke fixed the man with a withering glare. "Is there some part of the term 'threat assessment' you don't understand, Captain? I thought I made it sufficiently clear you're supposed to be telling ME what opposition to expect."

"Sorry, sir," the pilot said, and Rorke and Gerard took off their helmets and exited the aircraft.

They walked a safe distance away and watched the chopper ascend, headed toward the island only six miles away.

"Okay. I understand the threat assessment, but why the gun run?" Gerard asked.

"Because we're still not 'the enemy,' remember. We've been overflying them regularly, so I doubt they'll fire on an SRF chopper without provocation. That will change when we start shooting at them. If those damn sniper rifles still have ammo, they'll use them. I'd rather risk one chopper to find out than a dozen. If that chopper doesn't get blown out of the sky, it opens up all sorts of interesting possibilities."

The North Wall
Clark Island

Same Time

Hughes stood on the north wall, the acrid smell of the smoke from the grass fire in his nostrils as he gazed down at the dozer demolishing the external ramp, turning the berm into a sheer twenty-foot wall of dirt for its entire length. It would mean leaving the dozer outside and bringing the operator in with a ladder, but it couldn't be helped. They'd take the battery and disable the dozer in multiple other ways to prevent it being used against them.

"I guess we're about as ready as we'll ever be."

Hughes turned to find Georgia Howell beside him. "I didn't hear you come up."

"You looked pretty deep in thought," Howell said.

He sighed. "Always these days, none of them are pleasant, I'm afraid."

"We'll make it," Howell said. "Between the wall and cutting the bridge, we've got damn good defenses."

Hughes nodded absently. His first order of business upon hearing the bus engines fade had been removal of the bridge. The dozer cleared the damaged bus out of the way and came back to the island as a dozen willing volunteers broke the end of the pontoon bridge free from the east bank and let the bridge swing like a door on a hinge as the river current folded it back along the side of the *Cape Vincent*.

"We've beat the cons before and we'll keep beating them," Howell said.

Hughes shook his head. "Maybe, but not by throwing rocks, and we don't have much ammo left. Besides, it's not just the cons I'm worried about, because they didn't suddenly get a visit from the 'machine-gun fairy.' Also from what Kinsey said about the way those two machine guns set up on the bridge, that took training as well, something we haven't seen in the cons' tactics so far. The SRF is in the act here, whether we see them or not."

They both looked up at once at the distant thump of chopper blades and looked west to see the aircraft growing larger as it approached at high speed.

"Speak of the Devil, and it looks like he's coming from the direction of the prison," Howell said.

The chopper was over them in seconds, slowing slightly as it passed, obviously checking out the island. It continued well to the east before it turned and started back, crossing farther to the south now. Hughes could clearly see the machine gunner in the door and something in the man's posture made the hair rise on the back of his neck. He saw the gunner reach over and pull back the charging bolt.

"GEORGIA! DOWN!" Hughes screamed, but before she could react, he'd shoved her to the ground and fallen on top of her just as bullets whined through the space they'd occupied a scant second before.

The gunner raked the top of the wall, driving the defenders to cover, then as quickly as it had come, the chopper was past. Hughes lifted his head and saw it veer north and once again turn, obviously intent on another run.

"HE'S COMING BACK, PEOPLE," Hughes called. "FIRE AT WILL!"

Hughes immediately regretted his knee-jerk reaction as frightened defenders started blasting away frantically, wasting valuable ammunition. The positive result was that a few of the rounds must have pinged ineffectually off the chopper and he showed no appetite for more. He turned and left the way he'd come.

"CEASE FIRE!" Hughes yelled as he ran for the gangway of the nearest ship. He took the outside stairs two at a time as he tried desperately to reach the higher vantage point of the bridge wing before the chopper was out of sight. He got there in time to see it settle down, dropping out of sight behind a spread of distant pine trees.

Right at the prison complex.

Conference Room
Aryan Brotherhood of Texas HQ
Formerly Federal Correctional Complex
Knauth Road
Beaumont, Texas

"We'll give the cons their air support. I want ten armed choppers over here from Houston ASAP, and another ten on standby," Rorke said.

"I thought you didn't want us to have a visible role. Are you sure we want to be associated with these guys in case—" Gerard hesitated "—in case the future doesn't turn out quite like we expect. None of us wants to be facing some sort of atrocity trial."

"The chances of that are nonexistent. And as far as helping the cons more, things change. The President wants this taken care of, whatever it takes." He smiled. "Besides, do you think I'm really gonna keep playing patty-cake with these cons? I was willing to let them rule their little dung heap if they were useful, but as far as I can see, they're a bunch of incompetent clowns. We'll fly air cover on this op to soften up the opposition and give them a cakewalk, but after they take care of our friends in the fort, we'll 'discover' the massacre in progress. If in the process of coming to the aid of the defenders we blast the hell out of anything on the ground that moves, we just say we did our best in a very confused situation." Rorke shrugged. "With no witnesses to contradict us, we can spin it any way we want."

"That's why you want the second wave of choppers, to take out the cons," Gerard said, a statement rather than a question.

Rorke nodded. "We might not have them all collected in one place again, so we may as well take advantage of it. How long before you can get the first wave over here from Houston?"

"We only have four of the birds armed, so it'll take a while to get the guns in place on the others, and longer still for the ammo load out. We can probably have the first group here and ready to go in, say, four hours, but I'm not sure about the cons. McComb seems to be having problems getting things together," Gerard said.

Rorke's face clouded. "We'll see about that. Get that asshole in here."

Upper Cargo Deck
S/S *Cape Mendocino*
Clark Island
Neches River
Beaumont, Texas

Jordan Hughes looked out over the assembled population of their hastily constructed little fort. Five hundred and eighty-seven souls, that number swollen mostly by the families of the construction crew recruited by the Gillespie brothers. He'd left six lookouts in place and asked the others to gather on the cargo deck, a huge area out of sight below deck more than adequate to accommodate them all at once. They'd come without complaint, strangely silent as they'd filed in to the cavernous space.

The lights weren't on, but the massive stern door by the barge elevator was open, casting the whole space in a light not unlike the shade of a tree, and Hughes studied the attendees, HIS people whether he wanted them or not. He saw families with young children, and not a few aged parents, and felt a crushing responsibility unlike any he'd ever felt. He never signed up to make life-or-death decisions.

Matt Kinsey had insisted on attending, and Hughes was glad. The Coastie stood nearby, his arm bound to his chest to prevent his shoulder from moving. Laura and the girls stood on either side of Hughes, and Laura slipped her hand in his and gave a quick squeeze. She looked up at him.

"You can do this," she whispered.

Hughes snorted softly. "Then why the hell do I feel like Travis at the Alamo. All I need is a sword to draw a line in the sand."

Laura smiled and laid her head against his shoulder. "I don't think that would work on this steel deck, but I'll go look for some chalk if you like."

Hughes pulled her into a brief fierce hug, then released her and walked a few feet to step up on a low stack of wooden pallets so he could be seen and heard by the whole group. His hands were shaking, and he held them together behind his back and hoped no one would notice. He'd always thought pictures of historical figures in the same pose made them look like pompous pricks with a Napoleon complex and he suddenly wondered if they'd all been as terrified as he was right now. He took a deep breath and then began to speak.

"Okay, folks, thanks for coming, I won't keep you long. We beat back the cons again, but I'm sure they haven't given up, and each attack depletes our ammunition stocks further; we can't hold them off forever. Added to that are the facts they now have machine guns and the attack by the SRF helicopter a short while ago. Both Chief Kinsey and I believe the SRF is supplying the cons, and that they may even join in future attacks. With the Barrett ammo gone, we have no real air defense left, and the simple truth is we don't have a chance of surviving an attack with close air support."

"SO WHAT'S THE PLAN, CAPTAIN?" came a shout from the crowd, and Hughes recognized the voice of one of the former crewmen of the *Pecos Trader*.

He suppressed a sigh. They always thought he had a plan, when many times he didn't have a clue. Much of leadership seemed to consist of seeming confident when you were clueless. But there was no time for false confidence now, not with so many lives on the line.

"Not much of one, I'm afraid. We either run or stay here and fight it out as long as we can, not knowing what will happen to any survivors if we lose. From what I know of both the cons and the SRF, I'd say nothing good," he said.

"Run? How we gonna run? We're surrounded by water," Darius Green said.

Hughes nodded to where Lucius Wellesley stood. "If anyone wants to leave, we'll put you on a barge and Captain Wellesley will land you at a place of your choosing on either bank. But that has to be done quickly. We may be attacked again at any time."

"What do you mean 'land us'? What we gonna do ashore out in the open, with no food or water or weapons?" Darius Green asked.

"Anyone wanting to leave can take whatever weapons and ammunition they came in with, as well as a couple of days' food and water. You won't be able to carry much more than that anyway, since you'll be on foot," Hughes said.

"That's bullshit! Out there on foot with no defenses? Besides, if the SRF is with the cons like you say, they got choppers to hunt us down. That ain't no choice, man. That's a death sentence," Green said.

"I'm afraid it's the only choice I have to offer, Mr. Green. If we do it quickly enough and there are enough people and you all spread out when you land, some of you might escape. I think the only reason the SRF is involved is that we represent an organized threat to their power. If we disperse, they may decide to ignore us —"

"That's okay for you white folks, but you may have noticed those Aryan Brotherhood assholes are shooting us just for being black. So we all run away, and while the cons go after the black folks, the rest of y'all escape? Is that your plan, Hughes?" Green demanded.

There were angry shouts from the African-American members of the *Pecos Trader* crew, defending Hughes, and Green's group responded in kind. Tempers flared and the meeting dissolved into a shouting match as people ignored Hughes attempts to bring order.

BANG! BANG! BANG!

Thunderous banging filled the cavernous box of the cargo deck, echoing off the steel bulkheads. The crowd fell silent and looked toward the source of the sound, to see Matt Kinsey holding a fist-size steel shackle in his good hand and beating it against the steel bulkhead. When he was sure he had everyone's attention, Kinsey tossed the shackle back on deck where he'd found it and raised his voice.

"WE DON'T HAVE TIME FOR THIS, PEOPLE. CAPTAIN HUGHES WAS TALKING, SO SHUT THE HELL UP AND LISTEN TO HIM," Kinsey yelled.

The silence held and Hughes nodded to Kinsey and continued.

"To answer your last question, Mr. Green, no, that's not my plan. I intend to stay here and fight. However, that's not a decision I can make for any of you. Many of you have families with children, and as I said, I don't know what will happen to us if, more likely when, we lose. As you've pointed out, trying to escape will be equally dangerous, but all I can really do is present the two crappy options and let you all choose for yourselves. But I believe time is short, so everyone has to choose now," Hughes said.

A quiet fell over the crowd, replaced by a low murmuring as people discussed the choice in hushed tones. Darius Green spoke up first.

"Me and my folks are all staying. If we're gonna die, at least we can take some of them with us," Green said.

The other minorities were the next to indicate their choice to stay, because as Green had pointed out, fleeing held increased dangers for them. Kinsey indicated he was staying, and all the other Coasties followed suit. The rest seemed conflicted, no doubt weighing the chance of escape, however slight, against the almost certainty of dying or being captured by the cons.

"Okay, folks, we don't have much time and we need to get a head count so we can get things rolling. Would everyone staying please move to my left and those leaving move to my right," Hughes said.

Better than I expected, thought Hughes as he watched the crowd split into approximately equal groups, with indecision clearly showing on the faces of many of those who had not yet decided. When there was a clear separation between the two groups, a small figure stepped from the uncommitted side and spoke in a firm, clear voice belying her small stature.

"The Gillespies don't run. We'll all be staying," Dorothy Gillespie said as Jimmy Gillespie led the rest of the clan into the gap to stand behind his mother.

Dorothy Gillespie turned back to the uncommitted group. "The rest of y'all need to make your own decisions, but I ask you to think about what might be gained by running. These are wicked, evil men, and they'll find you eventually. Do we bow down to this evil and let it triumph? If we do, it appears to me we're already dead, it'll just take us a little longer to die, that's all. But if we stay, firm in our resolve, the Lord will provide."

"Mrs. Gillespie, I appreciate that sentiment, but I don't want anyone making a decision based on false hope. I doubt help will come," Hughes said.

Dorothy Gillespie smiled. "Then your faith is not strong enough, Captain, but that doesn't matter because I have enough for us both. '*We are hard-pressed on every side, but not crushed; perplexed, but not in despair; persecuted, but not abandoned; struck down, but not destroyed.*' Second Corinthians, verse four."

"PREACH IT, SISTER!" came a shout from among Darius Green's group.

Dorothy Gillespie looked over and smiled, then turned back to Hughes. "And the Lord helps those that help themselves, Captain Hughes, as he has so far, every time. So if he's running a little late this time, we'll just have to kick their sorry butts ourselves."

There was laughter from the crowd as Dorothy Gillespie led her family across the gap, quickly replaced by tension when no one else moved. Finally another person crossed the gap, followed by two more, and then the entire uncommitted group moved almost as one, closing the distance and eliminating the gap completely.

You could have heard a pin drop in the cavernous space of the cargo deck, and when Kinsey spoke, his words carried through the space.

"Well, I'll be damned," he said softly. "Remember the Alamo."

From the crowd came an unexpected reply.

"I do," Torres said. "We won, but don't worry, me and Alvarez are on y'all's side this time."

The laughter broke the tension completely, and as it died down, Hughes raised his hands for silence. "Thank you all. Whatever comes, we will face it together. Now everyone please get back to their posts."

Captain's Office
S/S *Cape Mendocino*

Ten Minutes Later

"I'm not going to debate this, Laura. I want you and the girls to take one of the fast fishing boats and head for Cormier's place on the bayou," Hughes said. "I have to stay, but I'll be damned if I'm going to sacrifice my family."

"So we're just supposed to slip away and leave everyone? How much moral authority do you think you'll have when the rest find out you saved your own family and left theirs in danger, especially after you just gave your 'stand with me' speech?" Laura asked.

"I don't give a damn. I didn't volunteer for this. I'll do the best I can, but sacrificing my family is too much to ask. Cormier's place is a long shot, but at least it's a chance. Kinsey can give us general directions, but we'll have to send a VHF message and hope Cormier receives it and comes out to find you and take you in. He might do it for you, but I doubt he'd consider it for six hundred people, most of whom he's never met. He's a good man, but there's no way he would strain his resources like that or risk taking in a group of total strangers who may even outnumber his own people." Hughes sighed. "Don't you understand, Laura, this might work for you and the girls, and maybe a few others Cormier knows, but for most of them it isn't an option. There are just too damn many people."

Laura said nothing, but gave Hughes an appraising look. "How long have you been planning this, Jordan Hughes? You didn't just think of it, I know that."

Hughes sat back in his chair and seemed to deflate. "I've been thinking of almost nothing else since it became clear we're going to be overrun. I actually thought more people would decide to leave, and depending on how many there were, I figured I'd change the plan a bit and put some of them in our small boats so everyone could take off on their own. The only difference is you and the girls would have a destination."

Laura smiled. "So you were undone by your own eloquence."

Hughes grimaced. "Actually I think Dot Gillespie threw me under the bus when she started quoting scripture."

"The girls won't want to leave, you know, any more than I do. In fact, I suspect they'll outright refuse. We'll likely have to bind and gag them to get them in a boat," Laura said.

Hughes' face hardened. "Whatever it takes. The thought of those filthy cons getting their hands on the girls — or you — makes my blood run cold."

Laura didn't respond but sat silent, a pensive look on her face.

"Do you think Cormier would take all of the kids?" she asked at last.

Hughes looked surprised. "I don't know, he might, I guess. He's a good man and it would be harder to turn down a bunch of kids than it would a group of mixed refugees. They don't eat as much and they're less likely to cause problems or upset whatever social dynamic the Cajuns have going. How many — "

"Forty-one below the age of twelve and six teenagers counting our twins," Laura replied, then smiled at the look on her husband's face. "I've been keeping the head count so Polack could calculate how long our stores will last, remember?"

"Do you think people would be willing to send their children off like that?"

"Aren't you?" Laura asked.

"Yeah, dumb question. But you can't handle forty-seven kids alone," he said.

"No, but our girls and the other teenagers can, and it changes the mission from 'running away' to 'helping the innocent children escape,'" Laura said. "I suspect that's the only way you're going to get our girls in a boat."

"We'll need several boats. Can the teenagers drive them?" Hughes asked.

Laura shook her head. "What about loading them all on *Judy Ann*? Cormier knows and trusts Lucius Wellesley, right? And that would give them VHF to keep calling Cormier as they get closer to Cajun country. If Lucius objects to leaving, we use the same 'saving the children' motivation we're using on our girls."

Hughes smiled. "Beautiful AND smart. Sounds like y'all will do just fine."

"Not 'y'all.' Just the girls. You're gonna need a doctor here, even if I am a horse doctor. I'm staying."

"Laura—"

"Don't even start, Jordan. I'm staying and that's it!"

"But the girls will need you," Hughes said.

"They're smart and independent young women, in case you hadn't noticed, and they'll have each other. Besides, they don't need me nearly as much as the younger children will need their own mothers, and then where do we draw the line? All of the mothers? All of the wives and grandparents? Then maybe some of the fathers as a protective detail?" Laura shook her head. "If we approach everyone and make this public, I HAVE to stay as an example; otherwise everyone is going to want to jump in the boats and go. If the SRF actually IS involved now, do you honestly think they're going to let a mass exodus happen? *Judy Ann* alone will probably be ignored, but they'll be well within range of the choppers until Cormier takes them in to his bayou hideaway. The SRF will spot a major evacuation for sure, and do you think they'll just let us set up elsewhere outside their control? You know they're likely to machine gun us on the water, or worse, we lead them to Cormier."

Laura's voice softened and she took Hughes' hand in hers. "Don't you think I WANT to go with them, Jordan? Don't you think my heart aches at the thought of forcing our fifteen-year-old kids to take on such a task? But times have changed and we have to accept that, and fifteen-year-olds will be doing things unimaginable to us just a few short months ago. This is the only chance to save them. Not just our girls, but ALL the kids. You know I'm right."

A lump rose in Hughes' throat, and he could only nod, squeezing Laura's hand as he did so. She moved into his arms and they shared a fierce embrace. Laura was the one to break it, gently disentangling herself and standing. She wiped a tear away.

"I'll start talking to the mothers and organizing the kids while you talk to Lucius. We have to get this moving fast if it's going to work," she said, and headed for the door before Hughes could object.

M/V *Judy Ann*

One Hour Later

Hughes stood in the little wheelhouse of the *Judy Ann*, watching the children descending the steep accommodation ladder under the supervision of his twin daughters and the other teens. The kids carried an assortment of makeshift luggage, mostly pillowcases and plastic garbage bags. Laura's common-sense rule for the hasty departure was one piece per passenger and, very young children excepted, the kids had to be able to carry their own bag.

The parents jumped at the chance to save their children. The older teens were harder to convince but, as Laura had surmised, won over by the very true argument they were the only chance to save the smaller children. Lucius Wellesley was the hardest sell, but in the end, he too succumbed to Laura's logic. He pared his crew down to only Jimmy Kahla, not only because he needed the chief engineer, but because Jimmy was an avid hunter and the best shot in *Judy Ann*'s crew.

"We'll give you what we can spare for firepower, but I'm afraid it's not much," Hughes said. "It's mainly the civilian stuff where the ammo isn't standard. All of the teenagers have some shooting experience, but I hope you don't need it."

"I hope we don't either, but I've seen your girls shoot, so I'm not too concerned. That Julie is something with that .308. I figure the only place we might have trouble is between here and the Intracoastal intersection, and if there are any cons on the water, I should be able to see 'em well ahead of time on the radar. I reckon if Jimmy and your two gals start layin' into them long distance, they'll turn tail soon enough. After we get in the canal headed east, I doubt they'd try to follow, they never have before anyway."

Hughes nodded and fished a smart phone out of his pocket and handed it to Wellesley.

Wellesley looked confused. "What's this?"

"Laura's phone. Some of the apps still work off-line. She kept it close, even during all our troubles; it has a lot of family pictures on it she couldn't bear losing," Hughes said.

Wellesley nodded. "You want me to give it to your girls after we get clear."

Hughes shook his head. "No … I mean yes, please do that, but that's not the reason I'm giving it to you. I used it to record a message about what's happening here. When you get clear of the cons, I'd appreciate it if you'd broadcast it over the VHF. Maybe the hams will spread it."

Wellesley looked doubtful. "Most of the hams have gone quiet since the government started triangulatin' 'em, and when they do transmit, it's only in short spurts. They'll likely all be listenin', but I doubt too many will risk re-transmitting. And to be straight up, Jordan, I doubt anyone will come riding to your rescue. I'll try to convince Cormier to send folks and bring 'em back myself, but I doubt there'll be enough of us or that we'll be in time."

Hughes shook his head. "You can't make a difference against armed choppers and I don't want any more lives wasted. Andrew's group has a chance for survival in the bayou if they lie low, so stay with them."

Wellesley looked down at the phone, confused. "Then what's the point?"

"Accountability," Hughes said. "Sooner or later some sort of real government will return, I have to believe that. When it does, I don't want anyone to be able to misrepresent what happened here. For all we know, they've wiped out Wilmington and been able to portray them as criminals and looters." Hughes' voice took on a hard edge. "We may not be able to hold out against these bastards, but I sure as hell want folks to know we were honorable people who did our best. I owe that to the folks on this island." He paused, struggling to control a flood of emotion. "And … and to the memory of those who died getting us this far."

Wellesley gave a solemn nod and slipped the phone into his pocket. "I'll see to it, my friend," he said softly.

"Thank you," Hughes said, then turned his attention back to the accommodation ladder in time to see Jana jump off the bottom step onto the deck of the towboat then turn to lift a little girl of perhaps three down after her.

"That's the last of them. I'll go down and hug the girls goodbye and be on my way," Hughes said, turning to extend his hand.

Wellesley pushed his hand down and wrapped him in a hug. "Give 'em hell, Jordan. I'll keep your girls safe and get your message out. You can count on it."

Hughes broke the embrace and nodded. He slapped Wellesley on the back a final time, then turned without speaking and went down the stairway to say his goodbyes.

CHAPTER TWENTY-SIX

Conference Room
Aryan Brotherhood of Texas HQ
Formerly Federal Correctional Complex
Knauth Road
Beaumont, Texas

One Hour Later

Rorke glared across the conference table at McComb. "What the hell do you mean you can't be ready today? I don't recall ASKING you if you could be ready, that was an order. Now get out of here and follow it."

McComb didn't back down. "I'm tryin' to follow it, General. You also told me to send everybody, which means I've stripped all of the posts and have damn near twelve hundred men, but I can't shit boats. We lost most of ours in the other attacks and we've run through all the barges we could get our hands on easily. Get as pissed off as you want, but it'll take time to round up enough boats to move that many people, and that's the bottom line. Ain't nothin' I can do about it I ain't already doing."

Rorke struggled to control his anger. He HAD to delay reporting to Crawford until he could report success, but each hour increased the risk Crawford might contact him first. The new president had been uncharacteristically silent in the last day or so, but that was unlikely to last; Crawford would be demanding an update soon.

"When?" Rorke asked.

McComb shrugged. "If we work through the night, maybe tomorrow sometime. Depends on whether we can turn up another barge or two, but—"

"Sunrise tomorrow and not one friggin' second later. Do you hear me, McComb?" Rorke said.

Captain's Office
S/S *Cape Mendocino*
Clark Island
Neches River
Beaumont, Texas

Matt Kinsey shifted in his chair and suppressed a groan as pain radiated from his left shoulder down his immobilized arm. Across the coffee table, Laura Hughes saw him grimace.

"Do you need something for the pain, Matt?" Laura asked. "Lucius left us the *Judy Ann*'s medical kit."

Kinsey shook his head. "Thanks, but I'm okay and we might need them later. Besides, meds put me in la-la land and I need to think clearly." Kinsey turned to Jordan Hughes. "Not that it matters, I guess; any way you slice it, we're clearly screwed."

"Maybe they won't have choppers," Hughes said.

"It doesn't really matter. Counting the north wall, we have over eight thousand feet of perimeter, which puts a defender every twenty feet or so if we spread out evenly, but we haven't had time to reinforce positions on deck, so we CAN'T spread them out evenly. Even if we use deck machinery and other things as cover, there'll be gaps. And we KNOW they have machine guns now, so they can chew us up, or at a minimum keep us cowering behind cover while they exploit the gaps," Kinsey said. "With those machine guns in play, we've got too much wall and not enough resources. We just haven't had the time we needed to complete the defenses."

"We have machine guns too, and Rich and I are working on more air cannons," Gowan said.

"Yeah. Exactly two machine guns with maybe ten minutes of ammo each if the gunners fire frugally," Kinsey said. "And with respect, Dan, your air cannons won't even last a fraction of that if they target you with machine-gun fire. It gets worse with choppers."

"How much worse?" Hughes asked.

"Orders of magnitude. We have no air defense except massed small-arms fire, which means a bunch of people pumping rounds up at the same moving target, hoping a few shots connect. It has a poor success rate and we don't have ammo to waste anyway. We could try using the machine guns, but elevating the muzzles enough to fire at an overhead chopper is problematic, and we'd end up with a gunfight with one gunner able to move in three dimensions and the other one a stationary target; it doesn't take too much imagination to figure out who'd win that fight." Kinsey sighed. "Choppers can just sit above us and rake our interior lines. We won't be able to bring them down and no one anywhere on the wall will be able to hide from them."

The group lapsed into silence.

Darius Green shifted from his position leaning against the wall, some distance from the others. He'd seemed wary when Hughes invited him to the meeting, and refused a seat when he'd arrived, preferring to stand against the wall a few feet away.

"So what we gonna do? Give up? 'Cause that's what it sounds like," Green said.

Hughes turned to Green. "No one's going to give up, Mr. Green. Chief Kinsey is just pointing out the problems. If we don't have a clear idea what we're up against, we can't figure out a way to beat them."

Green shrugged, but when he spoke his voice had a hard edge. "We all know we're not gonna beat 'em, you made that clear in your little John Wayne speech. Seems to me, all Kinsey here is sayin' is we can't keep 'em off the island, and we all know that too. The way I see it, the only thing we can do is kill as many of them as we can before they get us. We're not gonna do that by fighting on the walls and losing a bunch of folks doing it. The cons are comin' in, choppers or not, and if they DO bring choppers, everybody outside is gonna be shot to hell. So I say let 'em come. We give 'em a kick in the balls on their way in, then pull back and wait for 'em inside. If the choppers show up, they can't shoot what they can't see, and we'll be able to kill a lot more of the bastards while they're trying to root us out than we will in a stand-up fight on the wall." Green paused. "We all know the end of this story; otherwise nobody would have sent their kids away."

Kinsey nodded slowly. "He's right."

Green's voice softened. "I just had longer to think about it than y'all. Hiding in that warehouse, surrounded by the Aryan Brotherhood with no escape in sight, I didn't have much else to think about than how I wanted to go. I had hope when we came here, but turns out it's no different. Choppers or no choppers, they gonna win, all y'all know that. We gotta stop pretending there's even a tiny hope of anything else and concentrate on makin' them pay."

No one said anything for several seconds.

Hughes broke the silence with an audible sigh. "Does anyone disagree with that?"

Around the table and the room, there were head shakes.

"All right then, let's come up with a plan to make them pay. Any and all ideas are on the table, but we have to be quick. We don't have a helluva lot of time here," Hughes said.

Over Clark Island
Neches River
Beaumont, Texas

Day 49
May 19 - 4:20 a.m.
(The Next Day)

Rorke felt the thump of the chopper blades through his seat. It was a comforting vibration, and he was glad to be airborne again, now that they'd confirmed the sniper rifles weren't a threat. Or almost confirmed it, anyway; he was staying out of range until the island had been totally neutralized, just in case.

His chopper was west of the island, and in the barely lightening eastern sky, he could discern the outline of a second helicopter directly over the island.

The radio sounded in his earphones.

"Thunderbolt Actual, this is Recon One. Do you copy? Over."

Rorke keyed his mic. "Recon One, this is Thunderbolt Actual. I copy and request a sitrep. Over."

"IR scans confirmed by NV show five tangos spread along decks of ships, likely lookouts. No other heat signatures or activity detected. Over," came the reply.

Rorke mulled that over. He'd expected more activity, at least a token force along the wall to sound an alarm and hold until reinforced if attacked. But only five lookouts? Did they actually think their little victory yesterday settled the issue? Surely they couldn't be that naive. He keyed the mike again.

"Recon One, I copy five tangos on ships. Repeat five tangos on ships only. Please confirm there is no activity on north wall. Over," Rorke said.

"Thunderbolt Actual, I confirm zero activity, repeat, zero activity on north wall. It's wide open. Over."

"I copy, Recon One. What are the five tangos doing? Over," Rorke asked.

"Nothing. They looked up in our direction and a couple have NV gear, but mainly they're just staying put. Over."

Quentin Rorke had learned many things in his decades as a mercenary, one of which was that his adversaries were usually predictable. Even if the defenders inside the fort were negligent in not anticipating another attack, he was perplexed by the behavior of the lookouts. They'd obviously heard the chopper but weren't reacting. He would expect them to raise an alarm of some sort, to send defenders boiling out of their holes to man the defenses. He didn't like it when people acted unpredictably.

"I copy, Recon One. You may rejoin your attack squadron. Thunderbolt Actual out," Rorke said into his mic.

They were either incredibly lucky or walking into a trap, and he didn't much believe in luck. On the other hand, the defenders had no way of knowing they'd be facing an assault with a ten-chopper close air support force, and that was likely to trump whatever pathetic trap they had cobbled together. Still, it didn't hurt to be cautious. Rorke changed frequencies and keyed the mic again.

"Thunderbolt Actual to Riverine Actual. Do you copy? Over."

"This is Riverine Actual. I copy. Over," came McComb's voice.

"Riverine Actual, it's possible the landing may be unopposed. Put an advance scout force of fifty men on the north tip of the island at once to report what they find. Over," Rorke said.

McComb acknowledged the order and Rorke settled in to wait. Whatever trap they might have set, fifty men was probably enough bait to trip it. After all, the defenders wouldn't let TOO many men land directly in front of their most vulnerable area.

A long twenty minutes later, Rorke's radio squawked. "Riverine Actual to Thunderbolt Actual. Do you copy? Over."

"I copy, Riverine Actual. Go ahead. Over," Rorke said.

"The boys say it's wide open. There ain't a soul there. Ah … over," McComb said.

Rorke looked down at the island. It was getting light enough to see now, and if he HAD indeed caught the defenders napping, they were going to wake up to a very unpleasant surprise. He and Gerard had planned the assault, without McComb's input of course, and decided the north wall was still the preferred point of attack. Defenders on the wall would be completely in the open and exposed to fire from his gunships, and in any event, the cons seemed incapable of executing any sort of complex plan. It seemed far better to hammer one massive blow at the weakest point of the line. Besides, attacking the ships' sides in boats meant the cons might flee when the going got rough. He smiled; he'd have a bit more control of that after they'd landed on the island.

"Riverine Actual, looks like it's your lucky day. Commence landing full assault force now. Repeat, land full assault force now. I am activating air support. Over," Rorke said.

McComb acknowledged, and below Rorke saw the white wakes of over two hundred boats of all sizes and types rounding a bend upriver to close on Clark Island. He raised his mic and activated the air-assault force and glanced south to see the choppers rising from the prison complex. The choppers had no targets at the moment, but Rorke had no doubt the north wall would soon be jammed with defenders.

He watched with growing concern as more convicts boiled ashore, many carrying ladders, and the wall still remained empty of defenders. Encouraged by the lack of resistance, the cons were all running for the wall now, eager to get at the defenders on the other side. But there were no defenders. Something was very, very wrong.

Forepeak Tank
M/V *Cape Vincent*
Clark Island

Baker parted the plastic curtain and poked his binoculars through the crack to peer out at the bare dirt of the island below the north wall. It was swarming with cons, many carrying ladders as they rushed forward, and from his slightly elevated position he could see boats disgorging even more cons onto the low-lying island.

"Jeez," he said as he lowered the glasses, "there's a bunch of them."

Beside him, Torres raised his cheek from the stock of the M240. "Are they all off the boats yet?"

"Almost," Baker said, and raised the glasses again.

Two minutes later he lowered them again and looked back at Torres. "That's it. You ready?"

Torres fished earplugs from his pocket and tossed them to Baker before twisting a pair into his own ears.

"This is gonna be like shooting from inside a bass drum, noisy as hell. You'll need those. Pull the curtain whenever you're ready," Torres said.

Baker nodded, pushed the plugs into his ears, and ripped down the plastic curtain.

***

Task Force 'Kick in the Balls' was formed to make the most effective use of the defenders' two machine guns. They were positioned to do the most good, the most quickly — thanks to Dan Gowan and his cutting torch.

The north wall was anchored on either end against the hulls of the M/V *Cape Vincent* and her sister ship, the M/V *Cape Victory*, with the bows of both vessels extending out beyond the wall. Gowan and Rich Martin had climbed into the empty forepeak tanks and cut long horizontal firing ports through the hulls of both ships, allowing an uninterrupted view of the entire unfortified tip of the island from either ship. They hid their work with a curtain of black plastic garbage bags duct taped over the opening from the inside to match the black of the hull. The ruse wouldn't last long, but it didn't need to.

Torres and Alvarez manned the guns, each with a spotter/assistant, and were positioned well back in the tanks. They were hidden from above, or indeed, anyone who wasn't looking straight down their gun barrels.

***

"*Chinga tu madre*," Torres whispered as Baker ripped the garbage bags away, letting him see their attackers for the first time.

The field was filled with running cons spread across the ten acres as those unburdened with ladders outpaced the others. Torres shook off his momentary shock and opened fire, soon joined by Alvarez from the other ship. He first took out the faster men clustered at the base of the wall and awaiting the ladders, then swept the entire tip of the island, cons falling like ripe wheat.

The surprise was complete, and Torres held nothing back, the limited ammo supply not an issue, as his orders were to kill as many cons as possible in the shortest amount of time. If the choppers did come, they had no real idea as to how they would be outfitted, and even the Coasties' concealed firing positions could be taken out by missiles.

The cons began to dive for the dirt as soon as Torres had opened fire, and he swept the field again and again, zeroing in on any movement. He was burning through ammo at a terrific rate and barely conscious of Baker feeding fresh belts in time and again until his partner tapped his shoulder and signaled the last belt was going in.

Torres nodded and blazed away until the bolt clicked on an empty chamber. He lifted his head to gaze out on the carnage just as firing ceased from the other ship, Alvarez apparently out of ammo as well.

Men were down all over the field, some unmoving and others writhing in pain. Screams and curses filled the air, audible even through his earplugs. Here and there a head was raised tentatively.

He saw Baker's lips moving and pulled out an earplug.

"How many you think we got?" Baker asked,

Torres looked back toward the field and shook his head. "I dunno, maybe three hundred?"

But as he watched, men began to stand up, and he realized some of the unmoving bodies weren't casualties.

"But not enough," Torres said as he watched more and more men rise.

Then they started running. Some were moving for the wall, but here and there, a con started back toward the boats. Then the trickle became a flood and all of the cons were running back the way they came.

"Son of a bitch. They're running," Baker said.

Over Clark Island
Neches River
Beaumont, Texas

Rorke watched the carnage below with a growing sense of déjà vu. *Not this time!* He keyed his mic.

"Over-watch Actual, this is Thunderbolt Actual. Do you copy? over," Rorke said.

"This is Over-watch Actual. Go ahead, Thunderbolt. Over," came the reply.

"Over-watch, I want all units to shred those boats. Repeat. All units to take out those boats and anyone in them. Do you copy? Over," Rorke said.

There was a moment's hesitation, followed by the reply, "Thunderbolt Actual, I copy. Take out boats and anyone in them. Please confirm. Over."

"Affirmative, Over-watch. I say again, affirmative. Over."

Rorke listened as the flight leader passed commands, and in seconds the choppers had departed their slow orbit above the fortified portion of the island and turned to hover so their door gunners could target the north end. Most of the boats were still empty, but here and there a con was in a boat. One or two boats were actually moving away from the island, less than half-full, as their occupants showed no inclination to wait for any of their slower brethren.

The boats moving away were targeted first, the vessels and their occupants disappearing in a hail of massed machine-gun fire from at least four choppers. In seconds the only evidence of their passing were debris fields littered with floating body parts.

Then all the choppers turned their attention to the boats on the shore line, reducing them to splinters and shards of fiberglass as the cons in the boats attempted to get out of the boats—few were successful.

Rorke's radio squawked and McComb's voice came over the speaker, hysterical and any semblance of communication procedures forgotten.

"WHAT THE HELL'S THE MATTER WITH YOU, RORKE? YOU'RE KILLING MY MEN!"

"You should be killing them yourself, Riverine Actual, rather than standing around with your thumb up your ass, watching them desert under fire. So get it together, get over that wall, and take that island, because five minutes from now I'm going to have my choppers open fire on anyone still on the northern tip of the island. Do you copy? Over," Rorke said.

"I … I copy. McComb … I mean Riverine Actual out."

Upper Cargo Deck
S/S *Cape Mendocino*

Jordan Hughes looked over as Kinsey's radio squawked, echoing across the cavernous steel box of the cargo deck.

"Magician to *Jefe*. You copy? Over."

"Go ahead, Magician. Over," Kinsey said into his radio.

"Something strange going on. The choppers took out all the boats and the cons are coming back. They were slow turning around, but they're coming strong now. They'll be over the wall soon. Over."

"We copy, Magician. How many did you take out? Over," Kinsey asked.

"I'd say two to three hundred, but there's still a shitload of them. Over a thousand, I'd say. Over," Torres said.

Kinsey glanced over at Hughes, who nodded.

"Okay, Magician. Get in position. *Jefe* out," Kinsey said.

The echoes of the exchange faded as Hughes looked over to see Kinsey shaking his head.

"Worried about ammo?" Hughes asked.

Kinsey nodded. "There are a thousand left. Even combat veterans miss a lot of their shots, and at these odds we have to kill one of them with every second or third shot. That's not happening."

Hughes looked out over the little force of defenders gathered on the cargo deck, or at least one of the forces. There were similar groups hidden in the bowels of each of the other ships forming their improvised fort.

"Well, let's just hope our other methods get the job done," Hughes said.

Kinsey sighed and nodded, then raised his radio. "You should probably say something, Jordan. People will be nervous."

Hughes looked at the radio. What the hell could you say at a time like this? He was no warrior and he'd pretty much exhausted his supply of motivational speeches. He looked past Kinsey to where Dorothy Gillespie stood, holding her surviving son Jimmy's hand, her head not even reaching his shoulder. In her free hand, she held her late husband Earl's hunting rifle. Hughes caught her eye and motioned her over.

She approached, a quizzical look on her face.

Hughes held up the radio. "Dot, they'll be here any minute. I should say something, but I have no words. Could you ..."

Dorothy Gillespie started shaking her head before he finished the sentence, but as Hughes trailed off, she stopped, as if considering the request, then nodded slowly, holding her hand out for the radio.

Hughes passed it over, then showed her the transmit button. She nodded and raised the radio to her lips, the familiar words coming out clear and serene, echoing off the steel walls of the cargo deck.

"The Lord is my shepherd; I shall not want. He maketh me to lie down in green pastures; he leadeth me beside still waters."

Across the cargo deck and in engine rooms and mess rooms and other spaces on the twelve ships, people began to recite the familiar comforting words.

"He restoreth my soul; he leadeth me in the paths of righteousness for his name's sake."

Her voice stronger now, reinforced by fifty others, the prayer boomed through the cavernous space.

"Yea, though I walk through the valley of the shadow of death, I will fear no evil; for thou art with me; thy rod and thy staff they comfort me. Thou preparest a table before me in the presence of mine enemies; thou anointest my head with oil; my cup runneth over. Surely goodness and mercy shall follow me all the days of my life; and I will dwell in the house of the Lord for ever."

Dorothy Gillespie finished and absolute quiet prevailed. She looked at Hughes and he nodded his thanks, unable to speak. She handed him the radio and walked slowly back to her waiting family as Hughes composed himself and raised the radio.

"Amen," he said. "Get ready, folks. They're coming. Good luck."

CHAPTER TWENTY-SEVEN

Clark Island
Neches River
Beaumont, Texas

But luck had little to do with events as they unfolded. Focused by Darius Green's frank evaluation of their chances, Hughes and the others put all their energy into devising a plan to bleed their attackers, intent on making maximum use of 'home field advantage' to compensate for their meager supply of ammunition.

Their main advantage was familiarity. To a seaman, ships share certain characteristics that make it relatively easy to move around even a ship never before visited. But to landsmen such as their attackers, the ships would seem a confusing maze of intersecting passageways, engine and cargo spaces with multiple and widely separated entrances and exits, emergency escape passages, and myriad nooks and crannies that might hide a defender or a booby trap.

To capitalize on their advantage, Hughes broke the ship-savvy members of their defense force into twelve separate cadres, one to lead the defenses on each ship, filling out each group with landlubbers. The attackers thus faced not one force, but twelve, each independent and determined to bleed their attackers by making maximum use of whatever their particular ship had to offer.

S/S *Cape Flattery*

Dan Gowan raised his head just enough to peek over the bulwark at the cons boiling up over the north wall. A tall man in a sheriff's uniform seemed to be in charge, dividing the arriving cons into groups and sending them toward the various ships' gangways. Gowan nodded as the man directed eight or ten his way. *That's right; feed 'em in a bit at a time, they'll be much easier to kill that way.*

Leaving the gangways down had been a judgment call, and despite being against it initially, Gowan had to admit Kinsey had been right. Leaving twelve open paths was inviting the leader of the cons to split his force and he was being very cooperative. The sooner the cons could be lured belowdecks, the sooner they could start killing them.

The cons reached the gangway and started up. Gowan smiled. *Welcome to MY house, assholes.*

A daylight attack was an unexpected bonus. The attackers drove forward, hastily equipped and organized and fully expecting to overwhelm and cut down the defenders on the walls. They had given little thought to or preparation for any other scenario.

Gowan and his team fired on the arriving cons then fell back in seeming panic, luring their attackers into the engine room. Gowan doused the lights, plunging the cons into pitch darkness as the defenders grasped a guide rope and a Coastie with one of their precious sets of NV gear led them out to safety. They locked the engine room doors from the outside and then activated the CO_2 fire-fighting system, displacing all the oxygen in the engine room and suffocating the first attackers.

Ten down, God knows how many to go, thought Gowan as he heard running boots on the steel deck above him. Lots of boots.

***

Battles raged on each of the twelve ships, with the early advantage going to the defenders.

On the *Cape Florida*, Georgia Howell and the bosun Kenny Nunez lured two separate groups of cons onto the massive enclosed cargo deck from opposite directions, where Howell took a page from Gowan's book and keyed her radio to have a waiting crewman kill the lights at the electrical subpanel. Howell and Nunez then fired several bursts in the dark in both directions, provoking return fire from both groups of confused cons as the pair flattened themselves on the deck. Bullets flying over their heads, Howell and Nunez groped in the dark for the guide ropes they'd rigged earlier just inches off the deck, then crawled along them to a vertical escape trunk and safety as the cons murdered each other in the dark.

In the passageways of the aptly named *Equality State*, Darius Green and three of his men got some long overdue payback. They hid behind stairwell doors and in cleaning gear lockers or any other place they could find, peeking through tiny holes drilled in bulkheads and doors. When they saw stragglers, they let them pass, then emerged behind them, silent as ghosts to bludgeon the cons down with short-handled two-pound hammers they'd found in the engine room. With every deadly blow, Green thought of the faces of all the innocent victims of the Aryan Brotherhood.

Scenes of stealth, cunning, and uncommon valor played out on all the ships, each a microcosm and integral part of the larger battle. But the victories could not last, and as the defenders reached the bottom of their bag of ammo-conserving tricks and the cons started warning each other by radio, the momentum of the battle slowed.

The cons became wary, using SRF-supplied grenades with devastating effect to clear spaces before entry. More and more defenders found themselves cornered, cut off, and out of ammunition. But still they fought on, giving ground grudgingly and fighting with what they had, clubbing their rifles, or grabbing knives from the galley or tools from work areas, and finally feet, fists, and teeth. With nowhere to retreat and SRF guns at their own backs, the cons fought equally hard, knowing now what awaited any who ran. The fight on each ship became an hours-long game of cat and mouse—a desperate, dogged struggle in which the defenders would ambush a con or small group and retreat, or the cons would contain a group of defenders and finish them off with grenades.

But the issue was never really in doubt, as the cons' greater numbers, firepower, and grenades turned the tide. The surviving defenders became fugitives, making their way across decks slick with blood to prepared places of concealment in tanks or cargo holds or machinery spaces. On every ship they rallied for a last stand, counting their meager stocks of ammunition and plotting strategy, determined to take a few more cons with them. Defenders waited as the cons closed, tentatively probing the inky darkness, the now eerie quiet allowing them all to hear once more the constant *thump, thump, thump* of the orbiting choppers, a sound that brought solace to neither side.

Steering Gear Flat
S/S *Cape Mendocino*

Hughes sat on the deck with his back against a bulkhead and looked through the blackness at Laura kneeling by Kinsey, the red glow of her headlamp the only bit of light in the space. Kinsey had reopened his wound in the fighting and it was bleeding again. Badly.

"I need to stitch this up," Laura said.

Hughes saw Kinsey shake his head in the light of the headlamp. "Just pack it and wrap it tight so I can fight. It won't matter soon anyway."

Hughes saw Laura start to protest and then seem to think better of it and nod. He snapped on his own flashlight and played it around the space. They'd left many dead cons in their wake as they retreated to this space they'd prepared for their final stand. They'd broken contact before they got here, and he was grateful for the respite and time to regroup, though he doubted it would last.

Not a bad place for a last stand, he thought. The steering gear flat was in the extreme rear of the ship, accessible from the engine room only after a long transit through a series of oval openings through the webs of the vertical strength members that formed the foundation of the massive elevator system on the decks above. There were two such access ways from the engine room, one on each side of the ship, as well as a secondary access to the space via the emergency escape trunk and vertical ladder, which led to a hatch flush-mounted in the lower cargo deck above them. Gowan had welded a hook and eye on the inside of the emergency hatch so they could lock it from the inside, leaving the accesses from the engine room the only possible points of attack.

It was a bit of a fluke, really. Hughes hadn't considered grenades, but the cons seemed to have an ample supply, and the defenders' chosen refuge was at least somewhat grenade proof. Clearance through each of the fifteen oval man-way openings on the access paths was tight, and no one was likely to have the arm strength to hurl a grenade far enough, with enough accuracy, or with a flat enough trajectory to transit all the man-way holes and reach the steering gear flat. Better still, any attackers brave, or foolish, enough to attempt the access passageways would be sitting ducks, perfect targets silhouetted in each man-way as they approached. The space was a defensible haven. Or a tomb.

There were nine of them altogether, nine of more than fifty. They'd spread out to receive the attack, each small group with their own set of traps to spring to better inflict damage on their attackers. They were all meant to rally here for a last stand, but the gunfire, screams, and grenade explosions that echoed through the ship for hours had fallen silent thirty minutes ago. An eerie silence prevailed, unconsciously causing the survivors to move quietly and speak in hushed whispers, even though they knew they couldn't be heard outside their place of refuge. None of the others had made it back, and Hughes entertained no illusions that they would. *Not that it matters much*, he thought.

The group included not only Laura and Kinsey, but Bollinger and the five surviving adult members of the Gillespie clan. They were all suffering, a few from noncritical gunshot wounds Laura had done her best to treat, and others from painful bruises resulting from collisions in the dark with the hard unyielding steel of the ship or equipment.

They were battered but defiant. The place smelled of sweat and fear and there was an overwhelming sense of resignation. The plan, if it could be dignified with that name, was simple. They'd use their remaining ammo to prevent the cons from getting too close, and when the last of the ammo was gone, use a collection of knives and hand tools to dispatch the attacking cons as they were forced to enter the last tight entry man-way one at a time.

They sat in the dark and waited, the silence broken only by the distant thump of the chopper blades that seemed to vibrate through the steel hull. Hughes forced himself to his feet and moved to the starboard entrance, where Jimmy Gillespie crouched, peering down the access way into the darkness, a handgun holstered on his hip. At the far reaches of his flashlight beam, Hughes saw Jimmy's wife, Janet, guarding the port entrance, an AR in her hand. Her long red hair was tied up in a bandanna, with stray strands leaking out, catching the feeble light in strange ways. *Three months ago she was a happy soccer mom whose biggest worry was when Jimmy would be home from sea. What a screwed-up mess this is*, he thought as he dropped down beside Jimmy.

Jimmy looked over and nodded.

"How much ammo do we have left?" Hughes asked.

"Nine rounds for the Glock and eleven for the AR, Captain," Jimmy said.

Hughes nodded and was about to stand when Jimmy spoke.

"You think they got everyone else?" Jimmy asked.

Hughes hesitated. "There are plenty of hiding places on this ship, so I'm hoping they just got cut off and all found a place to hole up. And this is a big ship with a lot of steel between us and whatever may be happening. I doubt we hear anything unless it's close," Hughes said, his words a hopeful lie.

"We can hear the choppers," Jimmy said.

Hughes had no reply, but he could see the look of grim determination on Jimmy's face in the dim glow of his headlamp.

"If they don't find us, how long before we come out and hit 'em again?" Jimmy asked.

"If they don't find enough bodies, they'll be on edge for sure and keep looking. But our advantage is they don't really know how many of us there were to begin with or how we're spread out on the ships. If they don't find us, I think they'll drop their guard after maybe two or three days, and we stocked enough food and water here for that. When they get complacent, we'll slip out at night and see how many throats we can cut while they sleep, and how much food and ammo we can steal to bring back down here. That will work once anyway. Then for sure they'll keep looking until they find us," Hughes said.

Jimmy nodded. "As long as we can take some of them with us—"

Hughes laid a hand on Jimmy's shoulder. "You smell that?"

Jimmy sniffed the air and his eyes widened. "Smoke."

Just then the sounds of fighting started again, shouts and sporadic gunfire, increasing in volume.

"It sounds like there are some of us left elsewhere, and the cons are burning them out," Hughes said.

Over Clark Island
Neches River
Beaumont, Texas

Twenty Minutes Earlier

Rorke cursed as he stared down at the island. This was taking far longer than it should, and those useless cons were blowing it again. His chopper was circling the island at a high altitude, keeping well clear of the other choppers orbiting below. Useless choppers, as it turned out. With no visible targets except the occasional con who'd lost enthusiasm for the fight and come topside, looking for an escape route, his choppers weren't a factor.

Rorke looked down in frustration. McComb was not returning his radio calls, and he'd been able to follow the fight only by monitoring the confused jumble of transmissions between the cons, transmissions that weren't positive. He'd heard neither gunfire nor grenade concussions in several minutes and was about to try McComb again when his own pilot's voice sounded in his headphones with a notice he'd been expecting.

"General, be advised the attack squadron leader reports they are all bingo fuel. He requests permission to return to base," the pilot said.

Rorke considered his options. This should have been over by now. By his plan, the defenders should all be dead and his reserve chopper squadron should be wiping out what was left of the cons. He briefly considered dispensing with air cover for the hour or two it would take Squadron One to return to base and refuel, but dismissed the idea. Without the constant threat of the choppers overhead, he had no doubt the cons would start fleeing topside, away from the fight, thus delaying things even further. He'd just have to use his reserves a bit early.

"Very well. Permission granted for squadron one to RTB for refueling. Order squadron two at the prison to relieve squadron one on over-watch. How's our own fuel?" Rorke asked.

"We're not carrying the load of the other choppers. I estimate approximately fifteen more minutes on station before we have to return to base. Maybe twenty at the outside," the pilot said.

Rorke acknowledged the pilot, then keyed his mic. "Thunderbolt Actual to Riverine Actual. Do you copy? Over."

No response.

He repeated the call again. "Thunderbolt Actual to Riverine Actual. You'd better answer, McComb, if you'd like to live another day. Over."

The answer was immediate, and McComb sounded exhausted.

"Thunderbolt, this is Riverine. We're kinda busy down here. Over."

"Riverine, give me a sitrep. Over," Rorke said.

"Give you a what?"

"WHAT THE HELL IS GOING ON?" Rorke yelled.

"What's goin' on is most of my guys are dead. I got maybe three hundred left. The ship people are obviously low on ammo, but they're holed up in different places on all the ships and we can't root 'em out. That's what's happening, General. Over," McComb said.

"That's why I gave you grenades. Over," Rorke said.

"Yeah, well, not enough. We need some more. Over," McComb says.

Rorke lost it again. "THERE ARE NO MORE, YOU IDIOT. I GAVE YOU ALL WE HAD."

"Well, you better find some, 'cause we ain't chargin' into any more traps. And if you think you and the SRF can do any better, come on down. Over," McComb said.

Rorke struggled to contain his rage. *Soon, McComb, you'll regret that, but I still need you awhile yet,* he thought and didn't reply immediately. The 'ship people,' as McComb called them, had proved resourceful, but maybe it was time they did a bit of improvising themselves. He keyed the mic.

"Well, our friends seem to like fire, so maybe we should give them a taste of their own medicine. Set the ships on fire and then retreat topside. They'll either have to come out of their holes or die like rats." Rorke paused. "I presume you're at least competent enough to finish them off if you flush them into the open and have them outnumbered and outgunned. Over."

"We can do that. Just make sure your guys in the choppers ain't trigger-happy. Riverine out," McComb said, without waiting for a response.

Rorke started to chew him a new one, but thought better of it. He smiled. With the cons AND the ship people all up on deck fighting it out, his choppers could take them ALL out. Maybe this would work out after all.

"How long to refuel and get back here?" Rorke asked the pilot.

"Counting the round trip to Houston, at least an hour, maybe more," the pilot responded.

"Then let's get it done. The quicker we get to base and refuel, the quicker we can be back on station. I don't want to miss the last act of this little shit show," Rorke said.

CHAPTER TWENTY-EIGHT

Fort Box
Wilmington Container Terminal
Cape Fear River
Wilmington, North Carolina

Day 49
May 19 - 8:20 a.m.
(Eight Hours Earlier)

The Honorable Simon J. Tremble, President of the United States, struggled to control his impatience as Marine One circled Fort Box. In the few short hours he'd been president, he'd found he had considerably less power than he'd imagined, at least over the people responsible for his personal safety. The short trip to Fort Box became a major logistical effort, with layer upon layer of security, advance teams to check out and secure the destination, and endless details. *I'm surprised they let me go to the toilet by myself. I think it was easier to move around as a fugitive,* he thought as the chopper descended.

His eagerness to rush directly to Wilmington had been derailed initially, and wisely in retrospect, by his longtime friend Major General Joe Pinkney. Understanding the potential impact of the situation, Pinkney immediately moved Tremble and Anderson out of sight and began sending back-channel messages to trusted colleagues up and down his chain of command, alerting them that Tremble was indeed alive and had proof that first Gleason and now Crawford had subverted the Constitution.

When Tremble had protested this could all be done from Wilmington, a harried Pinkney had exploded.

"Goddamn it, Simon. We're basically conspiring against a sitting president, no matter how he got there. He's drinking like a fish and tilting toward bat-shit crazy and he still has control of the nuclear codes and all manner of power. We have to get everyone on the same page for this to work, and it has to be done quietly so the bastard doesn't get wind of it. 'Delicate' doesn't come close to what's needed here, so I'd appreciate a little patience while I try to keep this from becoming a bigger frigging mess than it already is, okay?"

Tremble had conceded the point, asked that a patrol be sent out to collect Keith and the others at Tuttle's camp, then accepted the offer of a shave and a haircut (real ones), a shower, and clean clothes for himself and Anderson—and begun to pace a trail in the carpet of the spacious VIP quarters where he and Anderson were sequestered.

He was distracted a few hours later by the arrival of Keith and the others, and convinced to try to get some rest, only to rise at sunrise after three hours of tossing and turning punctuated with brief catnaps. The whole of the following day had been restless torture, his anxiety mitigated to some degree by detailed briefings from Pinkney as to what had transpired during his isolation and the progress of the ongoing effort to secure his presidency.

Pinkney finally returned near sunrise the next morning, escorting a rumpled little man who was a justice of the peace in Bladen County, North Carolina. Or at least he HAD been a JP when there was anything like a functioning county government.

"Crawford has the last surviving Supreme Court justice, but we found a federal district court judge willing to review the facts and declare Crawford guilty of treason. It's a little sketchy, but everything is nowadays. We put a force into Mount Weather on the pretext of sending up a team to brief Crawford on the Wilmington operation. He's now in custody and the nuclear football is secured. Mr. Mays here will swear you in and make it official with me and the others in your group as witnesses," Pinkney said.

So in a living room of VIP housing at Fort Bragg, North Carolina, sworn in by a groggy, sleep-deprived justice of the peace representing a nonfunctional county government, the Honorable Simon J. Tremble became President of the United States—and still had to wait two hours to get his requested trip to Wilmington.

He rode now, still luxuriating in the feeling of being truly clean for the first time in months, and wearing khaki pants and a blue golf shirt with the presidential seal on the pocket. Seated across from him, Anderson looked considerably less comfortable in US Army ACUs bearing captain's bars. Anderson frowned as he stared out the large window of the chopper.

"You don't look too happy. What's the problem?" Tremble asked.

"You know the problem. I didn't volunteer in the first place and I sure as hell didn't volunteer to be an officer," Anderson said, belatedly adding, "Mr. President."

"Presidential prerogative. I needed an aide I could trust, so you're drafted. And a presidential aide has to have the appropriate rank, and captain was minimum. Besides, I didn't exactly volunteer to be president either, so quit bitching or I'll make you a major," Tremble said.

"I think I liked it better when I was your guard. No one asked me if I wanted that job either," Anderson muttered as the chopper bumped slightly as it settled to the ground.

Despite his complaint and to the annoyance of the Secret Service agents waiting outside the chopper, Anderson went into protective mode as soon as they touched down; he motioned Tremble to stay back and was first out of the chopper door, his head on a swivel. Only when he'd checked out the area did he look back into the chopper and nod for Tremble to exit.

This is going to get old real fast, Tremble thought as he exited the chopper and looked around. He'd been fully briefed before he left Bragg, but seeing the situation on the ground firsthand was still a shock. He stopped and looked over what was obviously a well-organized facility bounded by stout defensive walls of stacked shipping containers, with orderly 'streets' lined with RVs, travel trailers, and tents, radiating out like spokes of a wheel from a squat three-story building.

Or rather, he corrected himself, the REMAINS of a well-ordered facility. The whole area was dotted with charred spots where mortar rounds had hit. There were gaps in the neatly ordered streets as well, occupied by the blackened remains of tents, obvious victims of fires set by the incoming rounds. But the most overpowering feature was the smell, the acrid scent of smoke mixed with a faint whiff of CS gas. His eyes watered a bit even now.

"Welcome to Wilmington, Mr. President."

He turned to see a tall gray-haired man wearing admiral's stars standing nearby, holding a salute. Tremble returned the salute and walked over, his hand extended.

"Sam, good to see you again. It's been a long time," Tremble said as he shook the man's hand.

"You as well, Mr. President, and I'd like you to meet General Duncan Beasley." Wright gestured to the Marine standing beside him.

"General," Tremble said, offering his hand, "your reputation precedes you. Nice to meet you at last."

Beasley looked surprised. "What reputation would that be, Mr. President?"

Tremble's eyes narrowed. "The one that says you're a straight shooter." Tremble glanced at Wright. "I already know that's true of Admiral Wright here. And now, I want the no-bullshit version of what happened here. This isn't what I expected, and I believe your immediate superiors are equally baffled at the outcome."

Wright glanced at Beasley. "General Beasley and I discussed it at some length, Mr. President, and believe we followed your predecessor's orders to the letter, no matter how much we disagreed with them. He instructed us not to accept the surrender of the fort and made it quite clear that extended to individuals attempting to surrender as well. However, he did not order us to execute individuals who were captured by being knocked unconscious or otherwise neutralized while actively resisting. Executing defenseless or unarmed prisoners would, of course, be contrary to both US and international law."

"And just how did you ensure the defenders would be 'neutralized while actively resisting,'" Tremble asked.

"We figured they had limited night-vision capability and so would be more likely to light up the facility, so we took out all the lights. Our own one hundred percent NV capability put us at a huge advantage. Then we blanketed the fort with a mortar barrage, mixed tear gas and flash-bang rounds, and came in behind it with overwhelming force, equipped with gas masks. The defenders were largely blind and disoriented, and we estimate plus ninety percent of them were incapacitated by the CS barrage. We subdued the rest with nonlethal means, rubber bullets, beanbag rounds, and in a few instances Tasers," Beasley said.

"Casualties?" Tremble asked.

Wright sighed. "The defenders were using real bullets, I'm afraid. We had one KIA and a dozen wounded. All the wounded will recover. There were no KIAs among the defenders, but there were twenty or thirty injuries, mostly from breathing too much gas or broken bones. Our rounds were nonlethal, but, as you know, that doesn't mean harmless. I regret the loss of even one of our people, but as things go, it could have been much worse."

"I'd say that was a bit of an understatement, Admiral. But I'm curious, how did your troops react to being ordered to assault an entrenched position with nonlethal rounds?" Tremble asked.

"Actually the idea came from the ranks," Wright said. "A lot of the folks at Bragg have people here in the fort. We may have had a mutiny on our hands if we'd have done anything else." Wright paused. "And to be honest, Mr. President, I wouldn't have followed the clear INTENT of Crawford's order in any event. This is my hometown, and my brother's boy, Josh, was inside the walls."

Tremble nodded. "I can't argue with that. I'm just glad y'all came up with a creative interpretation of your orders. Now, where's Hunnicutt?"

"He took a beanbag round to the chest and cracked a couple of ribs. After he received medical attention, I had him confined to quarters, pending your orders, Mr. President," Beasley said.

"Take me to him," Tremble said.

"Yes, Mr. President. This way," Beasley said and pointed toward the flat-roofed building before starting in that direction.

Beasley led the way into the headquarters building and down a long hall. He was about to knock on a door when Tremble stopped him. "I can take it from here, gentlemen. I'd like a few minutes alone with Hunnicutt. I'll meet the rest of you back at the main entrance to the building in a few minutes and we can continue our discussions."

Wright and Beasley nodded and started down the hall, but Anderson stayed put. "I'll be here just outside the door if you need me, Mr. President."

Tremble looked at him. "So are you going to become my nanny, George?"

"You gave me the job, sir. Be careful what you wish for," Anderson said.

Tremble chuckled and shook his head, then knocked on the door.

"Come in," came the response, and Tremble went in to find Hunnicutt sitting at his desk, writing.

"Good afternoon, Colonel. I'm Simon —"

Hunnicutt sprang to his feet, almost upsetting his chair in the process. He stood straight and tried to snap a salute, but faltered and a look of pain shot across his face as the sudden movement tugged at his cracked ribs.

"As you were, Colonel. May I sit down?" Tremble asked.

"Of course, Mr. President. Here, take my desk chair, it's more comfortable," Hunnicutt said.

"This will do fine," Tremble said, moving to the straight-back chair across the desk.

He'd just sat down when he noticed Hunnicutt was still standing. He smiled. "I'd suggest you sit as well, Colonel. I feel a bit strange with you standing there looking at me."

"Yes, of course," Hunnicutt said as he sat back down behind his desk, obviously still stunned by the unexpected visit.

"What is that you're working on so intently, Colonel?" Tremble asked when Hunnicutt was settled in his chair.

"Not colonel, Mr. President, major. Colonel was just a temporary rank I ... I assumed to make room in the rank structure below me in ... in rather challenging circumstances. I never intended for it to be permanent," Hunnicutt said.

Tremble nodded. "Challenging circumstances is a bit of an understatement; we've all had more than our fair share of those of late. But Colonel Hunnicutt has a nice ring to it, so I think we'll make it permanent." He smiled. "I do have some influence there, you know. But you didn't answer my question."

Hunnicutt looked down at the yellow legal pad. "It's ... it's my after-action report, sir. Not just for this last engagement, but for the previous operations. I want to make it clear I bear full responsibility, and all my officers and troops were following my orders. Whatever sentence may be imposed should fall on me alone, and I —"

Tremble looked puzzled. "Sentence? What the hell are you talking about, Colonel? Sentence for what?"

"A lot of people died, sir, and they died on my orders and by my hand."

"It's my understanding they were either attacking you or preparing to attack you, is that not correct?" Tremble asked.

"Yes, Mr. President, but they still died by my hand —"

Tremble leaned across the desk and fixed Hunnicutt with a stare. "Yes, they died by your hand and at your orders, and it's something you're going to have to live with every single day for the rest of your life. But there will be no trial, because in my view and the view of others whose counsel I trust, none is warranted. I received a full intelligence briefing in the hours I was waiting to fly down here. While the regular military was not involved earlier, they were not unaware of what was happening here. In my view, your actions and the conduct of the people under your command were exemplary. I need you, Colonel. The country needs you, and more people like you. My greatest fear is that you will put YOURSELF on trial and find yourself guilty, again and again. There are many decisions we've made, and which we all have yet to make in the days ahead, which will weigh heavy on our consciences. But to be blunt, I can't allow you the luxury of wallowing in self-pity, because I have work for you to do. Is that clear?"

"Ah ... yes. Yes, Mr. President," Hunnicutt said.

"Good. I suggest you finish your report if you find it personally helpful as a therapeutic exercise, but I need no such justification. What I DO need is you back in harness not later than forty-eight hours from today," Tremble said.

"Yes, Mr. President," Hunnicutt said.

"Now. What's this I hear about your plan to unite the farms along the river. We need to get agriculture re-established and that sounds like a good model we might be able to duplicate elsewhere. How do you plan to —"

There was a tentative knock at the door. Hunnicutt looked at Tremble, who nodded.

"Come in," said Hunnicutt.

The door opened and Duncan Beasley stuck his head in the room. "Sorry to disturb you, Mr. President, but there's something coming over the radio I think you'll want to hear."

***

In 1831, twenty-one-year-old William Barret Travis arrived in the Mexican state of Texas, one step ahead of an arrest warrant in his native Alabama, where he was being hounded by creditors. Something of a malcontent and serial failure, young Travis had failed, first at establishing a law office and then a newspaper in Alabama. Like many men of the era in similar circumstances, he departed to reinvent himself in the greener pastures and more forgiving climate of Mexican Texas. He left behind a pregnant wife and young son.

Travis quickly gained a mixed reputation by clashing with unpopular Mexican authorities in Anahuac, an act which gained him both supporters and detractors. Supporters outnumbered detractors, it seemed, because five years later Travis, with little significant military experience, was commissioned a lieutenant colonel in the new Texan army. A series of chance events then placed him in command of an abandoned, tumbledown, and largely indefensible former mission called the Alamo in San Antonio de Bexar. The rest, as they say, is history.

A history that defined Travis not by his faults, which were many, but by the nature of his death. He died the epitome of resistance against overwhelming force, and his open letter of February 24, 1836, 'To the People of Texas & All Americans in the World,' is renowned as both a declaration of defiance and a masterpiece of American patriotism. The Alamo is remembered not only for the sacrifice of the men who died there, but largely due to Travis' letter informing the world of their desperate plight and their determination to resist at all costs, a letter that to this day forms part of the education of every Texas schoolchild.

The parallels were heavy on Jordan Hughes' mind when he contemplated how the government might 'spin' the events likely to transpire, and he was passionate that the truth about Clark Island and its defenders be told.

* * *

"What's this all about, General?" Tremble asked as he walked along beside Beasley at a brisk pace, both Anderson and Hunnicutt close behind.

"Ham radio traffic was a source of intel for us when we had orders to stay close to base, and it largely dried up when Crawford cracked down on it, but just an hour ago … well, Mr. President, I think you should hear for yourself," Beasley said.

Tremble was about to press the question when Beasley stopped in front of what was obviously a communications tent and stepped back so Tremble could enter. Inside he found Admiral Sam Wright standing beside an elaborate bank of radio gear, next to a seated operator wearing headphones. Wright looked up as Tremble entered.

"What's up, Sam?" Tremble asked.

Wright nodded toward the radio operator. "The corporal here says he first started picking this up about an hour ago, and now it's being transmitted more or less continually on every amateur frequency."

"WHAT'S being transmitted?" Tremble said.

Wright touched the radio operator on the shoulder. "Put it on the speaker again, Corporal."

The soldier pulled an earphone off one ear. "It's just about to repeat, sir. Let me catch it at the start."

Wright nodded and the operator pulled his headphone back on, waited perhaps ten seconds, and then flipped a toggle switch. A speaker came to life. The sound quality was poor, but the passion of the speaker came through the static.

"To all survivors, wherever you are. My name is Jordan Hughes and I'm with about five hundred survivors on Clark Island in the Neches River near Beaumont, Texas. We are besieged by a group of escaped convicts masquerading as police officers. We have survived previous attacks and have no doubt the convicts intend to kill or enslave us all. Another attack is imminent, and we will resist to our last breath, but our survival is doubtful. This is not a plea for help, as I believe no one can help us, at least in the short time remaining. Rather it is a warning.

705

"The convicts are being helped by FEMA Special Reaction Force troops, whose agenda is unknown. We have committed no crime, harmed no one, and helped anyone we were able to help. I can only conclude the government is in league with these criminals because our independence threatens the police state they seek to create.

"In a time when our world is descending into anarchy and barbarism, we MUST keep the spark of decency and humanity alive, else survival is meaningless. We may lose now, but someday we will rise. A dictatorship may be emerging now, but someday we will be a democracy again. All these things can come to pass only if we remember what we were, and what we can become again.

"We are only a few hundred souls, insignificant in the scheme of things, a single point of light and hope about to wink out. The government will no doubt lie about what happens here and cast us as criminals and looters, just as they've lied about recent events in Wilmington, North Carolina. DON'T LET THEM GET AWAY WITH IT. My fervent hope is that anyone hearing this message will pass it on so eventually the entire country can bear witness to what is happening here and elsewhere.

"We will hold out as long as we can and try to give a good accounting of ourselves. This spark will not be easily extinguished, though the final outcome is inevitable. We ask only to have our story told. Whether your own circumstances allow you to do so is up to you, and I fully understand the risks associated with doing as I ask; the government will likely deal harshly with anyone caught transmitting this message. But before you decide to do nothing, I ask you to consider these questions. If not you, who? If not now, when?

Remember Clark Island!

This is Jordan Hughes at Clark Island, Texas.

The corporal flipped the toggle switch and the voice died. "It's the same thing over and over on all the ham channels," he said. "From chatter in between, I think one operator will transmit, and then he'll stop and another will pick it up. I think they're doing that because they think FEMA is still triangulating them and each wants to stay on the air as short a time as possible."

The room grew silent.

"Is this legit?" Tremble asked.

"Absolutely, Mr. President. Captain Hughes was here with us until he took his group to Texas. I recognize his voice," Hunnicutt said.

"When was that recording made?" Tremble asked the radio operator.

"It's impossible to tell, Mr. President. I think the speaker was likely in a rush and he didn't include a date or time, and the quality of the recording varies from frequency to frequency. I'd say it's been re-recorded several times," the corporal said.

Tremble nodded and turned back to Sam Wright, more formal now. "Admiral, do we have assets in the area that could reach—"

"Already in motion, Mr. President," Wright said.

Steering Gear Flat
S/S *Cape Mendocino*

Hughes squatted beside Jimmy Gillespie, gazing down the access passage. The engine room was already full of thick white smoke, and it was boiling down the access ways to accumulate in the steering gear flat, forming a visible line as it filled the space from the top down. There was some visibility below the line, but the acrid smoke was irritating his eyes and making it difficult to breathe. Hughes stifled a cough and motioned for Jimmy to follow him as he crawled back to the others, staying low beneath the smoke. Just as they reached them, he heard gunshots, individual weapons soon joined by the jackhammer reports of machine guns.

Hughes looked over his little band of defenders sitting and squatting on the deck below the smoke. He saw mostly fear, their willingness of a short while ago to go down fighting now contending with the prospect of being suffocated without the chance to strike a blow. But they still clutched an assortment of knives, hammers, and improvised clubs.

"From the gunfire, I'd say they're flushing any other holdouts and attacking. We obviously can't stay here, but the only possible way out now is the emergency escape hatch and they may well be waiting for us at the top. If we do slip past them, we have to decide whether to try to find another hiding spot or to engage," Hughes said.

Matt Kinsey was shaking his head, a grimace of pain on his face. "If we find another hole, they'll just smoke us out there too. Realistically, they can just set all the ships on fire and leave, then let the choppers gun down anyone who manages to escape. I don't know what anyone else is going to do, but if we make it out that hatch, I'm going to fight."

"Me too," Bollinger said.

Dorothy Gillespie started to speak but was interrupted by a coughing spasm. She shook her head. "The Gillespies aren't hiding anymore," she gasped between coughs, to nods and signs of agreement from the rest of her clan.

Hughes looked at Laura. She gave him a wan smile. "You have to ask?"

He smiled and squeezed her hand.

"Okay then. Jimmy, you go up first with the Glock and unhook the hatch. The smoke's gonna be thick in that trunk, so hold your breath until you're out. That goes for all of you. I'll go next with the AR, and Jimmy and I will do what we can to defend the hatch if the cons catch us while we're exiting. I want the five ladies to come next, with Kinsey and Bollinger bringing up the rear. Bollinger, I want you to come up right behind Chief Kinsey. He's climbing one-handed, so he'll need you to hold him on the ladder when he changes grips."

"Got it," Bollinger said, and Hughes turned to Jimmy Gillespie.

"Any time you're ready, Jimmy," he said.

Jimmy nodded, kissed his wife, Janet, and then disappeared up the ladder through the smoke.

Laura reached over and wrapped Hughes in a fierce hug. "Is this it?" she whispered.

Hughes hugged her tightly. "I think so," he whispered back.

"I love you," Laura said.

"Me too you," Hughes said. "I guess this is—"

"CLEAR," came Jimmy's voice through the smoke, and Hughes kissed Laura and broke the embrace to crawl up the ladder, trying to keep the slung AR from banging in the tight confines of the escape trunk. His lungs were near bursting when he stuck his head through the hatch and took a breath. He dipped back down and unslung the rifle and passed it up to Jimmy so he could clear the hatch.

"CLEAR," he yelled down the hatch when he was out.

There were no attackers waiting, and Hughes considered their options as he and Jimmy stood guard at the top of the hatch as the others emerged. The cargo deck was in shadow, lit only by the ambient light coming in from the open stern door, but smoke was thickening there as well. The sounds of gunfire were intensifying on the open deck above them and he was confused. There couldn't be that many surviving defenders, and he'd already heard enough shots to kill them all several times over. As soon as everyone was out of the hatch, he turned to the group.

"Something strange is going on," Hughes said to the group. "Jimmy, swap me the Glock for the AR. I'm gonna check it out before we walk into an ambush."

Hughes looked at Kinsey. "Matt, if I'm not back in five minutes, you're in charge."

"I'll go, Captain," Jimmy said, but Hughes shook his head and then nodded toward the Gillespie women.

"When the time comes, your place is here, Jimmy," he said quietly.

Jimmy only nodded, and Hughes took off at a run across the cargo deck to the entrance to the living quarters. He opened the door slowly, expecting to find either cons or a raging fire, and finding neither. The passageway was pitch black and smelled of smoke, but not the choking accumulation he'd just endured. He took off his headlight, switched it on, and held it beside the Glock as he picked his way through the dark passageway. The gunfire was louder now, coming from the forward end of the ship, but diminishing in intensity—all individual weapons now and no machine-gun fire.

He made his way to the interior stairwell and up one deck. The gunfire had stopped completely by the time he got to the door opening onto the main deck. He switched off his headlamp and slipped it in his pocket, cracked the door open, and studied the area. There was no gunfire now, and he heard the thump of the blades of a single chopper, out of sight over his head. It seemed different somehow, and he craned his neck to see it, but it was almost directly overhead.

He opened the door more fully and exited, off in a crouching run to dive behind a set of mooring bitts at the ship side nearest the island. His heart sank as he looked over the side to see a dozen choppers on the ground surrounded by hundreds of uniformed men. The SRF had landed in force.

"FREEZE," yelled a voice behind him, and he spun, bringing up the Glock to face a man in full combat gear, pointing an M4 at him.

"CAPTAIN HUGHES! DON'T SHOOT!" screamed a voice to his left.

He hesitated, and the man holding the M4 lowered his weapon. "We're the good guys, Captain," the man said, and Hughes noticed for the first time the man wore woodland camo pattern, not the black battle dress utilities of the SRF.

Confused, he turned to the voice to see Georgia Howell, one side of her face bruised, and her short hair was in wild disarray. Her shirttail was out and her normally neat khakis looked like someone had dragged them through a grease pit with her in them, multiple times. But there was a look of triumph and relief on her bruised face.

"We did it, Cap. We held out," she said.

Captain's Office
S/S *Cape Mendocino*

The Marines from the USS *Makin Island* made short work of the Clark Island attackers. The SRF pilots turned tail as soon as they spotted the incoming Marine choppers, but they couldn't outrun the more capable aircraft or their autocannons and rockets. Those not blown out of the sky were forced down along the river. Rorke's chopper arrived back on scene just in time to lead the retreat and was thus among the first recipients of multiple rockets. The Marines of the assault force weren't particularly interested in acquiring more mouths to feed by taking prisoners. The surviving cons figured that out pretty quickly and decided to swim for it, not a particularly wise decision given the increasing numbers and aggressiveness of the local alligator population. No one shed any tears about the cons' poor judgment.

Hughes sat beside Laura on the settee in the captain's office, studying Georgia Howell as she sat across from them. The enormity of what they'd endured was still catching up with them all, but Howell had pressed forward on her own initiative, getting a head count of survivors—and she had begun the much grimmer task of collecting the dead.

"How many?" Hughes asked.

Georgia Howell shook her head. "It's too early to tell for sure. I initially figured we lost close to fifty percent, but I don't think it will be nearly that bad when it's all said and done."

"How many of our …" Hughes stopped himself. *They are all OUR people now,* he thought.

Howell picked up on his truncated question. "Among the original *Pecos Trader* crew we lost Tim Sutton, Jerry Gunter, and Billy Searcy, though several of the crewmen lost family members as well. And we lost …" She paused as if composing herself. "We lost Polak. He wasn't shot though. The folks with him said he just collapsed, so I figure it was his heart."

Hughes nodded, and Howell continued. "The Coasties lost Jefferson, Cahill, and Stevenson's wife. That's it for the original group from Wilmington. We lost Darius Green, and his folks took the biggest hit percentage wise; they threw themselves at the cons like crazy people, from what I hear."

Hughes nodded. "I'm not surprised. There was a lot of well-justified rage there. We owe Darius a debt, so make sure we help his survivors all we can."

"I was already thinking the same thing," Howell said. "And speaking of survivors, Major Arnold already has medivac choppers inbound to take our wounded back to the *Makin Island*. They have pretty extensive medical facilities."

"Good. Thank the major and make damn sure Matt Kinsey is on one of the first choppers. How about the fires?" Hughes asked.

"Fortunately they didn't find that much to burn. Mostly piled-up mattresses, paper, and scrap wood. Being in layup status, most of the ships didn't have much paint or solvent aboard and the cons apparently weren't smart enough to get at the fuel. With no cargo to burn and most everything in the quarters being fire retardant, the fires didn't get out of hand. Dan and Rich organized firefighting crews and they have things mostly contained, though some of the ship's living areas are uninhabitable for now," Howell said.

"How about the Marines? Did they have casualties?" Laura asked.

"Only two superficial wounds. Major Arnold has already returned to the *Makin Island*, but he left a small holding force in place here in radio contact. I have a team collecting the cons' abandoned weapons and ammo. Between the Marines and our folks, we should be okay against any immediate threats," Howell said as she stood. "And if that's all for now, Captain, I'd better get back to work."

"Thank you, Georgia," Hughes said, starting to stand. "You've done an outstanding job. I'll be down to give you a hand in—"

Howell waved him back to his seat. "Take a while to decompress, Cap. Dan and I have this for now."

Hughes nodded and sank back down on the settee as Howell left the room.

He sat alone with Laura on the settee, the adrenaline from the fight and elation from the rescue ebbing. He held his wife's hand in his as crushing exhaustion washed over him. He felt lifeless and weary to the bone. Laura squeezed his hand.

Hughes sat up on the edge of the settee. "I need to get back to work."

"Rest a while," Laura said.

Hughes eyed her suspiciously. "First Georgia, now you. Why is everyone being so damned solicitous? I haven't endured anything the rest of you haven't."

"Not true," Laura said. "You've had to make the decisions and your stress levels have been much higher. Look."

Laura put her hand on his back and gently pushed him forward so he could see his own reflection in the glass of the coffee table. A week before his thick hair had been dark with flecks of gray, but the face staring back at him was topped with snow-white hair.

Hughes stared at his reflection in shock. "I look like an old man."

"A wise old man I love and whose leadership we all need. You've done well, Jordan," Laura said softly.

He snorted. "Have I? There are a lot of dead people out there who say different. I'm not sure that's such a great accomplishment for my first term as emperor of the island."

"And how many would be alive if you HADN'T been in charge? No one could have done better. You can take that to the bank," Laura said.

Hughes looked over and gave her a wan smile. "I would, but all the banks are closed, along with everything else, remember?"

Laura said nothing for a long moment, but when she spoke, the look on her face alone filled him with hope. "They won't always be, Jordan. And we start back today."

EPILOGUE

The Wiggins Family Compound
Near Lewiston, Maine

July 4, 2021 - 8 a.m.
(14 Months Later)

Bill Wiggins stood on the back deck and watched Tex move through the garden, little Billy her ever-present shadow.

"There's a good one, Mommy! Can I pick it?" Billy asked.

Wiggins smiled. It had seemed strange at first, when Billy asked if he could call Tex Mommy, but it seemed so right now.

"Go ahead," he heard Tex say and saw Billy using both hands to pluck a juicy ripe tomato.

"You take that over to Nana and Papa's house and come back. We'll pick some stuff for the party," Tex said.

"Okay," Billy said, taking off like a streak for the elder Wigginses' house, clutching the tomato.

"And don't run!" Tex shouted as Billy disappeared around the corner of the house.

Bill Wiggins laughed. "A little late on that one, I think."

Tex smiled and walked, or rather waddled, toward the deck. Her baby bump preceded her up the short steps to the deck. Wiggins wrapped her in a hug and then put his hand gently on her stomach.

"Is the little stranger behaving today?" he asked.

"He's kicking the hell out of me as usual," Tex said. "I'd say this kid's been taking prenatal karate lessons."

"How do you know it's a HE?" Wiggins asked.

"'Cause I can already tell he's too ornery to be female," Tex said.

Wiggins laughed. "Maybe she takes after her mother, then."

"Ouch," he said as Tex jabbed him in the ribs. "Is that any way to treat the man of the house?"

"It is if he doesn't mind his manners," Tex said, then lifted her face for a kiss, which Wiggins gladly provided.

They broke the kiss and stood looking out over the neatly tended garden to the field beyond. There were two recreational vehicles and three travel trailers spread out in the field behind the house, with three log cabins in various stages of construction. The goal was to get everyone under a permanent roof by the first snowfall.

The new residents were a mix of Wigginses' relatives and family friends, all judged to be trustworthy and in need of a place to stay. The Wigginses' hundred acres had become that place of refuge, and more willing hands to do hard work and provide for the common defense had been welcome.

They were doing things the old way, salvaging antique steam-powered equipment from abandoned farms to use their endless supply of wood. They'd traded five gallons of their precious gasoline for a now-useless irrigation system on a neighboring farm and salvaged the pipe, using it to bring water from the woodland spring uphill to all the residences. The water was gravity flow at low pressure, but eliminating the need to carry water was a major labor saver.

They were making progress and sustaining themselves, through hunting, fishing, gathering, and growing what Maine's short season would allow them. Their only need for electricity was their radio, powered by solar-charged batteries.

Tex laid her head against Wiggins shoulder and sighed contentedly. "Happy Fourth of July."

"It is a happy one, isn't it? So what's the plan?" Wiggins asked.

"Everyone's supposed to bring a dish and start gathering mid-morning. I'm going to harvest what I can from the garden so it will be nice and fresh, and then take it over to your folks' house to help your mom in the kitchen. I think the plan is for you and your dad to get the fire going so it will burn down to coals in time to grill the venison. The rest of the guys are going to rig the awning and set up the tables and chairs. Your mom wants to eat at noon so we're done before President Tremble's radio address," Tex said.

"Sounds like a good schedule," Wiggins said.

Tex poked his chest and smiled. "Then see that you stick to it, mister. None of Jerry's home brew until AFTER your chores are complete."

Wiggins laughed. "What a buzz kill! You're just jealous because you can't have any."

Tex made a face. "Not really. I tasted that stuff and I don't think Jerry quite has it perfected yet. I'll stick with spring water."

Wiggins put a gentle hand on her stomach. "As well you should."

"How long do you think Billy will be at your folks' house?" Tex asked.

"He's never there less than a half hour. You know that," Wiggins said.

"Hmmm," she said, with a lascivious smile. "Does that suggest anything, Mr. Wiggins?"

He shot a look back toward his parents' house and returned her smile. "Why yes, Mrs. Wiggins. Yes, it does."

The Wiggins Family Compound
Near Lewiston, Maine

Same Day - 2 p.m.

The meal was over and its remains littered the center of the row of picnic tables placed end to end under the shade of the nylon tarp they'd rigged as an awning. The adults sat and laughed and joked while the older kids spread out on the lawn and busied themselves with setting up horseshoes and a variety of other yard games resurrected for the occasion, as the younger kids worked at annoying their older siblings. On the deck, Ray Wiggins fiddled with the radio set on the rail, the volume low as he fine-tuned it to reduce static. It was a scene from a happier time, one none of them ever thought they'd see again.

Suddenly, the elder Wiggins turned to face the others.

"Here it comes, folks," he said as he twisted the knob to increase the radio volume.

"*Repeat,*" boomed the radio. "*Stand by for a message from the President of the United States.*"

After a pause, the transmission continued with a now-familiar voice.

"*My friends and fellow Americans, this is Simon Tremble speaking to you from the White House on a beautiful Fourth of July. On this, the two hundred and forty-fifth anniversary of our nation's birth, we come together not so much in celebration, but in thanksgiving and* remembrance. Let us give thanks for all we've managed to accomplish while never forgetting our countrymen who perished in the terrible months following the global blackout.

"I come to you today in that spirit of thanksgiving and remembrance, but also to give you my insights into what may lie ahead. Since my elevation to this office, I've tried to be as transparent as possible, so today I offer not empty platitudes, but a candid assessment of the challenges we face and a plan for meeting those challenges.

"We are a resilient people, but never in the history of our nation have we been tested as we have during the recent disaster. An accurate census still eludes us, but our best estimates are that over ninety percent of our fellow citizens have perished since that terrible day in April not yet two years ago. There is no one within the sound of my voice who hasn't been a victim of this tragedy.

"Emotions aside, there are also obvious practical consequences. Ninety percent of our doctors and nurses, ninety percent of our engineers and skilled craftsmen, ninety percent of the workers in our power plants and oil refineries and factories, and ninety percent of our teachers are gone—in short, ninety percent of the people we relied on to produce all the products and services we once took for granted. They can't be replaced, at least in the near term.

"Our surviving population of approximately thirty million is roughly the same as the population of the United States on the eve of the Civil War in 1860, but it is spread over a much greater geographical area, further compounding the challenges faced by both individual communities and the nation as a whole. Restoration of our country is a daunting task, but we are not a nation of quitters, nor will we allow ourselves to become mired in a victim mentality.

"Politically, we are in an unprecedented situation. I am president as a result of circumstance rather than a free and fair election, and likewise the surviving members of Congress were elected by constituents now long dead. None of us represent the current will of the people and that must be corrected at the earliest possible opportunity. I have consulted with Congress and hereby announce my intention to hold new elections for all national offices three years hence during the regular election cycle of 2024. To those who might wonder at the delay, I would point out that less than a third of our state governments are functioning entities, and the percentage of functioning county and municipal governments is even lower. Without functioning local governments in place, there can be no elections, either local or national. The consensus is that it will take at least three years before we can restore local political infrastructures sufficiently stable to hold elections.

"Financially, there are equal challenges. As we've all learned in recent months, clean water, food, and the means to protect them are the real wealth in a time of want, and money, especially paper money, is useless. That said, no nation can grow and prosper with a barter economy alone; there must be a universally accepted method of exchange.

"Electronic banking will not return for a very long time, if ever, and acceptance of paper currency has always depended upon people's faith and belief in the government issuing the currency. That faith has been shaken as the disaster wiped out not only our own economy, but those of nations worldwide. On the plus side, there is no doubt this event has been a global reset, which has also wiped out our heretofore tremendous national debt. We are a debtor nation no longer, and I pledge to you to do my best to prevent us from ever again becoming one.

"To that end, last month I ordered the Secretary of the Treasury to complete a thorough inventory of the precious metals held at the United States Bullion Depository at Fort Knox and elsewhere, which revealed holdings in excess of four hundred billion dollars at pre-disaster prices of thirteen hundred dollars per ounce for gold and twenty dollars per ounce for silver. To save you the calculation, which I'm sure many of you are already doing, that works out to over thirteen thousand dollars each for every surviving American.

"Effective immediately, we are fixing the value of gold and silver at the previously mentioned prices and issuing new currency one hundred percent backed by our inventory of precious metal. The paper currency will be fully convertible to precious metal 'on demand' at regional exchanges to be established in more populated areas. To that end, we will also begin minting both gold and silver coins to redeem the currency and otherwise to be used as legal tender.

"We will use our precious metal reserves wisely to grow the economy until such time as it can support a just system of taxation that encourages rather than discourages production. The current government will be studying the nature and details of that system, but will not impose our will; final approval will rest with the newly elected president and Congress, three years hence.

"In the interim, acquisitions made by the federal government and the pay of US government and military personnel will be in the new currency. Additionally, as each state government comes back on line, they will receive a grant of new currency to cover expenses and pay workers, with an emphasis on those skills needed for our recovery. Pay scales will be lean and adjusted to reflect the realities of our situation, but no one who steps up to fulfill these vital jobs will starve.

"To be sure, a hard-money economy alone may prove insufficient to our needs, and we anticipate that a parallel barter economy will continue to exist for some time. We encourage such a development, as a hybrid economy will, in our judgment, be the healthiest and most robust option.

"To demonstrate our good faith and speed acceptance of the new currency, each American eighteen years old or older will receive a onetime grant of five hundred dollars, as will every citizen turning eighteen for the next three years. Our hope is that the injection of the new currency and confidence in it will help us more quickly reestablish a vibrant national economy.

"No nation worthy of the name can long exist if its citizens are isolated from one another, and transportation is now and will remain a challenge. We've had limited success in getting a refinery going on the Gulf Coast and are currently refining crude stocks that were in inventory at the time of the disaster, but fuel alone is only part of the transportation equation. A nation of thirty million souls with limited manpower cannot hope to maintain anything as complex as our national interstate and federal highway systems. Nor can we meet the demands of a large-scale commercial aviation industry and the sophisticated infrastructure it requires. Simply put, we don't intend to try, at least in the near term.

"We will revert to our system of the last centuries, where the majority of goods are moved via our extensive inland waterway system or via coastwise shipping. For communities in the interior of the country with no water transportation access, we will prioritize redevelopment of railroads and the proved simplicity and reliability of steam-powered locomotives.

"And finally, there is electrical power, a commodity we all now appreciate for the miracle it is. Much of the tragedy of the last months could have been avoided had those of us in power, and I include myself in that criticism, listened more carefully to the warnings regarding the potential impact of solar events. Solar storms are not a new phenomenon and there will be more. Perhaps not tomorrow, or next week, or even in our lifetimes. However, we owe it to all of our countrymen who died to ensure this very difficult lesson is never forgotten. We cannot and will not be caught unprepared again.

"As many of you know by now, the fault lies not with our means of producing power, but the method by which we distribute and transmit it over long distances. That system involves long transmission lines, which act as antennas for the electromagnetic surge produced by solar events, and massive transformers, which burn out as a result of the surge. It may be possible to protect such a system from solar events, but we will always lack the means to adequately test those safeguards. An untested system is a system at risk, and we refuse to once again gamble with the lives of our citizens. The alternative, or at least the alternative available to us with our current technology, lies not in attempting to protect our electrical grid, but eliminating it altogether.

"As reported previously, we have managed to restore power production at several of our nuclear facilities. We are also working to salvage the small percentage of high- and medium-voltage transformers that survived the solar storm. Our technical people advise me they will soon be able to route limited power to facilities nationwide, which we will convert to production of small energy systems. Pump factories will begin producing small water turbines, alternators can be salvaged from abandoned vehicles and converted to wind turbines. We will expand solar panel production as fast as possible. Likewise the millions of batteries now sitting dormant can be salvaged for their raw materials and turned into new battery banks for stand-alone systems. In short, we will prioritize the effort to make every community and every rural homestead energy self-sufficient.

"Nothing I have described here will be easy or fast, and as we all know, nothing ever goes entirely to plan. There will be missteps along the way, as there always are. What I offer here today is a start, a way forward to a promising future. Whether or not we can fulfill that promise lies not just with me or Congress, but with us all.

"It's natural in times like these to dwell on all we've lost, but as tragic as those losses have been, I challenge you instead to look at what we've gained. A fire has burned down our house, but also cleansed us of much that was wrong with our society. It is inevitable that forest and field will reclaim much of our country, and in so doing, heal many of the wounds we have inflicted on it. The air and water will be cleaner and nature's balance will be restored over much of the country.

"We are thirty million strong, and the vast natural resources of our country still await. Let us go forward together. Let us retain the core values of family, faith, hard work, and self-reliance that built the nation to start with. But this time, let us seize the opportunity to discard outmoded notions of the past and judge all people on, as a very great man once said, 'the content of their character' rather than the color of their skin or their gender. Let us use all of our talents and resources as we respect our differences. Let us leave behind the partisan politics that have so long divided us and come together to restore our country to its rightful place among nations. If we are to prosper, there are too few of us left to do anything else.

"Let us not look back at what was, but forward to the bright future to come.

"God bless you all, and God bless America."

Bridge
S/S Cape Mendocino
Clark Island
Neches River
Beaumont, Texas

Jordan Hughes stood on the wing of the bridge, looking down on the island, scarcely able to credit all they'd accomplished in the months since they'd fought for the very existence of their 'castle with a moat.' There was no raw dirt now, but berms sloping gently up to near the deck of each ship and continuing along the gap bridged by the northern wall, leaving the entire interior of the fort like a bowl, its raised sides providing a defense against man and nature. The effectiveness of the berm as a storm barrier was tested soon after it was completed, when a hurricane arrived unannounced, sending a six-foot storm surge up the Neches. The ballasted ships held in place like rocks and the berm didn't leak a drop.

And now in midsummer, it was a green bowl full of growing things. The hundred-acre interior of their refuge was sown with grass to stabilize the soil, the seed salvaged from a Tractor Supply store, where looters hadn't been interested in grass seed. The green expanse was dotted with large rectangles of neat garden plots, growing heirloom-variety vegetables from seeds salvaged from the Gillespie home and seed packets overlooked by looters in the stockrooms of retailers. The gardening operation was overseen by Dot Gillespie, who guarded her crops like a mother hen, insisting that half of each harvest be preserved as seed against the time when they could expand their agricultural operations and farm the unoccupied west bank of the river. With no treated seed and neither pesticides or herbicides available, they were doing things the old-fashioned way, and Hughes smiled when he saw Dot Gillespie's wide sun hat bobbing between the rows, inspecting her crops alone, the small army of children she'd dragooned for weeding duty granted a temporary reprieve for the holiday.

They'd managed to trade gasoline Wellesley had squirreled away from some of the barges for livestock, and there was a growing flock of chickens and several cages of rabbits now occupying one of the cargo decks of the *Cape Vincent*. But those were the future, and they hadn't touched them yet, intent on letting their chicken flock and rabbit herd multiply to sustainable levels before they started harvesting it.

Wellesley had proved prescient in other ways as well, because as they practiced restraint and let their sustainable food sources grow, the alligators that now cruised the river with impunity had become a welcome source of protein. Gator tail was frequently on the menu for their communal meals and, after some initial reluctance by the more squeamish members of the community, was now an established part of their diet.

The brackish river and its tributaries provided other food as well. Foraging parties down to Sabine Pass had turned up shrimp nets and scrounged more power boats to fish nearby Sabine Lake, where, free from any other fishing pressure, the shallow waters now teemed with new life. Shrimp, crabs, and fish of all sorts were a welcome addition to the community diet, and with Gowan keeping the power on, several of the walk-in freezers on the larger ships allowed them to preserve anything they couldn't eat against a rainy day.

It went on and on, with more things than seemed possible. The ever-energetic Gowan had found a water-well drilling rig just outside Vidor and induced the owner operator to bring it to the island, over the re-established pontoon bridge, and over the entry ramp up the berm to drill a water well straight down in the middle of the island so they had a good source of water from deep underground, free of any surface contamination. He then routed the well output through a setup he'd rigged up on one of the steamships to heat the water enough to kill any stray bacteria, thus ensuring them of a stable source of drinking water.

They needed it all, with a population now exceeding a thousand, augmented by selective inclusion of refugees with needed skill sets. They'd accomplished much and planned to do so much more, if only they had the time. And if only they could have done it all IN time. He heard a footstep on the steel deck behind him and turned as Laura approached and slipped her hand in his.

"I thought I'd find you up here. You just can't get the captain to leave the bridge, now can you?" she teased.

Hughes shook his head. "Well, not much need for a captain if the ship can't move."

She hugged him and lifted her face for a kiss and Hughes obliged.

She returned his kiss then pressed her cheek against his chest. "Oh, I don't know. I think you're plenty useful."

"Maybe," Hughes said.

"The President delivered a damn good speech. I think it will lift people's spirits," Laura said.

Hughes nodded and said nothing, and they lapsed into silence. After a long moment, Laura broke it.

"You shouldn't dwell on them, you know," she said into his chest.

"Who?"

"You know who," she said softly. "The refugees in the camp across the river who were wiped out when the storm hit. The others we couldn't take in when we were struggling ourselves, but could only give them what food we could spare and send them on their way, whether they wanted to go or not. The ones with typhus and typhoid and cholera and a half-dozen other Third World diseases we had no way to treat or protection from catching except forcing them to stay away. We survived, all of us have survived and our families survived, because we had to make hard decisions. Not just you, but all of us. We saved the ones we could, and I can't, I won't, punish myself for the ones we COULDN'T save. And you shouldn't either. We're in better shape today and able to help more people BECAUSE of those decisions."

He sighed. "Except there's almost no one left to help."

Laura raised her head, put a hand on his cheek, and gazed into his eyes. "Listen to me, Jordan. NOT. YOUR. FAULT. Captain or not. Do you understand?"

He sighed again. "I know, I know. I just can't keep from wishing it had been different."

She put her cheek back against his chest. "Well, it wasn't and there's nothing any of us can do about it. And while we're discussing captains, there's one more thing, and I don't want any argument. The last time we went back to the house, I brought back your uniform, the one with the shoulder boards. I think you should wear it this afternoon—"

"Damn it, Laura! You know I don't like to wear that thing. I'm not in the military and it just seems, I don't know, phony to me and—"

She looked up and brought her finger to his lips. "It's an important day and I think you should wear it. Not for you, but for … for the others. Will you do it for me?"

"That's really not playing fair, you know," Hughes said.

She looked up, smiled, and batted her eyes. "Why, Captain Hughes, I do declare you wound me with such an accusation," she said, in an exaggerated Southern belle accent.

Hughes laughed and pulled her close. "All right, all right. I'll wear the damn thing, but only for the ceremony."

The moment was broken as the VHF squawked and a familiar voice boomed across the bridge, with no semblance of communication protocol.

"Hughes, this is Cormier. You there, *cher?*"

Hughes grinned at Laura and walked to the radio.

"I'm here, Andrew. Where are you?" Hughes said.

"We just turnin' the corner at the Neches intersection. We'll be there in less than an hour, and we brought a lot of good stuff to eat and the best Cajun band on the bayou." He laughed. "Actually the only Cajun band left on the bayou."

"Thank you all for coming, Andrew," Hughes said.

"*Au contraire, mon ami!* Thank you for inviting us. It's past time for a *fais do-do* and we all gonna pass a good time," Cormier said.

Clark Island
Neches River
Beaumont, Texas

Same Day - 6:00 p.m

Hughes sat beside Laura under a sunshade rigged over the rough raised wooden stage, fidgeting in his uniform. In deference to the sweltering heat of July in Southeast Texas, they'd started the holiday celebrations later in the day. *Not that it made a helluva lot of difference*, thought Hughes as he wiped away sweat from his forehead.

He looked out over the group seated in front of the stage, under jury-rigged shade awnings of their own, marginally less hot than the overflow crowd, who stood in the sun. The former senior officers of *Pecos Trader* were in uniform as well, as were Kinsey and the rest of the Coasties. Hughes had no clue how they'd all managed that, but had no doubt it was somehow Laura's doing.

The rest of the crowd was gathering in their Sunday best, or what passed for Sunday best these days, anyway. He was seeing many of the women in skirts or dresses for the first time and actually didn't recognize some of them at first. Among the men there were fresh haircuts and neatly trimmed facial hair, attesting to the importance everyone placed on the ceremony.

Hughes' own mood was decidedly mixed; despite the community's many successes, responsibility for all that remained to be done and a great sense of loss sat on his shoulders like a ponderous weight, sapping his ability to celebrate success. The somber occasion before him did nothing to lessen that feeling. He unconsciously touched his shirt pocket holding the notes for his speech, wondering if it was adequate, before turning his gaze to the squat gray cube next to the stage, dead center in the middle of the island.

Cremation had been Gowan's idea. When the final count was made after the last terrible fight with the cons, the defenders had lost well over a hundred of their own. The dead cons went into the river as alligator food, but no one in the fort was willing to discard their own dead like trash. Conversely, burying so many within the confines of the fort would take up valuable real estate needed for food production, and there wasn't room on the small bluff downriver where they'd buried Earl Gillespie and the other fallen heroes.

But after cremation, the problem then became suitable disposition of the ashes. In the end, they decided to mix them with concrete to form a monument. Someone had pointed out that Pete Brown and Davy Jones were already cremated, and their ashes also went into the neat cube now sitting in the middle of the island with a brass plaque on top listing the names of the fallen.

A single exception to the 'inside' burial restriction was made. With unanimous approval of the inhabitants, the body of Earl Gillespie, the first to fall in defense of Clark Island, was re-interred beside the cube, one of its sides becoming his headstone. As Hughes had previously promised Dot, there was a place left beside Earl when her time came.

Hughes felt Laura's gentle touch on his arm.

"Everyone is here, Jordan. It's time," she whispered.

He nodded and rose. The murmur of conversation ceased as he stood, and all faces turned to him, their looks expectant. He reached for the notes in his pocket but stopped; there was little he could add after the President's speech, and he didn't need notes to begin the simple ceremony.

"Friends and neighbors, we're gathered here today to celebrate, to give thanks, to mourn, and to hope." He touched his shirt pocket. "I had a speech prepared for the occasion, but earlier today our president said much of what I intended to say, and undoubtedly said it better."

Hughes paused for scattered polite laughter then continued.

"But speeches aside, the real reason we're here today is to honor our fallen dead, without whose courage and sacrifice, none of us would be here today. Their ashes form a part of this monument, stubborn, solid and unyielding in death as they were in life. Copying machines are in short supply these days, so we have no printed programs for you, but each of the fallen has a friend or family member who will stand and say their name aloud as we honor them. I'm going to ask Dan Gowan to start and the rest of you just rise and say your hero's name as the opportunity presents itself. Dan?" Hughes turned and looked at Dan Gowan, who rose.

"Jake Kadowski, known to us all as Polak," Gowan said.

There was a pause and Matt Kinsey rose. "David Jones."

Then there was a steady sequence as reciters rose throughout the audience.

"Pete Brown."

"Darius Green."

"Libby Fowler."

On it went, the simple recitation more powerful than any speech he could have made, evoking emotion almost unbearable in its intensity. Across the crowd he could see it was having a similar effect, as there were muffled sobs, and some reciters were having difficulty getting their names out. Laura stood and stepped up beside him, taking his hand in hers. There were tears in her eyes.

The process was uneven, as each reciter waited a respectful interval before speaking, and occasionally two began to speak at once. Hughes lost track of the number, but finally the cadence slowed and Jimmy and Janet Gillespie rose together.

"B … Bobby Gillespie," Jimmy said.

"Mike Gillespie," said Janet.

Dot Gillespie rose in turn. "Earl Thomas Gillespie," she said, steel in her voice.

Hughes looked at the Gillespie family, all standing now, gathered around Dot: Jimmy and Janet, Mike's and Bobby's widows, and a passel of children whose names he could never keep straight. He flashed back to Earl volunteering to fight a battle he knew he couldn't win to buy Georgia Howell a chance to escape with the children. He remembered Mike and Bobby holding off the cons on their dozer, saving the fort. He knew in that instant they were the epitome of all that was right and good in this new world, and demonstrated more than anyone else what it would take to survive and prosper. And he knew what he must do. Calm settled over him, and when he spoke, his voice was clear and strong, carrying over the muffled sobs of the group.

"This was not on the program, folks, but I have a proposal. We've been calling our community Clark Island, simply because that was the name on the chart. That was the past, but all of us gathered here are the future, and we need a new name. None among us has fought harder or suffered and sacrificed more for our continued existence than the Gillespie family. I hereby propose that henceforth and forever more, this place be known as Fort Gillespie, Texas, in honor of that sacrifice."

There was a moment of shocked silence as the crowd digested the idea, and then a voice from the back of the crowd yelled, "HELL YES!" That was followed by other shouts of approval, which grew into a roar of acclamation, such that even Dot Gillespie's reserve broke, and a single tear ran down her cheek. Then the chant began.

"GIL-LES-PIE, GIL-LES-PIE, GIL-LES-PIE!"

Over and over from a thousand throats, the chant rose, both a cry of defiance and celebration of victory over near impossible odds. As it rose, it lifted with it some of the great weight from his shoulders. He couldn't predict the future, but these were good people, survivors all, and he knew now that, with him or without him, they would fulfill the bright promise of the President's vision.

Hughes pulled Laura into his arms and she looked up at him, her eyes glistening.

"It's going to be all right, isn't it?" she asked.

He nodded, almost unable to speak. "Yeah. Yeah, I think it is."

The End

Author's Notes

Thank you for reading *The Disruption Trilogy*. I do hope it lived up to your expectations. As my longtime readers know, I struggled to complete this one, not because of a lack of ideas, but because I had so many ideas, I couldn't keep them all 'in the box,' so to speak.

There were (and are), literally dozens of different ways this story could evolve and it was really tough trying to wind up all the various threads to arrive at a natural conclusion. That need to wind up this story in a trilogy (rather than eight or ten volumes), was driven largely by my own reading preferences. I feel a series that drags on too long, pulling the reader from cliffhanger to cliffhanger, becomes tedious. At some point, readers deserve a real ending, and I personally don't think they should have to read ten books to get there. That said, the first two books of this trilogy were cliffhangers by necessity. The story arc was incomplete, and each of those first books topped the scales at close to a very long 150,000 words, so I had to cut things off with unfinished business each time. I was happy with each of the first two books, but also a bit frustrated I couldn't give readers the closure they had every right to expect. That's what I struggled with in the third and final book, and I do hope you found the conclusion satisfying.

I ended the trilogy on a note of promise so readers could put down the book with a sense of closure. However, there are many unwritten stories in the post-apocalyptic world of Hughes, Kinsey, Hunnicutt, and all my other new friends (and enemies). I may revisit them at another time. If and when I do, I want you to be free to join me on that journey, confident that I will offer you exit points along the way. In the interim (and if you haven't already done so), I invite you to dive into my Dugan thrillers. The titles are listed on the last page of this book.

That's it for now. Thank you for your readership and support.

Best regards,

R.E. (Bob) McDermott
McDermott Publishing World HQ (aka our spare bedroom)
On the shores of beautiful Old Hickory Lake
Old Hickory, TN

Acknowledgments

As I've said before, the ranks of supportive people to whom I owe thanks grows with each book. That's especially true with *The Disruption Trilogy.*

As always, my wife, Andrea, was my first reader and sounding board, saving readers from any number of less than wonderful turns of phrase.

Longtime friends and former maritime industry colleagues, Captains Ken Varall, Seth Harris, William Heu, and Jorge Viso were all instrumental in helping me keep with the shipboard scenes. Longtime reader (and now friend) First Sergeant David Schoettle, of the US Army made sure the dialogue between soldiers rang true.

Worthy of special mention is Lt. Colonel Jerry Johnson (USMC-Retired), a new reader and now old friend who helped me make my helicopter combat scenes realistic. From the jungles of Southeast Asia to the oil patch in the Gulf of Mexico, Jerry has been on the 'pointy end of the spear,' and 'been there, done that.' No amount of internet research can replace the insights of a man who's piloted a chopper under heavy fire and walked away from a crash or two.

I am indebted to both Dave and Jerry for their help and service to our country.

Our son, Chris and daughter-in-law Jennifer read the final draft, which as it turned out, wasn't quite so final. Many thanks to them for catching multiple errors which had eluded me.

On the publishing front, Guido Henkel did his normal excellent job of formatting both the ebooks and the print books, and his lovely wife, Lieu, provided not only the stunning cover for *Promises To Keep*, but new covers for the earlier books in the trilogy as well, to pull them together under a common theme. The results were remarkable and I couldn't be more pleased.

Hundreds of readers volunteered to read the advance review copies of the books in this trilogy. Space prevents me from mentioning each by name, but you know who you are and you have my profound thanks.

Any errors made, despite all this excellent help and support, are mine and mine alone.

R.E. (Bob) McDermott
Old Hickory, Tennessee

Thanks and an Invitation!

There isn't any shortage of thrillers in the world, so I'm truly honored you chose to read one (or actually three) of mine and I sincerely hope you enjoyed it. If you did enjoy the *Disruption Trilogy*, I hope you'll check out my Dugan books (listed on the last page) and consider joining my Readers' Group. Group members receive early notice of new releases, as well as limited time opportunities to buy new releases at deeply discounted prices. You can learn more about my Readers' Group at:

www.remcdermott.com/join-my-readers-group

There's no obligation, so check it out.

With that out of the way, let me say I truly enjoy hearing from readers, and if you're so inclined, feel free to shoot me an email via my website at:

www.remcdermott.com/contact

And finally, independent authors live and die on the strength of our Amazon reviews, so for us those reviews are a very big deal. But it's not enough to just accumulate a lot of good reviews, as factors in the Amazon quality ratings also include both the frequency and timeliness of those reviews. Thus a book with a lot of great reviews will tumble in the ratings if reviews don't continue to accumulate on a regular basis. So the bottom line is, I regularly beg for reviews and appreciate every single one.

Reviews need not be lengthy, and a sentence or so with your opinion of the book is more than sufficient. Please consider returning to Amazon and leaving a brief review of *The Complete Disruption Trilogy* (or any of my other books). I will sincerely appreciate it.

On that note, and whatever your decision regarding a review, I'll close by thanking you once again for taking a chance on a new author, with the hope that I've entertained you at least a bit, and with the promise that I'll always strive to deliver a good story at a fair price.

Sincerely,

R.E. (Bob) McDermott

P.S. Don't forget to check out my Dugan books on the following page.

More Books by
R.E. McDermott

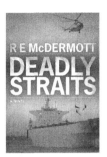

Deadly Straits - When marine engineer and very part-time spook Tom Dugan becomes collateral damage in the War on Terror, he's not about to take it lying down. Falsely implicated in a hijacking, he's offered a chance to clear himself by helping the CIA snare their real prey, Dugan's best friend, London ship owner Alex Kairouz. But Dugan has some plans of his own. Available in paperback on both Amazon and Barnes & Noble.

Deadly Coast - Dugan thought Somali pirates were bad news, then it got worse. As Tom Dugan and Alex Kairouz, his partner and best friend, struggle to ransom their ship and crew from murderous Somali pirates, things take a turn for the worse. A US Navy contracted tanker with a full load of jet fuel is also hijacked, not by garden variety pirates, but by terrorists with links to Al Qaeda, changing the playing field completely. Available in paperback on both Amazon and Barnes & Noble.

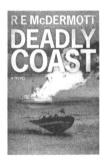

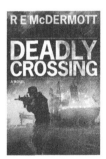

Deadly Crossing - Dugan's attempts to help his friends rescue an innocent girl from the Russian mob plunge him into a world he'd scarcely imagined, endangering him and everyone he holds dear. A world of modern day slavery and unspeakable cruelty, from which no one will escape, unless Dugan can weather a Deadly Crossing. Available in paperback on both Amazon and Barnes & Noble.

Made in United States
North Haven, CT
20 April 2025

68152138R00396